CW01465199

CRITICAL ACCLAIM FOR THE CICERO NOVELS

'The culmination of twelve years' work and a remarkable literary achievement ... A trilogy that is likely to stand alongside the works of Robert Graves and Mary Renault as an enduring imaginative vision of the ancient world.'
Observer

'One of the great triumphs of contemporary historical literature ... Thrillers are supposed to thrill, but few really do raise your heart rate and short-circuit your critical faculties ... Exhilarating ... This trilogy deserves the highest compliment that can be paid to a work of historical fiction: it is easily mistaken for history.'
The Times

'Triumphant, compelling and deeply moving ... the finest fictional treatment of Ancient Rome in the English language ... distinguished by a mastery of the sources, sympathetic imagination, political intelligence and narrative skill ... It's a wonderful, dramatic, story, wonderfully told.'
Scotsman

'Magnificent ... Better than Robert Graves's Claudius novels.'
Standpoint

'A superb trilogy which does full justice to one of Rome's most interesting, complex and humane statesmen.'
Evening Standard

'Sinuous, clever and compelling ... a magnificent trilogy.'
Metro

'A masterful story of political intrigue ... fascinating and absorbing.'
Financial Times

'A brutal tale of murder and mayhem and a tour de force of research and imagination.'
Daily Express

'The thrilling pace of the narrative does not let up from start to finish ... an utterly engrossing, suspense-filled read.'
Irish Times

'The events and political upheavals of these years are some of the most complicated in ancient history. Undaunted, Harris remains impressively faithful to the ancient sources, embellishing the gaps with terse dialogue, exhilarating exchanges and witty observations ... the best kind of narrative history.'
New Statesman

'A fascinating world, a world of subtle political machinations and fine oratory and nuanced debate, and complex legislation, and intrigue ... Extremely absorbing.'
Independent

Also by Robert Harris

---------------------FICTION---------------------

Fatherland

Enigma

Archangel

Pompeii

The Ghost

The Fear Index

An Officer and a Spy

Conclave

Munich

The Second Sleep

V2

---------------------NON–FICTION---------------------

A Higher Form of Killing (*with Jeremy Paxman*)

Gotcha! Media, the Government and the Falklands Crisis

The Making of Neil Kinnock

Selling Hitler

Good and Faithful Servant

ROBERT
HARRIS

THE CICERO TRILOGY

HUTCHINSON
HEINEMANN

7 9 10 8 6

Hutchinson Heinemann
20 Vauxhall Bridge Road
London SW1V 2SA

Hutchinson Heinemann is part of the Penguin Random House group of companies whose addresses can be found at global.penguinrandomhouse.com

Penguin Random House UK

First published as *The Cicero Trilogy* by Hutchinson Heinemann in 2021

www.penguin.co.uk

A CIP catalogue record for this book is available from the British Library.

ISBN 9781786332929

Typeset in 11.5/15 pt Dante MT Std
by Integra Software Services Pvt. Ltd, Pondicherry

Printed and bound in Great Britain by Clays Ltd, Elcograf S.p.A.

The authorised representative in the EEA is Penguin Random House Ireland, Morrison Chambers, 32 Nassau Street, Dublin D02 YH68.

To my family

CONTENTS

NORTH SEA
FURTHER GAUL
NEARER GAUL
ITALY
1.
FURTHER SPAIN
NEARER SPAIN
2.
SARDINIA
SICILY
MEDITERRA
MAURETANIA
NUMIDIA
3.
NG

THE ROMAN EMPIRE 44BC
1. Rome
2. Munda
3. Thapsus
4. Dyrrachium
5. Corcyra
6. Pharsalus
7. Patrae
8. Athens
9. Thessalonica
10. Rhodes
11. Laodicea
12. Carrhae
PANNONIA
DACIA
ILLYRICUM
MOESIA
BLACK SEA
BITHYNIA & PONTUS
THRACE
MACEDONIA
GALATIA
EPIRUS
Taurus Mountains
PHRYGIA
CILICIA
SYRIA
LYCIA
ACHAEA
CYPRUS
NEAN SEA
JUDEA
CYRENAICA
EGYPT

CICERO'S ITALY
Mutina
R. Rubicon
ADRIATIC SEA
Ancona
Rome
Tusculum
Arpinum
Astura
Formiae
Cumae
Puteoli
Bay of Naples
Pompeii
Brundisium
Tarentum
TYRRHENIAN SEA
Messina
Regium
Lilybaeum
IONIAN SEA
Syracuse
NG

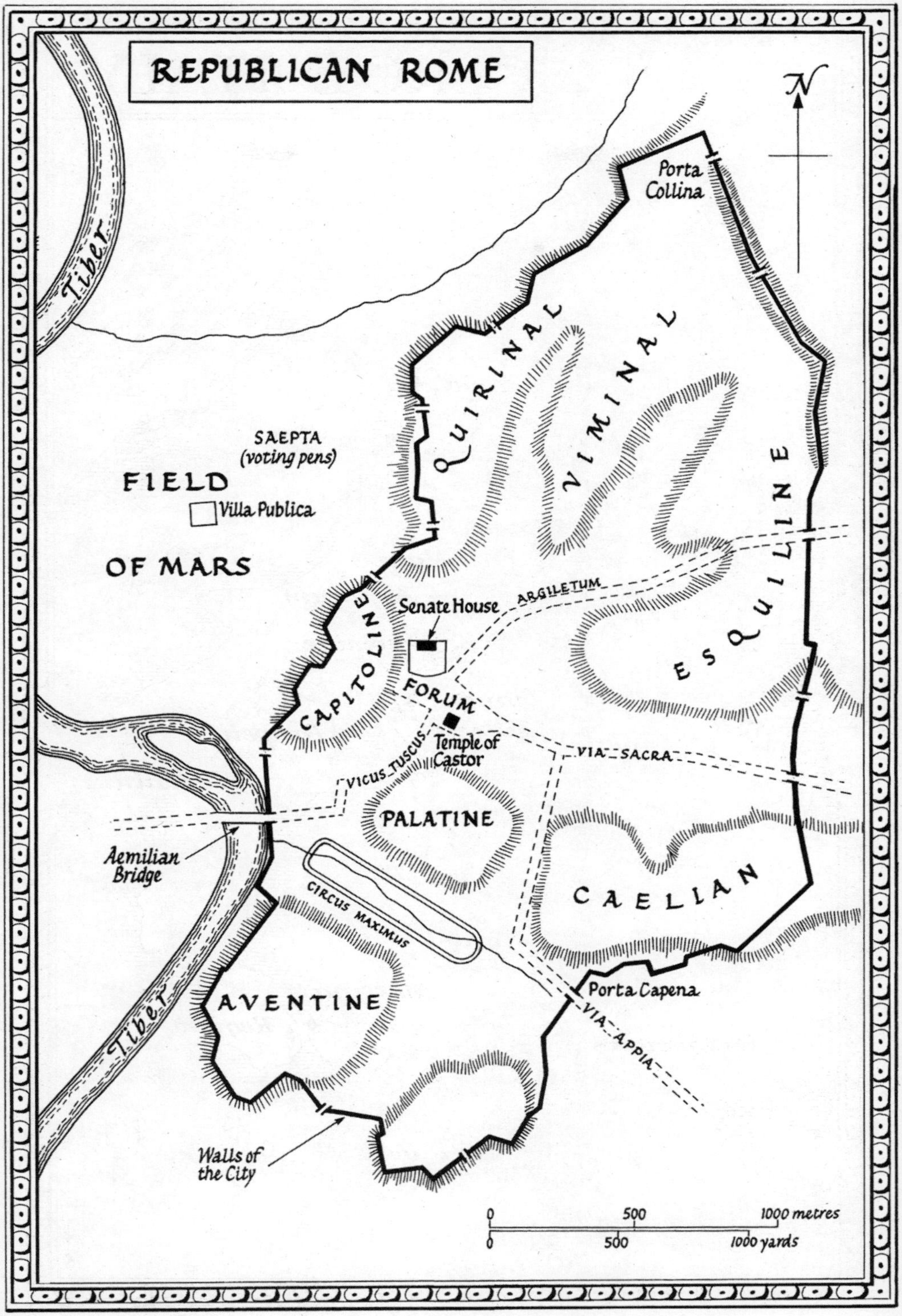
REPUBLICAN ROME
N
Porta Collina
Tiber
QUIRINAL
VIMINAL
SAEPTA
(voting pens)
FIELD
Villa Publica
OF MARS
ESQUILINE
ARGILETUM
Senate House
CAPITOLINE
FORUM
Temple of Castor
VIA SACRA
VICUS TUSCUS
PALATINE
Aemilian Bridge
CIRCUS MAXIMUS
CAELIAN
Porta Capena
AVENTINE
VIA APPIA
Tiber
Walls of the City
0
500
1000 metres
0
500
1000 yards

INTRODUCTION

The Cicero Trilogy consists of three novels which appeared at irregular intervals over the course of almost a decade: *Imperium* in 2006, *Lustrum* in 2009 and *Dictator* in 2015. Although each book was designed to be self-contained, focusing on a separate phase in Cicero's career – his rise to power, his time in power, and his struggle to survive after he lost power – in my mind I always saw them as a single-volume epic that could be read straight through. In a curious way, it now feels as though the work is actually appearing properly for the first time.

I can date the moment of its inception to 17 April 2003, when I received an advance copy of Tom Holland's now-classic account of the end of the Roman republic, *Rubicon*. I had just finished my first Roman novel, *Pompeii*, and was turning my mind to what I might tackle next. I had always wanted to write a political novel. But having spent several years happily immersed in the ancient world, I was reluctant to leave it behind. Sitting in the garden, it suddenly struck me that I could combine the two ambitions in 'a big, saga-type novel', as I noted in my diary that evening, 'tracing the interlinked lives of Cicero, Caesar, Pompey, Crassus, etc., with Cicero as the linking figure'.

Cicero appealed to me from the outset: a man from the provinces, always an outsider, constantly dodging and weaving between more powerful forces, who succeeded purely by the quickness of his wit and his ability as a speaker. He was the world's first professional politician, with a credo he expounds in the novel:

> *Politics? Boring? Politics is history on the wing! What other sphere of human activity calls forth all that is most noble in men's souls, and all that is most base? Or has such excitement? Or more vividly exposes our strengths and weaknesses? Boring? You might as well say that life itself is boring!*

Cicero also had the advantage of having been largely overlooked in popular culture. I cannot think of a film, a play or a novel in which he is the central, rather than merely a supporting, character, and often a sinister one at that. He is given just nine lines in Shakespeare's *Julius Caesar*. (When Cassius suggests involving Cicero in the plot to assassinate the dictator, Brutus briskly dismisses the idea: 'He will never follow any thing / That other men begin.') Even scholars have tended to be quite sniffy. The great nineteenth-century German scholar Theodor Mommsen – who gushed like a super-fan about Julius Caesar as 'the entire and perfect man' – sneered at Cicero as 'a weakling', and 'a journalist in the worst sense of the word'.

But that was what I liked about him. It is a quirk of my own nature always to be suspicious of the 'man of destiny' figure in history – the Caesars and Napoleons – and to prefer instead those less heroic, less sung, nimbler, crafty politicians, who at least try to avoid getting other people killed.

Cicero is perhaps the greatest example of this type. He detested soldiering. Even the deaths of the animals in the arena could upset him. There is no record of his ever being gratuitously cruel – a rare quality in that era. He was a defender in the law courts, never a prosecutor – apart from the one great case which made his name, and which takes up the first part of the *Trilogy*. He approached his political career assiduously and methodically, climbing each rung of the ladder in a way that seems strikingly modern. He would have risen in any nation, at any time, in any system. As Anthony Trollope wrote in 1881:

> *What a man he would have been for London life! How he would have enjoyed his club, picking up the news of the day from all lips, while he seemed to give it to all ears! How popular he would have been at the Carlton, and how men would have listened to him while every great or little crisis was discussed! How supreme he would have sat on the Treasury bench – or how unanswerable, how fatal, how joyous when attacking the Government from the opposite seats! How crowded would have been his rack with invitations to dinner! How delighted would have been the middle-aged countesses of the time to hold with him mild intellectual flirtations – and the girls of the period, how proud to get his autograph, how much prouder to have touched the lips of the great orator with theirs! How the pages of the magazines would have run over with little essays from his pen!*

Cicero had many faults. He was boastful, duplicitous, grasping, hypocritical and sometimes cowardly. ('Unchanging consistency of standpoint', he once blithely observed, 'has never been considered a virtue in great statesmen.') But he generally proved himself brave in the end, sometimes recklessly so. His was the most attractive kind of courage: to face danger, instinctively flinch, collect oneself, and then stand firm.

Having decided that Cicero would be the central character, the question then arose of how to tell his story. One obvious solution would have been to copy the example of Robert Graves in *I, Claudius*, and have him write a first-person autobiography. But Cicero, unlike Claudius, was a genius, and I shied away from the challenge of trying to imitate a genius's thought processes. Geniuses are best described from the outside. This led me naturally to his secretary, Tiro.

That there was such a man as Tiro, and that he published a biography of Cicero after his master's death, is well attested. 'Your services to me are beyond count,' Cicero once wrote to him, 'in my home and out of it, in Rome and abroad, in my studies and literary work …' (Letter, 7 November 50 BC). He was three years younger than Cicero, born a slave, but long outlived him, surviving – according to Saint Jerome – until his hundredth year. Tiro was the first person to record a speech in the senate verbatim: his shorthand system, known as *notae Tironianae,* was still in use in the Church in the sixth century. Indeed, some traces of it (the symbol *&*, the abbreviations *etc.*, *N.B.*, *i.e.*, *e.g.*) survive to this day. He also wrote several treatises on the development of Latin. His multi-volume life of Cicero is referred to as a source by the first-century historian Asconius Pedianus in his commentary on Cicero's speeches; Plutarch cites it twice. But, like the rest of Tiro's literary output, the book disappeared amid the collapse of the Roman Empire.

What kind of work might it have been? In 1985, Elizabeth Rawson, Fellow of Corpus Christi College, Oxford, speculated that it would probably have been in the Hellenistic tradition of biography – a literary form 'written in an unpretentious, unrhetorical style; it might quote documents, but it liked apophthegms by its subject, and it could be gossipy and irresponsible … It delighted in a subject's idiosyncrasies … Such biography was written not for statesmen and generals, but for what the Romans called *curiosi*.'

For me as a novelist, Tiro was a gift almost too good to be true – intimate yet set apart by his status as a slave, constantly at Cicero's side, plausibly taking down his letters, his speeches and his conversations verbatim – loyal, doting, awestruck and frequently appalled.

Most Roman novels tend to be about the emperors or soldiers. My aim was to bring to life in as much detail as possible the actual political machinery of the Roman republic – a kind of *West Wing on the Tiber*. How did a man, without benefit of amplification, command an audience of six hundred in the senate, and several thousand in the forum? How did he stand for election? How did he canvass for votes? And who exactly voted?

My happiest moments writing the novels were occasionally to look up and think, *Yes, it must have been something like that*. Of course, fiction is no substitute for scholarship. Inevitably it leaves the reader wondering how much of what they are reading is true. My rule in the *Trilogy* was never to write something that I knew for certain couldn't have happened. Mostly I didn't need to. The story was so remarkable it required little embellishment. By and large in the pages which follow, whenever something is described which seems absurd or fantastical, it is true; whenever it seems dull or prosaic, I made it up.

Finally, I should say that I have not revised the text, even though there are occasional nods towards New Labour or George W. Bush that nowadays probably mean little. When I started writing the novels it was not quite the cliché it has since become to compare the collapse of the Roman republic to the possible fate of modern America, or of democracy generally. As it turned out, the underlying theme of the *Trilogy* – how a greedy ruling elite came under attack by populist forces whipped up by rich and unscrupulous demagogues; how institutions that had lasted for centuries suddenly started to collapse – seems sharper in hindsight than it did at the time.

But enough self-justification. I am starting to sound as pompous as Cicero. The preliminaries are over. It is time to let the Games begin.

Robert Harris
February 2021

Nescire autem quid ante quam natus sis acciderit, id est semper esse puerum. Quid enim est aetas hominis, nisi ea memoria rerum veterum cum superiorum aetate contexitur?

To be ignorant of what occurred before you were born is to remain always a child. For what is the worth of human life, unless it is woven into the life of our ancestors by the records of history?

Cicero, *Orator*, 46 BC

THE CICERO TRILOGY

PART ONE

SENATOR

79–70 BC

'Urbem, urbem, mi Rufe, cole et in ista luce vive!'

'Rome! Stick to Rome, my dear Rufus, and
live in the limelight!'
Cicero, letter to Rufus, 26 June 50 BC

I

My name is Tiro. For thirty-six years I was the confidential secretary of the Roman statesman Cicero. At first this was exciting, then astonishing, then arduous, and finally extremely dangerous. During those years I believe he spent more hours with me than with any other person, including his own family. I witnessed his private meetings and carried his secret messages. I took down his speeches, his letters and his literary works, even his poetry – such an outpouring of words that I had to invent what is commonly called shorthand to cope with the flow, a system still used to record the deliberations of the senate, and for which I was recently awarded a modest pension. This, along with a few legacies and the kindness of friends, is sufficient to keep me in my retirement. I do not require much. The elderly live on air, and I am very old – almost a hundred, or so they tell me.

In the decades after his death, I was often asked, usually in whispers, what Cicero was really like, but always I held my silence. How was I to know who was a government spy and who was not? At any moment I expected to be purged. But since my life is almost over, and since I have no fear of anything any more – not even torture, for I would not last an instant at the hands of the carnifex or his assistants – I have decided to offer this work as my answer. I shall base it on my memory, and on the documents entrusted to my care. Because the time left to me inevitably must be short, I propose to write it quickly, using my shorthand system, on a few dozen small rolls of the finest paper – Hieratica, no less – which I have long hoarded for the purpose. I pray forgiveness in advance for all my errors and infelicities of style. I also pray to the gods that I may reach the end before my own end overtakes me. Cicero's final words to me were a request to tell the truth about him, and this I shall endeavour to do. If he does not always emerge as a paragon of virtue, well, so be it. Power brings a man many luxuries, but a clean pair of hands is seldom among them.

And it is of power and the man that I shall sing. By power I mean official, political power – what we know in Latin as *imperium* – the power of life and death, as vested by the state in an individual. Many hundreds of men have sought this power, but Cicero was unique in the history of the republic in that he pursued it with no resources to help him apart from his own talent. He was not, unlike Metellus or Hortensius, from one of the great aristocratic families, with generations of political favours to draw on at election time. He had no mighty army to back up his candidacy, as did Pompey or Caesar. He did not have Crassus's vast fortune to grease his path. All he had was his voice – and by sheer effort of will he turned it into the most famous voice in the world.

I was twenty-four years old when I entered his service. He was twenty-seven. I was a household slave, born on the family estate in the hills near Arpinum, who had never even seen Rome. He was a young advocate, suffering from nervous exhaustion, and struggling to overcome considerable natural disabilities. Few would have wagered much on either of our chances.

Cicero's voice at this time was not the fearsome instrument it later became, but harsh and occasionally prone to stutter. I believe the problem was that he had so many words teeming in his head that at moments of stress they jammed in his throat, as when a pair of sheep, pressed by the flock behind them, try at the same time to squeeze through a gate. In any case, these words were often too highfalutin for his audience to grasp. 'The Scholar', his restless listeners used to call him, or 'the Greek' – and the terms were not meant as compliments. Although no one doubted his talent for oratory, his frame was too weak to carry his ambition, and the strain on his vocal cords of several hours' advocacy, often in the open air and in all seasons, could leave him rasping and voiceless for days. Chronic insomnia and poor digestion added to his woes. To put it bluntly, if he was to rise in politics, as he desperately wished to do, he needed professional help. He therefore decided to spend some time away from Rome, travelling both to refresh his mind and to consult the leading teachers of rhetoric, most of whom lived in Greece and Asia Minor.

Because I was responsible for the upkeep of his father's small library, and possessed a decent knowledge of Greek, Cicero asked if he might borrow me, as one might remove a book on loan, and take me with him to the East. My job would be to supervise arrangements, hire transport, pay teachers and so forth, and after a year go back to my old master. In the end, like many a useful volume, I was never returned.

We met in the harbour of Brundisium on the day we were due to set sail. This was during the consulship of Servilius Vatia and Claudius Pulcher, the six hundred and seventy-fifth year after the foundation of Rome. Cicero then was nothing like the imposing figure he later became, whose features were so famous he could not walk down the quietest street unrecognised. (What has happened, I wonder, to all those thousands of busts and portraits, which once adorned so many private houses and public buildings? Can they really *all* have been smashed and burned?) The young man who stood on the quayside that spring morning was thin and round-shouldered, with an unnaturally long neck, in which a large Adam's apple, as big as a baby's fist, plunged up and down whenever he swallowed. His eyes were protuberant, his skin sallow, his cheeks sunken; in short, he was the picture of ill health. *Well, Tiro,* I remember thinking, *you had better make the most of this trip, because it is not going to last long.*

We went first to Athens, where Cicero had promised himself the treat of studying philosophy at the Academy. I carried his bag to the lecture hall and was in the act of turning away when he called me back and demanded to know where I was going.

'To sit in the shade with the other slaves,' I replied, 'unless there is some further service you require.'

'Most certainly there is,' he said. 'I wish you to perform a very strenuous labour. I want you to come in here with me and learn a little philosophy, in order that I may have someone to talk to on our long travels.'

So I followed him in, and was privileged to hear Antiochus of Ascalon himself assert the three basic principles of stoicism – that virtue is sufficient for happiness, that nothing except virtue is good, and that the emotions are not to be trusted – three simple rules which, if only men could follow them, would solve all the problems of the world. Thereafter, Cicero and I would often debate such questions, and in this realm of the intellect the difference in our stations was always forgotten. We stayed six months with Antiochus and then moved on to the real purpose of our journey.

The dominant school of rhetoric at that time was the so-called Asiatic method. Elaborate and flowery, full of pompous phrases and tinkling rhythms, its delivery was accompanied by a lot of swaying about and striding up and down. In Rome its leading exponent was Quintus Hortensius Hortalus, universally considered the foremost orator of the day, whose fancy footwork had earned him the nickname of 'the Dancing Master'. Cicero, with an eye to discovering his tricks, made a point of seeking out all Hortensius's mentors: Menippus of Stratonicea, Dionysius of Magnesia, Aeschylus of Cnidus, Xenocles of Adramyttium – the names alone give a flavour of their style. Cicero spent weeks with each, patiently studying their methods, until at last he felt he had their measure.

'Tiro,' he said to me one evening, picking at his customary plate of boiled vegetables, 'I have had quite enough of these perfumed prancers. You will arrange a boat from Loryma to Rhodes. We shall try a different tack, and enrol in the school of Apollonius Molon.'

And so it came about that, one spring morning just after dawn, when the straits of the Carpathian Sea were as smooth and milky as a pearl (you must forgive these occasional flourishes: I have read too much Greek poetry to maintain an austere Latin style), we were rowed across from the mainland to that ancient, rugged island, where the stocky figure of Molon himself awaited us on the quayside.

This Molon was a lawyer, originally from Alabanda, who had pleaded in the Rome courts brilliantly, and had even been invited to address the senate in Greek – an unheard-of honour – after which he had retired to Rhodes and opened his rhetorical school. His theory of oratory, the exact opposite of the Asiatics', was simple: don't move about too much, hold your head straight, stick to the point, make 'em laugh, make 'em cry, and when you've won their sympathy, sit down quickly – 'For nothing,' said Molon, 'dries more quickly than a tear.' This was far more to Cicero's taste, and he placed himself in Molon's hands entirely.

Molon's first action was to feed him that evening a bowl of hard-boiled eggs with anchovy sauce, and, when Cicero had finished that – not without some complaining, I can tell you – to follow it with a lump of red meat, seared over charcoal, accompanied by a cup of goat's milk. 'You need bulk, young man,' he told him, patting his own barrel chest. 'No mighty note was ever sounded by a feeble reed.' Cicero glared at him, but dutifully chewed until his plate was empty, and that night, for the first time in months, slept soundly. (I know this because I used to sleep on the floor outside his door.)

At dawn, the physical exercises began. 'Speaking in the forum,' said Molon, 'is comparable to running in a race. It requires stamina and strength.' He threw a fake punch at Cicero, who let out a loud '*Oof!*' and staggered backwards, almost falling over. Molon had him stand with his legs apart, his knees rigid, then bend from the waist twenty times to touch the ground on either side of his feet. After that, he made him lie on his back with his hands clasped behind his head and repeatedly sit up without shifting his legs. He made him lie on his front and raise himself solely by the strength of his arms, again twenty times, again without bending his knees. That was the regime on the first day, and each day afterwards more exercises were added and their duration increased. Cicero again slept soundly, and now had no trouble eating, either.

For the actual declamatory training, Molon took his eager pupil out of the shaded courtyard and into the heat of midday, and had him recite his exercise pieces – usually a trial scene or a soliloquy from Menander – while walking up a steep hill without pausing. In this fashion, with the lizards scattering underfoot and only the scratching of the cicadas in the olive trees for an audience, Cicero strengthened his lungs and learned how to gain the maximum output of words from a single breath. 'Pitch your delivery in the middle range,' instructed Molon. 'That is where the power is. Nothing too high or low.' In the afternoons, for speech projection, Molon took him down to the shingle beach, paced out eighty yards (the maximum range of the human voice) and made him declaim against the boom and hiss of the sea – the nearest thing, he said, to the murmur of three thousand people in the open air, or the background mutter of several hundred men in conversation in the senate. These were distractions Cicero would have to get used to.

'But what about the content of what I say?' Cicero asked. 'Surely I will compel attention chiefly by the force of my arguments?'

Molon shrugged. 'Content does not concern me. Remember Demosthenes: "Only three things count in oratory. Delivery, delivery, and again: delivery."'

'And my stutter?'

'The st-st-stutter does not b-b-bother me either,' replied Molon with a grin and a wink. 'Seriously, it adds interest and a useful impression of honesty. Demosthenes himself had a slight lisp. The audience identifies with these flaws. It is only perfection which is dull. Now, move further down the beach and still try to make me hear.'

Thus was I privileged, from the very start, to see the tricks of oratory passed from one master to another. 'There should be no effeminate bending of the neck, no twiddling of the fingers. Do not move your shoulders. If you must use your fingers for a gesture, try bending the middle finger against the thumb and extending the other three – that is it, that is good. The eyes of course are *always* turned in the direction of the gesture, except when we have to reject: "O gods, avert such plague!" or "I do not think that I deserve such honour."'

Nothing was allowed to be written down, for no orator worthy of the name would dream of reading out a text or consulting a sheaf of notes. Molon favoured the standard method of memorising a speech: that of an imaginary journey around the speaker's house. 'Place the first point you want to make in the entrance hall, and picture it lying there, then the second in the atrium, and so on, walking round the house in the way you would naturally tour it, assigning a section of your speech not just to each room, but to every alcove and statue. Make sure each site is well lit, clearly defined, and distinctive. Otherwise you will go groping around like a drunk trying to find his bed after a party.'

Cicero was not the only pupil at Molon's academy that spring and summer. In time we were joined by Cicero's younger brother Quintus, and his cousin Lucius, and also by two friends of his: Servius, a fussy lawyer who wished to become a judge, and Atticus – the dapper, charming Atticus – who had no interest in oratory, for he lived in Athens, and certainly had no intention of making a career in politics, but who loved spending time with Cicero. All marvelled at the change which had been wrought in his health and appearance, and on their final evening together – for now it was autumn, and the time had come to return to Rome – they gathered to hear the effects which Molon had produced on his oratory.

I wish I could recall what it was that Cicero spoke about that night after dinner, but I fear I am the living proof of Demosthenes' cynical assertion that content counts for nothing beside delivery. I stood discreetly out of sight, among the shadows, and all I can picture now are the moths whirling like flakes of ash around the torches, the wash of stars above the courtyard, and the enraptured faces of the young men, flushed in the firelight, turned towards Cicero. But I do remember Molon's words afterwards, when his protégé, with a final bow of his head towards the imaginary jury, sat down. After a long silence he got to his feet and said, in a hoarse voice: 'Cicero, I congratulate you and I am amazed at you. It is Greece and her fate that I am sorry for. The only glory that was left to us was the supremacy of our eloquence, and now you have taken that as well. Go back,' he said, and gestured with those three outstretched fingers, across the lamp-lit terrace to the dark and distant sea, 'go back, my boy, *and conquer Rome.*'

Very well, then. Easy enough to say. But how do you do this? How do you 'conquer Rome' with no weapon other than your voice?

The first step is obvious: you must become a senator.

To gain entry to the senate at that time it was necessary to be at least thirty-one years old and a millionaire. To be exact, assets of one million sesterces had to be shown to the authorities simply to qualify to be a candidate at the annual elections in July, when twenty new senators were elected to replace those who had died in the previous year or had become too poor to keep their seats. But where was Cicero to get a million? His father certainly did not have that kind of money: the family estate was small and heavily mortgaged. He faced, therefore, the three traditional options. But making it would take too long, and stealing it would be too risky. Accordingly, soon after our return from Rhodes, he married it. Terentia was seventeen, boyishly flat-chested, with a head of short, tight black curls. Her half-sister was a vestal virgin, proof of her family's social status. More importantly, she was the owner of two slum apartment blocks in Rome, some woodland in the suburbs, and a farm; total value: one and a quarter million. (Ah, Terentia: plain, grand and rich – what a piece of work you were! I saw her only a few months ago, being carried on an open litter along the coastal road to Naples, screeching at her bearers to make better speed: white-haired and walnut-skinned but otherwise quite unchanged.)

So Cicero, in due course, became a senator – in fact, he topped the poll, being generally now regarded as the second-best advocate in Rome, after Hortensius – and then was sent off for the obligatory year of government service, in his case to the province of Sicily, before being allowed to take his seat. His official title was quaestor, the most junior of the magistracies. Wives were not permitted to accompany their husbands on these tours of duty, so Terentia – I am sure to his deep relief – stayed at home. But I went with him, for by this time I had become a kind of extension of himself, to be used unthinkingly, like an extra hand or foot. Part of the reason for my indispensability was that I had devised a method of taking down his words as fast as he could utter them. From small beginnings – I can modestly claim to be the man who invented the ampersand – my system eventually swelled to a handbook of some four thousand symbols. I found, for example, that Cicero was fond of repeating certain phrases, and these I learned to reduce to a line, or even a few dots – thus proving what most people already know, that politicians essentially say the same thing over and over again. He dictated to me from his bath and his couch, from inside swaying carriages and on country walks. He never ran short of words and I never ran short of symbols to catch and hold them for ever as they flew through the air. We were made for one another.

But to return to Sicily. Do not be alarmed: I shall not describe our work in any detail. Like so much of politics, it was dreary even while it was happening, without revisiting it sixty-odd years later. What was memorable, and significant, was the journey home. Cicero purposely delayed this by a month, from March to April, to ensure he passed through Puteoli during the senate recess, at exactly the moment when all the smart political set would be on the Bay of Naples, enjoying the mineral baths. I was ordered to hire the finest twelve-oared rowing boat I could find, so that he could enter the harbour in style, wearing for the first time the purple-edged toga of a senator of the Roman republic.

For Cicero had convinced himself that he had been such a great success in Sicily, he must be the centre of all attention back in Rome. In a hundred stifling market squares, in the shade of a thousand dusty, wasp-infested Sicilian plane trees, he had dispensed Rome's justice, impartially and with dignity. He had purchased a record amount of grain to feed the electors back in the capital, and had dispatched it at a record cheap price. His speeches at government ceremonies had been masterpieces of tact. He had even feigned interest in the conversation of the locals. He knew he had done well, and in a stream of official reports to the senate he boasted of his achievements. I must confess that occasionally I toned these down before I gave them to the official messenger, and tried to hint to him that perhaps Sicily was not entirely the centre of the world. He took no notice.

I can see him now, standing in the prow, straining his eyes at Puteoli's quayside, as we returned to Italy. What was he expecting? I wonder. A band to pipe him ashore? A consular deputation to present him with a laurel wreath? There was a crowd, all right, but it was not for him. Hortensius, who already had his eye on the consulship, was holding a banquet on several brightly coloured pleasure-craft moored nearby, and guests were waiting to be ferried out to the party. Cicero stepped ashore – ignored. He looked about him, puzzled, and at that moment a few of the revellers, noticing his freshly gleaming senatorial rig, came hurrying towards him. He squared his shoulders in pleasurable anticipation.

'Senator,' called one, 'what's the news from Rome?'

Cicero somehow managed to maintain his smile. 'I have not come from Rome, my good fellow. I am returning from my province.'

A red-haired man, no doubt already drunk, said, 'Ooooh! My *good fellow*! He's returning from his *province* ...'

There was a snort of laughter, barely suppressed.

'What is so funny about that?' interrupted a third, eager to smooth things over. 'Don't you know? He has been in Africa.'

Cicero's smile was now heroic. 'Sicily, actually.'

There may have been more in this vein. I cannot remember. People began drifting away once they realised there was no city gossip to be had, and very soon Hortensius came along and ushered his remaining guests towards their boats. Cicero he nodded to, civilly enough, but pointedly did not invite to join him. We were left alone.

A trivial incident, you might think, and yet Cicero himself used to say that this was the instant at which his ambition hardened within him to rock. He had been humiliated – humiliated by his own vanity – and given brutal evidence of his smallness in the world. He stood there for a long time, watching Hortensius and his friends partying across the water, listening to the merry flutes, and when he turned away, he had changed. I do not exaggerate. I saw it in his eyes. *Very well*, his expression seemed to say, *you fools can frolic; I shall work.*

'This experience, gentlemen, I am inclined to think was more valuable to me than if I had been hailed with salvoes of applause. I ceased thenceforth from considering what the world was likely to hear about me: from that day I took care that I should be seen personally every day. I lived in the public eye. I frequented the forum. Neither my doorkeeper nor sleep prevented anyone from getting in to see me. Not even when I had nothing to do did I do nothing, and consequently absolute leisure was a thing I never knew.'

I came across that passage in one of his speeches not long ago and I can vouch for the truth of it. He walked away from the harbour like a man in a dream, up through Puteoli and out on to the main highway without once looking back. I struggled along behind him carrying as much luggage as I could manage. To begin with, his steps were slow and thoughtful, but gradually they picked up speed, until at last he was striding so rapidly in the direction of Rome I had difficulty keeping up.

And with this both ends my first roll of paper, and begins the real story of Marcus Tullius Cicero.

II

The day which was to prove the turning point began like any other, an hour before dawn, with Cicero, as always, the first in the household to rise. I lay for a little while in the darkness and listened to the thump of the floorboards above my head as he went through the exercises he had learned on Rhodes – a visit now six years in the past – then I rolled off my straw mattress and rinsed my face. It was the first day of November; cold.

Cicero had a modest two-storey dwelling on the ridge of the Esquiline Hill, hemmed in by a temple on one side and a block of flats on the other, although if you could be bothered to scramble up on to the roof you would be rewarded with a decent view across the smoky valley to the great temples on Capitol Hill about half a mile to the west. It was actually his father's place, but the old gentleman was in poor health nowadays and seldom left the country, so Cicero had it to himself, along with Terentia and their five-year-old daughter, Tullia, and a dozen slaves: me, the two secretaries working under me, Sositheus and Laurea, the steward, Eros, Terentia's business manager, Philotimus, two maids, a nurse, a cook, a valet and a doorkeeper. There was also an old blind philosopher somewhere, Diodotus the Stoic, who occasionally groped his way out of his room to join Cicero for dinner when his master needed an intellectual workout. So: fifteen of us in the household in all. Terentia complained endlessly about the cramped conditions, but Cicero would not move, for at this time he was still very much in his man-of-the-people phase, and the house sat well with the image.

The first thing I did that morning, as I did every morning, was to slip over my left wrist a loop of cord, to which was attached a small notebook of my own design. This consisted of not the usual one or two but four double-sided sheets of wax, each in a beechwood frame, very thin and so hinged that I could fold them all up and snap them shut. In this way I could take many more notes in a single session of dictation than the average secretary; but even so, such was Cicero's daily torrent of words, I always made sure to put spares in my pockets. Then I pulled back the curtain of my tiny room and walked across the courtyard into the tablinum, lighting the lamps and checking all was ready. The only piece of furniture was a sideboard, on which stood a bowl of chickpeas. (Cicero's name derived from *cicer*, meaning chickpea, and believing that an unusual name was an advantage in politics, he always took pains to draw attention to it.) Once I was satisfied, I passed through the atrium into the entrance hall, where the doorman was already waiting with his hand on the big metal lock. I checked the light through the narrow window, and when I judged it pale enough, gave a nod to the doorman, who slid back the bolts.

Outside in the chilly street, the usual crowd of the miserable and the desperate was already waiting, and I made a note of each man as he crossed the threshold. Most I recognised; those I did not, I asked for their names; the familiar no-hopers, I turned away. But the standing instruction was: 'If he has a vote, let him in', so the tablinum was soon well filled with anxious clients, each seeking a piece of the senator's time. I lingered by the entrance until I reckoned the queue had all filed in and was just stepping back when a figure with the dusty clothes, straggling hair and uncut beard of a man in mourning loomed in the doorway. He gave me a fright, I do not mind admitting.

'Tiro!' he said. 'Thank the gods!' And he sank against the door jamb, exhausted, peering out at me with pale, dead eyes. I guess he must have been about fifty. At first I could not place him, but it is one of the jobs of a political secretary to put names to faces, and gradually, despite his condition, a picture began to assemble in my mind: a large house overlooking the sea, an ornamental garden, a collection of bronze statues, a town somewhere in Sicily, in the north – Thermae, that was it.

'Sthenius of Thermae,' I said, and held out my hand. 'Welcome.'

It was not my place to comment on his appearance, nor to ask what he was doing hundreds of miles from home and in such obvious distress. I left him in the tablinum and went through to Cicero's study. The senator, who was due in court that morning to defend a youth charged with parricide, and who would also be expected to attend the afternoon session of the senate, was squeezing a small leather ball to strengthen his fingers, while being robed in his toga by his valet. He was listening to one letter being read out by young Sositheus, and at the same time dictating a message to Laurea, to whom I had taught the rudiments of my shorthand system. As I entered, he threw the ball at me – I caught it without thinking – and gestured for the list of callers. He read it greedily, as he always did. What had he caught overnight? Some prominent citizen from a useful tribe? A Sabatini, perhaps? A Pomptini? Or a businessman rich enough to vote among the first centuries in the consular elections? But today it was only the usual small fry and his face gradually fell until he reached the final name.

'Sthenius?' He interrupted his dictation. 'He's that Sicilian, is he not? The rich one with the bronzes? We had better find out what he wants.'

'Sicilians don't have a vote,' I pointed out.

'Pro bono,' he said, with a straight face. 'Besides, he does have bronzes. I shall see him first.'

So I fetched in Sthenius, who was given the usual treatment – the trademark smile, the manly double-grip handshake, the long and sincere stare into the eyes – then shown to a seat and asked what had brought him to Rome. I had started remembering more about Sthenius. We had stayed with him twice in Thermae, when Cicero heard cases in the town. Back then he had been one of the leading citizens of the province, but now all his vigour and confidence had gone. He needed help, he announced. He was facing ruin. His life was in terrible danger. He had been robbed.

'Really?' said Cicero. He was half glancing at a document on his desk, not paying too much attention, for a busy advocate hears many hard-luck stories. 'You have my sympathy. Robbed by whom?'

'By the governor of Sicily, Gaius Verres.' The senator looked up sharply.

There was no stopping Sthenius after that. As his story poured out, Cicero caught my eye and performed a little mime of note-taking – he wanted a record of this – and when Sthenius eventually paused to draw breath, he gently interrupted and asked him to go back a little, to the day, almost three months earlier, when he had first received the letter from Verres. 'What was your reaction?'

'I worried a little. He already had a ... *reputation*. People call him – his name meaning boar – people call him the Boar with Blood on his Snout. But I could hardly refuse.'

'You still have this letter?'

'Yes.'

'And in it did Verres specifically mention your art collection?'

'Oh yes. He said he had often heard about it and wanted to see it.'

'And how soon after that did he come to stay?'

'Very soon. A week at most.'

'Was he alone?'

'No, he had his lictors with him. I had to find room for them as well. Bodyguards are always rough types, but these were the worst set of thugs I ever saw. The chief of them, Sextius, is the official executioner for the whole of Sicily. He demands bribes from his victims by threatening to botch the job – you know, mangle them – if they do not pay up beforehand.' Sthenius swallowed and started breathing hard. We waited.

'Take your time,' said Cicero.

'I thought Verres might like to bathe after his journey, and then we could dine – but no, he said he wanted to see my collection straightaway.'

'You had some very fine pieces, I remember.'

'It was my life, Senator, I cannot put it plainer. Thirty years of travelling and haggling. Corinthian and Delian bronzes, pictures, silver – nothing I did not handle and choose myself. I had Myron's *The Discus Thrower* and *The Spear Bearer* by Polycleitus. Some silver cups by Mentor. Verres was complimentary. He said it deserved a wider audience. He said it was good enough for public display. I paid no attention till we were having dinner on the terrace and I heard a noise from the inner courtyard. My steward told me a wagon drawn by oxen had arrived and Verres's lictors were loading it with everything.'

Sthenius was silent again, and I could readily imagine the shame of it for such a proud man: his wife wailing, the household traumatised, the dusty outlines where the statues had once stood. The only sound in the study was the tap of my stylus on wax.

Cicero said: 'You did not complain?'

'Who to? The governor?' Sthenius laughed. 'No, Senator. I was alive, wasn't I? If he had just left it at that, I would have swallowed my losses, and you would never have heard a squeak from me. But collecting can be a sickness, and I tell you what: your Governor Verres has it badly. You remember those statues in the town square?'

'Indeed I do. Three very fine bronzes. But you are surely not telling me he stole those as well?'

'He tried. This was on his third day under my roof. He asked me whose they were. I told him they were the property of the town, and had been for centuries. You know they are four hundred years old? He said he would like permission to remove them to his residence in Syracuse, also as a loan, and asked me to approach the council. By then I knew what kind of a man he was, so I said I could not, in all honour, oblige him. He left that night. A few days after that, I received a summons for trial on the fifth day of October, on a charge of forgery.'

'Who brought the charge?'

'An enemy of mine named Agathinus. He is a client of Verres. My first thought was to face him down. I have nothing to fear as far as my honesty goes. I have never forged a document in my life. But then I heard the judge was to be Verres himself, and that he had already fixed on the punishment. I was to be whipped in front of the whole town for my insolence.'

'And so you fled?'

'That same night, I took a boat along the coast to Messana.'

Cicero rested his chin in his hand and contemplated Sthenius. I recognised that gesture. He was weighing the witness up. 'You say the hearing was on the fifth of last month. Have you heard what happened?'

'That is why I am here. I was convicted in my absence, sentenced to be flogged – and fined five thousand. But there is worse than that. At the hearing, Verres claimed fresh evidence had been produced against me, this time of spying for the rebels in Spain. There is to be a new trial in Syracuse on the first day of December.'

'But spying is a capital offence.'

'Senator – believe me – he plans to have me crucified. He boasts of it openly. I would not be the first, either. I need help. Please. Will you help me?'

I thought he might be about to sink to his knees and start kissing the senator's feet, and so, I suspect, did Cicero, for he quickly got up from his chair and started pacing about the room. 'It seems to me there are two aspects to this case, Sthenius. One, the theft of your property – and there, frankly, I cannot see what is to be done. Why do you think men such as Verres desire to be governors in the first place? Because they know they can take what they want, within reason. The second aspect, the manipulation of the legal process – that is more promising.

'I know several men with great legal expertise who live in Sicily – one, indeed, in Syracuse. I shall write to him today and urge him, as a particular favour to me, to accept your case. I shall even give him my opinion as to what he should do. He should apply to the court to have the forthcoming prosecution declared invalid, on the grounds that you are not present to answer. If that fails, and Verres goes ahead, your advocate should come to Rome and argue that the conviction is unsound.'

But the Sicilian was shaking his head. 'If it was just a lawyer in Syracuse I needed, Senator, I would not have come all the way to Rome.'

I could see Cicero did not like where this was leading. Such a case could tie up his practice for days, and Sicilians, as I had reminded him, did not have votes. Pro bono indeed!

'Listen,' he said reassuringly, 'your case is strong. Verres is obviously corrupt. He abuses hospitality. He steals. He brings false charges. He plots judicial murder. His position is indefensible. It can easily be handled by an advocate in Syracuse – really, I promise you. Now, if you will excuse me, I have many clients to see, and I am due in court in less than an hour.'

He nodded to me and I stepped forward, putting a hand on Sthenius's arm to guide him out. The Sicilian shook it off. 'But I need you,' he persisted.

'Why?'

'Because my only hope of justice lies here, not in Sicily, where Verres controls the courts. And everyone here tells me Marcus Cicero is the second-best lawyer in Rome.'

'Do they indeed?' Cicero's tone took on an edge of sarcasm: he hated that epithet. 'Well then, why settle for second best? Why not go straight to Hortensius?'

'I thought of that,' said his visitor artlessly, 'but he turned me down. He is representing Verres.'

I showed the Sicilian out and returned to find Cicero alone in his study, tilted back in his chair, staring at the wall, tossing the leather ball from one hand to the other. Legal textbooks cluttered his desk. *Precedents in Pleading* by Hostilius was one which he had open; Manilius's *Conditions of Sale* was another.

'Do you remember that red-haired drunk on the quayside at Puteoli, the day we came back from Sicily? "Ooooh! My *good fellow*! He's returning from his *province* ..."'

I nodded.

'That was Verres.' The ball went back and forth, back and forth. 'The fellow gives corruption a bad name.'

'I am surprised at Hortensius for getting involved with him.'

'Are you? I'm not.' He stopped tossing the ball and contemplated it on his outstretched palm. 'The Dancing Master and the Boar …' He brooded for a while. 'A man in my position would have to be mad to tangle with Hortensius and Verres combined, and all for the sake of some Sicilian who is not even a Roman citizen.'

'True.'

'True,' he repeated, although there was an odd hesitancy in the way he said it which sometimes makes me wonder if he had not just then glimpsed the whole thing – the whole extraordinary set of possibilities and consequences, laid out like a mosaic in his mind. But if he had, I never knew, for at that moment his daughter Tullia ran in, still wearing her nightdress, with some childish drawing to show him, and suddenly his attention switched entirely on to her and he scooped her up and settled her on his knee. 'Did you do this? Did you *really* do this all by yourself …?'

I left him to it and slipped away, back into the tablinum, to announce that we were running late and that the senator was about to leave for court. Sthenius was still moping around, and asked me when he could expect an answer, to which I could only reply that he would have to fall in with the rest. Soon after that Cicero himself appeared, hand in hand with Tullia, nodding good morning to everyone, greeting each by name ('The first rule in politics, Tiro: never forget a face'). He was beautifully turned out, as always, his hair pomaded and slicked back, his skin scented, his toga freshly laundered; his red leather shoes spotless and shiny; his face bronzed by years of pleading in the open air; groomed, lean, fit: he *glowed*. They followed him into the vestibule, where he hoisted the beaming little girl into the air, showed her off to the assembled company, then turned her face to his and gave her a resounding kiss on the lips. There was a drawn-out 'Ahh!' and some isolated applause. It was not wholly put on for show – he would have done it even if no one had been present, for he loved his darling Tulliola more than he ever loved anyone in his entire life – but he knew the Roman electorate were a sentimental lot, and that if word of his paternal devotion got around, it would do him no harm.

And so we stepped out into the bright promise of that November morning, into the gathering noise of the city – Cicero striding ahead, with me beside him, notebook at the ready; Sositheus and Laurea tucked in behind, carrying the document cases with the evidence he needed for his appearance in court; and, on either side of us, trying to catch the senator's attention, yet proud merely to be in his aura, two dozen assorted petitioners and hangers-on, including Sthenius – down the hill from the leafy, respectable heights of the Esquiline and into the stink and smoke and racket of Subura. Here the height of the tenements shut out the sunlight and the packed crowds squeezed our phalanx of supporters into a broken thread that still somehow determinedly trailed along after us. Cicero was a well-known figure here, a hero to the shopkeepers and merchants whose interests he had represented, and who had watched him walking past for years. Without once breaking his rapid step, his sharp blue eyes registered every bowed head, every wave of greeting, and it was rare for me to need to whisper a name in his ear, for he knew his voters far better than I.

I do not know how it is these days, but at that time there were six or seven law courts in almost permanent session, each set up in a different part of the forum, so that at the hour when they all opened one could barely move for advocates and legal officers hurrying about. To make it worse, the praetor of each court would always arrive from his house preceded by half a dozen lictors to clear his path, and as luck would have it, our little entourage debouched into the forum at exactly the moment that Hortensius – at this time a praetor himself – went parading by towards the senate house. We were all held back by his guards to let the great man pass, and to this day I do not think it was his intention to cut Cicero dead, for he was a man of refined, almost effeminate manners: he simply did not see him. But the consequence was that the so-called second-best advocate in Rome, his cordial greeting dead on his lips, was left staring at the retreating back of the so-called best with such an intensity of loathing I was surprised Hortensius did not start rubbing at the skin between his shoulder blades.

Our business that morning was in the central criminal court, convened outside the Basilica Aemilia, where the fifteen-year-old Caius Popillius Laenas was on trial accused of stabbing his father to death through the eye with a metal stylus. I could already see a big crowd waiting around the tribunal. Cicero was due to make the closing speech for the defence.

That was attraction enough. But if he failed to convince the jury, Popillius, as a convicted parricide, would be stripped naked, flayed till he bled, then sewn up in a sack together with a dog, a cock and a viper and thrown into the River Tiber. There was a whiff of bloodlust in the air, and as the onlookers parted to let us through, I caught a glimpse of Popillius himself, a notoriously violent youth, whose eyebrows merged to form a continuous thick black line. He was seated next to his uncle on the bench reserved for the defence, scowling defiantly, spitting at anyone who came too close. 'We really must secure an acquittal,' observed Cicero, 'if only to spare the dog, the cock and the viper the ordeal of being sewn up in a sack with Popillius.' He always maintained that it was no business of the advocate to worry whether his client was guilty or not: that was for the court. He undertook only to do his best, and in return the Popillii Laeni, who could boast four consuls in their family tree, would be obliged to support him whenever he ran for office.

Sositheus and Laurea set down the boxes of evidence, and I was just bending to unfasten the nearest when Cicero told me to leave it. 'Save yourself the trouble,' he said, tapping the side of his head. 'I have the speech up here well enough.' He bowed politely to his client – 'Good day, Popillius: we shall soon have this settled, I trust' – then continued to me, in a quieter voice: 'I have a more important task for you. Give me your notebook. I want you to go to the senate house, find the chief clerk, and see if there is a chance of having this put on the order paper this afternoon.' He was writing rapidly. 'Say nothing to our Sicilian friend just yet. There is great danger. We must take this carefully, one step at a time.'

It was not until I had left the tribunal and was halfway across the forum to the senate house that I risked taking a look at what he had written: *That in the opinion of this house the prosecution of persons in their absence on capital charges should be prohibited in the provinces.* I felt a tightening in my chest, for I saw at once what it meant. Cleverly, tentatively, obliquely, Cicero was preparing at last to challenge his great rival. I was carrying a declaration of war.

Gellius Publicola was the presiding consul for November. He was a blunt, delightfully stupid military commander of the old school. It was said, or at any rate it was said by Cicero, that when Gellius had passed through Athens with his army twenty years before, he had offered to mediate between the warring schools of philosophy: he would convene a conference at which they could thrash out the meaning of life once and for all, thus sparing themselves further pointless argument. I knew Gellius's secretary fairly well, and as the afternoon's agenda was unusually light, with nothing scheduled apart from a report on the military situation, he agreed to add Cicero's motion to the order paper. 'But you might warn your master,' he said, 'that the consul has heard his little joke about the philosophers, *and he does not much like it.*'

By the time I returned to the criminal court, Cicero was already well launched on his closing speech for the defence. It was not one of those which he afterwards chose to preserve, so unfortunately I do not have the text. All I can remember is that he won the case by the clever expedient of promising that young Popillius, if acquitted, would devote the rest of his life to military service – a pledge which took the prosecution, the jury, and indeed his client entirely by surprise. But it did the trick, and the moment the verdict was in, without pausing to waste another moment on the ghastly Popillius, or even to snatch a mouthful of food, he set off immediately westwards towards the senate house, still trailed by his original honour-guard of admirers, their number swelled by the spreading rumour that the great advocate had another speech planned.

Cicero used to say that it was not in the senate chamber that the real business of the republic was done, but outside, in the open-air lobby known as the senaculum, where the senators were obliged to wait until they constituted a quorum. This daily massing of white-robed figures, which might last for an hour or more, was one of the great sights of the city, and while Cicero plunged in among them, Sthenius and I joined the crowd of gawpers on the other side of the forum. (The Sicilian, poor fellow, still had no idea what was happening.)

It is in the nature of things that not all politicians can achieve greatness. Of the six hundred men who then constituted the senate, only eight could be elected praetor – to preside over the courts – in any one year, and only two of these could go on to achieve the supreme *imperium* of the consulship. In other words, more than half of those milling around the senaculum were doomed never to hold elected office at all. They were what the aristocrats sneeringly called the *pedarii*, the men who voted with their feet, shuffling dutifully to one side of the chamber or the other whenever a division was called. And yet, in their way, these citizens were the backbone of the republic: bankers, businessmen and landowners from all over Italy; wealthy, cautious and patriotic; suspicious of the arrogance and show of the aristocrats. Like Cicero, they were often 'new men', the first in their families to win election to the senate. These were his people, and observing him threading his way among them that afternoon was like watching a master-craftsman in his studio, a sculptor with his stone – here a hand resting lightly on an elbow, there a heavy arm clapped across a pair of meaty shoulders; with this man a coarse joke, with that a solemn word of condolence, his own hands crossed and pressed to his breast in sympathy; detained by a bore, he would seem to have all the hours of the day to listen to his dreary story, but then you would see his hand flicker out and catch some passer-by, and he would spin as gracefully as a dancer, with the tenderest backward glance of apology and regret, to work on someone else. Occasionally he would gesture in our direction, and a senator would stare at us, and perhaps shake his head in disbelief, or nod slowly to promise his support.

'What is he saying about me?' asked Sthenius. 'What is he going to do?'

I made no answer, for I did not know myself.

By now it was clear that Hortensius had realised something was going on, but was unsure exactly what. The order of business had been posted in its usual place beside the door of the senate house. I saw Hortensius stop to read it – *the prosecution of persons in their absence on capital charges should be prohibited in the provinces* – and turn away, mystified. Gellius Publicola was sitting in the doorway on his carved ivory chair, surrounded by his attendants, waiting until the entrails had been inspected and the auguries declared favourable before summoning the senators inside. Hortensius approached him, palms spread wide in enquiry. Gellius shrugged and pointed irritably at Cicero. Hortensius swung round to discover his ambitious rival surrounded by a conspiratorial circle of senators. He frowned, and went over to join his own aristocratic friends: the three Metellus brothers – Quintus, Lucius and Marcus – and the two elderly ex-consuls who really ran the empire, Quintus Catulus (whose sister was married to Hortensius), and the double-triumphator Publius Servilius Vatia Isauricus. Merely writing their names after all these years raises the hairs on my neck, for these were such men, stern and unyielding and steeped in the old republican values, as no longer exist. Hortensius must have told them about the motion, because slowly all five turned to look at Cicero. Immediately thereafter a trumpet sounded to signal the start of the session and the senators began to file in.

The old senate house was a cool, gloomy, cavernous temple of government, split by a wide central aisle of black and white tile. Facing across it on either side were long rows of wooden benches, six deep, on which the senators sat, with a dais at the far end for the chairs of the consuls. The light on that November afternoon was pale and bluish, dropping in shafts from the unglazed windows just beneath the raftered roof. Pigeons cooed on the sills and flapped across the chamber, sending small feathers and even occasionally hot squirts of excrement down on to the senators below. Some held that it was lucky to be shat on while speaking, others that it was an ill omen, a few that it depended on the colour of the deposit. The superstitions were as numerous as their interpretations. Cicero took no notice of them, just as he took no notice of the arrangement of sheep's guts, or whether a peal of thunder was on the left or the right, or the particular flight-path of a flock of birds – idiocy all of it, as far as he was concerned, even though he later campaigned enthusiastically for election to the College of Augurs.

By ancient tradition, then still observed, the doors of the senate house remained open so that the people could hear the debates. The crowd, Sthenius and I among them, surged across the forum to the threshold of the chamber, where we were held back by a simple rope. Gellius was already speaking, relating the dispatches of the army commanders in the field. On all three fronts, the news was good. In southern Italy, the vastly rich Marcus Crassus – he who once boasted that no man could call himself wealthy until he could keep a legion of five thousand solely out of his income – was putting down Spartacus's slave revolt with great severity. In Spain, Pompey the Great, after six years' fighting, was mopping up the last of the rebel armies. In Asia Minor, Lucius Lucullus was enjoying a glorious run of victories over King Mithradates. Once their reports had been read, supporters of each man rose in turn to praise his patron's achievements and subtly denigrate those of his rivals. I knew the politics of this from Cicero and passed them on to Sthenius in a superior whisper: 'Crassus hates Pompey and is determined to defeat Spartacus before Pompey can return with his legions from Spain to take all the credit. Pompey hates Crassus and wants the glory of finishing off Spartacus so that he can rob him of a triumph. Crassus and Pompey both hate Lucullus because he has the most glamorous command.'

'And whom does Lucullus hate?'

'Pompey and Crassus, of course, for intriguing against him.'

I felt as pleased as a child who has just successfully recited his lesson, for it was all just a game then, and I had no idea that we would ever get drawn in. The debate came to a desultory halt, without the need for a vote, and the senators began talking among themselves. Gellius, who must have been well into his sixties, held the order paper up close to his face and squinted at it, then peered around the chamber, trying to locate Cicero, who, as a junior senator, was confined to a distant back bench near the door. Eventually Cicero stood to show himself, Gellius sat, the buzz of voices died away, and I picked up my stylus. There was a silence, which Cicero allowed to grow, an old trick to increase tension. And then, when he had waited so long it seemed that something must be wrong, he began to speak – very quietly and hesitantly at first, forcing his listeners to strain their ears, the rhythm of his words hooking them without their even knowing it.

'Honourable members, compared to the stirring accounts of our men in arms to which we have lately listened, I fear what I say will sound small indeed.' And now his voice rose. 'But if the moment has come when this noble house no longer has ears for the pleas of an innocent man, then all those courageous deeds are worthless, and our soldiers bleed in vain.' There was a murmur of agreement from the benches beside him. 'This morning there came into my home just such an innocent man, whose treatment by one of our number has been so shameful, so monstrous and so cruel that the gods themselves must weep to hear of it. I refer to the honourable Sthenius of Thermae, recently resident in the miserable, misgoverned, misappropriated province of Sicily.'

At the word 'Sicily', Hortensius, who had been sprawling on the front bench nearest the consul, twitched slightly. Without taking his eyes from Cicero he turned and began whispering to Quintus, the eldest of the Metellus brothers, who promptly leaned behind him and beckoned to Marcus, the junior of the fraternal trio. Marcus squatted on his haunches to receive his instructions, then, after a brief bow to the presiding consul, came hurrying down the aisle towards me. For a moment I thought I was about to be struck – they were tough, swaggering fellows, those Metelli

– but he did not even look at me. He lifted the rope, ducked under it, pushed through the crowd and disappeared.

Cicero, meanwhile, was hitting his stride. After our return from Molon, with the precept 'Delivery, delivery, delivery' carved into his mind, he had spent many hours at the theatre, studying the methods of the actors, and had developed a considerable talent for mime and mimicry. Using only the smallest touch of voice or gesture, he could, as it were, populate his speeches with the characters to whom he referred. He treated the senate that afternoon to a command performance: the swaggering arrogance of Verres was contrasted with the quiet dignity of Sthenius, the long-suffering Sicilians shrank before the vileness of the public executioner, Sextius. Sthenius himself could hardly believe what he was witnessing. He had been in the city but a day, and here he was, the subject of a debate in the Roman senate itself. Hortensius, meanwhile, kept glancing towards the door, and as Cicero began to work towards his peroration – 'Sthenius seeks our protection, not merely from a thief, but from the very man who is supposed to punish thieves!' – he finally sprang to his feet. Under the rules of the senate, a serving praetor always took precedence over a humble member of the *pedarii*, and Cicero had no choice but to give way.

'Senators,' boomed Hortensius, 'we have sat through this long enough! This is surely one of the most flagrant pieces of opportunism ever seen in this noble house! A vague motion is placed before us, which now turns out to relate to one man only. No notice is given to us about what is to be discussed. We have no means of verifying whether what we are hearing is true. Gaius Verres, a senior member of this order, is being defamed with no opportunity to defend himself. I move that this sitting be suspended immediately!'

Hortensius sat to a patter of applause from the aristocrats. Cicero stood. His face was perfectly straight.

'The senator seems not to have read the motion,' he said, in mock puzzlement. 'Where is there any mention here of Gaius Verres? Gentlemen, I am not asking this house to vote on Gaius Verres. It would not be fair to judge Gaius Verres in his absence. Gaius Verres is not here to defend himself. And now that we have established that principle, will Hortensius please extend it to my client, and agree that he should not be tried in his absence either? Or is there to be one law for the aristocrats and another for the rest of us?'

That raised the temperature well enough and set the *pedarii* around Cicero and the crowd at the door roaring with delight. I felt someone pushing roughly behind me and Marcus Metellus shouldered his way back into the chamber and walked quickly up the aisle towards Hortensius. Cicero watched his progress, at first with an expression of puzzlement, and then with one of realisation. He quickly held up his hand for silence. 'Very well. Since Hortensius objects to the vagueness of the original motion, let us reframe it so that there can be no doubt. I propose an amendment: *That whereas Sthenius has been prosecuted in his absence, it is agreed that no trial of him in his absence shall take place, and that if any such trial has already taken place, it shall be invalid*. And I say: let us vote on it now, and in the highest traditions of the Roman senate save an innocent man from the dreadful punishment of crucifixion!'

To mingled cheers and cat-calls, Cicero sat and Gellius rose. 'The motion has been put,' declared the consul. 'Does any other member wish to speak?'

Hortensius, the Metellus brothers and a few others of their party, such as Scribonius Curio, Sergius Catilina and Aemilius Alba, were in a huddle around the front bench, and it briefly seemed that the house would move straight to a division, which would have suited Cicero perfectly. But when the aristocrats finally settled back in their places, the bony figure of Catulus was revealed to be still on his feet. 'I believe I shall speak,' he said. 'Yes, I believe I shall have something to say.' Catulus was as hard and heartless as flint – the great-great-great-great-great-grandson (I believe that is the correct number of greats) of that Catulus who had triumphed over Hamilcar in the First Punic War – and a full two centuries of history were distilled into his vinegary old voice. 'I shall speak,' he repeated, 'and what I shall say first is that that young man' – pointing at Cicero – 'knows nothing whatsoever about "the highest traditions of the Roman senate", for if he did he would realise that no senator ever attacks another, except to his face. It shows a lack of breeding. I look at him there, all clever and eager in his place, and do you know what I think, gentlemen? I think of the wisdom of the old saying: "An ounce of heredity is worth a pound of merit"!'

Now it was the aristocrats who were rocking with laughter. Catilina, of whom I shall have much more to say later, pointed at Cicero, and then drew his finger across his throat. Cicero flushed pink but kept his self-control. He even managed a thin smile. Catulus turned with delight to the benches behind him, and I caught a glimpse of his grinning profile, sharp and beak-nosed, like a head on a coin. He swivelled back to face the chamber. 'When I first entered this house, in the consulship of Claudius Pulcher and Marcus Perperna ...' His voice settled into a confident drone.

Cicero caught my eye. He mouthed something, glanced up at the windows, then gestured with his head towards the door. I understood at once what he meant, and as I pushed my way back through the spectators and into the forum, I realised that Marcus Metellus must have been dispatched on exactly the same errand. In those days, when time-keeping was cruder than it is now, the last hour of the day's business was deemed to begin when the sun dropped west of the Maenian Column. I guessed that must be about to happen, and sure enough, the clerk responsible for making the observation was already on his way to tell the consul. It was against the law for the senate to sit after sunset. Clearly, Hortensius and his friends were planning to talk out the remainder of the session, preventing Cicero's motion from being put to the vote. By the time I had quickly confirmed the sun's position for myself, run back across the forum and wriggled my way through the crowd to the threshold of the chamber, Gellius was making the announcement: 'The last hour!'

Cicero was instantly on his feet, wanting to make a point of order, but Gellius would not take it, and the floor was still with Catulus. On and on Catulus went, giving an interminable history of provincial government, virtually from the time since the she-wolf suckled Romulus. (Catulus's father, also a consul, had famously died by shutting himself up in a sealed room, kindling a charcoal fire, and suffocating himself with the fumes: Cicero used to say he must have done it to avoid listening to another speech by his son.) When he did eventually reach some sort of conclusion, he promptly yielded the floor to Quintus Metellus. Again Cicero rose, but again he was defeated by the seniority rule. Metellus had praetorian rank, and unless he chose to give way, which naturally he did not, Cicero had no right of speech. For a time Cicero stood his ground, against a swelling roar of protest, but the men on either side of him – one of whom was Servius, his lawyer friend, who had his interests at heart and could see he was in danger of making a fool of himself – pulled at his toga, and finally he surrendered and sat down.

It was forbidden to light a lamp or a brazier inside the chamber. As the gloom deepened, the cold sharpened and the white shapes of the senators, motionless in the November dusk, became like a parliament of ghosts. After Metellus had droned on for an eternity, and sat down in favour of Hortensius – a man who could talk on anything for hours – everyone knew the debate was over, and very soon afterwards Gellius dissolved the house. He limped down the aisle, an old man in search of his dinner, preceded by four lictors carrying his curule chair. Once he had passed through the doors, the senators streamed out after him and Sthenius and I retreated a short distance into the forum to wait for Cicero. Gradually the crowd around us dwindled. The Sicilian kept asking me what was happening, but I felt it wiser to say nothing, and we stood in silence. I pictured Cicero sitting alone on the back benches, waiting for the chamber to empty so that he could leave without having to speak to anyone, for I feared he had badly lost face. But to my surprise he strolled out chatting with Hortensius and another, older senator, whom I did not recognise. They talked for a while on the steps of the senate house, shook hands and parted.

'Do you know who that was?' asked Cicero, coming over to us. Far from being cast down, he appeared highly amused. 'That was Verres's father. He has promised to write to his son, urging him to drop the prosecution, if we agree not to bring the matter back to the senate.'

Poor Sthenius was so relieved, I thought he might die from gratitude. He dropped to his knees and began kissing the senator's hands. Cicero made a sour face and gently raised him to his feet. 'Really, my dear Sthenius, save your thanks until I have actually achieved something. He has only promised to write, that is all. It is not a guarantee.'

Sthenius said, 'But you will accept the offer?'

Cicero shrugged. 'What choice do we have? Even if I re-table the motion, they will only talk it out again.'

I could not resist asking why, in that case, Hortensius was bothering to offer a deal at all.

Cicero nodded slowly. 'Now that is a good question.' There was a mist rising from the Tiber, and the lamps in the shops along the Argiletum shone yellow and gauzy. He sniffed the damp air. 'I suppose it can only be because he is embarrassed. Which in his case, of course, takes quite a lot. Yet it seems that even *he* would prefer not to be associated too publicly with such a flagrant criminal as Verres. So he is trying to settle the matter quietly. I wonder how much his retainer is from Verres: it must be an enormous sum.'

'Hortensius was not the only one who came to Verres's defence,' I reminded him.

'No.' Cicero glanced back at the senate house, and I could see that something had just occurred to him. 'They are all in it together, aren't they? The Metellus brothers are true aristocrats – they would never lift a finger to help anyone apart from themselves, unless it was for money. As for Catulus, the man is frantic for gold. He has undertaken so much building on the Capitol over the past ten years, it is almost more of a shrine to him than it is to Jupiter. I estimate we must have been looking at half a million in bribes this afternoon, Tiro. A few Delian bronzes – however fine, Sthenius, forgive me – would not be sufficient to buy that kind of protection. What *is* Verres up to down there in Sicily?' He suddenly began working his signet ring over his knuckle. 'Take this to the National Archive, Tiro, and show it to one of the clerks. Demand in my name to see all the official accounts submitted to the senate by Gaius Verres.'

My face must have registered my dismay. 'But the National Archive is run by Catulus's people. He is sure to hear word of what you are doing.'

'That cannot be helped.'

'But what am I looking for?'

'Anything interesting. You will know it when you see it. Go quickly, while there is still some light.' He put his arm round the shoulders of the Sicilian. 'As for you, Sthenius – you will come to dinner with me tonight, I hope? It is only family, but I am sure my wife will be delighted to meet you.'

I rather doubted that, but naturally it was not my place to say so.

The National Archive, which was then barely six years old, loomed over the forum even more massively than it does today, for back then it had less competition. I climbed that great flight of steps up to the first gallery, and by the time I found an attendant my heart was racing. I showed him the seal, and demanded, on behalf of Senator Cicero, to see Verres's accounts. At first he claimed never to have heard of Cicero, and besides, the building was closing. But then I pointed in the direction of the Carcer and told him firmly that if he did not desire to spend a month in chains in the state prison for impeding official business, he had better fetch those records now. (One lesson I had learned from Cicero was how to hide my nerves.) He scowled a bit and thought about it, then told me to follow him.

The Archive was Catulus's domain, a temple to him and his clan. Above the vaults was his inscription – *Q. Lutatius Catulus, son of Quintus, grandson of Quintus, consul, by a decree of the Senate, commissioned the erection of this National Archive, and approved it satisfactory* – and beside the entrance stood his life-size statue, looking somewhat more youthful and heroic than he had appeared in the senate that afternoon. Most of the attendants were either his slaves or his freedmen, and wore his emblem, a little dog, sewn on to their tunics. I shall tell you the kind of man Catulus was. He blamed the suicide of his father on the populist praetor Gratidianus – a distant relative of Cicero – and after the victory of the aristocrats in the civil war between Marius and Sulla he took the opportunity for revenge. His young protégé, Sergius Catilina, at his behest, seized Gratidianus, and whipped him through the streets to the Catulus family tomb. There, his arms and legs were broken, his ears and nose cut off, his tongue pulled out of his mouth and severed, and his eyes gouged out. In this ghastly condition his head was then lopped off, and Catilina bore it in triumph to Catulus, who was waiting in the forum. Do you wonder now why I was nervous as I waited for the vaults to be opened?

The senatorial records were kept in fireproof strong-rooms, built to withstand a lightning strike, tunnelled into the rock of the Capitol, and when the slaves swung back the big bronze door I had a glimpse of thousands upon thousands of rolled papyri, receding into the shadows of the sacred hill. Five hundred years of history were encompassed in that one small space: half a millennium of magistracies and governorships, proconsular decrees and judicial rulings, from Lusitania to Macedonia, from Africa to Gaul, and most of them made in the names of the same few families: the Aemilii, the Claudii, the Cornelii, the Lutatii, the Metelli, the Servilii. This was what gave Catulus and his kind the confidence to look down upon such provincial equestrians as Cicero.

They kept me waiting in an antechamber while they searched for Verres's records, and eventually brought out to me a single document case containing perhaps a dozen rolls. From the labels on the ends I saw that these were all, with one exception, accounts from his time as urban praetor. The exception was a flimsy piece of papyrus, barely worth the trouble of unrolling, covering his work as a junior magistrate twelve years previously, at the time of the war between Sulla and Marius, and on which was written just three sentences: *I received 2,235,417 sesterces. I expended on wages, grain, payments to legates, the proquaestor, the praetorian cohort 1,635,417 sesterces. I left 600,000 at Ariminum.* Remembering the scores of rolls of meticulous accounts which Cicero's term as a junior magistrate on Sicily had generated, all of which I had written out for him, I could barely refrain from laughing.

'Is this all there is?'

The attendant assured me it was.

'But where are the accounts from his time in Sicily?'

'They have not yet been submitted to the treasury.'

'Not yet submitted? He has been governor for almost two years!'

The fellow looked at me blankly, and I could see that there was no point in wasting any more time with him. I copied out the three lines relating to Verres's junior magistracy and went out into the evening.

While I had been in the National Archive, darkness had fallen over Rome. In Cicero's house the family had already gone into dinner. But the master had left instructions with the steward, Eros, that I was to be shown straight into the dining room the moment I returned. I found Cicero lying on a couch beside Terentia. His brother, Quintus, was also there, with his wife, Pomponia. The third couch was occupied by Cicero's cousin Lucius and the hapless Sthenius, still clad in his dirty mourning clothes and squirming with unease. I could sense the strained atmosphere as soon as I entered, although Cicero was in good spirits. He always liked a dinner party. It was not the quality of the food and drink which mattered to him, but the company and the conversation. Quintus and Lucius, along with Atticus, were the three men he loved most.

'Well?' he said to me. I told him what had happened and showed him my copy of Verres's quaestorian accounts. He scanned it, grunted, and tossed the wax tablet across the table. 'Look at that, Quintus. The villain is too lazy even to lie adequately. Six hundred thousand – what a nice round sum, not a penny either side of it – and where does he leave it? Why, in a town which is then conveniently occupied by the opposition's army, so the loss can be blamed on them! And no accounts submitted from Sicily for *two years*? I am obliged to you, Sthenius, for bringing this rogue to my attention.'

'Oh yes, *so* obliged,' said Terentia, with savage sweetness. '*So* obliged – for setting us at war with half the decent families in Rome. But presumably we can socialise with Sicilians from now on, so that will be all right. Where did you say you came from again?'

'Thermae, your ladyship.'

'Thermae. I have never heard of it, but I am sure it is delightful. You can make speeches to the town council, Cicero. Perhaps you will even get elected there, now that Rome is forever closed to you. You can be the consul of Thermae and I can be the first lady.'

'A role I am sure you will perform with your customary charm, my darling,' said Cicero, patting her arm.

They could needle away at one another like this for hours. Sometimes I believe they rather enjoyed it.

'I still fail to see what you can do about it,' said Quintus. He was fresh from military service: four years younger than his brother, and possessed of about half the brains. 'If you raise Verres's conduct in the senate, they will talk it out. If you try to take him to court, they will make sure he is acquitted. Just keep your nose out of it is my advice.'

'And what do you say, cousin?'

'I say no man of honour in the Roman senate can stand by and see this sort of corruption going on unchecked,' replied Lucius. 'Now that you know the facts, you have a duty to make them public.'

'Bravo!' said Terentia. 'Spoken like a true philosopher who has never stood for office in his life.'

Pomponia yawned noisily. 'Can we talk about something else? Politics is so dull.'

She was a tiresome woman whose only obvious attraction, apart from her prominent bust, was that she was Atticus's sister. I saw the eyes of the two Cicero brothers meet and my master give a barely perceptible shake of his head: ignore her, his expression said, it is not worth arguing over. 'All right,' he conceded, 'enough of politics. But I propose a toast.' He raised his cup and the others did the same. 'To our old friend Sthenius. If nothing else, may this day have seen the beginning of the restoration of his fortunes. Sthenius!'

The Sicilian's eyes were wet with tears of gratitude.

'Sthenius!'

'And Thermae, Cicero,' added Terentia, her small dark eyes, her shrew's eyes, bright with malice over the rim of her drink. 'Do not let us forget Thermae.'

*

I took my meal alone in the kitchen and went exhausted to bed with my lamp and a book of philosophy which I was too tired to read. (I was free to borrow whatever I liked from the household's small library.) Later, I heard the guests all leave and the bolts slam shut on the front door. I heard Cicero and Terentia mount the stairs in silence and go their separate ways, for she had long since taken to sleeping in another part of the house to avoid being woken by him before dawn. I heard Cicero's footsteps on the boards above my head, and then I blew out my lamp, and that was the last sound I heard as I surrendered myself to sleep – his footsteps pacing, up and down, up and down.

It was six weeks later that we heard the news from Sicily. Verres had ignored the entreaties of his father. On the first day of December, in Syracuse, exactly as he had threatened, he had judged Sthenius in his absence, found him guilty of espionage, sentenced him to be crucified, and dispatched his officials to Rome to arrest him and return him for execution.

III

The governor of Sicily's contemptuous defiance caught Cicero off his guard. He had been convinced he had struck a gentlemen's agreement which would safeguard his client's life. 'But then of course,' he complained bitterly, 'none of them is a gentleman.' He stormed around the house in an uncharacteristic rage. He had been tricked! They had played him for a fool! He would march down to the senate house right there and then and expose their villainous lies! I knew he would calm down before long, for he was only too aware that he lacked the rank simply to demand a hearing in the senate: he would risk humiliation.

But there was no escaping the fact that he was under a heavy obligation to protect his client, and on the morning after Sthenius had learned his fate, Cicero convened a meeting in his study to determine how best to respond. For the first time that I can remember, all his usual callers were turned away, and six of us crammed into that small space: Cicero, brother Quintus, cousin Lucius, Sthenius, myself (to take notes), and Servius Sulpicius, already widely regarded as the ablest jurist of his generation. Cicero began by inviting Servius to give his legal opinion.

'In theory,' said Servius, 'our friend has a right of appeal in Syracuse, but only to the governor, that is to Verres himself; so that avenue is closed to us. To bring a prosecution against Verres is not an option: as a serving governor he has executive immunity; besides, Hortensius is the praetor of the extortion court until January; and besides both of these, the jury will be composed of senators who will never convict one of their own. You could table another motion in the senate, but you have already tried that, and presumably if you tried again you would merely meet with the same result. Continuing to live openly in Rome is not an option for Sthenius – anyone convicted of a capital crime is automatically subject to banishment from the city, so it is impossible for him to remain here. Indeed,

Cicero, you are liable to prosecution yourself if you harbour him under your roof.'

'So what is your advice?'

'Suicide,' said Servius. Sthenius let out a terrible groan. 'No, really, I am afraid you should consider it. Before they catch hold of you. You do not want to suffer the scourge, the hot irons, or the torments of the cross.'

'Thank you, Servius,' said Cicero, cutting him off swiftly before he had an opportunity to describe those torments in further detail. 'Tiro, we need to find Sthenius a place where he can hide. He cannot stay here any longer. It is the first place they will look. As for the legal situation, Servius, your analysis strikes me as faultless. Verres is a brute, but a cunning brute, which is why he felt strong enough to press ahead with the conviction. In short, having thought about the matter overnight, it seems to me that there is only one slim possibility.'

'Which is?'

'To go to the tribunes.'

This suggestion produced an immediate stir of unease, for the tribunes were at that time an utterly discredited group. Traditionally, they had checked and balanced the power of the senate by voicing the will of the common people. But ten years earlier, after Sulla had defeated the forces of Marius, the aristocrats had stripped them of their powers. They could no longer summon meetings of the people, or propose legislation, or impeach the likes of Verres for high crimes and misdemeanours. As a final humiliation, any senator who became a tribune was automatically disqualified from standing for senior office, that is the praetorship or the consulship. In other words, the tribuneship was designed to be a political dead end – a place to confine the ranting and the rancorous, the incompetent and the unpromotable: the effluent of the body politic. No senator of any nobility or ambition would go anywhere near it.

'I know your objections,' said Cicero, waving the room to be silent. 'But the tribunes still have one small power left to them, do they not, Servius?'

'That is true,' agreed Servius. 'They do have a residual *potestas auxilii ferendi*.' Our blank looks gave him obvious satisfaction. 'It means,' he explained with a smile, 'that they have the right to offer their protection to private persons against the unjust decisions of magistrates. But I must warn you, Cicero, that your friends, among whom I have long counted it an honour to number myself, will think much the less of you if you start dabbling in the politics of the mob. Suicide,' he repeated. 'Where is the objection? We are all mortal. For all of us it is only a matter of time. And this way you go with honour.'

'I agree with Servius about the danger we run if we approach the tribunes,' said Quintus. (It was usually 'we' when Quintus spoke about his elder brother.) 'Whether we like it or not, power in Rome nowadays lies with the senate and with the nobles. That's why our strategy has always been to build your reputation carefully, through your advocacy in the courts. We shall do ourselves irreparable damage with the men who really matter if the feeling gets around that you are merely another rabble-rouser. Also … I hesitate to raise this, Marcus, but have you considered Terentia's reaction if you were to follow this course?'

Servius guffawed at that. 'You will never conquer Rome, Cicero, if you cannot rule your wife.'

'Conquering Rome would be child's play, Servius, believe me, compared with ruling my wife.'

And so the debate went on. Lucius favoured an immediate approach to the tribunes, no matter what the consequences. Sthenius was too numb with misery and fear to have a coherent opinion on anything. At the very end, Cicero asked me what I thought. In other company this might have caused surprise, a slave's view not counting for much in most Romans' eyes, but these men were used to the way that Cicero sometimes turned to me for advice. I replied cautiously that it seemed to me that Hortensius would not be happy to learn of Verres's action, and that the prospect of the case becoming a public scandal might yet force him to put more pressure on his client to see sense: going to the tribunes was a risk, but on balance it was one worth taking. The answer pleased Cicero.

'Sometimes,' he said, summing up the discussion with an aphorism I have never forgotten, 'if you find yourself stuck in politics, the thing to do is start a fight – start a fight, even if you do not know how you are going to win it, because it is only when a fight is on, and everything is in motion, that you can hope to see your way through. Thank you, gentlemen.' And with that the meeting was adjourned.

There was no time to waste, for if the news from Syracuse had already reached Rome, it was a fair assumption that Verres's men were not far behind. Even while Cicero was talking, I had conceived an idea for a possible hiding place for Sthenius, and the moment the conference was over I went in search of Terentia's business manager, Philotimus. He was a plump and lascivious young man, generally to be found in the kitchen, pestering the maids to satisfy one or other, or preferably both, of his vices. I asked him if there was a spare apartment available in one of his mistress's tenement blocks, and when he replied that there was, I bullied him into giving me the key. I checked the street outside the house for suspicious loiterers, and when I was sure that it was safe I persuaded Sthenius to follow me.

He was in a state of complete dejection, his dreams of returning to his homeland dashed, in hourly terror of being arrested. And I fear that when he first saw the squalid building in Subura in which I said he would now have to live, he must have felt that even we had abandoned him. The stairs were rickety and gloomy. There was evidence of a recent fire on the walls. His room, on the fifth floor, was barely more than a cell, with a straw mattress in the corner and a tiny window which offered no view, except across the street to another, similar apartment, close enough for Sthenius to reach out and shake hands with his neighbour. For a latrine he had a bucket. But if it did not offer him comfort, it at least offered him security – dropped, unknown, into this warren of slums, it would be almost impossible for him to be found. He asked me, in a plaintive tone, to sit with him a while, but I had to get back and gather all the documents relating to his case, so that Cicero could present them to the tribunes. We were fighting time, I told him, and left at once.

The headquarters of the tribunes were next door to the senate house, in the old Basilica Porcia. Although the tribunate was only a shell, from which all the succulent flesh of power had been sucked, people still hung around its building. The angry, the dispossessed, the hungry, the militant – these were the denizens of the tribunes' basilica. As Cicero and I walked across the forum, we could see a sizeable crowd jostling on its steps to get a view of what was happening inside. I was carrying a document case, but still I cleared a way for the senator as best I could, receiving some kicks and curses for my pains, as these were not citizens with any great love for a purple-bordered toga.

There were ten tribunes, elected annually by the people, and they always sat on the same long wooden bench, beneath a mural depicting the defeat of the Carthaginians. It was not a large building, but packed, noisy and warm, despite the December cold outside. A young man, bizarrely barefoot, was haranguing the mob as we entered. He was an ugly, raw-faced youth with a brutal, grating voice. There were always plenty of cranks in the Basilica Porcia, and I took him at first to be just another, as his entire speech seemed to be devoted to arguing why one particular pillar should not, on any account, be demolished, or even moved one inch, to give the tribunes more room. And yet for some curious reason he compelled attention. Cicero began listening to him very carefully, and after a while he realised – from the constant references to 'my ancestor' – that this peculiar creature was none other than the great-grandson of the famous Marcus Porcius Cato who had originally built the basilica and given it his name.

I mention this here because young Cato – he was then twenty-three – was to become such an important figure, in both the life of Cicero and the death of the republic. Not that one would have guessed it at the time. He looked destined for nowhere more significant than the asylum. He finished his speech, and as he went by, wild-eyed and unseeing, he knocked into me. What remains in my mind is the animal stink of him, his hair matted with damp and the patches of sweat the size of dinner plates spreading under the armpits of his tunic. But he had won his point, and that pillar stayed absolutely in its place for as long as the building stood – which was not, alas, to be many years longer.

However, returning to my story, the tribunes were a poor lot on the whole, but there was one among them who stood out for his talent and his energy, and that was Lollius Palicanus. He was a proud man, but of low birth, from Picenum in the Italian north-east, the power base of Pompey the Great. It had been assumed that when Pompey returned from Spain he would use his influence to try to gain his fellow countryman a praetorship, and Cicero had been as surprised as everybody else earlier in the summer when Palicanus had suddenly announced his candidacy for the tribunate. But on this particular morning he looked happy enough with his lot. The fresh crop of tribunes always began their term of office on the tenth day of December, so he must have been very new in the job. 'Cicero!' he bellowed, the moment he saw us. 'I had been wondering when you would show up!'

He told us that he had already heard the news from Syracuse, and he wanted to talk about Verres. But he wanted to talk in private, for there was more at stake, he said mysteriously, than the fate of one man. He proposed meeting us at his house on the Aventine Hill in an hour, to which Cicero agreed, whereupon he immediately ordered one of his attendants to guide us, saying he would follow separately.

It turned out to be a rough and unpretentious place, in keeping with the man, close to the Lavernan Gate, just outside the city wall. The thing I remember most clearly is the larger-than-lifesize bust of Pompey, posed in the headgear and armour of Alexander the Great, which dominated the atrium. 'Well,' said Cicero, after he had contemplated it for a while, 'I suppose it makes a change from the Three Graces.' This was exactly the sort of droll but inappropriate comment which used to get repeated around the town, and which invariably found its way back to its victim. Luckily, only I was present on this occasion, but I took the opportunity to pass on what the consul's clerk had said regarding his joke about Gellius mediating between the philosophers. Cicero pretended to be sheepish and promised to be more circumspect in future – he knew, he said, that people liked their statesmen to be dull – but naturally he soon forgot his resolution.

'That was a good speech you made the other week,' said Palicanus, the moment he arrived. 'You have the stuff in you, Cicero, you really have, if I may say so. But those blue-blooded bastards screwed you over, and now you are in the shit. So what exactly are you planning to do about it?' (This was more or less how he spoke – rough words in a rough accent – and the aristocrats used to have some sport with him over his elocution.)

I opened my case and handed the documents to Cicero, and he quickly laid out the situation regarding Sthenius. When he had finished he asked what chance there was of receiving any help from the tribunes.

'That depends,' said Palicanus, with a quick lick of his lips and a grin. 'Come and sit down and let us see what is to be done.'

He took us through into another room, small and completely overwhelmed by a huge wall painting of a laurelled Pompey, this time dressed as Jupiter, complete with lightning bolts shooting from his fingers.

'Do you like it?' asked Palicanus.

'It is remarkable,' said Cicero.

'Yes, it is,' he said, with some satisfaction. '*That* is art.'

I took a seat in the corner, beneath the Picenean deity, while Cicero, whose eye I dared not meet, settled himself at the opposite end of the couch to our host.

'What I am about to tell you, Cicero, is not to be repeated outside this house. Pompey the Great' – Palicanus nodded to the painting, in case we were in any doubt as to whom he meant – 'will soon be returning to Rome for the first time in six years. He will come with his army, so there can be no fancy double-dealing from our noble friends. He will seek the consulship. And he will get the consulship. And he will get it unopposed.'

He leaned forward eagerly, expecting shock or surprise, but Cicero received this sensational intelligence as coolly as if he were being told the weather.

'So in return for your helping me over Sthenius, I am to support you over Pompey?'

'You are a canny one, Cicero, you have the stuff in you. What do you think?'

Cicero rested his chin in his hand and gazed at Palicanus. 'Quintus Metellus will not be happy, for a start. You know the old poem – "In Rome Metelli are, 'tis fate,/Elected to the consulate." He has been scheduled since birth to have his turn next summer.'

'Has he indeed? Well he can kiss my backside. How many legions did Quintus Metellus have behind him, the last time you looked?'

'Crassus has legions,' Cicero pointed out. 'So has Lucullus.'

'Lucullus is too far away, and besides, he has his hands full. As for Crassus – well, it is true that Crassus hates Pompey's guts. But the thing about Crassus is that he is not a proper soldier. He is a businessman, and that type always cuts a deal.'

'And then there is the little matter of its being completely unconstitutional. You have to be forty-two at the time of the consular election, and Pompey is how old?'

'Just thirty-four.'

'Indeed. Almost a year younger than me. And a consul is also required to have been elected to the senate and to have served as praetor, neither of which Pompey has achieved. He has never made a political speech in his life. To put the matter simply, Palicanus, seldom has a man been less qualified for the post.'

Palicanus made a dismissive gesture. 'All that may be true, but let us face facts – Pompey has run whole countries for years, and done it with proconsular authority to boot. He *is* a consul, in all but name. Be realistic, Cicero. You cannot expect a man such as Pompey to come back to Rome and start at the bottom, running for quaestor like some political hack. What would that do to his dignity?'

'I appreciate his feelings, but you asked my opinion, and I am giving it to you, and I tell you the aristocrats will not stand for it. All right, perhaps if he has ten thousand men outside the city they will have no choice but to let him become consul, but sooner or later his army will go home and then how will he— Ha!' Cicero suddenly threw back his head and started laughing. 'That is very clever.'

'You have seen it?' said Palicanus, with a grin.

'I have seen it.' Cicero nodded appreciatively. 'Very good.'

'Well, I am offering you the chance to be a part of it. And Pompey the Great does not forget his friends.'

At the time I had not the least idea of what they were talking about. Only when we were walking home afterwards did Cicero explain everything to me. Pompey was planning to seek the consulship on the platform of a full restoration of tribunician power. Hence Palicanus's surprising move in becoming a tribune. The strategy was not born of some altruistic desire on Pompey's part to give the Roman people greater liberty – although I suppose it is just possible he was occasionally pleased to lie in his bath in Spain and fancy himself a champion of citizens' rights – no: it was purely a matter of self-interest. Pompey, as a good general, saw that by advocating such a programme, he would trap the aristocrats in a pincer movement, between his soldiers encamped beyond the walls of Rome and the common people on the city's streets. Hortensius, Catulus, Metellus and the rest would have no choice but to concede both Pompey's consulship and the tribunes' restoration, or risk annihilation. And once they did, Pompey could send his army home, and if necessary rule by circumventing the senate and appealing directly to the people. He would be unassailable. It was, as Cicero described it to me, a brilliant stroke, and he had seen it in that flash of insight as he sat on Palicanus's couch.

'What exactly would be in it for me?' asked Cicero.

'A reprieve for your client.'

'And nothing else?'

'That would depend on how good you were. I cannot make specific promises. That will have to wait until Pompey himself gets back.'

'It is rather a weak offer, if I may say so, my dear Palicanus.'

'Well, you are in rather a weak position, if I may say so, my dear Cicero.'

Cicero stood. I could see he was put out. 'I can always walk away,' he said.

'And leave your client to die in agony on one of Verres's crosses?' Palicanus also stood. 'I doubt it, Cicero. I doubt you are that hard.' He took us out then, past Pompey as Jupiter, past Pompey as Alexander. 'I shall see you and your client at the basilica tomorrow morning,' he said, shaking hands with Cicero on the doorstep. 'After that you will be in our debt, and we shall be watching.' The door closed with a confident slam.

Cicero turned on his heel and stepped into the street. 'If that is the kind of art he puts on public display,' he said, 'what do you suppose he keeps in the latrine? And do not warn me to guard my tongue, Tiro, because I do not care who hears it.'

He walked on ahead of me through the city gate, his hands clasped behind his back, his head hunched forward, brooding. Of course, Palicanus was right. Cicero had no choice. He could not abandon his client. But I am sure he must have been weighing the political risks of moving beyond a simple appeal to the tribunes to a full-blooded campaign for their restoration. It would cost him the support of the moderates, such as Servius.

'Well,' he said with a wry smile, when we reached his house, 'I wanted to get into a fight, and it seems I have succeeded.'

He asked Eros, the steward, where Terentia was, and looked relieved when he learned she was still in her room. At least that saved him from having to tell her the news for a few more hours. We went into his study, and he had just started dictating to me his speech to the tribunes – 'Gentlemen, it is an honour to stand before you for the first time' – when we heard shouts and a thump from the entrance. Cicero, who always liked to think on his feet and was prowling around, ran out to find out what was happening. I hurried after him. Six rough-looking fellows were crowded in the vestibule, all wielding sticks. Eros was rolling on the ground, clutching his stomach, with blood pouring from a split lip. Another stranger, armed not with a stick but with an official-looking document, stepped up to Cicero and announced that he had the authority to search the house.

'The authority of whom?' Cicero was calm – calmer than I would have been in his shoes.

'Gaius Verres, pro-praetor of Sicily, issued this warrant in Syracuse on the first day of December.' He held it up before Cicero's face for an insultingly short time. 'I am searching for the traitor Sthenius.'

'You will not find him here.'

'I shall be the judge of that.'

'And who are you?'

'Timarchides, freedman of Verres, and I shall not be kept talking while he escapes. You,' he said, turning to the nearest of his men, 'secure the front. You two take the back. The rest of you come with me. We shall start with your study, Senator, if you have no objection.'

Very soon the house was filled with the sounds of the search – boots on marble tile and wooden board, the screams of the female slaves, harsh male voices, the occasional crash as something was knocked and broken. Timarchides worked his way through the study upending document cases, watched by Cicero from the door.

'He is hardly likely to be in one of those,' said Cicero. 'He is not a dwarf.'

Finding nothing in the study, they moved on up the stairs to the senator's spartan bedroom and dressing room. 'Be assured, Timarchides,' said Cicero, still keeping his cool, but obviously with greater difficulty as he watched his bed being overturned, 'that you and your master will be repaid for this, one hundredfold.'

'Your wife,' said Timarchides. 'Where does she sleep?'

'Ah,' said Cicero quietly. 'Now I really would not do that, if I were you.'

But Timarchides had his blood up. He had come a long way, was finding nothing, and Cicero's manner was chafing on his nerves. He ran along the passage, followed by three of his men, shouted, 'Sthenius! We know you're in there!' and threw open the door of Terentia's bedroom. The screech that followed and the sharp crack of her hand across the invader's face rang through the house. Then came such a volley of colourful abuse, delivered in such an imperious voice, and at such a volume, that Terentia's distant ancestor who had commanded the Roman line against Hannibal at Cannae a century and a half before must surely have sat bolt upright in his tomb. 'She fell on that wretched freedman,' Cicero used to say afterwards, 'like a tigress out of a tree. I almost felt sorry for the fellow.'

Timarchides must have realised his mission had failed and decided to cut his losses, for in short order he and his ruffians were retreating down the stairs, followed by Terentia, with little Tullia hiding behind her skirts and occasionally brandishing her tiny fists in imitation of her mother. We heard Timarchides calling to his men, heard a running of feet and the slam of the door, and after that the old house was silent except for the distant wailing of one of the maids.

'And this,' said Terentia, taking a deep breath and rounding on Cicero, her cheeks flushed, her narrow bosom rising and falling rapidly, '*this* is all because you spoke in the senate on behalf of that dreary Sicilian?'

'I am afraid it is, my darling,' he said sadly. 'They are determined to scare me off.'

'Well, you must not let them, Cicero.' She put her hands on either side of his head, gripped it tight – a gesture not at all of tenderness but of passion – and glared furiously into his eyes. 'You must *crush* them.'

The upshot was that the following morning, when we set out for the Basilica Porcia, Quintus was on one side of Cicero, Lucius was on the other, and behind him, magnificently turned out in the formal dress of a Roman matron and carried in a litter hired specially for the occasion, came Terentia. It was the first time she had ever troubled to see him speak, and I swear he was more nervous of appearing before her than he was of appearing before the tribunes. He had a big retinue of clients to back him up as he left the house, and we picked up more along the way, especially after we stopped off halfway down the Argiletum to retrieve Sthenius from his bolt-hole. A hundred or more of us must have surged across the forum and into the tribunes' hall. Timarchides followed at a distance with his gang, but there were far too many of us for him to risk an attack, and he knew that if he tried anything in the basilica itself he would be torn to bits.

The ten tribunes were on the bench. The hall was full. Palicanus rose and read the motion – *That in the opinion of this body the proclamation of banishment from Rome does not apply to Sthenius* – and Cicero stepped up to the tribunal, his face clenched white with nerves. Quite often he was sick before a major speech, as he had been on this occasion, pausing at the door to vomit into the gutter. The first part of his oration was more or less the same as the one he had given in the senate, except that now he could call his client to the front and gesture to him as need arose to stir the pity of the judges. And certainly a more perfect illustration of a dejected victim was never paraded before a Roman court than Sthenius on that day. But Cicero's peroration was entirely new, not at all like his normal forensic oratory, and marked a decisive shift in his political position. By the time he reached it, his nerves were gone and his delivery was on fire.

'There is an old saying, gentlemen, among the merchants in the Macellum, that a fish rots from the head down, and if there is something rotten in Rome today – and who can doubt that there is? – I tell you plainly that it has started in the head. It has started at the top. It has started in the senate.' Loud cheers and stamping of feet. 'And there is only one thing to do with a stinking, rotten fish-head, those merchants will tell you, and that is to cut it off – cut it off and throw it out!' Renewed cheers. 'But it will need quite a knife to sever this head, for it is an aristocratic head, and we all know what they are like!' Laughter. 'It is a head swollen with the poison of corruption and bloated with pride and arrogance. And it will need a strong hand to wield that knife, and it will need a steady nerve besides, because they have necks of brass, these aristocrats, I tell you: brass necks, all of them!' Laughter. 'But that man will come. He is not far away. Your powers will be restored, I promise you, however hard the struggle.' A few brighter sparks started shouting out Pompey's name. Cicero held up his hand, three fingers outstretched. 'To you now falls the great test of being worthy of this fight. Show courage, gentlemen. Make a start today. Strike a blow against tyranny. Free my client. And then free Rome!'

Later, Cicero was so embarrassed by the rabble-rousing nature of this speech that he asked me to destroy the only copy, so I must confess I am writing here from memory. But I recollect it very clearly – the force of his words, the passion of his delivery, the excitement of the crowd as he whipped them up, the wink he exchanged with Palicanus as he left the tribunal, and Terentia not moving a muscle, simply staring straight ahead as the common people around her erupted in applause. Timarchides, who had been standing at the back, slipped out before the ovation ended, no doubt to ride at full gallop to Sicily and report to his master what had happened – for the motion, I need hardly add, was passed by ten votes to nil, and Sthenius, as long as he stayed in Rome, was safe.

IV

Another of Cicero's maxims was that if you must do something unpopular, you might as well do it wholeheartedly, for in politics there is no credit to be won by timidity. Thus, although he had never previously expressed an opinion about Pompey or the tribunes, neither cause now had a more devoted adherent. And the Pompeians were naturally delighted to welcome such a brilliant recruit to their ranks.

That winter was long and cold in the city, and for no one, I suspect, more than Terentia. Her personal code of honour required her to support her husband against the enemies who had invaded her home. But having sat among the smelly poor, and listened to Cicero haranguing her own class, she now found her drawing room and dining room invaded at all hours by his new political cronies: men from the uncouth north who spoke with ugly accents and who liked to put their feet up on her furniture and plot late into the night. Palicanus was the chief of these, and on his second visit to the house in January he brought with him one of the new praetors, Lucius Afranius, a fellow senator from Pompey's homeland of Picenum. Cicero went out of his way to be charming, and in earlier years, Terentia, too, would have felt it an honour to have a praetor in her house. But Afranius had no decent family or breeding of any sort. He actually had the nerve to ask her if she liked dancing, and, when she drew back in horror, declared that personally he loved nothing more. He pulled up his toga, showed her his legs and demanded to know if she had ever seen a finer pair of calves.

These men were Pompey's representatives in Rome and they brought with them something of the whiff and manners of the army camp. They were blunt to the point of brutality; but then, perhaps, they had to be, given what they were planning. Palicanus's daughter, Lollia – a blowsy young piece, very much not to Terentia's taste – occasionally joined the menfolk, for she was married to Aulus Gabinius, another of Pompey's Picenean lieutenants, currently serving with the general in Spain. This Gabinius was a link with the legionary commanders, who in turn provided intelligence on the loyalty of the centuries – an important consideration, for, as Afranius put it, there was no point in bringing the army all the way to Rome to restore the powers of the tribunes, only to find that the legions would happily go over to the aristocrats if they were offered a big enough bribe.

At the end of January, Gabinius sent word that the final rebel strongholds of Uxama and Calagurris had been taken, and that Pompey was ready to march his legions home. Cicero had been active among the *pedarii* for weeks, drawing senators aside as they waited for debates, convincing them that the rebel slaves in the Italian north posed a gathering threat to their businesses and trade. He lobbied well. When the issue came up for discussion in the senate, despite the intense opposition of the aristocrats and the supporters of Crassus, the house voted narrowly to let Pompey keep his Spanish army intact and bring it back to the mother country to crush Spartacus's northern recruits. From that point on, the consulship was as good as his, and on the day the motion passed, Cicero came home smiling. True, he had been snubbed by the aristocrats, who now loathed him more than any other man in Rome, and the presiding consul, the super-snobbish Publius Cornelius Lentulus Sura, had even refused to recognise him when he tried to speak. But what did that matter? He was in the inner circle of Pompey the Great, and, as every fool knows, the quickest way to get ahead in politics is to get yourself close to the man at the top.

Throughout these busy months, I am ashamed to say, we neglected Sthenius of Thermae. He would often turn up in the mornings, and hang around the senator for the entire day in the hope of securing an interview. He was still living in Terentia's squalid tenement block. He had little money. He was unable to venture beyond the walls of the city, as his immunity ended at the boundaries of Rome. He had not shaved his beard nor cut his hair, nor, by the smell of him, changed his clothes since October. He reeked – not of madness exactly, but of obsession, forever producing small pieces of paper, which he would fumble and drop in the street.

Cicero kept making excuses not to see him. Doubtless he felt he had discharged his obligations already. But that was not the sole explanation. The truth is that politics is a country idiot, capable of concentrating only on one thing at a time, and poor Sthenius had become yesterday's topic. All anyone could talk about now was the coming confrontation between Crassus and Pompey; the plight of the Sicilian was a bore.

In the late spring, Crassus – having finally defeated the main force of Spartacus's rebels in the heel of Italy, killing Spartacus and taking six thousand prisoners – had started marching towards Rome. Very soon afterwards, Pompey crossed the Alps and wiped out the slave rebellion in the north. He sent a letter to the consuls which was read out in the senate, giving only the faintest credit to Crassus for his achievement and instead proclaiming that it was really he who had finished off the slave war 'utterly and entirely'. The signal to his supporters could not have been clearer: only one general would be triumphing that year, and it would not be Marcus Crassus. Finally, lest there be any remaining doubt, at the end of his dispatch Pompey announced that he too was moving on Rome. Little wonder that amid these stirring historical events, Sthenius was forgotten.

Sometime in May, it must have been, or possibly early June – I cannot find the exact date – a messenger arrived at Cicero's house bearing a letter. With some reluctance the man let me take it, but refused to leave the premises until he had received a reply: those, he said, were his orders. Although he was wearing civilian clothes, I could tell he was in the army. I carried the message into the study and watched Cicero's expression darken as he read it. He handed it to me, and when I saw the opening – *From Marcus Licinius Crassus, Imperator, to Marcus Tullius Cicero: Greetings* – I understood the reason for his frown. Not that there was anything threatening in the letter. It was simply an invitation to meet the victorious general the next morning on the road to Rome, close to the town of Lanuvium, at the eighteenth milestone.

'Can I refuse?' asked Cicero, but then he answered his own question. 'No, I can't. That would be interpreted as a mortal insult.'

'Presumably he is going to ask for your support.'

'Really?' said Cicero sarcastically. 'What makes you think that?'

'Could you not offer him some limited encouragement, as long as it does not clash with your undertakings to Pompey?'

'No. That is the trouble. Pompey has made that very clear. He expects absolute loyalty. So Crassus will pose the question: "Are you for me or against me?" and then I shall face the politician's worst nightmare: the requirement to give a straight answer.' He sighed. 'But we shall have to go, of course.'

We left soon after dawn the following morning, in a two-wheeled open carriage, with Cicero's valet doubling up as coachman for the occasion. It was the most perfect time of day at the most perfect time of year, already hot enough for people to be bathing in the public pool beside the Capena Gate, but cool enough for the air to be refreshing. There was none of the usual dust thrown up from the road. The leaves of the olive trees were a glossy fresh green. Even the tombs that line the Appian Way so thickly along that particular stretch just beyond the wall gleamed bright and cheerful in the first hour of the sun. Normally, Cicero liked to draw my attention to some particular monument and give me a lecture on it – the statue of Scipio Africanus, perhaps, or the tomb of Horatia, murdered by her brother for displaying excessive grief at the death of her lover. But on this morning his usual good spirits had deserted him. He was too preoccupied with Crassus.

'Half of Rome belongs to him – these tombs as well, I should not wonder. You could house an entire family in one of these! Why not? Crassus would! Have you ever seen him in operation? Let us say he hears there is a fire raging and spreading through a particular neighbourhood: he sends a team of slaves round all the apartments, offering to buy out the owners for next to nothing. When the poor fellows have agreed, he sends another team equipped with water-carts to put the fires out! That is just one of his tricks. Do you know what Sicinnius calls him – always bearing in mind, by the way, that Sicinnius is afraid of no one? He calls Crassus "the most dangerous bull in the herd".'

His chin sank on to his chest and that was all he said until we had passed the eighth milestone and were deep into open country, not far from Bovillae. That was when he drew my attention to something odd: military pickets guarding what looked like small timber yards. We had already passed four or five, spaced out at regular half-mile intervals, and the further down the road we went, the greater the activity seemed – hammering, sawing, digging. It was Cicero who eventually supplied the answer. The legionaries were making crosses. Soon afterwards, we encountered a column of Crassus's infantry tramping towards us, heading for Rome, and we had to pull over to the far side of the road to let them pass. Behind the legionaries came a long, stumbling procession of prisoners, hundreds of them, vanquished rebel slaves, their arms pinioned behind their backs

– a terrible, emaciated, grey army of ghosts, heading for a fate which we had seen being prepared for them, but of which they were presumably ignorant. Our driver muttered a spell to ward off evil, flicked his whip over the flanks of the horses and we jolted forwards. A mile or so later, the killing started, in little huddles off on either side of the road, where the prisoners were being nailed to the crosses. I try not to remember it, but it comes back to me occasionally in my dreams, especially, for some reason, the crosses with their impaled and shrieking victims being pulled upright by soldiers heaving on ropes, each wooden upright dropping with a thud into the deep hole that had been dug for it. That I remember, and also the moment when we passed over the crest of a hill and saw a long avenue of crosses running straight ahead for mile after mile, shimmering in the mid-morning heat, the air seeming to tremble with the moans of the dying, the buzz of the flies and the screams of the circling crows.

'So this is why he dragged me out of Rome,' muttered Cicero furiously, 'to intimidate me by showing me these poor wretches.' He had gone very white, for he was squeamish about pain and death, even when inflicted on animals, and for that reason tried to avoid attending the games. I suppose this also explains his aversion to all matters military. He had done the bare minimum of army service in his youth, and was quite incapable of wielding a sword or hurling a javelin; throughout his career he had to put up with the taunt that he was a draft-dodger.

At the eighteenth milestone, surrounded by a ditch and ramparts, we found the bulk of Crassus's legions encamped beside the road, giving off that dusty smell of sweat and leather which always lingers over an army in the field. Standards fluttered over the gate, beside which Crassus's own son, Publius, then a brisk young junior officer, was waiting to conduct Cicero to the general's tent. A couple of other senators were being shown out as we arrived, and suddenly there was Crassus himself at the entrance, instantly recognisable – 'Old Baldhead', as his soldiers called him – wearing the scarlet cloak of a commander, despite the heat. He was all affability, waving goodbye to his previous visitors, wishing them a safe journey, and greeting us equally heartily – even me, whose hand he shook as warmly as if I were a senator myself, rather than a slave who might in other circumstances have been howling from one of his crosses. And looking back on it, and trying to fix precisely what it was about him which made him so disconcerting, I think it was this: his indiscriminate and detached friendliness, which you knew would never waver or diminish even if he had just decided to have you killed. Cicero had told me he was worth at least two hundred million, but Crassus talked as easily to any man as a farmer leaning on a gate, and his army tent – like his house in Rome – was modest and unadorned.

He led us inside – me as well: he insisted – apologising for the gruesome spectacle along the Appian Way, but he felt it was necessary. He seemed particularly proud of the logistics which had enabled him to crucify six thousand men along three hundred and fifty miles of road, from the victorious battlefield to the gates of Rome, without, as he put it, 'any scenes of violence'. That was seventeen crucifixions to the mile, which meant one hundred and seventeen paces between each cross – he had a wonderful head for figures – and the trick was not to cause a panic among the prisoners, or else one would have had another battle on one's hands. So, after every mile – or sometimes two or three, varying it to avoid arousing suspicion – the requisite number of recaptured slaves would be halted by the roadside as the rest of the column marched on, and not until their comrades were out of sight did the executions begin. In this way the job had been done with the minimum amount of disruption for the maximum deterrent effect – the Appian Way being the busiest road in Italy.

'I doubt whether many slaves, once they hear of this, will rise against Rome in the future,' smiled Crassus. 'Would you, for example?' he said to me, and when I replied very fervently that I most certainly would not, he pinched my cheek and ruffled my hair. The touch of his hand made my flesh shrivel. 'Is he for sale?' he asked Cicero. 'I like him. I'd give you a good price for him. Let us see …' He named an amount that was at least ten times what I was worth, and for a terrible moment I thought the offer might be accepted and I would lose my place in Cicero's life – a banishment I could not have borne.

'He is not for sale, at any price,' said Cicero. The journey had upset him; there was a hoarseness to his voice. 'And to avoid any misunderstanding, Imperator, I believe I should tell you right away that I have pledged my support to Pompey the Great.'

'Pompey the who?' mocked Crassus. 'Pompey the *Great*? As great as what?'

'I would rather not say,' replied Cicero. 'Comparisons can be odious.' At which remark even Crassus, for all his ironclad bonhomie, drew back his head a little.

There are certain politicians who cannot stand to be in the same room as one another, even if mutual self-interest dictates that they should try to get along, and it quickly became apparent to me that Cicero and Crassus were two such men. This is what the Stoics fail to grasp when they assert that reason rather than emotion should play the dominant part in human affairs. I am afraid the reverse is true, and always will be, even – perhaps especially – in the supposedly calculating world of politics. And if reason cannot rule in politics, what hope is there for it in any other sphere? Crassus had summoned Cicero in order to seek his friendship. Cicero had come determined to keep Crassus's goodwill. Yet neither man could quite conceal his distaste for the other, and the meeting was a disaster.

'Let us get to the point, shall we?' said Crassus, after he had invited Cicero to sit down. He took off his cloak and handed it to his son, then settled on the couch. 'There are two things I would like to ask of you, Cicero. One is your support for my candidacy for the consulship. I am forty-four, so I am more than old enough, and I believe this ought to be my year. The other is a triumph. For both I am willing to pay whatever is your current market rate. Normally, as you know, I insist on an exclusive contract, but, given your prior commitments, I suppose I shall have to settle for half of you. Half of Cicero,' he added with a slight bow of his head, 'being worth twice as much as the entirety of most men.'

'That is flattering, Imperator,' responded Cicero, bridling at the implication. 'Thank you. My slave cannot be bought, but I can, is that it? Perhaps you will allow me to think about it.'

'What is there to think about? Every citizen has two votes for the consulship. Give one to me and one to whomever else you please. Just make sure your friends all follow your example. Tell them Crassus never forgets those who oblige him. Or those who disoblige him, for that matter.'

'I would still have to think about it, I am afraid.'

Some shadow moved across Crassus's friendly face, like a pike in clear water. 'And my triumph?'

'Personally, I absolutely believe you have earned the honour. But, as you know, to qualify for a triumph it is necessary for the military action concerned to have extended the dominion of the state. The senate has consulted the precedents. Apparently, it is not enough merely to regain territory that has been lost previously. For example, when Fulvius won back Capua after its defection to Hannibal, he was not allowed a triumph.' Cicero explained all this with what seemed genuine regret.

'But this is a technicality, surely? If Pompey can be a consul without meeting any of the necessary requirements, why cannot I at least have a triumph? I know you are unfamiliar with the difficulties of military command, or even,' he added sinuously, 'with military service, but surely you would agree that I have met all the other requirements – killed five thousand in battle, fought under the auspices, been saluted imperator by the legions, brought peace to the province, withdrawn my troops? If someone of influence such as yourself were to put down a motion in the senate, he would find me very generous.'

There was a long pause, and I wondered how Cicero would escape from his dilemma.

'*There* is your triumph, Imperator!' he said suddenly, pointing in the direction of the Appian Way. '*That* is the monument to the kind of man you are! For as long as Romans have tongues to speak, they will remember the name of Crassus as the man who crucified six thousand slaves over three hundred and fifty miles, with one hundred and seventeen paces between the crosses. None of our other great generals would ever have done such a thing. Scipio Africanus, Pompey, Lucullus …' He flicked them away with contempt. 'None of them would even have *thought* of it.'

Cicero sat back and smiled at Crassus; Crassus smiled in return. Time went on. I felt myself begin to sweat. It became a contest to see whose smile would crack first. Eventually, Crassus stood and held out his hand to Cicero. 'Thank you so much for coming, my young friend,' he said.

When the senate met a few days later to determine honours, Cicero voted with the majority to deny Crassus a triumph. The vanquisher of Spartacus had to settle for an ovation, an altogether second-class award. Rather than entering the city riding on a chariot drawn by four horses, he would have to walk in; the customary fanfare of trumpets would be replaced by the trilling of flutes; and instead of the usual wreath of laurel he would only be permitted to wear myrtle. 'If the man has any sense of honour,' said Cicero, 'he will turn it down.' I need hardly add that Crassus quickly sent word of his acceptance.

Once the discussion moved on to honours for Pompey, Afranius pulled a clever trick. He used his praetorian rank to rise early in the debate and declare that Pompey would accept with humble gratitude whatever the house chose to grant him: he would be arriving outside the city with ten thousand men the following day, and hoped to thank as many of the senators in person as possible. *Ten thousand men?* After that, even the aristocrats were unwilling publicly to snub the conqueror of Spain, and the consuls were instructed by a unanimous vote to attend on Pompey at his earliest convenience and offer him a full triumph.

The next morning Cicero dressed with even more care than usual and consulted with Quintus and Lucius as to what line he should take in his discussions with Pompey. He decided on a bold approach. The following year he would be thirty-six, just eligible to stand for an aedileship of Rome, four of which were elected annually. The functions of the office – the maintenance of public buildings and public order, the celebration of various festivals, the issuing of trading licences, distribution of grain and so on – were a useful means of consolidating political support. That was what he would ask for, it was agreed: Pompey's backing for an aedileship. 'I believe I have earned it,' said Cicero.

After that was settled, we joined the throngs of citizens heading west towards the Field of Mars, where it was rumoured that Pompey intended to halt his legions. (It was, at least in those days, illegal to possess military *imperium* within the sacred boundaries of Rome; thus both Crassus and Pompey were obliged, if they wanted to keep command of their armies, to do their scheming from beyond the city's walls.) There was intense interest in seeing what the great man looked like, for the Roman Alexander, as Pompey's followers called him, had been away fighting for nearly seven years. Some wondered how much he might have changed; others – of whom I was one – had never set eyes on him at all. Cicero had already heard from Palicanus that Pompey intended to set up his headquarters in the Villa Publica, the government guest house next to the voting enclosures, and that was where we made for – Cicero, Quintus, Lucius and I.

The place was encircled with a double cordon of soldiers, and by the time we had fought our way through the crowds to the perimeter wall, no one was being allowed into the grounds unless they had authorisation. Cicero was most offended that none of the guards had even heard of him, and we were lucky that Palicanus was at that moment passing close to the gate: he was able to fetch his son-in-law, the legionary commander Gabinius, to vouch for us. Once we were inside we found that half of official Rome was already there, strolling around the shaded colonnades, humming with curiosity at being this close to power.

'Pompey the Great arrived in the middle of the night,' Palicanus informed us, adding grandly: 'The consuls are with him now.' He promised to return with more information as soon as he had any, then disappeared, self-importantly, between the sentries into the house.

Several hours passed, during which there was no further sign of Palicanus. Instead we noted the messengers rushing in and out, hungrily witnessed food being delivered, saw the consuls leave, and then watched Catulus and Isauricus, the elder statesmen, arrive. Waiting senators, knowing Cicero to be a fervent partisan of Pompey and believing him to be in his inner counsels, kept coming up to him and asking what was really happening. 'All in good time,' he would reply, 'all in good time.' Eventually I guess he must have found this formula embarrassing, for he sent me off to find him a stool, and when I returned, he set it against a pillar, leaned back and closed his eyes. Towards the middle of the afternoon, Hortensius arrived, squeezing his way through the curious onlookers held back by the soldiers, and was admitted immediately into the villa. When he was followed soon afterwards by the three Metellus brothers, it was impossible even for Cicero to pretend this was anything other than a humiliation. Brother Quintus was dispatched to see if he could pick up any gossip outside the senate house, while Cicero paced up and down the colonnades and ordered me for the twentieth time to try to find Palicanus or Afranius or Gabinius – anyone who could get him in to that meeting.

I hung around the crowded entrance, rising on tiptoe, trying to see over all the jostling heads. A messenger came out and briefly left the door half open, and for a moment I glimpsed white-robed figures, laughing and talking, standing around a heavy marble table with documents spread across it. But then I was distracted by a commotion from the street. With shouts of 'Hail Imperator!' and much cheering and yelling, the gate was swung open and, flanked by bodyguards, in stepped Crassus. He took off his plumed helmet and handed it to one of his lictors, wiped his forehead and looked around him. His gaze fell upon Cicero. He gave him a slight nod of the head accompanied by another of his plain man's smiles, and that was one of the few occasions, I should say, when Cicero was entirely lost for words. Then Crassus swept his scarlet cloak around him – rather magnificently, it must be admitted – and marched into the Villa Publica, while Cicero plonked down heavily on his stool.

I have frequently observed this curious aspect of power: that it is often when one is physically closest to its source that one is least well informed as to what is actually going on. For example, I have seen senators obliged to step out of the senate chamber and dispatch their slaves to the vegetable market to find out what was happening in the city they were supposedly running. Or I have known of generals, surrounded by legates and ambassadors, who have been reduced to intercepting passing shepherds to discover the latest events on the battlefield. So it was that afternoon with Cicero, who sat within twenty feet of the room in which Rome was being carved up like a cooked chicken, but who had to hear the news of what had been decided from Quintus, who had picked it up from a magistrate in the forum, who had heard it from a senate clerk.

'It's bad,' said Quintus, although one could already tell that from his face. 'Pompey for consul and the rights of the tribunes restored, and with no opposition to be offered by the aristocrats. But in return – listen to this – *in return*, Hortensius and Quintus Metellus are to be consuls in the following year, with the full support of Pompey, while Lucius Metellus is to replace Verres as governor of Sicily. Finally, Crassus – *Crassus!* – is to rule with Pompey as joint consul, with both their armies to be dissolved on the day they take office.'

'But I should have been in there,' said Cicero, staring with dismay at the villa. *'I should have been in there!'*

'Marcus,' said his brother sadly, putting his hand on his shoulder, 'none of them would have you.'

Cicero looked stunned at the scale of this reversal – himself excluded, his enemies rewarded, Crassus elevated to the consulship – but then he shook his shoulder free and made angrily towards the doors. And perhaps his career might have been ended there by the sword of one of Pompey's sentries, for I believe, in his desperation, Cicero had resolved to force his way through to the negotiating table and demand his share. But it was too late. The big men, their deal struck, were already coming out, their aides scampering ahead of them, their guards stamping to attention as they passed. Crassus emerged first, and then, from the shadows, Pompey, his identity obvious at once not only from the aura of power around him

– the way the proximate air seemed almost to crackle as he moved – but from the cast of his features. He had a broad face, wide cheekbones, and thick wavy hair that rose in a quiff, like the prow of a ship. It was a face full of weight and command, and he possessed the body to go with it, wide shoulders and a strong chest – the torso of a wrestler. I could see why, when he was younger, and famed for his ruthlessness, he had been called the Butcher Boy.

And so off they went, Baldhead and the Butcher Boy, noticeably neither talking nor even looking at one another, heading towards the gate, which swung open as they approached. A stampede of senators, seeing what was happening, set off in pursuit, and we were swept along in the rush, borne out of the Villa Publica and into what felt like a solid wall of noise and heat. Twenty thousand people must have gathered on the Field of Mars that afternoon, all bellowing their approval. A narrow avenue had been cleared by the soldiers, straining arms chain-linked at the elbows, feet scrabbling in the dust to hold back the crowd. It was just wide enough for Pompey and Crassus to walk abreast, although what their expressions were and whether they had started talking I could not see, as we were far back in the procession. They made slow progress towards the tribunal, where the officials traditionally stand at election time. Pompey heaved himself up first, to a renewed surge of applause, which he basked in for a while, turning his wide and beaming face this way and that, like a cat in sunshine. Then he reached down and hauled Crassus up after him. At this demonstration of unity between the two notorious rivals, the crowd let out another roar, and it came again and even louder when Pompey seized hold of Crassus's hand and raised it above his head.

'What a sickening spectacle,' said Cicero. He had to shout into my ear to make himself heard. 'The consulship demanded and conceded at the point of the sword. We are witnessing the beginning of the end of the republic, Tiro, remember my words!' I could not help reflecting, however, that if *he* had been in that conference, and had helped engineer this joint ticket, he would now be hailing it as a masterpiece of statecraft.

Pompey waved at the crowd for quiet, then began speaking in his parade-ground voice. 'People of Rome! The leaders of the senate have graciously conveyed to me the offer of a triumph, and I am pleased to accept it. They have also told me that I will be allowed to stand as a candidate for the consulship, and I am pleased to accept that as well. The only thing that pleases me more is that my old friend Marcus Licinius Crassus will be my colleague.' He concluded by promising that the following year he would hold a great festival of games, dedicated to Hercules, in honour of his victories in Spain.

Well, these were fine words, no doubt, but he spoke them all too quickly, forgetting to leave the necessary pause after every sentence, which meant that those few who had managed to hear what he said had no opportunity to repeat it to those behind who had not. I doubt if more than a few hundred out of that vast assembly knew what he was saying, but they cheered in any case, and they cheered even more when Crassus immediately, and cunningly, upstaged him.

'I hereby dedicate,' he said, in the booming voice of a trained orator, 'at the same time as Pompey's games – on the same day as Pompey's games – one tenth of my fortune – one tenth of my *entire* fortune – to providing free food to the people of Rome – free food for every one of you, for *three months* – and a great banquet in the streets – a banquet for every citizen – a banquet in honour of Hercules!'

The crowd went into fresh ecstasies. 'The villain,' said Cicero admiringly. 'A tenth of his fortune is a bribe of twenty million! But cheap at the price. See how he turns a weak position into a strong one? I bet you were not expecting *that*,' he called out to Palicanus, who was struggling towards us from the tribunal. 'He has made himself look Pompey's equal. You should never have allowed him a platform.'

'Come and meet the imperator,' urged Palicanus. 'He wants to thank you in person.' I could see Cicero was in two minds, but Palicanus was insistent, tugging at his sleeve, and I suppose he thought he ought to try to salvage something from the day.

'Is he going to make a speech?' shouted Cicero, as we followed Palicanus towards the tribunal.

'He doesn't really make speeches,' replied Palicanus over his shoulder. 'Not yet, anyway.'

'That is a mistake. They will expect him to say something.'

'Well, they will just have to be disappointed, won't they?'

'What a waste,' Cicero muttered to me in disgust. 'What I would not give to have an audience such as this! How often do you see so many voters in one place?' But Pompey had little experience of public oratory, and besides, he was accustomed to commanding men, not pandering to them. With a final wave to the crowd, he clambered down from the platform. Crassus followed suit and the applause slowly died away. There was a palpable sense of anticlimax, as people stood around wondering what they should do next. 'What a waste,' repeated Cicero. '*I* would have given them a show.'

Behind the tribunal was a small enclosed area, where it was the custom for the magistrates to wait before going up to officiate on election-day. Palicanus conducted us into it, past the guards, and here, a moment or two later, Pompey himself appeared. A young black slave handed him a cloth and he began dabbing at his sweating face and wiping the back of his neck. A dozen senators waited to greet him and Palicanus thrust Cicero into the middle of the line, then drew back with Quintus, Lucius and myself to watch. Pompey was moving down the queue, shaking hands with each of the senators in turn, Afranius at his back to tell him who was who. 'Good to meet you,' said Pompey. 'Good to meet you. Good to meet you.' As he came closer I had a better opportunity to study him. He had a noble face, no question of it, but there was also a disagreeable vanity in those fleshy features, and his grand, distracted manner only emphasised his obvious boredom at meeting all these tedious civilians. He reached Cicero very quickly.

'This is Marcus Cicero, Imperator,' said Afranius.

'Good to meet you.'

He was about to move on, but Afranius took his elbow and whispered, 'Cicero is considered one of the city's foremost advocates, and was very useful to us in the senate.'

'Was he? Well, then – keep up the good work.'

'I shall,' said Cicero quickly, 'for I hope next year to be aedile.'

'Aedile?' Pompey scoffed at the very idea. 'No, no, I do not think so. I have other plans in that direction. But I'm sure we can always find a use for a clever lawyer.'

And with that he really did move on – 'Good to meet you ... Good to meet you ...' – leaving Cicero staring straight ahead and swallowing hard.

V

That night, for the first and last time in all my years in his service, Cicero drank too much. I could hear him arguing over dinner with Terentia – not one of their normal, witty, icily courteous disputes, but a row which echoed throughout the small house, as she berated him for his stupidity in ever trusting such an obviously dishonourable gang: Piceneans, all of them, not even proper Romans! 'But then of course, you are not a proper Roman either' – a dig at Cicero's lowly provincial origins which invariably got under his skin. Ominously, I did not hear what he said back to her – it was delivered in such a quiet, malevolent tone – but whatever it was, it must have been devastating, for Terentia, who was not a woman easily shaken, ran from the dining room in tears and disappeared upstairs.

I thought it best to leave him well alone. But an hour later I heard a crash, and when I went in Cicero was on his feet and swaying slightly, staring at a broken plate. The front of his tunic was stained with wine. 'I really do not feel well,' he said.

I got him up to his room by hooking his arm over my shoulder – not an easy procedure, as he was heavier than I – laid him on his bed, and unlaced his shoes. 'Divorce,' he muttered into his pillow, 'that is the answer, Tiro – divorce, and if I have to leave the senate because I can't afford it – well, so what? Nobody would miss me. Just another "new man" who came to nothing. Oh dear, Tiro!' I managed to get his chamber pot in front of him just before he was sick. Head down, he addressed his own vomit. 'We shall go to Athens, my dear fellow, and live with Atticus and study philosophy and no one here will miss us …' these last few words all running together into a long, self-pitying burble of slurred syllables and sibilant consonants which no shorthand symbol of mine could ever have reconstructed. I set the pot beside him, blew out the lamp and he was snoring even before I reached the door. I confess I went to bed that night with a troubled heart.

And yet, the next morning, I was woken at exactly the usual pre-dawn hour by the sound of him going through his exercises – a little more slowly than usual, perhaps, but then it was awfully early, for this was the height of summer, and he can hardly have had more than a few hours' sleep. Such was the nature of the man. Failure was the fuel of his ambition. Each time he suffered a humiliation – be it as an advocate in his early days when his constitution failed him, or on his return from Sicily, or now, with Pompey's offhand treatment – the fire in him was temporarily banked, but only that it might flare up again even more fiercely. 'It is perseverance,' he used to say, 'and not genius that takes a man to the top. Rome is full of unrecognised geniuses. Only perseverance enables you to move forward in the world.' And so I heard him preparing for another day of struggle in the Roman forum and felt the old, familiar rhythm of the house reassert itself.

I dressed. I lit the lamps. I told the porter to open the front door. I checked the callers. Then I went into Cicero's study and gave him his list of clients. No mention was ever made, either then or in the future, of what had happened the previous night, and I suspect this helped draw us even closer. To be sure, he looked a little green, and he had to screw up his eyes to focus on the names, but otherwise he was entirely normal. 'Sthenius!' he groaned, when he saw who was waiting, as usual, in the tablinum. 'May the gods have mercy upon us!'

'He is not alone,' I warned him. 'He has brought two more Sicilians with him.'

'You mean to say he is multiplying?' He coughed to clear his throat. 'Right. Let us have him in first and get rid of him once and for all.'

As in some curious recurring dream from which one cannot wake, I found myself yet again conducting Sthenius of Thermae into Cicero's presence. His companions he introduced as Heraclius of Syracuse and Epicrates of Bidis. Both were old men, dressed like him in the dark garb of mourning, with uncut hair and beards.

'Now listen, Sthenius,' said Cicero sternly, after he had shaken hands with the grim-looking trio, 'this has got to stop.'

But Sthenius was in that strange and remote private kingdom into which outside sounds seldom penetrate: the land of the obsessive litigant. 'I am most grateful to you, Senator. Firstly, now that I have obtained the court records from Syracuse,' he said, pulling a piece of paper from his leather bag and thrusting it into Cicero's hands, 'you can see what the monster has done. This is what was written before the verdict of the tribunes. And this,' he said, giving him another, 'is what was written afterwards.'

With a sigh, Cicero held the two documents side by side and squinted at them. 'So what is this? This is the official record of your trial for treason, in which I see it is written that you were present during the hearing. Well, we know that is nonsense. And here ...' his words began to slow as he realised the implications, 'here it says that you were *not* present.' He looked up, his bleary eyes starting to clear. 'So Verres is falsifying the proceedings of his own court, and then he is falsifying his own falsification?'

'Exactly!' cried Sthenius. 'When he realised you had produced me before the tribunes, and that all of Rome knew I could hardly have been in Syracuse on the first day of December, he had to obliterate the record of his lie. But the first document was already on its way to me.'

'Well, well,' said Cicero, continuing to scrutinise the paper, 'perhaps he is more worried than we thought. And I see it also says here that you had a defence attorney representing you that day: "Gaius Claudius, son of Gaius Claudius, of the Palatine tribe." You are a fortunate man, to have your very own Roman lawyer. Who is he?'

'He is Verres's business manager.'

Cicero studied Sthenius for a moment or two. 'What else do you have in that bag of yours?' he said.

Out it all came then, tipped over the study floor on that hot summer's morning: letters, names, scraps of official records, scribbled notes of gossip and rumours – seven months' angry labour by three desperate men, for it transpired that Heraclius and Epicrates had also been swindled out of their estates by Verres, one worth sixty thousand, the other thirty. In both cases, Verres had abused his office to bring false accusations and secure illegal verdicts. Both had been robbed at around the same time as Sthenius. Both had been, until then, the leading men in their communities. Both had been obliged to flee the island penniless and seek refuge in Rome. Hearing of Sthenius's appearance before the tribunes, they had sought him out and proposed cooperation.

'As single victims, they were weak,' said Cicero, years later, reminiscing about the case, 'but when they joined in common cause, they found they had a network of contacts which spread across the entire island: Thermae in the north, Bidis in the south, Syracuse in the east. These were men sagacious by nature, shrewd by experience, accomplished by education, and their fellow countrymen had opened up the secrets of their suffering to them, as they would never have done to a Roman senator.'

Outwardly, Cicero still seemed the calm advocate. But as the sun grew stronger and I blew out the lamps, and as he picked up one document after another, I could sense his gathering excitement. Here was the sworn affidavit of Dio of Halaesa, from whom Verres had first demanded a bribe of ten thousand to bring in a not guilty verdict, and then stolen all his horses, tapestries and gold and silver plate. Here were the written testimonies of priests whose temples had been robbed – a bronze Apollo, signed in silver by the sculptor Myron, and presented by Scipio a century and a half earlier, stolen from the shrine of Aesculapius at Agrigentum; a statue of Ceres carried away from Catina, and of Victory from Henna; the sacking of the ancient shrine of Juno in Melita. Here was the evidence of farmers in Herbita and Agyrium, threatened with being flogged to death unless they paid protection money to Verres's agents. Here was the story of the wretched Sopater of Tyndaris, seized in midwinter by Verres's lictors and bound naked to an equestrian statue in full view of the entire community, until he and his fellow citizens agreed to hand over a valuable municipal bronze of Mercury that stood in the local gymnasium. 'It is not a province Verres is running down there,' murmured Cicero, in wonder, 'it is a fully fledged criminal state.' There were a dozen more of these grim stories.

With the agreement of the three Sicilians, I bundled the papers together and locked them in the senator's strongbox. 'It is vital, gentlemen, that not a word of this leaks out,' Cicero told them. 'By all means continue to collect statements and witnesses, but please do it discreetly. Verres has used violence and intimidation many times before, and you can be sure he will use them again to protect himself. We need to take the rascal unawares.'

'Does that mean,' asked Sthenius, hardly daring to hope, 'that you will help us?'

Cicero looked at him but did not answer.

*

Later that day, when he returned from the law courts, the senator made up his quarrel with his wife. He dispatched young Sositheus down to the old flower market in the Forum Boarium, in front of the Temple of Portunus, to buy a bouquet of fragrant summer blooms. These he then gave to little Tullia, telling her solemnly that he had a vital task for her. She was to take them in to her mother and announce they had come for her from a rough provincial admirer. ('Have you got that, Tulliola? A rough provincial admirer.') She disappeared very self-importantly into Terentia's chamber, and I guess they must have done the trick, for that evening, when – at Cicero's insistence – the couches were carried up to the roof and the family dined beneath the summer stars, the flowers had a place of honour at the centre of the table.

I know this because, as the meal was ending, I was unexpectedly sent for by Cicero. It was a still night, without a flicker of wind to disturb the candles, and the night-time sounds of Rome down in the valley mingled with the scent of the flowers in the warm June air – snatches of music, voices, the call of the watchmen along the Argiletum, the distant barking of the guard dogs set loose in the precincts of the Capitoline Triad. Lucius and Quintus were still laughing at some joke of Cicero's, and even Terentia could not quite hide her amusement as she flicked her napkin at her husband and scolded him that that was quite enough. (Pomponia, thankfully, was away visiting her brother in Athens.)

'Ah,' said Cicero, looking round, 'now here is Tiro, the master politician of us all, which means I can proceed to make my little declaration. I thought it appropriate that he should be present to hear this as well. I have decided to stand for election as aedile.'

'Oh, very good!' said Quintus, who thought it was all still part of Cicero's joke. Then he stopped laughing and said in a puzzled way, 'But that is not funny.'

'It will be if I win.'

'But you can't win. You heard what Pompey said. He doesn't want you to be a candidate.'

'It is not for Pompey to decide who is to be a candidate. We are free citizens, free to make our own choices. I choose to run for aedile.'

'There is no sense in running and losing, Marcus. That is the sort of pointlessly heroic gesture Lucius here believes in.'

'Let us drink to pointless heroism,' said Lucius, raising his glass.

'But we cannot win against Pompey's opposition,' persisted Quintus. 'And what is the point of incurring Pompey's enmity?'

To which Terentia retorted: 'After yesterday, one might better ask, "What is the point of incurring Pompey's friendship?"'

'Terentia is right,' said Cicero. 'Yesterday has taught me a lesson. Let us say I wait a year or two, hanging on Pompey's every word in the hope of favour, running errands for him. We have all seen men like that in the senate – growing older, waiting for half-promises to be fulfilled. They are hollowed out by it. And before they even know it, their moment has passed and they have nothing left with which to bargain. I would sooner clear out of politics right now than let that happen to me. If you want power, there is a time when you have to seize it. This is my time.'

'But how is this to be accomplished?'

'By prosecuting Gaius Verres for extortion.'

So there it was. I had known he would do it since early morning, and so, I am sure, had he, but he had wanted to take his time about it – to try on the decision, as it were, and see how it fitted him. And it fitted him very well. I had never seen him more determined. He looked like a man who believed he had the force of history running through him. Nobody spoke.

'Come on!' he said with a smile. 'Why the long faces? I have not lost yet! And I do not believe I shall lose, either. I had a visit from the Sicilians this morning. They have gathered the most damning testimony against Verres, have they not, Tiro? We have it under lock and key downstairs. And when we do win – think of it! I defeat Hortensius in open court, and all this "second-best advocate" nonsense is finished for ever. I assume the rank of the man I convict, according to the traditional rights of the victorious prosecutor, which means I become a praetorian overnight – so no more jumping up and down on the back benches in the senate, hoping to be called. And I place myself so firmly before the gaze of the Roman people that my election as aedile is assured. But the best thing of all is that *I* do it – I, Cicero – and I do it without owing favours to anyone, least of all Pompey the Great.'

'But what if we lose?' said Quintus, finding his voice at last. 'We are defence attorneys. We never prosecute. You have said it yourself a hundred times: defenders win friends; prosecutors just make enemies. If you don't bring Verres down, there is a good chance he will eventually be elected consul. Then he will never rest until you are destroyed.'

'That is true,' conceded Cicero. 'If you are going to kill a dangerous animal, you had better make sure you do it with the first thrust. But then – don't you see? This way I can win everything. Rank, fame, office, dignity, authority, independence, a base of clients in Rome and Sicily. It opens my way clear through to becoming consul.'

This was the first time I had heard him mention his great ambition, and it was a measure of his renewed confidence that he felt able to utter the word at last. *Consul*. For every man in public life, this was the apotheosis. The very years themselves were distinguished from one another on all official documents and foundation stones by the names of the presiding consuls. It was the nearest thing below heaven to immortality. How many nights and days must he have thought of it, dreamed of it, nursed it, since his gawky adolescence? Sometimes it is foolish to articulate an ambition too early – exposing it prematurely to the laughter and scepticism of the world can destroy it before it is even properly born. But sometimes the opposite occurs, and the very act of mentioning a thing makes it suddenly seem possible, even plausible. That was how it was that night. When Cicero pronounced the word 'consul' he planted it in the ground like a standard for us all to admire. And for a moment we glimpsed the brilliant, starry future through his eyes, and saw that he was right: that if he took down Verres, he had a chance; that he might just – with luck – go all the way to the summit.

There was much to be done over the following months, and as usual a great deal of the work fell upon me. First, I drew up a large chart of the electorate for the aedileship. At that time, this consisted of the entire Roman citizenry, divided into their thirty-five tribes. Cicero himself belonged to the Cornelia, Servius to the Lemonia, Pompey to the Clustumina, Verres to the Romilia, and so forth. A citizen cast his ballot on the Field of Mars as a member of his tribe, and the results of each tribe's vote were then read out by the magistrates. The four candidates who secured the votes of the greatest number of tribes were duly declared the winners.

There were several advantages for Cicero in this particular electoral college. For one thing – unlike the system for choosing praetors and consuls – each man's vote, whatever his wealth, counted equally, and as Cicero's strongest support was among the men of business and the teeming poor, the aristocrats would find it harder to block him. For another, it was a relatively easy electorate to canvass. Each tribe had its own headquarters somewhere in Rome, a building large enough to lay on a show or a dinner. I went back through our files and compiled a list of every man Cicero had ever defended or helped over the past six years, arranged according to his tribe. These men were then contacted and asked to make sure that the senator was invited to speak at any forthcoming tribal event. It is surely amazing how many favours there are to be called in after six years of relentless advocacy and advice. Cicero's campaign schedule was soon filled with engagements, and his working day became even longer. After the courts or the senate had adjourned, he would hurry home, quickly bathe and change, and then rush out again to give one of his rousing addresses. His slogan was 'Justice and Reform'.

Quintus, as usual, acted as Cicero's campaign manager, while cousin Lucius was entrusted with organising the case against Verres. The governor was due to return from Sicily at the end of the year, whereupon – at the very instant he entered the city – he would lose his *imperium*, and with it his immunity from prosecution. Cicero was determined to strike at the first opportunity, and, if possible, give Verres no time to dispose of evidence or intimidate witnesses. For this reason, to avoid arousing suspicion, the Sicilians stopped coming to the house, and Lucius became the conduit between Cicero and his clients, meeting them in secret at various locations across the city. I thus came to know Lucius much better, and the more I saw of him the more I liked him. He was in many respects very similar to Cicero. He was almost the same age, clever and amusing, a gifted philosopher. The two had grown up together in Arpinum, been schooled together in Rome, and travelled together in the East. But there was one huge difference: Lucius entirely lacked worldly ambition. He lived alone, in a small house full of books, and did nothing all day except read and think – a most dangerous occupation for a man which in my experience leads invariably to dyspepsia and melancholy. But oddly enough, despite his solitary disposition, he soon came to relish leaving his study every day and was so enraged by Verres's wickedness that his zeal to bring him to justice eventually exceeded even Cicero's. 'We shall make a lawyer of you yet, cousin,' Cicero remarked admiringly, after Lucius had produced yet another set of damning affidavits.

Towards the end of December an incident occurred which finally brought together, and in dramatic fashion, all these separate strands of Cicero's life. I opened the door one dark morning to find, standing at the head of the usual queue, the man we had recently seen in the tribunes' basilica, acting as defence attorney for his great-grandfather's pillar – Marcus Porcius Cato. He was alone, without a slave to attend him, and looked as though he had slept out in the street all night. (I suppose he might have done, come to think of it, although Cato's appearance was usually dishevelled – like that of a holy man or mystic – so that it was hard to tell.) Naturally, Cicero was intrigued to discover why a man of such eminent birth should have turned up on his doorstep, for Cato, bizarre as he was, dwelt at the very heart of the old republican aristocracy, connected by blood and marriage to a webwork of Servilii, Lepidi and Aemilii. Indeed, such was Cicero's pleasure at having so high-born a visitor, he went out to the tablinum himself to welcome him, and conducted him into the study personally. This was the sort of client he had long dreamed of finding in his net one morning.

I settled myself in the corner to take notes, and young Cato, never a man for small talk, came straight to the point. He was in need of a good advocate, he said, and he had liked the way Cicero had handled himself before the tribunes, for it was a monstrous thing when any man such as Verres considered himself above the ancient laws. To put it briefly: he was engaged to be married to his cousin, Aemilia Lepida, a charming girl of eighteen, whose young life had already been blighted by tragedy. At the age of thirteen, she had been humiliatingly jilted by her fiancé, the haughty young aristocrat Scipio Nasica. At fourteen, her mother had died. At fifteen, her father had died. At sixteen, her brother had died, leaving her completely alone.

'The poor girl,' said Cicero. 'So I take it, if she is your cousin, that she must be the daughter of the consul of six years ago, Aemilius Lepidus Livianus? He was, I believe, the brother of your late mother, Livia?' (Like many supposed radicals, Cicero had a surprisingly thorough knowledge of the aristocracy.)

'That is correct.'

'Why, then, I congratulate you, Cato, on a most brilliant match. With the blood of those three families in her veins, and with her nearest relatives all dead, she must be the richest heiress in Rome.'

'She is,' said Cato bitterly. 'And that is the trouble. Scipio Nasica, her former suitor, who has just come back from Spain after fighting in the army of Pompey the so-called Great, has found out how rich she has become, now that her father and brother are gone, and he has reclaimed her as his own.'

'But surely it is for the young lady herself to decide?'

'She has,' said Cato. 'She has decided on him.'

'Ah,' replied Cicero, sitting back in his chair, 'in that case, you may be in some difficulties. Presumably, if she was orphaned at fifteen, she must have had a guardian appointed. You could always talk to him. He is probably in a position to forbid the marriage. Who is he?'

'That would be me.'

'You? You are the guardian of the woman you want to marry?'

'I am. I am her closest male relative.'

Cicero rested his chin in his hand and scrutinised his prospective new client – the ragged hair, the filthy bare feet, the tunic unchanged for weeks. 'So what do you wish me to do?'

'I want you to bring legal proceedings against Scipio, and against Lepida if necessary, and put a stop to this whole thing.'

'These proceedings – would they be brought by you in your role as rejected suitor, or as the girl's guardian?'

'Either.' Cato shrugged. 'Both.'

Cicero scratched his ear. 'My experience of young women,' he said carefully, 'is as limited as my faith in the rule of law is boundless. But even I, Cato, *even I* have to say that I doubt whether the best way to a girl's heart is through litigation.'

'A girl's heart?' repeated Cato. 'What has a girl's heart got to do with anything? This is a matter of principle.'

And money, one would have added, if he had been any other man. But Cato had that most luxurious prerogative of the very rich: little interest in money. He had inherited plenty, and gave it away without even noticing. No: it was principle that always motivated Cato – the relentless desire never to compromise on principle.

'We would have to go to the embezzlement court,' said Cicero, 'and lay charges of breach of promise. We would have to prove the existence of a prior contract between you and the Lady Lepida, and that she was therefore a cheat and a liar. We would have to prove that Scipio was a double-dealing, money-grubbing knave. I would have to put them both on the witness stand and tear them to pieces.'

'Do it,' said Cato, with a gleam in his eye.

'And at the end of all that, we would probably still lose, for juries love nothing more than star-crossed lovers, save perhaps for orphans – and she is both – and you would have been made the laughing-stock of Rome.'

'What do I care what people think of me?' said Cato scornfully.

'And even if we win – well, imagine it. You might end up having to drag Lepida kicking and screaming from the court through the streets of Rome, back to her new marital home. It would be the scandal of the year.'

'So this is what we have descended to, is it?' demanded Cato bitterly. 'The honest man is to step aside so that the rascal triumphs? And this is Roman justice?' He leapt to his feet. 'I need a lawyer with steel in his bones, and if I cannot find anyone to help me, then I swear I shall lay the prosecution myself.'

'Sit down, Cato,' said Cicero gently, and when Cato did not move, he repeated it: 'Sit, Cato, and I shall tell you something about the law.' Cato hesitated, frowned, and sat, but only on the edge of his chair, so that he could leap up again at the first hint that he should moderate his convictions. 'A word of advice, if I may, from a man ten years your senior. You must not take everything head-on. Very often the best and most important cases never even come to court. This looks to me like one of them. Let me see what I can do.'

'And if you fail?'

'Then you can proceed however you like.'

After he had gone, Cicero said to me: 'That young man seeks opportunities to test his principles as readily as a drunk picks fights in a bar.' Nevertheless, Cato had agreed to let Cicero approach Scipio on his behalf, and I could tell that Cicero relished the opportunity this would give him to scrutinise the aristocracy at first hand. There was literally no man in Rome with grander lineage than Quintus Caecilius Metellus Pius Cornelius Scipio Nasica – Nasica meaning 'pointed nose', which he carried very firmly in the air – for he was not only the natural son of a Scipio, but the adopted son of Metellus Pius, pontifex maximus and the titular head of the Metelli clan. Father and adopted son had only recently returned from Spain, and were presently on Pius's immense country estate at Tibur. They were expected to enter the city on the twenty-ninth day of December, riding behind Pompey in his triumph. Cicero decided to arrange a meeting for the thirtieth.

The twenty-ninth duly arrived, and what a day that was – Rome had not seen such a spectacle since the days of Sulla. As I waited by the Triumphal Gate it seemed that everyone in the city had turned out to line the route. First to pass through the gate from the Field of Mars was the entire body of the senate, including Cicero, on foot, led by the consuls and the other magistrates. Then the trumpeters, sounding the fanfares. Then the carriages and litters laden with the spoils of the Spanish war – gold and silver, coin and bullion, weapons, statues, pictures, vases, furniture, precious stones and tapestries – and wooden models of the cities Pompey had conquered and sacked, and placards with their names, and the names of all the famous men he had killed in battle. Then the massive, plodding white bulls, destined for sacrifice, with gilded horns hung with ribbons and floral garlands, driven by the slaughtering-priests. Then trudging elephants – the heraldic symbol of the Metellii – and lumbering ox-carts bearing cages containing the wild beasts of the Spanish mountains, roaring and tearing at their bars in rage. Then the arms and insignia of the beaten rebels, and then the prisoners themselves, the defeated followers of Sertorius and Perperna, shuffling in chains. Then the crowns and tributes of the allies, borne by the ambassadors of a score of nations. Then the twelve lictors of the imperator, their rods and axes wreathed in laurel. And now at last, to a tumult of applause from the vast crowd, the four white horses of the imperator's chariot came trotting through the gate, and there was Pompey himself, in the barrel-shaped, gem-encrusted chariot of the triumphator. He wore a gold-embroidered robe with a flowered tunic. In his right hand he held a laurel bough and in his left a sceptre. There was a wreath of Delphic laurel on his head, and his handsome face and muscled body had been painted with red lead, for on this day he truly was the embodiment of Jupiter. Standing beside him was his eight-year-old son, the golden-curled Gnaeus, and behind him a public slave to whisper in his ear that he was only human and all this would pass. Behind the chariot, riding on a black war-horse, came old Metellus Pius, his leg tightly bandaged, evidence of a wound incurred in battle. Next to him was Scipio, his adopted son – a handsome young fellow of twenty-four: no wonder, I thought, that Lepida preferred him to Cato – and then the legionary commanders, including Aulus Gabinius, followed by all the knights and cavalry, armour glinting in the pale December sun. And finally the legions of Pompey's infantry, in full marching order, thousand upon thousand of sunburnt veterans, the crash of their tramping boots seeming to shake the very earth, roaring at the top of their voices, *'Io Triumphe!'* and chanting hymns to the gods and singing filthy songs about their commander-in-chief, as they were traditionally permitted to do in this, the hour of his glory.

It took half the morning for them all to pass, the procession winding through the streets towards the forum, where, according to tradition, as Pompey ascended the steps of the Capitol to sacrifice before the Temple of the Jupiter, his most eminent prisoners were lowered into the depths of the Carcer and garrotted – for what could be more fitting than that the day which ended the military authority of the conqueror should also end the lives of the conquered? I could hear the distant cheering inside the city but spared myself that sight, and hung around the Triumphal Gate with the dwindling crowd to see the entry of Crassus for his ovation. He made the best of it, marching with his sons beside him, but despite the efforts of his agents to whip up some enthusiasm, it was a poor show after the magnificence of Pompey's dazzling pageant. I am sure he must have resented it mightily, picking his way between the horse shit and elephant dung left behind by his consular colleague. He did not even have many prisoners to parade, the poor fellow, having slaughtered almost all of them along the Appian Way.

The following day, Cicero set out for the house of Scipio, with myself in attendance, carrying a document case – a favourite trick of his to try to intimidate the opposition. We had no evidence; I had simply filled it with old receipts. Scipio's residence was on the Via Sacra, fronted by shops, although naturally these were not your average shops, but exclusive jewellers, who kept their wares behind metal grilles. Our arrival was expected, Cicero having sent notice of his intention to visit, and we were shown immediately by a liveried footman into Scipio's atrium. This has been described as 'one of the wonders of Rome', and indeed it was, even at that time. Scipio could trace his line back for at least eleven generations, nine of which had produced consuls. The walls around us were lined with the wax masks of the Scipiones, some of them centuries old, yellowed with smoke and grime (later, Scipio's adoption by Pius was to bring a further six consular masks crowding into the atrium), and they exuded that thin, dry compound of dust and incense which is to me the smell of antiquity. Cicero went round studying the labels. The oldest mask was three hundred and twenty-five years old. But naturally, it was that of Scipio Africanus, conqueror of Hannibal, which fascinated him the most, and he spent a long time bent down studying it. It was a noble, sensitive face – smooth, unlined, ethereal, more like the representation of a soul than of flesh and blood. 'Prosecuted, of course, by the great-grandfather of our present client,' sighed Cicero, as he straightened. 'Contrariness runs thick in the blood of the Catos.'

The footman returned and we followed him through into the tablinum. There, young Scipio lounged on a couch surrounded by a jumble of precious objects – statues, busts, antiques, rolls of carpet and the like. It looked like the burial chamber of some Eastern potentate. He did not stand when Cicero entered (an insult to a senator), nor did he invite him to sit, but merely asked him in a drawling voice to state his business. This Cicero proceeded to do, firmly but courteously, informing him that Cato's case was legally watertight, given that Cato was both formally betrothed to the young lady, and also her guardian. He gestured to the document case, which I held before me like a serving boy with a tray, and ran through the precedents, concluding by saying that Cato was resolved to bring an action in the embezzlement court, and would also seek a motion *obsignandi gratia*, preventing the young lady from having further contact with any person or persons material to the case. There was only one sure way of avoiding this humiliation, and that was for Scipio to give up his suit immedately.

'He really is a crackpot, isn't he?' said Scipio languidly, and lay back on his couch with his hands behind his head, smiling at the painted ceiling.

'Is that your only answer?' said Cicero.

'No,' said Scipio, 'this is my only answer. Lepida!' And at that, a demure young woman appeared from behind a screen, where she had obviously been listening, and moved gracefully across the floor to stand beside the couch. She slipped her hand into Scipio's. 'This is my wife. We were married yesterday evening. What you see around you are the wedding gifts of our friends. Pompey the Great came directly from sacrificing on the Capitol to be a witness.'

'Jupiter himself could have been a witness,' retorted Cicero, 'but that would not suffice to make the ceremony legal.' Still, I could see by the way his shoulders slumped slightly that the fight had gone out of him. Possession, as the jurists say, is nine tenths of the law, and Scipio had not merely the possession, but obviously the eager acquiescence, of his new bride. 'Well,' Cicero said, looking around at the wedding presents, 'on my behalf, I suppose, if not that of my client, I offer you both congratulations. Perhaps my wedding gift to you should be to persuade Cato to recognise reality.'

'That,' said Scipio, 'would be the rarest gift ever bestowed.'

'My cousin is a good man at heart,' said Lepida. 'Will you convey my best wishes, and my hopes that one day we shall be reconciled?'

'Of course,' said Cicero, with a gentlemanly bow, and he was just turning to go when he stopped abruptly. 'Now that is a pretty piece. That is a very pretty piece.'

It was a bronze statue of a naked Apollo, perhaps half the size of a man, playing on a lyre – a sublime depiction of graceful masculinity, arrested in mid-dance, with every hair of his head and string of his instrument perfectly delineated. Worked into his thigh in tiny silver letters was the name of the sculptor: Myron.

'Oh, that,' said Scipio, very offhand, 'that was apparently given to some temple by my illustrious ancestor, Scipio Africanus. Why? Do you know it?'

'If I am not mistaken, it is from the shrine of Aesculapius at Agrigentum.'

'That is the place,' said Scipio. 'In Sicily. Verres got it off the priests there and gave it to me last night.'

In this way Cicero learned that Gaius Verres had returned to Rome and was already spreading the tentacles of his corruption across the city. 'Villain!' exclaimed Cicero as he walked away down the hill. He clenched and unclenched his fists in impotent fury. 'Villain, villain, *villain*!' He had good cause to be alarmed, for it was fair to assume that if Verres had given a Myron to young Scipio, then Hortensius, the Metellus brothers and all his other prominent allies in the senate would have received even heftier bribes – and it was precisely from among such men that the jury at any future trial would be drawn. A secondary blow was the discovery that Pompey had been present at the same wedding feast as Verres and the leading aristocrats. Pompey had always had strong links with Sicily – as a young general he had restored order on the island, and had even stayed overnight in the house of Sthenius. Cicero had looked to him if not exactly for support – he had learned his lesson there – then at least for benign neutrality. The awful possibility now occurred to him that if he went ahead with the prosecution he might have every powerful faction in Rome united against him.

But there was no time to ponder the implications of that now. Cato had insisted on hearing the results of Cicero's interview immediately, and was waiting for him at the house of his half-sister, Servilia, which was also on the Via Sacra, only a few doors down from Scipio's residence. As we entered, three young girls – none I would guess more than five years old – came running out into the atrium, followed by their mother. This was the first occasion, I believe, on which Cicero met Servilia, who was later to become the most formidable woman among the many formidable women who lived in Rome. She was nearly thirty, handsome but not at all pretty, about five years older than Cato. By her late first husband, Marcus Brutus, she had given birth to a son when she was still only fifteen; by her second, the feeble Junius Silanus, she had produced these three daughters in quick succession. Cicero greeted them as if he had not a care in the world, squatting on his haunches to talk to them while Servilia looked on. She insisted that they meet every caller, and so become familiar with adult ways, for they were her great hope for the future, and she wished them to be sophisticated.

Eventually a nurse came and took the girls away and Servilia showed us through to the tablinum. Here, Cato was waiting with Antipater the Tyrian, a Stoic philosopher who seldom left his side. Cato took the news of Lepida's marriage quite as badly as one would have predicted, striding around and swearing, which reminds me of another of Cicero's witticisms – that Cato was always the perfect Stoic, as long as nothing went wrong.

'Do calm yourself, Cato,' said Servilia after a while. 'It is perfectly obvious the matter is finished, and you might as well get used to it. You did not love her – you do not know what love is. You do not even need her money – you have plenty of your own. She is a drippy little thing. You can find a hundred better.'

'She asked me to bring you her best wishes,' said Cicero, which provoked another outpouring of abuse from Cato.

'I shall not put up with it!' he shouted.

'Yes you will,' said Servilia. She pointed at Antipater, who quailed. 'You tell him, philosopher. My brother thinks his fine principles are all the product of his intellect, whereas they are simply girlish emotions tricked out by false philosophers as manly points of honour.' And then, to Cicero again: 'If he had had more experience of the female sex, Senator, he would see how foolish he is being. But you have never even lain with a woman, have you, Cato?'

Cicero looked embarrassed, for he always had the equestrian class's slight prudishness about sexual matters, and was unused to the free ways of the aristocrats.

'I believe it weakens the male essence, and dulls the power of thought,' said Cato sulkily, producing such a shriek of laughter from his sister that his face turned as red as Pompey's had been painted the previous day, and he stamped out of the room, trailing his Stoic after him.

'I apologise,' said Servilia, turning to Cicero. 'Sometimes I almost think he is slow-witted. But then, when he does get hold of a thing, he will never let go of it, which is a quality of sorts, I suppose. He praised your speech to the tribunes about Verres. He made you sound a very dangerous fellow. I rather like dangerous fellows. We should meet again.' She held out her hand to bid Cicero goodbye. He took it, and it seemed to me that she held it rather longer than politeness dictated. 'Would you be willing to take advice from a woman?'

'From you,' said Cicero, eventually retrieving his hand, 'of course.'

'My other brother, Caepio – my full brother, that is – is betrothed to the daughter of Hortensius. He told me that Hortensius was speaking of you the other day – that he suspects you plan to prosecute Verres, and has some scheme in mind to frustrate you. I know no more than that.'

'And in the unlikely event that I was planning such a prosecution,' said Cicero, with a smile, 'what would be your advice?'

'That is simple,' replied Servilia, with the utmost seriousness. 'Drop it.'

VI

Far from deterring him, this conversation with Servilia and his visit to Scipio convinced Cicero that he would have to move even more quickly than he had planned. On the first day of January, in the six hundred and eighty-fourth year since the foundation of Rome, Pompey and Crassus took office as consuls. I escorted Cicero to the inaugural ceremonies on Capitol Hill, and then stood with the crowd at the back of the portico. The rebuilt Temple of Jupiter was at that time nearing completion under the guiding hand of Catulus, and the new marble pillars shipped from Mount Olympus and the roof of gilded bronze gleamed in the cold sunshine. According to tradition, saffron was burnt on the sacrificial fires, and those crackling yellow flames, the smell of spice, the shiny clarity of the winter air, the golden altars, the shuffling creamy bullocks awaiting sacrifice, the white and purple robes of the watching senators – all of it made an unforgettable impression on me. I did not recognise him, but Verres was also there, Cicero told me afterwards, standing with Hortensius: he was aware of the two of them looking at him, and laughing at some shared joke.

For several days thereafter nothing could be done. The senate met and heard a stumbling speech from Pompey, who had never before set foot in the chamber, and who was only able to follow what was happening by constant reference to a bluffer's guide to procedure which had been written out for him by the famous scholar Varro, who had served under him in Spain. Catulus, as usual, was given the first voice, and he made a notably statesmanlike speech, conceding that, although he opposed it personally, the demand for the restoration of the tribunes' rights could not be resisted, and that the aristocrats had only themselves to blame for their unpopularity. ('You should have seen the looks on the faces of Hortensius and Verres when he said *that*,' Cicero told me later.) Afterwards, following the ancient custom, the new consuls went out to the Alban Mount to preside over the celebrations of the Latin Festival, which lasted four days. These were followed by another two days of religious observance, during which the courts were closed. So it was not until the second week of the new year that Cicero was finally able to begin his assault.

On the morning that Cicero planned to make his announcement, the three Sicilians – Sthenius, Heraclius and Epicrates – came openly to the house for the first time in half a year, and together with Quintus and Lucius they escorted Cicero down the hill into the forum. He also had a few tribal officials in his train, mainly from the Cornelia and the Esquilina, where his support was particularly strong. Some onlookers called out to Cicero as he passed, asking where he was going with his three strange-looking friends, and Cicero responded cheerfully that they should come along and see – they would not be disappointed. He always liked a crowd, and in this way he ensured he had one as he approached the tribunal of the extortion court.

In those days, this court always met before the Temple of Castor and Pollux, at the very opposite end of the forum to the senate house. Its new praetor was Acilius Glabrio, of whom little was known, except that he was surprisingly close to Pompey. I say surprisingly because as a young man he had been required by the dictator Sulla to divorce his wife, even though she was then pregnant with his child, and yield her in marriage to Pompey. Subsequently, this unfortunate woman, whose name was Aemilia, died in childbirth in Pompey's house, whereupon Pompey returned the infant – a son – to his natural father; the boy was now twelve, and the joy of Glabrio's life. This bizarre episode was said to have made the two men not enemies but friends, and Cicero gave much thought as to whether this was likely to be helpful to his cause or not. In the end he could not decide.

Glabrio's chair had just been set up for him, the signal that the court was ready to open for business, and it must have been cold, for I have a very clear memory of Glabrio wearing mittens and sitting beside a charcoal brazier. He was stationed on that platform which runs along the front of the temple, halfway up the stairs. His lictors, their bundled rods slung over their shoulders, were standing in line, stamping their feet, on the steps beneath him. It was a busy spot, for as well as housing the extortion court, the temple was also the venue of the Bureau of Standards, where tradesmen went to check their weights and measures. Glabrio looked surprised to see Cicero with his train of supporters advancing towards him, and many other curious passers-by turned to watch. The praetor waved to his lictors to let the senator approach the bench. As I opened the document case and handed Cicero the *postulatus*, I saw anxiety in his eyes, but also relief that the waiting was finally over. He mounted the steps and turned to address the spectators.

'Citizens,' he said, 'today I come to offer my life in service to the Roman people. I wish to announce my intention to seek the office of aedile of Rome. I do this not out of any desire for personal glory, but because the state of our republic demands that honest men stand up for justice. You all know me. You know what I believe in. You know that I have long been keeping an eye on certain aristocratic gentlemen in the senate!' There was a murmur of approval. 'Well, I have in my hand an application to prosecute – a *postulatus*, as we lawyers call it. And I am here to serve notice of my intention to bring to justice Gaius Verres for the high crimes and misdemeanours committed during his term as governor of Sicily.' He waved it above his head, finally extracting a few muted cheers. 'If he is convicted he will not only have to pay back what he has stolen; he will lose all civil rights as a citizen. Exile or death will be his only choices. He will fight like a cornered animal. It will be a long, hard battle, make no mistake, and on its outcome I hereby wager everything – the office I seek, my hopes for the future, the reputation which I have risen early and toiled in the heat to gain – but I do so in the firm conviction that right will prevail!'

And with that he swung round and marched up the remaining few steps to Glabrio, who was looking mightily bemused, and gave him his application to prosecute. The praetor glanced at it quickly, then passed it to one of his clerks. He shook Cicero's hand – and that was it. The crowd began to disperse and there was nothing left to do except walk back up to the house. I am afraid the whole business had fallen embarrassingly flat, the trouble being that Rome was constantly witnessing individuals declaring their intention to run for some office or another – at least fifty were elected annually – and nobody saw Cicero's announcement in quite the same historic terms as he did. As for the prosecution, it was more than a year since he had stirred up the original excitement about Verres, and people, as he frequently remarked, have short memories; they had forgotten all about the wicked governor of Sicily. I could see that Cicero was suffering a dreadful sense of anticlimax, which even Lucius, who was usually good at making him laugh, could not shake him out of.

We reached the house, and Quintus and Lucius tried to amuse him by picturing the responses of Verres and Hortensius when they learned that a charge had been laid: the slave running back from the forum with the news, Verres turning white, a crisis meeting summoned. But Cicero would have none of it. I guessed he was thinking of the warning Servilia had given him, and the way Hortensius and Verres had laughed at him on inauguration day. 'They knew this was coming,' he said. 'They have a plan. The question is: what? Do they know our evidence is too weak? Is Glabrio in their pocket? What?'

The answer was in his hands before the morning was out. It came in the form of a writ from the extortion court, served upon him by one of Glabrio's lictors. He took it with a frown, broke open the seal, read it quickly, and then said a soft 'Ah ...'

'What is it?' asked Lucius.

'The court has received a second application to prosecute Verres.'

'That is impossible,' said Quintus. 'Who else would want to do that?'

'A senator,' replied Cicero, studying the writ. 'Caecilius Niger.'

'I know him,' piped up Sthenius. 'He was Verres's quaestor, in the year before I had to flee the island. It was rumoured that he and the governor quarrelled over money.'

'Hortensius has informed the court that Verres has no objection to being prosecuted by Caecilius, on the grounds that he seeks "personal redress", whereas I, apparently, merely seek "public notoriety".'

We all looked at one another in dismay. Months of work seemed to be turning to dust.

'It is clever,' said Cicero ruefully. 'You have to say that for Hortensius. What a clever devil he is! I assumed he would try to have the whole case dismissed without a hearing. I never imagined that instead he would seek to control the prosecution as well as the defence.'

'But he cannot do that!' spluttered Quintus. 'Roman justice is the fairest system in the world!'

'My dear Quintus,' replied Cicero, with such patronising sarcasm it made me wince, 'where *do* you find these slogans? In nursery books? Do you suppose that Hortensius has dominated the Roman bar for the best part of twenty years by playing *fair*? This is a writ. I am summoned before the extortion court tomorrow morning to argue why I should be allowed to bring the prosecution rather than Caecilius. I have to plead my worth before Glabrio and a full jury. A jury, let me remind you, that will be composed of thirty-two senators, many of whom, you may be sure, will recently have received a new year's gift of bronze or marble.'

'But we Sicilians are the victims!' exclaimed Sthenius. 'Surely it must be for us to decide whom we wish to have as our advocate?'

'Not at all. The prosecutor is the official appointee of the court, and as such a representative of the Roman people. Your opinions are of interest, but they are not decisive.'

'So we are finished?' asked Quintus plaintively.

'No,' said Cicero, 'we are not finished,' and already I could see that some of the old fight was coming back into him, for nothing roused him to greater energy than the thought of being outwitted by Hortensius. 'And if we are finished, well then, at least let us go down with a fight. I shall start preparing my speech, and you, Quintus, will see if you can prepare me a crowd. Call in every favour. Why not give them your line about Roman justice being the fairest in the world, and see if you can persuade a couple of respectable senators to escort me to the forum? Some might even believe it. When I step up to that tribunal tomorrow, I want Glabrio to feel that the whole of Rome is watching him.'

No one can really claim to know politics properly until he has stayed up all night, writing a speech for delivery the following day. While the world sleeps, the orator paces around by lamplight, wondering what madness ever brought him to this occupation in the first place. Arguments are prepared and discarded. Versions of openings and middle sections and perorations lie in drifts across the floor. The exhausted mind ceases to have any coherent grip upon the purpose of the enterprise, so that often – usually an hour or two after midnight – there comes a point where failing to turn up, feigning illness and hiding at home seem the only realistic options. And then, somehow, under pressure of panic, just as humiliation beckons, the parts cohere, and there it is: a speech. A second-rate orator now retires gratefully to bed. A Cicero stays up and commits it to memory.

Taking only a little fruit and cheese and some diluted wine to sustain him, this was the process Cicero went through that evening. Once he had the sections in order, he released me to get some sleep, but I do not believe that he saw his own bed for even an hour. At dawn he washed in freezing-cold water to revive himself and dressed with care. When I went in to see him, just before we left for court, he was as restless as any prize-fighter limbering up in the ring, flexing his shoulders and rocking from side to side on the balls of his feet.

Quintus had done his job well, and immediately the door was opened we were greeted by a noisy crowd of well-wishers, jammed right the way up the street. In addition to the ordinary people of Rome, three or four senators with a particular interest in Sicily had turned out to demonstrate their support. I remember the taciturn Gnaeus Marcellinus, the righteous Calpurnius Piso Frugi – who had been praetor in the same year as Verres, and despised him as a scoundrel – and at least one member of the Marcelli clan, the traditional patrons of the island. Cicero waved from the doorstep, hoisted up Tullia and gave her one of his resounding kisses, and showed her to his supporters. Then he returned her to her mother, with whom he exchanged a rare public embrace, before Quintus, Lucius and I cleared a passage for him and he thrust his way into the centre of the throng.

I tried to wish him luck, but by then, as so often before a big speech, he was unreachable. He looked at people but he did not see them. He was primed for action, playing out some inner drama, rehearsed since childhood, of the lone patriot, armed only with his voice, confronting everything that was corrupt and despicable in the state. As if sensing their part in this fantastic pageant the crowd gradually swelled in number, so that by the time we reached the Temple of Castor there must have been two or three hundred to clap him vigorously into court. Glabrio was already in his place between the great pillars of the temple, as were the panel of jurors, among whom sat the menacing spectre of Catulus himself. I could see Hortensius on the bench reserved for distinguished spectators, examining his beautifully manicured hands and looking as calm as a summer morning. Next to him, also very easy with himself, was a man in his mid-forties with reddish, bristling hair and a freckled face, whom I realised must be Gaius Verres. It was curious for me actually to set eyes on this monster, who had occupied our thoughts for so long, and to find him so ordinary-looking – more fox, in fact, than boar.

Two chairs had been put out for the contesting prosecutors. Caecilius was already seated, with a bundle of notes in his lap, and did not look up when Cicero arrived, but nervously preoccupied himself with study. The court was called to order and Glabrio told Cicero that he, as the original applicant, must go first – a significant disadvantage. Cicero shrugged and rose, waited for absolute quiet, and started slowly as usual, saying that he assumed people might be surprised to see him in this role, as he had never before sought to enter any arena as a prosecutor. He had not wanted to do it now, he said. Indeed, privately he had urged the Sicilians to give the job to Caecilius. (I almost gasped at that.) But in truth, he said, he was not doing it simply for the Sicilians. 'What I am doing I do for the sake of my country.' And very deliberately he walked across the court to where Verres was sitting and slowly raised his arm to point at him. 'Here is a human monster of unparalleled greed, impudence and wickedness. If I bring this man to judgement, who can find fault with me for doing this? Tell me, in the name of all that is just and holy, what better service I can do my country at the present time!' Verres was not in the least put out, but grinned defiantly at Cicero, and shook his head. Cicero stared at him with contempt for a while longer, then turned to face the jury. 'The charge against Gaius Verres is that during a period of three years he has laid waste the province of Sicily – that he has plundered Sicilian communities, stripped bare Sicilian homes, and pillaged Sicilian temples. Could all Sicily speak with a single voice, this is what she would say: "All the gold, all the silver, all the beautiful things that once were in my cities, houses and temples: all these things you, Verres, have plundered and stolen from me; and on this account I sue you in accordance with the law for the sum of one million sesterces!" These are the words all Sicily would utter, if she could speak with a single voice, and as she cannot, she has chosen me to conduct her case for her. So what incredible impudence it is that *you*' – and now he finally turned to Caecilius – 'should dare to try to undertake their case when they have already said they will not have you!'

He strolled across to Caecilius, and stood behind him. He gave an exaggerated sigh of sadness. 'I am now going to speak to you as one friend to another,' he said, and patted Caecilius's shoulder, so that his rival had to twist round in his seat to see him – a fidgety movement which drew a good deal of laughter. 'I earnestly advise you to examine your own mind. Recollect yourself. Think of what you are, and what you are fit for. This prosecution is a very formidable and a very painful undertaking. Have you the powers of voice and memory? Have you the intelligence and the ability to sustain such a burden? Even if you had the advantage of great natural gifts, even if you had received a thorough education, could you hope to stand the strain? We shall find out this morning. If you can reply to what I am now saying, if you can use one single expression that is not contained in some book of extracts compiled from other people's speeches and given to you by your schoolteacher, then perhaps you will not be a failure at the actual trial.'

He moved towards the centre of the court, and now he addressed the crowd in the forum as well as the jury. '"Well," you may say, "what if that is so? Do *you* then possess all these qualities yourself?" Would that I did, indeed! Still, I have done my best, and worked hard from boyhood, in order to acquire them if I could. Everyone knows that my life has centred around the forum and the law courts; that few men, if any, of my age have defended more cases; that all the time I can spare from the business of my friends I spend in the study and hard work which this profession demands, to make myself fitter and readier for forensic practice. Yet even I, when I think of the great day when the accused man is summoned to appear and I have to make my speech, am not only anxious, but tremble physically from head to foot. *You*, Caecilius, have no such fears, no such thoughts, no such anxieties. You imagine that, if you can learn by heart a phrase or two out of some old speech, like "I beseech almighty and most merciful God" or "I could wish, gentlemen, had it only been possible", you will be excellently prepared for your entrance into court.

'Caecilius, you are nothing, and you count for nothing. Hortensius will *destroy* you! But he will never crush me with his cleverness. He will never lead me astray by any display of ingenuity. He will never employ his great powers to weaken and dislodge me from my position.' He looked towards Hortensius, and bowed to him in mock humility, to which Hortensius responded by standing and bowing back, eliciting more laughter. 'I am well acquainted with all this gentleman's methods of attack,' continued Cicero, 'and all his oratorical devices. However capable he may be, he will feel, when he comes to speak against me, that the trial is among other things a trial of his own capacities. And I give the gentleman fair warning well beforehand, that if you decide that I am to conduct this case, he will have to make a radical change in his methods of defence. If *I* conduct the case, he will have no reason to think that the court can be bribed without serious danger to a large number of people.'

The mention of bribery produced a brief uproar, and brought the normally equable Hortensius to his feet, but Cicero waved him back into his place. On and on he went, his rhetoric hammering down upon his opponents like the ringing blows of a blacksmith in a forge. I shall not quote it all: the speech, which lasted at least an hour, is readily available for those who wish to read it. He smashed away at Verres for his corruption, and at Caecilius for his previous links with Verres, and at Hortensius for desiring a second-rate opponent. And he concluded by challenging the senators themselves, walking over to the jury and looking each of them in the eye. 'It rests with you, then, gentlemen, to choose the man whom you think best qualified by good faith, industry, sagacity and weight of character to maintain this great case before this great court. If you give Quintus Caecilius the preference over me, I shall not think I have been beaten by the better man. But Rome may think that an honourable, strict and energetic prosecutor like myself was not what you desired, and not what senators would ever desire.' He paused, his gaze coming to rest at last on Catulus, who stared straight back at him, and then he said very quietly: 'Gentlemen, see that this does not happen.'

There was loud applause, and now it was Caecilius's turn. He had risen from very humble origins, much more humble than Cicero's, and he was not entirely without merit. One could even say he had some prior claim to prosecute, especially when he began by pointing out that his father had been a freed Sicilian slave, that he had been born in the province, and that the island was the place he loved most in the world. But his speech was full of statistics about falling agricultural production and Verres's system of accounting. He sounded peevish rather than impassioned. Worse, he read it all out from notes, and in a monotone, so that when, after an hour, he approached his peroration, Cicero slumped to one side and pretended to fall asleep. Caecilius, who was facing the jury and therefore could not see what everyone was laughing at, was seriously knocked off his stride. He struggled through to the end and then sat down, crimson with embarrassment and rage.

In terms of rhetoric, Cicero had scored a victory of annihilating proportions. But as the voting tablets were passed among the jury, and the clerk of the court stood ready with his urn to collect them, Cicero knew, he told me afterwards, that he had lost. Of the thirty-two senators, he recognised at least a dozen firm enemies, and only half as many friends. The decision, as usual, would rest with the floaters in the middle, and he could see that many of these were craning their necks for a signal from Catulus, intent on following his lead. Catulus marked his tablet, showed it to the men on either side of him, then dropped it in the urn. When everyone had voted, the clerk took the urn over to the bench, and in full view of the court tipped it out and began counting the tablets. Hortensius, aban-doning his pretence of coolness, was on his feet, and so was Verres, trying to see how the tally was going. Cicero sat as still as a statue. Caecilius was hunched in his chair. All around me people who made a habit of attending the courts and knew the procedure as well as the judges were whispering that it was close, that they were re-counting. Eventually the clerk passed the tally up to Glabrio, who stood and called for silence. The voting, he said, was fourteen for Cicero – my heart stopped: he had lost! – thirteen for Caecilius, with five abstentions, and that Marcus Tullius Cicero was therefore appointed special prosecutor (*nominis delator*) in the case of Gaius Verres. As the spectators applauded and Hortensius and Verres sat down stunned, Glabrio told Cicero to stand and raise his right hand, and then had him swear the traditional oath to conduct the prosecution in good faith.

The moment that was finished, Cicero made an application for an adjournment. Hortensius swiftly rose to object: why was this necessary? Cicero said he wished to travel to Sicily to subpoena evidence and witnesses. Hortensius interrupted to say it was outrageous for Cicero to demand the right to prosecute, only to reveal in his next breath that he lacked an adequate case to bring to court! This was a valid point, and for the first time I realised how unconfident Cicero must be of the strength of his position. Glabrio seemed inclined to agree with Hortensius, but Cicero pleaded that it was only now, since Verres had left his province, that his victims felt it safe to speak out. Glabrio pondered the issue, checked the calendar, then announced, reluctantly, that the case would stand adjourned for one hundred and ten days. 'But be sure you are ready to open immediately after the spring recess,' he warned Cicero. And with that, the court was dismissed.

⋆

To his surprise, Cicero later discovered that he owed his victory to Catulus. This hard and snobbish old senator was, nevertheless, a patriot to his marrow, which was why his opinions commanded such respect. He took the view that the people had the right, under the ancient laws, to see Verres subjected to the most rigorous prosecution available, even though Verres was a friend of his. Family obligations to his brother-in-law, Hortensius, naturally prevented him from voting for Cicero outright, so instead he abstained, taking four waverers with him.

Grateful to be still in 'the Boar Hunt', as he called it, and delighted to have outwitted Hortensius, Cicero now flung himself into the business of preparing his expedition to Sicily. Verres's official papers were sealed by the court under an order *obsignandi gratia*. Cicero laid a motion before the senate demanding that the former governor submit his official accounts for the past three years (he never did). Letters were dispatched to every large town on the island, inviting them to submit evidence. I reviewed our files and extracted the names of all the leading citizens who had offered Cicero hospitality when he was a junior magistrate, for we would need accommodation throughout the province. Cicero also wrote a courtesy letter to the governor, Lucius Metellus, informing him of his visit and requesting official cooperation – not that he expected anything other than official harassment, but he reasoned it might be useful to have the notification in writing, to show that he had at least tried. He decided to take his cousin with him – Lucius having worked on the case for six months already – and to leave his brother behind to manage his election campaign. I was to go, too, along with both of my juniors, Sositheus and Laurea, for there would be much copying and note-taking. The former praetor, Calpurnius Piso Frugi, offered Cicero the services of his eighteen-year-old son, Gaius – a young man of great intelligence and charm, to whom everyone soon took a liking. At Quintus's insistence, we also acquired four strong and reliable slaves, ostensibly to act as porters and drivers, but also to serve as bodyguards. It was lawless country down in the south at that time – many of Spartacus's followers still survived in the hills; there were pirates; and no one could be sure what measures Verres might adopt.

All of this required money, and although Cicero's legal practice was now bringing in some income – not in the form of direct payments, of course, which were forbidden, but in gifts and legacies from grateful clients – he had nothing like the amount of ready cash necessary to mount a proper prosecution. Most ambitious young men in his position would have gone to see Crassus, who always gave loans to rising politicians on generous terms. But just as Crassus liked to show that he rewarded support, so he also took care to let people see how he punished opposition. Ever since Cicero had declined to join his camp, he had gone out of his way to demonstrate his enmity. He cut him dead in public. He poor-mouthed him behind his back. Perhaps if Cicero had grovelled sufficiently, he would have condescended to change his mind: his principles were infinitely malleable. But, as I have already said, the two men found it difficult even to stand within ten feet of one another.

So Cicero had no choice but to approach Terentia, and a painful scene ensued. I only became involved because Cicero, in a rather cowardly way, at first dispatched *me* to see her business manager, Philotimus, to enquire how difficult it would be to raise one hundred thousand from her estate. With characteristic malevolence, Philotimus immediately reported my approach to his mistress, who stormed down to find me in Cicero's study, and demanded to know how I dared poke my nose into her affairs. Cicero came in while this was happening and was consequently obliged to explain why he needed the money.

'And how is this sum to be repaid?' demanded Terentia.

'From the fine levied on Verres once he is found guilty,' replied her husband.

'And you are sure he *will* be found guilty?'

'Of course.'

'Why? What is your case? Let me hear it.' And with that she sat down in his chair and folded her arms. Cicero hesitated, but knowing his wife and seeing she was not to be shifted, told me to open the strongbox and fetch out the Sicilians' evidence. He took her through it, piece by piece, and at the end of it she regarded him with unfeigned dismay. 'But that is not enough, Cicero! You have wagered everything on *that*? Do you really think a jury of senators will convict one of their own because he has rescued some important statues from provincial obscurity and brought them back to Rome – where they properly belong?'

'You may be right, my dear,' conceded Cicero. 'That is why I need to go to Sicily.'

Terentia regarded her husband – arguably the greatest orator and the cleverest senator in Rome at that time – with the sort of look a matron might reserve for a child who has made a puddle on the drawing room floor. She would have said something, I am sure, but she noticed I was still there, and thought the better of it. Silently, she rose and left the study.

The following day, Philotimus sought me out and handed me a small money chest containing ten thousand in cash, with authorisation to draw a further forty thousand as necessary.

'Exactly half of what I asked for,' said Cicero, when I took it in to him. 'That is a shrewd businesswoman's assessment of my chances, Tiro – and who is to say she is wrong?'

VII

We left Rome on the Ides of January, on the last day of the Festival of the Nymphs, with Cicero riding in a covered wagon so that he could continue to work – although I found it a torment even attempting to read, let alone write, in that rattling, creaking, lurching *carruca*. It was a miserable journey, freezing cold, with flurries of snow across the higher ground. By this time, most of the crosses bearing the crucified rebel slaves had been removed from the Appian Way. But some still stood as a warning, stark against the whitened landscape, with a few rotted fragments of bodies attached. Gazing at them, I felt as if Crassus's long arm had reached out after me from Rome and was once again pinching my cheek.

Because we had departed in such a hurry, it had proved impossible to arrange places to stay all along our route, and on three or four nights when no inns were available we were reduced to sleeping by the roadside. I lay with the other slaves, huddled around the campfire, while Cicero, Lucius and young Frugi slept in the wagon. In the mountains I would wake at dawn to find my clothes starched with ice. When at last we reached the coast at Velia, Cicero decided it would be quicker to board a ship and hug the coast – this despite the risk of winter storms and pirates, and his own marked aversion to travelling by boat, for he had been warned by a sibyl that his death would somehow be connected with the sea.

Velia was a health resort, with a well-known temple to Apollo Oulius, then a fashionable god of healing. But it was all shuttered up and out of season, and as we made our way down to the harbour front, where the grey sea battered against the wharf, Cicero remarked that he had seldom seen a less enticing holiday spot. Aside from the usual collection of fishing boats, the port contained one huge vessel, a cargo ship the size of a trireme, and while we were negotiating our journey with the local sailors, Cicero happened to ask to whom it belonged. It was, we were told, a gift from the citizens of the Sicilian port of Messana to their former governor, Gaius Verres, and had been moored here for a month.

There was something infinitely sinister about that great ship, sitting low in the water, fully crewed and ready to move at a moment's warning. Our appearance in the deserted harbour had clearly already been registered and was causing something of a panic. Even as Cicero led us cautiously towards the vessel, we heard three short blasts sounded on a trumpet, and saw it sprout oars, like some immense water beetle, and edge away from the quayside. It moved a short distance out to sea, and dropped anchor. As the ship turned into the wind, the lanterns at its prow and stern danced bright yellow in the gloomy afternoon, and figures deployed along its heaving decks. Cicero debated with Lucius and young Frugi what to do. In theory, his warrant from the extortion court gave him authority to board and search any vessel he suspected of connection with the case. In truth, we lacked the resources, and by the time reinforcements could be summoned, the ship would be long gone. What it showed beyond doubt was that Verres's crimes were on a scale vastly bigger than anything even Cicero had imagined. He decided we should press on south at redoubled speed.

I guess it must be a hundred and twenty miles from Velia down to Vibo, running straight along the shin bone to the toe of Italy. But with a favourable wind and strong rowing we did it in just two days. We kept always within sight of the shore, and put in for one night to sleep on the sandy beach, where we cut down a thicket of myrtle to make a campfire and used our oars and sail for a tent. From Vibo we took the coast road to Regium, and here we chartered a second boat to sail across the narrow straits to Sicily. It was a misty early morning when we set off, with a saturating drizzle falling. The distant island appeared on the horizon as a dreary black hump. Unfortunately, there was only one place to make for, especially in midwinter, and that was Verres's stronghold of Messana. He had bought the loyalty of its inhabitants by exempting them from taxes throughout all his three years as governor, and alone of the towns on the island it had refused to offer Cicero any cooperation. We steered towards its lighthouse, and as we drew closer realised that what we had perceived as a large mast at the entrance to the harbour was not part of a ship at all, but a cross, facing directly across the straits to the mainland.

'That is new,' said Cicero, frowning as he wiped the rain from his eyes. 'This was never a place of execution in our day.'

We had no option but to sail straight past it, and the sight fell across our waterlogged spirits like a shadow.

Despite the general hostility of the people of Messana towards the special prosecutor, two citizens of the town – Basiliscus and Percennius – had bravely agreed to offer him hospitality, and were waiting on the quayside to greet us. The moment he stepped ashore, Cicero queried them about the cross, but they begged to be excused from answering until they had transported us away from the wharf. Only when we were in the compound of Basiliscus's house did they feel it safe to tell the story. Verres had spent his last days as governor living full-time in Messana, supervising the loading of his loot aboard the treasure ship which the grateful town had built for him. There had been a festival in his honour about a month ago, and almost it seemed as part of the entertainment, a Roman citizen had been dragged from the prison, stripped naked in the forum, publicly flogged, tortured, and finally crucified.

'A Roman citizen?' repeated Cicero incredulously. He gestured at me to begin making notes. 'But it is illegal to execute a Roman citizen without a full trial. Are you sure that is what he was?'

'He cried out that his name was Publius Gavius, that he was a merchant from Spain, and that he had done military service in the legions. Throughout his whipping he screamed, "I am a Roman citizen!" every time he received a blow.'

'"I am a Roman citizen",' repeated Cicero, savouring the phrase. '"I am a Roman citizen ..." But what was alleged to be his crime?'

'Spying,' replied our host. 'He was on the point of boarding a ship for Italy. But he made the mistake of telling everyone he met that he had escaped from the Stone Quarries in Syracuse and was going straight to Rome to expose all Verres's crimes. The elders of Messana had him arrested and held until Verres arrived. Then Verres ordered him to be scourged, tortured with hot irons and executed on a cross looking out across the straits to Regium, so that he could see the mainland throughout his final agonies. Imagine that – being only five miles from safety! The cross has been left standing by the followers of Verres as a warning to anyone else who feels tempted to talk too freely.'

'There were witnesses to this crucifixion?'

'Of course. Hundreds.'

'Including Roman citizens?'

'Yes.'

'Could you identify any of them?'

He hesitated. 'Gaius Numitorius, a Roman knight from Puteoli. The Cottius brothers from Tauromenium. Lucceius – he is from Regium. There must have been others.'

I took down their names. Afterwards, while Cicero was having a bath, we gathered beside his tub to discuss this development. Lucius said, 'Perhaps this man Gavius really was a spy.'

'I would be more inclined to believe that,' replied Cicero, 'if Verres had not brought exactly the same charge against Sthenius, who is no more a spy than you or I. No, this is the monster's favoured method of operation: he arranges a trumped-up charge, then uses his position as supreme justice in the province to reach a verdict and pronounce sentence. The question is: why did he pick on Gavius?'

Nobody had an answer; nor did we have the spare time to linger in Messana and try to find one. Early the following morning we had to leave for our first official engagement, in the northern coastal town of Tyndaris. This visit set the pattern for a score which followed. The council came out to greet Cicero with full honours. He was conducted into the municipal square. He was shown the standard-issue statue of Verres, which the citizens had been obliged to pay for, and which they had now pulled down and smashed. Cicero made a short speech about Roman justice. His chair was set up. He listened to the complaints of the locals. He then selected those which were most eye-catching or most easily proved – in Tyndaris it was the story of Sopater, bound naked to a statue until the town yielded up its bronze of Mercury – and finally either I or one of my two assistants moved in to take statements, which would be witnessed and signed.

From Tyndaris we travelled on to Sthenius's home city of Thermae, where we saw his wife in his empty house, who sobbed as Cicero delivered letters from her exiled husband, and then ended the week in the fortress port of Lilybaeum, on the extreme western tip of the island. Cicero knew this place well, having been based here when he was a junior magistrate. We stayed, as so often in the past, at the home of his old friend Pamphilius. Over dinner on the first night, Cicero noticed that the usual decorations of the table – a beautiful jug and goblets, all family heirlooms – were missing, and when he asked what had become of them, was told that Verres had seized them. It quickly transpired that all the other guests in the dining room had similar tales to tell. Young Gaius Cacurius had been obliged to give up all his furniture, and Lutatius a citrus-wood table at which Cicero had regularly eaten. Lyso had been robbed of his precious statue of Apollo, and Diodorus of a set of chased silver cups by Mentor. The list was endless, and I should know, for I was the one summoned to compile it. After taking statements from each of them, and subsequently from all their friends, I began to think that Cicero had gone a little mad – did he plan to catalogue every stolen spoon and cream jug on the island? – but of course he was being cleverer than I, as events were to show.

We moved on a few days later, rattling down the unmade tracks from Lilybaeum to the temple city of Agrigentum, then up into the mountainous heart of the island. The winter was unusually harsh; the land and sky were iron. Cicero caught a bad cold and sat wrapped in his cloak in the back of our cart. At Henna, a town built precipitously into the cliffs and surrounded by lakes and woods, the ululating priests all came out to greet us, wearing their elaborate robes and carrying their sacred boughs, and took us to the shrine of Ceres, from which Verres had removed the goddess's statue. And here for the first time our escort became involved in scuffles with the lictors of the new governor, Lucius Metellus. These brutes with their rods and axes stood to one side of the market square and shouted threats of dire penalties for any witness who dared to testify against Verres. Nevertheless, Cicero persuaded three prominent citizens of Henna – Theodorus, Numenius and Nicasio – to undertake to come to Rome and give their evidence.

Finally, we turned south-east towards the sea again, into the fertile plains below Mount Aetna. This was state-owned land, administered on behalf of the Roman treasury by a revenue-collection company, which in turn awarded leases to local farmers. When Cicero had first been on the island, the plains of Leontini had been the granary of Rome. But now we drove past deserted farmhouses and grey, untended fields, punctuated by drifting columns of brown smoke, where the homeless former tenants now lived in the open. Verres and his friends in the tax company had fanned out across the region like a ravaging army, commandeering crops and livestock for a fraction of their true value, and raising rents far beyond what most could pay. One farmer who had dared to complain, Nymphodorus of

Centuripae, had been seized by Verres's tithe collector, Apronius, and hanged from an olive tree in the market place of Aetna. Such stories enraged Cicero, and drove him to fresh exertions. I still cherish the memory of this most urban of gentlemen, his toga hoisted around his knees, his fine red shoes in one hand, his warrant in the other, picking his way daintily across a muddy field in the pouring rain to take evidence from a farmer at his plough. By the time we came at last to Syracuse, after more than thirty days of arduous travels around the province, we had the statements of nearly two hundred witnesses.

Syracuse is by far the largest and fairest of Sicily's cities. It is four towns, really, which have merged into one. Three of these – Achradina, Tycha and Neapolis – have spread themselves around the harbour, and in the centre of this great natural bay sits the fourth settlement, known simply as the Island, the ancient royal seat, which is linked to the others by a bridge. This walled city-within-a-city, forbidden at night to Sicilians, is where the Roman governor has his palace, close by the great temples of Diana and Minerva. We had feared a hostile reception, given that Syracuse was said to be second only to Messana in its loyalty to Verres, and its senate had recently voted him a eulogy. In fact, the opposite was the case. News of Cicero's honesty and diligence had preceded him, and we were escorted through the Agrigentine gate by a crowd of cheering citizens. (One reason for Cicero's popularity was that, as a young magistrate, he had located in the overgrown municipal cemetery the one-hundred-and-thirty-year-old lost tomb of the mathematician Archimedes, the greatest man in the history of Syracuse. Typically, he had read somewhere that it was marked by a cylinder and a sphere, and once he had found the monument, he paid to have the weeds and brambles cleared away. He had then spent many hours beside it, pondering the transience of human glory. His generosity and respect had not been forgotten by the local population.)

But to resume. We were lodged in the home of a Roman knight, Lucius Flavius, an old friend of Cicero's, who had plenty of stories of Verres's corruption and cruelty to add to our already bulging stock. There was the tale of the pirate captain, Heracleo, who had been able to sail right into Syracuse at the head of a squadron of four small galleys, pillage the warehouses, and leave without encountering any resistance. Captured some weeks later, further up the coast at Megara, neither he nor his men had been paraded as prisoners, and there were rumours that Verres had exchanged him for a large ransom. Then there was the horrible business of the Roman banker from Spain, Lucius Herennius, who had been dragged into the forum of Syracuse one morning, summarily denounced as a spy and, on Verres's orders, beheaded – this despite the pleadings of his friends and business associates, who had come running to the scene when they heard what was happening. The similarity of Herennius's case to that of Gavius in Messana was striking: both Romans, both from Spain, both involved in commerce, both accused of spying, and both executed without a hearing or a proper trial.

That night, after dinner, Cicero received a messenger from Rome. Immediately he had read the letter, he excused himself, and took Lucius, young Frugi and myself aside. The dispatch was from his brother Quintus, and it contained grave news. It seemed that Hortensius was up to his old tricks again. The extortion court had unexpectedly given permission for a prosecution to be brought against the former governor of Achaia. The prosecutor, Dasianus, a known associate of Verres, had undertaken to travel to Greece and back and present his evidence two days before the deadline set for Cicero's return from Sicily. Quintus urged his brother to return to Rome as quickly as possible to retrieve the situation.

'It's a trap,' declared Lucius immediately, 'to make you panic, and cut short your expedition here.'

'Probably so,' agreed Cicero. 'But I can't afford to take the risk. If this other prosecution slips into the court's schedule ahead of ours, and if Hortensius spins it out as he likes to do, our case could be pushed back until after the elections. By then Hortensius and Quintus Metellus will be consuls-elect. That youngest Metellus brother will no doubt be a praetor-elect, and this third will still be governor here. How will that be for having the odds stacked against us?'

'So what are we going to do?'

'We have wasted too much time pursuing the small fry in this investigation,' said Cicero. 'We need to take the war into the enemy's camp, and loosen some tongues among those who really know what has been going on – the Romans themselves.'

'I agree,' said Lucius. 'The question is: how?'

Cicero glanced around and lowered his voice before replying. 'We shall carry out a raid,' he announced. 'A raid on the offices of the revenue collectors.'

Even Lucius looked slightly green at that, for short of marching up to the governor's palace and attempting to arrest Metellus, this was about the most provocative gesture Cicero could make. The revenue collectors were a syndicate of well-connected men, of equestrian rank, operating under statutory protection, whose investors would certainly include some of the wealthiest senators in Rome. Cicero himself, as a specialist in commercial law, had built up a network of supporters among exactly this class of businessman. He knew it was a risky strategy, but he was not to be dissuaded, for it was here, he was sure, that the dark heart of Verres's murderous corruption was to be found. He sent the messenger back to Rome that same night with a letter for Quintus, announcing that he had only one more thing left to do, and that he would depart from the island within a few days.

Cicero now had to make his preparations with great speed and secrecy. He deliberately timed his raid to take place two days hence, at the least-expected hour – just before dawn on a major public holiday, Terminalia. The fact that this is the day sacred to Terminus, the ancient god of boundaries and good neighbours, only made it more symbolically attractive as far as he was concerned. Flavius, our host, agreed to come with us to point out the location of the offices. In the interim, I went down to the harbour in Syracuse and found the same trusty skipper I had used years before, when Cicero made his ill-judged return to Italy. From him I hired a ship and crew and told him to be ready to sail before the end of the week. The evidence we had already collected was packed in trunks and stowed aboard. The ship was placed under guard.

None of us got much sleep on the night of the raid. In the darkness before dawn we positioned our hired ox-carts at either end of the street to block it, and when Cicero gave the signal we all jumped out carrying our torches. The senator hammered on the door, stood aside without waiting for a reply, and a couple of our burliest attendants took their axes to it. The instant it yielded, we poured through into the passage, knocking aside the elderly nightwatchman, and secured the company's records. We quickly formed a human chain – Cicero, too – and passed the boxes of wax tablets and papyrus rolls from hand to hand, out into the street and on to the back of our carts.

I learned one valuable lesson that day, which is that if you seek popularity, there is no surer way of achieving it than raiding a syndicate of tax collectors. As the sun rose and news of our activity spread through the neighbourhood, an enthusiastic honour guard of Syracusans formed themselves around us, more than large enough to deter the director of the company, Carpinatius, when he arrived to reoccupy the building with a detachment of legionaries lent to him for the purpose by Lucius Metellus. He and Cicero fell into a furious argument in the middle of the road, Carpinatius insisting that provincial tax records were protected by law from seizure, Cicero retorting that his warrant from the extortion court overrode such technicalities. In fact, as Cicero conceded afterwards, Carpinatius was right. 'But,' he added, 'he who controls the street controls the law' – and on this occasion, at least, it was Cicero who controlled the street.

In all, we must have transported more than four cartloads of records back to the house of Flavius. We locked the gates, posted sentries, and then began the wearying business of sorting through them. Even now, remembering the size of the task that confronted us, I find myself starting to break into a sweat of apprehension. These records, which went back years, not only covered all the state land on Sicily, but itemised every farmer's number and quality of grazing animals, and every crop he had ever sown, its size and yield. Here were details of loans issued and taxes paid and correspondence entered into. And it quickly became clear that other hands had already been through this mass of material, and removed every trace of the name of Verres. A furious message arrived from the governor's palace, demanding that Cicero appear before Metellus when the courts reopened the following day, to answer a writ from Carpinatius that he return the documents. Meanwhile, yet another large crowd had started gathering outside and was chanting Cicero's name. I thought of Terentia's prediction, that her husband and she would be ostracised by Rome and end their days as consul and first lady of Thermae, and never did a prophecy seem more prescient than at that moment. Only Cicero retained his cool. He had represented enough shady revenue collectors in his time to know most of their tricks. Once it became apparent that the files specifically relating to Verres had been excised, he dug out an old list of all the company's managers, and hunted through it until he came to the name of the firm's financial director during the period of Verres's governorship.

'I'll tell you one thing, Tiro,' he said to me. 'I have never come across a financial director yet who didn't keep an extra set of records for himself when he handed over to his successor, just to be on the safe side.'

And with that we set off on our second raid of the morning.

Our quarry was a man named Vibius, who was at that moment celebrating Terminalia with his neighbours. They had set up an altar in the garden and there was some grain upon it, also some honeycombs and wine, and Vibius had just sacrificed a sucking pig. ('Always very pious, these crooked accountants,' observed Cicero.) When he saw the senator bearing down upon him, he looked a little like a sucking pig himself, but once he had read the warrant, which had Glabrio's praetorian seal attached to it, he reluctantly decided there was nothing he could do except co-operate. Excusing himself from his bemused guests, he led us inside to his tablinum and opened up his strongbox. Among the title deeds, account books and jewellery, there was a little packet of letters marked 'Verres', and as Cicero broke it open, Vibius's face bore an expression of utter terror. I guess he must have been told to destroy it, and had either forgotten or had thought to make some profit out of it.

At first sight, it was nothing much – merely some correspondence from a tax inspector, Lucius Canuleius, who was responsible for collecting export duty on all goods passing through Syracuse harbour. The letters concerned one particular shipment of goods which had left Syracuse two years before, and upon which Verres had failed to pay any tax. The details were attached: four hundred casks of honey, fifty dining room couches, two hundred chandeliers and ninety bales of Maltese cloth. Another prosecutor might not have spotted the significance, but Cicero saw it at once.

'Take a look at that,' he said, handing it to me. 'These are not goods seized from a number of unfortunate individuals. *Four hundred* casks of honey? *Ninety* bales of foreign cloth?' He turned his furious gaze on the hapless Vibius. 'This is a *cargo*, isn't it? Your Governor Verres must have stolen *a ship*.'

Poor Vibius never stood a chance. Glancing nervously over his shoulder at his bewildered guests, who were staring open-mouthed in our direction, he confirmed that this was indeed a ship's cargo, and that Canuleius had been instructed never again to attempt to levy tax on any of the governor's exports.

'How many more such shipments did Verres make?' demanded Cicero.

'I am not sure.'

'Guess then.'

'Ten,' said Vibius fearfully. 'Perhaps twenty.'

'And no duty was ever paid? No records kept?'

'No.'

'And where did Verres acquire all these cargoes?' demanded Cicero.

Vibius was almost swooning with terror. 'Senator, please …'

'I shall have you arrested,' said Cicero. 'I shall have you transported to Rome in chains. I shall break you on the witness stand before a thousand spectators in the Forum Romanum and feed what's left of you to the dogs of the Capitoline Triad.'

'From ships, Senator,' said Vibius, in a little mouse voice. 'They came from ships.'

'What ships? Ships from where?'

'From everywhere, Senator. Asia. Syria. Tyre. Alexandria.'

'So what happened to these ships? Did Verres have them impounded?'

'Yes, Senator.'

'On what grounds?'

'Spying.'

'Ah, spying! Of course! Did ever a man,' said Cicero to me, 'root out so many spies as our vigilant Governor Verres? So tell us,' he said, turning back to Vibius, 'what became of the crews of these spy ships?'

'They were taken to the Stone Quarries, Senator.'

'And what happened to them then?'

He made no reply.

The Stone Quarries was the most fearsome prison in Sicily, probably the most fearsome in the world – at any rate, I never heard of a worse one. It was six hundred feet long and two hundred wide, gouged deep into the solid rock of that fortified plateau known as Epipolae, which overlooks Syracuse from the north. Here, in this hellish pit, from which no scream could carry, exposed without protection to the burning heat of summer and the cold downpours of winter, tormented by the cruelty of their guards and the debased appetites of their fellow prisoners alike, the victims of Verres suffered and died.

Cicero, with his notorious aversion to military life, was often charged with cowardice by his enemies, and certainly he was prone to nerves and squeamishness. But I can vouch that he was brave enough that day. He went back to our headquarters and collected Lucius, leaving young Frugi behind to continue his search of the tax records. Then, armed only with our walking sticks and the warrant issued by Glabrio, and followed by the now-usual crowd of Syracusans, we climbed the steep path to Epipolae. As always, the news of Cicero's approach and the nature of his mission had preceded him, and the captain of the guard, after receiving a withering harangue from the senator, threatening all manner of dire repercussions if his demands were not met, allowed us to pass through the perimeter wall and on to the plateau. Once inside, refusing to heed warnings that it was too dangerous, Cicero insisted on being allowed to inspect the Quarries himself.

This vast dungeon, the work of Dionysius the Tyrant, was already more than three centuries old. An ancient metal door was unlocked and we proceeded into the mouth of a tunnel, guided by prison guards who carried burning torches. The glistening walls, cankerous with lime and fungi, the scuttling of the rats in the shadows, the stench of death and waste, the cries and groans of the abandoned souls – truly this was a descent into Hades. Eventually we came to another massive door, and when this was unlocked and unbolted we stepped on to the floor of the prison. What a spectacle greeted our eyes! It was as if some giant had filled a sack with hundreds of manacled men and had then tipped them out into a hole. The light was weak, almost subaquatic, and everywhere, as far as one could see, there were prisoners. Some shuffled about, a few huddled in groups, but most lay apart from their fellows, mere yellowing sacks of bones. The day's corpses had not yet been cleared, and it was hard to distinguish the living skeletons from the dead.

We picked our way among the bodies – those who had already died, and those whose end had yet to come: there was no discernible difference – and occasionally Cicero stopped and asked a man his name, bending to catch the whispered reply. We found no Romans, only Sicilians. 'Is any man here a Roman citizen?' he demanded loudly. 'Have any of you been taken from ships?' There was silence. He turned and called for the captain of the watch and demanded to see the prison records. Like Vibius, the wretch struggled between fear of Verres and fear of the special prosecutor, but eventually he succumbed to Cicero's pressure.

Built into the rock walls of the quarry were separate special cells and galleries, where torture and execution were done, and where the guards ate and slept. (The favoured method of execution, we discovered afterwards, was the garrotte.) Here, too, was housed the administration of the prison, such as it was. Boxes of damp and musty rolls were fetched out for us, containing long lists of prisoners' names, with the dates of their arrival and departure. Some men were recorded as having been released, but against most was scratched the Sicilian word *edikaiothesan* – meaning 'the death penalty was inflicted upon them'.

'I want a copy of every entry for the three years when Verres was governor,' Cicero said to me, 'and you,' he said to the prison captain, 'when it is done, will sign a statement to say that we have made a true likeness.'

While I and the other two secretaries set to work, Cicero and Lucius searched through the records for Roman names. Although the majority of those held in the Quarries during Verres's time were obviously Sicilian, there was also a considerable proportion of races from all across the Mediterranean – Spaniards, Egyptians, Syrians, Cilicians, Cretans, Dalmatians. When Cicero asked why they had been imprisoned, he was told they were pirates – pirates and spies. All were recorded as having been put to death, among them the infamous pirate captain Heracleo. The Romans, on the other hand, were officially described as 'released' – including the two men from Spain, Publius Gavius and Lucius Herennius, whose executions had been described to us.

'These records are a nonsense,' said Cicero quietly to Lucius, 'the very opposite of the truth. No one saw Heracleo die, although the spectacle of a pirate on the cross invariably draws an enthusiastic crowd. But plenty saw the Romans executed. It looks to me as though Verres simply switched the two about – killed the innocent ships' crews and freed the pirates, no doubt on payment of a fat ransom. If Gavius and Herennius had discovered his treachery, that would explain why Verres had been so anxious to kill them quickly.'

I thought poor Lucius was going to be sick. He had surely come a long way from his philosophy books in sunlit Rome to find himself studying death lists by the guttering light of candles, eighty feet beneath the dripping earth. We finished as quickly as we could, and never have I been more glad to escape from anywhere than I was to climb the tunnel out of the Stone Quarries and rejoin humanity on the surface. A slight breeze had sprung up, blowing in across the sea, and I remember as if it were this afternoon rather than an afternoon more than half a century ago the way we all instinctively turned our faces to it and gratefully drank in the taste of that cold clear air.

'Promise me,' said Lucius after a while, 'that if ever you achieve this *imperium* you desire so much, you will never preside over cruelty and injustice such as this.'

'I swear it,' replied Cicero. 'And if ever, my dear Lucius, you should question why good men forsake philosophy to seek power in the real world, promise me in return that you will always remember what you witnessed in the Stone Quarries of Syracuse.'

By this time it was late afternoon, and Syracuse, thanks to Cicero's activities, was in a tumult. The crowd which had followed us up the steep slope to the prison was still waiting for us outside the walls of Epipolae. Indeed, it had grown larger, and had been joined by some of the most distinguished citizens of the city, among them the chief priest of Jupiter, all dressed up in his sacred robes. This pontificate, traditionally reserved for the highest-ranking Syracusan, was presently held by none other than Cicero's client, Heraclius, who had returned privately from Rome to help us – at considerable personal risk. He came with a request that Cicero should immediately accompany him to the city's senate chamber, where the elders were waiting to give him a formal civic welcome. Cicero was in two minds. He had much work to do, and not long left to do it, and it was undoubtedly a breach of protocol for a Roman senator to address a local assembly without the permission of the governor. However, it also promised to be a wonderful opportunity to further his enquiries. After a short hesitation, he agreed to go, and we duly set off on foot back down the hill with a huge escort of respectful Sicilians.

The senate chamber was packed. Beneath a gilded statue of Verres himself, the house's most senior senator, the venerable Diodorus, welcomed Cicero in Greek, and apologised for the fact that they had so far offered him no assistance: not until the events of today had they truly believed he was in earnest. Cicero, also speaking in Greek, and fired up by the scenes he had just witnessed, then proceeded to make a most brilliant off-the-cuff speech, in which he promised to dedicate his life to righting the injustices done to the people of Sicily. At the end of it, the Syracusan senators voted almost unanimously to rescind their eulogy to Verres (which they swore they had only agreed to after being pressured into it by Metellus). Amid loud cheers, several younger members threw ropes around the neck of Verres's statue and pulled it down, while others – more importantly – fetched out of the senate's own secret archives a wealth of new evidence which they had been collecting about Verres's crimes. These outrages included the theft of twenty-seven priceless portraits from the Temple of Minerva – even the highly decorated doors of the sanctuary had been carried away! – as well as details of all the bribes Verres had demanded to bring in 'not guilty' verdicts when he was a judge.

News of this assembly and the toppling of the statue had by now reached the governor's palace, and when we tried to leave the senate house we found the building ringed with Roman soldiers. The meeting was dissolved on Metellus's orders, Heraclius arrested, and Cicero ordered to report to the governor at once. There could easily have been a bloody riot, but Cicero leapt up on to the back of a cart and told the Sicilians to calm themselves, that Metellus would not dare to harm a Roman senator acting on the authority of a praetor's court – although he did add, and only half in jest, that if he had not emerged by nightfall, they might perhaps make enquiries as to his whereabouts. He then clambered down and we allowed ourselves to be conducted over the bridge and on to the Island.

The Metellus family were at this time approaching the zenith of their power. In particular, the branch of the clan that had produced the three brothers, Quintus, Lucius and Marcus – all then in their forties – looked set to dominate Rome for years to come. It was, as Cicero said, a three-headed monster, and this middle head – the second brother, Lucius – was in many ways the most formidable of all. He received us in the royal chamber of the governor's palace with the full panoply of his *imperium* – an imposing, handsome figure, seated in his curule chair beneath the unyielding marble gaze of a dozen of his predecessors, flanked by his lictors, with his junior magistrate and his clerks behind him, and an armed sentry on the door.

'It is a treasonable offence,' he began, without rising and without preliminaries, 'to foment rebellion in a Roman province.'

'It is also a treasonable offence,' retorted Cicero, 'to insult the people and senate of Rome by impeding their appointed representative in his duties.'

'Really? And what kind of Roman representative addresses a Greek senate in its native tongue? Everywhere you have gone in this province, you have stirred up trouble. I shall not have it! We have too small a garrison to keep order among so many natives. You are making this place ungovernable, with your damned agitation.'

'I assure you, Governor, the resentment is against Verres, not against Rome.'

'Verres!' Metellus banged the arm of his chair. 'Since when did you care about Verres? I shall tell you when. Since you saw a chance to use him as a way of advancing yourself, you shitty little seditious lawyer!'

'Take this down, Tiro,' Cicero said, without removing his steady gaze from Metellus. 'I want a verbatim record. Such intimidation is entirely admissible in court.'

But I was too frightened even to move, for there was a lot of shouting now from the other men in the room, and Metellus had jumped to his feet. 'I order you,' he said, 'to return the documents you stole this morning!'

'And I remind the governor,' replied Cicero calmly, 'with the greatest respect, that he is not on the parade ground, that he is addressing a free Roman citizen, and I shall discharge the duty I have been assigned!'

Metellus had his hands on his hips and was leaning forward, his broad chin thrust out. 'You will undertake to return those documents now, in private – or you will be ordered to return them tomorrow in court, before the whole of Syracuse!'

'I choose to take my chance in court, as always,' said Cicero, with a tiny inflection of his head. 'Especially knowing what an impartial and honourable judge I shall have in you, Lucius Metellus – the worthy heir of Verres!'

I know I have this conversation exactly right, because the moment we were outside the chamber – which was very soon after this last exchange – Cicero and I reconstructed it while it was still fresh in our memories, in case he did indeed have occasion to use it in court. (The fair copy remains to this day among his papers.)

'That went well,' he joked, but his hand and voice were trembling, for it was now plain that his whole mission, perhaps even his mortal safety, was in the gravest peril. 'But if you seek power,' he said, almost to himself, 'and if you are a new man, this is what you have to do. Nobody is ever going simply to hand it to you.'

We returned at once to the house of Flavius and worked all night, by the weak light of smoky Sicilian candles and stuttering oil lamps, to prepare for court the following morning. Frankly, I did not see what Cicero could possibly hope to achieve, except humiliation. Metellus was never going to award judgement in his favour, and besides – as Cicero had privately conceded – the right of law lay with the tax company. But fortune, as the noble Terence has it, favours the brave, and she certainly favoured Cicero that night. It was young Frugi who made the breakthrough. I have not mentioned Frugi as often in this narrative as I should have done, chiefly because he had that kind of quiet decency which does not attract much comment, and which is only noticed when its possessor has gone. He had spent the day on the tax company records, and in the evening, despite having caught Cicero's cold, he refused to go to bed, and switched his attention instead to the evidence collected by the Syracusan senate. It must have been long after midnight when I suddenly heard him utter a cry, and then he beckoned us all over to the table. Laid out across it was a series of wax tablets, detailing the company's banking activities. Taken on their own, the lists of names, dates and sums loaned meant little. But once Frugi compared it with the list compiled by the Syracusans of those who had been forced to pay a bribe to Verres, we could see they tallied exactly: his victims had raised the funds they needed to buy him off by borrowing. Better still was the effect produced when he laid out a third set of accounts: the company's receipts. On the same dates exactly the same sums had been redeposited with the tax company by a character named 'Gaius Verrucius'. The depositor's identity was so crudely forged, we all burst out laughing, for obviously the name originally entered had been 'Verres', but in every case the last two letters had been scraped off and 'ucius' added as a replacement.

'So Verres demanded a bribe,' said Cicero, with growing excitement, 'and insisted his victim borrow the necessary cash from Carpinatius – no doubt at an extortionate rate of interest. Then he reinvested the bribe with his friends in the tax company, so that he not only protected his capital but earned an extra share of the profits as well! Brilliant villain! Brilliant, greedy, stupid villain!' And after executing a brief dance of delight, he flung his arms around the embarrassed Frugi and kissed him warmly on both cheeks.

Of all Cicero's courtroom triumphs, I should say that the one he enjoyed the following day was among the sweetest – especially considering that technically it was not a victory at all but a defeat. He selected the evidence he needed to take back to Rome, and Lucius, Frugi, Sositheus, Laurea and

I each carried a box of documents down to the Syracusan forum, where Metellus had set up his tribunal. An immense throng of local people had already gathered. Carpinatius was sitting waiting for us. He fancied himself as quite a lawyer, and presented his own case, quoting all the relevant statutes and precedents establishing that tax records could not be removed from a province, and generally giving the impression that he was merely the humble victim of an over-mighty senator. Cicero hung his head and put on such a mime of dejection I found it hard to keep a straight face. When at last he got to his feet he apologised for his actions, conceded he was wrong in law, begged forgiveness from the governor, promised gladly to return the documents to Carpinatius, but – he paused – *but* there was one small point he did not understand, which he would be very grateful to have cleared up first. He picked up one of the wax tablets and studied it in bafflement. 'Who exactly is Gaius Verrucius?'

Carpinatius, who had been smiling happily, looked like a man struck in the chest by an arrow fired from very short range, while Cicero, in a puzzled manner, as if it were all a mystery far beyond his comprehension, pointed out the coincidence of names, dates and sums in the tax company's records and the claims of bribery compiled by the Syracusan senate.

'And there is another thing,' said Cicero pleasantly. 'This gentleman, who did so much business with you, does not appear in your accounts before his near-name-sake, Gaius Verres, came to Sicily, and he has not done any business with you since Gaius Verres left. But in those three years when Verres was here, he was your biggest client.' He showed the accounts to the crowd. 'And it is unfortunate – do you see? – that whenever the slave who wrote up your records came to put down his name, he always made the same slip of his stylus. But there we are. I am sure there is nothing suspicious about it. So perhaps you could simply tell the court who this Verrucius is, and where he can be found.'

Carpinatius looked helplessly towards Metellus, as someone in the crowd shouted, 'He does not exist!' 'There never was anyone in Sicily called Verrucius!' yelled another. 'It is Verres!' And the crowd started chanting: 'It is Verres! It is Verres!'

Cicero held up his hand for silence. 'Carpinatius insists I cannot remove these records from the province, and I concede in law he is correct. But nowhere in law does it say I cannot make a copy, as long as it is fair, and properly witnessed. All I need is help. Who here will help me copy these records, so that I can take them back to Rome and bring this swine Verres to justice for his crimes against the people of Sicily?'

A plantation of hands sprang up. Metellus tried to call for silence, but his words were lost in the din of people shouting their support. Cicero, with Flavius to help him, picked out all the most eminent men in the city – Sicilian and Roman alike – and invited them to come forward and take a share of the evidence, whereupon I handed each volunteer a tablet and stylus. I could see Carpinatius out of the corner of my eye frantically trying to struggle across to Metellus, and I could see Metellus with his arms folded scowling furiously down from his raised bench at the chaos of his court. Eventually, he simply turned on his heel and strode angrily up the steps and into the temple behind him.

Thus ended Cicero's visit to Sicily. Metellus, I am sure, would dearly have liked to have arrested him, or at least prevented him from removing evidence. But Cicero had won over too many adherents in both the Roman and the Sicilian communities. To have seized him would have caused an insurrection, and as Metellus had conceded, he did not have the troops to control the entire population. By the end of that afternoon, the copies of the tax company's records had been witnessed, sealed and transferred to our guarded ship in the harbour, where they joined the other trunks of evidence. Cicero himself remained only one more night on the Island, drawing up the list of witnesses he wished to bring to Rome. Lucius and Frugi agreed to remain behind in Syracuse to arrange their transportation.

The following morning they came down to the dock to see Cicero off. The harbour was packed with well-wishers, and he made a gracious speech of thanks. 'I know that I carry in this fragile vessel the hopes of this entire province. In so far as it lies within my power, I shall not let you down.' Then I helped him on to the deck, where he stood with fresh tears shining on his cheeks. Consummate actor that he was, I knew that he could summon any emotion at will, but I am sure that on that day his feelings were unfeigned. I wonder, indeed, looking back on it, if he somehow knew that he would never return to the island again. The oars dipped and stroked us out into the channel. The faces on the quayside blurred, the figures dwindled and disappeared, and slowly we headed out through the mouth of the harbour and into open water.

VIII

The journey back from Regium to Rome was easier than our progress south had been, for by now it was early spring, and the mainland was soft and welcoming. Not that we had much opportunity to admire the birds and flowers. Cicero worked every mile of the way, propped up, swaying and pitching in the back of his covered wagon, assembling the outline of his case against Verres. I would fetch documents from the baggage cart as he needed them, and trot along at the rear of his carriage taking down his dictation, which was no easy feat. His plan, as I understood it, was to separate the mass of evidence into four sets of charges – corruption as a judge, extortion in collecting taxes and official revenues, the plundering of private and municipal property, and, finally, illegal and tyrannical punishments. Witness statements and records were grouped accordingly, and even as he bounced along, he began drafting whole passages of his opening speech. (Just as he had trained his body to carry the weight of his ambition, so he had, by effort of will, cured himself of travel sickness, and over the years he was to do a vast amount of work while journeying up and down Italy.) In this manner, almost without his noticing where he was, we completed the trip in less than a fortnight and came at last to Rome on the Ides of March, exactly two months after we had left the city.

Hortensius, meanwhile, had not been idle, and an elaborate decoy prosecution was now underway. Of course, as Cicero had suspected, it had been designed partly as a trap to lure him into leaving Sicily early. Dasianus had not bothered to travel to Greece to collect any evidence. He had never even left Rome. But that had not stopped him from bringing charges against the former governor of Achaia in the extortion court, and the praetor, Glabrio, with nothing to do until Cicero returned, had found himself with little option but to let him proceed. And so there he was, day after day, this long-forgotten nonentity, droning away before a bored-looking jury of senators, with Hortensius at his side. And when Dasianus's loquacity flagged, the Dancing Master would rise in his graceful way, and pirouette about the court, making his own elaborate points.

Quintus, ever the well-trained staff officer, had prepared a daily campaign schedule while we had been away, and had set it up in Cicero's study. Cicero went to inspect it the moment he entered the house, and one glance revealed the shape of Hortensius's plan. Blobs of red dye marked the festivals when the court would not be sitting. Once those were removed, there were only twenty full working days until the senate went into recess. The recess itself lasted a further twenty days, and was followed immediately by the five-day Festival of Flora. Then there was the Day of Apollo, the Tarentine Games, the Festival of Mars, and so on. Roughly one day in four was a holiday. 'To put it simply,' said Quintus, 'judging by the way it is going, I think Hortensius will have no trouble occupying the court until almost the consular elections at the end of July. Then you yourself have to face the elections for aedile at the beginning of August. The earliest we are likely to be able to get into court, therefore, is the fifth. But then in the middle of August, Pompey's games begin – and they are scheduled to last for a full fifteen days. And then of course there are the Roman Games, and the Plebeian Games—'

'For pity's sake,' exclaimed Cicero, peering at the chart, 'does nobody in this wretched town do anything except watch men and animals kill one other?' His high spirits, which had sustained him all the way from Syracuse, seemed visibly to leak from him at that moment, like air from a bladder. He had come home ready for a fight, but Hortensius was far too shrewd to meet him head-on in open court. Blocking and attrition: these were to be his tactics, and they were nicely judged. Everyone knew that Cicero's resources were modest. The longer it took him to get his case to court, the more money it would cost him. Within a day or two, our first few witnesses would start arriving in Rome from Sicily. They would expect to have their travel and accommodation costs defrayed, and to be compensated for their loss of earnings. On top of this, Cicero was having to fund his election campaign for aedile. And assuming he won, he would then have to find the money to maintain himself in the office for a year, repairing public buildings and staging two more sets of official games. He could not afford to skimp these duties: the voters never forgave a cheapskate.

So there was nothing for it but to endure another painful session with Terentia. They dined alone together on the night of his return from Syracuse, and later I was summoned by Cicero and told to bring him the draft passages of his opening speech. Terentia was lying stiffly on her couch when I went in, stabbing irritably at her food; Cicero's plate, I noticed, was untouched. I was glad to hand him the document case and escape immediately. Already the speech was vast and would have taken at least two days to deliver. Later, I heard him pacing up and down, declaiming parts of it, and I realised she was making him rehearse his case, before deciding whether to advance him any more money. She must have liked what she heard, for the following morning Philotimus arranged for us to draw a line of credit for another fifty thousand. But it was humiliating for Cicero, and it is from around this time that I date his increasing preoccupation with money, a subject which had never previously interested him in the least.

I sense that I am dawdling in this narrative, having already reached my eighth roll of Hieratica, and need to speed it up a little, else either I shall die on the job, or you will be worn out reading. So let me dispense with the next four months very quickly. Cicero was obliged to work even harder than before. First of all in the mornings he had to deal with his clients (and of course there was a great backlog of casework to get through, which had built up while we were in Sicily). Then he had to appear in court or the senate, whichever was in session. He kept his head down in the latter, anxious in particular to avoid falling into conversation with Pompey the Great, fearful either that Pompey might ask him to drop his prosecution of Verres and give up his candidacy for aedile, or – worse – offer to help, which would leave him beholden to the mightiest man in Rome, an obligation he was determined to avoid. Only when the courts and senate adjourned for public holidays and recesses was he able to transfer all his energies to the Verres prosecution, sorting out and mastering the evidence, and coaching the witnesses. We were bringing around one hundred Sicilians to Rome, and as for virtually all of them it was their first visit, they needed to have their hands held, and this task fell to me. I became a kind of one-man tour agent, running around the city, trying to stop them falling prey to Verres's spies, or turning into drunks, or getting into fights – and a homesick Sicilian, let me tell you, is no easy charge. It was a relief when young Frugi returned from Syracuse to lend me a hand (cousin Lucius having remained in Sicily to keep the supply of witnesses and evidence flowing). Finally, in the early evenings, accompanied by Quintus, Cicero resumed his visits to the tribal headquarters to canvass for the aedileship.

Hortensius was also active. He kept the extortion court tied up with his tedious prosecution, using his mouthpiece Dasianus. Really, there was no end to his tricks. For example, he went out of his way to be friendly to Cicero, greeting him whenever they were standing around in the senaculum, waiting for a senate quorum, and ostentatiously steering him away for a private word about the general political situation. At first, Cicero was flattered, but then he discovered that Hortensius and his supporters were putting it about that he had agreed to take an enormous bribe deliberately to bungle the prosecution, hence the public embraces. Our witnesses, cooped up in their apartment blocks around the city, heard the rumours and started fluttering in panic, like chickens in a henhouse when a fox is about, and Cicero had to visit each in turn and reassure him. The next time Hortensius approached him with his hand outstretched, he showed him his back. Hortensius smiled, shrugged and turned away – what did he care? Everything was going his way.

I should perhaps say a little more about this remarkable man – 'the King of the Law Courts', as his claque of supporters called him – whose rivalry with Cicero lit up the Roman bar for a generation. The foundation of his success was his memory. In more than twenty years of advocacy, Hortensius had never been known to use a note. It was no trouble to him to memorise a four-hour speech, and deliver it perfectly, either in the senate or in the forum. And this phenomenal memory was not a dull thing, born of night-time study; it shone quick in the daylight. He had an alarming capacity to remember everything his opponents had said, whether in statement or cross-examination, and could hurl it back in their faces whenever he chose. He was like some doubly armoured gladiator in the arena of the law, lunging with sword and trident, protected by net and shield. He was forty-four years old that summer, and lived with his wife and teenaged son and daughter in an exquisitely decorated house on the Palatine Hill, next door to his brother-in-law, Catulus. *Exquisite* – that is the *mot juste* for Hortensius: exquisite in manners, exquisite in dress, in hairstyle, in scent, exquisite in his taste for all fine things. He never said a rude word to anyone. But his besetting sin was greed, which was already swelling to outrageous proportions – a palace on the Bay of Naples, a private zoo, a cellar containing ten thousand casks of the finest Chianti, a picture by Cydias bought for one hundred and fifty thousand, eels dressed in jewellery, trees watered with wine, the first man to serve peacock at dinner: the whole world knows the stories. It was this extravagance which had led him to form his alliance with Verres, who showered him with stolen gifts – the most notorious of which was a priceless sphinx, carved out of a single piece of ivory – and who paid for his campaign for the consulship.

Those consular elections were fixed to be held on the twenty-seventh day of July. On the twenty-third, the jury in the extortion court voted to acquit the former governor of Achaia of all the charges against him. Cicero, who had hurried down from working on his opening speech at home to await the result, listened impassively as Glabrio announced that he would begin hearing the case against Verres on the fifth day of August – 'when I trust your addresses to the court will be slightly shorter,' he said to Hortensius, who replied with a smirk. All that remained was to select a jury. This was accomplished the following day. Thirty-two senators, drawn by lot, was the number laid down by the law. Each side was entitled to make six objections, but despite using up all his challenges, Cicero still faced a dauntingly hostile jury, including – yet again – Catulus and his protégé Catilina, as well as that other grand old man of the senate, Servilius Vatia Isauricus; even Marcus Metellus slipped on to the panel. Apart from these aristocratic hard-liners, we had also to write off cynics such as Aemilius Alba, Marcus Lucretius and Antonius Hybrida, for they would invariably sell themselves to the highest bidder, and Verres was lavish with his funds. I do not think I ever knew the true meaning of that old expression about someone looking like the cat that got the cream until I saw Hortensius's face on the day that jury was sworn in. He had it all. The consulship was in the bag, and with it, he was now confident, the acquittal of Verres.

The days which followed were the most nerve-racking Cicero had endured in public life. On the morning of the consular election he was so dispirited he could hardly bring himself to go out to the Field of Mars to vote, but of course he had to be seen to be an active citizen. The result was never in doubt, from the moment the trumpets sounded and the red flag was hoisted over the Janiculum Hill. Hortensius and Quintus Metellus were backed by Verres and his gold, by the aristocrats, and by the supporters of Pompey and Crassus. Nevertheless, there was always a race-day atmosphere on these occasions, with the candidates and their supporters streaming out of the city in the early-morning sunshine towards the voting pens, and the enterprising shopkeepers piling their stalls with wine and sausages, dice and parasols, and all else necessary to enjoy a good election. Pompey, as senior consul, in accordance with the ancient custom, was already standing at the entrance to the returning officer's tent, with an augur beside him. The moment all the candidates for consul and praetor, perhaps twenty senators, had lined up in their whitened togas, he mounted the platform and read out the traditional prayer. Soon afterwards the voting started and there was nothing for the thousands of electors to do except mill around and gossip until it was their turn to enter the enclosures.

This was the old republic in action, the men all voting in their allotted centuries, just as they had in ancient times, when as soldiers they elected their commander. Now that the ritual has become meaningless, it is hard to convey how moving a spectacle it was, even for a slave such as I, who did not have the franchise. It embodied something marvellous – some impulse of the human spirit that had sparked into life half a millennium before among that indomitable race who dwelled amid the hard rocks and soft marshland of the Seven Hills: some impulse towards the light of dignity and freedom, and away from the darkness of brute subservience. This is what we have lost. Not that it was a pure, Aristotelian democracy, by any means. Precedence among the centuries – of which there were one hundred and ninety-three – was determined by wealth, and the richest classes always voted earliest and declared first: a significant advantage. These centuries also benefited by having fewer members, whereas the centuries of the poor, like the slums of Subura, were vast and teeming; as a consequence, a rich man's vote counted for more. Still, it was freedom, as it had been practised for hundreds of years, and no man on the Field of Mars that day would have dreamed that he might live to see it taken away.

Cicero's century, one of the twelve consisting entirely of members of the equestrian order, was called around mid-morning, just as it was starting to get hot. He strolled with his fellows into the roped-off enclosure and proceeded to work the throng in his usual way – a word here, a touch of the elbow there. Then they formed themselves into a line and filed by the table at which sat the clerks, who checked their names and handed them their voting counters. If there was to be any intimidation, this was generally the place where it occurred, for the partisans of each candidate could get up close to the voters and whisper their threats or promises. But on this day all was quiet, and I watched Cicero step across the narrow wooden bridge and disappear behind the boards to cast his ballot. Emerging on the other side, he passed along the line of candidates and their friends, who were standing beneath an awning, paused briefly to talk to Palicanus – the roughly spoken former tribune was standing for a praetorship – and then exited without giving Hortensius or Metellus a second glance.

Like all those before it, Cicero's century backed the official slate – Hortensius and Quintus Metellus for consul; Marcus Metellus and Palicanus for praetor – and now it was merely a question of going on until an absolute majority was reached. The poorer men must have known they could not affect the outcome, but such was the dignity conveyed by the franchise, they stood all afternoon in the heat, awaiting their turn to collect their ballots and shuffle over the bridge. Cicero and I went up and down the lines as he canvassed support for the aedileship, and it was marvellous how many he knew personally – not just the voters' names, but their wives' names and the number of their children, and the nature of their employment: all done without any prompting from me. At the eleventh hour, when the sun was just starting to dip towards the Janiculum, a halt was called at last and Pompey proclaimed the winners. Hortensius had topped the poll for consul, with Quintus Metellus second; Marcus Metellus had won most votes for praetor. Their jubilant supporters crowded round them, and now for the first time we saw the redheaded figure of Gaius Verres slip into the front rank – 'The puppet-master comes to take his bow,' observed Cicero – and one would have thought that *he* had won the consulship by the way the aristocrats shook his hand and pounded him on the back. One of them, a former consul, Scribonius Curio, embraced Verres and said, loudly enough for all to hear, 'I hereby inform you that today's election means your acquittal!'

There are few forces in politics harder to resist than a feeling that something is inevitable, for humans move as a flock, and will always rush like sheep towards the safety of a winner. On every side now, one heard the same opinion: Cicero was done for, Cicero was finished, the aristocrats were back in charge, no jury would ever convict Gaius Verres.

Aemilius Alba, who fancied himself a wit, told everyone he met that he was in despair: the bottom had dropped out of the market for Verres's jurors, and he could not sell himself for more than three thousand. Attention now switched to the forthcoming elections for aedile, and it was not long before Cicero detected Verres's hand at work behind the scenes here, as well. A professional election agent, Ranunculus, who was well disposed towards Cicero and was afterwards employed by him, came to warn the senator that Verres had called a night-time meeting at his own house of all the leading bribery merchants, and had offered five thousand to every man who could persuade his tribe not to vote for Cicero. I could see that both Cicero and his brother were worried. Worse was to follow. A few days later, on the eve of the actual election, the senate met with Crassus in the chair, to witness the praetors-elect draw lots to determine which courts they would preside over when they took office in January. I was not present, but Cicero was in the chamber, and he returned home afterwards looking white and limp. The unbelievable had happened: Marcus Metellus, already a juror in the Verres case, had drawn the extortion court!

Even in his darkest imaginings, Cicero had never contemplated such an outcome. He was so shocked he had almost lost his voice. 'You should have heard the uproar in the house,' he whispered to Quintus. 'Crassus must have rigged the draw. Everyone believes he did it, but nobody knows *how* he did it. That man will not rest until I am broken, bankrupt and in exile.' He shuffled into his study and collapsed into his chair. It was a stiflingly hot day, the third of August, and there was hardly room to move among all the accumulated material from the Verres case: the piles of tax records and affidavits and witness statements, roasting and dusty in the heat. (And these were only a fraction of the total: most were locked in boxes in the cellar.) His draft speech – his immense opening speech, which kept on growing and growing, like some proliferating madness – was stacked in tottering piles across his desk. I had long since given up trying to keep track of it. Only he knew how it might come together. It was all in his head, the sides of which he now began massaging with the tips of his fingers. He asked in a croaking voice for a cup of water. I turned away to fetch it, heard a sigh and then a thump, and when I looked round he had slumped forwards, knocking his skull against the edge of his desk. Quintus and I rushed to either side of him and pulled him up. His cheeks were dead grey, with a livid streak of bright red blood trickling from his nose; his mouth hung slackly open.

Quintus was in a panic. 'Fetch Terentia!' he shouted at me. 'Quickly!'

I ran upstairs to her room and told her the master was ill. She came down at once and was magnificent in the way she took command. Cicero by now was feebly conscious, his head between his knees. She knelt beside him, called for water, pulled a fan from her sleeve, and starting waving it vigorously to cool his cheeks. Quintus in the meantime, still wringing his hands, had dispatched the two junior secretaries to fetch whatever doctors were in the neighbourhood, and each soon returned with a Greek medic in tow. The wretched quacks immediately began arguing between themselves about whether it was best to purge or bleed. Terentia sent both packing. She also refused to allow Cicero to be carried up to bed, warning Quintus that word of this would quickly get around, and the widespread belief that her husband was finished would then become an accomplished fact. She made him rise unsteadily to his feet and, holding his arm, took him out into the atrium, where the air was fresher. Quintus and I followed. 'You are not finished!' I could hear her saying sternly to him. 'You have your case – now make it!' Cicero mumbled something in reply.

Quintus burst out: 'That is all very well, Terentia, but you do not understand what has just happened.' And he told her about Metellus's appointment as the new president of the extortion court, and its implications. There was no chance of a guilty verdict being returned once *he* was in the judge's chair, which meant their only hope was to have the hearing concluded by December. But that was impossible, given Hortensius's ability to spin it out. There was simply too much evidence for the time available: only ten days in court before Pompey's games, and Cicero's opening statement alone would take up most of it. No sooner would he have finished outlining his case than the court would be in recess for the best part of a month, and by the time they came back the jury would have forgotten his brilliant points. 'Not that it matters,' Quintus concluded gloomily, 'as most of them are in the pay of Verres already.'

'It's true, Terentia,' said Cicero. He looked around him distractedly, as if he had only just woken up and realised where he was. 'I must pull out of the election for aedile,' he muttered. 'It would be humiliating enough to lose, but even more humiliating to win and not be able to discharge the duties of the office.'

'Pathetic,' replied Terentia, and she angrily pulled her arm free of his. 'You don't deserve to be elected, if this is how you surrender at the first setback, without putting up a fight!'

'My dear,' said Cicero beseechingly, pressing his hand to his forehead, 'if you will tell me how I am supposed to defeat time itself, then I will fight it bravely. But what am I to do if I only have ten days to set out my prosecution before the court goes into recess for weeks on end?'

Terentia leaned in close to him, so that her face was only inches from his. 'Make your speech shorter!' she hissed.

After his wife had retired to her corner of the house, Cicero, still not fully recovered from his fit of nerves, retreated to his study and sat there for a long time, staring at the wall. We left him alone. Sthenius came by just before sunset to report that Quintus Metellus had summoned all the Sicilian witnesses to his house, and that a few of the more timid souls had foolishly obeyed. From one of these, Sthenius had obtained a full report of how Metellus had tried to intimidate them into retracting their evidence. 'I am consul-elect,' he had thundered at them. 'One of my brothers is governing Sicily, the other is going to preside over the extortion court. Many steps have been taken to ensure that no harm can befall Verres. We shall not forget those who go against us.' I took down the exact quotation and tentatively went in to see Cicero. He had not moved in several hours. I read out Metellus's words, but he gave no sign of having heard.

By this stage I was becoming seriously concerned, and would have fetched his brother or wife again, if his mind had not suddenly re-emerged from wherever it had been wandering. Staring straight ahead, he said in a grim tone: 'Go and make an appointment for me to see Pompey this evening.' When I hesitated, wondering if this was another symptom of his malady, he glared at me. 'Go!'

It was only a short distance to Pompey's house, which was in the same district of the Esquiline Hill as Cicero's. The sun had just gone down but it was still light, and swelteringly hot, with a torpid breeze wafting gently from the east – the worst possible combination at the height of summer, because it carried into the neighbourhood the stench of the putrefying corpses in the great common graves beyond the city wall. I believe the problem is not so acute these days, but sixty years ago the Esquiline Gate was the place where everything dead and not worth a proper funeral was taken to be dumped – the bodies of dogs and cats, horses, donkeys, slaves, paupers and still-born babies, all mixed up and rotting together, along with the household refuse. The stink always drew great flocks of crying gulls, and I remember that on this particular evening it was especially acute: a rancid and pervasive smell, which one tasted on the tongue as much as one absorbed it through the nostrils.

Pompey's house was much grander than Cicero's, with a couple of lictors posted outside and a crowd of sightseers gathered opposite. There were also half a dozen canopied litters set down in the lee of the wall, their bearers squatting nearby playing bones – evidence that a big dinner party was in progress. I gave my message to the gatekeeper, who vanished inside, and returned a little later with the praetor-elect, Palicanus, who was dabbing at his greasy chin with a napkin. He recognised me, asked what it was all about, and I repeated my message. 'Right you are,' said Palicanus, in his blunt way. 'You can tell him from me that the consul will see him immediately.'

Cicero must have known Pompey would agree to meet, for when I returned he had already changed into a fresh set of clothes and was ready to go out. He was still very pale. He exchanged a last look with Quintus, and then we set off. There was no conversation between us as we walked, because Cicero, who hated any reminder of death, kept his sleeve pressed to his mouth and nose to ward off the smell from the Esquiline Field. 'Wait here,' he said, when we reached Pompey's house, and that was the last I saw of him for several hours. The daylight faded, the massy purple twilight ripened into darkness and the stars began to appear in clusters above the city. Occasionally, when the door was opened, the muffled sounds of voices and laughter reached the street, and I could smell meat and fish cooking, although on that foul night they all reeked of death to me, and I wondered how Cicero could possibly find the stomach for it, for by now it was clear that Pompey had asked him to join his dinner party.

I paced up and down, leaned against the wall, attempted to think up some new symbols for my great shorthand system, and generally tried to occupy myself as the night went on. Eventually, Pompey's guests started reeling out, half of them too drunk to stand properly, and it was the usual crew of Piceneans – Afranius, the former praetor and lover of the dance; Palicanus, of course; and Gabinius, Palicanus's son-in-law, who also had a reputation for loving women and song – a real old soldiers' reunion, it must have been, and I found it hard to imagine that Cicero could have enjoyed himself much. Only the austere and scholarly Varro – 'the man who showed Pompey where the senate house was', in Cicero's cutting phrase – would have been remotely congenial company, especially as he at least emerged sober. Cicero was the last to leave. He set off up the street and I hurried after him. There was a good yellow moon and I had no difficulty in making out his figure. He still kept his hand up to his nose, for neither the heat nor the smell had much diminished, and when he was a decent distance from Pompey's house, he leaned against the corner of an alley and was violently sick.

I came up behind him and asked him if he needed assistance, at which he shook his head and responded, 'It is done.' That was all he said to me, and all he said to Quintus, too, who was waiting up anxiously for him at the house when he got in: 'It is done.'

At dawn the following day we made the two-mile walk back to the Field of Mars for the second round of elections. Although these did not carry the same prestige as those for the consulship and the praetorship, they nevertheless had the advantage of always being much more exciting. Thirty-four men had to be elected (twenty senators, ten tribunes and four aediles), which meant there were simply too many candidates for the poll to be easily controlled: when an aristocrat's vote carried no more weight than a pauper's, anything could happen. Crassus, as junior consul, was the presiding officer at this supplementary election – 'But presumably even he,' said Cicero darkly, as he pulled on his red leather shoes, 'cannot rig this ballot.'

He had woken in an edgy, preoccupied mood. Whatever had been agreed with Pompey the previous night had obviously disturbed his rest, and he snapped irritably at his valet that his shoes were not as clean as they ought to be. He donned the same brilliant white toga he had worn on this day six years earlier, when he had first been elected to the senate, and braced himself before the front door was opened, as if he were about to shoulder a great weight. Once again, Quintus had done a fine job, and a marvellous crowd was waiting to escort him out to the voting pens. When we reached the Field of Mars, we found it was packed right down to the river's edge, for there was a census in progress, and tens of thousands had come to the city to register. You can imagine the noisy roar of it. There must have been a hundred candidates for those thirty-four offices, and all across the vast open field one could see these gleaming figures passing to and fro, accompanied by their friends and supporters, trying to gather every last vote before polling opened. Verres's red head was also conspicuous, darting all over the place, with his father beside him, and his son, and his freedman, Timarchides – the creature who had invaded our house – making extravagant promises to any who would vote against Cicero. The sight seemed to banish Cicero's ill humour instantly, and he plunged in to canvass. I thought on several occasions that our groups might collide, but the crowd was so huge it never happened.

When the augur pronounced himself satisfied, Crassus came out of the sacred tent and the candidates gathered at the base of his tribunal. Among them, I should record, making his first attempt to enter the senate, was Julius Caesar, who stood beside Cicero and engaged him in friendly conversation. They had known one another a long time, and indeed it was on Cicero's recommendation that the younger man had gone to Rhodes to study rhetoric under Apollonius Molon. Much hagiography now clusters around Caesar's early years, to the extent that you would think he had been marked out by his contemporaries as a genius ever since the cradle. Not so, and anyone who saw him in his whitened toga that morning, nervously fiddling with his thinning hair, would have been hard put to distinguish him from any of the other well-bred young candidates. There was one great difference, though: few can have been as poor. To stand for election, he must have borrowed heavily, for he lived in very modest accommodation in the Subura, in a house full of women – his mother, his wife, and his little daughter – and I picture him at this stage not as the gleaming hero waiting to conquer Rome, but as a thirty-year-old man lying sleepless at night, kept awake by the racket of his impoverished neighbourhood, brooding bitterly on the fact that he, a scion of the oldest family in Rome, had been reduced to such circumstances. His antipathy towards the aristocrats was consequently far more dangerous to them than Cicero's ever was.

As a self-made man, Cicero merely resented and envied them. But Caesar, who believed he was a direct descendant of Venus, viewed them with contempt, as interlopers.

But now I am running ahead of myself, and committing the same sin as the hagiographers, by shining the distorting light of the future on to the shadows of the past. Let me simply record that these two outstanding men, with six years' difference in their ages but much in common in terms of brains and outlook, stood chatting amiably in the sun, as Crassus mounted the platform and read out the familiar prayer: 'May this matter end well and happily for me, for my best endeavours, for my office, and for the People of Rome!' And with that the voting started.

The first tribe into the pens, in accordance with tradition, were the Suburana. But despite all Cicero's efforts over the years, they did not vote for him. This must have been a blow, and certainly suggested Verres's bribery agents had earned their cash. Cicero, however, merely shrugged: he knew that many influential men who had yet to vote would be watching for his reaction, and it was important to wear a mask of confidence. Then, one after another, came the three other tribes of the city: the Esquilina, the Collina and the Palatina. Cicero won the support of the first two, but not the third, which was scarcely surprising, as it was easily the most aristocratically inclined of Rome's neighbourhoods. So the score was two–two: a tenser start than he would have liked. And now the thirty-one rustic tribes started lining up: the Aemilia, Camilia, Fabia, Galeria … I knew all their names from our office files, could tell you who were the key men in each, who needed a favour and who owed one. Three of these four went for Cicero. Quintus came up and whispered in his ear, and for the first time he could perhaps afford to relax, as Verres's money had obviously proved most tempting to those tribes composed of a majority of city-dwellers. The Horatia, Lemonia, Papiria, Menenia … On and on, through the heat and the dust, Cicero sitting on a stool between counts but always rising whenever the voters passed in front of him after casting their ballots, his memory working to retrieve their names, thanking them, and passing on his respects to their families. The Sergia, Voltina, Pupina, Romilia … Cicero failed in the last tribe, not surprisingly, as it was Verres's own, but by the middle of the afternoon he had won the support of sixteen tribes and needed only two more for victory. Yet still Verres had not given up, and could be seen in huddled groups with his son and Timarchides. For a terrible hour, the balance seemed to tilt his way. The Sabatini did not go for Cicero, and nor did the Publilia. But then he just scraped in with the Scaptia, and finally it was the Falerna from northern Campania who put him over the top: eighteen tribes out of the thirty which had so far voted, with five left to come – but what did they matter? He was safely home, and at some point when I was not looking Verres quietly removed himself from the election field to calculate his losses. Caesar, whose own elevation to the senate had just been confirmed, was the first to turn and shake Cicero's hand. I could see Quintus triumphantly brandishing his fists in the air, Crassus staring angrily into the distance. There were cheers from the spectators who had been keeping their own tallies – those curious zealots who follow elections as fervently as other men do chariot racing – and who appreciated what had just happened. The victor himself looked stunned by his achievement, but no one could deny it, not even Crassus, who would shortly have to read it out, even though the words must have choked him. Against all odds, Marcus Cicero was an aedile of Rome.

A big crowd – they are always bigger after a victory – escorted Cicero from the Field of Mars all the way back to his house, where the domestic slaves were assembled to applaud him over the threshold. Even Diodotus the blind Stoic put in a rare appearance. All of us were proud to belong to such an eminent figure; his glory reflected on every member of his household; our worth and self-esteem increased with his. From the atrium, Tullia darted forward with a cry of 'Papa!' and wrapped her arms around his legs, and even Terentia stepped up and embraced him, smiling. I still hold that image of the three of them frozen in my mind – the triumphant young orator with his left hand on the head of his daughter and his right clasped about the shoulders of his happy wife. Nature bestows this gift, at least, on those who rarely smile: when they do, their faces are transformed, and I saw at that moment how Terentia, for all her complaints about her husband, nonetheless relished his brilliance and success.

It was Cicero who reluctantly broke the embrace. 'I thank you all,' he declared, looking around at his admiring audience. 'But this is not the time for celebrations. That will only come when Verres is defeated. Tomorrow, at long last, I shall open the prosecution in the forum, and let us pray to the gods that before too many days have passed, fresh and far greater honour will descend upon this household. So what are you waiting for?' He smiled and clapped his hands. 'Back to work!'

Cicero retired with Quintus to his study, and beckoned to me to follow. He threw himself into his chair with a gasp of relief and kicked off his shoes. For the first time in more than a week the tension in his face seemed to have eased. I assumed he would now want to begin on the urgent task of pulling together his speech, but apparently he had other plans for me. I was to go back out into the city with Sositheus and Laurea, and between us we were to visit all the Sicilian witnesses, give them the news of his election, check that they were holding firm, and instruct them all to present themselves in court the following morning.

'All?' I repeated in astonishment. 'All one hundred?'

'That is right,' he replied. The old decisiveness was back in his voice. 'And tell Eros to hire a dozen porters – reliable men – to carry every box of evidence down to court at the same time as I go down tomorrow.'

'All the witnesses ... A dozen porters ... Every box of evidence ...' I was making a list of his orders. 'But this is going to take me until midnight,' I said, unable to conceal my bewilderment.

'Poor Tiro. But do not worry – there will be time enough to sleep when we are dead.'

'I am not worried about my sleep, Senator,' I said stiffly. 'I was wondering when I was going to have time to help you with your speech.'

'I shall not require your help,' he said with a slight smile, and raised a finger to his lips, to warn me that I must say nothing. But as I had no idea of the significance of his remark, there was hardly any danger of my revealing his plans, and not for the first time I left his presence in a state of some confusion.

IX

And so it came about that on the fifth day of August, in the consulship of Gnaeus Pompey Magnus and Marcus Licinius Crassus, one year and nine months after Sthenius had first come to see Cicero, the trial of Gaius Verres began.

Bear in mind the summer heat. Calculate the number of victims with an interest in seeing Verres brought to justice. Remember that Rome was, in any case, swarming with citizens in town for the census, the elections and the impending games of Pompey. Consider that the hearing pitched the two greatest orators of the day in head-to-head combat ('a duel of real magnitude', as Cicero later called it). Put all this together, and you may begin to guess something of the atmosphere in the extortion court that morning. Hundreds of spectators, determined to have a decent vantage point, had slept out in the forum overnight. By dawn, there was nowhere left to stand that offered any shade. By the second hour, there was nowhere left at all. In the porticoes and on the steps of the Temple of Castor, in the forum itself and in the colonnades surrounding it, on the rooftops and balconies of the houses, on the sides of the hills – anywhere that human beings could squeeze themselves into, or hang off, or perch on – there you would find the people of Rome.

Frugi and I scurried around like a pair of sheepdogs, herding our witnesses into court, and what an exotic and colourful assembly they made, in their sacred robes and native dress, victims from every stage of Verres's career, drawn by the promise of vengeance – priests of Juno and Ceres, the mystagogues of the Syracusan Minerva and the sacred virgins of Diana; Greek nobles whose descent was traced to Cecrops or Eurysthenes or to the great Ionian and Minyan houses, and Phoenicians whose ancestors had been priests of Tyrian Melcarth, or claimed kindred with the Zidonian Iah; eager crowds of impoverished heirs and their guardians, bankrupt farmers and grain merchants and ship owners, fathers bewailing their children carried off to slavery, children mourning for their parents dead in the governor's dungeons; deputations from the foot of Mount Taurus, from the shores of the Black Sea, from many cities of the Grecian mainland, from the islands of the Aegean and of course from every city and market town of Sicily.

I was so busy helping to ensure that all the witnesses were admitted, and that every box of evidence was in its place and securely guarded, that only gradually did I come to realise what a spectacle Cicero had stage-managed. Those evidence boxes, for example, now included public testimony collected by the elders of virtually every town in Sicily. It was only when the jurors started shouldering their way through the masses and taking their places on the benches that I realised – showman that he was – why Cicero had been so insistent on having *everything* in place at once. The impression on the court was overwhelming. Even the hard-faces, like old Catulus and Isauricus, registered astonishment. As for Glabrio, when he came out of the temple preceded by his lictors, he paused for a moment on the top step, and swayed half a pace backwards when confronted by that wall of faces.

Cicero, who had been standing apart until the last possible moment, squeezed through the crowd and climbed the steps to his place on the prosecutor's bench. There was a sudden quietness; a silent quiver of anticipation in the still air. Ignoring the shouts of encouragement from his supporters, he turned and shielded his eyes against the sun and scanned the vast audience, squinting to right and left, as I imagine a general might check the lie of the land and position of the clouds before a battle. Then he sat down, while I stationed myself at his back so that I could pass him any document he needed. The clerks of the court set up Glabrio's curule chair – the signal that the tribunal was in session – and everything was ready, save for the presence of Verres and Hortensius. Cicero, who was as cool as I had ever seen him, leaned back and whispered to me, 'After all that, perhaps he is not coming.' Needless to say, he *was* coming – Glabrio sent one of his lictors to fetch him – but Hortensius was giving us a foretaste of his tactics, which would be to waste as much time as possible. Eventually, perhaps an hour late, to ironic applause, the immaculate figure of the consul-elect eased through the press of spectators, followed by his junior counsel – none other than young Scipio Nasica, the love rival of

Cato – then Quintus Metellus, and finally came Verres himself, looking redder than usual in the heat. For a man with any shred of conscience, it would surely have been a vision out of hell, to see those ranks of his victims and accusers, all ranged against him. But this monster merely bowed at them, as if he were delighted to greet old acquaintances.

Glabrio called the court to order, but before Cicero could rise to begin his speech, Hortensius jumped up to make a point of order: under the Cornelian Law, he declared, a prosecutor was entitled to call no more than forty-eight witnesses, but this prosecutor had brought to court at least double that number, purely for the purpose of intimidation! He then embarked on a long, learned and elegant speech about the origins of the extortion court, which lasted for what felt like another hour. At length, Glabrio cut him off, saying there was nothing in the law about restricting the number of witnesses present in court, only the number giving verbal evidence. Once again, he invited Cicero to open his case, and once again, Hortensius intervened with another point of order. The crowd began to jeer, but he pressed on, as he did repeatedly whenever Cicero rose to speak, and thus the first few hours of the day were lost in vexatious legal point-scoring.

It was not until the middle of the afternoon, when Cicero was wearily getting to his feet for the ninth or tenth time, that Hortensius at last remained seated. Cicero looked at him, waited, then slowly spread his arms wide in mock-amazement. A wave of laughter went round the forum. Hortensius responded by gesturing with a foppish twirl of his hand to the well of the court, as if to say, 'Be my guest.' Cicero bowed courteously and came forward. He cleared his throat.

There could scarcely have been a worse moment at which to begin such an immense undertaking. The heat was unbearable. The crowd was now bored and restless. Hortensius was smirking. There were only perhaps two hours left before the court adjourned for the evening. And yet this was to be one of the most decisive moments in the history of our Roman law – indeed, in the history of all law, everywhere, I should not wonder.

'Gentlemen of the court,' said Cicero, and I bent my head over my tablet and noted the words in shorthand. I waited for him to continue. For almost the first time before a major speech, I had no idea what he was going to say. I waited a little longer, my heart thumping, and then nervously glanced up to find him walking across the court away from me. I thought he was going to stop and confront Verres, but instead he walked straight past him and halted in front of the senators in the jury.

'Gentlemen of the court,' he repeated, addressing them directly, 'at this great political crisis, there has been offered to you, not through man's wisdom but almost as the direct gift of heaven, the very thing you most need – a thing that will help more than anything else to mitigate the unpopularity of your order and the suspicion surrounding these courts. A belief has become established – as harmful to the republic as it is to yourselves – that these courts, with you senators as the jury, will never convict any man, however guilty, if he has sufficient *money*.'

He put a wonderful, contemptuous stress on the last word. 'You are not wrong there!' shouted a voice in the crowd.

'But the character of the man I am prosecuting,' continued Cicero, 'is such that you may use him to restore your own good name. Gaius Verres has robbed the treasury and behaved like a pirate and a destroying pestilence in his province of Sicily. You have only to find this man guilty, and respect in you will be rightly restored. But if you do not – if his immense wealth is sufficient to shatter your honesty – well then, I shall achieve one thing at least. The nation will not believe Verres to be right and me wrong – but they will certainly know all they need to know about a jury of Roman senators!'

It was a nice stroke to start off with. There was a rustle of approval from the great crowd that was like a wind moving through a forest, and in some curious sense the focus of the trial seemed to shift all at once twenty paces to the left. It was as if the senators, sweating in the hot sun and squirming uncomfortably on their wooden benches, had become the accused, while the vast press of witnesses, drawn from every corner of the Mediterranean, was the jury. Cicero had never addressed such an immense throng before, but Molon's training on the seashore stood him in good stead, and when he turned to the forum his voice rang clear and true.

'Let me tell you of the impudent and insane plan that is now in Verres's mind. It is plain to him that I am approaching this case so well prepared that I shall be able to pin him down as a robber and a criminal, not merely in the hearing of this court but in the eyes of the whole world. But in spite of this, he holds so low an opinion of the aristocracy, he believes the senatorial courts to be so utterly abandoned and corrupt, that he goes about boasting openly that he has bought the safest date for his trial, he has bought the jury, and just to be on the safe side he has also bought the consular election for his two titled friends who have tried to intimidate my witnesses!'

This was what the crowd had come to hear. The rustle of approval became a roar. Metellus jumped up in anger, and so did Hortensius – yes, even Hortensius, who normally greeted any taunt in the arena with nothing more strenuous than a raised eyebrow. They began gesticulating angrily at Cicero.

'What?' he responded, turning on them. 'Did you count on my saying nothing of so serious a matter? On my caring for anything, except my duty and my honour, when the country and my own reputation are in such danger? Metellus, I am amazed at you. To attempt to intimidate witnesses, especially these timorous and calamity-stricken Sicilians, by appealing to their awe of you as consul-elect, and to the power of your two brothers – if this is not judicial corruption, I should be glad to know what is! What would you not do for an innocent kinsman if you abandon duty and honour for an utter rascal who is no kin of yours at all? Because I tell you this: Verres has been going round saying that you were only made consul because of his exertions, and that by January he will have the two consuls and the president of the court to suit him!'

I had to stop writing at this point, because the noise was too great for me to hear. Metellus and Hortensius both had their hands cupped to their mouths and were bellowing at Cicero. Verres was gesturing angrily at Glabrio to put a stop to this. The jury of senators sat immobile – most of them, I am sure, wishing they were anywhere but where they were – while individual spectators were having to be restrained by the lictors from storming the court. Eventually, Glabrio managed to restore order, and Cicero resumed, in a much calmer voice.

'So these are their tactics. Today the court did not start its business until the middle of the afternoon – they are already reckoning that today does not count at all. It is only ten days to the games of Pompey the Great. These will occupy fifteen days and will be followed immediately by the Roman Games. So it will not be until after an interval of nearly forty days that they expect to begin their reply. They count on being able then, with the help of long speeches and technical evasions, to prolong the trial until the Games of Victory begin. These games are followed without a break by the Plebeian Games, after which there will be very few days, or none at all, on which the court can sit. In this way they reckon that all the impetus of the prosecution will be spent and exhausted, and that the whole case will come up afresh before Marcus Metellus, who is sitting there on this jury.

'So what am I to do? If I spend upon my speech the full time allotted me by law, there is the gravest danger that the man I am prosecuting will slip through my fingers. "Make your speech shorter" is the obvious answer I was given a few days ago, and that is good advice. But, having thought the matter over, I shall go one better. Gentlemen, *I shall make no speech at all.*'

I glanced up in astonishment. Cicero was looking at Hortensius, and his rival was staring back at him with the most wonderful frozen expression on his face. He looked like a man who has been walking through a wood cheerfully enough, thinking himself safely alone, and has suddenly heard a twig snap behind him and has stopped dead in alarm.

'That is right, Hortensius,' said Cicero. 'I am not going to play your game and spend the next ten days in the usual long address. I am not going to let the case drag on till January, when you and Metellus as consuls can use your lictors to drag my witnesses before you and frighten them into silence. I am not going to allow you gentlemen of the jury the luxury of forty days to forget my charges, so that you can then lose yourselves and your consciences in the tangled thickets of Hortensius's rhetoric. I am not going to delay the settlement of this case until all these multitudes who have come to Rome for the census and the games have dispersed to their homes in Italy. I am going to call my witnesses at once, beginning now, and this will be my procedure: I shall read out the individual charge. I shall comment and elaborate upon it. I shall bring forth the witness who supports it, and question him, and then you, Hortensius, will have the same opportunity as me for comment and cross-examination. I shall do all this and I shall rest my case within the space of ten days.'

All my long life I have treasured – and for what little remains of it I shall continue to treasure – the reactions of Hortensius, Verres, Metellus and Scipio Nasica at that moment. Of course, Hortensius was on his feet as soon as he had recovered his breath and was denouncing this break with precedent as entirely illegal. But Glabrio was ready for him, and told him brusquely that it was up to Cicero to present his case in whatever manner he wished, and that he, for one, was sick of interminable speeches, as he had made clear in this very court before the consular elections. His remarks had obviously been prepared beforehand, and Hortensius rose again to accuse him of collusion with the prosecution. Glabrio, who was an irritable man at the best of times, told him bluntly he had better guard his tongue, or he would have his lictors remove him from the court – consul-elect or no. Hortensius sat down furiously, folded his arms and scowled at his feet, as Cicero concluded his opening address, once again by turning on the jury.

'Today the eyes of the world are upon us, waiting to see how far the conduct of each man among us will be marked by obedience to his conscience and observance of the law. Even as you will pass your verdict upon the prisoner, so the people of Rome will pass its verdict upon yourselves. The case of Verres will determine whether, in a court composed of senators, the condemnation of a very guilty and very rich man can possibly occur. Because all the world knows that Verres is distinguished by nothing except his monstrous offences and his immense wealth. Therefore if he is acquitted it will be impossible to imagine any explanation except the most shameful. So I advise you, gentlemen, for your own sakes, to see that this does not occur.' And with that he turned his back on them. 'I call my first witness – Sthenius of Thermae.'

I doubt very strongly whether any of the aristocrats on that jury – Catulus, Isauricus, Metellus, Catilina, Lucretius, Aemilius and the rest – had ever been addressed with such insolence before, especially by a new man without a single ancestral mask to show on his atrium wall. How they must have loathed being made to sit there and take it, especially given the deliriums of ecstasy with which Cicero was received by the vast crowd in the forum when he sat down. As for Hortensius, it was possible almost to feel sorry for him. His entire career had been founded on his ability to memorise immense orations and deliver them with the aplomb of an actor. Now he was effectively struck mute; worse, he was faced with the prospect of having to deliver four dozen mini-speeches in reply to each of Cicero's witnesses over the next ten days. He had not done sufficient research even remotely to attempt this, as became cruelly evident when Sthenius took the witness stand. Cicero had called him first as a mark of respect for the originator of this whole fantastic undertaking, and the

Sicilian did not let him down. He had waited a long time for his day in court, and he made the most of it, giving a heart-wringing account of the way Verres had abused his hospitality, stolen his property, trumped up charges against him, fined him and tried to have him flogged, sentenced him to death in his absence and then forged the records of the Syracusan court – records which Cicero produced in evidence, and passed around the jury.

But when Glabrio called upon Hortensius to cross-examine the witness, the Dancing Master, not unnaturally, showed some reluctance to take the floor. The one golden rule of cross-examination is never, under any circumstances, to ask a question to which you do not know the answer, and Hortensius simply had no idea what Sthenius might say next. He shuffled a few documents, held a whispered consultation with Verres, then approached the witness stand. What could he do? After a few petulant questions, the implication of which was that the Sicilian was fundamentally hostile to Roman rule, he asked him why, of all the lawyers available, he had chosen to go straight to Cicero – a man known to be an agitator of the lower classes. Surely his whole motivation from the start was merely to stir up trouble?

'But I did not go straight to Cicero,' replied Sthenius in his ingenuous way. 'The first advocate I went to was you.'

Even some of the jury laughed at that.

Hortensius swallowed, and attempted to join in the merriment. 'Did you really? I can't say that I remember you.'

'Well you wouldn't, would you? You are a busy man. But I remember you, Senator. You said you were representing Verres. You said you didn't care how much of my property he had stolen – no court would ever believe the word of a Sicilian over a Roman.'

Hortensius had to wait for the storm of cat-calls to die down. 'I have no further questions for this witness,' he said in a grim voice, and with that the court was adjourned until the following day.

It had been my intention to describe in detail the trial of Gaius Verres, but now I come to set it down, I see there is no point. After Cicero's tactical masterstroke on that first day, Verres and his advocates resembled nothing so much as the victims of a siege: holed up in their little fortress, surrounded on every side by their enemies, battered day after day by a rain of missiles, and with tunnels undermining their crumbling walls. They had no means of fighting back. Their only hope was somehow to withstand the onslaught for the full nine days remaining, and then try to regroup during the lull enforced by Pompey's games. Cicero's objective was equally clear: to obliterate Verres's defences so completely that by the time he had finished laying out his case not even the most corrupt senatorial jury in Rome would dare to acquit him.

He set about this mission with his usual discipline. The prosecution team would gather before dawn. While Cicero performed his exercises, was shaved and dressed, I would read out the testimony of the witnesses he would be calling that day, and run through our schedule of evidence. He would then dictate to me the rough outline of what he intended to say. For an hour or two he would familiarise himself with the day's brief and thoroughly memorise his remarks, while Quintus, Frugi and I ensured that all his witnesses and evidence boxes were ready. We would then parade down the hill to the forum – and parades they were, for the general view around Rome was that Cicero's performance in the extortion court was the greatest show in town. The crowds were as large on the second and third days as they had been on the first, and the witnesses' performances were often heartbreaking, as they collapsed in tears recounting their ill treatment. I remember in particular Dio of Halaesa, swindled out of ten thousand sesterces, and two brothers from Agyrium forced to hand over their entire inheritance of four thousand. There would have been more, but Lucius Metellus had actually refused to let a dozen witnesses leave the island to testify, among them Heraclius of Syracuse, the chief priest of Jupiter – an outrage against justice which Cicero neatly turned to his advantage. 'Our allies' rights,' he boomed, 'do not even include permission to complain of their sufferings!' Throughout all this, Hortensius, amazing to relate, never said a word. Cicero would finish his examination of a witness, Glabrio would offer the King of the Law Courts his chance to cross-examine, and His Majesty would regally shake his head, or declare grandly, 'No questions for this witness.' On the fourth day, Verres pleaded illness and tried to be excused attendance, but Glabrio was having none of it, and told him he would be carried down to the forum on his bed if necessary.

It was on the following afternoon that Cicero's cousin Lucius at last returned to Rome, his mission in Sicily accomplished. Cicero was overjoyed to find him waiting at the house when we got back from court, and embraced him tearfully. Without Lucius's support in dispatching witnesses and boxes of evidence back to the mainland, Cicero's case would not have been half as strong. But the seven-month effort had clearly exhausted Lucius, who had not been a strong man to begin with. He was now alarmingly thin, and had developed a painful, racking cough. Even so, his commitment to bringing Verres to justice was unwavering – so much so that he had missed the opening of the trial in order to take a detour on his journey back to Rome. He had stayed in Puteoli and tracked down two more witnesses: the Roman knight Gaius Numitorius, who had witnessed the crucifixion of Gavius in Messana, and a friend of his, a merchant named Marcus Annius, who had been in Syracuse when the Roman banker Herennius had been judicially murdered.

'And where are these gentlemen?' asked Cicero eagerly.

'Here,' replied Lucius. 'In the tablinum. But I must warn you, they do not want to testify.'

Cicero hurried through to find two formidable men of middle age – 'The perfect witnesses from my point of view,' as he afterwards described them, 'prosperous, respectable, sober, and – above all – not Sicilian.' As Lucius had predicted, they were reluctant to get involved. They were businessmen, with no desire to make powerful enemies, and did not relish the prospect of taking starring roles in Cicero's great anti-aristocratic production in the Roman forum. But he wore them down, for they were not fools, either, and could see that in the ledger of profit and loss, they stood to gain most by aligning themselves with the side that was winning. 'Do you know what Pompey said to Sulla, when the old man tried to deny him a triumph on his twenty-sixth birthday?' asked Cicero. 'He told me over dinner the other night: "More people worship a rising than a setting sun."' This potent combination of name-dropping and appeals to patriotism and self-interest at last won them round, and by the time they went into dinner with Cicero and his family, they had pledged their support.

'I knew if I had them in your company for a few moments,' whispered Lucius, 'they would do whatever you wanted.'

I had expected Cicero to put them on the witness stand the very next day, but he was too smart for that. 'A show must always end with a climax,' he said. By now he was ratcheting up the level of outrage with each new piece of evidence, having moved on through judicial corruption, extortion and straightforward robbery, to cruel and unusual punishment. On the eighth day of the trial, he dealt with the testimony of two Sicilian naval captains, Phalacrus of Centuripa and Onasus of Segesta, who described how they and their men had only escaped floggings and executions by bribing Verres's freedman, Timarchides (present in court, I am glad to say, to experience his humiliation personally). Worse: the families of those who had not been able to raise sufficient funds to secure the release of their relatives had been told they would still have to pay a bribe to the official executioner, Sextius, or he would deliberately make a mess of the beheadings. 'Think of that unbearable burden of pain,' declaimed Cicero, 'of the anguish that racked those unhappy parents, thus compelled to purchase for their children by bribery not life but a speedy death!' I could see the senators on the jury shaking their heads at this, and muttering to one another, and each time Glabrio invited Hortensius to cross-examine the witnesses, and Hortensius simply responded yet again, 'No questions,' they groaned. Their position was becoming intolerable, and that night the first rumours reached us that Verres had already packed up the contents of his house and was preparing to flee into exile.

Such was the state of affairs on the ninth day, when we brought Annius and Numitorius into court. If anything, the crowd in the forum was bigger than ever, for there were now only two days left until Pompey's great games. Verres came late, and obviously drunk. He stumbled as he climbed the steps of the temple up to the tribunal, and Hortensius had to steady him as the crowd roared with laughter. As he passed Cicero's place, he flashed him a shattered, red-eyed look of fear and rage – the hunted, cornered look of an animal at bay. Cicero got straight down to business and called as his first witness Annius, who described how he had been inspecting a cargo down at the harbour in Syracuse one morning, when a friend had come running to tell him that their business associate, Herennius, was in chains in the forum and pleading for his life.

'So what did you do?'

'Naturally, I went at once.'

'And what was the scene?'

'There were perhaps a hundred people crying out that Herennius was a Roman citizen, and could not be executed without a proper trial.'

'How did you all know that Herennius was a Roman? Was he not a banker from Spain?'

'Many of us knew him personally. Although he had business in Spain, he had been born to a Roman family in Syracuse and had grown up in the city.'

'And what was Verres's response to your pleas?'

'He ordered Herennius to be beheaded immediately.' There was a groan of horror around the court.

'And who dealt the fatal blow?'

'The public executioner, Sextius.'

'And did he make a clean job of it?'

'I am afraid he did not, no.'

'Clearly,' said Cicero, turning to the jury, 'Herennius had not paid Verres and his gang of thieves a large enough bribe.'

For most of the trial, Verres had sat slumped in his chair, but on this morning, fired by drink, he jumped up and began shouting that he had never taken any such bribe. Hortensius had to pull him down. Cicero ignored him and went on calmly questioning his witness.

'This is an extraordinary situation, is it not? A hundred of you vouch for the identity of this Roman citizen, yet Verres does not even wait an hour to establish the truth of who he is. How do you account for it?'

'I can account for it easily, Senator. Herennius was a passenger on a ship from Spain which was impounded with all its cargo by Verres's agents. He was sent to the Stone Quarries, along with everyone else on board, then dragged out to be publicly executed as a pirate. What Verres did not realise was that Herennius was not from Spain at all. He was known to the Roman community in Syracuse and would be recognised. But by the time Verres discovered his mistake, Herennius could not be allowed to go free, because he knew too much about what the governor was up to.'

'Forgive me, I do not understand,' said Cicero, playing the innocent. 'Why would Verres want to execute an innocent passenger on a cargo ship as a pirate?'

'He needed to show a sufficient number of executions.'

'Why?'

'Because he was being paid bribes to let the real pirates go free.'

Verres was up on his feet again shouting that it was a lie, and this time Cicero did not ignore him, but took a few paces towards him. 'A lie, you monster? A lie? Then why in your own prison records does it state that Herennius was released? And why do they further state that the notorious pirate captain, Heracleo, was executed, when no one on the island ever saw him die? I shall tell you why – because you, the Roman governor, responsible for the safety of the seas, were all the while taking bribes from the very pirates themselves!'

'Cicero, the great lawyer, who thinks himself so clever!' said Verres bitterly, his words slurred by drink. 'Who thinks he knows everything! Well, here is something you don't know. I have Heracleo in my private custody, here in my house in Rome, and he can tell you all himself that it's a lie!'

Amazing now, to reflect that a man could blurt out something so foolish, but the facts are there – they are in the record – and amid the pandemonium in court, Cicero could be heard demanding of Glabrio that the famous pirate be fetched from Verres's house by the lictors and placed in official custody, 'for the public safety'. Then, while that was being done, he called as his second witness of the day Gaius Numitorius. Privately, I thought that Cicero was rushing it too much: that he could have milked the admission about Heracleo for more. But the great advocate had sensed that the moment for the kill had arrived, and for months, ever since we had first landed in Sicily, he had known exactly the blade he wished to use. Numitorius swore an oath to tell the truth and took the stand, and Cicero quickly led him through his testimony to establish the essential facts about Publius Gavius: that he was a merchant travelling on a ship from Spain; that his ship had been impounded and the passengers all taken to the Stone Quarries, from which Gavius had somehow managed to escape; that he had made his way to Messana to take a ship to the mainland, had been apprehended as he went aboard, and handed over to Verres when he visited the town. The silence of the listening multitudes was intense.

'Describe to the court what happened next.'

'Verres convened a tribunal in the forum of Messana,' said Numitorius, 'and then he had Gavius dragged before him. He announced to everyone that this man was a spy, for which there was only one just penalty. Then he ordered a cross set up overlooking the straits to Regium, so that the prisoner could gaze upon Italy as he died, and had Gavius stripped naked and publicly flogged before us all. Then he was tortured with hot irons. And then he was crucified.'

'Did Gavius speak at all?'

'Only at the beginning, to swear that the accusation was not true. He was not a foreign spy. He was a Roman citizen, a councillor from the town of Consa, and a former soldier in the Roman cavalry, under the command of Lucius Raecius.'

'What did Verres say to that?'

'He said that these were lies, and commanded that the execution begin.'

'Can you describe how Gavius met his dreadful death?'

'He met it very bravely, Senator.'

'Like a Roman?'

'Like a Roman.'

'Did he cry out at all?' (I knew what Cicero was after.)

'Only while he was being whipped, and he could see the irons being heated.'

'And what did he say?'

'Every time a blow landed, he said, "I am a Roman citizen."'

'Would you repeat what he said, more loudly please, so that all can hear.'

'He said, "I am a Roman citizen."'

'So just that?' said Cicero. 'Let me be sure I understand you. A blow lands' – he put his wrists together, raised them above his head and jerked forwards, as if his back had just been lashed – 'and he says, through gritted teeth, "I am a Roman citizen." A blow lands' – and again he jerked forwards – '"I am a Roman citizen." A blow lands. *"I am a Roman citizen –* "'

These flat words of mine cannot begin to convey the effect of Cicero's performance upon those who saw it. The hush around the court amplified his words. It was as if all of us now were witnesses to this monstrous miscarriage of justice. Some men and women – friends of Gavius, I believe – began to scream, and there was a growing swell of outrage from the masses in the forum. Yet again, Verres shook off Hortensius's restraining hand and stood up. 'He was a filthy spy!' he bellowed. 'A spy! He only said it to delay his proper punishment!'

'But he said it!' said Cicero, triumphantly, wheeling on him, his finger jabbing in outrage. 'You admit he said it! Out of your own mouth I accuse you – the man claimed to be a Roman citizen and you did nothing! This mention of his citizenship did not lead you to hesitate or delay, even for a little, the infliction of this cruel and disgusting death! If you, Verres, had been made a prisoner in Persia or the remotest part of India, and were being dragged off to execution, what cry would you be uttering, except that you were a Roman citizen? What then of this man whom you were hurrying

to his death? Could not that statement, that claim of citizenship, have saved him for an hour, for a day, while its truth was checked? No, it could not – not with you in the judgement seat! And yet the poorest man, of humblest birth, in whatever savage land, has always until now had the confidence to know that the cry "I am a Roman citizen" is his final defence and sanctuary. It was not Gavius, not one obscure man, whom you nailed upon that cross of agony: it was the universal principle that Romans are free men!'

The roar which greeted the end of Cicero's tirade was terrifying. Rather than diminishing after a few moments, it gathered itself afresh and rose in volume and pitch, and I became aware, at the periphery of my vision, of a movement towards us. The awnings under which some of the spectators had been standing as protection against the sun began to collapse with a terrible tearing sound. A man dropped off a balcony on to the crowd beneath. There were screams. What was unmistakably a lynch mob began storming the steps to the platform. Hortensius and Verres stood up so quickly in their panic that they knocked over the bench behind them. Glabrio could be heard yelling that the court was adjourned, then he and his lictors hastened up the remaining steps towards the temple, with the accused and his eminent counsel in undignified pursuit. Some of the jury also fled into the sanctuary of the holy building (but not Catulus: I distinctly remember him standing like a sharp rock, staring unflinchingly ahead, as the current of bodies broke and swirled around him). The heavy bronze doors slammed shut. It was left to Cicero to try to restore order by climbing on to his own bench and gesturing for calm, but four or five men, rough-looking fellows, ran up and seized his legs and lifted him away. I was terrified, for both his safety and my own, but he stretched out his arms as if he was embracing the whole world. When they had settled him on their shoulders they spun him around to face the forum. The blast of applause was like the opening of a furnace door and the chant of 'Cic-er-o! Cic-er-o! Cic-er-o! Cic-er-o!' split the skies of Rome.

And that, at last, was the end of Gaius Verres. We never learned exactly what went on inside the temple after Glabrio suspended the sitting, but Cicero's belief was that Hortensius and Metellus made it clear to their client that further defence was useless. Their own dignity and authority were in tatters: they simply had to cut him adrift before any more harm was done to the reputation of the senate. It no longer mattered how lavishly he had bribed the jury – no member of it would dare to vote to acquit him after the scenes they had just witnessed. At any rate, Verres slipped out of the temple when the mob had dispersed, and fled the city at nightfall – disguised, some say, as a woman – riding full pelt for southern Gaul. His destination was the port of Massilia, where exiles could traditionally swap their hard-luck stories over grilled mullet and pretend they were on the Bay of Naples.

All that remained to do now was to fix the level of his fine, and when Cicero returned home he convened a meeting to discuss the appropriate figure. Nobody will ever know the full value of what Verres stole during his years in Sicily – I have heard an estimate of forty million – but Lucius, as usual, was eager for the most radical course: the seizure of every asset Verres possessed. Quintus thought ten million would be about right. Cicero was curiously silent for a man who had just recorded such a stupendous victory, and sat in his study moodily toying with a metal stylus. Early in the afternoon, we received a letter from Hortensius, relaying an offer from Verres to pay one million into court as compensation. Lucius was particularly appalled – 'an insult', he called it – and Cicero had no hesitation in sending the messenger away with a flea in his ear. An hour later he was back, with what Hortensius called his 'final figure': a settlement of one and a half million. This time, Cicero dictated a longer reply:

From: Marcus Tullius Cicero
To: Quintus Hortensius Hortalus
Greetings!
In view of the ludicrously low sum your client is proposing as compensation for his unparalleled wickedness, I intend asking Glabrio to allow me to continue the prosecution tomorrow, when I shall exercise my right to address the court on this and other matters.

'Let us see how much he and his aristocratic friends relish the prospect of having their noses rubbed further into their own filth,' he exclaimed to me. I finished sealing the letter, and when I returned from giving it to the messenger, Cicero set about dictating the speech he proposed to deliver the next day – a slashing attack on the aristocrats for prostituting their great names, and the names of their ancestors, in defence of such a scoundrel as

Verres. Urged on by Lucius in particular, he poured out his loathing. 'We are aware with what jealousy, with what dislike, the merit and energy of "new men" are regarded by certain of the "nobles"; that we have only to shut our eyes for a moment to find ourselves caught in some trap; that if we leave them the smallest opening for any suspicion or charge of misconduct, we have to suffer for it at once; that we must never relax our vigilance, and never take a holiday. We have enemies – let us face them; tasks to perform – let us shoulder them; not forgetting that an open and declared enemy is less formidable than one who hides himself and says nothing!'

'There go another thousand votes,' muttered Quintus.

The afternoon wore on in this way, without any answer from Hortensius, until, at length, not long before dusk, there was a commotion from the street, and soon afterwards Eros came running into the study with the breathless news that Pompey the Great himself was in the vestibule. This was indeed an extraordinary turn-up, but Cicero and his brother had time to do no more than blink at one another before that familiar military voice could be heard barking, 'Where is he? Where is the greatest orator of the age?'

Cicero muttered an oath beneath his breath, and went out into the tablinum, followed by Quintus, then Lucius, and finally myself, just in time to see the senior consul come striding out of the atrium. The confines of that modest house made him bulk even larger than he did normally. 'And there he is!' he exclaimed. 'There is the man whom everyone comes to see!' He made straight for Cicero, threw his powerful arms around him, and embraced him in a bear hug. From where I was standing, just behind Cicero, I could see Pompey's crafty grey eyes taking in each of us in turn, and when he released his embarrassed host, he insisted on being introduced, even to me, so that I – a humble domestic slave from Arpinum – could now boast, at the age of thirty-four, that I had shaken hands with both the ruling consuls of Rome.

He had left his bodyguards out in the street and had come into the house entirely alone, a significant mark of trust and favour. Cicero, whose manners as always were impeccable, ordered Eros to tell Terentia that Pompey the Great was downstairs, and I was instructed to pour some wine.

'Only a little,' said Pompey, putting his large hand over the cup. 'We are on our way to dinner, and shall only stay a moment. But we could not pass our neighbour without calling in to pay our respects. We have been watching your progress, Cicero, over these past few days. We have been receiving reports from our friend Glabrio. Magnificent. We drink your health.' He raised his cup, but not a drop, I noticed, touched his lips. 'And now that this great enterprise is successfully behind you, we hope that we may see a little more of you, especially as I shall soon be merely a private citizen again.'

Cicero gave a slight bow. 'That would be my pleasure.'

'The day after tomorrow, for example – how are you placed?'

'That is the day of the opening of your games. Surely you will be occupied? Perhaps some other time ...'

'Nonsense. Come and watch the opening from our box. It will do you no harm to be seen in our company. Let the world observe our friendship,' he added grandly. 'You enjoy the games, do you not?'

Cicero hesitated, and I could see his brain working through the consequences, of both refusal and acceptance. But really he had no choice. 'I adore the games,' he said. 'I can think of nothing I would rather do.'

'Excellent,' beamed Pompey. At that moment Eros returned, with a message that Terentia was lying down, unwell, and sent her apologies. 'That is a pity,' said Pompey, looking slightly put out. 'But let us hope there will be some future opportunity.' He handed me his untouched wine. 'We must be on our way. No doubt you have much to do. Incidentally,' he said, turning on the threshold of the atrium, 'have you settled on the level of the fine yet?'

'Not yet,' replied Cicero.

'What have they offered?'

'One and a half million.'

'Take it,' said Pompey. 'You have covered them in shit. No need to make them eat it, too. It would be embarrassing to me personally and injurious to the stability of the state to proceed with this case further. You understand me?' He nodded in a friendly way and walked out. We heard the front door open and the commander of his bodyguard call his men to attention. The door closed. For a little while, nobody spoke.

'What a ghastly man,' said Cicero. 'Bring me another drink.' As I fetched the jug, I saw Lucius frowning.

'What gives him the right to talk to you like that?' he asked. 'He said it was a social visit.'

'A social visit! Oh, Lucius!' Cicero laughed. 'That was a visit from the rent collector.'

'The rent collector? What rent do you owe him?' Lucius might have been a philosopher, but he was not a complete idiot, and he realised then what had happened. 'Oh, I understand!' A look of disgust came across his face, and he turned away.

'Spare me your superiority,' said Cicero, catching his arm. 'I had no choice. Marcus Metellus had just drawn the extortion court. The jury was bribed. The hearing was fixed to fail. I was this far' – Cicero measured an inch with his thumb and forefinger – 'from abandoning the whole prosecution. And then Terentia said to me, "Make your speech shorter," and I realised that was the answer – to produce every document and every witness, and do it all in ten days, and *shame* them – that was it, Lucius: you understand me? – *shame* them before the whole of Rome, so they had no alternative except to find him guilty.'

In such a way did he speak, working all his persuasive powers upon his cousin, as if Lucius were a one-man jury which he needed to convince – reading his face, trying to find within it clues to the right words and arguments which would unlock his support.

'But *Pompey*,' said Lucius, bitterly. 'After what he did to you before!'

'All I needed, Lucius, was one thing – one tiny, tiny favour – and that was the assurance that I could proceed as I wished, and call my witnesses straight away. No bribery was involved; no corruption. I just knew I had to be sure to secure Glabrio's consent beforehand. But I could hardly, as the prosecutor, approach the praetor of the court myself. So I racked my brains: who could?'

Quintus said, 'There was only one man in Rome, Lucius.'

'Exactly!' cried Cicero. 'Only one man to whom Glabrio was honour-bound to listen. The man who had given him his son back, when his divorced wife died – Pompey.'

'But it was not a tiny favour,' said Lucius. 'It was a massive interference. And now there is a massive price to be paid for it – and not by you, but by the people of Sicily.'

'The people of Sicily?' repeated Cicero, beginning to lose his temper. 'The people of Sicily have never had a truer friend than me. There would never have been a prosecution without me. There would never have been an offer of one and a half million without me. By heaven, Gaius Verres would have been *consul* in two years' time but for me! You cannot reproach me for abandoning the people of Sicily!'

'Then refuse to pay his rent,' said Lucius, seizing hold of his hand. 'Tomorrow, in court, press for the maximum damages, and to hell with Pompey. You have the whole of Rome on your side. That jury will not dare to go against you. Who cares about Pompey? In five months' time, as he says himself, he will not even be consul. Promise me.'

Cicero clasped Lucius's hand fervently in both of his and gazed deep into his eyes – the old double-grip sincere routine, which I had seen so often in this very room. 'I promise you,' he said. 'I promise you I shall think about it.'

Perhaps he did think about it. Who am I to judge? But I doubt it can have occupied his mind for more than an instant. Cicero was no revolutionary. He never desired to set himself at the head of a mob, tearing down the state: and that would have been his only hope of survival, if he had turned Pompey against him as well as the aristocracy. 'The trouble with Lucius,' he said putting his feet up on the desk after his cousin had gone, 'is that he thinks politics is a fight for justice. Politics is a profession.'

'Do you think Verres bribed Pompey to intervene, to lower the damages?' asked Quintus, voicing exactly the possibility which had occurred to me.

'It could be. More likely he simply wants to avoid being caught in the middle of a civil war between the people and the senate. Speaking for myself, I would be happy to seize everything Verres possesses, and leave the wretch to live on Gaulish grass. But that is not going to happen,' he sighed, 'so we had better see how far we can make this one and a half million stretch.'

The three of us spent the rest of the evening compiling a list of the most worthy claimants, and after Cicero had deducted his own costs, of close to one hundred thousand, we reckoned he could just about manage to fulfil his obligations, at least to the likes of Sthenius, and to those witnesses who had travelled all the way to Rome. But what could one say to the priests? How could one put a price on looted temple statues made of gems and precious metals, long since broken up and melted down by Verres's goldsmiths? And what payment could ever recompense the families and friends of Gavius and Herennius and the other innocents he had murdered? The work gave Cicero his first real taste of what it is like to have power

– which is usually, when it comes down to it, a matter of choosing between equally unpalatable options – and fairly bitter he found it.

We went into court in the usual manner the following morning, and there was the usual big crowd in their usual places – everything the same, in fact, except for the absence of Verres, and the presence of twenty or thirty men of the magistrates' patrol, stationed around the perimeter of the tribunal. Glabrio made a short speech, opening the session and warning that he would not tolerate any disturbances similar to those which had occurred the previous day. Then he called on Hortensius to make a statement.

'Due to ill health,' Hortensius began, and there was the most wonderful shout of laughter from all sides. It was some time before he was able to proceed. 'Due to ill health,' he repeated, 'brought on by the strain of these proceedings, and wishing to spare the state any further disruption, my client Gaius Verres no longer proposes to offer a defence to the charges brought by the special prosecutor.'

He sat down. There was applause from the Sicilians at this concession, but little response from the spectators. They were waiting to take their lead from Cicero. He stood, thanked Hortensius for his statement – 'somewhat shorter than the speeches he is in the habit of making in these surroundings' – and demanded the maximum penalty under the Cornelian Law: a full loss of civil rights, in perpetuity, 'so that never again can the shadow of Gaius Verres menace his victims or threaten the just administration of the Roman republic'. This elicited the first real cheer of the morning.

'I wish,' continued Cicero, 'that I could undo his crimes, and restore to both men and gods all that he has robbed from them. I wish I could give back to Juno the offerings and adornments of her shrines at Melita and Samos. I wish Minerva could see again the decorations of her temple at Syracuse. I wish Diana's statue could be restored to the town of Segesta, and Mercury's to the people of Tyndaris. I wish I could undo the double injury to Ceres, whose images were carried away from both Henna and Catina. But the villain has fled, leaving behind only the stripped walls and bare floors of his houses here in Rome and in the country. These are the only assets which can be seized and sold. His counsel assesses the value of these at one and a half million sesterces, and this is what I must ask for and accept as recompense for his crimes.'

There was a groan, and someone shouted, 'Not enough!'

'It is not enough. I agree. And perhaps some of those in this court, who defended Verres when his star was rising, and others who promised him their support if they found themselves among his jurors, might inspect their consciences – might inspect, indeed, the contents of their villas!'

This brought Hortensius to his feet to complain that the prosecutor was talking in riddles.

'Well,' responded Cicero in a flash, 'as Verres provided him with an ivory sphinx, the consul-elect should find no difficulty solving riddles.'

It cannot have been a premeditated joke, as Cicero had no idea what Hortensius was going to say. Or perhaps, on second thoughts, having written that, I am being naïve, and it was actually part of that store of spontaneous witticisms which Cicero regularly laid up by candlelight to use should the opportunity arise. Whatever the truth, it was proof of how important humour can be on a public occasion, for nobody now remembers a thing about that last day in court except Cicero's crack about the ivory sphinx. I am not even sure, in retrospect, that it is particularly funny. But it brought the house down, and transformed what could have been an embarrassing speech into yet another triumph. 'Sit down quickly' – that was always Molon's advice when things were going well, and Cicero took it. I handed him a towel and he mopped his face and dried his hands as the applause continued. And with that, his exertions in the prosecution of Gaius Verres were at an end.

That afternoon, the senate met for its final debate before it went into a fifteen-day recess for Pompey's games. By the time Cicero had finished smoothing matters over with the Sicilians, he was late for the start of the session, and we had to run together from the Temple of Castor, right across the forum to the senate house. Crassus, as the presiding consul for the month, had already called the house to order and was reading the latest dispatch from Lucullus on the progress of the campaign in the East. Rather than interrupt him by making a conspicuous entry, Cicero stood at the bar of the chamber, and we listened to Lucullus's report. The aristocratic general had, by his own account, scored a series of crushing victories, entering the kingdom of Tigranes, defeating the king himself in battle, slaughtering tens of thousands of the enemy, advancing deeper into hostile territory to capture the city of Nisibisis, and taking the king's brother as hostage.

'Crassus must feel like throwing up,' Cicero whispered to me gleefully. 'His only consolation will be to know that Pompey is even more furiously jealous.' And, indeed, Pompey, sitting beside Crassus, his arms folded, did look sunk in a gloomy reverie.

When Crassus had finished speaking, Cicero took advantage of the lull to enter the chamber. The day was hot and the shafts of light from the high windows lit jewelled swirls of midges. He walked purposefully, head erect, watched by everyone, down the central aisle, past his old place in obscurity by the door, towards the consular dais. The praetorian bench seemed full, but Cicero stood patiently beside it, waiting to claim his rightful place, for he knew – and the house knew – that the ancient reward for a successful prosecutor was the assumption of the defeated man's rank. I do not know how long the silence went on, but it seemed an awfully long time to me, during which the only sound came from the pigeons in the roof. It was Afranius who finally beckoned to him to sit beside him, and who cleared sufficient space by roughly shoving his neighbours along the wooden seat. Cicero picked his way across half a dozen pairs of outstretched legs and wedged himself defiantly into his place. He glanced around at his rivals, and met and held the gaze of each. No one challenged him. Eventually, someone rose to speak, and in a grudging voice congratulated Lucullus and his victorious legions – it might have been Pompey, now I come to think of it. Gradually the low drone of background conversation resumed.

I close my eyes and I see their faces still in the golden light of that late-summer afternoon – Cicero, Crassus, Pompey, Hortensius, Catulus, Catilina, the Metellus brothers – and it is hard for me to believe that they, and their ambitions, and even the very building they sat in, are now all so much dust.

PART TWO

PRAETORIAN

68–64 BC

'Nam eloquentiam quae admirationem non habet nullam iudico.'

'Eloquence which does not startle I don't consider eloquence.'
Cicero, letter to Brutus, 48 BC

X

I propose to resume my account at a point more than two years after the last roll ended – an elision which I fear says much about human nature, for if you were to ask me: 'Tiro, why do you choose to skip such a long period in Cicero's life?' I should be obliged to reply: 'Because, my friend, those were happy years, and few subjects make more tedious reading than happiness.'

The senator's aedileship turned out to be a great success. His chief responsibility was to keep the city supplied with cheap grain, and here his prosecution of Verres reaped him a great reward. To show their gratitude for his advocacy, the farmers and grain merchants of Sicily not only helped him by keeping their prices low: on one occasion they even gave him an entire shipment for nothing. Cicero was shrewd enough to ensure that others shared the credit. From the aediles' headquarters in the Temple of Ceres, he passed this bounty on for distribution to the hundred or so precinct bosses who really ran Rome, and many, out of gratitude, became his clients. With their help, over the following months, he built an electoral machine second to none (Quintus used to boast that he could have a crowd of two hundred on the streets within an hour whenever he chose), and henceforth little occurred in the city which the Ciceros did not know about. If some builders or a shopkeeper, for example, needed a particular licence, or wished to have their premises put on to the water supply, or were worried about the state of a local temple, sooner or later their problems were likely to come to the notice of the two brothers. It was this laborious attention to humdrum detail, as much as his soaring rhetoric, which made Cicero such a formidable politician. He even staged good games – or, rather, Quintus did, on his behalf – and at the climax of the Festival of Ceres, when, in accordance with tradition, foxes were released into the Circus Maximus with flaming torches tied to their backs, the entire crowd of two hundred thousand rose to acclaim him in the official box.

'That so many people can derive so much pleasure from such a revolting spectacle,' he said to me when he returned home that night, 'almost makes one doubt the very premise on which democracy is based.' But he was pleased nevertheless that the masses now thought of him as a good sport, as well as 'the Scholar' and 'the Greek'.

Matters went equally well with his legal practice. Hortensius, after a typically smooth and untroubled year as consul, spent increasingly lengthy periods on the Bay of Naples, communing with his bejewelled fish and wine-soaked trees, leaving Cicero in complete domination of the Roman bar. Gifts and legacies from grateful clients soon began flowing in such profusion that he was even able to advance his brother the million he needed to enter the senate – for Quintus had belatedly set his heart on a political career, even though he was a poor speaker and Cicero privately believed that soldiering was better suited to his temperament. But despite his increasing wealth and prestige, Cicero refused to move out of his father's house, fearing it would tarnish his image as the People's Champion to be seen swanking around on the Palatine Hill. Instead, without consulting Terentia, he borrowed heavily against his future earnings to buy a grand country villa, thirteen miles from the prying eyes of the city voters, in the Alban Hills near Tusculum. She pretended to be annoyed when he took her out to see it, and maintained that the elevated climate was bad for her rheumatics. But I could tell that she was secretly delighted to have such a fashionable retreat, only half a day's journey from Rome. Catulus owned the adjoining property, and Hortensius also had a house not far away, but such was the hostility between Cicero and the aristocrats that, despite the long summer days he spent reading and writing in his villa's cool and poplared glades, they never once invited him to dine. This did not disturb Cicero; rather, it amused him, for the house had once belonged to the nobles' greatest hero, Sulla, and he knew how much it must irritate them to see it in the hands of a new man from Arpinum. The villa had not been redecorated for more than a decade, and when he took possession an entire wall was devoted to a mural showing the dictator receiving a military decoration from his troops. Cicero made sure all his neighbours knew that his first act as owner was to have it whitewashed over.

Happy, then, was Cicero in the autumn of his thirty-ninth year: prosperous, popular, well rested after a summer in the country, and looking forward to the elections the following July, when he would be old enough to stand for a praetorship – the final stepping-stone before the glittering prize of the consulship itself.

And at this critical juncture in his fortunes, just as his luck was about to desert him and his life become interesting again, my narrative resumes.

At the end of September it was Pompey's birthday, and for the third year in succession Cicero received a summons to attend a dinner in his honour. He groaned when he opened the message, for he had discovered that there are few blessings in life more onerous than the friendship of a great man. At first, he had found it flattering to be invited into Pompey's inner circle. But after a while he grew weary of listening to the same old military anecdotes – usually illustrated by the manoeuvring of plates and decanters around the dinner table – of how the young general had outwitted three Marian armies at Auximum, or killed seventeen thousand Numidians in a single afternoon at the age of twenty-four, or finally defeated the Spanish rebels near Valencia. Pompey had been giving orders since he was seventeen and perhaps for this reason had developed none of Cicero's subtlety of intellect. Conversation as the senator enjoyed it – spontaneous wit, shared gossip, sharp observations which might be spun off mutually into some profound or fantastic dissertation on the nature of human affairs – all this was alien to Pompey. The general liked to hold forth against a background of respectful silence, assert some platitude, and then sit back and bask in the flattery of his guests. Cicero used to say he would sooner have all his teeth drawn by a drunken barber in the Forum Boarium than listen to another of these mealtime monologues.

The root of the problem was that Pompey was bored. At the end of his consulship, as promised, he had retired into private life with his wife, young son and baby daughter. But then what? Lacking any talent for oratory, there was nothing to occupy him in the law courts. Literary composition held no interest for him. He could only watch in a stew of jealousy as Lucullus continued his conquest of Mithradates. Not yet forty, his future, as the saying went, seemed all behind him. He would make occasional forays down from his mansion and into the senate, not to speak but to listen to the debates – processions for which he insisted on an immense escort of friends and clients. Cicero, who felt obliged to walk at least part of the way with him, observed that it was like watching an elephant trying to make itself at home in an anthill.

But still, he was the greatest man in the world, with a huge following among the voters, and not to be crossed, especially with an election less than a year away. Only that summer he had secured a tribuneship for his crony Gabinius: he still kept a hand in politics. So on the thirtieth day of September, Cicero went off as usual to the birthday party, returning later in the evening to regale Quintus, Lucius and myself with an account of events. Like a child, Pompey delighted in receiving presents, and Cicero had taken him a manuscript letter in the hand of Zeno, the founder of stoicism, two centuries old and extremely valuable, which had been acquired for him in Athens by Atticus. He would dearly have loved to have kept it for his own library in Tusculum, but he hoped that by giving it to Pompey he could begin to tempt the general into an interest in philosophy. Instead, Pompey had barely glanced at it before setting it aside in favour of a gift from Gabinius, of a silver rhino horn containing some Egyptian aphrodisiac made of baboon excrement. 'How I wish I could have retrieved that letter!' groaned Cicero, flopping down on to a couch, the back of his hand resting on his forehead. 'Even now it's probably being used by some kitchen maid to light the fire.'

'Who else was there?' asked Quintus eagerly. He had only been back in Rome for a few days, following his term as quaestor in Umbria, and was avid for the latest news.

'Oh, the usual cohort. Our fine new tribune-elect Gabinius, obviously, and his father-in-law, the art connoisseur Palicanus; Rome's greatest dancer, Afranius; that Spanish creature of Pompey's, Balbus; Varro, the household polymath. Oh, and Marcus Fonteius,' he added lightly, but not so lightly that Lucius did not immediately detect the significance.

'And what did you talk about with Fonteius?' enquired Lucius, in the same clumsy attempt at an offhand manner.

'This and that.'

'His prosecution?'

'Naturally.'

'And who is defending the rascal?'

Cicero paused, and then said quietly, 'I am.'

I should explain, for those not familiar with the case, that this Fonteius had been governor of Further Gaul about five years earlier, and that one winter, when Pompey was particularly hard pressed fighting the rebels in Spain, he had sent the beleaguered general sufficient supplies and fresh recruits to enable him to survive until the spring. That had been the start of their friendship. Fonteius had gone on to make himself extremely rich, in the Verres manner, by extorting various illegal taxes out of the native population. The Gauls had at first put up with it, telling themselves that robbery and exploitation have ever been the handmaids of civilisation. But after Cicero's triumphant prosecution of the governor of Sicily, the chief of the Gauls, Induciomarus, had come to Rome to ask the senator to represent them in the extortion court. Lucius had been all for it; in fact it was he who had brought Induciomarus to the house: a wild-looking creature, dressed in his barbarian outfit of jacket and trousers – he gave me quite a shock when I opened the door to him one morning. Cicero, however, had politely declined. A year had passed, but now the Gauls had finally found a credible legal team in Plaetorius, who was a praetor-elect, and Marcus Fabius as his junior. The case would soon be in court.

'That is outrageous,' said Lucius, hotly. 'You cannot defend him. He is as guilty as Verres was.'

'Nonsense. He has neither killed anyone nor falsely imprisoned anyone either. The worse that can be said is that he once imposed excessive duties on the wine traders of Narbonne, and made some locals pay more than others to repair the roads. Besides,' added Cicero quickly, before Lucius could challenge this somewhat generous interpretation of Fonteius's activities, 'who are you or I to determine his guilt? It is a matter for the court to decide, not us. Or would you be a tyrant and deny him an advocate?'

'I would deny him *your* advocacy,' Lucius responded. 'You have heard from Induciomarus's own lips the evidence against him. Is all that to be cancelled out, simply because Fonteius is a friend of Pompey?'

'It has nothing to do with Pompey.'

'Then why do it?'

'Politics,' said Cicero, suddenly sitting up and swinging himself round so that his feet were planted on the floor. He fixed his gaze on Lucius and said very seriously: 'The most fatal error for any statesman is to allow his fellow countrymen, even for an instant, to suspect that he puts the interests of foreigners above those of his own people. That is the lie which my enemies spread about me after I represented the Sicilians in the Verres case, and that is the calumny which I can lay to rest if I defend Fonteius now.'

'And the Gauls?'

'The Gauls will be represented perfectly adequately by Plaetorius.'

'Not as well as they would be by you.'

'But you say yourself that Fonteius has a weak case. Let the weakest case be defended by the strongest advocate. What could be fairer than that?'

Cicero flashed him his most charming smile, but for once Lucius refused to be parted from his anger. Knowing, I suspect, that the only sure way to defeat Cicero in argument was to withdraw from the conversation altogether, he stood and limped across to the atrium. I had not realised until that moment how ill he looked, how thin and stooped; he had never really recovered from the strain of his efforts in Sicily. 'Words, words, words,' he said bitterly. 'Is there no end to the tricks you can make them perform? But, as with all men, your great strength is also your weakness, Marcus, and I am sorry for you, absolutely I am, because soon you will not be able to tell your tricks from the truth. And then you will be lost.'

'The truth,' laughed Cicero. 'Now there is a loose term for a philosopher to use!' But he was addressing his witticism to the air, for Lucius had gone.

'He will be back,' said Quintus.

But he did not come back, and over the following days Cicero went about his preparations for the trial with the determined expression of a man who has resigned himself to some distasteful but necessary surgical procedure. As for his client: Fonteius had been anticipating his prosecution for three years, and had used the time well, to acquire a mass of evidence to support his defence. He had witnesses from Spain and Gaul, including officers from Pompey's camp, and various sly and greedy tax farmers and merchants – members of the Roman community in Gaul, who would have sworn that night was day and land sea if it would have turned them a reasonable profit. The only trouble, as Cicero realised once he had mastered his brief, was that Fonteius was plainly guilty. He sat for a long time staring at the wall in his study, while I tiptoed around him, and it is important that I convey what he was doing, for it is necessary in order to understand his character. He was not merely trying, as a cynical and second-rate advocate might have done, to devise some clever tactic in order to outwit the prosecution. *He was trying to find something to believe in.* That was the core of his genius, both as an advocate and as a statesman. 'What convinces is conviction,' he used to say. 'You simply must believe the argument you are advancing, otherwise you are lost. No chain of reasoning, no matter how logical or elegant or brilliant, will win the case, if your audience senses that belief is missing.' Just one thing to believe in, that was all he needed, and then he could latch on to it, build out from it, embellish it, and transform it just for the space of an hour or two into the most important issue in the world, and deliver it with a passion that would obliterate the flimsy rationality of his opponents. Afterwards he would usually forget it entirely. And what did he believe in when it came to Marcus Fonteius? He gazed at the wall for many hours and concluded only this: that his client was a Roman, being assailed within his own city by Rome's traditional enemy, the Gauls, and that whatever the rights and wrongs of the case, that was a kind of treachery.

Such was the line which Cicero took when he found himself once again in the familiar surroundings of the extortion court before the Temple of Castor. The trial lasted from the end of October until the middle of November, and was most keenly fought, witness by witness, right up until the final day, when Cicero delivered the closing speech for the defence. From my place behind the senator, I had, from the opening day, kept an eye out for Lucius among the crowd of spectators, but it was only on that last morning that I fancied I saw him, a pale shadow, propped against a pillar at the very back of the audience. And if it was he – and I do not know it was – I have often wondered what he thought of his cousin's oratory, as he tore into the evidence of the Gauls, jabbing his finger at Induciomarus – 'Does he actually know what is meant by giving evidence? Is the greatest chief of the Gauls worthy to be set on the same level as even the meanest citizen of Rome?' – and demanding to know how a Roman jury could possibly believe the word of a man whose gods demanded human victims: 'For who does not know that to this very day they retain the monstrous and barbarous custom of sacrificing men?' What would he have said to Cicero's description of the Gaulish witnesses, 'swaggering from end to end of the forum, with proud and unflinching expressions on their faces and barbarian menaces upon their lips'? And what would he have made of Cicero's brilliant *coup de théâtre* at the very end, of producing in court, in the closing moments of his speech, Fonteius's sister, a vestal virgin, clad from head to toe in her official garb of a flowing white gown, with a white linen shawl around her narrow shoulders, and who raised her white veil to show the jury her tears – a sight which made her brother also break down weeping? Cicero laid his hand gently on his client's shoulder.

'From this peril, gentlemen, defend a gallant and blameless citizen. Let the world see that you place more confidence in the evidence of our fellow countrymen than in that of foreigners, that you have greater regard for the welfare of our citizens than for the caprice of our foes, that you set more store by the entreaties of she who presides over your sacrifices than by the effrontery of those who have waged war against the sacrifices and shrines of all the world. Finally, gentlemen, see to it – and here the dignity of the Roman people is most vitally engaged – see to it that you show that the prayers of a vestal maid have more weight with you than the threats of Gauls.'

Well, that speech certainly did the trick, both for Fonteius, who was acquitted, and for Cicero, who was never again regarded as anything less than the most fervent patriot in Rome. I looked up after I had finished making my shorthand record, but it was impossible to discern individuals in the crowd any more – it had become a single, seething creature, aroused by Cicero's technique to a chanting ecstasy of national self-glorification. Anyway, I sincerely hope that Lucius was not present, and there must surely be a chance that he was not, for it was only a few hours later that he was discovered at his home quite dead.

Cicero was dining privately with Terentia when the message came. The bearer was one of Lucius's slaves. Scarcely more than a boy, he was weeping uncontrollably, so it fell to me to take the news in to the senator. He looked up blankly from his meal when I told him, and stared straight at me, and said irritably, 'No,' as if I had offered him the wrong set of documents in court. And for a long time that was all he said: 'No, no.' He did not move; he did not even blink. The working of his brain seemed locked. It was Terentia who eventually spoke, and suggested gently that he should go and find out what had happened, whereupon he started searching dumbly for his shoes. 'Keep an eye on him, Tiro,' she said quietly to me.

Grief kills time. All that I retain of that night, and of the days which followed, are fragments of scenes, like some luridly brilliant hallucinations left behind after a fever. I recall how thin and wasted Lucius's body was when we found it, lying on its right side in his cot, the knees drawn up, the left hand laid flat across his eyes, and how Cicero, in the traditional manner, bent over him with a candle, to call him back to life. 'What was he seeing?' – that was what he kept asking: 'What was he seeing?' Cicero was not, as I have indicated, a superstitious man, but he could not rid himself of the conviction that Lucius had been presented with a vision of unparalleled horror at the end, and that this had somehow frightened him to death. As to how he died – well here I must confess to carrying a secret all these years, of which I shall be glad now to unburden myself. There was a pestle and mortar in the corner of that little room, with what Cicero – and I, too, at first – took to be a bunch of fennel lying beside it. It was a reasonable supposition, for among Lucius's many chronic ailments was poor digestion, which he attempted to relieve by a solution of fennel oil. Only later, when I was clearing the room, did I rub those lacy leaves with my thumb, and detect the frightful, musty, dead-mouse odour of hemlock. I knew then that Lucius had tired of this life, and for whatever reason – despair at its injustices, weariness with his ailments – had chosen to die like his hero, Socrates. This information I always meant to share with Cicero and Quintus. But for some reason, in the sadness of those days, I kept it to myself, and then the proper time for disclosure had passed, and it seemed better to let them continue to believe he had died involuntarily.

I also recall how Cicero spent such a great sum on flowers and incense that, after Lucius had been cleaned and anointed and laid on his funeral couch in his finest toga, his skinny feet pointing towards the door, he seemed, even in that drab November, to be in an Elysian grove of petals and fragrant scent. I remember the surprising number, for such a solitary man, of friends and neighbours who came to pay their respects, and the funeral procession at dusk out to the Esquiline Field, with young Frugi weeping so hard he could not catch his breath. I recall the dirges and the music, and the respectful glances of the citizens along the route – for this was a Cicero they were bearing to meet his ancestors, and the name now counted for something in Rome. Out on the frozen field, the body lay on its pyre under the stars, and the great orator struggled to deliver a brief eulogy. But his words would not perform their tricks for him on that occasion, and he had to give up. He could not even collect himself sufficiently to apply the torch to ignite the wood, and passed the task instead to Quintus. As the flames shot high the mourners threw their gifts of scent and spices on to the bonfire, and the perfumed smoke, flecked with orange sparks, curled up to the Milky Way. That night I sat with the senator in his study as he dictated a letter to Atticus, and it is surely a tribute to the affection which Lucius also inspired in that noble heart that this was the first of Cicero's hundreds of letters which Atticus chose to preserve:

'Knowing me as well as you do, you can appreciate better than most how deeply my cousin Lucius's death has grieved me, and what a loss it means to me both in public and in private life. All the pleasure that one human being's kindness and charm can give another I had from him.'

Despite having lived in Rome for many years, Lucius had always said that he wished to have his ashes interred in the family vault in Arpinum. Accordingly, on the morning after the cremation, the Cicero brothers set off with his remains on the three-day journey east, accompanied by their wives, having sent word ahead to their father of what had happened. Naturally, I went too, for although Cicero was in the mourning period, his legal and political correspondence could not be neglected. Nevertheless, for the first – and, I think, the only – time in all our years together, he transacted no official business on the road, but simply sat with his chin in his hand, staring at the passing countryside. He and Terentia were in one carriage, Quintus and Pomponia in another, endlessly bickering – so much so that I saw Cicero draw his brother aside and plead with him, for the sake of Atticus, if for no one else, to make the marriage work. 'Well,' retorted Quintus, with some justice, 'if the good opinion of Atticus is that important to you, why do *you* not marry her?' We stayed the first night at the villa in Tusculum, and had reached as far as Ferentium on the Via Latina when a message reached the brothers from Arpinum that their father had collapsed and died the previous day.

Given that he was in his sixties and had been ailing for many years, this was obviously less of a shock than the death of Lucius (the news of which had apparently proved the final blow to the old man's fragile health). But to leave one house festooned with the pine and cypress boughs of mourning and to arrive at another similarly adorned was the height of melancholy, made worse by the mischance that we reached Arpinum on the twenty-fifth day of November, that date kept sacred to Proserpina, Queen of Hades, who carries into effect the curses of men upon the souls of the dead. The Ciceros' villa lay three miles out of the town, down a winding stony road, in a valley ringed by high mountains. It was cold at this altitude, the peaks already draped with the vestal veils of snow which they would wear till May. I had not been back for ten years, and to see it all as I remembered aroused strange feelings in me. Unlike Cicero, I had always preferred the country to the town. I had been born here; my mother and father had both lived and died here; for the first quarter-century of my life, these springy meadows and crystal streams, with their tall poplars and verdant banks, had been the limit of my world. Seeing how much I was affected, and knowing how devoted I had been to the old master, Cicero invited me to accompany him and Quintus to the funeral couch, to say goodbye. In a way, I owed their father almost as much as they did, for he had taken a shine to me when I was a lad, and educated me so that I could help with his books, and then had given me the chance to travel with his son. As I bent to kiss his cold hand, I had a strong sense of returning home, and then the idea came to me that perhaps I could remain here, and act as steward, marry some girl of equal station, and have a child of my own. My parents, despite their status as domestic slaves rather than farm labourers, had both died in their early forties; I had to reckon on having, at best, only ten years left myself. (Little do we know how the fates will play us!) I ached to imagine that I might depart the earth without issue and I resolved to raise the matter with Cicero at the earliest opportunity.

Thus it was that I came to have rather a profound conversation with him. On the day after our arrival, the old master was buried in the family vault, then Lucius's ashes in their alabaster vase were interred beside him, and finally a pig was sacrificed to keep the spot holy. The next morning Cicero took a tour around his newly inherited estate, and I went with him in case he needed to dictate any notes, for the place (which was so heavily mortgaged as to be virtually worthless) was in a dilapidated state, and much work needed to be done. Cicero observed that it was originally his mother who had managed the property; his father had always been too much of a dreamer to cope with land agents and agricultural suppliers; after her death, he had slowly let it all go to ruin. This was, I think, the first time in more than a decade in his service that I had heard Cicero mention his mother. Helvia was her name. She had died twenty years earlier, when he was in his teens, by which time he had left for Rome to be educated. I could barely remember anything of her myself, except that she had a reputation for terrible strictness and meanness – the sort of mistress who marked the jars to check if the slaves had stolen anything, and took great pleasure in whipping them if she suspected that they had.

'Never a word of praise from her, Tiro,' he said, 'either for myself or my brother. Yet I tried so hard to please her.' He stopped and stared across the fields to the fast-moving, ice-cold river – the Fibrenus it was called – in the centre of which was a little island, with a wooded grove and a small pavilion, half tumbled down. 'That was where I used to go and sit as a boy,' he said wistfully. 'The hours I spent there! In my mind I was going to be another Achilles, albeit of the law courts rather than the battlefield. You know your Homer: "Far to excel, out-topping all the rest!"'

He was silent for a while, and I recognised this as my opportunity. And so I put my plan to him – I gabbled it out, fairly ineptly I suppose: that I might remain here and bring the farm back up to scratch for him – and all the while he kept looking at that childhood island of his. 'I know exactly what you mean,' he said with a sigh when I had finished. 'I feel it, too. This is the true fatherland of myself and my brother, for we are descended from a very ancient family of this place. Here are our ancestral cults, here is our race, here are many memorials of our forefathers. What more need I say?' He turned to look at me, and I noticed how very clear and blue his eyes were, despite all his recent weeping. 'But consider what we have seen this week – the empty, senseless shells of those we loved – and think what a terrible audit Death lays upon a man. Ah!' He shook his head vigorously, as if emptying it of a bad dream, then returned his attention to the landscape. After a while he said, in a very different voice: 'Well, I tell you, for my part, I do not propose to die leaving one ounce of talent unspent, or one mile of energy left in my legs. And it is your destiny, my dear fellow, to walk the road with me.' We were standing side by side; he prodded me gently in the ribs with his elbow. 'Come on, Tiro! A secretary who can take down my words almost as quickly as I can utter them? Such a marvel cannot be spared to count sheep in Arpinum! So let us have no more talk of such foolishness.'

And that was the end of my pastoral idyll. We walked back up to the house, and later that afternoon – or perhaps it was the following day: the memory plays such tricks – we heard the sound of a horse galloping very fast along the road from the town. It had started to rain, that much I do remember, and everyone was cooped up irritably indoors. Cicero was reading, Terentia sewing, Quintus practising drawing his sword, Pomponia lying down with a headache. (She still maintained that politics was 'boring', which drove Cicero into a quiet frenzy. 'Such a stupid thing to say!' he once complained to me. 'Politics? Boring? Politics is history on the wing! What other sphere of human activity calls forth all that is most noble in men's souls, and all that is most base? Or has such excitement? Or more vividly exposes our strengths and weaknesses? Boring? You might as well say that life itself is boring!') Anyway, at the noise of hooves clattering to a halt, I went out to greet the rider, and took from him a letter bearing the seal of Pompey the Great. Cicero opened it himself and let out a shout of surprise. 'Rome has been attacked!' he announced, causing even Pomponia to rouse herself briefly from her couch. He read on rapidly. The consular war fleet had been set on fire in its winter anchorage at Ostia. Two praetors, Sextilius and Bellinus, together with their lictors and staff, had been kidnapped. It was all the work of pirates and designed to spread terror, pure and simple. There was panic in the capital. The people were demanding action. 'Pompey wants me with him straightaway,' said Cicero. 'He is calling a council of war at his country estate the day after tomorrow.'

XI

Leaving the others behind and travelling hard in a two-wheeled carriage (Cicero never went on horseback if he could avoid it), we retraced our route, reaching the villa at Tusculum by nightfall the following day. Pompey's estate lay on the other side of the Alban Hills, only five miles to the south. The lazy household slaves were stunned to find their master back so quickly and had to scramble to put the place in order. Cicero bathed and went directly to bed, although I do not believe he slept well, for I fancied I heard him in the middle of the night, moving around his library, and in the morning I found a copy of Aristotle's *Nicomachean Ethics* half unrolled on his desk. But politicians are resilient creatures. When I went into his chamber he was already dressed and keen to discover what Pompey had in mind. As soon as it was light we set off. Our road took us around the great expanse of the Alban Lake, and when the sun broke pink over the snowy mountain ridge we could see the silhouettes of the fishermen pulling in their nets from the glittering waters. 'Is there any country in the world more beautiful than Italy?' Cicero murmured, inhaling deeply, and although he did not express it, I knew what he was thinking, because I was thinking it too: that it was a relief to have escaped the enfolding gloom of Arpinum, and that there is nothing quite like death to make one feel alive.

At length we turned off the road and passed through a pair of imposing gates on to a long driveway of white gravel lined with cypresses. The formal gardens to either side were filled with marble statues, no doubt acquired by the general during his various campaigns. Gardeners were raking the winter leaves and trimming the box hedges. The impression was one of vast, quiet, confident wealth. As Cicero strode through the entrance into the great house he whispered to me to stay close by, and I slipped in unobtrusively behind him, carrying a document case. (My advice to anyone, incidentally, who wishes to be inconspicuous, is always to carry documents: they cast a cloak of invisibility around their bearer that is the equal of anything in the Greek legends.) Pompey was greeting his guests in the atrium, playing the grand country seigneur, with his third wife, Mucia, beside him, and his son, Gnaeus – who must have been eleven by this time – and his infant daughter, Pompeia, who had just learned to walk. Mucia was an attractive, statuesque matron of the Metellus clan, in her late twenties and obviously pregnant again. One of Pompey's peculiarities, I later discovered, was that he always tended to love his wife, whoever she happened to be at the time. She was laughing at some remark which had just been made to her, and when the originator of this witticism turned I saw that it was Julius Caesar. This surprised me, and certainly startled Cicero, because up to this point we had seen only the familiar trio of Piceneans: Palicanus, Afranius and Gabinius. Besides, Caesar had been in Spain for more than a year, serving as quaestor. But here he was, lithe and well built, with his lean, intelligent face, his amused brown eyes, and those thin strands of dark hair which he combed so carefully across his sunburnt pate. (But why am I bothering to describe him? The whole world knows what he looked like!)

In all, eight senators gathered that morning: Pompey, Cicero and Caesar; the three Piceneans mentioned above; Varro, Pompey's house intellectual, then aged fifty; and Caius Cornelius, who had served under Pompey as his quaestor in Spain, and who was now, along with Gabinius, a tribune-elect. I was not as conspicuous as I had feared, as many of the principals had also brought along a secretary or bag-carrier of some sort; we all stood respectfully to one side. After refreshments had been served, and the children had been taken away by their nurses, and the Lady Mucia had graciously said goodbye to each of her husband's guests in turn – lingering somewhat over Caesar, I noticed – slaves fetched in chairs so that everyone could sit. I was on the point of leaving with the other attendants when Cicero suggested to Pompey that, as I was famous throughout Rome as the inventor of a marvellous new shorthand system – these were his words – I might stay and keep a minute of what was said. I blushed with embarrassment. Pompey looked at me suspiciously, and I thought he was going to forbid it, but then he shrugged and said, 'Very well. That might be useful. But there will only be one copy made, and I shall keep it. Is that acceptable to everyone?' There was a noise of assent, whereupon a stool was fetched for me and I found myself sitting in the corner with my notebook open and my stylus gripped in a sweaty hand. The chairs were arranged in a semicircle, and when all his guests were seated, Pompey stood. He was, as I have said, no orator on a public platform. But on his own ground, among those whom he thought of as his lieutenants, he radiated power and authority. Although my verbatim transcript was taken from me, I can still remember much of what he said, because I had to write it up from my notes, and that always causes a thing to stick in my mind. He began by giving the latest details of the pirate attack on Ostia: nineteen consular war triremes destroyed, a couple of hundred men killed, grain warehouses torched, two praetors – one of whom had been inspecting the granaries and the other the fleet – seized in their official robes, along with their retinues and their symbolic rods and axes. A ransom demand for their release had arrived in Rome yesterday. 'But for my part,' said Pompey, 'I do not believe we should negotiate with such people, as it will only encourage them in their criminal acts.' (Everyone nodded in agreement.) The raid on Ostia, he continued, was a turning point in the history of Rome. This was not an isolated incident, but merely the most daring in a long line of such outrages, which included the kidnapping of the noble Lady Antonia from her villa in Misenum (she whose own father had led an expedition against the pirates!), the robbery of temple treasures from Croton, and the surprise attacks on Brundisium and Caieta. Where would be struck next? What Rome was facing was a threat very different from that posed by a conventional enemy. These pirates were a new type of ruthless foe, with no government to represent them and no treaties to bind them. Their bases were not confined to a single state. They had no unified system of command. They were a worldwide pestilence, a parasite which needed to be stamped out, otherwise Rome – despite her overwhelming military superiority – would never again know security or peace. The existing national security system, of giving men of consular rank a single command of limited duration in an individual theatre, was clearly inadequate to the challenge.

'Long before Ostia, I had been devoting much careful study to this problem,' declared Pompey, 'and I believe this unique enemy demands a unique response. Now is our opportunity.' He clapped his hands and a pair of slaves carried in a large map of the Mediterranean, which they set up on a stand beside him. His audience leaned forwards to get a better look, for they could see mysterious lines had been drawn vertically across both sea and land. 'The basis of our strategy from now on must be to combine the military and the political spheres,' said Pompey. 'We hit them with everything.' He took up a pointer and rapped it on the painted board. 'I propose we divide the Mediterranean into fifteen zones, from the Pillars of Hercules here in the west to the waters of Egypt and Syria here in the east, each zone to have its own legate, whose task will be to scour his area clean of pirates and then to make treaties with the local rulers to ensure the brigands' vessels never return to their waters. All captured pirates are to be handed over to Roman jurisdiction. Any ruler who refuses to cooperate will be regarded as Rome's enemy. Those who are not with us are against us. These fifteen legates will all report to one supreme commander, who will have absolute authority over all the mainland for a distance of fifty miles from the sea. I shall be that commander.'

There was a long silence. It was Cicero who spoke first. 'Your plan is certainly a bold one, Pompey, although some might consider it a disproportionate response to the loss of nineteen triremes. You do realise that such a concentration of power in a single pair of hands has never been proposed in the entire history of the republic?'

'As a matter of fact, I *do* realise that,' replied Pompey. He tried to keep a straight face, but in the end he could not stop it breaking into a broad grin, and quickly everyone was laughing, apart from Cicero, who looked as if his world had just fallen apart – which in a sense it had, because this was, as he put it afterwards, a plan for the domination of the world by one man, nothing less, and he had few doubts where it would lead. 'Perhaps I should have walked out there and then,' he mused to me later on the journey home. 'That is what poor, honest Lucius would have urged me to do. Yet Pompey would still have gone ahead, either with me or without me, and all I would have done is earned his enmity, and that would have put paid to my chances of a praetorship. Everything I do now must be viewed through the prism of that election.'

And so, of course, he stayed, as the discussion meandered on over the next few hours, from grand military strategy to grubby political tactics. The plan was for Gabinius to place a bill before the Roman people soon after he took office, which would be in about a week, setting up the special command and ordering it be given to Pompey; then he and Cornelius would dare any of the other tribunes to veto it. (One must remember that in the days of the republic only an assembly of the people had the power to make laws; the senate's voice was influential, but not decisive; their task was to implement the people's will.)

'What do you say, Cicero?' asked Pompey. 'You have been very quiet.'

'I say that Rome is indeed fortunate,' replied Cicero carefully, 'to have a man with such experience and global vision as yourself to call on in her hour of peril. But we must be realistic. There will be huge resistance to this proposal in the senate. The aristocrats, in particular, will say that it is nothing more than a naked grab for power dressed up as patriotic necessity.'

'I resent that,' said Pompey.

'Well, you may resent it all you like, but you will still need to demonstrate that it is not the case,' retorted Cicero, who knew that the surest way to a great man's confidence, curiously enough, is often to speak harshly back to him, thus conveying an appearance of disinterested candour. 'They will also say that this commission to deal with the pirates is simply a stepping-stone to your true objective, which is to replace Lucullus as commander of the Eastern legions.' To that, the great man made no response other than a grunt – he could not, because that really was his true objective. 'And finally, they will set about finding a tribune or two of their own, to veto Gabinius's bill.'

'It sounds to me as though you should not be here, Cicero,' sneered Gabinius. He was something of a dandy, with thick and wavy hair slicked back in a quiff, in imitation of his chief. 'To achieve our objective will require bold hearts, and possibly stout fists, not the quibbles of clever lawyers.'

'You will need hearts and fists *and* lawyers before you are done, Gabinius, believe me,' responded Cicero. 'The moment you lose the legal immunity conferred by your tribuneship, the aristocrats will have you in court and fighting for your life. You will need a clever lawyer, well enough, and so will you, Cornelius.'

'Let us move on,' said Pompey. 'Those are the problems. Do you have any solutions to offer?'

'Well,' replied Cicero, 'for a start, I strongly urge that your name should not appear anywhere in the bill setting up the supreme command.'

'But it was my idea!' protested Pompey, sounding exactly like a child whose game was being taken over by his playmates.

'True, but I still say it would be prudent not to specify the actual name of the commander at the very outset. You will be the focus of the most terrible envy and rage in the senate. Even the sensible men, whose support we can normally rely on, will baulk at this. You must make the central issue the defeat of the pirates, not the future of Pompey the Great. Everyone will know the post is designed for you; there is no need to spell it out.'

'But what am I to say when I lay the bill before the people?' asked Gabinius. 'That any fool off the street can hold the office?'

'Obviously not,' said Cicero, with a great effort at patience. 'I would strike out the name "Pompey" and insert the phrase "senator of consular rank". That limits it to the fifteen or twenty living ex-consuls.'

'So who might be the rival candidates?' asked Afranius.

'Crassus,' said Pompey at once: his old enemy was never far from his thoughts. 'Perhaps Catulus. Then there is Metellus Pius – doddery, but still a force. Hortensius has a following. Isauricus. Gellius. Cotta. Curio. Even the Lucullus brothers.'

'Well, I suppose if you are really worried,' said Cicero, 'we could always specify that the supreme commander should be any ex-consul whose name begins with a P.' For a moment, no one reacted, and I was certain he had gone too far. But then Caesar threw back his head and laughed, and the rest – seeing that Pompey was smiling weakly – joined in. 'Believe me, Pompey,' continued Cicero in a reassuring tone, 'most of these are far too old and idle to be a threat. Crassus will be your most dangerous rival, simply because he is so rich and jealous of you. But if it comes to a vote you will defeat him overwhelmingly, I promise you.'

'I agree with Cicero,' said Caesar. 'Let us clear our hurdles one at a time. First, the principle of the supreme command; then, the name of the commander.' I was struck by the authority with which he spoke, despite being the most junior man present.

'Very well,' said Pompey, nodding judiciously. 'It is settled. The central issue must be the defeat of the pirates, not the future of Pompey the Great.' And on that note, the conference adjourned for lunch.

There now followed a squalid incident which it embarrasses me to recall, but which I feel I must, in the interests of history, set down.

For several hours, while the senators lunched, and afterwards strolled in the garden, I worked as rapidly as I could to translate my shorthand notes into a fair manuscript record of proceedings, which I could then present to Pompey. When I had finished, it occurred to me that perhaps I should check what I had written with Cicero, in case there might be something in it to which he objected. The chamber where the conference had been held was empty, and so was the atrium, but I could hear the senator's distinctive voice, and set off, clutching my roll of paper, in the direction from which I judged it was coming. I crossed a colonnaded courtyard, where a fountain played, then followed the portico round to another, inner garden. But now his voice had faded altogether. I stopped to listen. There was only bird-song, and the trickling of water. Then, suddenly, from somewhere very close, and loud enough to make me jump, I heard a woman groan, as if in agony. Like a fool, I turned, and took a few more steps, and through an open door was confronted by the sight of Caesar with Pompey's wife. The Lady Mucia did not see me. She had her head down between her forearms, her dress was bunched up around her waist, and she was bent over a table, gripping the edge so tightly her knuckles were white. But Caesar saw me well enough, for he was facing the door, thrusting into her from behind, his right hand cupped around her swollen belly, his left resting casually on his hip, like a dandy standing on a street corner. For exactly how long our eyes met I cannot say, but he stares back at me even now – those fathomless dark eyes of his gazing through the smoke and chaos of all the years that were to follow – amused, unabashed, challenging. I fled.

By this time, most of the senators had wandered back into the conference chamber. Cicero was discussing philosophy with Varro, the most distinguished scholar in Rome, of whose works on philology and antiquities I was deeply in awe. On any other occasion I would have been honoured to be introduced, but my head was still reeling from the scene I had just witnessed and I cannot remember a thing of what he said. I handed the minutes to Cicero, who skimmed them quickly, took my pen from me, and made a small amendment, all the while still talking to Varro. Pompey must have noticed what he was doing, for he came across with a big smile on his wide face, and pretended to be angry, taking the minutes away from Cicero and accusing him of inserting promises he had never made – 'though I think you can count on my vote for the praetorship,' he said, and slapped him on the back. Until a short while earlier, I had considered Pompey a kind of god among men – a booming, confident war hero – but now, knowing what I did, I thought him also sad. 'This is quite remarkable,' he said to me, as he ran his huge thumb down the columns of words. 'You have captured my voice exactly. How much do you want for him, Cicero?'

'I have already turned down an enormous sum from Crassus,' replied Cicero.

'Well, if ever there is a bidding war, be sure that I am included,' said Caesar, in his rasping voice, coming up behind us. 'I would dearly love to get my hands on Tiro.' But he said it in such a friendly way, accompanying it with a wink, that none of the others heard the menace in his words, while I felt almost faint with terror.

'The day that I am parted from Tiro,' said Cicero, prophetically as it turned out, 'is the day that I quit public life.'

'Now I am doubly determined to buy him,' said Caesar, and Cicero joined in the general laughter.

After agreeing to keep secret everything that had been discussed, and to meet in Rome in a few days' time, the group broke up. The moment we turned out of the gates and on to the road to Tusculum, Cicero let out a long-pent-up cry of frustration and struck the side of the carriage with the palm of his hand. 'A criminal conspiracy!' he said, shaking his head in despair. 'Worse – a *stupid* criminal conspiracy. This is the trouble, Tiro, when soldiers decide to play at politics. They imagine that all they need to do is issue an order, and everyone will obey. They never see that the very thing which makes them attractive in the first place – that they are supposedly these great patriots, above the squalor of politics – must ultimately defeat them, because either they *do* stay above politics, in which case they go nowhere, or they get down in the muck along with the rest of us, and show themselves to be just as venal as everyone else.' He stared out at the lake, darkening now in the winter light. 'What do you make of Caesar?' he said suddenly, to which I returned a noncommittal answer about his seeming very ambitious. 'He certainly is that. So much so, there were times today when it occurred to me that this whole fantastic scheme is actually not Pompey's at all, but Caesar's. That, at least, would explain his presence.'

I pointed out that Pompey had described it as his own idea.

'And no doubt Pompey thinks it is. But that is the nature of the man. You make a remark to him, and then you find it being repeated back to you, as if it were his own. "The central issue must be the defeat of the pirates, not the future of Pompey the Great." That is a typical example. Sometimes, just to amuse myself, I have argued against my own original assertion, and waited to see how long it was before I heard my rebuttal coming back at me too.' He frowned and nodded. 'I am sure I am right. Caesar is quite clever enough to have planted the seed and left it to flower on its own. I wonder how much time he has spent with Pompey. He seems very well bedded in.'

It was on the tip of my tongue then to tell him what I had witnessed, but a combination of fear of Caesar, my own shyness, and a feeling that Cicero would not think the better of me for spying – that I would in some sense be contaminated myself by describing the whole sordid business – caused me to swallow my words. It was not until many years later – after Caesar's death, in fact, when he could no longer harm me and I was altogether more confident – that I revealed my story. Cicero, then an old man, was silent for a long time. 'I understand your discretion,' he said at last, 'and in many ways I applaud it. But I have to say, my dear friend, that I wish you *had* informed me. Perhaps then things might have turned out differently. At least I would have realised earlier the kind of breathtakingly reckless man we were dealing with. But by the time I did understand, it was too late.'

The Rome to which we returned a few days later was jittery and full of rumours. The burning of Ostia had been clearly visible to the whole city as a red glow in the western night sky. Such an attack on the capital was unprecedented, and when Gabinius and Cornelius took office as tribunes on the tenth day of December, they moved quickly to fan the sparks of public anxiety into the flames of panic. They caused extra sentries to be posted at the city's gates. Wagons and pedestrians entering Rome were stopped and searched at random for weapons. The wharves and warehouses along the river were patrolled both day and night, and severe penalties were promulgated for citizens convicted of hoarding grain, with the inevitable result that the three great food markets of Rome in those days – the Emporium, the Macellum, and the Forum Boarium – immediately ran out of supplies. The vigorous new tribunes also dragged the outgoing consul, the hapless Marcius Rex, before a meeting of the people, and subjected him to a merciless cross-examination about the security lapses which had led to the fiasco at Ostia. Other witnesses were found to testify about the menace of the pirates, and that menace grew with every retelling. They had a thousand ships! They were not lone raiders at all, but an organised conspiracy! They had squadrons and admirals and fearsome weapons of poison-tipped arrows and Greek fire! Nobody in the senate dared object to any of this, for fear of seeming complacent – not even when a chain of beacons was built all along the road to the sea, to be lit if pirate vessels were seen heading for the mouth of the Tiber. 'This is absurd,' Cicero said to me, on the morning we went out to inspect these most visible symbols of the national peril. 'As if any sane pirate would dream of sailing twenty miles up an open river to attack a defended city!' He shook his head in dismay at the ease with which a timorous population can be moulded by unscrupulous politicians. But what could he do? His closeness to Pompey had trapped him into silence.

On the seventeenth day of December, the Festival of Saturn began and lasted for a week. It was not the most enjoyable of holidays, for obvious reasons, and although the Cicero family went through the normal rituals of exchanging gifts, even allowing us slaves to have the day off and sharing a meal with us, nobody's heart was in it. Lucius used to be the life and soul of these events, and he was gone. Terentia, I believe, had hoped she was pregnant, but had discovered she was not, and was becoming seriously worried that she would never bear a son. Pomponia nagged away at Quintus about his inadequacies as a husband. Even little Tullia could not cheer the mood.

As for Cicero, he spent much of Saturnalia in his study, brooding on Pompey's insatiable ambition, and the implications it had for the country and for his own political prospects. The elections for the praetorship were barely eight months away, and he and Quintus had already compiled a list of likely candidates. From whichever of these men was eventually elected, he could probably expect to find his rivals for the consulship. The two brothers spent many hours discussing the permutations, and it seemed to me, although I kept it to myself, that they missed the wisdom of their cousin. For although Cicero used to joke that if he wanted to know what was politically shrewd, he would ask Lucius his opinion and then do precisely the opposite, nevertheless he had offered a fixed star to steer by. Without him, the Ciceros had only one another, and despite their mutual devotion, it was not always the wisest of relationships.

It was in this atmosphere, around the eighth or ninth day of January, when the Latin Festival was over and serious politics resumed, that Gabinius finally mounted the rostra to demand a new supreme commander. I am talking here, I should explain, about the old republican rostra, which was very different to the wretched ornamental footstool we have today. This ancient structure, now destroyed, was the heart of Rome's democracy: a long, curved platform, twelve feet high, covered with the statues of the heroes of antiquity, from which the tribunes and the consuls addressed the people. Its back was to the senate house, and it faced out boldly across the widest expanse of the forum, with six ships' battering rams, or 'beaks' – those *rostra* which gave the platform its name – thrusting from its heavy masonry (the beaks had been captured from the Carthaginians in a sea battle nearly three centuries earlier). The whole of its rear was a flight of steps, if you can imagine what I am saying, so that a magistrate might leave the senate house or the tribunes' headquarters, walk fifty paces, ascend the steps, and find himself on top of the rostra, facing a crowd of thousands, with the tiered façades of the two great basilicas on either side of him and the Temple of Castor straight ahead. This was where Gabinius stood on that January morning and declared, in his smooth and confident way, that what Rome needed was a strong man to take control of the war against the pirates.

Cicero, despite his misgivings, had done his best, with the help of Quintus, to turn out a good-sized crowd, and the Piceneans could always be relied upon to drum up a couple of hundred veterans. Add to these the regulars who hung about the Basilica Porcia, and those citizens going about their normal business in the forum, and I should say that close on a thousand were present to hear Gabinius spell out what was needed if the pirates were to be beaten – a supreme commander of consular rank with *imperium* lasting for three years over all territory up to fifty miles from the sea, fifteen legates of praetorian rank to assist him, free access to the treasury of Rome, five hundred warships and the right to levy up to one hundred and twenty thousand infantry and five thousand cavalry. These were staggering numbers and the demand caused a sensation. By the time Gabinius had finished the first reading of his bill, and had handed it to a clerk to be pinned up outside the tribunes' basilica, both Catulus and Hortensius had come hurrying into the forum to find out what was going on. Pompey, needless to say, was nowhere to be seen, and the other members of the group of seven (as the senators around Pompey had taken to calling themselves) took care to stand apart from one another, to avoid any suggestion of collusion. But the aristocrats were not fooled. 'If this is your doing,' Catulus snarled at Cicero, 'you can tell your master he will have a fight on his hands.'

The violence of their reaction was to prove even worse than Cicero had predicted. Once a bill had been given its first reading, three weekly market days had to pass before it could be voted on by the people (this was to enable country-dwellers to come into the city and study what was proposed). So the aristocrats had until the beginning of February to organise against it, and they did not waste a moment. Two days later, the senate was summoned to debate the *lex Gabinia*, as it would be called, and despite Cicero's advice that he should stay away, Pompey felt that he was honour-bound to attend, and stake his claim to the job. He wanted a good-sized escort down to the senate house, and because there no longer seemed much point in secrecy, the seven senators formed an honour-guard around him. Quintus also joined them, in his brand-new senatorial toga: this was only his third or fourth visit to the chamber. As usual, I stayed close to Cicero. 'We should have known we were in trouble,' he lamented afterwards, 'when no other senator turned up.'

The walk down the Esquiline Hill and into the forum went well enough. The precinct bosses had played their part, delivering plenty of enthusiasm on the streets, with people calling out to Pompey to save them from the menace of the pirates. He waved to them like a landlord to his tenants. But the moment the group entered the senate house they were met by jeers from all sides, and a piece of rotten fruit flew across the chamber and splattered on to Pompey's shoulder, leaving a rich brown stain. Such a thing had never happened to the great general before, and he halted and looked around him in stupefaction. Afranius, Palicanus and Gabinius quickly closed ranks to protect him, just as if they were back on the battlefield, and I saw Cicero stretch out his arms to hustle all four to their places, no doubt reasoning that the sooner they sat down, the sooner the demonstration would be over. I was standing at the entrance to the chamber, held back with the other spectators by the familiar cordon of rope slung between the two doorposts. Of course, we were all supporters of Pompey, so the more the senators inside jeered him, the more we outside roared our approval, and it was a while before the presiding consul could bring the house to order.

The new consuls in that year were Pompey's old friend Glabrio, and the aristocratic Calpurnius Piso (not to be confused with the other senator of that name, who will feature later in this story, if the gods give me the strength to finish it). A sign of how desperate the situation was for Pompey in the senate was that Glabrio had chosen to absent himself, rather than be seen in open disagreement with the man who had given him back his son. That left Piso in the chair. I could see Hortensius, Catulus, Isauricus, Marcus Lucullus – the brother of the commander of the Eastern legions – and all the rest of the patrician faction poised to attack. The only ones no longer present to offer opposition were the three Metellus brothers: Quintus was abroad, serving as the governor of Crete, while the younger two, as if to prove the indifference of fate to the petty ambitions of men, had both died of the fever not long after the Verres trial. But what was most disturbing was that the *pedarii* – the unassuming, patient, plodding mass of the senate, whom Cicero had taken so much trouble to cultivate – even they were hostile, or at best sullenly unresponsive to Pompey's megalomania. As for Crassus, he was sprawled on the consular front bench opposite, with his arms folded and his legs casually outstretched, regarding Pompey with an expression of ominous calm. The reason for his sangfroid was obvious. Sitting directly behind him, placed there like a pair of prize animals just bought at auction, were two of that year's tribunes, Roscius and Trebellius. This was Crassus's way of telling the world that he had used his wealth to purchase not just one, but two vetoes, and that the *lex Gabinia*, whatever Pompey and Cicero chose to do, would never be allowed to pass.

Piso exercised his privilege of speaking first. 'An orator of the stationary or quiet type' was how Cicero condescendingly described him many years later, but there was nothing stationary or quiet about him that day. 'We know what you are doing!' he shouted at Pompey, as he came to the end of his harangue. 'You are defying your colleagues in the senate and setting yourself up as a second Romulus – slaying your brother so that you may rule alone! But you would do well to remember the fate of Romulus, who was murdered in his turn by his own senators, who cut up his body and carried the mangled pieces back to their homes!' That brought the aristocrats to their feet, and I could just make out Pompey's massive profile, stock still and staring straight ahead, obviously unable to believe what was happening.

Catulus spoke next, and then Isauricus. The worst, though, was Hortensius. For almost a year, since the end of his consulship, he had hardly been seen in the forum. His son-in-law, Caepio, the beloved elder brother of Cato, had recently died on army service in the East, leaving Hortensius's daughter a widow, and the word was that the Dancing Master no longer had the strength in his legs for the struggle. But now it seemed that Pompey's over-reaching ambition had brought him back into the arena revitalised, and listening to him reminded one of just how formidable he could be on a big set-piece occasion such as this. He never ranted or stooped to vulgarity, but eloquently restated the old republican case: that power must always be divided, hedged around with limitations, and renewed by annual votes, and that while he had nothing personally against Pompey – indeed, felt that Pompey was more worthy of supreme command than any other man in the state – it was a dangerous, un-Roman precedent that would be set by the *lex Gabinia*, and that ancient liberties were not to be flung aside merely because of some passing scare about pirates. Cicero was shifting in his place and I could not help but reflect that this was exactly the speech which he would have made if he had been free to speak his mind.

Hortensius had just about reached his peroration when the figure of Caesar rose from that obscure region at the back of the chamber, close to the door, which had once been occupied by Cicero, and asked Hortensius to give way. The respectful silence in which the great advocate had been heard fractured immediately, and one has to admit that it was brave of Caesar to take him on in such an atmosphere. Caesar stood his ground until at last he could be heard, and then he started to speak, in his clear, compelling, remorseless way. There was nothing un-Roman, he said, about seeking to defeat pirates, who were the scum of the sea; what was un-Roman was to will the end of a thing but not the means. If the republic functioned as perfectly as Hortensius said it did, why had this menace been allowed to grow? And now that it was grown monstrous, how was it to be defeated? He had himself been captured by pirates a few years back when he was on his way to Rhodes, and held to ransom, and when at last he had been released, he had gone back and hunted down every last man of his kidnappers, and carried out the promise he had made to them when he was their prisoner – had seen to it that the scoundrels were crucified! 'That, Hortensius, is the Roman way to deal with piracy – and that is what the *lex Gabinia* will enable us to do!'

He finished to a round of boos and cat-calls, and as he resumed his seat, with the most magnificent display of disdain, some kind of fight broke out at the other end of the chamber. I believe a senator threw a punch at Gabinius, who turned round and punched him back, and very quickly he was in difficulties, with bodies piling in on top of him. There was a scream and a crash as one of the benches toppled over. I lost sight of Cicero. A voice in the crowd behind me cried that Gabinius was being murdered and there was such a surge of pressure forwards that the rope was pulled from its fixings and we tumbled into the chamber. I was lucky to scramble to one side as several hundred of Pompey's plebeian supporters (who were a rough-looking lot, I must admit) poured down the aisle towards the consular dais and dragged Piso from his curule chair. One brute had him by the neck, and for a few moments it looked as though murder would be done. But then Gabinius managed to struggle free and pull himself up on to a bench to show that, although he had been somewhat knocked about, he was still alive. He appealed to the demonstrators to let go of Piso, and after a short argument the consul was reluctantly released. Rubbing his throat, Piso declared hoarsely that the session was adjourned without a vote and so, by the very narrowest of margins, for the moment at least, the commonwealth was saved from anarchy.

Such violent scenes had not been witnessed in the heart of Rome's governing district for more than fourteen years, and they had a profound effect on Cicero, even though he had managed to escape the mêlée with barely a ruffle in his immaculate dress. Gabinius was streaming blood from his nose and lip and Cicero had to help him from the chamber. They came out some distance after Pompey, who walked on, looking neither right nor left, with the measured tread of a man at a funeral. What I remember most is the silence as the mingled crowd of senators and plebeians parted to let him through. It was as if both sides, at the very last moment, had realised that they were fighting on a cliff-edge, had come to their senses and drawn back. We went out into the forum, with Pompey still not saying anything, and when he turned into the Argiletum, in the direction of his house, his supporters all followed him, partly for want of anything else to do. Afranius, who was next to Pompey, passed the word back that the general wanted a meeting. I asked Cicero if there was anything he required and he replied, with a bitter smile, 'Yes, that quiet life in Arpinum!'

Quintus came up and said urgently, 'Pompey must withdraw, or be humiliated!'

'He already has been humiliated,' retorted Cicero, 'and we with him. Soldiers!' he said to me in disgust. 'What did I tell you? I would not dream of giving them orders on the battlefield. Why should they believe they know better than I about politics?'

We climbed the hill to Pompey's house and filed inside, leaving the muted crowd in the street. Ever since that first conference I had been accepted as the minute-taker for the group, and when I settled into my usual place in the corner, no one gave me a second glance. The senators arranged themselves around a big table, Pompey at the head. The pride had entirely gone out of his massive frame. Slumped in his throne-like chair he reminded me of some great beast that had been captured, shackled, baffled and taunted in the arena by creatures littler than himself. He was utterly defeatist and kept repeating that it was all over – the senate would clearly never stand for his appointment, he had only the support of the dregs on the streets, Crassus's tame tribunes would veto the bill in any case: there was nothing left for it but death or exile. Caesar took the opposite view – Pompey was still the most popular man in the republic, he should go out into Italy and begin recruiting the legions he needed, his old veterans would provide the backbone of his new army, the senate would capitulate once he had sufficient force. 'There is only one thing to do if you lose a throw of the dice: double your stake and throw again. Ignore the aristocrats, and if necessary rule through the people and the army.'

I could see that Cicero was preparing himself to speak, and was sure he did not favour either of these extremes. But there is as much skill in knowing how to handle a meeting of ten as there is in manipulating a gathering of hundreds. He waited until everyone had had their say, and the discussion was exhausted, before coming fresh to the fray. 'As you know, Pompey,' he began, 'I have had some misgivings about this undertaking from the outset. But after witnessing today's débâcle in the senate, I have to tell you, they have vanished entirely. Now we simply have to win this fight – for your sake, for Rome's, and for the dignity and authority of all those of us who have supported you. There can be no question of surrender. You are famously a lion on the battlefield; you cannot become a mouse in Rome.'

'You watch your language, lawyer,' said Afranius, wagging his finger at him, but Cicero took no notice.

'Can you conceive of what will happen if you give up now? The bill has been published. The people are clamouring for action against the pirates. If you do not assume the post, someone else will, and I can tell you who it will be: Crassus. You say yourself he has two tame tribunes. He will make sure this law goes through, only with his name written into it instead of yours. And how will you, Gabinius, be able to stop him? By vetoing your own legislation? Impossible! Do you see? We cannot abandon the battle now!'

This was an inspired argument, for if there was one thing guaranteed to rouse Pompey to a fight, it was the prospect of Crassus stealing his glory. He drew himself up, thrust out his jaw and glared around the table. I noticed both Afranius and Palicanus give him slight nods of encouragement. 'We have scouts in the legions, Cicero,' said Pompey, 'marvellous fellows who can find a way through the most difficult terrain – marshes, mountain ranges, forests which no man has penetrated since time began. But politics beats any obstacle I have ever faced. If you can show me a route out of this mess, you will have no truer friend than me.'

'Will you place yourself in my hands entirely?'

'You are the scout.'

'Very well,' said Cicero. 'Gabinius, tomorrow you must summon Pompey to the rostra, to ask him to serve as supreme commander.'

'Good,' said Pompey belligerently, clenching his massive fist. 'And I shall accept.'

'No, no,' said Cicero, 'you will refuse absolutely. You will say you have done enough for Rome, that you have no ambitions left in public life, and are retiring to your estate in the country.' Pompey's mouth fell open. 'Don't worry. I shall write the speech for you. You will leave the city tomorrow afternoon, and you will not come back. The more reluctant you seem, the more frantic the people will be for your recall. You will be our Cincinnatus, fetched from his plough to save the country from disaster. It is one of the most potent myths in politics, believe me.'

Some of those present were opposed to such a dramatic tactic, considering it too risky. But the idea of appearing modest appealed to Pompey's vanity. For is this not the dream of every proud and ambitious man? That rather than having to get down in the dust and fight for power, the people should come crawling to him, begging him to accept it as a gift? The more Pompey thought about it, the more he liked it. His dignity and authority would remain intact, he would have a comfortable few weeks, and if it all went wrong, it would be someone else's fault.

'This sounds very clever,' said Gabinius, who was dabbing at his split lip. 'But you seem to forget that it is not the people who are the problem; it is the senate.'

'The senate will come round once they wake up to the implications of Pompey's retirement. They will be faced with a choice of either doing nothing about the pirates, or awarding the supreme command to Crassus. To the great majority, neither will be acceptable. Apply a little grease and they will slide our way.'

'That is clever,' said Pompey admiringly. 'Is he not clever, gentlemen? Did I not tell you he was clever?'

'These fifteen legateships,' said Cicero. 'I propose you should use at least half of them to win over support inside the senate.' Palicanus and Afranius, seeing their lucrative commissions in jeopardy, immediately objected loudly, but Pompey waved them to be quiet. 'You are a national hero,' continued Cicero, 'a patriot above petty political squabbles and intrigue. Rather than using your patronage to reward your friends, you should use it to divide your enemies. Nothing will split the aristocratic faction more disastrously than if some can be persuaded to serve under you. They will tear each other's eyes out.'

'I agree,' said Caesar, with a decisive nod. 'Cicero's plan is better than mine. Be patient, Afranius. This is only the first stage. We can wait for our rewards.'

'Besides,' said Pompey sanctimoniously, 'the defeat of Rome's enemies should be reward enough for all of us.' I could see that in his mind's eye, he was already at his plough.

Afterwards, as we were walking home, Quintus said, 'I hope you know what you are doing.'

'*I* hope I know what I am doing,' replied Cicero.

'The nub of the problem, surely, is Crassus and those two tribunes of his, and his ability to veto the bill. How are you going to get round that?'

'I have no idea. Let us hope that a solution presents itself. One usually does.'

I realised then just how much Cicero was relying on his old dictum that sometimes you have to start a fight to discover how to win it. He said good night to Quintus and walked on, head down in thought. From being a reluctant participant in Pompey's grand ambition, he had now emerged as its chief organiser, and he knew that this would put him in a hard place, not least with his own wife. In my experience, women are far less willing than men to forget past slights and it was inexplicable to Terentia that her husband should still be dancing attendance on the 'Prince of Picenum', as she derisively called Pompey, especially after that day's scenes in the senate, about which the whole city was talking. She was waiting for Cicero in the tablinum when we arrived home, all drawn up in full battle order and ready to attack. She flew at him immediately. 'I cannot believe things have reached such a pass! There is the senate on one side and the rabble on the other – and where is my husband to be found? As usual, with the rabble! Surely even you will sever your connection with him now?'

'He is announcing his retirement tomorrow,' Cicero soothed her.

'What?'

'It is true. I am going to write his statement myself this evening. Which means I shall have to dine at my desk, I am afraid, if you will excuse me.' He eased past her, and once we were in his study he said, 'Do you think she believed me?'

'No,' I replied.

'Nor do I,' he said, with a chuckle. 'She has lived with me too long!'

He was rich enough by now to have divorced her if he wanted, and he could have made himself a better match, certainly a more beautiful one. He was disappointed she had not been able to give him a son. And yet, despite their endless arguments, he stayed with her. Love was not the word for it – not in the sense that the poets use it. Some stranger, stronger compound bound them. She kept him sharp, that was part of it: the whetstone to his blade. At any rate, she did not bother us for the rest of that night, as Cicero dictated the words he thought that Pompey should say. He had never written a speech for anyone else before, and it was a peculiar experience. Nowadays, of course, most senators employ a slave or two to turn out their speeches; I have even heard of some who have no idea of what they are going to say until the text is placed in front of them: how these fellows can call themselves statesmen defeats me. But Cicero found that he rather enjoyed composing parts for others. It amused him to think of lines that great men ought to utter, if only they had the brains, and later he would use the technique to considerable effect in his books. He even thought of a phrase for Gabinius to deliver, which afterwards became quite famous: 'Pompey the Great was not born for himself alone, but for Rome!'

The statement was deliberately kept short and we finished it long before midnight, and early the following morning, after Cicero had performed his exercises and greeted only his most important callers, we went across to Pompey's house and gave him the speech. Overnight, Pompey had contracted a bad dose of cold feet, and now he fretted aloud whether retirement was such a good idea after all. But Cicero saw that it was nervousness about going up on to the rostra as much as anything else, and once Pompey had his prepared text in his hands, he began to calm down. Cicero then gave some notes to Gabinius, who was also present, but the tribune resented being handed his lines like an actor, and questioned whether he should really say that Pompey was 'born for Rome'. 'Why?' teased Cicero. 'Do you not believe it?' Whereupon Pompey gruffly ordered Gabinius to stop complaining and say the words as written. Gabinius fell silent, but he glowered at Cicero and from that moment I believe became his secret enemy – a perfect example of the senator's recklessness in causing offence by his repartee.

An enormous throng of spectators had gathered in the forum, eager to see the sequel to the previous day's performance. We could hear the noise as we came down the hill from Pompey's house – that awesome, oblivious swelling sound of a great excited multitude, which always reminds me of a huge sea rolling against a distant shore. I felt my blood begin to pulse faster in anticipation. Most of the senate was there, and the aristocrats had brought along several hundred supporters of their own, partly for their protection, and also to howl down Pompey when, as they expected, he declared his desire for the supreme command. The great man briefly entered the forum escorted, as before, by Cicero and his senatorial allies, but kept to the edge of it, and immediately went to the back of the rostra, where he paced around, yawned, blew on his freezing hands, and generally gave every indication of nerves, as the roar of the crowd increased in volume. Cicero wished him luck, then went round to the front of the rostra to stand with the rest of the senate, for he was keen to observe their reactions. The ten tribunes filed up on to the platform and sat on their bench, then Gabinius stepped forward and shouted dramatically, 'I summon before the people Pompey the Great!'

How important appearance is in politics, and how superbly Pompey was fashioned by nature to carry the look of greatness! As that broad and familiar figure came plodding up the steps and into view, his followers gave him the most tremendous ovation. He stood there as solid as a full-grown bull, his massive head tilted back slightly on his muscular shoulders, looking down on the upturned faces, his nostrils flared as if inhaling the applause. Normally, the people resented having speeches read to them rather than delivered with apparent spontaneity, but on this occasion there was something in the way that Pompey unrolled his short text and held it up that reinforced the sense that these were words as weighty as the man delivering them – a man above the smooth oratorical tricks of the law and politics.

'People of Rome,' he bellowed into the silence, 'when I was seventeen I fought in the army of my father, Gnaeus Pompeius Strabo, to bring unity to the state. When I was twenty-three I raised a force of fifteen thousand, defeated the combined rebel armies of Brutus, Caelius and Carrinas, and was saluted imperator in the field. When I was twenty-four I conquered Sicily. When I was twenty-five I conquered Africa. On my twenty-sixth birthday, I triumphed. When I was thirty, and not even a senator, I took command of our forces in Spain with proconsular authority, fought the rebels for six years, and conquered. When I was thirty-six I returned to Italy, hunted down the last remaining army of the fugitive slave Spartacus, and conquered. When I was thirty-seven I was voted consul and triumphed for a second time. As consul, I restored to you the ancient rights of your tribunes, and staged games. Whenever danger has threatened this commonwealth, I have served it. My entire life has been nothing but one long special command. Now a new and unprecedented menace has arisen to threaten the republic. And to meet that danger, an office with new and unprecedented authority is rightly proposed. Whoever you choose to shoulder this burden must have the support of all ranks and all classes, for a great trust is involved in bestowing so much power on a single man. It is clear to me, after the meeting of the senate yesterday, that I do not have their trust, and therefore I want to tell you that however much I am petitioned, I shall not consent to be nominated; and if nominated, I shall not serve. Pompey the Great has had his fill of special commands. On this day I renounce all ambition for public office and retire from the city to till the soil like my forefathers before me.'

After a moment of shock, a terrible groan of disappointment broke from the crowd, and Gabinius darted to the front of the rostra, where Pompey was standing impassively.

'This cannot be permitted! Pompey the Great was not born for himself alone, but for Rome!'

Of course, the line provoked the most tremendous demonstration of approval, and the chant of 'Pompey! Pompey! Rome! Rome!' bounced off the walls of the basilicas and temples until one's ears ached with the noise. It was some time before Pompey could make himself heard.

'Your kindness touches me, my fellow citizens, but my continued presence in the city can only impede your deliberations. Choose wisely, O people of Rome, from the many able former consuls in the senate! And remember that although I now quit Rome altogether, my heart will remain among your hearths and temples for ever. Farewell!'

He raised his roll of papyrus as if it were a marshal's baton, saluted the wailing crowd, turned, and trudged implacably towards the back of the platform, ignoring all entreaties to remain. Down the steps he went, watched by the astonished tribunes, first the legs sinking from view, and then the torso, and finally the noble head with its crowning quiff. Some people standing close to me began weeping and tearing at their hair and clothes, and even though I knew the whole thing was a ruse, it was all I could do not to break into sobs myself. The assembled senators looked as if some weighty missile had dropped among them – a few were defiant, many were shaken, the majority simply blank with wonder. For almost as long as anyone could remember, Pompey had been the foremost man in the state, and now he had – gone! Crassus's face in particular was a picture of conflicting emotions, which no artist ever born could have hoped to capture. Part of him knew that he must now, at last, after a lifetime in Pompey's shadow, be the favourite to seize the special command; the shrewder part knew that this had to be a trick, and that his whole position was threatened by some unforeseen jeopardy.

Cicero stayed just long enough to gauge the reactions to his handiwork, then hurried round to the back of the rostra to report. The Piceneans were there, and the usual crush of hangers-on. Pompey's attendants had brought a closed litter of blue and gold brocade to ferry him to the Capena Gate, and the general was preparing to clamber into it. He was like many men I have seen immediately after they have delivered a big speech, in the same breath both arrogant with exhilaration and anxious for reassurance. 'That went extremely well,' he said. 'Did you think it was all right?'

'Superb,' said Cicero. 'Crassus's expression is beyond description.'

'Did you like the line about my heart remaining among the hearths and temples of Rome for ever?'

'It was the consummate touch.'

Pompey grunted, highly pleased, and settled himself among the cushions of his litter. He let the curtain drop, then quickly pulled it aside again. 'You are sure this is going to work?'

'Our opponents are in disarray. That is a start.' The curtain fell, then parted once more.

'How long before the bill is voted on?'

'Fifteen days.'

'Keep me informed. Daily at the least.'

Cicero stepped aside as the canopied chair was hoisted on to the shoulders of its bearers. They must have been strong young fellows, for Pompey was a great weight, yet they set off at the double, past the senate house and out of the forum – the heavenly body of Pompey the Great trailing his comet's tail of clients and admirers. 'Did I like the line about hearths and temples?' repeated Cicero under his breath as he watched him go. 'Well, naturally I did, you great booby – I wrote it!' I guess it must have been hard for him to devote so much energy to a chief he did not admire and a cause he believed to be fundamentally specious. But the journey to the top in politics often confines a man with some uncongenial fellow passengers and shows him strange scenery, and he knew there was no turning back now.

XII

For the next two weeks there was only one topic in Rome, and that was the pirates. Gabinius and Cornelius, in the phrase of the time, 'lived on the rostra' – that is, every day they kept the issue of the pirate menace before the people by issuing fresh proclamations and summoning more witnesses. Horror stories were their speciality. For example, it was put about that if one of the pirates' prisoners announced that he was a Roman citizen, his captors would pretend to be frightened, and beg forgiveness. They would even fetch a toga for him to wear, and shoes for his feet, and bow whenever he passed, and this game would go on for a long time, until at last, when they were far out at sea, they would let down a ladder and tell him he was free to go. If their victim refused to walk, he would be flung overboard. Such tales enraged the audience in the forum, who were accustomed to the magical incantation 'I am a Roman citizen' guaranteeing deference throughout the world.

Cicero himself did not speak from the rostra. Oddly enough, he had never yet done so, having decided early on to hold back until a moment in his career when he could make the maximum impact. He was naturally tempted to make this the issue on which he broke his silence, for it was a popular stick with which to beat the aristocrats. But in the end he decided against it, reasoning that the measure already had such overwhelming backing in the streets, he would be better employed behind the scenes, plotting strategy and trying to tempt over waverers in the senate. For this reason, his crucial importance has been frequently neglected. Instead of the fiery public orator he played the moderate for a change, working his way up and down the senaculum, listening to the complaints of the *pedarii*, promising to relay messages of commiseration and entreaty to Pompey, and dangling – very occasionally – half-offers of preferment to men of influence. Each day a messenger came to the house from Pompey's estate in the Alban Hills bearing a dispatch containing some fresh moan or enquiry or instruction ('Our new Cincinnatus does not seem to be spending much time ploughing,' observed Cicero with a wry smile), and each day the senator would dictate to me a soothing reply, often giving the names of men it might be useful for Pompey to summon out for interview. This was a delicate task, since it was important to maintain the pretence that Pompey was taking no further part in politics. But a combination of greed, flattery, ambition, realisation that some kind of special command was inevitable, and fear that it might go to Crassus eventually brought half a dozen key senators into Pompey's camp, the most significant of whom was Lucius Manlius Torquatus, who had only just finished serving as praetor and was certain to run for the consulship the following year.

Crassus remained, as always, the greatest threat to Cicero's schemes, and naturally he was not idle during this time either. He, too, went around making promises of lucrative commissions, and winning over adherents. For connoisseurs of politics it was fascinating to observe the perennial rivals, Crassus and Pompey, so evenly poised. Each had two tame tribunes; each could therefore veto the bill; and each had a list of secret supporters in the senate. Crassus's advantage over Pompey was the support of most of the aristocrats, who feared Pompey more than any other man in the republic; Pompey's advantage over Crassus was the popularity he enjoyed among the masses on the streets. 'They are like two scorpions, circling each other,' said Cicero, leaning back in his chair one morning, after he had dictated his latest dispatch to Pompey. 'Neither can win outright, yet each can kill the other.'

'Then how will victory ever be achieved?'

He looked at me, then suddenly lunged forward and slammed his palm down on his desk with a speed that made me jump. 'By the one which strikes the other by surprise.'

At the time he made that remark, there were only four days left before the *lex Gabinia* was due to be voted on by the people. He still had not thought of a means of circumventing Crassus's veto. He was wearied and discouraged, and once again began to talk of our retiring to Athens and studying philosophy. That day passed, and the next, and the next, and still no solution presented itself. On the final day before the vote, I rose as usual at dawn and opened the door to Cicero's clients. Now that he was known to be so close to Pompey, these morning levees had doubled in size compared to the old days, and the house was crowded with petitioners and well-wishers at all hours, much to Terentia's annoyance. Some of them had famous names: for example, on this particular morning, Antonius Hybrida, who was the second son of the great orator and consul Marcus Antonius, and who had just finished a term as tribune; he was a fool and a drunk, but protocol dictated he would have to be seen first. Outside it was grey and raining and the callers had brought in with them a wet-dog smell of moist stale clothes and damp hair. The black and white mosaic floor was streaked with tracks of mud and I was just contem-plating summoning one of the household slaves to mop up when the door opened again and who should step in but Marcus Licinius Crassus himself. I was so startled, I briefly forgot to be alarmed, and gave him as natural a greeting as if he had been a nobody, come to request a letter of introduction.

'And a very good morning to you, Tiro,' he returned. He had only met me once, yet he still remembered my name, which frightened me. 'Might it be possible to have a word with your master?' Crassus was not alone but had brought with him Quintus Arrius, a senator who followed him around like a shadow, and whose ridiculously affected speech – always adding an aspirate to a vowel: 'Harrius' was how he pronounced his name – was to be so memorably parodied by that cruellest of poets, Catullus. I hurried through into Cicero's study, where he was doing his usual trick of dictating a letter to Sositheus while signing documents as quickly as Laurea could produce them.

'You will never guess who is here!' I cried.

'Crassus,' he replied, without looking up.

I was immediately deflated. 'You are not surprised?'

'No,' said Cicero, signing another letter. 'He has come to make a magnanimous offer, which is not really magnanimous at all, but which will show him in a better light when our refusal to agree to it becomes public. He has every reason to compromise, while we have none. Still, you had better show him in before he bribes all my clients away from me. And stay in the room and take a note, in case he tries to put words into my mouth.'

So I went out to fetch Crassus – who was indeed glad-handing his way around Cicero's tablinum, to the awed amazement of all concerned – and showed him into the study. The junior secretaries left, and there were just the four of us – Crassus, Arrius and Cicero all seated, and myself standing in the corner and taking notes.

'You have a very nice house,' said Crassus, in his friendly way. 'Small but charming. You must tell me if you think of selling.'

'If it ever catches fire,' responded Cicero, 'you will be the first to know.'

'Very droll,' said Crassus, clapping his hands and laughing with great good humour. 'But I am perfectly serious. An important man such as yourself should have a larger property, in a better neighbourhood. The Palatine, of course. I can arrange it. No, please,' he added, as Cicero shook his head, 'do not dismiss my offer. We have had our differences, and I should like to make a gesture of reconciliation.'

'Well, that is handsome of you,' said Cicero, 'but alas, I fear the interests of a certain gentleman still stand between us.'

'They need not. I have watched your career with admiration, Cicero. You deserve the place you have won in Rome. It is my view that you should achieve the praetorship in the summer, and the consulship itself two years after that. There – I have said it. You may have my support. Now what do you say in reply?'

This was indeed a stunning offer, and at that moment I grasped an important point about clever men of business – that it is not consistent meanness which makes them rich (as many vulgarly assume), but rather the capacity, when necessary, to be unexpectedly, even extravagantly generous. Cicero was entirely caught off balance. He was effectively being offered the consulship, his life's dream, on a platter – an ambition he had never even dared voice in the presence of Pompey, for fear of arousing the great man's jealousy.

'You overwhelm me, Crassus,' he said, and his voice was so thick with emotion he had to cough to clear it before he could continue. 'But fate has once again cast us on different sides.'

'Not necessarily. On the day before the people vote, surely the time has arrived for a compromise? I accept that this supreme command is Pompey's conception. Let us share it.'

'A shared supreme command is an oxymoron.'

'We shared the consulship.'

'Yes, but the consulship is a joint office, based on the principle that political power should always be shared. Running a war is entirely different, as you know far better than I. In warfare, any hint of division at the top is fatal.'

'This command is so huge, there is easily room enough for two,' said Crassus airily. 'Let Pompey take the east, and I the west. Or Pompey the sea and I the land. Or vice versa. I do not mind. The point is that between us we can rule the world, with you as the bridge that links us.'

I am sure that Cicero had expected Crassus to come in threatening and aggressive, tactics which a career in the law courts had long since taught him how to handle. But this unexpectedly generous approach had him reeling, not least because what Crassus was suggesting was both sensible and patriotic. It would also be the ideal solution for Cicero, enabling him to win the friendship of all sides. 'I shall certainly put your offer to him,' promised Cicero. 'He shall have it in his hands before the day is out.'

'That is no use to me!' scoffed Crassus. 'If it were a matter of merely putting a proposal, I could have sent Arrius here out to the Alban Hills with a letter, could I not, Arrius?'

'Hindeed you could.'

'No, Cicero, I need you actually to bring this about.' He leaned in close and moistened his lips; there was something almost lecherous about the way Crassus talked of power. 'I shall be frank with you. I have set my heart upon resuming a military career. I have all the wealth a man could want, but that can only be a means and not an end in itself. Can you tell me what nation ever erected a statue to a man because he was rich? Which of the earth's many peoples mingles the name of some long-dead millionaire in its prayers because of the number of houses he once possessed? The only lasting glory is on the page – and I am no poet! – or on the battlefield. So you see, you really must deliver the agreement of Pompey for our bargain to stick.'

'He is not a mule to be driven to market,' objected Cicero, whom I could see was starting to recoil again from the crudeness of his old enemy. 'You know what he is like.'

'I do. Too well! But you are the most persuasive man in the world. You got him to leave Rome – do not deny it! Now surely you can convince him to come back?'

'His position is that he will come back as the sole supreme commander, or he will not come back at all.'

'Then Rome will never see him again,' snapped Crassus, whose friendliness was beginning to peel away like a thin layer of cheap paint on one of his less salubrious properties. 'You know perfectly well what is going to happen tomorrow. It will unfold as predictably as a farce at the theatre. Gabinius will propose your law and Trebellius, on my behalf, will veto it.

Then Roscius, also on my instructions, will propose an amendment, setting up a joint command, and dare any tribune to veto *that*. If Pompey refuses to serve, he will look like a greedy child, willing to spoil the cake rather than share it.'

'I disagree. The people love him.'

'The people loved Tiberius Gracchus, but it did him no good in the end. That was a horrible fate for a patriotic Roman, which you might do well to remember.' Crassus stood. 'Look to your own interests, Cicero. Surely you can see that Pompey is leading you to political oblivion? No man ever became consul with the aristocracy united against him.' Cicero also rose and warily took Crassus's proferred hand. The older man grasped it hard and pulled him close. 'On two occasions,' he said in a very soft voice, 'I have offered the hand of friendship to you, Marcus Tullius Cicero. There will not be a third.'

With that, he strode out of the house, and at such a pace I could not get in front of him to show him out, or even open the door. I returned to the study to find Cicero standing exactly where I had left him, frowning at his hand. 'It is like touching the skin of a snake,' he said. 'Tell me – did I mishear him, or is he suggesting that Pompey and I might suffer the same fate as Tiberius Gracchus?'

'Yes: "a horrible fate for a patriotic Roman",' I read from my notes. 'What was the fate of Tiberius Gracchus?'

'Cornered like a rat in a temple and murdered by the nobles, while he was still tribune, and therefore supposedly inviolable. That must have been sixty years ago, at least. Tiberius Gracchus!' He clenched his hand into a fist. 'You know, for a moment, Tiro, he almost had me believing him. But I swear to you, I would sooner never be consul than feel that I had only achieved it because of Crassus.'

'I believe you, Senator. Pompey is worth ten of him.'

'A hundred, more like – for all his absurdities.'

I busied myself with a few things, straightening the desk and collecting the morning's list of callers from the tablinum, while Cicero remained motionless in the study. When I returned again, a curious expression had come over his face. I gave him the list and reminded him that he still had a houseful of clients to receive, including a senator. Absent-mindedly he selected a couple of names, among them Hybrida's, but then he suddenly said, 'Leave things here to Sositheus. I have a different task for you to perform. Go to the National Archive and consult the Annals for the consular year of Mucius Scaevola and Calpurnius Piso Frugi. Copy down everything relating to the tribuneship of Tiberius Gracchus and his agrarian bill. Tell nobody what you are doing. If anyone asks you, make something up. Well?' He smiled for the first time in a week and made a shooing gesture, flicking his fingers at me. 'Go on, man. Go!'

After so many years in his service I had become used to these bewildering and peremptory commands, and once I had wrapped myself up against the cold and wet I set off down the hill. Never had I known the city so grim and hard pressed – in the depths of winter, under a dark sky, freezing, short of food, with beggars on every corner, and even the occasional corpse in the gutter of some poor wretch who had died in the night. I moved quickly through the dreary streets, across the forum and up the steps to the Archive. This was the same building in which I had discovered the meagre official records of Gaius Verres and I had been back on many errands since, especially when Cicero was aedile, so my face was familiar to the clerks. They gave me the volume I needed without asking any questions. I took it over to a reading desk beside the window and unrolled it with my mittened fingers. The morning light was weak, it was very draughty, and I was not at all sure what I was looking for. The Annals, at least in those days before Caesar got his hands on them, gave a very straight and full account of what had happened in each year: the names of the magistrates, the laws passed, the wars fought, the famines endured, the eclipses and other natural phenomena observed. They were drawn from the official register that was written up each year by the pontifex maximus, and posted on the white board outside the headquarters of the college of priests.

History has always fascinated me. As Cicero himself once wrote: 'To be ignorant of what occurred before you were born is to remain always a child. For what is the worth of human life, unless it is woven into the life of our ancestors by the records of history?' I quickly forgot the cold and could have spent all day happily unwinding that roll, poring over the events of more than sixty years before. I discovered that in this particular year, Rome's six hundred and twenty-first, King Attalus III of Pergamon had died, bequeathing his country to Rome; that Scipio Africanus Minor had destroyed the Spanish city of Numantia, slaughtering all of its five thousand inhabitants, apart from fifty whom he saved to walk in chains in his triumph; and that Tiberius Gracchus, the famous radical tribune, had introduced a law to share out the public land among the common people, who were then, as always, suffering great hardship. Nothing changes, I thought. Gracchus's bill had infuriated the aristocrats in the senate, who saw it as threatening their estates, and they had persuaded or suborned a tribune named Marcus Octavius to veto the law. But because the people were unanimous in their support for the bill, Gracchus had argued from the rostra that Octavius was failing in his sacred duty to uphold their interests. He had therefore called upon the people to begin voting Octavius out of office, tribe by tribe, which they at once proceeded to do. When the first seventeen of the thirty-five tribes had voted overwhelmingly for Octavius's removal, Gracchus had suspended the polling and appealed to him to withdraw his veto. Octavius had refused, whereupon Gracchus had 'called upon the gods to witness that he did not willingly wish to remove his colleague', had balloted the eighteenth tribe, achieved a majority, and Octavius had been stripped of his tribuneship ('reduced to the rank of a private citizen he departed unobserved'). The agrarian law had then been passed. But the nobles, as Crassus had reminded Cicero, had exacted their revenge a few months later, when Gracchus had been surrounded in the Temple of Fides, beaten to death with sticks and clubs, and his body flung in the Tiber.

I unfastened the hinged notebook from my wrist and took out my stylus. I remember how I glanced around to make sure I was alone before I opened it and started copying the relevant passages from the Annals, for now I understood why Cicero had been so emphatic about the need for secrecy. My fingers were freezing and the wax was hard; the script I produced was atrocious. At one point, when Catulus himself, the patron of the Archive, appeared in the doorway and stared straight at me, I felt as if my heart would shatter the bones of my breast. But the old man was shortsighted, and I doubt he would have known who I was in any case; he was not that sort of politician. After talking for a while with one of his freedmen, he left. I finished my transcription and almost ran out of that place, down the icy steps and back across the forum towards Cicero's house, carrying my wax tablet pressed close to me, sensing I had never done a more significant morning's work in my life.

When I reached the house, Cicero was still ensconced with Antonius Hybrida, although as soon as he saw me waiting near the door, he drew their conversation to a close. Hybrida was one of those well-bred, fine-boned types, who had ruined himself and his looks with wine. I could smell his breath even from where I stood: it was like fruit rotting in a gutter. He had been thrown out of the senate a few years previously for bankruptcy and loose morals – specifically, corruption, drunkenness, and buying a beautiful young slave girl at an auction and living openly with her as his mistress. But the people, in that peculiar way of theirs, rather loved him for his rakish ways, and now that he had served a year as their tribune, he had worked his way back into the senate. I waited until he had gone before I gave Cicero my notes. 'What did he want?' I asked.

'My support in the elections for praetor.'

'He has a nerve!'

'I suppose he has. I promised to back him, though,' said Cicero carelessly, and seeing my surprise he explained: 'At least with him as praetor I shall have one fewer rival for the consulship.'

He laid my notebook on his desk and read it carefully. Then he put his elbows on either side of it, rested his chin in the palms of his hands, hunched forward and read it again. I pictured his quick thoughts running ahead in the way that water runs along the cracks in a tiled floor – first onwards, and then spreading to either side, blocked in one spot, advancing in another, widening and branching out, all the little possibilities and implications and likelihoods in shimmering fluid motion. Eventually, he said, half to himself and half to me, 'Such a tactic had never been tried before Gracchus used it, and has never been attempted since. One can see why. What a weapon to put into any man's hands! Win or lose, we should have to live with the consequences for years.' He looked up at me. 'I am not sure, Tiro. Perhaps it would be better if you erased it.' But when I made a move towards the desk, he said quickly, 'And then again perhaps not.' Instead, he told me to fetch Laurea and a couple of the other slaves and have them run around to all the senators in Pompey's inner group, asking them to assemble after the close of official business that afternoon. 'Not here,' he added quickly, 'but in Pompey's house.' Thereupon he sat down and began writing out, in his own hand, a dispatch to the general, which was sent off with a rider who had orders to wait and return with a reply. 'If Crassus wants to summon up the ghost of Gracchus,' he said grimly, when the letter had gone, 'he shall have him!'

Needless to say, the others were agog to hear why Cicero had summoned them, and once the courts and offices were shut for the day, everyone turned up at Pompey's mansion, filling all the seats around the table, except for the absent owner's great throne, which was left empty as a mark of respect. It may seem strange that such clever and learned men as Caesar and Varro were ignorant of the precise tactics which Gracchus had used as tribune, but remember that he had been dead by then for sixty-three years, that huge events had intervened, and that there was not yet the mania for contemporary history which was to develop over the coming decades. Even Cicero had forgotten it until Crassus's threat dislodged some distant memory from the time when he was studying for the bar. There was a profound hush as he read out the extract from the Annals, and when he had finished, an excited hubbub. Only the white-haired Varro, who was the oldest present, and who remembered hearing from his father about the chaos of the Gracchus tribunate, expressed reservations. 'You would create a precedent,' he said, 'by which any demagogue could summon the people, and threaten to dispose of any of his colleagues whenever he felt he had a majority among the tribes. Indeed, why stop at a tribune? Why not remove a praetor, or a consul?'

'*We* would not create the precedent,' Caesar pointed out impatiently. 'Gracchus created it for us.'

'Exactly,' said Cicero. 'Although the nobles may have murdered him, they did not declare his legislation illegal. I know what Varro means, and to a degree I share his unease. But we are in a desperate struggle, and obliged to take some risks.'

There was a murmur of assent, but in the end the most decisive voices in favour were those of Gabinius and Cornelius, the men who would actually have to stand before the people and push the legislation through, and who would, as a consequence, be chiefly liable to the nobles' retaliation, both physical and legal.

'The people overwhelmingly want this supreme command, and they want Pompey to be given it,' declared Gabinius. 'The fact that Crassus's purse is deep enough to buy two tribunes should not be allowed to frustrate their will.'

Afranius wanted to know if Pompey had expressed an opinion.

'This is the dispatch I sent to him this morning,' said Cicero, holding it up, 'and here on the bottom is the reply he sent back instantly, and which reached me here at the same time as you all did.' Everyone could see what Pompey had scrawled, in his large, bold script: the single word, *Agreed*. That settled the matter. Afterwards, Cicero instructed me to burn the letter.

The morning of the assembly was bitterly cold, with an icy wind whipping around the colonnades and temples of the forum. But the chill did not deter a vast assembly from turning out. On major voting days, the tribunes transferred themselves from the rostra to the Temple of Castor, where there was more space to conduct the ballot, and workmen had been busy overnight, erecting the wooden gangways up which the citizens would file to cast their votes. Cicero arrived early and discreetly, with only myself and Quintus in attendance, for as he said as he walked down the hill, he was only the stage manager of this production and not one of its leading performers. He spent a little while conferring with a group of tribal officers, then retreated with me to the portico of the Basilica Aemilia, from where he would have a good view of proceedings and could issue instructions as necessary.

It was a dramatic sight, and I guess I must be one of the very few left alive who witnessed it – the ten tribunes lined up on their bench, among them, like hired gladiators, the two matched pairs of Gabinius and Cornelius (for Pompey), versus Trebellius and Roscius (for Crassus); the priests and the augurs all standing at the top of the steps to the temple; the orange fire on the altar providing a flickering point of colour in the greyness; and spread out across the forum the great crowd of voters, red-faced in the cold, milling around the ten-foot-high standard of their particular tribe. Each standard carried its name proudly in large letters – *AEMILIA, CAMILIA, FABIA*, and so on – so that its members, if they wandered off, could see where they were supposed to be. There was much joking and horse-trading between the groups, until the trumpet of the herald called them to order. Then the official crier gave the legislation its second reading in a penetrating voice, after which Gabinius stepped forward and made a short speech. He had joyful news, he said: the news that the people of Rome had been praying for. Pompey the Great, deeply moved by the sufferings of the nation, was willing to reconsider his position, and serve as supreme commander – but only if it was the unanimous desire of them all. 'And is it your desire?' demanded Gabinius, to which there was a huge demonstration of enthusiasm. This went on for some time, thanks to the tribal officers. In fact, whenever it seemed the volume might be waning, Cicero would give a discreet signal to a couple of these officers, who would relay it across the forum, and the tribal standards would start waving again, rekindling the applause. Eventually Gabinius motioned them to be quiet. 'Then let us put it to the vote!'

Slowly – and one had to admire his courage in standing up at all, in the face of so many thousands – Trebellius rose from his place on the tribunes' bench and came forward, his hand raised to signal his desire to intervene. Gabinius regarded him with contempt, and then roared to the crowd, 'Well, citizens, should we let him speak?'

'No!' they screamed in response.

To which Trebellius, in a voice made shrill by nerves, shouted: 'Then I veto the bill!'

At any other time in the past four centuries, excepting the year when Tiberius Gracchus was tribune, this would have been the end of the legislation. But on that fateful morning, Gabinius motioned the jeering crowd to be silent. 'Does Trebellius speak for you all?'

'No!' they chanted back. 'No! No!'

'Does he speak for anyone here?' The only sound was the wind: even the senators who supported Trebellius dared not raise their voices, for they were standing unprotected among their tribes, and would have been set upon by the mob. 'Then, in accordance with the precedent set by Tiberius Gracchus, I propose that Trebellius, having failed to observe the oath of his office and represent the people, be removed as tribune, and that this be voted on immediately!'

Cicero turned to me. 'And now the play begins,' he said.

For a moment, the citizenry simply looked at one another. Then they started nodding, and a sound grew out of the crowd of realisation – that is how I think of it now, at any rate, as I sit in my little study with my eyes closed and try to remember it all – a realisation that they could do this, and that the grandees in the senate were powerless to stop them. Catulus, Hortensius and Crassus, in great alarm, started pushing their way towards the front of the assembly, demanding a hearing, but Gabinius had stationed a few of Pompey's veterans along the bottom steps and they were not allowed to pass. Crassus, in particular, had lost all his usual restraint. His face was red and contorted with rage as he tried to storm the tribunal, but he was pushed back. He noticed Cicero watching and pointed at him, and shouted something, but he was too far away and there was too much noise for us to hear. Cicero smiled at him benignly. The crier read out Gabinius's motion – 'That the people no longer desire Trebellius to be their tribune' – and the electoral clerks dispersed to their stations. As usual, the Suburana were the first to vote, filing up the gangplank two abreast to cast their ballots, then down the stone steps at the side of the temple and back into the forum. The city tribes followed one after the other, and every one of them voted for Trebellius to be stripped of his office. Then the rural tribes started balloting. This all took several hours, and throughout it Trebellius looked grey with anxiety, and frequently conferred with his companion, Roscius. At one point he disappeared from the tribunal. I did not see where he went, but I guess it must have been to plead with Crassus to release him from his obligation. All across the forum, small huddles of senators gathered as their tribes finished voting, and I noticed Catulus and Hortensius going, grim-faced, from group to group. Cicero also did the rounds, leaving me behind as he circulated among the senators, talking to some of those, such as Torquatus and his old ally Marcellinus, whom he had secretly persuaded to switch to Pompey's camp. At length, after seventeen tribes had voted to oust Trebellius, Gabinius ordered a pause in the balloting. He summoned Trebellius to the front of the tribunal and asked him whether he was prepared now to bow to the will of the people, and by so doing keep his tribunate, or whether it would be necessary to hold an eighteenth ballot and cast him out of office. This was Trebellius's chance to enter history as the hero of his cause, and I have often wondered whether, in his old age, he looked back on his decision with regret. But I suppose he still had hopes of a political career. After a short hesitation, he signalled his assent and his veto was withdrawn. I need hardly add that he was subsequently despised by both sides and never heard of again.

All eyes now turned to Roscius, Crassus's second tribune, and it was at this point, some time in the early afternoon, that Catulus appeared again at the foot of the temple steps, cupped his hands to his mouth, and shouted up to Gabinius, demanding a hearing. As I have mentioned before, Catulus commanded great respect among the people for his patriotism. It was therefore hard for Gabinius to refuse him, not least because he was regarded as the senior ex-consul in the senate. He gestured to the veterans to let him pass, and Catulus, despite his age, shot up the steps like a lizard. 'This is a mistake,' Cicero muttered to me.

Gabinius told Cicero afterwards that he thought the aristocrats, seeing that they had lost, might now be willing to concede in the interests of national unity. But not at all. Catulus railed against the *lex Gabinia* and the illegal tactics being used to drive it through. It was madness, he declared, for the republic to entrust its security to one man. Warfare was a hazardous business, especially at sea: what would happen to this special command if Pompey was killed? Who would be his replacement? A cry went up of 'You!' which, however flattering, was not at all the response that Catulus wanted. He knew he was far too old to go off soldiering. What he really wanted was a dual command – Crassus and Pompey – because even though he detested Crassus personally, he reckoned that the richest man in Rome would at least provide a counterweight to Pompey's power. But by now Gabinius had begun to realise his error in letting Catulus speak. The winter days were short. He needed to finish the voting by sunset. He roughly interrupted the former consul and told him he had had his say: it was time to put the matter to the ballot. Roscius thereupon sprang forward and tried to make a formal proposal splitting the supreme command in two, but the people were becoming exasperated, and refused to give him a hearing. In fact they set up such a deafening clamour it was said that the noise killed a raven flying overhead and sent it plummeting to the earth. All Roscius could do against the uproar was raise two fingers to veto the legislation and signify his belief that there should be two commanders. Gabinius knew that if he had to call yet another ballot to remove a tribune, he would lose the light, and with it the chance of establishing the supreme command that day – and who could tell what lengths the aristocrats might go to if they had a chance to regroup overnight? So he responded by turning his back on Roscius and ordering the bill to be put regardless.

'That's it,' said Cicero to me, as the voting clerks sprang to their stations. 'It's done. Run up to Pompey's house, and tell them to send a message to the general immediately. Write this down: "The bill is passed. The command is yours. You must set out for Rome at once. Be sure to arrive tonight. Your presence is required to secure the situation. Signed, Cicero."'

I checked I had his words correctly, then hurried off on my errand, while Cicero plunged back into the crowded forum to practise his art – cajoling, flattering, sympathising, even occasionally threatening – for there was nothing, according to his philosophy, that could not be made or undone or repaired by words.

Thus was passed, by a unanimous vote of all the tribes, the *lex Gabinia*, a measure which was to have immense consequences – for all those personally concerned, for Rome, and for the world.

As night fell, the forum emptied and the combatants retired to their respective headquarters – the aristocratic diehards to the home of Catulus, on the brow of the Palatine; the adherents of Crassus to his own, more modest dwelling, lower down the same hill; and the victorious Pompeians to the mansion of their chief, on the Esquiline. Success had worked its usual fecund magic, and I should think that at least twenty senators crammed themselves into Pompey's tablinum to drink his wine and await his victorious return. The room was brilliantly illuminated by candelabra, and there was that thick atmosphere of drink and sweat and the noisy racket of masculine conversation which often follows the release of tension. Caesar, Afranius, Palicanus, Varro, Gabinius and Cornelius were all present, but the newcomers outnumbered them. I cannot remember all their names. Lucius Torquatus and his cousin, Aulus, were certainly present, along with another notable young pair of bluebloods, Metellus Nepos and Lentulus Marcellinus. Cornelius Sisenna (who had been one of Verres's most enthusiastic supporters) made himself thoroughly at home, putting his feet up on the furniture, as did the two ex-consuls, Lentulus Clodianus and Gellius Publicola (the same Gellius who was still smarting from Cicero's joke about the philosophy conference). As for Cicero, he sat apart in an adjoining chamber, composing an acceptance speech for Pompey to deliver the next day. At the time, I could not understand his curious quietness, but with hindsight I believe he may have had an intuition that something had just cracked in the commonwealth which it would be hard even for his words to repair. From time to time he sent me out to the vestibule to check on Pompey's whereabouts.

Shortly before midnight, a messenger arrived to say that Pompey was approaching the city along the Via Latina. A score of his veterans had been stationed at the Capena Gate to escort him home by torchlight, in case his enemies resorted to desperate tactics, but Quintus – who had spent much of the night touring the city with the precinct bosses – reported to his brother that the streets were quiet. Eventually, cheering outside announced the great man's arrival, and suddenly there he was among us, bigger than ever, grinning, shaking hands, clapping backs; even I received a friendly punch on the shoulder. The senators clamoured for Pompey to make a speech, at which Cicero remarked, a touch too loudly, 'He cannot speak yet: I have not written what he should say.' Just for a moment I saw a shadow flash across Pompey's face, but yet again Caesar came to Cicero's rescue, howling with laughter, and when Pompey suddenly grinned and wagged his finger in mock-reproach, the atmosphere relaxed into the joshing humour of an officers' mess, where the triumphant commander expects to be ribbed.

Whenever I picture the word *imperium* it is always Pompey who comes into my mind – Pompey that night, hovering over his map of the Mediterranean, distributing dominion over land and sea as casually as he dispensed his wine ('Marcellinus, you can have the Libyan sea, while you, Torquatus, shall have eastern Spain …'), and Pompey the following morning, when he went down into the forum to claim his prize. The annalists later reckoned that twenty thousand crammed into the centre of Rome to see him anointed world commander. It was such a throng that even Catulus and Hortensius dared not commit some last act of resistance, although I am sure they would have liked to, but were instead obliged to stand with the other senators, putting the best face on it they could; Crassus, typically, could not even manage that, and stayed away altogether. Pompey did not say much, mostly a few protestations of humble gratitude, crafted by Cicero, and an appeal for national unity. But then he did not have to say anything: his presence alone had caused the price of grain in the markets to halve, such was the confidence he inspired. And he finished with the most wonderful theatrical flourish, which can only have come from Cicero: 'I shall now put on again that uniform once so dear and so familiar to me, the sacred red cloak of a Roman commander in the field, and I shall not take it off again until victory in this war is won – or I shall not survive the outcome!' He raised his hand in salute and left the platform – was wafted from the platform would be a better way of putting it, on a wind of acclamation. The applause was still going on when suddenly, beyond the rostra, he came into view again – steadily climbing the steps of the Capitol, now wearing the *paludamentum*, that bright scarlet cloak which is the mark of every Roman proconsul on active service. As the people went wild with enthusiasm, I glanced across to where Cicero was standing next to Caesar. Cicero's expression was one of amused distaste, but Caesar's was enraptured, as if he were already glimpsing his own future. Pompey carried on into the precincts of the Capitoline Triad, where he sacrificed a bull to Jupiter, and left the city immediately afterwards, without saying goodbye to Cicero or to anyone else. It was to be six years before he returned.

XIII

In the annual elections for praetor that summer, Cicero topped the poll. It was an ugly, scrappy campaign, fought in the aftermath of the struggle over the *lex Gabinia*, when trust between the political factions had broken down. I have before me the letter which Cicero wrote to Atticus that summer, expressing his disgust at all things in public life: 'It is unbelievable in how short a time how much worse you will find them than when you left.' Twice the balloting had to be abandoned halfway through when fighting broke out on the Field of Mars. Cicero suspected Crassus of hiring thugs to disrupt the voting, but could not prove it. Whatever the truth, it was not until September that the eight praetors-elect were finally able to assemble in the senate house to determine which court each would preside over in the coming year. The selection, as usual, was to be settled by drawing lots.

The most coveted office was that of urban praetor, who in those days ran the justice system and was ranked third in the state, behind the two consuls; he also had responsibility for staging the Games of Apollo. If that was the plum, then the post to be avoided at all costs was the embezzlement court, a job of stunning tedium. 'Of course, I should like the urban praetorship,' Cicero confided to me as we walked down to the senate that morning. 'And frankly, I should rather hang myself than sort out embezzlement for a year. But I shall willingly settle for anything in between.' He was in a buoyant mood. The elections were concluded at last and he had won the most votes. Pompey was gone not only from Rome but from Italy, so he had no great man looming over him. And he was getting very close to the consulship now – so close he could almost feel that ivory chair beneath him.

There was always a full chamber for these lot-drawing ceremonies, combining as they did high politics with a game of chance, and by the time we arrived the majority of the senators had already gone in. Cicero entered to a noisy reception, with cheers from his old supporters among the *pedarii* and abusive shouts from the aristocrats. Crassus, stretched out in his usual position on the consular front bench, regarded him through half-closed eyes, like a big cat pretending to be asleep while a little bird hops by. The election had turned out much as Cicero had expected, and if I give you here the names of the other praetors-elect, I believe you will have a good sense of how politics stood at that time. Apart from Cicero, there were only two other men of obvious ability waiting calmly to draw their lots. By far the most talented was Aquilius Gallus, who some say was a better lawyer even than Cicero, and who was already a respected judge; in fact, he was something of a paragon – brilliant, modest, just, kindly, a man of supreme taste, with a magnificent mansion on the Viminal Hill; Cicero had it in mind to approach the older man to be his running-mate for consul. Next to Gallus, at least in gravitas, was Sulpicius Galba, of a distinguished aristocratic family, who had so many consular masks in his atrium, it was inconceivable he would not be one of Cicero's rivals for the consulship; but although he was honest and able, he was also harsh and arrogant – that would count against him in a tight election. Fourth in talent, I suppose, although Cicero sometimes burst out laughing at his absurdities, was Quintus Cornificius, a rich religious fundamentalist, who talked endlessly about the need to revive Rome's declining morals – 'the candidate of the gods', Cicero called him. After that, I am afraid, there was a great shelving-away in ability: remarkably, all the other four praetors-elect were men who had previously been expelled from the senate, for deficiencies in either funds or morals. The oldest of these was Varinius Glaber, one of those clever, bitter men who expect to succeed in life and cannot believe it when they realise they have failed – already a praetor seven years earlier, he had been given an army by the senate to put down the revolt of Spartacus; but his legions were weak and he had been beaten repeatedly by the rebel slaves, eventually retiring from public life in humiliation. Then there was Caius Orchivius – 'all push and no talent', as Cicero characterised him – who had the support of a big voting syndicate. In seventh place when it came to brains Cicero placed Cassius Longinus – 'that barrel of lard' – who was sometimes called the fattest man in Rome. Which left, in eighth, none other than Antonius Hybrida, the drinker who kept a slave girl for a wife, whom Cicero had agreed to help in the elections on the grounds that here, at least, would be one praetor whose ambitions he would not have to worry about. 'Do you know why they call him "Hybrida"?' Cicero asked me one day. 'Because he's half man, half imbecile. I wouldn't award him the half, personally.'

But those gods to whom Cornificius was so devoted have a way of punishing such hubris, and they duly punished Cicero that day. The lots were placed in an ancient urn which had been used for this purpose for centuries, and the presiding consul, Glabrio, called up the candidates in alphabetical order, which meant that Antonius Hybrida went first. He dipped his trembling hand into the urn for a token and gave it to Glabrio, who raised an eyebrow and then read out: 'Urban praetor.' There was a moment of silence, and then the chamber rang with such a shout of laughter that the pigeons roosting in the roof all took off in a great burst of shit and feathers. Hortensius and some of the other aristocrats, knowing that Cicero had helped Hybrida, pointed towards the orator and clapped their sides in mockery. Crassus almost fell off his bench with delight, while Hybrida himself – soon to be the third man in the state – stood beaming all around him, no doubt misinterpreting the derision as pleasure at his good fortune.

I could not see Cicero's face, but I could guess what he was thinking: that his bad luck would surely now be completed by drawing embezzlement. Gallus went next and won the court which administered electoral law; Longinus the fat man received treason; and when candidate-of-the-gods Cornificius was awarded the criminal court, the odds were starting to look decidedly grim – so much so that I was sure the worst was about to happen. But thankfully it was the next man up, Orchivius, who drew embezzlement. When Galba was given responsibility for hearing cases of violence against the state, that meant there were only two possibilities left for Cicero – either his familiar stamping-ground of the extortion court, or the position of foreign praetor, which would have left him effectively the deputy of Hybrida: a grim fate for the cleverest man in the city. As he stepped up to the dais to draw his lot, he gave a rueful shake of his head – you can scheme all you like in politics, the gesture seemed to say, but in the end it all comes down to luck. He thrust his hand into the urn and drew out – extortion. There was a certain pleasing symmetry in that it was Glabrio, the former president of this very court in which Cicero had made his name, who read out the announcement. So that left the foreign praetorship to Varinius, the victim of Spartacus. Thus the courts were settled for the following year, and the preliminary field lined up for the consulship.

Amid all this rush of political events, I have neglected to mention that Pomponia had become pregnant in the spring – proof, as Cicero wrote triumphantly to Atticus when he passed on the news, that the marriage with Quintus must be working after all. Not long after the praetorian elections, the child was born, a healthy boy. It was a matter of great pride to me, and a mark of my growing standing within the family, that I was invited to attend the lustrical, on the ninth day following the birth. The ceremony was held at the Temple of Tellus, next to the family house, and I doubt whether any nephew could have had a more doting uncle than Cicero, who insisted on commissioning a splendid amulet from a silversmith as a naming-present. It was only after baby Quintus had been blessed by the priest with holy water, and Cicero took him in his arms, that I realised how much he missed having a boy of his own. A large part of any man's motivation in pursuing the consulship must surely have been that his son, and grandson, and sons of his sons to infinity, could exercise the right of *ius imaginum*, and display his likeness after death in the family atrium. What was the point in founding a glorious family name if the line was extinct before it even started? And glancing across the temple to Terentia, carefully studying her husband as he stroked the baby's cheek with the back of his little finger, I could see that the same thought was in her mind.

The arrival of a child often prompts a keen reappraisal of the future, and I am sure this was what led Cicero, shortly after the birth of his nephew, to arrange for Tullia to become betrothed. She was now ten years old, his cynosure as ever, and rare was the day, despite his legal and political work, when he did not clear a little space to read to her or play some game. And it was typical of his mingling of tenderness and cunning that he first raised his plan with her, rather than with Terentia. 'How would you like,' he said to her one morning, when the three of us were in his study, 'to get married one day?' When she replied that she would like that very much, he asked her whom in all the world she would most like to have as a husband.

'Tiro!' she cried, flinging her arms around my waist.

'I am afraid he is much too busy helping me to have time to take a wife,' he replied solemnly. 'Who else?'

Her circle of grown-up male acquaintances was limited, so it was not long before she raised the name of Frugi, who had spent so much time with Cicero since the Verres case, he was almost a part of the family.

'Frugi!' exclaimed Cicero, as if the idea had never before occurred to him. 'What a wonderful thought! And you are sure this is what you want? You are? Then let us go and tell your mama immediately.'

In this way Terentia found herself outmanoeuvred by her husband on her own territory as skilfully as if she had been some cretinous aristocrat in the senate. Not that she could have found much to object to in Frugi, who was a good enough match even for her – a gentle, diligent young man, now aged twenty-one, from an extremely distinguished family. But she was far too shrewd not to see that Cicero, by creating a substitute whom he could train and bring on to a public career, was doing the next best thing to having a son of his own. This realisation no doubt made her feel threatened, and Terentia always reacted violently to threats. The betrothal ceremony in November went smoothly enough, with Frugi – who was very fond of his fiancée, by the way – shyly placing a ring on her finger, under the approving gaze of both families and their households, with the wedding fixed for five years hence, when Tullia would be pubescent. But that night Cicero and Terentia had one of their most ferocious fights. It blew up in the tablinum before I had time to get out of the way. Cicero had made some innocuous remark about the Frugis being very welcoming to Tullia, to which Terentia, who had been ominously quiet for some time, responded that it was indeed very good of them, *considering*.

'Considering what?' asked Cicero wearily. He had obviously decided that arguing with her that night was as inevitable as vomiting after a bad oyster, and that he might as well get it out of the way at once.

'Considering the connection they are making,' she responded, and very quickly she was launched on her favourite line of attack – the shamefulness of Cicero's lackeying towards Pompey and his coterie of provincials, the way that this had set the family in opposition to all who were most honourable in the state, and the rise of mob rule which had been made possible by the illegal passage of the *lex Gabinia*. I cannot remember all of it, and in any case what does it matter? Like most arguments between husband and wife it was not about the thing itself, but a different matter entirely – that is, her failure to produce a son, and Cicero's consequent semi-paternal attachment to Frugi. Nevertheless, I do remember Cicero snapping back that, whatever Pompey's faults, no one disputed that he was a brilliant soldier, and that once he had been awarded his special command and had raised his troops and put to sea, he had wiped out the pirate threat in only forty-nine days. And I also recall her crushing retort, that if the pirates really had been swept from the sea in seven weeks, perhaps they had not been quite the menace that Cicero and his friends had made them out to be in the first place! At that point, I managed to slip out of the room and retreat to my little cubicle, so the rest was lost to me. But the mood in the house during the following days was as fragile as Neapolitan glass.

'You see how hard pressed I am?' Cicero complained to me the next morning, rubbing his forehead with his knuckles. 'There is no respite for me anywhere, either in my business or my leisure.'

As for Terentia, she became increasingly preoccupied with her supposed barrenness, and took to praying daily at the Temple of the Good Goddess on the Aventine Hill, where harmless snakes roamed freely in the precincts to encourage fertility and no man was allowed to set eyes upon the inner sanctum. I also heard from her maid that she had set up a small shrine to Juno in her bedroom.

Secretly, I believe Cicero shared Terentia's opinion of Pompey. There was something suspicious as well as glorious about the speed of his victory ('Organised at the end of winter,' as Cicero put it, 'started at the beginning of spring, and finished by the middle of the summer'), which made one wonder whether the whole enterprise could not have been handled perfectly well by a commander appointed in the normal way. Still, there was no denying his success. The pirates had been rolled up like a carpet, driven from the waters of Sicily and Africa eastwards, through the Illyrian Sea to Achaia, and then purged from the whole of Greece. Finally, they had been trapped by Pompey himself in their last great stronghold, Coracesium, in Cilicia, and in a huge battle on sea and land, ten thousand had been killed and four hundred vessels destroyed. Another twenty thousand had been captured. But rather than have them crucified, as no doubt Crassus would have done, Pompey had ordered the pirates to be resettled inland with their wives and families, in the depopulated towns of Greece and Asia Minor – one of which he renamed, with characteristic modesty, Pompeiopolis. All this he did without reference to the senate.

Cicero followed his patron's fantastic progress with mixed feelings ('Pompeiopolis! Dear gods, the *vulgarity* of it!'), not least because he knew that the more swollen with success Pompey became, the longer the shadow he would cast over his own career. Meticulous planning and overwhelming numerical superiority: these were Pompey's favourite tactics, both on the battlefield and in Rome, and as soon as phase one of his campaign – the destruction of the pirates – was completed, phase two began in the forum, when Gabinius started agitating to have the command of the Eastern legions stripped from Lucullus and awarded to Pompey. He used the same trick as before, employing his powers as tribune to summon witnesses to the rostra, who gave the people a sorry picture of the war against Mithradates. Some of the legions, unpaid for years, had simply refused to leave their winter camp. The poverty of these ordinary fighting men Gabinius contrasted with the immense wealth of their aristocratic commander, who had shipped back so much booty from the campaign that he had bought an entire hill just outside the gates of Rome and was building a great palace there, with all the state rooms named after the gods. Gabinius subpoenaed Lucullus's architects and had them brought to the rostra, where he forced them to show to the people all their plans and models. Lucullus's name from that time on became a synonym for outrageous luxury, and the angry citizens burned his effigy in the forum.

In December, Gabinius and Cornelius stood down as tribunes, and a new creature of Pompey's, the tribune-elect, Caius Manilius, took over the safeguarding of his interests in the popular assemblies. He immediately proposed a law granting command of the war against Mithradates to Pompey, along with the government of the provinces of Asia, Cilicia and Bithynia – the latter two held by Lucullus. Any thin hopes that Cicero might have entertained of lying low on the issue were destroyed when Gabinius came to see him bearing a message from Pompey. This briskly conveyed the general's good wishes, along with his hopes that Cicero would support the *lex Manilia* 'in all its provisions', not only behind the scenes but also in public, from the rostra.

'"In all its provisions",' repeated Gabinius, with a smirk. 'You know what that means.'

'I presume it means the clause which appoints you to the command of the legions on the Euphrates, thus giving you legal immunity from prosecution now that your term as tribune has expired.'

'You have it.' Gabinius grinned and did a passable impersonation of Pompey, drawing himself up and puffing out his cheeks: '"Is he not clever, gentlemen? Did I not tell you he was clever?"'

'Calm youself, Gabinius,' said Cicero wearily. 'I assure you there is no one I would rather see heading off to the Euphrates than you.'

It is dangerous in politics to find oneself a great man's whipping boy. Yet this was the role in which Cicero was now becoming trapped. Men who would never have dared directly to insult or criticise Pompey could instead land blows on his lawyer-surrogate with impunity, knowing that everyone would guess their real target. But there was no escaping a direct order from the commander-in-chief, and so this became the occasion of Cicero's first speech from the rostra. He took immense trouble over it, dictating it to me several days beforehand, and then showing it to Quintus and Frugi for their comments. From Terentia he prudently withheld it, for he knew he would have to send a copy to Pompey and it was therefore necessary for him to ladle on the flattery. (I see from the manuscript, for example, that Pompey's 'superhuman genius as a commander' was amended at Quintus's suggestion to 'Pompey's superhuman *and unbelievable* genius as a commander'.) He hit upon a brilliant slogan to sum up Pompey's success – 'one law, one man, one year' – and fretted over the rest of the speech for hours, conscious that if he failed on the rostra, his career would be set back and his enemies would say he did not have the common touch to move the plebs of Rome. When the morning came to deliver it, he was physically sick with nerves, retching again and again into the latrine while I stood next to him with a towel. He was so white and drawn that I actually wondered if he would have the legs to get all the way down to the forum. But it was his belief that a great performer, however experienced, must always be frightened before going on stage – 'the nerves should be as taut as bowstrings if the arrows are to fly' – and by the time we reached the back of the rostra he was ready. Needless to say, he was carrying no notes. We heard Manilius announce his name and the applause begin. It was a beautiful morning, clear and bright; the crowd was huge. He adjusted his sleeves, drew himself erect, and slowly ascended into the noise and light.

Catulus and Hortensius once again were the leaders of the opposition to Pompey, but they had devised no new arguments since the *lex Gabinia*, and Cicero had some sport with them. 'What is Hortensius saying?' he teased. 'That if one man is to be put in supreme command, the right man is Pompey, but that supreme command ought not to be given to one man? That line of reasoning is now out of date, refuted not so much by words as by events. For it was you, Hortensius, who denounced that courageous man Gabinius for introducing a law to appoint a single commander against the pirates. Now I ask you in Heaven's name – if on that occasion the Roman people had thought more of your opinion than of their own welfare and their true interests, should we today be in possession of our present glory and our worldwide empire?' By the same token, if Pompey wanted Gabinius as one of his legionary commanders, he should have him, for no man had done more, apart from Pompey, to defeat the pirates. 'Speaking for myself,' he concluded, 'whatever devotion, wisdom, energy or talent I possess, whatever I can achieve by virtue of the praetorship which you have conferred upon me, I dedicate to the support of this law. And I call on all the gods to witness – most especially the guardians of this hallowed spot who see clearly into the hearts of all who enter upon public life – that I am acting not as a favour to Pompey, nor in the hope of gaining favour from him, but solely in the cause of my country.' He left the rostra to respectful applause. The law was passed, Lucullus was stripped of his command and Gabinius was given his legateship. As for Cicero, he had surmounted another obstacle in his progress to the consulship, but was more hated than ever by the aristocrats.

Later, he had a letter from Varro, describing Pompey's reaction at the moment when he received the news that he now had complete control of Rome's forces in the East. As his officers crowded round him at his headquarters in Ephesus to congratulate him, he frowned, struck himself on the thigh, and said ('in a weary voice', according to Varro): 'How sad it makes me, this constant succession of labours! Really I would rather be one of those people whom no one has heard about, if I am never to have any relief from military service, and never to be able to escape from being envied so that I can live quietly in the country with my wife.' Such play-acting was hard to stomach, especially when the whole world knew how much he had desired the command.

*

The praetorship brought an elevation in Cicero's station. Now he had six lictors to guard him whenever he left the house. He did not care for them at all. They were rough fellows, hired for their strength and easy cruelty: if a Roman citizen was sentenced to be punished, they were the ones who carried it out, and they were adept at floggings and beheadings. Because their posts were permanent, some had been used to power for years, and they rather looked down on the magistrates they guarded as mere transitory politicians, here today and gone tomorrow. Cicero hated it when they cleared the crowds out of his way too roughly, or ordered passers-by to remove their headgear or dismount in the presence of a praetor, for the people being so humiliated were his voters. He instructed the lictors to show more politeness, and for a time they would, but they soon snapped back into their old ways. The chief of them, the *proximus lictor*, who was supposed to stand at Cicero's side at all times, was particularly obnoxious. I forget his name now, but he was always bringing Cicero tittle-tattle of what the other praetors were up to, gleaned from his fellow lictors, not realising that this made him deeply suspect in the eyes of Cicero, who was well aware that gossip is a trade, and that reports of his own actions would be being offered as currency in return. 'These people,' Cicero complained to me one morning, 'are a warning of what happens to any state which has a permanent staff of officials. They begin as our servants and end up imagining themselves our masters!'

My own status rose with his. I discovered that to be known as the confidential secretary of a praetor, even if one was a slave, was to enjoy an unaccustomed civility from those one met. Cicero told me beforehand that I could expect to be offered money to use my influence on behalf of petitioners, and when I insisted hotly that I would never accept a bribe, he cut me off. 'No, Tiro, you should have some money of your own. Why not? I ask only that you tell me who has paid you, and that you make it clear to whoever approaches you that my judgements are not to be bought, and that I will decide things on their merits. Aside from that, I trust you to use your own discretion.' This conversation meant a great deal to me. I had always hoped that eventually Cicero would grant me my freedom; permitting me to have some savings of my own I saw as a preparation for that day. The amounts which came in were small – fifty or a hundred here and there – and in return I might be required to bring a document to the praetor's attention, or draft a letter of introduction for him to sign.

The money I kept in a small purse, hidden behind a loose brick in the wall of my cubicle.

As praetor, Cicero was expected to take in promising pupils from good families to study law with him, and in May, after the senate recess, a new young intern of sixteen joined his chambers. This was Marcus Caelius Rufus from Interamnia, the son of a wealthy banker and prominent election official of the Velina tribe. Cicero agreed, largely as a political favour, to supervise the boy's training for two years, at the end of which it was fixed that he would move on to complete his apprenticeship in another household – that of Crassus, as it happened, for Crassus was a business associate of Rufus's father, and the banker was anxious that his heir should learn how to manage a fortune. The father was a ghastly money-lending type, short and furtive, who seemed to regard his son as an investment which was failing to show an adequate yield. 'He needs to be beaten regularly,' he announced, just before he brought him in to meet Cicero. 'He is clever enough, but wayward and dissolute. You have my permission to whip him as much as you like.' Cicero looked askance at this, having never whipped anyone in his life, but fortunately as it turned out he got on very well with young Rufus, who was as dissimilar to his father as it was possible to imagine. He was tall and handsome and quick-witted, with an indifference towards money and business which Cicero found amusing; I less so, for it generally fell to me to do all the humdrum tasks which were Rufus's responsibility, and which he shirked. But still, I must concede, looking back, that he had charm.

I shall not dwell on the details of Cicero's praetorship. This is not a textbook about the law, and I can sense your eagerness for me to get on to the climax of my story – the election for the consulship itself. Suffice it to say that Cicero was considered a fair and honest judge, and that the work was easily within his competence. If he encountered a particularly awkward point of jurisprudence, and needed a second opinion, he would either consult his old friend and fellow pupil of Molon, Servius Sulpicius, or go over to see the distinguished praetor of the election court, Aquilius Gallus, in his mansion on the Viminal Hill. The biggest case over which he had to preside was that of Caius Licinius Macer, a kinsman and supporter of Crassus, who was impeached for his actions as governor of Macedonia. The hearing dragged on for weeks, and at the end of it Cicero summed up very fairly, except that he could not resist one joke. The nub of the prosecution case was that Macer had taken half a million in illegal payments. Macer at first denied it. The prosecution then produced proof that the exact same sum had been paid into a money-lending company which he controlled. Macer abruptly changed his story and claimed that, yes, he remembered the payments, but thought that they were legal. 'Now, it may be,' said Cicero to the jury, as he was directing them on points of evidence, 'that the defendant believed this.' He left a pause just long enough for some of them to start laughing, whereupon he put on a mock-stern face. 'No, no, he may have believed it. In which case' – another pause – 'you may reasonably conclude perhaps that he was too *stupid* to be a Roman governor.' I had sat in sufficient courts by then to know from the gale of laughter that Cicero had just convicted the man as surely as if he had been the prosecuting counsel. But Macer – who was not stupid at all, but on the contrary, very clever: so clever that he thought everyone else a fool – did not see the danger, and actually left the tribunal while the jury was balloting in order to go home and change and have a haircut, in anticipation of his victory celebration that night. While he was absent, the jury convicted him, and he was just leaving his house to return to the court when Crassus intercepted him on his doorstep and told him what had happened. Some say he dropped dead on the spot from shock, others that he went straight back indoors and killed himself to spare his son the humiliation of his exile. Either way, he died, and Crassus – as if he needed one – had a whole new reason for hating Cicero.

The Games of Apollo on the sixth day of July traditionally marked the start of the election season, although in truth it always seemed to be election season in those days. No sooner had one campaign come to an end than the candidates began anticipating the start of the next. Cicero joked that the business of governing the state was merely something to occupy the time between polling days. And perhaps this is one of the things that killed the republic: it gorged itself to death on votes. At any rate, the responsibility for honouring Apollo with a programme of public entertainment always fell to the urban praetor, which in this particular year was Antonius Hybrida.

Nobody had been expecting much, or indeed anything at all, for Hybrida was known to have drunk and gambled away all his money. So it was a vast surprise when he staged not only a series of wonderful theatrical productions, but also lavish spectacles in the Circus Maximus, with a full programme of twelve chariot races, athletic competitions and a wild-beast hunt involving panthers and all manner of exotic animals. I did not attend, but Cicero gave me a full account when he came home that evening. Indeed, he could talk of nothing else. He flung himself down on one of the couches in the empty dining room – Terentia was in the country with Tullia – and described the parade into the Circus: the charioteers and the near-naked athletes (the boxers, the wrestlers, the runners, the javelin throwers and the discus men), the flute players and the lyre players, the dancers dressed as Bacchanalians and satyrs, the incense burners, the bulls and the goats and the heifers with their gilded horns plodding to sacrifice, the cages of wild beasts and the gladiators … He seemed dizzy with it. 'How much must it have all cost? That is what I kept asking myself. Hybrida must be banking on making it all back when he goes out to his province. You should have heard the cheers they gave to him when he entered and when he left! Well, I see nothing for it, Tiro. Unbelievable as it seems, we shall have to amend the list. Come.'

We went together into the study and I opened the strongbox and pulled out all the papers relating to Cicero's consular campaign. There were many secret lists in there – lists of backers, of donors, of supporters he had yet to win over, of towns and regions where he was strong and where he was weak. The key list, however, was of the men he had identified as possible rivals, together with a summary of all the information known about them, pro and anti. Galba was at the top of it, with Gallus next to him, and then Cornificius, and finally Palicanus. Now Cicero took my pen and carefully, in his neat and tiny writing, added a fifth, whose name he had never expected to see there: Antonius Hybrida.

And then, a few days later, something happened which was to change Cicero's fortunes and the future of the state entirely, although he did not realise it at the time. I am reminded of one of those harmless-looking specks which one occasionally hears about, that a man discovers on his skin one morning, and thinks little of, only to see it gradually swell over the following months into an enormous tumour. The speck in this instance was a message, received out of the blue, summoning Cicero to see the pontifex maximus, Metellus Pius. Cicero was mightily intrigued by this, since Pius, who was very old (sixty-four, at least) and grand, had never previously deigned even to speak to him, let alone demand his company. Accordingly, we set off at once, with the lictors clearing our way.

In those days, the official residence of the head of the state religion was on the Via Sacra, next to the House of the Vestal Virgins, and I remember that Cicero was pleased to be seen entering the premises, for this really was the sacred heart of Rome, and not many men ever got the chance to cross the threshold. We were shown to a staircase and conducted along a gallery which looked down into the garden of the vestals' residence. I secretly hoped to catch a glimpse of one of those six mysterious white-clad maidens, but the garden was deserted, and it was not possible to linger as the bow-legged figure of Pius was already waiting for us impatiently at the end of the gallery, tapping his foot, with a couple of priests on either side of him. He had been a soldier all his life and had the cracked and roughened look of something made of leather which has been left outside for years and only lately brought indoors. There was no handshake for Cicero, no invitation to be seated, no preliminaries of any sort. Pius merely said immediately, in his hoarse voice, 'Praetor, I need to talk to you about Sergius Catilina.'

At the mere mention of the name, Cicero stiffened, for Catilina was the man who had tortured to death his distant cousin, the populist politician Gratidianus, by breaking his limbs and gouging out his eyes and tongue. A jagged streak of violent madness ran through Catilina, like lightning across his brain. At one moment he could be charming, cultured, friendly; then a man would make some seemingly innocuous remark, or he would catch another looking at him in a way he thought disrespectful, and he would lose all self-restraint. During the proscriptions of Sulla, when death lists were posted in the forum, Catilina had been one of the most proficient killers with the hammer and knife – *percussores*, as they were known – and had made a lot of money out of the estates of those he executed. His own brother-in-law was among the men he had murdered. Yet he had an undeniable charisma, and for each person he repulsed by his savagery, he attracted two or three more by his equally reckless displays of generosity. He was also sexually licentious. Seven years previously, he had been prosecuted for having sexual relations with a vestal virgin – none other, in fact, than Terentia's half-sister, Fabia. This was a capital offence, not only for him but for her, and if he had been found guilty she would have suffered the traditional punishment for a vestal virgin who broke her sacred vows of chastity – burial alive in the tiny chamber reserved for the purpose beside the Colline Gate. But the aristocrats, led by Catulus, had rallied around Catilina and secured his acquittal, and his political career had continued uninterrupted. He had been praetor the year before last, and had then gone out to govern Africa, thus missing the turmoil surrounding the *lex Gabinia*. He had only just returned.

'My family,' continued Pius, 'have been the chief patrons of Africa since my father governed the province half a century ago. The people there look to me for protection, and I have to tell you, Praetor, I have never seen them more incensed by any man than they have been by Sergius Catilina. He has plundered that province from end to end – taxed them and murdered them, stolen their temple treasures and raped their wives and daughters. The Sergii!' he exclaimed in disgust, retching up a great gob of yellow phlegm into his mouth and spitting it on to the floor. 'Descended from the Trojans, or so they boast, and not a decent one among them for two hundred years! And now they tell me you are the praetor responsible for bringing his type to book.' He looked Cicero up and down. 'Amazing! I cannot say that I know who the hell you are, but there it is. So what are you going to do about it?'

Cicero was always cool when someone tried to insult him. He merely said, 'Do the Africans have a case prepared?'

'They do. They already have a delegation in Rome seeking a suitable prosecutor. Who should they go to?'

'That is hardly a matter for me. I must remain the impartial president of the court.'

'Blah blah. Spare me the lawyer's talk. Privately. Man-to-man.' Pius beckoned Cicero to come closer. He had left most of his teeth behind on various battlefields and his breath whistled when he tried to whisper. 'You know the courts these days better than I. Who could do it?'

'Frankly, it will not be easy,' said Cicero. 'Catilina's reputation for violence precedes him. It will take a brave man to lay a charge against such a brazen killer. And presumably he will be standing for the consulship next year. There is a powerful enemy in the making.'

'Consul?' Pius suddenly struck himself very hard on the chest. The thump made his priestly attendants jump. 'Sergius Catilina will not be consul – not next year or any year – not as long as this old body has any life left in it! There must be someone in this city who is man enough to bring him to justice. And if not – well, I am not quite such a senile fool that I have forgotten how to fight in Rome. You just make sure, Praetor,' he concluded, 'that you leave enough time in your calendar to hear the case,' and he shuffled off down the corridor, grumbling to himself, pursued by his holy assistants.

As he watched him go, Cicero frowned and shook his head. Not comprehending politics nearly as well as I should have done, even after thirteen years in his service, I was at a loss to understand why he should have found this conversation so troubling. But he certainly was shaken, and as soon as we were back on the Via Sacra, he drew me out of the keen hearing of the *proximus lictor* and said, 'This is a serious development, Tiro. I should have seen this coming.' When I asked why it mattered to him whether Catilina was prosecuted or not, he replied, in a withering tone, 'Because, *bird-brain*, it is illegal to stand for election if you have charges pending against you. Which means that if the Africans do find a champion, and if a charge is laid against Catilina, and if it drags on into next summer, he will be barred from standing for the consulship until the case is resolved. Which means that if by any chance he is acquitted, *I* shall have to fight him in *my* year.'

I doubt whether there was another senator in Rome who would have tried to peer so far into the future – who would have piled up so many *ifs* and discerned a reason for alarm. Certainly, when he explained his anxiety to Quintus, his brother dismissed it with a laugh: 'And *if* you were struck by lightning, Marcus, and *if* Metellus Pius were able to remember what day of the week it was …' But Cicero continued to fret, and he made discreet enquiries about the progress of the African delegation as they searched for a credible advocate. However, as he suspected, they were finding it hard going, despite the immense amount of evidence they had collected of Catilina's wrongdoing, and the fact that Pius had carried a resolution in the senate censuring the former governor. No one was anxious to take on such a dangerous opponent, and risk being discovered floating face-down in the Tiber late one night. So, for the time being at least, the prosecution languished, and Cicero put the matter to the back of his mind. Unfortunately, it was not to remain there for long.

XIV

At the end of his term as praetor, Cicero was entitled to go abroad and govern a province for a year. This was the normal practice in the republic. It gave a man the opportunity to gain administrative experience, and also to replenish his coffers after the expense of running for office. Then he would come home, assess the political mood, and if all seemed promising, stand for the consulship that summer: Antonius Hybrida, for example, who had obviously incurred tremendous liabilities by the cost of his Games of Apollo, went off to Cappadocia to see what he could steal. But Cicero did not take this course, and waived his right to a province. For one thing, he did not want to put himself in a position where a trumped-up charge might be laid against him and he would find himself with a special prosecutor dogging his footsteps for months. For another, he was still haunted by that year he had spent as a magistrate in Sicily, and ever afterwards he had hated to be away from Rome for longer than a week or two. There can seldom have been a more urban creature than Cicero. It was from the bustle of the streets and the courts, the senate and the forum that he drew his energy, and the prospect of a year of dreary provincial company, however lucrative, in Cilicia or Macedonia, was anathema to him.

Besides, he had committed himself to an immense amount of advocacy, starting with the defence of Caius Cornelius, Pompey's former tribune, who had been charged with treason by the aristocrats. No fewer than five of the great patrician senators – Hortensius, Catulus, Lepidus, Marcus Lucullus and even old Metellus Pius – lined up to prosecute Cornelius for his part in advancing Pompey's legislation, charging him with illegally ignoring the veto of a fellow tribune. Faced with such an onslaught, I was sure that he was bound to be sent into exile. Cornelius thought so too, and had actually packed up his house and was ready to leave. But Cicero was always inspired by the sight of Hortensius and Catulus on the other side, and he rose to the occasion, making a most effective closing speech for the defence. 'Are we really to be lectured,' he demanded, 'on the traditional rights of the tribunes by five gentlemen, all of whom supported the legislation of Sulla abolishing exactly those rights? Did any of these illustrious figures step forward to support the gallant Gnaeus Pompey when, as the first act of his consulship, he restored the tribunes' power of veto? Ask yourself, finally, this: is it really a new-found concern for the traditions of the tribunes which drags them from their fish-ponds and private porticoes into court? Or is it, rather, the product of certain other "traditions" much dearer to their hearts – their tradition of self-interest and their traditional desire for revenge?'

There was more in a similar vein, and by the time he had finished, the five distinguished litigants (who had made the mistake of all sitting in a row) were looking half their previous size, especially Pius, who obviously found it hard to keep up, and who had his hand cupped to his ear and kept twisting in his seat as his tormentor prowled around the court. This was to be one of the old soldier's last appearances in public before the long twilight of his illness descended upon him. After the jury had voted to acquit Cornelius of all the charges, Pius left the court to jeers and mocking laughter, wearing an expression of elderly bafflement which I fear nowadays I recognise all too well as the natural set of my own features. 'Well,' said Cicero, with a certain satisfaction, as we prepared to walk home, 'at any rate, I believe that now he knows who I am.'

I shall not mention every case which Cicero took on at this time because there were dozens, all part of his strategy to place as many influential men as possible under an obligation to support him at the consular election, and to keep his name constantly in the voters' minds. He certainly chose his clients carefully, and four of them at least were senators: Fundanius, who controlled a big voting syndicate; Orchivius, who had been one of his colleagues as praetor; Gallius, who was planning to run for a praetorship; and Mucius Orestinus, charged with robbery, who was hoping to become tribune, and whose case tied up the practice for many days.

I believe that never before had any candidate approached the business of politics as exactly that – a business – and every week a meeting was convened in Cicero's study to review the campaign's progress. Participants came and went, but the inner core consisted of five: Cicero himself, Quintus, Frugi, myself, and Cicero's legal apprentice, Rufus, who, although still very young (or perhaps because of it), was adept at picking up gossip around the city. Quintus was once again the campaign manager, and insisted on presiding. He liked to suggest, by the occasional indulgent smile or raised eyebrow, that Cicero, genius though he was, could be something of an airy-fairy intellectual, and needed the blunt common sense of his brother to keep his feet on the earth; and Cicero, with a reasonably good grace, played along.

It would make an interesting study, if only I had the life left in me to write it: the story of brothers in politics. There were the Gracchi, of course, Tiberius and Caius, who devoted themselves to distributing wealth from the rich to the poor, and who both perished violently as a result. And then in my own time there were Marcus and Lucius Lucullus, patrician consuls in successive years, as well as any number of siblings from the Metellus and Marcellus clans. In a sphere of human activity in which friendships are transitory and alliances made to be broken, the knowledge that another man's name is forever linked to yours, however the fates may play, must be a powerful source of strength. The relationship between the Ciceros, like that between most brothers, I expect, was a complicated mixture of fondness and resentment, jealousy and loyalty. Without Cicero, Quintus would have been a dull and competent officer in the army, and then a dull and competent farmer in Arpinum, whereas Cicero without Quintus would still have been Cicero. Knowing this, and knowing that his brother knew it too, Cicero went out of his way to conciliate him, generously wrapping him in the glittering mantle of his fame.

Quintus spent a long time that winter compiling an election handbook, a distillation of his fraternal advice to Cicero, which he liked to quote from whenever possible, as if it were Plato's *Republic*. *Consider what city this is,* it began, *what it is you seek, and who you are. Every day, when you go down to the forum, repeat to yourself: 'I am a new man. I seek the consulship. This is Rome.'* I can still recall some of the other little homilies it preached. *All things are full of deceit, snares and treachery. Hold fast to the saying of Epicharmus, that the bone and sinew of wisdom is 'Never trust rashly' ... See to it that you show off both the variety and number of your friends ... I am very anxious that you should always have a crowd about you ... If someone asks you to do something, do not decline, even if you cannot do it ... Lastly, see that your canvass is a fine show, brilliant, resplendent and popular; and also, if it can be managed, that there should be scandalous talk about the crimes, lusts and briberies of your competitors.*

Quintus was very proud of his handbook, and many years later he actually had it published, much to the horror of Cicero, who believed that political mastery, like great art, depends for its effects on the concealment of all the cunning which lies behind it.

In the spring Terentia celebrated her thirtieth birthday and Cicero arranged a small dinner party in her honour. Quintus and Pomponia came, and Frugi and his parents, and fussy Servius Sulpicius and his unexpectedly pretty wife, Postumia; there must have been others, but the flow of time has washed them from my memory. The household was assembled briefly by Eros the steward to convey our good wishes, and I remember thinking, when Terentia appeared, that I had never seen her looking quite so fine, or in a more cheerful mood. Her short dark curly hair was lustrous, her eyes bright, and her normally bony frame seemed fuller and softer. I said as much to her maid after the master and mistress had led their guests in to dinner, at which she glanced around to check that no one was observing us, linked her hands and made a circular gesture outwards over her stomach. At first I did not understand, which gave her a fit of the giggles, and it was only after she had run back upstairs, still laughing, that I realised what a fool I had been; and not just me, of course. A normal husband would surely have noticed the symptoms sooner, but Cicero was invariably up at dawn and back at dusk, and even then there was always a speech to write or a letter to be sent – the miracle was that he should have found time to perform his conjugal duties at all. Anyway, midway through the dinner, a loud shout of excitement, followed by applause, confirmed that Terentia had taken the opportunity of the celebration to announce her pregnancy.

Later that evening, Cicero came into the study with a wide smile. He acknowledged my congratulations with a bow. 'She is certain it is a boy. Apparently, the Good Goddess has informed her of the fact, by means of certain supernatural signs understood only by women.' He rubbed his hands vigorously in anticipation; he really could not stop smiling. 'Always a wonderful addition at election time, Tiro, a baby – suggestive of a virile candidate, and a respectable family man. Talk to Quintus about scheduling the infant's campaign appearances.' He pointed to my notebook. 'I am joking, you idiot!' he said, seeing my dumbstruck expression, and pretended to cuff my ear. But I am undecided whom it says more about, him or me, that I am still not entirely convinced he *was* joking.

From this time on, Terentia became much stricter in her observance of religious rituals, and on the day following her birthday she made Cicero accompany her to the Temple of Juno on Capitol Hill, where she bought a small lamb for the priest to sacrifice, in gratitude for her pregnancy and marriage. Cicero was delighted to oblige her, for he was genuinely overjoyed at the prospect of another child, and besides, he knew how much the voters lapped up these public displays of piety.

And now I fear I must return to the growing tumour that was Sergius Catilina.

A few weeks after Cicero's summons to see Metellus Pius, that year's consular elections were held. But such was the flagrant use of bribery by the winning ticket, the result was swiftly annulled and in October the poll was held again. On this occasion Catilina submitted his name as a candidate. Pius swiftly put a stop to his chances – I suppose it must have been the last successful battle the old warrior fought – and the senate ruled that only those whose names were on the original ballot would be permitted to stand. This drove Catilina into one of his furies, and he began hanging around the forum with his violent friends, making all kinds of threats, which were taken sufficiently seriously by the senate that they voted an armed bodyguard to the consuls. Not surprisingly, no one had been brave enough to come forward and take up the Africans' case in the extortion court. I actually suggested it to Cicero one day, wondering if it might be a popular cause for him to espouse – after all, he had brought down Verres, and that had made him the most famous advocate in the world. But Cicero shook his head. 'Compared to Catilina, Verres was a kitten. Besides, Verres was not a man anyone much liked, whereas Catilina undeniably has a following.'

'Why is he so popular?' I asked.

'Dangerous men always attract a following, although that is not what concerns me. If it were simply a question of the mob in the street, he would be less of a threat. It is the fact that he has widespread aristocratic support – Catulus certainly, which probably also means Hortensius.'

'I should have thought him much too uncouth for Hortensius.'

'Oh, Hortensius knows how to make use of a street fighter when the occasion demands it. Many a cultured house is protected by a savage dog. And Catilina is also a Sergius, do not forget, so they approve of him on snobbish grounds. The masses and the aristocracy: that is a potent combination in politics. Let us hope he can be stopped in the consular elections this summer. I am only grateful that the task does not look like falling to me.'

I thought at the time that this was the sort of remark which proves there are gods, because whenever, in their celestial orbits, they hear such complacency, it amuses them to show their power. Sure enough, it was not long afterwards that Caelius Rufus brought Cicero some disturbing news. Rufus by this time was seventeen, and, as his father had stated, quite ungovernable. He was tall and well built and could easily have passed for a man in his early twenties, with his deep voice and the small goatee beard which he and his fashionable friends liked to sport. He would slip out of the house when it was dark and Cicero was preoccupied with his work and everyone else was asleep; often he would not return until just before dawn. He knew that I had a little money put by, and was always pestering me to advance him small loans; one evening, after I had refused yet again, I retired to my cubicle to discover that he had found my hiding place and taken everything I possessed. I spent a miserable, sleepless night, but when I confronted him the next morning and threatened to report him to Cicero, tears came into his eyes and he promised to pay me back. And, in fairness to him, he did, and with generous interest; so I changed my hiding place and never said a word about it.

He drank and whored around the city at night with a group of very disreputable young noblemen. One of them was Gaius Curio, a twenty-year-old whose father had been consul and a great supporter of Verres. Another was Mark Antony, the nephew of Hybrida, who I reckon must then have been eighteen. But the real leader of the gang, chiefly because he was the eldest and richest and could show the others ways of getting into mischief they had never even dreamed of, was Clodius Pulcher. He was in his middle twenties and had been away for eight years on military service in the East, getting into all sorts of scrapes, including leading a mutiny against Lucullus – who also happened to be his brother-in-law – and then being captured by the very pirates he was supposed to be fighting. But now he was back in Rome, and looking to make a name for himself, and one night he announced that he knew exactly how he was going to do it – it would be a lark, a dare, risky and amusing (these were his actual words, according to Rufus) – *he would prosecute Catilina.*

When Rufus rushed in to tell Cicero the following morning, the senator at first refused to believe him. All he knew of Clodius were the scandalous rumours, widely circulating, that he had slept with his own sister – indeed these rumours had lately taken on a more substantial form, and had been cited by Lucullus himself as one of the grounds on which he had divorced his wife. 'What would such a creature be doing in the law courts,' scoffed Cicero, 'except as a defendant?' But Rufus, in his cheeky way, retorted that if Cicero wanted proof of what he was saying, he need only pay a visit to the extortion court in the next hour or two, when Clodius was planning to submit his application to prosecute. Needless to say, this was a spectacle Cicero could not resist, and once he had seen his more important clients, he went down to his old haunt at the Temple of Castor, taking me and Rufus with him.

Already, in that mysterious way it does, news that something dramatic was about to happen had spread, and there was a crowd of a hundred or more hanging around the foot of the steps. The current praetor, a man named Orbius, afterwards governor of Asia, had just sat down in his curule chair and was looking around him, no doubt wondering what was up, when a group of six or seven smirking youths appeared, strolling from the direction of the Palatine, apparently without a care between them. They clearly fancied themselves the height of fashion, and I suppose they were, with their long hair and their little beards, and their thick, embroidered belts worn loosely around their waists. 'By heavens, what a spectacle!' muttered Cicero, as they pushed past us, trailing a fragrant wake of crocus oil and saffron unguents. 'They look more like women than men!' One of their number detached himself from the rest and climbed the steps to the praetor. Midway up, he paused, and turned to the crowd. He was, if I may express it vulgarly, 'a pretty boy', with long blond curls, thick, wet red lips and a bronzed skin – a kind of young Apollo. But his voice when he spoke was surprisingly firm and masculine, marred only by his slangy, mock-plebeian accent, which rendered his family name as 'Clodius' instead of 'Claudius': another of his fashionable affectations.

'I am Publius Clodius Pulcher, son of Appius Claudius Pulcher, consul, grandson of consuls in the direct line for the past eight generations, and I come this morning to lay charges in this court against Sergius Catilina for the crimes he lately committed in Africa.' At the mention of Catilina's name there was some muttering and whistling, and a big brute standing close to us shouted, 'You want to watch your backside, girlie!'

But Clodius did not seem in the least concerned. 'May my ancestors and the gods bless this undertaking, and bring it to a fruitful conclusion.' He trotted briskly up to Orbius and gave him the *postulatus*, all neatly bound up in a cylinder, with a seal and a red ribbon, while his supporters applauded noisily, Rufus among them, until Cicero silenced him with a look. 'Run and find my brother,' he said to him. 'Inform him of what has happened, and tell him we need to meet at once.'

'That is a job for a slave,' objected Rufus, with a pout, no doubt worried about losing face in front of his friends. 'Surely Tiro here could go and fetch him?'

'Do as you are ordered,' snapped Cicero, 'and while you are at it, find Frugi as well. And be grateful I have not yet told your father of the disreputable company you are keeping.' That made Rufus shift himself, and he disappeared out of the forum towards the Temple of Ceres, where the plebeian aediles were normally to be found at that hour of the morning. 'I have spoiled him,' Cicero said wearily, as we climbed the hill back to the house, 'and do you know why? It is because he has charm, that most cursed of all the gifts, and I never can stop myself indulging someone with charm.'

As punishment, and also because he no longer fully trusted him, Cicero refused to let Rufus attend the day's campaign meeting, but sent him off instead to write up a brief. He waited until he was out of the way before describing the morning's events to Quintus and Frugi. Quintus was inclined to take a sanguine view, but Cicero was absolutely convinced that he would now have to fight Catilina for the consulship. 'I have checked the calendar of the extortion court – you remember what that is like – and the truth is there is simply no chance of Catilina's case being heard until July, which makes it impossible for him to be a consular candidate in this year. Therefore he comes inevitably into mine.' He suddenly pounded his fist on the desk and swore – a thing he rarely did. 'I predicted exactly this outcome a year ago – Tiro is my witness.'

Quintus said, 'Perhaps Catilina will be found guilty and sent into exile?'

'With that perfumed creature as his prosecutor? A man whom every slave in Rome knows to have been the lover of his own sister? No, no – you were right, Tiro. I should have taken down Catilina myself, when I had the chance. He would have been easier to beat in court than he will be in the ballot.'

'Perhaps it is not too late,' I suggested. 'Perhaps Clodius could be persuaded to yield the prosecution to you.'

'No, he will never do that,' said Cicero. 'You had only to look at him – the arrogance of the fellow – a typical Claudian. This is his chance for glory, and he will not let it slip. You had better bring out our list of potential candidates, Tiro. We need to find ourselves a credible running-mate – and quickly.'

In those days consular candidates usually submitted themselves to the electorate in pairs, for each citizen cast two votes for consul and it was obviously good tactics to form an alliance with a man who would complement one's own strengths during the canvass. What Cicero needed to balance his ticket was someone with a distinguished name who had wide appeal among the aristocracy. In return, he could offer them his own popularity among the *pedarii* and the lower classes, and the support of the electoral machine which he had built up in Rome. He had always thought that this would be easy enough to arrange when the time came. But now, as we reviewed the names on the list, I saw why he was becoming so anxious. Palicanus would bring nothing to the ticket. Cornificius was an electoral no-hoper. Hybrida had only half a brain. That left Galba and Gallus. But Galba was so aristocratic, he would have nothing to do with Cicero, and Gallus – despite all Cicero's pleadings – had said firmly that he had no interest in becoming consul.

'Can you believe it?' complained Cicero, as we huddled around his desk, studying the list of likely runners. 'I offer the man the greatest job in the world, and he has to give me nothing in return except to stand at my side for a day or two. Yet he still says he would prefer to concentrate on jurisprudence!' He took up his pen and crossed out Gallus's name, then added Catilina's to the bottom of the list. He tapped his pen beside it idly, underlined it, circled it, then glanced at each of us. 'Of course, there is one other potential partner we have not mentioned.'

'And who is that?' asked Quintus.

'Catilina.'

'Marcus!'

'I am perfectly serious,' said Cicero. 'Let's think it through. Suppose, instead of attempting to prosecute him, I offer to defend him. If I secure his acquittal, he will be under an obligation to support me for consul. On the other hand, if he is found guilty, and goes into exile – then that is the end of him. Either outcome is acceptable as far as I am concerned.'

'You would defend *Catilina*?' Quintus was well used to his brother, and it took a great deal to shock him, but on that day he was almost speechless.

'I would defend the blackest devil in hell if he was in need of an advocate. That is our system of law.' Cicero frowned and shook his head irritably. 'But we went over all this with poor Lucius just before he died. Come on, brother – spare me the reproachful face! You wrote the book: "I am a new man. I seek the consulship. This is Rome." Those three things – they say it all. I am a new man, therefore there is no one to help me but myself, and you few friends. I seek the consulship, which is immortality – a prize worth fighting for, yes? And this is Rome – *Rome* – not some abstract place in a work of philosophy, but a city of glory built on a river of filth. So yes, I will defend Catilina, if that is what is necessary, and then I will break with him as soon as I can. And he would do the same to me. That is the world we live in.' Cicero sat back in his chair and raised his hands. 'Rome.'

Cicero did not make a move immediately, preferring to wait and see whether the prosecution of Catilina would definitely go ahead. There was a widespread view that Clodius was simply showing off, or perhaps trying to distract attention from the shame of his sister's divorce. But in the lumbering way of the law, as the summer came on, the process passed through all its various stages – the *postulatio*, *divinatio*, and *nominis delatio* – a jury was selected and a date was fixed for the start of the trial in the last week of July. There was no chance now that Catilina would be free of litigation in time for the consular elections; nominations had already closed.

At this point, Cicero decided to let Catilina know that he might be interested in acting as his advocate. He gave much thought as to how to convey the offer, for he did not wish to lose face by being rebuffed, and he also wanted to be able to deny ever making an approach in case he was challenged in the senate. In the end he hit upon a characteristically subtle scheme. He called Rufus to his study, swore him to secrecy, and announced that he had it in mind to defend Catilina: what did he think? ('But not a word to anyone, mind!') This was exactly the sort of gossip which Rufus most delighted in, and naturally he could not resist sharing the confidence with his friends, among them Mark Antony – who, as well as being the nephew of Hybrida, was also the adopted son of Catilina's close friend, Lentulus Sura.

I guess it must have taken all of a day and a half for a messenger to turn up on Cicero's doorstep, bearing a letter from Catilina asking him if he would care to visit, and proposing – in the interests of confidentiality – that the rendezvous be conducted after dusk. 'And so the fish bites,' said Cicero, showing me the letter, and he sent back with the slave a verbal reply that he would attend on Catilina in his house that same night.

Terentia was now very close to parturition, and was finding the heat of Rome in July insufferable. She lay, restless and groaning, on a couch in the stifling dining room, Tullia on one side reading to her in a piping voice, a maid with a fan on the other. Her temper, warm in the best of circumstances, was in these days permanently inflamed. As darkness fell and the candelabra were lit, she saw that Cicero was preparing to leave, and immediately demanded to know where he was going. When he gave a vague reply, she tearfully insisted that he must have taken a concubine and was visiting her, for why else would a respectable man go out of doors at this hour? And so, reluctantly, he told her the truth, that he was calling on Catilina. Of course this did not mollify her in the slightest, but only enraged her further. She demanded to know how he could bear to spend a moment in the company of the monster who had debauched her own sister, a vestal virgin, to which Cicero responded with some quip about Fabia having always been 'more vestal than virgin'. Terentia struggled to rise but failed and her furious invective pursued us all the way out of the house, much to Cicero's amusement.

It was a night very like the one on the eve of the elections for aedile, when he had gone to see Pompey. There was the same oppressive heat and feverish moonlight; the same slight breeze stirred the smell of putrefaction from the burial fields beyond the Esquiline Gate and spread it over the city like an invisible moist dust. We went down into the forum, where the slaves were lighting the street lamps, past the silent, darkened temples, and up on to the Palatine, where Catilina had his house. I was carrying a document case, as usual, and Cicero had his hands clasped behind his back and was walking with his head bowed in thought. Back then the Palatine was less built up than it is today, and the buildings were spaced further apart. I could hear the sound of a stream nearby and there was a scent of honeysuckle and dog rose. 'This is the place to live, Tiro,' said Cicero, halting on the steps. 'This is where we shall come when there are no more elections to be fought, and I need take less account of what the people think. A place with a garden to read in – imagine that – and where the children can play.' He glanced back in the direction of the Esquiline. 'It will be a relief to all concerned when this baby arrives. It is like waiting for a storm to break.'

Catilina's house was easy to find, for it was close by the Temple of Luna, which was painted white and lit up at night by torches, in honour of the moon goddess. A slave was waiting in the street to guide us, and he took us straight into the vestibule of the mansion of the Sergii, where a most beautiful woman greeted Cicero. This was Aurelia Orestilla, the wife of Catilina, whose daughter he was supposed to have seduced initially, before moving on to the mother, and for whose sake, it was rumoured, he had murdered his own son by his first marriage (the lad having threatened to kill Aurelia rather than accept such a notorious courtesan into the family). Cicero knew all about her, and cut off her effusive greeting with a curt nod. 'Madame,' he said, 'it is your husband I have come to see, not you,' at which she bit her lip and fell silent. It was one of the most ancient houses in Rome, and its timbers creaked as we followed the slave into the interior, which smelled of dusty old drapes and incense. One curious feature I remember was that it had been stripped almost bare, and obviously recently, for one could see the blurred rectangular outlines of where pictures had once hung, and circles of dust on the floor marked the absence of statues. All that remained in the atrium were the dingy wax effigies of Catilina's ancestors, jaundiced by generations of smoke. This was where Catilina himself was standing. The first surprise was how tall he was when one got close up – at least a head higher than Cicero – and the second was the presence behind him of Clodius. This must have been a terrific shock to Cicero, but he was far too cool a lawyer to show it. He shook hands quickly with Catilina, and then with Clodius, politely refused an offer of wine, and the three men turned straight to business.

Looking back, I am struck by how alike Catilina and Clodius were. This was the only time I ever saw them in a room together, and they might have been father and son, with their drawling voices, and the way they stood together so languidly, as if the world was theirs to own. I suppose this is what is called 'breeding'. It had taken four hundred years of intermarriage between the finest families in Rome to produce those two villains – as thoroughbred as Arab bloodstock, and just as quick and headstrong and dangerous.

'This is the deal as we see it,' said Catilina. 'Young Clodius here will make a brilliant speech for the prosecution and everyone will say he is the new Cicero and I am bound to be convicted. But then you, Cicero, will make an even more brilliant argument for the defence in reply, and therefore no one will be surprised when I am acquitted. At the end of it, we shall have put on a good show and we shall all emerge with our positions enhanced. I am declared innocent before the people of Rome. Clodius is acknowledged as the brave and coming man. And you will have won yet another splendid triumph in the courts, defending someone a cut above your usual run of clients.'

'And what if the jury decides differently?'

'You need not be concerned about them.' Catilina patted his pocket. 'I have taken care of the jury.'

'The law is *so* expensive,' said Clodius with a smile. 'Poor Catilina has had to sell his heirlooms to be sure of justice. It really is a scandal. How *do* people manage?'

'I shall need to see the trial documents,' said Cicero. 'How soon before the hearing opens?'

'Three days,' said Catilina, and he gestured to a slave who was standing at the door. 'Does that give you long enough to prepare?'

'If the jury has already been convinced, I can make the speech in six words: "Here is Catilina. Let him go."'

'Oh, but I want the full Ciceronian production!' protested Catilina. 'I want: "This n-n-noble m-m-man … the b-b-blood of centuries … behold the tears of his w-w-wife and f-f-friends …"' He had his hand in the air and was twirling it expressively, crudely imitating Cicero's almost imperceptible stutter. Clodius was laughing; they were both slightly drunk. 'I want "African s-s-savages s-s-sullying this ancient c-c-court ..." I want Carthage and Troy to be conjured before us, and Dido and Aeneas—'

'You will get,' said Cicero, coldly cutting him off, 'a professional job.' The slave had returned with the papers for the trial and I began rapidly piling them into my document case, for I could sense the atmosphere beginning to worsen as the drink took hold and I was anxious to get Cicero out of there. 'We shall need to meet to discuss your evidence,' he continued, in the same chilly tone. 'Tomorrow it had better be, if that is convenient to you.'

'By all means. I have nothing better to do. I had been expecting to stand for the consulship this summer, as you well know, until this young mischief-maker put a stop to it.'

It was the agility that was so shocking in a man of such height. He suddenly lunged forward and wrapped his powerful right arm around Clodius's neck and dragged the younger man's head down, so that Clodius was bent double. Poor Clodius – who was no weakling, incidentally – let out a muffled cry, and his fingers clawed feebly at Catilina's arm. But the strength of Catilina was appalling, and I wonder if he might not have broken his visitor's neck with a quick upward flick of his forearm, if Cicero had not said calmly, 'I must advise you, Catilina, as your defence attorney, that it would be a grievous mistake to murder your prosecutor.'

On hearing that, Catilina swung round and frowned at him, as if he had momentarily forgotten who Cicero was. Then he started laughing. He ruffled Clodius's blond curls and let him go. Clodius staggered backwards, coughing and massaging the side of his head and throat, and for an instant he gave Catilina a look of pure murder, but then he too started laughing, and straightened up. They embraced, Catilina called for some more wine, and we left them to it. 'What a pair,' exclaimed Cicero, as we passed by the Temple of Luna on our way back home. 'With any luck they will have killed one another by morning.'

By the time we had returned to Cicero's house, Terentia was in labour. There was no mistaking it.

We could hear the screams from the street. Cicero stood in the atrium, white with shock and alarm, for he had been away when Tullia was born, and nothing in his philosophy books had prepared him for what was happening. 'Dear heavens, it sounds as though she is being tortured. Terentia!' He started towards the staircase which led to her room, but one of the midwives intercepted him.

We passed a long vigil in the dining room. He asked me to stay with him, but was at first too anxious to do any work. Sometimes he lay stretched out on the same couch Terentia had been occupying when we left, and then, when he heard another scream, he would jump up and pace around. The air was hot and heavy, the candle flames motionless, their black threads of smoke as rigid as plumb-lines suspended from the ceiling. I busied myself by emptying my case of the court papers I had carried back from Catilina's house and sorting them into categories – charges, depositions, summaries of documentary evidence. Eventually, to distract himself, Cicero, still prone on the couch, stretched out a hand and started reading, picking up one roll after another and holding it to the lamp which I placed beside him. He kept flinching and wincing, but I could not tell whether it was the continuing howls from upstairs or the horrific allegations against Catilina, for these were indeed the most appalling accounts of violence and rape, dispatched by almost every town in Africa, from Utica to Thaenae, and from Thapsus to Thelepte. After an hour or two, he tossed them aside in disgust and asked me to fetch some paper so that he could dictate a few letters, beginning with one to Atticus. He lay back and closed his eyes in an effort to concentrate. I have the very document before me now.

It is a long time since I had a line from you. I have already written to you in detail about my election campaign. At the moment I am proposing to defend my fellow candidate Catilina. We have the jury we want, with full cooperation from the prosecution. If he is acquitted I hope he will be more inclined to work with me in the campaign. But should it go otherwise, I shall bear it philosophically.

'Ha! That is certainly true enough.' He closed his eyes again.

I need you home pretty soon. There is a decidedly strong belief going around that your noble friends are going to oppose my election.

And at that point my writing stops, because instead of a scream we heard a different sound from above us – the gurgling cry of a baby. Cicero sprang from the couch and ran upstairs to Terentia's room. It was some time before he reappeared, and when he did he silently took the letter from me and wrote across the top in his own hand:

I have the honour to inform you that I have become the father of a little son. Terentia is well.

How transformed a house is by the presence of a healthy newborn baby! I believe, although it is seldom acknowledged, that this must be because it is a double blessing. The unspoken dreads which attend all births – of agony, death and deformity – are banished, and in their place comes this miracle of a fresh life. Relief and joy are intertwined.

Naturally, I was not permitted upstairs to see Terentia, but a few hours later Cicero brought his son down and proudly showed him off to the household and his clients. To be frank, there was not much that was visible, apart from an angry little red face and a lick of fine dark hair. He was wrapped up tight in the woollen swaddling clothes which had performed the same service for Cicero more than forty years earlier. The senator also had a silver rattle preserved from his infancy which he tinkled above the tiny face. He carried him tenderly into the atrium and pointed to the spot where he dreamed that one day his consular image would hang. 'And then,' he whispered, 'you will be Marcus Tullius Cicero, son of Marcus Tullius Cicero the *consul* – how does that sound? Not bad, eh? There will be no taunts of "new man" for you! Here you are, Tiro – make the acquaintance of a whole new political dynasty.' He offered the bundle to me, and I held it nervously, in that way the childless do when handed a baby, and was relieved when the nurse took him from me.

Cicero meanwhile was once again contemplating the blank spot on his atrium wall, and had fallen into one of his reveries. I wonder what it was he was seeing there: his death mask, perhaps, staring back at him, like a face in the mirror? I enquired after the health of Terentia, and he said, distractedly, 'Oh, she is very well. Very strong. You know what she is like. Strong enough, at least, to resume belabouring me for making an alliance with Catilina.' He dragged his gaze away from the empty wall. 'And now,' he sighed, 'I suppose we had better keep our appointment with the villain.'

When we reached the house of Catilina, we found the former governor of Africa in a charming humour. Cicero later made a list of his 'paradoxical qualities' and I give it here, for it was nicely put: 'To attach many by friendship, and to retain them by devotion; to share what he possessed with all, and to be at the service of all his friends in time of need, with money, influence, effort, and – if necessary – with reckless crime; to control his natural temper as occasion required, and to bend and turn it this way and that; to be serious with the strict, easy with the liberal, grave with the old, amiable with the young, daring with criminals, dissolute with the depraved …' This was the Catilina who was waiting for us that day. He had already heard about the birth of Cicero's son, and pumped his advocate's hand in warm congratulation, and then produced a beautiful calfskin box, which he insisted Cicero open. Inside was a baby's silver amulet which Catilina had acquired in Utica. 'It is merely a local trinket to ward off ill health and evil spirits,' he explained. 'Please give it to your lad with my blessing.'

'Well,' replied Cicero, 'this is handsome of you, Catilina.' And it was indeed quite exquisitely engraved, certainly no mere trinket: when Cicero held it to the light I saw all manner of exotic wild animals chasing each another, linked by a motif of curling serpents. For one last moment he toyed with it, and weighed it in his palm, but then he replaced it in its box and handed it back to Catilina. 'I am afraid I cannot accept it.'

'Why?' asked Catilina, with a puzzled smile. 'Because you are my advocate, and advocates cannot be paid? Such integrity! But this is only a trifle for a baby!'

'Actually,' said Cicero, drawing in his breath, 'I have come to tell you I am not going to be your advocate.'

I was in the act of unpacking all the legal documents on to a small table which stood between the two men. I had been watching them in a sideways fashion but now I put my head down and carried on. After what seemed to me a long silence, I heard Catilina say, in a quiet voice, 'And why is that?'

'To speak frankly: because you are so obviously guilty.'

Another silence, and then Catilina's voice, when it came, was once again very calm. 'But Fonteius was guilty of extortion against the Gauls, and you represented him.'

'Yes. But there are degrees of guilt. Fonteius was corrupt but harmless. You are corrupt and something else entirely.'

'That is for the court to decide.'

'Normally I would agree. But you have purchased the verdict in advance, and that is not a charade I wish to be a part of. You have made it impossible for me to convince myself that I am acting honourably. And if I cannot convince myself, then I cannot convince anyone else – my wife, my brother; and now, perhaps more importantly, my son, when he is old enough to understand.'

At this point I risked a look at Catilina. He was standing completely motionless, his arms hanging loosely by his sides, and I was reminded of an animal that has suddenly come across a rival – it was a type of predatory stillness: watchful and ready to fight. He said lightly, but it seemed to me the lightness was now more strained: 'You realise this is of no consquence to me, but only to yourself? It does not matter who is my advocate; nothing changes for me. I shall be acquitted. But for you now – instead of my friendship, you will have my enmity.'

Cicero shrugged. 'I prefer not to have the enmity of any man, but when it is unavoidable, I shall endure it.'

'You will never have endured an enmity such as mine, I promise you that. Ask the Africans.' He grinned. 'Ask Gratidianus.'

'You removed his tongue, Catilina. Conversation would be difficult.'

Catilina swayed forward slightly, and I thought he might do to Cicero what he had only half done to Clodius the previous evening, but that would have been an act of madness, and Catilina was never wholly mad: things would have been far easier if he had been. Instead he checked himself and said, 'Well then, I suppose I must let you go.'

Cicero nodded. 'You must. Leave the papers, Tiro. We have no need of them now.'

I cannot remember if there was any further conversation; I do not believe there was. Catilina and Cicero simply turned their backs on one another, which was the traditional means of signalling enmity, and so we left that ancient, empty, creaking mansion, and went out into the heat of the Roman summer.

XV

Now began a most difficult and anxious period in Cicero's life, during which I am sure he often regretted that he had made such an enemy of Catilina, and had not simply found some excuse to wriggle out of his commitment to defend him. For there were, as he often observed, only three possible outcomes to the coming election, and none was pleasant. Either he would be consul and Catilina would not – in which case who could tell what lengths his resentful and defeated rival might be willing to go to? Or Catilina would be consul and he would not, and all the resources of the office would be turned against him. Or – and this, I think, alarmed him most of all – he and Catilina might be consuls together, in which case his dream of supreme *imperium* would degenerate into a year-long running battle, and the business of the republic would be paralysed by their acrimony.

The first shock came when the trial of Catilina opened a couple of days later, because who should step forward to act as chief defence advocate but the senior consul himself, Lucius Manlius Torquatus, head of one of the oldest and most respected patrician families in Rome. Catilina was escorted into court by all the traditional old guard of the aristocracy – Catulus, of course, but also Hortensius, Lepidus and the elder Curio. The only consolation for Cicero was that Catilina's guilt was utterly manifest, and Clodius, who had his own reputation to consider, actually made quite a decent job of drawing out the evidence. Although Torquatus was an urbane and precise attorney, he could only (to use the crude phrase of the time) apply so much perfume to this particular turd. The jury had been bribed, but the record of Catilina's behaviour in Africa was sufficiently shocking that they very nearly found him guilty, and he was only acquitted *per infamiam* – that is, he was dishonourably discharged from the court. Clodius, fearful of retaliation from Catilina and his supporters, departed the city soon afterwards, to serve on the staff of Lucius Murena, the new governor of Further Gaul. 'If only I had prosecuted Catilina myself!' groaned Cicero. 'He would be with Verres in Massilia by now, watching the waves coming in!' But at least he had avoided the dishonour of serving as Catilina's defender – for which, incidentally, he gave much credit to Terentia, and thereafter he was always more willing to listen to her advice.

Cicero's campaign strategy now called for him to leave Rome for four months, and travel north to canvass, all the way up to the borders of Italy in Nearer Gaul. No consular candidate, as far as I am aware, had ever done such a thing before, but Cicero, even though he loathed to leave the city for so long, was convinced it was worth it. When he stood for aedile, the number of registered electors was some four hundred thousand; but now those rolls had been revised by the censors, and with the extension of the franchise as far north as the River Po, the electorate had increased to almost one million. Very few of these citizens would ever bother to travel all the way to Rome to cast their votes in person. But Cicero reckoned that if he could only persuade just one in ten of those he met to make the effort, it could give him a decisive edge on the Field of Mars.

He fixed his departure for after the Roman Games, which began that year as usual on the fifth day of September. And now came Cicero's second – I will not call it a shock exactly, but it was certainly more troubling than a mere surprise. The Roman Games were always given by the curule aediles, one of whom was Caesar. As with Antonius Hybrida, nothing much was expected of him, for he was known to be hard up. But Caesar took the whole production over, and in his lordly way declared that the games were in honour not only of Jupiter, but of his dead father. For days beforehand he had workmen in the forum building colonnades, so that people could stroll around and see the wild beasts he had imported, and the gladiators he had bought – no fewer than three hundred and twenty pairs, clad in silver armour: the greatest number ever produced for a public spectacle. He laid on banquets, held processions, staged plays, and on the morning of the games themselves the citizens of Rome woke to discover that he had, overnight, erected a statue of the populist hero, Marius – the aristocrats' great hate-figure – within the precincts of the Capitol.

Catulus immediately insisted that a session of the senate be called, and tabled a motion demanding that the statue be removed at once. But Caesar replied to him with contempt, and such was his popularity in Rome, the senate did not dare to press the matter further. Everyone knew that the only man who could possibly have lent Caesar the money for such an extravaganza was Crassus, and I remember how Cicero returned from the Roman Games in the same dejected manner that he had come back from Hybrida's Games of Apollo. It was not that Caesar, six years his junior, was ever likely to run against him personally in an election, but rather that Crassus was clearly up to something, and he could not work out what. Cicero described to me that night a part of the entertainment. 'Some poor wretch, a criminal, was led out naked into the centre of the Circus, armed with a wooden sword, and then they released a panther and a lion to attack him, which no doubt they had starved for weeks. And actually he put on a reasonable show, using the only advantage he had – his brains – dashing this way and that, and for a while it looked as though he might succeed in making the beasts attack one another instead of him. The crowd were cheering him on. But then he tripped and the creatures tore him to pieces. And I looked to one side of me at Hortensius and the aristocrats, all laughing and applauding, and at Crassus and Caesar side by side on the other, and I thought to myself, Cicero: that man is you.'

His personal relations with Caesar were always cordial, not least because Caesar enjoyed his jokes, but he had never trusted him, and now that he suspected he was in alliance with Crassus, he began to keep a greater distance. There is another story I should tell about Caesar. Around this time Palicanus came to call, seeking Cicero's support for his own bid for the consulship. Oh dear – poor Palicanus! He was a cautionary lesson in what can happen in politics if one becomes too dependent on the favour of a great man. He had been Pompey's loyal tribune, and then his loyal praetor, but he had never been given his share of the spoils once Pompey had achieved his special commands, for the simple reason there was nothing left he could offer in return; he had been bled dry. I picture him, day after day sitting in his house, staring at his gigantic bust of Pompey, or dining alone beneath that mural of Pompey as Jupiter – truthfully, he had about as much chance of becoming consul as I did. But Cicero tried to let him down kindly, and said that although he could not form an electoral alliance with him, he would at least try to do something for him in the future (of course, he never did). At the end of the interview, just as Palicanus was rising, Cicero, keen to end on a friendly note, asked to be remembered to his daughter, the blowsy Lollia, who was married to Gabinius.

'Oh, do not talk to me about that whore!' responded Palicanus. 'You must have heard? The whole city is talking about it! She is being screwed every day by Caesar!'

Cicero assured him he had not heard.

'Caesar,' said Palicanus bitterly. 'Now there is a duplicitous bastard! I ask you: is that any time to bed a comrade's wife – when he is a thousand miles away, fighting for his country?'

'Disgraceful,' agreed Cicero. 'Mind you,' he observed to me after Palicanus had gone, 'if you are going to do such a thing, I should have thought that was the ideal time. Not that I am an expert on such matters.' He shook his head. 'Really, though, one has to wonder about Caesar. If a man would steal your wife, what else wouldn't he take from you?'

Yet again I almost told him what I had witnessed in Pompey's house; and yet again I thought the better of it.

It was on a clear autumn morning that Cicero bade a tearful goodbye to Terentia, Tullia and little Marcus, and we left the city to begin his great campaign tour of the north. Quintus, as usual, remained behind to nurse his brother's political interests, while Frugi was entrusted with the legal casework. As for young Rufus, this became the occasion of his finally leaving Cicero and going to the household of Crassus to complete his internship.

We travelled in a convoy of three four-wheeled carriages, pulled by teams of mules – one carriage for Cicero to sleep in, another specially fitted out as an office, and a third full of luggage and documents; other, smaller vehicles trailed behind for the use of the senator's retinue of secretaries, valets, muleteers, cooks, and heaven knows who else, including several thick-set men who acted as bodyguards. We left by the Fontinalian Gate, with no one to see us off. In those days, the hills to the north of Rome were still pine-clad, apart from the one on which Lucullus was just completing his notorious palace. The patrician general had now come back from the East, but was unable to enter the city proper without forfeiting his military *imperium* and with it his right to a triumph. So he was lingering out here amid his spoils of war, waiting for his aristocratic cronies to assemble a majority in the senate to vote him *triumphator*, but the supporters of Pompey, among them Cicero, kept blocking it. Mind you, even Cicero glanced up from his letters long enough to take a look at this colossal structure, the roof of which was just visible over the tree-tops, and I secretly hoped that we might catch a glimpse of the great man himself, but of course he was nowhere to be seen. (Incidentally, Quintus Metellus, the sole survivor of the three Metelli brothers, had also recently returned from Crete, and was also holed up outside the city in anticipation of a triumph which, again, the ever-jealous Pompey would not allow. The plight of Lucullus and Metellus was a source of endless amusement to Cicero: 'A traffic jam of generals,' he called them, 'all trying to get into Rome through the Triumphal Gate!') At the Mulvian Bridge we paused while Cicero dashed off a final note of farewell to Terentia. Then we crossed the swollen waters of the Tiber and turned north on to the Flaminian Way.

We made extremely good time on that first day, and shortly before nightfall we reached Ocriculum, about thirty miles north of the city. Here we were met by a prominent local citizen who had agreed to give Cicero hospitality, and the following morning the senator went into the forum to begin his canvass. The secret of effective electioneering lies in the quality of the staff work done in advance, and here Cicero was very fortunate to have attached to his campaign two professional agents, Ranunculus and Filum, who travelled ahead of the candidate to ensure that a decent crowd of supporters would always be waiting in each town when we arrived. There was nothing about the electoral map of Italy which these two rascals did not know: who among the local knights would be offended if Cicero did not stop to pay his respects, and who should be avoided; which were the most important tribes and centuries in each particular district, and which were most likely to come his way; what were the issues which most concerned the citizens, and what were the promises they expected in return for their votes. They had no other topic of conversation except politics, yet Cicero could sit with them late into the night swapping facts and stories, as happily as he could converse with a philosopher or a wit.

I would not weary you with all the details of the campaign, even if I could remember them. Dear gods! What a heap of ash most political careers amount to, when one really stops to consider them! I used to be able to name every consul for the past one hundred years, and most praetors for the past forty. Now, they have almost entirely faded out of my memory, quenched like lights at midnight around the Bay of Naples. Little wonder that the towns and crowds of Cicero's consular campaign have all merged into one generalised impression of hands shaken, stories listened to, bores endured, petitions received, jokes told, undertakings given, and local worthies smoothed and flattered. The name of Cicero was famous by this time, even outside Rome, and people turned out to see him en masse, especially in the larger towns where law was practised, for the speeches he had prepared for the prosecution of Verres – even those he had not delivered – had been extensively copied and circulated. He was a hero to both the lower classes and the respectable knights, who saw him as a champion against the rapacity and snobbery of the aristocracy. For this reason, there were not many grand houses which opened their doors to him, and we had to endure taunts and even occasionally missiles whenever we passed close to the estates of one or other of the great patricians.

We pressed on up the Flaminian Way, devoting a day to each of the decent-sized towns – Narnia, Carsulae, Mevania, Fulginiae, Nuceria, Tadinae and Cales – before finally reaching the Adriatic coast about two weeks after leaving Rome. It was some years since I had gazed upon the sea, and when that line of glittering blue appeared above the dust and scrub I felt as thrilled as a child. The afternoon was cloudless and balmy, a straggler left behind by a distant summer which had long since retreated. On impulse, Cicero ordered that the wagons be halted so that we could all walk on the beach. How odd the things which *do* lodge in one's mind, for although I cannot now recall much of the serious politics, I can still remember every detail of that hour-long interlude – the smell of the seaweed and the taste of salt spray on my lips, the warmth of the sun on my cheeks, the rattle of the shingle as the waves broke and the hiss as they receded, and Cicero laughing as he tried to demonstrate how Demosthenes was supposed to have improved his elocution by rehearsing his speeches with a mouth full of pebbles.

A few days later, at Ariminum, we picked up the Aemilian Way and swung west, away from the sea, and into the province of Nearer Gaul. Here we could feel the nip of winter coming on. The black and purple mountains of the Apenninus rose sheer to our left, while to our right, the Po delta stretched grey and flat to the horizon. I had a curious sensation that we were mere insects, creeping along the foot of a wall at the edge of some great room. The passionate political issue in Nearer Gaul at that time was the franchise. Those who lived to the south of the River Po had been given the vote; those who lived to the north had not. The populists, led by Pompey and Caesar, favoured extending citizenship across the river, all the way to the Alps; the aristocrats, whose spokesman was Catulus, suspected a plot further to dilute their power, and opposed it. Cicero, naturally, was in favour of widening the franchise to the greatest extent possible, and this was the issue he campaigned on.

They had never seen a consular candidate up here before, and in every little town crowds of several hundred would turn out to listen to him. Cicero usually spoke from the back of one of the wagons, and gave the same speech at every stop, so that after a while I could move my lips in synchronicity with his. He denounced as nonsense the logic which said that a man who lived on one side of a stretch of water was a Roman and that his cousin on the other was a barbarian, even though they both spoke Latin. 'Rome is not merely a matter of geography,' he would proclaim. 'Rome is not defined by rivers, or mountains, or even seas; Rome is not a question of blood, or race, or religion; Rome is an ideal. Rome is the highest embodiment of liberty and law that mankind has yet achieved in the ten thousand years since our ancestors came down from those mountains and learned how to live as communities under the rule of law.' So if his listeners had the vote, he would conclude, they must be sure to use it on behalf of those who had not, for that was their fragment of civilisation, their special gift, as precious as the secret of fire. Every man should see Rome once before he died. They should go next summer, when the travelling was easy, and cast their ballots on the Field of Mars, and if anyone asked them why they had come so far, 'You can tell them Marcus Cicero sent you!' Then he would jump down, and pass among the crowd while they were still applauding, doling out handfuls of chickpeas from a sack carried by one of his attendants, and I would make sure I was just behind him, to catch his instructions and write down names.

I learned much about Cicero while he was out campaigning. Indeed, I would say that despite all the years we had spent together I never really knew him until I saw him in one of those small towns south of the Po – Faventia, say, or Claterna – with the late autumn light just starting to fade, and a cold wind blowing off the mountains, and the lamps being lit in the little shops along the main street, and the upturned faces of the local farmers gazing in awe at this famous senator on the back of his wagon, with his three fingers outstretched, pointing towards the glory of

Rome. I realised then that, for all his sophistication, he was really still one of them – a man from a small provincial town with an idealised dream of the republic and what it meant to be a citizen, which burned all the fiercer within him because he, too, was an outsider.

For the next two months Cicero devoted himself entirely to the electors of Nearer Gaul, especially those around the provincial capital of Placentia, which actually lies on the banks of the Po and where whole families were divided by the vexed question of citizenship. He was given great assistance in his campaigning by the governor, Piso – that same Piso, curiously enough, who had threatened Pompey with the fate of Romulus if he pressed ahead with his desire for the special command. But Piso was a pragmatist, and besides, his family had commercial interests beyond the Po. He was thus in favour of extending the vote; he even gave Cicero a special commission on his staff, to enable him to travel more freely. We spent the festival of Saturnalia at Piso's headquarters, imprisoned by snow, and I could see the governor becoming more and more charmed by Cicero's manners and wit, to the extent that one evening, after plenty of wine, he clapped him on the shoulder and declared, 'Cicero, you are a good fellow after all. A better fellow and a better patriot than I realised. Speaking for myself, I would be willing to see you as consul. It is only a pity it will never happen.'

Cicero looked taken aback. 'And why are you so sure of that?'

'Because the aristocrats will never stand for it, and they control too many votes.'

'It is true they have great influence,' conceded Cicero. 'But I have the support of Pompey.'

Piso roared with laughter. 'And much good may it do you! He is lording it around at the other end of the world, and besides – haven't you noticed? – he never stirs for anyone except himself. Do you know who I would watch out for if I were you?'

'Catilina?'

'Yes, him too. But the one who should really worry you is Antonius Hybrida.'

'But the man is a halfwit!'

'Cicero, you disappoint me. Since when has idiocy been a bar to advancement in politics? You take it from me – Hybrida is the man the aristocrats will rally around, and then you and Catilina will be left to fight it out for second place, and do not look to Pompey for help.'

Cicero smiled and affected unconcern, but Piso's remarks had obviously struck home, and as soon as the snowfall melted we set off back to Rome at maximum speed.

We reached the city in the middle of January, and to begin with all seemed well. Cicero resumed his hectic round of advocacy in the courts, and his campaign team once again met weekly under the supervision of Quintus, who assured him his support was holding firm. We were minus young Rufus, but his absence was more than made up for by the addition of Cicero's oldest and closest friend, Atticus, who had returned to live in Rome after an absence in Greece of some twenty years.

I must tell you a little about Atticus, whose importance in Cicero's life I have so far only hinted at, and who was about to become extremely significant indeed. Already rich, he had recently inherited a fine house on the Quirinal Hill together with twenty million in cash from his uncle, Quintus Caecilius, one of the most loathed and misanthropic money-lenders in Rome, and it says much about Atticus that he alone remained on reasonable terms with this repulsive old man right up to his death. Some might have suspected opportunism, but the truth was that Atticus, because of his philosophy, had made it a principle never to fall out with anyone. He was a devoted follower of the teachings of Epicurus – 'that pleasure is the beginning and end of living happily' – although I hasten to add that he was an Epicurean not in the commonly misunderstood sense, as a seeker after luxury, but in the true meaning, as a pursuer of what the Greeks call *ataraxia*, or freedom from disturbance. He consequently avoided arguments and unpleasantness of any kind (needless to say, he was unmarried) and desired only to contemplate philosophy by day and dine by night with his cultured friends. He believed that all mankind should have similar aims, and was baffled that they did not: he tended to forget, as Cicero occasionally reminded him, that not everyone had inherited a fortune. He never for an instant contemplated undertaking anything as upsetting or dangerous as a political career, yet at the same time, as an insurance against future mishap, he had taken pains to cultivate every aristocrat who passed through Athens – which, over two decades, was a lot – by drawing up their family trees, and presenting them as gifts, beautifully illustrated by his slaves. He was also extremely shrewd with money. In short, there can never have been anyone quite so worldly in their pursuit of unworldliness as Titus Pomponius Atticus.

He was three years older than Cicero, who stood somewhat in awe of him, not only because of his wealth but also because of his social connections, for if there is one man guaranteed to enjoy an automatic entrée into smart society it is a rich and witty bachelor in his middle forties with an unfeigned interest in the genealogy of his host and hostess. This made him invaluable as a source of political intelligence, and it was from Atticus that Cicero now began to realise how formidable was the opposition to his candidacy. First, Atticus heard over dinner from his great friend Servilia – the half-sister of Cato – that Antonius Hybrida was definitely running for the consulship. A few weeks after that, Atticus reported a comment of Hortensius (another of his acquaintances) to the effect that Hybrida and Catilina were planning to run on a joint ticket. This was a serious blow, and although Cicero tried to make light of it – 'Oh well, a target that is double the size is twice as easy to hit' – nevertheless I could see that he was shaken, for he had no running-mate of his own, and no serious prospect at this stage of finding one.

But the really bad news came just after the senatorial recess in the late spring. Atticus sent a message that he needed to see the Cicero brothers urgently, so when the courts had closed for the day all three of us made our way up to his house. This was a perfect bachelor set-up, built on a promontory next to the Temple of Salus – not large, but with the most wonderful views across the city, especially from the library, which Atticus had made the centrepiece of the house. There were busts of the great philosophers around the walls, and many little cushioned benches to sit on, for Atticus's rule was that while he would never lend a book, any of his friends were free whenever they liked to come up and read or even make their own copies. And it was here, beneath a head of Aristotle, that we found Atticus reclining that afternoon, dressed in the loose white tunic of a Greek, and reading, if I remember rightly, a volume of *Kyriai doxai*, the principal doctrines of Epicurus.

He came straight to the point. 'I was at dinner last night on the Palatine, at the home of Metellus Celer and the Lady Clodia, and among the other guests was our former consul, no less an aristocrat than' – he blew on an imaginary trumpet – 'Publius Cornelius Lentulus Sura.'

'By heavens,' said Cicero with a smile, 'the company you keep!'

'Did you know that Lentulus is trying to make a comeback, by standing for a praetorship this summer?'

'Is he really?' Cicero frowned and rubbed his forehead. 'He is of course a great friend of Catilina. I suppose they must be in alliance. See how the gang of rascals grows?'

'Oh yes, it is quite a political movement – he, and Catilina and Hybrida, and I got the impression there were others, but he would not give me their names. At one point, he produced a piece of paper with the prediction of some oracle written upon it, that he would be the third of the Cornelii to rule as dictator in Rome.'

'Old Sleepy-Head? Dictator? I trust you laughed in his face.'

'No, I did not,' replied Atticus. 'I took him very seriously. You ought to try it some time, Cicero, instead of just delivering one of your crushing witticisms which simply shuts everybody up. No, I encouraged him to ramble on, and he drank more of Celer's excellent wine, and I listened more, and he drank more, and eventually he swore me to secrecy and he told me his great secret.'

'Which is?' said Cicero, leaning forward in his seat, for he knew that Atticus would not have summoned us for nothing.

'They are being backed by Crassus.'

There was a silence.

'Crassus is voting for them?' asked Cicero, which I think was the first time I had ever heard him say something seriously stupid: I ascribe it to the shock.

'No,' said Atticus irritably. 'He is backing them. You know what I mean. Financing them. Buying them the whole election, according to Lentulus.'

Cicero seemed temporarily deprived of the power of speech. After another long pause it was Quintus who spoke up. 'I do not believe it. Lentulus must have been well in his cups to make such a ridiculous boast. What possible reason would Crassus have for wanting to see such men in power?'

'To spite me,' said Cicero, recovering his voice.

'Nonsense!' exclaimed Quintus angrily. (Why was he so angry? I suppose because he was frightened that the story was true, in which case he would look a fool, especially in the light of all the assurances he had given his brother that the campaign was in the bag.) 'Absolute nonsense!' he repeated, although with slightly less certainty. 'We already know that Crassus is investing heavily in Caesar's future. How much would it cost him in addition to buy two consulships and a praetorship? You are talking not just about a million, but four million, five million. He hates you, Marcus, everyone knows it. But does he hate you so much more than he loves his money? I doubt it.'

'No,' said Cicero firmly, 'I am afraid you are wrong, Quintus. This story has the ring of truth, and I blame myself for not recognising the danger earlier.' He was on his feet now, and pacing around, as he always did when he was thinking hard. 'It started with those Games of Apollo given by Hybrida – Crassus must have paid for those. The games were what brought Hybrida back from the political dead. And could Catilina really have raised the funds to bribe his jury simply by selling a few statues and pictures? Of course not. And even if he did, who is paying his campaign expenses now? Because I have been inside his house and I can tell you: that man is bankrupt.' He wheeled around, his gaze darting to right and left, bright and unseeing, his eyes working as rapidly as his thoughts. 'I have always known in my bones that there was something wrong about this election. I have sensed some invisible force against me from the very outset. Hybrida and Catilina! These creatures should never even have been *candidates* in any normal canvass, let alone the front-runners. They are merely the tools of someone else.'

'So we are fighting Crassus?' said Quintus, sounding resigned to it at last.

'Crassus, yes. Or is it really Caesar, using Crassus's money? Every time I look around, I seem to see a flash of Caesar's cloak, just disappearing out of view. He thinks he is cleverer than anyone, and perhaps he is. But not on this occasion. Atticus –' Cicero stopped in front of him, and took his hands in both of his '– my old friend. I cannot thank you enough.'

'For what? I merely listened to a bore, and then plied him with a little drink. It was hardly anything.'

'On the contrary, the ability to listen to bores requires stamina, and such stamina is the essence of politics. It is from the bores that you really find things out.' Cicero squeezed his hands warmly, then swung around to his brother. 'We need to find some evidence, Quintus. Ranunculus and Filum are the men who can sniff it out – not much moves at election time in this city that those two are not aware of.'

Quintus agreed, and in this way the shadow-boxing of the consular election finally ended, and the real fight began.

XVI

To discover what was going on, Cicero devised a trap. Rather than simply asking around about what Crassus was up to – which would have got him nowhere, and would also have alerted his enemies that he was suspicious – he called Ranunculus and Filum to him, and told them to go out into the city and let it be known that they were representing a certain anonymous senator who was worried about his prospects in the forthcoming consular ballot, and was willing to pay fifty sesterces per vote to the right electoral syndicate.

Ranunculus was a runtish, almost half-formed creature, with a flat, round face at the end of a feeble body, who well deserved his nickname of 'Tadpole'. Filum was a giant spindle, an animated candlestick. Their fathers and grandfathers had been bribery agents before them. They knew the score. They disappeared into the back streets and bars, and a week or so later reported back to Cicero that something very strange was going on. All the usual bribery agents were refusing to cooperate. 'Which means,' as Ranunculus put it, in his squeaky voice, 'either that Rome is full of honest men for the first time in three hundred years, or that every vote that was up for sale has already been bought.'

'There must be someone who will crack for a higher price,' insisted Cicero. 'You had better do the rounds again, and this time offer a hundred.'

So back they went, and back they returned after another week with the same story. Such was the huge amount that the bribery agents were already being paid, and such was their nervousness about antagonising their mysterious client, that there was not a single vote to be had, and not a breath of rumour as to who that client might be. Now you might well wonder, given the thousands of votes involved, how such an immense operation could remain so tight a secret. The answer is that it was very cleverly organised, with perhaps only a dozen agents, or *interpretes* as they were called, knowing the identity of the buyer (I regret to say that both Ranunculus and Filum had acted as *interpretes* in the past). These men would contact the officials of the voting syndicates and strike the initial bargain – such-and-such a price for fifty votes, say, or five hundred, depending on the size of the syndicate. Because naturally no one trusted anyone else in this game, the money would then be deposited with a second category of agent, known as the *sequestres*, who would hold the cash available for inspection. And finally, when the election was over and it was time to settle up, a third species of criminal, the so-called *divisores*, would distribute it. This made it extremely difficult to bring a successful prosecution, for even if a man was arrested in the very act of handing over a bribe, he might genuinely have no idea of who had commissioned the corruption in the first place. But still Cicero refused to accept that someone would not talk. 'We are dealing with bribery agents,' he shouted, in a rare show of anger, 'not an ancient order of Roman knights! Somewhere you will find a man who will betray even as dangerous a paymaster as Crassus, if the money is good enough. Go and track him down and find his price – or must I do everything myself?'

By this time – I suppose it must have been well into June, about a month before the election – everyone knew that something strange was going on. It was turning into one of the most memorable and closely fought campaigns in living memory, with a field of no fewer than seven for the consulship, a reflection of the fact that many men fancied their chances that year. The three front-runners were reckoned to be Catilina, Hybrida and Cicero. Then came the snobbish and acerbic Galba, and the deeply religious Cornificius. The two no-hopers were the corpulent ex-praetor Cassius Longinus, and Gaius Licinius Sacerdos, who had been governor of Sicily even before Verres, and who was at least a decade older than his rivals. (Sacerdos was one of those irritating candidates who enter elections 'not out of any personal ambition', as they like to say, but solely with the intention of 'raising issues' – 'Always beware of the man who says he is not seeking office for himself,' said Cicero, 'for he is the vainest of the lot.') Realising that the bribery agents were unusually active, the senior consul, Marcius Figulus, was prevailed upon by several of these candidates to bring before the senate a severe new law against electoral malpractice: what he hoped would become the *lex Figula*. It was already illegal for a candidate to offer a bribe; the new bill also made it a criminal offence for a voter to accept one.

When the time came for the measure to be debated in the senate, the consul first went round each of the candidates in turn to ask for his opinion. Sacerdos, as the senior man, spoke first, and made a pious speech in favour; I could see Cicero squirming with irritation at his platitudes. Hybrida naturally spoke against, but in his usual bumbling and unmemorable way – no one would ever have believed his father had once been the most eagerly sought advocate in Rome. Galba, who was going to lose badly in any case, took this opportunity to withdraw from the election, loftily announcing that there was no glory in participating in such a squalid contest, which disgraced the memory of his ancestors. Catilina, for obvious reasons, also spoke against the *lex Figula*, and I must concede that he was impressive. Utterly without nerves, he towered over the benches around him, and when he came to the end of his remarks he pointed at Cicero and roared that the only men who would benefit from yet another new piece of legislation were the lawyers, which drew the usual cheers from the aristocrats. Cicero was in a delicate position, and as he rose I wondered what he would say, because obviously he did not wish to see the legislation fail, but nor, on the eve of the most important election of his life, did he want to alienate the voting syndicates, who naturally regarded the bill as an attack on their honour. His response was adroit.

'In general I welcome this bill,' he said, 'which can only be a terror to those who are guilty. The honest citizen has nothing to fear from a law against bribery, and the dishonest should be reminded that a vote is a sacred trust, not a voucher to be cashed in once a year. But there is one thing wrong with it: an imbalance which needs to be redressed. Are we really saying that the poor man who succumbs to temptation is more to be condemned than the rich man who deliberately places temptation in his way? I say the opposite: that if we are to legislate against the one, we must strengthen the sanctions against the other. With your permission, therefore, Figulus, I wish to propose an amendment to your bill: *That any person who solicits, or seeks to solicit, or causes to be solicited, the votes of any citizen in return for money should be liable to a penalty of ten years' exile.*' That produced an excited and long-drawn-out 'Oohh!' from all around the chamber.

I could not see Crassus's face from where I was standing, but Cicero delightedly assured me afterwards that it turned bright red, for that phrase, *or causes to be solicited*, was aimed directly at him, and everyone knew it. The consul placidly accepted the amendment, and asked if any member wished to speak against it. But the majority of the house were too surprised to react, and those such as Crassus who stood to lose most dared not expose themselves in public by openly opposing it. Accordingly, the amendment was carried without opposition, and when the house divided on the main bill, it was passed by a large margin. Figulus, preceded by his lictors, left the chamber, and all the senators filed out into the sunshine to watch him mount the rostra and give the bill to the herald for an immediate first reading. I saw Hybrida make a move towards Crassus, but Catilina caught his arm, and Crassus walked rapidly away from the forum, to avoid being seen with his nominees. The usual three weekly market days would now have to elapse before the bill could be voted upon, which meant that the people would have their say almost on the eve of the consular election.

Cicero was pleased with his day's work, for the possibility now opened up that if the *lex Figula* passed, and if he lost the election because of bribery, he might be in a position to launch a prosecution not only against Catilina and Hybrida, but also against his arch-enemy Crassus himself. It was only two years, after all, since a previous pair of consul-select had been stripped of their offices for electoral malpractice. But to succeed in such an action he would require evidence, and the pressure to find it became even more intense. Every waking hour he now spent canvassing, going about with a great crowd of supporters, but never with a *nomenclator* at his elbow to whisper the names of the voters: unlike his opponents Cicero took great pride in being able to remember thousands of names, and on the rare occasion when he met someone whose identity he had forgotten, he could always bluff his way through.

I admired him greatly at this time, for he must have known that the odds were heavily against him and the chances were that he was going to lose. Piso's prediction about Pompey had proved amply correct, and the great man had not lifted a finger to assist Cicero during the campaign. He had established himself at Amisus, on the eastern edge of the Black Sea – which is about as far away from Rome as it is possible to get – and there, like some great Eastern potentate, he was receiving homage from no fewer than twelve native kings. Syria had been annexed. Mithradates was in headlong retreat. Pompey's house on the Esquiline had been decorated with the captured beaks of fifty pirate triremes and was nowadays known as the *domus rostra* – a shrine to his admirers all across Italy. What did Pompey care any more about the pygmy struggles of mere civilians? Cicero's letters to him went unanswered. Quintus railed against his ingratitude, but Cicero was fatalistic: 'If it is gratitude you want, get a dog.'

Three days before the consular election, and on the eve of the vote on the bribery law, there was at last a breakthrough. Ranunculus came rushing in to see Cicero with the news that he had found a bribery agent named Gaius Salinator, who claimed to be in a position to sell three hundred votes for five hundred sesterces apiece. He owned a bar in the Subura called the Bacchante, and it had been agreed that Ranunculus would go to see him that very night, give him the name of the candidate for whom the bribed electors were to vote, and at the same time hand over the money to one of the *sequestres*, who was trusted by them both. When Cicero heard about this he became very excited, and insisted that he would accompany Ranunculus to the meeting, with a hood pulled down to conceal his well-known face. Quintus was against the plan, considering it too dangerous, but Cicero was insistent that he needed to gather evidence at first hand. 'I shall have Ranunculus and Tiro with me for protection,' he said (I assume this was one of his jokes), 'but perhaps you could arrange for a few loyal supporters to be drinking in the neighbourhood, just in case we need more assistance.'

I was by this time almost forty, and after a life devoted exclusively to clerical duties my hands were as soft as a maiden's. In the event of trouble it would be Cicero, whose daily exercises had given him an imposing physique, who would be called upon to protect *me*. Nevertheless, I opened up the safe in his study and began counting out the cash we needed in silver coin. (He had a well-stocked campaign fund, made up of gifts from his admirers, which he drew on to pay for such expenses as his tour of Nearer Gaul: this money was not bribes, as such, although obviously it was comforting for the donors to know that Cicero was a man who famously never forgot a name.) Anyway, this silver was fitted into a money belt which I had to strap around my waist, and with a heavy tread, in both senses of the phrase, I descended with Cicero at dusk into the Subura. He cut a curious figure wearing a hooded tunic borrowed from one of his slaves, for the night was very warm. But in the crowded slums of the poor, the bizarrely dressed are an everyday sight, and when people saw a man with a hood pulled down low over his face they gave him a wide berth, perhaps fearing that he had leprosy or some disfiguring complaint which they might catch. We followed Ranunculus, who darted, appropriately tadpole-like, through the labyrinth of narrow, squalid alleys which were his natural habitat, until at last we came to a corner where men were sitting leaning against the wall, passing back and forth a jar of wine. Above their heads, beside the door, was a painting of Bacchus with his groin thrust out, relieving himself, and the spot had the smell to match the sign. Ranunculus stepped inside and led us behind the counter and up some narrow wooden stairs to a raftered room, where Salinator was waiting, along with another man, the *sequester*, whose name I never learned.

They were so anxious to see the money, they paid little attention to the hooded figure behind me. I had to take off my belt and show them a handful of coins, whereupon the *sequester* produced a small pair of scales and began weighing the silver. Salinator, who was a flabby, lank-haired, pot-bellied creature, watched this for a while, then said to Ranunculus, 'That seems well enough. Now you had better give me the name of your client.'

'I am his client,' said Cicero, throwing back his hood. Needless to say, Salinator recognised him at once, and stepped back in alarm, crashing into the *sequester* and his scales. The bribery agent struggled to recover, hopelessly trying to turn his stumble into a sequence of bows, and began some improvised speech about what an honour it was and so forth to help the senator in his campaign, but Cicero shut him up quickly. 'I do not require any help from the likes of you, wretch! All I require is information.'

Salinator had just begun to whine that he knew nothing when suddenly the *sequester* dropped his scales and made a dive for the staircase. He must have got about halfway down before he ran into the solid figure of Quintus, who spun him around, hauled him up by his collar and the seat of his tunic and threw him back into the room. I was relieved to see, coming up the stairs behind Quintus, a couple of stout young lads who often served as Cicero's attendants. At the sight of so many, and confronted by the most famous advocate in Rome, Salinator's resistance began to weaken. What finished it altogether was when Cicero threatened to hand him over to Crassus for trying to sell the same votes twice. He was more scared of retribution at Crassus's hands than of anything, and I was reminded of that phrase about Old Baldhead which Cicero had repeated years before: 'the most dangerous bull in the herd'.

'Your client is Crassus, then?' asked Cicero. 'Think carefully before you deny it.'

Salinator's chin twitched slightly: the nearest he dared come to a nod.

'And you were to deliver three hundred votes to Hybrida and Catilina for the consulship?'

Again he gave the ghost of a nod. 'For them,' he said, 'and the others.'

'Others? You mean Lentulus Sura for praetor?'

'Yes. Him. And the others.'

'You keep saying "the others",' said Cicero, frowning. 'Who are these "others"?'

'Keep your mouth shut!' shouted the *sequester*, but Quintus kicked him in the stomach and he groaned and rolled over.

'Ignore him,' said Cicero affably. 'He is a bad influence. I know the type. You can tell me.' He put an encouraging hand on the bribery agent's arm. 'The others?'

'Cosconius,' said Salinator, casting a nervous glance at the figure writhing on the floor. Then he took a breath and said rapidly, in a quiet voice: 'Pomptinus. Balbus. Caecilius. Labienus. Faberius. Gutta. Bulbus. Calidius. Tudicius. Valgius. And Rullus.'

As each new name was mentioned, Cicero looked more and more astonished. 'Is that it?' he said, when Salinator had finished. 'You are sure there is no one left in the senate you have forgotten?' He glanced across at Quintus, who was looking equally amazed.

'That is not just two candidates for consul,' said Quintus. 'That is three candidates for praetor and *ten* for tribune. Crassus is trying to buy the entire government!'

Cicero was not a man who liked to show surprise, but even he could not disguise it that night. 'This is completely absurd,' he protested. 'How much is each of these votes costing?'

'Five hundred for consul,' replied Salinator, as if he were selling pigs at market. 'Two hundred for praetor. One hundred for tribune.'

'So you are telling me,' said Cicero, frowning as he performed the calculation, 'that Crassus is willing to pay three quarters of a million merely for the three hundred votes in your syndicate?'

Salinator nodded, this time more vigorously, even happily, and with a certain professional pride. 'It has been the most magnificent canvass anyone can remember.'

Cicero turned to Ranunculus, who had been keeping watch at the window in case of any trouble in the street. 'How many votes do you think Crassus will have bought altogether at this sort of price?'

'To feel confident of victory?' replied Ranunculus. He pondered the matter judiciously. 'It must be seven or eight thousand.'

'*Eight thousand?*' repeated Cicero. 'Eight thousand would cost him *twenty million*. Have you ever heard the like? And at the end of it, he is not even in office himself, but has filled the magistracies with ninnies like Hybrida and Lentulus Sura.' He turned back to Salinator. 'Did he give you any reason for such an immense exercise?'

'No, Senator. Crassus is not a man much given to answering questions.'

Quintus swore. 'Well, he will answer some fucking questions now,' he said, and to relieve his frustration he aimed another kick at the belly of the *sequester*, who had just started to rise, and sent the fellow groaning and crashing back to the floor.

Quintus was all for beating the last scrap of information out of the two hapless agents, and then either marching them round to the house of Crassus and demanding that he put a stop to his schemes, or dragging them before the senate, reading out their confessions, and calling for the elections to be postponed. But Cicero kept a cooler head. With a straight face he thanked Salinator for his honesty, told Quintus to have a cup of wine and calm down, and me to gather up our silver. Later, when we had returned home, he sat in his study and tossed that little leather exercise ball of his from one hand to the other, while Quintus raged that he had been a fool to let the two bribery agents go, that they would surely now alert Crassus or flee the city.

'They will not do either,' replied Cicero. 'To go to Crassus and tell him what has happened would be to sign their own death warrants. Crassus would never leave such incriminating witnesses alive, and they know it. And flight would merely bring about the same result, except that it would take him longer to track them down.' Back and forth, back and forth went the ball. 'Besides, no crime has been committed. Bribery is hard enough to prove at the best of times – impossible to establish when not a vote has been cast. Crassus and the senate would merely laugh at us. No, the best thing is to leave them at liberty, where at least we know where to find them again, and be ready to subpoena them if we lose the election.' He threw the ball higher and caught it with a swiping motion. 'You were right about one thing, though, Quintus.'

'Was I really?' said Quintus bitterly. 'How kind of you to say so.'

'Crassus's action has nothing to do with his enmity for me. He would not spend twenty million simply to frustrate *my* hopes. He would only invest twenty million if the likely return were *huge*. What can it be? On that issue I must confess myself baffled.' He stared at the wall for a while. 'Tiro, you always got on well with young Caelius Rufus, didn't you?'

I remembered the shirked tasks which I had been obliged to complete for him, the lies I had told to keep him out of trouble, the day he stole my savings and persuaded me not to report his thieving to Cicero. 'Reasonably well, Senator,' I replied cautiously.

'Go and talk to him tomorrrow morning. Be subtle about it. See if you can extract any clues from him about what Crassus is up to. He lives under the same roof, after all. He must know something.'

I lay awake long into the night, pondering all of this, and feeling increasingly anxious for the future. Cicero did not sleep much either. I could hear him pacing around upstairs. The force of his concentration seemed almost to penetrate the floorboards, and when sleep did at last come to me, it was restless and full of portents.

The following morning I left Laurea to deal with Cicero's press of visitors and set off to walk the mile or so to the house of Crassus. Even today, when the sky is cloudless and the mid-July heat feels oppressive even before the sun is up, I whisper to myself, 'Election weather!' and feel again that familiar clench of excitement in my stomach. The sound of hammering and sawing rose from the forum, where the workmen were finishing the erection of the ramps and fences around the Temple of Castor, for this was the day on which the bribery bill was to be put to the vote of the people. I cut through behind the temple and paused to take a drink from the tepid waters of the fountain of Juturna. I had no idea what I was going to say to Rufus. I am a most inexpert liar – I always have been – and I realised I should have asked Cicero to advise me on some line to take, but it was too late now. I climbed the path to the

Palatine, and when I reached the house of Crassus I told the porter that I had an urgent message for Caelius Rufus. He offered to let me wait inside but I declined. Instead, while he went off to fetch the young man, I crossed the street and tried to make myself as inconspicuous as possible.

Crassus's house, like the man himself, presented a very modest façade to the world, although I had been told that this was deceptive, and that once you got inside it went back a long way. The door was dark, low and narrow, but stout, flanked by two small, barred windows. Ivy climbed across peeling walls of light ochre. The terracotta roof was also ancient, and the edges of the tiles where they overhung the pavement were cracked and black, like a row of broken teeth. It might have been the home of an unwise banker, or some hard-up country landowner who had allowed his town house to fall into disrepair. I suppose this was Crassus's way of showing that he was so fabulously rich, he had no need to keep up a smart appearance, but of course in that street of millionaires it only drew attention to his wealth, and there was something almost vulgar in this studied lack of vulgarity. The dark little door was constantly opening and shutting as visitors scurried in and out, revealing the extent of the activity within: it put me in mind of a buzzing wasps' nest, which shows itself only as a tiny hole in the masonry. None of these men was recognisable to me until Julius Caesar stepped out. He did not see me, but walked straight off down the street in the direction of the forum, trailed by a secretary carrying a document case. Shortly afterwards, the door opened again and Rufus appeared. He paused on the threshold, cupped his hand above his eyes to shield them from the sun and squinted across the street towards me. I could see at once that he had been out all night as usual, and was not in a good humour at being woken. Thick stubble covered his handsome chin, and he kept sticking out his tongue, swallowing and wincing, as if the taste of it was too horrible to hold it in his mouth. He walked carefully towards me, and when he asked me what in the name of the gods I wanted, I blurted out that I needed to borrow some money.

He squinted at me in disbelief. 'What for?'

'There is a girl,' I replied helplessly, simply because it was the sort of thing he used to say to me when he wanted money and I had not the wit to come up with anything else. I tried to steer him along the street a little way, anxious that Crassus might come out and see us together. But he shook me off and stood swaying in the gutter.

'A girl?' he repeated incredulously. 'You?' And then he began to laugh, but that obviously hurt his head, so he stopped and put his fingers gently to his temple. 'If I had any money, Tiro, I should give it to you willingly – it would be a gift, bestowed simply for the pleasure of seeing you with any living person other than Cicero. But that could never happen. You are not the type for girls. Poor Tiro – you are not any kind of type, that I can see.' He peered at me closely. 'What do you really need it for?' I could smell the stale wine hot on his breath, and could not prevent myself flinching, which he mistook for an admission of guilt. 'You are lying,' he said, and then a grin spread slowly across his stubbled face. 'Cicero sent you to find out something.'

I pleaded with him to move away from the house, and this time he did. But the motion of walking evidently did not agree with him. He halted again, turned very white and held up a warning finger. Then his eyes and throat bulged, he gave an alarming groan, and out came such a heavy gush of vomit it reminded me of a chambermaid emptying a bucket out of an upstairs window into the street. (Forgive these details, but the scene just came entirely back into my mind after an absence of sixty years, and I could not help but laugh at the memory.) Anyway, this seemed to act as a purge; his colour returned and he became much brighter. He asked me what it was that Cicero wanted to know.

'What do you think?' I replied, a little impatiently.

'I wish I could help you, Tiro,' he said, wiping his mouth with the back of his hand. 'You know I would if I could. It is not nearly as pleasant living with Crassus as it was with Cicero. Old Baldhead is the most awful shit – worse even than my father. He has me learning accountancy all day, and a duller business was never invented, except for commercial law, which was last month's torture. As for politics, which does amuse me, he is careful to keep me away from all that side of things.'

I tried asking him a few more questions, for instance about Caesar's visit that morning, but it quickly became clear that he was genuinely ignorant of Crassus's plans. (I suppose he might have been lying, but given his habitual garrulity, I doubted it.) When I thanked him anyway and turned to leave, he grabbed my elbow. 'Cicero must be really desperate,' he said, with an expression of unaccustomed seriousness, 'to ask for help from me. Tell him I am sorry to hear it. He is worth a dozen of Crassus and my father put together.'

*

I did not expect to be seeing Rufus again for a while, and banished him from my mind for the remainder of the day, which was entirely given over to the vote on the bribery bill. Cicero was very active among the tribes in the forum, going from one to another with his entourage, and urging the merits of Figula's proposal. He was especially pleased to find, under the standard marked *VETURIA*, several hundred citizens from Nearer Gaul, who had responded to his campaign and turned out to vote for the first time. He talked to them for a long while about the importance of stamping out bribery, and as he turned away he had the glint of tears in his eyes. 'Poor people,' he muttered, 'to have come so far, only to be mocked by Crassus's money. But if we can get this bill through, I may yet have a weapon to bring the villain down.'

My impression was that his canvassing was proving effective, and that when it came to a vote the *lex Figula* would pass, for the majority were not corrupt. But simply because a measure is honest and sensible does not guarantee that it will be adopted; rather the opposite, in my experience. Early in the afternoon, the populist tribune Mucius Orestinus – he, you may remember, who had formerly been a client of Cicero's on a charge of robbery – came to the front of the rostra and denounced the measure as an attack by the aristocrats on the integrity of the plebs. He actually singled out Cicero by name as a man 'unfit to be consul' – those were his precise words – who posed as a friend of the people, but never did anything for them unless it furthered his own selfish interests. That set half the crowd booing and jeering and the other half – presumably those who were accustomed to selling their votes, and wished to continue doing so – yelling their approval.

This was too much for Cicero. He had, after all, only the year before, secured Mucius's acquittal, and if such a glossy rat as this was leaving his sinking ship, it really must be halfway to the sea bed already. He shouldered his way to the steps of the temple, his face red with the heat and with anger, and demanded to be allowed to answer. 'Who is paying for *your* vote, Mucius?' he shouted, but Mucius pretended not to hear. The crowd around us were now pointing to Cicero, pushing him forward and calling on the tribune to let him speak, but obviously that was the last thing Mucius wanted. Nor did he want a vote on the bill which he might lose. Raising his arm, he solemnly announced that he was vetoing the legislation, and amid scenes of pandemonium, with scuffles between the rival factions, the *lex Figula* was lost. Figulus immediately announced that he would summon a meeting of the senate the following day to debate what should be done.

It was a bitter moment for Cicero, and when at last we reached his house and he was able to close the door on the crowd of his supporters in the street, I thought he might collapse again, as on the eve of the elections for aedile. For once he was too tired to play with Tullia. And even when Terentia came down with little Marcus, and showed him how the infant had learned to take a wobbly step or two unaided, he did not hoist him up and toss him into the air, which was his usual greeting, but simply patted his cheek and squeezed his ear in an absent-minded way, and then passed on towards his study – only to stop dead in surprise on the threshold, for who should be sitting at his desk but Caelius Rufus.

Laurea, who was waiting just inside the door, apologised to Cicero and explained that he would have told Rufus to wait in the tablinum, like every other visitor, but he had been insistent that his business was so confidential he could not be seen in the public rooms.

'That is all right, Laurea. I am always pleased to see young Rufus. Although I fear,' he added, shaking Rufus's hand, 'that you will find me dull company at the end of a long and dispiriting day.'

'Well then,' said Rufus with a grin, 'perhaps I might have just the news to cheer you up.'

'Crassus is dead?'

'On the contrary,' laughed Rufus, 'very much alive, and planning a great conference tonight in anticipation of his triumph at the polls.'

'Is he indeed?' said Cicero, and immediately, at this touch of gossip, I saw him start to revive a little, like some wilted flower after a sprinkle of rain. 'And who will be at this conference?'

'Catilina. Hybrida. Caesar. I am not sure who else. But the chairs were being set out as I left. I have all this from one of Crassus's secretaries, who went around the city with the invitations while the popular assembly was in progress.'

'Well, well,' murmured Cicero. 'What I would not give to have an ear at that keyhole!'

'But you could have,' responded Rufus. 'This meeting is in the chamber where Crassus transacts all his business affairs. Often – but not tonight, I am told by my informant – he likes to keep a secretary close at hand, to make a note of what is said, but without the other person being aware of it. For that purpose he has had a small listening post constructed. It is just a simple cubicle, hidden behind a tapestry. He showed it to me when he was giving me lessons in how to be a man of business.'

'You mean to tell me that Crassus eavesdrops on *himself*?' asked Cicero in wonder. 'What sort of statesman would do that?'

'"There is many a rash promise made by a man who thinks there are no witnesses" – that was what he said.'

'So you think that you could hide yourself in there, and make an account of what is said?'

'Not me,' scoffed Rufus. 'I am no secretary. I was thinking of Tiro here,' he said, clapping me on the shoulder, 'with his miraculous shorthand.'

I would like to be able to boast that I volunteered readily for this suicidal assignment. But it would not be true. On the contrary, I threw up all manner of practical objections to Rufus's scheme. How would I enter Crassus's house undetected? How would I leave it? How would I determine which speaker was which from the babble of voices if I was concealed behind a screen? But to all my questions Rufus had answers. The essential fact was that I was terrified. 'What if I am caught,' I protested to Cicero, finally coming to the crux of what really bothered me, 'and tortured? I cannot claim to be so courageous that I would not betray you.'

'Cicero can simply deny any knowledge of what you were doing,' said Rufus – unhelpfully, I thought, from my point of view. 'Besides, everyone knows that evidence obtained under torture is unreliable.'

'I am beginning to feel faint,' I joked feebly.

'Compose yourself, Tiro,' said Cicero, who had become increasingly excited the more he heard. 'There would be no torture and no trial. I would make sure of that. If you were detected, I would negotiate your release, and I would pay any price to see that you were unharmed.' He took both my hands in that sincere double grip of his, and looked deep into my eyes. 'You are more my second brother than my slave, Tiro, and have been ever since we sat and learned philosophy together in Athens all those years ago – do you remember? I should have discussed your freedom with you before now, but somehow there has always seemed to be some fresh crisis to distract me. So let me tell you now, with Rufus here as my witness, that it is my intention to give you your liberty – yes, and that simple life in the country you have long desired so much. And I see a day when I shall ride over from my place to your little farm, and sit in your garden, and as we watch the sun go down over some distant, dusty olive grove or vineyard, we shall discuss the great adventures we have had together.' He let go of my hands, and this rustic vision trembled on the warm dusky air an instant longer, then faded. 'Now,' he said briskly, 'this offer of mine is not conditional in any way on your undertaking this mission – let me make that clear: you have earned it many times over already. I would never order you to put yourself in danger. You know how badly my cause stands tonight. You must do whatever you think best.'

Those were very nearly his exact words: how could I forget them?

XVII

The conference was set for nightfall, which meant there was no time to be lost. As the sun vanished behind the brow of the Esquiline, and as I climbed the slope of the Palatine Hill for the second time that day, I had a disturbing premonition that I was walking into a trap. For how could I, or Cicero for that matter, be certain that Rufus had not transferred his loyalty to Crassus? Indeed, was 'loyalty' not an absurd word to apply to whatever shifting, temporary focus of amusement seized the fancy of my young companion? But there was nothing to be done about it now. Rufus was already leading me down a small alley towards the back of Crassus's house. Pulling aside a thick curtain of trailing ivy, he uncovered a tiny, iron-studded door, which looked to have long since rusted shut. But a sharp jab from his shoulder caused it to swing silently open and we jumped down into an empty storeroom.

Like Catilina's, the house was very old, and had been added to over the centuries, so that I quickly lost track of our route as we followed the winding passages. Crassus was famous for the number of highly skilled slaves he owned – he hired them out, as a kind of employment agent – and with so many swarming around on duty it seemed impossible that we could reach our destination undetected. But if Rufus had developed any skill during his years of legal study in Rome, it was for illicit entry and exit. We cut across an inner courtyard, hid in an antechamber while a maid went by, then stepped into a big, deserted room, hung with fine tapestries from Babylon and Corinth. Perhaps twenty gilt chairs had been arranged in the centre in a semicircle, and numerous lamps and candelabra were lit around the perimeter. Rufus quickly seized one of the lamps, crossed the floor and lifted the edge of a heavy woollen tapestry depicting Diana bringing down a stag with a spear. Behind it was an alcove, of the sort in which a statue might stand, just high enough and deep enough to take a man, with a little ledge near the top for a lamp. I stepped inside smartly, for I could hear loud male voices coming closer. Rufus put a finger to his lips, winked at me, and carefully replaced the tapestry. His rapid footsteps faded and I was alone.

To begin with I was blind, but gradually I became used to the weak glow of the oil lamp just behind my shoulder. When I put my eye to the tapestry I found that there were tiny spyholes, bored through the thick material in such a way as to give me a complete view of the room. I heard more footsteps, and then abruptly my vision was obscured by the back of a wrinkled bald pink head, and Crassus's voice rang very loud in my ears – so loud I almost stumbled forward in shock – calling genially to his visitors to follow him. He moved away, and the shapes of other men passed by on their way to take their places: the loose-limbed Catilina; Hybrida, with his drinker's face; Caesar, looking sleek and dandified; the impeccable Lentulus Sura; Mucius, the hero of the afternoon; and a couple of notorious bribery agents – these I recognised, together with various other senators who were seeking the tribuneship. They all seemed in an excellent mood, joking with one another, and Crassus had to clap his hands to get their attention.

'Gentlemen,' he said, standing before them with his back to me, 'thank you for attending. We have much to discuss and not long in which to do it. The first item on the agenda is Egypt. Caesar?'

Crassus sat, and Caesar stood. He stroked back a stray sparse hair and tucked it behind his ear with his index finger. Very carefully, so as not to make a sound, I opened my notebook, withdrew my stylus, and, as Caesar started to speak in that unmistakable harsh voice of his, started to write.

It is, if you will forgive a little immodesty at this juncture, the most wonderful invention, my shorthand system. Although I concede that Xenophon had some primitive version nearly four centuries before me, that was more of a private aid to composition than proper stenography, and besides, it was only suitable for Greek, whereas mine compresses the whole of Latin, with its large vocabulary and complex grammar, into four thousand symbols. And it does so, moreover, in such a way that the system can be taught to any willing pupil; in theory even a woman could become a stenographer.

As those who have the skill will know, few things wreak greater havoc with shorthand than trembling fingers. Anxiety renders the digits as dextrous as Lucanian sausages, and I had feared my nervousness that night would be an impediment to a fast script. But once I was underway I found the process oddly soothing. I did not have time to stop and consider what I was writing. I heard the words – Egypt, colonists, public land, commissioners – without remotely comprehending their meaning; my ambition was merely to keep pace with their delivery. In fact, the greatest practical difficulty I had was the heat: it was like a furnace in that confined place; the sweat ran in stinging rivulets into my eyes and the perspiration from my palms made my stylus slippery to grip. Only occasionally, when I had to lean forward and press my eye to the fabric to check the identity of the speaker, did I realise the enormity of the risk I was taking. Then I experienced a sensation of terrifying vulnerability, made worse by the fact that the audience often seemed to be staring directly at me. Catilina in particular appeared fascinated by the scene on the tapestry which concealed me, and my worst moment of the night by far came right at the end, when Crassus declared the conference over. 'And when we meet again,' he said, 'the destiny of all of us, and of Rome, will have been changed for ever.' The moment the applause was finished, Catilina rose from his seat and walked directly towards me, and as I shrank back against the wall, he ran his palm down the tapestry, barely a hand's breadth from my sweating face. The way that bulge travelled before my gaze still has the power to wake me in the night with a shout. But all he wished to do was compliment Crassus on the workmanship, and after a brief discussion about where it had been purchased, and – inevitably with Crassus – how much it had cost, the two men moved away.

I waited a long time, and when at last I dared to look out through my spyhole, I saw that the room was empty. Only the disarrangement of the chairs proved that there had been a meeting at all. It took an effort to restrain myself from wrenching aside the tapestry and making a run for the door. But the agreement was that I would wait for Rufus, so I forced myself to sit hunched in that narrow space, my back to the wall, my knees drawn up and my arms clasped around them. I have no idea how long the conference had lasted, except that it was long enough to fill the four notebooks I had brought with me, nor how long I sat there. It is even possible I fell asleep, because when Rufus returned, the lamps and candles, including my own, had all burned away to darkness. I jumped when he pulled back the tapestry. Without speaking, he put out his hand to help me, and together we crept back through the sleeping house to the storeroom. After I had scrambled up stiffly into the alley, I turned to whisper my thanks.

'No need,' he whispered in return. I could just make out the excited gleam of his eyes in the moonlight – eyes so wide and bright that when he added, 'I enjoyed it,' I knew that it was not mere bravado, but that the young fool was telling the truth.

It was well after midnight when I finally returned home. Everyone else was asleep, but Cicero was waiting up for me in the dining room. I could tell he had been there for hours by the scattering of books around the couch. He sprang up the moment I appeared. 'Well?' he said, and when I nodded to signify my mission had succeeded, he pinched my cheek and declared me the bravest and cleverest secretary any statesman ever had. I pulled the notebooks from my pocket to show him. He flipped one open and held it to the light. 'Ah, of course, they are all your damned hieroglyphics,' he said with a wink. 'Come and sit down and I shall fetch you some wine, and you can tell me everything. Would you like something to eat?' He looked around vaguely; the role of waiter was not one which came naturally to him. Soon I was sitting opposite him with an untouched cup of wine and an apple, my notebooks spread before me, like a schoolboy called to recite his lesson.

I no longer possess those wax tablets, but Cicero kept my subsequent transcription among his most secret papers, and looking at it now I am not surprised that I could not follow the original discussion. The conspirators had obviously met many times before, and their deliberations that night presupposed a good deal of knowledge. There was much talk of legislative timetables, and amendments to drafts of bills, and divisions of responsibilities. So you must not imagine that I simply read out what I had written and all was clear. It took the two of us many hours of puzzling over various cryptic remarks, and fitting this to that, until at last we had the whole thing plainly in sight. Every so often Cicero would exclaim something like 'Clever devils! They are such clever devils!' and get up and prowl around, then return to work some more. And to cut it short, and give you the gist, it turned out that the plot which Caesar and Crassus must have been hatching over many months fell into four parts. First, they aimed to seize control of the state by sweeping the board in the general elections, securing not only both consulships, but also all ten tribunates, and a couple of praetorships besides: the bribery agents reported that the thing was more or less a fait accompli, with Cicero's support slipping daily. The second stage called for the introduction by the tribunes of a great land reform bill in December, which would demand the breaking up of the big publicly owned estates, in particular the fertile plains of Campania, and their immediate redistribution as farms to five thousand of the urban plebs. The third step involved the election in March of ten commissioners, headed by Crassus and Caesar, who would be given immense powers to sell off conquered land abroad, and to use the funds thereby released to compulsorily purchase further vast estates in Italy, for an even greater programme of resettlement. The final stage demanded nothing less than the annexation of Egypt the following summer, using as a pretext the disputed will of one of its dead rulers, King Ptolemy the something-or-other, drawn up some seventeen years earlier, by which he had supposedly bequeathed his entire country to the Roman people; again, the revenue from this was to be given to the commissioners, for further acquisition of land in Italy.

'Dear gods: it is a *coup d'état* disguised as an agrarian reform bill!' cried Cicero, when we finally reached the end of my record. 'This commission of ten, led by Crassus and Caesar, will be the real masters of the country; the consuls and the other magistrates will be mere ciphers. And their domination at home will be maintained in perpetuity by the proceeds of extortion abroad.' He sat back and was silent for a long while, his arms folded, his chin on his chest.

I was drained by what I had endured and longed only for sleep. Yet the early summer light now beginning to seep into the room showed we had worked right through the night and it was already election eve. I was aware of the dawn chorus starting up outside, and soon after that heard the tread of someone coming down the stairs. It was Terentia in her nightdress, her hair awry, her unmade-up face soft with sleep, a shawl drawn around her narrow shoulders. I stood respectfully and looked away in embarrassment. 'Cicero!' she exclaimed, taking no notice of me. 'What on earth are you doing down here at this hour?'

He looked up at her and wearily explained what had happened. She had a very quick mind for anything political or financial – had she not been born a woman, and given her spirit, there is no telling what she might have done – and naturally, the moment she grasped it, she was horrified, for Terentia was an aristocrat to her core, and the notion of privatising state land and giving it to the plebs was, to her, a step on the road to the destruction of Rome.

'You must lead the fight against it,' she urged Cicero. 'This could win you the election. All the decent men will rally to you.'

'Ah, but will they?' Cicero picked up one of my notebooks. 'Outright opposition to this could rebound on me badly. A large faction in the senate, half of them patriotic and the other half just plain greedy, has always favoured seizing Egypt. And out on the streets, the cry of "Free farms for all!" is far more likely to gain Catilina and Hybrida votes than cost them. No, I am trapped.' He stared at the transcript of the conference and shook his head slowly, like an artist ruefully contemplating the work of some talented rival. 'It really is an extraordinary scheme – a stroke of true political genius. Only Caesar could have dreamed it up. And as for Crassus – for a down-payment of just twenty million, he can expect to gain control of most of Italy and the whole of Egypt. Even you would concede that that is a good return on your investment.'

'But you have to do *something*,' persisted Terentia. 'You cannot simply allow it to happen.'

'And what exactly would you have me do?'

'And you are supposed to be the cleverest man in Rome?' she asked in exasperation. 'Is it not obvious? Go to the senate this morning and expose what they are plotting. Denounce them!'

'A brilliant tactic, Terentia,' responded Cicero sarcastically. (I was beginning to find my position between them increasingly uncomfortable.) 'I both reveal the existence of a popular measure and denounce it at the same time. You are not listening to me: the people who stand to benefit the most from this are *my* supporters.'

'Well then, you have only yourself to blame for depending on such a rabble in the first place! This is the problem with your demagoguery, Cicero – you may think you can control the mob, but the mob will always end up devouring you. Did you seriously believe you could beat men like Crassus and Catilina when it came to a public auction of principles?' Cicero grunted irritably; however, I noticed he did not argue with her. 'But tell me,' she continued, needling away at him, 'if this "extraordinary scheme", as you call it – or "criminal enterprise", as I should prefer it – really is as popular as you say, why all this skulking around at night? Why do they not come out with it openly?'

'Because, my dear Terentia, the aristocrats think like you. They would never stand for it. First it will be the great public estates that are broken up and redistributed, next it will be their private domains. Every time Caesar and Crassus give a man a farm, they will create another client for themselves. And once the patricians start to lose control of the land, they are finished. Besides, how do you think Catulus or Hortensius would react to being ordered around by a ten-man commission elected by the people? The people! To them it would seem like a revolution – Tiberius Gracchus all over again.' Cicero threw the notebook back on to the dining table. 'No, they would scheme and bribe and kill to preserve the status quo, just as they always have done.'

'And they would be right!' Terentia glowered down at him. Her fists were clenched; I almost expected her to hit him. 'They were right to take away the powers of the tribunes, just as they were right to try to stop that provincial parvenu Pompey. And if you had any sense, you would go to them now with this, and you would say to them, "Gentlemen, this is what Crassus and Caesar are proposing to do – support me and I shall try to put a stop to it!"'

Cicero sighed in exasperation and slumped back on to the couch. For a while he was silent. But then he suddenly glanced up at her. 'By heavens, Terentia,' he said quietly, 'what a clever shrew you are.' He jumped up and kissed her on the cheek. 'My brilliant, clever shrew – you are quite correct. Or rather, half correct, for there is actually no need for *me* to do anything with it at all. I should simply pass it to Hortensius. Tiro, how long would it take you to make a fair copy of this transcript – not of all of it necessarily, just enough to whet Hortensius's appetite?'

'A few hours,' I said, bewildered by his dramatic change of mood.

'Quick!' he said, more alive with excitement than I can ever remember seeing him. 'Fetch me a pen and paper!'

I did as I was ordered. He dipped the nib in the inkpot, thought about it for a moment, and then wrote the following, as Terentia and I watched over his shoulder:

From: Marcus Tullius Cicero
To: Quintus Hortensius Hortalus
Greetings!
I feel it is my patriotic duty to share with you in confidence this record of a meeting held last night at the home of M. Crassus, involving G. Caesar, L. Catilina, G. Hybrida, P. Sura, and various candidates for the tribuneship whose names will be familiar to you. I intend to tackle certain of these gentlemen in a speech to the senate today, and if you would care to discuss the matter further, I shall be afterwards at the home of our esteemed mutual friend T. Atticus.

'That should do the trick,' he said, blowing on the ink to dry it. 'Now, Tiro, make as full a copy of your notes as you can, being sure to include all the passages which will make their blue blood run cold, and deliver it, together with my letter, personally into the hands of Hortensius – personally, mark you: not to any aide – at least an hour before the senate meets. Also, send one of the lads with a message to Atticus, asking him to call on me before I leave.' He gave me the letter and hurried out of the door.

'Do you want me to ask Sositheus or Laurea to bring in your clients?' I called after him, for by now I could hear them queuing outside in the street. 'When do you want the doors opened?'

'No clients in the house this morning!' he shouted in reply, already halfway up the stairs. 'They can accompany me to the senate if they wish. You have work to do and I have a speech to compose.'

His footsteps thumped along the boards above our heads to his room and I found myself alone with Terentia. She touched her hand to her cheek where her husband had kissed her and looked at me in puzzlement. 'Speech?' she said. 'What speech is he talking about?'

But I had to confess that I had no idea, and thus can claim no hand in, or even prior knowledge of, that extraordinary piece of invective which all the world knows by the name of *In toga candida*.

*

I wrote as quickly and as neatly as my tiredness would allow, setting out my document like the script of a play, with the name of the speaker first, and then his remarks. I excised a great deal of what I considered irrelevant material, but then at the end I wondered if I was really competent enough to judge. Therefore I decided to keep my notebooks with me, in case I might need to refer to them during the day. Once it was done, I sealed it and placed it in a cylinder, and set off. I had to push my way through the throng of clients and well-wishers blocking the street, who clutched at my tunic and demanded to know when the senator would appear.

Hortensius's house on the Palatine was subsequently bought, many years later, by our dear and beloved emperor, so that gives you an idea of how fine it was. I had never been to it before and I had to stop several times and ask for directions. It was right at the top of the hill, on the southwestern side overlooking the Tiber, and one might have been in the country rather than the city, with its view over the dark green trees to the gentle silver curve of the river and the fields beyond. His brother-in-law Catulus, as I think I have mentioned, owned the house next door, and the whole spot – fragrant with the scent of honeysuckle and myrtle, and silent save for the twittering of the birds – was redolent of good taste and old money. Even the steward looked like an aristocrat, and when I said I had a personal message for his master from Senator Cicero, you might have thought I had farted, such an exquisite expression of distaste spread across his bony face at the mention of the name. He wanted to take the cylinder from me, but I refused, so he bade me wait in the atrium, where the masks of all Hortensius's consular ancestors stared down at me with their blank, dead eyes. Displayed on a three-legged table in the corner was a sphinx, wonderfully carved from a single huge piece of ivory, and I realised that this must be the very sphinx which Verres had given to his advocate all those years ago, and which Cicero had made his joke about. I was just stooping to examine it when Hortensius came into the room behind me.

'Well,' he said, as I stood up, feeling guilty, 'I never thought to see a representative of Marcus Cicero under the roof of my ancestors. What is all this about?'

He was wearing his full senatorial rig, but with slippers on his feet instead of shoes, and was obviously still getting ready to depart for the morning's debate. It seemed strange to me, too, to see the old enemy unarmoured, as it were, outside the arena. I gave him Cicero's letter, which he broke open and read in front of me. Immediately he saw the names it mentioned he gave me a sharp glance, and I could tell that he was hooked, although he was too well bred to show it.

'Tell him I shall inspect it at my leisure,' he said, taking the document from me, and strolled back the way he had come, as if nothing less interesting had ever been placed in his manicured hands – although I am sure that the moment he was out of sight he must have run to his library and broken open the seal. For myself, I went back out into the fresh air and descended to the city by the Caci Steps, partly because I had time to kill before the senate convened and could afford to take a long way round, and partly because the other route took me nearer to the house of Crassus than I cared to go. I came out into that district on the Etruscan road where all the perfume and incense shops are located, and the scented air and the weight of my tiredness combined to make me feel almost drugged. My mood was oddly separated from the real world and its concerns. By this time tomorrow, I remember thinking, the voting on the Field of Mars would be well underway, and we would probably know whether Cicero was to be consul or not, and in either event the sun would shine and in the autumn it would rain. I lingered in the Forum Boarium and watched the people buying their flowers and their fruit and all the rest of it, and wondered what it would be like not to have any interest in politics, but simply to live, as the poet has it, *vita umbratilis*, 'a life in the shade'. That was what I planned to do when Cicero gave me my freedom and my farm. I would eat the fruit I grew and drink the milk of the goats I reared; I would shut my gate at night and never give a fig for another election. It was the closest to wisdom I have ever come.

By the time I eventually reached the forum, two hundred or more senators had assembled in the senaculum and were being watched by a crowd of curious gawpers – out-of-towners to judge by their rustic dress, who had come to Rome for the elections. Figulus was sitting on his consular chair in the doorway of the senate house, the augurs beside him, waiting for a quorum, and every so often there was a minor commotion as a candidate erupted into the forum with his corona of supporters. I saw Catilina arrive, with his curious mixture of young aristocrats and the dregs of the streets, and then Hybrida, whose rackety assemblage of debtors and gamblers, such as Sabidius and Panthera, seemed quite respectable by comparison. The senators began to file into the chamber, and I was just beginning to wonder if some mishap had befallen Cicero when, from the direction of the Argiletum, came the noise of drums and flutes and then two columns of young men rounded the corner into the forum, carrying freshly cut boughs above their heads, with children scampering excitedly all around them. These were followed by a mass of respectable Roman knights led by Atticus, and then came Quintus with a dozen or so back-bench senators. Some maids were scattering rose petals. It was a vastly better show than any of its rivals had managed, and the crowd around me greeted it with applause. At the centre of all this whirling activity, as in the eye of a tornado, walked the candidate himself, clad in the gleaming *toga candida* which had already seen him through three victorious election campaigns. It was rare that I was able to watch him from a distance – usually I was tucked in behind him – and for the first time I appreciated what a natural actor he was, in that when he donned his costume he found his character. All those qualities which the traditional whiteness was supposed to symbolise – clarity, honesty, purity – seemed to be personified in his solid frame and steady gaze as he walked, unseeing, past me. I could tell by the way he moved, and his air of detachment, that he was heavy with a speech. I fell in at the back of the procession and heard the cheers from his supporters as he entered the chamber, and the answering cat-calls of his opponents.

We were kept back until the last of the senators had gone in, and then permitted to run to the bar of the house. I secured myself my usual decent vantage point beside the door jamb and was immediately aware of someone squeezing in beside me. It was Atticus, looking white with nerves. 'How does he find it within himself to do this?' he asked, but before I could say anything, Figulus got up to report on the failure of his bill at the popular assembly. He droned on for a while, and then called on Mucius to explain his conduct in vetoing a measure which had been adopted by the house. There was an oppressive, restless air in the chamber. I could see Catilina and Hybrida among the aristocrats, with Catulus seated just in front of them on the consular bench, and Crassus a few places along from him. Caesar was on the same side of the chamber, on the bench reserved for ex-aediles. Mucius got up and in a dignified way explained that his sacred office called on him to act in the interests of the people, and that the *lex Figula*, far from protecting those interests, was a threat to their safety and an insult to their honour.

'Nonsense!' shouted a voice from the opposite side of the aisle, which I recognised at once as Cicero's. 'You were bought!'

Atticus gripped my arm. 'Here he goes!' he whispered.

'My conscience—' continued Mucius.

'Your conscience had nothing to do with it, you liar! You sold yourself like a whore!'

There came that low grumble of noise which is caused by several hundred men all muttering to one another at once, and suddenly Cicero was on his feet, his arm outstretched, demanding the floor. At that same moment I heard a voice behind me calling to be let through, and we shuffled out of the way to allow a late-arriving senator, who proved to be Hortensius, access to the chamber. He hurried down the aisle, bowed to the consul, and took his place next to Catulus, with whom he quickly struck up a whispered conversation. By this time Cicero's supporters among the *pedarii* were bellowing that he should be allowed to speak, which, given that he was a praetorian, and outranked Mucius, he was undeniably entitled to do. Very reluctantly, Mucius allowed himself to be pulled down by the senators seated around him, whereupon Cicero pointed at him – his white-draped arm held out straight and rigid, like some statue of avenging Justice – and declared: 'A whore you are, Mucius – yes, and a treacherous one at that, for only yesterday you declared to the popular assembly that I was not fit to be consul – I, the first man to whom you turned when you were prosecuted for robbery! Good enough to defend you, Mucius, but not good enough to defend the Roman people, is that it? But why should I care what you say about me, when the whole world knows you were paid to slander me?'

Mucius turned scarlet. He shook his fist and started shouting insults in return, but I could not make them out over the general tumult. Cicero regarded him with contempt, then held up his hand for silence. 'But who is Mucius in any case?' he said, spitting out the name and dismissing it with a flick of his fingers. 'Mucius is just one solitary whore in a whole hired troupe of common prostitutes. Their master is a man of noble birth, bribery his chosen instrument – and believe me, gentlemen, he plays it like a flute! He is a briber of juries, a briber of voters and a briber of tribunes. Little wonder he loathed our bill against bribery, and that the method he used to stop it should have been – bribery!' He paused and lowered his voice. 'I should like to share some information with the house.' The senate now went very quiet. 'Last night, Antonius Hybrida and Sergius Catilina met, together with others, at the house of this man of noble birth—'

'Name him!' shouted someone, and for a moment I thought that Cicero might actually do so. He stared across the aisle at Crassus with such calculated intensity that he might as well have gone over and touched him on the shoulder, so clear was it whom he had in mind. Crassus sat up slightly in his seat and slowly leaned forward, never taking his eyes from Cicero: he must have wondered what was coming. One could feel the entire chamber holding its breath. But Cicero had different quarry to chase, and with an almost palpable effort of will, he dragged his gaze away from Crassus.

'This man, as I say, of noble birth, having bribed away the bribery bill, has a new scheme in mind. He intends now to bribe his way to the consulship, not for himself but for his two creatures, Hybrida and Catilina.'

Naturally, both men instantly jumped up to protest, as Cicero must have calculated they would. But as their rank was no higher than his, he was entitled to leave them standing. 'Well, there they are,' he said, turning to the benches behind him, 'the best that money can buy!' He let the laughter build and chose the perfect moment to add: 'As we lawyers say – *caveat emptor*!'

Nothing is more injurious to a politician's dignity and authority than to be mocked, and if it happens it is vitally important to appear entirely unconcerned. But Hybrida and Catilina, buffeted by gusts of merriment from every side, could not decide whether to remain defiantly standing or to sit and feign indifference. They ended up trying to do both, bobbing up and down like a pair of workmen at either end of a pump-handle, which only increased the general hilarity. Catilina in particular was obviously losing his temper, for like many arrogant men the one thing he could not abide was to be teased. Caesar tried to come to their rescue, rising to demand what point Cicero was trying to make, but Cicero refused to acknowledge his intervention and the consul, enjoying himself like everyone else, declined to call Cicero to order.

'Let us take the lesser first,' continued Cicero, after both his targets had finally sunk back in to their seats. 'You, Hybrida, should never even have been elected praetor, and would not have been had I not taken pity on you, and recommended you to the centuries. You live openly with a courtesan, you cannot speak in public, you can barely remember your own name without the assistance of a *nomenclator*. You were a thief under Sulla, and a drunkard thereafter. You are, in short, a joke; but a joke of the worst sort – a joke that has gone on too long.'

The chamber was much quieter now, for these were insults which would oblige a man to be your enemy for life, and as Cicero turned towards Catilina, Atticus's anxious grip on my arm tightened. 'As for you, Catilina, is it not a prodigy and a portent of evil times that you should hope for, or even think of, the consulship? For from whom do you ask it? From the chiefs of the state, who, two years ago, refused even to allow you to stand for it? Do you ask it from the order of knights which you have slaughtered? Or from the people, who still remember the monstrous cruelty with which you butchered their leader – my kinsman – Gratidianus, and carried his still-breathing head through the streets to the Temple of Apollo? Do you ask it from the senators, who by their own authority had almost stripped you of all your honours, and surrendered you in chains to the Africans?'

'I was acquitted!' roared Catilina, leaping back to his feet.

'Acquitted!' mocked Cicero. 'You? Acquitted? You – who disgraced yourself by every sort of sexual perversion and profligacy; who dyed your hands in the wickedest murder, who plundered the allies, who violated the laws and the courts of justice? You, who married in adultery the mother of the daughter you first debauched? Acquitted? Then I can only imagine that Roman knights must have been liars; that the documentary evidence of a most honourable city was false; that Quintus Metellus Pius told lies; that Africa told lies. Acquitted! O wretched man, not to see that you were not acquitted by that decision, but only reserved for some more severe tribunal, and some more fearful punishment!'

This would have been too much even for an equable man to sit through, but in Catilina it induced nothing short of murderous insanity. He gave an animal's bellow of primitive rage and launched himself over the bench in front of him, crashing between Hortensius and Catulus, and diving across the aisle in an effort to reach his tormentor. But of course this was precisely the reaction Cicero had been trying to goad him into. He flinched but stood his ground as Quintus and a few other ex-soldiers scrambled to form a cordon around him – not that there was any need, for Catilina, big though he was, had been seized at once by the consul's lictors. His friends, among them Crassus and Caesar, quickly had him by the arms and started dragging him back to his seat as he writhed and roared and kicked in fury. The whole of the senate was on its feet, trying to see what was happening, and Figulus had to suspend the session until order was restored.

When the sitting resumed, Hybrida and Catilina, as custom dictated, were given the opportunity to respond, and each man, quivering with outrage, tipped a bucketful of the usual insults over Cicero's head – ambitious, untrustworthy, scheming, 'new man', foreigner, evader of military service, coward – while their supporters cheered them dutifully. But neither had Cicero's flair for invective, and even their most dedicated partisans must have been dismayed by their failure to answer his central charge: that their candidacies were based on bribery by a mysterious third party. It was noticeable that Hortensius and even Catulus offered them only the most half-hearted applause. As for Cicero, he put on a professional mask and sat smiling and unconcerned throughout their shrill tirades, seemingly no more concerned than a duck in a rainstorm. Only afterwards – after Quintus and his military friends had escorted him rapidly out of the chamber to prevent a further assault by Catilina, and only after we had reached the safety of Atticus's house on the Quirinal and the door had been locked and barred – only then did he appear to realise the enormity of what he had done.

XVIII

There was nothing left for Cicero now except to wait for the reaction of Hortensius. We passed the hours in the dry stillness of Atticus's library, surrounded by all that ancient wisdom, under the gaze of the great philosophers, while beyond the terrace the day ripened and faded and the view over the city became yellower and dustier in the heat of the July afternoon. I should like to record that we took down the occasional volume and spent the time swapping the thoughts of Epicurus or Zeno or Aristotle, or that Cicero said something profound about democracy. But in truth no one was much in the mood for political theory, least of all Quintus, who had scheduled a campaign appearance in the busy Porticus Aemilia and fretted that his brother was losing valuable canvassing time. We relived the drama of Cicero's speech – 'You should have seen Crassus's face when he thought I was about to name him!' – and pondered the likely response of the aristocrats. If they did not take the bait, Cicero had placed himself in a highly dangerous position. Every so often, he would ask me if I was absolutely certain that Hortensius had read his letter, and yet again I would reply that I had no doubt, for he had done so right in front of me. 'Then we shall give him another hour,' Cicero would say, and resume his restless pacing, occasionally stopping to make some cutting remark to Atticus: 'Are they always this punctual, these smart friends of yours?' or 'Tell me, is it considered a crime against good breeding to consult a clock?'

It was the tenth hour by Atticus's exquisite sundial when at last one of his slaves came into the library to announce that Hortensius's steward had arrived.

'So now we are supposed to negotiate with his servants?' muttered Cicero. But he was so anxious for news that he hurried out into the atrium himself, and we all went with him. Waiting there was the same bony, supercilious fellow whom I had encountered at Hortensius's house that morning; he was not much more polite now. His message was that he had come in Hortensius's two-seater carriage to collect Cicero and convey him to a meeting with his master.

'But I must accompany him,' protested Quintus.

'My orders are simply to bring Senator Cicero,' responded the steward. 'The meeting is highly sensitive and confidential. Only one other person is required – that secretary of his, who has the quick way with words.'

I was not at all happy about this, and nor was Quintus – I out of a cowardly desire to avoid being cross-examined by Hortensius, he because it was a snub, and also perhaps (to be more charitable) because he was worried for his brother's safety. 'What if it is a trap?' he asked. 'What if Catilina is there, or intercepts you on your journey?'

'You will be under the protection of Senator Hortensius,' said the steward stiffly. 'I give you his word of honour in the presence of all these witnesses.'

'It will be all right, Quintus,' said Cicero, laying a reassuring hand on his brother's arm. 'It is not in Hortensius's interests for any injury to befall me. Besides,' he smiled, 'I am a friend of Atticus here, and what better guarantee of safe passage is there than that? Come along, Tiro. Let us find out what he has to say.'

We left the relative safety of the library and went down into the street, where a smart *carpentum* was waiting, with Hortensius's livery painted on its side. The steward sat up at the front next to the driver, while I sat in the back with Cicero and we lurched off down the hill. But instead of turning south towards the Palatine, as we had expected, we headed north, towards the Fontinalian Gate, joining the stream of traffic leaving the city at the end of the day. Cicero had pulled the folds of his white toga up over his head, ostensibly to shield himself from the clouds of dust thrown up by the wheels, but actually to avoid any of his voters seeing him travelling in a vehicle belonging to Hortensius. Once we were out of the city, however, he pulled his hood down. He was clearly not at all happy to be leaving the precincts of Rome, for despite his brave words he knew that a fatal accident out here would be very easy to arrange. The sun was big and low, just beginning to set behind those massive family tombs which line the road. The poplars threw elongated shadows which fell jet black across our path, like crevasses. For a while we were stuck behind a plodding bullock cart. But then the coachman cracked his whip and we raced forward, just narrowly managing to overtake it before a chariot rattled past us, heading towards the city. I guess we both must have realised by then where we were going, and Cicero pulled his hood up again and folded his arms, his head down. What thoughts must have been spinning through his mind! We turned off the road and began climbing a steep hillside, following a driveway freshly laid with gravel. It took us on a winding journey over gushing brooks and through gloomy, scented pine groves where pigeons called to one another in the dusk, until eventually we came to a huge pair of open gates, and beyond them an immense villa set in its own park, which I recognised from the model Gabinius had displayed to the jealous mob in the forum as the palace of Lucullus.

For years thereafter, whenever I smelt fresh cement and wet paint, I would think of Lucullus and that echoing mausoleum he had built for himself beyond the walls of Rome. What a brilliant, melancholy figure he was – perhaps the greatest general the aristocrats had produced for fifty years, yet robbed of ultimate victory in the East by the arrival of Pompey, and doomed by the political intrigues of his enemies, among them Cicero, to linger outside Rome for years, unhonoured and unable even to attend the senate, for by crossing the city's boundaries he would forfeit his right to a triumph. Because he still retained military *imperium*, there were sentries in the grounds, and lictors with their bundles of rods and axes waited sullenly in the hall – so many lictors, in fact, that Cicero calculated that a second general on active service must be on the premises. 'Do you think it's possible that Quintus Metellus is here as well?' he whispered, as we followed the steward into the cavernous interior. 'Dear gods, I think he must be!'

We passed through various rooms stuffed with loot from the war until at last we reached the great chamber known as the Room of Apollo, where a group of six were talking beneath a mural of the deity shooting a fiery arrow from his golden bow. At the sound of our footsteps on the marble floor, the conversation ceased and there was a loud silence. Quintus Metellus was indeed among them – stouter, greyer and more weatherbeaten following his years of command in Crete, but still very much the same man who had attempted to intimidate the Sicilians into dropping their case against Verres. On one side of Metellus was his old courtroom ally Hortensius, whose bland and handsome face was expressionless, and on the other, Catulus, as thin and sharp as a blade. Isauricus, the grand old man of the senate, was also present – seventy years old he must have been on that July evening, but he did not look it (he was one of those types who never look it: he was to live to be ninety, and attend the funerals of almost everyone else in the room); I noticed he was holding the transcript I had delivered to Hortensius. The two Lucullus brothers completed the sextet. Marcus, the younger, I knew as a familiar figure from the senate front bench. Lucius, the famous general, paradoxically I did not recognise at all, for he had been away fighting for eighteen out of the past twenty-three years. He was in his middle fifties, and I quickly saw why Pompey was so passionately jealous of him – why they had literally come to blows when they met in Galatia to effect the handover in the Eastern command – for Lucullus had a chilly grandeur which made even Catulus seem slightly common.

It was Hortensius who ended the embarrassment, and who stepped forward to introduce Cicero to Lucullus. Cicero extended his hand, and for a moment I thought Lucullus might refuse to shake it, for he would only have known Cicero as a partisan of Pompey, and as one of those populist politicians who had helped engineer his dismissal. But finally he took it, very gingerly, as one might pick up a soiled sponge in a latrine. 'Imperator,' said Cicero, bowing politely. He nodded to Metellus as well: 'Imperator.'

'And who is that?' demanded Isauricus, pointing at me.

'That is my secretary, Tiro,' said Cicero, 'who recorded the meeting at the house of Crassus.'

'Well, I for one do not believe a word of it,' replied Isauricus, brandishing the transcript at me. 'No one could have written down all of this as it was uttered. It is beyond human capacity.'

'Tiro has developed his own system of stenography,' explained Cicero. 'Let him show you the actual records he made last night.'

I pulled out the notebooks from my pocket and handed them around.

'Remarkable,' said Hortensius, examining my script intently. 'So these symbols substitute for sounds, do they? Or for entire words?'

'Words mostly,' I replied, 'and common phrases.'

'Prove it,' said Catulus belligerently. 'Take down what I say.' And giving me barely a moment to open a fresh notebook and take up my stylus, he went on rapidly: 'If what I have read here is true, the state is threatened with civil war as a result of a criminal conspiracy. If what I have read is false, it is the wickedest forgery in our history. For my own part, I do not believe it is true, because I do not believe such a record could have been produced by a living hand. That Catilina is a hothead, we all know well enough, but he is a true and noble Roman, not a devious and ambitious outsider, and I will take his word over that of a new man – always! What is it you want from us, Cicero? You cannot seriously believe, after all that has happened between us, that I could possibly support you for the consulship? So what is it?'

'Nothing,' replied Cicero pleasantly. 'I came across some information which I thought might be of interest to you. I passed it along to Hortensius, that is all. You brought me out here, remember? I did not ask to come. I might more appropriately ask: What do *you* gentlemen want? Do you want to be trapped between Pompey and his armies in the East, and Crassus and Caesar and the urban mob in Italy, and gradually have the life squeezed out of you? Do you want to rely for your protection on the two men you are backing for consul – the one stupid, the other insane – who cannot even manage their own households, let alone the affairs of the nation? Is that what you want? Well, good then. I at least have an easy conscience. I have done my patriotic duty by alerting you to what is happening, even though you have never been any friends of mine. I also believe I have demonstrated by my courage in the senate today my willingness to stand up to these criminals. No other candidate for consul has done it, or will in the future. I have made them my enemies and shown you what they are like. But from you, Catulus, and from all of you, *I* want *nothing*, and if all you wish to do is insult me, I bid you a good evening.'

He spun around and began walking towards the door, with me in tow, and I guess that must have felt to him like the longest walk he ever took, because we had almost reached the shadowy antechamber – and with it, surely, the black void of political oblivion – when a voice (it was that of Lucullus himself) shouted out: 'Read it back!' Cicero halted, and we both turned around. 'Read it back,' repeated Lucullus. 'What Catulus said just now.'

Cicero nodded at me, and I fumbled for my notebook. '"If what I have read here is true",' I began, reciting in that flat, strange way of stenography being read back, '"the state is threatened with civil war as a result of a criminal conspiracy if what I have read is false it is the wickedest forgery in our history for my own part I do not believe it is true because I do not believe such a record could have been produced by a living hand—"'

'He could have memorised that,' objected Catulus. 'It is all just a cheap trick, of the sort you might see done by a conjuror in the forum.'

'And the latter part,' persisted Lucullus. 'Read out the last thing your master said.'

I ran my finger down my notation. '"... never been any friends of mine I also believe I have demonstrated by my courage in the senate today my willingess to stand up to these criminals no other candidate for consul has done it or will in the future I have made them my enemies and shown you what they are like but from you Catulus and from all of you I want nothing and if all you wish to do is insult me I bid you a good evening."'

Isauricus whistled. Hortensius nodded, and said something like 'I told you' or 'I warned you' – I cannot remember exactly – to which Metellus responded, 'Yes, well, I have to say, that is proof enough for me.' Catulus merely glared at me.

'Come back, Cicero,' said Lucullus, beckoning to him. 'I am satisfied. The record is genuine. Let us put aside for the time being the question of who needs whom the most, and start from the premise that each of us needs the other.'

'I am still not convinced,' grumbled Catulus.

'Then let me convince you with a single word,' said Hortensius impatiently. 'Caesar. Caesar – with Crassus's gold, two consuls and ten tribunes behind him!'

'So, really, we must talk with such people?' Catulus sighed. 'Well, Cicero perhaps,' he conceded. 'But we certainly do not need *you*,' he snapped, pointing at me, just as I was moving, as always, to follow my master. 'I do not want that creature and his tricks within a mile of me, listening to what we say, and writing everything down in his damned untrustworthy way. If anything is to pass between us, it must never be divulged.'

Cicero hesitated. 'All right,' he said reluctantly, and he gave me an apologetic look. 'Wait outside, Tiro.'

I had no business to feel aggrieved. I was merely a slave, after all: an extra hand, a tool – a 'creature', as Catulus put it. But nevertheless I felt my humiliation keenly. I folded up my notebook and walked into the antechamber, and then kept on walking, through all those echoing, freshly stuccoed state rooms – Venus, Mercury, Mars, Jupiter – as the slaves in their cushioned slippers moved silently with their glowing tapers among the gods, lighting the lamps and candelabra. I went out into the soft warm dusk of the park, where the cicadas were singing, and for reasons which I cannot even now articulate I found that I was weeping, but I suppose I must have been very tired.

It was almost dawn when I awoke, stiff in my limbs and damp with cold from the dew. For a moment I had no idea where I was or how I had got there, but then I realised I was on a stone bench close to the front of the house, and that it was Cicero who had woken me. His face looming over me was grim. 'We have finished here,' he said. 'We must get back to the city quickly.' He glanced across to where the carriage was waiting, and put his finger to his lips to warn me not to say anything in front of Hortensius's steward. So it was in silence that we clambered into the *carpentum*, and as we left the park I remember turning for a final look at the great villa, the torches still burning along its terraces, but losing their sharpness now as the pale morning light came up; of the other aristocrats there was no sign.

Cicero, conscious that in little more than two hours he would have to leave his house to go down to the Field of Mars for the election, kept urging the driver to make better speed, and those poor horses must have been whipped until their hides were raw. But we were lucky that the roads were empty, save for a few very early voters walking into town for the election, and we hurtled along at a great speed, reaching the Fontinalian Gate just as it was opening, and then rattled up the paved slopes of the Esquiline Hill faster than a man could sprint. Just before the Temple of Tellus, Cicero told the driver to stop and let us out, so that we could walk the last part of the way – an order which puzzled me, until I realised that he wanted to avoid being seen by the crowd of his supporters which was already beginning to assemble in the street outside his front door. He strode on ahead of me in that way of his, with his hands clasped behind his back, still keeping his thoughts to himself, and I noticed that his once-brilliant white toga was stained with dirt. We went down the side of the house and through the little door at the back which the servants used, and there we bumped into Terentia's business manager, the odious Philotimus, who was obviously on his way back from some nocturnal assignation with one of the slave girls. Cicero did not even see him, so preoccupied was he with what had happened and what was to come. His eyes were red with tiredness, his face and hair brown with dust from the journey. He told me to go and open up the door and let the people in. Then he went upstairs.

Among the first across the threshold was Quintus, who naturally demanded to know what was happening. He and the others had waited for our return in Atticus's library until nearly midnight, and he was furious and anxious in equal measure. This put me in an awkward spot, and I could only stammer that I would prefer it if he addressed his questions directly to his brother. To be honest, seeing Cicero and his bitterest enemies all together in such a setting now seemed so unreal to me, I could almost have believed I had dreamed it. Quintus was not satisfied, but fortunately I was saved further embarrassment by the sheer number of visitors pouring through the door. I escaped by pretending I had to check everything was ready in the tablinum, and from there I slipped into my little cubicle and rinsed my neck and face with tepid water from my basin.

When I next saw Cicero, an hour later, he once again demonstrated those remarkable powers of recuperation which I have observed to be the distinguishing mark of all successful politicians. Watching him come down the stairs in a freshly laundered white toga, his face washed and shaved and his hair combed and scented, no one could have guessed that he had not slept for the past two nights. The cramped house by this time was packed with his supporters. Cicero had the infant Marcus, whose first birthday it was, carefully balanced on his shoulders, and such a cheer went up when the two of them appeared, it must have shaken off several roof tiles: no wonder the poor child started crying. Cicero quickly lifted him down, lest this be seen as a bad omen for the day, and handed him to Terentia, who was standing behind him on the stairs. He smiled at her, and said something, and at that moment I realised for the first time just how close they had become over the years: that what had started as a marriage of convenience was now a most formidable partnership. I could not hear what passed between them, and then he came down into the crowd.

So many people had turned out it was hard for him to struggle through the tablinum to the atrium, where Quintus, Frugi and Atticus were surrounded by a very decent showing of senators. Among those present to demonstrate their support were Cicero's old friend Servius Sulpicius; Gallus, the renowned scholar of judisprudence, who had refused to run himself; the elder Frugi, with whom Cicero was forming a family connection; Marcellinus, who had supported him ever since the Verres trial; and all those senators he had represented in the courts, such as Cornelius, Fundanius, Orchivius, and also Fonteius, the corrupt ex-governor of Gaul. Indeed, as I struggled through the rooms after Cicero, it was as if the past ten years had all sprung back to life, so many half-forgotten courtroom struggles were represented there; even Popillius Laenas, whose nephew Cicero had rescued from a charge of parricide on the day Sthenius came to see us. The atmosphere was more akin to a family festival than an election day, and Cicero as ever was in his element on these occasions: I doubt if there was one supporter whose hand he did not shake, and with whom he did not establish one brief moment of rapport, sufficient to leave the other man feeling he had been specially singled out.

Just before we left, Quintus pulled him to one side to ask, quite angrily as I recall it, where on earth he had been all night – he had almost sent men out looking for him – to which Cicero, conscious of the people all around him, replied quietly that he would tell him later. But that only made Quintus more aggrieved. 'Who do you think I am?' he demanded. 'Your maid? Tell me now!' And so Cicero told him then very rapidly about the journey out to the palace of Lucullus and the presence there of Metellus and Catulus, as well as Hortensius and Isauricus.

'The whole patrician gang!' whispered Quintus excitedly, his irritation entirely forgotten. 'My gods, whoever would have thought it? And are they going to support us?'

'We talked for hour after hour, but in the end they would not commit themselves until they had spoken to the other great families,' replied Cicero, glancing nervously around in case anyone was listening, but the din was too great for him to be overheard. 'Hortensius, I think, would have agreed on the spot. Catulus remains instinctively opposed. The others will do what self-interest dictates. We shall just have to wait and see.'

Atticus, who had heard all this, said, 'But they believed in the truth of the evidence you showed them?'

'I think so, yes. Thanks to Tiro. But we can discuss all this later. Put on your bravest faces, gentlemen,' he said, gripping the hands of each of us in turn, 'we have an election to win!'

Seldom can a candidate have staged a more splendid show than Cicero did during his walk down to the Field of Mars, and for that much credit must go to Quintus. We made up a parade of three or four hundred, with musicians, young men carrying green boughs wound with ribbons, girls with rose petals, actor friends of Cicero's from the theatre, senators, knights, merchants, stall-holders, regular spectators from the law courts, guild officers, legal clerks, representatives from the Roman communities in Sicily and Nearer Gaul. We set up a terrific noise of cheering and whistling as we came on to the campus and there was a great surge of voters towards us. It is always said of elections, in my experience, that whichever one is in progress at the time is the most significant there has ever been, and on that day, at least, it was arguably true, with the added excitement that no one knew how it would turn out, given the activity among the bribery agents, the sheer number of candidates and the enmity between them following Cicero's attack on Catilina and Hybrida in the senate.

We had anticipated trouble, and Quintus had taken the precaution of stationing some of our heftier supporters immediately behind and in front of his brother. As we approached the voting pens I felt increasingly worried, for I could see Catilina and his followers up ahead, waiting beside the returning officer's tent. Some of these ruffians jeered us as we arrived at the enclosure, but Catilina himself, after a brief and contemptuous glance in Cicero's direction, resumed talking to Hybrida. I muttered to young Frugi that I was surprised he did not at least put on a show of intimidation – that, after all, was his usual tactic – to which Frugi, who was no fool, responded: 'He does not feel he needs to – he is so confident of victory.' His words filled me with unease.

But then a very remarkable thing happened. Cicero and all the other senators seeking either the consulship or the praetorship – perhaps two dozen men – were standing in the small area reserved for the candidates, surrounded by a low sheep fence to separate them from their supporters. The presiding consul, Marcius Figulus, was talking to the augur, checking that all was propitious for the ballot to begin, when just at that moment Hortensius appeared, followed by a retinue of about twenty men. The crowd parted to let him through. He approached the fence and called to Cicero, who interrupted his conversation with one of the other candidates – Cornificius, I think it was – and went over to him. This in itself surprised people, for it was known that there was little love lost between the two old rivals, and there was a stir among the onlookers; Catilina and Hybrida certainly both turned to stare. For a moment or two, Cicero and Hortensius regarded one another, then simultaneously they nodded, and each reached out and slowly shook the hand of the other. No word was uttered, and with the handclasp still in place, Hortensius half turned to the men behind him and raised Cicero's arm above his head. A great shout of applause, mingled with some boos and groans, broke out from the watching crowd, for there was no doubt what the gesture meant: I certainly never expected to see anything like it. *The aristocrats were supporting Cicero!* Immediately, Hortensius's attendants turned and disappeared into the throng, presumably to spread the word among the nobles' agents in the centuries that they were to switch their support. I risked a look at Catilina and saw on his face an expression of puzzlement rather than anything else, for the incident, though obviously significant – people were still buzzing about it – was so fleeting that Hortensius was already walking away. An instant later, Figulus called to the candidates to follow him to the platform so that the voting could begin.

You can always spot a fool, for he is the man who will tell you he knows who is going to win an election. But an election is a living thing – you might almost say, the most vigorously alive thing there is – with thousands upon thousands of brains and limbs and eyes and thoughts and desires, and it will wriggle and turn and run off in directions no one ever predicted, sometimes just for the joy of proving the wiseacres wrong. This much I learnt on the Field of Mars that day, when the entrails were inspected, the skies were checked for suspicious flights of birds, the blessings of the gods were invoked, all epileptics were asked to leave the field (for in those days an attack of epilepsy, or *morbus comitialis*, automatically rendered proceedings void), a legion was deployed on the approaches to Rome to prevent a surprise attack, the list of candidates was read, the trumpets were sounded, the red flag was hoisted over the Janiculum Hill, and the Roman people began to cast their ballots.

The honour of being the first of the one hundred and ninety-three centuries to vote was decided by lot, and to be a member of this *centuria praerogativa*, as it was known, was considered a rare blessing, for its decision often set the pattern for what followed. Only the richest centuries were eligible for the draw, and I remember how I stood and watched as that year's winners, a stalwart collection of merchants and bankers, filed self-importantly over the wooden bridge and disappeared behind the screens. Their ballots were quickly counted, Figulus came to the front of his tribunal and announced that they had put Cicero in first place and Catilina second. At once a gasp went up, for all those fools I was speaking of had predicted it would be Catilina first and Hybrida second, and then the gasp quickly turned into cheers as Cicero's supporters, realising what had happened, began a noisy demonstration which spread across the Field of Mars. Cicero was standing under the awning beneath the consul's platform. He permitted himself only the most fleeting of smiles, and then, such was the actor in the man, he composed his features into an expression of dignity and authority appropriate to a Roman consul. Catilina – who was as far away from Cicero as it was possible to get, with all the other candidates lined up between them – looked as if he had been struck in the face. Only Hybrida's expression was blank – whether because he was drunk as usual or too stupid to realise what was happening I cannot say. As for Crassus and Caesar, they had been loitering and chatting together near to the place where the voters emerged after casting their ballots, and I could have laughed aloud as they looked at one another in disbelief. They held a hurried consultation and then darted off in different directions, no doubt to demand how the expenditure of twenty million sesterces had failed to secure the *centuria praerogativa*.

If Crassus really had purchased the eight thousand votes which Ranunculus had estimated, that would normally have been enough to swing the election. But this ballot was unusually heavy, thanks to the interest aroused all across Italy, and as the voting went on throughout the morning it became apparent that the briber-in-chief had fallen just short of his target. Cicero had always had the equestrian order firmly behind him, plus the Pompeians and the lower orders. Now that Hortensius, Catulus, Metellus, Isauricus and the Lucullus brothers were delivering the blocs of voters controlled by the aristocrats, he was winning a vote from every century, either as their first or second preference, and soon the only question was who would be his consular colleague. Throughout the morning, it looked as if it would be Catilina, with my notes (which I found the other day) showing that at noon the voting was:

Cicero	81 centuries
Catilina	34 centuries
Hybrida	29 centuries
Sacerdos	9 centuries
Longinus	5 centuries
Cornificius	2 centuries

But then came the voting of the six centuries composed exclusively of the aristocrats, the *sex suffragia*, and they really put the knife into Catilina, so that if I retain one image above all from that memorable day it is of the patricians, having cast their ballots, filing past the candidates. Because the Field of Mars lies outside the city limits, there was nothing to stop Lucius Lucullus, and Quintus Metellus with him, both in their scarlet cloaks and military uniforms, turning out to vote, and their appearance caused a sensation – but nothing like as great an uproar as greeted the announcement that their century had voted Cicero first and then Hybrida. After them came Isauricus, the elder Curio, Aemilius Alba, Claudius Pulcher, Junius Servilius – the husband of Cato's sister, Servilia – old Metellus Pius, the pontifex maximus, too sick to walk but carried in a litter, followed by his adopted son, Scipio Nasica ... And again and again the announcement was the same: Cicero first, and next Hybrida; Cicero first, and next Hybrida; Cicero first ... When, finally, Hortensius and Catulus passed by, it was noticeable that neither man could bring himself to look Catilina in the eye, and once it was declared that their century, too, had voted for Cicero and Hybrida, Catilina must have realised his chances were finished. At that point Cicero had eighty-seven centuries to Hybrida's thirty-five and Catilina's thirty-four – for the first time in the day, Hybrida had eased in front of his running-mate, but more importantly, the aristocrats had publicly turned on one of their own, and in the most brutal manner. After that, Catilina's candidacy was effectively dead, although one had to give him high marks for his conduct. I had anticipated that he would storm off in a rage, or lunge at Cicero and try to murder him with his bare hands. But instead he stood throughout that long, hot day, as the citizens went past him and his hopes of the consulship sank with the sun, and he maintained a look of imperturbable calm, even when Figulus came forward for the final time to read the result of the election:

Cicero	193 centuries
Hybrida	102 centuries
Catilina	65 centuries
Sacerdos	12 centuries
Longinus	9 centuries
Cornificius	5 centuries

We cheered until our throats ached, although Cicero himself seemed very preoccupied for a man who had just achieved his life's ambition, and I felt oddly uneasy. He was now permanently wearing what I later came to recognise as his 'consular look': his chin held ever-so-slightly high, his mouth set in a determined line, and his eyes seemingly directed towards some glorious point in the distance. Hybrida held out his hand to Catilina, but Catilina ignored it, and stepped down from the podium like a man in a trance. He was ruined, bankrupt – surely it would be only a year or two before he was thrown out of the senate altogether. I searched around for Crassus and Caesar, but they had quit the field hours earlier, once Cicero had passed the number of centuries needed for victory. So, too, had the aristocrats. They had gone home for the day the instant Catilina had been safely disposed of, like men who had been required to perform some distasteful duty – put down a favourite hunting-dog, say, which had become rabid – and who now wanted nothing more than the quiet comfort of their own hearths.

Thus did Marcus Tullius Cicero, at forty-two, the youngest age allowable, achieve the supreme *imperium* of the Roman consulship – and achieve it, amazingly, by a unanimous vote of the centuries, and as a 'new man', without family, fortune or force of arms to assist him: a feat never accomplished before or afterwards. We returned that evening from the Field of Mars to his modest home, and once he had thanked his supporters and sent them away, and received the congratulations of his slaves, he ordered that the couches from the dining room be carried up on to the roof, so that he could dine beneath the open sky, as he had done on that night – so long ago it seemed – when he had first disclosed his ambition to become consul. I was honoured to be invited to join the family group, for Cicero was insistent that he would never have achieved his goal without me. For a delirious moment I thought he might be about to award me my freedom and give me that farm right there and then, but he said nothing about it, and it did not seem the appropriate time or setting to bring it up. He was on one couch with Terentia, Quintus was with Pomponia, Tullia was with her fiancé, Frugi, and I reclined with Atticus. I can recall little at my great age of what we ate or drank, or any of that, but I do remember that we each went over our particular memories of the day, and especially of that extraordinary spectacle of the aristocracy voting en masse for Cicero.

'Tell me, Marcus,' said Atticus, in his worldly way, once plenty of good wine had been consumed, 'how did you manage to persuade them? Because, although I know you are a genius with words, these men despised you – absolutely loathed everything you said and stood for. What did you offer them, besides stopping Catilina?'

'Obviously,' replied Cicero, 'I had to promise that I will lead the opposition to Crassus and Caesar and the tribunes when they publish this land reform bill of theirs.'

'That will be quite a task,' said Quintus.

'And that is all?' persisted Atticus. (It is my belief, looking back, that he was behaving like a good cross-examiner, and that he knew the answer to the question before he asked it, probably from his friend Hortensius.) 'You really agreed to nothing else? Because you were in there for many hours.'

Cicero winced. 'Well, I did have to undertake,' he said reluctantly, 'to propose in the senate, as consul, that Lucullus should be awarded a triumph, and also Quintus Metellus.'

Now at last I understood why Cicero had seemed so grim and preoccupied when he left his conference with the aristocrats. Quintus put down his plate and regarded him with undisguised horror. 'So first they want you to turn the people against you by blocking land reform, and then they demand that you should make an enemy out of Pompey by awarding triumphs to his greatest rivals?'

'I am afraid, brother,' said Cicero wearily, 'that the aristocracy did not acquire their wealth without knowing how to drive a hard bargain. I held out as long as I could.'

'But why did you agree?'

'Because I needed to win.'

'But to win what, exactly?'

Cicero was silent.

'Good,' said Terentia, patting her husband's knee. 'I think all those policies are good.'

'Well, you would!' protested Quintus. 'But within weeks of taking office, Marcus will have no supporters left. The people will accuse him of betrayal. The Pompeians will do the same. And the aristocrats will drop him just as soon as he has served his purpose. Who will be left to defend him?'

'I shall defend you,' said Tullia, but for once no one laughed at her precocious loyalty, and even Cicero could only manage a faint smile. But then he rallied.

'Really, Quintus,' he said, 'you are spoiling the whole evening. Between two extremes there is always a third way. Crassus and Caesar have to be stopped: I can make that case. And when it comes to Lucullus, everyone accepts that he deserves a triumph a hundred times over for what he achieved in the war against Mithradates.'

'And Metellus?' cut in Quintus.

'I am sure I shall be able to find something to praise even in Metellus, if you give me sufficient time.'

'And Pompey?'

'Pompey, as we all know, is simply a humble servant of the republic,' replied Cicero, with an airy wave of his hand. 'More importantly,' he added, deadpan, 'he is not here.'

There was a pause, and then, reluctantly, Quintus started to laugh. 'He is not here,' he repeated. 'Well, that is true.' After a while, we all laughed; one had to laugh, really.

'That is better!' Cicero smiled at us. 'The art of life is to deal with problems as they arise, rather than destroy one's spirit by worrying about them too far in advance. Especially tonight.' And then a tear came into his eye. 'Do you know who we should drink to? I believe we should raise a toast to the memory of our dear cousin, Lucius, who was here on this roof when we first talked of the consulship, and who would so much have wanted to see this day.' He raised his cup, and we all raised ours with him, although I could not help remembering the last remark Lucius ever made to him: *Words, words, words. Is there no end to the tricks you can make them perform?*

Later, after everyone had gone, either to their home or to their bed, Cicero lay on his back on one of the couches, with his hands clasped behind his head, staring up at the stars. I sat quietly on the opposite couch with my notebook ready in case he needed anything. I tried to stay alert. But the night was warm and I was swooning with tiredness, and when my head nodded forward for the fourth or fifth time, he looked across at me and told me to go and get some rest: 'You are the private secretary of a consul-elect now. You will need to keep your wits as sharp as your pen.' As I stood to take my leave, he settled back into his contemplation of the heavens. 'How will posterity judge us, eh, Tiro?' he said. 'That is the only question for a statesman. But before it can judge us, it must first remember who we are.' I waited for a while in case he wanted to add something else, but he seemed to have forgotten my existence, so I went away and left him to it.

PART THREE

CONSUL

63 BC

'O condicionem miseram non modo administrandae verum etiam conservandae rei publicae!'

'The preservation of the republic no less than governing it – what a thankless task it is!'

Cicero, speech, 9 November 63 BC

XIX

Two days before the inauguration of Marcus Tullius Cicero as consul of Rome, the body of a child was pulled from the River Tiber, close to the boat sheds of the republican war fleet.

Such a discovery, though tragic, would not normally have warranted the attention of a consul-elect. But there was something so grotesque about this particular corpse, and so threatening to civic peace, that the magistrate responsible for keeping order in the city, C. Octavius, sent word to Cicero asking him to come at once.

Cicero at first was reluctant to go, pleading pressure of work. As the consular candidate who had topped the poll, it fell to him, rather than his colleague, to preside over the opening session of the senate, and he was writing his inaugural address. But I knew there was more to it than that. He had an unusual squeamishness about death. Even the killing of animals in the games disturbed him, and this weakness – for alas in politics a soft heart is always perceived as a weakness – had started to be noticed. His immediate instinct was to send me in his place.

'Of course I shall go,' I replied carefully. 'But …' I let my sentence trail away.

'But?' he said sharply. 'But what? You think it will look bad?'

I held my tongue and continued transcribing his speech. The silence lengthened.

'Oh, very well,' he groaned at last. He heaved himself to his feet. 'Octavius is a dull dog, but steady enough. He wouldn't summon me unless it was important. In any case I need to clear my head.'

It was late December and from a dark grey sky blew a wind that was quick enough and sharp enough to steal your breath. Outside in the street a dozen petitioners were huddled, hoping for a word, and as soon as they saw the consul-elect stepping through his front door they ran across the road towards him. 'Not now,' I said, pushing them back. 'Not today.' Cicero threw the edge of his cloak over his shoulder, tucked his chin down on to his chest and set off briskly down the hill.

We must have walked about a mile, I suppose, crossing the forum at an angle and leaving the city by the river gate. The waters of the Tiber were fast and high, flexed by yellowish-brown whirlpools and writhing currents. Up ahead, opposite Tiber Island, amid the wharfs and cranes of the Navalia, we could see a large crowd milling around. (You will get a sense of how long ago all this happened by the way – more than half a century – when I tell you that the Island was not yet linked by its bridges to either bank.) As we drew closer, many of the onlookers recognised Cicero, and there was a stir of curiosity as they parted to let us through. A cordon of legionaries from the marine barracks was protecting the scene. Octavius was waiting.

'My apologies for disturbing you,' said Octavius, shaking my master's hand. 'I know how busy you must be, so close to your inauguration.'

'My dear Octavius, it is a pleasure to see you at any time. You know my secretary, Tiro?'

Octavius glanced at me without interest. Although he is remembered today only as the father of Augustus, he was at this time aedile of the plebs and very much the coming man. He would probably have made consul himself had he not died prematurely of a fever some four years after this encounter. He led us out of the wind and into one of the great military boat-houses, where the skeleton of a liburnian, stripped for repair, sat on huge wooden rollers. Next to it on the earth floor an object lay shrouded in sailcloth. Without pausing for ceremony, Octavius threw aside the material to show us the naked body of a boy.

He was about twelve, as I remember. His face was beautiful and serene, quite feminine in its delicacy, with traces of gold paint glinting on the nose and cheeks, and with a bit of red ribbon tied in his damp brown curls. His throat had been cut. His body had been slashed open all the way down to the groin and emptied of its organs. There was no blood, only that dark, elongated cavity, like a gutted fish, filled with river mud. How Cicero managed to contemplate the sight and maintain his composure, I do not know, but he swallowed hard and kept on looking. Eventually he said hoarsely, 'This is an outrage.'

'And that's not all,' said Octavius. He squatted on his haunches, took hold of the lad's skull between his hands and turned it to the left. As the head moved, the gaping wound in the neck opened and closed obscenely, as if it were a second mouth trying to whisper a warning to us. Octavius seemed entirely indifferent to this, but then of course he was a military man and no doubt used to such sights. He pulled back the hair to reveal a deep indentation just above the boy's right ear, and pressed his thumb into it. 'Do you see? It looks as if he was felled from behind. I'd say by a hammer.'

'His face painted. His hair beribboned. Felled from behind by a hammer,' repeated Cicero, his words slowing as he realised where his logic was leading him. 'Then his throat cut. And finally his body ... eviscerated.'

'Exactly,' said Octavius. 'His killers must have wanted to inspect his entrails. He was a sacrifice – a human sacrifice.'

At those words, in that cold, dim place, the hairs on the nape of my neck stirred and spiked, and I knew myself to be in the presence of Evil – Evil as a palpable force, as potent as lightning.

Cicero said, 'Are there any cults in the city you have heard of that might practise such an abomination?'

'None. There are always the Gauls, of course – they are said to do such things. But there aren't many of them in town at the moment, and those that are here are well behaved.'

'And who is the victim? Has anyone claimed him?'

'That's another reason I wanted you to come and see for yourself.' Octavius rolled the body over on to its stomach. 'There's a small owner's tattoo just above his backside, do you see? Those who dumped the body may have missed it. "C.Ant.M.f.C.n." Caius Antonius, son of Marcus, grandson of Caius. There's a famous family for you! He was a slave of your consular colleague, Antonius Hybrida.' He stood and wiped his hands on the sailcloth, then casually threw the cover back over the body. 'What do you want to do?'

Cicero was staring at the pathetic bundle on the floor as if mesmerised. 'Who knows about this?'

'Nobody.'

'Hybrida?'

'No.'

'What about the crowd outside?'

'There's a rumour going round that there's been some kind of ritual killing. You above all know what crowds are like. They're saying it's a bad omen on the eve of your consulship.'

'They may be right.'

'It's been a hard winter. They could do with calming down. I thought we might send word to the College of Priests and ask them to perform some kind of ceremony of purification—'

'No, no,' said Cicero quickly, pulling his gaze away from the body. 'No priests. Priests will only make it worse.'

'So what shall we do?'

'Tell no one else. Burn the remains as quickly as possible. Don't let anyone see them. Forbid anyone who has seen them from disclosing the details, on pain of imprisonment.'

'And the crowd?'

'You deal with the body. I'll deal with the crowd.'

Octavius shrugged. 'As you wish.' He sounded unconcerned. He had only one day left in office – I should imagine he was glad to be rid of the problem.

Cicero went over to the door and inhaled a few deep breaths, bringing some colour back to his cheeks. Then I saw him, as I had so often, square his shoulders and clamp a confident expression on his face. He stepped outside and clambered up on to a stack of timber to address the crowd.

'People of Rome, I have satisfied myself that the dark rumours running through the city are false!' He had to bellow into that biting wind to make himself heard. 'Go home to your families and enjoy the rest of the festival.'

'But I saw the body!' shouted a man. 'It was a human sacrifice, to call down a curse on the republic.'

The cry was taken up by others: 'The city is cursed!' 'Your consulship is cursed!' 'Fetch the priests!'

Cicero raised his hands. 'Yes, the corpse was in a dreadful state. But what do you expect? The poor lad had been in the water a long time. The fish are hungry. They take their food where they can. You really want me to bring a priest? To do what? To curse the fish? To *bless* the fish?' A few people began to laugh. 'Since when did Romans become frightened of *fish*? Go home. Enjoy yourselves. The day after tomorrow there will be a new year, with a new consul – one who you can be sure will always guard your welfare!'

It was no great oration by his standards but it did what was required. There were even a few cheers. He jumped down. The legionaries cleared a path for us through the mob and we retreated quickly towards the city. As we neared the gate, I glanced back. At the fringes of the crowd people were already beginning to wander away in search of fresh diversions. I turned to Cicero to congratulate him on the effectiveness of his remarks, but he was leaning over the roadside ditch, vomiting.

Such was the state of the city on the eve of Cicero's consulship – a vortex of hunger, rumour and anxiety; of crippled veterans and bankrupt farmers begging at every corner; of roistering bands of drunken young men terrorising shopkeepers; of women from good families openly prostituting themselves outside the taverns; of sudden conflagrations, violent tempests, moonless nights and scavenging dogs; of fanatics, soothsayers, beggars, fights. Pompey was still away commanding the legions in the East, and in his absence an uneasy, shifting mood swirled around the streets like river fog, giving everyone the jitters. There was a sense that some huge event was impending, but no clear idea what it might be. The new tribunes were said to be working with Caesar and Crassus on a vast and secret scheme for giving away public land to the urban poor. Cicero had tried to find out more about it but had been rebuffed. The patricians were certain to resist it, whatever it was. Goods were scarce, food hoarded, shops empty. Even the moneylenders had stopped making loans.

As for Cicero's colleague as consul, Antonius Hybrida – Antonius the Half-Breed: Half-Man, Half-Beast – he was both wild and stupid, as befitted a candidate who had run for office on a joint ticket with Cicero's sworn enemy, Catilina. Nevertheless, knowing the perils they would face, and feeling the need for allies, Cicero had made strenuous efforts to get on good terms with him. Unfortunately his approaches had come to nothing, and I shall say why. It was the custom for the two consuls-elect to draw lots in October to decide which province each would govern after his year in office. Hybrida, who was steeped in debt, had set his heart on the rebellious but lucrative lands of Macedonia, where a vast fortune was waiting to be made. However to his dismay he drew instead the peaceful pastures of Nearer Gaul, where not even a field mouse was stirring. It was Cicero who drew Macedonia, and when the result was announced in the senate, Hybrida's face had assumed such a picture of childish resentment and surprise that the entire chamber had been convulsed by laughter. He and Cicero had not spoken since.

Little wonder then that Cicero was finding it so hard to compose his inaugural address, and that when we returned to his house from the river and he tried to resume his dictation his voice kept on trailing off. He would stare into the distance with a look of abstraction on his face and repeatedly wonder aloud why the boy had been killed in such a manner, and of what significance it was that he belonged to Hybrida. He agreed with Octavius: the likeliest culprits were the Gauls. Human sacrifice was certainly one of their cults. He sent a message to a friend of his, Q. Fabius Sanga, who was the Gauls' principal patron in the senate, asking in confidence if he thought such an outrage was possible. But Sanga sent rather a huffy letter back within the hour saying of course not, and that the Gauls would be gravely offended if the consul-elect persisted in such damaging speculation. Cicero sighed, threw the letter aside, and attempted to pick up the threads of his thoughts. But he could not weave them together into anything coherent, and shortly before sunset he called again for his cloak and boots.

I had assumed his intention was to take a turn in the public gardens not far from the house, where he often went when he was composing a speech. But as we reached the brow of the hill, instead of turning right he pressed on towards the Esquiline Gate, and I realised to my amazement that he intended to go outside the sacred boundary to the place where the corpses were burned – a spot he usually avoided at all costs. We passed the porters with their handcarts waiting for work just beyond the gate, and the squat official residence of the carnifex, who, as public executioner, was forbidden to live within the precincts of the city. Finally we entered the sacred grove of Libitina, filled with cawing crows, and approached the temple. In those days this was the headquarters of the undertakers' guild: the place where one could buy all that was needed for a funeral, from the utensils with which to anoint a body to the bed on which the corpse was cremated. Cicero asked me for some money and went ahead and spoke to a priest. He handed him the purse, and a couple of official mourners appeared. Cicero beckoned me over. 'We are just in time,' he said.

What a curious party we must have made as we crossed the Esquiline Field in single file, the mourners first, carrying jars of incense, then the consul-elect, then me. All around us in the dusk were the dancing flames of funeral pyres, the cries of the bereaved, and the sickly smell of incense – strong, yet not quite strong enough to disguise the stink of burning death. The mourners led us to the public *ustrina*, where a pile of corpses on a handcart were waiting to be thrown on to the flames. Devoid of clothes and shoes, these unclaimed bodies were as destitute in death as they had been in life. Only the murdered boy's was covered: I recognised it by the sailcloth shroud into which it had now been tightly sewn. As a couple of attendants tossed it easily on to the metal grille, Cicero bowed his head and the hired mourners set up a particularly noisy lamentation, no doubt in the hope of a good tip. The flames roared and flattened in the wind, and very quickly that was it: he had gone to whatever fate awaits us all.

It was a scene I have never forgotten.

Surely the greatest mercy granted us by Providence is our ignorance of the future. Imagine if we knew the outcome of our hopes and plans, or could see the manner in which we are doomed to die – how ruined our lives would be! Instead we live on dumbly from day to day as happily as animals. But all things must come to dust eventually. No human being, no system, no age is impervious to this law; everything beneath the stars will perish; the hardest rock will be worn away. Nothing endures but words.

And with this in mind, and in the renewed hope that I may live long enough to see the task through, I shall now relate the extraordinary story of Cicero's year in office as consul of the Roman republic, and what befell him in the four years afterwards – a span of time we mortals call a lustrum, but which to the gods is no more than the blinking of an eye.

XX

The following day, inaugural eve, it snowed – a heavy fall, of the sort one normally sees only in the mountains. It clad the temples of the Capitol in soft white marble and laid a shroud as thick as a man's hand across the whole of the city. I had never witnessed such a phenomenon before, and nor, despite my great age, have I heard of the like again. Snow in Rome? This surely had to be an omen. But of what?

Cicero stayed firmly in his study, beside a small coal fire, and continued to work on his speech. He placed no faith in portents. When I burst in and told him of the snow, he merely shrugged, 'What of it?' and when tentatively I began to advance the argument of the stoics in defence of augury – that if there are gods, they must care for men, and that if they care for men, they must send us signs of their will – he cut me off with a laugh: 'Surely the gods, given their immortal powers, should be able to find more articulate means of communication than snowflakes. Why not send us a letter?' He turned back to his desk, shaking his head and chuckling at my credulity. 'Really, go and attend to your duties, Tiro, and make sure no one else bothers me.'

Chastened, I went away and checked the arrangements for the inaugural procession, and then made a start on his correspondence. I had been his secretary for sixteen years by this time and there was no aspect of his life, public or private, with which I was not familiar. My habit in those days was to work at a folding table just outside his study, fending off unwanted visitors and keeping an ear open for his summons. It was from this position that I could hear the noises of the household that morning: Terentia marching in and out of the dining room, snapping at the maids that the winter flowers were not good enough for her husband's new status, and berating the cook about the quality of that night's menu; little Marcus, now well into his second year, toddling unsteadily after her, and shouting in delight at the snow; and darling Tullia, thirteen and due to be married in the autumn, practising her Greek hexameters with her tutor.

Such was the extent of my work, it was not until after noon that I was able to put my head out of doors again. Despite the hour, the street for once was empty. The city felt muffled, ominous; as still as midnight. The sky was pale, the snowfall had stopped, and frost had formed a glittering white crust over the surface. Even now – for such are the peculiarities of memory in the very old – I can recall the sensation of breaking it with the tip of my shoe. I took a last breath of that freezing air and was just turning to go back in to the warmth when I heard, very faint in the hush, the crack of a whip and the sound of men crying and groaning. A few moments later a litter borne by four liveried slaves came swaying around the corner. An overseer trotting alongside waved his whip in my direction.

'Hey, you!' he shouted. 'Is that Cicero's house?'

When I replied that it was, he called over his shoulder – 'This is the street!' – and lashed out at the slave nearest him with such force the poor fellow nearly stumbled. To get through the snow he had to pull his knees up high to his waist, and in this way he floundered on towards me. Behind him a second litter appeared, then a third, and a fourth. They drew up outside the house, and the instant they had set down their burdens the porters all sank down in the snow, collapsing over the shafts like exhausted rowers at their oars. I did not care for the look of this at all.

'It may be Cicero's house,' I protested, 'but he is not receiving visitors.'

'He will receive us!' came a familiar voice from inside the first litter, and a bony hand clawed back the curtain to reveal the leader of the patrician faction in the senate, Q. Lutatius Catulus. He was wrapped in animal skins right up to his pointed chin, giving him the appearance of a large and malevolent weasel.

'Senator,' I said, bowing, 'I shall tell him you're here.'

'And not just I,' said Catulus.

I looked along the street. Clambering stiffly out of the next litter, and cursing his old soldier's bones, was the conqueror of Olympus and father of the senate, Vatia Isauricus, while nearby stood Cicero's great rival in the law courts, the patricians' favourite advocate, Q. Hortensius. He in turn was holding out his hand to a fourth senator, whose shrivelled, nut-brown, toothless face I could not place. He looked very decrepit. I guessed he must have stopped attending debates a long while ago.

'Distinguished gentlemen,' I said, in my most unctuous manner, 'please follow me and I shall inform the consul-elect.'

I whispered to the porter to show them into the tablinum and hurried towards Cicero's study. As I drew close, I could hear his voice in full declamatory flow – 'To the Roman people I say, enough!' – and when I opened the door I found him standing with his back to me, addressing my two junior secretaries, Sositheus and Laurea, his hand outstretched, his thumb and middle finger formed into a circle. 'And to you, Tiro,' he continued, without turning round, 'I say: not another damned interruption! What sign have the gods sent us now? A shower of frogs?'

The secretaries sniggered. On the brink of achieving his life's ambition, he had put the perturbations of the previous day out of his mind and was in a great good humour.

'There's a delegation from the senate to see you.'

'Now that's what I call an ominous portent. Who's in it?'

'Catulus, Isauricus, Hortensius, and another I don't recognise.'

'The cream of the aristocracy? Here?' He gave me a sharp look over his shoulder. 'And in this weather? It must be the smallest house they've ever set foot in! What do they want?'

'I don't know.'

'Well, be sure you make a thorough note.' He gathered his toga around him and stuck out his chin. 'How do I look?'

'Consular,' I assured him.

He stepped over the discarded drafts of his speech and made his way into the tablinum. The porter had fetched chairs for our visitors but only one was seated – the trembling old senator I did not recognise. The others stood together, each with his own attendant close at hand, clearly uncomfortable at finding themselves on the premises of this low-born 'new man' they had so reluctantly backed for consul. Hortensius actually had a handkerchief pressed to his nose, as if Cicero's lack of breeding might be catching.

'Catulus,' said Cicero affably, as he came into the room. 'Isauricus. Hortensius. I'm honoured.' He nodded to each of the former consuls, but when he reached the fourth senator I could see even his prodigious memory temporarily fail him. 'Rabirius,' he concluded after a brief struggle. 'Gaius Rabirius, isn't it?' He held out his hand but the old man did not react and Cicero smoothly turned the gesture into a sweeping indication of the room. 'Welcome to my home. This is a pleasure.'

'There's no pleasure in it,' said Catulus.

'It's an outrage,' said Hortensius.

'It's war,' asserted Isauricus, 'that's what it is.'

'Well, I'm very sorry to hear it,' replied Cicero pleasantly. He did not always take them seriously. Like many rich old men they tended to regard the slightest personal inconvenience as proof of the end of the world.

Hortensius clicked his fingers, and his attendant handed Cicero a legal document with a heavy seal. 'Yesterday the Board of Tribunes served this writ on Rabirius.'

At the mention of his name, Rabirius looked up. 'Can I go home?' he asked plaintively.

'Later,' said Hortensius in a stern voice, and the old man bowed his head.

'A writ on Rabirius?' repeated Cicero, looking at him with bemusement. 'And what conceivable crime is he capable of?' He read the writ aloud so I could make a note of it. '"The accused is herein charged with the murder of the tribune L. Saturninus and the violation of the sacred precincts of the senate house."' He looked up in puzzlement. 'Saturninus? It must be – what? – forty years since he was killed.'

'Thirty-six,' corrected Catulus.

'And Catulus should know,' said Isauricus, 'because he was there. As was I.'

Catulus spat out his name as if it were poison. 'Saturninus! What a rogue! Killing him wasn't a crime – it was a public service.' He gazed into the distance as if surveying some grand historical mural on the wall of a temple: *The Murder of Saturninus in the Senate House*. 'I see him as plainly as I see you, Cicero. A rabble-rousing tribune of the very worst kind. He murdered our candidate for consul and the senate declared him a public enemy. After that, even the plebs deserted him. But before we could lay our hands on him, he and some of his gang barricaded themselves up on the Capitol. So we blocked the water pipes! That was your idea, Vatia.'

'It was.' The old general's eyes gleamed at the memory. 'I knew how to conduct a siege, even then.'

'Of course they surrendered after a couple of days, and were lodged in the senate house till their trial. But we didn't trust them not to escape again, so we got up on the roof and tore off the tiles and pelted them. There was no hiding place. They ran to and fro squealing like rats in a ditch. By the time Saturninus stopped twitching, you could barely tell who he was.'

'And Rabirius was with you both on the roof?' asked Cicero. Glancing up from my notes at the old man – his expression vacant, his head trembling slightly – it was impossible to imagine him involved in such an action.

'Oh yes, he was there,' confirmed Isauricus. 'There must have been about thirty of us. Those were the days,' he added, bunching his fingers into a gnarled fist, 'when we still had some juice in us!'

'The crucial point,' said Hortensius wearily – he was younger than his companions and obviously bored of hearing the same old story – 'is not whether Rabirius was there or not. It's the crime with which he is being charged.'

'Which is what? Murder?'

'*Perduellio*.'

I must confess I had never even heard of it, and Cicero had to spell it out for me. '*Perduellio*,' he explained, 'is what the ancients called treason.' He turned to Hortensius. 'Why use such an obsolete law? Why not just prosecute him with treason, pure and simple, and have done with it?'

'Because the sentence for treason is exile, whereas for *perduellio* it's death – and not by hanging, either.' Hortensius leaned forward to emphasise his words. 'If they find him guilty, Rabirius will be crucified.'

'What is this place?' demanded Rabirius, getting to his feet. 'Where am I?'

Catulus gently pressed him down into his seat. 'Calm yourself, Gaius. We're your friends.'

'But no jury is going to find *him* guilty,' objected Cicero quietly. 'The poor fellow's clearly lost his brains.'

'*Perduellio* isn't heard before a jury. That's what's so cunning. It's heard before two judges, specially appointed for the purpose.'

'Appointed by whom?'

'Our new urban praetor, Lentulus Sura.'

Cicero grimaced at the name. Sura was a former consul, a man of great ambition and boundless stupidity, two qualities which in politics often go together.

'And whom has Old Sleepy-Head chosen as judges? Do we know?'

'Caesar is one. And Caesar is the other.'

'*What?*'

'Gaius Julius Caesar and his cousin Lucius are to be selected to hear the case.'

'*Caesar* is behind this?'

'Naturally the verdict is a foregone conclusion.'

'But there must be a right of appeal,' insisted Cicero, now thoroughly alarmed. 'A Roman citizen cannot be executed without a proper trial.'

'Oh yes,' said Hortensius bitterly. 'If Rabirius is found guilty, of course he has the right of appeal. But here's the catch. Not to a court – only to the entire people, drawn up in full assembly, on the Field of Mars.'

'And what a spectacle that will be!' broke in Catulus. 'Can you imagine it? A Roman senator on trial for his life in front of the mob? They'll never vote to acquit him – it would rob them of their entertainment.'

'It will mean civil war,' said Isauricus flatly, 'because we won't stand for it, Cicero. D'you hear us?'

'I hear you,' he replied, his eyes rapidly scanning the writ. 'Which of the tribunes has laid the charge?' He found the name at the foot of the document. 'Labienus? He's one of Pompey's men. He's not normally a troublemaker. What's he playing at?'

'Apparently his uncle was killed alongside Saturninus,' said Hortensius with great contempt, 'and his family honour demands vengeance. It's nonsense. The whole thing is just a pretext for Caesar and his gang to attack the senate.'

'So what do you propose to do?' said Catulus. 'We voted for you, remember? Against the better judgement of some of us.'

'What do you want me to do?'

'What do you think? Fight for Rabirius's life! Denounce this wickedness in public, then join Hortensius as his defence counsel when the case comes before the people.'

'Well, that would be a novelty,' said Cicero, eyeing his great rival, 'the two of us appearing together.'

'The prospect is no more appealing to me than it is to you,' rejoined Hortensius coldly.

'Now, now, Hortensius, don't take offence. I'd be honoured to act as your colleague in court. But let's not rush into their trap. Let's try to see if we can settle this matter without a trial.'

'How can it be avoided?'

'I'll go and talk to Caesar. Discover what he wants. See if we can reach a compromise.' At the mere mention of the word 'compromise', the three ex-consuls all started to object at once. Cicero held up his hands. 'He must want something. It will do us no harm at least to hear his terms. We owe it to the republic. We owe it to Rabirius.'

'I want to go home,' said Rabirius plaintively. 'Please can I go home now?'

Cicero and I left the house less than an hour later, the unfamiliar snow crunching and squeaking beneath our boots as we descended the empty street towards the city. Once again we went alone, which I now find remarkable to contemplate – this must have been one of the last occasions when Cicero was able to venture out in Rome without a bodyguard. He did however pull up the hood of his cloak to avoid being recognised. Even the busiest thoroughfares in daylight could not be counted safe that winter.

'They will have to compromise,' he said. 'They may not like it, but they have no choice.' He suddenly swore, and kicked at the snow in his frustration. 'Is this what my consulship is going to consist of, Tiro? A year spent running back and forth between the patricians and the populists, trying to stop them tearing one another to pieces?' I could think of no hopeful reply, so we trudged on in silence.

Caesar's home at this time stood some way beneath Cicero's, in Subura. The building had been in his family for at least a century and had no doubt been fine enough in its day. But by the time Caesar had come to inherit it, the neighbourhood was impoverished. Even the virginal snow, smudged with the soot of burned-out fires and dotted with human shit thrown from the tenement windows, somehow served only to emphasise the squalor of the narrow streets. Beggars held out trembling hands for money, but I had brought none with me. I recall urchins pelting an elderly, shrieking whore with snowballs, and twice we saw fingers and feet poking out from beneath the icy mounds that marked where some poor wretch had frozen to death in the night.

And it was down here in Subura, like some great shark attended by shoals of minnows hoping for his scraps, that Caesar lurked and awaited his chance. His house was at the end of a street of shoemakers, flanked by two tottering apartment blocks, seven or eight storeys high. The frozen washing strung between them made it seem as though a pair of drunks with torn sleeves were embracing above his roof. Outside the entrance a dozen rough-looking fellows stamped their feet around an iron brazier. I felt their hungry, crafty eyes stripping the clothes from my back even as we waited to be admitted.

'Those are the citizens who will be judging Rabirius,' muttered Cicero. 'The old fool doesn't stand a chance.'

The steward took our cloaks and showed us into the atrium, then went to tell his master of Cicero's arrival, leaving us to inspect the death masks of Caesar's ancestors. Strangely, there were only three consuls in Caesar's direct line, a thin tally for a family that claimed to go back to the foundation of Rome and to have its origins in the womb of Venus. The goddess herself was represented by a small bronze. The statue was exquisite but scratched and shabby, as were the carpets, the frescoes, the faded tapestries and the furniture: all told a story of a proud family fallen on hard days. We had plenty of leisure to appreciate these heirlooms as time passed and still Caesar did not appear.

'You can't help but admire the fellow,' said Cicero, after he had paced around the room three or four times. 'Here am I, about to become the pre-eminent man in Rome, while he hasn't even made it to praetor yet. But I am the one who must dance attendance on him!'

After a while I became aware that we were being watched from behind a door by a solemn-faced girl of about ten who must have been Caesar's daughter, Julia. I smiled at her and she darted away. A little while later, Caesar's mother, Aurelia, emerged from the same room. Her narrow, dark-eyed, watchful face, like Caesar's, had something of the bird of prey about it, and she exuded a similar air of chilly cordiality. Cicero had been acquainted with her for many years. All three of her brothers, the Cottas, had been consul, and if Aurelia had been born a man, she would certainly have achieved the rank herself, for she was shrewder and braver than any of them. As it was, she had to content herself with furthering the career of her son, and when her eldest brother died she fixed it so that Caesar would take his place as one of the fifteen members of the College of Priests – a brilliant move, as I shall soon describe.

'Forgive him, Cicero, for his rudeness,' she said. 'I've reminded him you're here, but you know how he is.' There was a footstep and we glanced behind us to see a woman in the passage leading to the door. No doubt she had hoped to slip past unnoticed, but one of her shoes must have come undone. Leaning against the wall to refasten it, her auburn hair awry, she glanced guiltily in our direction, and I do not know who was the more embarrassed: Postumia – which was the woman's name – or Cicero, for he knew her very well as the wife of his great friend the jurist and senator Servius Sulpicius. Indeed, she was due to have dinner with Cicero that very evening.

He quickly turned his attention back to the bronze of Venus and pretended to be in the middle of a conversation – 'This is very fine: is it a Myron?' – and did not look up until she had gone.

'That was tactfully done,' said Aurelia approvingly, then her expression darkened and she shook her head. 'I don't reproach my son for his liaisons – men will be men – but some of these modern women are shameless beyond belief.'

'What are you two gossiping about?'

It was a trick of Caesar's, in both war and peace, to appear unexpectedly from the rear, and at the sound of that flint-dry voice we all three turned. I can see him now, his large head looming skull-like in the dimming afternoon light. People ask me about him all the time: 'You met Caesar? What was he like? Tell us what he was like – the great god Caesar!' Well, I remember him most as a curious combination of hard and soft – the muscles of a soldier within the loosely belted tunic of an effete dandy; the sharp sweat of the exercise yard laid over by the sweet scent of crocus oil; pitiless ambition sheathed in honeyed charm. 'Be wary of her, Cicero,' he continued, emerging from the shadows. 'She's twice the politician we are, aren't you, Mama?' He caught her by the waist from behind and kissed her beneath her ear.

'Now stop that,' she said, freeing herself and pretending to be annoyed. 'I've played the hostess long enough. Where's your wife? It's not seemly for her to be out unaccompanied all the time. Send her to me the moment she returns.' She inclined her head graciously towards Cicero. 'My best wishes to you for tomorrow. It's a remarkable achievement to be the first in one's family to achieve the consulship.'

Caesar watched her go admiringly. 'Seriously, Cicero,' he said, 'the women in this city are far more formidable than the men, your own wife being a fine example.'

Was Caesar hinting by this remark that he desired to seduce Terentia? I doubt it. The most hostile tribe of Gaul would have been a less gruelling conquest. But I could see Cicero bridling. 'I'm not here to discuss the women of Rome,' he said, 'expert though you may be.'

'Then why have you come?'

Cicero nodded to me. I opened my document case and handed Caesar the writ.

'Are you trying to corrupt me?' responded Caesar with a smile, handing it straight back to me. 'I can't discuss this. I'm to be a judge.'

'I want you to acquit Rabirius of these charges.'

Caesar chuckled in that mirthless way of his, and tucked a thin strand of hair behind his ear. 'No doubt you do.'

'Now, Caesar,' said Cicero with an edge of impatience in his voice, 'let's speak plainly. Everyone knows that you and Crassus give the tribunes their orders. I doubt whether Labienus even knew the name of this wretched uncle of his until you put it into his head. As for Sura – he would have thought *perduellio* was a fish unless someone told him otherwise. This is yet another of your designs.'

'Really, I cannot speak about a case I have to judge.'

'Admit it: the true purpose of this prosecution is to intimidate the senate.'

'You must direct your questions to Labienus.'

'I'm directing them to you.'

'Very well, since you press me, I'd rather call it a reminder to the senate that if they trample on the dignity of the people by killing their representatives, the people will have their vengeance, however long it takes.'

'And you really think you'll enhance the dignity of the people by terrorising a helpless old man? I've just come from Rabirius. His wits have been entirely withered by age. He has no idea what's going on.'

'If he's no idea what's going on, how can he be terrorised?'

There was quite a long pause, then Cicero said, in a different tone, 'Listen, my dear Gaius, we've been good friends for many years.' (This was putting it a bit strong, I thought.) 'May I give you some friendly advice, in the manner of an older brother to his junior? A glittering career lies ahead of you. You're young—'

'Not that young! I'm already three years older than Alexander the Great was when he died.'

Cicero laughed politely; he thought Caesar was joking. 'You're young,' he repeated. 'You have a powerful reputation. Why jeopardise it by provoking such a confrontation? Killing Rabirius will not only set the people against the senate, it will be a stain on your honour. It might play well with the mob today, but it will count against you tomorrow with all the sensible men.'

'I'll take the risk.'

'You do realise that as consul I'll be obliged to defend him?'

'Well, that would be a grave error, Marcus – if I may respond with equal friendliness? Consider the balance of forces that will be ranged against you. We have the support of the people, the tribunes, half the praetors – why, even Antonius Hybrida, your own consular colleague, is on our side! Who does that leave you with? The patricians? But they despise you. They'll throw you over the moment you're of no use to them. As I see it, you have only one choice.'

'Which is?'

'To join us.'

'Ah.' Cicero had a habit when he was weighing someone up of resting his chin in the palm of his hand. He contemplated Caesar in this way for a while. 'And what would that entail?'

'Support for our bill.'

'And in return?'

'I dare say my cousin and I can find it in our hearts to show some compassion to poor Rabirius, on the grounds of his impaired mind.' Caesar's thin lips smiled but his dark eyes stayed fixed on Cicero. 'What do you say?'

Before Cicero could respond, we were interrupted by the arrival home of Caesar's wife. Some say that Caesar married this woman, whose name was Pompeia, purely at the urging of his mother, for the girl had useful family connections in the senate. But on the basis of what I saw that afternoon, I should say her attractions belonged to a more obvious sphere. She was much younger than he, barely twenty, and the cold had imparted a pretty blush to her creamy throat and cheeks, and a sparkle to her large grey eyes. She embraced her husband, arching against him like a cat, and then made an almost equal fuss of Cicero, flattering him for his speeches and even a volume of his poetry she claimed to have read. It occurred to me that she was drunk. Caesar regarded her with amusement.

'Mama wants to see you,' he said, at which she pouted like a girl. 'Well, go on,' he commanded, 'don't make a sour face. You know what she's like,' and he gave her a pat on her rear to send her on her way.

'So many women, Caesar,' observed Cicero drily. 'Where will they emerge from next?'

Caesar laughed. 'I fear you'll take away a bad impression of me.'

'My impression is quite unchanged, I assure you.'

'So, then: do we have a bargain?'

'It depends on what your bill contains. All we have so far are election slogans. "Land for the landless." "Food for the hungry." I'll need a few more details than that. And also perhaps some concessions.' But Caesar did not respond. His expression was blank. After a while the silence became embarrassing, and it was Cicero who ended it by grunting and turning aside. 'Well, it's getting dark,' he said to me. 'We should go.'

'So soon? You'll take no refreshment? Then let me show you out.' Caesar was entirely affable: his manners were always impeccable, even when he was condemning a man to death. 'Think of it,' he continued, as he led us down the shabby passage. 'If you join us, how easy your term of office will be. This time next year your consulship will be over. You'll leave Rome. Live in a governor's palace. Make enough money in Macedonia to set you up for life. Come home. Buy a house on the Bay of Naples. Study philosophy. Write your memoirs. Whereas—'

The doorkeeper stepped forward to help Cicero on with his cloak, but Cicero waved him away and turned on Caesar. 'Whereas? Whereas what? If I don't join you? What then?'

Caesar put on an expression of pained surprise. 'None of this is aimed at you personally. I hope you understand that. We mean you no harm. In fact I want you to know that if ever you find yourself in personal danger, you can always rely on my protection.'

'*I* can always rely on *your* protection?' Seldom did I see Cicero at a loss for words. But on that freezing day, in that cramped and faded house, in that scruffy neighbourhood, I watched him struggle to find the language that would adequately convey his feelings. In the end he couldn't manage it. Draping his cloak over his shoulders, he stepped out into the snow, and under the sullen gaze of the band of ruffians still lingering in the street, he bade Caesar a curt farewell.

'*I* can always rely on *his* protection?' repeated Cicero as we trudged back up the hill. 'Who is he to talk to me in such a way?'

'He's very confident,' I ventured.

'Confident? He treats me as if I were his client!'

The day was ending, and with it the year, fading swiftly in that way of winter afternoons. In the windows of the tenements lamps were being lit. People were shouting to one another above our heads. There was a lot of smoke from the fires, and I could smell food cooking. At the street corners the pious had put out little dishes of honey cakes as new-year offerings to the neighbourhood gods – for we worshipped the spirits of the crossroads in those days rather than the great god Augustus – and the hungry birds were pecking at them, rising and fluttering and settling again as we hurried past.

'Do you want me to send a message to Catulus and the others?' I asked.

'And tell them what? That Caesar has undertaken to spare Rabirius if I betray them behind their backs, and that I'm going away to consider his proposal?' He was striding ahead, his irritation lending strength to his legs. I was sweating to keep up. 'I noticed you weren't making a note of what he said.'

'It didn't seem appropriate.'

'You must always make a note. From now on, everything is to be written down.'

'Yes, Senator.'

'We're heading into dangerous waters, Tiro. Every reef and current must be charted.'

'Yes, Senator.'

'Can you remember the conversation?'

'I think so. Most of it.'

'Good. Write it all down as soon as we get back. I want to keep a record by me. But don't say a word to anyone – especially not in front of Postumia.'

'Do you think she'll still come to dinner?'

'Oh yes, she'll come – if only to report back to her lover. She's quite without shame. Poor Servius. He's so proud of her.'

As soon as we reached the house, Cicero went upstairs to change while I retired to my little room to write down everything I could remember. I have that roll here now as I compose my memoir: Cicero preserved it among his secret papers. Like me it has become yellowish and brittle and faded with age. But again, like me, it is still comprehensible, just about, and when I hold it up close to my eyes I hear again Caesar's rasping voice in my ear. *'You can always rely on my protection ...'*

It took me an hour or more to finish my account by which time Cicero's guests had arrived and gone in for dinner. After I had done I lay down on my narrow cot and thought of all I had witnessed. I do not mind admitting I was uneasy, for Nature had not equipped me with the nerves for public life. I would have been happy to have stayed on the family estate: my dream was always to have a small farm of my own, to which I could retire and write. I had some money saved up, and secretly I had been hoping Cicero might give me my freedom when he won the consulship. But the months had gone by and he had never mentioned it, and now I was past forty and beginning to worry that I might die in servitude. The last night of the year is often a melancholy time. Janus looks backward as well as forward, and sometimes each prospect seems equally unappealing. But that evening I felt particularly sorry for myself.

Anyway, I kept out of Cicero's way until very late, when I reasoned the meal must be close to finishing, then went to the dining room and stood beside the door where Cicero could see me. It was a small but pretty room, freshly decorated with frescoes designed to give the diners the impression that they were in Cicero's garden at Tusculum. There were nine around the table, three to a couch – the perfect number. Postumia had turned up, exactly as Cicero had predicted. She was in a loosenecked gown and looked serene, as if the embarrassment of the afternoon had never occurred. Next to her reclined her husband Servius, one of Cicero's oldest friends and the most eminent jurist in Rome: no mean achievement in that city full of lawyers. But immersing oneself in the law is a little like bathing in freezing water – bracing in moderation, shrivelling in excess – and Servius over the years had become ever more hunched and cautious, whereas Postumia remained a beauty. Still, he had a following in the senate, and his ambition – and hers – burned strong. He planned to stand for consul himself in the summer, and Cicero had promised to support him.

The only friend of Cicero's of longer standing than Servius was Atticus. He was lying beside his sister, Pomponia, who was married – unhappily, alas – to Cicero's younger brother, Quintus. Poor Quintus: he looked as if he had taken refuge from her shrewish taunts in the wine as usual. The final guest was young Marcus Caelius Rufus, who had been Cicero's pupil, and who kept up a stream of jokes and stories. As for Cicero, he reclined between Terentia and his beloved Tullia and was putting on a show of such nonchalance, laughing at Rufus's gossip, you would never have guessed he had a care. But it is one of the tricks of the successful politician, to be able to hold many things in mind at once and to switch between them as the need arises, otherwise life would be insupportable. After a while he glanced towards me and nodded. 'Friends,' he said, loudly enough to cut through the general chatter, 'it is getting late, and Tiro has come to remind me I have an inaugural address to make in the morning. Sometimes I think he should be the consul and I the secretary.' There was laughter, and I felt the gaze of everyone turn on me. 'Ladies,' he continued, 'if you would forgive me, I wonder if the gentlemen might join me in my study for a moment.'

He dabbed the corners of his mouth with his napkin and threw it on to the table, then stood and offered his hand to Terentia. She took it with a smile all the more striking because it was so rare. She was like some twiggy winter plant that had suddenly put forth a bloom, warmed by the sun of Cicero's success – so much so that she had actually set aside her lifelong parsimony and dressed herself in a manner befitting the wife of a consul and future governor of Macedonia. Her brand-new gown was sewn with pearls, and other newly purchased jewels glinted all about her: at her narrow throat and thin bosom, at her wrists and on her fingers, even woven into her short dark curls.

The guests filed out, the women turning towards the tablinum, the men moving into the study. Cicero told me to close the door. Immediately the pleasure drained from his face.

'What's all this about, brother?' asked Quintus, who was still holding his wine glass. 'You look as if you've eaten a bad oyster.'

'I hate to spoil a pleasant evening, but a problem has arisen.' Grimly Cicero produced the writ that had been served on Rabirius, then described the afternoon's delegation from the senate and his subsequent visit to Caesar. 'Read out what the rascal said, Tiro,' he ordered.

I did as he asked, and when I came to the final part – Caesar's offer of protection – all four exchanged glances.

'Well,' said Atticus, 'if you turn your back on Catulus and his friends after all the promises you made to them before the election, you may have need of his protection. They'll never forgive you.'

'Yet if I keep my word to them, and oppose the populists' bill, then Caesar will find Rabirius guilty, and I'll be obliged to defend him on the Field of Mars.'

'And that you simply must not do,' said Quintus. 'Caesar's quite right. Defeat is certain. At all costs, leave his defence to Hortensius.'

'But that's impossible! I can hardly stay neutral as the president of the senate while a senator is crucified. What kind of consul would that make me?'

'A live one, rather than a dead one,' replied Quintus, 'because if you throw in your lot with the patricians, believe me, you'll be in real danger. Almost everyone will be against you. Even the senate won't be united – Hybrida will see to that. There are plenty on those benches just waiting for an opportunity to bring you down, Catilina first among them.'

'I've an idea,' said young Rufus. 'Why don't we smuggle Rabirius out of the city and hide him in the country somewhere till this blows over?'

'Could we?' Cicero pondered the suggestion, then shook his head. 'No. I admire your spirit, Rufus, but it wouldn't work. If we deny Caesar Rabirius, he's perfectly capable of trumping up a similar charge against Catulus or Isauricus – and can you imagine the consequences of *that*?'

Servius meanwhile had picked up the writ and was studying it intently. His eyesight was weak and he had to hold the document so close to the candelabrum I feared it might catch fire. '*Perduellio*,' he muttered. 'That's a strange coincidence. I was planning to propose in the senate this very month that the statute of *perduellio* be repealed. I'd even looked up all the precedents. I have them laid out on my desk at home.'

'Perhaps that's where Caesar got the idea,' said Quintus. 'Did you mention it to him?'

Servius's face was still pressed to the writ. 'Of course not. I never speak to him. The fellow's an utter scoundrel.' He glanced up to discover Cicero staring at him. 'What is it?'

'I think I know how Caesar might have heard of *perduellio*.'

'How?'

Cicero hesitated. 'Your wife was at Caesar's house when we arrived this afternoon.'

'Don't be absurd. Why would Postumia visit Caesar? She barely knows him. She was with her sister all day.'

'I saw her. So did Tiro.'

'Well then, maybe you did, but I'm sure there's some innocent explanation.' Servius pretended to carry on reading. After a while he said, in a low and resentful voice, 'I was puzzled why you'd waited till after dinner to discuss Caesar's proposal. Now I understand. You felt unable to speak openly in front of my wife, in case she ran to his bed and repeated what you said!'

It was a horribly embarrassing moment. Quintus and Atticus both stared at the floor; even Rufus held his tongue for a change. 'Servius, Servius, old friend,' said Cicero, taking him by the shoulders. 'You're the man in Rome I most wish to see succeed me as consul. My trust in you is absolute. Never doubt it.'

'But you have insulted the honour of my wife, which is also an insult to me, so how can I accept your trust?' He pushed Cicero's hands away and walked with dignity out of the room.

'Servius!' called Atticus, who could not bear any kind of unpleasantness. But the poor cuckold had already gone, and when Atticus moved to follow him, Cicero said quietly, 'Leave him, Atticus. It's his wife he needs to speak to, not us.'

There was a long silence, during which I strained my ears for the sound of raised voices in the tablinum, but the only noise was of dishes being cleared from the dining room. Eventually, Rufus gave a roar of laughter. 'So that's why Caesar is always one step ahead of his enemies! He has spies in all your beds!'

'Shut up, Rufus,' said Quintus.

'Damn Caesar!' cried Cicero suddenly. 'There's nothing dishonourable about ambition. I'm ambitious myself. But his lust for power is not of this world. You look into those eyes of his, and it's like staring into some dark sea at the height of a storm!' He flung himself into his chair and sat drumming his fingertips against the arms. 'I don't see what choice I have. At least if I agree to his terms I can gain myself some time. They've already been working on this damned bill of theirs for months.'

'What's so wrong with giving free farms to the poor anyway?' asked Rufus, who, like many of the young, had populist sympathies. 'You've been out on the streets. You've seen what it's like this winter. People are starving.'

'I agree,' said Cicero. 'But it's food they need, not farms. Farming demands years of skill, and back-breaking labour. I'd like to see those layabouts I met outside Caesar's house today working the fields from dawn till dusk! If we're forced to rely on them for food, we'll all be starving in a year.'

'At least Caesar is concerned about them—'

'*Concerned* about them? Caesar is concerned about no man except himself. Do you really think Crassus, the richest man in Rome, is *concerned* about the poor? They want to dole out the public land – at no expense to themselves, by the way – to create an army of supporters so huge it will keep them in power for ever. Crassus has his eyes on Egypt. The gods alone know what Caesar wants – the entire planet, probably. *Concerned!* Really, Rufus, you do talk like a young fool sometimes. Have you learnt nothing since you came to Rome except how to gamble and whore?'

I do not think Cicero meant his words to sound as harsh as they did, but I could tell they struck Rufus like a slap, and when he turned away his eyes were shining with suppressed tears – and not merely of humiliation, either, but of anger, for he was no longer the charming adolescent idler Cicero had taken in as a pupil, but a young man of growing ambition: a change Cicero had failed to notice. Even though the discussion went on for a while longer, Rufus took no further part in it.

'Tiro,' said Atticus, 'you were there at Caesar's house. What do you think your master should do?'

I had been waiting for this moment, for I was invariably the last to be asked his opinion in these inner councils, and I always tried to prepare something to say. 'I think that by agreeing to Caesar's proposal, it may be possible to gain some concessions in the bill. These can then be presented to the patricians as a victory.'

'And then,' mused Cicero, 'if they refuse to accept them, the blame will clearly be theirs, and I shall be released from my obligation. It's not a bad idea.'

'Well said, Tiro!' declared Quintus. 'Always the wisest man in the room.' He yawned excessively. 'Now, come on, brother.' He reached down and pulled Cicero to his feet. 'It's getting late and you have a speech to make tomorrow. You must get some sleep.'

By the time we made our way through the house to the vestibule, the place was silent. Terentia and Tullia had retired to bed. Servius and his wife had gone home. Pomponia, who hated politics, had refused to wait for her husband and had departed with them, according to the porter. Outside, Atticus's carriage was waiting. The snow gleamed in the moonlight. From somewhere down in the city rose the familiar cry of the night-watchman, calling the midnight hour.

'A new year,' said Quintus.

'And a new consul,' added Atticus. 'Well done, my dear Cicero. I am proud to be your friend.'

They shook his hand and slapped his back, and eventually – but only grudgingly, I could not help noticing – Rufus did the same. Their words of warm congratulation flickered briefly in the icy air and vanished. Afterwards, Cicero stood in the street, waving to their carriage until it rounded the corner. As he turned to go back indoors he stumbled slightly, and plunged his foot into the snowdrift piled against the doorstep. He pulled out his wet shoe, shook it crossly and swore, and it was on the tip of my tongue to say it was an omen; but wisely, I think, I held my peace.

XXI

I do not know how the ceremony goes these days, when even the most senior magistrates are merely errand boys, but in Cicero's time the first visitor to call upon the new consul on the day of his swearing-in was always a member of the College of Augurs. Accordingly, just before dawn, Cicero stationed himself in the atrium alongside Terentia and his children to await the augur's arrival. I knew he had not slept well for I had heard him moving about upstairs, pacing up and down, which is what he always did when he was thinking. But his powers of recuperation were miraculous, and he looked fit and keen enough as he stood with his family, like an Olympian who has been training his whole life for one particular race and at last is about to run it.

When all was ready I signalled to the porter and he opened the heavy wooden door to admit the keepers of the sacred chickens, the *pularii* – half a dozen skinny little fellows, looking a bit like chickens themselves. Behind this escort loomed the augur, tapping the floor with his curved staff: a veritable giant in his full rig of tall conical cap and abundant purple robe. Little Marcus shrieked when he saw him coming down the passageway and hid behind Terentia's skirts. The augur that day was Quintus Caecilius Metellus Celer, and I should say something of him, for he was to be an important figure in Cicero's story. He was just back from fighting in the East – a real soldier, something of a war hero, in fact, after beating off an enemy attack on his winter quarters while greatly outnumbered. He had served under the command of Pompey the Great, who also happened to be married to his sister, which had not exactly hindered his promotion. Not that it mattered. He was a Metellus, and therefore more or less predestined to be consul himself in a couple of years; that day he was due to be sworn in as praetor. His wife was the notorious beauty Clodia, a member of the Claudian family: all in all you could not have got much better connected than Metellus Celer, who was by no means as stupid as he looked.

'Consul-Elect, good morning!' he barked, as if addressing his legionaries at reveille. 'So the great day has come at last. What will it hold, I wonder?'

'You're the augur, Celer. You tell me.'

Celer threw back his head and laughed. I found out later he had no more faith in divination than Cicero had, and was only a member of the College of Augurs out of political expediency. 'Well, I can predict one thing, and that is that there will be trouble. There was a crowd outside the Temple of Saturn when I passed just now. It looks as though Caesar and his friends may have posted their great bill overnight. What an amazing rogue he is!'

I was standing directly behind Cicero so I couldn't see his face, but I could tell by the way his shoulders stiffened that this news immediately set him on his guard.

'Right,' continued Celer, ducking to avoid a low beam, 'which way is your roof?'

Cicero ushered the augur towards the stairs, and as he passed me he whispered urgently, 'Go and find out what's going on, as quickly as you can. Take the boys. I need to know every clause.'

I beckoned to Sositheus and Laurea to join me, and led by a couple of slaves with torches we set off down the hill. It was hard to find our way in the darkness, and the ground was treacherous with snow. But as we came out into the forum I saw a few lights glinting ahead, and we headed for those. Celer was right. A bill had been nailed up in its traditional place outside the Temple of Saturn. Despite the hour and the cold, such was the public excitement a couple of dozen citizens had already gathered to read the text. It was very long, several thousand words, arranged on six large boards, and was proposed in the name of the tribune Rullus, although everyone knew that the authors were really Caesar and Crassus. I set Sositheus on the beginning part, Laurea on the end, while I took the middle.

We worked quickly, ignoring the people behind us complaining that we were blocking their view, and by the time we had it all down, the night was nearly over and the first day of the new year had arrived. Even without studying all the details I could tell it would cause Cicero great trouble. The republic's state land in Campania was to be compulsorily seized and divided into five thousand farms, which would be given away free. An elected commission of ten men would decide who got what, and would have sweeping powers to raise taxes abroad and buy and sell more land in Italy as they saw fit, without reference to the senate. The patricians would be incensed, and the timing of the promulgation – just hours before Cicero had to give his inaugural address – was obviously meant to put the maximum amount of pressure on the incoming consul.

When we got back to the house Cicero was still on the roof, seated for the first time on his ivory curule chair. It was bitterly cold up there, with snow still on the tiles and parapet. He was swaddled in a rug, almost up to his chin, and wore a curious hat made of rabbit fur, with flaps that covered his ears. Celer stood nearby with the *pularii* clustered around him. He was sectioning the sky with his wand, wearily checking the heavens for birds and lightning. But the air was very still and clear and he was obviously having no success. The instant Cicero saw me he seized the tablets with his mittened hands and began flicking through them rapidly. The hinged wooden frames clattered over, *click click click*, as he absorbed each page.

'Is it the populists' bill?' asked Celer, alerted by the noise and turning round.

'It is,' replied Cicero, his eyes scanning the writing with great rapidity, 'and they could not have designed a piece of legislation more likely to tear the republic apart.'

'Will you have to respond to it in your inaugural address?' I asked.

'Of course. Why else do you think they've published it now?'

'They've certainly picked their moment well,' said Celer. 'A new consul. His first day in office. No military experience. No great family behind him. They're testing your mettle, Cicero.' A shout came from down in the street. I looked over the parapet. A crowd was forming to escort Cicero to his inauguration. Across the valley, the temples of the Capitol were beginning to stand out sharply against the morning sky. 'Was that lightning?' said Celer to the nearest sacred chicken-keeper. 'I hope to Jupiter it was. My balls are freezing off.'

'If you saw lightning, Augur,' replied the chicken-keeper, 'lightning there must have been.'

'Right then, lightning it was, and on the left side, too. Write it down, boy. Congratulations, Cicero – a propitious omen. We'll be on our way.'

But Cicero seemed not to have heard. He was sitting motionless in his chair, staring straight ahead. Celer put his hand on his shoulder as he passed. 'My cousin Quintus Metellus sends his regards, by the way, along with a gentle reminder that he's still outside the city waiting for that triumph you promised him in return for his vote. So is Licinius Lucullus, come to that. Don't forget, they've hundreds of veterans they can call on. If this thing comes to civil war – as it well may – they're the ones who can come in and restore order.'

'Thank you, Celer. Bringing soldiers into Rome – that's certainly the way to avoid civil war.'

The remark was meant to be sarcastic, but sarcasm bounces off the Celers of this world like a child's arrow off armour. He left Cicero's roof with his self-importance quite undented. I asked Cicero if there was anything I could get him. 'Yes,' he said gloomily, 'a new speech. Leave me alone for a while.' I did as he asked and went downstairs, trying not to think about the task that now confronted him: speaking extempore to six hundred senators on a complicated bill he had only just seen, with the certainty that whatever he said was bound to infuriate one faction or the other. It was enough to turn my stomach liquid.

The house was filling quickly, not just with clients of Cicero's but with well-wishers walking in off the street. Cicero had ordered that no expense be spared on his inauguration, and whenever Terentia raised her concerns about the cost, he would always answer with a smile, 'Macedonia will pay.' So everyone who turned up was presented on arrival with a gift of figs and honey. Atticus, who was a leader of the Order of Knights, had brought a large detachment of Cicero's equestrian supporters; these, together with Cicero's closest colleagues in the senate, marshalled by Quintus, were all being given mulled wine in the tablinum. Servius was not among them. I managed to tell both Atticus and Quintus that the populists' bill had been posted, and that it was bad.

Meanwhile the hired flautists were also enjoying the household's food and drink, as were the percussionists and dancers, the agents from the precincts and the tribal headquarters, and of course the officials who came with the consulship: the scribes, summoners, copyists and criers from the treasury, along with the twelve lictors provided by the senate to ensure the consul's protection. All that was missing from the show was its leading actor, and as time went on it became harder and harder for me to explain his absence, for everyone by this time had heard of the bill and wanted to know what Cicero was planning to say about it. I could only reply that he was still taking the auspices and would be down directly. Terentia, decked out in her new jewels, hissed at me that I had better take control of the situation before the house was entirely stripped bare, and so I hit on the ruse of sending two slaves up to the roof to fetch the curule chair, with instructions to tell Cicero that the symbol of his authority was required to lead the procession – an excuse that also had the merit of being true.

This did the trick, and shortly afterwards Cicero descended – divested, I was glad to see, of his rabbit-fur hat. His appearance provoked a raucous cheer from the packed crowd, many of whom were now very merry on his mulled wine. Cicero handed me back the wax tablets on which the bill was written. 'Bring them with you,' he whispered. Then he climbed on to a chair, gave the company a cordial wave and asked all those present who were on the staff of the treasury to raise their hands. About two dozen did so; astonishing as it now seems, this was the total number of men who at that time administered the Roman empire from its centre.

'Gentlemen,' he said, resting his hand on my shoulder, 'this is Tiro, who has been my chief private secretary since before I was a senator. You are to regard an order from him as an order from me, and all business that it is to be discussed with me may also be raised with him. I prefer written to oral reports. I rise early and work late. I won't tolerate bribes, or corruption in any form, or gossip. If you make a mistake, don't be afraid to tell me, but do it quickly. Remember that, and we shall get along well enough. And now: to business!'

After this little speech, which left me blushing, the lictors were handed their new rods along with a purse of money for each man, and finally Cicero's curule chair was brought down from the roof and displayed to the crowd. It drew gasps and a round of applause all to itself, as well it might, for it was carved from Numidian ivory, and had cost over a hundred thousand sesterces ('Macedonia will pay!'). Then everyone drank more wine – even little Marcus took some from an ivory beaker – the flute-players started up, and we went out into the street to begin the long walk across the city.

It was still icy cold, but the sun was coming up, breaking over the rooftops in lines of gold, and the effect of the light on the snow was to give Rome a celestial radiance such as I had never seen before. The lictors led the parade; four of them carried aloft the curule chair on an open litter. Cicero walked beside Terentia. Tullia was behind him, accompanied by her fiancé, Frugi. Quintus carried Marcus on his shoulders, while on either side of the consular family marched the knights and the senators in gleaming white. The flutes piped, the drums beat, the dancers leaped. Citizens lined the streets and hung out of their windows to watch. There was much cheering and clapping, but also – to be honest – some booing, especially in the poorer parts of Subura, as we paraded along the Argiletum towards the forum. Cicero nodded from side to side, and occasionally raised his right hand in salute, but his expression was very grave, and I knew he must be turning over in his mind what lay ahead. In the period before a big speech a part of him was always unreachable. Occasionally I saw both Atticus and Quintus try to speak to him, but he shook his head, wishing to be left alone with his thoughts.

When we reached the forum it was packed with crowds. We passed the rostra and the empty senate house and finally began our ascent of the Capitol. The smoke from the altar fires was curling above the temples. I could smell the saffron burning, and hear the lowing of the bulls awaiting sacrifice. As we neared the Arch of Scipio I looked back, and there was Rome – her hills and valleys, towers and temples, porticoes and houses all veiled white and sparkling with snow, like a bride in her gown awaiting her groom.

We entered the Area Capitolina to find the remainder of the senate waiting for us, arrayed before the Temple of Jupiter. I was ushered along with Cicero's family and the rest of the household to the wooden stand that had been erected for spectators. A trumpet blast echoed off the walls, and the senators turned as one to watch as Cicero passed through their ranks – all those crafty faces, reddened by the cold, their covetous eyes studying the consul-elect: the men who had never won the consulship and knew they never would, the men who desired it and feared they might fail, and those who had held it once and still believed it was rightly theirs. Hybrida, Cicero's fellow consul, was already in position at the foot of the temple steps. Above the scene the great bronze roof looked molten in the brilliant winter sunshine. Without acknowledging one another, the two consuls-elect slowly mounted to the altar, where the chief priest, Metellus

Pius, lay on a litter, too sick to get to his feet. Surrounding Pius were the six Vestal Virgins and the other fourteen pontiffs of the state religion. I could clearly make out Catulus, who had rebuilt the temple on behalf of the senate, and whose name appeared above the door ('greater than Jove', some wags called him in consequence). Next to him was Isauricus. I recognised also Scipio Nasica, Pius's adopted son; Junius Silanus, who was the husband of Servilia, the cleverest woman in Rome; and finally, standing slightly apart from the rest, incongruous in his priestly garments, I spotted the thin and broad-shouldered figure of Julius Caesar, but unfortunately I was too far away to read his expression.

There was a long silence. The trumpet sounded again. A huge creamy bull with red ribbons tied to its horns was led towards the altar. Cicero pulled up the folds of his toga to shroud his head, and then in a loud voice recited from memory the state prayer. The instant he had finished, the attendant stationed behind the bull felled it with such a hammer blow that the crack echoed round the portico. The creature crashed on to its side and, as the attendants sawed open its stomach, the vision of the dead boy rose disconcertingly before my eyes. They had its entrails on the altar for inspection even before the wretched animal had died. There was a groan from the congregation, who interpreted the bull's thrashings as ill luck, but when the haruspices presented the liver to Cicero for his inspection, they declared it unusually propitious. Pius – who was quite blind in any case – nodded weakly in agreement, the innards were flung on the fire, and the ceremony was over. The trumpet wailed into the cold clear air for a final time, a gust of applause carried across the enclosed space, and Cicero was consul.

The senate's first session of the new year was always held in the Temple of Jupiter, with the consul's chair placed on a dais directly beneath the great bronze statue of the Father of the Gods. No citizen, however eminent, was permitted entry to the senate unless he was a member. But because I had been charged by Cicero with making a shorthand record of proceedings – the first time this had ever been done – I was allowed to sit near him during debates. You may well imagine my feelings as I followed him up the wide aisle between the wooden benches. The white-robed senators poured in behind us, their animated speculation like the roar of an incoming tide. Who had read the populists' bill? Had anyone spoken to Caesar? What would Cicero say?

As the new consul reached the dais, I turned to watch those figures I knew so well coming in to take their seats. To the right of the consular chair flowed the patrician faction – Catulus, Isauricus, Hortensius and the rest – while to the left headed those who supported the populists' cause, notably Caesar and Crassus. I searched for Rullus, in whose name the bill had been laid, and spotted him with the other tribunes. Until very recently he had been just another rich young dandy, but now he had taken to wearing the clothes of a poor man, and had grown a beard, to show his populist sympathies. Further along I saw Catilina fling himself down on one of the front benches reserved for praetorians, his powerful arms spread wide, his long legs outstretched. His expression was heavy with thought; no doubt he was reflecting that but for Cicero it would have been he in the consul's chair that day. His acolytes took their places behind him – men like the bankrupt gambler Curius, and the immensely fat Cassius Longinus, whose flab occupied the space of two normal senators.

I was so interested in noting who was present and how they were behaving that I briefly took my eyes off Cicero, and when I looked around he had disappeared. I wondered if he might have gone outside to throw up, which he often did when he was nervous before a difficult speech. But when I went behind the dais I found him, hidden from view, standing at the back of the statue of Jupiter, engaged in an intense discussion with Hybrida. He was staring deep into Hybrida's bloodshot blue eyes, his right hand gripping his colleague's shoulder, his left making forceful gestures. Hybrida was nodding slowly in response, as if dimly understanding something. Finally a slow smile spread across his face. Cicero released him and the two men shook hands, then they both stepped out from behind the statue. Hybrida went off to take his place, while Cicero brusquely asked if I had remembered the transcription of the bill. I replied that I had. 'Good,' he said. 'Then let us begin.'

I found my place on a stool at the bottom of the dais, opened my tablet, pulled out my stylus, and prepared to take down what would be the first official shorthand record of a senate session. Two other clerks, trained by myself, were in position on either side of the chamber, to transcribe their own versions: afterwards we would compare notes so as to produce a complete summary. I still had no idea how Cicero was planning to handle the occasion. I knew he had been trying for days to craft a speech appealing for consensus, but that it had proved so hopelessly bland he had thrown away draft after draft in disgust. Nobody could be sure how he was going to react. The anticipation in the chamber was intense. When he mounted the dais, the chatter dropped away at once, and one could sense the entire senate leaning forward to hear what he had to say.

'Gentlemen,' he began, in his usual quiet manner of opening a speech, 'it is the custom that magistrates elected to this great office should start with some expression of humility, recalling those ancestors of theirs who have also held the rank, and expressing the hope that they may prove worthy of their example. In my case such humility, I am pleased to say, is not possible.' That drew some laughter. 'I am a new man,' he proclaimed. 'I owe my elevation not to family, or to name, or to wealth, or to military renown, but to the people of Rome, and as long as I hold this office I will be the people's consul.'

It was a wonderful instrument, that voice of Cicero's, with its rich tone and its hint of a stutter – an impediment that somehow made each word seem fought for and more precious – and his words resonated in the hush like a message from Jove. Tradition demanded that he should talk first about the army, and as the great carved eagles looked down from the roof, he lauded the exploits of Pompey and the Eastern legions in the most extravagant terms, knowing his words would be relayed by the fastest means possible to the great general, who would study them with keen interest. The senators stamped their feet and roared in prolonged approval, for every man present knew that Pompey was the most powerful man in the world and no one, not even his jealous enemies among the patricians, wanted to seem reluctant in his praise.

'As Pompey upholds our republic abroad, so we must play our part here at home,' continued Cicero, 'resolute to protect its honour, wise in charting its course, just in pursuit of domestic harmony.' He paused. 'Now, you all know that this morning, before the sun had even risen, the bill of the tribune Servilius Rullus, for which we have been waiting so long, was finally posted in the forum. And the moment I heard of this, by my instructions, a number of copyists came running up all together, to bring an exact transcript of it to me.' He stretched down his arm and I passed him the three wax tablets. My hand was shaking, but his never wavered as he held them aloft. 'Here is the bill, and I earnestly assure you that I have examined it as carefully as is possible in the circumstances of today and in the time allowed me, and that I have reached a firm opinion.'

He waited, and looked across the chamber – to Caesar in his place on the second bench, staring impassively at the consul, and to Catulus and the other patrician ex-consuls on the front bench opposite.

'It is nothing less,' he said, 'than a dagger, pointed towards the body politic, that we are being invited to plunge into our own heart!'

His words produced an immediate eruption – of shouted anger and dismissive gestures from the populists' benches and a low, masculine rumble of approval from the patricians'.

'A dagger,' he repeated, 'with a long blade.' He licked his thumb and flicked open the first notebook. 'Clause one, page one, line one. The election of the ten commissioners ...'

In this way he cut straight through the posturing and sentiment to the nub of the issue, which was, as it always is, power. 'Who proposes the commission?' he asked. 'Rullus. Who determines who is to elect the commissioners? Rullus. Who summons the assembly to elect the commissioners? Rullus ...' The patrician senators began joining in, chanting the unfortunate tribune's name after every question. 'Who declares the results?'

'Rullus!' boomed the senate.

'Who alone is guaranteed a place as a commissioner?'

'Rullus!'

'Who wrote the bill?'

'*Rullus!*' And the house collapsed in tears of laughter at its own wit, while poor Rullus flushed pink and looked this way and that as if seeking somewhere to hide. Cicero must have gone on for half an hour in this fashion, clause by clause, quoting the bill and mocking it and shredding it, in such savage terms that the senators around Caesar and on the tribunes' bench began to look distinctly grim. To think that he had had only an hour or so to collect his thoughts was marvellous. He denounced it as an attack on Pompey – who could not stand for election to the commission *in absentia* – and as an attempt to re-establish the kings in the guise of commissioners. He quoted freely from the bill – '*The ten commissioners shall settle any colonists they like in whatever towns and districts they choose, and assign them lands wherever they please*' – and made its bland language sound like a call for tyranny.

'What then? What kind of settlement will be made in those lands? What will be the method and arrangement of the whole affair? "Colonies will be settled there," Rullus says. Where? Of what kind of men? In what places? Did you, Rullus, think that we should hand over to you, and to the real architects of your schemes' – and here he pointed directly at Caesar and Crassus – 'the whole of Italy unarmed, that you might strengthen it with garrisons, occupy it with colonies, and hold it bound and fettered by every kind of chain?'

There were shouts of 'No!' and 'Never!' from the patrician benches. Cicero extended his hand and averted his gaze from it, in the classic gesture of rejection. 'Such things as these I will resist passionately and vigorously. Nor will I, while I am consul, allow men to set forth those plans against the state which they have long had in mind. I have decided to carry on my consulship in the only manner in which it can be conducted with dignity and freedom. I will never seek to obtain a province, any honours, any distinctions or advantage, nor anything that a tribune of the people can prevent me from obtaining.'

He paused to emphasise his meaning. I had my head down, writing, but at that I looked up sharply. *I will never seek to obtain a province.* Had he really just said that? I could not believe it. As the implications of his words sank in, the senators began to murmur.

'Yes,' said Cicero, over the swelling notes of disbelief, 'your consul, on this first of January, in a crowded senate, declares that, if the republic continues in its present state, and unless some danger arises that he cannot honourably avoid meeting, he will not accept the government of a province.'

I glanced across the aisle to where Quintus was sitting. He looked as if he had just swallowed a wasp. Macedonia – that shimmering prospect of wealth and luxury, of independence from a lifetime of drudgery in the law courts – was gone!

'Our republic has many hidden wounds,' declared Cicero, in the sombre tone he always used in peroration. 'Many wicked designs of evil citizens are being formed. Yet there is no external danger. No king, no people, no nation is to be feared. The evil is confined entirely within our gates. It is internal and domestic. It is the duty of each of us to remedy it to the best of our power. If you promise me your zeal in upholding the common dignity, I will certainly fulfil the most ardent wish of the republic – that the authority of this order, which existed in the time of our ancestors, may now, after a long interval, be seen to be restored to the state.' And with that he sat down.

Well, it certainly was a memorable address, and accorded with Cicero's first law of rhetoric, that a speech must always contain at least one surprise. But the shocks were not over yet. It was the custom when the presiding consul had finished his opening remarks for him to call next upon his colleague to give his opinion. The loud applause of the majority, and the catcalls from the benches around Catilina and Caesar, had barely died away, when Cicero shouted out, 'The house recognises Antonius Hybrida!'

Hybrida, who was sitting on the front bench nearest Cicero, glanced sheepishly across at Caesar, then got to his feet. 'This bill that's been proposed by Rullus – from what I've seen of it – I have to say – in my opinion – given the state of the republic it's really not such a good idea.' He opened and closed his mouth a couple of times. 'So I'm against it,' he said, and sat down abruptly.

After a moment's silence a great noise poured out from the senate, made up of all kinds of emotions – derision, anger, pleasure, shock. It was clear that Cicero had just pulled off a remarkable political coup, for everyone had taken it as certain that Hybrida would support his allies the populists. Now he had reversed himself entirely, and his motivation could not be more obvious – with Cicero ruling himself out of the running for a province, Macedonia would be his after all! The patrician senators on the benches behind Hybrida were leaning forward and clapping him on the back in sarcastic congratulations, and he was squirming at their taunts and looking nervously across the aisle at his erstwhile friends. Catilina seemed stupefied, like a man turned to stone. As for Caesar, he simply leaned back and folded his arms and studied the ceiling of the temple, shaking his head and smiling slightly, while the pandemonium continued.

The rest of the session was an anticlimax. Cicero worked his way down the list of praetors and then began calling the former consuls, asking each his opinion of Rullus's bill. They split exactly along factional lines. Cicero did not even call Caesar: he was still too junior, having not yet held imperium. The only really menacing note was struck by Catilina. 'You have called yourself the people's consul,' he sneered at Cicero, when at long last his turn came to speak. 'Well, we shall see what the people have to say about that!'

But the day belonged to the new consul, and when the light began to fade and he declared the session adjourned until after the Latin Festival, the patricians escorted him out of the temple and across the city to his home as if he were one of their own, rather than a despised 'new man'.

Cicero was in a great good humour as he stepped across the threshold, for nothing is more pleasing in politics than to catch your opponents off guard, and the defection of Hybrida was all that anyone could talk about. Quintus, however, was furious, and the moment the house was at last emptied of well-wishers, he turned on his brother with an anger I had never before witnessed. It was all the more embarrassing because Atticus and Terentia were also present.

'Why did you not consult any of us before giving away your province?' he demanded.

'What does it matter? The effect is what counts. You were sitting opposite them. Whom did you think looked sicker – Caesar or Crassus?'

But Quintus was not to be deflected. 'When was this decided?'

'To be honest, I've had it in mind ever since I drew the lot for Macedonia.'

At this, Quintus threw up his hands in exasperation. 'Do you mean to say that when we were talking to you last night, you'd already made up your mind?'

'More or less.'

'But why didn't you tell us?'

'First, because I knew you'd disagree. Second, because I thought there was still just a chance Caesar might produce a bill I could support. And third, because what I choose to do with my province is my business.'

'No, it's not just *your* business, Marcus, it's *our* business. How are we to pay off our debts without the income from Macedonia?'

'You mean, how are *you* to finance *your* campaign for the praetorship this summer?'

'That's unfair!'

Cicero seized Quintus's hand. 'Brother, listen to me. You will have your praetorship. And you won't acquire it through bribery, but through the good name of the Cicero family, which will make the triumph all the sweeter. You must see I had to separate Hybrida from Caesar and the tribunes? My only hope of piloting the republic through this storm is to keep the senate united. I can't have my colleague plotting behind my back. Macedonia had to go.' He appealed to Atticus and Terentia. 'Who wants to govern a province, in any case? You know I couldn't bear to leave you all behind in Rome.'

'And what's to stop Hybrida simply taking Macedonia off you and supporting the prosecution of Rabirius?' persisted Quintus.

'Why would he bother? His only reason for joining their schemes was money. Now he can pay off his debts without them. Besides, nothing's signed and sealed – I can always change my mind. And meanwhile by this noble gesture I show the people I'm a man of principle who puts the welfare of the republic ahead of his own personal gain.'

Quintus looked at Atticus. Atticus shrugged. 'The logic is sound,' he said.

'And what do you think, Terentia?' asked Quintus.

Cicero's wife had kept very quiet, which was unlike her. Even now she did not say anything, but continued to stare at her husband, who stared back at her impassively. Slowly she reached up to her hair, and from those tight dark curls she plucked the diadem that was fastened there. Still without taking her eyes from Cicero's face she removed the necklace from her throat, unclipped the emerald brooch from her breast, and slid the gold bracelets from each of her wrists. Finally, grimacing with the effort, she pulled the rings off her fingers. When she had finished, she cupped all this newly purchased jewellery in her two hands, and let it fall. The glittering gems and precious metal scattered noisily across the mosaic floor. Then she turned and walked out of the room.

XXII

We had to leave Rome at first light the next morning, part of that great exodus of magistrates, their families and retainers required to attend the Latin Festival on the Alban Mount. Terentia accompanied her husband, and the atmosphere between them inside their carriage was as chilly as the January mountain air outside. The consul kept me busy, dictating first a long dispatch to Pompey, describing political affairs in Rome, and then a series of shorter letters to each of the provincial governors, while Terentia kept her eyes averted from him and pretended to sleep. The children travelled with their nurse in another carriage. Behind us stretched a great convoy of vehicles conveying the elected rulers of Rome – first Hybrida and then the praetors: Celer, Cosconius, Pompeius Rufus, Pomptinus, Roscius, Sulpicius, Valerius Flaccus. Only Lentulus Sura, as urban praetor, stayed behind in the city to guard its welfare. 'The place will burn to the ground,' observed Cicero, 'with that idiot in charge.'

We reached Cicero's house at Tusculum early in the afternoon, but there was little time to rest, as he had to leave almost at once to judge the local athletes. The highlight of the Latin Games was traditionally the swinging competition, with so many points awarded for height, so many for style, and so many for strength. Cicero had not a clue which competitor was the best, and so ended up announcing that all were equally worthy victors and that he would award a prize to everyone, paid for out of his own pocket. This gesture won warm applause from the assembled country folk. As he rejoined Terentia in the carriage, I heard her remark to him, 'Presumably Macedonia will pay?' He laughed, and that was the beginning of a thaw between them.

The main ceremony took place at sunset on the summit of the mountain, which was accessible only by a steep and twisting road. As the sun sank, it grew brutally cold. Snow lay ankle-deep on the rocky ground.

Cicero walked at the head of the procession, surrounded by his lictors. Slaves carried torches. From all the branches of the trees and in the bushes the locals had hung small figures or faces made of wood or wool, a reminder of a time when human sacrifice had been practised and a young boy would be strung up to speed the end of winter. There was something indescribably melancholy about the whole scene – the bitter chill, the gathering twilight, and those sinister emblems rustling and turning in the wind. On the highest piece of ground the altar fire spat out orange sparks against the stars. An ox was sacrificed to Jupiter, and libations of milk from the nearby farms were also offered. 'Let the people refrain from strife and quarrelling,' proclaimed Cicero, and the traditional words seemed weighted with an extra meaning that evening.

By the time the ceremony was over, an immense full moon had risen like a blue sun and was casting an unhealthy light across the scene. It did at least have the merit of illuminating our path very clearly as we turned to descend, but then occurred two events that were to be talked about for weeks afterwards. First, the moon was suddenly and inexplicably blotted out, exactly as if it had been plunged into a black pool, and the procession, which had been relying on its light, was obliged to come to an abrupt and undignified halt while more torches were lit. The interruption did not last long, but it is strange how being stranded on a mountain path in darkness can work on one's imagination, especially if the vegetation around one is sown with hanging effigies. Quite a few voices were raised in panic, not least when it was realised that all the other stars and constellations were still shimmering brightly. I raised my eyes to the heavens with the rest, and that was when we saw a shooting star – pointed at the tip like a flaming spear – spurt across the night sky to the west, exactly in the direction of Rome, where it faded and vanished. Loud exclamations of wonder were followed by more mutterings in the dark as to what all this portended.

Cicero said nothing, but waited patiently for the procession to resume. Later that night, after we had safely reached Tusculum, I asked him what he made of it all. 'Nothing,' he replied, warming his chilled bones at the fire. 'Why should I? The moon went behind a cloud and a star crossed the sky. What else is there to be said?'

The following morning a message arrived from Quintus, who was looking after Cicero's interests back in Rome. Cicero read the letter and then showed it to me. It reported that a great wooden cross had been erected on the Field of Mars, rising starkly over the snowy plain, and that the plebs were flocking out of the city to look at it. 'Labienus is going around openly saying that the cross is for Rabirius, and that the old man will be hanging from it by the end of the month. You should return as soon as possible.'

'I will say one thing for Caesar,' said Cicero. 'He doesn't waste much time. His court hasn't even heard any evidence yet, but he wants to keep up the pressure on me.' He stared into the fire. 'Is the messenger still here?'

'He is.'

'Send a note ahead to Quintus and tell him we'll be back by nightfall, and another to Hortensius. Say I appreciated his visit the other day. Tell him I have thought the matter over and I shall be delighted to appear beside him in defence of Gaius Rabirius.' He nodded to himself. 'If it's a fight Caesar wants, he shall have one.' When I reached the door he called me back. 'Also, send one of the slaves to find Hybrida, and ask him if he would care to travel back with me in my carriage to Rome, to settle our arrangement. I need to have something in writing before Caesar gets to him and persuades him to change his mind.'

Thus I found myself later that day seated opposite one consul and next to the other, trying to write down the terms of their agreement as we bounced along the Via Latina. An escort of lictors rode ahead of us. Hybrida brought out a small flask of wine from which he took regular nips, occasionally offering it with a shaky hand to Cicero, who declined politely. I had never seen Hybrida for an extended period at such close quarters before. His once-noble nose was red and squashed – broken in battle he always claimed, but everyone knew he had got it in a tavern brawl – his cheeks were purple and his breath smelt so strongly of drink I felt I should go dizzy from the fumes. Poor Macedonia, I thought, to have such a creature as its governor. Cicero proposed that they should simply swap provinces, which would save having to put the matter to a vote in the senate. ('As you want,' said Hybrida. 'You're the lawyer.') In return for receiving Macedonia, Hybrida undertook to oppose the populists' bill and to support the defence of Rabirius. He also agreed to pay Cicero one quarter of the revenue he derived as governor. Cicero, for his part, promised to do his best to ensure that Hybrida's term was extended to two or three years, and to act as his defence counsel in the event that he was afterwards prosecuted for corruption. He hesitated over this last condition, as the chances of Hybrida being put on trial, given his character, were plainly high, but in the end he gave an undertaking and I wrote it down.

When the haggling was concluded, Hybrida produced his flask again, and this time Cicero consented to take a sip. I could tell by his expression that the wine was undiluted and not to his taste, but he pretended to find it pleasant, and then the two consuls settled back in their seats, seemingly satisfied at a job well done.

'I always thought,' said Hybrida, suppressing a burp, 'that you rigged that ballot for our provinces.'

'How could I have done that?'

'Oh, there are plenty of ways, as long as the consul's in on it. You can have the winning token hidden in your palm and substitute it for the one you draw. Or the consul can do it for you when he announces what you've got. So you really didn't do that?'

'No,' said Cicero, slightly affronted. 'Macedonia was mine by right.'

'Is that a fact?' Hybrida grunted and raised his flask. 'Well, we've fixed it now. Let's drink to fate.'

We had reached the plain, and the fields beyond the road stretched flat and bare. Hybrida started humming to himself.

'Tell me, Hybrida,' said Cicero after a while, 'did you lose a boy a few days ago?'

'A what?'

'A boy. About twelve years old.'

'Oh, him,' replied Hybrida, in an offhand way, as if he were in the regular habit of losing boys. 'You heard about that?'

'I didn't just hear about it, I saw what was done to him.' Cicero was suddenly staring at Hybrida with great intensity. 'As a mark of our new friendship, will you tell me what happened?'

'I'm not sure I should do that.' Hybrida gave Cicero a crafty look. Drunkard he might have been, but he was not without cunning, even in his cups. 'You've said some hard things about me in the past. I've got to get used to trusting you.'

'If you mean by that remark, will anything you say privately go beyond the two of us, let me put your mind at ease. We are now bound together, Hybrida, whatever may have happened between us earlier. I shan't do anything to jeopardise our alliance, which is at least as precious to me as it is to you, even if you tell me you killed the boy yourself. But I feel I need to know.'

'Very prettily put.' Hybrida burped again and nodded to me. 'And the slave?'

'He is utterly trustworthy.'

'Then have another drink,' said Hybrida, once more holding out the flask, and when Cicero hesitated he shook it in his face. 'Go on. I can't abide a man who stays sober while others drink.' So Cicero swallowed his distaste and took another gulp of wine, while Hybrida described what had happened to the boy as cheerfully as if he were relating a tale from a hunting trip. 'He was a Smyrnan. Very musical. I forget his name. He used to sing to my guests at dinner. I lent him to Catilina for a party just after Saturnalia.' He took another swig. 'Catilina really hates you, doesn't he?'

'I expect so.'

'Me, I'm easier by nature. But Catilina? Oh no! He's a Sergius through and through. Can't bear the thought that he was beaten to the consulship by a common man, and a provincial to boot.' He pursed his lips and shook his head. 'After you won the election, I swear he lost his mind. Anyway, at this party he was pretty wild, and to cut a long tale short, he suggested we should swear an oath, a sacred oath, which required a sacrifice appropriate to the undertaking. He had my boy summoned, and told him to start singing. And then he got behind him and' – Hybrida made a sweeping gesture with his fist – 'bang. That was it. Quick at least. The rest I didn't stay for.'

'Are you telling me Catilina killed the boy?'

'He split his skull.'

'Dear gods! A Roman senator! Who else was present?'

'Oh, you know – Longinus, Cethegus, Curius. The usual gang.'

'So four members of the senate – five including you?'

'You can leave me out of it. I was sickened, I can tell you. That lad cost me thousands.'

'And what kind of oath "appropriate" to such an abomination did he have you all swear?'

'Actually, it was to kill you,' said Hybrida cheerfully, and raised his flask. 'Your health.' Then he burst out laughing. He laughed so much, he spluttered the wine. It leaked from his battered nose and trickled down his stubbled chin and stained the front of his toga. He brushed at it ineffectively, and then gradually the motions ceased. His hand dropped, he slowly nodded forwards, and very soon after that he fell asleep.

This was the first occasion on which Cicero heard of any conspiracy against him, and to begin with he was unsure how to respond. Was it just some piece of drunken, bestial debauchery, or was it to be taken as a serious threat? As Hybrida started snoring, Cicero gave me a look of infinite revulsion and passed the remainder of the journey in silence with his arms folded, a brooding expression on his face. As for Hybrida, he slept all the way to Rome, so deeply that when we reached his house he had to be lifted out of the carriage by the lictors and laid out in the vestibule. His slaves seemed entirely used to receiving their master in this fashion, and as we left, one was tipping a jug of water over the consul's head.

Quintus and Atticus were waiting when we arrived home, and Cicero quickly told them what he had heard from Hybrida. Quintus was all for making the story public at once, but Cicero was not convinced. 'And then what?' he asked.

'The law should be allowed to take its course. The perpetrators must be publicly accused, prosecuted, disgraced and exiled.'

'No,' said Cicero. 'A prosecution would stand no chance of success. First, who would be mad enough to bring one? And if, by a miracle, some brave and foolhardy soul were willing to take on Catilina, where would he find the evidence for a conviction? Hybrida will refuse to be a witness, even with a promise of immunity – you may be sure of that. He'll simply deny the whole thing ever happened, and break off his alliance with me. And the corpse has gone, remember? Indeed there are witnesses to the fact that I've already made a speech assuring the people there has been no ritual killing!'

'So we do nothing?'

'No, we watch, and we wait. We need to get a spy in Catilina's camp. He won't trust Hybrida any more.'

'We should also take extra precautions,' said Atticus. 'How long do you have the lictors?'

'Until the end of January, when Hybrida starts his term as president of the senate. They come back to me again in March.'

'I suggest we ask for volunteers from the Order of Knights to protect you in public while they're not around.'

'A private bodyguard? People will say I'm putting on airs. It will have to be done discreetly.'

'It will be, don't worry. I'll arrange it.'

So it was agreed, and in the meantime Cicero set about trying to find an agent who might gain the confidence of Catilina, and who could then report back in secret on what he was up to. He first broached the matter a couple of days later with young Rufus. He summoned him to the house and began by apologising for his rudeness after dinner. 'You must understand, my dear Rufus,' he explained, walking him around the atrium with his arm across his shoulders, 'that it is one of the failings of the old always to see the young for what they were rather than for what they have become. I treated you as that tearaway who came into my household as a boy three years ago, whereas I now realise you are a man of nearly twenty, making his way in the world and deserving of greater respect. I am truly sorry for any offence, and hope none has been taken.'

'The fault was mine,' responded Rufus. 'I won't pretend I agree with your policies. But my love and respect for you is unshaken, and I won't allow myself to think ill of you again.'

'Good lad.' Cicero pinched his cheek. 'Did you hear that, Tiro? He loves me! So you wouldn't want to kill me?'

'Kill you? Of course not! Whatever made you think I would?'

'Others who share your views have talked of killing me – Catilina to name but one,' and he described to Rufus the killing of Hybrida's slave and the terrible oath Catilina had made his confederates swear.

'Are you certain?' asked Rufus. 'I've never heard him mention such a thing.'

'Well, he has undoubtedly spoken of his desire to murder me – Hybrida assures me of it – and if ever he does again, I'd like to think you'd give me warning.'

'Oh, I see,' said Rufus, looking at Cicero's hand on his shoulder. 'That's why you've brought me up here – to ask me to be your spy.'

'Not a spy, a loyal citizen. Or has our republic sunk to such a level that killing a consul comes second to friendship?'

'I'd neither kill a consul nor betray a friend,' replied Rufus, detaching himself from Cicero's embrace, 'which is why I'm glad that the shadow over our friendship has been lifted.'

'An excellent lawyer's answer. I taught you better than I realised.'

After he had gone, Cicero said thoughtfully, 'That young man is on his way to repeat every word I've just said to Catilina' – an observation that may well have been true, for certainly from that day onwards Rufus kept clear of Cicero but was often to be seen in Catilina's company. It was an ill-assorted gang he had joined: high-spirited young bloods like Cornelius Cethegus, out for a fight; ageing and dissolute noblemen like Marcus Laeca and Autronius Paetus, whose public careers had been frustrated by their private vices; mutinous ex-soldiers led by rabble-rousers like Caius Manlius, who had been a centurion under Sulla. What bound them together was loyalty to Catilina – who could be quite charming when he was not trying to kill you – and a desire to see the existing state of affairs in Rome smashed to pieces. Twice when Cicero had to address public assemblies, as part of his opposition to Rullus's bill, they set up a constant racket of jeers and whistles, and I was glad that Atticus had made arrangements to protect him, especially as the Rabirius affair was now catching fire.

Rullus's bill, Rabirius's prosecution, Catilina's death threat – you must remember that Cicero was having to contend with all these three at once, as well as coping with the general business of running the senate. Historians in my opinion often overlook this aspect of politics. Problems do not queue up outside a statesman's door, waiting to be solved in an orderly fashion, chapter by chapter, as the books would have us believe; instead they crowd in en masse, demanding attention. Hortensius, for example, arrived to discuss tactics for the defence of Rabirius only a few hours after Cicero had been howled down at the public assembly on Rullus's bill. And there was a further consequence of this overwork. Because Cicero was so preoccupied, Hortensius, who had little else to do, had effectively taken control of the case. Settling himself in Cicero's study and looking very pleased with himself, he announced that the matter was solved.

'Solved?' repeated Cicero. 'How?'

Hortensius smiled. He had employed a team of scribes, he said, to gather evidence, and they had turned up the intriguing fact that a ruffian named Scaeva, the slave of a senator, Q. Croton, had been given his freedom immediately after Saturninus's murder. The scribes had enquired further in the state archives. According to Scaeva's papers of manumission, he was the one who had 'struck the fatal blow' that killed Saturninus, and for this 'patriotic act' had been rewarded with his liberty by the senate. Both Scaeva and Croton were long since dead, but Catulus, once his memory had been jogged, claimed to remember the incident well enough, and had sworn an affidavit that after Saturninus had been stoned unconscious, he had seen Scaeva climb down to the floor of the senate house and finish him off with a knife.

'And that,' said Hortensius in conclusion, passing Catulus's affidavit to Cicero, 'I think you will agree, destroys Labienus's case against our client, and with a bit of luck will bring this wretched business to a swift conclusion.' He sat back in his chair and looked about him with an air of great satisfaction. 'Don't tell me you disagree?' he added, noticing Cicero's frown.

'In principle of course you are right. But I wonder in practice whether this will help us much.'

'Of course it will! Labienus has no case left. Even Caesar will have to concede that. Really, Cicero,' he said with a smile and the tiniest wag of a manicured finger, 'I could almost believe you're jealous.'

Cicero remained unconvinced. 'Well, we shall see,' he remarked to me after this conference. 'But I fear Hortensius has no idea of the forces ranged against us. He still imagines Caesar to be just another ambitious young senator on the make. He has not yet glimpsed his depths.'

Sure enough, on the very day Hortensius submitted his evidence to Caesar's special court, Caesar and his fellow judge – his elder cousin – without even hearing any witnesses, pronounced Rabirius guilty, and sentenced him to death by crucifixion. The news spread through Rome's cramped streets like a firestorm, and it was a very different Hortensius who appeared in Cicero's study the following morning.

'The man is a monster! A complete and utter swine!'

'And how has our unfortunate client reacted?'

'He doesn't yet know what's happened. It seemed kinder not to tell him.'

'So now what do we do?'

'We have no alternative. We appeal.'

Hortensius duly lodged an immediate appeal with the urban praetor, Lentulus Sura, who in turn referred the question to an assembly of the people, summoned for the following week on the Field of Mars. This was ideal terrain from the prosecution's point of view: not a court with a respectable jury, but a great swirling multitude of citizens. To enable them all to vote on Rabirius's fate, the entire proceedings would have to be crammed into one short winter's day. And as if that wasn't enough,

Labienus was also able to use his powers as tribune to stipulate that no defence speech should last for longer than half an hour. On hearing of this restriction, Cicero observed, 'Hortensius needs half an hour merely to clear his throat!' and as the date of the hearing drew closer, he and his fellow counsel bickered more frequently. Hortensius saw the matter in purely legal terms. The main thrust of his speech, he declared, would be to establish that the real killer of Saturninus was Scaeva. Cicero disagreed, seeing the trial as wholly political. 'This isn't a court,' he reminded Hortensius. 'This is the mob. Do you seriously imagine, in all the noise and excitement, with thousands of people milling about, that anybody is going to care a fig that the actual fatal blow was struck by some wretched slave who's been dead for years?'

'What line would you take, then?'

'I think we must concede at the outset that Rabirius was the killer, and claim that the action was legally sanctioned.'

Hortensius threw up his hands. 'Really, Cicero, I know you've a reputation as a tricky fellow and all that, but now you're simply being perverse.'

'And I'm afraid you spend too much time on the Bay of Naples talking to your fish. You no longer know this city as I do.'

Since they were unable to reach an agreement, it was decided that Hortensius would speak first and Cicero last, and each would argue as he pleased. I was glad that Rabirius was too feebleminded to grasp what was going on, because otherwise he would have been in despair, especially as Rome was anticipating his trial as if it were a circus. The cross on the Field of Mars had become a regular meeting place and was festooned with placards demanding justice, land and bread. Labienus also got hold of a bust of Saturninus and set it up on the rostra, garlanded with laurel. It did not help that Rabirius had a reputation as a vicious old skinflint; even his adopted son was a moneylender. Cicero was in no doubt that the verdict would go against him, and decided at least to try to save his life. He therefore laid an emergency resolution before the senate reducing the penalty for *perduellio* from crucifixion to exile. Thanks to Hybrida's support, this was narrowly passed, despite angry opposition from Caesar and the tribunes. Metellus Celer went out of the city late that night with a party of slaves and tore down the cross, smashed it up and burned it.

This, then, was how matters stood on the morning of the trial. Even as Cicero was checking his speech and dressing to go down to the Field of Mars, Quintus turned up in his chamber and urged his brother to withdraw as defence counsel. He had done all he could, argued Quintus, and would only suffer an unnecessary loss of prestige when Rabirius was found guilty. It might also be physically dangerous for him to confront the populists outside the city walls. I could see that Cicero was tempted by these arguments. But not the least of the reasons why I loved him, despite his faults, was that he possessed that most attractive form of courage: the bravery of a nervous man. After all, any rash fool can be a hero if he sets no value on his life, or hasn't the wit to appreciate danger. But to understand the risks, perhaps even to flinch at first, but then to summon the strength to face them down – that in my opinion is the most commendable form of valour, and that was what Cicero displayed that day.

Labienus was already in place on the platform when we reached the Field of Mars, alongside his precious stage prop, the bust of Saturninus. He was an ambitious soldier, one of Pompey's fellow countrymen from Picenum, and he affected to copy the great general in all things – his girth, his swaggering gait, even his hair, which he wore swept back in a Pompeian wave. When he saw Cicero and his lictors approaching, he put his fingers in his mouth and let out a derisive whistle, and this was taken up by the crowd, which must have numbered about ten thousand. It was an intimidating noise, and it intensified as Hortensius appeared leading Rabirius by the hand. The old fellow did not look frightened so much as bewildered by the racket and the numbers pressing forward to get a glimpse of him. I was pushed and shoved as I struggled to stay close to Cicero. I noticed a line of legionaries, their helmets and breastplates glinting in the bright January light, and behind them, sitting in a stand on a row of seats reserved for distinguished spectators, the military commanders Quintus Metellus, conqueror of Crete, and Licinius Lucullus, Pompey's predecessor in the East. Cicero made a face at me when he saw them, for he had promised both aristocratic generals triumphs in return for their support at election time, and had so far done nothing about it.

'It must be a crisis,' Cicero whispered to me, 'if Lucullus has left his palace on the Bay of Naples to mingle with the common herd!'

He clambered up the ladder on to the platform, along with Hortensius, and finally Rabirius, who had such difficulty mounting the rungs his advocates finally had to reach down and haul him up. All three glistened with the spittle that had been showered on them. Hortensius looked especially appalled, for obviously he had not realised how unpopular the senate had become during that hard winter. The orators sat down on their bench, with Rabirius between them. A trumpet sounded, and across the river the red flag was hoisted over the hill of Janiculum to signal that the city was in no peril of assault and the assembly could begin.

As the presiding magistrate, Labienus both controlled proceedings and acted as prosecutor, and this gave him a tremendous advantage. A bully by nature, he elected to speak first, and was soon shouting abuse at Rabirius, who sank lower and lower in his seat. Labienus did not bother to summon witnesses. He did not need to: he had the votes already. He finished with a stern peroration about the arrogance of the senate and the greed of the small clique that controlled it, and the necessity to make a harsh example of Rabirius, so that never in the future would any consul dare to imagine he could sanction the murder of a fellow citizen and hope to escape unpunished. The crowd roared in agreement. 'I realised then,' Cicero confided in me afterwards, 'with the force of a revelation, that the true target of this lynch mob of Caesar's was not Rabirius at all, but me, as consul, and that somehow I had to regain control of the situation before my authority to deal with the likes of Catilina was destroyed entirely.'

Hortensius went next, and did his best, but those great orotund purple passages for which he was so famous belonged to another setting – and, in truth, another era. He was past fifty, had more or less retired, was out of practice – and it showed. Some in the audience near the platform actually began to talk over him, and I was close enough to see the panic in his face as Hortensius gradually realised that he – the great Hortensius, the Dancing Master, the King of the Law Courts – was actually losing his audience! The more frantically he flung out his arms and patrolled the platform and swivelled his noble head, the more risible he seemed. Nobody was interested in his arguments. I could not hear all of what he said, as the din was tremendous, with thousands of citizens milling around and chatting to one another while they waited to vote. He broke off, sweating despite the cold, and wiped his face with his handkerchief, then called his witnesses, first Catulus and next Isauricus. Each came up to the platform and was heard respectfully. But the moment Hortensius resumed his speech, the racket of conversation started up again. By then he could have combined the tongue of Demosthenes with the wit of

Plautus – it would not have made a difference. Cicero stared straight ahead into the din, white-faced, immobile, as if chiselled out of marble.

At length Hortensius sat down and it was Cicero's turn to speak. Labienus called on him to address the assembly, but such was the volume of noise he did not rise at first. Instead he examined his toga carefully, and brushed away a few invisible specks. The hubbub continued. He checked his fingernails. He folded his arms. He looked around him. He waited. It went on a long time. And amazingly a kind of sullen, respectful silence did eventually fall over the Field of Mars. Only then did Cicero nod, as if in approval, and slowly get to his feet.

'Although it is not my habit, fellow citizens,' he said, 'to begin a speech by explaining why I am appearing on behalf of a particular individual, nonetheless in defending the life, the honour and the fortunes of Gaius Rabirius, I consider it my duty to lay before you an explanation. For this trial is not really about Rabirius – old, infirm and friendless as he is. This trial, gentlemen, is nothing less than an attempt to ensure that from now on there should be no central authority in the state, no concerted action of good citizens against the frenzy and audacity of wicked men, no refuge for the republic in emergencies, and no security for its welfare. Since this is so,' he continued, his voice becoming louder, his hands and his gaze rising slowly to the heavens, 'I beg of most high and mighty Jupiter and all the other immortal gods and goddesses to grant me their grace and favour, and I pray that by their will this day that has dawned may see the salvation of my client and the rescue of the constitution!'

Cicero used to say that the bigger a crowd the more stupid it is, and that a useful trick with an immense multitude is always to call on the supernatural. His words carried like a rolling drum across the hushed plain. There was still some chatter at the periphery, but it was too far away to drown him out.

'Labienus, you summon this assembly as a great populist. But of the two of us, which is really the people's friend? You, who think it right to threaten Roman citizens with the executioner even in the midst of their assembly; who, on the Field of Mars, give orders for the erection of a cross for the punishment of citizens? Or I, who refuse to allow this assembly to be defiled by the presence of the executioner? What a friend of the people our tribune is, what a guardian and defender of its rights and liberties!'

Labienus waved his hand at Cicero, as if he were a horsefly to be swiped away, but there was petulance in the gesture: like all bullies, he was better at handing out injuries than absorbing them.

'You maintain,' continued Cicero, 'that Gaius Rabirius killed Lucius Saturninus, a charge that Quintus Hortensius, in the course of his most ample defence, has proved to be false. But if it were up to me, I would brave this charge. In fact I would admit it. I would plead guilty to it!' A rumble of anger began to spread among the crowd, but Cicero shouted over their jeers. 'Yes, yes, I would admit it! I only wish I could proclaim that my client's *was* the hand that struck down that public enemy Saturninus!' He pointed dramatically at the bust, and it was some while before he could carry on, such was the volume of the hostility directed at him. 'You say your uncle was there, Labienus. Well, suppose he was. And suppose he was there not because his ruined fortunes left him no choice, but because his intimacy with Saturninus led him to put his friend before his country. Was that a reason for Gaius Rabirius to desert the republic and disobey the command and authority of the consul? What should I do, gentlemen, if Labienus, like Saturninus, caused a massacre of the citizens, broke from prison, and seized the Capitol with an armed force? I tell you what I should do. I should do as the consul did then. I should bring a motion before the senate, exhort you to defend the republic, and take arms myself to oppose, with your help, an armed enemy. And what would Labienus do? *He would have me crucified!*'

Yes, it was a brave performance, and I hope I have given here some flavour of the scene: the orators on the platform with their querulous client, the lictors lined up around the base to protect the consul, the teeming citizenry of Rome – plebs and knights and senators all pressed together – the legionaries in their plumed helmets and the generals in their scarlet cloaks, the sheep pens set out and made ready for the vote; the noise of it, the temples gleaming on the distant Capitol, and the bitter January cold. I kept a lookout for Caesar, and occasionally I thought I glimpsed his lean face peering from the crowd. Catilina was certainly there with his claque, including Rufus, who was yelling his share of insults at his former patron. Cicero finished, as he always did, by standing with his hand on the shoulder of his client and appealing for the mercy of the court – 'He does not ask you to grant him a happy life but only an honourable death' – and then it was all over and Labienus gave orders for the voting to begin.

Cicero commiserated with the dejected Hortensius, then jumped down from the platform and came over to where I was standing. He was still full of fire, as always after a big speech, breathing deeply, his eyes shining, his nostrils flared, like a horse at the end of a gruelling race. It had been a stirring performance. I remember one phrase in particular: 'Narrow indeed are the bounds within which Nature has confined our lives, but those of our glory are infinite.' Unfortunately, fine words are no substitute for votes, and when Quintus joined us he announced grimly that all was lost. He had just come from observing the first ballots cast – the centuries were voting unanimously to condemn Rabirius, which meant that the old man would be obliged to leave Italy immediately, his house would be pulled down, and all his property confiscated.

'This is a tragedy,' swore Cicero.

'You did your best, brother. At least he is an old man and has lived his life.'

'I'm not thinking of Rabirius, you idiot, but of my consulship!' Just as he was speaking, we heard a shout and a scream. A scuffle had started nearby, and when we turned we could clearly see the tall figure of Catilina in the thick of it, laying about him with his fists. Some of the legionaries ran to separate the combatants. Beyond them, Metellus and Lucullus had risen to their feet to watch. The augur, Celer, who was standing beside his cousin Metellus, had his hands cupped to his mouth and was urging the soldiers on. 'Just look at Celer there,' said Cicero, with a hint of admiration, 'simply itching to join in. He loves a fight!' He became thoughtful and then said suddenly, 'I'm going to talk to him.'

He set off so abruptly that his lictors had to scramble to get ahead of him to clear a path. When the two generals saw the consul approaching, they glowered at him. Both had been stuck outside the city for a long while waiting for the senate to vote them their triumphs – years, in the case of Lucullus, who had whiled away his time building a vast retreat at Misenum on the Bay of Naples as well as his mansion north of Rome. But the senate was reluctant to accede to their demands, chiefly because both had quarrelled with Pompey. So they were trapped. Only holders of imperium could have a triumph; but entering Rome to argue for a triumph would automatically end their imperium. One could sympathise with their frustration.

'Imperator,' said Cicero, raising his hand in salute to each man in turn. 'Imperator.'

'We have matters we need to discuss with you,' began Metellus in a menacing tone.

'I know exactly what you are about to say, and I assure you I shall keep my promise and argue your case in the senate to the full extent of my powers. But that's for another day. Do you see how hard pressed I am at the moment? I need some assistance, not for my sake but for the nation's. Celer, will you help me save the republic?'

Celer exchanged glances with his cousin. 'I don't know. That depends on what you want me to do.'

'It's dangerous work,' warned Cicero, knowing full well that this would make the challenge irresistible to a man such as Celer.

'I've never been called a coward. Tell me.'

'I want you to take a detachment of your cousin's excellent legionaries, cross the river, climb the Janiculum and haul down the flag.'

Even Celer swayed back on his heels at that, for the lowering of the flag – signalling the approach of an enemy army – would automatically suspend the assembly, and the Janiculum was always heavily protected by guards. Both he and his cousin turned to Lucullus, the senior of the trio, and I watched as that elegant patrician calculated the odds. 'It's a fairly desperate trick, Consul,' he said.

'It is. But if we lose this vote, it will be a disaster for Rome. No consul will ever again be sure he has the authority to suppress an armed rebellion. I don't know why Caesar wishes to set such a precedent, but I do know we can't afford to let him.'

In the end, it was Metellus who said, 'He's right, Lucius. Let's give him the men. Quintus,' he said to Celer, 'are you willing?'

'Of course.'

'Good,' said Cicero. 'The guards should obey you as praetor, but in case they make trouble, I'll send my secretary with you,' and to my dismay he pulled his ring from his finger and pressed it into my hand. 'You're to tell the commander that the consul says an enemy threatens Rome,' he said to me, 'and the flag must be lowered. My ring is the proof that you are my emissary. Do you think you can do that?'

I nodded. What else could I do? Metellus meanwhile was beckoning to the centurion who had weighed in against Catilina, and very soon afterwards I found myself panting along behind a contingent of thirty legionaries, their swords drawn, moving at the double, with Celer and the centurion at their head. Our mission – let us be frank about this – was to disrupt the Roman people in a lawful assembly, and I remember thinking, Never mind Rabirius, *this* is treason.

We left the Field of Mars and trotted across the Sublician Bridge, over the swollen brown waters of the Tiber, then traversed the flat plain of the Vaticanum, which was filled with the squalid tents and small makeshift huts of the homeless. At the foot of the Janiculum the crows of Juno watched from the bare branches of their sacred grove – such a mass of gnarled black shapes that when we passed and sent them crying into the air it was as if the very wood itself had taken flight. We toiled on up the road to the summit, and never did a hill seem so steep. Even as I write, I can feel again the thump of my heart and the searing of my lungs as I sobbed for breath. The pain in my side was as sharp as a spear tip being pressed into my flesh.

On the ridge of the hill, at the highest point, stands a shrine to Janus, with one face turned to Rome and the other to the open country, and above this, atop a high pole, flew a huge red flag, flapping and cracking in the stiff wind. About twenty legionaries were huddled around two large braziers, and before they could do anything to stop us we had them surrounded.

'Some of you men know me!' shouted Celer. 'I am Quintus Caecilius Metellus Celer – praetor, augur, lately returned from the army of my brother-in-law, Pompey the Great. And this fellow,' he said, gesturing to me, 'comes with the ring of our consul, Cicero. His orders are to lower the flag. Who's in command here?'

'I am,' said a centurion, stepping forward. He was an experienced man of about forty. 'And I don't care whose brother-in-law you are, or what authority you have, that flag stays flying unless an enemy threatens Rome.'

'But an enemy does threaten Rome,' said Celer. 'See!' And he pointed to the countryside west of the city, which was all spread out beneath us. The centurion turned to look, and in a flash, Celer had seized him from behind by his hair and had the edge of his sword at the soldier's throat. 'When I tell you there's an enemy coming,' he hissed, 'there's an enemy coming, understand? And do you know how I know there's an enemy coming, even though you can't see anything?' He gave the man's hair a vicious tug, which made him grunt. 'Because I'm a fucking *augur*, that's why. Now take down that flag, and sound the alarm.'

Nobody argued after that. One of the sentries unfastened the rope and hauled down the flag, while another picked up his trumpet and blew several piercing blasts. I looked across the river to the Field of Mars and the thousands all standing around there, but the distance was too great to judge immediately what was happening. Only gradually did it become apparent that the crowd was draining away, and that the clouds of dust rising at the edge of the field were being raised by people fleeing to their homes. Cicero described to me afterwards the effect of the trumpet and the realisation that the flag was coming down. Labienus had tried to calm the crowd and assure them it was a trick, but people in a mass are as stupid and easily frightened as a school of fish or a herd of beasts. In no time word spread that the city was about to be attacked. Despite the pleas of Labienus and his fellow tribunes, voting had to be abandoned. Many of the fences of the sheep pens were smashed by the stampeding citizens. The stand where Lucullus and Metellus had been sitting was knocked over and trampled to pieces. There was a fight. A pickpocket was stabbed to death. The pontifex maximus, Metellus Pius, suffered some kind of seizure and had to be rushed back to the city, unconscious. According to Cicero, only one man remained calm, and that was Gaius Rabirius, rocking back and forth on his bench, alone on the deserted platform amid the chaos, his eyes closed, humming to himself some strange and discordant tune.

For a few weeks after the uproar on the Field of Mars it seemed that Cicero had won. Caesar in particular went very quiet, and made no attempt to renew the case against Rabirius. On the contrary: the old man retired to his house in Rome, where he lived on, in a world of his own, entirely unmolested, until a year or so later, when he died. It was the same story with the populists' bill. Cicero's coup in buying off Hybrida had the effect of encouraging other defections, including one of the tribunes, who was bribed by the patricians to switch sides. Blocked in the senate by Cicero's coalition, and threatened with a veto in the popular assembly, Rullus's immense bill, the product of so much labour, was never heard of again.

Quintus was in a great good humour. 'If this were a wrestling match between you and Caesar,' he declared, 'it would all be over. Two falls decide the winner, and you have now laid him out flat twice.'

'Unfortunately,' replied Cicero, 'politics is neither as clean as a wrestling match, nor played according to fixed rules.'

He was absolutely certain that Caesar was up to something, otherwise his inactivity made no sense. But what was it? That was the mystery.

At the end of January, Cicero's first month as president of the senate was completed. Hybrida took over the curule chair and Cicero busied himself with his legal work. His lictors gone, he went down to the forum escorted by a couple of stout fellows from the Order of Knights. Atticus was as good as his word: they stayed close, but not so conspicuously that anyone suspected they were other than the consul's friends. Catilina made no move. Whenever he and Cicero encountered one another, which was inevitable in the cramped conditions of the senate house, he would ostentatiously turn his back. Once I thought I saw him draw his finger across his throat as Cicero passed by, but nobody else seemed to notice. Caesar, needless to say, was all affability, and indeed congratulated Cicero on the power of his speeches and the skill of his tactics. That was a lesson to me. The really successful politician detaches his private self from the insults and reverses of public life, so that it is almost as if they happen to someone else; Caesar had that quality more than any man I ever met.

Then one day came the news that Metellus Pius, the pontifex maximus, had died. It was not entirely a surprise. The old soldier was nearer seventy than sixty and had been ailing for several years. He never regained consciousness after the stroke he suffered on the Field of Mars. His body lay in state in his official residence, the old palace of the kings, and Cicero, as a senior magistrate, took his turn as one of the guard of honour standing watch over the corpse. The funeral was the most elaborate I had ever seen. Propped on his side, as though at a dinner, and dressed in his priestly robes, Pius was carried on a flower-decked litter by eight fellow members of the College of Priests, among them Caesar, Silanus, Catulus and Isauricus. His hair had been combed and pomaded, his leathery skin massaged with oil, his eyes were wide open; he seemed much more alive now that he was dead. His adopted son, Scipio, and his widow, Licinia Minor, walked behind the bier, followed by the Vestal Virgins and the chief priests of the official deities. Then came the chariots bearing the leaders of the Metelli, Celer at the front, and to see the family all together – and to see as well the actors parading behind them in the death masks of Pius's ancestors – was to be reminded that this was still the most powerful political clan in Rome.

The immense cortège passed along the Via Sacra, through the Fabian Arch (which was draped in black for the occasion) and across the forum to the rostra, where the litter was raised upright, so that the mourners could gaze on the body for a final time. The centre of Rome was packed. The entire senate wore togas dyed black. Spectators clustered on the temple steps, on balconies and roofs and the bases of the statues, and they stayed all the way through the eulogies, even though these lasted for hours. It was as if we all knew that in bidding farewell to Pius – stern, stubborn, haughty, brave, and perhaps a little stupid – we were bidding farewell to the old republic, and that something else was struggling to be born.

Once the bronze coin had been placed in Pius's mouth and he had been borne off to lie with his ancestors, the question naturally arose: who should be his successor? By universal consent the choice lay between the two most senior members of the senate: Catulus, who had rebuilt the Temple of Jupiter, and Isauricus, who had triumphed twice and was even older than Pius. Both coveted the office; neither would yield to the other. Their rivalry was comradely but intense. Cicero, who had no preference, at first took little interest in the contest. The electorate was in any case confined to the fourteen surviving members of the College of Priests. But then, about a week after Pius's funeral, while he was waiting outside the senate house with the others for the session to begin, he chanced upon Catulus and casually asked if any decision on filling the post had yet been reached.

'No,' said Catulus. 'And it won't be soon, either.'

'Really? Why is that?

'We met yesterday and agreed that in view of the fact that there are two candidates of equal merit, we should go back to the old method, and let the people choose.'

'Is that wise?'

'I certainly think so,' said Catulus, tapping the side of his beaky nose and giving one of his thin smiles, 'because I believe that in a tribal assembly I shall win.'

'And Isauricus?'

'He also believes that *he* will win.'

'Well, good luck to you both. Rome will be the winner whoever is the victor.' Cicero began to move away but then checked himself, and a slight frown crossed his face. He returned to Catulus. 'One more thing, if I may? Who proposed this widening of the franchise?'

'Caesar.'

Although Latin is a language rich in subtlety and metaphor, I cannot command the words, either in that tongue or even in Greek, to describe Cicero's expression at that moment. 'Dear gods,' he said in a tone of utter shock. 'Is it possible he means to stand himself?'

'Of course not. That would be ridiculous. He's far too young. He's thirty-six. He's not yet even been elected praetor.'

'Yes, but even so, in my opinion, you would be well advised to reconvene your college as quickly as possible and go back to the existing method of selection.'

'That is impossible.'

'Why?'

'The bill to change the franchise was laid before the people this morning.'

'By whom?'

'Labienus.'

'Ah!' Cicero clapped his hand to his forehead.

'You're alarming yourself unnecessarily, Consul. I don't believe for an instant that Caesar would be so foolish as to stand, and if he did he would be *crushed*. The Roman people are not entirely mad. This is a contest to be head of the state religion. It demands the utmost moral rectitude. Can you imagine Caesar responsible for the Vestal Virgins? He has to live among them. It would be like entrusting your hen-coop to a fox!'

Catulus swept on, but I could see that the tiniest flicker of doubt had entered his eyes, and soon the gossip started that Caesar was indeed intending to stand. All the sensible citizens were appalled at the notion, or made ribald jokes and laughed out loud. Still, there was something about it – something breathtaking about the sheer cheek of it, I suppose – that even his enemies could not help but admire. 'That fellow is the most phenomenal gambler I have ever encountered,' remarked Cicero. 'Each time he loses, he simply doubles his stake and rolls the dice again. Now I understand why he gave up on Rullus's bill and the prosecution of Rabirius. He saw that the chief priest was unlikely to recover, calculated the odds, and decided that the pontificate was a much better bet than either.' He shook his head in wonder and set about doing what he could to make sure this third gamble also failed. And it would have done, but for two things.

The first was the incredible stupidity of Catulus and Isauricus. For several weeks Cicero went back and forth between them, trying vainly to make them see that they could not both stand, that if they did they would split the anti-Caesar vote. But they were proud and irritable old men. They would not yield, or draw lots, or agree on a compromise candidate, and in the end both their names went forward.

The other decisive factor was money. It was said at the time that Caesar bribed the tribes with so much cash the coin had to be transported in wheelbarrows. Where had he found it all? Everyone said the source must be Crassus. But even Crassus would surely have baulked at the twenty million – *twenty million!* – Caesar was rumoured to have laid out to the bribery agents. Whatever the truth, by the time the vote was held on the Ides of March, Caesar must have known that defeat would mean his ruin. He could never have repaid such a sum if his career had been checked. All that would have been left to him were humiliation, disgrace, exile, possibly even suicide. That is why I am inclined to believe the famous story that on the morning of the poll, as he left his little house in Subura to walk to the Field of Mars, he kissed his mother goodbye and announced that he would either return as pontifex maximus or he would not return at all.

The voting lasted most of the day, and by one of those ironies that abound in politics, it fell to Cicero, who was once again in March the senior presiding magistrate, to announce the result. The early spring sun had fallen behind the Janiculum, and the sky was streaked in horizontal lines of purple, red and crimson, like blood seeping through a sodden bandage. Cicero read out the returns in a monotone. Of the seventeen tribes polled, Isauricus had won four, Catulus six, and Caesar had been backed by seven. It could scarcely have been closer. As Cicero climbed down from the platform, obviously sick to his stomach, the victor flung back his head and raised his arms to the heavens. He looked almost demented with delight – as well he might, for he knew that, come what may, he would now be pontifex maximus for life, with a huge state house on the Via Sacra and a voice in the innermost councils of the state. In my opinion, everything that happened subsequently to Caesar really stemmed from this amazing victory. That crazy outlay of twenty million was actually the greatest bargain in history: it would buy him the world.

XXIII

From this time on men began to look upon Caesar differently. Although Isauricus accepted his defeat with the stoicism of an old soldier, Catulus – who had set his heart on the chief pontificate as the crown of his career – never entirely recovered from the blow. The following day he denounced his rival in the senate. 'You are no longer working underground, Caesar!' he shouted in such a rage his lips were flecked with spittle. 'Your artillery is planted in the open and it is there for the capture of the state!' Caesar's only response was a smile. As for Cicero, he was in two minds. He agreed with Catulus that Caesar's ambition was so reckless and gargantuan it might one day become a menace to the republic. 'And yet,' he mused to me, 'when I notice how carefully arranged his hair is, and when I watch him adjusting his parting with one finger, I can't imagine that he could conceive of such a wicked thing as to destroy the Roman constitution.'

Reasoning that Caesar now had most of what he wanted, and that everything else – a praetorship, the consulship, command of an army – would come in due course, Cicero decided the time had come to try to absorb him into the leadership of the senate. For example, he felt it was unseemly to have the head of the state religion bobbing up and down during debates, alongside senators of the second rank, trying to catch the consul's eye. Therefore he resolved to call upon Caesar early, straight after the praetorians. But this conciliatory approach immediately landed him with a fresh political embarrassment – and one that showed the extent of Caesar's cunning. It happened in the following way.

Very soon after Caesar was elected – it must have been within three or four days at most – the senate was in session, with Cicero in the chair, when suddenly there was a shout at the far end of the chamber. Pushing his way through the crowd of spectators gathered at the door was a bizarre apparition. His hair was wild and disordered and powdery with dust. He had hastily thrown on a purple-edged toga, but it did not entirely conceal the military uniform he was wearing underneath. In place of red shoes his feet were clad in a soldier's boots. He advanced down the central aisle, and whoever was speaking halted in mid-sentence as all eyes turned on the intruder. The lictors, standing near me just behind Cicero's chair, stepped forward in alarm to protect the consul, but then Metellus Celer shouted out from the praetorian benches: 'Stop! Don't you see? It's my brother!' and sprang up to embrace him.

Observing this, a great murmur of wonder and then alarm went round the chamber, for everyone knew that Celer's younger brother, Quintus Caecilius Metellus Nepos, was one of Pompey's legates in the war against King Mithradates, and his dramatic and dishevelled appearance, obviously fresh from the scene of war, might well mean that some terrible calamity had befallen the legions.

'Nepos!' cried Cicero. 'What is the meaning of this? Speak!'

Nepos disentangled himself from his brother. He was a haughty man, very proud of his handsome features and fine physique. (They say he preferred to lie with men rather than women, and certainly he never married or left issue; but that is just gossip, and I should not repeat it.) He threw back his magnificent shoulders and turned to face the chamber. 'I come directly from the camp of Pompey the Great in Arabia!' he declared. 'I have travelled by the swiftest boats and the fastest horses to bring you great and joyful tidings. The tyrant and foremost enemy of the Roman people, Mithradates Eupator, in the sixty-eighth year of his life, is dead. The war in the East is won!'

There followed that peculiar instant of startled silence that always succeeds dramatic news, and then the whole of the chamber rose in thunderous acclamation. For a quarter of a century Rome had been fighting Mithradates. Some say he massacred eighty thousand Roman citizens in Asia; others allege one hundred and fifty thousand. Whichever is true, he was a figure of terror. For as long as most could remember, the name of Mithradates had been used by Roman mothers to frighten their children into good behaviour. And now he was gone! And the glory was Pompey's! It did not matter that Mithradates had actually committed suicide rather than been killed by Roman arms. (The old tyrant had taken poison, but because of all the precautionary antidotes he had swallowed over the years it had had no effect, and he had been obliged to call in a soldier to finish him off.) It did not matter either that most knowledgeable observers credited Lucius Lucullus, still waiting outside the gates for his triumph, as the strategist who had really brought Mithradates to his knees. What mattered was that Pompey was the hero of the hour, and Cicero knew what he had to do. The moment the clamour died down, he rose and proposed that in honour of Pompey's genius, there should be five days of national thanksgiving. This was warmly applauded. Then he called on Hybrida to utter a few inarticulate words of praise, and next he allowed Celer to laud his brother for travelling a thousand miles to bring the glad tidings. That was when Caesar got up; Cicero gave him the floor in honour of his status as chief priest, assuming he was going to offer ritual thanks to the gods.

'With all due respect to our consul, surely we are being niggardly with our gratitude?' said Caesar silkily. 'I move an amendment to Cicero's motion. I propose the period of thanksgiving be doubled to ten full days, and that for the rest of his life Gnaeus Pompey be permitted to wear his triumphal robes at the Games, so that the Roman people even in their leisure will ever be reminded of the debt they owe him.'

I could almost hear Cicero's teeth grinding behind his fixed smile as he accepted the amendment and put it to the vote. He knew that Pompey would mark well that Caesar had been twice as generous as he. The motion passed with only one dissenting voice: that of young Marcus Cato, who declared in a furious voice that the senate was treating Pompey as if he were a king, crawling to him and flattering him in a way that would have sickened the founders of the republic. He was jeered, and a couple of senators sitting near to him tried to pull him down. But looking at the faces of Catulus and the other patricians, I could tell how uncomfortable his words had made them.

Of all these great figures from the past who roost like bats in my memory and flutter from their caves at night to disturb my dreams, Cato is the strangest. What a bizarre creature he was! He was not much more than thirty at this time, but his face was already that of an old man. He was very angular. His hair was unkempt. He never smiled, and rarely bathed: he gave off a ripe smell, I can tell you. Contrariness was his religion. Even though he was immensely rich, he never rode in a litter or a carriage but went everywhere on foot, and frequently refused to wear shoes, or sometimes even a tunic – he desired, he said, to train himself to care nothing for the opinion of the world on any matter, trivial or great. The clerks at the treasury were terrified of him. He had served there as a junior magistrate for a year and they often told me how he had made them justify every item of expenditure, down to the tiniest sum. Even after he had left the department he always came into the senate chamber carrying a full set of treasury accounts, and there he would sit, in his regular place on the furthest back bench, hunched forward over the figures, gently rocking back and forth, oblivious to the laughter and talk of the men around him.

The day after the news about the defeat of Mithradates, Cato came to see Cicero. The consul groaned when I told him Cato was waiting. He knew him of old, having acted briefly as his advocate when Cato – in another of his other-worldly impulses – had resolved to sue his cousin, Lepida, in order to force her to marry him. Nevertheless, he ordered me to show him in.

'Pompey must be stripped of his command immediately,' announced Cato the moment he entered the study, 'and summoned home at once.'

'Good morning, Cato. That seems a little harsh, don't you think, given his recent victory?'

'The victory is precisely the trouble. Pompey is supposed to be the servant of the republic, but we are treating him as our master. He will return and take over the entire state if we're not careful. You must propose his dismissal tomorrow.'

'I most certainly will not! Pompey is the most successful general Rome has produced since Scipio. He deserves all the honours we can grant him. You're falling into the same error as your great-grandfather, who hounded Scipio out of office.'

'Well, if you won't stop him, I shall.'

'You?'

'I intend to put myself forward for election as tribune. I want your support.'

'Do you, indeed!'

'As tribune I shall veto any bill that may be introduced by one of Pompey's lackeys to further his designs. It is my intention to be a politician entirely different to any who has gone before.'

'I am sure you will be,' replied Cicero, glancing over the young man's shoulder at me, and giving me the very slightest wink.

'I propose to bring to public affairs for the first time the full rigour of a coherent philosophy, subjecting each issue as it arises to the maxims and precepts of stoicism. You know that I have living in my household none other than Athenodorus Cordylion – whom I think you will agree is the leading scholar of the stoics. He will be my permanent adviser. The republic is drifting, Cicero, that is how I see it – drifting towards disaster on the winds and currents of easy compromise. We should never have given Pompey his special commands.'

'I supported those commands.'

'I know, and shame on you! I saw him in Ephesus on my way back to Rome a year or two ago, all puffed up like some Eastern emperor. Where's his authorisation for all these cities he's founded and provinces he's occupied? Has the senate discussed it? Have the people voted?'

'He's the commander on the spot. He must be allowed a degree of autonomy. And having defeated the pirates, he needed to set up bases to secure our trade. Otherwise the brigands would simply have come back again when he left.'

'But we are meddling in places we know nothing about! Now we have occupied Syria. Syria! What business do we have in Syria? Next it will be Egypt. This is going to require permanent legions stationed overseas. And whoever commands the legions needed to control this empire, be it Pompey or someone else, will ultimately control Rome, and whoever raises a voice against it will be condemned for his lack of patriotism. The republic will be finished. The consuls will simply manage the civilian side of things, on behalf of some generalissimo overseas.'

'No one doubts that there are dangers, Cato. But this is the business of politics – to surmount each challenge as it appears and be ready to deal with the next. The best analogy for statesmanship in my opinion is navigation – now you use the oars and now you sail, now you run before a wind and now you tack into it, now you catch a tide and now you ride it out. All this takes years of skill and study, not some manual written by Zeno.'

'And where does it take you, this voyage of yours?'

'A very pleasant destination called survival.'

'Ha!' Cato's laugh was as disconcerting as it was rare: a kind of harsh, humourless bark. 'Some of us hope to arrive at a more inspiring land than that! But it will require a different kind of seamanship to yours. These will be my precepts,' he said, and he proceeded to count them off on his long and bony fingers: 'Never be moved by favour. Never appease. Never forgive a wrong. Never differentiate between things that are wrong – what is wrong is wrong, whatever the size of the misdemeanour, and that is the end of the matter. And finally, never compromise on any of these principles. "The man who has the strength to follow them—"'

'"—is always handsome however misshapen, always rich however needy, always a king however much a slave." I am familiar with the quotation, thank you, and if you want to go and live a quiet life in an academy somewhere, and apply your philosophy to your chickens and your fellow pupils, it might possibly even work. But if you want to run this republic, you will need more books in your library than a single volume.'

'This is a waste of time. It is obvious you will never support me.'

'On the contrary, I shall certainly vote for you. Watching you as a tribune promises to be one of the most entertaining spectacles Rome will ever have seen.'

After Cato had gone, Cicero said to me, 'That man is at least half mad, and yet there is something to him.'

'Will he win?'

'Of course. A man with the name of Marcus Porcius Cato will always rise in Rome. And he has a point about Pompey. How do we contain him?' He thought for a while. 'Send a message to Nepos enquiring if he has recovered from his journey, and inviting him to attend a military council at the end of tomorrow's session of the senate.'

I did as commanded, and the message duly came back that Nepos was at the consul's disposal. So after the house was adjourned the following afternoon, Cicero asked a few senior ex-consuls with military experience to remain behind, in order to receive a more detailed report from Nepos of Pompey's plans. Crassus, who had tasted the delights both of the consulship and of the power that flows from great wealth, was increasingly obsessed with the one thing he had never had – military glory – and he was anxious to be included in this council of war. He even lingered around the consul's chair in the hope of an invitation. But Cicero despised him more than anyone except Catilina, and delighted in this opportunity to snub his old adversary. He ignored him so pointedly that eventually Crassus stamped off in a rage, leaving a dozen or so grey-headed senators gathered around Nepos. I stood discreetly to one side, taking notes.

It was shrewd of Cicero to include in this conclave men like Gaius Curio, who had won a triumph a decade earlier, and Marcus Lucullus, Lucius's younger brother, for my master's gravest weakness as a statesman was his ignorance of military affairs. In his youth, in delicate health, he had hated everything about military life – the raw discomfort, the bone-headed discipline, the dull camaraderie of the camp – and had retreated as soon as possible to his studies. Now he felt his inexperience keenly, and he had to leave it to the likes of Curio and Lucullus, Catulus and Isauricus, to question Nepos. They soon established that Pompey had a force of eight well-equipped legions, with his personal headquarters encamped – at any rate the last time Nepos had seen him – south of Judaea, a few hundred miles from the city of Petra. Cicero invited opinions.

'As I see it, there are two options for the remainder of the year,' said Curio, who had fought in the East under Sulla. 'One is to march north to the Cimmerian Bosphorus, aim for the port of Pantikapaion, and bring the Caucasus into the empire. The other, which personally I would favour, is to strike east and settle affairs with Parthia once and for all.'

'There is a third choice, don't forget,' added Isauricus. 'Egypt. It's ours for the taking, after Ptolemy left it to us in his will. I say he should go west.'

'Or south,' suggested M. Lucullus. 'What's wrong with pressing on to Petra? There's very fertile land beyond the city, down on that coast.'

'North, east, west or south,' summed up Cicero. 'It seems Pompey is spoilt for choice. Do you know which he favours, Nepos? I am sure the senate will ratify his decision, whatever it may be.'

'Actually, I understand he favours withdrawing,' said Nepos.

The deep silence that followed was broken by Isauricus. '*Withdrawing?*' he repeated in astonishment. 'What do you mean, *withdrawing*? He has forty thousand seasoned men at his disposal, with nothing to stop them in any direction.'

'"Seasoned" is your word for them. "Exhausted" would be more accurate. Some of them have been fighting and marching out there for more than a decade.'

There was another pause as the implications of this settled over the gathering.

Cicero said, 'Do you mean to tell us he wants to bring them all back to Italy?'

'Why not? It is their home, after all. And Pompey has signed some extremely effective treaties with the local rulers. His personal prestige is worth a dozen legions. Do you know what they now call him in the East?'

'Please tell us.'

'"The Warden of Land and Sea."'

Cicero glanced around the faces of the former consuls. Most wore expressions of incredulity. 'I think I speak for all of us, Nepos, when I tell you that the senate would not be happy with a complete withdrawal.'

'Absolutely not,' said Catulus, and all the grey heads nodded in agreement.

'In which case, what I propose is this,' continued Cicero. 'That we send a message back with you to Pompey, conveying – obviously – our pride and delight and gratitude for his mighty feats of arms, but also our desire that he should leave the army in place for a fresh campaign. Of course, if he wants to lay down the burden of command, after so many years of service, the whole of Rome would understand, and warmly welcome home her most distinguished son—'

'You can suggest whatever you like,' interrupted Nepos rudely, 'but I shan't be carrying the message. I'm staying in Rome. Pompey has discharged me from military service, and it is my intention to canvass for election as tribune. And now, if you'll excuse me, I have other business to attend to.'

Isauricus swore as he watched the young officer swagger out of the chamber. 'He wouldn't have dared talk like that if his father had still been alive. What kind of generation have we bred?'

'And if that's how a puppy like Nepos speaks to us,' said Curio, 'imagine what his master will be like, with forty thousand legionaries behind him.'

'"The Warden of Land and Sea"', murmured Cicero. 'I suppose we should be grateful he's left us the air.' That drew some laughter. 'I wonder what pressing matter Nepos has to attend to that's more important than talking to us.' He beckoned me over, and whispered in my ear, 'Run after him, Tiro. See where he goes.'

I hurried down the aisle and reached the door in time to glimpse Nepos and his retinue of attendants heading across the forum in the direction of the rostra. It was around the eighth hour of the day, still busy, and amid the bustle of the city I had no trouble hiding myself – not that Nepos was the type of man much given to looking over his shoulder. His little entourage passed the Temple of Castor, and it was lucky I had moved up close behind it, because a little way up the Via Sacra they abruptly vanished, and I realised they had stepped into the official residence of the pontifex maximus.

My first impulse was to head back to Cicero and tell him, but then a shrewder instinct checked me. There was a row of shops opposite the great mansion, and I pretended to browse for jewellery, all the time keeping an eye on Caesar's door. I saw his mother arrive in a litter, and then his wife leave by the same means, looking very young and beautiful. Various people went in and out, but no one I recognised. After about an hour the impatient shopkeeper announced that he wished to close, and he ushered me out on to the street just as the unmistakable bald head of Crassus emerged from a small carriage and darted through the doorway into Caesar's home. I lingered for a while but no one else appeared, and not wishing to push my luck any further, I slipped away to give Cicero the news.

He had left the senate house by this time, and I found him at home, working on his correspondence. 'Well, at least that clears up one mystery,' he said, when I described what I had seen. 'We now know where Caesar got the twenty million to buy his office. It didn't all come from Crassus. A lot of it must have come from the Warden of Land and Sea.' He tilted back in his chair and became very pensive, for, as he later observed, 'When the chief general in the state, the chief moneylender and the chief priest all start meeting together, the time has come for everyone else to be on their guard.'

It was around this time that Terentia began to play an important role in Cicero's consulship. People often wondered why Cicero was still married to her after fifteen years, for she was excessively pious and had little beauty and even less charm. But she had something rarer. She had character. She commanded respect, and increasingly as the years went on he sought her advice. She had no interest in philosophy or literature, no knowledge of history; not much learning of any sort, in fact. However, unburdened by education or natural delicacy, she did possess a rare gift for seeing straight through to the heart of a thing, be it a problem or a person, and saying exactly what she thought. To begin with, not wishing to alarm her, Cicero did not mention Catilina's oath to murder him. But it was typical of Terentia's shrewdness that she soon discovered it for herself. As a consul's wife she had supervision of the cult of the Good Goddess. I cannot tell you what this entailed, as everything to do with the goddess and her serpent-infested temple on the Aventine is closed to men. All I know is that one of Terentia's fellow priestesses, a patriotic woman of noble family, came to her one day in a tearful state and warned her that Cicero's life was in danger, and that he should be on his guard. She refused to say more. But naturally Terentia would not leave it at that, and by a combination of flattery, cajolery and threats which must have been worthy of her husband, she slowly extracted the truth. Having done so, she then forced the unfortunate woman to come back to the house and repeat her story to the consul.

I was working with Cicero in his study when Terentia threw open the door. She did not knock; she never did. Being both richer than Cicero and more nobly born, she tended not to show the customary deference of wife to husband. Instead, she simply announced: 'There is someone here you must see.'

'Not now,' he said, without looking up. 'Tell them to go away.'

But Terentia stood her ground. 'It's ——,' she said, and here she named the lady, whose identity I shall conceal, not for her sake (she is long dead) but for the honour of her descendants.

'And why should I see *her*?' grumbled Cicero, and for the first time he glanced up irritably at his wife. But then he noticed the grimness of her expression and his tone changed. 'What is it, woman? What's wrong?'

'You need to listen for yourself.' She stood aside to reveal a matron of rare if fading beauty whose eyes were red and puffy from weeping. I made as if to leave, but Terentia ordered me very firmly to stay where I was. 'The slave is a highly skilled note-taker,' she explained to the visitor, 'and entirely discreet. If he so much as breathes a word to anyone, I can assure you I shall have him skinned alive.' And she gave me a look that left me in no doubt that she would do precisely that.

The subsequent meeting was almost as embarrassing for Cicero, who had a prudish streak, as it was for the lady, who was obliged, under prompting from Terentia, to confess that for several years she had been the mistress of Quintus Curius. He was a dissolute senator and friend of Catilina. Already expelled once from the senate for immorality and bankruptcy, he seemed certain to be thrown out again at the next census, and was in desperate straits.

'Curius has been in debt as long as I've known him,' explained the lady, 'but never as badly as now. His estate is mortgaged three times over. One moment he threatens to kill us both rather than endure the disgrace of bankruptcy, the next he boasts of all the fine things he's going to buy for me. Last night I laughed at him. I said, "How could *you* afford to buy *me* anything? It's *I* who has to give money to *you*!" I provoked him. We argued. Eventually he said, "By the end of the summer we shall have all the money we need." That was when he told me of Catilina's plans.'

'Which are?'

She glanced down at her lap for a moment, then straightened herself and gazed steadily at Cicero. 'To murder you, and then to seize control of Rome. To cancel all debts, confiscate the property of the rich, and divide the magistracies and priesthoods among his followers.'

'Do you believe they mean it?'

'I do.'

Terentia interrupted. 'But she's left out the worst part! To bind them to him more closely, Catilina made them swear a blood oath on the body of a child. They slaughtered him like a lamb.'

'Yes,' confessed Cicero, 'I know,' and he held up his hand to forestall her protest. 'I'm sorry. I didn't know how seriously to take it. There seemed no point in upsetting you over nothing.' To the lady he said: 'You must give up the names of all those involved in this conspiracy.'

'No, I can't—'

'What's said can't be unsaid. I must have their names.'

She wept for a while. She must have known she was trapped. 'At least will you give me your word you'll protect Curius?'

'I can't promise that. I'll see what I can do. Come, madam: the names.'

It took her some time to speak, and when she did I could hardly hear her. 'Cornelius Cethegus,' she whispered. 'Cassius Longinus. Quintus Annius Chilo. Lentulus Sura and his freedman Umbrenus ...' The names suddenly started to tumble out, as if by reciting them quickly she could shorten her ordeal. 'Autronius Paetus, Marcus Laeca, Lucius Bestia, Lucius Vargunteius—'

'Wait!' Cicero was gazing at her in astonishment. 'Did you just say Lentulus Sura – the urban praetor – and his freedman Umbrenus?'

'—Publius Sulla, and his brother Servius.' She stopped abruptly.

'And that is all?'

'Those are all the senators I've heard him mention. There are others outside the senate.'

Cicero turned to me. 'How many is that?'

'Ten,' I counted. 'Eleven, if you add Curius. Twelve, if you include Catilina.'

'*Twelve senators?*' I had seldom seen Cicero more flabbergasted. He blew out his cheeks and sat back in his chair as if he had been struck. He let out a long breath. 'But men like the Sulla brothers and Sura don't even have the excuse of bankruptcy! This is just treason, plain and simple!' Suddenly he was too agitated to sit still. He jumped to his feet and started pacing the narrow floor. 'Dear gods! What's going on?'

'You should have them arrested,' said Terentia.

'No doubt I should. But once I started down that path, even if I could do it – which I can't – where would it end? There are these twelve, and who knows how many more dozens beside? I can certainly think of plenty of others who might be involved. There's Caesar, for a start – where does he stand in all this? He backed Catilina for the consulship last year and we know he's close to Sura – it was Sura, remember, who allowed the prosecution of Rabirius. And Crassus – what about him? I wouldn't put anything past him! And Labienus – he's Pompey's tribune – is Pompey involved?'

Back and forth, back and forth he went.

'They can't *all* be plotting to kill you, Cicero,' Terentia pointed out, 'otherwise you'd have been dead long ago.'

'They may not plot together, but they all see an opportunity in chaos. Some are willing to kill to bring chaos about, and others just desire to stand back and watch chaos take hold. They are like boys with fire, and Caesar is the worst of the lot. It's a kind of madness – there's madness in the state.' He went on in this style for some time, his eyes, as it were, turned inward, his imagination aflame with prophetic visions of Rome in ruins, the Tiber red with blood, the forum strewn with hacked-off heads, which he laid out for us in graphic detail. 'I must prevent it. I have to stop it. There must be a means of stopping it …'

Throughout all this, the lady who had brought him the information sat watching him in wonder. At length he halted in front of her, bent low and clasped her hands. 'Madam, it can't have been an easy thing for you to come to my wife with this tale, but thank Providence you did! It's not just me, it is Rome herself who stands for ever in your debt.'

'But what am I to do now?' she wept. Terentia gave her a handkerchief and she dabbed at her eyes. 'I can't go back to Curius after this.'

'You have to,' said Cicero. 'You're the only source I have.'

'If Catilina discovers I've betrayed his plans to you, he'll kill me.'

'He'll never know.'

'And my husband? My children? What do I say to them? To have consorted with another man is bad enough – but with a traitor?'

'If they knew your motives, they'd understand. Look upon this as your atonement. It's vital you act as if nothing has happened. Find out all you can from Curius. Draw him out. Encourage him, if necessary. But you mustn't risk coming here again – that's far too dangerous. Pass on what you learn to Terentia. You two can easily meet and talk together privately in the precincts of the temple without arousing suspicion.'

She was naturally reluctant to enmesh herself in such a net of betrayal. But Cicero could persuade anyone to do anything if he set his mind to it. And when, without promising actual immunity to Curius, he made it clear that he would do all he could to show leniency to her lover, she surrendered. Thus the lady went away to act as his spy, and Cicero began to lay his plans.

XXIV

At the beginning of April, the senate rose for the spring recess. The lictors once again returned to Hybrida, and Cicero decided it would be safer if he took his family out of Rome to stay by the sea. We slipped away at first light, whilst most of the other magistrates were preparing to attend the theatre, and set off south along the Via Appia, accompanied by a bodyguard of knights. I suppose there must have been thirty of us in all. Cicero reclined on cushions in his open carriage, alternately being read to by Sositheus and dictating letters to me. Little Marcus rode on a mule with a slave walking beside him. Terentia and Tullia each had a litter to herself, carried by porters armed with concealed knives. Each time a group of men passed us on the road, I feared it might be a gang of assassins, and by the time we reached the edge of the Pontine Marshes at twilight, after a hard day's travelling, my nerves were fairly well shredded. We put up for the night at Tres Tabernae, and the croaking of the marsh frogs and the stench of stagnant water and the incessant whine of the mosquitoes robbed me of all rest.

The next morning we resumed our journey by barge. Cicero sat enthroned in the prow, his eyes closed, his face tilted towards the warm spring sun. After the noise of the busy highway, the silence of the canal was profound, the only sound the steady clop of the horses' hoofs on the towpath. It was most unlike Cicero not to work. At the next stop a pouch of official dispatches awaited us, but when I tried to give it to him he waved me away. It was the same story when we reached his villa at Formiae. He had bought this place a couple of years earlier – a handsome house on the coastline, facing out to the Mediterranean Sea, with a wide terrace where he usually wrote, or practised his speeches. But for the whole of our first week in residence he did little except play with the children, taking them fishing for mackerel, and jumping the waves on the little beach beneath the low stone wall. Given the gravity of his problems, I was puzzled at the time by his behaviour. Now I realise, of course, that he *was* working, only in the way that a poet works: he was clearing his mind, and hoping for inspiration.

At the beginning of the second week, Servius Sulpicius came to dine, accompanied by Postumia. He had a villa just around the bay, at Caieta. He had barely spoken to Cicero since the revelation of his wife's dalliance with Caesar, but he turned up looking cheerful for once, whereas she seemed unusually morose. The reason for their contrasting humours became clear just before dinner, when Servius drew Cicero aside for a private word. Fresh from Rome, he had a most delicious morsel of gossip to impart. He could hardly contain his glee. 'Caesar has taken a new mistress: Servilia, the wife of Junius Silanus!'

'So Caesar has a new mistress? You might as well tell me there are fresh leaves on the trees.'

'But don't you see? Not only does it put paid to all those groundless rumours about Postumia and Caesar, it also makes it much harder for Silanus to beat me in the consular election this summer.'

'And why do you think that?'

'Caesar wields a great block of populist votes. He's hardly going to throw them behind his mistress's husband, is he? Some of them might actually come to me. So with the approval of the patricians and with your support as well, I really do believe I'm home and dry.'

'Well then, I congratulate you, and I shall be proud to pronounce you the winner in three months' time. Do we know yet how many candidates there are likely to be?'

'Four are certain.'

'You and Silanus, and who else?'

'Catilina.'

'Catilina's definitely standing, then?'

'Oh yes. No question of it. Caesar's already let it be known he'll be backing him again.'

'And the fourth?'

'Licinius Murena,' said Servius, naming a former legate of Lucullus who was presently the governor of Further Gaul. 'But he's too much of a soldier to have a following in the city.'

They dined that night under the stars. From my quarters I could hear the sighing of the sea against the rocks, and occasionally the voices of the quartet carried to me on the warm salty air, along with the pungent smell of their grilled fish. In the morning, very early, Cicero came himself to wake me. I was startled to find him sitting at the end of my narrow mattress, still wearing his clothes from the previous evening. It was barely light. He did not appear to have slept. 'Get dressed, Tiro. It's time we were moving.'

As I pulled on my shoes, he told me what had happened. At the end of dinner, Postumia had found an excuse to speak with him alone. 'She took my arm and asked me to walk a turn with her along the terrace, and I thought for a moment I was about to be invited to replace Caesar in her bed, for she was a little drunk and that dress of hers was practically open to her knees. But no: it seems her feelings for Caesar have curdled from lust to the bitterest hatred, and all she wanted to do was betray him. She says Caesar and Servilia are made for one another: "Two colder-hearted creatures there never were created." She says – and here I quote her ladyship verbatim – "Servilia wants to be a consul's wife, and Caesar likes to fuck consuls' wives, so what union could be more perfect? Don't take any notice of what my husband tells you. Caesar is going to do everything he can to make sure Silanus wins."'

'Is that such a bad thing?' I asked stupidly, for I was still half asleep. 'I thought you always said Silanus was dull but respectable, and so perfect for high office.'

'I do want him to win, you dunderhead! And so do the patricians, and so it now seems does Caesar. Silanus is therefore unstoppable. The real fight is going to be for the second consulship – and that, unless we are very careful, is going to be won by Catilina.'

'But Servius is so confident—'

'Not confident – complacent, which is exactly what Caesar wants him to be.'

I splashed some cold water on my face. I was at last beginning to wake up. Cicero was already halfway out of the door.

'May I ask where we are going?' I called.

'South,' he replied over his shoulder, 'to the Bay of Naples, to see Lucullus.'

He left a note of explanation for Terentia and we were gone before she woke. We travelled fast in a closed carriage to avoid being recognised

– a necessary precaution since it seemed that half the senate, weary of Rome's unusually long winter, was en route to the warm spas of Campania. We reduced the escort to make better speed and only two men guarded the consul: a great ox of a knight called Titus Sextus and his equally hefty brother, Quintus; they rode on horseback fore and aft of us.

As the sun rose higher, the air became warmer, the sea bluer, and the aromas of mimosa blossom, and of sun-dried herbs and fragrant pines, gradually infiltrated the carriage. From time to time I would part the curtain and gaze out at the landscape, and I vowed to myself that if ever I did get that little farm I so desired, it would be down here in the south. Cicero meanwhile saw nothing. He slept throughout the entire journey and only woke towards the end of the afternoon as we jolted down the narrow lane to Misenum, where Lucullus had his – well, I was going to call it a house, but the word hardly fits that veritable palace of pleasure, the Villa Cornelia, which he had bought and extended on the coast. It stood on the promontory where the herald of the Trojans lies buried, and commanded perhaps the most exquisite view in Italy, from the island of Prochyta all the way across the wondrous blueness of the Bay of Naples to the mountains of Caprae. A gentle breeze rustled the tops of an avenue of cypresses, and we descended from our dusty carriage as if into Paradise.

On hearing who was in his courtyard, Lucullus himself wafted out to greet us. He was in his middle fifties, very languid and affected, and just beginning to run to fat: seeing him in his silken slippers and Greek tunic, you would never have believed he was a great general, the greatest for over a century; he looked more like a retired dancing-master. But the detachment of legionaries guarding his house and the lictors sprawled in the shade of the plane trees served as a reminder that he had been hailed as imperator in the field by his victorious soldiers and still commanded military imperium. He insisted Cicero must dine with him, and stay the night, but that first he must bathe and rest. Such was either his chilliness or his exquisite manners that he expressed not the slightest curiosity as to why Cicero had turned up on his doorstep uninvited.

The consul and his escort were led away by flunkeys, and I assumed I would be consigned to the slaves' quarters. But not at all: as the consul's private secretary, I too was conducted to a guest room, fresh clothes were fetched for me, and then a most remarkable thing occurred, which I blush to remember but must set down if this is to be an honest account. A young female slave appeared. She was Greek, I discovered, so I was able to converse with her in her own tongue. She was in her twenties, and very charming, in a short-sleeved dress – slender, olive-skinned, with a mass of long black hair all pinned up and waiting to fall in a soft cascade. Her name was Agathe. With much giggling and insistent gesturing she persuaded me to undress and step into a small windowless cubicle, which was entirely covered in mosaics of sea creatures. I stood there for a moment, feeling somewhat foolish, until all at once the ceiling seemed to dissolve and begin pouring forth warm fresh water. This was my first experience of one of Sergius Orata's famous shower baths, and I luxuriated in it for a long while before Agathe returned and led me into the next-door room to be cleansed and massaged – and oh, what sweet delight was that! Her smile revealed teeth as white as ivory and a mischievous pink tongue. When I met up with Cicero on the terrace an hour or so later, I asked if he had tried out one of these extraordinary showers.

'Certainly not! Mine came equipped with a young whore. I never heard of such degeneracy,' and then he peered at me and said in disbelief, 'Don't tell me you did!' I turned scarlet, at which he started laughing very loudly, and for many months thereafter, whenever he wished to tease me, he would bring up the episode of Lucullus's shower bath.

Before we dined, our host took us on a tour of his palace. The main part of the house was a century old, and had been built by Cornelia, mother of the Gracchi brothers, but Lucullus had tripled it in size, adding wings and terraces and a swimming pool – all of it hewn out of the solid rock. The views on every side were astounding, the rooms sumptuous. We were led into a tunnel lined with torches that cast their light on glistening mosaics of Theseus in the labyrinth. Steps took us down to the sea and out on to a platform positioned just above the lapping waves. Here was Lucullus's particular pride – a great expanse of man-made pools, filled with every species of fish you could name, including huge eels decorated with jewellery, which came at the sound of his call. He knelt and a slave handed him a silver bucket full of food, which he gently tipped into the water. Immediately the surface roiled with smooth and powerful bodies. 'They all have names,' he said, and pointed to a particularly fat and repulsive creature with gold rings in its fins. 'I call that one Pompey.'

Cicero laughed politely. 'And whose place is that?' he asked, nodding across the water to another huge villa with a fish farm.

'That belongs to Hortensius. He thinks he can breed better fish than I, but he will never manage it. Good night, Pompey,' he said to the eel in a caressing voice. 'Sleep well.'

I thought we must have seen everything, but Lucullus had saved the climax till last. We ascended by a different route, a wide staircase tunnelled into the bowels of the dripping rock beneath the house. We passed through several heavy iron gates manned by sentries, until we came at last to a series of chambers, each of which was crammed with the treasure Lucullus had carted back from the Mithradatic war. Attendants passed their torches over glittering heaps of jewel-encrusted armour, shields, dinner plates, beakers, ladles, basins, gold chairs and gold couches. There were heavy silver ingots and chests full of millions of tiny silver coins, and a golden statue of Mithradates more than six feet high. After a while our exclamations of wonder dwindled to silence. The riches were stupefying. Then, as we went back into the tunnel, there came a very faint scuffling noise from somewhere close at hand, which at first I thought was rats, but which Lucullus explained was the noise of the sixty prisoners – friends of Mithradates, and some of his generals – whom he had been keeping down here for the past five years in readiness for his triumphal parade, at the end of which they would be strangled.

Cicero put his hand to his mouth and cleared his throat. 'Actually, imperator, it's about your triumph that I've come to see you.'

'I thought it might be,' said Lucullus, and in the torchlight I saw the briefest of smiles pass over his fleshy face. 'Shall we eat?'

Naturally we dined on fish – oysters and sea bass, crab and eel, grey and red mullet. It was all too rich for me: I was accustomed to plainer fare and took little. Nor did I utter a word during dinner, but kept a subtle distance between myself and the other guests, to signify my awareness that my presence was a special favour. The Sextus brothers ate greedily, and from time to time one or the other would rise from the table and go into the garden to vomit noisily, to clear space for the next course. Cicero as usual was sparing in his consumption, while Lucullus chewed and swallowed steadily but without any apparent pleasure.

I found myself secretly observing him, for he fascinated me, and still does. In truth I believe he was the most melancholy man I ever met. The blight of his life was Pompey, who had replaced him as supreme commander in the East and who had then, through his allies in the senate, blocked Lucullus's hopes of a triumph. Many men would have accepted this, but not Lucullus. He had everything in the world he wanted except the one thing he most desired. So he flatly refused to enter Rome or surrender his command, and instead diverted his talents and ambition into creating ever more elaborate fish ponds. He became bored and listless, his domestic life unhappy. He was married twice, the first time to one of the sisters of Clodius, from whom he separated in scandalous circumstances, alleging that she had committed incest with her brother, who had then encouraged a mutiny against Lucullus in the East. The second marriage, which still endured, was to a sister of Cato, but she was also said to be flighty and unfaithful: I never set eyes on her, so I cannot judge. I did however meet her child, Lucullus's young son, then two years old, who was brought out by his nurse to kiss his father good night. Seeing the way Lucullus treated him, I could tell he loved the lad deeply. But the moment the child had gone away to bed, the veils came down once more over Lucullus's large blue eyes and he resumed his joyless chomping.

'So,' he said eventually, between mouthfuls, 'my triumph?' There was a fragment of fish stuck on his cheek that he didn't know about. It was peculiarly distracting.

'Yes,' repeated Cicero, 'your triumph. I was thinking of laying a motion before the senate straight after the recess.'

'And will it pass?'

'I don't believe in calling votes that I can't win.'

The *chomp, chomp* continued for a while longer.

'Pompey won't be pleased.'

'Pompey will have to accept that others are allowed to triumph in this republic as well as he.'

'And what's in it for you?'

'The honour of proposing your eternal glory.'

'Balls.' Lucullus finally wiped his mouth and the particle of fish disappeared. 'You've really travelled fifty miles in a day just to tell me this? You can't expect me to believe it.'

'Oh dear, you're too shrewd for me, Imperator! Very well, I confess I also wanted to have a political talk with you.'

'Go on.'

'I believe we are drifting towards calamity.' Cicero pushed away his plate and, summoning all his eloquence, proceeded to describe the state of the republic in the starkest terms, dwelling especially on Caesar's support for Catilina, and Catilina's revolutionary programme of cancelling debts and seizing the property of the rich. He did not have to point out what a threat this posed to Lucullus, reclining in his palace amid all his silk and gold: it was perfectly obvious. Our host's face became grimmer and grimmer, and when Cicero had finished, he took his time before replying.

'So it is your firm opinion that Catilina could win the consulship?'

'It is. Silanus will take the first place and he the second.'

'Well then, we have to stop him.'

'I agree.'

'So what do you propose?'

'That is why I've come. I'd like you to stage your triumph just before the consular elections.'

'Why?'

'For the purpose of your procession, I assume you plan to bring into Rome several thousand of your veterans from all across Italy?'

'Naturally.'

'Whom you will entertain lavishly, and reward generously out of the spoils of your victory?'

'Of course.'

'And who will therefore listen to your advice about whom to support in the consular elections?'

'I would like to think so.'

'In which case, I know just the candidate they should vote for.'

'I thought you might,' said Lucullus with a cynical smile. 'You have in mind your great ally Servius.'

'Oh no. Not him. The poor fool doesn't stand a chance. No, I'm thinking of your old legate – and their former comrade-in-arms – Lucius Murena.'

Accustomed though I was to the twists and turns of Cicero's stratagems, it had never crossed my mind that he might abandon Servius so readily. For a moment I could not believe what I had just heard. Lucullus looked equally surprised. 'I thought Servius was one of your closest friends?'

'This is the Roman republic, not a coterie of friends. My heart certainly urges me to vote for Servius. But my head tells me he can't beat Catilina. Whereas Murena, with your backing, might just be able to manage it.'

Lucullus frowned. 'I have a problem with Murena. His closest lieutenant in Gaul is that depraved monster, my former brother-in-law – a man whose name is so disgusting to me I refuse to pollute my mouth by even uttering it.'

'Well then, let me utter it for you. Clodius is not a man I have any great liking for myself. But in politics one cannot always pick and choose one's enemies, let alone one's friends. To save the republic, I must abandon an old and dear companion. To save the republic, you must embrace the ally of your bitterest foe.' He leaned across the table, and added softly, 'Such is politics, Imperator, and if ever the day comes when we lack the stomach for such work, we should get out of public life *and stick to breeding fish*!'

For a moment I feared he had gone too far. Lucullus threw down his napkin and swore that he would not be blackmailed into betraying his principles. But as usual Cicero had judged his man well. He let Lucullus rant on for a while, and when he had finished he made no response, but simply gazed across the bay and sipped his wine. The silence seemed to go on for a very long time. The moon above the water cast a path of shimmering silver. Finally, in a voice leaden with suppressed anger, Lucullus said that he supposed Murena might make a decent enough consul if he was willing to take advice, whereupon Cicero promised to lay the issue of his triumph before the senate as soon as the recess ended.

Neither man having much appetite left for further conversation, we all retired early to our rooms. I had not long been in mine when I heard a gentle knocking at the door. I opened it, and there stood Agathe. She came in without a word. I assumed she had been sent by Lucullus's steward, and told her it was not necessary, but as she climbed into my bed she assured me it was of her own volition, and so I joined her. We talked between caresses, and she told me something of herself – of how her parents, now dead, had been led back as slaves from the East as part of Lucullus's war booty, and how she could just vaguely remember the village in Greece where they had lived. She had worked in the kitchens, and now she looked after the imperator's guests. In due course, as her looks faded, she would return to the kitchens, if she was lucky; if not, it would be the fields, and an early death. She talked about all this without any self-pity, as one might describe the life of a horse or a dog. Cato called himself a stoic, I thought, but this girl really was one, smiling at her fate and armoured against despair by her dignity. I said as much to her, and she laughed.

'Come, Tiro,' she said, holding up her arms and beckoning me to her, 'no more solemn words. Here is my philosophy: enjoy such brief ecstasy as the gods permit us, for it is only in these moments that men and women are truly not alone.'

When I awoke with the dawn she had gone.

Do I surprise you, reader? I remember I surprised myself. After so many years of chastity, I had ceased even to imagine such things and was content to leave them to the poets: 'What life is there, what delight, without golden Aphrodite?' Knowing the words was one thing; I never expected to know their meaning.

I had hoped we might stay for one more night at least, but the next morning Cicero announced that we were leaving. Secrecy was absolutely vital to his plans, and the longer he lingered in Misenum, the more he feared his presence would become known. So after a final brief conference with Lucullus, we set off back in the closed carriage. As we descended towards the coastal road, I stared back at the house over my shoulder. There were many slaves to be seen, working in the gardens and moving beneath the various parts of the great villa, preparing it for another perfect spring day. Cicero was also looking back.

'They flaunt their wealth,' he murmured, 'and then they wonder why they are so hated. And if that is how stupendously rich Lucullus has become, who never actually defeated Mithradates, can you imagine the colossal wealth that Pompey must now possess?'

I could not imagine it, and nor did I wish to. It sickened me. Never before had the pointlessness of piling up treasure for its own sake been more apparent to me than it was on that warm blue morning as the house receded behind me.

Now that he had settled on his strategy, Cicero was eager to pursue it, and for that we needed to return to Rome. As far as he was concerned, the holiday was over. Reaching the seaside villa at Formiae at dusk, we rested overnight, and then set off again at first light. If Terentia was irritated by this neglect of her and the children, she did not show it. She knew he would travel quicker without them. We were back in Rome by the Ides of April, and Cicero at once set about making discreet contact with Murena. The governor was still in his province of Further Gaul, but it turned out he had sent back his lieutenant, Clodius, to start planning his election campaign. Cicero hummed and hawed about what to do, for he did not trust Clodius, and nor did he want to tip off his plans to Caesar and Catilina by going openly to the young man's house. Eventually he decided to approach him via his brother-in-law, the augur Metellus Celer, and this led to a memorable encounter.

Celer lived up on the Palatine Hill, on Victory Rise, close to the house of Catulus, in a street of fine residences overlooking the forum. Cicero reasoned that nobody would find it surprising to see a consul dropping by to visit a praetor. But when we entered the mansion, we discovered that its master was away for the day on a hunting trip. Only his wife was at home, and it was she who came out to greet us, accompanied by several maids. As far as I am aware, this was the first occasion on which Cicero met Clodia, and she made a striking impression on him of beauty and of cleverness. She was thirty or thereabouts, famous for her large brown eyes with long lashes – 'Lady Ox-Eyes', Cicero used to call her – which she employed to great effect, giving men flirtatious sidelong glances, or fixing them with beguiling and intimate stares. She had an expressive mouth and a caressing voice, pitched for gossip. Like her brother, she affected a fashionable 'urban' accent. But woe betide the man who tried to be too familiar with her – she was capable of turning in an instant into a true Claudian: haughty, ruthless, cruel. A rake named Vettius, who had tried to seduce her and failed, circulated quite a good pun about her: *in triclinio Coa, in cubiculo nola* ('a silky island in the dining room, a rocky fortress in bed'), with the result that two of her other admirers, M. Camurtius and M. Caesernius, took revenge on her behalf: they beat him up, and then, to make the punishment fit the crime, they buggered him half to death.

One would have thought this a world utterly alien to Cicero, and yet there was a part of his character – a quarter of him, let us say – that was irresistibly drawn to the rakish and the outrageous, even while the other three quarters thundered in the senate against loose morals. Perhaps it was the streak of the actor in him; he always loved the company of theatre people. He also liked men and women who were not boring, and no one could ever say that Clodia was that. At any rate, each expressed great pleasure at meeting the other, and when Clodia, with one of her wide-eyed sideways looks, asked in her breathy voice if there was anything – anything at all – she could do for Cicero in her husband's absence, he replied that actually there was: he would like to have a private word with her brother.

'Appius or Gaius?' she asked, assuming he must mean one of the older two, each of whom was as stern and humourless and ambitious as the other.

'Neither. I wanted to talk to Publius.'

'Publius! The wicked boy! You have picked my favourite.' She sent a slave at once to fetch him, no doubt from whichever gambling den or brothel was his current haunt, and while they awaited his arrival, she and Cicero strolled around the atrium, studying the death masks of Celer's consular ancestors. I withdrew quietly into the shadows and therefore I could not hear what they were saying, but I heard their laughter, and I realised that the source of their amusement was the frozen, waxy faces of generation after generation of Metelli – who were, it must be admitted, famed for their stupidity.

At length Clodius swept into the house, gave a low and (I thought) sarcastic bow to the consul, kissed his sister lovingly on the mouth, and then stood with his arm around her waist. He had been in Gaul for more than a year, but had not changed much. He was still as pretty as a woman, with thick golden curls, loose clothes, and a drooping way of looking at the world that was full of condescension. To this day I cannot decide whether he and Clodia really were lovers, or whether they simply enjoyed outraging respectable society. But I learnt afterwards that Clodius behaved this way with all three of his sisters in public, and certainly Lucullus had believed the rumours of incest.

Anyway, if Cicero was shocked, he did not show it. Smiling his apologies to Clodia, he asked if he might be allowed a word with her younger brother in private. 'Well, all right,' she replied with mock reluctance, 'but I am very jealous,' and after a final lingering, flirtatious handshake with the consul, she disappeared into the interior of the great house, leaving the three of us alone. Cicero and Clodius exchanged a few pleasantries about Further Gaul and the arduousness of the journey across the Alps, and then Cicero said, 'Now tell me, Clodius, is it true that your chief, Murena, is going to seek the consulship?'

'It is.'

'That's what I'd heard. It surprised me, I must confess. How do you think he can possibly win?'

'Easily. There are any number of ways.'

'Really? Give me one.'

'Obligation: the people still remember the generous games he staged before he was elected praetor.'

'Before he was elected praetor? My dear fellow, that was three years ago! In politics, three years is ancient history. Believe me, Murena is entirely forgotten here. Out of sight is out of mind, as far as Rome is concerned. I ask again: where do you propose to find the votes?'

Clodius maintained his smile. 'I believe many of the centuries will support him.'

'Why? The patricians will vote for Silanus and Servius. The populists will vote for Silanus and Catilina. Who will be left to vote for Murena?'

'Give us time, Consul. The new campaign hasn't even started yet.'

'The new campaign started the moment the old one ended. You should have been going around all year. And who will run this miraculous canvass?'

'I shall.'

'You?'

Cicero uttered the word with such derision I winced, and even Clodius's arrogance seemed briefly dented. 'I have some experience.'

'What experience? You're not even a member of the senate.'

'Well then, damn you! Why did you bother even coming to see me if you're so certain we're going to lose?'

His expression was one of such outrage, Cicero burst out laughing. 'Who said anything about losing? Did I? Young fellow,' he continued, putting his arm around Clodius's shoulders, 'I know a thing or two about winning elections, and I can tell you this: you have every chance of winning – just as long as you do exactly as I tell you. But you need to wake up before it's too late. *That* is why I wanted to see you.'

And so saying, he walked Clodius round and round the atrium and explained his plan, while I followed with my notebook open and took down his directions.

XXV

Cicero informed only the most trusted senators of his intention to propose a triumph for Lucullus – men like his brother Quintus; the former consul C. Piso; the praetors Pomptinus and Flaccus; friends such as Gallus, Marcellinus and the elder Frugi; and the patrician leaders Hortensius, Catulus and Isauricus. They in turn initiated others into the scheme. All were sworn to secrecy, told on which day to attend the chamber and requested above everything to keep together, whatever happened, until the house adjourned. Cicero did not tell Hybrida.

On the appointed date the senate house was unusually crowded. Elderly nobles who had not attended for many years were present, and I could see that Caesar scented danger of some kind, for he had a habit at such moments of almost literally sniffing the air, tilting his head back slightly and peering around him suspiciously (he did exactly that, I remember, moments before he was murdered). But Cicero had arranged the whole thing masterfully. A very tedious bill was at that time making its way on to the statute book, restricting the right of senators to claim expenses for unofficial trips to the provinces. This is precisely the sort of self-interested legislation that excites every elected bore in politics, and Cicero had lined up an entire bench of them and promised each he could speak for as long as he liked. The moment he read out the order of business some senators groaned and rose to leave, and after about an hour of listening to Q. Cornificius – a very dreary speaker at the best of times – attendance was thinning fast. Some of our side pretended to go, but actually lingered in the streets close to the senate house. Eventually even Caesar could stand it no longer and departed, together with Catilina.

Cicero waited a little longer, then stood and announced that he had received a new motion that he would like to place before the house. He called on Lucullus's brother Marcus to speak, who thereupon read out a letter from the great general requesting that the senate grant him a triumph before the consular elections. Cicero declared that Lucullus had waited long enough for his just reward and he would now put the matter to a vote. By this time the patrician benches had filled up again with those who had been lurking nearby, whilst on the populists' side there was hardly anyone to be seen. Messengers ran off to fetch Caesar. Meanwhile, all who favoured a triumph for Lucullus moved to stand around his brother, and after heads had been counted, Cicero duly declared that the motion had been passed by 120 to 16 and that the house should stand adjourned. He hurried down the aisle, preceded by his lictors, just as Caesar and Catilina arrived at the door. They obviously realised that they had been ambushed and had lost something significant, but it would take them an hour or two to work out exactly what. For now they could only stand aside and let the consul's procession pass. It was a delicious moment, and Cicero relived it again and again over dinner that night.

The trouble really started the following day in the senate. Belatedly the populists' benches were packed, and it was a rowdy house. Crassus, Catilina and Caesar had by this time worked out what Cicero was up to, and one after the other they rose to demand that the vote be taken again. But Cicero would not be intimidated. He ruled that there had been a proper quorum, Lucullus deserved his triumph, and the people were in need of a spectacle to cheer them up: as far as he was concerned, the issue was closed. Catilina, however, refused to sit down, and continued to demand a re-vote. Calmly Cicero tried to move on to the bill about travel expenses. As the uproar continued I thought the session might have to be suspended. But Catilina still had not entirely given up hope of winning power by the ballot box rather than the sword, and he recognised that the consul was right in one respect at least: the urban masses always enjoyed a triumph, and would not understand why they had been promised the pleasure one day only to be deprived of it the next. At the last moment he threw himself heavily back on to the front bench, sweeping his arm dismissively at the chair in a gesture of anger and disgust. Thus it was settled: Lucullus would have his day of glory in Rome.

That night Servius came to see Cicero. He brusquely rejected the offer of a drink and demanded to know if the rumours were true.

'What rumours?'

'The rumours that you've abandoned me and are supporting Murena.'

'Of course they're not true. I'll vote for you, and shall say as much to anyone who asks me.'

'Then why have you arranged to ruin my chances by filling the city with Murena's old legionaries in the week of the poll?'

'The question of when Lucullus holds his triumph is entirely a matter for him' – an answer that, while true in a strictly legal sense, was grossly misleading in every other. 'Are you sure you won't have a drink?'

'Do you really think I'm such a fool as that?' Servius's stooped frame was quivering with emotion. 'It's bribery, plain and simple. And I give you fair warning, Consul: I intend to lay a bill before the senate making it illegal for candidates, or their surrogates, to hold either banquets or games just before an election.'

'Listen, Servius, may I give you some advice? Money, feasting, entertainment – these have always been a part of an election campaign, and always will be. You can't just sit around waiting for the voters to come to you. You need to put on a show. Make sure you go everywhere in a big crowd of supporters. Spread a little money around. You can afford it.'

'That's bribing the voters.'

'No, it's *enthusing* them. Remember, these are poor citizens for the most part. They need to feel their vote has value, and that great men have to pay them some attention, if only once a year. It's all they have.'

'Cicero, you completely amaze me. Never did I think to hear a Roman consul say such a thing. Power has entirely corrupted you. I shall introduce my bill tomorrow. Cato will second the motion and I expect you to support it – otherwise the country will draw its own conclusions.'

'Typical Servius – always the lawyer, never the politician! Don't you understand? If people see you going around not to canvass but to collect evidence for a prosecution, they'll think you've given up hope. And there's nothing more fatal during an election campaign than to appear unconfident.'

'Let them think what they like. The courts will decide. That is what they're there for.'

The two men parted badly. Nevertheless, Servius was right in one respect: Cicero, as consul, could hardly let himself be seen to condone bribery. He was obliged to support the campaign finance reform bill when Servius and Cato laid it before the senate the next day.

Election canvasses normally lasted four weeks; this one went on for eight. The amount of money expended was amazing. The patricians set up a war chest to fund Silanus into which they all paid. Catilina received financial support from Crassus. Murena was given one million sesterces by Lucullus. Only Servius made a point of spending nothing at all, but went around with a long face, accompanied by Cato and a team of secretaries recording every example of illegal expenditure. Throughout this time Rome slowly filled with Lucullus's veterans, who camped out on the Field of Mars by day and came into the city at night to drink and gamble and whore. Catilina retaliated by bringing in supporters of his own, mostly from the north-west, in particular Etruria. Ragged and desperate, they materialised out of the primeval forests and swamps of that benighted region: ex-legionaries, brigands, herdsmen. Publius Cornelius Sulla, nephew of the former dictator, who supported Catilina, paid for a troop of gladiators, ostensibly to entertain but really to intimidate. At the head of this sinister assembly of professional and amateur fighters was the former centurion Gaius Manlius, who drilled them in the meadows across the river from the Field of Mars. There were terrible running battles between the two sides. Men were clubbed to death; men drowned. When Cato, in the senate, accused Catilina of organising this violence, Catilina slowly got to his feet.

'If a fire is raised to consume my fortunes,' he said very deliberately, turning to look at Cicero, 'then I will put it out – not with water but by demolition.'

There was a silence, and then, as the meaning of his words sank in, a shocked chorus of 'Oh!' rang round the chamber – 'Oh!' – for this was the first time Catilina had hinted publicly that he might be willing to use force. I was taking a shorthand record of the debate, sitting in my usual place, below and to the left of Cicero, who was in his curule chair. He immediately spotted his opportunity. He stood and held up his hand for silence.

'Gentlemen, this is very serious. There should be no mistake as to what we have just heard. Clerk, read back to the chamber the words of Sergius Catilina.'

I had no time to feel nervous as for the first and only time in my life I addressed the senate of the Roman republic: '"If a fire is raised to consume my fortunes,"' I read from my notes, '"then I will put it out – not with water but by demolition."'

I spoke as loudly as I could and sat down quickly, my heart pounding with such violence it seemed to shake my entire body. Catilina, still on his feet, his head on one side, was looking at Cicero with an expression I find it hard to describe – a sneer of insolence was part of it, and contempt, and blazing hatred obviously, and even perhaps a hint of fear: that twitch of alarm that can drive a desperate man to desperate acts. Cicero, his point made, gestured to Cato to resume his speech, and only I was close enough to see that his hand was shaking. 'Marcus Cato still has the floor,' he said.

That night Cicero asked Terentia to speak to her highly placed informant, the mistress of Curius, to try to find out exactly what Catilina meant. 'Obviously he's realised he's going to lose, which makes this a dangerous moment. He might be planning to disrupt the poll. "Demolition"? See if she knows why he used that particular phrase.'

Lucullus's triumph was to take place the following day, and in this atmosphere Quintus naturally worried about the arrangements for Cicero's security. But nothing could be done. There was no chance of varying the route, which was fixed by solemn tradition. The crowds would be immense. It was only too easy to imagine a determined assassin darting forwards, thrusting a long blade into the consul, and disappearing into the throng. 'But there it is,' said Cicero. 'If a man is set on killing you, it's hard to stop him, especially if he's willing to die in the attempt. We shall just have to trust to Providence.'

'And the Sextus brothers,' added Quintus.

Early the next morning Cicero led the entire senate out to the Field of Mars, to the Villa Publica, where Lucullus was lodging prior to entering the city, surrounded by the pitched tents of his veterans. With characteristic arrogance, Lucullus kept the delegation waiting for a while, and when he appeared, he presented a gaudy apparition, robed in gold, his face painted in red lead. Cicero recited the official proclamation of the senate, then handed him a laurel wreath, which Lucullus held aloft and showed to his veterans, slowly turning full circle to roars of approval before delicately placing it on his head. Because I was now on the staff of the treasury, I was given a place in the parade, behind the magistrates and senators, but ahead of the war booty and the prisoners, who included a few of Mithradates's relatives, a couple of minor princes, and half a dozen generals. We passed into Rome through the Triumphal Gate, and my chief recollections are of the oppressive heat of that summer day, and the contorted faces of the crowds lining the streets, and the rank smell of the beasts – the oxen and mules, dragging and carrying all that bullion and those works of art – their animal grunts and bellows mingling with the shouts of the spectators, and far behind us, like distant rolling thunder, the tramp of the legionaries' boots. It was quite disgusting, I have to say – the whole city stinking and shrieking like a vivarium – and no more so than after we had passed through the Circus Maximus and had come back along the Via Sacra to the forum, where we had to wait until the rest of the procession caught up with us. Standing outside the Carcer was the public executioner, surrounded by his assistants. He was a butcher by training, and looked it, squat and broad in his leather apron. This was where the crowd was thickest, drawn as always by the shivering thrill of close proximity to death. The miserable prisoners, yoked at the neck, their faces burned red by this sudden exposure to the sun after years of darkness, were led up one by one to the carnifex, who took them down into the Carcer and strangled them – thankfully out of sight, but still I could see that Cicero was keeping his face averted, and talking fixedly to Hybrida. A few rows back, Catilina watched Cicero with almost lascivious interest.

Such are my principal memories of the triumph, although I must recount one other, which is that when Lucullus drove across the forum in his chariot, he was followed on horseback by Murena, who had finally arrived in Rome for the election, having left his province to the care of his brother. He received a great ovation from the multitudes. The consular candidate looked the very picture of a war hero, in his gleaming breastplate and gorgeous scarlet-plumed helmet, even though he had not fought in the army for years and had grown rather plump in Further Gaul. Both men dismounted and started climbing the steps to the Capitol, where Caesar waited with the College of Priests. Lucullus was ahead, of course, but his legate was only a few paces behind, and I appreciated then Cicero's genius in laying on what was in effect an immense election rally for Murena. Each of the veterans received a bounty of nine hundred and fifty drachmas, which in those days was about four years' pay, and then the entire city and the surrounding neighbourhoods were treated to a lavish banquet. 'If Murena can't win after this,' Cicero observed to me, as he set off for the official dinner, 'he doesn't deserve to live.'

The next day, the public assembly voted the bill of Servius and Cato into law. When Cicero returned home, he was met by Terentia. Her face was white and trembling but her voice was calm. She had just come from the Temple of the Good Goddess, she said. She had some terrible news. Cicero must brace himself. Her friend, that noble lady who had come to her to warn her of the plot against his life, had that morning been discovered dead in the alley beside her house. Her head had been smashed in from behind by a hammer, her throat cut and her organs removed.

As soon as he had recovered from the shock, Cicero summoned Quintus and Atticus. They came at once and listened, appalled. Their first concern was for the consul's safety. It was agreed that a couple of men would stay in the house overnight and patrol the downstairs rooms. Others would escort him in public during the day. He would vary his route to and from the senate. A fierce dog would be acquired to guard the door.

'And how long must I go on living like a prisoner? Until the end of my life?'

'No,' responded Terentia, displaying her rare gift for getting to the heart of the matter, 'until the end of Catilina's life, because as long as he's in Rome, you'll never be safe.'

He saw the wisdom of this, reluctantly grunted his assent, and Atticus went off to send a message to the Order of Knights. 'But why did he have to *kill* her?' Cicero wondered aloud. 'If he suspected she was my informant, why couldn't he simply have warned Curius not to speak openly in front of her?'

'Because,' said Quintus, 'he likes killing people.'

Cicero thought for a while, then turned to me. 'Send one of the lictors to find Curius, and tell him I want to see him, straight away.'

'You mean to invite into your house someone who is part of a plot to murder you?' exclaimed Quintus. 'You must be mad!'

'I won't be alone. You'll be here. He probably won't come. But if he does, at least we may find out something.' He glanced around at our worried expressions. 'Well? Does anyone have a better idea?'

Nobody did, so I went out to the lictors, who were playing bones in a corner of the atrium, and ordered the most junior to find Curius and bring him back to the house.

It was one of those endless hot summer days when the sun seems reluctant to sink, and I remember how still it was, the motes of dust motionless in the shafts of fading light. On such evenings, when the only sounds even in the city are the drone of insects and the soft trilling of the birds, Rome seems older than anywhere in the world; as old as the earth itself; entirely beyond time. How impossible it was to believe that forces were at work at its very heart – in the order of the senate – that might destroy it! We sat around quietly, too tense to eat the meal that had been set upon the table. The additional bodyguards ordered by Atticus arrived and stationed themselves in the vestibule. When, after an hour or two, the lengthening shadows made the house gloomy, and the slaves went round lighting the candles, I assumed that Curius either had not been found, or had refused to come. But then at last we heard the front door open and slam shut, and the lictor came in with the senator, who looked around him suspiciously – first at Cicero, then at Atticus, Quintus, Terentia and me, and then back at Cicero again. He certainly was a handsome figure: one had to give him that. Gambling was his vice, not drink, and I suppose throwing dice leaves less of a mark upon a man.

'Well, Curius,' said Cicero quietly, 'this is a terrible business.'

'I'll talk to you alone, not in front of others.'

'Not talk in front of others? By the gods, you'll talk in front of the entire Roman people if I say so! Did you kill her?'

'Damn you, Cicero!' Curius swore, and lunged towards the consul, but Quintus was on his feet in a moment and blocked his way.

'Steady, Senator,' he warned.

'Did you kill her?' repeated Cicero.

'No!'

'But you know who did?'

'Yes! You!' Once more he tried to push his way past Quintus, but Cicero's brother was an old soldier, and stopped him easily. 'You killed her, you bastard,' he shouted again, struggling against Quintus's restraining arms, 'by making her your spy!'

'I'm prepared to bear my share of guilt,' replied Cicero, gazing at him coolly. 'Will you?'

Curius muttered something inaudible, pulled himself free of Quintus and turned away.

'Does Catilina know you're here?'

Curius shook his head.

'Well, that at least is something. Now listen to me. I'm offering you a chance, if you've brains enough to take it. You've hitched your fate to a madman. If you didn't know it before, you must realise it now. How did Catilina know she'd been to see me?'

Again Curius mumbled something no one could hear. Cicero cupped his hand to his ear. 'What? What are you saying?'

'Because I told him!' Curius glared at Cicero with tearful eyes. He struck his breast with his fist. 'She told me, and I told him!' And he struck himself again – hard, hard, hard blows – in the manner of some Eastern holy man lamenting the dead.

'I need to know everything. Do you understand me? I need names, places, plans, times. I need to know who exactly will strike at me, and in what location. It's treason if you don't tell me.'

'And treachery if I do!'

'Treachery against evil is a virtue.' Cicero got to his feet. He put his hands on Curius's shoulders and stared hard into his face. 'When your lady came to see me, it was your safety as much as mine that was her concern. She made me promise, on the lives of my children, that I would grant you immunity if this plot was ever exposed. Think of her, Curius, lying there – beautiful, brave, broken. Be worthy of her love and her memory, and act now as you know she would have wanted.'

Curius wept; indeed, I could hardly restrain my own tears, such was the pitiful vision Cicero conjured up: that, and the promise of immunity, did the trick. When Curius had pulled himself together sufficiently, he promised to get word to Cicero the moment he heard any definite news of Catilina's plans. Thus Cicero's thin line of information from the enemy's camp remained intact.

He did not have long to wait.

The following day was election eve, and Cicero was due to preside over the senate. But because of the fear of an ambush, he had to follow a circuitous route, along the Esquiline and down to the Via Sacra. The journey took twice as long as usual, and it was mid-afternoon by the time we arrived. His curule chair was placed on the doorstep and he sat there in the shade, reading through some letters, surrounded by his lictors, waiting for the auguries to be taken. Several senators wandered over to ask if he had heard what Catilina was supposed to have said that morning. Apparently he had addressed a meeting in his house in the most inflammatory terms. Cicero replied that he had not, and sent me off to see if I could discover anything. I walked around the senaculum and approached one or two senators with whom I was on friendly terms. The place was certainly buzzing with rumours. Some said that Catilina had called for the richest men in Rome to be murdered, others that he had urged an uprising. I jotted a few sentences down, and was just returning to Cicero when Curius brushed past me and slipped into my hand a note. He was sickly white with terror. 'Give this to the consul,' he whispered, and before I could reply he was gone. I looked around. A hundred or more senators were talking in small groups. As far as I could tell, no one had seen the encounter.

I hurried over to Cicero and handed him the message. I bent to his ear and whispered, 'It's from Curius.'

He opened it, studied it for a moment, and his face tensed. He passed it up to me. It said, *You will be murdered tomorrow during the elections*. At just that moment the augurs came up and declared that the auspices were propitious. 'Are you certain about that?' asked Cicero in a grim voice. Solemnly they assured him that they were. I could see him weighing in his mind what best to do. Finally he stood and indicated to his lictors that they should pick up his chair, and he followed them into the cool shadows of the senate chamber. The senators filed in behind us. 'Do we know what Catilina actually said this morning?'

'Not in any detail.'

As we walked up the aisle he said to me quietly, 'I fear this warning may have some substance to it. If you think about it, it's the one time when they can be sure precisely where I'll be – on the Field of Mars, presiding over the ballot. And with all those thousands of people milling around, how easy it would be for ten or twenty armed men to hack their way through to me and take me down.' By this time we had reached the dais and the benches were filling. He glanced back, searching the white-robed figures. 'Is Quintus here?'

'No, he's canvassing.' Indeed, a great many senators were absent. All the candidates for consul, and most of those for tribune and praetor – including Quintus and Caesar – had chosen to spend the afternoon meeting voters rather than attending to the business of the state. Only Cato was in his place, reading his treasury accounts. Cicero grimaced and tightened his fist, crushing Curius's message. He stood that way for quite some time until he became conscious that the house was watching him. He mounted the steps to his chair.

'Gentlemen,' he announced, 'I have just been informed of a grave and credible conspiracy against the republic, involving the murder of your leading consul.' There was a gasp. 'In order that the evidence may be examined and debated, I propose that the start of the elections tomorrow be postponed, until the nature of this threat has been properly assessed. Are there any objections?' In the excited murmur that followed, no clear voice could be heard. 'In that case, the senate will stand adjourned until first light tomorrow,' and with these words he swept down the aisle followed by his lictors.

Rome was now plunged into a state of great confusion. Cicero went straight back to his house and immediately set about trying to find out precisely what Catilina had said, dispatching clerks and messengers to potential informants across the city. I was ordered to fetch Curius from his house on the Aventine. At first his doorkeeper refused to admit me – the senator was seeing no one, he said – but I sent a message to him on behalf of Cicero and eventually was allowed in. Curius was in a state of nervous collapse, torn between his fear of Catilina and his anxiety not to be implicated in the murder of a consul. He flatly refused to go with me and meet Cicero face to face, saying it was too dangerous. It was only with great difficulty that I persuaded him to describe the meeting at Catilina's house.

All Catilina's henchmen were there, he said: some eleven senators in total, including himself. There were also half a dozen members of the Order of Knights – he named Nobilior, Statilius, Capito and Cornelius – as well as the ex-centurion Manlius and scores of malcontents from Rome and all across Italy. The scene was dramatic. The house was stripped entirely bare of possessions – Catilina was bankrupt and the place mortgaged – apart from a silver eagle that had once been the consul Marius's personal standard when he fought against the patricians. As for what Catilina had actually said, according to Curius it went something like this (I took it down as he dictated it):

'Friends, ever since Rome rid itself of kings it has been ruled by a powerful oligarchy that has had control of everything – all the offices of state, the land, the army, the money raked in by taxes, our provinces overseas. The rest of us, however hard we try, are just a crowd of nobodies. Even those of us who are high-born have to bow and scrape to men who in a properly run state would stand in awe of us. You know who I mean. All influence, power, office and wealth are in their hands; all they leave for us is danger, defeat, prosecutions and poverty.

'How long, brave comrades, will we endure it? Is it not better to die courageously and have done with it, than to drag out lives of misery and dishonour as the playthings of other men's insolence? But it need not be like this. We have the strength of youth and stout hearts, while our enemies are enfeebled by age and soft living. They have two, three or four houses joined together, when we have not a home to call our own. They have pictures and statues and fish ponds, while we have destitution and debts. Misery is all we have to look forward to.

'Awake, then! Before you glimmers the chance for liberty – for honour and glory and the prizes of victory! Use me in whatever way you like, as a commander or as a soldier in your ranks, and remember the rich spoils that can be won in war! This is what I shall do for you if I am consul. Refuse to be slaves! Be masters! And let us show the world at last that we are men!'

That, or something very like it, was the burden of Catilina's speech, and after he had delivered it he withdrew to an inner room for a more private discussion with his closest comrades, including Curius. Here, with the door firmly closed, he reminded them of their solemn blood oath, declared that the hour had come to strike, and proposed that they should kill Cicero on the Field of Mars during the confusion of the elections the following day. Curius claimed to have stayed only for part of this discussion before slipping away to pass on the warning to Cicero. He refused to swear an affidavit confirming this story. He absolutely insisted he would not be a witness. His name had to be kept out of it at all costs. 'You must tell the consul that if he calls on me, I shall deny everything.'

By the time I got back to Cicero's house, the door was barred and only those visitors who were known and trusted were being admitted. A crowd had gathered in the street. When I went into his study, Quintus and Atticus were already there. I relayed Curius's message, and showed Cicero his description of what Catilina had said. 'Now I have him!' he said. 'He's gone too far this time!' And he sent for the leaders of the senate. At least a dozen came during the course of that afternoon and evening, among them Hortensius and Catulus. Cicero showed them what Catilina was supposed to have said, along with the unsigned death threat. But when he refused to divulge his source ('I have given my word'), I could see that several – particularly Catulus, who had at one time been a great friend of Catilina – became sceptical. Indeed, knowing Cicero's cleverness, they obviously wondered if he might be making the whole thing up in order to discredit his enemy. Unnerved by their reaction, Cicero began to lose confidence.

There are times in politics, as in life generally, when whatever one does is wrong; this was just such an occasion. To have gone ahead with the elections and said nothing would have been a mad gamble. On the other hand, postponing them without adequate evidence now looked jittery. Cicero passed a sleepless night worrying about what he should say in the senate, and for once in the morning it showed. He looked like a man under appalling strain.

That day when the senate reassembled there was not an inch of space on the benches. Senators lined the walls and crammed the gangways. The auspices had been read and the doors opened soon after daybreak. It was the earliest session that anyone could remember. Yet already the summer heat was building. The question was: would the consular election go ahead or not? Outside, the forum was packed with citizens, mostly Catilina's supporters, and their angry chants, demanding to be allowed to vote, could be heard in the chamber. Beyond the city walls on the Field of Mars the sheep pens and ballot urns were set up and waiting. Inside the senate house it felt as if two gladiators were about to fight. As Cicero stood, I could see Catilina in his place on the front bench, his cronies around him, as coolly insolent as ever, with Caesar close by, his arms folded.

'Gentlemen,' Cicero began, 'no consul lightly intervenes in the sacred business of an election – especially not a consul such as I, who owes everything he has to election by the Roman people. But yesterday I was given warning of a plot to desecrate this most holy ritual – a plot, an intrigue, a conspiracy of desperate men, to take advantage of the tumult of polling day to murder your consul, foment chaos in the city, and so enable them to take control of the state. This despicable scheme was hatched not in some foreign land, or low criminal's hovel, but in the heart of the city, in the house of Sergius Catilina.'

The senators listened in absolute stillness as Cicero read out the anonymous note from Curius (*'You will be murdered tomorrow during the elections'*), followed by Catilina's words (*'How long, brave comrades, will we endure it? ...'*) and when he had finished there was not a pair of eyes directed anywhere other than at Catilina. 'At the end of this seditious rant,' concluded Cicero, 'Catilina retired with others to consider, not for the first time, how best I might be killed. Such is the extent of my knowledge, gentlemen, which I felt it my duty to lay before you, so that you might decide how best to proceed.'

He sat down, and after a pause someone called out, 'Answer!' and then others took up the cry, angrily hurling the word like a javelin at Catilina: 'Answer! Answer!' Catilina gave a shrug, and a kind of half-smile, and heaved himself to his feet. He was a huge man. His physical presence alone was sufficient to intimidate the chamber into silence.

'Back in the days when Cicero's ancestors were still fucking goats, or however it is they amuse themselves in the mountains he comes from—' He was interrupted by laughter; some of it, I have to say, from the patrician benches around Catulus and Hortensius. 'Back in those days,' he continued, once the racket had died down, 'when my ancestors were consuls and this republic was younger and more virile, we were led by fighters, not lawyers. Our learned consul here accuses me of sedition. If that is what he chooses to call it, sedition it is. For my part, I call it the truth. When I look at this republic, gentlemen, I see two bodies. One,' he said, gesturing to the patricians and from them up to Cicero, sitting dead still in his chair, 'is frail, with a weak head. The other' – he pointed to the door and the forum beyond it – 'is strong, but has no head at all. I know which body I prefer, and it won't go short of a head as long as I'm alive!'

Looking at those words written down now, it seems amazing to me that Catilina wasn't seized and accused of treason on the spot. But he had powerful backers, and no sooner had he resumed his seat than Crassus was on his feet. Ah, yes, Marcus Licinius Crassus – I have not devoted nearly enough space to him so far in this portion of my narrative! But let me rectify that. This hunter of old ladies' legacies; this lender of money at usurious rates; this slum landlord; this speculator and hoarder; this former consul, as bald as an egg and as hard as a piece of flint – this Crassus was a most formidable speaker when he put his cunning mind to it, which he did on that July morning.

'Forgive my obtuseness, colleagues,' he said. 'Perhaps it's just me, but I've been listening intently and I've yet to hear a solitary piece of evidence that justifies postponing the elections by a single instant. What does this so-called conspiracy actually amount to? An anonymous note? Well, the consul himself could have written it, and there are plenty who wouldn't put it past him! The report of a speech? It didn't sound particularly remarkable to me. Indeed, it reminded me of nothing so much as the sort of speech that that radical new man Marcus Tullius Cicero used to make before he threw in his lot with my patrician friends on the benches opposite!'

It was an effective point. Crassus grasped the front of his toga between his thumbs and forefingers, and spread his elbows, in the manner of a country gentleman delivering his opinion of sheep at market.

'The gods know, and you all know – and I thank Providence for it – I am not a poor man. I have nothing to gain from the cancellation of all debts; very much the reverse. But I do not think that Catilina can be barred from being a candidate, or these elections delayed an hour longer, purely on the basis of the feeble evidence we've just heard. I therefore propose a motion: *That the elections begin immediately, and that this house do adjourn and repair to the Field of Mars.*'

'I second the motion!' said Caesar, springing to his feet. 'And I ask that it be put to the vote at once, so that no more of the day may be wasted by these delaying tactics, and the election of the new consuls and praetors may be concluded by sunset, in accordance with our ancient laws.'

Just as a pair of scales that are finely balanced may suddenly be plunged one way or another by the addition of a few grains of wheat, so the whole atmosphere of the senate that morning abruptly tilted. Those who had been howling down Catilina only a short while earlier now began clamouring for the elections to start, and Cicero wisely decided not even to put the matter to a vote. 'The mood of the house is clear,' he said, in a stony voice. 'Polling will begin at once.' And he added, quietly: 'May the gods protect our republic.' I don't think many people heard him, certainly not Catilina and his gang, who didn't even observe the normal courtesy of letting the consul leave the chamber first. Fists in the air, roaring in triumph, they pushed their way down the crowded aisle and out into the forum.

Cicero was now in a fix. He could hardly go home, like a coward. He had to follow Catilina, for nothing could happen until he, as the presiding magistrate, arrived on the Field of Mars to take control of proceedings. Quintus, whose concern for his brother's safety was always paramount, and who had foreseen exactly this outcome, had brought along his old army breastplate, and he insisted that Cicero wear it beneath his toga. I could tell that Cicero was reluctant, but in the drama of the moment he allowed himself to be persuaded, and while a group of senators stood around to shield him, I helped him out of his toga, assisted Quintus in strapping on the bronze armour, and then readjusted the toga. Naturally, the rigid shape of the metal was clearly visible beneath the white wool, but Quintus reassured him that far from being a problem this was all to the good: it would act as a deterrent to any assassin. Thus protected, and with a tight escort of lictors and senators surrounding him, Cicero walked, head erect, from the senate house and into the glare and noise of election day.

The population was streaming westwards towards the Field of Mars, and we were carried with the flow. More and more supporters emerged and adhered around Cicero, until I should say that a protective layer of at least four or five men stood between him and the general throng. A huge crowd can be a terrifying sight – a monster, unconscious of its own strength, with subterranean impulses to stampede this way or that, to panic and to crush. The crowd on the election field that day was immense, and we drove into it like a wedge into a block of wood. I was next to Cicero, and we were jostled and pushed along by our escort until at last we reached the area set aside for the consul. This consisted of a long platform with a ladder up to it, and a tent behind it where he could rest. To one side, behind sheep fencing, was the enclosure for the candidates, of whom there were perhaps twenty (both the consulships and the eight praetorships all had to be decided that day). Catilina was talking to Caesar, and when they saw Cicero arrive, red-faced from the heat and wearing armour, they both laughed heartily and began gesturing to the others to look. 'I should never have worn this damn thing,' Cicero muttered. 'I'm sweating like a pig, and it doesn't even protect my head and neck.'

Nevertheless, as the elections were already running late, he had no time to take it off, but immediately had to go into a conclave with the augurs. They declared that the auspices were good, so Cicero gave the order for proceedings to begin. He mounted the platform, followed by the candidates, and recited all the prayers in a firm voice and without a hitch. The trumpets sounded, the red flag was hoisted up its staff above the Janiculum, and the first century trooped over the bridge to cast its ballots. Thereafter it was a matter of keeping the lines of voters moving, hour after hour, as the sun burned its fiery arc across the sky and Cicero boiled like a lobster in his breastplate.

For what it is worth, I believe that he would have been assassinated that day if he had not taken the course he did. Conspiracies thrive in darkness, and by shining such a strong light on the plotters he had temporarily frightened them off. Too many people were watching: if Cicero had been struck down, it would have been obvious who was responsible. And in any case, because he had raised the alarm, he was now surrounded by such a number of friends and allies, it would have taken scores of determined men to get to him.

So the business of the day went on as usual, with no hand raised against him. He had one small satisfaction at least, which was to declare his brother elected praetor. But Quintus's vote was smaller than expected, whereas Caesar topped the poll by a mile. The results for the consulship were as expected: Junius Silanus came in first and Murena second, with Servius and Catilina tied in last place. Catilina gave a mocking bow to Cicero and left the field with his supporters: he had not expected a different outcome. Servius, on the other hand, took his defeat badly, and came to see Cicero in his tent after the declaration to pour out a tirade against him for permitting the most corrupt campaign in history. 'I shall challenge it in the courts. My case is overwhelming. This battle is not over yet, by any means!' He stamped off, followed by his attendants carrying their document cases full of evidence. Cicero, slumped with exhaustion on his curule chair, swore as he watched him leave. I tried to make some consoling remarks, but he told me roughly to be quiet and to do something useful for a change by helping him take off that damned breastplate. His skin had been chafed raw by the metal edges, and the moment he was free of it he seized it in both hands and hurled it in a fury to the other side of the tent, where it landed with a clatter.

XXVI

A terrible melancholy now overcame Cicero, of a depth I had never seen before. Terentia went off with the children to spend the rest of the summer in the higher altitudes and cooler glades of Tusculum, but the consul stayed in Rome, working. The heat was more than usually oppressive, the stink of the great drain beneath the forum rose to envelop the hills, and many hundreds of citizens were carried off by the sweating fever, the stench of their corpses adding to the noisome atmosphere. I have often wondered what history would have found to say about Cicero if he had also succumbed to a fatal illness at that time – and the answer is 'very little'. At the age of forty-three he had won no military victories. He had written no great books. True, he had achieved the consulship, but then so had many nonentities, Hybrida being the most obvious example. The only significant law he had carried on to the statute book was Servius's campaign finance reform act, which he heartily disliked. In the meantime Catilina was still at liberty and Cicero had lost a great deal of prestige by what was seen as his panicky behaviour on the eve of the poll. As the summer turned to autumn, his consulship was almost three quarters done and dribbling away to nothing – a fact he realised more keenly than anybody.

One day in September I left him alone with a pile of legal papers to read. It was almost two months after the elections. Servius had made good his threat to prosecute Murena and was seeking to have his victory declared null and void. Cicero felt he had little choice except to defend the man whom he had done so much to make consul. Once again he would appear alongside Hortensius, and the amount of evidence to be mastered was immense. But when I returned some hours later the documents were still untouched. He had not moved from his couch, and was clutching a cushion to his stomach. I asked if he was ill. 'I have a dryness of the heart,' he said. 'What's the point of going on with all this work and striving? No one will ever remember my name – not even in a year's time, let alone in a thousand. I'm finished – a complete failure.' He sighed and stared at the ceiling, the back of his hand resting on his forehead. 'Such dreams I had, Tiro – such hopes of glory and renown. I meant to be as famous as Alexander. But it's all gone awry somehow. And do you know what most torments me as I lie awake at night? It's that I cannot see what I could have done differently.'

He continued to keep in touch with Curius, whose grief at the death of his mistress had not abated; in fact he had become ever more obsessed. From him Cicero learned that Catilina was continuing to plot against the state, and now much more seriously. There were disturbing reports of covered wagons full of weapons being moved under cover of darkness along the roads outside Rome. Fresh lists of possibly sympathetic senators had been drawn up, and according to Curius these now included two young patrician senators, M. Claudius Marcellus and Q. Scipio Nasica. Another ominous sign was that G. Manlius, Catilina's wild-eyed military lieutenant, had disappeared from his usual haunts in the back streets of Rome and was rumoured to be touring Etruria, recruiting armed bands of supporters. Curius could produce no written evidence for any of this – Catilina was much too cunning for that – and eventually, after asking a few too many questions, he came under suspicion from his fellow conspirators and began to be excluded from their inner circle. Thus Cicero's only first-hand source of information gradually ran dry.

At the end of the month he decided to risk his credibility once again by raising the matter in the senate. It was a disaster. 'I have been informed—' he began, but could proceed no further because of the gusts of merriment that blew around the chamber. 'I have been informed' was exactly the formulation he had used twice before when raising the spectre of Catilina, and it had become a kind of satirical catchphrase. Wags in the street would shout it after him as he went by: 'Oh, look! There goes Cicero! Has he been informed?' His enemies in the senate yelled it out while he was speaking: 'Have you informed yourself yet, Cicero?' And now inadvertently he had said it again. He smiled weakly and affected not to care, but of course he did. Once a leader starts to be laughed at as a matter of routine, he loses authority, and then he is finished. 'Don't go out without your armour!' someone called as he processed from the chamber, and the house was convulsed with mirth. He locked himself away in his study soon after that and I did not see much of him for several days. He spent more time with my junior, Sositheus, than he did with me; I felt oddly jealous.

There was another reason for his gloom, although few would have guessed it, and he would have been embarrassed if they had. In October his daughter was to be married – an occasion, he confided to me, that he was dreading. It was not that he disliked her husband, young Gaius Frugi, of the Piso clan: on the contrary, it was Cicero, after all, who had arranged the betrothal, years earlier, to bring in the votes of the Pisos. It was simply that he loved his little Tulliola so much that he could not bear the thought of their being parted. When, on the eve of the wedding, he saw her packing her childhood toys away as tradition demanded, tears came into his eyes and he had to leave the room. She was just fourteen. The following morning the ceremony took place in Cicero's house, and I was honoured to be asked to attend, along with Atticus and Quintus, and a whole crowd of Pisos (by heavens, what an ugly and lugubrious crowd they were!). I must confess that when Tullia was led down the stairs by her mother, all veiled and dressed in white, with her hair tied up and the sacred belt knotted around her waist, I cried myself; I cry now, remembering her girlishly solemn face as she recited that simple vow, so weighted with meaning: 'Where you are Gaius, I am Gaia.' Frugi placed the ring on her finger and kissed her very tenderly. We ate the wedding cake and offered a portion to Jupiter, and then at the wedding breakfast, while little Marcus sat on his sister's knee and tried to steal her fragrant wreath, Cicero proposed the health of the bride and groom.

'I give to you, Frugi, the best that I have to give: no nature kinder, no temper sweeter, no loyalty fiercer, no courage stronger, no—'

He could not go on, and under cover of the loud and sympathetic applause he sat down.

Afterwards, hemmed in as usual by his bodyguards, he joined the procession to Frugi's family home on the Palatine. It was a cold day. Not many people were about; few joined us. When we reached the mansion, Frugi was waiting. He hoisted his bride into his arms and, ignoring Terentia's mock entreaties, carried her over the threshold. I had one last glimpse of Tullia's wide, fearful eyes staring out at us from the interior, and then the door closed. She was gone, and Cicero and Terentia were left to walk slowly home in silence, hand in hand.

That night, sitting at his desk before he went to bed, Cicero remarked for the twentieth time on how empty the place seemed without her. 'Only one small member of the household gone, and yet how diminished it is! Do you remember how she used to play at my feet, Tiro, when I was working? Just here.' He gently tapped his foot against the floor beneath his table. 'How often did she serve as the first audience for my speeches – poor uncomprehending creature! Well, there it is. The years sweep us on like leaves before a gale, and it cannot be helped.'

Those were his last words to me that evening. He went off to his bed and I, after I had blown out the candles in the study, retired to mine. I said good night to the guards in the atrium and carried my lamp to my tiny room. I placed it on the night-stand beside my cot, undressed, and lay awake as usual thinking over the events of the day, until slowly I felt my mind beginning to dissolve into sleep.

It was midnight – very quiet.

I was woken by fists pounding on the front door. I sat up with a start. I could only have been asleep for a few moments. The distant hammering came again, followed by ferocious barking, shouts and running feet. I seized my tunic and pulled it on as I hurried into the atrium. Cicero, fully dressed, was already descending the stairs from his bedroom, preceded by two guards with drawn swords. Behind him, wrapped in a shawl, was Terentia, with her hair in curlers. The banging resumed again, sharper now – sticks or shoes beating against the heavy wood. Little Marcus started howling in the nursery. 'Go and ask who it is,' Cicero told me, 'but don't open the door,' and then, to one of the knights: 'Go with him.'

Cautiously I advanced along the passage. We had a guard dog by this time – a massive black and brown mountain dog named Sargon, after the Assyrian kings. He was snarling and barking and yanking on his chain with such ferocity I thought he would tear it from the wall. I called out, 'Who's there?'

The reply was faint but audible: 'Marcus Licinius Crassus!'

Above the noise of the dog I called to Cicero: 'He says it's Crassus!'

'And is it?'

'It sounds like him.'

Cicero thought about it for a moment. I guessed he was calculating that Crassus would cheerfully see him dead, but also that it was hardly likely that a man of Crassus's eminence would try to murder a serving consul. He drew back his shoulders and smoothed down his hair. 'Well then, if he says it's Crassus, and it sounds like Crassus, you'd better let him in.'

I opened the door a crack to see a group of a dozen men holding torches. The bald head of Crassus shone in the yellow light like a harvest moon. I opened the door wider. Crassus eyed the snarling dog with distaste, then edged past it into the house. He was carrying a scruffy leather document case. Behind him came his usual shadow, the former praetor Quintus Arrius, and two young patricians, friends of Crassus who had only lately taken their seats in the senate – Claudius Marcellus and Scipio Nasica, whose names had featured on the most recent list of Catilina's potential sympathisers. Their escort tried to follow them in but I told them to wait outside: four enemies at one time was quite enough, I decided. I relocked the door.

'So what's all this about, Crassus?' asked Cicero as his old foe stepped into the atrium. 'It's too late for a social call and too early for business.'

'Good evening, Consul.' Crassus nodded coldly. 'And good evening to you, madam,' he said to Terentia. 'Our apologies for disturbing you. Don't let us keep you from your bed.' He turned his back on her and said to Cicero, 'Is there somewhere private we can talk?'

'I'm afraid my friends get nervous if I leave their sight.'

'Are you suggesting we're assassins?'

'No, but you keep company with assassins.'

'Not any longer,' said Crassus with a thin smile, and patted his document case. 'That's why we're here.'

Cicero hesitated. 'All right, in private, then.' Terentia started to protest. 'Don't alarm yourself, my dear. My guards will be right outside the door, and the strong arm of Tiro will be there to protect me.' (This was a joke.)

He ordered some chairs to be taken to his study, and the six of us just about managed to squeeze into it. I could see that Cicero was nervous. There was something about Crassus that always made his flesh crawl. Still, he was polite enough. He asked his visitors if they would like some wine, but they declined. 'Very well,' he said. 'Sober is better than drunk. Out with it.'

'There's trouble brewing in Etruria,' began Crassus.

'I know the reports. But as you saw when I tried to raise the matter, the senate won't take it seriously.'

'Well, they need to wake up quickly.'

'You've certainly changed your tune!'

'That's because I've come into possession of certain facts. Tell him, Arrius.'

'Well,' said Arrius, looking shifty. He was a clever fellow, an old soldier, low-born, and Crassus's creature in all matters. He was much mocked behind his back for his silly way of speaking, adding an 'h' to some of his vowels, presumably because he thought it made him sound educated. 'I was in Hetruria up till yesterday. There are bands of fighters gathering right across the region. I hunderstand they're planning to hadvance on Rome.'

'How do you know that?'

'I served with several of the ringleaders in the legions. They tried to persuade me to join them, and I let them think I might – purely to gather hintelligence, you hunderstand,' he added quickly.

'How many of these fighters are there?'

'I should say five thousand, maybe ten.'

'As many as that?'

'If there aren't that many now, there will be soon enough.'

'Are they armed?'

'Some. Not all. They have a plan, though.'

'And what is this plan?'

'To surprise the garrison at Praeneste, seize the town, fortify it, and use it as a base to rally their forces.'

'Praeneste is almost impregnable,' put in Crassus, 'and less than a day's march from Rome.'

'Manlius has also sent supporters the length and breadth of Hitaly to stir up hunrest.'

'My, my,' said Cicero, looking from one to the other, 'how well informed *you* are!'

'You and I have had our disagreements, Consul,' said Crassus coldly, 'but I'm a loyal citizen, first and last. I don't want to see a civil war. That's why we're here.' He placed the document case on his lap, opened it and pulled out a bundle of letters. 'These messages were delivered to my house earlier this evening. One was addressed to me; two others were for my friends here, Marcellus and young Scipio, who happened to be dining with me. The rest are addressed to various other members of the senate. As you can see, the seals on those are still unbroken. Here you are. I want there to be no secrets between us. Read the one that came for me.'

Cicero gave him a suspicious look, glanced through the letter quickly and then handed it to me. It was very short: *The time for talking is over. The moment for action has arrived. Catilina has drawn up his plans. He wishes to warn you there will be bloodshed in Rome. Spare yourself and leave the city secretly. When it is safe to return, you will be contacted.* There was no signature. The handwriting was neat and entirely without character: a child could have done it.

'You see why I felt we had to come straight away,' said Crassus. 'I've always been a supporter of Catilina. But we want no part of this.'

Cicero put his chin in his hand and said nothing for a while. He looked from Marcellus to Scipio. 'And the warnings to you both? Are they exactly the same?' The two young senators nodded. 'Anonymous?' More nods. 'And you've no idea who they're from?' They shook their heads. For two such arrogant young Roman noblemen, they were as docile as lambs.

'The identity of the sender is a mystery,' declared Crassus. 'My door-keeper brought the letters in to us when we'd finished dinner. He didn't see who delivered them – they were left on the step and whoever was the courier ran away. Naturally Marcellus and Scipio read theirs at the same time as I read mine.'

'Naturally. May I see the other messages?'

Crassus reached into his document case and gave him the unopened letters one at a time. Cicero examined each address in turn and showed it to me. I remember a Claudius, an Aemilius, a Valerius and others of that ilk, including Hybrida: about eight or nine in total; all patricians.

'He seems to be warning his hunting companions,' said Cicero, 'for old times' sake. It's strange, is it not, that they should all be sent to you? Why is that, do you think?'

'I have no idea.'

'It's certainly an odd conspiracy that approaches a man who says he doesn't even belong to it and asks him to act as its messenger.'

'I can't pretend to explain it.'

'Perhaps it's a hoax.'

'Perhaps. But when one considers the alarming developments in Etruria, and then remembers how close Catilina is to Manlius … No, I think one has to take it seriously. I fear I owe you an apology, Consul. It seems Catilina may be a menace to the republic after all.'

'He's a menace to everyone.'

'Anything I can do to help – you have only to ask.'

'Well, for a start, I'll need those letters, all of them.'

Crassus exchanged looks with his companions, but then he stuffed the letters into the document case and gave it to Cicero. 'You'll be producing them in the senate, I assume?'

'I think I must, don't you? I'll also need Arrius to make a statement about what he's discovered in Etruria. Will you do that, Arrius?'

Arrius looked to Crassus for guidance. Crassus gave a slight nod. 'Habsolutely,' he confirmed.

Crassus said, 'And you'll be seeking the senate's authority to raise an army?'

'Rome must be protected.'

'May I just say that if you require a commander for such a force, you need look no further? Don't forget I was the one who put down the revolt of Spartacus. I can put down the revolt of Manlius just as well.'

As Cicero afterwards observed, the brazenness of the man was astonishing. Having helped create the danger in the first place by supporting Catilina, he now hoped to claim the credit for destroying it! Cicero made a non-committal reply, to the effect that it was rather late at night to be imagining armies into being and appointing generals, and that he would like to sleep on matters before deciding how to respond.

'But when you make your statement, you'll give me credit for my patriotism in coming forward, I hope?'

'You may rely on it,' said Cicero, ushering him out of the study and into the atrium, where the guards were waiting.

'If there's anything more I can do …' said Crassus.

'Actually there is one matter I'd appreciate your help on,' said Cicero, who never missed an opportunity to press home an advantage. 'This prosecution of Murena, if it succeeds, would rob us of a consul at a very dangerous moment. Will you join Hortensius and me in defending him?'

Of course this was the last thing Crassus wanted to do, but he made the best of it. 'It would be an honour.'

The two men shook hands. 'I cannot tell you,' said Cicero, 'how pleased I am that any misunderstandings that may have existed between us in the past are now cleared up.'

'I feel exactly the same, my dear Cicero. This has been a good night for both of us – and an ever better night for Rome.'

And with many mutual protestations of friendship, trust and regard, Cicero conducted Crassus and his companions to the door, bowed to him, wished him a sound night's sleep, and promised to talk to him in the morning.

'What a complete and utter lying shit that bastard is!' he exclaimed the moment the door had closed.

'You don't believe him?'

'What? That Arrius just happened to be in Etruria and by chance fell into idle conversation with men who are taking up arms against the state and who then on a whim urged him to join them? No I don't. Do you?'

'Those letters are very odd. Do you think he wrote them himself?'

'Why would he do that?'

'I suppose so that he could come to you in the middle of the night and play the part of the loyal citizen. They do give him the perfect excuse to withdraw his support from Catilina.' Suddenly I became excited, for I thought I saw the truth. 'That's it! He must have sent Arrius out to take a look at what was happening in Etruria, and then when Arrius came back and told him what was going on, he took fright. He's decided Catilina's certain to lose, and wants publicly to distance himself.'

Cicero nodded approvingly. 'That's clever.' He wandered back along the passage and into the atrium, his hands clasped behind his back, his head hunched forward, thinking. Suddenly he stopped. 'I wonder …' he began.

'What?'

'Well, look at it the other way round. Imagine that Catilina's plan works: that Manlius's ragamuffin army does indeed capture Praeneste and then advances on Rome, gathering support in every town and village through which it passes. There's panic and slaughter in the capital. The senate house is stormed. I am killed. Catilina effectively takes control of the republic. It's not impossible – the gods know, we have few enough here to defend us, while Catilina has many supporters living within our walls. Then what would happen?'

'I don't know. It's a nightmare.'

'I can tell you precisely what would happen. The surviving magistrates would have no option except to summon home the one man who could save the nation: Pompey the Great, at the head of his Eastern legions.

With his military genius, and with forty thousand trained men under his command, he'd finish off Catilina in no time, and once he'd done that, nothing would stand between him and the dictatorship of the entire world. And which of his rivals does Crassus fear and hate more than any other?'

'Pompey?'

'Pompey. Exactly. That's it. The situation must be much more perilous even than I thought. Crassus came to see me tonight to betray Catilina not because he's worried he might fail but because he's frightened he'll succeed.'

The next morning at first light we left the house accompanied by four knights including the Sextus brothers, who henceforth would seldom leave the consul's side. Cicero kept the hood of his cloak well up and his head well down, while I carried the case of letters. Every few paces I had to take an extra step to keep up with his long stride. When I asked him where we were going, he replied: 'We need to find ourselves a general.'

It seems odd to relate, but overnight all Cicero's recent misery and despair had left him. Faced with this immense crisis he seemed – not happy: that would be absurd to say, but invigorated. He almost bounded up the steps to the Palatine, and when we turned into Victory Rise I realised our destination must be the house of Metellus Celer. We passed the portico of Catulus and drew into the doorway of the next house, which stood vacant, its windows and entrance boarded up. Determined not to be seen, Cicero said that he would wait here while I went next door and announced that the consul wished to see the praetor alone and in the strictest confidence. I did as he asked, and Celer's steward quickly reported back that his master would join us as soon as he could get away from his morning levee. When I returned to fetch Cicero, I found him talking to the watchman of the empty house. 'This place belongs to Crassus,' he told me as we walked away. 'Can you believe it? It's worth a fortune but he's leaving it empty so that he can get a better price next year. No wonder he doesn't want a civil war – it's bad for business!'

Cicero was conducted by a servant down an alleyway between the two houses, through the rear door and directly into the family apartments. There, Celer's wife Clodia, alluring in a silken robe over her nightdress, and with the musky smell of the bedchamber still upon her, waited to greet him.

'When I heard you were coming clandestinely through the back door I hoped it was to see *me*,' she said reproachfully, fixing him with her sleepy eyes, 'but now I hear it's my husband you want, which really is too boring of you.'

'I fear everyone is a bore,' said Cicero, bowing to kiss her hand, 'compared to she who reduces us all, however eloquent, to stammering wrecks.'

It was a measure of Cicero's revived spirits that he had the energy to flirt, and the contact between his lips and her skin seemed to last far longer than was necessary. What a scene: the great and prudish orator bent over the hand of the most titled trollop in Rome! It actually flashed into my mind – a wild, fantastical notion – that Cicero might one day leave Terentia for this woman, and I was glad when Celer came bustling into the room in his usual hearty military manner and the intimate atmosphere was instantly dissolved.

'Consul! Good morning! What can I do for you?'

'You can raise an army and save your country.'

'An army? That's a good one!' But then he saw that Cicero was serious. 'What are you talking about?'

'The crisis I have for so long predicted is upon us at last. Tiro, show the praetor the letter addressed to Crassus.' I did so, and watched Celer's face grow rigid as he read the words.

'This was sent to Crassus?'

'So he says. And these others were also delivered to him last night for distribution across the city.' Cicero gestured to me and I handed Celer the bundle of letters. He read a couple and compared them. When he had finished, Clodia lifted them from his hands and studied them herself. He made no effort to stop her, and I made a note in my mind to remember that she was privy to all his secrets. 'And that's only the half of it,' continued Cicero. 'According to Quintus Arrius, Etruria is swarming with Catilina's men. Manlius is raising a rebel army equivalent to two legions. They plan to seize Praeneste, and Rome will be next. I want you to take command of our defences. You'll need to move swiftly if we're to stop them.'

'What do you mean by swiftly?'

'You'll leave the city today.'

'But I have no authority—'

'I'll get you the authority.'

'Hold on, Consul. There are things I need to think about before I go off raising troops and rampaging through the countryside.'

'Such as?'

'Well, first I must certainly consult my brother Nepos. And then I have my other brother – my brother by marriage – Pompey the Great, to think about—'

'We haven't the time for all that! If every man starts considering his family's interests ahead of his nation's, we'll never get anywhere. Listen, Celer,' Cicero said, softening his tone in that way I'd heard him do so often, 'your courage and firm action have already saved the republic once when Rabirius was in peril. Ever since then I've known that history has cast you to play the hero's part. There's glory as well as peril in this crisis. Remember Hector: "No sluggard's fate, ingloriously to die / But daring that which men to be shall learn." Besides, if you don't do it, Crassus will.'

'Crassus? He's no general! All he knows about is money.'

'Maybe, but he's already sniffing round the chance for military glory. Give him a day or two and he'll have bought himself a majority in the senate.'

'If there's military glory to be had, Pompey will want it, and my brother has come back to Rome expressly to ensure he gets it.' Celer gave me back the letters. 'No, Consul – I appreciate your faith in me, but I can't accept without their approval.'

'I'll give you Nearer Gaul.'

'What?'

'Nearer Gaul – I'll give it you.'

'But Nearer Gaul isn't yours to give.'

'Yes it is. It's presently my allotted province, swapped with Hybrida for Macedonia, if you recall. It was always my intention to renounce it. You can have it.'

'But it's not a basket of eggs! There'll have to be a fresh ballot among the praetors.'

'Yes, which you will win.'

'You'll rig the ballot?'

'*I* shan't rig the ballot. That would be most improper. No, no, I'll leave that side of things to Hybrida. He may not have many talents, but rigging ballots I believe is one of them.'

'What if he refuses?'

'He won't. We have an understanding. Besides,' said Cicero, flourishing the anonymous letter addressed to Hybrida, 'I'm sure he'd prefer it if this wasn't made public.'

'Nearer Gaul,' said Celer, rubbing his broad chin. 'It's better than Further Gaul.'

'Darling,' said Clodia, putting her hand on her husband's arm, 'it really is a very good offer, and I'm sure Nepos and Pompey will understand.'

Celer grunted, and rocked back and forth on his heels a few times. I could see the greed in his face. Eventually he said, 'How soon d'you think I could be given this province?'

'Today,' said Cicero. 'This is a national emergency. I shall argue that there must be no uncertainty about commands anywhere in the empire, and that my place is in Rome, just as yours is in the field, putting down the rebel forces. We'll be partners in defence of the republic. What do you say?'

Celer glanced at Clodia. 'It will put you ahead of all your contemporaries,' she said. 'Your consulship will be guaranteed.'

He grunted again, and turned back to Cicero. 'Very well,' he replied, and extended his massive muscled arm towards the consul. 'For the sake of my country, I say yes.'

From Celer's house, Cicero walked the few hundred paces to Hybrida's, roused the presiding consul from his habitual drunken stupor, sobered him up, told him about the rebel army gathering in Etruria, and gave him his lines for the day. Hybrida baulked at first when told he would have to rig the ballot for Nearer Gaul, but then Cicero showed him the letter from the conspirators with his name written on it. His glassy, red-veined eyes almost popped out of his head and he began to sweat and shake in alarm.

'I swear to you, Cicero, I knew nothing about it!'

'Yes, but unfortunately, my dear Hybrida, as you well know, this city is full of jealous and suspicious minds that might easily be persuaded to believe otherwise. If you really want to prove your loyalty beyond question, I suggest you oblige me in this matter of Nearer Gaul, and you may rely on my absolute support.'

So that took care of Hybrida, and then it was simply a matter of squaring the right senators, which Cicero proceeded to do before the afternoon session while the auspices were being taken. By now the city was awash with rumours about a rebel assault and a plot to murder the leading magistrates. Catulus, Isauricus, Hortensius, the Lucullus brothers, Silanus, Murena, even Cato, who was now a tribune-elect alongside Nepos – each was drawn aside and given a whispered briefing. Cicero at these moments looked like nothing so much as a crafty carpet salesman in a crowded bazaar, glancing furtively over his customer's shoulder and then backwards over his own, his voice low, his hands moving expressively as he sought to close a deal. Caesar watched him from a distance, and I in turn watched Caesar. His expression was unreadable. There was no sign of Catilina.

When the senators all trooped in for the start of the session, Cicero took his place at the end of the front bench nearest to the consular dais, which was where he always sat when he was not presiding; Catulus was on his other side. From this vantage point, by a series of nods and eye gestures at Hybrida and occasional audible whispers, Cicero was normally able to control proceedings even in those months when he did not have the chair. To be fair to him, Hybrida was almost credible when he had a script to read out, as he had that day. With his broad shoulders squared and his noble head thrown back, and in a voice that had been pickled rich in wine, he declared that public events had taken a grave turn overnight, and called upon Quintus Arrius to make a statement.

Arrius was one of those senators who did not speak often but when he did was listened to with respect. I don't know why. Perhaps the absurdity of his voice seemed to lend it a peculiar sincerity. He rose now and delivered a very full report of what he had seen happening in the countryside: that armed bands were congregating in Etruria, recruited by Manlius; that their numbers might soon swell to ten thousand; that he understood their intention was to attack Praeneste; that the security of Rome itself was threatened; and that similar uprisings were planned in Apulia and Capua. By the time he resumed his seat, there was an audible and growing swell of panic. Hybrida thanked him and next called on Crassus, Marcellus and Scipio to read aloud the messages they had received the previous evening. He gave the letters to the clerks, who passed them to their original recipients. Crassus was first on his feet. He described the mysterious arrival of the warnings and how he had gone at once with the others to see Cicero. Then he read his out in a firm, clear voice: '*The time for talking is over. The moment for action has arrived. Catilina has drawn up his plans. He wishes to warn you there will be bloodshed in Rome. Spare yourself and leave the city secretly. When it is safe to return, you will be contacted.*'

Can you imagine the cumulative effect of those words, gravely intoned by Crassus and then repeated, more nervously, by Scipio and Marcellus?

The shock was all the greater as Crassus was known to have supported Catilina for the consulship not once but twice. There was a profound hush, and then someone shouted, 'Where is he?' The cry was taken up by others. 'Where is he? Where is he?' In the pandemonium, Cicero briefly whispered something to Catulus, and the old patrician took the floor.

'In view of the appalling news this house has just received,' declared Catulus, 'and in accordance with the ancient prerogatives of this order, I propose that the consuls should be empowered to take all necessary measures for the defence of the realm, under the provisions of the Final Act. These powers shall include, but not be limited to, the authority to levy troops and conduct war, to apply unlimited force to allies and citizens alike, and to exercise supreme command and jurisdiction both at home and abroad.'

'Quintus Lutatius Catulus has proposed that we adopt the Final Act,' said Hybrida. 'Does anyone wish to oppose it?'

All heads now turned to Caesar, not least because the legitimacy of the Final Act was the central issue at the heart of the prosecution of Rabirius. But Caesar, for the first time in my experience, looked utterly overwhelmed by events. He noticeably did not exchange a word with his neighbour, Crassus, or even glance at him – a rare occurrence, as normally they were very thick together – and I deduced from this that Crassus's betrayal of Catilina had taken him entirely by surprise. He made no gesture of any sort, but stared straight ahead into the middle distance, thus giving some of us an early preview of those marble busts of him that gaze impassively with sightless eyes across every public building in Italy.

'Then if no one opposes it,' said Hybrida, 'the motion passes, and the chair recognises Marcus Tullius Cicero.'

Only now did Cicero rise, to a deep rumble of acclaim from those selfsame senators who just a few weeks earlier had been mocking him for his alarmism. 'Gentlemen,' he said, 'I wish to congratulate Antonius Hybrida for the very firm manner in which he has handled this crisis today.' The senators murmured in approval; Hybrida beamed. 'For my own part, trusting in the shield provided by my friends and allies, I shall remain in Rome and continue to defy this murderous madman Catilina, as I always have. Because no one can say how long this threat will continue, I hereby ask formally to be relieved of my allotted province, in accordance with the promise I made at the start of my consulship – a promise all the more urgent in this hour of trial for our republic.'

Cicero's patriotic self-sacrifice was warmly approved, and Hybrida at once produced the sacred urn and put into it one marked token representing Nearer Gaul and seven blanks – or so it appeared. In fact, I learned later, he had put in only blanks. The eight praetors then came forward. The first to try his luck was the haughty figure of Lentulus Sura, whom Cicero knew to be deeply involved in Catilina's schemes. Sura, one of the most inbred boobies in the senate, was closely related to Hybrida in all sorts of ways: for one thing, he had married the widow of Hybrida's brother, and was bringing up the son of that union, Mark Antony, as his own; and this same Mark Antony was engaged to Hybrida's daughter, Antonia. So I watched Hybrida closely, to see if he would be able to go through with the deception he had promised. But politics has loyalties all of its own, and they greatly supersede those to in-laws. Sura thrust his arm deep into the urn and handed his token to Hybrida, who announced it blank and showed it to the chamber. Sura shrugged and turned away; it wasn't a province he was after in any case, but Rome itself.

Pomptinus went next, and then Flaccus, with the same result. Celer was fourth to draw a lot. He looked very cool as he made his way to the dais and picked his token. Hybrida took it from him and seemed to turn away, towards the light, to read it carefully, and that is when he must have made the switch, for when he held it up for inspection, everyone nearby could clearly see the cross that was marked upon it.

'Celer draws Nearer Gaul!' he announced. 'May the gods favour his appointment.'

There was applause. Cicero was on his feet at once.

'I propose that Quintus Caecilius Metellus Celer be now invested with full military imperium, and be given the authority to raise an army to defend his province.'

'Does anyone object?' asked Hybrida.

For a moment I thought Crassus was going to get to his feet. He seemed to half lean forwards, hesitate, and then think better of it.

'The motion is passed unanimously.'

After the senate adjourned, Cicero and Hybrida convened a council of war with all the praetors to issue the necessary edicts for the defence of the city. A message was dispatched at once to the commander of the garrison at Praeneste, ordering him to strengthen the guard. A long-standing offer from the prefect of Reate to send a hundred men was accepted. In Rome the gates were to be closed an hour earlier than usual. There would be a curfew at the twelfth hour and street patrols throughout the night. The ancient prohibition on carrying arms within the precincts of the city would be suspended in the case of soldiers loyal to the senate. Wagons would be searched at random. Access to the Palatine would be blocked at sunset. All the gladiator schools in and around the capital would be closed and the fighters dispersed to distant towns and colonies. Huge rewards, of up to one hundred thousand sesterces, were to be offered to anyone – slaves as well as freemen – with information about potential traitors. Celer would leave at first light to begin mustering fresh levies of troops. Finally it was agreed that various reliable men should be approached and asked to bring a prosecution against Catilina for violence against the state, in return for guarantees of their personal protection.

Throughout all this Lentulus Sura sat calmly, with his freedman Publius Umbrenus seated beside him taking notes, and afterwards Cicero complained bitterly to me of this absurdity: that two of the chief plotters should be able to attend the innermost security council of the state and report back on its decisions to their fellow criminals! But what could he do? It was the same old story: he had no evidence.

Cicero's guards were anxious to get him home before darkness fell, and so once the business was concluded we went out cautiously into the thickening twilight and then hurried across the forum, through Subura and up the Esquiline Hill. About an hour later, Cicero was in his study composing dispatches notifying the provincial governors of the senate's decisions when the guard dog set up its infernal barking again. Moments later the porter came in to tell us that Metellus Celer had arrived to see the consul and was waiting in the atrium.

It was obvious straight away that Celer was agitated. He was pacing around the room and cracking his knuckles, while Quintus and Titus Sextus kept a careful watch on him from the passageway.

'Well, Governor,' said Cicero, seeing at once that his visitor needed calming down, 'the afternoon went smoothly enough, I thought.'

'From your point of view, perhaps, but my brother isn't happy. I told you there'd be trouble. Nepos says that if the rebels in Etruria are as serious as we make out, Pompey himself should be brought home to deal with them.'

'But we haven't the time to wait for Pompey and his army to travel a thousand miles back to Rome. We'll all be slaughtered in our beds long before he gets here.'

'So *you* say, but Catilina swears he means no threat to the state, and insists those letters have nothing to do with him.'

'You've spoken to him?'

'He came to see me just after you left the senate. To prove his peaceful intentions he's offered to surrender himself into my personal custody for as long as I wish.'

'Ha! What a rogue! You sent him away with a flea in his ear, I trust?'

'No, I've brought him here to see you.'

'*Here*? He's in my *house*?'

'No, he's waiting in the street. I think you should talk to him. He's alone and unarmed – I'll vouch for him.'

'Even if he is, what possible good can come of talking to him?'

'He's a Sergius, Consul,' said Celer icily, 'descended from the Trojans. He deserves some respect for his blood, if nothing else.'

Cicero glanced at the Sextus brothers. Titus shrugged. 'If he's on his own, Consul, we can handle him.'

'Fetch him in then, Celer,' said Cicero, 'and I'll hear what he has to say. But I promise you, we're wasting our time.'

I was horrified that Cicero would take such a risk, and while Celer went off to get Catilina, I actually dared to remonstrate with him. But he cut me off. 'It will show good faith on my part if I can announce in the senate that at least I was willing to receive the villain. Who knows, anyway? Perhaps he's come to apologise.'

He forced a smile, but I could tell that this unexpected development had strained his nerves. As for me, I felt like one of the condemned men in the Games, when the tiger is let into the arena, for that was how Catilina came prowling into that room – wild and wary, full of barely suppressed fury: I half expected him to spring at Cicero's throat. The Sextus brothers stepped in close behind him as he came to a halt a couple of paces in front of Cicero. He raised his hand in mock salute. 'Consul.'

'Say your piece, Senator, and then get out.'

'I hear you've been spreading lies about me again.'

'You see?' said Cicero, turning to Celer. 'What did I tell you? This is pointless.'

'Just hear him out,' said Celer.

'Lies,' repeated Catilina. 'I don't know a damned thing about these letters people are saying I sent last night. I'd have to be a rare fool to dispatch such messages all across the city.'

'I'm willing to believe that you personally didn't send them,' replied Cicero, 'but there are plenty of men around you stupid enough to do such a thing.'

'Balls! They're blatant forgeries. D'you know what I think? I think you wrote them yourself.'

'You'd do better to direct your suspicions towards Crassus – he's the one who's used them as an excuse to turn his back on you.'

'Old Baldhead is playing his own game, the same as he always does.'

'And the rebels in Etruria? Are they nothing to do with you either?'

'They're poor and starving wretches, driven to desperate lengths by the moneylenders – they have my sympathy, but I'm not their leader. I'll make the same offer to you I've made to Celer. I'll surrender myself into your custody and live in this house where you and your guards can keep an eye on me, and then you can see how innocent I am.'

'That is not an offer but a joke! If I don't feel safe living in the same city as you, I'll hardly feel safe under the same roof.'

'So there's nothing I can do that will satisfy you?'

'Yes. Remove yourself from Rome and Italy entirely. Go into exile. Never return.'

Catilina's eyes glittered and his large hands contracted into fists. 'My first ancestor was Sergestus, companion of Aeneas, the founder of our city – and *you* dare to tell *me* to leave?'

'Oh, spare us the family folklore! Mine at least is a serious offer. If you go into exile, I'll see to it that no harm befalls your wife and children. Your sons won't suffer the shame of having a father who is condemned – because you will be condemned, Catilina, be in no doubt about that. You'll also escape your creditors, which I'd have thought was another consideration.'

'And what about my friends? How long will they be subjected to your dictatorship?'

'My dictatorship, as you call it, is only in force to protect us all against *you*. Once you're gone it won't be needed, and I for one would be pleased to start afresh and offer a clean slate to all men. Voluntary exile would be a noble course, Catilina – one worthy of those ancestors you're always talking about.'

'So now the grandson of a chickpea farmer presumes to lecture a Sergius on what is noble? He'll be telling you next, Celer!' Celer stared stiffly ahead, like a soldier on parade. 'Look at him,' sneered Catilina. 'Typical Metelli – they always prosper whatever happens. But you realise, Cicero, that secretly he despises you? They all do. I at least have the guts to say to your face what they only whisper behind your back. They may use you to protect their precious property. But once you've done their dirty work they'll want nothing more to do with you. Destroy me if you will; in the end you'll only destroy yourself.'

He turned on his heel, pushed past the Sextus brothers, and strode out of the house. Cicero said, 'Why is it he always seems to leave a smell of sulphur behind him?'

'Do you think he'll go into exile?' asked Celer.

'He might. I don't think he knows from one moment to the next what he's going to do. He's like an animal: he'll follow whatever impulse seizes him. The main thing is to maintain our guard and vigilance – I in the city, you in the countryside.'

'I'll leave at first light.' Celer made a move towards the door, then stopped and turned. 'By the way, all that stuff about us despising you – there's not a word of truth in it, you know.'

'I know that, Celer, thank you.' Cicero smiled at him, and maintained the smile until he heard the door close, at which point it slowly faded from his face. He sank back on to the nearest chair and held out his hands, palms upward, contemplating them in wonder, as if their violent trembling was the strangest thing he had ever seen.

XXVII

The following day, Quintus came to see Cicero in great excitement, bearing a copy of a letter that had been posted outside the offices of the tribunes. It was addressed to a number of prominent senators, among them Catulus, Caesar and Lepidus, and was signed by Catilina: *Unable to withstand that group of enemies who have persecuted me with false charges, I have departed for exile in Massilia. I leave not because I am guilty of the heinous crimes of which I am accused but to preserve the peace of the state and to spare the republic the bloodshed that would ensue if I struggled against my fate. I commend my wife and family to your care and my honour to your memories. Farewell!*

'Congratulations, brother,' said Quintus, clapping him on the back. 'You've seen him off.'

'But is this certain?'

'As certain as can be. He was seen early this morning riding out of the city with a few companions. His house is locked and deserted.'

Cicero winced and tugged at his ear lobe. 'Even so, something about it smells wrong to me.'

Quintus, who had hurried up the hill specially to convey the good news, was irritated by his caution. 'Catilina's been obliged to flee. It's tantamount to a confession. You've beaten him.'

And slowly, as the days passed and nothing was heard of Catilina, it did begin to seem that Quintus was right. Nevertheless, Cicero refused to relax the security restrictions in Rome; indeed, he went around with even more protection than before. Accompanied by a dozen men, he ventured outside the city to see Quintus Metellus, who still possessed military imperium, and asked him to go to the heel of Italy and take charge of the region of Apulia. The old man grumbled, but Cicero swore that after this last mission his triumph was assured, and Metellus – secretly glad to have something to occupy him, I suspect – set off at once. Another former consul also hoping for a triumph, Marcius Rex, went north to Faesulae. The praetor Q. Pompeius Rufus, whom Cicero trusted, was ordered to go to Capua to raise troops. Meanwhile Metellus Celer continued recruiting an army in Picenum.

At some point during this time, the rebel leader Manlius sent a message to the senate: *We call on gods and men to witness that our object in taking up arms was not to attack our country or endanger others, but to protect ourselves from wrong. We are poor needy wretches; the cruel harshness of moneylenders has robbed most of us of our homes, and all of us have lost reputation and fortune.* He demanded that every debt contracted in silver (as most debts were) be repaid in copper: an effective relief of three quarters. Cicero proposed sending a stern reply that there could be no negotiations until the rebels laid down their arms. The motion carried in the senate, but many outside whispered that the rebels' cause was just.

October gave way to November. The days began to be dark and cold; the people of Rome grew weary and depressed. The curfew had put a stop to many of those entertainments with which they normally warded off the encroaching gloom of winter. The taverns and the baths closed early; the shops were bare. Informers, eager for the huge rewards for denouncing traitors, took the opportunity to pay back scores against their neighbours. Everyone suspected everyone else. Matters became so serious that eventually Atticus bravely took it upon himself to talk to Cicero.

'Some citizens are saying you've deliberately exaggerated the threat,' he warned his friend.

'And why would I do that? Do they think it gives me pleasure to turn Rome into a gaol in which I'm the most closely guarded prisoner?'

'No, but they think you're obsessed with Catilina and have lost all sense of proportion; that your fears for your own personal safety are making their lives intolerable.'

'Is that all?'

'They believe you're acting like a dictator.'

'Do they really?'

'They also say you're a coward.'

'Well then, damn the people!' exclaimed Cicero, and for the first time I saw him treat Atticus coldly, refusing to respond to his further attempts at conversation with anything more than monosyllables.

Eventually his friend wearied of this frosty atmosphere, rolled his eyes at me and went away.

Late on the evening of the sixth day of November, long after the lictors had gone off for the night, Cicero was reclining in the dining room with Terentia and Quintus. He had been reading dispatches from magistrates all over Italy, and I was just handing him some letters for his signature when Sargon started barking furiously. The noise made us all jump; everyone's nerves were shredded by then. Cicero's three guards all got to their feet. We heard the front door open and the sound of an urgent male voice, and suddenly into the room strode Cicero's former pupil, Caelius Rufus. It was his first appearance on the premises for months, all the more startling because he had gone over to Catilina at the start of the year. Quintus jumped up, ready for a fight.

'Rufus,' said Cicero calmly, 'I thought you were a stranger to us these days.'

'I'll never be a stranger to you.'

He took a step forward, but Quintus put his hand on his chest and stopped him. 'Arms up!' he commanded, and nodded to the guards. Rufus hastily raised both hands, while Titus Sextus searched him. 'I expect he's come to spy on us,' said Quintus, who had never cared much for Rufus, and often asked me why I thought his brother tolerated the presence of such a tearaway.

'I've not come to spy. I've come to warn: Catilina's back.'

Cicero banged his fist on the table. 'I knew it! Put your hands down, Rufus. When did he return?'

'This evening.'

'And where is he now?'

'At the home of Marcus Laeca, on the street of the scythe-makers.'

'Who's with him?'

'Sura, Cethegus, Bestia – the whole gang. I've only just got away.'

'And?'

'They're going to kill you at sunrise.'

Terentia put her hand to her mouth.

'How?' demanded Quintus.

'Two men, Vargunteius and Cornelius, will call on you at dawn to pledge their loyalty and claim they've deserted Catilina. They'll be armed. There'll be others at their backs to overpower your guards. You mustn't admit either of them.'

'We won't,' said Quintus.

'But I'd have admitted them,' said Cicero. 'A senator and a knight – of course I would. I'd have offered them the hand of friendship.' He seemed amazed at how close to disaster he had come despite all his precautions.

'How do we know the lad isn't lying?' said Quintus. 'It could be a trick to divert us from the real threat.'

'He has a point, Rufus,' said Cicero. 'Your loyalty is as fixed as a weathercock.'

'It's the truth.'

'Yet you support their cause?'

'Their cause, yes, not their methods – not any longer.'

'What methods are these?'

'They've agreed to carve up Italy into military regions. The moment you're dead, Catilina will go to the rebel army in Etruria. Parts of Rome will be set alight. There'll be a massacre of senators on the Palatine, and then the city gates will be opened to Manlius and his mob.'

'And Caesar? Does he know all this?'

'He wasn't there tonight, but I sense he knows what's planned. Catilina talks to him quite often.'

This was the first time Cicero had received direct intelligence of Catilina's intentions. His expression was appalled. He bent his head and rubbed his temples with his knuckles. 'What to do?' he muttered.

'We need to get you out of this house tonight,' said Quintus, 'and hide you somewhere they can't get at you.'

'You could go to Atticus,' I suggested.

Cicero shook his head. 'That's the first place they'd look. The only safe refuge is out of Rome. Terentia and Marcus at least could go to Tusculum.'

'I'm not going anywhere,' said Terentia, 'and neither should you. The Roman people will respect many kinds of leader, but they'll never respect a coward. This is your home and your father's home before you – stay in it and dare them to do their worst. I know I should if I were a man.'

She glared at Cicero and I feared we were about to be treated to another of their stupendous rows, which had so often split that modest house like claps of thunder. But then Cicero nodded. 'You're right. Tiro, send a message to Atticus telling him we need reinforcements urgently. We'll barricade the doors.'

'And we should get some barrels of water on the roof,' added Quintus, 'in case they try to burn us out.'

'I'll stay and help,' said Rufus.

'No, my young friend,' said Cicero. 'You've done your part, and I'm grateful for it. But you should leave the city at once. Go back to your father's house in Interamna until all this is settled, one way or the other.' Rufus started to protest, but Cicero cut him off. 'If Catilina fails to kill me tomorrow, he may suspect you of betraying him; if he succeeds, you'll be sucked into the whirlpool. Either way, you're better off a long way from Rome.'

Rufus tried to argue, but to no avail. After he had gone, Cicero said, 'He's probably on our side, but who can tell? In the end, the only safe place to put a Trojan horse is outside your walls.'

I dispatched one of the slaves to Atticus with a plea for help. Then we barred the door and dragged a heavy chest and a couch across it. The rear entrance was also locked and bolted; as a second line of defence we wedged an upended table to block the passageway. Together with Sositheus and Laurea I carried up bucket after bucket of water to the roof, along with carpets and blankets to smother any fires. Within this makeshift citadel we had, to protect the consul, a garrison of three bodyguards, Quintus, myself, Sargon and his handler, a gatekeeper, and a few male slaves armed with knives and sticks. And I must not forget Terentia, who carried a heavy iron candle-holder at all times, and who would probably have been more effective than any of us. The maids cowered in the nursery with Marcus, who had a toy sword.

Cicero put on a display of great calmness. He sat at his desk, thinking and making notes and writing out letters in his own hand. From time to time he asked me whether there was any reply yet from Atticus. He wanted to know the moment the extra men appeared, so I armed myself with a kitchen knife, went up on to the roof again, wrapped myself in a blanket, and kept watch on the street. It was dark and silent; nothing moved. As far as I could tell, the whole of Rome was slumbering. I thought back to the night that Cicero won the consulship, and how I had joined the family up here to dine by starlight in celebration. He had realised from the start that his position was weak and that power would be fraught with dangers; he could hardly have imagined such a scene as this.

Several hours passed. I heard dogs bark occasionally but no human voices, apart from the watchman down in the valley calling the divisions of the night. The cocks crowed as usual then fell silent, and the air actually seemed to grow darker and very cold. Laurea called up that the consul wanted to see me. I went downstairs and found him seated in his curule chair in the atrium, with a drawn sword resting across his knees.

'You're sure you definitely requested those extra men from Atticus?'

'Of course.'

'And you stressed the urgency?'

'Yes.'

'And the messenger was trustworthy?'

'Very.'

'Well then,' said Cicero, 'Atticus won't let me down; he never has.' But he sounded as if he was trying to reassure himself, and I am sure that he was remembering the circumstances of their last meeting, and their chilly parting. It was nearly dawn. The dog started barking wildly again. Cicero looked at me with exhausted eyes. His face was very strained. 'Go and see,' he said.

I climbed back up to the roof and peered carefully over the parapet. At first I could make out nothing. But gradually I realised that the shadows on the far side of the street were moving. A line of men was approaching, keeping close to the wall. My first thought was that our reinforcements had arrived. But then Sargon set up his infernal barking again. The shadows halted and a man's voice whispered. I hurried back down to Cicero. Quintus was standing next to him with his sword unsheathed. Terentia clutched her candlestick.

'The attackers are here,' I said.

'How many?' asked Quintus.

'Ten. Perhaps twelve.'

There was a loud knock on the front door. Cicero swore. 'If a dozen men are determined to get into this house, they'll do it.'

'The door will hold them for a while,' said Quintus. 'It's fire that worries me.'

'I'll go back to the roof,' I said.

There was a very faint grey tinge to the sky by this time, and when I looked down into the street I could see the dark shapes of heads huddled around the front of the house. They seemed intent on something. There was a flash, and abruptly they all drew back as a torch flared. Someone must have seen my face looking down, because a man shouted, 'Hey, you up there! Is the consul in?' I pulled back out of sight.

Another man called up, 'This is Senator Lucius Vargunteius, to see the consul! I have urgent information for him!'

Just then I heard a crash and voices from the back of the house. A second group was trying to break in at the rear. I was halfway across the roof when suddenly a torch sailed over the edge of the parapet, twisting and roaring in flight. It buzzed close to my ear and clattered on to the tiles next to me, the burning pitch breaking and scattering into a dozen flaming pieces. I shouted down the stairwell for help, grabbed a heavy carpet and just about managed to throw it over the little fires, stamping out the ones I missed as best I could. Another torch roared through the air, landed with a crash and disintegrated; then another; and another. The roof, which was made of old timber as well as terracotta, glimmered in the darkness like a field of stars, and I saw that Quintus was right: if this went on much longer, they would burn us out and slaughter Cicero in the street.

Filled with a fury born of fear, I seized the handle of the nearest torch, which still had a sizeable piece of burning pitch attached to it, darted to the edge of the roof, took careful aim and hurled it at the men below. It hit one fellow square on the head, setting his hair on fire. While he was screaming, I ran back for another. By now Sositheus and Laurea had come up on to the roof to help stamp out the fires, and they must have thought I was demented as I jumped up on to the parapet, screaming with rage, and threw another burning missile at our attackers. Out of the corner of my eye I saw that more shadowy figures with torches were pouring into the street. I thought we were certain to be overwhelmed. But suddenly from beneath me came the sound of angry cries, the ring of steel on steel, and the echo of running feet. 'Tiro!' shouted a voice, and by the flaring yellow light I recognised the upturned face of Atticus. The street was jammed with his men. 'Tiro! Is your master safe? Let us in!'

I ran downstairs and along the passageway, with the consul and Terentia at my heels, and together with Quintus and the Sextus brothers we dragged away the chest and the couch and unbarred the door. The moment it was open, Cicero and Atticus fell into one another's arms, to the cheers and applause from the street of some thirty members of the Order of Knights.

*

By the time it was fully light, the approaches to Cicero's house were blocked and guarded. Any visitor wishing to see him, even senior members of the senate, had to wait at one of the armed checkpoints until word had been sent to the consul. Then, if Cicero wanted to meet them, I would go out to confirm their identity and escort them into his presence. Catulus, Isauricus, Hortensius and both of the Lucullus brothers were all admitted in this way, along with the consuls-elect Silanus and Murena. They brought with them the news that throughout Rome Cicero was now regarded as a hero. Sacrifices had been made in his honour and prayers of thanks offered up for his safety, while rocks had been hurled at Catilina's empty house. All morning a steady procession of gifts and goodwill messages was carried up the Esquiline Hill – flowers, wine, cakes, olive oil – until the atrium looked like a market stall. Clodia sent him a basket of luxuriant fruit from her orchard on the Palatine. But this was intercepted by Terentia before it reached her husband, and I watched a look of suspicion darken her face as she read Clodia's note; she ordered the steward to throw the fruit away, 'for fear of poison', she said.

A warrant was issued by Cicero for the arrest of Vargunteius and Cornelius. The leaders of the senate also urged him to order the capture of Catilina, dead or alive. But Cicero hesitated. 'It's all very well for them,' he said to Quintus and Atticus after the deputation had gone, 'their names wouldn't be on the warrant. But if Catilina is killed illegally on my orders, I'll be fighting off prosecutors for the rest of my days. Besides, it would only be a short-term remedy. It would still leave his supporters in the senate.'

'You're not suggesting he should be allowed to carry on living in Rome?' protested Quintus.

'No, I just want him to leave – leave and take his treasonous friends with him, and let them all join the rebel army and be killed on the field of battle, preferably a hundred miles away from me. By heavens, I'd give them a pass of safe conduct and a guard of honour to escort them out of the city if they wanted it – anything they liked so long as they'd just clear out.'

But however much he paced around, he could not see a way of bringing this about, and in the end he decided his only course was to call a meeting of the senate. Quintus and Atticus immediately objected that this would be dangerous: how could they guarantee his safety? Cicero pondered further and then came up with a clever idea. Rather than convene the senate in its usual chamber, he gave orders that the benches should be carried across the forum to the Temple of Jupiter the Protector. This had two advantages. First, because the temple was on the lower slopes of the Palatine, it could more easily be defended against an attack by Catilina's supporters. Second, it would have great symbolic value. According to legend, the temple had been vowed to Jupiter by Romulus himself at a critical juncture in the war against the Sabine tribes. Here was the very spot on which Rome had stood and rallied in her earliest hour of danger: here she would stand and rally in her latest, led by her new Romulus.

By the time Cicero set off for the temple, tightly protected by lictors and bodyguards, an atmosphere of real dread hung over the city, as tangible as the grey November mist rising from the Tiber. The streets were deathly quiet. Nobody applauded or jeered; they simply hid indoors. In the shadows of their windows the citizenry gathered, white-faced and silent, to watch the consul pass.

When we reached the temple, we found it ringed by members of the Order of Knights, some quite elderly, all armed with lances and swords. Within this security perimeter several hundred senators stood around in muted groups. They parted to let us through and a few patted Cicero on the back and whispered their good wishes. Cicero nodded in acknowledgement, took the auspices very quickly, and then he and the lictors led the way into the large building. I had never set foot inside before, and it presented a most sombre scene. Centuries old, every wall and corner was crammed with relics of military glory from the earliest days of the republic – bloodied standards, dented armour, ships' beaks, legionary eagles, and a statue of Scipio Africanus painted up to look so lifelike it actually seemed he stood among us. I was some distance back in Cicero's retinue, the senators pouring in behind me, and because I was so busy craning my neck at all the memorabilia, I must have dawdled a little. At any rate, it wasn't until I had nearly reached the dais that I became aware, to my embarrassment, that the only sound in the building was the *click click* of my footsteps on the stone floor. The senate, I realised, had fallen entirely still.

Cicero was fiddling with a roll of papyrus. He turned to find out what was happening and I saw his face transfix with astonishment. I spun round in alarm myself – only to see Catilina calmly taking his place on one of the benches. Almost everyone else was still on their feet, watching him. Catilina sat, whereupon all the men nearest to him started edging away, as if he had leprosy. I never saw such a demonstration in my life. Even Caesar wouldn't go near him. Catilina took no notice, but folded his arms and thrust out his chin. The silence lengthened, until eventually I heard Cicero's voice, very calm, behind me.

'How much longer, Catilina, will you try our patience?'

All my life people have asked me about Cicero's speech that day. 'Did he write it out beforehand?' they want to know. 'Surely he must at least have planned what he was going to say?' The answer to both questions is 'no'. It was entirely spontaneous. Fragments of things he had long wanted to say, lines he had practised in his head, thoughts that had come to him in the sleepless nights of the last few months – all of it he wove together while he was on his feet.

'How much longer must we put up with your madness?'

He descended from his dais and started to advance very slowly along the aisle to where Catilina was sitting. As he walked, he extended both his arms and briefly gestured to the senators to take their places, which they did, and somehow that schoolmasterly gesture, and their instant compliance, established his authority. He was speaking for the republic.

'Is there no end to your arrogance? Don't you understand that we know what you're up to? Don't you appreciate that your conspiracy is uncovered? Do you think there's a man among us who doesn't know what you did last night – where you were, who came to your meeting, and what you agreed?' He stood at last in front of Catilina, his arms akimbo, looked him up and down, and shook his head. 'Oh, what times are these,' he said in a voice of utter disgust, 'and oh, what morals! The senate knows everything, the consul knows everything, and yet – *this man is still alive*!'

He wheeled around. 'Alive? Not just alive, gentlemen,' he cried, moving on down the aisle from Catilina and addressing the packed benches from the centre of the temple, 'he attends the senate! He takes part in our debates. He listens to us. He watches us – and all the time he's deciding who he's going to kill! Is this how we serve the republic – simply by sitting here, hoping it's not going to be us? How very brave we are! It's been twenty days since we voted ourselves the authority to act. We have the sword – but we keep it sheathed! You ought to have been executed immediately, Catilina. Yet still you live. And as long as you live, you don't give up your plotting – you increase it!'

I suppose by now even Catilina must have realised the size of his mistake in coming into the temple. In terms of physical strength and sheer effrontery he was much more powerful than Cicero. But the senate was not the arena for brute force. The weapons here were words, and no one ever knew how to deploy words as well as Cicero. For twenty years, whenever the courts were in session, scarcely a day had gone by that hadn't seen Cicero practising his craft. In a sense, his whole life had been but a preparation for this moment.

'Let's go over the events of last night. You went to the street of the scythe-makers – I'll be precise – to the house of Marcus Laeca. There you were joined by your criminal accomplices. Well, do you deny it? Why the silence? If you deny it, I'll prove it. In fact, I see some of those who were with you here in the senate. In heaven's name, where in the world are we? What country is this? What city are we living in? Here, gentlemen – here in our very midst, in this, the most sacred and important council in the world, there are men who want to destroy us, destroy our city, and extend that destruction to the entire world!

'You were at the house of Laeca, Catilina. You carved up the regions of Italy. You decided where you wanted each man to go. You said you would go yourself as soon I was dead. You chose parts of the city to be burnt. You sent two men to kill me. So I say to you, why don't you finish the journey you have begun? At long last really leave the city! The gates are open. Be on your way! The rebel army awaits its general. Take all your men with you. Cleanse the city. Put a wall between us. You cannot remain among us any longer – I cannot, I will not, I *must not* permit it!'

He thumped his right fist against his chest and cast his eyes to the roof of the temple as the senate came to its feet, bellowing its approval. 'Kill him!' someone shouted. 'Kill him! Kill him!' The cry was passed from man to man. Cicero waved them back down on to their benches.

'If I give an order for you to be killed, there will remain in the state the rest of the conspirators. But if, as I have long been urging, you leave the city, you will drain from it that flood of sewage that for you are your accomplices and for the rest of us our deadly enemies. Well, Catilina? What are you waiting for? What's left that can give you any pleasure in this city now? Beyond that conspiracy of ruined men, there isn't a single person who doesn't fear you, not one who doesn't hate you.'

There was much more in this vein, and then Cicero moved into his peroration. 'Let the traitors, then, depart!' he concluded. 'Go forth, Catilina, to your iniquitous and wicked war, and so bring sure salvation to the republic, disaster and ruin on yourself, and destruction to those who have joined you. Jupiter, you will protect us,' he thundered, reaching out his hand to the statue of the deity, 'and visit on these evil men, alive or dead, your punishment eternal!'

He turned away and stalked up the aisle to the dais. Now the chant was 'Go! Go! Go!' In an effort to retrieve the situation, Catilina leapt to his feet and began waving his arms about and shouting at Cicero's back. But it was far too late for him to undo the damage, and he didn't have the skill. He was flayed, humiliated, exposed, finished. I caught the words 'immigrant' and 'exile,' but the din was too great for him to be heard, and in any case his fury rendered him almost incomprehensible. As the cacophony of sound raged around him he fell silent, breathing deeply, and stood there for a short while longer, turning this way and that, like a once great ship lashed by a terrible storm, mastless and twisting at anchor, until something in him seemed to give way. He shuddered and stepped out into the aisle, at which point several senators, including Quintus, jumped across the benches to protect the consul. But even Catilina was not that demented: had he lunged at his enemy he would have been torn to pieces. Instead, with a final contemptuous glance around him – a glance that no doubt took in all those ancient glories in which his ancestors had played their part – he marched out of the senate. Later that same day, accompanied by twelve followers whom he called his lictors, and preceded by the silver eagle that had once belonged to Marius, he left the city and went to Arretium, where he formally proclaimed himself consul.

There are no lasting victories in politics, there is only the remorseless grinding forward of events. If my work has a moral, this is it. Cicero had scored an oratorical triumph over Catilina that would be talked about for years. With the whip of his tongue he had driven the monster from Rome. But the sewage, as he called it, did not, as he had hoped, drain away with him. On the contrary, after their leader had departed, Sura and the others remained calmly in their places, listening to the rest of the debate. They sat together, presumably on the principle of safety in numbers: Sura, Cethegus, Longinus, Annius, Paetus, the tribune-elect Bestia, the Sulla brothers, even Marcus Laeca, from whose house the assassins had been dispatched. I could see Cicero staring at them and I wondered what was going through his mind. Sura actually rose at one point and suggested in his sonorous voice that Catilina's wife and children be placed under the protection of the senate! The discussion meandered on. Then the tribune-elect Metellus Nepos demanded the floor. Now that Catilina had left the city, he said, presumably to lead the insurrection, surely the most prudent course would be to invite Pompey the Great back to Italy to take charge of the senatorial forces? Caesar quickly stood and seconded the proposal. Nimble-witted as ever, Cicero saw a chance to drive a wedge between his opponents, and with an innocent air of genuine interest he asked Crassus, who had been consul alongside Pompey, for his opinion. Crassus got up reluctantly.

'Nobody has a higher opinion of Pompey the Great than I,' he began, and then had to stop for a while, tapping his foot irritably as the temple shook with mocking laughter. 'Nobody has a higher opinion than I,' he repeated, 'but I have to say to the tribune-elect, in case he hasn't noticed, that it's nearly winter, the very worst time to transport troops by sea. How can Pompey possibly be here before the spring?'

'Then let us have Pompey the Great without his army,' countered Nepos. 'Travelling with a light escort he can be with us in a month. His name alone is worth a dozen legions.'

This was too much for Cato. He was on his feet in an instant. 'The enemies we face will not be defeated by *names*,' he mocked, 'even *names* that end in "Great". What we need are armies: armies in the field – armies like the one being raised at this very moment by the tribune-elect's own brother. Besides, if you ask me, Pompey has too much power as it is.'

That drew a loud and shocked 'Oh!' from the assembly.

'If this senate will not vote Pompey the command,' said Nepos, 'then I give you fair warning that I shall lay a bill before the people as soon as I take office as tribune demanding his recall.'

'And I give you fair warning,' retorted Cato, 'that I shall veto your bill.'

'Gentlemen, gentlemen!' cried Cicero, having to shout to make himself heard. 'We shall do neither the state nor ourselves any good by bickering at a time of national emergency! Tomorrow there will be a public assembly. I shall report to the people on our deliberations, and I hope,' he added, staring hard at Sura and his cronies, 'that those senators whose bodies may be with us but whose loyalties lie elsewhere will search their hearts overnight and act accordingly. This house stands adjourned.'

Normally after a session ended Cicero liked to stand outside for a while so that any senator who wished to speak to him could do so. It was one of those tools by which he exerted his control over the chamber, this knowledge he had of every man, however minor – his strengths and weaknesses, what he desired and what he feared, what he would put up with and what he would not stomach under any circumstances. But that afternoon he hurried away, his face rigid with frustration. 'It's like fighting the Hydra!' he complained furiously when we got home. 'No sooner do I lop off one head than another two grow back in its place! So while Catilina storms out, his henchmen all sit there as calm as you please, and now Pompey's faction are starting to stir! I have one month,' he ranted, 'just one month – if I can survive that long – before the new tribunes come into office. Then the agitation for Pompey's recall will really get started. And in the meantime we can't even be sure we'll actually have two new consuls in January because of this *fucking lawsuit*!' And with that he swept his arm across his desk and sent all the documents relating to Murena's prosecution flying across the floor.

In such a mood he was quite unreasonable, and I had learned from long experience that there was no point in attempting to reply. He waited irritably for me to respond and then, failing to get satisfaction, he stamped out in search of someone else to shout at, while I knelt and calmly gathered up all the rolls of evidence. I knew he would come back sooner or later, in order to prepare his address to the people for the following day, but the hours passed, dusk fell and the lamps and candles were lit, and I began to feel alarmed. Afterwards I discovered he had gone with his guards and lictors to the nearby gardens and spent the time pacing round and round so ceaselessly they thought he would wear a groove in the stones. When at last he came back, his face was very pale and grim. He had devised a plan, he told me, and he did not know which frightened him more: the thought that it might fail or the possibility that it might succeed.

*

The following morning he invited Q. Fabius Sanga to come and see him. Sanga, you may recall, was the senator to whom he had written on the day the murdered boy's body was discovered, requesting information about human sacrifice and the religion of the Gauls. Sanga was about fifty and immensely rich from his investments in Nearer and Further Gaul. He had never aspired to rise beyond the back benches and treated the senate purely as a place in which he could protect his business interests. He was very respectable and pious, lived modestly and was rumoured to be strict with his wife and children. He only spoke in debates about Gaul, on which he was, to be frank, an immense bore: once he started talking about its geography, climate, tribes, customs and so forth, he could empty the chamber quicker than a shout of 'Fire!'

'Are you a patriot, Sanga?' asked Cicero the moment I showed him in.

'I like to think I am, Consul,' replied Sanga cautiously. 'Why?'

'Because I wish you to play a vital part in the defence of our beloved republic.'

'Me?' Sanga looked very alarmed. 'Oh dear. I am rather afflicted by gout ...'

'No, no, nothing like that. I merely want you to ask a man to speak to a man, and then to tell me what he replies.'

Sanga noticeably relaxed. 'Well yes, I believe I could do that. Who are these men?'

'One is Publius Umbrenus, a freedman of Lentulus Sura, who often acts as his secretary. He used to live in Gaul, I believe. Perhaps you know him?'

'I do indeed.'

'The other fellow simply needs to be a Gaul of some sort. I don't mind from what region of Gaul especially. Someone known to you. An emissary of one of the tribes would be ideal. A credible figure here in Rome, and one whom you trust absolutely.'

'And what do you want this Gaul to do?'

'I want him to contact Umbrenus and offer to organise an uprising against Roman rule.'

When Cicero had first explained his plan to me the night before, I had been privately appalled, and I anticipated that the strait-laced Sanga would feel the same way: that he would throw up his hands and perhaps even storm out of the room at hearing such a monstrous suggestion. But businessmen, I have since come to realise, are the least shockable of characters, far less so than soldiers and politicians. You can propose almost anything to a businessman and he will usually be willing at least to think about it. Sanga merely raised his eyebrows. 'You want to lure Sura into an act of treason?'

'Not necessarily treason, but I do want to discover if there are any limits to the wickedness that he and his confederates are willing to envisage. We already know that they cheerfully plot assassination, massacre, arson and armed rebellion. The only heinous crime left that I can think of is collusion with Rome's enemies – not,' he added quickly, 'that I regard the Gauls as enemies, but you understand what I mean.'

'Do you have any particular tribe in mind?'

'No. I'll leave that up to you.'

Sanga was silent, turning the matter over. He had a very crafty face. His thin nose twitched. He tapped at it and pulled at it. You could tell he was smelling money. 'I have many trading interests in Gaul, and trade depends on peaceful relations. The last thing I want is to make my Gallic friends any less popular in Rome than they are already.'

'I can assure you, Sanga, if they help me expose this conspiracy, then by the time I've finished they'll be national heroes.'

'And I suppose there's also the question of my own involvement …'

'Your role will be kept entirely secret, except, of course, with your permission, from the governors of Further and Nearer Gaul. They're both good friends of mine and I'm sure they'll want to recognise your contribution.'

At the prospect of money, Sanga smiled for the first time that morning. 'Well, seeing as you put it like that, there *is* a tribe that might fit the bill. The Allobroges, who control the Alpine passes, have just sent a delegation to the senate to complain about the level of taxes they have to submit to Rome. They arrived in the city a couple of days ago.'

'Are they warlike?'

'Very. If I could hint to them that their petition might be looked at favourably, I'm sure they'd be willing to do something in return …'

After he had gone, Cicero said to me: 'You disapprove?'

'It's not my place to pass judgement, Consul.'

'Oh, but you do disapprove! I can see it in your face! You think it's somehow dishonourable to lay a trap. But shall I tell you what's dishonourable, Tiro? What's dishonourable is to go on living in a city that you are secretly plotting to destroy! If Sura has no treasonous intentions, he will send those Gauls packing. But if he agrees to consider their proposals, I shall have him, and then I shall take him personally to the gates of the city and fling him out, and let Celer and his armies finish him off. And no one can say there is anything dishonourable about that!'

He spoke with such vehemence he almost convinced me.

XXVIII

The trial of the consul-elect, Licinius Murena, on a charge of electoral corruption, began on the Ides of November and was scheduled to last two weeks. Servius and Cato led for the prosecution; Hortensius, Cicero and Crassus for the defence. It was a huge affair, staged in the forum, the jury alone numbering nine hundred. These jurors were made up of equal proportions of senators, knights and respectable citizens; there were too many members for the jury to be rigged, which was the intention behind having such a large number, but it also made it hard to tell which way they would vote. The prosecution certainly laid out a formidable case. Servius had plenty of evidence of Murena's bribery, which he presented in his dry legal manner, and he went on at great length about Cicero's betrayal of their friendship by appearing for the accused. Cato took the stoic line and inveighed against the rottenness of an age in which office could be bought by feasts and games. 'Did you not,' he thundered at Murena, 'seek supreme power, supreme authority, the very government of the state, by pandering to men's senses, bewitching their minds and plying them with pleasures? Did you think you were asking a gang of spoilt youths for a job as a pimp or the Roman people for world dominion?'

Murena was not at all happy with this, and had to be calmed throughout by young Clodius, his campaign manager, who sat beside him day after day and tried to keep his spirits up with witty remarks. As for his defence counsel – well, Murena could hardly have hoped for better. Hortensius, still bruised from his mauling during the trial of Rabirius, was determined to show he could still command a court, and he had a great deal of sport at Servius's expense. Crassus, it was true, was not much of an advocate, but his mere presence on the defence's bench carried weight in itself. As for Cicero, he was being kept in reserve for the final day of the trial, when he was due to make the summing-up to the jury.

Throughout the hearing he sat on the rostra, reading and writing, and only occasionally looking up and pretending to be shocked or amused by what had just been said. I squatted behind him, handing him documents and receiving instructions. Little of this was to do with the case, for as well as having to attend the court each day, Cicero was now in sole charge of Rome, and was sunk up to his ears in administration. From the entire length of Italy came reports of disturbances: in the heel and in the toe, in the knee and in the thigh. Celer had his hands full arresting malcontents in Picenum. There were even rumours that Catilina might be about to take the ultimate step and recruit slaves to the rebel army in return for emancipation – if that happened, the whole country would soon be in flames. More troops had to be levied and Cicero persuaded Hybrida to take command of a new army. He did this partly to show a united front, but chiefly to get Hybrida out of the city, for he was still not entirely convinced of his colleague's loyalty and did not want him in Rome if Sura and the other conspirators decided to make their move. It seemed to me madness to give an entire army to a man he did not trust, but Cicero was no fool. He appointed a senator with almost thirty years' military experience, M. Petreius, as Hybrida's second in command, and gave Petreius sealed orders that were only to be opened in the event that the army looked likely to have to fight.

As the winter arrived, the republic seemed to be on the brink of collapse. At a public assembly, Metellus Nepos made a violent attack on Cicero's consulship, accusing him of every possible crime and folly – dictatorship, weakness, rashness, cowardice, complacency, incompetence. 'How long,' he demanded, 'must the people of Rome be denied the services of the one man who could deliver them from this miserable situation – Gnaeus Pompey, so rightly surnamed "the Great"?' Cicero did not attend the assembly but was given a full report of what was said.

Just before the end of Murena's trial – I think it must have been the first day of December – Cicero received an early-morning visit from Sanga. The senator came in with his little eyes shining, as well they might, because he brought momentous news. The Gauls had done as he had requested and had approached Sura's freedman, Umbrenus, in the forum. Their conversation had been entirely friendly and natural. The Gauls had bemoaned their lot, cursed the senate, and declared that they agreed with the words of Catilina: death was preferable to living in this condition of slavery. Pricking up his ears, Umbrenus had suggested they continue their discussion somewhere more private, and had taken them to the home of Decimus Brutus, which was close by. Brutus himself – an aristocrat who had been consul some fourteen years previously – had nothing to do with the conspiracy and was away from Rome, but his wife, a clever and sinuous woman, was one of Catilina's many amours, and it was she who suggested they should make common cause. Umbrenus went off to fetch one of the leaders of the plot, and returned with the knight Capito, who swore the Gauls to secrecy and said that the uprising in the city would be starting any day now. As soon as Catilina and the rebels were close to Rome, the newly elected tribune Bestia would call a public assembly and demand that Cicero be arrested. This would be the signal for a general uprising. Capito and a fellow knight, Statilius, at the head of a large body of arsonists, would start fires in twelve locations. In the ensuing panic the young senator Cethegus would lead the death squad that had volunteered to murder Cicero; others would assassinate the various victims allotted to them; many young men would kill their fathers; the senate house would be stormed.

'And how did the Gauls respond?' asked Cicero.

'As instructed, they asked for a list of men who supported the conspiracy,' replied Sanga, 'so they could gauge its chances of success.' He produced a wax tablet, crammed with names written in tiny letters. 'Sura,' he read, 'Longinus, Bestia, Sulla—'

'We know all this,' interrupted Cicero, but Sanga held up his finger.

'—Caesar, Hybrida, Crassus, Nepos—'

'But this is a fantasy, surely?' Cicero took the tablet from Sanga's hand and scanned the list. 'They want to make themselves sound stronger than they are.'

'That I can't judge. I can only tell you that those were the names Capito provided.'

'A consul, the chief priest, a tribune and the richest man in Rome, who has already denounced the conspiracy? I don't believe it.' Nevertheless, Cicero threw the tablet to me. 'Copy them out,' he ordered, and then he shook his head. 'Well, well – be careful of what questions you ask, for fear of what answers you may receive.' It was one of his favourite maxims from the law courts.

'What should I tell the Gauls to do next?' asked Sanga.

'If that list is correct, I should advise them to join the conspiracy! When exactly did this meeting take place?'

'Yesterday.'

'And when are they due to meet again?'

'Today.'

'So obviously they are in a hurry.'

'The Gauls got the impression that matters would come to a head in the next few days.'

Cicero fell silent, thinking. 'Tell them they should demand written proof of the involvement of as many of these men as possible: letters, fixed with personal seals, that they can take back and show to their fellow countrymen.'

'And if the conspirators refuse?'

'The Gauls should say it will be impossible for their tribe to take such a hazardous step as going to war with Rome without hard evidence.'

Sanga nodded, and then he said: 'I'm afraid that after this my involvement in this affair will have to end.'

'Why?'

'Because it's becoming far too dangerous to remain in Rome.' As a final favour he agreed to return with the conspirators' answer as soon as the Gauls had received it; then he would leave. In the meantime, Cicero had no alternative but to go down to Murena's trial. Sitting on the bench next to Hortensius, he put on an outward show of calm, but from time to time I would catch his gaze drifting around the court, resting occasionally on Caesar – who was one of the jurors – on Sura, who was sitting with the praetors, and finally and most often on Crassus, who was only two places further along the bench. He must have felt extremely lonely, and I noticed for the first time that his hair was flecked with grey, and that there were ridges of dark skin under his eyes. The crisis was ageing him. At the seventh hour, Cato finished his summing-up of the prosecution case, and the judge, whose name was Cosconius, asked Cicero if he would like to conclude for the defence. The question seemed to catch him by surprise, and after a moment or two of shifting through his documents he rose and requested an adjournment until the next day, so that he could gather his thoughts. Cosconius looked irritable, but conceded that the hour was getting late. He grudgingly agreed to Cicero's request, and the conclusion of Murena's trial was postponed.

We hurried home in the now-familiar cocoon of guards and lictors, but there was no sign of Sanga, nor any message from him. Cicero went silently into his study and sat with his elbows on his desk, his thumbs pressed hard to his temples, surveying the piles of evidence laid across it, rubbing at his flesh, as if he might somehow drive into his skull the speech he needed to deliver. I had never felt sorrier for him. But when I took a step towards him to offer my help, he flicked his hand at me without looking up, wordlessly dismissing me from his presence. I did not see him again that evening. Instead Terentia drew me to one side to express her worries about the consul's health. He was not eating properly, she said, or sleeping. Even the morning exercises he had practised since he was a young man had been abandoned. I was surprised she should talk to me in this intimate way, as the truth was she had never much liked me, and took out on me much of the frustration she felt with her husband. I was the one who spent the most time sequestered with him, working. I was the one who disturbed their rare moments of leisure together by bringing him piles of letters and news of callers. Nevertheless, for once she spoke to me politely and almost as a friend. 'You must reason with him,' she said. 'I sometimes believe you are the only one he will listen to, while I can only pray for him.'

When the next morning arrived and there was still no word from Sanga, I began to fear that Cicero would be too nervous to make his speech. Remembering Terentia's plea, I even suggested he might ask for a further postponement. 'Are you mad?' he snapped. 'This isn't the time to show weakness. I'll be fine. I always am.' Despite his bravado, I had never seen him shake more at the start of a speech, or begin more inaudibly. The forum was packed and noisy, even though great masses of cloud were rolling over Rome, releasing occasional flurries of rain across the valley. But as it turned out, Cicero put a surprising amount of humour into that speech, memorably contrasting the claims of Servius and Murena for the consulship.

'You are up before dawn to rally your clients,' he said to Servius, 'he to rally his army. You are woken by the call of cocks, he by the call of trumpets. You draw up a form of proceedings, he a line of battle. He understands how to keep off the enemy's forces, you rainwater. He has been engaged in extending boundaries, you in defining them.' The jury loved that. And they laughed even longer when he poked fun at Cato and his rigid philosophy. 'Rest assured that the superhuman qualities we have seen in Cato are innate; his failings due not to Nature but to his master.

For there was a man of genius called Zeno, and the disciples of his teaching are called stoics. Here are some of his precepts: the wise man is never moved by favour and never forgives anyone's mistakes; only a fool feels pity; all misdeeds are equal, the casual killing of a cock no less a crime than strangling one's father; the wise man never assumes anything, never regrets anything, is never wrong, never changes his mind. Unfortunately Cato has seized on this doctrine not just as a topic for discussion but as a way of life.'

'What a droll fellow our consul is,' sneered Cato in a loud voice as everybody laughed. But Cicero hadn't finished yet.

'Now I must admit when I was younger I also took some interest in philosophy. My masters, though, were Plato and Aristotle. They don't hold violent or extreme views. They say that favour can sometimes influence the wise man; that a good man can feel pity; that there are different degrees of wrongdoing and different punishments; that the wise man often makes assumptions when he doesn't know the facts, and is sometimes angry, and sometimes forgives, and sometimes changes his mind; that all virtue is saved from excess by a so-called mean. If you had studied these masters, Cato, you might not be a better man or braver – that would be impossible – but you might be a little more kind.

'You say that the public interest led you to start these proceedings. I don't doubt it. But you slip up because you never stop to think. I am defending Lucius Murena not because of friendship, but for the sake of peace, quiet, unity, liberty, our self-preservation – in short, the very lives of us all. Listen, gentlemen,' he said, turning to the jury, 'listen to a consul who spends all his days and nights in non-stop thinking about the republic. It is vital that there are two consuls in the state on the first day of January. Plans have been laid by men among us now to destroy the city, slaughter the citizens and obliterate the name of Rome. I give you warning. My consulate is reaching its dying days. Don't take from me the man whose vigilance should succeed mine.' He rested his hand on Murena's shoulder. 'Don't remove the man to whom I wish to hand over the republic still intact, for him to defend against these deadly perils.'

He spoke for three hours, stopping only now and again to sip a little diluted wine or to mop the rain from his face. His delivery became more and more powerful as he went on, and I was reminded of some strong and graceful fish that had been tossed, apparently dead, back into the water – inert at first and belly-up; but then suddenly, on finding itself returned to its natural element, with a flick of its tail, it revives. In the same way Cicero gathered strength from the very act of speaking, and he finished to prolonged applause not only from the crowd but from the jury. It proved to be a good omen: when their ballots were counted, Murena was acquitted by a huge majority. Cato and Servius left at once in a state of great dejection. Cicero lingered on the rostra just long enough to congratulate the consul-elect, and to receive many slaps on the back from Clodius, Hortensius and even Crassus, and then we headed home.

The instant we came into the street, we noticed a fine carriage drawn up outside the house. As we came closer, we saw that it was crammed with silver plate, statues, carpets and pictures. A wagon behind it was similarly laden. Cicero hurried forward. Sanga was waiting just inside the front door, his face as grey as an oyster.

'Well?' demanded Cicero.

'The conspirators have written their letters.'

'Excellent!' Cicero clapped his hands. 'Have you brought them with you?'

'Wait, Consul. There's more to it than that. The Gauls don't actually have the letters yet. They've been told to go to the Fontinalian Gate at midnight, and be ready to leave the city. They'll be met there by an escort, who'll give them the letters.'

'And why do they need an escort?'

'He'll take them to meet Catilina. And then from Catilina's camp they are to go directly to Gaul.'

'By the gods, if we can get hold of those letters, we will have them at last!' Cicero strode up and down the narrow passageway. 'We must lay an ambush,' he said to me, 'and catch them red-handed. Send for Quintus and Atticus.'

'You'll need soldiers,' I said, 'and an experienced man to command them.'

'He must be someone we can trust absolutely.'

I took out my notebook and stylus. 'What about Flaccus? Or Pomptinus?' Both men were praetors with long experience in the legions, and both had proved steadfast throughout the crisis.

'Good. Get them both here now.'

'And the soldiers?'

'We could use that century from Reate. They're still in their barracks. But they're to be told nothing of their mission. Not yet.'

He called for Sositheus and Laurea and rapidly issued the necessary instructions, then he turned to say something to Sanga, but the passageway behind him was empty, the front door open, and the street deserted. The senator had fled.

Quintus and Atticus arrived within the hour, and shortly afterwards the two praetors also turned up, greatly bemused by this dramatic summons. Without going into details, Cicero said simply that he had information that a delegation of Gauls would be leaving the city at midnight, together with an escort, and that he had reason to believe they were on their way to Catilina with incriminating documents. 'We need to stop them at all costs, but we need to let them get far enough along the road that there can be no doubt that they're leaving the city.'

'In my experience an ambush at night is always more difficult than it sounds,' said Quintus. 'In the darkness some are bound to escape – taking your evidence with them. Are you sure we can't simply seize them at the gate?'

But Flaccus, who was a soldier of the old school, having seen service under Isauricus, said immediately, 'What rubbish! I don't know what army you served in, but it should be easy enough. In fact I know just the spot. If they're taking the Via Flaminia, they'll have to cross the Tiber at the Mulvian Bridge. We'll trap them there. Once they're halfway across, there's no chance of escape, unless they're willing to throw themselves into the river and drown.'

Quintus looked very put out, and from that moment on effectively washed his hands of the whole operation, so much so that when Cicero suggested he should join Flaccus and Pomptinus at the bridge, he replied sulkily that it was clear his advice was not needed.

'In that case I shall have to go myself,' said Cicero, but everyone immediately objected to that on the grounds that it was not safe. 'Then it will have to be Tiro,' he concluded, and seeing my look of horror, he added: 'Someone has to be there who isn't a soldier. I shall need a clear account written up by an eyewitness that I can give to the senate tomorrow, and Flaccus and Pomptinus will be too busy directing operations.'

'What about Atticus?' I suggested – somewhat impertinently, I realise now, but fortunately for me, Cicero was too preoccupied to notice.

'He'll be in charge of my security in Rome, as usual.' Behind his back, Atticus shrugged at me apologetically. 'Now, Tiro, make sure you write down everything they say, and above all else, secure those letters with their seals unbroken.'

We set off on horseback well after darkness fell: the two praetors, their eight lictors, another four guards, and finally and reluctantly, me. To add to my woes I was a terrible rider. I bounced up and down in my saddle, an empty document case banging against my back. We clattered over the stones and through the city gate at such speed, I had to wind my fingers into the mane of my poor mare to stop myself falling off. Fortunately she was a tolerant beast, no doubt especially reserved for women and idiots, and as the road stretched down the hill and across the plain, she plunged on without requiring guidance from me, and so we managed to keep pace with the horses ahead of us.

It was one of those nights when the sky is an adventure all to itself, a brilliant moon racing through motionless oceans of silvery cloud. Beneath this celestial odyssey, the tombs lining the Via Flaminia silently flickered as if in a lightning storm. We trotted along steadily until, after about two miles, we came to the river. We drew to a halt and listened. In the darkness I could hear rushing water, and looking ahead I could just make out the flat roofs of a couple of houses and the silhouettes of trees, sharp against the hurtling sky. From somewhere close by a man's voice demanded the password. The praetors replied – 'Aemilius Scaurus!' – and suddenly, from both sides of the road, the men of the Reate century rose out of the ditches, their faces blackened with charcoal and mud. The praetors quickly divided this force in two. Pomptinus with his men was to remain where he was, while Flaccus led forty legionaries over to the opposite bank. For some reason it seemed to me safer to be with Flaccus, and I followed him on to the bridge. The river was wide and shallow and flowing very fast across the big flat rocks. I peered over the edge of the parapet to where the waters crashed and foamed against the pillars more than forty feet below, and I realised what an effective trap the bridge made, that jumping in to avoid capture would be an act of suicide.

In the house on the far bank there was a family asleep. At first they refused to let us in, but their door soon flew open when Flaccus threatened to break it down. They had irritated him so he locked them in the cellar. From the upstairs room we had a clear view of the road, and here we settled down to wait. The plan was that all travellers, from whichever direction, would be allowed on to the bridge, but that once they reached the other side they would be challenged and questioned before being allowed off it. Long hours passed and not a soul approached, and the conviction steadily grew in me that we must have been tricked. Either there was no party of Gauls heading out of the city that night, or they had already gone, or they had chosen a different route. I expressed these doubts to Flaccus, but he shook his grizzled head. 'They will come,' he said, and when I asked why he was so certain, he replied: 'Because the gods protect Rome.' Then he folded his large hands over his broad stomach and went to sleep.

I must have drifted off myself. At any rate, the next thing I remember is a hand on my shoulder and a voice hissing in my ear that there were men on the bridge. Straining my eyes into the darkness, I heard the sound of the horses' hoofs before I could make out the shapes of the riders – five, ten men or more, crossing at a leisurely pace. 'This is it!' whispered Flaccus, jamming on his helmet, and with surprising speed for a man of his girth, he jumped down the stairs three at a time and ran out on to the road. As I ran after him I heard whistles and a trumpet blaring, and legionaries with drawn swords and some with torches began appearing from all directions and surging on to the bridge. The oncoming horses shied and stopped. A man yelled out that they must fight their way through. He spurred his horse and charged our line, heading straight for the spot where I was standing, slashing right and left with his sword. Someone next to me reached out to grab his reins, and to my amazement I saw the outstretched hand cleanly severed and land almost at my feet. Its owner screamed and the rider, realising there were too many to hack his way past, wheeled around and headed back the way he had come. He shouted to the others to follow, and the entire party now attempted to retreat towards Rome. But Pomptinus's men were flooding on to the bridge from the opposite side. We could see their torches and hear their excited cries. All of us ran in pursuit – even I, my fear entirely forgotten in my desire to seize those letters before they could be thrown into the river.

By the time we reached the middle of the bridge, the fighting was almost over. The Gauls, distinctive by their long hair and beards and their wild dress, were throwing down their weapons and dismounting; they must have been expecting an ambush such as this. Soon only the impetuous rider who had tried to break past us was still in his saddle, urging his companions to show some resistance. But it turned out they were slaves, with no stomach for a fight: they knew that even to raise a hand against a Roman citizen would mean crucifixion. One by one they surrendered. Eventually their leader also threw down his bloodied sword, then I saw him bend and hurriedly begin unfastening the straps of his saddlebag, at which I had the rare presence of mind to dart forward and seize the bag. He was young and very strong and almost managed to hurl it into the river, and would have done so had not other willing hands reached up and dragged him off his horse. I guess these men must have been friends of the soldier whose hand he had cut off, for they gave him quite a kicking before Flaccus wearily intervened and told them to stop. He was dragged up by his hair and Pomptinus, who knew him, identified him as Titus Volturcius, a knight from the town of Croton. I meanwhile had his bag in my hand, and I called over a soldier with a torch so that I could search it properly. Inside were six letters, all sealed.

I sent a messenger at once to Cicero to tell him that our mission had borne fruit. Then, once our prisoners had all been bound with their hands behind their backs and roped in a line at the neck – all except the Gauls, who were treated with the respect due to ambassadors – we started back to Rome.

We entered the city just before dawn. A few people were already up. They stopped and gawped at our sinister little procession as we crossed the forum and headed up the hill to Cicero's house. We left the prisoners outside in the street under close guard. Inside, the consul received us flanked by Quintus and Atticus. He listened to the praetors' accounts, thanked them warmly, and then asked to see Volturcius. He was pushed and dragged in, looking bruised and frightened, and immediately launched into some absurd story about being asked by Umbrenus to convey the Gauls out of the city, and at the last moment being given some letters to carry, and not knowing their contents.

'Then why did you put up such a fight on the bridge?' demanded Pomptinus.

'I thought you were highwaymen.'

'Highwaymen in army uniform? Commanded by praetors?'

'Take the villain away,' ordered Cicero, 'and don't bring him back until he's ready to tell the truth.'

After the prisoner had been dragged out, Flaccus said, 'We need to act quickly, before the news is all over Rome.'

'You're right,' agreed Cicero. He asked to see the letters and we examined them together. Two I easily recognised as belonging to the urban praetor, Lentulus Sura: his seal included a portrait of his grandfather, who had been consul a century earlier. The other four we worked out from the names on our lists as probably having come from the young senator Cornelius Cethegus, and the three knights Capito, Statilius and Caeparius. The praetors watched us impatiently.

'Surely there's an easy way to settle this?' said Pomptinus. 'Why don't we just open the letters?'

'That would be tampering with evidence,' replied Cicero, continuing his minute perusal of the letters.

'With respect, Consul,' growled Flaccus, 'we're wasting time.'

I realise now of course that wasting time was precisely Cicero's intention. He knew how awkward his position would be if he had to decide the conspirators' fate. He was giving them a final chance to flee. His preferred solution was still for them to be dealt with by the army in battle. But he could only delay for so long, and eventually he told us to go and fetch them. 'Mind you, I don't want them arrested,' he cautioned. 'Simply tell them the consul would be grateful for an opportunity to clear up a few matters, and ask them to come and see me.'

The praetors clearly thought he was being feeble but they did as they were commanded. I was sent to accompany Flaccus to the homes of Sura and Cethegus, who lived on the Palatine; Pomptinus went off to locate the others. I remember how odd it felt to approach Lentulus Sura's grand ancestral house and discover life there going on entirely as normal. He had not fled; quite the opposite. His clients were waiting patiently in the public rooms to see him. When he heard we were at the door, he sent out his stepson, Mark Antony, to discover what we wanted. Antony was then just twenty, very tall and strong, with a fashionable goatee beard and a face still thickly covered in pimples. It was the first time I had ever met him, and I wish I could remember more about this encounter, but I'm afraid all I can recall are his spots. He went off and gave his stepfather the message, and returned to say that the praetor would call on the consul as soon as he had finished his morning levee.

It was the same story at the home of Caius Cethegus, that fiery young patrician who, like his kinsman Sura, was a member of the Cornelian clan. Petitioners were queuing to talk to him, but he at least paid us the compliment of coming into the atrium himself. He looked Flaccus up and down as if he were a stray dog, heard what he had to say, and replied that it was not his habit to go running to anyone when called, but out of respect for the office, if not the man, he would attend on the consul very shortly.

We went back to Cicero, who was clearly amazed to hear that the two senators were still in Rome. 'What are they thinking of?' he muttered to me.

In fact it turned out that only one of the five – Caeparius, a knight from Terracina – had actually run away from the city. The rest all arrived separately at Cicero's house over the next hour or so, such was their supreme confidence that they were untouchable. I often wonder when it was they started to realise that they had made an appalling miscalculation. Was it when they reached the street where Cicero lived and discovered it jammed with armed men, prisoners and curious onlookers? Was it when they went inside to find not just Cicero but the two consuls-elect, Silanus and Murena, and the principal leaders of the senate – Catulus, Isauricus, Hortensius, Lucullus and several others – all of whom Cicero had summoned to witness proceedings? Or was it, perhaps, when they saw their letters laid out on the table, with the seals unbroken? Or noticed the Gauls being treated as honoured guests in an adjoining room? Or was it when Volturcius abruptly changed his mind and decided to save himself by testifying against them, in return for the promise of a pardon? I imagine it might have felt rather like drowning – a dawning realisation that they had ventured out of their depth, and were being carried further and further away from the shore with every passing moment. Only when Volturcius accused Cethegus to his face of boasting that he would murder Cicero and then storm the senate house did Cethegus at last jump to his feet and declare he would not stay here and listen to this a moment longer. But he found his exit blocked by two legionaries of the Reate century, who returned him very forcefully to his chair.

Cicero turned to his new star witness. 'And what about Lentulus Sura? What exactly did he say to you?'

'He said that the Sibylline Books had prophesied that Rome would be ruled by three members of the Cornelian family; that Cinna and Sulla had been the first two; and that he himself was the third and would soon be master of the city.'

'Is this true, Sura?' But Sura made no reply and merely stared straight ahead, blinking rapidly. Cicero sighed. 'An hour ago you could have left the city unmolested. Now I'd be as guilty as you are if I dared to let you go.' He beckoned to the soldiers standing in the atrium. They filed in and stationed themselves in pairs behind the conspirators.

'Open Sura's letters!' cried Catulus, who could not contain his fury any longer at this betrayal of the republic by the direct descendant of one of the six founding families of Rome. 'Open the letters and let's discover how far the treasonous swine was prepared to go!'

'Not yet,' said Cicero. 'We'll do that in front of the senate.' He looked sadly at the conspirators who were now his prisoners. 'Whatever happens, I don't want anyone ever to be able to say I forged evidence or coerced testimony.'

It was now the middle of the morning. Incongruously, the house was starting to fill with flowers and greenery in preparation for the annual ceremony of the Good Goddess, over which Terentia was due to preside that night as the wife of the senior magistrate. As slaves carried in baskets of mistletoe, myrtle and winter roses, Cicero issued a decree that the senate should meet that afternoon not in their usual chamber but in the Temple of Concordia, so that the spirit of the goddess of national harmony might guide their deliberations. He also gave orders that a newly completed statue of Jupiter, originally destined for the Capitol, should be put up at once in the forum in front of the rostra. 'I shall surround myself with a bodyguard of deities,' he said to me. 'Because mark my words, by the time this is over, I may well have need of all the protection I can get.'

The five conspirators were kept under guard in the atrium while Cicero went to his study to question the Gauls. Their testimony was, if anything, even more damning than that of Volturcius, for it turned out that just before leaving Rome, the ambassadors had been taken to the house of Cethegus and shown a stockpile of weapons that were to be distributed when the signal for the massacre was given. I was sent along with Flaccus to make an inventory of this arsenal, which we discovered in the tablinum, stacked in boxes from floor to ceiling. The swords and knives were unused, gleaming and of a curious curved design, with strange carvings on their hilts. Flaccus said they looked foreign-made to him. I rested my thumb on the blade of one sword. It was as sharp as a razor, and I thought with a shiver that not only might Cicero's throat have been cut with it, but very probably mine as well.

By the time I had finished examining the boxes and returned to Cicero's house, it was time to leave for the senate. The downstairs rooms were festooned with sweet-smelling flora, and numerous amphorae of wine were being carried in from the street. Clearly, whatever other mysteries it might entail, the ceremony of the Good Goddess was not abstemious. Terentia drew her husband to one side and embraced him. I could not hear what she said, and nor did I try to, but I did see her take his arm and grip it fiercely. Then we set off, surrounded by legionaries, with each conspirator escorted down to the Temple of Concordia by a man of consular rank. They were all very subdued now; even Cethegus had lost his arrogance. None of us knew what to expect. As we entered the forum, Cicero took Sura by the hand as a mark of respect, but the patrician appeared too dazed by events to notice. I was walking just behind them, carrying the box of letters. What was remarkable was not so much the size of the crowds – needless to say, almost the entire population had flocked to the forum to watch what was going on – but their complete silence. The temple was ringed by armed men. The waiting senators looked on in amazement as they saw Cicero leading Sura. Once inside, the conspirators were locked into a small storeroom near the entrance, while Cicero went straight to the makeshift dais where his chair had been placed beneath the statue of Concordia. 'Gentlemen,' he began, 'earlier today, shortly before first light, the gallant praetors Lucius Flaccus and Gaius Pomptinus, acting on my orders, at the head of a large body of armed men, apprehended a group of riders on the Mulvian Bridge heading in the direction of Etruria ...' Nobody whispered; nobody even coughed. It was a silence such as I had never heard before in the senate – fearful, ominous, oppressive. Occasionally I was able to glance up from my note-taking at Caesar and Crassus. Both men were leaning forward in their seats, concentrating on Cicero's every word. 'Thanks to the loyalty of our allies, the envoys of the Gauls, who were appalled by what was proposed, I had already received warning of the treasonous activities of some of our fellow citizens, and was able to take the necessary precautions ...'

When the consul finished his account, which included a description of the plot to set fire to parts of the city and massacre many senators and other prominent figures, there was a kind of collective sigh or groan.

'The question now arises, gentlemen, of what we are supposed to do with these villains. I propose that as a first step we consider the evidence against the accused, and hear what they have to say for themselves. Send in the witnesses!'

The four Gauls entered first. They looked around them in wonder at the long rows of white-robed senators, whose appearance was such a dramatic contrast with their own. Titus Volturcius came in next, trembling so much he could hardly walk down the aisle. Once they were in position, Cicero called out to Flaccus, who was stationed at the entrance: 'Bring in the first of the prisoners!'

'Which do you wish to question first?' Flaccus shouted in reply.

'Whichever is to hand,' said Cicero grimly, and so it was that Cethegus, escorted by a pair of guards, was brought from the storeroom to the far end of the temple, where Cicero waited. Finding himself before an audience of his peers, the young senator recovered some of his old spirit. He almost sauntered down the aisle, and when the consul showed him the letters and asked him to identify which seal was his, he picked it up casually.

'This one is mine, I believe.'

'Give it to me.'

'If you insist,' said Cethegus, handing it over. 'I must say, I was always taught it was the height of bad manners for one gentleman to read another gentleman's mail.'

Cicero ignored him, broke open the letter and read it out loud: '*From Caius Cornelius Cethegus to Catugnatus, chief of the Allobroges – greetings! By this letter I give you my word that I and my companions will keep the promises we have made to your envoys, and that if your nation rises against your unjust oppressors in Rome, it will have no more loyal allies than us.*'

On hearing this, the assembled senators let out a great bellow of outrage. Cicero held up his hand. 'Is this your writing?' he asked Cethegus.

The young senator, clearly taken aback by his reception, mumbled something I could not hear.

'Is this your writing?' repeated Cicero. 'Speak up!'

Cethegus hesitated, then said quietly, 'It is.'

'Well, young man, clearly we had different tutors, for I was always taught that the true height of bad manners was not reading another man's mail, but plotting treason with a foreign power! Now,' continued Cicero, consulting his notes, 'at your house this morning we discovered an armoury of a hundred swords and the same number of daggers. What do you have to say for yourself?'

'I'm a collector of weapons—' began Cethegus. He may have been trying to be witty; if he was, it was a foolish joke, and also his last. The rest of his words were lost in the angry protests that came from every corner of the temple.

'We've heard enough from you,' said Cicero. 'Your guilt is self-confessed. Take him away and bring in the next.'

Cethegus was led off, not quite so jaunty now, and Statilius was marched down the aisle. The same process was repeated: he identified his seal, the letter was broken open and read (the language was almost identical to that used by Cethegus), he confirmed that the handwriting was his; but when he was asked to explain himself, he claimed that the letter was not meant seriously.

'Not meant seriously?' repeated Cicero in wonder. 'An invitation to an alien tribe to slaughter Roman men, women and children – not meant seriously?' Statilius could only hang his head.

Capito's turn followed, with the same result, and then Caeparius made a dishevelled appearance. He was the one who had tried to escape at dawn, but he had been captured on his way to Apulia with messages for the rebel forces. His confession was the most abject of all. Finally there remained only Lentulus Sura to confront, and this was a moment of great drama, for you must remember that Sura was not only the urban praetor, and therefore the third most powerful magistrate in the state, but also a former consul: a man in his middle fifties of the most distinguished lineage and appearance. As he entered, he looked around with appealing eyes at colleagues he had sat with for a quarter of a century in the highest council of the state, but none would meet his gaze. With great reluctance he identified the last two letters, both of which bore his seal. The one to the Gauls was the same as those that had been read out earlier. The second was addressed to Catilina. Cicero broke it open.

'You will know who I am from the bearer of this message,' he read. *'Be a man. Remember how critical your position is. Consider what you must now do and enlist aid wherever you find it – even from the lowest of the low.'* Cicero held out the letter to Sura. 'Your writing?'

'Yes,' replied Sura with great dignity, 'but there's nothing criminal about it.'

'This phrase, "the lowest of the low" – what do you mean by it?'

'Poor people – shepherds, tenant farmers and suchlike.'

'Isn't it rather a lordly way for a so-called champion of the poor to refer to our fellow citizens?' Cicero turned to Volturcius: 'You were supposed to convey this letter to Catilina at his headquarters, were you not?'

Volturcius lowered his eyes. 'I was.'

'What precisely does Sura mean by this phrase, "the lowest of the low"? Did he tell you?'

'Yes, he did, Consul. He means that Catilina should encourage an uprising of slaves.'

The roars of fury that greeted this revelation were almost physical in their force. To encourage an uprising of slaves so soon after the havoc wrought by Spartacus and his followers was worse even than making an alliance with the Gauls. 'Resign! Resign! Resign!' the senate chorused at the urban praetor. Several senators actually ran across the temple and began wrenching off Sura's purple-bordered toga. He fell to the ground and briefly disappeared in a crowd of assailants and guards. Large pieces of his toga were borne away, and very quickly he was reduced to his undergarments. His nose was bleeding, and his hair, normally oiled and coiffed, was standing on end. Cicero called out for a fresh tunic to be brought, and when one was found, he actually went down and helped Sura put it on.

After some kind of calm had been restored, Cicero took a vote on whether or not Sura should be stripped of his office. The senate roared back an overwhelming 'Aye!' which was of great significance, as it meant Sura was no longer immune from punishment. Dabbing at his nose, he was taken away, and the consul resumed his questioning of Volturcius: 'We have here five conspirators, fully revealed at last, unable any longer to hide from public gaze. To your certain knowledge, are there more?'

'There are.'

'And what are their names?'

'Autronius Paetus, Servius Sulla, Cassius Longinus, Marcus Laeca, Lucius Bestia.'

Everyone looked around the temple to see if any of the named men were present; none was.

'The familiar roll-call,' said Cicero. 'Does the house agree that these men should also be arrested?'

'Aye!' they chorused back.

Cicero turned back to Volturcius. 'And were there any others?'

'I did hear of others.'

'And their names?'

Volturcius hesitated and glanced nervously around the senate. 'Gaius Julius Caesar,' he said quietly, 'and Marcus Licinius Crassus.'

There were gasps and whistles of astonishment. Both Caesar and Crassus angrily shook their heads.

'But you have no actual evidence of their involvement?'

'No, Consul. It was only ever rumours.'

'Then strike their names from the record,' Cicero instructed me. 'We shall deal in evidence, gentlemen,' he said, having to raise his voice to be heard above the swelling murmur of excitement, 'evidence and not speculation!'

It was a while before he could continue. Caesar and Crassus continued to shake their heads and protest their innocence with exaggerated gestures to the men seated around them. Occasionally they turned to look at Cicero, but it was hard to read their expressions. The temple was gloomy even on a sunny day. But now the winter afternoon light was fading fast, and even faces quite close by were becoming difficult to see.

'I have a proposal!' shouted Cicero, clapping his hands to try to regain order. 'I have a proposal, gentlemen!' At last the noise began to die away. 'It's obvious that we cannot settle the fate of these men today. Therefore they must be kept guarded overnight until we can agree a course of action. To keep them all in the same place would invite a rescue attempt. Therefore what I propose is this. The prisoners should be separated and each entrusted to the custody of a different member of the senate, a man of praetorian rank. Does anyone have any objections to that?' There was silence. 'Very well.' Cicero squinted around the darkening temple. 'Who will volunteer for this duty?' Nobody raised his hand. 'Come now, gentlemen – there's no danger. Each prisoner will be guarded. Quintus Cornificius,' he said at last, pointing to a former praetor of impeccable reputation, 'will you be so good as to take charge of Cethegus?'

Cornificius glanced around, then got to his feet. 'If that is what you want, Consul,' he replied reluctantly.

'Spinther, will you take Sura?'

Spinther stood. 'Yes, Consul.'

'Terentius – would you house Caeparius?'

'If that is the will of the senate,' replied Terentius in a glum voice.

Cicero continued to peer around for more potential custodians, and finally his gaze alighted on Crassus. 'In which case,' he said, as if the idea had only just occurred to him, 'Crassus, what better way for you to prove your innocence – not to me, who requires no proof, but to that tiny number who might doubt it – than for you to take custody of Capito? And by the same token, Caesar – you are a praetor-elect – perhaps you will take Statilius into the residence of the chief priest?' Both Crassus and Caesar looked at him with their mouths agape. But what else could they do except nod their assent? They were in a trap. Refusal would have been tantamount to a confession of guilt; so would allowing their prisoners to escape. 'Then that is settled,' declared Cicero, 'and until we reconvene tomorrow, this house stands adjourned.'

'Just a moment, Consul!' came a sharp voice, and with a discernible cracking of his elderly knees, Catulus got to his feet. 'Gentlemen,' he said, 'before we depart to our homes for the night to ponder how we may vote tomorrow, I feel it necessary to recognise that one among us has been consistent in his policy, has been consistently attacked for it, and has also, as events have proved, been consistently wise. Therefore I wish to propose the following motion: In recognition of the fact that Marcus Tullius Cicero has saved Rome from burning, its citizens from massacre and Italy from war, this house decrees a three-day public thanksgiving at every shrine to all the immortal gods for having favoured us at such a time with such a consul.'

I was stunned. As for Cicero, he was quite overwhelmed. This was the first time in the history of the republic that a public thanksgiving had been proposed for anyone other than a victorious general. There was no need to put the motion to the vote. The house rose in acclamation. One man alone remained frozen in his seat, and that was Caesar.

XXIX

I come now to the crux of my story, that hinge around which Cicero's life, and the lives of so many of us, was to revolve for ever after – the decision about the fate of the prisoners.

Cicero left the senate with the applause, as it were, still ringing in his ears. The senators poured out after him, and he went immediately across the forum to the rostra to deliver a report to the people. Hundreds of citizens were still standing around in the chilly twilight, hoping to discover what was going on, and among them I noticed many friends and family of the accused. In particular I recognised young Mark Antony going from group to group, trying to rouse support for his stepfather, Sura.

The speech that Cicero afterwards had published was very different to the one he actually delivered – a matter I shall come to in due course. Far from singing his own praises, he gave an entirely matter-of-fact report, almost identical to the one he had just relayed to the senate. He told the crowd about the conspirators' plot to set fire to the city and to murder the magistrates, about their desire to make a pact with the Gauls, and the ambush on the Mulvian Bridge. Then he described the opening of the letters and the reactions of the accused. The people listened in a silence that was either rapt or sullen depending on how one chose to interpret it. Only when Cicero announced that the senate had just voted a three-day national holiday to celebrate his achievement did they finally break into applause. Cicero mopped the sweat from his face and beamed and waved, but he must have known that the cheers were really for the holiday rather than for him. He finished by pointing to the large statue of Jupiter, which he had arranged to have put up quickly that morning. 'Surely the very fact that this statue was being erected when the conspirators and witnesses were taken on my orders through the forum to the Temple of Concordia is clear proof of the intervention of Jupiter, Best and Greatest? If I were to say that I foiled them entirely alone I would be taking too much credit for myself. It was Jupiter, the mighty Jupiter, who foiled them; it was Jupiter who secured the salvation of the Capitol, of these temples, of the whole city and of you all.'

The respectful applause that greeted this remark was no doubt intended for the deity rather than the speaker, but at least it meant that Cicero was able to leave the platform with a semblance of dignity. Wisely he did not linger. As soon as he came down the steps his bodyguard closed around him, and with the lictors clearing the way, we pushed and struggled across the forum in the direction of the Quirinal Hill. I mention this in order to show that the situation in Rome as night fell was very far from stable, and that Cicero was not nearly as sure of what he ought to do as he later pretended. He would have liked to have returned home and consulted Terentia, but as chance would have it, this was the one occasion in his entire life when he was not allowed to cross his own threshold: during the nocturnal rites of the Good Goddess, no member of the male sex was allowed under the same roof as the priestesses of the cult; even little Marcus had been sent away. Instead we had to climb the Via Salutaris to the house of Atticus, where it had been arranged that the consul would spend the evening.

Here it was, therefore, with armed guards ringing the house and with all manner of people – senators, knights, treasury officials, lictors, messengers – bustling in and out from the crowded atrium, that Cicero issued various orders to protect the city. He also sent a note to Terentia to inform her of what had happened. Then he retreated to the quiet of the library to try to decide what to do with the five conspirators. From the four corners of the room, freshly garlanded busts of Aristotle and Plato, Zeno and Epicurus gazed down on his deliberations, unperturbed.

'If I sanction the execution of the traitors, I shall be pursued by their supporters for the rest of my days – you saw how sullen that crowd was. On the other hand, if I let them simply go into exile, those same supporters will agitate constantly for their return; I shall never know safety, and this whole fever will quickly recur.' He gazed dejectedly at the head of Aristotle. 'The philosophy of the golden mean does not seem to fit this particular predicament.'

Exhausted, he sat on the edge of his chair, leaning forward, with his hands clasped behind the back of his neck, staring at the floor. He did not lack advice. His brother Quintus urged a hard line: the conspirators were so clearly guilty, the whole of Rome – the whole world, come to that – would think him a weakling if he didn't punish them with death. This was a time of war! The gentle Atticus's view was entirely the opposite: if Cicero had stood for anything throughout his political career, it was surely the rule of law. For centuries every citizen had had the right of appeal against arbitrary sentence. What else had the Verres case been about if not this? *Civis Romanus sum!* As for me, I am afraid that when my turn came to speak, I advocated the coward's way out. Cicero had only another twenty-six days in office. Why not lock the prisoners away somewhere and leave it to his successors to determine their fate? Both Quintus and Atticus threw up their hands at this, but Cicero could see the merits in it, and years later he told me that actually I had been right. 'But that is with hindsight,' he said, 'which is of course the irredeemable flaw of history. If you remember the circumstances of the time, with soldiers on the streets and armed bands congregating, and with rumours that Catilina might attack the city at any moment in an attempt to free his associates – how could I have avoided taking a stand?'

The most extreme advice of all came from Catulus, who turned up late in the evening, just as Cicero was about to retire to bed, with a group of former consuls, including the two Lucullus brothers, Lepidus, Torquatus and the former governor of Nearer Gaul, C. Piso. They came to demand that Caesar be arrested.

'On what evidence?' asked Cicero, rising wearily to his feet to greet the delegation.

'Treason, of course,' replied Catulus. 'Do you have the least particle of doubt that he's had a hand in this business from the start?'

'None. But that's not the same as having evidence.'

'Then make the evidence,' said the senior Lucullus smoothly. 'All that's required is a more detailed statement from Volturcius implicating Caesar, and we shall have him at last.'

'I guarantee you a majority of the senate will vote to arrest him,' said Catulus. His companions murmured in agreement.

'And then what?'

'Execute him along with the others.'

'Execute the head of the state religion on a trumped-up charge? There'll be a civil war!'

Lucullus said, 'There's likely to be a civil war one day anyway, thanks to Caesar, but if you act now, you can prevent it. Remember your authority. You've just been granted a thanksgiving. Your prestige in the senate has never been higher.'

'I was not granted a thanksgiving in order to go round like a tyrant butchering my opponents!'

'No, you were granted it,' retorted Catulus, 'because I proposed it.'

'And you are so blinded with hatred for Caesar because he robbed you of the pontificate that you can no longer see straight!' I had never heard Cicero speak in such a way to one of the old patricians, and Catulus's whole body seemed to give a jerk, as if he had stepped on something sharp. 'Now listen to me,' the consul continued, pointing his finger. 'Listen to me, all of you. I have Caesar precisely where I want him. I have that Leviathan by the tail at last. If he lets his prisoner escape tonight, I agree – we can arrest him, because he will have given us proof of his guilt. But for that very reason he won't let him escape. He'll obey the will of the senate for a change. And I mean to make sure it's a habit he gets used to.'

'Until he does the same thing again,' said Piso, who had only recently survived an attempt by Caesar to have him exiled for corruption.

'Then we'll just have to outwit him again,' said Cicero. 'And again. And again. And we'll have to go on doing it for as long as is necessary. But I believe I have his measure now, and my handling of this crisis over the past year has shown that my judgement about such matters is not usually wrong.'

His visitors lapsed into silence. He was the man of the hour. His prestige was at its zenith. For once nobody felt able to contradict him, not even Lucullus. Eventually Piso said, 'And the conspirators?'

'That is for the senate to decide, not me.'

'They will look to you for a lead.'

'Then they will look in vain. Dear gods, have I not done enough?' Cicero shouted suddenly. 'I have exposed the conspiracy. I have stopped Catilina from becoming consul. I have driven him from Rome. I have foiled an attempt to burn down half the city and massacre us in our homes. I have delivered the traitors into custody. Am I now supposed to shoulder all the opprobrium for killing them as well? It's time you gentlemen started playing your part.'

'What is it you want us to do?' asked Torquatus.

'Stand up in the senate tomorrow and say what you want done with the conspirators. Show a lead to the rest of them. Don't expect me to carry the whole burden any longer. I'll call you one by one. State your view – death it must be, I suppose: I can't see any way out of it – but state it loud and clear, so that at least when I go before the people I can say I am the instrument of the senate and not a dictator.'

'You can rely on us for that,' said Catulus, glancing around at the others. They all nodded in agreement. 'But you're wrong about Caesar. We'll never get a better chance than this to stop him. Think on it overnight, I urge you.'

After they had gone, certain grim contingencies needed to be faced. If the senate voted for the death penalty, when would the condemned men be killed, and how, and where, and by whom? There was no precedent for such an action. When was easy enough: immediately judgement was passed, to forestall a rescue. And by whom was also obvious: the public executioner would do the dispatching, to establish that they were common criminals. Where and how were harder. They could scarcely be flung from the Tarpeian Rock – that would invite a riot. Cicero consulted the head of his official bodyguard, the proximate lictor, who told him that the best place – because the most easy to protect – would be the execution chamber beneath the Carcer, which was conveniently next door to the Temple of Concordia. The space was too cramped and the light too poor for decapitation, he announced, so by a process of elimination it was settled that the conspirators would have to be strangled. The lictor went off to make sure that the carnifex and his assistants would be standing by.

I could tell Cicero was upset by this conversation. He refused to eat, saying he had no appetite. He did consent to drink a little of Atticus's wine, from one of his exquisite Neapolitan glass beakers, but unfortunately his hand was shaking so much he dropped it, shattering the glass on the mosaic floor. After that had been cleared up Cicero decided he needed some fresh air. Atticus called for a slave to unlock the doors, and we stepped out from the library on to the narrow terrace. Down in the valley, the effect of the curfew was to make Rome seem as dark and fathomless as a lake. Only the Temple of Luna, lit up by torches on the slopes of the Palatine, was distinctly visible. It seemed to hover, suspended in the night, like some white-hulled vessel descended from the stars to inspect us. We leaned against the balustrade and vainly contemplated what we could not see.

Cicero sighed and said, more to himself than to any of us, 'I wonder what men will make of us a thousand years from now. Perhaps Caesar is right – this whole republic needs to be pulled down and built again. I tell you, I have grown to dislike these patricians as much as I dislike the mob – and they haven't the excuse of poverty or ignorance.' And then again, a few moments later: 'We have so much – our arts and learning, laws, treasure, slaves, the beauty of Italy, dominion over the entire earth – and yet why is it that some ineradicable impulse of the human mind always impels us to foul our own nest?' I surreptitiously made a note of both remarks.

That night I slept very badly, in a cubicle adjoining Cicero's room. The tramp of the sentries' boots as they patrolled the garden and their whispered voices intermingled with my dreams. Seeing Lucullus had stirred a remembrance of Agathe, and I had a nightmare in which I asked him about her and he told me he had no idea whom I meant but that all his slaves in Misenum were dead. When I woke exhausted to the grey dawn, I had a heavy feeling of dread, as if a rock had been laid on my chest. I looked into Cicero's room, but his bed was empty. I found him sitting motionless in the library, with the shutters closed and only a small lamp beside him. He asked if it was dawn yet. He wanted to go home to speak with Terentia.

We left soon afterwards, escorted by a new detachment of bodyguards under the command of Clodius. Ever since the crisis began, this notorious reprobate had regularly volunteered to accompany the consul, and these demonstrations of his loyalty, matched by Cicero's stout defence of Murena, had strengthened the bond between them. I guess what drew Clodius to Cicero was the opportunity to learn the art of politics from a master – he intended to stand for the senate himself the following year – while Cicero was amused by Clodius's youthful indiscretions. At any rate, much as I distrusted him, I was glad to see him on duty that morning, for I knew he would lift the consul's mood with some distracting gossip. Sure enough, he started at once.

'Have you heard that Murena's getting married again?'

'Really?' said Cicero in surprise. 'To whom?'

'Sempronia.'

'Isn't Sempronia already married?'

'She's getting divorced. Murena will be her third husband.'

'Three husbands! What a hussy.'

They walked on a little further. 'She has a fifteen-year-old daughter from her first marriage,' said Clodius thoughtfully. 'Did you know that?'

'I did not.'

'I'm considering marrying the girl. What do you think?'

'So Murena would become your stepfather-in-law?'

'That's it.'

'Not a bad idea. He can help your career a lot.'

'She's also immensely rich. She's the heiress of the Gracchi estate.'

'Then what are you waiting for?' asked Cicero, and Clodius laughed.

By the time we reached Cicero's house, the female worshippers were emerging blearily into the cold morning, led by the Vestal Virgins. A crowd of bystanders had gathered to watch them go. Some, like Caesar's wife, Pompeia, looked very unsteady, and had to be supported by their maids. Others, including Caesar's mother, Aurelia, seemed entirely unmoved by whatever it was they had experienced. She swept past Cicero, stone-faced, without a glance in his direction, which suggested to me that she knew what had happened in the senate the previous afternoon. In fact an amazing number of the women coming out of the house had some connection with Caesar. In all I counted at least three of his former mistresses – Mucia, the wife of Pompey the Great; Postumia, the wife of Servius; and Lollia, who was married to Aulus Gabinius. Clodius looked on agog at this perfumed parade. Finally, Caesar's current and greatest amour, Servilia, the wife of the consul-elect, Silanus, stepped over the doorstep and into the street. She was not especially beautiful: her face was handsome – mannish, I suppose one would call it – but full of intelligence and strength of character. And it was typical of her that she, alone of all the wives of the senior magistrates, actually stopped to ask Cicero what he thought would happen that day.

'It will be for the senate to decide,' he replied guardedly.

'And what do you think their decision will be?'

'That is up to them.'

'But you will give them a lead?'

'If I do – forgive me – I shall announce it in the senate later rather than now on the street.'

'You don't trust me?'

'I do indeed, madam. But others may somehow get to hear of our conversation.'

'I don't know what you mean by that!' Her voice sounded offended but her piercing blue eyes shone with malicious humour.

'She is by far the cleverest of his women,' observed Cicero once she had moved on, 'even shrewder than his mother, and that's saying something. He'd do well to stick with her.'

The rooms of Cicero's house were still warm from the women's presence, the air moist with the scent of perfume and incense, of sandalwood and juniper. Female slaves were sweeping the floors and clearing away leftovers; on the altar in the atrium was a pile of white ash. Clodius made no attempt to hide his curiosity. He went round picking up objects and examining them and was obviously bursting to ask all manner of questions, especially when Terentia appeared. She was still wearing the robes of the high priestess, but even these were forbidden to the eyes of men, so she concealed them beneath a cloak that she kept tightly clasped at her throat. Her face was flushed; her voice was high and strange.

'There was a sign,' she announced, 'not an hour ago, from the Good Goddess herself!' Cicero looked dubious, but she was too enraptured to notice. 'I have received a special dispensation from the Vestal Virgins to inform you of what we saw. There,' she gestured dramatically, 'on the altar, the fire had entirely burned out. The ash was quite cold. But then a great bright flame shot up. It was the most extraordinary portent anyone could ever remember.'

'And what do they think it means, this portent?' enquired Cicero, clearly interested despite himself.

'It is a sign of favour, sent directly to your home on a day of great importance, to promise you safety and glory.'

'Is it indeed?'

'Be bold,' she said, taking his hand. 'Do the brave thing. You will be honoured for ever. And no harm will come to you. That is the message from the Good Goddess.'

I have often wondered in the years since whether this affected Cicero's judgement at all. True, he had repeatedly derided auguries and omens to me as childish nonsense. But then I have found that even the greatest sceptics, *in extremis*, will pray to every god in the firmament if they think it might help them. Certainly I could tell that Cicero was pleased. He kissed Terentia's hand and thanked her for her piety and concern for his interests. Then he went upstairs to prepare for the senate as news of the portent was spread, on his instructions, to the crowd in the street. Clodius, meanwhile, had found a woman's shift lying beneath one of the couches, and I watched him put it to his nose and inhale deeply.

On the orders of the consul, the prisoners were not brought to the senate but were left where they had been confined overnight. Cicero said this was for reasons of security, but in my opinion it was because he could not bear to look at their faces. Once again the session was held in the Temple of Concordia, and all the leading men of the republic attended except for Crassus, who sent word that he was ill. In reality he wished to avoid casting a vote either for or against the death penalty. He may also have been fearful of assault: there were plenty among the patricians and the Order of Knights who thought he too should have been arrested. Caesar, however, turned up as cool as you please, his sharp wide shoulders pushing past the guards, ignoring their oaths and insults. He squeezed into his seat on the front bench, settled back and thrust out his legs far into the gangway. Cato's narrow skull was directly opposite him: his head was bent reading the treasury accounts as usual. It was very cold. The doors at the far end of the temple had been left wide open for the crowd of spectators, and a veritable gale was blowing down the aisle. Isauricus wore a pair of old grey mittens, there was much coughing and sneezing, and when Cicero stood to call the house to order, his breath billowed out like steam from a cooking pot.

'Gentlemen,' he declared, 'this is the most solemn assembly of our order that I can ever remember. We meet to determine what should be done with the criminals who have threatened our republic. I intend that every man here who desires to speak shall have the chance to do so. I do not mean to express a view myself—' He held up his hand to quell the objections. 'No one can say I have not played the part of leader in this matter. But henceforth I wish to be the senate's servant, and whatever you decide, you may be sure I shall put into effect. I would rule only that your decision must be reached today, before nightfall. We cannot delay. Your punishment, whatever form it takes, must be a swift one. I now call Decimus Junius Silanus to give his opinion.'

It was the privilege of the senior consul-elect always to speak first in debates, but I am sure that on that particular day it was an honour Silanus would happily have forgone. Up to now I have not had much to say about

Silanus, in part because I find it hard to remember him: in an age of giants, he was a dwarf – respectable, grey, dull, prone to bouts of ill health and enervating gloom. He would never have won the prize in a thousand years but for the energy and ambition of Servilia, who was so determined that her three daughters should have a consul for a father, she made herself Caesar's mistress to further her husband's career. Glancing occasionally with nervous eyes along the front bench to the man who was cuckolding him, Silanus spoke haltingly of the competing claims of justice and mercy, of security and liberty, of his friendship with Lentulus Sura and his hatred of traitors. What was he driving at? It was impossible to tell. Finally Cicero had to ask him directly what penalty he was recommending. Silanus took a deep breath and closed his eyes. 'Death,' he said.

The senate stirred as the dreadful word was spoken. Murena was called next. I could see why Cicero had favoured him to be consul over Servius at a time of crisis. There was something solid and four-square about him as he stood with his legs apart and his pudgy hands on his hips. 'I am a soldier,' he said. 'Rome is at war. Out in the countryside women and children are being ravished, temples pillaged, crops destroyed; and now our vigilant consul has discovered that similar chaos was being plotted in the mother city. If I found men in my camp planning to set it afire and murder my officers, I would not hesitate for an instant to order their execution. The penalty for the traitors is always, must be – and can only be – death.'

Cicero worked his way along the front bench, calling one ex-consul after another. Catulus made a blood-curdling speech about the horrors of butchery and arson and also came out firmly in support of death; so did the two Lucullus brothers, Piso, Curio, Cotta, Figulus, Volcacius, Servilius, Torquatus and Lepidus; even Caesar's cousin Lucius came down reluctantly for the supreme penalty. Taken together with Silanus and Murena, that made fourteen men of consular rank all arguing for the same punishment. No voice was raised against. It was so one-sided, Cicero later told me he feared he might be accused of rigging the vote. After several hours during which nothing had been heard except demands for death, he rose and asked if there was any man who wished to propose a different sentence. All heads naturally turned to Caesar. But it was an ex-praetor, Tiberius Claudius Nero, who was the first on his feet. He had been one of Pompey's commanders in the war against the pirates, and he spoke on his chief's behalf. 'Why are we in such a hurry, gentlemen? The conspirators are safely under lock and key. I believe we should summon Pompey the Great home to deal with Catilina. Once the leader is defeated, then we can decide at our leisure what to do with his minions.'

When Nero had finished, Cicero asked, 'Does anyone else wish to speak against an immediate sentence of death?'

That was when Caesar slowly uncrossed his legs and rose to his feet. Immediately a great cacophony of shouts and jeering rang out, but Caesar had obviously anticipated this and had prepared his response. He stood with his hands behind his back, patiently waiting until the noise had died down. 'Whoever, gentlemen, is pondering a difficult question,' he said in his quietly threatening voice, 'ought to clear his mind of all hatred and anger, as well as affection and compassion. It isn't easy to discern the truth if one gives way to emotion.' He uttered the last word with such stinging contempt, it had the effect of briefly silencing his opponents. 'You may ask why I oppose the death penalty—'

'Because you're also guilty!' someone shouted.

'If I were guilty,' retorted Caesar, 'how better to hide it than to clamour for death with all the rest of you? No, I don't oppose death because these men were once my friends – in public life one must set aside such feelings. Nor do I oppose it because I regard their offences as trivial. Frankly, I think that any torture would be less than these men deserve. But people have short memories. Once criminals have been brought to justice, their guilt is soon forgotten, or becomes a matter of dispute. What's never forgotten is their punishment, especially if it's extreme. I'm sure Silanus makes his proposal with the best interests of his country at heart. Yet it strikes me – I won't say as harsh, for in dealing with such men nothing could be too harsh, but as out of keeping with the traditions of our republic.

'All bad precedents have their origins in measures that at the time seem good. Twenty years ago, when Sulla ordered the execution of Brutus and other criminal adventurers, who among us did not approve his action? The men were villains and troublemakers; it was generally agreed that they deserved to die. But those executions proved to be the first step on the path to a national calamity. Before long, anyone who coveted another man's land or villa – or in the end merely his dishes and clothes – could have him killed by denouncing him as a traitor. So those who rejoiced in the death of Brutus found themselves being hauled off to execution, and the killings didn't stop till Sulla had glutted all his followers with riches. Of course I'm not afraid that any such action will be taken by Marcus Cicero. But in a great nation like ours there are many men, with many different characters, and it may be that on some future occasion, when another consul has, like him, an armed force at his disposal, a false report will be accepted as true. If so, with this precedent set, who will there be to restrain him?'

At the mention of his own name, Cicero intervened. 'I have been listening to the remarks of the chief priest with great attention,' he said. 'Is he proposing that the prisoners simply be released to join Catilina's army?'

'By no means,' responded Caesar. 'I agree that they have forfeited the right to breathe the same air and see the same light as the rest of us. But death has been ordained by the immortal gods not as a means of punishment but as a relief from our toil and woe. If we kill them, their suffering ceases. I therefore propose a harsher fate: *that the prisoners' goods shall be confiscated and that they shall be imprisoned, each in a separate town, for the remainder of their lives; against this sentence the condemned shall have no right of appeal, and any attempt by any person to make an appeal on their behalf shall be regarded as an act of treason*. Life, gentlemen,' he concluded, 'will mean life.'

What an astonishing piece of effrontery this was – but also how clever and effective! Even as I wrote Caesar's motion down and handed it up to Cicero, I could hear the excited whispers running around the senate. The consul took it from me with a worried expression. He sensed his enemy had made a cunning move but was not quite sure of all its implications, or how to respond. He read Caesar's proposal aloud and asked if anyone wished to comment upon it, whereupon who should stand up but consul-elect and cuckold-in-chief Silanus.

'I have been deeply moved by the words of Caesar,' he declared, with an unctuous rubbing of his hands. 'So moved, in fact, that I shall not vote for my own proposal. Instead of death, I too believe that a more appropriate punishment would be imprisonment for life.'

That provoked a low exclamation of surprise, followed by a kind of rustling along the benches, which I recognised immediately as the wind of sensible opinion changing its direction. In a choice between death and exile, most senators favoured death. But if the choice became one between death and incarceration for life, they were able to adjust their calculation. And who could blame them? It seemed to offer the perfect solution: the conspirators would be punished horribly, but the senate would escape the odium of having blood on its hands. Cicero looked around him anxiously for supporters of the death penalty, but now speaker after speaker rose to urge the merits of perpetual imprisonment. Hortensius supported Caesar's motion; so, surprisingly, did Isauricus. Metellus Nepos declared that execution without the right of appeal would be illegal, and echoed Nero's demands for Pompey to be recalled. After this had gone on for another hour or two, with only a few voices now hankering after death, Cicero called a brief adjournment before the vote to allow some senators to go outside and relieve themselves and others to take refreshment. In the meantime, he held a quick private conclave with Quintus and me. It was already starting to get gloomy again and there was nothing we could do to alleviate it – lighting a fire or any kind of lamp within the walls of a temple was of course forbidden. Suddenly I realised there was not much time left. 'Well,' Cicero asked us softly, leaning out of his chair, 'what do you think?'

'Caesar's motion will pass,' answered Quintus in a whisper, 'no question of it. Even the patricians are weakening.'

Cicero groaned. 'So much for their promises …'

'Surely this is good for you,' I said eagerly, for I was all in favour of a compromise. 'It lets you off the hook.'

'But his proposal is a nonsense!' hissed Cicero, with an angry glance in Caesar's direction. 'No senate can pass a law that will bind its successors in perpetuity, and he well knows it. What if a magistrate lays a motion next year to say that it isn't treason to agitate for the prisoners' release after all, and it passes through a public assembly? He just wants to keep the crisis alive for his own ends.'

'Then at least it will become your successors' problem,' I answered, 'and not yours.'

'You'll look weak,' warned Quintus. 'What will history say? You'll have to speak.'

Cicero's shoulders sagged. This was precisely the predicament he had dreaded. I had never seen him in such an agony of indecision. 'You're right,' he concluded, 'although I can see no outcome from this that isn't ruinous to me.'

Accordingly, when the adjournment ended, he announced that he would give his view after all. 'I see that your faces and eyes, gentlemen, are all turned upon me, so I shall say what as consul I must say. We have before us two proposals: one of Silanus – though he will no longer vote for it – urging death for the conspirators; the other of Caesar for life imprisonment – an exemplary punishment for a heinous crime. It is, as he says, far worse than death, for Caesar removes even hope, the sole consolation of men in their misfortune. He further orders that their property be confiscated, to add poverty to their other torments. The only thing he leaves these wicked men is their life – whereas if he had taken that from them, he would in one painful act have relieved them of much mental and bodily suffering.

'Now, gentlemen, it is clear to me where my own interest lies. If you adopt the motion of Caesar, since he is a populist, I shall have less reason to fear the attacks of the people, because I shall be doing what he has proposed. Whereas if you adopt the alternative, I fear that more trouble may be brought down upon my head. But let the interests of the republic count for more than considerations of danger to myself. We must do what is right. Answer me this: if the head of a household were to find his children killed by a slave, his wife murdered and his house burned, and did not inflict the supreme penalty in return, would he be thought kindly and compassionate or the most inhuman and cruel of men not to avenge their suffering? To my mind, a man who does not soften his own grief and suffering by inflicting similar distress upon the man responsible is unfeeling and has a heart of stone. I support the proposal of Silanus.'

Caesar quickly rose to intervene. 'But surely the flaw in the consul's argument is that the accused have not committed any such acts – they are being condemned for their intentions, rather than for anything they have done.'

'Exactly!' cried a voice from the other side of the chamber, and all heads turned to Cato.

If the vote had been taken at this point, I have little doubt that Caesar's proposal would have carried the day, regardless of the consul's view. The prisoners would have been packed off across Italy, to rot or be reprieved according to the caprices of politics, and Cicero's future would have worked out very differently. But just as the outcome seemed assured, there arose from the benches near the back of the temple a familiar gaunt and ill-kempt apparition, his hair all awry, his shoulders bare despite the cold, his sinewy arm stretched out to indicate his desire to intervene.

'Marcus Porcius Cato,' said Cicero uneasily, for one could never be sure which way Cato's rigid logic would lead him. 'You wish to speak?'

'Yes, I wish to speak,' said Cato. 'I wish to speak because someone has to remind this house of exactly what it is we're facing. The whole point, gentlemen, is precisely that we're *not* dealing with crimes that have been committed, but with crimes that are *planned*. For that very reason it will be no good trying to invoke the law afterwards – we shall all have been slaughtered!' There was a murmur of acknowledgement: he spoke the truth. I glanced up at Cicero. He was also nodding. 'Too many sitting here,' proclaimed Cato, his voice rising, 'are more concerned for their villas and their statues than they are for their country. In heaven's name, men, wake up! Wake up while there's still time, and lend a hand to defend the republic! Our liberty and lives are at stake! At such a time does anyone here dare talk to me of clemency and compassion?'

He came down the gangway barefoot and stood in the aisle, that harsh and remorseless voice grating away like a blade on a grindstone. It was as if his famous great-grandfather had just stepped out of his grave and was shaking his furious grey locks at us.

'Do not imagine, gentlemen, that it was by force of arms that our ancestors transformed a petty state into this great republic. If it were so, it would now be at the height of its glory, since we have more subjects and citizens, more arms and horses, than they ever had. No, it was something else entirely that made them great – something we entirely lack. They were hard workers at home, just rulers abroad, and to the senate they brought minds that were not racked by guilt or enslaved by passion. That is what we've lost. We pile up riches for ourselves while the state is bankrupt and we idle away our lives, so that when an assault is made upon the republic there's no one left to defend it.

'A plot has been hatched by citizens of the highest rank to set fire to their native city. Gauls, the deadliest foes of everything Roman, have been called to arms. The hostile army and its leader are ready to descend upon us. And you're still hesitating and unable to decide how to treat public enemies taken within your own walls?' He literally spat out his sarcasm, showering the senators nearest him with phlegm. 'Why then, I suggest you take pity on them – they are young men led astray by ambition. Armed though they are, let them go. But mind what you're doing with your clemency and compassion – if they draw the sword, it will be too late to do anything about it. Oh yes, you say, the situation is certainly ugly, but you're not afraid of it. Nonsense! You're quaking in your shoes! But you're so indolent and weak that you stand irresolute, each waiting for someone else to act – no doubt trusting to the gods. Well, I tell you, vows and womanish supplications won't secure divine aid. Only vigilance and action can achieve success.

'We're completely encircled. Catilina and his army are ready to grip us by the throat. Our enemies are living in the very heart of the city. That is why we must act quickly. This therefore is my proposal, Consul. Write it down well, scribe: *Whereas by the criminal designs of wicked citizens the republic has been subjected to serious danger; and whereas, by testimony and confession, the accused stand convicted of planning massacre, arson and other foul atrocities against their fellow citizens: that, having admitted their criminal intention, they should be put to death as if they had been caught in the actual commission of capital offences, in accordance with ancient custom.*'

For thirty years I attended debates in the senate and I witnessed many great and famous speeches. But I never saw one – not one: not even close – that rivalled in its effects that brief intervention by Cato. What is great oratory, after all, except the distillation of emotion into exact words? Cato said what a majority of men were feeling but had not the language to express, even to themselves. He admonished them, and they loved him for it. All across the temple, senators rose from their seats applauding and went to stand beside their hero to indicate that he had their support. He was no longer the eccentric on the back bench. He was the rock and bone and sinew of the old republic. Cicero looked on in astonishment. As for Caesar, he jumped up demanding the right to reply, and actually started making a speech. But everyone could see that his true intention was to talk out Cato's motion and prevent a vote, for the light was very low now and shadows were deep across the chamber. There were shouts of rage from those around Cato, and some jostling, and several of the knights who had been watching from the doorway rushed in with their swords drawn. Caesar was twisting his shoulders back and forth to throw off the hands that were trying to pull him down, and still he kept on speaking. The knights looked to Cicero for instruction. All it would have taken was a nod from him, or a raised finger, and Caesar would have been run through on the spot. And for the briefest of instants he did hesitate. But then he shook his head, Caesar was released, and in the chaos he must have rushed from the temple, for I lost sight of him after that. Cicero came down off his dais. Striding along the aisle, shouting at the senators, he and his lictors separated the combatants, pushed a few of them back into their places, and when some sort of order had been restored he returned to his chair.

'Gentlemen,' he said, his face as white as milk in the darkness, his voice very thin and strained, 'the sentiment of the house is clear. Marcus Cato's motion passes. The sentence is death.'

Speed was now vital. The condemned men had to be moved quickly to the execution chamber before their friends and supporters realised their fate. To fetch each prisoner, Cicero placed a former consul at the head of a detachment of guards: Catulus went for Cethegus, Torquatus for Capito, Piso for Caeparius and Lepidus for Statilius. After settling the details, and requesting that the other senators remain in their places while the deed was done, he himself went off last of all to collect the most senior of the accused, Lentulus Sura.

Outside, the sun had just gone down. The forum was ominously crowded, yet the people parted at once to let us through. They reminded me of spectators at a sacrifice – solemn, respectful, filled with awe at the mysteries of life and death. We went with our escort up on to the Palatine, to the home of Spinther, who was a kinsman of Sura, and found our prisoner in the atrium playing dice with one of the men assigned to guard him. He had just made his throw: the dice clattered on to the board as we came in. He must have realised at once from Cicero's expression that it was all over for him. He glanced down to inspect his score, then looked back up at us and gave a bleak smile. 'I seem to have lost,' he said.

I cannot reproach Sura for his behaviour. His grandfather and his great-grandfather had both been consuls and they would have been proud of his conduct in this last hour at least. He handed over a purse with some money to be distributed among his guards, then walked out of the house as calmly as if he were going to take a bath. He offered only the mildest of reproaches. 'I believe you laid a trap for me,' he said.

'You trapped yourself,' replied Cicero.

Sura didn't say another word as we crossed the forum, but trod steadily with his chin thrust out. He still wore the plain tunic he had been given the previous day. Yet from their demeanours one would have guessed that the deathly pale Cicero, despite his consular purple, was the condemned man and Sura his captor. I felt the eyes of the vast crowd upon us; they were as curious and docile as sheep. At the foot of the steps leading up to the Carcer, Sura's stepson Mark Antony ran out in front of the guards, crying out to know what was happening.

'I have a short appointment,' replied Sura calmly. 'It will all be over soon. Go and comfort your mother. She will have more need of you now than I.'

Antony bellowed with grief and anger and tried to reach out to touch Sura, but he was pushed out of the way by the lictors. We passed on up the steps between the pickets of troops, ducked through a doorway that was low but very thick, almost like a tunnel, and into a windowless circular stone chamber lit by torches. The air was close, noxious with the stink of death and human waste. As my eyes adjusted to the gloom, I recognised Catulus, Piso, Torquatus and Lepidus, with the folds of their togas pressed to their noses, and also the short and broad figure of the state executioner, the carnifex, in his leather apron, attended by half a dozen assistants. The other prisoners were already lying on the ground with their arms tightly pinioned behind their backs. Capito, who had spent the day with Crassus, was crying softly. Statilius, who had been held at Caesar's official residence, was insensible from the effects of wine. Caeparius was lost to the world, curled up in a ball with his eyes closed. Cethegus was protesting loudly that this was illegal and demanding the right to address the senate; someone kicked him in the ribs and he went quiet. The carnifex seized Sura's arms and bound them quickly at the wrists and elbows.

'Consul,' said Sura, wincing as he was trussed, 'will you give me your word that no harm will befall my wife and family?'

'Yes, I promise you that.'

'And will you surrender our bodies to our families for burial?'

'I will.' (Afterwards Mark Antony claimed that Cicero had denied this final request: yet another of his innumerable lies.)

'This was not supposed to be my destiny. The auguries were quite clear.'

'You allowed yourself to be suborned by wicked men.'

Moments later the tying-up was finished and Sura looked around him. 'I die a Roman nobleman,' he shouted defiantly, 'and a patriot!'

That was too much even for Cicero. 'No,' he said curtly, nodding to the carnifex, 'you die a traitor.'

At those words, Sura was dragged towards the large black hole in the centre of the floor that was the only means of entrance to the execution chamber beneath us. Two powerful fellows lowered him into it, and I had a last glimpse of his handsome, baffled, stupid face in the torchlight. Then strong hands must have taken hold of him from beneath, for abruptly he disappeared. Statilius's limp form was let down immediately after Sura; then it was quickly the turn of Capito, who was shaking so much his teeth were rattling; then Caeparius, still in a swoon of terror; and finally Cethegus, who screamed and sobbed and put up such a tremendous struggle that two men had to sit on him while a third tied his wildly thrashing legs – in the end they tipped him through the hole head first and he fell with a thud. Nothing more was to be heard after that, apart from some occasional scuffling sounds; eventually those also ceased. I was told later that they were hanged in a row from hooks fixed in the ceiling. After what seemed an eternity, the carnifex called up that the job was done, and Cicero went reluctantly to the hole and peered down. A torch was flourished over the victims. The five strangled men lay in a row, gazing up at us with bulging sightless eyes. I felt no pity: I was remembering the violated body of the boy they had sacrificed to seal their pact. Cato was right, I thought: they deserved to die; and that remains my opinion to this day.

Once he had assured himself that the conspirators were dead, Cicero could not wait to get away from that 'antechamber to hell', as he afterwards called it. We squeezed back out through the narrow tunnel of a doorway and straightened into the fresh night air – only to find that a most amazing sight awaited us. In the dusk, the whole of the forum was lit by torches – a great carpet of flickering yellow light. In every direction people were standing, motionless and silent, including the whole of the senate, which had now emerged from the Temple of Concordia, just next door to the prison. Everyone was looking towards Cicero. Obviously he had to announce what had happened, although he had no idea what the reaction might be, and he also had another peculiar difficulty, which showed the unprecedented nature of what had just occurred: it was a superstition in those days that a magistrate must never utter the words 'death' or 'died' in the forum, lest he bring down a curse on the city. So Cicero thought for a moment, cleared his throat of whatever thick bile had accumulated in the Carcer, threw back his shoulders and proclaimed, very loudly, *'They have lived!'*

His voice echoed off the buildings and was followed by a silence so profound that I feared the vast crowd might be hostile after all and we would be the next to be hanged. But I suppose they were just working out what he meant. A few senators started clapping. Others joined in. The clapping turned to cheers. And slowly the cheers began spreading across the vast throng. 'Hail, Cicero!' they called. 'Hail, Cicero!' 'Thank the gods for Cicero!' 'Cicero – the saviour of the republic!'

Standing only a foot away from him, I saw the tears well up into his eyes. It was as if some dam had broken in him and all the emotions that had been accumulating behind it, not only during the past few hours but throughout his consulship, were suddenly allowed to burst forth. He tried to say something but could not, which only increased the volume of applause. Finally there was nothing for it but to descend the steps, and by the time he reached the level of the forum, with the cheers of friends and opponents alike ringing in his ears, he was weeping freely. Behind us, the bodies of the prisoners were being dragged out by hooks.

The story of Cicero's last few days as consul may be swiftly told. No civilian in the history of the republic had ever been as lauded as he was at this time. After months of holding its breath, the city seemed to let out a great sigh of relief. On the night the conspirators were executed, the consul was escorted home from the forum by the whole of the senate in a great torchlit procession and was cheered every step of the way. His house was brilliantly illuminated to welcome him back; the entrance where Terentia waited for him with his children was decked with laurel; his slaves lined up to applaud him into the atrium. It was a strange homecoming. He was too exhausted to sleep, too hungry to eat, too eager to forget the horrible business of the executions to be capable of talking about anything else. I assumed he would recover his equilibrium in a day or two. Only later did I realise that something in him had changed for ever: had snapped, like an axle. The following morning, the senate bestowed upon him the title 'Father of his Country'. Caesar chose not to attend the session, but Crassus came and voted with the rest, and praised Cicero to the skies.

Not every voice was raised in acclamation. Metellus Nepos, on taking up his tribunate a few days later, continued to insist that the executions were illegal. He predicted that when Pompey returned to Italy to restore order he would deal not only with Catilina but with this petty tyrant Cicero as well. Despite his immense popularity, Cicero was sufficiently worried to go to Clodia and ask her to tell her brother-in-law privately that if he persisted in this course, Cicero would prosecute him for his own links to Catilina. Clodia's lustrous brown eyes widened with delight at this opportunity to meddle in affairs of state. But Nepos coolly ignored the warning, reasoning correctly that Cicero would never dare to move against Pompey's closest political ally. All now depended, therefore, on how swiftly Catilina could be defeated.

When the salutary news of the execution of Sura and the others reached Catilina's camp, a large number of his followers at once deserted him. (I doubt they would have done so if the senate vote had been for life imprisonment.) Realising that Rome was now secure against them, he and Manlius decided to take the rebel army north, with the intention of crossing the Alps into Further Gaul and creating a mountainous enclave in which they might hold out for years. But winter was coming, and the lower passes were blocked by Metellus Celer at the head of three legions. Meanwhile, in hard pursuit at the rebels' rear was the senate's other army, under the command of Hybrida. This was the opponent Catilina chose to turn and fight, picking his ground in a narrow plain to the east of Pisae.

Not surprisingly, suspicions arose, which persist to this day, that Catilina and his old ally Hybrida had been in secret contact all along. Cicero had foreseen this, and when it became clear that battle was to be joined, Hybrida's veteran military legate, M. Petreius, opened the sealed orders he had been given in Rome. These appointed him the operational commander and directed that Hybrida should plead illness and take no part in the fighting; if he refused, Petreius was to arrest him. When the matter was put to Hybrida, he swiftly agreed, and announced that he was suffering from gout. In this way Catilina unexpectedly found himself facing one of the most able commanders in the Roman army, who was at the head of a force much larger and better equipped than his own.

On the morning of the battle, Catilina addressed his soldiers, many of whom were armed only with pitchforks and hunting spears, in the following terms: 'Men, we fight for our country, our freedom and our life, whereas our opponents fight for a corrupt oligarchy. Their numbers may be greater but our spirit is stronger, and we will prevail. But if for any reason we do not, and Fortune turns against us, do not allow yourselves to be slaughtered like cattle, but fight like men and make sure that bloodshed and mourning are the price that the enemy will pay for victory.' The trumpets then sounded and the front lines advanced towards one another.

It was a terrible carnage and Catilina was in the thick of it all day. Not one of his lieutenants surrendered. They fought with the ferocious abandon of men with nothing to lose. Only when Petreius sent in a crack praetorian cohort did the rebel army finally collapse. Every one of Catilina's followers, including Manlius, died where he stood; afterwards their wounds were found to be entirely in the front and none in the back. At nightfall, after the battle, Catilina was discovered deep inside his opponents' lines, surrounded by the corpses of the enemies he had hacked to pieces. He was still just breathing, but died soon afterwards from terrible wounds. On Hybrida's instructions his head was sent back to Rome in a barrel of ice and presented to the senate. But Cicero, who had left the consulship a few days earlier, refused to look at it, and thus ended the conspiracy of Lucius Sergius Catilina.

PART FOUR

PATER PATRIAE

62–58 BC

'Nam Catonem nostrum non tu amas plus quam ego; sed tamen ille optimo animo utens et summa fide nocet interdum rei publicae; dicit enim tamquam in Platonis politeia, non tamquam in Romuli faece, sententiam.'

'As for our friend Cato, I have as warm a regard for him as you. But the fact remains that with all his patriotism and integrity he is sometimes a political liability. He speaks in the senate as though he were living in Plato's Republic rather than Romulus's shit hole.'
Cicero, letter to Atticus, 3 June 60 BC

XXX

For the first few weeks after he ceased to be consul, everyone clamoured to hear the story of how Cicero had foiled the conspiracy of Catilina. There was not a fashionable dinner table in Rome that was not open to him. He went out often; he hated to be alone. Frequently I would accompany him, standing with other members of his entourage behind his couch as he regaled his fellow diners with extracts from his speeches, or the story of how he had escaped assassination on polling day on the Field of Mars, or the trap he had set on the Mulvian Bridge for Lentulus Sura. Usually he illustrated these tales by moving plates and cups around, in the manner of Pompey describing an old battle. If someone interrupted him or tried to raise another subject, he would wait impatiently for a gap in their conversation, give them a hard look and then resume: '*As* I was saying ...' Every morning the grandest of the grand families would flock to his levees and he would point to the very spot where Catilina had stood on the day he offered to be his prisoner, or to the exact pieces of furniture that had been used to barricade the door when the conspirators laid siege to the house. In the senate, whenever he rose to speak, a respectful hush fell over the assembly, and he never missed a chance to remind them that they were only meeting together at all because he had saved the republic. He became, in short – and whoever would have imagined saying this of Cicero? – a bore.

It would have been so much better for him if he had left Rome for a year or two to govern a province; his mystique would have grown with his absence; he would have become a legend. But he had given away his governorships to Hybrida and Celer and there was nothing for him to do except to stay in the city and resume his legal practice. Familiarity makes even the most fascinating figure dull: one would probably be bored with Jupiter Himself if one passed Him on the street every day.

Slowly Cicero's lustre faded. For several weeks he busied himself dictating to me an immense report on his consulship, which he wanted to present to Pompey. It was the size of a book and justified his every action in minute detail. I knew it was a mistake and tried all the tactics I could think of to delay sending it – to no avail. Off it went by special courier to the East, and while he awaited the great man's reply, Cicero set about editing and publishing the speeches he had delivered during the crisis. He inserted many purple passages about himself, especially in the public address he had made from the rostra on the day the plotters were arrested. I was sufficiently worried that one morning, when Atticus was leaving the house, I drew him aside and read out a couple of sections.

'*This day on which we are saved is, I believe, as bright and joyous as the day on which we were born. And just as we thank the gods for the man who founded this city, so you and your descendants will be able to hold in honour the man who has saved the city.*'

'What?' exclaimed Atticus. 'I don't remember him saying that.'

'Well he didn't,' I replied. 'For him to have compared himself to Romulus at such a moment would have seemed absurd. And listen to this.' I lowered my voice and looked around to make sure Cicero was nowhere near. '*In recognition of such great services, citizens, I shall demand of you no reward for my valour, no signal mark of distinction, no monument in my honour, except that this day be remembered for all time, and that the immortal gods should be thanked that there have arisen at such a moment in our history two men, one of whom has carried your empire to the limits not of earth but of heaven, and one who has preserved the home and seat of this empire ...*'

'Let me see that,' demanded Atticus. He grabbed the speech from my hands and read it through, shaking his head in disbelief. 'Putting yourself on the same level as Romulus is one thing: comparing yourself with Pompey is quite another. It would be dangerous enough if someone else said it about him, but for him to say it about *himself* ...? Let's just hope Pompey doesn't get to hear of it.'

'He's bound to.'

'Why?'

'I've been ordered to send him a copy.' Once again I checked that no one was listening. 'Forgive me, sir, if I am speaking out of turn,' I said, 'but I'm becoming quite concerned about him. He's not been the same since the executions. He isn't sleeping well, he won't listen to anyone, and yet he can't bear to spend even an hour by himself. I think the sight of the dead men has affected him – you know how squeamish he is.'

'It's not his delicate stomach that's troubling him, it's his conscience. If he were entirely satisfied that what he did was right, he wouldn't feel the need to justify himself so endlessly.'

It was a shrewd remark, and I feel sorrier for Cicero in retrospect than I did at the time, for it must be a lonely business trying to turn oneself into a public monument. However, by far his greatest folly was not the vainglorious letter to Pompey, or the endless boasting, or the amended speeches: it was a house.

Cicero was not the first politician, and I am sure he will not be the last, to covet a house beyond his means. In his case the property was the boarded-up mansion on the Palatine next to Celer's on Victory Rise that he had noticed when he went to persuade the praetor to take command of the army against Catilina. It now belonged to Crassus, but before that it had been the property of the immensely wealthy tribune M. Livius Drusus. The story went that the architect who built it had promised Drusus he would make sure he was not overlooked by any of his neighbours. 'No,' responded Drusus, 'rather construct it so that all my fellow citizens may see everything I do.' That was the sort of place it was: high up on the hill, tall, wide and ostentatious, easily visible from every part of the forum and the Capitol. Celer's house was on one side of it, and on the other was a large public garden and a portico that had been put up by Catulus's father. I do not know who planted the idea of buying the house in Cicero's head. I fancy it might have been Clodia. Certainly she told him over dinner one night that it was still on the market and that it would be 'wonderfully amusing' to have him as a next-door neighbour. Naturally that was enough to set Terentia dead against the purchase from the start.

'It is modern and it is vulgar,' she told him. 'It is a parvenu's idea of where a gentleman might live.'

'I am the Father of the Nation. The people will like the idea that I am looking down on them in a paternal manner. And it's where we deserve to be, up there among the Claudii, the Aemilii Scauri, the Metelli – the Ciceros are a great family now. Besides, I thought you hated this place.'

'It's not moving in principle I object to, husband; it's moving *there*. And how can you possibly afford it? It's one of the largest houses in Rome – it must be worth at least ten million.'

'I shall go and talk to Crassus. Maybe he'll let me have it cheap.'

Crassus's own mansion, which was also on the Palatine, was deceptively modest on the outside, especially for a man who was rumoured to have eight thousand amphorae filled with silver coin. Inside he sat with his abacus and his account books and the team of slaves and freedmen who ran his business interests. I accompanied Cicero when he went to see him, and after a little preliminary talk about the political situation, Cicero broached the subject of the Drusus house.

'Do you want to buy it?' asked Crassus, suddenly alert.

'I might. How much is it?'

'Fourteen million.'

'Ouch! That's too expensive for me, I fear.'

'I'd let you have it for ten.'

'That's generous, but it's still out of my range.'

'Eight?'

'No, really, Crassus – I appreciate it, but I should never have brought the subject up.' Cicero started to rise from his chair.

'Six?' offered Crassus. 'Four?'

Cicero sat down again. 'I could possibly manage three.'

'Shall we settle on three and a half?'

Afterwards, as we were walking home, I tried gently to suggest that taking possession of such a house for a quarter of its true value would not go down well with the voters. They would smell something fishy about it. 'Who cares about the voters?' replied Cicero. 'I'm barred from standing for the consulship for the next ten years whatever I do. In any case, they need never know how much I paid for it.'

'It will get out somehow,' I warned.

'For gods' sake, will you stop lecturing me about how I am to live? It is bad enough hearing it from my wife, without taking it from my secretary! Haven't I earned the right to some luxury at long last? Half this town would be nothing but charred brick and ashes if it weren't for me! Which reminds me – have we heard back from Pompey yet?'

'No,' I said, bowing my head.

I let the matter drop, but I continued to be troubled. I was absolutely certain that Crassus would expect something in return for his money; either that, or he hated Cicero so much he was willing to forfeit ten million simply to make the people envy and resent him. My secret hope was that Cicero would come to his senses in a day or two, not least because I knew that actually he did not have three and a half million sesterces, or anything like it. But Cicero always took the view that income should adjust to meet expenditure rather than the other way round. He had set his heart on moving up to Victory Rise to dwell among the pantheon of the great names of the republic, and was determined to find the cash somehow. He soon discovered a way.

Almost every day at this time one of the surviving conspirators was to be found on trial in the forum. Autronius Paetus, Cassius Longinus, Marcus Laeca, the two would-be assassins Vargunteius and Cornelius, and many more passed through the courts in a dismal procession. In each case Cicero was a witness for the prosecution, and such was his prestige that a word from him was invariably sufficient to sway the court. One after another they were found guilty – although, fortunately for them, because the emergency was now over, they were not sentenced to death. Instead, each was stripped of his citizenship and property and sent destitute into exile. Cicero was feared and hated by the conspirators and their families almost more than ever, and it remained necessary for him to go around with guards.

Perhaps the most keenly awaited trial of all was that of Publius Cornelius Sulla, who had been immersed in the conspiracy right up to his noble neck. As the date for his hearing approached, his advocate – inevitably it was Hortensius – came to see Cicero.

'My client has a favour to ask of you,' he said.

'Don't tell me: he would like me to refuse to appear as a witness against him?'

'That's right. He's entirely innocent and has always had the highest regard—'

'Oh, spare me all the hypocrisy. He's guilty and you know it.' Cicero scrutinised Hortensius's bland face, weighing him up. 'Actually, you can tell him I might be willing to hold my tongue in his particular case, but on one condition.'

'And what is that?'

'He gives me a million sesterces.'

I was making my usual note of the conversation, but I must say my hand froze when I heard that. Even Hortensius, who after thirty years at the Roman bar was not shocked by much, looked taken aback. Still, he went off and saw Sulla and came back later that same day.

'My client wishes to make a counter-offer. If you are willing to give the closing speech in his defence, he will pay you two million.'

'Agreed,' said Cicero without any hesitation.

There is little doubt that if Cicero had not struck this bargain, Sulla would have been condemned to exile like all the rest; indeed, it was said he had already transferred a large part of his fortune abroad. So when, on the opening day of the trial, Cicero turned up and sat on the bench reserved for the defence, the prosecuting counsel, Torquatus – an old ally of Cicero – could hardly contain his fury and disappointment. In the course of his summing-up he made a bitter attack on Cicero, accusing him of being a tyrant, of setting himself up as judge and jury, of having been the third foreign-born king of Rome, after Tarquin and Numa. It was painful to hear, and worse, it drew some applause from the spectators in the forum. This expression of popular opinion penetrated even Cicero's carapace of self-regard, and when the time came for him to deliver the closing speech he did venture a kind of apology. 'Yes,' he said, 'I suppose my achievements have made me too proud and bred in me a sort of arrogance. But of those glorious and deathless achievements, I can say only this: I shall be amply rewarded for saving this city and the lives of its citizens if no danger falls upon my person for this great service to all mankind. The forum is full of those men whom I have driven from your throats, gentlemen, but have not removed from mine.'

The speech was effective and Sulla was duly acquitted. But Cicero would have done well to heed these signals of a coming storm. Instead, such was his delight at raising most of the money he needed to buy his new house, he quickly shrugged off the incident. He was now only one and a half million short of the full sum, and for this he turned to the moneylenders. They required security, and therefore he told at least two of them, in confidence, of his agreement with Hybrida and his expectation of a share of the revenues from Macedonia. It was good enough to clinch the deal, and towards the end of the year we moved in to Victory Rise.

The house was as grand inside as out. Its dining room had a panelled ceiling with gilded rafters. In the hall were golden statues of young men, whose outstretched hands were designed to hold flaming torches. Cicero swapped his cramped study, where we had spent so many memorable hours, for a fine library. Even I had a larger room, which, though it was below ground, was not at all damp, and had a small barred window through which I could smell the flowers in the garden and hear the birdsong early in the morning. I would have preferred to have had my freedom, of course, and a place of my own, but Cicero had never mentioned it, and I was too bashful – and in a curious way, too proud – to ask.

After I had laid out my few belongings and found a hiding place for my life savings, I went and joined Cicero on a tour of the grounds. The colonnaded path took us past a fountain and a summer house, under a pergola and into a rose garden. The few blooms left were fleshy and faded; when Cicero reached out to pluck one, the petals came away. I felt that we were under inspection from the whole of the city: it made me uncomfortable, but that was the price one paid for the open view, which was indeed amazing. Beyond the Temple of Castor one could clearly see the rostra, and beyond that the senate house itself, and if one looked in the other direction one could just about make out the back of Caesar's official residence. 'I have done it at last,' said Cicero, gazing down at this with a slight smile. 'I have a better house than he has.'

The ceremony of the Good Goddess fell as usual on the fourth day of December. It was exactly a year since the arrest of the conspirators and just a week after we had moved into our new quarters. Cicero had no appointments in court; the senate's order of business was dull. He told me that for once we would not be going down into the city. Instead we would spend the day working on his memoirs.

He had decided to write one version of his autobiography in Latin, for the general reader, and another in Greek for more restricted circulation. He was also trying to persuade a poet to turn his consulship into a verse epic. His first choice, Archias, who had done a similar job for Lucullus, was reluctant to take it on; he said he was too old at sixty to do justice to such an immense theme. Cicero's preferred alternative, the fashionable Thyillus, replied humbly that his meagre skills as a versifier were simply not up to the task. 'Poets!' grumbled Cicero. 'I don't know what is the matter with them. The story of my consulship is an absolute gift to anyone with the slightest spark of imagination. It is beginning to look,' he continued darkly, in a phrase that struck fear into my heart, 'as though I shall have to write this poem myself.'

'Is that altogether wise?' I asked.

'What do you mean?'

I felt myself beginning to sweat. 'Well, after all, even Achilles needed his Homer. His story might not have had quite the same – what should one say? – *epic resonance* if he had told it from his own point of view.'

'I solved that problem in bed last night. My plan is to tell my tale in the voices of the gods, each taking it in turn to recount my career to me as they welcome me as an immortal on to Mount Olympus.' He jumped up and cleared his throat. 'I'll show you what I mean.

Torn from your studies in youth's early dawn, your
country recalled you,
Giving you place in the thick of the struggle for public
preferment;
Yet in seeking release from the worries and cares that
oppress you,
Time that the state leaves free you devote to us and to
learning ...'

Dear heavens, it was terrible stuff! The gods must have wept to hear it. But when the mood seized him, Cicero could lay down hexameters as readily as a bricklayer could throw up a wall: three, four, even five hundred lines a day was nothing to him. He paced around the great open space of his library, acting out the roles of Jupiter and Minerva and Urania, the words pouring out of him so freely I had difficulty keeping up, even in shorthand. When eventually Sositheus tiptoed in and announced that Clodius was waiting outside, I must confess I was greatly relieved. By now it was quite late in the morning – the sixth hour at least – and Cicero was so seized by inspiration he almost sent his visitor packing. But he knew that Clodius would probably be bearing some choice morsel of gossip, and curiosity got the better of him. He told Sositheus to show him in, and Clodius duly strolled into the library, his golden curls elegantly coiffed, his goatee trimmed, his bronzed limbs trailing a scent of crocus oil. He was thirty by now, a married man, having wed the fifteen-year-old heiress Fulvia in the summer, at the same time as he was elected a magistrate. Not that married life detained him much. Her dowry had bought them a large house on the Palatine, and there she sat alone most evenings while he continued with his roistering ways in the taverns of Subura.

'Tasty news,' announced Clodius. He held up a finger with a highly polished nail. 'But you mustn't tell a soul.'

Cicero gestured to him to take a seat. 'You know how discreet I am.'

'You will simply adore this,' said Clodius, settling himself down. 'This will make your day.'

'I hope it lives up to its billing.'

'It will.' Clodius tugged at his little beard with glee. 'The Warden of Land and Sea is divorcing.'

Cicero had been lounging back in his chair with a half-smile on his face, his usual posture when gossiping with Clodius. But now he slowly straightened. 'Are you absolutely sure?'

'I just heard it from your next-door neighbour, my darling sister – who sends her love, by the way – who received the news by special messenger from husband Celer last night. Apparently Pompey has written to Mucia telling her not to be in the house by the time he gets back to Rome.'

'Which will be when?'

'In a few weeks. His fleet is off Brundisium. He may even have landed by now.'

Cicero let out a low whistle. 'So he's coming home at last. After six years I was beginning to think I'd never see him again.'

'Hoping you'd never see him again, more like.'

It was an impertinent remark, but Cicero was too preoccupied with Pompey's impending return to notice. 'If he's divorcing, that must mean he's remarrying. Does Clodia know who he has in mind?'

'No, only that Mucia's out on her pretty little pink ear and the children go with Pompey, even though he hardly knows them. Her brothers are both up in arms, as you can imagine. Celer swears he's been betrayed. Nepos swears it even more. Clodia naturally finds it very funny. But still, what an insult, eh, after all they've done for him – to have their sister publicly cast aside for adultery.'

'And *was* she an adulteress?'

'*Was she an adulteress?*' Clodius gave a surprisingly high-pitched giggle. 'My dear Cicero, the bitch has been rolling around on her back waving her legs in the air ever since he left! Don't tell me you haven't had her? If so, you must be the only man in Rome who hasn't!'

'Are you drunk?' demanded Cicero. He leaned across and sniffed at Clodius, then wrinkled his nose. 'You are, damn you. I suggest you go away and sober up, and mind your manners in future.'

For a moment I thought Clodius might hit him. But then he smirked, and started wiggling his head from side to side derisively. 'Oh, I am a terrible man. A terrible, terrible man ...'

He looked so comical that Cicero forgot his anger and started laughing at him. 'Go on,' he said. 'Clear off, and take your mischief somewhere else.'

That was Clodius before he changed: a moody boy – a moody, spoilt, charming boy. 'That fellow amuses me,' Cicero remarked after the young patrician had gone, 'but I can't say I really care for him. Still,' he added, 'I'll forgive any man a coarse remark who brings me such intriguing news.' From then on he was too preoccupied trying to work out all the implications of Pompey's homecoming and potential remarriage to resume dictating his poem. I was grateful to Clodius for that at least, and thought no more about his visit for the remainder of the day.

A few hours later, Terentia came into the library to say goodbye to her husband. She was leaving to celebrate the Good Goddess's nocturnal rites. She would not be back until the morning. Relations between her and Cicero were cool. Despite the elegance of her private apartments on the upper floor, she still hated the house, especially the late-night comings and goings of Clodia's louche salon next door, and the proximity of the noisy crowds in the forum who gaped up at her whenever she went on to the terrace with her maids. To try to placate her, Cicero was going out of his way to be friendly.

'And where is the Good Goddess to be worshipped tonight? If,' he added with a smile, 'a mere man can be entrusted with such sacred information?' (The ritual was always held in the house of a senior magistrate, whose wife was responsible for organising it; they took it in turns.)

'At Caesar's house.'

'Aurelia presiding?'

'Pompeia.'

'I wonder if Mucia will be there.'

'I expect so. Why shouldn't she be?'

'She might be too ashamed to show her face.'

'Why?'

'It seems Pompey is divorcing her.'

'No?' Despite herself, Terentia was unable to conceal her interest. 'Where did you hear that?'

'Clodius came round to tell me.'

Immediately her lips compressed into a firm line of disapproval. 'Then it probably isn't true. You really ought to keep better company.'

'I shall keep what company I like.'

'No doubt, but do you really have to inflict it on the rest of us? It's bad enough living so close to the sister, without having the brother under our roof as well.'

She turned without saying goodbye and stalked off across the marble floor. Cicero pulled a face at her narrow back. 'First the old house was too far away from everyone, now the new one is too close. You're lucky you're not married, Tiro.'

I was tempted to reply that I had been given little choice in the matter.

He had been invited weeks ago to dine that evening with Atticus. Quintus had also been asked, and so, curiously enough, had I: our host's plan was that the four of us should reassemble in exactly the same place and at exactly the same time as last year, and drink a toast in celebration of the fact that we, and Rome, had survived. Cicero and I turned up at his house as darkness fell. Quintus was already there. But although the food and the wine were good enough, and there was Pompey to gossip about, and the library was conducive to conversation, the occasion was not a success. Everyone seemed out of sorts. Cicero had been put into a bad mood by his encounter with Terentia and was perturbed at the thought of Pompey's return. Quintus, coming to the end of his term as praetor, was heavily in debt and apprehensive about what province he might draw in the forthcoming lottery. Even Atticus, whose Epicurean sensibilities were normally unruffled by the outside world, was preoccupied with something. As usual, I took my mood from theirs, and only spoke when asked a question. We drank to the glorious fourth of December, but for once not even Cicero could bring himself to reminisce. Suddenly it did not seem appropriate to celebrate the deaths of five men, however villainous. The past fell like a clammy shadow across us, chilling all conversation. Finally Atticus said, 'I'm thinking of going back to Epirus.'

For a moment or two nobody spoke.

'When?' asked Cicero quietly.

'Directly after Saturnalia.'

'You're not *thinking* of going,' said Quintus with a nasty edge to his voice, 'you've already made up your mind. You're *telling* us.'

Cicero said, 'Why do you want to go now?'

Atticus played around with the stem of his glass. 'I came back to Rome two years ago to help you win the election. I've stayed ever since to support you. But now things seem to have settled down, I don't think you need me any more.'

'I most certainly do,' insisted Cicero.

'Besides, I have business interests over there I have to attend to.'

'Ah,' said Quintus into his glass, '*business interests*. Now we get to the bottom of it.'

'What do you mean by that?' asked Atticus.

'Nothing.'

'No, please – say what's on your mind.'

'Leave it, Quintus,' warned Cicero.

'Only this,' said Quintus. 'That somehow Marcus and I seem to run all the dangers of public life, and shoulder all the hard work, while you are free to flit between your estates and attend to your *business interests* at will. You prosper through your connection with us, yet we seem permanently short of money. That's all.'

'But you enjoy the rewards of a public career. You have fame and power and will be remembered by history, whereas I am a nobody.'

'A nobody! A nobody who knows everybody!' Quintus took another drink. 'I don't suppose there's any chance of you taking your sister back with you to Epirus, is there?'

'Quintus!' cried Cicero.

'If your marriage is unhappy,' said Atticus mildly, 'then I am sorry for you. But that is hardly my fault.'

'And there we are again,' said Quintus. 'You've even managed to avoid marriage. I swear this fellow has the secret of life! Why don't you bear your share of domestic suffering like the rest of us?'

'That's enough,' said Cicero, getting to his feet. 'We should leave you, Atticus, before any more words are uttered that aren't really meant. Quintus?' He held out his hand to his brother, who scowled and looked away. 'Quintus!' he repeated angrily, and thrust out his hand again. Quintus turned reluctantly and glanced up at him, and just for an instant I saw such a flash of hatred in his eyes it made me catch my breath. But then he threw aside his napkin and stood. He swayed a little and almost fell back on to the table, but I grabbed his arm and he recovered his balance. He lurched out of the library and we followed him into the atrium.

Cicero had ordered a litter to take us home, but now he insisted that Quintus have it. 'You ride home, brother. We shall walk.' We helped him into the chair, and Cicero told the bearers to carry him to our old house on the Esquiline, next to the Temple of Tellus, into which Quintus had moved when Cicero moved out. Quintus was asleep even before the litter set off. As we watched him go, I reflected that it was no easy matter being the younger brother of a genius, and that all the choices in Quintus's life – his career, his home, even his wife – had been made in accordance with the demands of his brilliant, ambitious sibling, who could always talk him into anything.

'He means no harm,' said Cicero to Atticus. 'He's worried about the future, that's all. Once the senate has decided which provinces are to be put into this year's ballot and he knows where he's going, he'll be happier.'

'I'm sure you're right. But I fear he believes at least some of what he says. I hope he doesn't speak for you as well.'

'My dearest friend, I am perfectly aware that our relationship has cost you far more than you have ever profited from it. We have simply chosen to tread different paths, that's all. I have sought public office while you have yearned for honourable independence, and who's to say which of us is right? But in every quality that really matters I put you second to no man, myself included. There now – are we clear?'

'We are clear.'

'And you will come and see me before you leave, and write to me often afterwards?'

'I shall.'

With that Cicero kissed him on the cheek and the two friends parted, Atticus retreating into his beautiful house with its books and treasures, while the former consul trudged down the hill towards the forum with his guards. On this question of the good life and how to lead it – purely theoretical in my own case, of course – my sympathies were all with Atticus. It seemed to me at the time – and still does now, only even more so – an act of madness for a man to pursue power when he could be sitting in the sunshine and reading a book. But then, even if I had been born into freedom, I know I would not have possessed that overweening force of ambition without which no city is created, no city destroyed.

As chance would have it, our route home took us past the scenes of all Cicero's triumphs, and he fell very quiet as we walked, no doubt pondering his conversation with Atticus. We passed the locked and deserted senate house, where he had made such memorable speeches; the curving wall of the rostra, surmounted by its multitude of heroic statues, from which he had addressed the Roman people in their thousands; and finally the Temple of Castor, where he had presented his case to the extortion court in the long legal battle against Verres that had launched his career. The great public buildings and monuments, so quiet and massive in the darkness, nevertheless seemed to me that night as substantial as air. We heard voices in the distance, and occasional scuffling noises closer by, but it was only rats in the heaps of rubbish.

We left the forum, and ahead of us were the myriad lights of the Palatine, tracing the shape of the hill – the yellow flickering of the torches and braziers on the terraces, the dim pinpricks of the candles and lamps in the windows amid the trees. Suddenly Cicero halted. 'Isn't that our house?' he asked, pointing to a long cluster of lights. I followed his outstretched arm and replied that I thought it was. 'But that's very odd,' he said. 'Most of the rooms seem to be lit. It looks as though Terentia is home.'

We set off quickly up the hill. 'If Terentia has left the ceremony early,' said Cicero breathlessly over his shoulder, 'it won't be of her own volition. Something must have happened.' He almost ran along the street towards the house and hammered on the door. Inside, we found Terentia standing in the atrium surrounded by a cluster of maids and womenfolk, who seemed to twitter and scatter like birds at Cicero's approach. Once again she was wearing a cloak fastened tightly at the throat to conceal her sacred robes. 'Terentia?' he demanded, advancing towards her. 'What's wrong? Are you all right?'

'I am well enough,' she replied, her voice cold and trembling with rage. 'It is Rome that is sick!'

That so much harm could flow from so farcical an episode will doubtless strike future generations as absurd. In truth, it seemed absurd at the time: fits of public morality generally do. But human life is bizarre and unpredictable. Some joker cracks an egg, and from it hatches tragedy.

The basic facts were simple. Terentia recounted them to Cicero that night, and the story was never seriously challenged. She had arrived at Caesar's residence to be greeted by Pompeia's maid, Abra – a girl of notoriously easy virtue, as befitted the character of her mistress, and of her master too, for that matter, although he of course was not on the premises at the time. Abra showed Terentia into the main part of the house, where Pompeia, the hostess for the evening, and the Vestal Virgins were already waiting, along with Caesar's mother, Aurelia. Within the hour, most of the senior wives of Rome were congregated in this spot and the ritual began. What exactly they were doing, Terentia would not say, only that most of the house was in darkness when suddenly they were interrupted by screams. They ran to discover the source and immediately came across one of Aurelia's freedwomen having a fit of hysterics. Between sobs she cried out that there was an intruder in the house. She had approached what she thought was a female musician, only to discover that the girl was actually a man in disguise! It was at this point that Terentia realised that Pompeia had disappeared.

Aurelia at once took charge of the situation and ordered that all the holy things be covered and that the doors be locked and watched. Then she and some of the braver females, including Terentia, began a thorough search of the huge house. In due course, in Pompeia's bedroom, they found a veiled figure dressed in women's clothes, clutching a lyre and trying to hide behind a curtain. They chased him down the stairs and into the dining room, where he fell over a couch and his veil was snatched away. Nearly everyone recognised him. He had shaved off his small beard and had put on rouge, black eye make-up and lipstick, but that was hardly sufficent to disguise the well-known pretty-boy features of Publius Clodius Pulcher – 'Your friend Clodius,' as Terentia bitterly described him to Cicero.

Clodius, who was plainly drunk, realising he was discovered, then jumped on to the dining table, pulled up his gown, exposing himself to all the assembled company, including the Vestal Virgins, and finally, while his audience was shrieking and swooning, ran out of the room and managed to escape from the house via a kitchen window. Only now did Pompeia appear, with Abra, whereupon Aurelia accused her daughter-in-law and her maid of collusion in this sacrilege. Both denied it tearfully, but the senior Vestal Virgin announced that their protests did not matter: a desecration had occurred, the sacred rites would have to be abandoned, and the devotees must all disperse to their homes at once.

Such was Terentia's story, and Cicero listened to it with a mixture of incredulity, disgust and painfully suppressed amusement. Obviously he would have to take a stern moral line in public and in front of Terentia – it *was* shocking, he agreed with her absolutely – but secretly he also thought it one of the funniest things he had ever heard. In particular, the image of Clodius waving his private parts in the horrified faces of Rome's stuffiest matrons made him laugh until his eyes watered. But that was for the seclusion of his library. As far as the politics were concerned, he thought Clodius had finally shown himself to be an irredeemable idiot – 'he's thirty, in the name of heaven, not thirteen' – and that his career as a magistrate was finished before it had even started. He also suspected, gleefully, that Caesar might be in trouble as well: the scandal had happened in his house, it had involved his wife; it would not look good.

This was the spirit in which Cicero went down to the senate the following morning, one year to the day after the debate on the fate of the conspirators. Many of the senior members had heard from their wives what had happened, and as they stood around in the senaculum waiting for the auspices to be taken, there was only one topic of discussion, or at least there was by the time Cicero had finished his rounds. The Father of the Nation moved solemnly from group to group, wearing an expression of piety and grave seriousness, his arms folded inside his toga, shaking his head and reluctantly spreading the news of the outrage to those who had not already heard it. 'Oh look,' he would say in conclusion, with a glance across the senaculum, 'there's poor Caesar now – this must be a terrible embarrassment for him.'

And Caesar did indeed look grey and grim, the young chief priest, standing alone on that bleak day in December, at the absolute nadir of his fortunes. His praetorship, now drawing to its close, had not been a success: at one point he was actually suspended, and had been lucky not to be hauled into court along with Catilina's other supporters. He was anxiously waiting to hear which province he would be allotted: it would need to be lucrative, as he was greatly in debt to the moneylenders. And now this ludicrous affair involving Clodius and Pompeia threatened to turn him into a figure of ridicule. It was almost possible to feel sorry for him as he watched, with hawkish eyes, Cicero going around the senaculum, relaying the gossip. Rome's cuckolder-in-chief: a cuckold! A lesser man would have stayed away from the senate for the day, but that was never Caesar's style. When the auspices had been read, he walked into the chamber and sat on the praetors' bench, two places along from Quintus, while Cicero went over to join the other ex-consuls on the opposite side of the aisle.

The session had barely begun when the former praetor Cornificius, who regarded himself as a custodian of religious probity, jumped up on a point of order to demand an emergency debate on the 'shameful and immoral' events that were said to have occurred overnight at the official residence of the chief priest. Looking back, this could have been the end for Clodius right then and there. He was not yet even eligible to take his seat in the senate. But fortunately for him, the consul presiding in December was none other than his stepfather-in-law, Murena, and whatever his private feelings on the subject, he had no intention of adding to the family's embarrassment if he could avoid it.

'This is not a matter for the senate,' ruled Murena. 'If anything has happened, it is the responsibility of the religious authorities to investigate.'

This brought Cato to his feet, his eyes ablaze with excitement at the thought of such decadence. 'Then I propose that this house asks the College of Priests to conduct an inquiry,' he said, 'and report back to us as soon as possible.'

Murena had little choice except to put the motion to the vote, and it passed without discussion. Earlier, Cicero had told me he was not going to intervene ('I'll let Cato and the others make hay if they want to; I'm going to keep out of it; it's more dignified'). However, when it came to the point, he could not resist the opportunity. Rising gravely to his feet, he looked directly at Caesar. 'As the alleged outrage occurred under the chief priest's own roof, perhaps he could save us all the trouble of waiting for the outcome of an inquiry and tell us now whether or not an offence was committed.'

Caesar's face was so clenched that even from my old position by the door – to which I had been obliged to return now that Cicero was no longer consul – I could see the muscle twitching in his jaw as he got up to reply. 'The rites of the Good Goddess are not a matter for the chief priest, as he is not even allowed to be present at the time they are celebrated.' He sat down.

Cicero put on a puzzled expression and rose again. 'But surely the chief priest's own wife was presiding over the ceremony? He must have at least some knowledge of what occurred.' He lapsed back into his seat.

Caesar hesitated for a fraction, then got up and said calmly, 'That woman is no longer my wife.'

An excited whisper went around the chamber. Cicero got up again. Now he sounded genuinely puzzled. 'So we may take it, therefore, that an outrage *did* occur.'

'Not necessarily,' replied Caesar, and once again sat down.

Cicero stood. 'But if an outrage did not occur, then why is the chief priest divorcing his wife?'

'Because the wife of the chief priest must be above suspicion.' There was a good deal of amusement at the coolness of this reply. Cicero did not rise again, but signalled to Murena that he no longer wished to pursue the matter. Afterwards, as we were walking home, he said to me, not without a hint of admiration, 'That was the most ruthless thing I ever saw in the senate. How long would you say Caesar and Pompeia have been married?'

'It must be six or seven years.'

'And yet I'm certain he only made up his mind to divorce her when I asked him that question. He realised it was the best way to get himself out of a tight corner. You have to hand it to him – most men wouldn't abandon their dog so casually.'

I thought sadly of the beautiful Pompeia and wondered if she was aware yet that her husband had just publicly ended their marriage. Knowing how swiftly Caesar liked to act, I suspected she would be out of his house by nightfall.

When we got home, Cicero went at once to his library to avoid running into Terentia, and lay down on a couch. 'I need to hear some pure Greek to wash away the dirt of politics,' he said. Sositheus, who normally read to him, was ill, so he asked if I would do the honours, and at his request I fetched a copy of Euripides from its compartment, and unrolled it beside the lamp. It was *The Suppliant Women* he asked to hear, I suppose because on that day the execution of the conspirators was uppermost in his mind, and he hoped that at least in yielding up the bodies of his enemies for an honourable burial he had played the part of Theseus. I had just got to his favourite lines – *Rashness in a leader causes failure; the sailor of a ship is calm, wise at the proper time. Yes, and forethought: this too is bravery* – when a slave came in and said that Clodius was in the atrium.

Cicero swore. 'Go and tell him to get out of my house. I can't be seen to have anything more to do with him.'

This was not a job I relished, but I laid aside Euripides and went out into the atrium. I had expected to find Clodius in a state of some distress. Instead he wore a rueful smile. 'Good day, Tiro. I thought I had better come and see my teacher straight away and get my punishment over and done with.'

'I'm afraid my master is not in.'

Clodius's smile faltered a little, because of course he guessed that I was lying. 'But I have worked the whole thing up for him into the most wonderful story. He simply has to hear it. No, this is ridiculous. I won't be sent away.'

He pushed past me and walked across the wide hall and into the library. I followed, wringing my hands. But to his surprise and mine the room was empty. There was a small door in the opposite corner for the slaves to come and go, and even as we looked, it closed gently. The Euripides lay where I had left it. 'Well,' said Clodius, sounding suddenly uneasy, 'make sure you tell him I called.'

'I certainly shall,' I replied.

XXXI

Around this time, exactly as Clodius had predicted, Pompey the Great returned to Italy, making land at Brundisium. The senate's messengers raced in relays nearly three hundred miles to Rome to bring the news. According to their dispatches, twenty thousand of Pompey's legionaries had disembarked with him, and the following day he addressed them in the town's forum. 'Men,' he was reported to have said, 'I thank you for your service. We have put an end to Mithradates, the republic's greatest enemy since Hannibal, and performed heroic deeds together that the world will remember for a thousand years. It is a bitter day that sees us part. But ours is a nation of laws, and I have no authority from the senate and people to maintain an army in Italy. Disperse to your native cities. Go back to your homes. I promise you your services will not go unrewarded. There will be money and land for all of you. You have my word. And in the meantime, stand ready for my summons to join me in Rome, where you will receive your bounty and we shall celebrate the greatest triumph the mother-city of our newly enlarged empire has ever seen!'

With that, he set off on the road to Rome, accompanied by only his official escort of lictors and a few close friends. As news of his humble entourage spread, it had the most amazing effect. People had feared he would move north with his army, leaving a swathe of countryside behind them stripped bare as if by locusts. Instead, the Warden of Land and Sea merely ambled along in a leisurely fashion, stopping to rest in country inns, as if he were nothing more grand than a sightseer returning from a foreign holiday. In every town along the route – in Tarentum and in Venusia, across the mountains and down on to the plains of Campania, in Capua and in Minturnae – the crowds turned out to cheer him. Hundreds decided to leave their homes and follow him, and soon the senate was receiving reports that as many as five thousand citizens were on the march with him to Rome.

Cicero read of all this with increasing alarm. His long letter to Pompey was still unacknowledged, and even he was beginning to perceive that his boasting about his consulship might have done him harm. Worse, he now learned from several sources that Pompey had formed a bad impression of Hybrida, having travelled through Macedonia on his journey back to Italy, witnessing at first hand his corruption and incompetence, and that when he reached Rome he would press for the governor's immediate recall. Such a move would threaten Cicero with financial ruin, not least because he had yet to receive a single sesterce from Hybrida. He called me to his library and dictated a long letter to his former colleague: *I shall try to protect your back with all my might, provided I do not seem to be throwing my trouble away. But if I find that it gets me no thanks, I shall not let myself be taken for an idiot – even by you.* A few days after Saturnalia there was a farewell dinner for Atticus, at the end of which Cicero gave him the letter and asked him to deliver it to Hybrida personally. Atticus swore to discharge this duty the moment he reached Macedonia, and then, amid many tears and embraces, the two best friends said their farewells. It was a source of deep sadness to both men that Quintus had not bothered to come and see him off.

With Atticus gone from the city, worries seemed to press in on Cicero from every side. He was deeply concerned, and I even more so, by the worsening health of his junior secretary, Sositheus. I had trained this lad myself, in Latin grammar, Greek and shorthand, and he had become a much-loved member of the household. He had a melodious voice, which was why Cicero came to rely on him as a reader. He was twenty-six or thereabouts, and slept in a small room next to mine in the cellar. What started as a hacking cough developed into a fever, and Cicero sent his own doctor down to examine him. A course of bleeding did no good; nor did leeches. Cicero was very much affected, and most days he would sit for a while beside the young man's cot, holding a cold wet towel to his burning forehead. I stayed up with Sositheus every night for a week, listening to his rambling nonsense talk and trying to calm him down and persuade him to drink some water.

It is often the case with these dreadful fevers that the final crisis is preceded by a lull. So it was with Sositheus. I remember it very well. It was long past midnight. I was stretched out on a straw mattress beside his cot, huddled against the cold under a blanket and a sheepskin. He had gone very quiet, and in the silence and the dim yellow light cast by the lamp, I nodded off myself. But something woke me, and when I turned, I saw that he was sitting up and staring at me with a look of great terror.

'The letters,' he said.

It was so typical of him to be worried about his work, I nearly wept. 'The letters are taken care of,' I replied. 'Everything is up to date. Go back to sleep now.'

'I copied out the letters.'

'Yes, yes, you copied out the letters. Now go to sleep.' I tried gently to press him back down, but he wriggled beneath my hands. He was nothing but sweat and bone by this time, as feeble as a sparrow. Yet he would not lie still. He was desperate to tell me something.

'Crassus knows it.'

'Of course Crassus knows it.' I spoke soothingly. But then I felt a sudden sense of dread. 'Crassus knows what?'

'The letters.'

'What letters?' Sositheus made no reply. 'You mean the anonymous letters? The ones warning of violence in Rome? *You* copied those out?' He nodded. 'How does Crassus know?' I whispered.

'I told him.' His fragile claw of a hand scrabbled at my arm. 'Don't be angry.'

'I'm not angry,' I said, wiping the sweat from his forehead. 'He must have frightened you.'

'He said he knew already.'

'You mean he tricked you?'

'I'm so sorry ...' He stopped, and gave an immense groan – a terrible noise, for one so frail – and his whole body trembled. His eyelids drooped, then opened wide for one last time, and he gave me such a look as I have never forgotten – there was a whole abyss in those staring eyes – and then he fell back in my arms unconscious. I was horrified by what I saw, I suppose because it was like gazing into the blackest mirror – nothing to see but oblivion – and I realised at that instant that I too would die like Sositheus, childless and leaving behind no trace of my existence. From then on I redoubled my resolve to write down all the history I was witnessing, so that my life might at least have this small purpose.

Sositheus lingered on all through that night, and into the next day, and on the last evening of the year he died. I went at once to tell Cicero.

'The poor boy,' he sighed. 'His death grieves me more than perhaps the loss of a slave should. See to it that his funeral shows the world how much I valued him.' He turned back to his book, then noticed that I was still in the room. 'Well?'

I was in a dilemma. I felt instinctively that Sositheus had imparted a great secret to me, but I could not be absolutely sure if it was true, or merely the ravings of a fevered man. I was also torn between my responsibility to the dead and my duty to the living – to respect my friend's confession, or to warn Cicero? In the end, I chose the latter. 'There's something you should know,' I said. I took out my tablet and read to him Sositheus's dying words, which I had taken the precaution of writing down.

Cicero studied me as I spoke, his chin in his hand, and when I finished, he said, 'I knew I should have asked you to do that copying.'

I had not quite been able to bring myself to believe it until that moment. I struggled to hide my shock. 'And why didn't you?'

He gave me another appraising look. 'Your feelings are bruised?'

'A little.'

'Well, they shouldn't be. It's a compliment to your honesty. You sometimes have too many scruples for the dirty business of politics, Tiro, and I would have found it hard to carry off such a deception under your disapproving gaze. So I had you fooled, then, did I?' He sounded quite proud of himself.

'Yes,' I replied, 'completely,' and he had: when I remembered his apparent surprise on the night Crassus brought the letters round with Scipio and Marcellus, I was forced to marvel at his skills as an actor, if nothing else.

'Well, I regret I had to trick you. However, it seems I didn't trick Old Baldhead – or at least he isn't tricked any longer.' He sighed again. 'Poor Sositheus. Actually, I'm fairly sure I know when Crassus extracted the truth from him. It must have been on the day I sent him over to collect the title deeds to this place.'

'You should have sent me!'

'I would have done but you were out and there was no one else I trusted. How terrified he must have been when that old fox trapped him into confessing! If only he had told me what he'd done – I could have set his mind at rest.'

'But aren't you worried what Crassus might do?'

'Why should I be worried? He got what he wanted, all except the command of an army to destroy Catilina – that he should even have *thought* of asking for that amazed me! But as for the rest – those letters Sositheus wrote at my dictation and left on his doorstep were a gift from the gods as far as he was concerned. He cut himself free of the conspiracy and left me to clear up the mess and stop Pompey from intervening. In fact I should say Crassus derived far more benefit from the whole affair than I did. The only ones who suffered were the guilty.'

'But what if he makes it public?'

'If he does, I'll deny it – he has no proof. But he won't. The last thing he wants is to open up that whole stinking pit of bones.' He picked up his book again. 'Go and put a coin in the mouth of our dear dead friend, and let us hope he finds more honesty on that side of the eternal river than exists on this.'

I did as he commanded, and the following day Sositheus's body was burnt on the Esquiline Field. Most of the household turned out to pay their respects, and I spent Cicero's money very freely on flowers and flautists and incense. All in all it was as well done as these occasions ever can be: you would have thought we were bidding farewell to a freedman, or even a citizen. Thinking over what I had learned, I did not presume to judge Cicero for the morality of his action, nor did I feel much wounded pride that he had been unwilling to trust me. But I did fear that Crassus would try to seek revenge, and as the thick black smoke rose from the pyre to merge with the low clouds rolling in from the east, I felt full of apprehension.

Pompey approached the city on the Ides of January. The day before he was due, Cicero received an invitation to attend upon the imperator at the Villa Publica, which was then the government's official guest house. It was respectfully phrased. He could think of no reason not to accept. To have refused would have been seen as a snub. 'Nevertheless,' he confided to me as his valet dressed him the next morning, 'I cannot help feeling like a subject being summoned out to greet a conqueror, rather than a partner in the affairs of state arranging to meet another on equal terms.'

By the time we reached the Field of Mars, thousands of citizens were already straining for a glimpse of their hero, who was now rumoured to be only a mile or two away. I could see that Cicero was slightly put out by the fact that for once the crowds all had their backs to him and paid him no attention, and when we went into the Villa Publica his dignity received another blow. He had assumed he was going to meet Pompey privately, but instead he discovered several other senators with their attendants already waiting, including the new consuls, Pupius Piso and Valerius Messalla. The room was gloomy and cold, in that way of official buildings that are little used, and yet although it smelled strongly of damp, no one had troubled to light a fire. Here Cicero was obliged to settle down to wait on a hard gilt chair, making stiff conversation with Pupius, a taciturn lieutenant of Pompey's whom he had known for many years and did not like.

After about an hour, the noise of the crowd began to grow and I realised that Pompey must have come into view. Soon the racket was so intimidating the senators gave up trying to talk and sat mute, like strangers thrown together by chance while seeking shelter from a thunderstorm. People ran to and fro outside, and cried and cheered. A trumpet sounded. Eventually we heard the clump of boots filling the antechamber next door, and a man said, 'Well, you can't say the people of Rome don't love you, Imperator!' And then Pompey's booming voice could be heard clearly in reply: 'Yes, that went well enough. That certainly went well enough.'

Cicero rose along with the other senators, and a moment later into the room strode the great general, in full uniform of scarlet cloak and glittering bronze breastplate on which was carved a sun spreading its rays. He handed his plumed helmet to an aide as his officers and lictors poured in behind him. His hair was as improbably thick as ever and he ran his meaty fingers through it, pushing it back in the familiar cresting wave that peaked above his broad, sunburnt face. He had changed little in six years except to have become – if such a thing were possible – even more physically imposing. His torso was immense. He shook hands with the consuls and the other senators, and exchanged a few words with each, while Cicero looked on awkwardly. Finally he moved on to my master. 'Marcus Tullius!' he exclaimed. Taking a step backwards, he appraised Cicero carefully, gesturing in mock-wonder first at his polished red shoes and then up the crisp lines of his purple-bordered toga to his neatly trimmed hair. 'You look very well. Come then,' he said, beckoning him closer, 'let me embrace the man but for whom I would have no country left to return to!' He flung his arms around Cicero, crushing him to his breastplate in a hug, and winked at us over his shoulder. 'I know that must be true, because it's what he keeps on telling me!' Everyone laughed, and Cicero tried to join in. But Pompey's clasp had squeezed all the air out of him, and he could only manage a mirthless wheeze. 'Well, gentlemen,' continued Pompey, beaming around the room, 'shall we sit?'

A large chair was carried in for the imperator and he settled himself into it. An ivory pointer was placed in his hand. A carpet was unrolled at his feet into which was woven a map of the East, and as the senators gazed down, he began gesturing at it to illustrate his achievements. I made some notes as he talked, and afterwards Cicero spent a long while studying them with an expression of disbelief. In the course of his campaign, Pompey claimed to have captured one thousand fortifications, nine hundred cities, and fourteen entire countries, including Syria, Palestine, Arabia, Mesopotamia and Judaea. The pointer flourished again. He had established no fewer than thirty-nine new cities, only three of which he had allowed to name themselves Pompeiopolis. He had levied a property tax on the East that would increase the annual revenues of Rome by two thirds. From his personal funds he proposed to make an immediate donation to the treasury of two hundred million sesterces. 'I have doubled the size of our empire, gentlemen. Rome's frontier now stands on the Red Sea.'

Even as I was writing this down, I was struck by the singular tone in which Pompey gave his account. He spoke throughout of 'my' this and 'my' that. But were all these states and cities, and these vast amounts of money, really his, or were they Rome's?

'I shall require a retrospective bill to legalise all this, of course,' he concluded.

There was a pause. Cicero, who had just about recovered his breath, raised an eyebrow. 'Really? Just *one* bill?'

'One bill,' affirmed Pompey, handing his ivory stick to an attendant, 'which need be of just one sentence: "The senate and people of Rome hereby approve all decisions made by Pompey the Great in his settlement of the East." Naturally, you can add some lines of congratulation if you wish, but that will be the essence of it.'

Cicero glanced at the other senators. None met his gaze. They were happy to let him do the talking. 'And is there anything else you desire?'

'The consulship.'

'When?'

'Next year. A decade after my first. Perfectly legal.'

'But to stand for election you will need to enter the city, which will mean surrendering your imperium. And surely you intend to triumph?'

'Of course. I shall triumph on my birthday, in September.'

'But then how can this be done?'

'Simple. Another bill. One sentence again: "The senate and people of Rome hereby permit Pompey the Great to seek election to the office of consul *in absentia*." I hardly need to canvass for the post, I think. People know who I am!' He smiled and looked around him.

'And your army?'

'Disbanded and dispersed. They will need rewarding, of course. I've given them my word.'

The consul Messalla spoke up. 'We received reports that you promised them land.'

'That's right.' Even Pompey could detect the hostility in the silence that followed. 'Listen, gentlemen,' he said, leaning forward in his throne-like chair, 'let's talk frankly. You know I could have marched with my legionaries to the gates of Rome and demanded whatever I wanted. But it's my intention to serve the senate, not to dictate to it, and I've just travelled up through Italy in the most humble manner to demonstrate exactly that. And I want to go on demonstrating it. You have all heard that I've divorced?' The senators nodded. 'Then how would it be if I made a marriage that tied me to the senatorial party for ever?'

'I think I speak for us all,' said Cicero cautiously, checking with the others, 'when I say that the senate desires nothing more than to work with you, and that a marriage alliance would be of the greatest help. Do you have a candidate in mind?'

'I do, as a matter of fact. I'm told Cato is a force in the senate these days, and Cato has nieces and daughters of marriageable age. My plan is that I should take one of these girls as my wife and my eldest son should take another. There.' He sat back contentedly. 'How does that strike you?'

'It strikes us very well,' responded Cicero, again after a quick glance around his colleagues. 'An alliance between the houses of Cato and Pompey will secure peace for a generation. The populists will all be prostrated with shock and the good men will all rejoice.' He smiled. 'I congratulate you on a brilliant stroke, Imperator. What does Cato say?'

'Oh, he doesn't know of it yet.'

Cicero's smile became fixed. 'You have divorced Mucia and severed your connections with the Metelli in order to marry a connection of Cato – but you have not yet enquired what Cato's reaction might be?'

'I suppose you could put it that way. Why? Do you think there'll be a problem?'

'With most men I would say no, but with Cato – well, one can never be sure where the undeviating arrow flight of his logic may lead him. Have you told many other people of your intentions?'

'A few.'

'In that case, might I suggest, Imperator, that we suspend our discussions for the time being, while you send an emissary to Cato as quickly as possible?'

A dark cloud had passed over Pompey's hitherto sunny expression – it had obviously never entered his mind that Cato might refuse him: if he did, it would mean a terrible loss of face – and in a distracted tone he agreed to Cicero's suggestion. By the time we left, he was already holding an urgent consultation with Lucius Afranius, his closest confidant. Outside, the crowds were as dense as ever, and even though Pompey's guards opened the gates only just wide enough to let us depart, they very nearly found themselves overwhelmed by the numbers pressing to get in. People shouted out to Cicero and the consuls as they struggled back towards the city: 'Have you spoken to him?' 'What does he say?' 'Is it true he has become a god?'

'He was not a god the last time I looked,' replied Cicero cheerfully, 'although he is not far off it! He is looking forward to rejoining us in the senate. What a farce,' he added to me, out of the corner of his mouth. 'Plautus could not have come up with a more absurd scenario.'

It did indeed turn out exactly as Cicero had feared. Pompey sent that very day for Cato's friend Munatius, who conveyed the great man's offer of a double marriage to Cato's house, where as it happened his family were all gathered for a feast. The womenfolk were overjoyed at the prospect, such was the status of Pompey as Rome's greatest war hero, and the renown of his magnificent physique. But Cato flew into an immediate rage, and without pausing for thought or consulting anyone made the following reply: 'Go, Munatius: go and tell Pompey that Cato is not to be captured by way of women's apartments. He greatly prizes Pompey's goodwill, and if Pompey behaves properly will grant him a friendship more to be relied upon than any marriage connection. But he will not give hostages for the glory of Pompey to the detriment of his country!'

Pompey, by all accounts, was stunned by the rudeness of the reply ('if Pompey behaves properly'!) and quit the Villa Publica at once in a very ill humour to go to his house in the Alban Hills. But even here he was pursued by tormenting demons determined to puncture his dignity. His daughter, then aged nine, whom he had not seen since she could barely speak, had been coached by her tutor, the famous grammarian Aristodemus of Nyssa, to greet her father with some passages from Homer. Unfortunately, the first line she spoke as he came through the door was that of Helen to Paris: 'You came back from the war; I wish you had died there.' Too many people witnessed the episode for it not to become public, and I am afraid that Cicero found it so funny he too played his part in spreading the story across Rome.

In the midst of all this tumult it was possible to believe that the affair of the Good Goddess might be forgotten. More than a month had now passed since the outrage, and Clodius had been careful to keep out of public view. People had started to talk of other things. But a day or two after the return of Pompey, the College of Priests finally handed its judgement on the incident to the senate. Pupius, who was the leading consul, was a friend of Clodius, and keen to hush up the scandal. Nevertheless, he was obliged to read out the priests' report, and their verdict was unambiguous. Clodius's action was a clear case of *nefas* – an impious deed, a sin, a crime against the goddess, an abomination.

The first senator on his feet was Lucullus, and what a sweet moment this must have been for him as, with great solemnity, he declared that his former brother-in-law had besmirched the traditions of the republic and had risked bringing the wrath of the gods down upon the city. 'Their anger can only be appeased,' he said, 'by the sternest punishment of the offender,' and he formally proposed that Clodius be charged with violating the sanctity of the Vestal Virgins – an offence for which the penalty was to be beaten to death. Cato seconded the motion. The two patrician leaders, Hortensius and Catulus, both rose in support, and it was clear that the mood of the house was strongly with them. They demanded that the most powerful magistrate in Rome after the consuls, the urban praetor, should convene a special court, appoint a hand-picked jury drawn from the senate, and try the case as speedily as possible. With such men in control, the result would be pre-ordained. Pupius agreed reluctantly to draw up a bill to this effect and by the time the session was over, Clodius looked to be a dead man.

Late that night, when I heard someone knock on the front door, I was sure in my bones that it must be Clodius. Despite Cicero's snub on the day after the Good Goddess fiasco, the young man had continued to make regular return visits to the house in the hope of a meeting. But I was under strict instructions to refuse him admittance: much to his irritation, he had never got further than the atrium. Now, as I crossed the hall, I braced myself for another unpleasant scene. But to my astonishment, when I unlocked the door, the person I found standing on the step was Clodia. Normally she voyaged around the city amid a flotilla of maids, but on this night she was unescorted. She asked in a very cool voice if my master was in, and I replied that I would check. I showed her into the hall and invited her to wait and then almost ran into the library, where Cicero was working. When I announced who had come to see him, he laid down his pen and thought for a moment or two.

'Has Terentia gone up to her room?'

'I believe so.'

'Then show her in.' I was amazed that he should take such a risk, and he must have realised the dangers himself, for just as I was leaving, he said, 'Make sure you don't leave us alone together.'

I went and fetched her. The moment she entered the library she crossed to where Cicero was standing and quickly knelt at his feet. 'I have come to plead for your support,' she said, bowing her head. 'My poor boy is beside himself with fear and remorse, yet he is too proud to try to ask you for help again, so I am here alone.' She took the hem of his toga in her hands and kissed it. 'My dear friend, it takes a great deal for a Claudian to kneel, but I am begging for your help.'

'Get up off the floor, Clodia,' replied Cicero, glancing anxiously at the door. 'Someone may see you, and the story will be all over Rome.' When she did not respond, he added, more gently, 'I won't even talk to you unless you *get on your feet*!' Clodia rose, her head still bowed. 'Now listen to me,' said Cicero. 'I'll say this once and then you must leave. You want me to help your brother, yes?' Clodia nodded. 'Then tell him he must do precisely what I say. He must write letters to every one of those women whose honour he has outraged. He must tell them he is sorry, it was a fit of madness, he is no longer worthy to breathe the same air as them and their daughters, and so on and so forth – believe me, he cannot be too obsequious. Then he must renounce his quaestorship. Leave Rome. Go into exile. Stay away from the city for a few years. When things calm down, he can come back and start again. It's the best advice I can offer. Goodbye.'

He began to turn away from her, but she grabbed his arm.

'Leaving Rome will kill him!'

'No, madam, staying in Rome will kill him. There is bound to be a trial and he is bound to be found guilty. Lucullus will see to that. But Lucullus is old and lazy, and your brother is young and energetic. Time is his greatest ally. Tell him I said that, and that I wish him well, and tell him to go tomorrow.'

'If he stays in Rome, will you join in the attacks on him?'

'I will do my best to keep out of it.'

'And if it comes to a trial,' she said, still holding his arm, 'will you defend him?'

'No, that is completely impossible.'

'Why?'

'Why?' Cicero gave an incredulous laugh. 'Any one of a thousand reasons.'

'Is it because you believe he is guilty?'

'My dear Clodia, the whole world *knows* he is guilty!'

'But you defended Cornelius Sulla, and the whole world knew he was guilty, too.'

'But this is different.'

'Why?'

'My wife, for one thing,' said Cicero softly, with another glance at the door. 'My wife was present. She witnessed the entire episode.'

'You are saying your wife would divorce you if you defended my brother?'

'Yes, I believe she would.'

'Then take another wife,' said Clodia, and stepping back but still staring at him she quickly untied her cloak and let it fall from her shoulders. Beneath it she was naked. The dark smoothness of her oiled skin glistened in the candlelight. I was standing almost directly behind her. She knew I was watching, yet she no more minded my presence than if I had been a table or a footstool. The air seemed to thicken. Cicero stood perfectly still. Thinking back on it, I am reminded of that moment in the senate, in the chaos after the debate on the conspirators, when a single word or gesture of assent from him would have led to Caesar's death, and the world – our world – would have been entirely different. So it was now. After a long pause he gave the very slightest shake of his head, and, stooping, he retrieved her cloak and held it out to her.

'Put it back on,' he said quietly.

She ignored it. Instead she put her hands on her hips. 'You really prefer that pious old broomstick to me?'

'Yes.' He sounded surprised by his own answer. 'When it comes to it, I believe I do.'

'Then what a fool you are,' she said, and turned around so that Cicero could drape the cloak across her shoulders. The gesture was as casual as if she were going home after a dinner party. She caught me looking at her and her eyes flashed me such a look that I quickly dropped my gaze. 'You will think back on this moment,' she said, briskly fastening her cloak, 'and regret it for the rest of your life.'

'No I won't, because I shall put it out of my mind, and I suggest you do the same.'

'Why should I want to forget it?' She smiled and shook her head. 'How my brother will laugh when he hears about it.'

'You'll tell him?'

'Of course. It was his idea.'

'Not a word,' said Cicero after Clodia had gone. He held up a warning hand. He did not want to discuss it, and we never did. Rumours that something had occurred between them circulated for many years, but I always refused to comment on the gossip. I have kept this secret for half a century.

Ambition and lust are often intertwined. In some men, such as Caesar and Clodius, they are as tightly plaited as a rope. With Cicero it was the opposite case. I believe he had a passionate nature, but it frightened him. Like his stutter or his youthful illnesses or his unsteady nerves, he viewed passion as a handicap, to be overcome by discipline. He therefore learned to separate this strand in his nature, and to avoid it. But the gods are implacable, and despite his resolution not to have anything to do with Clodia and her brother, he soon found himself being sucked into the quickening whirlpool of the scandal.

It is hard to comprehend at this great distance how completely the Good Goddess affair gripped public life in Rome, so that eventually all government business came to a halt. On the surface, Clodius's cause seemed hopeless. Plainly he had committed this ludicrous offence, and almost the whole of the senate was set on his punishment. But sometimes in politics a great weakness can be turned into a strength, and from the moment that Lucullus's motion was passed, the Roman people began to mutter against it. What was the young man guilty of, after all, except an excess of high spirits? Was a fellow to be beaten to death merely because of a lark? When Clodius ventured into the forum, he found that citizens, rather than wanting to pelt him with ordure, actually wished to shake his hand.

There were still thousands of plebeians in Rome who were disaffected with the renewed authority of the senate and who looked back with nostalgia to the days when Catilina ruled the streets. Clodius attracted these people by the score. They would gather around him in crowds. He took to jumping up on to a nearby cart or trader's stall and inveighing against the senate. He had learned well from Cicero the tricks of political campaigning: keep your speeches short, remember names, tell jokes, put on a show; above all, render an issue, however complex, into a story anyone can grasp. Clodius's tale was the simplest possible: he was the lone citizen unjustly persecuted by the oligarchs. 'Take care, my friends!' he would cry. 'If it can happen to me, a patrician, it could happen to any one of you!' Soon he was holding daily public meetings at which order was kept by his friends from the taverns and the gambling dens, many of whom had been supporters of Catilina.

Clodius attacked Lucullus, Hortensius and Catulus repeatedly by name, but when it came to Cicero he confined himself merely to repeating the old joke that the former consul had kept himself 'fully informed'. Cicero was often tempted to respond, and Terentia urged him to do so, yet he was mindful of his promise to Clodia and managed to keep his temper in check. However, the controversy kept on swelling regardless of his silence. I was with him on the day the senate's bill to set up the special court was laid before the people in a popular assembly. Clodius's gangs of toughs took control of the meeting, occupying the gangways and seizing the ballot boxes. Their clamour so unnerved the consul, Pupius, that he actually spoke against his own bill – in particular the clause that allowed the urban praetor to select the jury. Many senators turned to Cicero, expecting him to take control of the situation, but he remained on his bench, glowering with anger and embarrassment, and it was left to Cato to deliver a lashing attack on the consul. The meeting was abandoned. The senators promptly trooped back to their chamber and voted by 400 votes to 15 to press on with the bill despite the dangers of civil unrest. Fufius, a tribune who was sympathetic to Clodius, promptly announced that he would veto the legislation. The affair was now seriously out of hand, and Cicero hurried out of the chamber and up to his house, crimson in the face.

The turning point came when Fufius decided to convene a public assembly outside the city walls so that Pompey could be summoned and asked his views on the affair. Grumbling mightily at this intrusion on his time and dignity, the Warden of Land and Sea had no choice but to lumber over from the Alban Hills to the Flaminian Circus and submit himself to a series of insolent questions from the tribune, watched by a huge market-day crowd that temporarily set aside their bargaining and clustered round to gawp at him.

'Are you aware of the so-called outrage committed against the Good Goddess?' asked Fufius.

'I am.'

'Do you support the senate's proposal that Clodius be prosecuted?'

'I do.'

'Do you believe he should be tried by a jury of senators selected by the urban praetor?'

'I do.'

'Even though the urban praetor will also be his judge?'

'I suppose so, if that is the procedure the senate has settled on.'

'And where is the justice in that?'

Pompey glared at Fufius as if he were some buzzing insect that would not leave him alone. 'I hold the senate's authority in the highest respect,' he declared, and proceeded to deliver a lecture on the Roman constitution that might have been written for him by a fourteen-year-old. I was standing with Cicero at the front of the huge throng and could sense the audience behind us losing interest as he droned on. Soon they started shuffling about and talking. The vendors of hot sausages and pastries on the edge of the crowd began doing a busy trade. Pompey was a boring speaker at the best of times, but standing on that platform he must have felt as if he were in a bad dream. All those visions of a triumphant homecoming he had entertained as he lay at night in his tent beneath the burning stars of Arabia – and in the end what had he returned to? A senate and people obsessed not with his achievements but with a young man dressed in women's clothes!

When the public assembly was mercifully over, Cicero conducted Pompey across the Flaminian Circus to the Temple of Bellona, where the senate had convened specially to greet him. The ovation he received was respectful, and he sat down next to Cicero on the front bench and waited for the praise to begin. Instead, he found himself once again cross-examined from the chair about his views on the sacrilege issue. He repeated what he had just said outside, and when he resumed his place I saw him turn and mutter something irritably to Cicero. (His actual words, Cicero told me afterwards, were, 'I hope we can now talk about something else.') I had been keeping an eye throughout all this on Crassus, who was sitting on the edge of his bench, ready to jump up the moment he got a chance. There was something about his determination to speak, and a kind of happy craftiness in his expression, for which I did not much care.

'How wonderful it is, gentlemen,' he said, when at last he was called, 'to have with us beneath this sacred roof the man who has expanded our empire, and sitting next to him the man who has saved our republic. May the gods be blessed who have brought this to pass. Pompey I know stood ready with his army to come to the aid of the fatherland if it was necessary – but praise the heavens he was spared the task by the wisdom and foresight of our consul at that time. I hope I take nothing away from Pompey when I say that it is to Cicero that I feel I owe my status as a senator and a citizen; to him I owe my freedom and my life. Whenever I look upon my wife and my house, or upon the city of my birth, what I see is a gift that was granted me by Cicero …'

There was a time when Cicero would have spotted such an obvious trap a mile off. But I fear there is in all men who achieve their life's ambition only a narrow line between dignity and vanity, confidence and delusion, glory and self-destruction. Instead of staying in his seat and modestly disavowing such praise, Cicero rose and made a long speech agreeing with

Crassus's every word, whilst beside him Pompey gently cooked in a stew of jealousy and resentment. Watching from the door, I wanted to run forward and cry out to Cicero to stop, especially when Crassus stood and asked him if, as the Father of the Nation, he recognised in Clodius a second Catilina.

'How can I not,' responded Cicero, unable to resist this opportunity to rekindle the glory days of his leadership of the senate in front of Pompey, 'when the same debauched men who followed the one now flock to the other, and when the same tactics are daily employed? Unity, gentlemen, is our only hope of salvation, now as it was then – unity between this senate and the Order of Knights; unity between all classes; unity across Italy. As long as we remember that glorious concord that existed under my consulship, we need have no fear, for the spirit that saw off Sergius Catilina will most assuredly see off his bastard son!'

The senate cheered and Crassus sat back on his bench, beaming at a job well done, because of course the news of what Cicero had said spread across Rome immediately and quickly reached the ears of Clodius. At the end of the session, when Cicero walked back home with his entourage, Clodius was waiting in the forum surrounded by a gang of his own supporters. They blocked our path and I was sure some heads were going to be broken, but Cicero remained calm. He halted his procession. 'Offer them no provocation!' he called out. 'Give them no excuse to start a riot.' And turning to Clodius he said, 'You would have done well to have heeded my advice and gone into exile. The road you have started down can only end in one place.'

'And where is that?' sneered Clodius.

'Up there,' said Cicero, pointing at the Carcer, 'at the end of a rope.'

'Not so,' responded Clodius, and he gestured in the other direction, to the rostra, with its ranks of life-sized statues. 'One day I shall be up there, among the heroes of the Roman people.'

'Really? And tell me, will you be sculpted wearing women's clothing and carrying a lyre?' We all started to laugh. 'P. Clodius Pulcher: the first hero of the Order of Transvestites? I rather doubt it. Get out of my way.'

'Willingly,' said Clodius, with a smile. But as he stood aside to let Cicero pass, I was struck by how much he had changed. It was not merely that he seemed physically bigger and stronger: there was a glint of resolution in his eyes that had not been there before. He was feeding on his notoriety,

I realised: drawing energy from the mob. 'Caesar's wife was one of the best I ever had,' he said softly, as Cicero went by. 'Almost as good as Clodia.' He seized his elbow and added loudly, 'I was willing to be your friend. You should have been mine.'

'Claudians make unreliable friends,' replied Cicero, pulling himself free.

'Yes, but we make very reliable enemies.'

He proved to be as good as his word. From that day on, whenever he spoke in the forum he would always gesture to Cicero's new house, sitting on the Palatine high above the heads of the crowd, as a perfect symbol of dictatorship. 'Look how mightily the tyrant who butchered citizens without a proper trial has prospered by his handiwork – no wonder he is thirsty for fresh blood!' Cicero responded in kind. The mutual insults grew more and more deadly. Sometimes Cicero and I used to stand on the terrace and watch the tyro demagogue at work, and although we were too far away to hear exactly what he said, the applause of the crowd was audible and I recognised what we were seeing: the monster Cicero had thought he had slain had begun to twitch back into life.

XXXII

Around the middle of March, Hortensius came to see Cicero. He trailed Catulus after him, and when the old patrician shuffled in, he looked more than ever like a tortoise without its shell. Catulus had recently had the last of his teeth removed, and the trauma of the extraction, the long months of agony that had preceded it and the distortion of his mouth that had resulted all combined to make him look every one of his sixty years. He seemed unable to stop drooling and carried a large handkerchief that was sodden and yellowish. He reminded me of someone: I could not think who at first, and then I remembered – Rabirius. Cicero sprang up to help him to a chair, but Catulus waved him away, mumbling that he was perfectly all right.

'This wretched affair with Clodius cannot be allowed to drag on any longer,' Hortensius began.

'I agree with you,' said Cicero, who privately, I knew, was beginning to feel uncomfortable about the damaging war of words he was locked in with Clodius. 'The government is at a standstill. Our enemies are laughing at us.'

'We need to bring it to trial as soon as possible. I propose we should give up our insistence that the jury be selected by the urban praetor.'

'So how would it be selected?'

'In the usual way, by lot.'

'But might we not then find ourselves with quite a few dubious characters on the jury? We don't want the rascal to be acquitted. That really would be a disaster.'

'Acquittal is utterly impossible. Once any jury sees the weight of the evidence against him, he's bound to be convicted. All we need is a bare majority. We must have some faith in the good sense of the Roman people.'

'He must be crushed by the facts,' put in Catulus, holding his stained handkerchief to his mouth, 'and the sooner the better.'

'Will Fufius agree to drop his veto if we give up the clause about the jury?'

'He assures me he will, on condition we also reduce the penalty from death to exile.'

'What does Lucullus say?'

'He just wants a trial on any terms. You know he's been preparing for this day for years. He has all manner of witnesses lined up ready to testify to Clodius's immorality – even the slave girls who changed the sheets on his bed in Misenum after he had intercourse with his sisters.'

'Dear gods! Is it wise to have that kind of detail aired in public?'

'I never heard of such disgusting behaviour,' drooled Catulus. 'The whole Augean stable needs cleaning out, or it will be the ruin of us.'

'Even so …' Cicero frowned and did not complete the sentence. I could see he was not convinced, and for the first time I believe he sniffed danger to himself. Exactly what it was he could not say, simply that something about it smelled ominous. He continued to raise objections for a little longer – 'Wouldn't it be better just to drop the whole bill? Haven't we made our point? Don't we risk making a martyr of the young fool?' – before reluctantly giving Hortensius his assent. 'Well, I suppose you will have to do whatever you think is right. You've taken the lead in this thing from the start. However, I must make one thing clear – I want no part in it.'

I was vastly relieved to hear him utter those words: it seemed to me almost the first sensible decision he had made since leaving the consulship. Hortensius looked disappointed, having doubtless hoped that Cicero would lead for the prosecution, but he did not try to argue the matter, and duly went off to make the deal with Fufius. Thus the bill was passed and the people of Rome licked their lips and prepared for what promised to be the most scandalous trial in the republic's history.

The normal business of government was now able to resume, beginning with the drawing of lots by the praetors for their provinces. A few days before the ceremony, Cicero went out to the Alban Hills to see Pompey, and asked him as a favour not to press for the recall of Hybrida.

'But the man is a disgrace to our empire,' objected Pompey. 'I have never heard of such thievery and incompetence.'

'I am sure he is not as bad as all that.'

'Are you doubting my word?'

'No. But I would be grateful if you could oblige me in this matter. I gave him my assurance that I'd support him.'

'Ah, so I assume he's cutting you in?' Pompey winked and rubbed his thumb and forefinger together.

'Certainly not. I simply feel honour-bound to protect him, in return for all the help he gave me in saving the republic.'

Pompey looked unconvinced. But then he grinned and clapped Cicero on the shoulder. What was Macedonia after all? A mere vegetable plot to the Warden of Land and Sea! 'All right, let him have another year. But in return I expect you to do everything in your power to get my three bills through the senate.'

Cicero agreed, and thus when the lot drawing took place in the chamber of the senate, Macedonia, the most valuable prize, was not on the table. Instead there were just five provinces to be divided among the eight former praetors. The rivals all sat in a row on the front bench, Caesar at the end furthest from Quintus. Vergilius went first, if I remember rightly, and drew Sicily, and Caesar was the next to step up to try his luck. This was an important moment for him. Because of his divorce he had been obliged to hand back Pompeia's dowry and was being hard-pressed by his creditors: there was talk he was no longer solvent and might even be forced to leave the senate. He put his hand into the urn and gave the token to the consul. When the result was read out – 'Caesar draws Further Spain!' – he grimaced. Unfortunately for him, there was no war to be had in that distant land; he would much have preferred Africa or even Asia, where there was a greater chance of making money. Cicero managed to suppress a smile of triumph, but only for a moment or two, because shortly afterwards Asia went to Quintus, and Cicero was the first on his feet to congratulate his brother. Once again he let his tears flow freely. There seemed every possibility that Quintus might return from his province and become consul in his turn. Theirs was a dynasty in the making, and joyous was the family celebration that evening, to which I was once again invited. Cicero and Caesar were now on opposite sides of Fortune's wheel, with Cicero at the top and Caesar very firmly at the bottom.

Normally the new governors would have set off for their provinces immediately: in fact they should have left months earlier. But on this occasion the senate refused to allow them to leave Rome until the trial of Clodius had been concluded, in case they might be needed to restore public order.

The court duly convened in May, the prosecution being mounted by three young members of the Cornelius Lentulus family – Crus, Marcellinus and Niger, the latter being also the chief priest of Mars. They were great rivals of the Claudian clan, and had a particular grudge against Clodius, who had seduced several of their womenfolk. As his chief defender Clodius relied upon a former consul, Scribonius Curio, who was the father of one of his closest friends. Curio had made his fortune in the East as a soldier under Sulla, but was rather slow-witted, with a poor memory. As an orator he was known as 'The Fly-Swatter' because of his habit of throwing his arms around when he spoke. To weigh the evidence was a jury of fifty-six citizens, drawn by lot. They were of all types and conditions, from patrician senators down to such notorious low-life figures as Talna and Spongia. Originally eighty jurors had been empanelled, but the defence and prosecution each had twelve challenges, which they quickly used up, the defence rejecting the respectable and the prosecution the rough. Those who had survived this winnowing sat uneasily together.

A sex scandal will always draw a crowd, but a sex scandal involving the ruling classes is titillating beyond measure. To accommodate the numbers who wished to watch, it was necessary to hold the trial in front of the Temple of Castor. A special section of seats was set aside for the senate, and that was where Cicero took his place on the opening day, on the bench next to Hortensius. Caesar's ex-wife had prudently withdrawn from Rome to avoid giving evidence, but the chief priest's mother, Aurelia, and his sister, Julia, both came forward to act as witnesses, and identified Clodius as the man who had invaded the sacred rites. Aurelia made an especially strong impression, as she pointed her talon-like finger at the accused, sitting no more than ten feet from her, and insisted in her hard voice that the Good Goddess must be placated by his exile or disaster would descend on Rome. That was the first day.

On the second, Caesar followed her on to the witness stand, and I was struck again by the similarities between mother and son – tough and sinewy, and confident beyond mere arrogance, to a point where all men, aristocrat or plebeian, were deemed equally beneath them in their gaze. (This, I think, was why he was always so popular with the people: he was far too superior to be a snob.) Under cross-examination he responded that he could not say what had happened that night, as he had not been present. He added, very coldly, that he bore no particular ill will towards Clodius – in whose direction, however, he did not once look – because he had no idea whether he was guilty or not; clearly, he loathed him. As to his divorce, he could only repeat the answer he had given Cicero in the senate: he had set Pompeia aside not necessarily because she was guilty but because, as the chief priest's wife, she could not be tainted by suspicion. As everyone in Rome knew of Caesar's own reputation, not least his conquest of Pompey's wife, this fine piece of casuistry provoked long and mocking laughter, which he had to endure behind his habitual mask of supreme indifference.

He finished giving evidence and stepped down from the tribunal, coincidentally at exactly the same moment as Cicero rose to leave the audience. They almost walked into one another, and there was no chance of avoiding at least a brief exchange.

'Well, Caesar, you must be glad your testimony is over.'

'Why do you say that?'

'I presume it must have been awkward for you.'

'I never feel awkward. But yes, you're right, I am delighted to put this absurd affair behind me, because now I can set off for Spain.'

'When are you planning to leave?'

'Tonight.'

'But I thought the senate had forbidden the new governors to leave for their provinces until the trial was over?'

'True, but I haven't a moment to lose. The moneylenders are after me. Apparently I somehow have to make twenty-five million sesterces just to own nothing.' He gave a shrug – a gambler's shrug: I remember he seemed quite unconcerned – and sauntered off towards his official residence. Within the hour, accompanied by a small entourage, he was gone, and it was left to Crassus to stand surety for his debts.

Caesar's evidence was entertaining enough. But the real highlight of the proceedings came on the third day of Clodius's trial with the appearance of Lucullus. It is said that at the entrance to Apollo's shrine at Delphi three things are written: 'Know thyself '; 'Desire nothing too much' and 'Never go to law'. Did ever a man so wilfully ignore these precepts as Lucullus in this affair? Forgetting that he was supposed to be a military hero, he ascended the platform trembling with his desire to ruin Clodius, and very soon began to describe how he had surprised his wife in bed with her brother during a vacation when Clodius had been a guest in his house on the Bay of Naples more than a decade earlier. By then he had been watching them together for many weeks, said Lucullus – oh yes, the way they touched one another, and whispered when they thought his back was turned: they took him for a fool – and he had ordered his wife's maids to bring her sheets to him each morning for his inspection and report to him everything he saw. These female slaves, six in all, were summoned into court, and as they filed in, clearly nervous and with their eyes lowered, I saw among them my beloved Agathe, whose image had rarely left my mind in the two years since we were together.

They stood meekly as their depositions were produced, and I willed her to look up and glance in my direction. I waved. I even whistled. The people standing around me must have thought I had gone mad. Finally I cupped my hands to my mouth and yelled her name. She did raise her eyes at that, but there were so many thousands of spectators crammed into the forum, and the noise was so intense, and the glaring sunshine so bright, there can have been little chance of her seeing me. I tried to struggle forward through the packed crowd, but the people in front of me had queued for hours for their places, and they refused to let me pass. In an agony I heard Clodius's counsel announce that they did not wish to challenge these witnesses, as their testimony was not relevant to the case, and the maids were ordered to leave the platform. I watched Agathe turn with the others and descend out of sight.

Lucullus resumed giving evidence and I felt a great hatred well up in me at the sight of this decaying plutocrat who unthinkingly possessed a treasure for which, at that moment, I would have given my life. I was so preoccupied that I briefly lost track of what he was saying, and it was only when I realised that the crowd had started to gasp and laugh with delight that I took notice of his evidence. He was describing how he had concealed himself in his wife's bedchamber and observed her and her brother in the act of fornication: 'dog on bitch', as he put it. Nor, continued Lucullus, ignoring the noise of the crowd, did Clodius confine his base appetites to one sister, but boasted of his conquests of the other two. Bearing in mind that Clodia's husband Celer had just returned from Nearer Gaul to stand for the consulship, this allegation caused a particular sensation. Clodius sat through it all smiling broadly at his former brother-in-law, clearly aware that whatever damage Lucullus imagined he was doing to him, he was actually inflicting far more harm on his own reputation. That was the third day, and at the end of it the prosecution rested its case. I lingered after the court had been adjourned in the hope of seeing Agathe again, but she had been taken away.

On the fourth day, the defence began the job of trying to extricate Clodius from this morass of filth. It seemed a hopeless task, for no one, not even Curio, was in serious doubt of his client's guilt of the actual offence. Nevertheless, he did his best. The core of his case was that the whole episode had been a simple matter of mistaken identity. The lights had been dim, the women hysterical, the intruder disguised – how could anyone be sure it was Clodius? It was hardly a convincing line. But then, just as the morning was nearing its end, Clodius's side produced a surprise witness. A man named C. Causinius Schola, a seemingly respectable citizen from the town of Interamna, some ninety miles from Rome, came forward to say that on the night in question, Clodius had actually been with him in his home. Even under cross-examination he was quite unshakeable on this point, and although his was only one voice set against a dozen on the other side, including the firm testimony of Caesar's own mother, he cut a strangely believable figure.

Cicero, who was watching from the senators' benches, beckoned me over to him. 'This fellow is either lying or insane,' he whispered. 'On the day of the Good Goddess ceremony, surely Clodius came to see me? I recall having an argument with Terentia about his visit.'

Now that he mentioned the occasion, I remembered it as well, and I confirmed he was correct.

'What's all this?' asked Hortensius, who was, as usual, sitting next to Cicero and had been trying to listen to our conversation. Cicero turned to him. 'I was saying that Clodius was in my house that day, so how could he possibly have reached Interamna by nightfall? His alibi is preposterous.' He spoke entirely without premeditation; had he thought about the implications of what he was saying, he would have been more cautious.

'Then you must testify,' responded Hortensius at once. 'This witness needs to be destroyed.'

'Oh no,' said Cicero quickly, 'I told you at the start, I want no part of it,' and beckoning to me to follow, he got up at once and left the forum, accompanied by the two well-muscled slaves who these days acted as his guard. 'That was stupid of me,' he said as we climbed the hill to his house. 'I must be getting old.' Behind us I could hear the crowd laughing at some point made by one of Clodius's supporters: the weight of evidence might be against him, but the mob was all on his side. I sensed that Cicero was uneasy with the day's proceedings. Quite unexpectedly, the defence seemed to be taking charge.

Once the trial had adjourned for the day, all three of the prosecutors came to see Cicero, along with Hortensius. The instant I saw them I knew what they wanted, and I secretly cursed Hortensius for putting Cicero in this position. I showed them into the garden, where he was sitting with Terentia, watching little Marcus play with a ball. It was a perfect late afternoon in early summer. The air was fragrant with blossom and the sounds rising from the forum were as drowsy and indistinct as insects humming in a meadow.

'We need you to testify,' began Crus, who was the lead counsel.

'I suspected you were going to say that,' replied Cicero, with an angry look at Hortensius. 'And I think you can guess my reply. There must be a hundred people apart from me who saw Clodius in Rome earlier that day.'

'None that we can find,' said Crus. 'At least none that is willing to testify.'

'Clodius has frightened them off,' said Hortensius.

'And certainly none that has your authority,' added Marcellinus, who had always been a supporter of Cicero, right back to the days of the Verres prosecution. 'If you can do this favour for us tomorrow, and confirm that Clodius was with you, the jury will have no choice except to convict him. That alibi is the only thing standing between him and exile.'

Cicero looked at them in disbelief. 'Just a moment, gentlemen. Are you telling me that without my testimony you think he might *walk free*?' They hung their heads. 'How has this happened? Never has a more guilty man been set before a court.' He rounded on Hortensius. 'You said that acquittal was "utterly impossible". "Have some faith in the good sense of the Roman people" – wasn't that what you told me?'

'He has become very popular. And those who don't actually love the man at the very least fear his supporters.'

'We were also damaged by Lucullus,' said Crus. 'All that business about sheets and hiding behind screens has turned us into a laughing stock. Even some of the jury are saying that Clodius is no more perverted than the men prosecuting him.'

'So now it is my responsibility to make good your damage?' Cicero threw up his hands in exasperation.

Terentia had been nursing Marcus on her lap. Suddenly she set him down and told him to go indoors. Turning to her husband she said, 'You may not like it but you must do it – if not for the republic's sake, then for your own.'

'I said before: I want no part of it.'

'But nobody stands to gain more from sending Clodius into exile than you. He has become your greatest enemy.'

'Yes he has – indeed he has! – and whose fault is that?'

'Yours – for encouraging his career in the first place!'

They argued back and forth for a while longer as the senators watched, bemused. It was already widely known in Rome that Terentia was not the usual humble, obedient kind of wife and this scene was bound to be widely reported. But although Cicero must have resented her for contradicting him in front of his colleagues, I knew that he would have to agree with her in the end. His anger stemmed from his recognition that he had no choice: he was trapped. 'Very well,' he said finally. 'I'll do my duty for Rome, as always, although it may be at some cost to my personal safety. But then I suppose I should be used to that. I shall see you in the morning, gentlemen,' and with an irritated wave of his hand he dismissed them.

After they had gone, he sat brooding. 'You realise that this is a trap?'

'A trap for whom?' I asked.

'For me, of course.' He turned to Terentia. 'Consider it: out of the whole of Italy, it finally turns out that only one man is in a position to challenge Clodius's alibi – and that man is Cicero. Do you think that is a coincidence?' Terentia did not respond; nor had it occurred to me until he mentioned it. He said to me, 'This witness of theirs from Interamna – this Causinius Schola, or whatever his name is – we ought to find out more about him. Who do we know from Interamna?'

I thought for a moment, and then with a sick feeling in my heart I said, 'Caelius Rufus.'

'Caelius Rufus,' repeated Cicero, striking the side of his chair, 'of course.'

'Another man you should never have brought into our house,' said Terentia.

'When was the last time we saw him?'

'Months ago,' I answered.

'Caelius Rufus! He was a drinking and whoring companion of Clodius back when he first became my pupil.' The longer Cicero pondered it, the more certain he became. 'First he runs with Catilina and then he takes up with Clodius. What a snake that boy has been to me! This wretched witness from Interamna will turn out to be a client of his father's, you can rely upon it.'

'So you think Rufus and Clodius have plotted between them to entrap you?'

'Do you doubt they're capable of it?'

'No. But I wonder why they would go to all the trouble of creating a false alibi purely in order to lure you on to the witness stand to destroy it. Clodius wants his alibi to go unchallenged, surely?'

'So you think that someone else is behind it?' I hesitated.

'Who?' demanded Terentia.

'Crassus.'

'But Crassus and I are entirely reconciled,' said Cicero. 'You heard the way he praised me to the skies in front of Pompey. And then he let me have this house so cheaply—' He was going to say something else, but then he stopped.

Terentia turned the full force of her scrutiny on to me. 'Why would Crassus go to such lengths to cause your master trouble?'

'I don't know,' I lied. I could feel my face turning red.

Cicero said quietly, 'You might as well ask, why does the scorpion sting? Because that is what scorpions do.'

The conversation broke up soon afterwards. Terentia went off to attend to Marcus. I retired to the library to attend to the senator's correspondence. Only Cicero remained on the terrace, staring thoughtfully across the forum to the Capitol as the shades of evening began to spread.

The following morning, pale and silent with nerves – for he knew full well what kind of reception he was likely to receive – Cicero went down into the forum, escorted by the same number of bodyguards he used to have around him in the days of Catilina. Word had got out that the prosecution was unexpectedly calling him as a witness, and the moment Clodius's supporters saw him pushing his way towards the platform they set up a gale of booing and catcalling. As he climbed the temple steps towards the tribunal, some eggs and dung were thrown, which provoked the most remarkable counter-demonstration. Almost the whole of the jury got to their feet and formed a cordon to protect Cicero from the missiles. Some even turned to the crowd, pulled down their collars and pointed to their bare throats, as if to say to Clodius's lynch mob, 'You will have to kill us before you can kill him.'

Cicero was well used to giving evidence on the witness stand. He had done it in at least a dozen cases against Catilina's co-conspirators in the last year alone. But never had he faced a cockpit such as this, and the urban praetor had to suspend the court until order could be restored. Clodius sat looking at Cicero with his arms folded and a grim expression on his face: the behaviour of the jury must have been deeply troubling to him. Sitting by Clodius's side for the first time in the trial was his wife, Fulvia. It was a cunning move on the defence's part to produce her, for she was only sixteen and looked more like his daughter than a married woman – exactly the sort of vulnerable young girl guaranteed to melt a jury's heart. She was also a descendant of the Gracchi family, who were immensely popular with the people. She had a hard, mean face, but then being married to Clodius would surely have been enough to curdle even the sweetest nature.

When at last the chief prosecutor, Lentulus Crus, was called on to examine the witness, an anticipatory silence fell. He crossed the court to Cicero. 'Although the whole world knows who you are, would you please state your name?'

'Marcus Tullius Cicero.'

'Do you swear by all the gods to tell the truth?'

'I swear.'

'You are familiar with the accused?'

'I am.'

'Where was he between the sixth and seventh hours on the day of the ritual of the Good Goddess last year? Can you give the court that information?'

'I can. I remember it very well.' Cicero turned from his questioner to the jury. 'He was in my house.'

An excited murmur ran around the spectators and the jury. Clodius said very loudly, 'Liar!' and his claque set up a fresh chorus of jeering. The praetor, whose name was Voconius, called for order. He gestured to the prosecutor to continue.

'There is no doubt about this?' asked Crus.

'None whatever. Others in my household saw him, as well as I.'

'What was the purpose of the visit?'

'It was a social call.'

'Would it have been possible, in your opinion, for the accused to have left your house and been in Interamna by nightfall?'

'Not unless he put on wings as well as women's clothes.'

There was much laughter at this. Even Clodius smiled.

'Fulvia, the wife of the accused, who is also sitting there, claims to have been with her husband in Interamna that same evening. What do you say to that?'

'I would say that the delights of married life have obviously so affected her judgement that she no longer knows what day of the week it is.'

The laughter was even more prolonged, and again Clodius joined in, but Fulvia stared ahead of her with a face that was like a child's fist, small and white and clenched: she was a terror even then.

Crus had no further questions and returned to the prosecutors' bench, yielding the floor to Clodius's advocate, Curio. He was no doubt a brave man on the battlefield, but the courtroom was not his natural arena, and he approached the great orator in the manner of a nervous schoolboy poking a snake with a stick. 'My client has long been an enemy of yours, I believe?'

'Not at all. Until he committed this act of sacrilege we enjoyed friendly relations.'

'But then he was accused of this crime and you deserted him?'

'No, his senses deserted him, and then he committed the crime.'

Again there was laughter. The defence counsel looked annoyed. 'You say that on the fourth day of December last year my client came to see you?'

'I do.'

'It is suspiciously convenient, is it not, that you should suddenly remember that Clodius came to see you on that date?'

'I should have said that the convenience in the matter of dates was all on his side.'

'What do you mean by that?'

'Well, I doubt he spends many nights of the year in Interamna. But by a remarkable coincidence, the one night he does happen to find himself in that distant spot is also the night a dozen witnesses swear to have seen him cavorting in women's dress in Rome.'

As the amusement spread, Clodius stopped smiling. Clearly he had had enough of watching his advocate being batted around the court, and he gestured to him to come over to his bench for a consultation. But Curio, who was nearing sixty and unused to ridicule, was losing his temper and had started waving his arms around.

'Some fools no doubt will think this is all very witty wordplay, but I put it to you that you have made a mistake, and that my client came to see you on another day entirely.'

'I have no doubt about the date – and for a very good reason. It was the first anniversary of my salvation of the republic. Believe me, I shall always have particular reason for remembering the fourth day of December.'

'And so will the wives and children of the men you had murdered!' shouted Clodius. He leapt to his feet. Voconius at once appealed for order, but Clodius refused to sit and continued yelling insults. 'You behaved as a tyrant then, as you do now!' Turning to his supporters standing in the forum, he gestured to them to join in. They needed little encouragement. Almost to a man they surged forward, jeering. A fresh flight of missiles raked the platform. For the second time that morning, the jury came to Cicero's aid, surrounding him and trying to cover his head. The urban praetor shouted out to Curio, demanding to know if the defence had any further questions for the witness. Curio, who looked utterly dismayed at the way the jury were again protecting Cicero, signalled that he had finished, and the court was hastily adjourned. A combination of jurymen, bodyguards and clients cleared a path for Cicero through the forum and up the Palatine Hill to his home.

I had expected to find Cicero badly shaken by the whole experience, and certainly at first sight he looked it. His hair was standing up in tufts, his toga was streaked with dirt. But otherwise he was unscathed. Indeed, he was exultant, striding around his library, reliving the highlights of his testimony. He felt he had defeated Catilina for a second time. 'Did you see the way that jury closed ranks around me? If ever you wished for a symbol of all that is best about Roman justice, Tiro, you saw it this morning.' Still, he decided against going back to the court to hear the closing speeches, and it was not until two days later, when the verdict was due to be delivered, that he ventured down to the Temple of Castor to see Clodius sentenced.

The jury by this time had requested armed protection from the senate, and a century of troops guarded the steps up to the platform. As Cicero approached the section of seats reserved for senators, he raised his arm to the jury and a few saluted him back, but many glanced nervously in the other direction. 'I suppose they must be afraid of showing their feelings in front of Clodius's mob,' Cicero said to me. 'After they have cast their votes, do you think I should go and stand with them, to show my support? There is bound to be trouble, even with an armed guard.' I was not at all sure this was wise, but there was no time for me to reply, as the praetor was already coming out of the temple. I left Cicero to take his place on the bench and went to join the crowd nearby.

The prosecution and defence having rested their cases, it now remained only for Voconius to sum up their arguments and direct the jury on points of law. Clodius was once again seated beside Fulvia. He turned and whispered to her occasionally, while she stared hard at the men who would shortly decide her husband's fate. Everything in court always takes longer than one expects – questions have to be answered, statutes consulted, documents found – and it must have been at least an hour later that the court officials finally began handing out the wax voting tokens to the jurymen. On one side was scratched an A for acquittal, and on the other a C for condemnation. The system was designed for maximum secrecy: it was the work of a moment to use one's thumb to wipe a letter clear and then drop the vote into the urn as it was handed round. When every token had been collected, the urn was carried over to the table in front of the praetor and emptied out. All around me the crowd stood on tiptoe, straining to see what was happening. For some, the tension of the silence was too much, and they felt compelled to puncture it by shouting out banalities – 'Come on, Clodius!' 'Long live Clodius!' – cries that produced little flurries of applause in the teeming multitude. An awning had been set up above the court to keep off the weather, and I remember how the canvas snapped like a sail in the stiff May breeze. At last the reckoning was done and the tally was handed to the praetor. He stood, and the court all did the same. Fulvia gripped Clodius's arm. I closed my eyes tight shut and prayed. We needed just twenty-nine votes to send Clodius into exile for the rest of his life.

'There voted in favour of condemnation twenty-five, and in favour of acquittal thirty-one. The verdict of this court is therefore that Publius Clodius Pulcher is not guilty of the charges laid against him, and the case—'

The praetor's final words were lost in the roar of approval. For me, the earth seemed to tilt. I felt myself sway, and when I opened my eyes, blinking in the glare, Clodius was making his way around the court, shaking hands with the jurors. The legionaries had linked arms to prevent anyone storming the platform. The mob were cheering and dancing. On either side of me Clodius's supporters insisted on shaking my hand, and I tried to force a smile as I did so, otherwise they might have beaten me up, or worse. In the midst of this noisy jubilation, the senatorial benches sat as white and still as a field of freshly fallen snow. I could make out a few expressions – Hortensius stricken, Lucullus uncomprehending, Catulus slack-mouthed with dismay. Cicero wore his professional mask and gazed statesmanlike into the distance.

After a few moments Clodius came to the front of the platform. He ignored the praetor's shouts that this was a court of law and not a public assembly and held up his hands for quiet. At once the noise fell away.

'My fellow citizens,' he said, 'this is not a victory for me. This is a victory for you, the people.' Another great swell of applause carried forward and broke against the temple, and he turned his face towards it, Narcissus to his mirror. This time he let the adulation go on for a long time. 'I was born a patrician,' he continued eventually, 'but the members of my own class turned against me. It is you who have supported and sustained me. It is to you I owe my life. I am of you. I wish to be among you. And henceforth I shall dedicate myself to you. Let it be known, therefore, on the day of this great victory, that it is my resolve to disavow my inheritance of blood as a patrician, and to seek adoption as a plebeian.' I glanced at Cicero. The statesmanlike look had vanished. He was staring at Clodius in open astonishment. 'And if I am successful, I shall follow a path of ambition not through the senate – filled as it is with the bloated and the corrupt – but as a people's representative – as one of you – as a tribune!' More massive applause followed, which again he quieted with a stroke of his hand. 'And if you, the people, choose me as a tribune, I make you this pledge and this promise, my friends – those who have taken the lives of Roman citizens without trial will very soon know what it is to taste the people's justice!'

*

Afterwards, Cicero retired to his library to mull over the verdict with Hortensius, Catulus and Lucullus, while Quintus went off to see if he could discover what had happened. As the senators sat in shock, Cicero told me to fetch some wine. 'Four votes,' he murmured. 'Just four votes cast the other way, and that irresponsible reprobate would even now be on his way out of Italy for ever. *Four votes!*' He could not stop repeating it.

'Well, this is the end for me, gentlemen,' announced Lucullus. 'I shall retire from public life.' From a distance he seemed still to possess his usual cold demeanour, but when one came close to him, as I did when I handed him a cup of wine, one could see that he was blinking uncontrollably. He had been humiliated. It was intolerable to him. He drank the wine quickly and held out his cup for more.

'Our colleagues will be in a panic,' observed Hortensius.

Catulus said, 'I feel quite faint.'

'Four votes!'

'I shall tend my fish, study philosophy and compose myself for death. This republic holds no place for me any longer.'

Presently, Quintus arrived with news from the court. He had spoken to the prosecutors, he said, and to three of the jurors who had voted to condemn. 'It seems there has never been such bribery in the history of Roman justice. There are rumours that some of the key men were offered four hundred thousand to make sure the verdict went Clodius's way.'

'*Four hundred thousand?*' repeated Hortensius in disbelief. 'But where did Clodius get such sums?' demanded Lucullus.

'That little bitch of a wife is rich, but even so …'

Quintus said, 'The rumour is that the money was put up by Crassus.'

For the second time that day, the solid earth seemed to melt beneath my feet. Cicero glanced briefly in my direction.

'I find that hard to believe,' said Hortensius. 'Why would Crassus want to pay out a fortune to rescue Clodius, of all people?'

'Well, I can only report what is being said,' replied Quintus. 'Crassus had twenty of the jury round to his house last night, one after the other, and asked each of them what they wanted. He settled bills for some. To others he gave contracts. The rest took cash.'

'That is still not a majority of the jury,' pointed out Cicero.

'No, the word is that Clodius and Fulvia were also busy,' said Quintus, 'and not just with their gold. Beds were creaking in some noble houses in Rome last night, for those jurors who chose to take their payment in a different coin – male or female. I'm told that Clodia herself worked hard for several votes.'

'Cato has been right all along,' exclaimed Lucullus. 'The core of our republic is utterly rotten. We're finished. And Clodius is the maggot who will destroy us.'

'Can you imagine a *patrician* transferring to the *plebs*?' asked Hortensius in a tone of wonder. 'Can you imagine *wanting* to do such a thing?'

'Gentlemen, gentlemen,' said Cicero, 'we've lost a trial, that's all – don't let's lose our nerve. Clodius isn't the first guilty man to walk free from a court of law.'

'He will come after you, brother,' warned Quintus. 'If he transfers to the plebs, you can be sure he will be elected tribune – he's too popular now to be stopped – and once he has the powers of that office at his disposal, he can cause you a great deal of trouble.'

'It will never happen,' said Cicero. 'The state authorities will never allow him to transfer. And if by some amazing mischance they do, do you really think that I – after all that I've achieved in this city, starting from nothing – do you honestly believe that I can't handle a giggling puerile pervert such as our Little Miss Beauty? I could snap his spine in a single speech!'

'You're right,' said Hortensius, 'and I want you to know that we will never abandon you. If he does dare to attack you, you will always have our complete support. Is that not so, Lucullus?'

'Of course.'

'Don't you agree, Catulus?' But the old patrician did not answer. 'Catulus?' Again there was no reply. Hortensius sighed. 'I'm afraid he's grown very old of late. Wake him, will you, Tiro?'

I put my hand on Catulus's shoulder and shook him gently. His head lolled over on to one side and I had to grab him to stop him sliding to the floor. His head flopped back so that his leathery old face was suddenly staring up into mine. His eyes were open. His mouth hung loose, leaking spit. I snatched away my hand in shock, and it was Quintus who had to step forward to feel his neck and pronounce him dead.

*

Thus passed from this world Quintus Lutatius Catulus, in the sixty-first year of his life: consul, pontiff, and fierce upholder of the prerogatives of the senate. He was of an earlier, sterner era, and I look back on his death, as I do on that of Metellus Pius, as a milestone in the demise of the republic. Hortensius, who was Catulus's brother-in-law, took a candle from Cicero and held it to the old man's face, and softly tried to call him back to life. Never have I seen the point of the ancient tradition more clearly than at that moment, for it really did seem as if Catulus's spirit had just slipped out of the room and could easily return if properly summoned. We waited to see if he might revive, but of course he did not, and after a while Hortensius kissed his forehead and closed his eyes. He wept a little, and even Cicero looked red-eyed, for although he and Catulus had started out as enemies, they had ended up making common cause, and he had come to respect the old man for his integrity. Only Lucullus appeared unmoved, but by then I believe he had reached a stage where he preferred fish to human beings.

Naturally, all discussion of the trial was ended. Catulus's slaves were summoned to carry their master's corpse the short distance to his house, and once this had been done, Hortensius went off to break the news to his own household, while Lucullus retired to dine alone, no doubt on larks' wings and the tongues of nightingales, in his vast Room of Apollo. As for Quintus, he announced that he was to depart at dawn the next morning on the start of his long journey to Asia. Cicero knew that his brother was under orders to leave as soon as the jury returned its verdict, but even so I could tell that this was the hardest of all the blows he had endured that day. He summoned Terentia and little Marcus to say goodbye, and then abruptly withdrew to his library alone, leaving me to accompany Quintus to the door.

'Goodbye, Tiro,' Quintus said, taking my hand in both of his. He had hard, calloused palms; not like Cicero's soft lawyer's hands. 'I shall miss your counsel. Will you write to me often and tell me how my brother is faring?'

'Gladly.'

He seemed about to step into the street, but then he turned and said, 'He should have given you your freedom when he ceased to be consul. That was his intention. Did you know that?'

I was stunned by this revelation. 'He had stopped talking about it,' I stammered. 'I assumed he had changed his mind.'

'He says he is frightened of how much you know.'

'But I would never utter to anyone a word I had learned in confidence!'

'I know that, and in his heart so does he. Don't be concerned. It's really just an excuse. The truth is he's scared of the thought that you might leave him too, just as Atticus and I are doing. He relies on you more than you know.'

I was too overcome to speak.

'When I return from Asia,' he continued, 'you shall have your freedom, I promise you. You belong to the family, not just to my brother. In the meantime, look out for his safety, Tiro. There's something happening in Rome that I don't like the smell of.'

He raised his hand in farewell and, accompanied by his attendants, set off down the street. I stood on the step and watched his familiar sturdy figure, with its broad shoulders and steady tread, stride down the hill until it was out of sight.

XXXIII

Clodius was supposed to go straight off to Sicily as a junior magistrate. Instead he chose to linger in Rome to savour his victory. He even had the nerve to take his seat in the senate, to which he was now entitled. It was the Ides of May, two days after the trial, and the house was debating the political situation in the aftermath of the fiasco. Clodius entered the chamber just as Cicero was speaking. Greeted by loud hisses, he smiled to himself, as if he found the hostility amusing, and when no senator would budge along their bench to make room for him, he leaned against the wall and folded his arms, regarding the speaker with a smirk. Crassus, sitting in his usual place on the front row, looked distinctly uncomfortable, and pretended to examine a scratch on his red leather shoe. Cicero simply ignored Clodius and continued with his speech.

'Gentlemen,' he said, 'we must not flag or falter because of a single blow. I agree we have to recognise that our authority has been weakened, but that doesn't mean we should panic. We would be fools to ignore what has happened, but cowards to let it frighten us. The jury may have let loose an enemy upon the state—'

Clodius called out, 'I was acquitted not as an enemy of the state but as the man to clean up Rome!'

'Clodius, you are mistaken,' said Cicero calmly, not even deigning to look at him. 'The jury has preserved you not for the streets of Rome but for the death cell. They don't want to keep you with us, but rather to deprive you of the chance of exile.' He resumed his speech. 'And so, gentlemen, take heart and maintain your dignity—'

'And where's *your* dignity, Cicero?' shouted Clodius. 'You take bribes!'

'The political consensus of honest men still holds—'

'You took a bribe so that you could buy a house!'

Now Cicero turned to face him. 'At least,' he said, 'I didn't buy a jury.'

The senate rang with laughter, and I was reminded of an old lion cuffing an unruly cub. Still Clodius pressed on: 'I'll tell you why I was acquitted – because your evidence was a lie, and the jury didn't credit it.'

'On the contrary, twenty-five members of that jury gave me credit and thirty-one gave you none – they demanded their money in advance.'

It may not sound especially funny now, but at the time one would have thought that Cicero had made the wittiest remark in history. I suppose the senate laughed so much because they wanted to show him their support, and each time Clodius tried to respond they laughed even louder, so that in the end he gave up irritably and left the chamber. This sally was considered a great success for Cicero, especially as a couple of days later Clodius left Rome to go off to Sicily, and for the next few months he was able to put 'Little Miss Beauty' out of his mind.

It was made clear to Pompey the Great that if he wanted to stand for a second consulship he would have to give up his hopes of a triumph and come into Rome to campaign, and this he could not bring himself to do, for much as he relished the substance of power, he loved the show of it even more – the gaudy costumes, the blaring trumpets, the roar and stink of the wild beasts in their cages, the tramping boots and raucous cheers of his soldiers, the adulation of the crowd.

So he abandoned the idea of becoming consul, and the date of his triumphal entry into the city was fixed, at his request, to coincide with his forty-fifth birthday, at the end of September. Such was the scale of his achievement, however, that the parade – which it was reckoned would extend for at least twenty miles – had to be spread over two whole days. Therefore it was actually on the eve of the imperator's birthday that Cicero and the rest of the senate went out to the Field of Mars to greet the conqueror formally. Not only had Pompey coloured his face red for the occasion, he had dressed himself in the most fabulous golden armour, and was wearing a magnificent cloak that had once belonged to Alexander the Great. Drawn up around him were thousands of his veterans guarding hundreds of wagons laden with booty.

Until this point, Cicero had not really grasped the extent of Pompey's wealth. As he remarked to me: 'One million, or ten million, or a hundred million – what are these? Mere words. The imagination cannot comprehend their meaning.' But Pompey had gathered these riches all in one place, and by doing so revealed his power. For example, a skilled man at that time might work an entire day in Rome and at the end of it count himself lucky if he had earned one silver drachma. Pompey had laid out open chests on glistening display that morning which contained *seventy-five million* silver drachmae: more than the annual tax revenue of the entire Roman world. And that was just the cash. Towering over the parade, and requiring a team of four oxen to pull it, was a solid gold statue of Mithradates that was twelve feet tall. There was Mithradates's throne and his sceptre, also gold. There were thirty-three of his crowns, made of pearl, and three golden statues of Apollo, Minerva and Mars. There was a mountain shaped like a pyramid and made of gold, with deer and lions and fruit of every variety, and a golden vine entwined all around it. There was a chequered gaming board, three feet long by four feet broad, made of precious green and blue stones, with a solid gold moon upon it weighing thirty pounds. There was a sundial made of pearls. Another five wagons were required to carry the most precious books from the royal library. It made a profound impression on Cicero, who recognised that such wealth was bound to have unforeseeable consequences for Rome and its politics. He took great delight in going over to Crassus and teasing him. 'Well, Crassus, you once had the distinction of being the richest man in Rome – but not any more, I fancy. After this, even you will be applying to Pompey for a loan!' Crassus gave a crooked smile; one could tell the sight was choking him.

Pompey sent all this into the city on the first day, but remained himself outside the gates. On the second day, his birthday, the Triumphal parade proper began with the prisoners he had brought back from the East: first the army commanders, then the officials of Mithradates's household, then a group of captured pirate chiefs, then the King of the Jews, followed by the King of Armenia with his wife and son, and finally, as the highlight of this part of the procession, seven of Mithradates's children and one of his sisters. The thousands of Romans in the Forum Boarium and the Circus Maximus jeered and flung lumps of shit and earth at them, so much so that by the time they finally stumbled down the Via Sacra towards the Carcer they looked like clay figures come to life. There they were made to wait beneath the gaze of the carnifex and his assistants, trembling at the thought of their fate, while the distant roars from the direction of the Triumphal Gate signalled that at last their conqueror had entered the city.

Cicero waited too, with the rest of his colleagues, outside the senate house. I was on the opposite side of the forum, and as the parade passed between us, I kept losing sight of him amid all that torrent of glory. There were wagons with gaudy tableaux depicting each of the nations Pompey had subdued – Albania, Syria, Palestine, Arabia and so forth – followed by some of the eight hundred heavy bronze ramming beaks of the pirate ships he had captured, and the glittering heaps of armour and shields and swords he had seized from Mithradates's armies. Behind all this tramped Pompey's soldiers, chanting bawdy verses about their commander, and then at last Pompey himself came into the forum, riding in his jewel-studded chariot, wearing a purple toga embroidered with golden stars, and of course the cloak of Alexander. Clinging on to the platform behind him was the slave traditionally charged with intoning in his ear that he was only human. I did not envy that poor fellow his job, and he was clearly starting to get on Pompey's nerves, because the moment the charioteer pulled the horses up outside the Carcer and the parade came to a halt, Pompey pushed him roughly off the platform and turned his broad red-painted face to address the muddy apparitions of the prisoners.

'I, Pompey the Great, conqueror of three hundred and twenty-four nations, having been granted the power of life and death by the senate and people of Rome, do hereby declare that you, as vassals of the Roman empire, shall immediately' – he paused – 'be granted a full pardon and set free to return to the lands of your birth. Go, and tell the world of my mercy!'

It was as magnificent as it was unexpected, for Pompey had been known in his youth as 'The Butcher Boy', and had seldom showed much clemency to anyone. The crowd seemed disappointed at first, but then began to applaud, while the prisoners, when they were told what he had said, stretched out their hands and cried out to Pompey in a babble of foreign tongues. Pompey acknowledged their gratitude with a twirling gesture of his hand, then jumped down from his chariot and walked towards the Capitol, where he was due to sacrifice to Jupiter. The senate, Cicero included, trailed after him, and I was about to follow when I made a most remarkable discovery.

Now that the parade had ended, the wagons laden with arms and armour were queuing to leave the forum, and for the first time I saw at close quarters some of the swords and knives. I was no expert when it came to soldiering, but even I could recognise that these brand-new weapons, with their curved Oriental blades and mysterious engravings on their hilts, were exactly the same as the ones that Cethegus had been hoarding in his house, and of which I had made an inventory on the eve of his execution. I made a move to pick one up, intending to take it back and show it to Cicero, but the legionary who was guarding the wagon shouted at me roughly to keep my distance. I was on the point of telling him who I was and why I needed it when good sense checked my tongue. I turned without a word and hurried away, and when I looked back the legionary was still watching me suspiciously.

Cicero had been obliged to attend Pompey's great official banquet following the sacrifice, and it was not until late in the evening that he returned home – in a bad mood, as he usually was after spending much time with Pompey. He was surprised to find me waiting up for him, and listened intently as I explained my discovery. I was inordinately pleased with my cleverness and expected him to congratulate me. Instead, he became increasingly irritated. 'Are you trying to tell me,' he demanded, after he had heard me out, 'that Pompey sent back captured weapons from Mithradates in order to arm Catilina's conspiracy?'

'All I know is that the markings and the design were identical—'

Cicero cut me off. 'This is treasonous talk! I cannot have you saying such things! You've seen how powerful Pompey is. Don't ever mention it again, do you hear me?'

'I'm sorry,' I said, gulping with embarrassment. 'Forgive me.'

'Besides, how would Pompey have got them to Rome? He was a thousand miles away.'

'I wondered if perhaps they came back with Metellus Nepos.'

'Go to bed,' he said angrily. 'You're talking nonsense.' But he obviously must have thought about it overnight, because the next morning his attitude was more subdued. 'I suppose you could be right that the weapons came from Mithradates. After all, the entire royal arsenal was captured, and it's plausible that Nepos might have brought a consignment with him to Rome. However, that's not the same thing as saying that Pompey was actively assisting Catilina.'

'Of course not,' I said.

'That would simply be too appalling to contemplate. Those blades were intended to cut my throat.'

'Pompey would never do anything to harm either you or the state,' I assured him.

The following day Pompey asked Cicero to come and see him.

The Warden of Land and Sea had taken up residence again in his old house on the Esquiline Hill. Over the summer its appearance had been transformed. Dozens of the ramming beaks from captured pirates' warships now bristled from the walls. Some were fashioned in bronze to look like gorgons' heads. Others bore the snouts and horns of animals. Cicero had not seen them before, and regarded them with great distaste. 'Imagine having to sleep here every night,' he said as we waited for the porter to open the door. 'It's like the death chamber of a pharaoh.' And from this time on he often privately referred to Pompey as 'The Pharaoh' or sometimes 'The Shah'.

A large crowd stood outside, admiring the house. Inside, the public rooms were thronged with petitioners hoping to find space to feed at Pompey's golden trough. Some were bankrupt senators looking to sell their votes. Others were businessmen with schemes in which they hoped to persuade Pompey to invest. There were ship-owners and horse-trainers and furniture-makers and jewellers, and some who were plainly just beggars, out to catch Pompey's sympathy with a hard-luck story. Much to their envy, we were shown straight past all these mendicants and into a large private room. In one corner was a tailor's dummy displaying Pompey's triumphal toga and the cloak of Alexander; in another a large head of Pompey made entirely of pearls, which I recognised from the triumphal parade. And in the centre, set up on two trestles, was an architect's model of an immense complex of buildings, over which loomed Pompey, holding a pair of toy wooden temples in either hand. A group of men behind him seemed to be waiting anxiously for his decision.

'Ah,' he said, looking up, 'here is Cicero. He's a clever fellow. He will have a view. What do you think, Cicero? Should I build four temples here, or three?'

'I always build my temples in fours,' replied Cicero, 'providing I have the space.'

'Excellent advice!' exclaimed Pompey. 'Four it will be,' and he set them down in a row, to the applause of his audience. 'We shall decide which gods they are to be dedicated to later. Well?' he said to Cicero, gesturing to the model. 'What do you think?'

Cicero peered down at the elaborate construction. 'Most impressive. What is it? A palace?'

'A theatre, with seating for ten thousand. Here will be public gardens, surrounded by a portico. And here temples.' He turned to one of the men behind him, who I realised must be architects. 'Remind me again: how big is it going to be?'

'The whole construction will extend for a quarter of a mile, Excellency.'

Pompey grinned and rubbed his hands. 'A building a quarter of a mile in length! Imagine it!'

'And where is it to be built?' asked Cicero.

'On the Field of Mars.'

'But where will the people vote?'

'Oh, here somewhere,' said Pompey, waving his hand vaguely, 'or down here by the river. There'll still be plenty of room. Take it away, gentlemen,' he ordered, 'take it away and start digging the foundations, and don't worry about the cost.'

After they had gone, Cicero said, 'I don't wish to sound pessimistic, Pompey, but I fear you may have trouble over this with the censors.'

'Why?'

'They've always forbidden the building of a permanent theatre in Rome, on moral grounds.'

'I've thought of that. I shall tell them I'm building a shrine to Venus. It will be incorporated into the stage somehow – these architects know what they're doing.'

'You think the censors will believe you?'

'Why wouldn't they?'

'A shrine to Venus a quarter of a mile long? They might think you're taking your piety to extreme lengths.'

But Pompey was in no mood for teasing, especially not by Cicero. All at once his generous mouth shrank into a pout. His lips quivered. He was famous for his short temper, and for the first time I witnessed just how quickly he could lose it. 'This city!' he cried. 'It's so full of *little* men – just jealous *little* men! Here I am, proposing to donate to the Roman people the most marvellous building in the history of the world, and what thanks do I receive? None. *None!*' He kicked over one of the trestles. I was reminded of little Marcus in his nursery after he had been made to put away his games. 'And speaking of little men,' he said menacingly, 'why hasn't the senate given me any of the legislation I asked for? Where's the bill to ratify my settlements in the East? And the land for my veterans – what's become of that?'

'These things take time ...'

'I thought we had an understanding: I would support you in the matter of Hybrida, and you would secure my legislation for me in the senate. Well, I've done my part. Where's yours?'

'It is not an easy matter. I can hardly carry these bills on my own. I'm only one of six hundred senators, and unfortunately you have plenty of opponents among the rest.'

'Who? Name them!'

'You know who they are better than I. Celer won't forgive you for divorcing his sister. Lucullus is still resentful that you took over his command in the East. Crassus has always been your rival. Cato feels that you act like a king—'

'Cato! Don't mention that man's name in my presence! It's entirely thanks to Cato that I have no wife!' The roar of Pompey's voice was carrying through the house, and I noticed that some of his attendants had crept up to the door and were standing watching. 'I put off raising this with you until after my triumph, in the hope that you'd have made some progress. But now I am back in Rome and I demand that I am given the respect I'm due! Do you hear me? I demand it!'

'Of course I hear you. I should imagine the dead can hear you. And I shall endeavour to serve your interests, as your friend, as I always have.'

'Always? Are you sure of that?'

'Name me one occasion when I was not loyal to your interests.'

'What about Catilina? You could have brought me home then to defend the republic.'

'And you should thank me I didn't, for I spared you the odium of shedding Roman blood.'

'I could have dealt with him like *that*!' Pompey snapped his fingers.

'But only after he had murdered the entire leadership of the senate, including me. Or perhaps you would have preferred that?'

'Of course not.'

'Because you know that was his intention? We found weapons stored within the city for that very purpose.'

Pompey glared at him, and this time Cicero stared him out: indeed, it was Pompey who turned away first. 'Well, I know nothing about any weapons,' he muttered. 'I can't argue with you, Cicero. I never could. You've always been too nimble-witted for me. The truth is, I'm more used to army life than politics.' He forced a smile. 'I suppose I must learn that I can no longer simply issue a command and expect the world to obey it. "Let arms to toga yield, laurels to words" – isn't that your line? "O, happy Rome, born in my consulship" – there, you see? There's another. You can tell what a student I have become of your work.'

Pompey was not normally a man for poetry, and it was immediately clear to me that the fact that he could recite these lines from Cicero's consular epic – which had just started to be read all over Rome – was proof that he was dangerously jealous. Still, he somehow managed to bring himself to pat Cicero on the arm, and his courtiers exhaled with relief. They drifted away from the entrance, and gradually the sounds of the house resumed, whereupon Pompey – whose bonhomie could be as abrupt and disconcerting as his rages – suddenly announced that they should drink some wine. It was brought in by a very beautiful woman, whose name, I discovered afterwards, was Flora. She was one of the most famous courtesans in Rome and was living under Pompey's roof while he was between wives. She always wore a scarf around her neck, to conceal, she said, the bite marks Pompey inflicted when he was making love. She poured the wine demurely and then withdrew, while Pompey showed us Alexander's cloak, which had, he said, been found in Mithradates's private apartments. It looked very new to me, and I could see that Cicero was having difficulty keeping a straight face. 'Imagine,' he said in a hushed voice, feeling the material with great reverence, 'three hundred years old, and yet it looks as though it was made less than a decade ago.'

'It has magical properties,' said Pompey. 'As long as I keep it by me, I am told no harm can befall me.' He became very serious as he showed Cicero to the door. 'Speak to Celer, will you, and the others, on my behalf? I promised my veterans that I would give them land, and Pompey the Great can't be seen to go back on his word.'

'I'll do everything I can.'

'I'd prefer to work through the senate, but if I have to find my friends elsewhere, I shall. You can tell them I said that.'

As we walked home, Cicero said, 'Did you hear him? "I know nothing about any weapons"! Our Pharaoh may be a great general, but he is a terrible liar.'

'What are you going to do?'

'What else can I do? Support him, of course. I don't like it when he says he might try to find his friends elsewhere. At all costs I must try to keep him out of the arms of Caesar.'

And so Cicero put aside his distaste and his suspicions and did the rounds on Pompey's behalf, just as he had done years before when he was merely a rising senator. It was yet another lesson to me in politics – an occupation that, if it is to be pursued successfully, demands the most extraordinary reserves of self-discipline, a quality that the naive often mistake for hypocrisy.

First, Cicero invited Lucullus to dinner and spent several fruitless hours trying to persuade him to abandon his opposition to Pompey's bills; but Lucullus would never forgive The Pharaoh for taking all the credit for the defeat of Mithradates, and flatly refused to co-operate. Next, Cicero tried Hortensius, and received the same response. He even went to see Crassus, who, despite clearly wishing to destroy his visitor, nevertheless received him very civilly. He sat back in his chair with the tips of his fingers pressed together and his eyes half closed, listening to Cicero's appeal and relishing every word.

'So,' he summarised, 'Pompey fears he will lose face if his bills don't pass, and he asks me to set aside past enmities and give him my support, for the sake of the republic?'

'That's it.'

'Well, I have not forgotten the way he tried to take the credit for defeating Spartacus – a victory that was entirely mine – and you can tell him that I would not raise a hand to help him even if my life depended on it. How is your new house, by the way?'

'Very fine, thank you.'

After that Cicero decided to approach Metellus Celer, who was now consul-elect. It took him a while to summon up the nerve to go next door: this would be the first time he had stepped over the threshold since Clodius committed his outrage at the Good Goddess ceremony. In fact, like Crassus,

Celer could not have been friendlier. The prospect of power suited him – he had been bred for it, like a racehorse – and he too listened judiciously as Cicero made out his case.

'I no more care for Pompey's hauteur than you do,' concluded Cicero, 'but the fact remains that he is by far the most powerful man in the world, and it will be a disaster if he ends up alienated from the senate. But that is what will happen if we don't try to give him his legislation.'

'You think he will retaliate?'

'He says he will have no option except to find his friends elsewhere, which obviously means the tribunes or, even worse, Caesar. And if he follows that route, we'll have popular assemblies, vetoes, riots, paralysis, the people and the senate at one another's throats – in short, a disaster.'

'That's a grim picture, I agree,' said Celer, 'but I'm afraid I cannot help you.'

'Even for the sake of the country?'

'By divorcing my sister in such a public fashion, Pompey humiliated her. He also insulted me, my brother and all my family. I've learned what sort of man he is: utterly untrustworthy, interested only in himself. You should beware of him, Cicero.'

'You have good cause for grievance, no one can doubt that. But think what magnanimity it would show if you were able to say in your inaugural address that for the good of the nation Pompey should be accommodated.'

'It would not show magnanimity. It would show weakness. The Metelli may not be the oldest family in Rome, or the grandest, but we have become the most successful, and we have done it by never yielding an inch to our enemies. Do you know that creature we have as our heraldic symbol?'

'The elephant?'

'The elephant, that's right. We have it because our ancestors beat the Carthaginians, but also because an elephant is the animal our family most resembles. It is massive, it moves slowly, it never forgets, and it always prevails.'

'Yes, and it is also quite stupid, and therefore easily caught.'

'Maybe,' agreed Celer, with a twitch of annoyance. 'But then you set too great a store by cleverness, in my opinion,' and he stood to signal that the interview was over.

He led us into the atrium with its huge display of consular death masks, and as we crossed the marbled floor he gestured to his ancestors, as if all those massed bland, dead faces proved his point more eloquently than any words. We had just reached the entrance hall when Clodia appeared with her maids. I have no idea whether this was coincidental or deliberate, but I suspect the latter, for she was very elaborately coiffed and made up, considering the hour of the morning: 'In full night-time battle rig,' as Cicero said afterwards. He bowed his head to her.

'Cicero,' she responded, 'you have become a stranger to me.'

'True, alas, but not by choice.'

Celer said, 'I was told you two had become great friends while I was away. I'm glad to see you speaking again.' When I heard those words, and the casual way he uttered them, I knew at once that he had no idea of his wife's reputation. He possessed that curious innocence about the civilian world which I have noticed in many professional soldiers.

'You are well, I trust, Clodia?' enquired Cicero politely.

'I am prospering.' She looked at him from under her long lashes. 'And so is my brother in Sicily – despite your efforts.'

She flashed him a smile that was as warm as a blade and swept on, leaving the faintest wash of perfume in her wake. Celer shrugged and said, 'Well, there it is. I wish she talked to you as much as she does to this damned poet who's always trailing round after her. But she's very loyal to Clodius.'

'And does he still plan to become a plebeian?' asked Cicero. 'I wouldn't have thought having a pleb in the family would have gone down at all well with your illustrious ancestors.'

'It will never happen.' Celer checked to see that Clodia was out of earshot. 'Between you and me, I think the fellow is an absolute disgrace.'

This exchange, at least, cheered Cicero, but otherwise all his politicking had come to nothing, and the following day, as a last resort, he went to see Cato. The stoic lived in a fine but artfully neglected house on the Aventine, which smelled of stale food and unwashed clothes and offered nothing to sit on except hard wooden chairs. The walls were undecorated. There were no carpets. Through an open door I caught a glimpse of two plain and solemn teenage girls at work on their sewing, and I wondered if those were the daughters or nieces Pompey had wanted to marry. How different Rome would have been if only Cato had consented to the match! We were shown by a limping porter into a small and gloomy chamber, where Cato conducted his official business beneath a bust of Zeno. Once again Cicero laid out the case for making a compromise with Pompey, but Cato, like the others before him, would have none of it.

'He has too much power as it is,' said Cato, repeating his familiar complaint. 'If we let his veterans form colonies throughout Italy, he'll have a standing army at his beck and call. And why in the name of heaven should we be expected to confirm all his treaties without examining them one by one? Are we the supreme governing body of the Roman republic or little girls to be told where to sit and what to do?'

'True,' said Cicero, 'but we have to face reality. When I went to see him, he could not have made his intentions plainer: if we won't work with him, he'll get a tribune to lay the legislation he wants before a popular assembly, and that will mean endless conflict. Or, worse, he'll throw in his lot with Caesar when he gets back from Spain.'

'What are you afraid of? Conflict can be healthy. Nothing good comes except through struggle.'

'There's nothing good about a struggle between people and senate, believe me. It will be like Clodius's trial, only worse.'

'Ah!' Cato's fanatical eyes widened. 'You are confusing separate issues there. Clodius was acquitted not because of the mob but because of a bribed jury. And there's an obvious remedy for jury-bribing, which I intend to pursue.'

'What do you mean by that?'

'I intend to lay a bill before the house that will remove from all jurors who are not senators their traditional immunity to prosecution for bribery.'

Cicero clutched his hair. 'You can't do *that*!'

'Why not?'

'Because it will look like an attack by the senate on the people!'

'It's no such thing. It's an attack by the senate on dishonesty and corruption.'

'Maybe so, but in politics, how things look is often more important than what they are.'

'Then politics needs to change.'

'At least, I beg you, don't do it now – not on top of everything else.'

'It's never too soon to right a wrong.'

'Now listen to me, Cato. Your integrity may be second to none, but it obliterates your good sense, and if you carry on like this, your noble intentions will destroy our country.'

'Better destroyed than reduced to a corrupt monarchy.'

'But Pompey doesn't want to be a monarch! He's disbanded his army. All he's ever tried to do is work with the senate, yet all he's received is rejection. And far from corrupting Rome, he has done more to extend its power than any man alive!'

'No,' said Cato, shaking his head, 'no, you are wrong. Pompey has subjugated peoples with whom we had no quarrel, he has entered lands in which we have no business, and he has brought home wealth we have not earned. He is going to ruin us. It is my duty to oppose him.'

From this impasse, not even Cicero's agile brain could devise a means of escape. He went to see Pompey later that afternoon to report his failure, and found him in semi-darkness, brooding over the model of his theatre. The meeting was too short even for me to take a note. Pompey listened to the news, grunted, and as we were leaving called after Cicero, 'I want Hybrida recalled from Macedonia at once.'

This threatened Cicero with a serious personal crisis, for he was being hard-pressed by the moneylenders. Not only did he still owe a sizeable sum for the house on the Palatine; he had also bought several new properties, and if Hybrida stopped sending him a share of his spoils in Macedonia – which he had at last begun to do – he would be seriously embarrassed. His solution was to arrange for Quintus's term as governor of Asia to be extended for another year. He was then able to draw from the treasury the funds that should have gone to defray his brother's expenses (he had full power of attorney) and hand the whole lot over to his creditors to keep them quiet. 'Now don't give me one of your reproachful looks, Tiro,' he warned me, as we came out of the Temple of Saturn with a treasury bill for half a million sesterces safely stowed in my document case. 'He wouldn't even *be* a governor if it weren't for me, and besides, I shall pay him back.' Even so, I felt very sorry for Quintus, who was not enjoying his time in that vast, alien and disparate province and was very homesick.

Over the next few months, everything played out as Cicero had predicted. An alliance of Crassus, Lucullus, Cato and Celer blocked

Pompey's legislation in the senate, and Pompey duly turned to a friendly tribune named Fulvius, who laid a new land bill before the popular assembly. Celer then attacked the proposal with such violence that Fulvius had him committed to prison. The consul responded by having the back wall of the gaol dismantled so that he could continue to denounce the measure from his cell. This display of resolution so delighted the people, and discredited Fulvius, that Pompey actually abandoned the bill. Cato then alienated the Order of Knights entirely from the senate by stripping them of jury immunity and also refusing to cancel the debts many had incurred by unwise financial speculation in the East. In both of these actions he was absolutely right morally whilst being at the same time utterly wrong politically.

Throughout all this, Cicero made few public speeches, confining himself entirely to his legal practice. He was very lonely without Quintus and Atticus, and I often caught him sighing and muttering to himself when he thought he was alone. He slept badly, waking in the middle of the night and lying there with his mind churning, unable to nod off again until dawn. He confided to me that during these intervals, for the first time in his life, he was plagued with thoughts of death, as men of his age – he was forty-six – frequently are. 'I am so utterly forsaken,' he wrote to Atticus, 'that my only moments of relaxation are those I spend with my wife, my little daughter and my darling Marcus. My worldly, meretricious friendships may make a fine show in public, but in the home they are barren things. My house is crammed of a morning, I go down to the forum surrounded by droves of friends, but in all the crowds I cannot find one person with whom I can exchange an unguarded joke or let out a private sigh.'

Although he was too proud to admit it, the spectre of Clodius also disturbed his rest. At the beginning of the new session, a tribune by the name of Herennius introduced a bill on the floor of the senate proposing that the Roman people should meet on the Field of Mars and vote on whether or not Clodius should be permitted to become a pleb. That did not alarm Cicero: he knew the measure would swiftly be vetoed by the other tribunes. What did disturb him was that Celer spoke up in support of it, and after the senate was adjourned he sought him out.

'I thought you were opposed to Clodius transferring to the plebs?'

'I am, but Clodia nags me morning and night about it. The measure won't pass in any case, so I hope this will give me a few weeks' peace. Don't worry,' he added quietly. 'If ever it comes to a serious fight, I shall say what I really feel.'

This answer did not entirely reassure Cicero, and he cast about for some means of binding Celer to him more closely. As it happened, a crisis was developing in Further Gaul. A huge number of Germans – one hundred and twenty thousand, it was reported – had crossed the Rhine and settled on the lands of the Helvetii, a warlike tribe, whose response was to move westwards in their turn, into the interior of Gaul, looking for fresh territory. This situation was deeply troubling to the senate, and it was decided that the consuls should at once draw lots for the province of Further Gaul, in case military action proved necessary. It promised to be a glittering command, full of opportunites for wealth and glory. Because both consuls were competitors for the prize – Pompey's clown, Afranius, was Celer's colleague – it fell to Cicero to conduct the ballot, and while I will not go so far as to say he rigged it – as he had once before for Celer – nevertheless it was Celer who drew the winning token. He quickly repaid the debt. A few weeks later, when Clodius returned to Rome from Sicily after his quaestorship was over, and stood up in the senate to demand the right to transfer to the plebs, it was Celer who was the most violent in his opposition.

'You were born a patrician,' he declared, 'and if you reject your birthright you will destroy the very codes of blood and family and tradition on which this republic rests!'

I was standing at the door of the senate when Celer made his about-turn, and the expression on Clodius's face was one of total surprise and horror. 'I may have been born a patrician,' he protested, 'but I do not wish to die one.'

'You most assuredly will die a patrician,' retorted Celer, 'and if you continue on your present course, I tell you frankly, that inevitability will befall you sooner rather than later.'

The senate murmured with astonishment at this threat, and although Clodius tried to brush it off, he must have known that his chances of becoming a pleb, and thus a tribune, lay at that moment in ruins.

Cicero was delighted. He lost all fear of Clodius and from then on foolishly took every opportunity to taunt him and jeer at him. I remember in particular an occasion not long after this when he and Clodius found themselves walking together into the forum to introduce candidates at election time. Unwisely, for plenty around them were listening, Clodius took the opportunity to boast that he had now taken over from Cicero as the patron of the Sicilians, and henceforth would be providing them with seats at the Games. 'I don't believe you were ever in a position to do that,' he sneered.

'I was not,' conceded Cicero.

'Mind you, space is hard to come by. Even my sister, as consul's wife, says she can only give me one foot.'

'Well, I wouldn't grumble about one foot in your sister's case,' replied Cicero. 'You can always hoist the other.'

I had never before heard Cicero make a dirty joke, and afterwards he rather regretted it as being 'unconsular'. Still, it was worth it at the time for the roars of laughter it elicited from everyone standing around, and also for the effect it had on Clodius, who turned a fine shade of senatorial purple. The remark became famous and was repeated all over the city, although mercifully no one had the courage to relay it back to Celer.

And then, in an instant, everything changed, and as usual the man responsible was Caesar – who, although he had been away from Rome for almost exactly a year, had never been far from Cicero's thoughts.

One afternoon towards the end of May, Cicero was sitting on the front bench in the senate house next to Pompey. He had arrived late for some reason, otherwise I am sure he would have got wind of what was coming. As it was, he heard it at the same time as everyone else. After the auguries had been taken, Celer got to his feet to declare that a dispatch had just arrived from Caesar in Further Spain, which he now proposed to read.

'To the senate and people of Rome, from Gaius Julius Caesar, imperator—'

At the word 'imperator', a stir of excitement went around the chamber, and I saw Cicero abruptly sit up and exchange looks with Pompey.

'*From Gaius Julius Caesar*, imperator,' repeated Celer, with greater emphasis, '*greetings. The army is well. I have taken a legion and three cohorts across the mountains called Herminius and pacified the lands on either side of the river Durius. I have dispatched a flotilla from Gades seven hundred miles north and captured Brigantium. I have subdued the tribes of Callaecia and Lusitania and been saluted imperator in the field by the army. I have concluded treaties that will yield annual revenues of twenty million sesterces to the treasury. The rule of Rome now extends to the furthermost shores of the Atlantic sea. Long live our republic.'*

Caesar's language was always terse, and it took a moment for the senate to grasp the momentous nature of what they had just been told. Caesar had been sent out merely to govern Further Spain, a province thought to be more or less pacified, but had somehow contrived to conquer the neighbouring country! His financial backer Crassus immediately jumped to his feet and proposed that Caesar's achievement be rewarded with three days of national thanksgiving. For once, even Cato was too dazed to object, and the motion was carried unanimously. Afterwards, the senators spilled out into the bright sunshine. Most were talking excitedly about this brilliant feat. Not so Cicero: in the midst of that animated throng, he walked with the slow tread and downcast eyes of a man at a funeral. 'After all his scandals and near-bankruptcies, I thought he was finished,' he muttered to me as he reached the door, 'at least for a year or two.'

He beckoned me to follow, and we went and stood in a shady spot in the senaculum, where presently we were joined by Hortensius, Lucullus and Cato; all three looked equally mournful.

'So, what is next for Caesar?' asked Hortensius gloomily. 'Will he try for the consulship?'

'I should say it's certain, wouldn't you?' replied Cicero. 'He can easily afford the campaign – if he's giving twenty million to the treasury, you can be sure he's keeping much more for himself.'

At that moment Pompey walked past, looking thoughtful, and the group fell silent until he was far enough away not to be able to hear them.

Cicero said quietly, 'There goes The Pharaoh. I expect that great ponderous mind of his will be grinding like a mill-wheel. I certainly know what conclusion I'd come to in his place.'

'What's that?' asked Cato.

'I'd make a deal with Caesar.'

The others all shook their heads in disagreement. 'That will never happen,' said Hortensius. 'Pompey can't abide to see another man getting a share of the glory.'

'He'll put up with it this time, though,' said Cicero. 'You gentlemen won't help him get his laws through, but Caesar will promise him the earth – anything in return for Pompey's support in the elections.'

'Not this summer, at least,' said Lucullus firmly. 'There are too many mountains and rivers between here and the Atlantic. Caesar can't get back in time to put his name on the ballot.'

'And there's another thing,' added Cato. 'Caesar will want to triumph, and he'll have to stay outside the city until he does.'

'And we can hold him up for years,' said Lucullus, 'just as he made me wait for half a decade. My revenge for that insult is going to taste better than any meal.'

Cicero however did not look convinced. 'Well, maybe, but I have learned by hard experience never to underestimate our friend Gaius.'

It was a wise remark, because about a week later a second dispatch reached the senate from Further Spain. Again, Celer read it aloud to the assembled senators: in view of the fact that his newly conquered territory was entirely subdued, Caesar announced that he was returning to Rome.

Cato got up to object. 'Provincial governors should remain at their posts until this house gives them permission to do otherwise,' he said. 'I move that we tell Caesar to stay where he is.'

'It's a bit late for that!' someone next to me shouted from the doorway. 'I've just seen him on the Field of Mars!'

'That is impossible,' insisted Cato, looking flustered. 'The last time we heard from him, he was boasting that he was on the Atlantic coast.'

Nevertheless, Celer took the precaution of sending a slave out on to the Field of Mars to check the rumour, and he returned an hour later to announce that it was true: Caesar had overtaken his own messenger and was staying at the home of a friend outside the city.

The news threw Rome into a frenzy of hero-worship. The next day Caesar sent an emissary to the senate to ask that he be granted his triumph in September, and that in the interim he be permitted to stand for the consulship *in absentia*. There were plenty in the senate willing to grant him his wish, for they recognised that Caesar's renown, combined with his new wealth, had made his candidacy well-nigh unstoppable. If a vote had been called, his supporters would probably have won it. Accordingly, day after day, whenever the motion was brought before the house, Cato rose and talked it out. He droned on about the overthrow of the kings of Rome. He bored away about the ancient laws. He wearied everyone with the importance of asserting senatorial control over the legions. He repeatedly warned of the dangerous precedent it would set if a candidate were allowed to seek office at election time whilst still holding military imperium: 'Today Caesar asks for the consulship, tomorrow he may demand it.'

Cicero did not take part himself, but signalled his support for Cato by coming into the chamber whenever he spoke and sitting on the front bench nearest to him. Time was running out for Caesar, and it looked certain that he would miss the deadline for submitting his nomination. Naturally everyone expected that he would choose to triumph rather than become a candidate: Pompey had done that; every victorious general in Rome's history had done it; there was surely nothing to equal the glory of a triumph. But Caesar was never a man to mistake power's show for its substance. Late one afternoon on the fourth day of Cato's filibuster, when the chamber was almost empty and the long green summer shadows were creeping over the deserted benches, into the senate house strolled Caesar. The twenty or so senators who were present could not believe their eyes. He had taken off his uniform and put on a toga.

Caesar bowed to the chair and took his place on the front bench opposite Cicero. He nodded politely across the aisle to my master and settled down to listen to Cato. But for once the great didact was lost for words. Having no further motivation to talk, he sat down abruptly, and the following month Caesar was elected consul by a unanimous vote of all the centuries – the first candidate to achieve this feat since Cicero.

XXXIV

The whole of Rome now waited to see what Caesar would do. 'The only thing we can expect,' said Cicero, 'is that it will be unexpected.' And so it was. It took five months, but when Caesar made his move it was masterly.

One day towards the end of the year, in December, shortly before Caesar was due to be sworn in, Cicero received a visit from the eminent Spaniard Lucius Cornelius Balbus.

This remarkable creature was then forty years old. Born in Gades of Phoenician extraction, he was a trader, and very rich. His complexion was dark, his hair and beard as black as jet, his teeth and the whites of his eyes as bright as polished ivory. He had a very quick way of talking, and he laughed a lot, throwing back his small neat head in delight, so that the most boring men in Rome all fancied themselves great wits after a short time in his company. He had a particular gift for attaching himself to powerful figures – first to Pompey, under whom he served in Spain, and who arranged to make him a Roman citizen, and then to Caesar, who picked him up in Gades when he was governor, appointed him his chief engineer during his conquest of Lusitania, and then brought him back to Rome to run his errands. Balbus knew everyone, even if at first they did not know him, and he bustled in to see Cicero on that December morning with his hands held wide as if he were meeting his closest friend.

'My dear Cicero,' he said in his thickly accented Latin, 'how are you? You look as well as I have ever seen you – and I have never seen you looking anything other than well!'

'Then I suppose I am very much the same as ever.' Cicero gestured to Balbus to take a seat. 'And how is Caesar?'

'He is marvellous,' replied Balbus, 'completely marvellous. He asks me to give you his very warmest regards, and his absolute assurance that he is your greatest and most sincere friend in the world.'

'Time for us to start counting our spoons, then, Tiro,' said Cicero, and Balbus clapped his hands and pulled up his knees and literally rocked with laughter.

'Well, that is very funny – "count the spoons" indeed! I shall tell him you said that, and he will be most amused. The spoons!' He wiped his eyes and recovered his breath. 'Oh dear! But seriously, Cicero, when Caesar offers his friendship to a man, it is not an empty thing. He takes the view that deeds, not words, are what count in this world.'

Cicero had a mountain of legal documents to read. 'Balbus,' he said wearily, 'you have obviously come here to say something – so would you kindly just say it?'

'Of course. You are busy, I can see that. Forgive me.' He pressed his hand to his heart. 'Caesar wishes me to tell you that he and Pompey have reached an agreement. They intend to settle this question of land reform once and for all.'

Cicero gave me a quick look: it was exactly as he had predicted. To Balbus he said: 'On what terms is this to be settled?'

'The public lands in Campania will be divided between Pompey's demobbed legionaries and those among the Roman poor who wish to farm. The whole scheme will be administered by a commission of twenty. Caesar hopes very much to have your support.'

Cicero laughed in disbelief. 'But this is almost precisely the bill he tried to bring in at the start of my consulship and which I opposed!'

'There will be one great difference,' said Balbus with a grin. 'This is between us, please. Yes?' His eyebrows danced in delight. He ran his small pink tongue over the edges of his large white teeth. 'The official commission will be of twenty, but there will be an inner commission of just five magistrates who will take all the decisions. Caesar would be most honoured – most honoured indeed – if you would agree to join it.'

That caught Cicero off his guard. 'Would he indeed? And who would be the other four?'

'Apart from yourself, there would be Caesar, Pompey, one other still to be decided, and' – Balbus paused for effect, like a conjuror about to produce an exotic bird from an empty basket – 'and Crassus.'

Up to that point, Cicero had been treating the Spaniard with a kind of friendly disdain – as a joke figure: one of those self-important go-betweens who often crop up in politics. Now he gazed at him in wonder. '*Crassus?*' he repeated. 'But Crassus can barely abide to be in the same *city* as Pompey. How is he going to sit beside him on a committee of five?'

'Crassus is a dear friend of Caesar. And also Pompey is a dear friend of Caesar. So Caesar played the marriage-broker, in the interests of the state.'

'The interests of themselves more like! It will never work.'

'It most certainly will work. The three have met and agreed it. And against such an alliance, nothing else in Rome will stand.'

'If it has already been agreed, why am I needed?'

'As Father of the Nation, you have a unique authority.'

'So I am to be brought in at the last moment to provide a covering of respectability?'

'Not at all, not at all. You would be a full partner, absolutely. Caesar authorises me to say that no major decision in the running of the empire would be made without consulting you first.'

'So this inner commission would, in effect, act as the executive government of the state?'

'Precisely.'

'And how long would it exist?'

'I am sorry?'

'When will it dissolve?'

'It will never dissolve. It will be permanent.'

'But this is outrageous! There is no precedent in our history for such a body. It would be the first step on the road to a dictatorship!'

'My dear Cicero, really!'

'Our annual elections would become meaningless. The consuls would be puppets, the senate might as well not exist. This inner group would control the allocation of all land and taxes—'

'It would bring stability—'

'It would be a kleptocracy!'

'Are you actually *rejecting* Caesar's offer?'

'Tell your master I appreciate his consideration and I have no desire to be anything other than his friend, but this is not something I can countenance.'

'Well,' said Balbus, plainly shocked, 'he will be disappointed – indeed he will be sorrowful – and so will Pompey and Crassus. Obviously they would like your assurance that you will not oppose them.'

'I am sure they would!'

'Yes, they would. They desire no unpleasantness. But if opposition is offered, you must understand, it will have to be met.'

With great effort, Cicero controlled his temper. 'You can tell them I have struggled for more than a year on Pompey's behalf to secure a fair settlement for his veterans – in the teeth, I might add, of strenuous opposition from Crassus. You can tell them I won't go back on that. But I want no part of any secret deal to establish a government by cabal. It would make a mockery of everything I have ever stood for in my public life. You can see yourself out, I think.'

After Balbus had gone, Cicero sat silent in his library as I tiptoed around him arranging his correspondence into piles. 'Imagine,' he said eventually, 'sending that Mediterranean carpet salesman to offer me a fifth share of the republic at a knock-down price! Our Caesar fancies himself to be a great gentleman, but really he is the most awful vulgar crook.'

'There may be trouble,' I warned.

'Well then, let there be trouble. I am not afraid.' But clearly he was afraid, and suddenly here it was again, that quality I admired the most about him – his reluctant, nervous resolution in the end to do the right thing. Because he must have known that from this time on his position in Rome would start to become untenable. After another long period of reflection, he said: 'All the time that Spanish pimp was talking, I kept thinking of what Calliope says to me in my poetic autobiography. Do you recall her lines?' He closed his eyes and recited:

> 'Meantime the paths which you from earliest days did seek –
> Yes, and when consul too, as mood and virtue called –
> These hold, and foster still your fame and good men's praise.

'I have my faults, Tiro – you know them better than any man: no need to point them out – but I am not like Pompey, or Caesar or Crassus. Whatever I've done, whatever mistakes I've made, I've done for my country; and whatever they do, they do for themselves, even if it means helping a traitor like Catilina.' He gave a long sigh. He seemed almost surprised at his own principled stand. 'Well, there it all goes, I suppose – a peaceful old age, reconciliation with my enemies, power, money, popularity with the mob ...' He folded his arms and contemplated his feet.

'It's a lot to throw away,' I said.

'It is a lot. Perhaps you should run after Balbus and tell him I've changed my mind.'

'Shall I?' My tone was eager – I was desperate for a quiet life – but Cicero did not seem to hear me. He continued to brood on history and heroism, and after a while I went back to arranging his correspondence.

I had thought that 'The Beast with Three Heads', as the triumvirate of Caesar, Pompey and Crassus came to be known, might renew its offer, but Cicero heard no more. The following week Caesar became consul and quickly laid his land bill before the senate. I was watching from the door with a large crowd of jostling spectators when he started asking the senior members for their opinions on the proposed law. He began with Pompey. Naturally the great man approved at once, and so did Crassus. Cicero was called on next, and with Caesar watching him keenly, and with many reservations, added his assent. Hortensius rejected it. Lucullus rejected it. Celer rejected it. And when eventually Caesar worked his way down the list of the great and the good and came to Cato, he too stated his disapproval. But instead of simply giving his view like the others and then sitting down, Cato continued with his denunciation, reaching far back into antiquity for precedents to argue that common land was held in trust for all the nation and was not to be parcelled out by unscrupulous 'here today and gone tomorrow' politicians for their own gain. After an hour it became clear he had no intention of resuming his place and was resorting to his old trick of talking out the day's business.

Caesar grew more and more irritated, tapping his foot impatiently. At last he stood. 'We have heard enough from you,' he said, interrupting Cato in mid-sentence. 'Sit down, you damned sanctimonious windbag, and let someone else speak.'

'Any senator has the right to talk for as long as he wishes,' retorted Cato. 'You should look up the laws of this house if you want to preside over it,' and so saying, he carried on talking.

'Sit down!' bellowed Caesar.

'I shall not be intimidated by you,' replied Cato, and he refused to yield the floor.

Have you ever seen a bird of prey tilt its head from one side to the other, as it detects a potential kill? Well, that was very much how Caesar looked at that instant. His avian profile bent first to the left and then to the right, and then he extended a long finger and beckoned to his chief lictor. He pointed to Cato. 'Remove him,' he rasped. The proximate lictor looked unwilling. 'I said,' repeated Caesar in a terrible voice, *'remove him!'*

The terrified fellow did not need telling twice. Gathering half a dozen of his colleagues, he set off down the aisle towards Cato, who continued to speak even as the lictors clambered over the benches to seize him. Two men took hold of each of his arms and dragged him towards the door, and another picked up all his treasury accounts, while the senate watched in horror.

'What shall we do with him?' called the proximate lictor.

'Throw him in the Carcer,' commanded Caesar, 'and let him address his wisdom to the rats for a night or two.'

As Cato was bundled from the chamber, some senators began objecting to his treatment. The great stoic was carried directly past me, unresisting but continuing to shout out some obscure point about the Scantian forests. Celer rose from the front bench and hurried out after him, closely trailed by Lucullus, and then by Caesar's own consular colleague, Marcus Bibulus. I should think thirty or forty senators must have joined this demonstration. Caesar came down off his dais and tried to intercept a few of those departing. I remember him catching hold of the arm of old Petreius, the commander who had defeated Catilina's army at Pisae. 'Petreius!' he said. 'You are a soldier like me. Why are you leaving?'

'Because,' said Petreius, pulling himself free, 'I would rather be in prison with Cato than here with you!'

'Go then!' Caesar shouted after him. 'Go, all of you! But remember this: as long as I am consul, the will of the people will not be frustrated by procedural tricks and ancient customs! This bill will be placed before the people, whether you gentlemen like it or not, and it will be voted on by the end of the month.' He strode back up the aisle to his chair and glared around the chamber, defying anyone else to challenge his authority.

Cicero stayed uncomfortably in his place as the roll call resumed, and after the session was over he was intercepted outside the senate house by

Hortensius, who demanded to know in a reproachful voice why he had not walked out with the others. 'Don't blame me for the mess you have landed us in,' replied Cicero. 'I warned you what would happen if you continued to treat Pompey with contempt.' Nevertheless, I could tell he was embarrassed, and as soon as he could he escaped to his home. 'I have contrived the worst of all worlds for myself,' he complained to me as we climbed the hill. 'I gain no benefit from supporting Caesar, yet I am denounced by his enemies as a turncoat. What a political genius I have turned out to be!'

In any normal year, Caesar would have either failed with his bill, or at the very least been obliged to compromise. His measure was opposed, first and foremost, by his fellow consul, M. Bibulus, a proud and irascible patrician whose misfortune throughout his career had been to hold office at the same time as Caesar, and who in consequence had been so entirely overshadowed that people usually forgot his name. 'I am tired of playing Pollux to his Castor,' he declared angrily, and he vowed that now he was consul it would be different. Also ranged against Caesar were no fewer than three tribunes: Ancharius, Calvinus and Fannius, each of whom wielded a veto. But Caesar was determined to get his way, whatever the price, and now began his deliberate destruction of the Roman constitution – an act for which I trust he will be cursed by humanity until the end of time.

First, he inserted into the bill a clause requiring every senator to swear an oath – on pain of death – that they would never try to repeal the law once it was on the statute book. Then he called a public assembly at which both Crassus and Pompey appeared. Cicero stood with the other senators and watched as Pompey, for the first time in his long career, was prevailed upon to issue a direct threat. 'This bill is just,' he declared. 'My men have shed their blood for Roman soil, and it is only right that when they return they should be given a share of that soil as their reward.'

'And what,' Caesar asked him disingenuously, 'if those who oppose this bill resort to violence?'

'If anyone comes with the sword, I shall bring my shield,' responded Pompey, before adding with menacing emphasis, 'and I shall also bring a sword of my own.'

The crowd roared in delight. Cicero could not bear to watch any more. He turned and pushed his way past his fellow senators and out of the public assembly.

Pompey's words were effectively a call to arms. Within days Rome began to fill with his veterans. He paid for them to come from all over Italy, and he put them up in tents outside the city, or in cheap lodgings around the town. They smuggled in illegal weapons, which they kept concealed, in anticipation of the last day in January, when the law was to be voted upon by the people. Senators who were known to oppose the legislation were jeered at in the street and their houses stoned.

The man who organised this intimidation on behalf of the Beast with Three Heads was the tribune P. Vatinius, who was known as the ugliest man in Rome. He had contracted scrofula as a boy, and his face and neck were covered in pendulous purplish-blue lumps. His hair was sparse and his legs were rickety, so that he walked with his knees wide apart, as if he had just dismounted after a long ride, or had soiled himself. Curiously, he also had great charm, and did not care at all what anyone said about him: he would always cap an enemy's joke about his appearance with a funnier one of his own. Pompey's men were devoted to him, and so were the plebs. He called many public meetings in support of Caesar's law, and on one occasion summoned the consul Bibulus to be cross-examined on the tribunes' platform. Bibulus was bad-tempered at the best of times, and Vatinius, knowing this, got his followers to lash together some wooden benches and run a bridge from the tribunes' platform straight up to the Carcer. When in due course under questioning Bibulus denounced the land bill in violent language – 'You will not have your law this year, not even if you all want it!' – Vatinius arrested him and had him paraded along the bridge to the jail, like a prisoner of the pirates being made to walk the plank.

Cicero watched much of this from his garden, huddled in a cloak against the January chill. He felt very wretched and tried to keep out of it. Besides, he soon had more pressing problems of his own.

One morning in the midst of these tumultuous events, I opened the door to find Antonius Hybrida waiting outside in the street. It was more than three years since I had last set eyes on him, and at first I did not recognise him. He had grown very stout on the meats and vines of Macedonia, and even more florid, as if he had been coated in an extra layer of mottled red fat. When I took him into the library, Cicero jumped as if he had seen a ghost, which in a sense he had, for this was his past come back to haunt him – and with a vengeance. At the start of his consulship, when the two men had concluded their deal, Cicero had given a written undertaking to Hybrida that if he was ever prosecuted, he would appear as his advocate: now his former colleague had come to collect on that promise. He had brought a slave with him who carried the indictment, and Hybrida passed it across to Cicero with a hand that trembled so violently, I thought he was having a seizure. Cicero took it over to the light to study it.

'When was this served?'

'Today.'

'You realise what this is, don't you?'

'No. That's why I've brought the wretched thing straight round to you. I never could get the hang of all this legal talk.'

'This is a writ for treason.' Cicero scanned the document with an expression of increasing puzzlement. 'Odd. I would have thought they would have come after you for corruption.'

'I say, Cicero, there's no chance of some wine, is there?'

'Just a moment. Let's try to keep our heads clear for business for a little while longer. It says here that you lost an army in Histria.'

'Only the infantry.'

'Only the infantry!' Cicero laughed. 'When was that?'

'A year ago.'

'Who is the prosecutor? Has he been appointed yet?'

'Yes, he was sworn in yesterday. He's that protégé of yours – young Caelius Rufus.'

The news came as a complete shock. That Rufus had become completely estranged from his former mentor was no secret. But that he should choose as his first significant foray into public life the prosecution of Cicero's consular colleague – that was an act of real treachery. Cicero actually sat down, he was so taken aback. He said, 'I thought it was Pompey who was most determined to have you put on trial?'

'He is.'

'Then why is he letting Rufus cut his teeth on such an important case?'

'I don't know. What about that wine now?'

'Forget the damned wine for a minute.' Cicero rolled up the writ and sat tapping it against the palm of his hand. 'I don't like the sound of this. Rufus knows a lot about me. He could bring up all kinds of things.' He threw it back into Hybrida's lap. 'I think you should get someone else to defend you.'

'But I want you! You're the best. We had an agreement, remember? I would give you a share of the money and you would shield me from prosecution.'

'I agreed to defend you if ever you were charged with corruption. I never said anything about treason.'

'That's not true. You're breaking your word.'

'Look, Hybrida, I'll appear as a witness in your support, but this could be an ambush – laid by Caesar, probably, or Crassus – and I'd be a fool to walk straight into it.'

Hybrida's eyes, though now buried deep in his flesh, were still very blue, like sapphires pressed into a lump of red clay. 'People tell me you've come up in the world,' he said. 'Houses everywhere.'

Cicero made a weary gesture. 'Don't try to threaten me.'

'All this,' said Hybrida, pointing around the library. 'Very nice. Do people know how you got the money to pay for it?'

'I warn you: I could as readily appear as a witness for the prosecution as for the defence.'

But the threat sounded hollow, and Cicero must have known it, for he suddenly wiped his hand across his face, as if trying to expunge some disturbing vision.

'I think you should join me in that cup of wine,' said Hybrida, with deep satisfaction. 'Things always look better after a little drink.'

On the evening before the vote on Caesar's land bill, we could hear loud noises rising from the forum – hammering and sawing, drunken singing, cheers, cries, the breaking of pots. At dawn, a shroud of brown smoke hung over the area beyond the Temple of Castor where the voting was to take place.

Cicero dressed carefully and went down to the forum, accompanied by two guards, two members of his household staff – myself and another secretary – and half a dozen clients who wished to be seen with him. All the streets and alleys leading to the voting ground were crammed with citizens. Many, when they recognised Cicero, stood out of the way to let him through. But at least an equal number deliberately blocked his path and had to be pushed out of the way by his guards. It was a struggle for us to make progress, and by the time we found a spot with a view of the temple steps, Caesar was already speaking. It was impossible to hear more than a few words. A great press of bodies, thousands of them, stretched between us and him. The majority looked to be old soldiers who had been there all night, and who had lit fires to cook and keep themselves warm. 'These men are not attending this assembly,' Cicero observed, 'they are occupying it.'

After some time we became aware of scuffling in the direction of the Via Sacra, on the opposite side of the crowd to where we were standing, and the word quickly went round that Bibulus had arrived with the three tribunes who were intending to veto the bill. It was a tremendously brave action on their part. All around us men began pulling out from beneath their clothing knives and even swords. Bibulus and his supporters were clearly having difficulty reaching the temple steps. We could not see them; we could follow their progress only by the origin of the shouts and the line of flailing fists. The tribunes were felled early on and carried away, but somehow Bibulus – and behind him, Cato, who had been released from prison – did at last manage to reach his objective.

Shaking off the hands that were trying to restrain him, he climbed up on to the platform. His toga had been torn away, leaving his shoulder bare, and blood was running down his face. Caesar glanced at him briefly, and carried on speaking. The fury of the crowd was deafening. Bibulus pointed to the heavens and made a cutting gesture across his throat. He repeated this several times until his meaning was obvious – as consul, he had observed the heavens and was declaring that the auguries were unfavourable and no public business could be transacted. Still Caesar ignored him. And then two stout fellows climbed on to the platform carrying a big half-barrel, of the sort used to collect rainwater. They hoisted it above Bibulus's head and tipped it over him. I guess the crowd must have been shitting into it all night, for it was brimful of noxious brown liquid, and Bibulus was completely drenched. He tried to back away, skidded, his legs shot out from under him and he fell heavily on his backside. For a moment he was too winded to move. But then he saw that another barrel was being carried up on to the platform, and he scrambled away – I did not blame him – to the derisive laughter of thousands of citizens. He and his followers escaped from the forum and eventually found sanctuary in the Temple of Jupiter the Protector – the same building from which Cicero by his oratory had driven Sergius Catilina.

Thus, in the most contemptible of circumstances, was carried on to the statute book Caesar's great land reform act, which awarded farms to twenty thousand of Pompey's veterans and afterwards to those among the urban poor who could show they had more than three children. Cicero did not stay for the voting, which was a foregone conclusion, but slunk back to his house, where – such was his depression – he shunned all company, even Terentia's.

The following day, Pompey's soldiers were back on the streets again. They had spent the night celebrating and now they had shifted their attention to the senate house, crowding into the forum, waiting to see if the senate would dare to challenge the legality of what had happened. They left a narrow gangway through their ranks, wide enough for three or four men to walk abreast, and I found it intimidating to pass among them beside Cicero, even though the greetings they called out were friendly enough: 'Come on, Cicero!' 'Cicero – don't forget us!' Inside, I had never seen a more dejected assembly. It was the first day of the new month, and Bibulus, who had a bandage around his forehead, was in the chair. He rose at once and demanded that the house condemn the disgraceful violence of the previous day. He further insisted that the law be declared invalid because the auguries had been unfavourable. But nobody was willing to take such a step – not with several hundred armed men outside. Confronted by their silence, Bibulus lost his temper.

'The government of this republic has become a travesty,' he shouted, 'and I shall take no further part in it! You have shown yourselves unworthy of the name of the Roman senate. I shall not summon you to meet on any day when I am consul. Stay in your homes, gentlemen, as I shall do, and look into your souls, and ask yourselves if you have played your parts with honour.'

Many of his listeners bowed their heads in shame. But Caesar, who was sitting between Pompey and Crassus, and who had been listening to this with a faint smile, immediately rose and said, 'Before Marcus Bibulus and his soul depart the chamber and this house is adjourned for a month, I would remind you gentlemen that this law obliges us all to swear an oath to uphold it. I therefore propose that we should go together now, as a body, to the Area Capitolina and take that oath, so that we may show publicly our unity with the people.'

Cato jumped up. He had his arm in a sling. 'This is an outrage!' he protested, no doubt stung to find the moral high ground temporarily taken from him by Bibulus. 'I shan't sign your illegal law!'

'And nor shall I,' echoed Celer, who had delayed setting out for Further Gaul in order to oppose Caesar. Several others called out the same – among them I noticed young Marcus Favonius, who was an acolyte of Cato's, and the ex-consul Lucius Gellius, who was well into his seventies.

'Then on your own heads be it,' said Caesar with a shrug. 'But remember: the penalty for refusing to comply with the law may be death.'

I had not expected Cicero to speak, but very slowly he got to his feet, and it was a tribute to his authority that the whole chamber was immediately stilled. 'I do not mind this man's law,' he said, staring directly at Caesar, 'although I deplore and condemn absolutely the methods by which he has forced it upon us. Nevertheless,' he continued, turning to the rest of the chamber, 'the law it is, and the people want it, and it requires us to take this oath. Therefore I say to Cato and to Celer, and to any other of my friends who contemplate making dead heroes of themselves: the people will not understand your action, for you cannot oppose illegality by illegality and hope to command respect. Hard times lie ahead, gentlemen, and although you may not feel you need Rome any more, Rome has need of you. Preserve yourselves for the battles yet to come rather than sacrificing yourselves uselessly in one that is already lost.'

It was a most effective speech, and when the senators filed out of the chamber, almost all of them followed the Father of the Nation towards the Capitol, where the oath was to be sworn. Once Pompey's soldiers saw what the senate intended to do, they cheered them loudly (Bibulus, Cato and Celer went up later, when no one was looking). The sacred stone of Jupiter, which had fallen from the heavens many centuries earlier, was fetched out from the great temple, and the senators lined up to place their hands on it and promise to obey the law. But Caesar, even though they were all doing what he wanted, was clearly troubled. I saw him go up to Cicero and take him to one side and speak to him with great seriousness. Afterwards I asked Cicero what he had said. 'He thanked me for my leadership in the senate,' Cicero replied, 'but said he did not care for the tone of my remarks, and hoped that I did not plan to cause him and Pompey and Crassus any trouble, for if I did he would be obliged to retaliate, and that would pain him. He had given me my chance, he said, to join his administration and I had rejected it, and now I must bear the consequences. How do you like that for a piece of effrontery?' He swore roundly, which was unusual for him, and added, 'Catulus was right: I should have beheaded that snake when I had the chance.'

XXXV

Despite his resentment, Cicero kept out of public life for the whole of the next month – an easy matter, as it turned out, as the senate did not meet. Bibulus locked himself away in his house and refused to move, whereupon Caesar declared that he would govern through assemblies of the people, which Vatinius, as tribune, would summon on his behalf. Bibulus retaliated by letting it be known that he was perpetually on his roof, studying the auguries, and that they were consistently unfavourable – thus no official business could legally be transacted. Caesar responded by organising noisy demonstrations in the street outside Bibulus's home, and by continuing to pass his laws via the public assemblies regardless of what his colleague said. (Cicero wittily remarked that Rome seemed to be living under the joint consulship of Julius and Caesar.) It sounded legitimate when one put it that way – governing through the people: what could be fairer? – but really 'the people' were the mob, controlled by Vatinius, and any who opposed what Caesar wanted were quickly silenced. Rome had become a dictatorship in all but name, and most respectable senators were appalled. But with Pompey and Crassus supporting Caesar, few dared speak out against him. Cicero would have preferred to stay in his library and continue to avoid trouble. But in the midst of all this turmoil, towards the end of March, he was obliged to go down to the treason tribunal in the forum to defend Hybrida. To his huge embarrassment, the hearing was scheduled to be held in the comitium itself, just outside the senate house. The curved steps of the rostra, rising like the seats of an amphitheatre, had been cordoned off to form the court, and a large crowd was already clustered around it, eager to see what possible defence the famous orator could come up with for a client who was so manifestly guilty. 'Well, Tiro,' Cicero said to me under his breath as I opened the document case and handed him his notes, 'here is the proof that the gods have a sense of humour – that I should have to appear in this place, as the advocate for this rogue!' He turned and smiled at Hybrida, who was himself at that moment climbing laboriously up on to the platform. 'Good morning to you, Hybrida. I trust you have avoided the wine at breakfast, as you promised? We shall need to keep clear wits about us today.'

'Of course,' replied Hybrida. But it was obvious from the way he stumbled on the steps, as well as from his slurred speech, that he had not been as abstemious as he claimed.

Apart from me and his usual team of clerks, Cicero had also brought along his son-in-law, Frugi, to act as his junior. Rufus, in contrast, appeared alone, and the moment I saw him striding across the comitium towards us, with only one secretary in attendance, I felt what little confidence I had evaporate. Rufus was not yet twenty-three and had just completed a year in Africa on the staff of the governor. A youth had gone out, a man had returned, and I reckoned the contrast between this tall and sunburnt prosecutor and the fleshy, ruined Hybrida was worth a dozen jury votes even before the trial had started. Nor did Cicero come well out of the comparison. He was twice the age of Rufus, and when he went over to his opponent to shake his hand and wish him good luck, he appeared stooped and care-worn. It was like a tableau on the wall of the baths: Juventus versus Senex, with sixty jurymen arrayed in tiers behind them, and the praetor, the haughty Cornelius Lentulus Clodianus, seated between them in the judge's chair.

Rufus was called on first to lay out his case, and it was soon obvious that he had been a more attentive pupil in Cicero's chambers than any of us had realised. The burden of his prosecution was fivefold: first, that Hybrida had concentrated all his energies on extorting as much money as he could from Macedonia; second, that the revenue that should have gone to his army had been diverted into his own pocket; third, that he had neglected his duties as military commander during an expedition to the Black Sea to punish rebellious tribes; fourth, that he had demonstrated cowardice on the field of battle by fleeing from the enemy; and finally fifth, that as a result of his incompetence, the empire had lost the region around Histria on the Lower Danube. Rufus laid these charges with a mixture of moral outrage and malicious humour that was worthy of the Master at his best. I remember in particular his graphic account of

Hybrida's dereliction of duty on the morning of the battle against the rebels. 'They found the man himself stretched out in a drunken stupor,' he said, walking around the back of Hybrida and gesturing to him as if he were an exhibit, 'snoring with all the force of his lungs, belching repeatedly, while the distinguished ladies who shared his quarters sprawled over every couch, and the other women were lying on the floor all around. Half dead with terror, and aware now of the enemy's approach, they tried to rouse up Hybrida; they shouted his name, and tried in vain to hoist him up by his neck; some whispered blandishments in his ear, one or two gave him an energetic slap. He recognised all their voices and their touch and tried to put his arms round the neck of whoever was nearest to him. He was too much aroused to sleep, and too drunk to stay awake; dazed and half asleep, he was thrown around in the arms of his centurions and his concubines.'

And all this, mark you, delivered without a note. It was murderous enough for the defence by itself. But the prosecution's main witnesses – including several of Hybrida's army commanders, a pair of his mistresses, and his quartermaster – were even worse. At the end of the day Cicero congratulated Rufus on his performance, and that evening he frankly advised his gloomy client to sell his property in Rome for the best price he could get, and convert his assets into jewellery or anything portable that he could carry into exile. 'You must brace yourself for the worst.'

I shall not describe all the details of the trial. Suffice it to say that even though Cicero tried every trick he knew to discredit Rufus's case, he barely left a scratch on it, and the witnesses Hybrida produced in his own defence were uniformly feeble – mostly his old drinking companions, or officials he had bribed to lie. By the end of the fourth day, the only question was: should Cicero call on Hybrida to testify, in the hope at least of eliciting some sympathy from the jury; or should Hybrida cut his losses, leave Rome quietly before the verdict, and thus spare himself the humiliation of being jeered out of the city? Cicero took Hybrida into his library to make a decision.

'What do you think I should do?' asked Hybrida.

'I would leave,' answered Cicero, who was desperate to put an end to his own ordeal. 'It's possible your testimony could make matters even worse. Why give Rufus the satisfaction?'

Hybrida broke down. 'What did I ever do to that young man that he should seek to destroy me in such a fashion?' Tears of self-pity trickled down his plump cheeks.

'Now, Hybrida, compose yourself and remember your illustrious ancestors.' Cicero reached across and patted his knee. 'Besides, it's nothing personal. He's simply a clever young man from the provinces, ambitious to rise in the world. In many ways, he reminds me of myself at that age. Unfortunately, you just happen to provide him with the best means of making his name – just as Verres did for me.'

'Damn him,' said Hybrida suddenly, straightening his back. 'I shall testify.'

'Are you certain you are up to it? Cross-examination can be a brutal business.'

'You undertook to defend me,' said Hybrida, at last showing some of his old spirit, 'and I want to put up a defence, even if I lose.'

'Very well,' said Cicero, doing his best to disguise his disappointment. 'In that case we must rehearse your testimony, and that will take us some time. Tiro, you had better bring the senator some wine.'

'No,' said Hybrida firmly. 'No wine. Not tonight. I spent my entire career drunk; I shall at least end it sober.'

And so we worked late into the night, practising what Cicero would ask and how Hybrida would respond. After that, Cicero played the part of Rufus, throwing the most unpleasant questions he could devise at his former colleague, and helping him frame the least incriminating answers. I was surprised by how quick on the uptake Hybrida was when he put his mind to it. The two men went to bed at midnight – Hybrida sleeping under Cicero's roof – and got up at dawn to resume their preparation. Afterwards, as we were walking down to the court with Hybrida and his attendants ahead of us, Cicero said, 'I begin to see why he rose so high in the first place. If only he could have shown such grip earlier, he would not now be facing ruin.'

When we reached the comitium, Hybrida called out cheerfully, 'This is how it was in the time of our joint consulship, Cicero, when we stood shoulder to shoulder to save the republic!' The two men then went up on to the platform, where the court was waiting, and when Cicero announced that he would be calling Hybrida as his final witness, a stir of anticipation ran through the jury. I saw Rufus sit forward on his bench and whisper something in the ear of his secretary, and the man picked up his stylus.

Hybrida was quickly sworn in, and Cicero took him through the questions they had rehearsed, beginning with his military experience under Sulla a quarter of a century before, and dwelling especially on his loyalty to the state at the time of Catilina's conspiracy.

'You laid aside considerations of past friendship, did you not,' asked Cicero, 'to take command of the senate's legions that finally crushed the traitor?'

'I did.'

'And you sent back the monster's head to the senate as proof of your actions?'

'I did.'

'Mark that well, gentlemen,' said Cicero, addressing the jury. 'Is that the action of a traitor? Young Rufus over there supported Catilina – let him deny it – and then fled from Rome to avoid sharing in his fate. Yet now he has the nerve to come creeping back into the city and accuse of treason the very man who rescued us from ruin!' He turned back to Hybrida. 'After crushing Catilina, you relieved me of the burden of governing Macedonia, so that I could devote myself to extinguishing the last embers of the conspiracy?'

'I did.'

And so it went on, with Cicero leading his client through his testimony like a father leading a child by the hand. He prompted him to describe how he had raised revenue in Macedonia through entirely legal means, accounted for every penny, raised and equipped two legions, and led them on a hazardous expedition eastwards through the mountains to the Black Sea. He painted a terrifying picture of warlike tribes – Getians, Bastarns, Histrians – harrying the Roman column as it marched along the Danube valley.

'The prosecution alleges that when you heard there was a large enemy force ahead, you split your force in two, taking the cavalry with you to safety and leaving the infantry undefended. Is that true?'

'Not at all.'

'You were in fact bravely pursuing the Histrian army, is that correct?'

'That's right.'

'And while you were away, the Bastarn forces crossed the Danube and attacked the infantry from the rear?'

'True.'

'And there was nothing you could do?'

'I am afraid there was not.' Hybrida lowered his head and wiped his eyes, as Cicero had instructed him.

'You must have lost many friends and comrades at the hands of the barbarians.'

'I did. A great many.'

After a long pause, during which there was complete silence in the court, Cicero turned to the jury. 'The fortunes of war, gentlemen,' he said, 'can be cruel and capricious. But that is not the same as treason.'

As he resumed his seat there was prolonged applause, not only from the crowd but among the jury, and for the first time I dared to hope that Cicero's skill as an advocate might once again have saved the day. Rufus smiled to himself and took a sip of wine and water before getting to his feet. He had an athlete's way of loosening his shoulders by linking his hands behind his head and rotating his upper torso from side to side. Watching him do it then, just before he started his cross-examination, the years seemed to fall away, and suddenly I remembered how Cicero used to send him running errands across the city and tease him for the looseness of his clothes and the length of his hair. And I recalled how the boy would steal money from me and stay out all night drinking and gambling, and yet how hard it was to feel angry with him for long. What pattern of ambition's twisting paths had brought us each to this place?

Rufus sauntered over to the witness stand. He was entirely without nerves. He might have been meeting a friend at a tavern. 'Do you have a good memory, Antonius Hybrida?'

'I do.'

'Well then, I expect you remember a slave of yours who was murdered on the eve of your consulship.'

A look of great mystification passed across Hybrida's face and he glanced across in puzzlement towards Cicero. 'I'm not sure that I do. One's had so many slaves over the years ...'

'But you must remember this slave?' persisted Rufus. 'A Smyrnan? Twelve years old or thereabouts? His body was dumped in the Tiber. Cicero was there when his remains were discovered. His throat had been cut and his intestines removed.'

There was a gasp of horror around the court, and I felt my mouth go dry, not only at the memory of that poor lad, but at the realisation of where this chain of questioning might lead. Cicero saw it too. He jumped up in alarm and appealed to the praetor, 'This is irrelevant, surely? The death of a slave more than four years ago can have nothing to do with a lost battle on the shores of the Black Sea.'

'Let the prosecutor ask his question,' ruled Clodianus, and then added philosophically: 'I have found in life that all sorts of things are often linked.'

Hybrida was still looking hopelessly at Cicero. 'I believe perhaps I do remember something of the sort.'

'I should hope so,' responded Rufus. 'It's not every day that a human sacrifice is performed in one's presence! Even for you, I would have thought, with all your abominations, that must have been a rarity.'

'I know nothing about any human sacrifice,' muttered Hybrida. 'Catilina did the killing, and then required you and others present to swear an oath.'

'Did he?' Hybrida screwed up his face as if he were trying to remember some long-forgotten acquaintance. 'No, I don't think so. No, you are mistaken.'

'Yes he did. You swore an oath on the blood of that slaughtered child to murder your own colleague as consul – the man who now sits beside you as your advocate!'

These words produced a fresh sensation, and when the cries had died away, Cicero got up. 'Really, this is a pity,' he said, with a regretful shake of his head, 'a great pity, because my young friend was not doing a bad job as prosecutor up to this moment – he was my pupil once, gentlemen, so actually I flatter myself as well as him by conceding it. Unfortunately now he has gone and ruined his own case with an insane allegation. I fear I shall have to take him back to the classroom.'

'I know it is true, Cicero,' retorted Rufus, smiling even more broadly, 'because you told me about it yourself.'

For the barest flicker of an instant, Cicero hesitated, and I saw to my horror that he had forgotten his conversation with Rufus all those years ago. 'You ungrateful wretch,' he spluttered. 'I did no such thing.'

'In the first week of your consulship,' said Rufus, 'two days after the Latin Festival you called me to your house and asked if Catilina had ever talked in my presence of killing you. You told me that Hybrida had confessed to swearing an oath with Catilina on a murdered boy to do precisely that. You asked me to keep my ears open.'

'That is a complete lie!' shouted Cicero, but his bluster did little to dispel the effect of Rufus's cool and precise recollection.

'This is the man you took into your confidence as consul,' continued Rufus, with deadly calmness, pointing at Hybrida. 'This is the man you foisted on the people of Macedonia as their governor – a man you knew to have taken part in a bestial murder, and who had desired your own death. And yet this is the man you defend today. Why?'

'I don't have to answer your questions, boy.'

Rufus strolled over to the jury. 'That is the question, gentlemen: why does Cicero, of all men, who made his reputation attacking corrupt provincial governors, now destroy his good name by defending this one?'

Once again Cicero stretched out a hand to the praetor. 'Clodianus, I am asking you, for heaven's sake, to control your court. This is supposed to be a cross-examination of my client, not a speech about me.'

'That is true, Rufus,' said the praetor. 'Your questions must relate to the case in hand.'

'But they do. My case is that Cicero and Hybrida came to an agreement.'

Cicero said, 'There is no proof of that.'

'Yes there is,' retorted Rufus. 'Less than a year after you dispatched Hybrida to the long-suffering people of Macedonia, you bought yourself a new house – there!' He gestured to it, gleaming on the Palatine in the spring sunshine, and the jurymen all turned their heads to look. 'One much like it sold soon afterwards for fourteen million sesterces. *Fourteen million!* Ask yourselves, gentlemen: where did Cicero, who prided himself on his humble origins, acquire such a fortune, if not from the man he both blackmailed and protected, Antonius Hybrida? Is that not the truth,' he demanded, turning back to the accused, 'that you diverted part of the money you extorted from your province to your partner in crime in Rome?'

'No, no,' protested Hybrida. 'I may have sent Cicero a gift or two from time to time, but that is all.' (This was the explanation they had agreed on the previous evening, in case Rufus had evidence of money passing between them.)

'*A gift?*' repeated Rufus. With exaggerated slowness he looked once more at Cicero's house, raising his hand to protect his eyes from the sun. A woman with a parasol was strolling along the terrace, and I realised it must be Terentia. 'That is quite a gift!'

Cicero sat very still. He watched Rufus closely. Several members of the jury were shaking their heads. From the audience in the comitium came the sound of jeering.

'Gentlemen,' said Rufus, 'I believe I have made my case. I have shown how Hybrida lost a whole region from our empire by his treasonable negligence. I have proved his cowardice and incompetence. I have revealed how money that should have gone to the army went instead into his own coffers. The ghosts of his legionaries, abandoned by their chief and cruelly murdered by the barbarians, cry out to us for justice. This monster should never have been permitted to hold such a high position, and would not have done so without the collusion of his consular colleague. His career is soaked in blood and depravity – the murder of that child is but a small part of it. It is too late to bring the dead back to life, but let us at least remove this man and his stench from Rome. Let us send him into exile tonight.'

Rufus sat down to prolonged applause. The praetor looked somewhat surprised, and asked if that was the conclusion of the prosecution's case. Rufus signalled that it was.

'Well, well. I thought we had at least another day to go,' said Clodianus. He turned to Cicero. 'Do you wish to make your closing speech for the defence immediately, or would you prefer the court to adjourn overnight so that you can prepare your remarks?'

Cicero was looking very flushed, and I knew at once that it would be a grave mistake for him to speak before he had had a chance to calm down. I was sitting in the space set aside for the clerks, just below the podium, and I actually rose and went up the couple of steps to plead with him to accept the adjournment. But he waved me aside before I could utter a word. There was a curious light in his eyes. I am not sure he even saw me.

'Such lies,' he said with utter disgust. He rose to his feet. 'Such lies are best squashed dead at once, like cockroaches, and not left alive to breed overnight.'

The area in front of the court had been full before, but now people began to stream into the comitium from all across the forum. Cicero on his feet was one of the great sights of Rome, and no one wanted to miss it. Not one of the Three Heads of the Beast was present, but here and there in the crowd I could see their surrogates: Balbus for Caesar, Afranius for Pompey, Arrius for Crassus. I did not have time to look for anyone else: Cicero had started speaking and I had to take down his words.

'I must confess,' he said, 'I had not much relished the prospect of coming down to this court to defend my old friend and colleague Antonius Hybrida, for such obligations as these are numerous and rest heavily on a man who has been in public life as long as I have. Yes, Rufus: "obligations" – that is a word you do not understand, otherwise you would not have addressed me in such a fashion. But now I welcome this duty – I relish it, I am glad for it – because it enables me to say something that has needed to be said for years. Yes, I made common cause with Hybrida, gentlemen – I do not deny it. I sought him out. I overlooked the differences in our styles of life and views. I overlooked many things, in fact, because I had no choice. If I was to save this republic I needed allies, and could not be too particular about where they came from.

'Cast your minds back to that terrible time. Do you think that Catilina acted alone? Do you think that one man, however energetic and inspired in his depravity, could have proceeded as far as Catilina did – could have brought this city and our republic to the edge of destruction – if he had not had powerful supporters? And I do not mean that ragbag of bankrupt noblemen, gamblers, drunkards, perfumed youths and layabouts who flocked around him – among whom, incidentally, our ambitious young prosecutor was once numbered.

'No, I mean men of substance in our state – men who saw in Catilina an opportunity to advance their own dangerous and deluded ambitions. These men were not justly executed on the orders of the senate on the fifth day of December, nor did they die on the field of battle at the hands of the legions commanded by Hybrida. They were not sent into exile as a result of my testimony. They walk free today. No, more than that: *they control this republic!*'

Up to this point in his speech, Cicero had been heard in silence. But now a great many people drew in their breath, or turned to their neighbours to express their astonishment. Balbus had started making notes on a wax tablet. I thought, *Does he realise what he is doing?* and I risked a glance at Cicero. He barely seemed conscious of where he was – oblivious to the court, to his audience, to me, to political calculation: he was intent only on getting out his words. 'These men made Catilina what he was. He would have been nothing without them. They gave him their votes, their money, their assistance and their protection. They spoke up for him in the senate and in the law courts and in the popular assemblies. They shielded him and they nurtured him and they even supplied him with the weapons he needed to slaughter the government.' (Here my notes record more loud exclamations from the audience.) 'Until this moment, gentlemen, I did not realise the extent to which there were two conspiracies I had to fight. There was the conspiracy that I destroyed, and then there was the conspiracy behind that conspiracy – and that inner one prospers still. Look around you, Romans, and you can see how well it prospers! Rule by secret conclave and by terror on the streets. Rule by illegal methods and by bribery on a massive scale – dear gods, you accuse Hybrida of corruption? He is as guileless and as helpless as a baby by comparison with Caesar and his friends!

'This trial itself is the proof. Do you think that Rufus is the sole author of this prosecution? This neophyte who has barely grown his first beard? What nonsense! These attacks – this so-called evidence – all of it is designed to discredit not just Hybrida, but me – my reputation, my consulship, and the policies I pursued. The men behind Rufus seek to destroy the traditions of our republic for their own wicked ends, and to accomplish that – forgive me if I flatter myself: it is not the first time, I know – to achieve that aim they need to destroy me first.

'Well, gentlemen, here in this court, on this day, at this defining hour, you have a chance for immortal glory. That Hybrida made mistakes I do not doubt. That he has indulged himself more than was wise for him, I sadly concede. But look beyond his sins and you will see the same man who stood with me against the monster who threatened this city four years ago. Without his support, I would have been struck down by an assassin very early in my term. He did not desert me then, and I shall not abandon him now. Acquit him by your votes, I pray you; keep him here in Rome, and by the grace of our ancient gods we shall once again restore the light of liberty to this city of our forefathers!'

Thus spoke Cicero, but when he sat down there was very little applause, mostly just a buzz of amazement around the court at what he had said. Those who agreed with him were too frightened to be seen to support him. Those who disagreed with him were too cowed by the impact of his rhetoric to protest. The rest – the majority, I should say – were simply bewildered. I looked for Balbus in the crowd, but he had slipped away. I went up to Cicero with my notebook and congratulated him on the force of his remarks.

'Did you get it all down?' he asked, and when I replied that I had, he told me to copy out the speech as soon as we got home and hide it in a safe place. 'I expect a version is on its way to Caesar even now,' he added. 'I saw that reptile Balbus writing almost as quickly as I could speak. We must make sure we have an accurate transcript in case this is raised in the senate.'

I could not stay to talk to him further, as the praetor was ordering that the jury should be balloted at once. I glanced at the sky. It was the middle of the day; the sun was high and warm. I returned to my place and watched the urn as it was passed from hand to hand and filled with tokens. Cicero and Hybrida sat watching as well, side by side, too nervous to speak, and I thought of all the other trials I had sat through, and how they always ended in exactly this way, with this horrible period of waiting. Eventually the clerks completed their tally and the result was passed up to the praetor. He stood, and we all followed suit.

'The question before the court is whether Caius Antonius Hybrida is to be condemned for treason in connection with his governorship of the province of Macedonia. There voted in favour of condemnation forty-seven, and in favour of acquittal twelve.' There was a great cheer from the crowd. Hybrida bowed his head. The praetor waited until the sounds had died away. 'Caius Antonius Hybrida is therefore stripped of all rights of property and citizenship in perpetuity, and from midnight is to be denied fire and water anywhere within the lands, cities and colonies of Italy, and any who seek to assist him shall be subject to the same punishment. This court is adjourned.'

Cicero did not lose many cases, but on the rare occasions that he did, he was usually scrupulous in congratulating his opponents. Not this time. When Rufus came over to commiserate, Cicero pointedly turned his back on him, and I was pleased to see that the young rogue was left with his hand extended in mid-air, looking a fool. Eventually he shrugged and turned away. As for Hybrida, he was philosophical. 'Well,' he said to Cicero in my hearing, as he was preparing to be led away by the lictors, 'you warned me the way the wind was blowing, and thankfully I have a little money put by to see me through my old age. Besides, I am told that the southern coast of Gaul looks very like the Bay of Naples. So do not concern yourself with my fate, Cicero. After that speech, it is your own you ought to worry about.'

*

It must have been about two hours later – certainly no more – that the door to Cicero's house was suddenly thrown open and Metellus Celer appeared in a state of great agitation, demanding to see my master. Cicero was dining with Terentia and I was still transcribing his speech. But I could see it was supremely urgent so I took him through at once.

Cicero was reclining on a couch, describing the end of Hybrida's trial, when Celer burst into the room and interrupted him.

'What did you say in court about Caesar this morning?'

'Good day to you, Celer. I told a few truths, that's all. Will you join us?'

'Well, they must have been pretty dangerous truths, for Gaius is exacting a mighty revenge.'

'Is he really?' replied Cicero, with an attempt at sangfroid. 'And what is to be my punishment?'

'He is in the senate house as we speak, arranging for that swine of a brother-in-law of mine to become a plebeian!'

Cicero sat up in such alarm he knocked his glass over. 'No, no,' he said, 'that cannot be right. Caesar would never lift a finger to help Clodius – not after what Clodius did to his wife.'

'You are wrong. He is doing it right now.'

'How do you know?'

'My own darling wife just took great pleasure in telling me.'

'But how is it possible?'

'You forget Caesar is the chief priest. He has summoned an emergency meeting of the curia to approve an adoption.'

Terentia said, 'Is that legal?'

'Since when did legality matter,' asked Cicero bitterly, 'when Caesar is involved?' He started rubbing his forehead very hard, as if he could somehow magic forth a solution. 'What about getting Bibulus to pronounce the auguries unfavourable?'

'Caesar's thought of that. He has Pompey with him—'

'Pompey?' Cicero looked stunned. 'This gets worse every moment!'

'Pompey is an augur. He's observed the skies and declared that all's well.'

'But you're an augur. Can't you overrule him?'

'I can try. At the very least we ought to get down there.'

Cicero needed no further urging. Still wearing his slippers, he hurried out of the house after Celer, while I panted along at their backs with their attendants. The streets were quiet: Caesar had moved so quickly, no word of what was happening had filtered through to the people. Unfortunately, by the time we had sprinted across the forum and thrown open the doors of the senate house, the ceremony was just finishing – and what a shameful scene it was that met our eyes. Caesar was on the dais at the far end of the chamber, dressed in his robes as chief priest and surrounded by his lictors. Pompey was beside him, absurd in his augural cap and carrying a divining wand. Several other pontiffs were also standing around, among them Crassus, who had been co-opted into the college at Caesar's behest to replace Catulus. Clustered together on the wooden benches, like penned sheep, was the curia, the thirty elderly greyheads who were the chiefs of the tribes of Rome. And finally, to complete the picture, the golden-curled Clodius was kneeling in the aisle next to another man. Everyone turned at the noise of our entrance, and never have I forgotten the smirk of triumph on Clodius's face when he realised Cicero was watching – it was a look of almost childish devilment – although it was quickly replaced by an expression of terror as his brother-in-law strode towards him, followed by Cicero.

'What the fuck is going on here?' shouted Celer.

'Metellus Celer,' responded Caesar in a firm voice, 'this is a religious ceremony. Do not profane it.'

'A religious ceremony! With Rome's profaner-in-chief kneeling here – the man who fucked your own wife!' He aimed a kick at Clodius, who scrambled away from him towards Caesar's feet. 'And who is this boy?' he demanded, looming over the other cowering man. 'Let's see who's joined the family!' He hauled him to his feet by the scruff of his neck and turned him round to show us – a shivering, pimply youth of twenty or so.

'Show some respect to my adopted father,' said Clodius, who, despite his fear, could not stop himself laughing.

'You disgusting—' Celer dropped the youth and returned his attention to Clodius, drawing back his huge fist to strike him, but Cicero caught his arm. 'No, Celer. Don't give them an excuse to arrest you.'

'Wise advice,' said Caesar.

After a moment, Celer reluctantly lowered his hand. 'So your father is younger than you are? What a farce this is!'

Clodius smirked. 'He was the best that could be found at short notice.'

Precisely what the tribal elders – none of whom was under fifty – must have made of this spectacle, I cannot imagine. Many were old friends of

Cicero. We learned later that they had been turfed from their homes and places of business by Caesar's henchmen, frogmarched to the senate house and more or less ordered to approve Clodius's adoption.

'Have we finished here yet?' asked Pompey. He not only looked ridiculous in his augural outfit but plainly was embarrassed.

'Yes, we have finished,' said Caesar. He held out a hand as if bestowing a blessing at a wedding. 'Publius Clodius Pulcher, by the powers of my office as pontifex maximus, I declare that you are now the adopted son of Publius Fonteius, and will be entered into the state's records as a plebeian. Your change of status having immediate effect, you may therefore contest the elections for tribune if you wish. Thank you, gentlemen.' Caesar nodded their dismissal, the curia rose to their feet, and the first consul and chief priest of Rome lifted his robes a fraction and stepped down from the dais, his afternoon's work done. He moved past Clodius with his head averted in distaste, as one might pass a carcass in the street. 'You should have heeded my warning,' he hissed at Cicero as he went by. 'Now look what you've forced me to do.' He processed with his lictors towards the door, followed by Pompey, who still could not bring himself to meet Cicero's eyes; only Crassus permitted himself a slight smile.

'Come along, Father,' said Clodius, putting his arm around Fonteius's shoulders, 'let me help you home.' He gave another of his unnerving, girlish laughs, and after a bow to his brother-in-law and to Cicero, they joined the end of the cortège.

'*You* may have finished, Caesar,' Celer called after them, 'but I have not! I am the governor of Further Gaul, remember, and I command legions, whereas you have none! *I* have not even started yet!'

His voice was loud. It must have carried halfway across the forum. Caesar, however, passed from the chamber and into the daylight without giving any sign that he had heard. Once he and the rest had gone and we were alone, Cicero slumped heavily on to the nearest bench and put his head in his hands. Up in the rafters the pigeons flapped and cooed – to this day I cannot hear those filthy birds without thinking of the old senate house – while the sounds of the street outside seemed strangely disconnected from me: unearthly, as if I were already in prison.

'No despairing, Cicero,' said Celer briskly after some time had passed. 'He's not even a tribune yet – and won't be, if I can help it.'

'Crassus I can beat,' replied Cicero. 'Pompey I can outwit. Even Caesar I have managed to hold in check in the past. But all three combined, and with Clodius as their weapon?' He shook his head wearily. 'How am I to live?'

That evening Cicero went to see Pompey, taking me with him, partly to show that this was a business call and not in any way social, and also I suspect to bolster his nerve. We found the great man drinking in his bachelor den with his old army comrade and fellow Picenian Aulus Gabinius. They were examining the model of Pompey's theatre complex when we were shown in, and Gabinius was gushing with enthusiasm. He was the man who, as an ambitious tribune, had proposed the laws that secured Pompey his unprecedented military powers, and he had duly been rewarded with a legateship under Pompey in the East. He had been away for several years, during which time – unknown to him – Caesar had been conducting an affair with his wife, the blowsy Lollia (at the same time as he had been sleeping with Pompey's wife, come to think of it). But now Gabinius was back in Rome – just as ambitious, a hundred times as rich, and determined to become consul.

'Cicero, my dear fellow,' said Pompey, rising to embrace him, 'will you join us for some wine?'

'I shall not,' said Cicero stiffly.

'Oh dear,' said Pompey to Gabinius, 'do you hear his tone? He's come to upbraid me for that business this afternoon I was telling you about,' and turning back to Cicero he said, 'Do I really need to explain to you that it was all Caesar's idea? I tried to talk him out of it.'

'Really? Then why didn't you?'

'He was of the view – and I must say I have to agree with him – that the tone of your remarks in court today was grossly offensive to us, and merited a public rebuke of some kind.'

'So you open the way for Clodius to become a tribune – knowing that his stated intention once he gains that office is to bring a prosecution against me?'

'I would not have gone that far, but Caesar was set on it. Are you sure I cannot tempt you to some wine?'

'For many years,' said Cicero, with a terrible calmness, 'I have supported you in everything you wanted. I have asked for nothing in return except your friendship, which has been more precious to me than anything in my public life. And now at last you have shown your true regard for me to all the world – by helping to give my deadliest enemy the weapon he needs to destroy me!'

Pompey's lip quivered and his oyster eyes filled with tears. 'Cicero, I am appalled. How can you say such things? I would never stand aside and see you destroyed. My position is not an easy one, you know – trying to exert a calming influence on Caesar is a sacrifice I make on behalf of the republic every day of my life.'

'But not today, apparently.'

'He felt that his dignity and authority were threatened by what you said.'

'Not half as threatened as they will be if I reveal all I know about this Beast with Three Heads and its dealings with Catilina!'

Gabinius broke in. 'I don't think you should speak to Pompey the Great in that tone.'

'No, no, Aulus,' said Pompey sadly, 'what Cicero says is right. Caesar has gone too far. The gods know I have tried to do as much as I can to moderate his actions behind the scenes. When Cato was flung in prison, I had him released at once. And poor Bibulus would have suffered a much worse fate than having a barrel of shit poured over him if it hadn't been for me. But on this occasion I failed. I was bound to one day. I'm afraid Caesar is just so ... *relentless*.' He sighed and picked up one of the toy temples from his model theatre and contemplated it thoughtfully. 'Perhaps the time is coming,' he said, 'when I shall have to break with him.' He gave Cicero a crafty look – his eyes had quickly dried, I noticed. 'What do you think of that?'

'I think it cannot come soon enough.'

'You may be right.' Pompey took the temple between his fat thumb and forefinger and replaced it with surprising delicacy in its former position. 'Do you know what his new scheme is?'

'No.'

'He wishes to be awarded a military command.'

'I'm sure he does. But the senate has already decreed that there will be no provinces for the consuls this year.'

'The senate has, yes. But Caesar doesn't care about the senate. He is going to get Vatinius to propose a law in the popular assembly.'

'What?'

'A law granting him not just one province, but two – Nearer Gaul and Bithynia – with the authority to raise an army of two legions. And it won't just be a one-year appointment, either – he wants five years.'

'But the award of provinces has always been decided by the senate, not the people,' protested Cicero. 'And *five years*! This will smash our constitution to pieces.'

'Caesar says not. Caesar says to me, "What is wrong with trusting the people?"'

'It isn't the people! It's a mob, controlled by Vatinius.'

'Well,' said Pompey, 'now perhaps you can understand why I agreed to watch the skies for him this afternoon. Of course I should have refused. But I have to keep a larger picture in view. Someone must control him.'

Cicero put his head in his hands in despair. Eventually he said, 'May I tell some of my friends your reasons for going along with him today? Otherwise they will think I no longer have your support.'

'If you must – in the strictest confidence. And you may tell them – with Aulus here as a witness – that no harm will befall Marcus Tullius Cicero as long as Pompey the Great still breathes in Rome.'

Cicero was very silent and thoughtful as we walked home. Instead of going straight to his library, he took several turns around his garden in the darkness, while I sat at a table nearby with a lamp and quickly wrote down as much of Pompey's conversation as I could remember. When I had finished, Cicero told me to come with him, and we went next door to see Metellus Celer.

I was worried that Clodia might be present, but there was no sign of her. Instead Celer was sitting in his dining room alone, lit by a solitary candelabrum, chewing morosely on a cold chicken leg, with a jug of wine beside him. Cicero refused a drink for the second time that evening and asked me to read out what Pompey had just said. Celer was predictably outraged.

'So I shall have Further Gaul – which is where the fighting will have to be done – and he Nearer, yet each of us is to have two legions?'

'Yes, except that he will hold his province for an entire lustrum, while you will have to give up yours by the end of the year. You may be sure that if there's any glory to be had, Caesar will have it all.'

Celer let out a bellow of rage and shook his fists. 'He *must* be stopped! I don't care if there *are* three of them running this republic. There are hundreds of us!'

Cicero sat down on the couch beside him. 'We don't need to beat all three,' he said quietly. 'Just one will do. You heard what Pompey said. If we can somehow take care of Caesar, I don't think he'll do much about it. All Pompey cares about is his own dignity.'

'And what about Crassus?'

'Once Caesar is off the scene, he and Pompey won't be allies for another hour – they can't abide one another. No: Caesar is the stone that holds this arch together. Remove him and the structure falls.'

'So what do you propose we should do?'

'Arrest him.'

Celer gave Cicero a sharp look. 'But Caesar's person is inviolable, not once, but twice – first as chief priest, and then as consul.'

'You really think he'd worry about the law if he were in our place? When his every act as consul has been illegal? We either stop him now, while there's time, or we leave it until he's picked us all off one by one and there's nobody left to oppose him.'

I was amazed by what I was hearing. Until that afternoon I am sure that Cicero would never have entertained for a moment the thought of such a desperate action. It was a measure of the chasm he now saw opening up before him that he should actually have given voice to it.

'How would this be done?' asked Celer.

'You're the one with an army. How many men do you have?'

'I have two cohorts camped outside the city, preparing to march with me to Gaul.'

'How loyal are they?'

'To me? Absolutely.'

'Would they be willing to seize Caesar from his residence after dark and hold him somewhere?'

'No question, if I gave the order. But surely it would be better just to kill him?'

'No,' said Cicero. 'There would have to be a trial. On that I insist. I want no "accidents". We would have to put through a bill to set up a special tribunal to try him for his illegal actions. I'd lead for the prosecution. Everything would have to be open and clear.'

Celer looked dubious. 'As long as you agree there could only be one verdict.'

'And Pompey would have to approve – don't imagine for a moment you could go back to your old habit of opposing him on everything he wants. We would have to guarantee that his men could keep their farms, confirm his Eastern settlements – maybe even give him a second consulship.'

'That's a lot to swallow. Wouldn't we just be swapping one tyrant for another?'

'No,' said Cicero with great force. 'Caesar is of a different category of man altogether. Pompey merely wants to rule the world. Caesar longs to smash it to pieces and remake it in his own image. And there's something else.' He paused, searched for the words.

'What? He's cleverer than Pompey, I'll give him that.'

'Oh yes, yes, of course, he's a hundred times cleverer. No, it's not that – it's more – I don't know – there's a kind of divine recklessness about him – a contempt, if you like, for the world itself – as if he thinks it's all a joke. Anyway, this – whatever it is: this quality – it makes him hard to stop.'

'That's all very philosophical, but I'll tell you how we stop him. It's easy. We put a sword through his throat, and you'll find he'll die the same as any man. But we have to do it to him as he would do it to us – fast, and ruthlessly, and when he least expects it.'

'When would you suggest?'

'Tomorrow night.'

'No, that's too soon,' said Cicero. 'We can't do this entirely alone. We shall have to bring in others.'

'Then Caesar is bound to get to hear of it. You know how many informants he has.'

'I'm only talking about half a dozen men, if that. All reliable.'

'Who?'

'Lucullus. Hortensius. Isauricus – he still carries a lot of weight, and he's never forgiven Caesar for becoming chief priest. Possibly Cato.'

'Cato!' scoffed Celer. 'We'll still be discussing the ethics of the matter long after Caesar has died of old age!'

'I'm not so sure. Cato was the loudest in his clamour for action against Catilina's gang. And the people respect him almost as much as they love Caesar.'

A floorboard creaked and Celer put a warning finger to his lips. He called out, 'Who's there?' The door opened. It was Clodia. I wondered how long she had been listening and how much she might have heard. The same thought had obviously occurred to Celer. 'What are you doing?' he demanded.

'I heard voices. I was on my way out.'

'Out?' he said suspiciously. 'At this time? What are you going out for?'

'Why do you think? To see my brother the plebeian. To celebrate!'

Celer cursed and grabbed the wine jug and hurled it at her.

But she had already gone and it smashed harmlessly against the wall. I held my breath to see if she would respond, but then I heard the front door open and close.

'How soon can you get the others together?' asked Celer. 'Tomorrow?'

'Better make it the day after,' replied Cicero, who was plainly still marvelling at this exchange, 'otherwise it will seem as if there's some emergency, and Caesar may get wind of it. Let us meet at my house, at close of public business, the day after tomorrow.'

The following morning Cicero wrote out the invitations himself and had me go around the city delivering them in person into the hands of the recipients. All four were mightily intrigued, especially because by then everyone had heard of Clodius's transfer to the plebs. Lucullus actually said to me, with one of his bleak, supercilious smiles, 'What is it your master wishes to plot with me? A murder?' But each agreed to come – even Cato, who was not normally very sociable – for they were all alarmed by what was happening. Vatinius's bill proposing that Caesar be given two provinces and an army for five years had just been posted in the forum. The patricians were enraged, the populists jubilant, the mood in the city was stormy. Hortensius took me aside and told me that if I wanted to know how bad things were becoming, I should go and look at the tomb of the Sergii, which stands at the crossroads just outside the Capena Gate. This was where the head of Catilina had been interred. I went and found it piled high with fresh flowers.

I decided not to tell Cicero about these floral tributes: he was tense enough as it was. On the day of the meeting he shut himself away in his library and did not emerge until the appointed hour approached. Then he bathed, dressed in clean clothes, and fussed about the arrangement of the chairs in the tablinum. 'The truth is, I am too much of a lawyer for this kind of thing,' he confided to me. I murmured my assent, but actually I don't think it was the legality that was troubling him – it was his squeamishness again.

Cato was the first to arrive, in his usual malodorous rig of unwashed toga and bare feet. His nose twitched with distaste at the luxury of the house, but he readily consented to take some wine, for he was a heavy drinker: it was his only vice. Hortensius came next, full of sympathy for Cicero's deepening worries about Clodius; he assumed that this was what the meeting had been called to discuss. Lucullus and Isauricus, the two old generals, arrived together. 'This is quite a conspiracy,' said Isauricus, glancing at the others. 'Is anyone else coming?'

'Metellus Celer,' replied Cicero.

'Good,' said Isauricus. 'I approve of him. I reckon he's our best hope in the times to come. At least the fellow knows how to fight.'

The five sat in a circle. I was the only other person in the room. I went around with a jug of wine, and then retreated to the corner. Cicero had ordered me not to take notes but to try to remember as much as I could and write it up afterwards. I had attended so many meetings with these men over the years that no one any longer even noticed me.

'May we know what this is about?' asked Cato.

'I think we can guess,' said Lucullus.

Cicero said, 'I suggest we wait until Celer arrives. He is the one with most to contribute.'

The group sat in silence, until at last Cicero could stand it no longer and told me to go next door and find out why Celer was delayed.

I do not pretend to possess powers of divination, but even as I approached Celer's house I sensed that something was wrong. The exterior was too quiet; there was none of the normal coming and going. Inside there was that awful hush that always accompanies catastrophe. Celer's steward, whom I knew tolerably well, met me with tears in his eyes and told me that his master had been seized by terrible pains the previous day, and that although the doctors were unable to agree what was wrong with him, they concurred that it could well be fatal. I felt sick myself at the news and begged him to go to Celer and ask if he had any message for Cicero, who was waiting at home to see him. The steward went away and came back with a single word, which apparently was all that Celer had been able to gasp: 'Come!'

I ran back to Cicero's house. When I went into the tablinum, naturally the senators all turned to look at me, assuming I was Celer. There were groans of impatience when I gestured to Cicero that I needed to speak with him in private.

'What are you playing at?' he whispered angrily, when I got him into the atrium. His nerves were clearly stretched to breaking point. 'Where's Celer?'

'Gravely ill,' I replied. 'Perhaps dying. He wants you to come at once.'

Poor Cicero. That must have been a blow. He seemed literally to stagger back from it. Without exchanging a word we went straight round to Celer's house, where the steward was waiting for us, and he led us towards the private apartments. I shall never forget those gloomy passageways, with their dim candles and the sickly smell of incense being burned to cover the still more powerful odours of vomit and bodily decay. So many doctors had been called to attend upon Celer, they blocked the door to his bedchamber, talking quietly in Greek. We had to force our way inside. It was stiflingly hot, and so dark that Cicero was obliged to pick up a lamp and take it over to where the senator lay. He was naked apart from the bandages that marked where he had been bled. Dozens of leeches were attached to his arms and the insides of his legs. His mouth was black and frothy: I learned afterwards that he had been fed charcoal, as part of some crackpot cure. It had been necessary to tie him to his bed because of the force of his convulsions.

Cicero knelt beside him. 'Celer,' he said in a voice of great tenderness, 'my dear friend, who has done this to you?'

Hearing Cicero's voice, Celer turned his face to him, and tried to speak, but all that emerged was an unintelligible gurgle of black bubbles. He surrendered after that. He closed his eyes, and by all accounts he never opened them again.

Cicero lingered for a little while, and asked the doctors various questions. They disagreed about everything, in the way of medical men, but on one point they were unanimous: none had ever seen a healthy body succumb to a disease more quickly.

'A disease?' said Cicero incredulously. 'Surely he has been poisoned?'

Poisoned? The doctors recoiled at the very word. No, no – this was a ravaging sickness, a virulent distemper, the result of a snake bite: anything except poisoning, which was simply too appalling a possibility to be discussed. Besides, who would want to poison the noble Celer?

Cicero left them to it. That Celer had been murdered he never doubted, although whether Caesar had a hand in it, or Clodius, or both, he never discovered, and the truth remains a mystery to this day. There was, however, no question in his mind as to who had administered the fatal dose, for as we left that house of death we met coming in through the front door Clodia, accompanied by – of all people – young Caelius Rufus, fresh from his triumph over Hybrida. And although they both hastily assumed grave expressions, one could tell that they had been laughing a moment earlier; and although they quickly stood apart, it was clear that they were lovers.

XXXVI

Celer's body was burned on a funeral pyre set up in the forum as a mark of national mourning. His face in death was tranquil, that coal-black mouth as clean and pink as a rosebud. Caesar and all the senate attended. Clodia looked beautiful in mourning and shed many a widow's tear. Afterwards his ashes were interred in the family mausoleum, and Cicero sank into a deep gloom. He sensed that any hopes of stopping Caesar had died with Celer.

Seeing her husband's depression, Terentia insisted on a change of scene. Cicero had acquired a new property out on the coast at Antium, a day and a half 's journey from Rome, and that was where the family went for the start of the spring recess. On the way we passed close to Solonium, where the Claudian family had long owned a great country estate. Behind its high ochre walls, Clodius and Clodia were said to be closeted together in a family conference with their two brothers and two sisters. 'Six of them all together,' said Cicero, as we rattled past in our carriage, 'like a litter of puppies – the litter from hell! Imagine them in there, tumbling around in bed with one another and plotting my destruction.' I did not contradict him, although it was hard to imagine those two stiff-necked older brothers, Appius and Gaius, getting up to any such mischief.

When we reached Antium, the weather was inclement, with squalls of rain blowing in off the sea. Cicero sat out on the terrace, regardless of the conditions, gazing over the thundering waves at the grey horizon, trying to find a way out of his predicament. Eventually, after a day or two of that, with his head much clearer, he retreated to his library. 'What are the only weapons I possess, Tiro?' he asked me, and then he answered his own question. 'These,' he said, gesturing to his books. 'Words. Caesar and Pompey have their soldiers, Crassus his wealth, Clodius his bullies on the street. My only legions are my words. By language I rose, and by language I shall survive.'

Accordingly we began work on what he called 'The Secret History of My Consulship' – the fourth and final version of his autobiography, and by far the truest, a book he intended to be the basis of his defence if he was put on trial, which has never been published, and which I have drawn on to write this memoir. In it, he set out all the facts about Caesar's relationship with Catilina; about the way in which Crassus had defended Catilina, financed him and finally betrayed him; and about how Pompey had used his lieutenants to try to prolong and worsen the crisis so that he could use it as an excuse to come home with his army. It took us two weeks to compile, and I made an extra copy as we went along. When we had finished, I wrapped each roll of the original in a linen sheet and then in oilcloth and put them in an amphora, which we sealed tight with wax. Then Cicero and I rose early one morning, while the rest of the household was asleep, and took it into the nearby woods and buried it between a hornbeam and an ash. 'If anything happens to me,' Cicero instructed, 'dig it up and give it to Terentia, and tell her to use it as she thinks fit.'

As far as he could see, he had only one real hope left of avoiding being put on trial: that Pompey's disenchantment with Caesar would widen into an open breach. Given their characters, it was not an unreasonable expectation, and he was constantly on the lookout for any scrap of promising news. All letters from Rome were eagerly opened. All acquaintances on their way south to the Bay of Naples were closely questioned. There were bits of intelligence that seemed encouraging. As a gesture to Cicero, Pompey had asked Clodius to undertake a mission to Armenia rather than stand for tribune. Clodius had refused. Pompey had thereupon taken offence and fallen out with Clodius. Caesar had sided with Pompey. Clodius had argued with Caesar, even to the extent of threatening, when he became tribune, to rescind the triumvirate's legislation. Caesar had lost his temper with Clodius. Pompey had rebuked Caesar for landing them with this ungovernable patrician-cum-plebeian in the first place. Some even whispered that the two great men had stopped speaking. Cicero was delighted. 'Mark my words, Tiro: all regimes, however popular or powerful, pass away eventually.' There were signs that this one might be collapsing already. And perhaps it would have done if Caesar had not taken a dramatic step to preserve it.

The blow fell on the first day of May. It was in the evening, after dinner, and Cicero had just nodded off on his couch, when a letter arrived from

Atticus. I should explain that we were in the villa in Formiae by this time, and that Atticus had returned briefly to his house in Rome, whence he was sending Cicero more or less daily all the intelligence he could discover. Of course it was no substitute for actually seeing Atticus, but neverthless it was agreed between them that he should stay there, for he was of more service picking up gossip than counting waves on the seashore. Terentia was doing her embroidery in a corner of the room, all was peaceful, and I debated whether or not to wake Cicero. But he had already heard the noise of the messenger, and his hand rose imperiously from the couch. 'Give it me,' he said. I handed him the letter and went out on to the terrace. I could see a tiny light on a boat out at sea, and I was wondering what manner of fish had to be caught in darkness, or if this was the setting of traps for lobsters or whatnot – I am a terrible landlubber – when I heard a great groan from the couch behind me.

Terentia looked up in consternation. 'Whatever is it?' she asked.

I went inside. Cicero had the letter crumpled on his chest. 'Pompey has married again,' he said in a hollow voice. *'He has married Caesar's daughter!'*

Against the workings of history Cicero could deploy many weapons: logic, cunning, irony, wit, oratory, experience, his profound knowledge of law and men. But against the alchemy of two naked bodies in a bed in the darkness, and against all the complex longings and attachments and commitments such intimacy might arouse, he had nothing with which to fight. Strange as it may seem, the prospect of a marriage between the two had never occurred to him. Pompey was nearly forty-seven. Julia was fourteen. Only Caesar, raged Cicero, could have prostituted his child in a manner so cynical and repulsive and depraved. He railed against it for an hour or two – 'Imagine it: *him*, and *her*: *together*!' – and then, when he had calmed down, wrote a letter of congratulations to the bride and groom. As soon as he returned to Rome, he went to see them with a gift. I carried it in for him in a sandalwood box, and after he had delivered his prepared speech about the celestial radiance of their union, I placed it in his hands.

'Now who is in charge of receiving the presents in this household?' he asked with a smile, and he took half a step towards Pompey, who naturally reached out to take it, before Cicero abruptly turned away and gave the box to Julia with a bow. She laughed, and so after a moment or two did Pompey, although he wagged his finger at Cicero and called him a mischievous fellow. I must say that Julia had grown up to be a most charming young woman – pretty, graceful and obviously kind, and yet the peculiar thing was that one could see her father in every line of her face and gesture of her body. It was as if all the gaiety had been sucked out of him and blown into her. And the other amazing thing was that she was very clearly in love with Pompey. She opened the box and took out Cicero's gift – it was an exquisite silver dish, if I remember rightly, with their entwined initials engraved upon it – and when she showed it to Pompey, she held his hand and stroked his cheek. He beamed and kissed her on her forehead. Cicero regarded the happy couple with the fixed smile of a dinner guest who has just swallowed something very unpleasant but does not want to reveal the fact to his hosts.

'You must come and see us again soon,' said Julia. 'I wish to know you better. My father says you are the cleverest man in Rome.'

'He's very gracious, but alas, I must yield that prize to him.'

Pompey insisted on showing Cicero to the door himself. 'Isn't she delightful?'

'Very.'

'I tell you frankly, Cicero, I am happier with her than with any woman I have ever known. She makes me feel quite twenty years younger. Or even thirty.'

'At this rate you will soon be in your infancy,' joked Cicero. 'Congratulations again.' We had reached the atrium – to which, I noticed, the cloak of Alexander the Great and the pearl-encrusted head of Pompey had now been banished. 'And I assume relations with your new father-in-law are equally close?'

'Oh, Caesar's not such a bad fellow once you know how to handle him.'

'You are entirely reconciled?'

'We were never estranged.'

'And what about me?' blurted out Cicero, unable to conceal his true feelings any longer. He sounded like a discarded lover. 'What am I supposed to do about this monster Clodius you two have created to torment me?'

'My dear friend, don't worry about him for an instant! He talks a lot but it doesn't mean anything. If ever it really did come to a serious fight, he would have to step over my dead body to get at you.'

'Really?'

'Absolutely.'

'Is that a firm commitment?'

Pompey looked hurt. 'Have I ever let you down?'

Soon afterwards the marriage bore its first fruit. Pompey rose in the senate and read out a motion: that in view of the grievous loss, etc., etc., of Metellus Celer, the province he had been allotted before his death – Further Gaul – should be transferred to Julius Caesar, who had already been granted Nearer Gaul by a vote of the people; that this unified command would henceforth make it easier to crush any future rebellions; and that in view of the unsettled nature of the region, Caesar should be given an additional legion, bringing the total strength at his disposal to five.

Caesar, who was in the chair, asked if there were any objections. He swivelled his head left and right a couple of times, checking if anyone wished to speak, and was just about to move on to 'any other business' when Lucullus got to his feet. The old patrician general was nearing sixty by this time – disdainful, feline, but still magnificent in his way.

'Forgive me, Caesar,' he said, 'but will you also retain the province of Bithynia?'

'I will.'

'So you will now have three provinces?'

'I will.'

'But Bithynia is a thousand miles from Gaul!' Lucullus gave a mocking laugh and looked around the chamber for others to share his amusement. Nobody joined in.

Caesar said quietly, 'We all know our geography, Lucullus, thank you. Now does anyone else wish to speak?'

But Lucullus refused to stop. 'And your term of office,' he persisted, 'will it still be for five years?'

'It will. The people have decreed it. Why? Do you wish to oppose the will of the people?'

'But this is absurd!' cried Lucullus. 'Gentlemen, we cannot allow a single individual, however able, to control twenty-two thousand men on the very borders of Italy for *five years*. What if he were to move against Rome?'

Cicero was one of a number of senators who shifted uncomfortably on their hard wooden bench. But not one of them – not even Cato –

wanted to pick a fight on this issue, for there was not a chance of winning. Lucullus, plainly surprised by the lack of support, sat down grumpily and folded his arms.

Pompey said, 'I fear our friend Lucullus has spent too long with his fish. Things have changed in Rome of late.'

'Clearly,' muttered Lucullus, loud enough for all to hear, '*and not for the better.*'

At that Caesar rose. His expression was fixed and cold: almost inhuman, like a Thracian mask. 'I think Lucius Lucullus has forgotten that he commanded more legions than I in his time, and for longer than five years, and yet still the job of defeating Mithradates had to be finished off by my gallant son-in-law.' The supporters of the Beast with Three Heads gave a loud roar of approval. 'I think Lucius Lucullus's period as commander-in-chief might well bear investigation, perhaps by a special court. I think Lucius Lucullus's finances would certainly bear scrutiny – the people would be interested to know where he obtained his great wealth. And I think in the meantime that Lucius Lucullus should apologise to this house for his insulting insinuation.'

Lucullus glanced around. No one returned his gaze. To be hauled before a special court at his age, and with so much to explain, would be unbearable. Swallowing hard, he stood. 'If my words have offended you, Caesar—' he began.

'On his knees!' bellowed Caesar.

Lucullus looked suddenly very old and baffled. 'What?' he asked.

'He should apologise *on his knees*!' repeated Caesar.

I could not bear to watch, and yet at the same time it was impossible to tear one's eyes away, for the ending of a great career is an awesome thing to behold, like the felling of a mighty tree. For a moment or two longer, Lucullus remained upright. Then, very creakily, with joints stiff from years of military campaigning, he got down first on one knee and then on the other, and bowed his head to Caesar, while the senate looked on in silence.

A few days later, Cicero had to dip into his purse again to buy another wedding present, this time for Caesar.

Everyone had assumed that if Caesar remarried it would be to Servilia, who had been his mistress for several years, and whose husband, the former consul, Junius Silanus, had recently died. Indeed, around this time, such a marriage was rumoured actually to have taken place, when Servilia attended a dinner wearing a pearl that she announced the consul had given her, and which was worth sixty thousand gold pieces. But no: the very next week, Caesar took as his bride the daughter of Lucius Calpurnius Piso – a long, thin, plain girl of twenty, of whom no one had ever heard. After some deliberation, Cicero decided not to send his wedding gift round to Caesar by courier, but to hand it to him personally. Again it was a dish of silver with engraved initials; again it was in a sandalwood box; and again I was charged with looking after it. I duly waited with it outside the senate until the session was over, and when Caesar and Cicero strolled out together I took it over to them.

'This is just a small gift from Terentia and me to you and Calpurnia,' said Cicero, taking it out of my hands and giving it to Caesar, 'to wish you both a long and happy marriage.'

'Thank you,' said Caesar, 'that is thoughtful of you,' and without looking at it he passed the box to one of his attendants. 'Perhaps,' he added, 'while you're in this generous mood, you could also give us your vote.'

'My vote?'

'Yes, my wife's father is standing for the consulship.'

'Ah,' said Cicero, a look of comprehension spreading across his face, 'now it all makes sense. Frankly, I had wondered why you were marrying Calpurnia.'

'Rather than Servilia?' Caesar smiled and shrugged. 'That's politics.'

'And how is Servilia?'

'She understands.' Caesar seemed about to move on, then checked himself, as if he had just remembered something. 'Incidentally, what are you planning to do about our mutual friend Clodius?'

'I never give him a moment's thought,' replied Cicero. (This was a lie, of course: in truth he thought of little else.)

'That's wise,' nodded Caesar. 'He isn't worth the waste of one's mental processes. Still, I wonder what he will do when he becomes tribune.'

'I expect he will bring a prosecution against me.'

'That shouldn't worry you. You could beat him in any court in Rome.'

'He must know that too. Therefore I expect he will choose ground more favourable to him. A special court of some kind – one that ensures I am judged by the whole of the Roman people on the Field of Mars.'

'That would be harder for you.'

'I have armed myself with the facts and stand ready to defend myself. Besides, I seem to remember I beat you on the Field of Mars, when you brought a charge against Rabirius.'

'Don't bring that up! I still bear the scars!' Caesar's sharp and mirthless laughter stopped as abruptly as it had started. 'Listen, Cicero, if he does become a threat, never forget that I would stand ready to help you.'

Obviously taken aback by the offer, Cicero enquired, 'Really? How?'

'With this combined command I shall be heavily involved in military campaigning. I'll need a legate to handle civil administration in Gaul. You would fill the post ideally. You wouldn't actually have to spend much time there – you could come back to Rome as often as you liked. But if I put you on my staff, it would give you immunity from prosecution. Think about it. Now, if you will excuse me?' And with a polite nod he moved off to deal with the dozen or so other senators who were clamouring for a word with him.

Cicero watched him go with amazement. 'That's a handsome offer,' he said, 'very handsome indeed. We must send him a letter saying we'll bear it in mind, just so we have it on the record.'

That was what we did. And when Caesar replied the same day confirming that the legateship was Cicero's if he wanted it, Cicero for the first time began to feel more confident.

That year's elections were held later than usual, thanks to Bibulus's repeated intercessions claiming that the auguries were unfavourable. But the evil day could not be postponed for ever, and in October Clodius achieved his heart's ambition and topped the poll for tribune of the plebs. Cicero spared himself the torment of going down to the Field of Mars to listen to the result. In any case he did not need to: we could hear the roars of excitement without leaving the house.

On the tenth day of December, Clodius was sworn in as tribune. Again Cicero kept to his library. But the cheers were such that we could not escape them even with the doors closed and the windows shuttered, and presently word came up from the forum that Clodius had already posted details of his proposed legislation on the walls of the Temple of Saturn. 'He's not wasting his time,' said Cicero with a grim expression. 'Very well, Tiro. Go down and find out what fate Little Miss Beauty has in mind for us.'

My state of mind as I descended the steps to the forum was, as you can imagine, one of great trepidation. The meeting was over, but small groups of people stood around discussing what they had just heard. There was an excited atmosphere, as if they had all witnessed some spectacular event and needed to share their impressions with one another. I went over to the Temple of Saturn and had to shoulder my way through the crowds to see what all the fuss was about. Four bills had been pinned up. I took out my stylus and wax tablet. One was designed to stop any consul in the future behaving like Bibulus, by restricting the ancient right to proclaim unfavourable auguries. The second reduced the censors' powers to remove senators. The third allowed neighbourhood clubs to resume meeting (such associations had been banned by the senate six years previously for rowdy behaviour). And the fourth – the one that obviously had got everyone talking – entitled every citizen, for the first time in Rome's history, to a free monthly dole of bread.

I copied down the gist of each bill and hurried home to Cicero to report on their contents. He had his secret consular history unrolled on the table in front of him, and was ready to begin work on his defence. When I told him what Clodius was proposing, he sat back in his chair, thoroughly mystified. 'So, no word about me at all?'

'None.'

'Don't tell me he's planning to leave me alone after all his threatening talk.'

'Perhaps he's not as confident as he pretends.'

'Read me those bills again.' I did as he asked, and he listened with his eyes half closed, concentrating on every word. 'This is all very popular stuff,' he observed when I had finished. 'Free bread for life. A party on every street corner. No wonder it has gone down well.' He thought for a while. 'Do you know what he expects me to do, Tiro?'

'No.'

'He expects me to oppose these laws, merely because he is the one who has put them forward. He wants me to, in fact. Then he can turn round and say, "Look at Cicero, the friend of the rich! He thinks it is fine for senators to eat well and make merry, but woe betide the poor if they ask for a bit of bread and a chance to relax after their hard day's work!" You see? He plans to lure me into opposing him, then drag me before the plebs on the Field of Mars and accuse me of acting like a king. Well damn him! I shan't give him the satisfaction. I'll show him I can play a cleverer game than that.'

I am still not sure, if Cicero had set his mind to it, how much of Clodius's legislation he could have stopped. He had a tame tribune, Ninnius Quadratus, ready to use a veto on his behalf, and plenty of respectable citizens in the senate and among the equestrians would have come to his aid. These were the men who believed that free bread would make the poor dependent on the state and rot their morals. It would cost the treasury one hundred million sesterces a year and make the state itself dependent on revenues from abroad. They also thought that neighbourhood clubs fostered immoral pursuits, and that the organising of communal activities was best left to the official religious cults. In all this they may well have been right. But Cicero was more flexible. He recognised that times had changed. 'Pompey has flooded this republic with easy money,' he told me. 'That's what they forget. A hundred million is nothing to him. Either the poor will have their share or they will have our heads – and in Clodius they have found a leader.'

Cicero therefore decided not to raise his voice against Clodius's bills, and for one last brief moment – like the final flare of a guttering candle – he enjoyed something of his old popularity. He told Quadratus to do nothing, refused himself to condemn Clodius's plans, and was cheered in the street when he announced that he would not challenge the proposed laws. On the first day of January, when the senate met under the new consuls, he was awarded third place in the order of speaking after Pompey and Crassus – a signal honour. And when the presiding consul, Caesar's father-in-law, Calpurnius Piso, called on him to give his opinions, he used the occasion to make one of his great appeals for unity and reconciliation. 'I shall not oppose, or obstruct, or seek to frustrate,' he said, 'the laws that have been placed before us by our colleague Clodius, and I pray that out of difficult times, a new concord between senate and people may be forged.'

These words were met with a great ovation, and when the time came for Clodius to respond, he made an equally fulsome reply. 'It is not so long ago that Marcus Cicero and I enjoyed the friendliest of relations,' he said, with tears of sincere emotion in his eyes. 'I believe that mischief was made between us by a certain person close to him' – this was generally taken as a reference to Terentia's rumoured jealousy of Clodia – 'and I applaud his statesmanlike attitude to the people's just demands.'

Two days later, when Clodius's bills became law, the hills and valleys of Rome echoed with excitement as the neighbourhood clubs met to celebrate their restoration. It was not a spontaneous demonstration, but carefully organised by Clodius's man of affairs, a scribe named Cloelius. Poor men, freedmen and slaves alike chased pigs through the streets and sacrificed them without any priests to supervise the rites, then roasted the meat on the street corners. They did not stop their revels as night fell, but lit torches and braziers and continued to sing and dance. (It was unseasonably warm, and that always swells a crowd.) They drank until they vomited. They fornicated in the alleyways. They formed gangs and fought one another till blood ran in the gutters. In the smarter neighbourhoods, especially on the Palatine, the well-to-do cowered in their houses and waited for these Dionysian convulsions to pass. Cicero watched from his terrace, and I could see he was already wondering if he had made a mistake. But when Quadratus came to him and asked if he should gather some of the other magistrates from around the city and try to disperse the crowds, he replied that it was too late – the water was well and truly boiling now, and the lid would no longer fit back on the cooking pot.

Around midnight the racket began to subside. The streets became quiet, apart from some loud snoring in odd parts of the forum, which rose from the darkness like the noise of bullfrogs in a swamp. I went gratefully to my bed. But an hour or two later, something woke me. The sound was very distant, and in the daytime one would never have paid it any attention: it was only the hour and the surrounding silence that made it ominous. It was the noise of hammers being swung against brick.

I took a lamp and climbed the steps to the ground floor, unlocked the back door and went out on to the terrace. The city was still very dark, the air mild. I could see nothing. But the noise, which was coming from the eastern end of the forum, was more distinct outside, and when I listened hard I could pick out individual hammers being wielded – sometimes isolated, more often falling in a kind of peal, metal on stone, that rang out across the sleeping city. It was so continuous, I reckoned there must be at least a dozen teams labouring away. Occasionally there were shouts, and suddenly the sound of rubble being tipped. That was when I realised this was not building work I was hearing; it was demolition.

Cicero rose soon after dawn, as was his habit, and as usual I went to him in his library to see if he needed anything. 'Did you hear that hammering noise in the night?' he asked me. I replied that I had. He cocked his head, listening. 'Yet now it's silent. I wonder what mischief has been happening. Let's go down and see what the rogues have been up to.'

It was too early even for Cicero's clients to have begun assembling, and the street was empty. We went down to the forum accompanied by one of his burly attendants, and at first all seemed normal, apart from the heaps of rubbish left after the previous night's carousing, and the odd body sprawled in a drunken stupor. But as we approached the Temple of Castor, Cicero stopped and cried out in horror. It had been quite hideously disfigured. The steps leading up to the pillared façade had been taken down, so that anyone wishing to enter the building was now confronted by a ragged wall, twice the height of a man. The rubble had been formed into a parapet, and the only access to the temple was via a couple of ladders, each of which was guarded by men with sledgehammers. The newly exposed red brickwork was ugly and raw and naked, like an amputation. Various large placards were nailed to it. One read: 'P. CLODIUS PROMISES THE PEOPLE FREE BREAD.' A second proclaimed: 'DEATH TO THE ENEMIES OF THE ROMAN PEOPLE.' A third said: 'BREAD & LIBERTY.' There were other more detailed notices posted lower down at eye level that looked from a distance to be draft bills, and three or four dozen citizens were milling around reading them. Up above their heads on the podium of the temple was a line of men, motionless, like figures in a frieze. As we came closer, I recognised various of Clodius's lieutenants – Cloelius, Patina, Scato, Pola Servius: a lot of the rogues who had run with Catilina back in the old times. Further along I glimpsed Mark Antony and Caelius Rufus, and then Clodius himself.

'This is a monstrosity,' said Cicero, shaking with anger, 'a sacrilege, an outrage …'

Suddenly I realised that if we could see the men who had done this, they most assuredly could see us. I touched Cicero on the arm. 'Why don't you wait here, Senator,' I suggested, 'and let me go and see what those bills say? It might be unwise for you to stray too close. They are a rough-looking lot.'

I made my way quickly across to the wall, beneath the gaze of Clodius and his associates. On either side, men with heavily tattooed arms and close-cropped heads leaned on their sledge-hammers and stared at me belligerently. I quickly scanned the notices on the wall. As I guessed, they were new bills, a pair of them in fact. One was concerned with the allocation of consular provinces for the following year, and awarded Macedonia to Calpurnius Piso, and Syria (I think it was) to Aulus Gabinius. The other bill was very short, no more than a line: 'It shall be a capital offence to offer fire and water to any person who has put Roman citizens to death without a trial.'

I stared at it stupidly, not grasping its significance at first. That it was directed against Cicero was obvious enough. But it did not name him. It seemed more designed to frighten and harass his supporters than to threaten him directly. But then, like a great turning inside-out of my heart, I saw the devilish cunning in it, and felt the gorge rise into my mouth, so that I had to swallow the bitter taste to stop myself from vomiting. I stepped back from that wall as if the jaws of Hades had opened before me, and I kept stumbling backwards, unable to take my eyes from the words, increasing the distance and willing them to disappear. When I glanced up, I saw Clodius very plainly looking down at me, a smile on his face, enjoying every moment, and then I turned and hurried back to Cicero.

He saw at once in my expression that it was bad. 'Well?' he said anxiously. 'What is it?'

'Clodius has published a bill about Catilina.'

'Aimed at me?'

'Yes.'

'It cannot surely be as bad as your face suggests! What in the name of heaven does it say about me?'

'It doesn't even mention you.'

'Then what kind of bill is it?'

'It makes it a capital offence to offer fire or water to anyone who has put Roman citizens to death without a trial.'

His mouth dropped open. He was always much quicker on the uptake than I. He understood the implications at once. 'And that is *all*? One line?'

'That is all.' I bowed my head. 'I am very sorry.'

Cicero grabbed my arm. 'So the actual crime will be to help keep me alive? They won't even give me a *trial*?'

Suddenly his gaze flickered past me, over my shoulder, to the disfigured temple. I turned and saw Clodius waving at him – a slow and mocking gesture, as if he were waving goodbye to someone on a ship, leaving for a long journey. At the same time some of the tribune's henchmen started to climb down the ladders. 'I think we should get out of here,' I said. Cicero did not react. His mouth was working, but only a faint croak was emerging. It was as if he was being strangled. I looked back at the temple again. The men were on the ground now and moving towards us. 'Senator,' I said firmly, 'we really must get you out of here.' I gestured to his bodyguard to take his other arm, and together we propelled him out of the forum and back up the steps towards the Palatine. The gang of ruffians pursued us, and pieces of rubble from the temple started to fly past our ears. A sharp piece of brick caught Cicero on the back of his head, and he gave a cry. The cascade of missiles did not stop until we were halfway up the hill.

When we reached the safety of the house, we found it full of his morning callers. Not knowing what had happened, they moved at once towards Cicero as they always did, with their wretched letters and their petitions and their humble beseeching faces. Cicero gazed at them, blank with shock, and bleakly told me to send them away – 'all away' – then stumbled upstairs to his bedroom.

Once the clients had been thrown out, I gave orders for the front entrance to be locked and barred, and then I prowled around the empty public rooms, wondering what I should do. I kept waiting for Cicero to come down and give me orders, but the hours passed and there was no sign of him. Eventually Terentia sought me out. She was twisting a handkerchief between her hands, winding it tightly around her bony ringless fingers. She demanded to know what was going on. I replied that I was not entirely sure.

'Don't lie to me, slave! Why is your master collapsed on his bed and refusing to move?'

I quailed before her rage. 'He has – he has – made an error,' I stammered.

'An error? What manner of error?'

I hesitated. I did not know where to begin. There were so many errors: they stretched back like islands behind us, an archipelago of folly. Or perhaps 'errors' was the wrong word. Perhaps it was more accurate to call them consequences: the ineluctable consequences of a deed done by a great man for honourable motives – is that not, after all, how the Greeks define tragedy?

I said, 'He has allowed his enemies to take control of the centre of Rome.'

'And they are doing what, exactly?'

'They are preparing legislation that will make him an outlaw.'

'Well then, he must pull himself together and fight them!'

'It is very dangerous for him to venture out of the house.'

Even as I spoke, I could hear the mob in the street outside chanting, 'Death to the tyrant!' Terentia heard them too. As she listened, I could see the fear tauten her face. 'So what are we to do?'

'We could perhaps wait for nightfall and leave Rome,' I suggested. She stared at me and, frightened though she was, just for a moment I saw in her dark eyes a glint of that ancestor of hers – the one who had commanded a cohort against Hannibal. 'At the very least,' I went on hurriedly, 'we should restore all the precautions we took while Catilina was alive.'

'Send out messages to his colleagues,' she ordered. 'Ask Hortensius, Lucullus – any you can think – to come immediately. Fetch Atticus. Arrange everything else necessary to secure our safety. And summon his doctors.'

I did as she ordered. The shutters were fastened. The Sextus brothers hurried over. I even summoned the guard dog, Sargon, from his retirement on a farm just outside the city. By early afternoon the house had begun to fill with friendly faces, although most arrived shaken by the experience of passing through the chanting crowd. Only the doctors refused to come: they had heard about Clodius's bill and they claimed to fear prosecution.

Atticus went up to see Cicero and came down tearful. 'He has his face turned to the wall,' he told me. 'He refuses to speak.'

'They have robbed him of his voice,' I replied, 'and what is Cicero without his voice?'

A meeting was convened in the library to discuss what could be done: Terentia, Atticus, Hortensius, Lucullus, Cato. I forget who else was present. I sat there silent, stunned, in the room in which I had spent so many hours with Cicero. I listened to the others and wondered how they could hold a conversation about his future without his presence. It was as if he was already dead. The whole animating spark of that household – the wit, the quick intelligence, the guiding ambition – seemed to have fled out of the door, as it does when someone passes from the earth. Terentia had the coolest head present. 'Is there any chance that this law won't pass?' she asked Hortensius at one point.

'Very little,' he said. 'Clodius has copied Caesar's tactics to perfection, and clearly means to use the mob to control the popular assembly.'

'What about the senate?'

'We can adopt a resolution in his support. I'm sure we shall – I'll propose it myself – but Clodius will take no notice. Now if Pompey or Caesar were to come out against the bill, of course, that *would* make a difference. Caesar has an army less than a mile from the forum. Pompey's influence is immense.'

'And if it passes,' said Terentia, 'where will that leave me?'

'His property will all be seized – this house, its contents, everything. If you try to assist him in any way, you'll be arrested. I fear his only chance is to leave Rome at once, as soon as he is well, and get clear of Italy before the bill becomes law.'

'Could he stay at my house in Epirus?' asked Atticus.

'Then you would be liable to prosecution in Rome. It will be a brave man who gives him shelter. He will have to travel anonymously, and keep moving from place to place before his identity is discovered.'

'So that rules out any of my houses, I'm afraid,' said Lucullus. 'The mob would love to prosecute me.' He rolled his eyes, like a frightened horse. He had never recovered from his humiliation in the senate.

'May I speak?' I asked.

Atticus said, 'Of course, Tiro.'

'There is another option.' I glanced towards the ceiling. I was not sure whether Cicero would want me to reveal it to the others or not. 'In the summer, Caesar offered to appoint the master his legate in Gaul, which would give him immunity.'

Cato looked horrified. 'But that would put Cicero in his debt and make Caesar even more powerful than he is already! In the interests of the state, I very much hope Cicero would turn that down.'

'In the interests of friendship,' said Atticus, 'I hope he takes it. What do you say, Terentia?'

'My husband will decide,' she said simply.

After the others had gone, promising to return the following day, she went up to see Cicero again, then came down and called me to her. 'He is refusing to eat,' she said. Her eyes were watery but she jabbed her narrow chin towards me as she spoke. 'Well, he may give in to despair if he must, but I have to safeguard the interests of this family, and we do not have much time. I want you to arrange to have all the contents of the house packed up and removed. Some we can store in our old home – there is plenty of room as Quintus is away – and the rest Lucullus is willing to look after for us. This place is being watched, so it needs to be done piece by piece, to avoid arousing suspicion, the most valuable items first.'

And that was what we did, beginning that very evening, and continuing over the days and nights that followed. It was a relief to have something to do, while Cicero stayed in his room and refused to see anyone. We hid jewellery and coins in amphorae of wine and olive oil and carted them across the city. We concealed gold and silver dishes beneath our clothes and walked as normally as we could to the house on the Esquiline, where we divested ourselves with a clatter. Antique busts were swaddled in shawls and carried out cradled in the arms of slave girls as if they were babies. Some of the larger pieces of furniture were dismantled and wheeled away like firewood. Rugs and tapestries were wrapped in sheets and trundled off in the direction of the laundry, and then secretly diverted to their hiding place in Lucullus's mansion, which was beyond the Fontinalian Gate, just north of the city.

I took sole charge of emptying Cicero's library, filling sacks with his most private documents and carrying them myself to the cellar of our old house. On these journeys I always took care to skirt Clodius's headquarters in the Temple of Castor, where gangs of his men loitered ready to chase down Cicero if he dared to show his face. Once I stood at the back of a crowd and listened to Clodius himself denounce Cicero from the tribunes' platform. His domination of the city was absolute. Caesar was with his army on the Field of Mars, preparing to march to Gaul. Pompey had withdrawn from the city and was living in connubial bliss with Julia in his mansion in the Alban Hills. The consuls were beholden to Clodius for their provinces. Clodius had learned how to stimulate the mob as a gigolo might caress his lover. He had them chanting in ecstasy. I could not bear to watch for long.

We saved the transfer of the most valuable of Cicero's possessions until almost the very end. This was a citrus-wood table he had been given by a client, and which was said to be worth half a million sesterces. We could not dismantle it, so we decided to take it under cover of darkness to Lucullus's house, where it would easily fit in with all the other opulent furniture. We put it on the back of an ox cart, covered it in bales of straw, and set off on the journey of two miles or so. Lucullus's overseer met us at the door carrying a short whip, and told us that a slave girl would show us where to put it. It took four of us to lift that table down, and then the slave led us through the huge, echoing rooms of the house until she pointed to a spot and told us to set it there. My heart was beating fast, and not just from the weight of our burden, but because I had recognised her by then. How could I not? Most nights I had gone to sleep with her face in my mind. Of course I wanted to ask her a hundred questions, but I feared drawing attention to her in front of the overseer. We followed her back the way we had come, retracing our steps to the grand entrance hall, and I could not help noticing how underfed she seemed, the exhausted stoop of her shoulders, and the grey hairs that had appeared among the dark. She was clearly enduring a harsher existence than she had been used to in Misenum – a capricious life, the life of a slave, determined not so much by the status itself as the character of the master: Lucullus would not even have noticed she existed. The front door was open. The others passed through it. Just before I followed, I whispered, 'Agathe!' and she turned round wearily and peered at me in surprise that anyone knew her name, but there was no trace of recognition in those lifeless eyes.

XXXVII

The following morning I was talking to Cicero's steward when I glimpsed Cicero cautiously coming downstairs for the first time in two weeks. I caught my breath. It was like seeing a spectre. He had dispensed with his customary toga and was wearing an old black tunic to show he was in mourning. His cheeks were gaunt, his hair straggling, his growth of white beard made him look like an old tramp. When he reached the ground floor he stopped. By this time the house had been almost entirely emptied of its contents. He squinted in bewilderment at the bare walls and floors of the atrium. He shuffled into his library. I followed him and watched from the doorway as he inspected the empty cabinets. He had been left with only a chair and a small table. Without looking round, he said in a voice all the more awful for being so quiet, 'Who has done this?'

'The mistress thought it a sensible precaution,' I replied.

'A sensible precaution?' He ran his hand over the empty wooden shelving. It was all made of rosewood, beautifully carpentered to his own design. 'A stab in the back, more like!' He inspected the dust on his fingertips. 'She never did care for this place.' And then, still without looking at me, he said, 'Have a carriage made ready.'

'Of course.' I hesitated. 'May I know the destination, so I can tell the driver where he is to go?'

'Never mind the destination. Just get me the damned carriage.' I went and told the ostler to bring the carriage round to the front door, then I found Terentia and warned her that the master was planning to go out. She stared at me in alarm and hurried downstairs into the library. Most of the household had heard that Cicero had got out of bed at last, and they were standing around in the atrium, fascinated and fearful, not even pretending to work. I did not blame them: their fates, like mine, were all tied up with his. We heard the sound of raised voices, and soon afterwards Terentia ran out of the library with tears pouring down her cheeks. She said to me, 'Go with him,' and fled upstairs. Cicero emerged moments later, scowling, but at least looking much more his old self, as if having a heated argument with his wife had acted as a kind of tonic. He walked towards the front door and ordered the porter to open it. The porter looked at me, as if seeking my approval. I nodded quickly.

As usual there were demonstrators in the street, but far fewer than when the bill forbidding Cicero fire and water had first been promulgated. Most of the mob, like a cat at a mousehole, had grown weary of waiting for their victim to appear. Still, what the remainder lacked in numbers they made up for in venom, and they set up a great racket of 'Tyrant!' and 'Murderer!' and 'Death!' and as Cicero appeared they surged forwards. He stepped straight into the carriage, and I followed. A bodyguard was sitting up on the roof with the driver, and he leaned down to me to ask where we were to go. I looked at Cicero.

'To Pompey's house,' he said.

'But Pompey's not in Rome,' I protested. By this time, fists were pounding against the side of the carriage.

'Where is he, then?'

'At his place in the Alban Hills.'

'All the better,' replied Cicero. 'He will not be expecting me.'

I shouted up to the driver that we should head for the Capena Gate, and with a crack of his whip, and a final flurry of shouts and thumps on the wooden panels, we lurched forward.

The journey must have taken us at least two hours, and in the whole of that time Cicero did not utter a word, but sat hunched in the corner of the carriage, his legs turned away from me, as if he wished to compress himself into the smallest space possible. Only when we turned off the highway on to Pompey's long gravelled drive did he uncoil his body and peer out of the window at the opulent grounds, with their topiary and statuary. 'I shall shame him into protecting me,' he said, 'and if he still refuses I shall kill myself at his feet and he will be cursed by history for his cowardice for ever. You think I don't mean it? I am perfectly serious.' He put his hand in the pocket of his tunic and showed me a small knife, its blade no wider than his hand. He grinned at me. He seemed to have gone quite mad.

We pulled up in front of the great country villa, and Pompey's household steward sprang forward to open the carriage door. Cicero had been here countless times. The slave knew him very well. But his smile of greeting shrivelled as he saw Cicero's unkempt face and black tunic, and he took a step backwards in shock. 'Do you smell that, Tiro?' asked Cicero, offering me the back of his hand. He raised it to his own nostrils and sniffed. 'That's the smell of death.' He gave an odd laugh, then climbed down from the carriage and strode towards the house, saying to the steward over his shoulder, 'Tell your master I'm here. I know where to go.'

I hastened after him, and we went into a long salon filled with antique furniture, tapestries and carpets. Souvenirs of Pompey's many campaigns were on display in cabinets – red-glazed pottery from Spain, ebony carvings from Africa, chased silverware from the East. Cicero sat on a high-backed couch covered in ivory silk while I stood apart, near to one of the doors, which opened on to a terrace lined with busts of great men from antiquity. Beyond the terrace a gardener pushed a wheelbarrow piled with dead leaves. I could smell the fragrance of a bonfire somewhere, out of sight. It was a scene of such settled order and civilisation – such an oasis in the wilderness of all our terrors – that I have never forgotten it. Presently there was a little patter of footsteps and Pompey's wife appeared, accompanied by her maids, all of whom were older than her. She looked like a doll in her dark ringlets and simple green dress. She had a scarf round her neck. Cicero stood and kissed her hand.

'I am very sorry,' said Julia, 'but my husband has been called away.' She blushed and glanced at the door. She was obviously not accustomed to lying.

Cicero's face sagged slightly, but then he rallied. 'That does not matter,' he said. 'I shall wait.'

Julia looked anxiously at the door again, and I had a sudden instinct that Pompey was just beyond it, signalling to her what she should do. She said, 'I am not sure how long he is going to be.'

'I am confident he will come,' said Cicero loudly, for the benefit of any eavesdroppers. 'Pompey the Great cannot be seen to go back on his word.' He sat, and after some hesitation she did the same, folding her small white hands neatly in her lap.

Eventually she said, 'Was your journey comfortable?'

'Very pleasant, thank you.'

There was another long silence. Cicero put his hand in the pocket of his tunic, where his little knife was. I could see that he was turning it round in his fingers.

Julia said, 'Have you seen my father recently?'

'No. I have not been well.'

'Oh? I am sorry to hear that. I have not seen him for a while either. He will be leaving for Gaul any day. Then I really don't know when I shall see him again. I am lucky I won't be left on my own. It was horrid when he was in Spain.'

'And is married life suiting you?'

'Oh, it is wonderful!' she exclaimed, with genuine delight. 'We stay here all the time. We never go anywhere. It is a world of our own.'

'That must be pleasant. How charming that is. A carefree existence. I envy you.' There was a slight crack in Cicero's voice. He withdrew his hand from his pocket and raised it to his forehead. He looked down at the carpet. His body began to shake slightly, and I realised to my horror that he was weeping. Julia stood up quickly. 'It's nothing,' he said. 'Really. This damned illness …'

Julia hesitated, then reached over and touched his shoulder. She said softly, 'I shall tell him again that you are here.'

She left the room with her maids. After she had gone, Cicero sighed, wiped his nose on his sleeve and stared ahead. The aromatic smoke of the bonfire drifted over the terrace. Time passed. The light began to fade, and Cicero's face, emaciated by his long period of fasting, filled with shadows. Eventually I whispered in his ear that if we did not leave soon, we would never reach Rome by nightfall. He nodded, and I helped him to his feet.

As we drove away from the villa I glanced back, and to this day I am sure I saw the pale full moon of Pompey's face staring down at us from an upper window.

Once news of Pompey's betrayal became known, Cicero was seen to be finished, and I discreetly started packing in anticipation of a rapid exit from Rome. That is not to say that everyone shunned him. Hundreds donned mourning to show their solidarity, and the senate voted narrowly to dress in black to show their sympathy. A great demonstration of knights from all over Italy was organised on the Capitol by Aelius Lamia, and a delegation led by Hortensius went to call on the consuls to urge them to defend Cicero. But Piso and Gabinius both refused. They knew that Clodius had it in his power to determine which, if any, province they would receive, and they were anxious to show him their support. They actually forbade the senate to put on mourning and expelled the gallant Lamia from the city on the grounds that he threatened civic peace.

Whenever Cicero tried to venture out, he swiftly found himself surrounded by a jeering mob, and despite the protection organised by Atticus and the Sextus brothers, the experience was unpleasant and dangerous. Clodius's followers threw stones and excrement at him, forcing him to retreat indoors to shake the filth out of his hair and tunic. He sought out the consul, Piso, and eventually found him in a tavern, where he pleaded with him to intercede, to no avail. After that he stayed at home. But even here there was little respite. During the day, demonstrators would gather in the forum and chant slogans at the house, calling Cicero a murderer. Our nights were endlessly disturbed by the echo of running feet in the street, shouted insults, and the rattle of missiles on the roof. At a huge public meeting called by the tribunes outside the city, Caesar was asked his opinion of Clodius's bill. He declared that while he had opposed the execution of the conspirators, he also disapproved of retrospective legislation. It was an answer of great political dexterity: Cicero, when told of it, could only nod in rueful admiration. From that point on he knew he had no hope, and although he did not actually retire to his bed again, a great lethargy took hold of him, and often he refused to see his visitors.

There was one important exception, however. On the day before Clodius's bill was due to become law, Crassus came to call, and to my surprise Cicero agreed to receive him. I suppose he was in such a hopeless state by then, he was willing to take help from whatever quarter it was offered. The villain came in full of concerned words. Yet all the time he spoke of his shock at what had happened and of his disgust at Pompey's disloyalty, his eyes were flickering around the bare walls and checking what fixtures were left. 'If there is anything I can do,' he said, 'anything at all …'

'I don't think there is much, thank you,' said Cicero, who plainly regretted ever letting his old enemy through the door. 'We both know how politics is played. Sooner or later failure comes to us all. At least,' he added, '*my* conscience is clear. Really, don't let me detain you any longer.'

'What about money? A poor substitute, I know, for the loss of all one holds dear in life, but money would be useful in exile, and I would be willing to advance you a considerable sum.'

'That is very thoughtful of you.'

'I could give you, say, two million. Would that be of any help?'

'Naturally it would. But if I am in exile, what hope would I have of ever paying you back?'

Crassus looked around as if searching for a solution. 'You could give me the deeds to this house, I suppose.'

Cicero stared at him in disbelief. 'You want this house, for which I paid you three and a half million?'

'And a great bargain it was. You can't dispute that.'

'Well then, all the more reason for me not to sell it back to you for two million.'

'I fear property is only worth what someone is willing to pay for it, and this house will be valueless the day after tomorrow.'

'Why do you say that?'

'Because Clodius intends to burn it down and build a shrine to the goddess Liberty, and neither you nor anyone else will be able to lift a finger to stop him.'

Cicero paused, and then said quietly, 'Who told you that?'

'I make it my business to know these things.'

'And why would you want to pay two million sesterces for a patch of scorched earth containing a shrine to Liberty?'

'That is the kind of risk one has to take in business.'

'Goodbye, Crassus.'

'Think it over, Cicero. Don't be a stubborn fool. It's two million or nothing.'

'I said goodbye, Crassus.'

'All right, two and a half million?' Cicero did not respond. Crassus shook his head. 'That,' he said, rising to his feet, 'is exactly the sort of arrogant folly that has brought you to this pass. I shall warm my hands at your fire.'

*

On the next day, a meeting of Cicero's principal supporters was called to decide what he should do. It was to be held in the library, and I had to scour the house for chairs so that everyone should have a place to sit. I put out twenty. Atticus arrived first, then Cato, followed by Lucullus and, after a long interval, Hortensius. They all had to endure a hard passage through the mob that had occupied the neighbouring streets, especially Hortensius, who was roughed up quite badly, his face scratched, his toga splattered with shit. It was unnerving to see a man normally immaculate in his appearance so shaken and despoiled. We waited to see if anyone else would come, but nobody did. Tullia had already left Rome with her husband for the safety of the country, after an emotional scene with Cicero, so the only member of the family present was Terentia. I took notes.

If Cicero was dismayed that the vast crowds he had once commanded had dwindled to this small band, he did not show it. 'On this bitter day,' he said, 'I wish to thank all of you who have so bravely struggled to support my cause. Adversity is a part of life – not one I necessarily recommend, you understand' – my notes record laughter – 'but still: at least it shows us men's true natures, and just as I have shown my weakness, so I have seen your strength.' He stopped, and cleared his throat. I thought he was going to break down again. But this time he carried on. 'So the law will take effect at midnight? There is no doubt of that, I take it?' He glanced around. All four shook their head.

'No,' said Hortensius, 'none whatever.'

'Then what options are open to me?'

'It seems to me you have three,' said Hortensius. 'You can ignore the law and remain in Rome, and hope your friends will continue to support you, although from tomorrow that will be even more dangerous than it is now. You can leave the city tonight, while it is still legal for people to help you, and hope to get out of Italy unmolested. Or you could go to Caesar and ask if his offer of a legateship still stands, and claim immunity.'

Cato said, 'He does have a fourth option, of course.'

'Yes?'

'He could kill himself.'

There was a profound silence, and then Cicero said, 'What would be the benefit of that?'

'From the stoic point of view, suicide has always been considered a logical act of defiance for a wise man. It is also your natural right to put an end to your anguish. And frankly, it would set an example of resistance to tyranny that would stand for all time.'

'Do you have a particular method in mind?'

'I do. In my opinion you should brick yourself into this house and starve yourself to death.'

'I disagree,' said Lucullus. 'If it's martyrdom you seek, Cicero, why bother to do the deed yourself? Why not stay in the city and dare your enemies to do their worst? You have a chance of surviving. And if you don't, at least the opprobrium of murder falls on them.'

'Being murdered requires no courage,' retorted Cato with contempt, 'whereas suicide is a manly, conscious act.'

'And what is your own advice, Hortensius?' asked Cicero.

'Leave the city,' he replied at once. 'Keep yourself alive.' He touched his fingertips briefly to his forehead and felt along the rusty line of dried blood. 'I went to see Piso today. Privately he has some sympathy for the way you have been treated. Allow us the time to work for the repeal of Clodius's law while you are in voluntary exile. I am certain you will come back in triumph one day.'

'Atticus?'

'You know my view,' said Atticus. 'You would have saved yourself a lot of trouble if you had accepted Caesar's offer in the first place.'

'And Terentia? What do you say, my dear?'

She had put on mourning, like her husband, and in her black weeds, with her deathly pale face, she had become our Electra. She spoke with great force. 'Our present existence is intolerable. Voluntary exile smacks to me of cowardice. And try explaining suicide to your six-year-old son. You have no choice. Go to Caesar.'

It was late afternoon – a red sun dipping behind the bare trees, a warm spring breeze carrying the incongruous chant of 'Death to the tyrant!' from the forum. The other senators with their attendants left by the front door, serving as decoys to draw the attention of the mob, while Cicero and I crept out through the back. Cicero had a tattered old brown blanket draped over his head and looked exactly like a beggar. We hurried down the Caci Steps to the Etruscan Road, and then joined the crowds heading out of the city through the river gate. Nobody molested us, or even gave us a second glance.

I had sent a slave ahead with a message for Caesar that Cicero wished to see him, and one of his officers in a red-plumed helmet was waiting for us at the gate. He was very much taken aback by Cicero's appearance, but managed to recover sufficiently to give him a kind of half-salute, and then escorted us out to the Field of Mars. Here a huge tented city had been pitched to accommodate Caesar's newly mustered Gallic legions, and as we passed through it I noticed everywhere signs that the army was striking camp and preparing to depart: waste pits were being filled in, earth ramparts levelled, wagons loaded with supplies. The officer told Cicero that their orders were to begin marching north before dawn the next day. He led us to a tent much larger than the others and set apart on slightly higher ground, with a legionary eagle planted beside it. He asked us to wait, and then lifted the flap and went inside, leaving Cicero, bearded, and in his old tunic with his blanket draped around his shoulders, to gaze around the camp.

'This is how it always seems to be with Caesar,' I remarked, trying to lighten the silence. 'He likes to keep his visitors waiting.'

'We had better get used to it,' replied Cicero in a grim voice. 'Look at that,' he said, nodding beyond the camp towards the river. Rising from the plain in the dusty light was a great rickety edifice of scaffolding. 'That must be the Pharaoh's theatre.' He contemplated it for a long time, chewing the inside of his lip.

Eventually the flap parted again and we were shown into the tent. The interior was Spartan. A thin straw mattress lay on the ground, with a blanket thrown across it; near to it was a wooden chest on which stood a mirror, a set of hairbrushes, a jug of water and a basin, together with a miniature portrait of a woman in a gold frame (I am almost certain it was Servilia, but I was not close enough to be sure). At a folding table piled with documents sat Caesar. He was signing something. Two secretaries stood motionless behind him. He finished what he was doing, looked up, rose, and advanced towards Cicero with his hand outstretched. It was the first time I had seen him in military uniform. It fitted him as naturally as his skin, and I realised that in all the years I had observed him I had never actually seen him in the arena for which he was best suited. That was a sobering thought.

'My dear Cicero,' he said, examining his visitor's appearance, 'it truly grieves me to see you reduced to this condition.' With Pompey there was always hugging and back-slapping, but Caesar did not go in for that kind of thing. After the briefest of handshakes he gestured to Cicero to sit. 'How can I help?'

'I have come to accept the position of your legate,' replied Cicero, perching himself on the edge of the chair, 'if the offer still stands.'

'Have you indeed!' Caesar's mouth turned down. 'I must say you have left it very late.'

'I admit I would have preferred not to have come to you in these circumstances.'

'Clodius's law takes effect at midnight?'

'It does.'

'So in the end the choice has come down to me, or death, or exile?'

Cicero looked uncomfortable. 'You could put it like that.'

'Well, that's hardly very flattering!' Caesar gave one of his sharp laughs and lolled back in his chair. He studied Cicero. 'When I made the offer to you in the summer, your position was infinitely stronger than it is now.'

'You said that if Clodius ever became a threat to my safety, I could come to you. He is a threat. Here I am.'

'Six months ago he was a threat. Now he is your master.'

'Caesar, if you are asking me to beg …'

'I am not asking you to beg. Of course I am not asking you to beg. I would merely like to hear from your own lips what benefit you think you can bring to me by serving as my legate.'

Cicero swallowed hard. I could barely imagine how painful this was for him. 'Well, if you ask me to spell it out, I would say that while you obviously enjoy huge support among the people, you have far less in the senate, whereas my position is the opposite: weak at present with the people but still strong among our colleagues.'

'So you would guard my interests in the senate?'

'I would represent your views to them, yes, and perhaps occasionally I could relay their views back to you.'

'But your loyalty would be exclusively to me?'

I could almost hear Cicero grinding his teeth. 'I hope that my loyalty, as it has always been, would be to my country, which I would serve by reconciling your interests with those of the senate.'

'But I don't care about the interests of the senate!' exclaimed Caesar. He suddenly pitched forward on his chair and in one fluid motion sprang to his feet. 'I'll tell you something, Cicero. Let me explain myself to you. The other year, when I was on my way to Spain, I had to cross the mountains, and I went on ahead with a group of my staff to scout the way, and we came to this very small village. It was raining, and it was the most miserable-looking place you can possibly imagine. Hardly anyone lived there. Really, you had to laugh at such a dump. And one of my officers said to me, as a joke, "Yet, you know, even here there are probably men pushing themselves forward to gain office, and there will be fierce competition and jealous rivalries over who will win first place." And do you know what I replied?'

'No.'

'I said, "As far as I am concerned, I would rather be the first man here than the second in Rome." And I meant it, Cicero – I really did. Do you understand what I am trying to say?'

'I believe I do,' said Cicero, nodding slowly.

'That is a true story. That is who I am.'

Cicero said, 'Until this conversation, you have always been a puzzle to me, Caesar, but now perhaps I begin to understand you for the first time, and I thank you at least for your honesty.' He started to laugh. 'It really is quite funny.'

'What is?'

'That I should be the one being driven from Rome for seeking to be a king!'

Caesar scowled at him for an instant, and then he grinned. 'You are right,' he said. 'It is amusing.'

'Well,' said Cicero, getting to his feet, 'there is little point in carrying on with this interview. You have a country to conquer and I have other matters to attend to.'

'Don't say that!' cried Caesar. 'I was only setting out the facts. We need to know where we both stand. You can have the damned legateship – it's yours. And you can discharge it in whatever fashion you like. It would amuse me to see more of you, Cicero – really.' He held out his hand.

'Come. Most men in public life are so dull. We who are not must stick together.'

'I thank you for your consideration,' replied Cicero, 'but it would never work.'

'Why not?'

'Because in this village of yours, I, too, would aspire to be the first man, but failing that I would at least aspire to be a free man, and what is wicked about you, Caesar – worse than Pompey, worse than Clodius, worse even than Catilina – is that you won't rest until we are all obliged to go down on our knees to you.'

It was dark by the time we re-entered the city. Cicero did not even bother to put the blanket over his head. The light was too gloomy for him to be recognised, and besides, people were hurrying home with more important things to worry about than the fate of an ex-consul – their dinner, for example, and their leaking roof, and the thieves who were plaguing Rome more and more each day.

In the atrium Terentia was waiting with Atticus, and when Cicero told her that he had rejected Caesar's offer, she let out a great howl of pain and sank to the floor, squatting on her haunches with her hands covering her head. Cicero knelt next to her and put his arm around her shoulder. 'My dear, you must leave now,' he said. 'Take Marcus with you, and spend the night at Atticus's house.' He glanced up at Atticus, and his old friend nodded. 'It's too dangerous to stay here beyond midnight.'

She pulled away from him. 'And you?' she said. 'What will you do? Will you kill yourself?'

'If that is what you want – if that will make it easier.'

'Of course it is not what I want!' she shouted at him. 'I want my life returned to me!'

'That, I fear, is what I cannot give you.'

Once again Cicero reached out to her, but she pushed him away and got to her feet. 'Why?' she demanded, glaring down at him, her hands on her hips. 'Why are you putting your wife and children through this torment, when you could end it tomorrow by allying yourself with Caesar?'

'Because if I did, I would cease to exist.'

'What do you mean, you would cease to exist? What stupid, clever nonsense of yours is that?'

'My body would exist, but I, Cicero, I – whatever I am – would be dead.'

Terentia turned her back on him in despair and looked at Atticus for support. Atticus said, 'With respect, Marcus, you are starting to sound as inflexible as Cato. What's wrong with making a temporary alliance with Caesar?'

'There would be nothing temporary about it! Does no one in this city understand? That man won't stop until he is master of the world – he more or less just told me exactly that – and I would either have to go along with him as his junior accomplice or break with him at some later stage, and then I would be absolutely finished.'

Terentia said coldly, 'You are absolutely finished now.'

'So, Tiro,' said Cicero, after she had gone to fetch Marcus from the nursery to say goodbye, 'as my last act in this city, I would like to give you your freedom. I really should have done it years ago – at the very least when I left the consulship – and the fact that I didn't was not because I set no value on your services, but on the contrary because I valued them too much, and could not bear to lose you. But now, as I am losing everything else, it's only fair that I should say goodbye to you as well. Congratulations, my friend,' he said, shaking my hands, 'you have earned it.'

For years I had waited for this moment – I had yearned for it and dreamed of it and planned what I would do – and now it had arrived, almost casually it seemed, out of all this ruin and disaster. I was too overwhelmed with emotion to speak. Cicero smiled at me, and then embraced me as I wept, patting my back as if I was a child that needed comforting, and then Atticus, who was standing watching, took my hand and shook it warmly.

I managed to say a few words of thanks, and added that of course my first act as a free man would be to dedicate myself to his service, and that I would stay at his side to share his ordeal whatever happened.

'I am afraid that is impossible,' Cicero responded sadly. 'Slaves can be my only company from now. If a freedman were to help me, he would be guilty under Clodius's law of aiding a murderer. You must stay well clear of me from now on, Tiro, or they will crucify you. Now go and collect your belongings. You should leave with Terentia and Atticus.'

The intensity of my joy was replaced by an equally sharp stab of grief. 'But how will you cope without me?'

'Oh, I have other slaves,' he replied, making a feeble effort to sound unconcerned. 'They can accompany me out of the city.'

'Where will you go?'

'South. To the coast – Brundisium, perhaps – and find a boat. After that – the winds and currents will decide my fate. Now fetch your things.'

I went down to my room and gathered together my few possessions into a small bag, and then I pulled out the two loose bricks behind which I had hollowed out a safe. This was where I kept my savings. Sewn into a money belt, I had exactly two hundred and twenty-seven gold pieces, which it had taken me more than a decade to acquire. I put on the belt and went upstairs to the atrium, where Cicero was now saying goodbye to Marcus, watched by Atticus and a raw-eyed Terentia. He loved that boy – his only son, his joy, his hope for the future – and with immense self-discipline he somehow managed to keep their parting casual, so that the lad would not be too upset. He held him in his arms and swung him round, and Marcus begged him to do it again, which he did, and when Marcus begged for a third time, he said no and told him to go to his mother. Then he embraced Terentia and said, 'I am sorry that marriage to me has brought you to such a sad state.'

'Marriage to you has been the only purpose of my life,' she replied, and with a nod in my direction she walked firmly from the room.

Cicero next embraced Atticus, and entrusted his wife and son to his care, and then moved to say farewell to me, but I told him there was no need, that I had made my decision, and that I would remain at his side at the cost of my freedom and if necessary of my life. Naturally he expressed his gratitude, but he did not seem surprised, and I realised he had never thought seriously for a moment that I would accept his offer. I took off my money belt and gave it to Atticus.

'I wonder if I might ask you to do something for me,' I said.

'Of course,' he replied. 'You want me to look after this for you?'

'No,' I said. 'There is a slave of Lucullus, a young woman named Agathe, who has come to mean a lot to me, and I wonder if you would ask

Lucullus, as a favour to you, to free her. I am sure there is more than enough money here to buy her liberty and to provide for her thereafter.'

Atticus looked surprised, but said that of course he would do as I asked.

'Well, you certainly kept that secret,' said Cicero, studying me closely. 'Perhaps I don't know you as well as I think I do.'

After the others had gone, Cicero and I were left alone in the house, together with his guards and a few members of his household. We could no longer hear any chanting; the whole city seemed to have gone very quiet. He went upstairs to rest and put on some stout shoes, and when he came back down he took a candelabrum and moved from room to room – through the empty dining hall with its gilded roof, through the great hall with its marble statues that were too heavy to move, and into the bare library – as if committing the place to memory. He lingered so long I began to wonder if he had decided not to leave after all, but then the watchman in the forum called midnight, and he blew out the candles and said that we should go.

The night was moonless, and as we reached the top of the steps we could see beneath us at least a dozen torches slowly ascending the hill. Someone in the distance let out a peculiar bird cry, and it was answered by a similar shriek from a spot very close behind us. I felt my heart begin to pound. 'They are on their way,' said Cicero softly. 'He does not mean to miss a moment.' We hurried down the steps, and at the foot of the Palatine turned left into a narrow alley. Keeping close to the walls, we made a careful loop past shuttered shops and slumbering houses until we came out into the main street just by the Capena Gate. The porter was bribed to open up the pedestrian door, and waited impatiently as we exchanged whispered farewells with our protectors. Then Cicero stepped through the narrow portal, followed by me and by three other young slaves, who carried his luggage.

We did not speak or rest until we had walked for at least two hours and had got clear of the monumental tombs that line that stretch of road – in those days, notorious hiding places for robbers. Then Cicero decided it was safe to stop, and he sat down on a milestone and looked back at Rome. A faint red glow, too early for the dawn, crimson at its centre and dissolving into bands of pink, suffused the sky, outlining the low black humps of the city's hills. It was amazing to think that the burning of just one house could create such an immense celestial effect. Had I not known better, I would have said it was an omen. At the same time, faint on the still night air, came a curious sound, harsh and intermittent, pitched somewhere between a howl and a wail. I could not place it at first, but then Cicero said it must be trumpets on the Field of Mars, and that it was Caesar's army preparing to move off to Gaul. I could not make out his face in the darkness as he said this, which perhaps was just as well, but after a moment or two he stood and brushed the dust off his old tunic, and resumed his journey, in the opposite direction to Caesar's.

PART FIVE

EXILE

58–47 BC

'Nescire autem quid ante quam natus sis acciderit, id est semper esse puerum. Quid enim est aetas hominis, nisi ea memoria rerum veterum cum superiorum aetate contexitur?'

'To be ignorant of what occurred before you were born is to remain always a child. For what is the worth of human life, unless it is woven into the life of our ancestors by the records of history?'

Cicero, *Orator*, 46 BC

XXXVIII

I remember the cries of Caesar's war-horns chasing us over the darkened fields of Latium – their yearning, keening howls, like animals on heat – and how when they stopped there was only the slither of our shoes on the icy road and the urgent panting of our breath.

It was not enough for the immortal gods that Cicero should be spat at and reviled by his fellow citizens; not enough that in the middle of the night he be driven from the hearths and altars of his family and ancestors; not enough even that as we fled from Rome on foot he should look back and see his house in flames. To all these torments they deemed it necessary to add one further refinement: that he should be forced to hear his enemy's army striking camp on the Field of Mars.

Even though he was the oldest of our party Cicero kept up the same fast pace as the rest of us. Not long ago he had held Caesar's life in the palm of his hand. He could have crushed it as easily as an egg. Now their fortunes led them in entirely opposite directions. While Cicero hurried south to escape his enemies, the architect of his destruction marched north to take command of both provinces of Gaul.

He walked with his head down, not uttering a word and I imagined it was because he was too full of despair to speak. Only at dawn, when we rendezvoused with our horses at Bovillae and were about to embark on the second stage of our escape, did he pause with his foot in the doorway of his carriage and say suddenly, 'Do you think we should turn back?'

The question caught me by surprise. 'I don't know,' I said. 'I hadn't considered it.'

'Well, consider it now. Tell me: why are we fleeing Rome?'

'Because of Clodius and his mob.'

'And why is Clodius so powerful?'

'Because he's a tribune and can pass laws against you.'

'And who made it possible for him to become a tribune?'

I hesitated. 'Caesar.'

'Exactly. Caesar. Do you imagine that man's departure for Gaul at that precise hour was a coincidence? Of course not! He waited till his spies had reported I'd left the city before ordering his army to move. Why? I'd always assumed his advancement of Clodius was to punish me for speaking out against him. But what if his real aim all along was to drive me out of Rome? What scheme requires him to be certain I've gone before he can leave too?'

I should have grasped the logic of what he was saying. I should have urged him to turn back. But I was too exhausted to reason clearly. And if I am honest there was more to it than that. I was too afraid of what Clodius's thugs might do to us if they caught us re-entering the city.

So instead I said, 'It's a good question, and I can't pretend I have the answer. But wouldn't it look indecisive, after bidding goodbye to everyone, suddenly to reappear? In any case, Clodius has burned your house down now – where would we return to? Who would take us in? I think you'd be wiser to stick to your original plan and get as far away from Rome as you can.'

He rested his head against the side of the carriage and closed his eyes. In the pale grey light I was shocked by how haggard he appeared after his night on the road. His hair and beard had not been cut for weeks. He was wearing a toga dyed black. Although he was only in his forty-ninth year, these public signs of mourning made him look much older – like some ancient, mendicant holy man. After a while he sighed. 'I don't know, Tiro. Perhaps you're right. It's so long since I slept I'm too tired to think any more.'

And so the fatal error was made – more through indecision than decision – and we continued to press on southwards for the remainder of that day and for the twelve days that followed, putting what we thought was a safe distance between ourselves and danger.

We travelled with a minimal entourage to avoid attracting attention – just the carriage driver and three armed slaves on horseback, one in front and two behind. A small chest of gold and silver coins that Atticus, Cicero's oldest and closest friend, had provided to pay for our journey was hidden under our seat. We stayed only in the houses of men we trusted, no more than a night in each, and steered clear of those places where Cicero might have been expected to stop – for example at his seaside villa at Formiae, the first place any pursuers would look for him, and along the Bay of Naples, already filling with the annual exodus from Rome in search of winter sun and warm springs. Instead we headed as fast as we could towards the toe of Italy.

Cicero's plan, conceived on the move, was to make for Sicily and stay there until the political agitation against him in Rome subsided. 'The mob will turn on Clodius eventually,' he predicted. 'Such is the unalterable nature of the mob. He will always be my mortal enemy but he won't always be tribune – we must never forget that. In nine months his term of office will expire and then we can go back.'

He was confident of a friendly reception from the Sicilians, if only because of his successful prosecution of the island's tyrannical governor, Verres – even though that brilliant victory, which launched his political career, was now twelve years in the past and Clodius had more recently been a magistrate in the province. I sent letters ahead giving notice of his intention to seek sanctuary, and when we reached the harbour at Regium we hired a little six-oared boat to row us across the straits to Messina.

We left the harbour on a clear cold winter morning of searing blues – the sea and the sky; one light, one dark; the line dividing them as sharp as a blade; the distance to Messina a mere three miles. It took us less than an hour. We drew so close we could see Cicero's supporters lined up on the rocks to welcome him. But stationed between us and the entrance to the port was a warship flying the red and green colours of the governor of Sicily, Gaius Vergilius, and as we approached the lighthouse it slipped its anchor and moved slowly forwards to intercept us. Vergilius stood at the rail surrounded by his lictors and, after visibly recoiling at Cicero's dishevelled appearance, shouted down a greeting, to which Cicero replied in friendly terms. They had known one another in the Senate for many years.

Vergilius asked him his intentions.

Cicero called back that naturally he intended to come ashore.

'That's what I'd heard,' replied Vergilius. 'Unhappily I can't allow it.'

'Why not?'

'Because of Clodius's new law.'

'And what new law would that be? There are so many, one loses count.'

Vergilius beckoned to a member of his staff who produced a document and leaned down to pass it to me and I then gave it to Cicero. To this day I can remember how it fluttered in his hands in the slight breeze as if it were a living thing; it was the only sound in the silence. He took his time and when he had finished reading it he handed it to me without comment.

Lex Clodia in Ciceronem

Whereas M. T. Cicero has put Roman citizens to death unheard and uncondemned; and to that end forged the authority and decree of the Senate; it is hereby ordained that he be interdicted from fire and water to a distance of four hundred miles from Rome; that nobody should presume to harbour or receive him, on pain of death; that all his property and possessions be forfeit; that his house in Rome be demolished and a shrine to Liberty consecrated in its place; and that whoever shall move, speak, vote or take any step towards recalling him shall be treated as a public enemy, unless those whom Cicero unlawfully put to death should first spring back to life.

It must have been the most terrible blow. But he found the composure to dismiss it with a flick of his hand. 'When,' he enquired, 'was this nonsense published?'

'I'm told it was posted in Rome eight days ago. It came into my hands yesterday.'

'Then it's not law yet, and can't be law until it's been read a third time. My secretary will confirm it. Tiro,' he said, turning to me, 'tell the governor the earliest date it can be passed.'

I tried to calculate. Before a bill could be put to a vote it had to be read aloud in the Forum on three successive market days. But my reasoning was so shaken by what I had just read I couldn't remember what day of the week it was now, let alone when the market days fell. 'Twenty days from today,' I hazarded, 'perhaps twenty-five?'

'You see?' cried Cicero. 'I have three weeks' grace even if it passes, which I'm sure it won't.' He stood up in the prow of the boat, bracing his legs against the rocking of the hull, and spread his arms wide in appeal. 'Please, my dear Vergilius, for the sake of our past friendship, now that I have come so far, at least allow me to land and spend a night or two with my supporters.'

'No, as I say, I'm sorry, but I cannot take the risk. I've consulted my experts. They say even if you travelled to the very western tip of the island, to Lilybaeum, you'd still be within three hundred and fifty miles of Rome, and then Clodius would come after *me*.'

At that, Cicero ceased to be so friendly. He said coldly, 'You have no right under the law to impede the journey of a Roman citizen.'

'I have every right to safeguard the tranquillity of my province. And here, as you know, my word *is* the law ...'

He was apologetic. I dare say he was even embarrassed. But he was immovable, and after a few more angry exchanges there was nothing for it but to turn round and row back to Regium. Our departure provoked a great cry of dismay from the shoreline and I could see that Cicero for the first time was seriously worried. Vergilius was a friend of his. If this was how a friend reacted then soon the whole of Italy would be closed against him. Returning to Rome to oppose the law was much too risky. He had left it too late. Apart from the physical danger such a journey would entail, the bill would almost certainly pass, and then we would be stranded four hundred miles from the legal limit it prescribed. To comply safely with the terms of his exile he would have to flee abroad immediately. Obviously Gaul was out of the question because of Caesar. So it would have to be somewhere in the East – Greece perhaps, or Asia. But unfortunately we were on the wrong side of the peninsula to make our escape in the treacherous winter seas. We needed to get over to the opposite coast, to Brundisium on the Adriatic, and find a big ship capable of making a lengthy voyage. Our predicament was exquisitely vile – as no doubt Caesar, the original sponsor and creator of Clodius, had intended.

It took us two weeks of arduous travel to cross the mountains, often in heavy rain and mostly along bad roads. Every mile seemed fraught with the hazard of ambush, although the primitive little towns we passed through were welcoming enough. At night we slept in smoky, freezing inns and dined on hard bread and fatty meat made scarcely more palatable by sour wine. Cicero's mood veered between fury and despair. He saw clearly now that he had made a terrible mistake by leaving Rome. It had been madness for him to quit the city and leave Clodius free to spread the calumny that he had put citizens to death 'unheard and uncondemned' when in fact each of the five Catiline conspirators had been allowed to speak in his own defence and their execution had been sanctioned by the entire Senate. But his flight was tantamount to an admission of guilt. He should have obeyed his instinct and turned back when he heard Caesar's departing trumpets and first began to realise his error. He wept at the disaster his folly and timidity had brought upon his wife and children.

And when he had finished lashing himself, he turned his scourge on Hortensius 'and the rest of the aristocratic gang', who had never forgiven him for rising from his humble origins to the consulship and saving the republic: they had deliberately urged him to flee in order to ruin him. He should have heeded the example of Socrates, who said that death was preferable to exile. Yes, he should have killed himself! He snatched up a knife from the dining table. He *would* kill himself! I said nothing. I didn't take the threat seriously. He couldn't stand the sight of others' blood, let alone his own. All his life he had tried to avoid military expeditions, the games, public executions, funerals – anything that might remind him of mortality. If pain frightened him, death terrified him – which, although I would never have been impertinent enough to point it out, was the principal reason we had fled Rome in the first place.

When finally we came within sight of the fortified walls of Brundisium, he decided not to venture inside. The port was so large and busy, so full of strangers, and so likely to be his destination, he was convinced it was the obvious spot for his assassination. Instead we sought sanctuary a little way up the coast, in the residence of his old friend Marcus Laenius Flaccus. That night we slept in decent beds for the first time in three weeks, and the next morning we went down to the beach. The waves were much rougher than on the Sicilian side. A strong wind was hurling the Adriatic relentlessly against the rocks and shingle. Cicero loathed sea voyages at the best of times; this one promised to be especially treacherous. Yet it was our only means of escape. One hundred and twenty miles beyond the horizon lay the shore of Illyricum.

Flaccus, noticing his expression, said, 'Fortify your spirits, Cicero – perhaps the bill won't pass, or one of the other tribunes will veto it. There must be *someone* left in Rome willing to stand up for you – Pompey, surely?'

But Cicero, his gaze still fixed out to sea, made no reply, and a few days later we heard that the bill had indeed become law and that Flaccus was therefore guilty of a capital offence simply by having a convicted exile on his premises. Even so he tried to persuade us to stay. He insisted that Clodius didn't frighten *him*. But Cicero wouldn't hear of it: 'Your loyalty moves me, old friend, but that monster will have dispatched a team of his hired fighters to hunt me down the moment his law passed. There is no time to lose.'

I had found a merchant ship in the harbour at Brundisium whose hard-pressed master was willing to risk a winter voyage across the Adriatic in return for a huge fee, and the next morning at first light, when no one was around, we went on board. She was a sturdy, broad-beamed vessel, with a crew of about twenty, used to ply the trade route between Italy and Dyrrachium. I was no judge of these things, but she looked safe enough to me. The master estimated the crossing would require a day and a half – but we needed to leave quickly, he said, and take advantage of the favourable wind. So while the sailors made her ready and Flaccus waited on the quayside, Cicero quickly dictated a final message to his wife and children: *It has been a fine life, a great career – the good in me, nothing bad, has brought me down. My dear Terentia, loyalest and best of wives, my darling daughter Tullia, and little Marcus, our one remaining hope – goodbye!* I copied it out and passed it up to Flaccus. He raised his hand in farewell. Then the sail was unfurled, the cables cast off, the oarsmen pushed us away from the harbour wall, and we set off into the pale grey light.

At first we made good speed. Cicero stood high above the deck on the steersmen's platform, leaning on the stern rail, watching the great lighthouse of Brundisium recede behind us. Apart from his visits to Sicily, it was the first time he had left Italy since his youth, when he went to Rhodes to learn oratory from Molon. Of all the men I ever knew, Cicero was the least equipped by temperament for exile. To thrive he needed the appurtenances of civilised society – friends, news, gossip, conversation, politics, dinners, plays, baths, books, fine buildings; to watch all these dwindle away must have been an agony for him.

Nevertheless, in little more than an hour they had gone, swallowed up in the void. The wind drove us forwards strongly, and as we cut through the whitecaps I thought of Homer's 'dark blue wave / foaming at the bow'. But then around the middle of the morning the ship seemed gradually to lose propulsion. The great brown sail became slack-bellied and the two steersmen standing at their levers on either side of us began exchanging anxious looks. Soon dense black clouds started to mass on the horizon, and within an hour they had closed over our heads like a trapdoor. The light became shadowy; the temperature dropped. The wind got up again, but this time the gusts were in our faces, driving the cold spray off the surface of the waves. Hailstones raked the heaving deck.

Cicero shuddered, leaned forwards and vomited. His face was as grey as a corpse. I put my arm around his shoulders and indicated that we should descend to the lower deck and seek shelter in the cabin. We were halfway down the ladder when a flash of lightning split the gloom, followed instantly by a deafening, sickening crack, like a bone snapping or a tree splintering, and I was sure we must have lost the mast, for suddenly we seemed to be tumbling over and over while all around us great glistening black mountains of jet towered and toppled in the lightning flashes. The shriek of the wind made it impossible to speak or hear. In the end I simply pushed Cicero into the cabin, fell in after him and closed the door.

We tried to stand, but the ship was listing. The deck was ankle-deep in water. Our feet slid from under us. The floor tilted first one way and then the other. We clutched at the walls as we were pitched back and forth in the darkness amid loose tools and jars of wine and sacks of barley, like dumb beasts in a crate on our way to slaughter. Eventually we wedged ourselves in a corner and lay there soaked and shivering as the boat shook and plunged. I was sure we were doomed and closed my eyes and prayed to Neptune and all the gods for deliverance.

A long time passed. How long I cannot say – certainly it was the remainder of that day, and the whole of the night, and part of the day that followed. Cicero seemed quite unconscious; on several occasions I had to touch his cold cheek to reassure myself he was still alive. Each time his eyes opened briefly and then closed again. Afterwards he said he had fully resigned himself to drowning but such was the misery of his seasickness he felt no fear: rather he saw how Nature in her mercy spares those *in extremis* from the terrors of oblivion and makes death seem a welcome release. Almost the greatest surprise of his life, he said, was when he awoke on the second day and realised the storm was over and his existence would continue after all: 'Unfortunately my situation is so wretched, I almost regret it.'

Once we were sure the storm had blown itself out, we went back on deck. The sailors were just at that moment tipping over the side the corpse of some poor wretch whose head had been smashed by a swinging boom. The Adriatic was oily-smooth and still, of the same grey shade as the sky, and the body slid into it with scarcely a splash. There was a smell on the cold wind I didn't recognise, of something rotten and decaying. About a mile away I noticed a wall of sheer black rock rising above the surf. I assumed we had been blown back home again and that it must be the coast of Italy. But the captain laughed at my ignorance and said it was Illyricum, and that those were the famous cliffs that guard the approaches to the ancient city of Dyrrachium.

Cicero had at first intended to make for Epirus, the mountainous country to the south, where Atticus owned a great estate that included a fortified village. It was a most desolate region, having never recovered from the terrible fate decreed it by the Senate a century earlier, when, as a punishment for siding against Rome, all seventy of its towns had been razed to the ground simultaneously and its entire population of one hundred and fifty thousand sold into slavery. Nevertheless, Cicero claimed he wouldn't have minded the solitude of such a haunted spot. But just before we left Italy Atticus had warned him – 'with regret' – that he could only stay for a month lest word of his presence become known: if it did, under clause two of Clodius's bill, Atticus himself would be liable to the death penalty for harbouring the exile.

Even as we stepped ashore at Dyrrachium Cicero remained in two minds about which direction to take – south to Epirus, temporary refuge though it would be, or east to Macedonia, where the governor, Apuleius Saturninus, was an old friend of his, and from Macedonia on to Greece and Athens. In the event, the decision was made for him. A messenger was waiting on the quayside – a young man, very anxious. Glancing around to make sure he was not observed, he drew us quickly into a deserted warehouse and produced a letter. It was from Saturninus, the governor. I do not have it in my archives because Cicero seized it and tore it to pieces the moment I had read it out loud to him. But I can still remember the gist of what it said: that 'with regret' (that phrase again!), despite their years of friendship, Saturninus would not be able to receive Cicero in his household as it would be 'incompatible with the dignity of a Roman governor to offer succour to a convicted exile'.

Hungry, damp and exhausted from our crossing, having hurled the fragments of the letter to the ground, Cicero sank on to a bale of cloth with his head in his hands. That was when the messenger said nervously, 'Your Excellency, there is another letter ...'

It was from one of the governor's junior magistrates, the quaestor Gnaeus Plancius. His family were old neighbours of the Ciceros from their ancestral lands around Arpinum. Plancius said that he was writing secretly and sending his letter via the same courier, who was to be trusted; that he disagreed with his superior's decision; that it would be an honour for him to take the Father of the Nation under his protection; that secrecy was vital; that he had already set out on the road to meet him at the Macedonian border; and that in the meantime he had arranged for a carriage to transport Cicero out of Dyrrachium 'immediately, in the interests of your personal safety; I plead with you not to delay by so much as an hour; I shall explain more when I see you'.

'Do you trust him?' I asked.

Cicero stared at the floor and in a low voice replied, 'No. But what choice do I have?'

With the messenger's help I arranged for our luggage to be transferred from the boat to the quaestor's carriage – a gloomy contraption, little better than a cell on wheels, without suspension and with metal grilles nailed over the windows so that its fugitive occupant could look out but no one could see him. We clattered up from the harbour into the city and joined the traffic on the Via Egnatia, the great highway that runs all the way to Byzantium. It started to sleet. There had been an earthquake a few days earlier and the place was wretched in the downpour, with corpses of the native tribespeople unburied by the roadside and here and there little groups of survivors sheltering in makeshift tents among the ruins, huddled over smoking fires. It was this odour of destruction and despair that I had smelt out at sea.

We travelled across the plain towards the snow-covered mountains and spent the night in a small village hemmed in by the encroaching peaks. The inn was squalid, with goats and chickens in the downstairs rooms. Cicero ate little and said nothing. In this strange and barren land, with its savage-looking people, he had at last fallen into the full depths of despair, and it was only with difficulty that I roused him from his bed the next morning and persuaded him to continue our journey.

For two days the road climbed into the mountains, until we came to the edge of a wide lake, fringed with ice. On the far side was a town,

Lychnidos, that marked the border with Macedonia, and it was here, in its forum, that Plancius awaited us. He was in his early thirties, strongly built, wearing military uniform, with half a dozen legionaries at his back, and there was a moment when they all began to stride towards us that I experienced a rush of panic and feared we had blundered into a trap. But the warmth with which Plancius embraced Cicero, and the tears in his eyes, convinced me immediately that he was genuine.

He could not disguise his shock at Cicero's appearance. 'You need to recover your strength,' he said, 'but unfortunately, we must leave here straight away.' And then he told us what he had not dared put into his letter: that he had received reliable intelligence that three of the traitors Cicero had sent into exile for their parts in Catilina's conspiracy – Autronius Paetas, Cassius Longinus and Marcus Laeca – were all out looking for him, and had sworn to kill him.

Cicero said, 'Then there is nowhere in the world where I am safe. How are we to live?'

'Under my protection, as I said. In fact come back with me to Thessalonica, and stay under my very roof. I was military tribune until last year and I'm still on active service, so there'll be soldiers to guard you as long as you stay within the frontiers of Macedonia. My house is no palace, but it's secure and it's yours for as long as you need it.'

Cicero stared at him. Apart from the hospitality of Flaccus, it was the first real offer of help he had received for weeks – for months, in fact – and that it should have come from a young man he barely knew, when old allies such as Pompey had turned their backs on him, moved him deeply. He tried to speak, but the words choked in his throat and he had to look away.

The Via Egnatia runs for one hundred and fifty miles across the mountains of Macedonia before descending to the plain of Amphaxis, where it enters the port of Thessalonica, and this was where our journey ended, two months after leaving Rome, in a secluded villa off a busy thoroughfare in the northern part of the town.

Five years earlier, Cicero had been the undisputed ruler of Rome, second only to Pompey the Great in the affections of the people. Now he had lost everything – reputation, position, family, possessions, country; even at times the balance of his mind. For reasons of security he was confined to the villa during the hours of daylight. His presence was kept secret. A guard was posted at the entrance. Plancius told his staff that his anonymous guest was an old friend suffering from acute grief and melancholia. Like all the best lies it had the merit of being partly true. Cicero barely ate, or spoke, or left his room; sometimes his fits of weeping could be heard from one end of the house to the other. He would not receive visitors, not even his brother Quintus, who was passing nearby on his way back to Rome after completing his term as governor of Asia: *You would not have seen your brother the man you knew*, he pleaded in mitigation, *not a trace or semblance of him but only the likeness of a breathing corpse*. I tried my best to console him, without success, for how could I, a slave, understand his sense of loss, having never possessed anything worth losing in the first place? Looking back, I can see that my attempts to offer solace through philosophy must only have added to his aggravation. Indeed on one occasion, when I tried to advance the Stoic argument that possessions and rank are unnecessary, given that virtue alone is sufficient for happiness, he threw a stool at my head.

We had arrived in Thessalonica at the beginning of spring, and I took it upon myself to send letters to Cicero's friends and family letting them know, in confidence, where he was hiding, and asking them to write in response using Plancius as a poste restante. It took three weeks for these messages to reach Rome, and a further three weeks before we started to receive replies, and the news they brought was anything but encouraging. Terentia described how the charred walls of the family house on the Palatine hill had been demolished so that Clodius's shrine to Liberty – the irony! – could be erected on the site. The villa at Formiae had been pillaged, the country estate in Tusculum also invaded, and even some of the trees in the garden carted off by the neighbours. Homeless, at first she had taken refuge with her sister in the House of the Vestal Virgins.

But that impious wretch Clodius, in defiance of all the sacred laws, broke into the temple, and dragged me to the Basilica Porcia, where in front of the mob he had the impertinence to question me about my own property! Of course I refused to answer. He then demanded that I hand over our little son as a hostage to my good behaviour. In answer I pointed to the painting that shows Valerius defeating the Carthaginians and reminded him that my ancestors fought in that very battle and that as my family had never feared Hannibal, we most certainly would not be intimidated by him.

It was the plight of his son that most upset Cicero: 'The first duty of any man is to protect his children, and I am helpless to fulfil it.' Marcus and Terentia were now sheltering in the home of Cicero's brother, while his adored daughter, Tullia, was sharing a roof with her in-laws. But although Tullia, like her mother, tried to make light of her troubles, it was easy enough to read between the lines and recognise the truth: that she was nursing her sick husband, the gentle Frugi – whose health, never robust, seemed to have collapsed under the strain. *Ah, my beloved, my heart's longing!* Cicero wrote to his wife. *To think that you, dearest Terentia, once everybody's refuge in trouble, should now be so tormented! You are before my eyes night and day. Goodbye, my absent loves, goodbye.*

The political outlook was equally bleak. Clodius and his supporters were continuing their occupation of the Temple of Castor in the southern corner of the Forum. Using this fortress as their headquarters, they could intimidate the voting assemblies and pass or block whatever bills they chose. One new law we heard about, for example, demanded the annexation of Cyprus and the taxation of its wealth, 'for the good of the Roman people' – that is, to pay for the free dole of corn Clodius had instituted for every citizen – and charged Marcus Porcius Cato with accomplishing this piece of theft. Needless to say, it passed, for what group of voters ever refused to levy a tax on someone else, especially if it benefited themselves? At first Cato refused to go. But Clodius threatened him with prosecution if he disobeyed the law. As Cato held the constitution to be sacred above all things, he felt he had no choice but to comply. He sailed off for Cyprus, along with his young nephew, Marcus Junius Brutus, and with his departure Cicero lost his most vocal supporter in Rome.

Against Clodius's intimidation, the Senate was powerless. Even Pompey the Great ('the Pharaoh', as Cicero and Atticus privately called him) was now becoming frightened of the over-mighty tribune he had helped Caesar create. He was rumoured to spend most of his time making love to his young wife Julia, the daughter of Caesar, while all the time his public standing declined. Atticus wrote gossipy letters about him to cheer Cicero up, one of which survives:

You remember that when the Pharaoh restored the King of Armenia to his throne a few years back, he brought his son to Rome as a hostage to ensure the old man behaved himself? Well, just after your departure, bored of having the young fellow under his own roof, Pompey decided to lodge him with Lucius Flavius, the new praetor. Naturally, our Little Miss Beauty [Cicero's nickname for Clodius] soon got to hear of it, where upon he invited himself round to Flavius's for dinner, asked to see the prince, and then took him away with him at the end of the meal, as if he were a napkin! Why? I hear you ask. Because Clodius has decided to put the prince on the throne of Armenia in place of his father, and take all the revenues of Armenia away from Pompey and have them for himself! Unbelievable – but it gets better: the prince is duly sent back to Armenia on a ship. There is a storm. The ship returns to harbour. Pompey tells Flavius to get himself down to Antium straight away and recapture his prize hostage. But Clodius's men are waiting. There is a fight on the Via Appia. Many are killed – among them Pompey's dear friend Marcus Papirius.

Since then, things have gone from bad to worse for the Pharaoh. The other day, when he was in the Forum attending the trial of one of his supporters (Clodius is prosecuting them left, right and centre), Clodius called together a gang of his criminals and started a chant. 'What's the name of the lecherous imperator? What's the name of the man who is trying to find a man? Who is it who scratches his head with one finger?' After each question he made a sign by shaking the folds of his toga – in that way the Pharaoh does – and the mob, like a circus chorus, all roared out the answer: 'Pompey!'

No one in the Senate lifts a finger to help him, as they all think his harassment is eminently deserved for the way he abandoned you ...

But if Atticus thought such news would bring comfort to Cicero, he was wrong. On the contrary, it served only to make him feel more isolated and helpless. With Cato gone, Pompey cowed, the Senate impotent, the voters bribed and Clodius's mob in control of all law-making, Cicero despaired of ever having his exile rescinded. He chafed against the conditions in which we were obliged to exist. Thessalonica may be nice enough for a short stay in the springtime. But as the months passed, summer came – and Thessalonica in the summer becomes a hell of humidity and mosquitoes. No breath of a breeze stirs the brittle vegetation. The air is suffocating. And because the walls of the town retain the heat, the nights can be even more sweltering than the days. I slept in the room next to Cicero's – or rather, I tried to sleep. Lying in my tiny cubicle, I felt as if I were a roasting pig in a brick oven, and that the sweat pooling beneath my back was my melted flesh. Often after midnight I would hear Cicero stumbling around in the dark, his door opening, his bare feet slapping across the mosaic tiles. Then I would slip out after him and watch from a distance to make sure he was all right. He would sit in the courtyard on the edge of the dried-up pool with its dust-clogged fountain, and stare up at the brilliant stars, as if he could read in their alignment some clue as to why his good fortune had so spectacularly deserted him.

The next morning he would often summon me to his room. 'Tiro,' he would whisper, his fingers gripping my arm tightly, 'I've got to get out of this shithole. I'm losing all sense of myself.' But where could we go? He dreamed of Athens, or possibly Rhodes. But Plancius would not hear of it: the danger of assassination, he insisted, was, if anything, even greater than before, as rumours of Cicero's presence in the region spread. After a while I began to suspect that he quite enjoyed having such a famous figure in his power and was reluctant to let us leave. I voiced my suspicions to Cicero, who said: 'He's young and ambitious. Perhaps he's calculating that the situation in Rome will change and he might eventually get some political credit for shielding me. If so, he deludes himself.'

And then late one afternoon, when the ferocity of the day's heat had subsided a little, I happened to go into town with a packet of letters for dispatch to Rome. It was hard to persuade Cicero even to raise the energy to reply to his correspondence, and when he did so, it was mostly a list of complaints. *I am still stuck here with no one to talk to and nothing to think about. There could be no less suitable spot in which to bear calamity in such a state of grief as I am in.* But write he did, and to supplement the occasional trusted traveller who would carry our letters, I had arranged to hire couriers provided by a local Macedonian merchant named Epiphanes, who ran an import/export business with Rome.

He was an inveterate lazy crook, of course, as are most people in that part of the world. But I reckoned the bribes I paid him ought to have been enough to buy his discretion. He had a warehouse up the slope from the harbour, on the higher ground close to the Egnatian Gate, where a haze of red-grey dust hung permanently over the clustered roofs, thrown up by the traffic from Rome to Byzantium. To reach his office one had to cross a yard where his wagons were loaded and unloaded. And there, that afternoon – with its shafts resting on blocks and its horses unhitched and drinking noisily from a water trough – was a chariot. It was so unlike the usual ox carts that the sight of it brought me up short and I went over to give it a closer look. Obviously it had been ridden hard: it was so filthy from the road it was impossible to tell its original colour. But it was fast and strong and built for fighting – a war chariot – and when I found Epiphanes upstairs I asked him whose it was.

He gave me a crafty look. 'The driver did not say his name. He just asked me to look after it.'

'A Roman?'

'Undoubtedly.'

'Alone?'

'No, he had a companion – a gladiator, perhaps: both young men, strong.'

'When did they arrive?'

'An hour ago.'

'And where are they now?'

'Who can say?' He shrugged and bared his yellow teeth.

A terrible realisation gripped me. 'Have you been opening my letters? Have you had me followed?'

'Sir, I am shocked. Really …' He spread his hands to show his innocence and glanced around as if in silent appeal to some invisible jury. 'How could such a thing even be suggested?'

Epiphanes! For a man who made his living by lying, he was remarkably bad at it. I turned and ran out of that room and down those steps and didn't stop running until I was within sight of our villa, where a pair of rough-looking villains were loitering in the street. My footsteps slowed as the two strangers turned to look at me and I knew in my bones they had been sent to kill Cicero. One had a puckered scar that split the side of his face from his eyebrow to his jaw (Epiphanes was right: he was a fighter straight from the gladiator barracks), while the other could have been a blacksmith – given his swagger, he could have been Vulcan himself – with bulging sunburnt calves and forearms and a face as black as a Negro's. He called out to me, 'We're looking for the house where Cicero is living!' And when I started to plead ignorance, he cut me off and added, 'Tell him Titus Annius Milo has come to pay his compliments, all the way from Rome.'

Cicero's room was dark, his candle expiring for want of air. He lay on his side, facing the wall.

'Milo?' he repeated in a monotone. 'What sort of a name is that? Is he Greek, or what?' But then he rolled over on to his back and raised himself up on his elbows. 'Wait – hasn't a candidate of that name just been elected tribune?'

'It's the same man. He's here.'

'But if he's a tribune-elect, why isn't he in Rome? His term of office begins in three months.'

'He says he wants to talk to you.'

'It's a long way to come just for a chat. What do we know of him?'

'Nothing.'

'Maybe he's come to kill me?'

'Maybe – he has a gladiator with him.'

'That doesn't inspire confidence.' Cicero lay back and thought it over. 'Well, what does it matter? I might as well be dead in any case.'

He had skulked in his room so long that when I opened the door, the daylight blinded him and he had to put up his hand to protect his eyes. Stiff-limbed and waxen, half starved, with straggling grey hair and beard, he looked like a corpse freshly risen from its tomb. It was scarcely surprising that when he first came into the room, supported on my arm, Milo failed to recognise him. It was only when he heard that familiar voice bidding him good day that our visitor gasped, pressed his hand to his heart, bowed his head and declared this to be the greatest moment and the greatest honour of his life, that he had heard Cicero speak countless times in the law courts and from the rostra but had never thought to meet him, the Father of the Nation, in person, let alone be in a position (he dared to hope) to render him some service …

There was a lot more in this vein, and eventually it elicited from Cicero something I had not seen from him in months: laughter. 'Yes, very well, young man, that's enough. I understand: you're pleased to see me! Come.' And with that he stepped forward, arms open, and the two men embraced.

In later years, Cicero was to be much criticised for his friendship with Milo. And it is true that the young tribune-elect was headstrong, violent and reckless, but there are times when these traits are more to be prized than prudence, calmness and caution – and these were such times. Besides, Cicero was touched that Milo should have come so far to see him; it made him feel he was not entirely finished. He invited him to stay for dinner and to save whatever he had to say until then. He even tidied himself up a little for the occasion, combing his hair and changing into less funereal garb.

Plancius was away upcountry in Tauriana, judging the local assizes, so therefore only the three of us gathered to eat. (Milo's gladiator, a murmillo named Birria, took his meal in the kitchen; even a man as easy-going as Cicero, who had been known occasionally to tolerate the presence of an actor at his dinner table, drew the line at a gladiator.) We lay in the garden in a kind of fine-mesh tent designed to keep out the mosquitoes, and over the next few hours we learned something of Milo, and why he had made such an arduous journey of seven hundred miles. He came, he said, of a noble but hard-up family. He had been adopted by his maternal grandfather. Even so, there was little money and he had been obliged to earn a living as the owner of a gladiator school in Campania, supplying fighters for funeral games in Rome. ('No wonder we've never heard of him,' Cicero remarked to me afterwards.) His work brought him often to the city. He had been appalled, he claimed, by the violence and intimidation unleashed by Clodius. He had wept to see Cicero harried and pilloried and eventually driven from Rome. Given his occupation, he fancied himself to be in a unique position to help restore order, and through intermediaries he had approached Pompey with an offer. 'What I am about to disclose is in the strictest confidence,' he said, with a sideways glance at me. 'No word of it must go beyond us three.'

'Who am I to tell?' retorted Cicero. 'The slave who empties my chamber pot? The cook who brings my meals? I assure you I see no one else.'

'Very well,' said Milo, and then he told us what he had offered Pompey: to place at his disposal one hundred pairs of highly trained fighting men to recapture the centre of Rome and end Clodius's control of the legislative assembly. In return he had asked for a certain sum to cover expenses, and also Pompey's support in the elections for tribune: 'I couldn't just do this as a private citizen, you understand – I'd be prosecuted. I told him I needed the inviolability of the office.'

Cicero was studying him closely. He had barely touched his food. 'And what did Pompey say to that?'

'At first he brushed me off. He said he'd think about it. But then came the business with the Prince of Armenia, when Papirius was killed by Clodius's men. Did you hear about that?'

'We heard something of it.'

'Well, the killing of his friend seemed to make Pompey do that bit of extra thinking, because the day after Papirius was put on the pyre, he called me to his house. "That idea of your becoming tribune – you've got yourself a deal."'

'And how has Clodius reacted to your election? He must know what you have in mind.'

'Well that's why I'm here. And this you won't have heard about, because I left Rome straight after it happened, and no messenger could have got here quicker than I.' He stopped and held out his cup for more wine. He had come a long way to tell his story; he was obviously a raconteur; he meant to do it in his own time. 'It was about two weeks ago, not long after the elections. Pompey was doing a little business in the Forum when he ran into a gang of Clodius's men. There was some pushing and shoving, and one of them dropped a dagger. A lot of people saw it, and a great shout went up that they were going to murder Pompey. His attendants hustled him out of there fast, and back to his house, and barricaded him in – and that's where he is still, as far as I know, with only the Lady Julia for company.'

Cicero said in astonishment, 'Pompey the Great is barricaded in his own house?'

'I don't blame you if you find it funny. Who wouldn't? There's rough justice in it, and Pompey knows it. In fact he said to me that the greatest mistake of his life was letting Clodius drive you out of the city.'

'Pompey said that?'

'That's why I've raced across three countries, barely stopping to eat or sleep – to give you the news that he's going to do everything he can to get your exile overturned. His blood is up. He wants you back in Rome, you and me and him, fighting side by side, to save the republic from Clodius and his gang! What do you say to that?'

He was like a dog that has just laid a kill at its master's feet; if he'd had a tail, it would have been thumping against the fabric of the couch. But if Milo had expected either delight or gratitude, he was to be disappointed. Depressed in spirit and ragged in appearance though he might be, Cicero had nevertheless seen straight through to the heart of the matter. He swilled his wine around in his cup, frowning before he spoke.

'And does Caesar agree to this?'

'Ah now,' said Milo, shifting slightly on his couch, 'that's for you to settle with him. Pompey will play his part, but you must play yours. It would be hard for him to campaign to bring you back if Caesar were to object very strongly.'

'So he wants me to reconcile with him?'

'His word was to *reassure* him.'

It had grown dark while we were talking. The household slaves had lit lamps around the perimeter of the garden; their gleams were clouded with moths. But no light was on the table, so I couldn't properly make out Cicero's expression. He was silent for a long while. It was terrifically hot as usual, and I was conscious of the night sounds of Macedonia – the cicadas and the mosquitoes, the occasional dog bark, the voices of local people in the street, speaking in their strange, harsh foreign tongue. I wondered if Cicero was thinking the same as I was – that another year in such a place as this would kill him. Perhaps he was, because eventually he let out a sigh of resignation and said, 'And in what terms am I supposed to "reassure" him?'

'That's up to you. If any man can find the right words, it's you. But Caesar has made it clear to Pompey that he needs something in writing before he'll even think of reconsidering his position.'

'Am I supposed to give you a document to take back to Rome?'

'No, this part of the arrangement has to be between you and Caesar. Pompey thinks it would be best if you sent your own private emissary to Gaul – someone you trust, who could deliver some form of written undertaking into Caesar's hands personally.'

Caesar – everything seemed to come back to him eventually. I thought again of the sound of his trumpets leaving the Field of Mars, and in the stifling gloom I sensed rather than saw that both men had turned to look at me.

XXXIX

How easy it is for those who play no part in public affairs to sneer at the compromises required of those who do. For two years Cicero had stuck to his principles and refused to join with Caesar, Pompey and Crassus in their 'triumvirate' to control the state. He had denounced their criminality in public; they had retaliated by making it possible for Clodius to become a tribune; and when Caesar had offered him a legateship in Gaul that would have given him legal immunity from Clodius's attacks, Cicero had refused it, because acceptance would have made him Caesar's creature.

But the price of upholding those principles had been banishment, poverty and heartbreak. 'I have made myself powerless,' he said to me, after Milo had gone off to bed, leaving us alone to discuss Pompey's offer, 'and where is the virtue in that? What use am I to my family or my principles stuck in this dump for the rest of my life? Oh, no doubt one day I could become some kind of shining example to be taught to bored pupils: the man who refused ever to compromise his conscience. Perhaps after I'm safely dead they might even put up a statue of me at the back of the rostra. But I don't want to be a monument. My skill is statecraft, and that requires me to be alive and in Rome.' He fell silent. 'Then again, the thought of having to bend the knee to Caesar is scarcely bearable. To have suffered all this, and then to have to go creeping back to him like some dog that's learnt its lesson …'

He was still undecided when he retired for the night, and the following morning, when Milo called to ask him what answer he should take back to Pompey, I could not have predicted what he would say. 'You can tell him this,' responded Cicero. 'That my whole life has been dedicated to the service of the state, and that if the state demands of me that I should reconcile with my enemy – then reconcile I shall.'

Milo embraced him and then immediately set off back to the coast in his war chariot with his gladiator standing beside him – such a pair of brutes longing for a fight that one could only tremble for Rome and all the blood that was bound to be spilt.

It was settled that I should leave Thessalonica on my mission to Caesar at the end of the summer, as soon as the military campaigning season was over. To have set off before then would have been pointless, as Caesar was with his legions deep inside Gaul, and his habit of rapid forced marches made it impossible to say with any certainty where he might be.

Cicero spent many hours working on his letter. Years later, after his death, our copy was seized by the authorities, along with all the other correspondence between Cicero and Caesar, presumably in case it contradicted the official history that the Dictator was a genius and that all who opposed him were stupid, greedy, ungrateful, shortsighted and reactionary. I assume it has been destroyed; at any rate, I have never heard of it since. However, I still possess my shorthand notes, covering most of the thirty-six years I worked for Cicero – such a vast mass of unintelligible hieroglyphics that the ignorant operatives who ransacked my archive doubtless assumed them to be harmless gibberish and left them untouched. It is from these that I have been able to reconstruct the many conversations, speeches and letters that make up this memoir of Cicero – including his humiliating appeal to Caesar that summer, which is not lost after all.

Thessalonica

From M. Cicero to G. Caesar, Proconsul, greetings.

I hope you and the army are well.

Many misunderstandings have unfortunately arisen between us in recent years but there is one in particular which, if it exists, I wish to dispel. I have never wavered in my admiration for your qualities of intelligence, resourcefulness, patriotism, energy and command. You have justly risen to a position of great eminence in our republic, and I wish only to see your efforts crowned with success both on the battlefield and in the counsels of state, as I am sure they will be.

Do you remember, Caesar, that day when I was consul, when we debated in the Senate the punishment of those five traitors who were plotting the destruction of the republic, including my own murder? Tempers were high. Violence was in the air. Each man distrusted his neighbour. Suspicion even unjustly fell upon you, astonishingly, and had I not intervened, the flower of your glory might have been cut off before it had a chance to bloom. You know this to be true; swear otherwise if you dare.

The wheel of fate has now reversed our positions, but with this difference: I am not a young man now, as you were then, with golden prospects. My career is over. If the Roman people were ever to vote for my return from exile, I should not seek any office. I should not put myself at the head of any party or faction, especially one injurious to your interests. I should not seek to overturn any of the legislation enacted during your consulship. In what little earthly time remains to me, my life will be devoted solely to restoring the fortunes of my poor family, supporting my friends in the law courts, and rendering such service as I can to the well-being of the commonwealth. On this you may rest assured.

I am sending you this letter via my confidential secretary M. Tiro, whom you may remember, and who can be relied upon to convey in confidence any reply you may wish to make.

'Well, there it is,' said Cicero, when it was finished, 'a shameful document, and yet if one day it were to be read aloud in court, I don't believe I would need to blush too deeply.' He copied it out carefully in his own hand, sealed it, and handed it to me. 'Keep your eyes open, Tiro. Observe how he seems and who is with him. I want an exact account. If he asks after my condition, hesitate, speak with reluctance, and then confide that I am utterly broken in body and spirit. The more certain he is I'm finished, the more likely he is to let me return.'

By the time the letter was done, our situation had in fact become much more precarious again. In Rome, the senior consul, Lucius Calpurnius Piso, who was Caesar's father-in-law and an enemy of Cicero's, had been awarded the governorship of Macedonia in a public vote rigged by Clodius. He would take office at the start of the new year: an advance guard from his staff was expected in the province shortly. If they caught Cicero they might kill him on the spot. Another door was starting to close on us. My departure could no longer be put off.

I dreaded the emotion of our parting, and so, I knew, did Cicero; therefore we colluded to avoid it. On the night before I left, when we had dined together for the final time, he pretended to be tired and retired to bed early, while I assured him I would wake him in the morning to say a final goodbye. In fact I slipped away before dawn, while the house was still in darkness, without a fuss, as he would have wanted.

Plancius had arranged an escort to conduct me back over the mountains to Dyrrachium, and there I took ship and sailed to Italy – not straight across to Brundisium this time, but north-west, to Ancona. It was a much longer voyage than our original crossing and took almost a week. But it was still quicker than going overland, with the added advantage that I would not encounter any of Clodius's agents. I had never before travelled such a long distance on my own, let alone by ship. My terror of the sea was not the same as Cicero's – of shipwreck and of drowning. It was rather of the vast emptiness of the horizon during the day and the glittering, indifferent hugeness of the universe at night. I was at this time forty-six, and conscious of the void into which we all are voyaging; I thought of death often while sitting out on deck. I had witnessed so much; ageing in body though I was, in spirit I was even older. Little did I realise that actually I had lived less than half my life, and was destined to see things that would make all the wonders and dramas that had gone before seem quite pallid and insignificant.

The weather was favourable, and we landed at Ancona without incident. From there I took the road north, crossing the Rubicon two days later and formally entering the province of Nearer Gaul. This was territory familiar to me: I had toured it with Cicero six years earlier, when he was seeking election as consul and canvassing the towns along the Via Aemilia. The vineyards beside the road had all been harvested weeks before; now the vines were being cut back for winter, so that as far as one could see, columns of white smoke from the burning vegetation were rising over the flat terrain, as if some retreating army had scorched the earth behind it.

In the little town of Claterna, where I stayed the night, I learned that the governor had returned from beyond the Alps and had set up his winter headquarters in Placentia, but that with typical restless energy he was already touring the countryside holding assizes: he was due in the neighbouring town of Mutina the next day. I left early, reached it at noon, passed through the heavily fortified walls, and made for the basilica on the forum. The only clue to Caesar's presence was a troop of legionaries at the entrance. They made no attempt to ask my business, and I went straight inside. A cold grey light from the clerestory windows fell upon a hushed queue of citizens waiting to present their petitions. At the far end – too far away for me to make out his face – seated between pillars, dispensing judgement from his magistrate's chair, in a toga so white it stood out brightly amid the locals' drab winter plumage, was Caesar.

Uncertain how to approach him, I found myself joining the line of petitioners. Caesar was issuing his rulings at such a rate that we shuffled forwards almost continuously, and as I drew closer I saw that he was doing several things at once – listening to each supplicant, reading documents as they were handed to him by a secretary, and conferring with an army officer who had taken off his helmet and was bending down to whisper in his ear. I took out Cicero's letter so that I would have it ready. But then it struck me that this was not perhaps the proper place to hand over the appeal: that it was unconducive somehow to the dignity of a former consul for his request to be considered alongside the domestic complaints of all these farmers and tradespeople, worthy folk though they no doubt were. The officer finished his report, straightened, and was just walking past me towards the door, fastening his helmet, when his eyes met mine and he stopped in surprise. 'Tiro?'

I glimpsed his father in him before I could put a name to the young man himself. It was M. Crassus's son, Publius, now a cavalry commander on Caesar's staff. Unlike his father he was a cultured, gracious, noble man, and an admirer of Cicero, whose company he used to seek out. He greeted me with great affability – 'What brings you to Mutina?' – and when I told him, he volunteered at once to arrange a private interview with Caesar and insisted I accompany him to the villa where the governor and his entourage were staying.

'I'm doubly glad to see you,' he said as we walked, 'for I've often thought of Cicero, and the injustice done to him. I've talked to my father about it and persuaded him not to oppose his recall. And Pompey, as you know, supports it too – only last week he sent Sestius, one of the tribunes-elect, up here to plead his cause with Caesar.'

I could not help observing, 'It seems that everything these days depends upon Caesar.'

'Well, you have to understand his position. He feels no personal animosity towards your master – very much the opposite. But unlike my father and Pompey, he's not in Rome to defend himself. He's concerned about losing political support while his back is turned, and being recalled before his work here is complete. He sees Cicero as the greatest threat to his position. Come inside – let me show you something.'

We passed the sentry and went into the house, and Publius conducted me through the crowded public rooms to a small library where, from an ivory casket, he produced a series of dispatches, all beautifully edged in black and housed in purple slip-cases, with the word *Commentaries* picked out in vermilion in the title line.

'These are Caesar's own personal copies,' Publius explained, handling them carefully. 'He takes them with him wherever he goes. They are his record of the campaign in Gaul, which he has decided to send regularly to be posted up in Rome. One day he intends to collect them all together and publish them as a book. It's perfectly marvellous stuff. See for yourself.'

He plucked out a roll for me to read:

There is a river called the Saone, which flows through the territories of the Aedui and Sequani into the Rhone with such incredible slowness that it cannot be determined by the eye in which direction it flows. This the Helvetii were crossing by rafts and boats joined together. When Caesar was informed by spies that the Helvetii had already conveyed three parts of their forces across that river, but that the fourth part was left behind on this side of the Saone, he set out from the camp with three legions. Attacking them, encumbered with baggage, and not expecting him, he cut to pieces a great part of them ...

I said, 'He writes of himself with wonderful detachment.'

'He does. That's because he doesn't want to sound boastful. It's important to strike the right note.'

I asked if I might be allowed to copy some of it, and show it to Cicero. 'He misses the regular news from Rome. What reaches us is sparse, and late.'

'Of course – it's all public information. And I'll make sure you get in to see Caesar. You'll find he's in a tremendously good mood.'

He left me alone and I settled to work.

Even allowing for a degree of exaggeration, it was plain from the *Commentaries* that Caesar had enjoyed an astonishing run of military successes. His original mission had been to halt the migration of the Helvetii and four other tribes who were trekking westwards across Gaul to the Atlantic in search of new territory. He had followed their immense column, which consisted both of fighting men and of the elderly and women and children, with a new army he had mostly raised himself of five legions. Finally he had lured them into battle at Bibracte. As a guarantee to his new legions that neither he nor his officers would abandon them if things went wrong, he had all their horses sent far away to the rear. They fought on foot with the infantry, and in the event Caesar, by his own account, did not merely halt the Helvetii – he slaughtered them. Afterwards a list giving the total strength of the migration had been discovered in the enemy's abandoned camp:

Helvetii	*263,000*
Tulingi	*36,000*
Latobrigi	*14,000*
Rauraci	*23,000*
Boii	*32,000*
	368,000

Of these, according to Caesar, the total number who returned alive to their former homeland was 110,000.

Then – and this was what no one else surely would have dreamed of attempting – he had force-marched his weary legions back across Gaul to confront 120,000 Germans who had taken advantage of the Helvetii's migration to cross into Roman-controlled territory. There had been another terrific battle, lasting seven hours, in which young Crassus had commanded the cavalry, and by the end of it the Germans had been entirely annihilated. Hardly any had been left alive to flee back across the Rhine, which for the first time became the natural frontier of the Roman Empire. Thus, if Caesar's account was to be believed, almost one third of a million people had either died or disappeared in the space of a single summer. To round off the year, he had left his legions in their new winter camp, a full one hundred miles north of the old border of Further Gaul.

By the time I had finished my copying it was beginning to get dark, but the villa was still noisy with activity – soldiers and civilians wanting an appointment with the governor, messengers rushing in and out. As I could no longer see to write, I put away my tablet and stylus and sat in the gloom. I wondered what Cicero would have made of it all had he been in Rome. To have condemned the victories would have seemed unpatriotic; at the same time, such sweeping cleansing of populations and adjustments to the frontier, without the authorisation of the Senate, were illegal. I also pondered what Publius Crassus had said: that Caesar feared Cicero's presence in Rome lest he be 'recalled before his work here is complete'. What did 'complete' mean in this context? The phrase seemed ominous.

My reverie was interrupted by the arrival of a young officer, barely more than thirty, with tight blond curls and an improbably immaculate uniform, who introduced himself as Caesar's aide-de-camp, Aulus Hirtius. He said that he understood I had a letter for the governor from Cicero, and that if I would be so kind as to give it to him, he would see that he received it. I replied that I was under firm instructions to give it to Caesar personally. He said that was impossible. I said that in that case I would follow the governor from town to town until such time as I got the chance to speak to him. Hirtius scowled at me and tapped his neatly shod foot, then went away again. An hour passed before he reappeared and curtly asked me to follow him.

The public part of the house was still thronged with callers, even though it was now night-time. We went down a passage, through a stout door and into a warm, heavily scented, thickly carpeted room, brilliantly lit by a hundred candles, in the centre of which on a table lay Caesar, flat on his back and entirely naked, having oil worked into his skin by a Negro masseur. He glanced at me briefly and held out his hand. I gave Cicero's letter to Hirtius, who broke the seal and handed it to Caesar. I directed my gaze to the floor as a mark of respect.

Caesar said, 'How was your journey?'

I replied, 'Good, Excellency, thank you.'

'And are you being looked after?'

'I am, thank you.'

I dared then to look at him properly for the first time. His body was glistening, well muscled, and plucked entirely hairless in every respect – a disconcerting affectation which had the effect of emphasising his numerous scars and bruises, presumably picked up on the battlefield. His face was undeniably striking – angular and lean, dominated by dark and penetrating eyes. The overall effect was one of great power, of both the intellect and the will. One could see why men and women alike fell easily under his spell. He was then in his forty-third year. He turned on to his side towards me – there was no spare flesh, I noticed: his stomach was entirely hard – propped himself up on his elbow and gestured to Hirtius, who produced a portable inkstand and carried it over to him.

He said, 'And how is Cicero's health?'

'It's very poor, I'm afraid.'

He laughed. 'Oh no, I don't believe a word of *that*! He'll outlive us all – or me, at any rate.'

He dipped his pen in the inkpot, scrawled something on the letter, and gave it back to Hirtius, who sprinkled sand on the wet ink, blew away the residue, rolled the document up again, and returned it to me without expression.

Caesar said, 'If you need anything during your stay, be sure to ask.' He lay on his back once more and the masseur resumed his kneading.

I hesitated. I had come such a long way. I felt there should be something more, if only by way of an anecdote for me to take back to Cicero. But Hirtius touched my arm and nodded towards the door.

As I reached it, Caesar called after me, 'Do you still practise that shorthand of yours?'

'I do.'

He made no further comment. The door closed and I followed Hirtius back up the passage. My heart was pounding, as if I had survived a sudden fall. It wasn't until I had been shown to the room where I was to sleep overnight that I thought to check what he had written on the letter. Two words only – either elegantly brief or typically contemptuous, depending on how you chose to interpret them: *Approved. Caesar.*

When I rose the following morning, the house was silent; Caesar had already left with his entourage for the next town. My mission concluded, I too set off on my long return journey.

When I reached the harbour at Ancona, I found a letter from Cicero waiting for me: the first of Piso's soldiers had just arrived in Thessalonica and therefore as a precaution he was departing immediately for Dyrrachium – which, as it lies in the province of Illyricum, was beyond Piso's influence. He hoped to meet me there. Depending on Caesar's answer and on developments in Rome, we would then decide where to go next: *Like Callisto, it seems we are doomed to wander throughout eternity.*

I had to wait ten days for a favourable wind and did not reach Dyrrachium until the festival of Saturnalia. The City Fathers had placed at Cicero's disposal a well-defended house up in the hills with a view across the sea, and this was where I found him, gazing at the Adriatic. He turned at my approach. I had forgotten how much exile had aged him. My dismay must have shown in my expression, because his own face fell the moment he saw me, and he said bitterly, 'So I take it the answer was no?'

'On the contrary.'

I showed him his original letter with Caesar's scrawl in the margin. He held it in his hands and studied it for a long while.

'"Approved. Caesar",' he said. 'Will you look at that? "Approved. Caesar"! He's doing something he doesn't want to do and he's as sulky about it as a child.'

He sat on a bench under an umbrella pine and made me recount my visit in every detail, and then he read the extracts I had copied from Caesar's *Commentaries*. When he had finished, he said, 'He writes very well in his brutal way. Such artlessness requires some art – it will add to his reputation. But where will his campaigning take him next, I wonder? He could grow strong – very strong. If Pompey is not careful, he will wake up to find a monster on his back.'

There was nothing we could do now but wait, and whenever I think of Cicero at this time, I always picture him in the same way: on that terrace, leaning over the balustrade, a letter bearing the latest news from Rome clenched in his hand, staring grimly at the horizon, as if somehow by sheer willpower he could see all the way to Italy and impose himself on events.

First we heard from Atticus of the swearing-in of the new tribunes, eight of whom were Cicero's supporters and only two his declared enemies – but two was enough to impose a veto on any law repealing his exile. Then from Cicero's brother, Quintus, we learned that Milo, as tribune, had brought a prosecution against Clodius for violence and intimidation, and that Clodius's response had been to order his bullies to attack Milo's house. On New Year's Day the new consuls took office. One, Lentulus

Spinther, was already a firm supporter of Cicero. The other, Metellus Nepos, had long been considered his enemy. But someone must have got at him, because in the inaugural debate of the new Senate, Nepos declared that while he still did not care for Cicero personally, he would not oppose his recall. Two days later, a motion to repeal Cicero's exile, drawn up by Pompey, was laid by the Senate before the people.

At that moment it was possible to believe that Cicero's banishment would soon be over, and I began to make discreet preparations for our departure to Italy. But Clodius was a resourceful and vindictive enemy. On the night before the people were due to meet, he and his supporters occupied the Forum, the comitium, the rostra – in sum, the whole legislative heart of the republic – and when Cicero's friends and allies arrived to vote, they attacked them without mercy. Two tribunes, Fabricius and Cispius, were set upon and their attendants murdered and flung in the Tiber. When Quintus tried to get up on to the rostra, he was dragged off and beaten up so badly he only survived by pretending to be dead. Milo responded by unleashing his own squad of gladiators. Soon the centre of Rome was a battlefield, and the fighting went on for days. But although Clodius for the first time suffered severe punishment, he was not entirely driven out, and he still had the two tribunes with their vetoes. The law to bring Cicero home had to be abandoned.

When Cicero received Atticus's account of what had happened, he fell into a despair almost as great as that which had gripped him in Thessalonica. *From your letter*, he wrote back, *and from the facts themselves I see that I am utterly finished. In matters where my family needs your help I beg you not to fail us in our misery.*

However, there is always this to be said for politics: it is never static. If the good times do not last, neither do the bad. Like Nature, it follows a perpetual cycle of growth and decay, and no statesman, however cunning, is immune to this process. If Clodius had not been so arrogant, reckless and ambitious, he never would have achieved the heights he did. But being all those things, and subject to the laws of politics, he was bound to overreach and topple eventually.

In the spring, during the Festival of Flora, when Rome was crowded with visitors from all over Italy, Clodius's mob found itself for once outnumbered by ordinary citizens who despised their bullying tactics. Clodius himself was actually jeered at the theatre. Unused to anything other than adulation from the people, according to Atticus he looked around him in astonishment at the slow handclapping, taunts, whistles and obscene gestures, and realised – almost too late – that he was in danger of being lynched. He retreated hastily, and that was the beginning of the end of his domination, for the Senate now recognised how he could be beaten: by appealing over the heads of the urban plebs to the population at large.

Spinther duly laid a motion calling for the entire citizenry of the republic to be summoned together in its most sovereign body, the electoral college of one hundred and ninety-three centuries, and for them to determine the fate of Cicero once and for all. The motion passed in the Senate by four hundred and thirteen votes to one, the one being Clodius. It was further agreed that the vote on Cicero's recall should take place at the same time as the summer elections, when the centuries would already be assembled on the Field of Mars.

The moment he heard what had been decided, Cicero was so certain he was reprieved he arranged for a sacrifice to be made to the gods. Those tens of thousands of ordinary citizens from across Italy were the solid, sensible foundation on which he had built his career; he was sure they would not let him down. He sent word to his wife and family asking them to meet him in Brundisium, and rather than lingering in Illyricum to await the result, which would take two weeks to reach us, he decided to sail for home on the day the vote was held. 'If there is a tide flowing in one's direction, one must catch it early, and not allow it time to ebb. Besides, it will look good if I show confidence.'

'If the vote goes against you, you will be breaking the law by returning to Italy.'

'But it won't. The Roman people will never vote to keep me in exile – and if they do, well there's no point in going on, is there?'

And so, fifteen months to the day after we had landed in Dyrrachium, we went down to the harbour to begin the journey back to life. Cicero had shaved off his beard and cut his hair and had put on a white toga with the purple stripe of a senator. As chance would have it, our return crossing was on the same merchant ship that had brought us over. But the contrast between the two journeys could not have been more marked. This time we skimmed across a flat sea all day with a favourable wind, spent the night lying out on the open deck, and the following morning came in sight of Brundisium. The entrance to the greatest harbour in Italy opens like an immense pair of outstretched arms, and as we passed between the booms and approached the crowded quayside, it felt as if we were being clasped to the heart of a dear and long-lost friend. The whole town seemed to be at the harbour and *en fête*, with pipes and drums playing, young girls carrying flowers, and youths waving boughs decorated with coloured ribbons.

I thought they were for Cicero, and said so in great excitement, but he cut me off and told me not to be a fool. 'How would they have known we were coming? Besides, have you forgotten everything? Today is the anniversary of the founding of the colony of Brundisium, and therefore a local holiday. You would have known that once, when I was running for office.'

Nevertheless, some of the people had noticed his senatorial toga and quickly realised who he was. The word was passed. Soon a sizeable crowd was shouting his name and cheering. Cicero, standing on the upper deck as we glided towards our berth, raised his hand in acknowledgement and turned this way and that so all could see him. Among the multitude I spotted his daughter, Tullia. She was waving with the rest and calling out to him, even jumping up and down to attract his attention. But Cicero was sunning himself in the applause, his eyes half closed, like a prisoner released from a dungeon into the light, and in the noise and tumult of the crowd he did not see her.

XL

That Cicero did not recognise his only daughter was less peculiar than it may seem. She had changed greatly in the time we had been away. Her face and arms, once plump and girlish, were thin and pale; her fair hair was covered by the dark headdress of mourning. The day of our arrival was her twentieth birthday, although I am ashamed to say that I had forgotten it and so had failed to remind Cicero.

His first act on stepping down from the gangplank was to kneel and kiss the soil. Only after this patriotic act had been loudly cheered did he look up and notice his daughter watching him in her widow's weeds. He stared at her and burst into tears, for he truly loved her, and he had loved her husband too, and now he saw by the colour and style of her dress that he was dead.

He enfolded her in his arms, to the crowd's delight, and after a long embrace took a step back to examine her. 'My dearest child, you cannot imagine how much I have yearned for this moment.' Still holding her hands, he switched his gaze to the faces behind her and scanned them eagerly. 'Is your mother here, and Marcus?'

'No, Papa, they're in Rome.'

This was hardly surprising – in those days it was an arduous journey, especially for a woman, of two or three weeks from Rome to Brundisium, with a serious risk of robbery in the remoter stretches; if anything, the surprise was that Tullia *had* come, and come alone at that. But Cicero's disappointment was obvious although he tried to hide it.

'Well, it's no matter – no matter at all. I have you, and that's the main thing.'

'And I have you – and on my birthday.'

'It's your birthday?' He gave me a reproachful look. 'I almost forgot. Of course it is. We shall celebrate tonight!' And he took her by the arm and led her away from the harbour.

Because we did not yet know for certain that his exile had been repealed, it was decided that we should not set off for Rome until we had official confirmation, and once again Laenius Flaccus volunteered to put us up at his estate outside Brundisium. Armed men were stationed around the perimeter for Cicero's protection, and he spent much of the next few days with Tullia, strolling through the gardens and along the beach, learning at first hand how difficult her life had been during his exile – how, for example, her husband, Frugi, had been set upon by Clodius's henchmen when he was trying to speak on Cicero's behalf, stripped naked and pelted with filth and driven from the Forum, and how his heart had ceased to beat properly afterwards until, a few months later, he died in her arms; how, because she was childless, she had been left with nothing except a few pieces of jewellery and her returned dowry, which she had given to Terentia to help pay off the family's debts; how Terentia had been obliged to sell a large part of her own property, and had even steeled herself to plead with Clodius's sister to intercede with her brother to grant her and her children some mercy, and how Clodia had mocked her and boasted that Cicero had tried to have an affair with her; how families they had always thought of as friends had closed their doors on them in fear; and so on and so forth.

Cicero told me all this sadly one night after Tullia had gone to bed. 'Little wonder Terentia isn't here. It seems she avoids going out in public as much as she can and prefers to stay cooped up in my brother's house. As for Tullia, we need to find her a new husband as soon as possible, while she's still young enough to give a man some children safely.' He rubbed his temples, as he always did at times of stress. 'I'd thought that coming back to Italy would mark the end of my troubles. Now I see it is merely the beginning.'

It was on our sixth day as Flaccus's guests that a messenger arrived from Quintus with the news that despite a last-minute demonstration by Clodius and his mob, the centuries had voted unanimously to restore to Cicero his full rights of citizenship, and that he was accordingly a free man once more. Oddly, the news did not seem to give him much joy, and when I remarked on his indifference he replied: 'Why should I rejoice? I have merely had returned to me something that should never have been taken away in the first place. Otherwise, I am weaker than I was before.'

We began our journey to Rome the next day. By then the news of his rehabilitation had spread among the people of Brundisium, and a crowd of several hundred had gathered outside the gates of the villa to see him off. He got down from the carriage he was sharing with Tullia, greeted each well-wisher with a handshake, made a short speech, and then we resumed our journey. But we had not gone more than five miles when we encountered another large group at the next settlement, also clamouring for the opportunity to shake his hand. Once again he obliged. And so it went on throughout that day, and the days that followed, always the same, except that the crowds grew steadily larger as word preceded us that Cicero would be passing through. Soon people were coming from miles around, even walking down from the mountains to stand by the roadside. By the time we reached Beneventum, the numbers were in their thousands; in Capua, the streets were entirely blocked.

To begin with, Cicero was touched by these unfeigned demonstrations of affection, then delighted, then amazed, and finally thoughtful. Was there some means, he wondered, of turning this astonishing popularity among the ordinary citizens of Italy into political influence in Rome? But popularity and power, as he well knew, are separate entities. Often the most powerful men in a state can pass down a street unrecognised, while the most famous bask in feted impotence.

This was brought home to us soon after we left Campania, when Cicero decided we should call in at Formiae and inspect his villa on the seashore. He knew from Terentia and Atticus that it had been attacked, and was braced to find a ruin. In fact, when we turned off the Via Appia and entered the grounds, the shuttered property appeared perfectly intact, albeit the Greek statuary had gone. The garden was neatly tended. Peacocks still strutted between the trees and we could hear the distant motion of the sea. As the carriage halted and Cicero climbed out, members of the household began to materialise from various parts of the property, as if they had been in hiding. Seeing their master again, they flung themselves to the ground, crying with relief. But when he began to move towards the front door, several tried to block his path, pleading with him not to go inside. He gestured to them to move out of the way and ordered the door to be unlocked.

The first shock to confront us was the smell – of smoke and damp and human waste. And then there was the sound – empty and echoing, broken only by the crunch of plaster and pottery beneath our feet, and the cooing of the pigeons in rafters. As the shutters started to come down, the summer afternoon sunlight revealed a vista of room after room stripped bare. Tullia put her hand to her mouth in horror and Cicero gently told her to go and wait in the carriage. We moved on into the interior. All the furniture was gone, all the pictures, the fixtures. Here and there sections of the ceilings were hanging down; even the mosaic floors had been prised up and carted away; weeds grew out of bare earth amid the bird shit and human faeces. The walls were scorched where fires had been lit, and covered with the most obscene drawings and graffiti, all executed in dripping red paint.

In the dining room a rat scuttled along the side of the wall and squeezed itself down a hole. Cicero watched it disappear with a look of infinite disgust on his face. Then he marched out of the house, clambered back into his carriage, and ordered the driver to rejoin the Via Appia. He did not speak for at least an hour.

Two days later we reached Bovillae, on the outskirts of Rome.

We woke the next morning to find yet another crowd waiting to escort us into the city. As we stepped out into the heat of that summer morning, I was apprehensive: the state of the villa at Formiae had unnerved me. It was also the eve of the Roman Games, a public holiday. The streets would be packed, and reports had already reached us of a shortage of bread that had led to rioting. I was sure Clodius would use the pretext of the disorder to attempt some kind of ambush. But Cicero was calm. He believed the people would protect him. He asked for the roof to be removed from the carriage, and with Tullia holding a parasol seated beside him, and me stationed up on the bench next to the driver, we set off.

I do not exaggerate when I say that every yard of the Via Appia was lined with citizens and that for nearly two hours we were borne northwards on a wave of continuous applause. Where the road passes over the River Almo, by the Temple of the Great Mother, the crowd was three or four deep. Further on, they occupied the steps of the Temple of Mars so densely it resembled a stand at the games. And just outside the city walls, along that stretch where the aqueduct runs beside the highway, young men were perched precariously on the tops of the arches, or clinging to the palm trees. They waved, and Cicero waved back. The din and the heat and the dust were terrific. Eventually we were forced to a halt just outside the Capena Gate, where the press of humanity was simply too great for us to go on.

I jumped down with the intention of opening the door, and tried to push my way round to the side of the carriage. But a surge of people, desperate to get closer to Cicero, pinned me against it so hard I could neither move nor breathe. The carriage shifted and threatened to topple, and I do believe that Cicero might have been killed by an excess of love just ten paces short of Rome, had not his brother Quintus appeared at that moment from the recesses of the gate along with a dozen attendants who pushed the crowd back and cleared a space for Cicero to descend.

It was four years since the two had last met, and Quintus no longer appeared the younger brother. His nose had been broken during the fighting in the Forum. He was obviously drinking too much. He looked like a beaten-down old boxer. He held out his arms to Cicero and they locked hold of one another, unable to speak for emotion, tears pouring down their cheeks, each silently pounding the back of the other.

When they separated, Quintus told him what he had arranged, and then we entered the city on foot, Cicero and Quintus walking hand in hand, with Tullia and me behind them, a file of attendants on either side. Quintus, who used to be Cicero's campaign manager, had devised the route in order to show off his brother to as many supporters as possible. We passed the Circus Maximus, its flags already flying in anticipation of the games, and as we progressed slowly along the crowded valley between the Palatine and the Caelian hills, it seemed as if everyone Cicero had ever represented in the law courts, or helped out with a favour, or even just shaken hands with at election time had come out to bid him welcome. Even so, I noticed that not all were cheering, and that here and there small groups of sullen plebeians scowled at us or turned their backs, especially as we drew close to the Temple of Castor, where Clodius had his headquarters. Fresh slogans had been daubed across it, in the same angry red paint that had been used at Formiae: *M. CICERO STEALS THE PEOPLE'S BREAD*; *WHEN THE PEOPLE ARE HUNGRY THEY KNOW WHO TO BLAME*. One man spat at us. Another slyly drew back the folds of his tunic to show me his knife. Cicero affected not to notice.

A crowd of several thousand cheered us all the way across the Forum and up the Capitoline steps to the Temple of Jupiter, where a fine white bull was waiting to be sacrificed. At every moment I feared an assault, despite my reason telling me it would have been suicidal: any attacker would have been torn apart by Cicero's supporters, even assuming he could have got close enough to strike a blow. Nevertheless, I would have preferred it if we could have got into a place with walls and a door. But that was impossible: on this day Cicero belonged to Rome. First we had to listen to the priests recite their prayers, then Cicero had to cover his head and step forward to deliver his ritual thanks to the gods, and stand and watch while the beast was killed and its entrails examined until the auspices were pronounced propitious. Then he entered the temple and laid offerings at the feet of a small statue of Minerva he had placed there before his exile. Finally, when he emerged, he was surrounded by many of those senators who had campaigned hardest for his restoration – Sestius, Cestilius, Curtius, the Cispius brothers and the rest, led by the senior consul, Lentulus Spinther – each of whom had to be thanked individually. Many were the tears shed and the kisses exchanged, and it must have been well after noon before he was able to start walking home, and even then Spinther and the others insisted on accompanying him; Tullia, unnoticed by any of us, had already gone on ahead.

'Home' of course was no longer his own fine mansion on the slopes of the Palatine: looking up, I could see that it had been entirely demolished to make room for Clodius's shrine to Liberty. Instead we were to be lodged just below it, in the house of Quintus, where we would live until such time as Cicero could get the site restored to him and begin rebuilding. This street, too, was packed with well-wishers, and Cicero had to struggle to reach the threshold. Beyond it, in the shade of the courtyard, waited his wife and children.

I knew, because he had so often spoken of it, how much Cicero had looked forward to this moment. And yet there was an awkwardness to it that made me want to hide my face. Terentia, decked out in her finery, had plainly been waiting for him for several hours, and in the interim little Marcus had grown bored and fretful. 'So, husband,' she said, with a thin smile, tugging savagely at the boy to make him stand up properly, 'you are home at last! Go and greet your father,' she instructed Marcus, and pushed him forwards, but immediately he darted around her and hid behind her skirts. Cicero stopped some distance short, his arms outstretched to the boy, uncertain how to respond, and in the end the situation was only retrieved by Tullia, who ran to her father, kissed him, led him over to her mother and gently pressed her parents together, and in this way at last the family was reunited.

Quintus's villa was large, but not sufficiently spacious to accommodate two full households in any comfort, and from that first day there was friction. Out of respect for his brother's superior age and rank, Quintus, with typical generosity, had insisted that Cicero and Terentia should take over the master's quarters, which he usually shared with his wife, Pomponia, the sister of Atticus. It was clear she had objected bitterly to this, and could barely bring herself to give Cicero a civil greeting.

It is not my intention to dwell on personal gossip: such matters fall beneath the dignity of my subject. Nevertheless, I cannot give a proper account of Cicero's life without mentioning what happened, for this was when his domestic unhappiness really started, and it was to have an effect upon his political career.

He and Terentia had been married for more than twenty years. They had often argued. But underlying their disputes was a mutual respect. She was a woman of independent wealth: that was why he had married her; it was certainly not for her looks or the sweetness of her temper. It was Terentia's fortune that had enabled him to enter the Senate. In return, his success had increased her social standing. Now the disaster of his fall had exposed the inherent weaknesses of this partnership. Not only had she been obliged to sell a good part of her property in order to protect the family in his absence, she had been reviled and insulted and reduced to lodging with her in-laws – a family she snobbishly considered far beneath her own. Yes, Cicero was alive and he was back in Rome and I am sure she was glad for that. But she made no secret of her view that his days of political power were over, even if he – still floating on the clouds of popular adulation – had failed to grasp the fact.

I was not asked to dine with the family that first evening, and given the tensions between them, I cannot say I minded especially. I was, however, dismayed to find that I had been given a bed in the slaves' quarters in the cellar, sharing a cubicle with Terentia's steward, Philotimus. He was an oily, avaricious creature of middle age: we had never liked one another, and I should guess he was no happier to see me than I him. Still, his love of money at least made him a diligent manager of Terentia's business affairs, and it must have pained him to see her fortune depleted month after month. The bitterness with which he assailed Cicero for placing her in this situation infuriated me, and after a while I told him curtly to shut his mouth and show some respect, or I would make sure the master gave him a whipping. Later, as I lay awake listening to his snores, I wondered how many of the complaints I had just heard were his, and how many he was merely repeating from the lips of his mistress.

The next day, because of my restlessness, I overslept and woke in a panic. Cicero was due to attend the Senate that morning to express his formal thanks for their support. Normally he learnt his speeches by heart and delivered them without a note. But it was so long since he had spoken in public he feared he might stumble over his words, therefore this oration had had to be dictated and written out during the journey from Brundisium. I took it from my dispatch box, checked I had the full text, and hurried upstairs, at the same time as Quintus's secretary, Statius, was showing two visitors into the tablinum. One was Milo, the tribune who had visited us in Thessalonica; the other was Lucius Afranius, Pompey's principal lieutenant, who had been consul two years after Cicero.

Statius said to me, 'These gentlemen wish to see your master.'

'I'll see if he's available.'

At which Afranius remarked, in a tone I didn't much care for, 'He'd better be available!'

I went at once to the principal bedroom. The door was closed. Terentia's maid put her finger to her lips and told me Cicero wasn't there. Instead she directed me along the passage to the dressing room, where I found him being helped into his toga by his valet. As I was describing who had come to see him, I noticed over his shoulder a small makeshift bed. He caught my glance and muttered, 'Something's wrong but she won't tell me what it is,' and then, perhaps regretting his candour, brusquely ordered me to go and fetch Quintus so that he too could hear what his visitors had come to say.

At first the meeting was friendly. Afranius announced that he brought with him the warmest regards of Pompey the Great, who hoped soon to welcome Cicero back to Rome in person. Cicero thanked him for the message and thanked Milo for all that he had done to bring about his recall. He described the enthusiasm of his reception in the countryside and of the crowds that had turned out to see him in Rome the previous day: 'I feel it is a whole new life that I am beginning. I hope Pompey will be in the Senate to hear me praise him with such poor eloquence as I can muster.'

'Pompey won't be attending the Senate,' Afranius said bluntly.

'I'm sorry to hear it.'

'He doesn't feel it appropriate, in view of the new law that is to be proposed.' Whereupon he opened a small bag and handed over a draft bill, which Cicero read with evident surprise and then gave to Quintus, who eventually handed it to me.

> *Whereas the people of Rome are being denied access to a sufficient supply of grain; and to the extent that this constitutes a grave threat to the well-being and security of the state; and mindful of the principle that all Roman citizens are entitled to the equivalent of at least one free loaf of bread per day – it is hereby ordained that Pompey the Great shall be granted the power as Commissioner of Grain to purchase, seize or similarly obtain throughout the entire world enough grain to secure a plentiful supply for the city; that this power should be his for a term of five years; and that to assist him in this task he shall have the right to appoint fifteen lieutenant commissioners of grain to carry out such duties as he directs.*

Afranius said, 'Naturally, Pompey would like you to have the honour of proposing the legislation when you address the Senate today.'

Milo said, 'It's a cunning stroke, you must agree. Having retaken the streets from Clodius, we shall now remove his ability to buy votes with bread.'

'Is the shortage really so serious it demands an emergency law?' asked Cicero. He turned to Quintus.

Quintus said, 'It's true, there's little bread to be had, and what there is has risen to an extortionate price.'

'Even so, these are astonishing, unprecedented powers over the nation's food supply to bestow upon one man. I'd really need to find out more about the situation before I offered an opinion, I'm afraid.'

He tried to hand the draft bill back to Afranius, who refused to take it. He folded his arms and glared at Cicero. 'I must say, we expected a little more gratitude than that – after all we've done for you.'

'It goes without saying,' added Milo, 'that you'd be one of the fifteen lieutenant commissioners.' And he rubbed his finger and thumb together to indicate the lucrative nature of the appointment.

The ensuing silence became uncomfortable. Eventually Afranius said, 'Well, we'll leave the draft with you, and when you address the Senate we'll listen to your words with interest.'

After they had gone, it was Quintus who spoke first. 'At least now we know their price.'

'No,' said Cicero gloomily, 'this isn't their price. This is merely the first instalment of their price – a loan that in their eyes will never be repaid, however much I give them.'

'So what will you do?'

'Well, it's a devil's alternative, is it not? Propose the bill, and everyone will say I'm Pompey's creature; say nothing, and he'll turn against me. Whatever I do, I lose.'

As was often the case, he had not decided which course to take even when we set off to attend the Senate. He always liked to take the temperature of the chamber before he spoke – to listen to its heartbeat like a doctor with a patient. Birria, the scarred gladiator who had accompanied Milo when he visited us in Macedonia, acted as a bodyguard, along with three of his comrades. In addition, I suppose there must have been twenty or thirty of Cicero's clients, who served as a human shield; we felt quite safe. As we walked, Birria boasted to me of their strength: he said that Milo and Pompey had a hundred pairs of gladiators on standby in a barracks on the Field of Mars, ready to deploy at a moment's notice if Clodius tried any of his tricks.

When we reached the Senate building, I handed Cicero the text of his speech. On entering he touched the ancient doorpost and looked around him at what he called 'the greatest room in the world' in thankful amazement that he should have lived to see it again. As he approached his customary position on the front bench nearest to the consuls' dais, the neighbouring senators rose to shake his hand. It was an ill-attended house – not just Pompey was absent, I noticed, but also Clodius, and Marcus Crassus, whose pact with Pompey and Caesar was still the most powerful force in the republic. I wondered why they had stayed away.

The presiding consul that day was Metellus Nepos, the long-standing enemy of Cicero who was nevertheless now publicly reconciled with him

– albeit only grudgingly and under pressure from the majority of the Senate. He made no acknowledgement of Cicero's presence but instead rose to announce that a new dispatch had just arrived from Caesar in Further Gaul. The chamber fell silent and the senators listened intently as he read out Caesar's account of yet more brutal encounters with savage and exotically named tribes – the Viromandui, the Atrebates and the Nervii – fought out amid those gloomy echoing forests and swollen impassable rivers. It was clear that Caesar had pushed much further north than any Roman commander before him, almost to the cold north sea, and again his victory was little short of an annihilation: of the sixty thousand men who had made up the army of the Nervii, he claimed to have left alive only five hundred. When Nepos had finished, the house seemed to let out its breath; only then did the consul call on Cicero to speak.

It was a difficult moment to make a speech, and in the event Cicero mostly restricted himself to a list of thanks. He thanked the consuls. He thanked the Senate. He thanked the people. He thanked the gods. He thanked his brother. He thanked just about everybody except Caesar, whom he did not mention. He thanked especially Pompey ('whose courage, fame and achievements are unapproached in the records of any nation or any age') and Milo ('his whole tribunate was nothing but a firm, unceasing, brave and undaunted championship of my well-being'). But he did not raise either the grain shortage or the proposal to give Pompey extra powers, and as soon as he sat down, Afranius and Milo promptly got up from their places and left the building.

Afterwards, as we walked back to Quintus's house, I noticed that Birria and his gladiators were no longer with us, which I thought was odd, for the danger had hardly gone away. There were a great many beggars among the streams of spectators milling around, and perhaps I was mistaken, but it seemed to me that the number of hostile looks and gestures Cicero attracted was substantially greater than before.

Once we were safely indoors, Cicero said, 'I couldn't do it. How could I take the lead in a controversy I know nothing about? Besides, it wasn't the proper occasion to make a proposal of that sort. All anyone could talk about was Caesar, Caesar, Caesar. Perhaps now they'll leave me alone for a while.'

The day was long and sunny, and Cicero spent much of it in the garden reading or throwing a ball for the family dog, a terrier named Myia, whose antics greatly delighted young Marcus and his nine-year-old cousin, Quintus Junior, the only child of Quintus and Pomponia. Marcus was a sweet, straightforward lad whereas Quintus, spoilt by his mother, had a streak of something nasty in him. But they played together happily enough. Occasionally the roar of the crowd in the Circus Maximus carried up from the valley on the other side of the hill – a hundred thousand voices crying out or groaning in unison: a sound at once exhilarating and frightening, like the growl of a tiger; it made the hairs tingle on my neck and arms. In the middle of the afternoon Quintus suggested that perhaps Cicero should go down to the Circus and show himself to the audience and watch at least one of the races. But Cicero preferred to stay where he was: 'I am tired of exhibiting myself to strangers.'

Because the boys were reluctant to go to bed and Cicero, having been away so long, wished to indulge them, dinner was not served until late. This time, to Pomponia's obvious irritation, he invited me to join them. She did not approve of slaves eating with their masters, and doubtless felt it was her prerogative, not her brother-in-law's, to decide who should be present at her own table. In the event we were six: Cicero and Terentia on one couch, Quintus and Pomponia on another, Tullia and I on the third. Normally Pomponia's brother, Atticus, would have joined us. He was Cicero's closest friend. But a week before Cicero's return he had abruptly left Rome for his estates in Epirus. He pleaded urgent business but I suspect he foresaw the looming family arguments. He always preferred a quiet life.

It was dusk and the slaves were just bringing in tapers to light the lamps and candles when from somewhere in the distance arose a cacophony of whistles, drums, horn blasts and chanting. At first we dismissed it as a passing procession connected with the games. But the noise seemed to come from directly outside the house, where it remained.

Finally Terentia said, 'What on earth is that, do you suppose?'

'You know,' replied Cicero, in a tone of scholarly interest, 'I wonder if it might not be a *flagitatio*. Now there's a quaint custom! Tiro, would you take a look?'

I don't suppose such a thing exists any more, but back in the days of the republic, when people were free to express themselves, a *flagitatio* was the right of citizens who had a grievance, but were too poor to use the courts, to demonstrate outside the house of the person they held responsible.

Tonight the target was Cicero. I could hear his name mingled among their chants, and when I opened the door I got the message clear enough:

Whoreson Cicero where's our bread?
Whoreson Cicero stole our bread!

A hundred people packed the narrow street, repeating the same phrases over and over, with occasional and saltier variations on the word 'whoreson'. When they noticed me looking at them, a terrific jeer went up. I closed the door, bolted it and went back to the dining room to report.

Pomponia sat up in alarm. 'But what shall we do?'

'Nothing,' said Cicero calmly. 'They're entitled to make their noise. Let them get it off their chests, and when they tire of it they'll go away.'

Terentia asked, 'But why are they accusing *you* of stealing their bread?'

Quintus said, 'Clodius blames the lack of bread on the size of the crowds coming into Rome to support your husband.'

'But the crowds aren't here to support my husband – they've come to watch the games.'

'Brutally honest, as always,' agreed Cicero, 'and even if they *were* here for me, the city has never to my knowledge run short of food on a festival day.'

'So why has it happened now?'

'I imagine someone has sabotaged the supply.'

'Who would do that?'

'Clodius, to blacken my name; or perhaps even Pompey, to give himself a pretext to take over distribution. In any case, there's nothing we can do about it. So I suggest we eat our meal and ignore them.'

But although we tried to carry on as if nothing was happening, and even made jokes and laughed about it, our conversation was strained, and every time there was a lull, it was filled by the angry voices outside:

Cocksucker Cicero stole our bread!
Cocksucker Cicero ate our bread!

Eventually Pomponia said, 'Will they go on like that all night?'

Cicero said, 'Possibly.'

'But this has always been a quiet and respectable street. Surely you can do something to stop them?'

'Not really. It's their right.'

'Their right!'

'I believe in the people's rights, if you remember.'

'Good for you. But how am I to sleep?'

Cicero's patience finally gave in. 'Why not put some wax in your ears, madam?' he suggested, then added under his breath, 'I'm sure I'd put some in mine if I were married to you.'

Quintus, who had drunk plenty, tried to stifle his laughter. Pomponia turned on him at once. 'You'll allow him to speak to me in that way?'

'It was only a joke, my dear.'

Pomponia put down her napkin, rose with dignity from her couch and announced that she would go and check on the boys. Terentia, after a sharp look at Cicero, said that she would join her. She beckoned to Tullia to follow.

When the women had gone, Cicero said to Quintus, 'I'm sorry. I shouldn't have spoken in that way. I'll go and find her and apologise. Besides, she's right: I've brought trouble on your house. We'll move out in the morning.'

'No you won't. I'm master here, and my roof will be your roof for as long as I'm alive. Insults from that rabble are of no concern to me.'

We listened again.

Bumfucker Cicero where's our bread?
Bumfucker Cicero sold *our bread!*

Cicero said, 'It's a marvellously flexible metre, I'll give them that. I wonder how many more versions they can come up with.'

'You know we could always send word to Milo. Pompey's gladiators would clear the street in no time.'

'And put myself even further in their debt? I don't think so.'

We went our separate ways to bed, although I doubt any of us slept much. The demonstration did not cease as Cicero had predicted; if anything, by the following morning it had increased in volume, and certainly in violence, for the mob had started digging up the cobblestones and were hurling them against the walls, or lobbing them over the parapet so that they landed with a crash in the atrium or the garden. It was clear our situation was becoming parlous, and while the women and children sheltered indoors, I climbed up on to the roof with Cicero and Quintus to estimate the danger. Peering cautiously over the ridge tiles, it was possible to see down into the Forum. Clodius's mob was occupying it in force. The senators trying to get to the chamber for the day's session had to run a gauntlet of abuse and chanting. The words drifted up to us, accompanied by the banging of cooking utensils:

Where's our bread?
Where's our bread?
Where's our bread?

Suddenly there was a scream from the floor beneath us. We scrabbled down from the roof and descended to the atrium in time to see a slave fishing out a black-and-white object, like a pouch or a small bag, that had just dropped through the aperture in the roof and fallen into the impluvium. It was the mangled body of Myia, the family dog. The two boys crouched in the corner of the atrium, hands over their ears, crying. Heavy stones battered against the wooden door. And now Terentia turned on Cicero with a bitterness I had never before witnessed: 'Stubborn man! Stubborn, foolish man! Will you do something at last to protect your family? Or must I crawl out yet again on my hands and knees and plead with this scum not to hurt us?'

Cicero swayed backwards in the face of her fury. Just then there was a fresh bout of childish sobbing and he looked across to where Tullia was comforting her brother and cousin. That seemed to settle the issue. He said to Quintus, 'Do you think you can smuggle a slave out through a window at the back?'

'I'm sure we can.'

'In fact best send two, in case one doesn't get through. They should go to Milo's barracks on the Field of Mars and tell the gladiators we need help immediately.'

The messengers were dispatched, and in the meantime Cicero went over to the boys and distracted them by putting his hands around their shoulders and telling them stories of the bravery of the heroes of the republic. After what seemed a long interval, during which the assault on the door increased in fury, we heard a fresh wave of roars from the street, followed by screaming. The gladiators controlled by Milo and Pompey had arrived, and in this way Cicero saved himself and his family, for I do believe that Clodius's men, finding they were unopposed, were fully intending to break into the house and massacre us all. As it was, after only a short battle in the street, the besiegers, who were not nearly so well armed or trained, fled for their lives.

Once we were sure the street was clear, Cicero, Quintus and I went up on to the roof again and watched as the fighting spilled down into the Forum. Columns of gladiators ran in from either side and started laying about them with the flats of their swords. The mob scattered but did not break entirely. A barricade built of trestle tables, benches and shutters from the nearby stores was thrown up between the Temple of Castor and the Grove of Vesta. This line held, and at one point I saw the blond-headed figure of Clodius himself directing the fighting, wearing a cuirass over his toga and brandishing a long iron spike. I know it was him because he had his wife, Fulvia, beside him – a woman as fierce and cruel and fond of violence as any man. Here and there fires were lit, and the smoke drifting in the summer heat added to the confusion of the melee. I counted seven bodies, although whether they were dead or merely injured I could not tell.

After a while, Cicero could not bear to watch any longer. Leaving the roof, he said quietly, 'It is the end of the republic.'

We stayed in the house all day as the skirmishing continued in the Forum, and what is most striking to me now is that throughout all this time, less than a mile away, the Roman Games continued uninterrupted, as if nothing unusual were happening. Violence had become a normal part of politics. By nightfall it was peaceful again, although Cicero prudently decided not to venture out of doors until the following morning, when he walked together with Quintus and an escort of Milo's gladiators to the Senate house. The Forum now was full of citizens who were supporters of Pompey. They called out to Cicero to make sure they had bread again by sending for Pompey to solve the crisis. Cicero, who carried with him the draft of the bill to make Pompey commissioner of grain, made no response.

It was another ill-attended house. Because of the unrest, more than half the senators had stayed away. The only former consuls on the front bench apart from Cicero were Afranius and M. Valerius Messalla. The presiding consul, Metellus Nepos, had been hit by a stone while crossing the Forum the previous day and was wearing a bandage. He brought up the grain riots as the first item on the order paper, and several of the magistrates actually suggested that Cicero himself should take control of the city's supply, at which Cicero made a modest gesture and shook his head.

Nepos said reluctantly, 'Marcus Cicero, do you wish to speak?'

Cicero nodded and rose. 'We none of us needs to be reminded,' he began, 'least of all the gallant Nepos, of the frightful violence that gripped the city yesterday – violence which has at its core a shortage of that most basic of human needs, bread. Some of us believe it was an ill day when our citizens were granted a free dole of corn in the first place, for it is human nature that what starts as gratitude quickly becomes dependency and ends as entitlement. This is the pass we have reached. I do not say we should rescind Clodius's law – it is too late for that: the public's morals are already corrupted, as no doubt he intended. But we must at least ensure that the supply of bread is continuous if we are to have civil order. And there is only one man in our state with the authority and genius of organisation to ensure such a thing, and that is Pompey the Great. Therefore I wish to propose the following resolution ...'

And here he read out the draft bill I have already quoted, and that part of the chamber which was packed with Pompey's lieutenants rose in acclamation. The rest sat solemn-faced, or muttered angrily, for they had always feared Pompey's lust for power. The cheering was heard outside and taken up by the crowds waiting in the Forum. When they learned that it was Cicero who had proposed the new law, they started clamouring for him to come and address them from the rostra, and all the tribunes – save for two supporters of Clodius – duly sent an invitation to him to speak. When the request was read out in the Senate, Cicero protested that he was not prepared for such an honour. (In fact I had with me a speech he had already written out, and which I was able to give him just before he mounted the steps to the platform.)

He was met by a tremendous ovation, and it was some time before he could make himself heard. When the applause died away, he started to speak, and had just reached the passage in which he thanked the people for their support – *Had I experienced nothing but an unruffled tranquillity, I should have missed the incredible and well-nigh superhuman transports of delight which your kindness now permits me to enjoy* – when who should appear at the edge of the crowd but Pompey. He stood ostentatiously alone – not that he had any need of bodyguards when the Forum was full of his gladiators – and pretended that he had come merely as an ordinary citizen to listen to what Cicero had to say. But of course the people would not permit that, so he allowed himself to be thrust forward to the rostra, which he mounted, and where he embraced Cicero. I had forgotten what a massive physical presence he was: that majestic torso and manly bearing, the famous thick quiff of still-dark hair rising like the beak of a warship above his broad and handsome face.

The occasion demanded flattery, and Cicero rose to it. 'Here is a man,' he said, lifting Pompey's arm, 'who has had, has, and will have, no rival in virtue, sagacity and renown. He gave to me all that he had given to the republic, what no other has ever given to a private friend – safety, security, dignity. To him, fellow citizens, I owe a debt such as it is scarce lawful for one human being to owe to another.'

The applause was prolonged, and Pompey's beam of pleasure was as wide and warm as the sun.

Afterwards he consented to walk back with Cicero to Quintus's house and take a cup of wine. He made no reference to Cicero's exile, no enquiries after his health, no apology for his failure years before to help Cicero stand up to Clodius, which was what had opened the door to the whole disaster in the first place. He talked only of himself and of the future, childlike in his eager anticipation of his grain commissionership and the opportunities it would give him for travel and patronage. 'And you, of course, my dear Cicero, must be one of my fifteen legates – whichever one you like, wherever you want to go. Sardinia? Sicily? Egypt? Africa?'

'Thank you,' said Cicero. 'It is generous of you, but I must decline. My priority now has to be my family – restoring us to our property, comforting my wife and children, revenging us on our enemies and trying to recover our fortune.'

'You'll recover your fortune quicker in the grain business than any other, I assure you.'

'Even so, I must remain in Rome.'

The broad face fell. 'I'm disappointed, I can't pretend otherwise. I want the name of Cicero attached to this commission. It will add weight. What about you?' he said, turning to Quintus. 'You could do it, I suppose.'

Poor Quintus! The last thing he wanted, having returned from two tours of duty in Asia, was to go abroad again and deal with farmers and grain merchants and shipping agents. He squirmed. He protested his unfitness for the office. He looked to Cicero for support. But Cicero could hardly deny Pompey a second request, and this time he said nothing.

'All right: it's done.' Pompey clapped his hands on the armrests of his chair to signal that the matter was settled, and pushed himself up on to his feet. He grunted with the effort and I noticed he was getting rather stout. He was in his fiftieth year, the same age as Cicero. 'Our republic is passing through the most strenuous times,' he said, putting his arms around the brothers' shoulders. 'But we shall come through them, as we always have, and I know that you will both play your part.' He clasped the two men tightly, squeezed them, and held them there, pinned on either side of his commodious chest.

XLI

Early the following morning, Cicero and I walked up the hill to inspect the ruins of his house. The palatial building in which he had invested so much of his wealth and prestige had been entirely pulled down; nine tenths of the huge plot was weeds and rubble; it was barely possible to discern the original layout of the walls through the tangled overgrowth. Cicero stooped to pick up one of the scorched bricks poking from the ground. 'Until this place is restored to me, we shall be entirely at their mercy – no money, no dignity, no independence … Every time I step outdoors I shall have to look up here and be reminded of my humiliation.' The edges of the brick crumbled in his hands and the red dust trickled through his fingers like dried blood.

At the far end of the plot a statue of a young woman had been set up on top of a high plinth. Fresh offerings of flowers were piled around the base. By consecrating the site as a shrine to Liberty, Clodius believed he had made it inviolable and thus impossible for Cicero to reclaim. The marble figure was shapely in the morning light, with long tresses and a diaphanous dress slipping down to expose a naked breast. Cicero regarded her with his hands on his hips. Eventually he said, 'Surely Liberty is always depicted as a matron with a cap?' I agreed. 'So who, pray, is this hussy? Why, she is no more the embodiment of a goddess than I am!'

Until that moment he had been sombre, but now he started to laugh, and when we returned to Quintus's house he set me the task of discovering where Clodius had acquired the statue. That same day he petitioned the College of Pontiffs to return his property to him on the grounds that the site had been improperly consecrated. A hearing was fixed for the end of the month, and Clodius was summoned to defend his actions.

When the day arrived, Cicero admitted he felt ill-prepared and out of practice. Because his library was still in storage, he had been unable to consult all the legal sources he needed. He was also, I am sure, nervous at the prospect of confronting Clodius face to face. To be beaten by his enemy in a street brawl was one thing; to lose to him in a legal dispute would be a calamity.

The headquarters of the pontifical college were then in the old Regia, said to be the most ancient building in the city. It stood like its modern successor at the point where the Via Sacra divides and enters the Forum, although the noise of that busy spot was entirely deadened by the thickness of its high and windowless walls. The candlelit gloom of the interior made one forget that outside it was bright and sunny. Even the chilly, tomblike air smelt sacred, as if it had been undisturbed for more than six hundred years.

Fourteen of the fifteen pontiffs were seated at the far end of the crowded chamber, waiting for us. The only absentee was their chief, Caesar: his chair, grander than the others, stood empty. Among the priests were several I knew well – Spinther, the consul; Marcus Lucullus, brother of the great general, Lucius, who was said to have lately lost his reason and to be confined to his palace outside Rome; and the two rising young aristocrats, Q. Scipio Nasica and M. Aemilius Lepidus. And here at last I saw the third triumvir, Crassus. The curious conical hat of animal fur the pontiffs were required to wear robbed him of his most distinctive feature, his baldness. His crafty face was quite impassive.

Cicero took a seat facing them while I sat on a stool at his back, ready to pass any documents he required. Behind us was an audience of eminent citizens, including Pompey. Of Clodius there was no sign. Whispered conversations gradually ceased. The silence grew oppressive. Where was he? Perhaps he might not come. With Clodius one never knew. But then at last he swaggered in, and I felt myself turn cold at the sight of the man who had caused us so much anguish. 'Little Miss Beauty', Cicero used to call him, but in middle age he had outgrown the insult. His luxuriant blond curls were nowadays cut as tight to his skull as a golden helmet; his thick red lips had lost their pout. He appeared hard, lean, disdainful – a fallen Apollo. As is often the case with the bitterest of enemies, he had started out as a friend. But then he had outraged law and morality once too often, by disguising himself as a woman and defiling the sacred rite of the Good Goddess. Cicero had been obliged to give evidence against him, and from that day on Clodius had sworn vengeance. He sat on a chair barely three paces from Cicero, but Cicero continued to stare straight ahead, and the two men never once looked at one another.

The senior pontiff by age was Publius Albinovanus, who must have been eighty. In a quavering voice he read out the point at issue – 'Was the shrine to Liberty, lately erected on the property claimed by M. Tullius Cicero, consecrated in accordance with the rites of the official religion or not?' – and invited Clodius to speak first.

Clodius left it just long enough to indicate his contempt for the whole proceeding, and then slowly got to his feet. 'I am appalled, holy fathers,' he began in his slangy patrician drawl, 'and dismayed, but not surprised, that the exiled murderer Cicero, having brazenly slaughtered Liberty during the time of his consulship, should now seek to compound the offence by tearing down her image ...'

He brought up every slander that had ever been made against Cicero – his illegal killing of the Catiline conspirators ('the sanction of the Senate is no excuse for executing five citizens without a trial'), his vanity ('if he objects to this shrine, it is mostly out of jealousy since he regards himself as the only god worth worshipping') and his political inconsistency ('this is the man whose return was supposed to mean the restoration of senatorial authority, and yet whose first act was to betray it by winning dictatorial powers for Pompey'). It was not without impact. It would have played well in the Forum. But it failed entirely to address the legal point at issue: was the shrine properly consecrated or not?

He argued for an hour, and then it was Cicero's turn, and it was a measure of how effective Clodius had been that he was obliged to speak extempore to begin with, defending his support for Pompey's grain commission. Only after he had answered that could he turn to making his main case: that the shrine could not be held to be consecrated because Clodius was not legally a tribune when he dedicated it. 'Your transfer from patrician to pleb was sanctioned by no decree of this college, was entered upon in defiance of all pontifical regulations, and must be held to be null and void; and if that is invalid your entire tribunate falls to the ground.' This was dangerous territory: everyone knew it was Caesar who had organised Clodius's adoption as a pleb. I saw Crassus lean forwards listening intently. Sensing the danger, and perhaps remembering his undertaking to Caesar, Cicero swerved away: 'Does this mean I am saying that all Caesar's laws were illegal? By no means; for none of them any longer affects my interests, apart from those aimed with hostile intent against my own person.'

He pressed on, switching to an attack on Clodius's methods, and now his oratory took flight – his arm outstretched, his finger pointing at his enemy, the words almost tumbling from his mouth in his passion: 'Oh, you abominable plague spot of the state, you public prostitute! What harm had you suffered at the hands of my unhappy wife that you harassed, plundered and tortured her so brutally? Or from my daughter, who lost her beloved husband? Or from my little son, who still lies awake weeping at night? But it was not just my family you attacked – you waged a bitter war against my very walls and doorposts!'

However his real coup was to reveal the origins of the statue Clodius had set up. I had tracked down the workmen who had erected it and learnt that the piece had been donated by Clodius's brother Appius, who had carried it off from Tanagra, in Boeotia, where it had graced the tomb of a well-known local courtesan.

The whole room roared with laughter when Cicero revealed this fact. 'So this is his idea of Liberty – a courtesan's likeness, erected over a foreign tomb, stolen by a thief and set up again by a sacrilegious hand! And *she* is the one who drives me from my house? Holy fathers, this property cannot be lost to me without inflicting disgrace upon the state. If you believe that my return to Rome has been a source of pleasure to the immortal gods, to the Senate, to the Roman people and to all of Italy, then let it be your hands that reinstall me in my home.'

Cicero sat to loud murmurs of approval from the distinguished audience. I stole a look at Clodius. He was scowling at the floor. The pontiffs leaned in to confer. Crassus seemed to be doing most of the talking. We had expected a decision at once. But Albinovanus straightened and announced that the college would need more time to consider their verdict: it would be relayed to the Senate the following day. This was a blow. Clodius stood, bent down to Cicero as he passed and hissed, through a false smile, just loud enough for me to hear, 'You will die before that place is rebuilt.' He left the chamber without another word. Cicero pretended nothing had happened. He lingered to chat with many old friends, with the result that we were among the last to leave the building.

Outside the chamber was a courtyard containing the famous white board on which the chief priest by tradition in those days published the state's official news. This was where Caesar's agents posted his *Commentaries*, and here was where we found Crassus standing – ostensibly reading the latest dispatch but in truth waiting to intercept Cicero. He had taken off his cap; here and there little wisps of brown fur still adhered to his high-domed skull.

'So, Cicero,' he said in his unsettlingly jovial manner, 'you were pleased with the effect of your speech?'

'Reasonably, thank you. But my opinion has no value. It's for you and your colleagues to decide.'

'Oh, I thought it effective enough. My only regret is that Caesar wasn't present to hear it.'

'I shall send him a copy.'

'Yes, be sure that you do. Mind you, reading is all very well. But how would he *vote* on the issue? That's what I have to decide.'

'And why do you have to decide that?'

'Because he wishes me to act as his proxy and cast his vote as I think fit. Many colleagues will follow my lead. It is important I get it right.'

He grinned, showing yellow teeth.

'I have no doubt you will. Good day to you, Crassus.'

'Good day, Cicero.'

We passed out of the gate, Cicero cursing under his breath, and had gone only a few paces when Crassus suddenly called out after him, and hurried to catch us up. 'One last thing,' he said. 'In view of these tremendous victories that Caesar has won in Gaul, I wondered if you would be good enough to support a proposal in the Senate for a period of public celebration in his honour.'

'Why does it matter if I support it?'

'Obviously it would add weight, given the history of your relations with Caesar. People would notice. And it would be a noble gesture on your part. I'm sure Caesar would appreciate it.'

'How long would this period of celebration last?'

'Oh … fifteen days should just about do it.'

'*Fifteen days*? That's nearly twice as long as Pompey was voted for conquering Spain.'

'Yes, well one could argue that Caesar's victories in Gaul are twice as important as Pompey's in Spain.'

'I'm not sure Pompey would agree.'

'Pompey,' retorted Crassus with emphasis, 'must learn that a triumvirate consists of three men, not one.'

Cicero gritted his teeth and bowed. 'It would be an honour.'

Crassus bowed in return. 'I knew you would do the patriotic thing.'

The following day, Spinther read out the pontiffs' judgement to the Senate: unless Clodius could provide written proof that he had consecrated the shrine on instructions from the Roman people, 'the site can be restored to Cicero without sacrilege'.

A normal man now would have given up. But Clodius wasn't normal. Though he might pretend to be a pleb, he was still a Claudian – a family who took pride in hounding their enemies to the grave. First he lied and told a meeting of the people that the judgement had actually gone in his favour and called on them to defend 'their' shrine. Then, when the consul-designate Marcellinus proposed a motion in the Senate to return to Cicero his three properties – in Rome, Tusculum and Formiae, 'with compensation to restore them to their former state' – Clodius tried to talk out the session, and would have succeeded had he not, after three hours on his feet, been howled down by an exasperated Senate. Nor were his tactics entirely without effect. Frightened of antagonising the plebs, and to Cicero's dismay, the Senate agreed to pay compensation of only two million sesterces to rebuild the house on the Palatine, and just half a million and a quarter of a million respectively for the repairs at Tusculum and Formiae – far below the actual costs.

For the past two years most of Rome's builders and craftsmen had been employed on Pompey's immense development of public buildings on the Field of Mars. Grudgingly – because anyone who has ever employed builders learns quickly never to let them out of one's sight – Pompey agreed to transfer a hundred of his men to Cicero. Work on restoring the Palatine house began at once, and on the first morning of construction Cicero had the great pleasure of swinging an axe at the head of Liberty and smashing it clean off, then crating up the remains and having them delivered to Clodius with his compliments.

I knew Clodius would retaliate, and one morning soon afterwards, when Cicero and I were working on some legal papers in Quintus's tablinum, we heard what sounded like heavy footsteps clumping across the roof. I went out into the street and was lucky not to be struck on the head by bricks dropping from the sky. Panicking workmen came running round the corner and shouted that a gang of Clodius's toughs had overrun the site and were demolishing the new walls and hurling the debris down on to Quintus's house. Just then Cicero and Quintus came out to see what the trouble was, and yet again they had to send a messenger to Milo to request the assistance of his gladiators. It was just as well, for no sooner had the runner gone than there was a series of flashes overhead, and burning brands and lumps of flaming pitch started landing all around us. Fires broke out on the roof. The terrified household had to be evacuated, and everyone, including Cicero and even Terentia, was pressed into service to pass buckets of water, drawn from the street fountains, from hand to hand to try to prevent the house from burning down.

Crassus had a monopoly of the city's fire services, and fortunately for us, he was at his home on the Palatine. He heard the commotion, came out into the street, saw what was going on, and turned up himself in a shabby tunic and slippers, with one of his teams of fire slaves dragging a water tender equipped with pumps and hoses. But for them the building would have been lost; as it was, the damage caused by the water and smoke rendered the place uninhabitable, and we had to move out while it was repaired. We loaded our luggage into carts and, with night coming on, made our way across the valley to the Quirinal hill, to seek temporary refuge in the house of Atticus, who was still away in Epirus. His narrow, ancient house was fine for an elderly bachelor of fixed and moderate habits; it was less ideal for two families with extensive households and warring spouses. Cicero and Terentia slept in separate parts of the building.

Eight days later, as we were walking along the Via Sacra, we heard an outburst of shouts and the sound of running feet behind us, and turned to see Clodius and a dozen of his henchmen flourishing cudgels and even swords, sprinting to attack us. We had the usual bodyguard of Milo's men and they hustled us into the doorway of the nearest house. In their panic, Cicero was pushed to the ground and gashed his head and twisted his ankle but otherwise was unharmed. The startled owner of the house in which we sought refuge, Tettius Damio, took us in and gave us a cup of wine, and Cicero talked calmly to him of poetry and philosophy until we were told that our attackers had been driven off and the coast was clear; then he said his thanks and we continued on our way home.

Cicero was in that state of elation that sometimes follows a close brush with death. His appearance, however, was a different matter – limping, with a bloodied forehead and torn and dirty clothes – and the instant Terentia saw him she cried out in shock. Useless for him to protest that it was nothing, that Clodius had been put to flight, and that his descent to such tactics showed how desperate he was becoming: Terentia would not listen. The siege, the fire and now this: she insisted that they all should leave Rome at once.

Cicero replied mildly, 'You forget, Terentia: I've tried that once, and see where it left us. Our only hope is to stay here and win back our position.'

'And how are you to do that when you can't even walk in safety down a busy street in broad daylight?'

'I shall find a way.'

'And in the meantime, what lives do the rest of us have?'

'Normal lives!' Cicero suddenly shouted back at her. 'We defeat them by leading normal lives! We sleep together as man and wife for a start.'

I glanced away in embarrassment.

Terentia said, 'You wish to know why I keep you from my room? Then look!'

And to Cicero's astonishment and certainly to mine, this most pious of Roman matrons began to unfasten the belt of her dress. She called to her maid to come and help. Turning her back to her husband, she opened her gown and her maid pulled it down all the way from the nape of her neck to the base of her spine, exposing the pale flesh between her thin shoulders, which was savagely crisscrossed by at least a dozen livid red welts.

Cicero stared at the scars, transfixed. 'Who did this to you?'

Terentia pulled the dress back up and her maid knelt to fasten her belt.

'Who did this?' repeated Cicero quietly. 'Clodius?'

She turned to face him. Her eyes were not wet but dry and full of fire. 'Six months ago I went to see his sister, as one woman to another, to plead on your behalf. But Clodia is not a woman: she is a Fury. She told me I was no better than a traitor myself – that my presence defiled her house. She summoned her steward and had him whip me off the premises. She had her louche friends with her. They laughed at my shame.'

'*Your* shame?' cried Cicero. 'The only shame is theirs! You should have told me!'

'Told *you*? You, who greeted the whole of Rome before he greeted his own wife?' She spat out the words. 'You may stay and die in the city if you wish. I shall take Tullia and Marcus to Tusculum and see what lives we can have there.'

The following morning, she and Pomponia left with the children, and a few days later, amid much mutual shedding of tears, Quintus also departed to buy grain for Pompey in Sardinia. Prowling round the empty house, Cicero was keenly aware of their absence. He told me he felt every blow that Terentia had endured as if it were a lash upon his own back, and he tortured his brain to find some means of avenging her, but he could see no way through, until one day, quite unexpectedly, the glimmer of an opportunity presented itself.

It happened that around this time, the distinguished philosopher Dio of Alexandria was murdered in Rome while under the roof of his friend and host, Titus Coponius. The assassination caused a great scandal. Dio had come to Italy supposedly with diplomatic protection, as the head of a delegation of one hundred prominent Egyptians to petition the Senate against the restoration of their exiled pharaoh, Ptolemy XII, nicknamed 'the Flute Player'.

Suspicion naturally fell on Ptolemy himself, who was staying with Pompey at his country estate in the Alban hills. The Pharaoh, detested by his people for the taxes he levied, was offering the stupendous reward of six thousand gold talents if Rome would secure his restoration, and the effect of this bribe upon the Senate was as dignified as if a rich man had thrown a few coins into a crowd of starving beggars. In the scramble for the honour of overseeing Ptolemy's return, three main candidates had emerged: Lentulus Spinther, the outgoing consul, who was due to become governor of Cilicia and therefore would legally command an army on the borders of Egypt; Marcus Crassus, who yearned to possess the same wealth and glory as Pompey and Caesar; and Pompey himself, who feigned disinterest in the commission but behind the scenes was the most active of the three in trying to secure it.

Cicero had no desire to become embroiled in the affair. There was nothing in it for him. He was obliged to support Spinther, in return for Spinther's efforts to end his exile, and lobbied discreetly behind the scenes on his behalf. But when Pompey asked him to come out and meet the Pharaoh to discuss the death of Dio, he felt unable to turn the summons down.

The last time we had visited the house was almost two years earlier, when Cicero had gone to plead for help in resisting Clodius's attacks. On that occasion Pompey had pretended to be out to avoid seeing him. The memory of his cowardice still rankled with me, but Cicero refused to dwell on it: 'If I do, I shall become bitter, and a man who is bitter hurts no one but himself. We must look to the future.' Now, as we rattled up the long drive to the villa, we passed several groups of olive-skinned men wearing exotic robes and exercising those sinister yellowish prick-eared greyhounds so beloved of the Egyptians.

Ptolemy awaited Cicero with Pompey in the atrium. He was a short, plump, smooth figure, dark-complexioned like his courtiers, and so quietly spoken that one found oneself bending forward to catch what he was saying. He was dressed Roman-style in a toga. Cicero bowed and kissed his hand, and I was invited to do the same. His perfumed fingers were fat and soft like a baby's, but the nails I noticed with disgust were broken and dirty. Coyly peering around him with her arms clasped across his stomach was his young daughter. She had huge charcoal-black eyes and a painted ruby mouth – an ageless slattern's mask even at the age of eleven, or so it seems to me now, but perhaps I am being unfair and allowing my memory to be distorted by what was to come, for this was the future Queen Cleopatra, later to cause such mischief.

Once the niceties were out of the way and Cleopatra had departed with her maids, Pompey came to the point: 'This killing of Dio is starting to become embarrassing, both to me and to His Majesty. And now to cap it all, a murder charge has been brought by Titus Coponius, Dio's host when he was killed, and by his brother Gaius. The whole thing is ridiculous, of course, but apparently they are not to be persuaded out of it.'

'Who is the accused?' enquired Cicero.

'Publius Asicius.'

Cicero paused to remember the name. 'Isn't he one of your estate managers?'

'He is. That's what makes it embarrassing.'

Cicero had the tact not to ask whether Asicius was guilty or not. He considered the matter purely as a lawyer. He said to Ptolemy, 'Until this matter blows over, I would strongly advise Your Majesty to remove yourself as far away from Rome as possible.'

'Why?'

'Because if I were the Coponius brothers, the first thing I should do is issue a subpoena summoning you to give evidence.'

'Can they do that?' asked Pompey.

'They can try. To save His Majesty the embarrassment, I would advise him to be miles away when the writ is served – out of Italy, if possible.'

'But what about Asicius?' said Pompey. 'If he's found guilty, that could look very bad for me.'

'I agree.'

'Then he must be acquitted. You'll take the case, I hope? I'd regard it as a favour.'

This was not what Cicero wanted. But Pompey was insistent, and in the end, as usual, he had no option but to accede. Before we left, Ptolemy, as a token of his thanks, presented Cicero with a small and ancient jade statue of a baboon, which he explained was Hedj-Wer, the god of writing. I expect it was quite valuable, but Cicero couldn't abide it – 'What do I want with their primitive mud gods?' he complained to me afterwards, and he must have thrown it away; I never saw it again.

Asicius, the accused man, came to see us. He was a former legionary commander who had served with Pompey in Spain and the East. He looked eminently capable of murder. He showed Cicero his summons. The charge was that he had visited Coponius's house early in the morning with a forged letter of introduction. Dio was in the act of opening it when Asicius whipped out a small knife he had concealed in his sleeve and stabbed the elderly philosopher in the neck. The blow had not been immediately fatal. Dio's cries had brought the household running. According to the writ, Asicius had been recognised before he managed to slash his way out of the house.

Cicero did not enquire about the truth of the matter. He merely advised Asicius that his best chance of acquittal lay in a good alibi. Someone would need to vouch that he was with them at the time of the murder – and the more witnesses he could produce and the less connection they had with Pompey, or indeed Cicero, the better.

Asicius said, 'That's easy enough. I have just the fellow lined up: a man known to be on bad terms both with Pompey and yourself.'

'Who?'

'Your old protégé Caelius Rufus.'

'Rufus? What's he doing mixed up in this business?'

'Does it matter? He'll swear I was with him at the hour the old man was killed. And he's a senator nowadays, don't forget – his word carries weight.'

I half expected Cicero to tell Asicius to find another advocate, such was his distaste for Rufus. But to my surprise he said, 'Very well, tell him to come and see me and we'll depose him.'

After Asicius had gone, Cicero said, 'Surely Rufus is a close friend of Clodius? Doesn't he live in one of his apartments? In fact, isn't Clodia his mistress?'

'She certainly used to be.'

'That was what I thought.' The mention of Clodia made him thoughtful. 'So what is Rufus doing offering an alibi to an agent of Pompey?'

Later that same day, Rufus came to the house. At twenty-five, he was the youngest member of the Senate, and very active in the law courts. It was odd to see him swaggering through the door wearing the purple-striped toga of a senator. Only nine years before, he had been Cicero's pupil. But then he had turned on his former mentor, and eventually beaten him in court by prosecuting Cicero's consular colleague, Hybrida. Cicero could have forgiven him that – he always liked to see a young man on the rise as an advocate – but his friendship with Clodius was a betrayal too far. So he greeted him very icily and pretended to read various documents while Rufus dictated his statement to me. Cicero must have been listening keenly, however, for when Rufus described how he was entertaining Asicius in his house at the time of the killing, and gave as his home address a property on the Esquiline, Cicero suddenly looked up and said, 'But don't you rent a property from Clodius on the Palatine?'

'I've moved,' replied Rufus casually, but there was something too offhand in his tone, and Cicero detected it at once.

He pointed his finger at him and said, 'You've quarrelled.'

'Not at all.'

'You've quarrelled with that devil and his sister from hell. That's why you're doing this favour for Pompey. You always were the most hopeless liar, Rufus. I see through you as clearly as if you were made of water.'

Rufus laughed. He had great charm: he was said to be the most handsome young man in Rome. 'You seem to forget, I don't live in your house any more, Marcus Tullius. I don't have to give an account of my friendships to you.' He swung himself easily on to his feet. He was also very tall. 'Now I've given your client his alibi, as was requested, and our business here is done.'

'Our business will be done when I say it is,' Cicero called after him cheerfully. He did not bother to rise. I showed Rufus out, and when I returned, he was still smiling. 'This is what I've been waiting for, Tiro. I can feel it. He's fallen out with those two monsters, and if that's the case, they won't rest until they've destroyed him. We need to ask around town. Discreetly. Spread some money around if we have to. But we must find out why he's left that house!'

The trial of Asicius ended the day it began. The case boiled down to the word of a few household slaves against that of a senator, and on hearing Rufus's affidavit, the praetor directed the jury to acquit. This was the first of many legal victories for Cicero following his return, and he was soon in high demand, appearing in the Forum most days, just as in his prime.

Throughout this time the violence in Rome worsened. On some days the courts could not sit because of the risks to public safety. A few days after setting upon Cicero in the Via Sacra, Clodius and his followers attacked the house of Milo and attempted to burn it down. Milo's gladiators drove them off and retaliated by occupying the voting pens on the Field of Mars in a vain attempt to prevent Clodius's election as aedile.

Cicero sensed opportunity in the chaos. One of the new tribunes, Cannius Gallus, laid a bill before the people demanding that Pompey alone should be entrusted with restoring Ptolemy to the throne of Egypt. The bill so incensed Crassus that he actually paid Clodius to organise a popular campaign against Pompey. And when Clodius eventually won the aedileship, he used his powers as a magistrate to summon Pompey to give evidence in an action he brought against Milo.

The hearing took place in the Forum in front of many thousands. I watched it with Cicero. Pompey mounted the rostra, but had hardly uttered more than a few sentences when Clodius's supporters started to drown him out with catcalls and slow handclaps. There was a kind of heroism in the way that Pompey simply put his shoulders down and went on reading out his text, even though no one could hear him. This must have gone on for an hour or more, and then Clodius, who was standing a few feet along the rostra, started really working up the crowd against him.

'Who's starving the people to death?' he shouted.

'Pompey!' roared his followers.

'Who wants to go to Alexandria?'

'Pompey!'

'Whom do you want to go?'

'Crassus!'

Pompey looked as if he had been struck by lightning. Never had he been insulted in such a way. The crowd started heaving like a stormy sea, one side pushing against the other, with little eddies of scuffles breaking out here and there, and suddenly from the back, ladders appeared and were passed rapidly over our heads to the front, where they were thrown up against the rostra and a group of ruffians began scaling it – Milo's ruffians, it transpired, for the moment they reached the platform they charged at Clodius and hurled him off it, a good twelve feet down on to the spectators. There were cheers and screams. I didn't see what happened after that, as Cicero's attendants hustled us out of the Forum and away from danger, but we learned later that Clodius had escaped unharmed.

The following evening, Cicero went off to dine with Pompey and came home rubbing his hands with pleasure. 'Well, if I'm not mistaken, that's the beginning of the end of our so-called triumvirate, at least as far as Pompey's concerned. He swears Crassus is behind a plot to murder him, says he'll never trust him again, threatens that if necessary Caesar will have to return to Rome to answer for his mischief in creating Clodius in the first place and destroying the constitution. I've never seen him in such a rage. As for me, he couldn't have been friendlier, and assures me that whatever I do, I can rely on his support.

'But better even than that – when he was deep in his cups, he finally told me why Rufus has switched allegiance. I was right: there's been the most tremendous falling-out between him and Clodia – so much so that she's claiming he tried to poison her! Naturally, Clodius has taken his sister's side, thrown Rufus out of his house and called in his debts. So

Rufus has had to turn to Pompey in the hope of some Egyptian gold to pay off what he owes. Isn't it all marvellous?'

I agreed it was all marvellous, though I couldn't see why it warranted quite such ecstasies of joy.

Cicero said, 'Bring me the praetors' lists, quick!'

I went and fetched the schedule of court cases that were due to be heard over the next seven days. Cicero told me to look up when Rufus was next due to appear. I ran my finger down the various courts and cases until I found his name. He was scheduled to begin a prosecution in the constitutional court for bribery in five days' time.

Cicero said, 'Who is he prosecuting?'

'Bestia.'

'Bestia! That villain!'

Cicero lay back on the couch in his familiar posture when cooking up a scheme, with his hands clasped behind his head, staring at the ceiling. L. Calpurnius Bestia was an old enemy of his, one of Catilina's tame tribunes, lucky not to have been executed for treason with his five fellow conspirators. Yet here he was, apparently still active in public life, being prosecuted for buying votes during the recent praetorian elections. I wondered what possible interest Bestia could hold for Cicero, and after a long period during which he said nothing, I ventured to ask him.

His voice seemed to come from a long way away, as if I had interrupted him in a dream. 'I was just thinking,' he said slowly, 'that I might offer to defend him.'

XLII

The next morning, Cicero went to call on Bestia, taking me with him. The old rogue had a house on the Palatine. His expression when Cicero was shown in was comical in its astonishment. He had with him his son Atratinus, a clever lad who had only just donned the toga of manhood and was eager to begin his career. When Cicero announced that he wished to discuss his impending prosecution, Bestia naturally assumed he was about to receive another writ and grew quite menacing. It was only thanks to the intervention of the boy, who was in awe of Cicero, that he was persuaded to sit down and listen to what his distinguished visitor had to say.

Cicero said, 'I have come here to offer my services in your defence.'

Bestia gaped at him. 'And why in the name of the gods would you do that?'

'I have undertaken later in the month to appear on behalf of Publius Sestius. Is it true that you saved his life during the fighting in the Forum when I was in exile?'

'I did.'

'Well then, Bestia, chance for once throws us on the same side. If I appear for you, I can describe the incident at great length and that will help me lay the ground for Sestius's defence, which will be heard by the same court. Who are your other advocates?'

'Herennius Balbus to open, and then my son here to follow.'

'Good. Then with your agreement I'll speak third and do the winding-up – my usual preference. I'll put on a good show, don't worry. We should have the whole thing wrapped up in a day or two.'

Bestia by this time had moved from an attitude of deep suspicion to one of hardly being able to believe his luck that the greatest advocate in Rome was willing to speak on his behalf. And when Cicero strolled into court a couple of days later, his appearance provoked gasps of surprise.

Rufus in particular was stunned. The very fact that Cicero, of all people – whom Bestia had once plotted to murder – should now appear as his supporter more or less guaranteed his acquittal. And so it proved. Cicero made an eloquent speech, the jury voted, and Bestia was found not guilty.

As the court was rising, Rufus came over to Cicero. For once his normal charm was gone. He had been counting on an easy victory; instead his career had been checked. He said bitterly, 'Well I hope you're satisfied, although such a triumph brings you nothing but dishonour.'

'My dear Rufus,' replied Cicero, 'have you learnt nothing? There is no more honour in a legal dispute than there is in a wrestling match.'

'What I've *learnt*, Cicero, is that you still bear me a grudge and will stop at nothing to gain revenge on your enemies.'

'Oh my dear, poor boy, I don't regard *you* as my enemy. You're not important enough. I have bigger fish to catch.'

That really infuriated Rufus. He said, 'Well, you can tell your client that as he insists on continuing as a candidate, I shall bring a second charge against him tomorrow – and the next time you rise in his defence, if you dare, I give you fair warning: I shall be waiting for you!'

He was as good as his word: very soon afterwards, Bestia and his son brought the new writ round to show Cicero. Bestia said hopefully, 'You'll defend me again, I hope?'

'Oh no, that would be very foolish. One can't spring the same surprise twice. No, I'm afraid I can't be your advocate again.'

'So what's to be done?'

'Well, I can tell you what *I'd* do in your place.'

'And what's that?'

'I'd lay a counter-suit against him.'

'For what?'

'Political violence. That takes precedence over bribery cases. Therefore you'll have the advantage of putting him on trial first, before he can get you into court.'

Bestia conferred with his son. 'We like the sound of it,' he announced. 'But can we really make a case against him? Has he actually committed political violence?'

'Of course,' said Cicero. 'Didn't you hear? He was involved in the murder of several of those Egyptian envoys. Ask around town,' he continued. 'You'll find lots of people willing to tell tales. There's one man in particular you should go to see, although of course you never heard the name from me: you'll understand why the moment I say it. You should talk to Clodius, or better still to that sister of his. I hear Rufus used to be her lover, and when his ardour cooled, he tried to get rid of her with poison. You know what that family is like – they love their vengeance. You should offer to let them join your suit. With the Claudii beside you, you'll be unbeatable. But remember – you never got any of this from me.'

I had worked very closely with Cicero for many years. I had grown used to his clever tricks. I did not think him capable of surprising me any more. That day proved me wrong.

Bestia thanked him profusely, swore to be discreet and went off full of purpose. A few days later, a notice to prosecute was posted in the Forum: he and Clodius had combined forces to charge Rufus with both the attacks on the Alexandrian envoys and the attempted murder of Clodia. The news caused a sensation. Almost everyone believed that Rufus would be found guilty and sentenced to exile for life, and that the career of Rome's youngest senator was over.

When I showed him the list of charges, Cicero said, 'Oh dear. Poor Rufus. He must be feeling very wretched. I think we should visit him and cheer him up.'

And so we set off to find the house that Rufus was renting. Cicero, who at the age of fifty was starting to feel stiff in his limbs on cold winter mornings, rode in a litter, while I walked alongside him. Rufus turned out to be lodging on the second floor of an apartment block in the less fashionable part of the Esquiline, not far from the gate where the undertakers ply their trade. The place was gloomy even at midday, and Cicero had to ask the slaves to light candles. In the dim light we discovered their master in a drunken sleep, curled up beneath a pile of blankets on a couch. He groaned and rolled over and begged to be left alone, but Cicero dragged away his covers and told him to get up on his feet.

'What's the point? I'm finished!'

'You're not finished. Quite the contrary: we have that woman exactly where we want her.'

'We?' repeated Rufus, squinting up at Cicero through bloodshot eyes. 'When you say "we", does that imply you're on my side?'

'Not merely on your side, my dear Rufus. I am going to be your advocate!'

'Wait,' said Rufus. He touched his hand gently to his forehead, as if checking it was still intact. 'Wait a moment – did you *plan* all this?'

'Consider yourself to have been given a political education. And now let us agree that the slate is wiped clean between us, and concentrate on beating our common enemy.' Rufus began to swear. Cicero listened for a while, then interrupted him. 'Come, Rufus. This is a good bargain for us both. You'll get that harpy off your back once and for all, and I'll satisfy the honour of my wife.'

Cicero held out his hand. At first Rufus recoiled. He pouted and shook his head and muttered. But then he must have realised he had no choice. At any rate, eventually he extended his own hand, Cicero shook it warmly, and with that the trap he had laid for Clodia snapped shut.

The trial was scheduled to take place at the start of April, which meant it would coincide with the opening of the Festival of the Great Mother, with its famous parade of castrated holy men. Even so, there was no doubting which would be the greater attraction, especially when Cicero's name was announced as one of Rufus's advocates. The others were to be Rufus himself, and Crassus, in whose household Rufus had also served an internship as a young man. I am certain Crassus would have preferred not to have performed this service for his former protégé, especially given the presence of Cicero on the bench beside him, but the rules of patronage placed him under a heavy obligation. On the other side once again were young Atratinus and Herennius Balbus – both furious at Cicero's duplicity, not that he cared a fig for their opinion – and Clodius, representing the interests of his sister. No doubt he too would have preferred to be at the Great Mother's festivities, which he, as aedile, was supposed to oversee, but he could hardly have backed out of the trial when his family's honour was at stake.

I cherish my memories of Cicero at this time, in the weeks before Rufus's trial. He seemed once again to hold all the threads of life in his hands, just as he had in his prime. He was active in the courts and in the Senate. He went out to dinner with his friends. He even moved back in to the house on the Palatine. True, it was not entirely finished. The place still reeked of lime and paint; workmen trailed mud in from the garden. But Cicero was so delighted to be back in his own home, he did not care. His furniture and books were fetched out of storage, the household gods were placed on the altar, and Terentia was summoned back from Tusculum with Tullia and Marcus.

Terentia entered the house cautiously and moved between the rooms with her nose wrinkled in distaste at the pungent smell of fresh plaster. She had never much cared for the place from the start, and was not about to change her opinion now. But Cicero persuaded her to stay: 'That woman who caused you so much pain will never harm you again. She may have laid a hand on you. But I promise you: I shall flay her alive.'

He also, to his great delight, after two years' separation, heard that Atticus had at last returned from Epirus. The moment he reached the city gates, he came straight round to inspect Cicero's rebuilt house. Unlike Quintus, Atticus had not changed at all. His smile was still as constant, his charm as thickly laid-on – 'Tiro, *my dear fellow*, thank you *so much* for taking care of my oldest friend *so devotedly*' – his figure as trim, his silvery hair as sleek and well cut. The only difference was that now he trailed a shy young woman at least thirty years his junior, whom he introduced to Cicero … as his fiancée! I thought Cicero might faint with shock. Her name was Pilia. She was of an obscure family, with no money and no particular beauty either – just a quiet, homely country girl. But Atticus was besotted. At first Cicero was greatly put out. 'It's ridiculous,' he grumbled to me when the couple had gone. 'He's three years older even than I am! Is it a wife he's after or a nurse?' I suspect he was mostly offended because Atticus had never mentioned her before, and worried that she might disrupt the easy intimacy of their friendship. But Atticus was so obviously happy, and Pilia so modest and cheerful, that Cicero soon came round to her, and sometimes I saw him glancing at her in an almost wistful way, especially when Terentia was being shrewish.

Pilia quickly became a close friend and confidante of Tullia. They were the same age and of similar temperaments, and I often saw them walking together, holding hands. Tullia had been a widow by this time for a year and encouraged by Pilia now declared herself ready to take a new husband. Cicero made enquiries about a suitable match and soon came up with Furius Crassipes – a young, rich, good-looking aristocrat, of an ancient but undistinguished family, eager for a career as a senator. He had also recently inherited a handsome house and a park just beyond the city walls. Tullia asked me for my opinion.

I said, 'What I think doesn't matter. The question is: do you like him?'

'I think I do.'

'Do you *think* you do or are you sure?'

'I'm sure.'

'Then that is enough.'

In truth I thought Crassipes was more in love with the idea of Cicero as a father-in-law than Tullia as a wife. But I kept this view to myself. A wedding date was fixed.

Who knows the secrets of another's marriage? Certainly not I. Cicero, for example, had long complained to me of Terentia's peevishness, of her obsession with money, of her superstition and her coldness and her rude tongue. And yet the whole of this elaborate legal spectacle he had contrived to be enacted in the centre of Rome was for her – his means of making amends for all the wrongs she had suffered because of the failure of his career. For the first time in their long marriage, he laid at her feet the greatest gift he had to offer her: his oratory.

Not that she wanted to listen to it, mind you. She had hardly ever heard him speak in public, and never in the law courts, and had no desire to start now. It took considerable amounts of Cicero's eloquence simply to persuade her to leave the house and come down to the Forum on the morning he was due to speak.

By this time the trial was in its second day. The prosecution had already laid out its case, Rufus and Crassus had responded, and only Cicero's address remained to be heard. He had sat through the other speeches with barely concealed impatience; the details of the case were irrelevant to him and the advocates bored him. Atratinus, in his disconcertingly piping voice, had portrayed Rufus as a libertine, addicted to pleasure, sunk in debt, 'a pretty-boy Jason in perpetual search of a golden fleece' who had been paid by Ptolemy to intimidate the Alexandrian envoys and arrange the murder of Dio. Clodius had spoken next and described how his sister, 'this chaste and distinguished widow', had been tricked by Rufus into giving him gold out of the goodness of her heart – money she had thought was to finance public entertainment but which he had used to bribe Dio's assassins – and how Rufus had then provided poison to her slaves to kill her and so cover his traces. Crassus, in his plodding way, and Rufus, with typical verve, had rebutted each of the charges. But the balance of opinion was that the prosecution had made its case and that the young reprobate was likely to be found guilty. This was the state of play when Cicero arrived in the Forum.

I conducted Terentia to her seat while he made his way through the thousands of spectators and went up the steps of the temple to the court. Seventy-five jurors had been empanelled. Beside them sat the praetor Domitius Calvinus with his lictors and scribes. To the left was the prosecution, with their witnesses arrayed behind them. And there in the front row, modestly attired but very much the centre of attention, was Clodia. She was almost forty but still beautiful, a grande dame with those famous huge dark eyes of hers that could invite intimacy one moment and threaten murder the next. She was known to be excessively close to Clodius – so much so that they had often been accused of incest. I saw her head turn very slightly to follow Cicero as he walked across to his place. Her expression was one of disdainful indifference. But she must have wondered what was coming.

Cicero adjusted the folds of his toga. He had no notes. A hush fell over the vast throng. He glanced across to where Terentia was sitting. Then he turned to the jury. 'Gentlemen, anyone who doesn't know our laws and customs might wonder why we are here, during a public festival, when all the other courts are suspended, to judge a young man of hard work and brilliant intellect – especially when it turns out he is being attacked by a person he once prosecuted, and by the wealth of a courtesan.'

At that, a great roar went rolling around the Forum, like the sound the crowd makes at the start of the games when a famous gladiator makes his first thrust. This was what they had come to see! Clodia stared straight ahead as if she had been turned to marble. I am sure that she and Clodius would never have brought their prosecution if they had thought there was a chance of Cicero being against them; but there was no escape now.

Having laid down a marker of what was to come, Cicero then proceeded to build his case. He conjured a picture of Rufus that was unrecognisable to those of us who knew him – of a sober, hard-working servant of the commonwealth whose main misfortune was to be 'born not unhandsome', and thus to have come to the attention of Clodia, 'the Medea of the Palatine', into whose neighbourhood he had moved. He stood behind the seated Rufus and clasped his hand on his shoulder. 'His change of residence has been for this young man the cause of all his misfortunes and of all the gossip, for Clodia is a woman not only of noble birth but of notoriety, of whom I will say no more than what is necessary to refute the charges.'

He paused to allow the sense of anticipation to build. 'Now, as many of you will know, I am on terms of great personal enmity with this woman's husband ...' He stopped and snapped his fingers in exasperation. 'I meant to say brother: I always make that mistake.'

His timing was perfect, and to this day even people who otherwise know nothing of Cicero still quote that joke. Almost everyone in Rome had felt the arrogance of the Claudii at some point down the years; to see them ridiculed was irresistible. Its effect not just on the audience but on the jury and even the praetor was wonderful to behold.

Terentia turned to me in puzzlement. 'Why is everyone laughing?'

I did not know what to reply.

When order was restored, Cicero continued, with menacing friendliness: 'Well, I am truly sorry to have to make this woman an enemy, especially as she is every other man's friend. So let me first ask her whether she prefers me to deal with her severely, in the old-fashioned manner, or mildly, in the modern way?'

And then, to her evident horror, Cicero actually started walking across the court towards her. He was smiling, hand extended, inviting her to choose – the tiger playing with its prey. He halted barely a pace away from her.

'If she prefers the old method, then I must call up from the dead one of those full-bearded men of antiquity to rebuke her ...'

I have often pondered what Clodia should have done at this point. On reflection I believe her best course would have been to laugh along with Cicero – to try to win over the sympathy of the crowd by some piece of pantomime that would have shown she was entering into the spirit of the joke. But she was a Claudian. Never before had anyone dared openly to laugh at her, let alone the common people in the Forum. She was outraged, probably panicking, and so she responded in the worst way possible: she turned her back on Cicero like a sulky child.

He shrugged. 'Very well, let me call up a member of her own family – to be specific, Appius Claudius the Blind. He will feel the least sorrow since he won't be able to see her. If he were to appear, this is what he would say ...'

And now Cicero addressed her in a ghostly voice, his eyes closed, his arms raised straight out in front of him; even Clodius started laughing. 'Oh woman, what hast thou to do with Rufus, this stripling who is young enough to be thy son? Why hast thou been either so intimate with him as to give him gold, or caused such jealousy as to warrant the administering of poison? Why was Rufus so closely connected with thee? Is he a kinsman? A relative by marriage? A friend of thine late husband? None of these! What else could it have been then between you two except reckless passion? O woe! Was it for this that I brought water to Rome, that thou mightest use it after thy incestuous debauches? Was it for this that I built the Appian Way, that thou mightest frequent it with a train of other women's husbands?'

With that, the ghost of old Appius Claudius evaporated and Cicero addressed Clodia's turned back in his normal voice. 'But if you prefer a more congenial relative, let us speak to you in the voice of your youngest brother over there, who loves you *most* dearly – who, as a boy, in fact, being of a nervous disposition and prey to night terrors, always used to get into bed with his big sister. Imagine him saying to you' – and now Cicero perfectly imitated Clodius's fashionable slouching stance and plebeian drawl – 'what's there to worry about, sister? So what if you fancied some young fellow. He was handsome. He was tall. You couldn't get enough of him. You knew you were old enough to be his mother. But you were rich. So you bought him things to purchase his affection. It didn't last long. He called you a hag. Well, forget him – just find yourself another one, or two, or ten. After all, that's what you usually do.'

Clodius was no longer laughing. He looked at Cicero as if he would like to clamber over the benches of the court and strangle him. But the audience were laughing right enough. I glanced around and saw men and women with tears running down their cheeks. Empathy is the essence of the orator's art. Cicero had that immense crowd entirely on his side, and after he had made them laugh with him, it was easy for him to make them share his outrage as he moved in for the kill.

'I am now forgetting, Clodia, the wrongs you have done me; I am putting aside the memory of what I have suffered; I pass over your cruel actions towards my family during my absence; but I ask you this: if a woman without a husband opens her house to all men's desires, and publicly leads the life of a courtesan; if she is in the habit of attending dinner parties with men who are perfect strangers; if she does this in Rome, in her park outside the city walls, and amid all those crowds on the Bay of Naples; if her embraces and caresses, her beach parties, her water parties, her dinner parties, proclaim her to be not only a courtesan, but also a shameless and wanton courtesan – if she does all that and a young man should be discovered consorting with this woman, should he be considered the corrupter or the corrupted, the seducer or the seduced?

'This whole charge arises from a hostile, infamous, merciless, crime-stained, lust-stained house. An unstable and angry wanton of a woman has forged this accusation. Gentlemen of the jury: do not allow Marcus Caelius Rufus to be sacrificed to her lust. If you restore Rufus in safety to me, to his family, to the state, you will find in him one pledged, devoted and bound to you and to your children; and it is you above all, gentlemen, who will reap the rich and lasting fruits of all his exertions and labours.'

And with that it was over. For a moment Cicero stood there – one hand stretched towards the jury, the other towards Rufus – and there was silence. Then some great subterranean force seemed to rise from beneath the Forum, and an instant later the air began to tremble as several thousand pairs of feet stamped the ground and the crowd roared their approval. Someone started pointing repeatedly at Clodia and shouting, 'Whore! Whore! Whore!' and very quickly the chant was taken up all around us, the arms flashing out again and again: 'Whore! Whore! Whore!'

Clodia looked out blank-faced with incredulity across this sea of hatred. She didn't seem to notice that her brother had moved across the court and was standing beside her. But then he grasped her elbow and that seemed to jolt her out of her reverie. She glanced up at him, and finally, after some gentle coaxing, she allowed herself to be led off the platform and out of sight and into an obscurity from which it is fair to say she never again emerged as long as she lived.

Thus did Cicero exact his revenge on Clodia and reclaim his place as the dominant voice in Rome. It is hardly necessary to add that Rufus was acquitted and that Clodius's loathing of Cicero was redoubled. 'One day,' he hissed, 'you will hear a sound behind you, and when you turn, I shall be there, I promise you.' Cicero laughed at the crudeness of the threat, knowing he was too popular for Clodius to dare to attack him – at least for now. As for Terentia, although she deplored the vulgarity of Cicero's jokes and was appalled by the rudeness of the mob, nevertheless she was pleased by the utter social annihilation of her enemy, and as she and Cicero walked home, she took his arm – the first time I had witnessed such a public gesture of affection for years.

The following day, when Cicero went down the hill to attend a meeting of the Senate, he was mobbed both by the ordinary people and by the scores of senators waiting outside the chamber for the session to begin. As he received the congratulations of his peers, he looked exactly as he had done in his days of power, and I could see that he was quite intoxicated by his reception. As it happened, this was the Senate's final meeting before it rose for its annual vacation, and there was a febrile mood in the air. After the haruspices had ruled the heavens propitious, and just as the senators started to file in for the start of the debate, Cicero beckoned me over and pointed on the order paper to the main subject to be discussed that day: the grant of forty million sesterces from the treasury to Pompey, to finance his grain purchases.

'This could be interesting.' He nodded to the figure of Crassus, just then stalking in to the chamber, wearing a grim expression. 'I had a word with him about it yesterday. First Egypt, now this – he's in a rage at Pompey's megalomania. The thieves are at one another's throats, Tiro: there could be an opportunity for mischief here.'

'Be careful,' I warned him.

'Oh dear, yes: "Be careful!"' he mocked, and tapped me on the head with the rolled-up order paper. 'Well, I have a little power after yesterday, and you know what I always say: power is for using.'

With that he went off cheerfully into the Senate building.

I had not been intending to stay for the session, having much work to do in preparing Cicero's speech of the previous day for publication. But now I changed my mind and went and stood at the doorway. The presiding consul was Cornelius Lentulus Marcellinus, a patriotic aristocrat of the old sort – hostile to Clodius, supportive of Cicero and suspicious of Pompey. He made sure to call a series of speakers who all denounced the granting of such a huge sum to Pompey. As one pointed out, there was no money available in any case, every spare copper being swallowed up implementing Caesar's law that gave the Campanian lands to Pompey's veterans and the urban poor. The house grew rowdy. Pompey's supporters heckled his opponents. His opponents shouted back. (Pompey himself was not allowed to be present, as the grain commission conveyed imperium – a power that barred its holders from entering the Senate.) Crassus looked gratified with the way things were going. Finally, Cicero indicated that he wished to speak, and the house became quiet as senators leaned forwards to hear what he had to say.

'Honourable members,' he said, 'will recall that it was on my proposal that Pompey was given this grain commission in the first place, so I am hardly going to oppose it now. We cannot order a man to do a job one day, and then deny him the means with which to accomplish it the next.' Pompey's supporters murmured loud assent. Cicero held up his hand. 'However, as has been eloquently pointed out, our resources are finite. The treasury cannot pay for everything. We cannot be expected to buy grain all over the world to feed our citizens for nothing and at the same time give free farms to soldiers and plebs. When Caesar passed his law, even he, with all his great powers of foresight, can hardly have imagined that a day was coming – and coming very soon – when veterans and the urban poor would have no need of farms to grow grain, because the grain would simply be given to them for nothing.'

'Oh!' shouted the benches of the aristocrats in delight. 'Oh! Oh!' And they pointed at Crassus, who, along with Pompey and Caesar, was one of the architects of the land laws. Crassus was staring hard at Cicero, although his face was impassive and it was impossible to tell what he was thinking.

'Would it not be prudent,' continued Cicero, 'in the light of changing circumstances, for this noble house to look again at the legislation passed during the consulship of Caesar? Now is obviously not the right occasion to discuss it fully, complex as the question is, and conscious as I am that the house is eager to rise for the recess. I would therefore propose that the issue be placed on the order paper at the first available opportunity when we reconvene.'

'I second that!' shouted Domitius Ahenobarbus, a patrician who was married to Cato's sister, and who hated Caesar so much he had recently called for him to be stripped of his command in Gaul.

Several dozen other aristocrats also jumped up clamouring to add their support. Pompey's men seemed too confused to react: after all, the main thrust of Cicero's speech had seemed to be in support of their chief. It was indeed a tidy piece of mischief that Cicero had wrought, and when he sat down and glanced along the aisle in my direction, I almost fancy he winked at me. The consul held a whispered conference with his scribes and then announced that in view of the obvious support for Cicero's motion, the issue would be debated on the Ides of May. With that the house was adjourned and the senators started moving towards the exit – none quicker than Crassus, who almost knocked me flying in his eagerness to get away.

Cicero, too, was determined to have a holiday, feeling he deserved one after seven months of non-stop strain and labour, and he had in mind the ideal destination. A wealthy tax farmer for whom he had done much legal work had lately died, leaving Cicero some property in his will – a small villa on the Bay of Naples, at Cumae, between the sea and the Lucrine Lake. (In those days, I should add, it was illegal to accept direct payment for one's services as an advocate, but permissible to receive legacies; the rule was not always strictly observed.) Cicero had never seen the place but had heard that it enjoyed one of the loveliest aspects in the region. He proposed to Terentia that they should travel to inspect it together, and she agreed, although when she discovered I was to be included in the party, she plunged into another of her sulks.

'I know how it will be,' I overheard her complaining to Cicero. 'I shall be left alone all day while you are closeted with your official wife!'

He made some soothing reply to the effect that no such thing would happen, and I was careful to keep out of her way.

On the eve of our departure, Cicero gave a dinner for his future son-in-law, Crassipes, who happened to mention that Crassus, to whom he was very close, had left Rome in a hurry the previous day, telling no one where he was going. Cicero said, 'No doubt he's heard of some elderly widow in a remote spot who is at death's door and who might be persuaded to part with her property cheaply.'

Everyone laughed apart from Crassipes, who looked very prim. 'I am sure he is simply taking a vacation, like everyone else.'

'Crassus doesn't take holidays – there's no profit in them.' Then Cicero raised his cup and proposed a toast to Crassipes and Tullia. 'May their union be long and happy and blessed with many children – for preference I should like three at least.'

'Father!' exclaimed Tullia. She laughed and blushed and looked away.

'What?' asked Cicero, with an air of innocence. 'I have the grey hairs and now I need the grandchildren to go with them.'

He rose from the table early. Before he left for the south he wanted to see Pompey. In particular he wanted to plead the case for Quintus to be allowed to relinquish his legateship and return home from Sardinia. He travelled to Pompey's in a litter but ordered the porters to go slowly so that I could walk alongside and we could have some conversation. It was getting dark. We had to travel a mile or so, beyond the city walls, to the Pincian hill, where Pompey had his new suburban villa – or palace would be a better word for it – looking down on his vast complex of temples and theatres then nearing completion on the Field of Mars.

The great man was dining alone with his wife, and we had to wait for them to finish. In the vestibule a team of slaves was busy transferring piles of luggage to half a dozen wagons drawn up in the courtyard – so many trunks of clothes and boxes of tableware and carpets and furniture and even statues that it looked as if Pompey were planning to set up a new home somewhere. Eventually the couple appeared and Pompey presented Julia to Cicero, who in turn presented me to her.

'I remember you,' she said to me, although I'm sure she didn't. She was only seventeen but very gracious. She possessed her father's exquisite manners, and also something of his piercing way of looking at one, so that I had a sudden, disconcerting memory of Caesar's naked hairless torso reclining on the massage table at his headquarters in Mutina: I had to shut my eyes to banish it.

She left almost at once, pleading the need to get a good night's sleep before her travels the next day. Pompey kissed her hand – he was famously devoted to her – and took us through into his study. This was a vast room the size of a house, crammed with trophies from his many campaigns, including what he insisted was the cloak of Alexander the Great. He sat on a couch made out of a stuffed crocodile, which he said Ptolemy had given him, and invited Cicero to take the seat opposite.

Cicero said, 'You look as though you are embarking on a military expedition.'

'That's what comes of travelling with one's wife.'

'Might I ask where you're going?'

'Sardinia.'

'Ah,' said Cicero, 'that's a coincidence. I wanted to ask you about Sardinia.' And he proceeded to make an eloquent case for his brother to be allowed home, citing three reasons in particular – the length of time he had been away, his need to spend time with his son (who was turning into a troubled boy) and his preference for military rather than civil command.

Pompey heard him out, stroking his chin, reclining on his Egyptian crocodile. 'If that's what you want,' he said. 'Yes, he can come back. You're right anyway – he isn't much good at administration.'

'Thank you. I'm obliged to you, as always.'

Pompey regarded Cicero with crafty eyes. 'So I hear you caused a stir in the Senate the other day.'

'Only on your behalf – I was simply trying to secure the funds for your commission.'

'Yes, but by challenging Caesar's laws.' He wagged his finger in reproach. 'That's naughty of you.'

'Caesar is not a god, infallible; his laws have not come down to us from Mount Olympus. Besides, if you'd been there and seen the pleasure Crassus was taking in all the attacks on you, I believe you would have wanted me to find some way to wipe the smile from his face. And by criticising Caesar, I certainly did that.'

Pompey brightened at once. 'Oh well, I'm with you there!'

'Believe me, Crassus's ambition and disloyalty to you have been far more destabilising to the commonwealth than anything *I* have done.'

'I agree entirely.'

'In fact I'd suggest that if your alliance with Caesar is threatened by anyone, it's him.'

'How is that?'

'Well, I don't understand how Caesar can stand back and allow him to plot against you in this way, especially letting him employ Clodius. Surely as your father-in-law he owes his first duty to you? If Crassus carries on like this, he will sow much discord, I predict it now.'

'He will.' Pompey nodded. He looked crafty again. 'You're right, of course.' He stood, and Cicero followed suit. He took Cicero's hand in both his immense paws. 'Thank you for coming to see me, my old friend. You have given me much food for thought during my voyage to Sardinia. We must write to one another often. Where exactly will you be?'

'Cumae.'

'Ah! I envy you. Cumae – the most beautiful spot in Italy.'

Cicero was well pleased with his night's work. On the way home he said to me, 'This triple alliance of theirs can't last. It defies nature. All I have to do is keep chipping away at it, and sooner or later the whole rotten edifice will come crashing down.'

We left Rome at first light – Terentia, Tullia and Marcus all in the same carriage, along with Cicero, who was in great good humour – and made quick progress, stopping first for a night at Tusculum, which Cicero was glad to find habitable again, and then at the family estate in Arpinum, where we remained for a week. Finally from those cold high peaks of the Apennines we descended south to Campania.

With every mile the clouds of winter seemed to lift, the sky became bluer, the temperature warmer, the air more fragrant with the scent of pines and herbs, and when we joined the coastal road, the breeze off the sea was balmy. Cumae was then a much smaller and quieter town than it is today. At the Acropolis I gave a description of our destination and was directed by a priest to the eastern side of the Lucrine Lake, to a spot low in the hills, looking out across the lagoon and the narrow spit of land to the variegated blueness of the Mediterranean. The villa itself was small and dilapidated, with half a dozen elderly slaves to look after it. The wind blew through open walls; a section of the roof was missing. But it was worth every discomfort simply for the panorama. Down on the lake, little rowing boats moved among the oyster beds, while from the garden at the back there rose a majestic view of the lush green pyramid of Vesuvius. Cicero was enchanted, and set to work at once with the local builders, commissioning a great programme of renovation and redecoration. Marcus played on the beach with his tutor. Terentia sat on the terrace and sewed. Tullia read her Greek. It was a family holiday of a sort they had not taken for many years.

There was one puzzle, however. That whole stretch of coast from Cumae to Puteoli, then as now, was dotted with villas belonging to members of the Senate. Naturally Cicero assumed that once word spread he was in residence, he would begin to receive callers. But nobody came. At night he stood on the terrace and looked up and down the seashore and peered up into the hills and complained he could see hardly any lights. Where were the parties, the dinners? He patrolled the beach, a mile in either direction, and not once did he spot a senatorial toga.

'Something must be happening,' he said to Terentia. 'Where are they all?'

'I don't know,' she replied, 'but speaking for myself, I am happy there is no one with whom you can discuss politics.'

The answer came on our fifth morning.

I was on the terrace answering Cicero's correspondence when I noticed that a small group of horsemen had turned off the coastal road and were coming up the track towards the house. My immediate thought was *Clodius*! I stood to get a better view and saw to my dismay that the sun was glinting on helmets and breastplates. Five riders: soldiers.

Terentia and the children had gone off for the day to visit the sibyl who was said to live in a jar in a cave at Cumae. I ran inside to alert Cicero, and by the time I found him – he was choosing the colour scheme for the dining room – the horsemen were already clattering into the courtyard. Their leader dismounted and took off his helmet. He was a fearsome apparition: dust-rimed, like some harbinger of death. The whiteness of his nose and forehead was in contrast to the grime of the rest of his face. He looked as if he wore a mask. But I knew him. He was a senator, albeit not a very distinguished one – a member of that tame, dependable class of pedarii who never spoke but merely voted with their feet. Lucius Vibullius Rufus was his name. He was one of Pompey's officers from Pompey's home region of Picenum naturally.

'Could I have a word?' he said gruffly.

'Of course,' said Cicero. 'Come inside, all of you. Come and have something to eat and drink, I insist.'

Vibullius said, 'I'll come in. They'll wait out here and make sure we're not disturbed.' He moved very stiffly, a clay effigy come to life.

Cicero said, 'You look all in. How far have you ridden?'

'From Luca.'

'Luca?' repeated Cicero. 'That must be three hundred miles!'

'More like three hundred and fifty. We've been on the road a week.' As he lowered himself to a seat, he gave off a shower of dust. 'There's been a meeting concerning you, and I've been sent to inform you of its conclusions.' He glanced at me. 'I need to speak in confidence.'

Cicero, baffled and plainly wondering if he was dealing with a madman, said, 'He's my secretary. You can say all you have to say in front of him. What meeting?'

'As you wish.' Vibullius tugged off his gloves, unbuckled the side of his breastplate, reached under the metal and pulled out a document, which he carefully unwrapped. 'The reason I've come from Luca is because that's where Pompey, Caesar and Crassus have been meeting.'

Cicero frowned. 'No, that's impossible. Pompey is going to Sardinia – he told me so himself.'

'A man can do both, can he not?' replied Vibullius affably. 'He can go to Luca and then go to Sardinia. I can tell you in fact how it came about. After your little speech in the Senate, Crassus travelled up to see Caesar in Ravenna to tell him what you'd said. Then they both crossed Italy to intercept Pompey before he took ship at Pisa. The three of them spent several days together, discussing many matters – among them what's to be done about *you*.'

I felt suddenly queasy. Cicero was more robust: 'There's no need to be impertinent.'

'And the gist of it is this: *shut up, Marcus Tullius!* Shut up in the Senate about Caesar's laws. Shut up trying to cause trouble between the Three. Shut up about Crassus. Shut up generally, in fact.'

'Have you finished?' asked Cicero calmly. 'Do I need to remind you – you are a guest in my house?'

'Not quite finished, no.' Vibullius paused and consulted his notes. 'Also present for part of the conference was Sardinia's governor, Appius Claudius. He was there to make certain undertakings on behalf of his brother, the upshot of which is that Pompey and Clodius are to be publicly reconciled.'

'Reconciled?' repeated Cicero. Now he sounded uncertain.

'In future they will stand together in the best interests of the commonwealth. Pompey wishes me to tell you that he's very unhappy with you, Marcus Tullius: very unhappy. I am quoting his exact words now. He believes he demonstrated great loyalty to you in campaigning for your recall from exile, in the course of which he made certain personal undertakings about your future conduct to Caesar – undertakings, he reminds you, which you repeated to Caesar in writing, and have now broken. He feels let down. He feels embarrassed. He insists, as a test of friendship, that you withdraw your motion on Caesar's land laws from the Senate, and that you do not pronounce on the issue again until you have consulted him in person.'

'I only spoke as I did in Pompey's interest—'

'He would like you to write him a letter confirming that you will do as he asks.' Vibullius rolled up his document and tucked it away under his cuirass. 'That's the official part. What I am about to tell you next is strictly confidential. You understand what I'm saying?'

Cicero made a weary gesture. He understood.

'Pompey wishes you to appreciate the scale of the forces at work: that is why the others gave him permission to inform you. Later this year, both he and Crassus will put their names forward in the consular elections.'

'They'll lose.'

'If the elections were to be held as usual in the summer, you might be right. But the elections will be postponed.'

'Why?'

'Because of violence in Rome.'

'What violence?'

'Clodius will provide the violence. As a result, the elections won't take place until the winter, by which time the campaigning season in Gaul will be over and Caesar will be able to send thousands of his veterans to Rome to vote for his colleagues. *Then* they will be elected. At the end of their terms as consul, Pompey and Crassus will both take up proconsular commands – Pompey in Spain, Crassus in Syria. Instead of the usual one year, these commands will last for five years. Naturally, in the interests of fairness, Caesar's proconsular command in Gaul will also be extended for another five years.'

'This is quite unbelievable—'

'And at the end of his extended term, Caesar will come back to Rome and be elected consul in his turn – Pompey and Crassus making sure *their* veterans are on hand to vote for him. Those are the terms of the Luca Accord. It is designed to last for seven years. Pompey has promised Caesar you will abide by it.'

'And if I do not?'

'He will no longer guarantee your safety.'

XLIII

'Seven years,' said Cicero with great contempt after Vibullius and his men had gone. 'Nothing in politics can be planned in advance for *seven years*. Is Pompey entirely lacking in sense? Does he not see how this devils' pact works entirely in Caesar's favour? In effect, he promises to protect Caesar's back until such time as Caesar has finished pillaging Gaul, whereupon the conqueror will return to Rome and take control of the whole republic – Pompey included.'

He sat slumped on the terrace in despair. From the shore below came the lonely cries of seabirds as the oyster fishermen landed their catch. We knew now why the neighbourhood was so deserted. According to Vibullius, half the Senate had got wind of what was happening in Luca and more than a hundred had gone north to try to get their share of the spoils. They had forsaken the sun of Campania to bask in the warmest sun of all: power.

'I am a fool,' said Cicero, 'to be counting the waves down here while the future of the world is being decided at the other end of the country. Let's face it, Tiro. I am a spent force. Every man has his season, and I have had mine.'

Later in the day Terentia returned from her visit to the sibyl's cave in Cumae. She noticed the dust on the carpets and the furniture and asked who had been in the house. Reluctantly Cicero described what had happened. Her eyes shone. She said excitedly, 'How strange that you should tell me this! The sibyl prophesied this very outcome. She said that first Rome would be ruled by three, and then by two, and then by one, and then by none.'

Even Cicero, who regarded the notion of a sibyl living in a jar and predicting the future as entirely fatuous, was impressed. 'Three, two, one, none … Well we know who the three are – that's obvious. And I can guess who the one will be. But who will be the two? And what does she mean by none? Is that her way of predicting chaos? If so, I agree – that's what will follow if we allow Caesar to tear up the constitution. But for the life of me I can't see how I am to stop him.'

'Why should *you* be the one to stop him?' demanded Terentia.

'I don't know. Who else is there?'

'But why does it always fall to *you* to block Caesar's ambitions when Pompey, the most powerful man in the state, will do nothing to assist you? Why is it your responsibility?'

Cicero fell silent. Eventually he responded, 'It's a good question. Perhaps it's just conceit on my part. But can I really, with honour, stand back and do nothing, when every instinct tells me the nation is heading for disaster?'

'Yes!' she cried with passion. 'Yes! Absolutely! Haven't you suffered enough for your opposition to Caesar? Is there another man in the world who has endured more? Why not let others take up the fight? Surely you've earned the right to some peace at last?' Then quietly she added, 'I am sure that I have.'

Cicero did not answer for a long time. The truth, I suspect, is that from the moment he learnt about the Luca agreement, he knew in his heart that he could not continue opposing Caesar – not if he wanted to live. All he needed was for someone to put the issue to him bluntly, as Terentia had just done.

Finally he sighed with a weariness I had never before heard. 'You're right, my wife. At least no one will ever be able to reproach me for not having seen Caesar for what he is, and for not trying to stop him. But you are right – I'm too old and tired to fight him any longer. My friends will understand and my enemies will denounce me whatever I do, so why should I care what they think? Why shouldn't I enjoy some leisure at last down here in the sun with my family?'

And he reached over and took her hand.

Nevertheless, he was ashamed of his capitulation. I know that, because although he wrote a long letter to Pompey in Sardinia setting out his change of heart – his 'palinode', he called it – he never let me see it and kept no copy. Nor did he show it to Atticus. At the same time he wrote to the consul Marcellinus announcing that he wished to withdraw his motion calling on the Senate to re-examine Caesar's land laws. He offered no explanation; he did not need to; everyone recognised that the political firmament had shifted and the new alignment was against him.

We returned to a Rome full of rumours. Few knew for sure what Pompey and Crassus were planning, but gradually word got around that they were intending to run on a joint ticket for the consulship, just as they had in the past, even though everyone knew they had always loathed one another. Some senators, however, were determined to fight back against the cynicism and arrogance of the Three. A debate was scheduled on the allocation of consular provinces, and one motion called for Caesar to be stripped of both Nearer and Further Gaul. Cicero knew that if he attended the chamber, he would be asked his views. He considered staying away. But then he reasoned that he would have to recant publicly sooner or later: he might as well get it over with. He began working on his speech.

And then, on the eve of the debate, after more than two years away in Cyprus, Marcus Porcius Cato returned to Rome. He arrived in fine style, in a flotilla of treasure ships, sailing up the Tiber from Ostia, accompanied by his nephew, Brutus, a young man of whom great things were expected. The whole of the Senate, and all of the magistrates and priests, as well as most of the population, turned out to welcome Cato home. There was a landing stage with painted poles and ribbons where he was supposed to disembark and meet the consuls, but he sailed on past them, standing in the prow of a royal galley that had six banks of oars, his bony profile fixed straight ahead, wearing a shabby black tunic. The crowds at first gasped and groaned with disappointment at his high-handedness, but then his treasure started to be unloaded – ox wagon after ox wagon of it, seven thousand silver talents' worth in all, that wound in procession from the Navalia all the way to the state treasury in the Temple of Saturn. With this one contribution, Cato transformed the finances of the nation – it was enough to provide free grain to the citizenry for five years – and the Senate went into immediate session to vote him an honorary praetorship, together with the right to wear a special purple-bordered toga.

Called upon by Marcellinus to respond, Cato scornfully denounced what he called 'these corrupt baubles': 'I have discharged the duty placed upon me by the Roman people – an assignment I never requested and would have preferred not to have undertaken. Now that it is done, I need no Eastern flattery or showy garments to puff myself up: the knowledge that I have performed my duty is reward enough for me, as it should be for any man.'

He was back in the chamber for the next day's debate on the provinces, as if he had never been away – sitting in his customary position, going through a set of the treasury's accounts as he always did to make sure there was no waste in public expenditure. Only when Cicero rose to speak did he put them aside.

It was quite late on in the session and most ex-consuls had already given their opinions. Even so, Cicero managed to spin out the suspense a little longer by devoting the first part of his speech to an attack on his old enemies Piso and Gabinius, governors of Macedonia and Syria respectively. Then the consul, Marcius Philippus, who was married to Caesar's niece, and who was growing restless like many others, interrupted him to ask why he spent all his time attacking those two puppets when the man who had really instigated the campaign that led to his exile was Caesar. This gave Cicero precisely the opening he wanted. 'Because,' he said, 'I am taking account of the public welfare rather than my own grievances. It is this old and unfailing loyalty of mine to the republic which restores, reconciles and reinstates me in friendship with Gaius Caesar.

'For me,' he went on, having to shout now to be heard above the jeers, 'it is impossible not to be the friend of one who renders good service to the state. Under Caesar's command we have fought a war in Gaul, whereas before we merely repelled attacks. Unlike his predecessors he believes the whole of Gaul should be brought under our rule. And so he has, with brilliant success, crushed in battle the fiercest and greatest tribes of Germania and Helvetia; the rest he has terrified, checked and subdued and taught to submit to the rule of the Roman people.

'But the war is not yet won. If Caesar is removed, the embers may yet burst out again into flame. Therefore, as a senator – even as the man's personal enemy, if you like – I must lay aside private grievances for the sake of the state, for how can I be the enemy of this man, whose dispatches, whose fame, whose envoys fill our ears every day with fresh names of races, peoples and places?'

It was not his most convincing performance, and towards the end he rather tripped himself up by trying to pretend that he and Caesar had never really been enemies at all, a piece of sophistry that was greeted with derision. Still, he got through it. The motion to replace Caesar was defeated and at the end of the session, even though the most passionate anti-Caesareans – men like Ahenobarbus and Bibulus – pointedly turned their backs on him in contempt, Cicero walked towards the exit with his head unbowed. That was when Cato intercepted him. I was waiting by the door and was able to overhear their whole exchange.

Cato: 'I am beyond disappointed in you, Marcus Tullius. Your desertion has just cost us what may have been our last chance to stop a dictator.'

Cicero: 'Why should I want to stop a man who is winning victory after victory?'

Cato: 'But who is he winning these victories for? Is it for the republic or is it for himself? And when did it become national policy to conquer Gaul in any case? Has the Senate or the people ever authorised this war of his?'

Cicero: 'Then why don't you put down a motion to end it?'

Cato: 'Perhaps I shall.'

Cicero: 'Yes – and see how far it gets you! Welcome home, incidentally.'

But Cato was in no mood for such pleasantries and stamped off to talk to Bibulus and Ahenobarbus. From this time on it was he who led the opposition to Caesar, while Cicero retreated to his house on the Palatine, and to a quieter life.

There was nothing heroic in what Cicero had done. He realised his loss of face. *Good night to principle, sincerity and honour!* was how he summed it up in a letter to Atticus.

Yet even after all these years, and even with the wisdom of hindsight, I do not see what else he could have done. It was easier for Cato to spit defiance at Caesar. He was from a rich and powerful family, and he did not have the constant threat of Clodius hanging over him.

Everything now proceeded exactly as the Three had planned, and Cicero could not have stopped it even if he had sacrificed his life. First, Clodius and his ruffians disrupted the canvassing for the consular elections so that the campaign came to a stop. Then they threatened and intimidated the other candidates until they withdrew. Finally the elections had to be postponed. Only Ahenobarbus, with the support of Cato, had the courage to continue to stand for the consulship against Pompey and Crassus. Most of the Senate put on mourning in protest.

That winter, for the first time, the city was filled with Caesar's veterans – drinking, whoring and threatening any who refused to salute the effigy of their leader when they set it up at crossroads. On the eve of the postponed poll, Cato and Ahenobarbus went down by torchlight to the voting pens to try to stake out their canvassing position. But they were attacked en route, either by Clodius's men or Caesar's and their torch-bearer was killed. Cato was stabbed in his right arm, and although he entreated Ahenobarbus to stand firm, the candidate fled back to his house and barricaded the door and refused to come out. The next day Pompey and Crassus were elected consuls, and soon after that, as agreed at Luca, they made sure they were allotted the provinces they desired to govern at the end of their joint term of office: Spain for Pompey, Syria for Crassus, both commands awarded for five years instead of the normal one, with a further five-year extension for Caesar as proconsul in Gaul. Pompey never even left Rome, but governed Spain through his subordinates.

Throughout all this, Cicero kept clear of politics. On the days when he had no engagements in the law courts, he stayed at home and supervised the schooling of his son and nephew in grammar, Greek and rhetoric. He dined quietly most evenings with Terentia. He composed poetry. He began to write a book on the history and practice of oratory.

'I am still an exile,' he remarked to me, 'only now my exile is in Rome.'

Caesar quickly heard reports of Cicero's about-face in the Senate and immediately sent him a letter of thanks. I recall Cicero's surprise when it arrived, delivered by one of Caesar's superbly swift and reliable military couriers. As I have explained, nearly all their correspondence has since been seized. But I remember the opening, because it was always the same:

From: G. Caesar, Imperator, to M. Cicero, greetings.
I and the army are well ...

And this particular letter had one other passage I have never forgotten: *It pleases me to know I have a place in your heart. There is not a man in Rome whose opinion I prize more than yours. You may rely on me in all things.* Cicero was torn between feelings of gratitude and shame, relief and despair. He showed the letter to his brother Quintus, who had just returned from Sardinia.

Quintus said, 'You have done the right thing. Pompey has proved a fickle friend. Caesar may be more loyal.' And then he added, 'To be honest, Pompey treated me with such contempt while I was away that I wondered if I might not do better to throw in my own lot with Caesar.'

'And how would you do that?'

'Well, I am a soldier, am I not? Perhaps I could ask for a position on his staff. Or perhaps you could ask for a commission on my behalf.'

At first Cicero was uncertain: he had no desire to beg for favours from Caesar. But then he saw how unhappy Quintus was to be back in Rome. There was his miserable marriage to Pomponia, of course, but it was more than that. He was not an advocate or orator like his elder brother. Neither the law courts nor the Senate held much appeal. He had already served as praetor and as a governor in Asia. The sole remaining step for him in politics was a consulship, and he would never gain that unless he enjoyed some spectacular stroke of good fortune or patronage. And then again, the only sphere in which such a transformation might come his way was on the battlefield ...

The possibility seemed remote, but by such reasoning the brothers convinced themselves that they should further tie their fortunes to those of Caesar. Cicero wrote to him requesting a commission for Quintus, and Caesar replied at once that he would be delighted to oblige. Not only that: he asked Cicero in return if he would help supervise the great rebuilding programme he was planning in Rome to rival Pompey's. Some hundred million sesterces was to be spent on laying out a new forum in the centre of the city and creating a covered walkway a mile long on the Field of Mars. As recompense for his efforts Caesar gave Cicero a loan of eight hundred thousand sesterces at two and a quarter per cent interest, half the market rate.

That was how he was. He was like a whirlpool. He sucked men in by the sheer force of his energy and power until almost the whole of Rome was mesmerised by him. Whenever his *Commentaries* were posted up outside the Regia, crowds would gather and remain there all day reading of his exploits. That year his young protégé Decimus defeated the Celts in a great naval battle in the Atlantic, after which Caesar caused their entire nation to be sold into slavery and their leaders executed. Brittany was conquered, the Pyrenees pacified, Flanders suppressed. Every community in Gaul was required to pay a levy, even after he had sacked their towns and carted off all their ancient treasures. A vast but peaceful German migration of 430,000 members of the Usipetes and Tencteri tribes crossed the Rhine and was lulled by Caesar into a false sense of security when he pretended to agree a truce; then he annihilated them. His engineers erected a bridge across the Rhine and he and his legion rampaged about through Germany for eighteen days before withdrawing back into Gaul and dismantling the bridge behind them. Finally, as if this were not enough, he put to sea with two legions and landed on the barbarian shores of Britain – a place that many in Rome had refused to believe even existed, and which certainly lay beyond the limits of the known world – burned a few villages, captured some slaves, and then sailed home before the winter storms trapped him.

To celebrate his victories Pompey summoned a meeting of the Senate to vote his father-in-law a further twenty days of public supplication, whereupon a scene ensued that I have never forgotten. One after another the senators rose to praise Caesar, Cicero dutifully among them, until at last there was no one left for Pompey to call except Cato.

'Gentlemen,' said Cato, 'yet again you have all taken leave of your senses. By Caesar's own account he has slaughtered four hundred thousand men, women and children – people with whom we had no quarrel, with whom we were not at war, in a campaign not authorised by a vote either of this Senate or of the Roman people. I wish to lay two counter-proposals for you to consider: first, that far from holding celebrations, we should sacrifice to the gods that they do not turn their wrath for Caesar's folly and madness upon Rome and the army; and second, that Caesar, having shown himself a war criminal, should be handed over to the tribes of Germany for them to determine his fate.'

The shouts of rage that greeted this speech were like howls of pain: 'Traitor!' 'Gaul-lover!' 'German!' Several senators jumped up and started shoving Cato this way and that, causing him to stumble backwards. But he was a strong and wiry man. He regained his balance and stood his ground, glaring at them like an eagle. A motion was proposed that he be taken directly by the lictors to the Carcer and imprisoned until such time as he apologised. Pompey, however, was too shrewd to permit his martyrdom. 'Cato by his words has done himself more harm than any punishment we can inflict,' he declared. 'Let him go free. It does not matter. He will stand forever condemned in the eyes of the Roman people for such treacherous sentiments.'

I too felt that Cato had done himself great damage among all moderate and sensible opinion; I remarked as much to Cicero as we walked home. Given his new-found closeness to Caesar, I expected him to agree. But to my surprise he shook his head. 'No, you are quite wrong. Cato is a prophet. He blurts out the truth with the clarity of a child or a madman. Rome will rue the day it tied its destiny to Caesar's. And so shall I.'

I make no claim to be a philosopher, but this much I have observed: that whenever a thing seems at its zenith, you may be sure its destruction has already started.

So it was with the triumvirate. It towered above the landscape of politics like some granite monolith. Yet it had weaknesses that none could see and which were only to be revealed with time. Of these the most dangerous was the inordinate ambition of Crassus.

For years he had been feted as the richest man in Rome, with a fortune of some eight thousand talents, or nearly two hundred million sesterces. But latterly this had come to seem almost paltry compared to the wealth of Pompey and Caesar, who each had the resources of entire countries at their disposal. Therefore Crassus had set his heart on going out to Syria not to administer it but to use it as a base from which to mount a military expedition against the Parthian empire. Those who knew anything of the treacherous sands and cruel peoples of Arabia thought the plan was hugely risky – not least, I am sure, Pompey. But such was his detestation of Crassus that he did nothing to dissuade him. As for Caesar, he too encouraged him. He sent Crassus's son Publius – whom I had met in Mutina – back to Rome from Gaul with a detachment of one thousand highly trained cavalry so that he could join his father as deputy commander-in-chief.

Cicero despised Crassus more than he did any other man in Rome. Even for Clodius he could occasionally summon a certain reluctant respect. But Crassus he considered cynical, grasping and duplicitous, all traits that he covered over with a slippery and false bonhomie. The two had a furious argument in the Senate around this time, when Cicero denounced the retiring governor of Syria, Gabinius – his old enemy – for finally succumbing to Ptolemy's bribe and restoring the Pharaoh to the Egyptian throne. Crassus defended the man he was about to replace. Cicero accused Crassus of putting his personal interests above those of the republic. Crassus jeered that Cicero was an exile. 'Sooner an honourable exile,' retorted Cicero, 'than a pampered thief.' Crassus stalked over to him and thrust out his chest, and the two ageing statesmen had to be physically prevented from exchanging blows.

Pompey took Cicero aside and told him he would not tolerate such abuse of his consular colleague. Caesar wrote a stern letter from Gaul that he regarded any attack on Crassus as an insult to himself. What worried them, I believe, was that Crassus's expedition was proving so unpopular with the people, it was beginning to undermine the authority of the Three. Cato and his followers denounced it as illegal and immoral to make war on a country with which the republic had treaties of friendship; they produced auguries to show it was offensive to the gods and would bring ruin down on Rome.

Crassus was sufficiently concerned to seek a public reconciliation with Cicero. He approached him via Furius Crassipes, his friend who was also Cicero's son-in-law. Crassipes offered to host a dinner for them both on the eve of Crassus's departure. To have refused the invitation would have shown disrespect to Pompey and Caesar; Cicero had to go. 'But I want you to be on hand as a witness,' he said to me. 'This villain will put words in my mouth and invent endorsements I never gave.'

Naturally I was not present for the meal itself. Still, I remember some parts of the evening very clearly. Crassipes had a fine suburban house set in the middle of a park about a mile south of the city, on the banks of the Tiber. Cicero and Terentia were the first to arrive so that they could spend some time with Tullia, who had recently miscarried. She looked pale, poor child, and thin, and I noticed how coldly her husband treated her, criticising her for such domestic oversights as the wilting flower arrangements and the poor quality of the canapés. Crassus turned up an hour later in a veritable convoy of carriages that clattered to a halt in the courtyard. With him was his wife Tertulla – an elderly sour-faced lady, almost as bald as he was – together with their son Publius and Publius's new bride Cornelia, a very gracious seventeen-year-old, the daughter of Scipio Nasica and considered to be the most eligible heiress in Rome.

Crassus also trailed a retinue of adjutants and secretaries who seemed to have no function except to hurry back and forth with messages and documents, conveying a general impression of importance. When the principals went in to dinner and the coast was clear, they lolled about on Crassipes's furniture and drank his wine, and I was struck by the contrast between these unmilitary amateurs and Caesar's efficient, battle-hardened staff.

After the meal, the men went into the tablinum to discuss military strategy – or rather Crassus held forth and the others listened. He was very deaf by this time – he was sixty – and talked too loudly. Publius was embarrassed – 'It's all right, Father, there's no need to shout, we're not in the other room' – and once or twice he glanced at Cicero and raised his eyebrows in silent apology. Crassus announced that he would head east through Macedonia, then Thrace, the Hellespont, Galatia, and the northern part of Syria, traverse the desert of Mesopotamia, cross the Euphrates and thrust deep into Parthia.

Cicero said, 'They must be well aware you're coming. Aren't you worried you will lack the element of surprise?'

Crassus scoffed, 'I have no need of the element of surprise. I prefer the element of certainty. Let them tremble as we approach.'

He had his eye on various rich pickings along the way – he cited the temples of the goddess Derceto at Hierapolis and of Jehovah at Jerusalem, the jewelled effigy of Apollo at Tigraocerta, the golden Zeus of Nicephorium and the treasure houses of Seleucia. Cicero joked that it sounded less a military campaign than a shopping expedition, but Crassus was too deaf to hear.

At the end of the evening the two old enemies shook hands warmly and expressed profound satisfaction that any slight misunderstandings that might have arisen between them had been put to rest at last. 'These are mere figments of the imagination,' declared Cicero, with a twirl of his fingers. 'Let them be utterly eradicated from our memories. Between two such men as you and I, whose lot has fallen on the same political ground, I would hope that alliance and friendship will continue to the credit of both. In all matters affecting you during your absence, my devoted and indefatigable service and any influence I command are absolutely and unreservedly at your disposal.'

'What an utter villain that fellow is,' said Cicero as we settled into the carriage to drive home.

A day or so later – and a full two months before the expiry of his term as consul, so eager was he to be off – Crassus left Rome wearing the red cloak and full uniform of a general on active service. Pompey, his fellow consul, came out of the Senate house to see him off. The tribune Ateius Capito attempted to arrest him in the Forum for his illegal war-making, and when he was knocked aside by Crassus's lieutenants he ran ahead to the city gate and set up a brazier. As Crassus passed by he threw incense and libations on to the flames and called down curses on him and upon his expedition, mingling his incantations with the names of strange and terrible deities. The superstitious people of Rome were appalled and cried out to Crassus not to go. But he laughed at them, and with a final jaunty wave turned his back on the city and spurred his horse.

Such was Cicero's life at this period, walking on tiptoe between the three great men in the state, endeavouring to keep on good terms with all of them, doing their bidding, privately despairing of the future of the republic, but waiting and hoping for better times.

He sought refuge in his books, especially philosophy and history, and one day, soon after Quintus had gone off to join Caesar in Gaul, he announced to me that he had decided to produce a work of his own. It was too dangerous, he said, to write an open attack on the current state of politics in Rome. But he could approach it in a different way, by updating Plato's *Republic* and setting out what an ideal state might look like: 'Who could object to that?' The answer, I thought, was a large number of people, but I kept my opinion to myself.

I look back on the writing of that work, which took us in the end almost three years, as one of the most satisfying periods of my life. Like most literary compositions, it entailed much heartbreak and many false starts. Originally he planned to write it in nine rolls, but then reduced that to six. He decided to cast it in the form of an imagined conversation between a group of historical characters – chief among them one of his heroes, Scipio Aemilianus, the conqueror of Carthage – who gather in a villa on a religious holiday to discuss the nature of politics and how societies should be organised. He reasoned that no one would mind if dangerous notions were placed in the mouths of the legendary figures of Roman history.

He started dictating it in his new villa in Cumae during the senatorial recess. He consulted all the ancient texts, and on one particularly memorable day we rode over to the villa of Faustus Cornelius Sulla, the son of the former dictator, who lived a little way along the coast. Cicero's ally Milo, who was rising in politics, had just married Sulla's twin sister Fausta, and at the wedding breakfast, which Cicero attended, Sulla had invited him to use his library whenever he liked. It was one of the most valuable collections in Italy. The volumes had been carted back by Sulla the Dictator from Athens almost thirty years earlier, and amazingly included most of the original manuscripts of Aristotle, written in his own hand three centuries earlier. I shall never forget as long as I live the sensation of unrolling each of the eight books of Aristotle's *Politics*: tiny cylinders of minute Greek characters, the edges slightly damaged by damp from the caves in Asia Minor where they had been hidden for many years. It was like reaching back through time and touching the face of a god.

But I am wandering too far from my subject. The essential point was that Cicero for the first time laid out his political credo in black and white, and I can summarise it in a sentence: that politics is the most noble of all callings ('there is really no other occupation in which human virtue approaches more closely the august function of the gods'); that there is 'no nobler motive for entering public life than the resolution not to be ruled by wicked men'; that no individual, or combination of individuals, should be allowed to become too powerful; that politics is a profession, not a pastime for dilettantes (nothing is worse than rule by 'clever poets'); that a statesman should devote his life to studying 'the science of politics, in order to acquire in advance all the knowledge that it may be necessary for him to use at some future time'; that authority in a state must always be divided; and that of the three known forms of government – monarchy, aristocracy and people – the best is a mixture of all three, for each one taken on its own can lead to disaster: kings can be capricious, aristocrats self-interested, and 'an unbridled multitude enjoying unwonted power more terrifying than a conflagration or a raging sea'.

Often today I reread *On the Republic*, and always I am moved, especially by the passage at the end of book six, when Scipio describes how his grandfather appears to him in a dream and takes him up into the heavens to show him the smallness of the earth in comparison to the grandeur of the Milky Way, where the spirits of dead statesmen dwell as stars. The description was inspired by the vast, clear night skies above the Bay of Naples:

> *I gazed in every direction and all appeared wonderfully beautiful. There were stars which we never see from earth, and they were all larger than we have ever imagined. The starry spheres were much greater than the earth; indeed the earth itself seemed to me so small that I was scornful of our empire, which covers only a single point, as it were, upon its surface.*

'If only you will look on high,' the old man tells Scipio, 'and contemplate this eternal home and resting place, you will no longer bother with the gossip of the common herd or put your trust in human reward for your exploits. Nor will any man's reputation endure very long, for what men say dies with them and is blotted out with the forgetfulness of posterity.'

Composing such passages was Cicero's chief comfort in the lonely days of his wilderness years. But the prospect that he might ever again have the chance to put his principles into effect seemed remote indeed.

Three months after Cicero began writing *On the Republic*, in the summer of Rome's seven hundredth year, Pompey's wife Julia gave birth to a baby boy. The moment he was brought the news at his morning levee, Cicero hastened round to see the happy couple bearing a gift, for the son of Pompey and the grandson of Caesar would be a mighty presence in the years to come, and he wanted to be among the first with his congratulations.

It was not long after dawn yet already hot. In the valley beneath Pompey's house loomed his newly opened theatre, with its temples and gardens and porticoes, its fresh white marble dazzling in the sun. Cicero had attended its dedication ceremony just a few months earlier – a spectacle that had included fights involving five hundred lions, four hundred panthers, eighteen elephants and the first rhinoceros ever seen in Rome. He had found it all revolting, especially the slaughter of the elephants: *What pleasure can a cultivated man get out of seeing a weak human being torn to pieces by a powerful animal or a noble creature transfixed by a hunting spear?* But naturally he had kept his feelings to himself.

From the moment we entered the immense house it was clear something terrible had occurred. Senators and clients of Pompey stood in worried, silent groups. Someone whispered to Cicero that no announcement had been made, but Pompey's failure to appear, and an earlier glimpse of several of Julia's maids fleeing, weeping, across an inner courtyard, suggested the worst. Suddenly from the interior there was a flutter of activity, a curtain parted and Pompey emerged in the midst of a retinue of slaves. He stopped, as if shocked by the number of people waiting for him, and searched for a familiar face. His eye fell on Cicero. He raised his hand and walked towards him. Everyone watched. At first he seemed entirely calm and clear-eyed. But then as he reached his old ally the effort at self-control abruptly became too much. His whole body and face seemed to sag and with a terrible choking sob he cried out, 'She's dead!'

A great groan went round the vast room – of genuine shock and grief, I have no doubt, but also of alarm, for these were politicians and this was a much bigger thing than the death of one young woman, tragic though it was. Cicero, in tears himself, put his arms round Pompey and tried to comfort him, and after a few moments Pompey asked him to come and see the body. Knowing how squeamish Cicero was about death, I thought he might try to refuse. But that would have been impossible. He was not being invited purely as a friend. He was to be an official witness on behalf of the Senate in what was a matter of state. He went off holding Pompey's hand, and when he returned shortly afterwards, the others gathered round.

'She started bleeding again soon after the birth,' reported Cicero, 'and the flow could not be stopped. The end was peaceful and she was brave, as befits her lineage.'

'And the child?'

'He will not last the day.'

More groans greeted this announcement and then everyone left to spread the news across the city. Cicero said to me, 'The poor girl was whiter than the sheet in which they'd wound her. And the boy was blind and limp. I am truly sorry for Caesar. She was his only child. It's as if Cato's prophecies of the gods' rage are starting to come true.'

We went back to the house and Cicero wrote Caesar a letter of consolation. As ill luck would have it, Caesar was in the most inaccessible place it was possible for him to be, having crossed over to Britain again, this time with an invasion force of twenty-seven thousand men, including Quintus. It was not until he returned to Gaul several months later that he found the packets of letters informing him of his daughter's death. He showed by all accounts not a tremor of emotion but retired to his quarters, never spoke of it, and after three days of official mourning went on with his normal duties. It was, I guess, the secret of his achievements that he was quite indifferent to the death of anyone – enemy or friend, his only child or even ultimately himself – a coldness of nature that he concealed beneath his famous layers of charm.

Pompey was at the opposite end of the human spectrum. All his depths were on the surface. He loved his various wives with great (some said excessive) tenderness, and Julia most of all. At her funeral – which was, despite Cato's objections, a state occasion held in the Forum – he found it hard to deliver the eulogy through his tears, and generally gave every appearance of being broken in spirit. The ashes were afterwards interred in a mausoleum in the precincts of one of his temples on the Field of Mars.

It must have been perhaps two months later that he asked Cicero to come and see him and showed him the letter he had just received from Caesar. After commiserating with him on the loss of Julia, and thanking him for his condolences, Caesar proposed a new marital alliance, but of double the strength: he would give his sister's granddaughter, Octavia, to Pompey, and Pompey in return would give him the hand of his daughter, Pompeia.

'What do you make of this?' demanded Pompey. 'I believe the barbarian air of Britain must have affected his brain! For one thing, my daughter's already betrothed to Faustus Sulla – what am I supposed to tell him? "Very sorry, Sulla, someone more important has just come along"? And then Octavia of course is married – and not to just some nobody, either, but to Caius Marcellus: how's he going to feel about my stealing his wife? Damn it all, Caesar's married himself, come to that, to that poor little drab Calpurnia! All these lives to be turned upside down, and meanwhile dear little Julia's side of our bed is not yet cold! Do you know, I haven't even had the heart to clear out her hairbrushes?'

Cicero for once found himself speaking up for Caesar: 'I'm sure he's only thinking of the stability of the republic.'

But Pompey was not to be pacified. 'Well I shan't do it. If I marry for a fifth time, it will be to a woman of my choice; and as for Caesar, he will have to find himself a different bride.'

Cicero, who loved gossip, could not resist describing Caesar's letter to several friends, swearing each to secrecy. Naturally, after extracting a similar oath, each friend mentioned it to several others, and so it went on until the news of Caesar's proposal was the talk of Rome. Marcellus especially was outraged that his wife was being spoken of by Caesar as if she were his chattel. Caesar was embarrassed when he heard what was being said; he blamed Pompey for revealing his plans. Pompey was unapologetic; he in turn blamed Caesar for the clumsiness of his matchmaking. Another crack had appeared in the monolith.

XLIV

The following year during the Senate recess Cicero set off as usual with his family for Cumae in order to continue work on his political book; and I, as usual, went with him. It was not long before my fiftieth birthday.

For most of my life I had enjoyed good health. But when, to break the journey, we reached the cold mountain heights of Arpinum, I started to shiver, and the next morning I could barely move my limbs. When I tried to continue with the others I fainted and had to be carried to bed. Cicero could not have been kinder. He postponed his departure in the hope I would recover. But my fever worsened and I was told afterwards he spent long hours at my bedside. In the end he had to leave me behind, along with instructions to the household slaves that I should receive exactly the same care they would give to him. From Cumae two days later he wrote to say that he was sending me his Greek doctor, Andricus, and also a cook: *If you care for me, see that you get well and join us when you are thoroughly strong again. Goodbye.*

Andricus purged and bled me. The cook produced delicious meals that I was too ill to eat. Cicero wrote constantly.

> *You cannot imagine how anxious I feel about your health. If you relieve my mind on this score, I shall relieve yours of every worry. I should write more if I thought you could read with any pleasure. Put your clever brain, which I value so highly, to the job of preserving yourself for us both.*

After about a week, the fever eased. By then it was too late to travel to Cumae. Cicero wrote telling me to join him instead at Formiae, on his way back to Rome.

Let me find you there, my dear Tiro, well and strong. My (our) literary brainchildren have been drooping their heads missing you. Atticus is staying with me, enjoying himself in cheerful mood. He wanted to hear my compositions but I told him that in your absence my tongue of authorship is tied completely. You must get ready to restore your services to my Muses. My promise will be performed on the appointed day. Now mind you get thoroughly well. I shall be with you soon. Goodbye.

I shall relieve your mind of every worry ... My promise will be performed on the appointed day ... I read the letters over and over, trying to make sense of those two phrases. I deduced that he must have said something to me when I was delirious, but I had no recollection of what it was.

As arranged, I arrived at the villa in Formiae on the afternoon of my fiftieth birthday, the twenty-eighth day of April. It was cold and blustery, not at all propitious, with rain gusting off the sea. I still felt frail. The effort of hurrying into the house so as not to be soaked left me dizzy. The place appeared deserted and I wondered if I had misunderstood my instructions. I went from room to room, calling out, until I heard a young boy's stifled laughter coming from the triclinium. I pulled back the curtain and discovered the whole dining room crammed full of people trying to stay silent: Cicero, Terentia, Tullia, Marcus, young Quintus Cicero, all the household staff, and (even more bizarrely) the praetor Caius Marcellus with his lictors – that same noble Marcellus whose wife Caesar had tried to bestow on Pompey, and who had a villa nearby. At the sight of my astonished face they all started laughing, then Cicero took me by the hand and led me into the centre of the room while the others made space for us. I felt my knees weaken.

Marcellus said, 'Who wishes this day to free this slave?'

Cicero replied, 'I do.'

'You are the legal owner?'

'I am.'

'Upon what grounds is he to be freed?'

'He has shown great loyalty and given exemplary service to our family ever since he was born into the condition of slavery, and to me in particular, and also to the Roman state. His character is sound and he is worthy of his freedom.'

Marcellus nodded. 'You may proceed.'

The lictor briefly touched his rod of office to my head. Cicero stepped in front of me, grasped my shoulders and recited the simple legal formula: 'This man is to be free.' He had tears in his eyes; so had I. Gently he turned me round until I had my back to him, and then he let me go, as a father might release a child to take its first steps.

It is difficult for me to describe the joy of becoming free. Quintus expressed it best when he wrote to me from Gaul: *I could not be more delighted, my dear Tiro, believe me. Before you were our slave but now you are our friend.* Outwardly, nothing much changed. I continued to live under Cicero's roof and to perform the same duties. But in my heart I was a different man. I exchanged my tunic for a toga – a cumbersome garment that I wore without ease or comfort, but with intense pride. And for the first time I began to make plans of my own. I started to compile a comprehensive dictionary of all the symbols and abbreviations used in my shorthand system, together with instructions on how to use it. I drew up a scheme for a book on Latin grammar. I also went back through my boxes of notes whenever I had a spare hour and copied down particularly amusing or clever quotations thrown out by Cicero over the years. He greatly approved of the idea of a book of his wit and wisdom. Often after a particularly fine remark he would stop and say, 'Note that down, Tiro – that's one for your compendium.' Gradually it became understood between us that if I outlived him, I would write his biography.

I asked him once why he had waited so long to set me free, and why he had decided to do it at that moment. He answered, 'Well, you know I can be a selfish man, and I rely on you entirely. I thought to myself, "If I free him, what's to stop him going off and transferring his allegiance to Caesar or Crassus or someone? They'd certainly pay him plenty for all he knows about me." Then when you fell ill in Arpinum I realised how unjust it would be if you died in servitude, and so I made my pledge to you, even though you were too feverish to understand it. If ever there was a man who deserved the nobility of freedom, it is you, dear Tiro. Besides,' he added with a wink, 'nowadays I have no secrets worth selling.'

Love him though I did, I nevertheless wanted to end my days under my own roof. I had some savings and now was paid a salary; I dreamed of buying a smallholding near Cumae where I could keep a few goats and chickens and grow my own vines and olives. But I feared loneliness. I suppose I could have gone down to the slave market and bought myself a companion, but the idea repulsed me. I knew with whom I wanted to share this dream of a future life: Agathe, the Greek slave girl whom I had met in the household of Lucullus and whose freedom I had asked Atticus to purchase on my behalf before I went into exile with Cicero. Atticus confirmed he had done as I asked and that she had been manumitted. But although I made enquiries as to what had happened to her, and always kept an eye out whenever I walked through Rome, she had vanished into the teeming multitudes of Italy.

I did not have long to enjoy my freedom in tranquillity. My modest plans, like everyone else's, were about to be mocked by the immensity of events. As Plautus has it:

Whatever the mind may hope for
The future is in the hands of the gods.

A few weeks after my liberation, in the month that was then named Quintilis but that we are now required to call July, I was hurrying along the Via Sacra, trying not to trip over my new toga, when I saw a crowd gathered ahead. They were deathly still – not at all animated as they usually were when news of one of Caesar's victories was posted on the white board. I thought immediately that he must have suffered a terrible defeat. I joined the back of the throng and asked the man in front of me what was happening. Irritated, he glanced over his shoulder and muttered in a distracted voice, 'Crassus has been killed.'

I stayed just long enough to pick up the few details that were available. Then I hastened back to tell Cicero. He was working in his study. I gasped out the news and he quickly stood up, as if such grave information should not be acknowledged sitting down.

'How did it happen?'

'In battle, it's reported – in the desert, near a town in Mesopotamia named Carrhae.'

'And his army?'

'Defeated – wiped out.'

Cicero stared at me for a few moments. Then he shouted to one slave to bring his shoes and another to arrange a litter. I asked him where he was going. 'To see Pompey, of course – come too.'

It was a sign of Pompey's pre-eminence that whenever there was a major crisis in the state, it was to his house that people always flocked – be it the ordinary citizens, who that day crowded the surrounding streets in silent, watchful multitudes; or the senior senators, who even now were arriving in their litters and being ushered by Pompey's attendants into his inner sanctum. As luck would have it, both the elected consuls, Calvinus and Messalla, were under indictment for bribery and had been unable to take up office. Present instead was the informal leadership of the Senate, including senior ex-consuls such as Cotta, Hortensius and the elder Curio, and prominent younger men like Ahenobarbus, Scipio Nasica and M. Aemilius Lepidus. Pompey took command of the meeting. No one knew the eastern empire better than he: after all, much of it he had conquered. He announced that a dispatch had just been received from Crassus's legate, G. Cassius Longinus, who had managed to escape from enemy territory and get back into Syria, and that if everyone was in agreement he would now read it out.

Cassius was a cold, austere man – 'pale and thin', as Caesar later complained – not given to boastfulness or lying, so his words were heard with all the greater respect. According to him, the Parthian king, Orodes II, had sent an envoy to Crassus on the eve of the invasion to say that he was willing to take pity on him as an old man and allow him to return in peace to Rome. But Crassus had boastfully replied that he would give his answer in the Parthian capital, Seleucia, at which the envoy had burst out laughing and pointed to the palm of his upturned hand, saying, 'Hair will grow here, Crassus, before you set eyes on Seleucia!'

The Roman force of seven legions, plus eight thousand cavalry and archers, had bridged the Euphrates at Zeugma in a thunderstorm – itself a bad omen – and at one point during the traditional offerings to placate the gods, Crassus had dropped the entrails of the sacrificial animal into the sand. Although he had tried to make a joke of it – 'That's what comes of being an old man, lads, but I can grip my sword tightly enough!' – the soldiers groaned, remembering the curses that had accompanied their departure from Rome. *Already*, wrote Cassius, *they sensed that they were doomed.*

From the Euphrates [he continued] we advanced ever deeper into the desert, with insufficient supplies of water and no clear sense of a route or objective. The land is trackless, flat, with no living tree to offer shade. After wading for fifty miles with full packs through soft sand in desert storms during which hundreds of our men succumbed to thirst and heat, we reached a river called the Balissus. Here for the first time our scouts sighted elements of the enemy's forces on the opposite bank. On the orders of M. Crassus we crossed the river at noon and set off in pursuit. But by now the enemy had entirely disappeared again. We marched for several more hours until we were in the midst of a wilderness. Suddenly from all around us we heard the beating of kettle drums. At that moment, as if springing out of the sand, arose in every direction an immense horde of mounted archers. The silken banners of the Parthian commander, Sillaces, were visible behind.

Against the advice of more experienced officers, M. Crassus ordered the army to be drawn up in a single large square, twelve cohorts across. Our archers were then sent forward to engage the enemy. However, they were soon obliged to retreat in the face of the Parthians' vastly superior forces and speed of manoeuvre. Their arrows spread much slaughter through our packed ranks. Nor did death come easily or quickly. In the convulsion and agony of their pain, our men would writhe as the arrows struck them; they would snap them off in their wounds and then lacerate their flesh by trying to tear out the barbed arrowheads that had pierced through their veins and muscles. Many died in this way, and even the survivors were in no state to fight. Their hands were pinioned to their shields and their feet nailed through to the ground so that they were incapable of either running away or defending themselves. Any hopes that this murderous rain would exhaust itself were dashed by the sight of fresh supplies of arrows appearing on the battlefield on heavily laden camel trains.

Apprehending the danger that the army would soon be entirely wiped out, P. Crassus applied to his father for permission to take his cavalry, together with some infantry and archers, and pierce the encircling line. M. Crassus endorsed the plan. This breakout force of some six thousand men moved forwards and the Parthians quickly withdrew. But although Publius had been expressly ordered not to pursue the enemy, he disobeyed these instructions. His men advanced out of sight of the main army, whereupon the Parthians reappeared behind them. Rapidly surrounded, Publius withdrew his men to a narrow ridge, where they presented an easy target. Once again the enemy's archers did their murderous work. Perceiving the situation to be hopeless and fearing capture, Publius bade his men farewell and told them to look after their own safety. Then, since he was unable to use his hand, which had been pierced through with an arrow, he presented his side to his shieldbearer and ordered him to run him through with his sword. Most of his officers followed his example and put themselves to death.

Once they had overrun the Roman position, the Parthians cut off the head of Publius and mounted it on a spear. They then carried it back to the main Roman army and rode up and down our lines, taunting M. Crassus to come and look upon his son. Seeing what had happened, he addressed our men as follows: 'Romans, this grief is a private thing of my own. But in you, who are safe and sound, abide the great fortune and the glory of Rome. And now, if you feel any pity for me, who have lost the best son that any father has ever had, show it in the fury with which you face the enemy.'

Regrettably, they paid no heed. On the contrary, this sight more than all the other dreadful things that had happened broke the spirit and paralysed the energies of our forces. The airborne slaughter resumed, and it is a certainty that the entire army would have been annihilated had not night fallen and the Parthians withdrawn, shouting that they would give Crassus the night to grieve for his son and would return to finish us off in the morning.

This provided us with an opportunity. M. Crassus being prostrate with grief and despair, and no longer capable of issuing orders, I took over the direction of our forces, and in silence and under cover of darkness those who could walk made a forced march to the town of Carrhae, leaving behind, amidst the most piteous cries and pleadings, some four thousand wounded who were either massacred or enslaved by the Parthians the following day.

At Carrhae our forces divided. I led five hundred men in the direction of Syria while M. Crassus took the bulk of our surviving army towards the mountains of Armenia. Intelligence reports indicate that outside the fortress of Sinnaca he was confronted by an army led by a subordinate of the Parthian king, who offered a truce. M. Crassus was compelled by his mutinous legionaries to go forward and negotiate, even though he believed it to be a trap. As he went, he turned and spoke these words: 'I call upon all you Roman officers present to see that I am being forced to go this way. You are eyewitnesses of the shameful and violent treatment that I have received. But if you escape and get home safely, tell them all that Crassus died because he was deceived by the enemy, not because he was handed over to the Parthians by his own countrymen.'

These are his last known words. He was killed along with his legionary commanders. I am informed that afterwards his severed head was delivered personally to the king of the Parthians by Sillaces during a performance of The Bacchae *and that it was used as a prop on stage. Afterwards the king caused Crassus's mouth to be filled with molten gold, remarking: 'Gorge yourself now with that metal for which in life you were so greedy.'*

I await the Senate's orders.

When Pompey finished reading, there was silence.

Finally Cicero said, 'How many men have we lost, do we have any idea?'

'I estimate thirty thousand.'

There was a groan of dismay from the assembled senators. Someone said that if that were true, then it was the worst defeat since Hannibal had wiped out the Senate's army at Cannae, one hundred and fifty years before.

'This document,' said Pompey, waving Cassius's dispatch, 'must go no further than this room.'

Cicero said, 'I agree. Cassius's frankness is admirable in private, but a less alarming version must be prepared for the people, stressing the bravery of our legionaries and their commanders.'

Scipio, who was Publius's father-in-law, said, 'Yes, they all died heroes – that's what we must tell everyone. That's what I'm going to tell my daughter, certainly. The poor girl is a widow at nineteen.'

Pompey said, 'Please give her my condolences.'

Then Hortensius spoke up. The ex-consul was in his sixties and mostly retired, but still listened to with respect. 'What happens next? Presumably the Parthians won't leave it at that. Knowing our weakness, they'll invade Syria in retaliation. We can barely muster a legion in its defence and we have no governor.'

'I would propose we make Cassius acting governor,' said Pompey. 'He's a hard, unsparing man – exactly what this emergency demands. As for an army – well, he must raise and train a new one locally.'

Ahenobarbus, who never lost an opportunity to undermine Caesar, said, 'All our best fighting men are in Gaul. Caesar has ten legions – a huge number. Why don't we order him to send a couple to Syria to fill the breach?'

At the mention of Caesar's name there was a perceptible stirring of hostility in the room.

'He recruited those legions,' pointed out Pompey. 'I agree they would be more useful in the east. But he regards those men as his own.'

'Well he needs to be reminded they are not his own. They exist to serve the republic, not him.'

Looking round at the senators all nodding vigorously in agreement, Cicero said afterwards that it was only at that moment that he realised the true significance of Crassus's death. 'Because, dear Tiro, what have we learned while writing our *Republic*? Divide power three ways in a state and tension is balanced; divide it in two and sooner or later one side must seek to dominate the other – it is a natural law. Disgraceful as he was, Crassus at least preserved the equilibrium between Pompey and Caesar. But with him gone, who will do it now?'

And so we drifted towards calamity. At times, Cicero was shrewd enough to see it. 'Can a constitution devised centuries ago to replace a monarchy, and based upon a citizens' militia, possibly hope to run an empire whose scope is beyond anything ever dreamed of by its framers? Or must the existence of standing armies and the influx of inconceivable wealth inevitably destroy our democratic system?'

And then at other times he would dismiss such apocalyptic talk as excessively gloomy and argue that the republic had endured all manner of disasters in the past – invasions, revolutions, civil wars – and had always somehow survived them: why should this time be any different?

But it was.

The elections that year were dominated by two men. Clodius sought to be praetor. Milo ran for the consulship. The violence and the bribery of the campaign were beyond anything the city had ever seen, and yet again polling day had to be postponed repeatedly. It was now more than a year since the republic had elected legitimate consuls. The Senate was presided over by an interrex, often a nonentity, on a rolling five-day mandate; the fasces of the consuls were placed symbolically in the Temple of Libitina, goddess of the dead. *Hurry back to Rome,* Cicero wrote to Atticus, who was on another of his business trips. *Come and look at the empty husks of the real old Roman Republic we used to know.*

It was a measure of how desperate things were becoming that Cicero vested all his hopes in Milo, even though Milo was entirely his opposite: crude and brutal, lacking in eloquence or indeed any political skill apart from the staging of gladiatorial games to enthuse the voters, the costs of which had left him bankrupt. Milo had outlived his usefulness to Pompey, who would have nothing more to do with him, and who was supporting his opponents, Scipio Nasica and Plautius Hypsaeus. But Cicero still needed him. *I have firmly concentrated all my efforts, all my time, care, diligence and thought, my whole mind in short, on winning the consulship for Milo.* He saw him as the best bulwark against the eventuality he dreaded most: Clodius's election to the consulship.

Cicero often asked me to perform small services for Milo during that campaign. For example, I went back through our files and prepared lists of our old supporters for him to canvass. I also set up meetings between him and Cicero's clients in the various tribal headquarters. I even took him bags of money that Cicero had raised from wealthy donors.

One day in the new year, Cicero asked me, as a favour, if I would spend a short time observing Milo's campaign at first hand. 'To put the matter bluntly, I'm worried he's going to lose. You know elections as well as I do. Watch him with the voters. See if anything can be done to improve his prospects. If he loses and Clodius wins, I don't need to tell you it will be a disaster for me.'

I cannot pretend that I was delighted with the assignment, but I did as I was asked, and on the eighteenth day of January I turned up at Milo's house, which was on the steepest part of the Palatine, behind the Temple of Saturn. A listless crowd was gathered outside, but of the would-be consul himself there was no sign. I knew then that Milo's candidacy was in trouble. If a man is standing for election and feels himself to have a chance of winning, he works every hour of the day. But Milo did not emerge until the middle of the morning, and when he did, he took me to one side to complain about Pompey, who he said was entertaining Clodius that very morning at his country house in the Alban Hills.

'The man's ingratitude is unbelievable! Do you remember how he used to be so frightened of Clodius and his gang that he daren't even set foot out of doors until I brought in my gladiators to clear the streets? And now he has taken that snake under his roof, yet he won't even bid me good morning!'

I sympathised – we all knew what Pompey was like: a great man, but entirely preoccupied with himself – and then tried tactfully to steer the conversation back to Milo's campaign. There was not long until polling day. Where did he plan to spend these precious final hours?

'Today,' he announced, 'I am going to Lanuvium, my adopted grandfather's ancestral home.'

I could scarcely believe it. 'You're leaving Rome, this close to the actual vote?'

'It's only twenty miles. A new priest is to be nominated for the Temple of Juno the Saviour. She is the municipal deity, which means that the ceremony will be huge – you'll see, hundreds of voters will be there.'

'Even so, surely these voters are already committed to you, given your family connection to the town? Wouldn't your time be better spent pursuing voters who are undecided?'

But Milo refused to discuss it further. Indeed his refusal was so absolute that now, when I look back on it, I wonder if he hadn't already given up hope of winning the election in the voting pens and decided to go looking for trouble instead. After all, Lanuvium is also in the Alban Hills, and the road to it would take us practically past Pompey's gates. He must have calculated there was a good chance we would meet Clodius on the way. It would have been just the sort of opportunity for a fight he relished.

By the time we set out that afternoon he had gathered together a considerable wagon train of luggage and servants, protected by his usual small private army of slaves and gladiators armed with swords and javelins. Milo rode in a carriage at the head of this menacing column together with his wife, Fausta. He invited me to join them but I preferred the discomfort of horseback to sharing a carriage with those two, whose tempestuous relationship was notorious. We clattered off down the Via Appia, arrogantly forcing all the other traffic out of our way – again, I noted, poor electoral tactics – and had been going for about two hours when of course, on the outskirts of Bovillae, we duly encountered Clodius heading in the opposite direction, back to Rome.

Clodius was on horseback with perhaps thirty attendants – less well armed than Milo's, and far less numerous. I was in the middle of our column. As he passed, he caught my eye. He knew me pretty well as Cicero's secretary. He certainly gave me a foul look.

The rest of his party followed him. I averted my gaze. I wanted no trouble. But moments later, from behind me, there was a shout and then the clash of steel hitting steel. I turned and saw that a fight had broken out between our gladiators, who were bringing up the rear, and some of Clodius's men. Clodius himself had already gone a little way further along the road. He drew up his horse and turned, and at that moment Birria, the gladiator who had sometimes acted as a bodyguard to Cicero, hurled a javelin at him. It did not hit him full on, but rather in his side as he was in the act of turning, and the force of it almost knocked him from his saddle. The barbed tip buried itself deep in his flesh. He looked at it in astonishment, and screamed and clutched at the shaft with both hands, his whitened toga turning crimson with blood.

His bodyguards spurred their horses and surrounded him. Our convoy halted. I noticed we were close to a tavern – the same place, by bizarre coincidence, where we had stopped to pick up our horses on the night Cicero fled Rome. Milo jumped out of his carriage with his sword drawn and walked down the side of the road to see what was going on. All along the column men were dismounting. By now Clodius's attendants had pulled the javelin from his ribs and were helping him towards the tavern. He was sufficiently conscious to be able to half walk supported on the arms of his companions. Meanwhile small groups of men were fighting hand-to-hand along the road and in the fields next to it – desperate, hacking struggles, some on horseback, some on foot – such a confused melee that I could not at first distinguish our men from theirs. But gradually I perceived that ours were winning, for we outnumbered them three to one. I saw several of Clodius's men, despairing of victory, fling up their arms in surrender or fall to their knees. Others simply threw aside their weapons, turned and ran, or galloped off. No one bothered to pursue them.

The struggle over, Milo, with his arms akimbo, surveyed the carnage, then gestured to Birria and a few others to go and fetch Clodius from the tavern.

I got down from my horse. I had no idea what would happen next. I walked towards Milo. Just then there was a shout, or rather a scream from the tavern, and Clodius was carried out by four gladiators, each holding an arm or a leg. Milo had a calculation to make: would he let Clodius live and take the consequences, or kill him and have done with it? They laid him on the road at his feet. Milo took a javelin from the man standing next to him, checked the tip with his thumb, placed it in the centre of Clodius's chest, grasped the shaft and plunged it in with all his force. Clodius's mouth fountained blood. After that, they all took turns in slashing at the corpse, but I could not bring myself to watch.

I was no horseman, yet I believe I galloped back to Rome at a speed a cavalryman would have been proud of. I urged my exhausted mount up to the Palatine, and for the second time in half a year I found myself blurting out to Cicero the news that one of his enemies – the greatest of them all – was dead.

He gave no sign of pleasure. He was ice-cold, calculating. He drummed his fingers and then said, 'Where is Milo now?'

'I believe he carried on to Lanuvium for the ceremony as planned.'

'And Clodius's body?'

'The last time I saw it, it was still by the roadside.'

'Milo made no attempt to conceal it?'

'No, he said there was no point – there were too many witnesses.'

'That's probably true – it's a busy spot. Were *you* seen by many people?'

'I don't think so. Clodius recognised me, but not the others.'

He gave a hard smile. 'Clodius at least we no longer have to worry about.' He thought it over and nodded. 'That's good – good that you weren't seen. I think it would be better if we agree you were here with me all afternoon.'

'Why?'

'It wouldn't be wise for me to be implicated in this business, even indirectly.'

'You anticipate this will cause you trouble?'

'Oh, I am quite certain of it. The question is: how much?'

We settled down to wait for word of what had happened to reach Rome. In the fading light of the afternoon I found it difficult to banish from my mind the image of Clodius dying like a stuck pig. I had witnessed death before, but that was the first time I had seen a man killed in front of me.

About an hour before darkness, a woman's piercing shriek arose from some place nearby. It went on and on – a frightening, other-worldly ululation.

Cicero walked over and opened the door to his terrace and listened. 'The Lady Fulvia,' he said judiciously, 'if I am not mistaken, has just learned she is a widow.'

He sent a servant up the hill to find out what was happening. The man came back and reported that Clodius's body had arrived in Rome on a litter belonging to the senator Sextus Tedius, who had discovered it beside the Via Appia. The corpse had been conveyed to Clodius's house and received by Fulvia. In her grief and fury she had stripped it naked, apart from its sandals, propped it up, and was now sitting beside it in the street beneath flaming torches, crying out that everyone should come and see what had been done to her husband.

Cicero said, 'She means to whip up the mob.' He ordered the guard on the house to be doubled overnight. The following morning it was judged far too dangerous for Cicero or any other prominent senator to venture out. We watched from the terrace as a huge crowd led by Fulvia escorted the body on its bier down to the Forum and placed it on the rostra, and then we listened as Clodius's lieutenants worked the plebs up to a fury. At the end of the bitter eulogies the mourners broke into the Senate house and carried Clodius's corpse inside, then went back across the Forum to the Argiletum and started dragging out benches and tables and chests full of volumes from the booksellers' shops. To our horror we realised they were constructing a funeral pyre.

Around midday, smoke began to issue from the small windows set high up in the walls of the Senate chamber. Sheets of orange flame and scraps of burning books whirled against the sky, while from inside came a terrifying and uninterrupted roar, as if a vent had been opened to the underworld. An hour later the roof split from end to end; thousands of tiles and spars of fiery timber plunged soundlessly from view; there was a strange interval of silence; and then the noise of the crash passed over us like a hot wind.

The fountain of smoke and dust and ashes lingered above the centre of Rome in a pall for several days, until the rain washed it away; and in this manner the last mortal vestiges of Publius Clodius Pulcher and the ancient assembly building he had reviled all his life vanished together from the face of the earth.

XLV

The destruction of the Senate house had a powerful effect on Cicero. He went down the next day under heavy guard, grasping a stout stick, and clambered around the smouldering ruins. The blackened brickwork was still warm to the touch. The wind howled through the gaping holes, and from time to time from above our heads some piece of debris would dislodge and fall with a soft thump into the drifts of ash. Six hundred years that temple had stood there – a witness to the greatest moments in Rome's existence, and his own – and now it had gone in less than half an afternoon.

Everyone, including Cicero, assumed that Milo would now go into voluntary exile, or at any rate that he would keep well clear of Rome. But that was to underrate the bravado of the man. Far from lying low, he put himself at the head of an even larger force of gladiators and re-entered the city that same afternoon, barricading himself in his house. The grieving supporters of Clodius immediately laid siege to it. But they were easily driven off by arrows. They then went in search of a less formidable fortress on which to vent their anger, and found one in the home of the interrex, Marcus Aemilius Lepidus.

Although he was only thirty-six, and not yet even praetor, Lepidus was a member of the College of Pontiffs, and in the absence of any elected consuls that was enough to make him temporary chief magistrate. The damage inflicted on his property was slight – his wife's nuptial couch was broken up and her weaving destroyed – but the assault created a sense of outrage and panic in the Senate.

Lepidus, ever conscious of his dignity, played up the incident for all it was worth; indeed, this was the beginning of his rise to prominence. (Cicero used to say that Lepidus was the luckiest politician he knew: every time he made a mess of something he was showered with rewards – 'He is a sort of genius of mediocrity.') The young interrex summoned a meeting of the Senate to be held outside the city walls, on the Field of Mars, in Pompey's new theatre – a large chamber within the complex had to be specially consecrated for the occasion – and he invited Pompey to attend.

This was three days after the burning of the Senate house.

Pompey duly obliged, sweeping down the hill from his palace surrounded by two hundred legionaries in full battle array – an entirely legal display of force, as he held military imperium as governor of Spain. But still – nothing like it had been seen since the days of Sulla. He left them picketed in the portico of the theatre while he went inside and listened modestly as his supporters demanded that he be appointed dictator for six months so that he could take the steps necessary to restore order: call up all the military reservists in Italy, put Rome under curfew, suspend the imminent elections and bring the killers of Clodius to justice.

Cicero saw the danger at once and rose to speak. 'No one has greater respect for Pompey than I,' he began, 'but we must be careful not to do our enemies' work for them. To argue that to preserve our freedoms we must suspend our freedoms, that to safeguard elections we must cancel elections, that to defend ourselves from dictatorship we must appoint a dictator – what logic is this? We have elections scheduled. We have candidates on the ballot. The canvass is completed. The best way for us to show confidence in our institutions is to allow them to function normally and to elect our magistrates as our ancestors taught us in the olden time.'

Pompey nodded, as if he could not have put the issue better himself, and at the end of the session he made an elaborate show of congratulating Cicero on his staunch defence of the constitution. But Cicero was not fooled. He saw exactly what Pompey was up to. That night, Milo came to visit him for a council of war. Also present was Caelius Rufus, now a tribune and a long-term supporter and close friend of Milo. From down in the valley came the sound of scuffling, of dogs barking and occasional shouts and cries. A group of men carrying flaming torches ran across the Forum. But most citizens were too afraid to venture out and stayed in their houses behind barred doors. Milo seemed to think he had the election in the bag. After all, he had rid the state of Clodius, for which most decent people were grateful, and the burning-down of the Senate house and the violence in the streets had appalled the majority of voters.

Cicero said, 'I agree that if there were a ballot tomorrow, Milo, you would probably win it. But there is not going to be a ballot. Pompey will see to that.'

'How can he?'

'He'll use the campaign as a cover to manufacture an atmosphere of hysteria so that the Senate and the people will be forced to turn to him to abort the elections.'

Rufus said, 'He's bluffing. He doesn't have the power.'

'Oh, he has the power, and he knows it. All he has to do is sit tight and wait for things to come to him.'

Milo and Rufus both dismissed Cicero's fears as the nervousness of an old man, and the next day resumed campaigning with fresh energy. But Cicero was right: the mood in Rome was too jittery for normal electioneering and Milo walked straight into Pompey's trap. One morning soon after their meeting Cicero received an urgent summons to see Pompey. He found the great man's house ringed with soldiers and Pompey himself in an elevated part of the garden with double his normal bodyguard. Seated in the portico with him was a man Pompey introduced as Licinius, the owner of an eating house near the Circus Maximus. Pompey ordered Licinius to repeat his tale to Cicero, and Licinius duly described how he had overheard a group of Milo's gladiators plotting at his counter to murder Pompey, and how, when they realised he was listening, they had tried to silence him by stabbing him: as proof he showed Cicero a minor flesh wound just beneath his ribs.

Of course, as Cicero said to me afterwards, the whole story was absurd. 'For a start, whoever heard of such feeble gladiators? If that kind of man wishes to silence you, you are silenced.' But it didn't matter. The eating-house plot, as it became known, joined all the other rumours now circulating about Milo – that he had turned his house into an arsenal filled with swords, shields and javelins; that he had stocks of brands hidden throughout the city in order to burn it down; that he had shipped arms along the Tiber to his villa at Ocriculum; that the assassins who had murdered Clodius would be turned loose on his opponents in the election ...

The next time the Senate met, no less a figure than Marcus Bibulus, Caesar's former consular colleague and passionate lifelong enemy, rose to propose that Pompey should hold office by emergency decree as sole consul. This was remarkable enough; what no one had anticipated was the reaction of Cato. A hush fell over the chamber as he got to his feet. 'I would not have proposed this motion myself,' he said, 'but seeing as it has been laid before us, I propose we accept it as a sensible compromise. Some government is better than no government; a sole consulship is better than a dictatorship; and Pompey is more likely to rule wisely than anyone else.'

Coming from Cato, this was almost unbelievable – he had used the word 'compromise' for the first time in his life – and no one looked more stunned than Pompey. Afterwards, so the story went, he invited Cato back to his house to thank him personally and to ask him in future to be his private adviser in all matters of state. 'You have no need to thank me,' replied Cato, 'for I only did what I believed to be in the best interests of the republic. If you wish to talk to me alone I shall certainly be at your disposal. But I shall say nothing to you in private that I wouldn't say anywhere else, and I shall never hold my tongue in public to please you.'

Cicero observed their new closeness with deep foreboding. 'Why do you think men like Cato and Bibulus have suddenly thrown in their lot with Pompey? Do you imagine they believe all this nonsense about a plot to murder him? Do you think they've suddenly changed their minds about him? Not at all! They've given him sole authority because they see him as their best hope of checking the ambitions of Caesar. I'm sure Pompey recognises this and believes he can control them. But he's wrong. Don't forget I know him. His vanity is his weakness. They will flatter him and load him down with powers and honours, and he won't even notice what they're doing, until one day it will be too late – they will have set him on a collision course with Caesar. And then we shall have war.'

Cicero went straight from the Senate meeting to find Milo, and told him in blunt terms that he must now abandon his campaign for the consulship. 'If you send a message to Pompey before nightfall and announce that you are withdrawing your candidacy in the interests of national unity, you might just head off a prosecution. If you don't, you're finished.'

'And if I *am* prosecuted,' responded Milo slyly, 'will you defend me?'

I had expected Cicero to say it was impossible. Instead he sighed and ran his hand through his hair. 'Listen to me, Milo – listen carefully. When I was at the lowest point of my life, six years ago in Thessalonica, you were the only one who offered me hope. Therefore you can rest assured, whatever happens I shan't turn my back on you now. But for pity's sake, don't let it come to that. Write to Pompey today.'

Milo promised to think about it, although naturally he did not withdraw. The vaulting ambition that had carried him, in a mere half-dozen years, from ownership of a gladiator school to the brink of the consulship, was hardly likely at this late stage to be bridled by caution and good sense. Besides, his campaign debts were so enormous (some said the amount he owed was seventy million sesterces) that he was facing exile whatever he did; he gained nothing by giving up now. So he continued with his canvass and Pompey moved ruthlessly to destroy him by setting up an inquiry into the events of the eighteenth and nineteenth of January – including the murder of Clodius, the burning of the Senate house and the attack on the home of Lepidus – under the chairmanship of Domitius Ahenobarbus. The slaves of Milo and Clodius were put to the torture to ascertain the facts, and I feared that some poor wretch, in his desperation, might remember my presence at the scene, which would have been embarrassing to Cicero. But I seem to have been blessed with the sort of personality that nobody notices – the reason perhaps why I have survived to write this account – and nobody mentioned me.

The inquiry led to Milo's trial for murder at the beginning of April and Cicero was required to honour his pledge to defend him. It was the only time I ever saw him prostrated by nerves. Pompey had filled the centre of the city with soldiers to guarantee order. But the effect was the opposite of reassuring. They blockaded every approach to the Forum and guarded the main public buildings. All the shops were closed. An atmosphere of tension and dread lay over the city. Pompey himself came to watch proceedings and took a seat high up on the steps of the Temple of Saturn, surrounded by troops. Yet despite the show of force, the vast pro-Clodian crowd was allowed to intimidate the court. They jeered both Milo and Cicero whenever they tried to speak and made it difficult for the defence to be heard. All outrage and emotion was on their side – the brutality of the crime, the spectacle of the weeping widow and her fatherless children, and above all perhaps that curious retrospective sanctity that settles over the reputation of any politician, however worthless, if his career is cut off in its prime.

As chief defence advocate, allowed under the special rules of the court only two hours to speak, Cicero had an almost impossible task. He could hardly pretend that Milo, who had openly boasted of what he had done, was innocent of the crime. Indeed some of Milo's supporters, such as Rufus, thought that Cicero should make a virtue of it and argue that the murder was not a crime at all but a public service. Cicero recoiled from that line of reasoning. 'What are you saying? That any man can be condemned to death without trial and summarily executed by his enemies if it suits enough people? That's mob rule, Rufus – exactly what Clodius believed in – and I refuse to stand up in a Roman court and make such a case.'

The only feasible alternative was to argue that the killing was justified on the grounds of self-defence – but that was difficult to reconcile with the evidence that Clodius had been dragged out of the tavern and finished off in cold blood. Still, it was not impossible. I had known Cicero win from weaker positions. And he wrote a good speech. However, on the morning he was due to deliver it, he woke gripped by a terrible anxiety. At first I took no notice. He was often nervous before a big oration, and suffered from loose bowels and vomiting. But this morning was different. He was not gripped by fear, which he sometimes called 'cold strength' and had learned how to harness; rather he was simply in a funk and could not remember a word of what he was supposed to say.

Milo suggested he should go down to the Forum in a closed litter and wait somewhere out of sight, calmly composing himself until it was time for him to speak; and this was what we tried. Cicero, at his request, had been provided with a bodyguard by Pompey for the duration of the trial, and they cordoned off a part of the Grove of Vesta and kept everyone away while the orator reclined beneath the thick embroidered canopy, trying to commit his speech to memory and occasionally leaning out to retch on the sacred earth. But although he could not see the crowd, he could hear it chanting and roaring nearby, and that was almost worse. When the praetor's clerk finally came to fetch us, Cicero's legs were so weak he could barely stand. As we walked into the Forum, the noise was terrific, and the sunlight glinting on the armour and weapons of the soldiers dazzled our eyes.

The Clodians jeered Cicero when he appeared and jeered him all the louder when he tried to speak. His nerves were so obvious he actually confessed them in his opening sentence – 'I am afraid, gentlemen of the jury: an unseemly condition in which to begin a speech in defence of the bravest of men, but there it is' – and blamed his fear squarely on the rigged nature of the hearing: 'Wherever I look, I look in vain for the familiar environment of the courts and the traditional procedure of the law.'

Unfortunately, complaining about the rules of a contest is always a sure sign of a man who knows he is about to lose it, and although Cicero made some effective points – 'Suppose, gentlemen, I could induce you to acquit Milo, but only on condition that Clodius comes back to life again: why all those terrified glances?' – a speech is only as good as its delivery. By thirty-eight votes to thirteen the jury found Milo guilty, and he was sent into exile for life. His property was hastily auctioned at knock-down prices to pay his creditors, and Cicero directed Terentia's steward, Philotimus, to buy a lot of it anonymously so that it could be disposed of later and the profits handed to Milo's wife, Fausta: she had made it clear she would not be accompanying her husband into exile. A day or two later Milo went off with remarkable cheerfulness to Massilia in southern Gaul. His departure was very much in the spirit of a gladiator who knew he would lose eventually and was simply grateful to have lived so long. Cicero tried to make amends by publishing the speech he would have given if his nerves hadn't got the better of him. He sent a copy to Milo, who replied charmingly a few months later that he was glad Cicero hadn't spoken it, *for otherwise I should not be eating such wonderful Massilian mullets*.

Soon after Milo left Rome, Pompey invited Cicero to dinner to show there were no hard feelings. Cicero went off grumbling and reeled home afterwards in such a state of amazement that he came and woke me up, for who should have been at the dinner table but the widow of Publius Crassus, the teenaged Cornelia – and Pompey had married her!

Cicero said, 'Well, naturally I congratulated him – she's a beautiful and accomplished girl, even if she is young enough to be his granddaughter – and then I asked him, by way of conversation, what Caesar had made of the match. He looked at me with great disdain and said that he hadn't even told Caesar: what business was it of Caesar's? He was fifty-three years old and he would marry whomever he pleased!

'I replied, as gently as I could, that perhaps Caesar might take a different view – after all, he had sought a marital alliance and been rebuffed, and the bride's father has not exactly shown himself a friend of Caesar's. To which Pompey replied, "Oh, don't worry about Scipio, he's entirely friendly. I'm appointing him my consular colleague for the remainder of my term!" Is the man mad, do you suppose? Caesar is going to look at Rome and think that the whole place has been taken over by the aristocratic party, with Pompey at their head.' Cicero groaned and closed his eyes; I guessed he had drunk rather a lot. 'I told you this would happen. I am Cassandra – doomed to see the future yet destined never to be believed.'

Cassandra or not, there was one consequence of Pompey's special consulship that Cicero had not foreseen. To help end electoral corruption, Pompey had decided to reform the laws relating to the fourteen provincial commands. Up to this point, consuls and praetors had always left Rome immediately upon the expiry of their term of office to take up their allotted province; and because of the huge sums that could be extorted from such commands, a practice had arisen of candidates borrowing against their expected earnings in order to fund their election campaigns. Pompey, with amazing hypocrisy considering his own abuse of the system, decided to put a stop to all that. Henceforth, a period of five years would have to elapse between holding office in Rome and taking up a governorship overseas. To fill such positions in the interim it was decreed that every senator of praetorian rank who had never done their turn as governor would have to draw lots for the vacant provinces.

To his horror, Cicero now realised he was in danger of having to do what he had always sworn to avoid: sweating it out in some corner of the empire, administering justice to the natives. He went to see Pompey to plead to be excused. His health was poor, he said. He was getting old. He even suggested that the time he had spent in exile might be counted as his term abroad.

Pompey wouldn't hear of it. Indeed he seemed to take a malicious pleasure in running through all the possible commands that might now fall to Cicero, with their various unique drawbacks – extreme distance from Rome, rebellious tribesmen, ferocious customs, hostile climates, savage wild beasts, impassable roads, incurable local diseases and so forth. Lots to determine who went where were drawn at a special session of the Senate, with Pompey in the chair. Cicero went up and plucked his token from the urn and handed it to Pompey, who read out the result with a smile: 'Marcus Tullius draws Cilicia.'

Cilicia! Cicero could barely conceal his dismay. This mountainous, primitive homeland of pirates at the extreme eastern edge of the Mediterranean – which included within its administration the island of Cyprus – was about as far away from Rome as it was possible to get. It also shared a border with Syria, and so was within range of the Parthian army, if Cassius was unable to hold them in check. Finally, to cap Cicero's woes, the current governor was Clodius's brother, Appius Clodius Pulcher, who could be relied upon to make his successor's life as difficult as possible.

I knew he would expect me to go with him and I tried desperately to think of excuses why I should stay behind. He had just completed *On the Republic*. I told him that in my view I would be more use to him in Rome, overseeing its publication.

'Nonsense,' he said, 'Atticus will take care of copying and circulation.'

'There's also my health,' I continued, 'I've never really recovered from that fever I contracted at Arpinum.'

'In that case a sea voyage will do you good.'

And so it went on. My every objection was met by an answer. He started to become offended. But I had a bad feeling about this expedition. Although he swore we would only be gone a year, I sensed it would be longer. Rome felt strangely impermanent to me. Perhaps it was a consequence of having to pass the burnt-out shell of the Senate house every day, or maybe it was my knowledge of the widening split between Pompey and Caesar. Whatever the reason, I had a superstitious dread that if I left I might never come back, and that even if I did return it would be to a different city.

Eventually Cicero said, 'Well, I cannot force you to come – you're a free man now. But I feel you owe me this one last service, and I'll make a bargain with you. When we return, I'll give you the money to buy that farm you've always wanted, and I shan't press you to perform any more duties for me. The rest of your life will be your own.'

I could hardly refuse such an offer, and so I tried to ignore my forebodings and set about helping him plan his administration.

As governor of Cilicia, Cicero would have command of a standing army of about fourteen thousand men, with every prospect of having to fight a war. He decided therefore to appoint two legates with military experience. One was his old comrade Caius Pomptinus, the praetor who had helped him round up Catilina's co-conspirators. For the second he turned to his brother Quintus, who had expressed a strong desire to quit Gaul. At first his service under Caesar had been a great success. He had taken part in the invasion of Britain, and on his return Caesar had placed him in command of a legion that soon afterwards was attacked in its winter camp by a vastly superior force of Gauls. The fighting had been fierce: nine tenths of the Romans had been wounded. But Quintus, although ill and exhausted, had kept a cool head and the legion had survived the siege long enough for Caesar to arrive and relieve them; afterwards he had been singled out for praise by Caesar in his *Commentaries*.

The following summer he was promoted to command of the newly formed Fourteenth Legion. This time, however, he had disobeyed Caesar's orders. Instead of keeping all his men in camp, he had sent out several hundred raw recruits to forage for food. They had been cut off by an invading force of Germans. Caught in the open, they had stood gaping at their commanders, unsure of what to do, and half of them had been massacred when they tried to make a run for it. *All my previous good standing with Caesar has been destroyed*, Quintus wrote sadly to his brother. *He treats me to my face with civility but I detect a certain coldness, and I know he goes behind my back to consult with my junior officers; in short I fear I may never fully regain his trust.* Cicero wrote to Caesar asking if his brother might be allowed to join him in Cilicia; Caesar readily agreed; and two months later Quintus arrived back in Rome.

As far as I am aware, Cicero never uttered a word of reproach to his brother. Nevertheless, something was altered in their relationship. I believe Quintus felt a keen sense of failure. He had hoped to find fame and fortune and independence in Gaul; instead he came back tarnished, out of pocket and more dependent than ever on his famous sibling. His marriage remained bitter. He was still drinking heavily. And his only son, young Quintus, who was now fifteen, had all the charms of that particular age, being sullen, secretive, insolent and duplicitous. Cicero believed the boy needed more of his father's attention and suggested he should accompany us to Cilicia, along with his own son, Marcus. My expectations of our trip, already low, receded further.

When we left Rome at the start of the senatorial recess, we were a huge party. Cicero had been invested with imperium and was obliged to travel with six lictors as well as a great retinue of slaves carrying all our baggage for the voyage abroad. Terentia came part of the way to see her husband off, and so did Tullia, who had just been divorced by Crassipes. She was closer to her father than ever and read him poetry on the journey. Privately he fretted to me about her future: twenty-five years old, no child, no husband … We stopped off at Tusculum to say goodbye to Atticus, and Cicero asked him as a favour to keep an eye on Tullia and try to find her a new match while he was away.

'Of course I shall,' Atticus replied, 'and would you in return do a favour for me? Will you try to make Quintus just a little kinder to my sister? I know Pomponia is a difficult woman, but he has returned from Gaul in a permanent foul temper, and their constant arguments are having a bad effect on their boy.'

Cicero agreed, and when we met up with Quintus and his family at Arpinum, he took his brother aside and repeated what Atticus had said. Quintus promised to do his best. But Pomponia, I'm afraid, was quite impossible, and it was not long before the couple were refusing to speak to one another, let alone share a bed, and they parted very coldly.

Relations between Terentia and Cicero were more civil, apart from the one vexed area that had been a source of antagonism between them all their married life – money. In contrast to her husband, Terentia had welcomed his appointment as governor, seeing in it a wonderful opportunity for enrichment. She had even brought her steward, Philotimus, along on the journey south so that he could give Cicero the benefit of his various ideas for skimming off a profit. Cicero kept postponing the conversation and Terentia kept nagging him to have it until at last on their final day together he lost his temper.

'This fixation of yours with making money is really most unseemly.'

'This fixation of yours with spending it gives me no choice!'

Cicero paused for a moment to control his irritation and then tried to explain the matter calmly. 'You don't seem to understand – a man in my position cannot risk the slightest impropriety. My enemies are just waiting for an opportunity to prosecute me for corruption.'

'So you intend to be the only provincial governor in history not to come home richer than he went out?'

'My dear wife, if you ever read a word I wrote, you would know I am just about to publish a treatise on good government. How will that sit with a reputation for thievery in office?'

'Books!' said Terentia with great contempt. 'Where is the money in *books*?'

They repaired their quarrel sufficiently to dine together that night, and to humour her Cicero agreed that at some stage in the coming year he would at least listen to Philotimus's business proposals – but only on condition they were legal.

The next morning the family parted, with many tears and much embracing – Cicero and Marcus, who was now fourteen, setting off on horseback together side by side, while Terentia and Tullia stood at the gate of the family farm, waving. I remember that just before the road carried us out of sight I took a final look over my shoulder. Terentia had gone in by then but Tullia was still there watching us, a fragile figure against the majesty of the mountains.

We were due to embark on the first leg of our voyage to Cilicia from Brundisium, and it was while we were on the road there, at Venusia, that Cicero received an invitation from Pompey. The great man was taking the winter sun at his villa in Tarentum and suggested that Cicero should come and stay for a couple of days 'to discuss the political situation'. As Tarentum was only forty miles from Brundisium, and as our route would take us practically past the door, and as Pompey was not a man to whom it was easy to say no, Cicero had little option but to accept.

Once again we found Pompey living in a state of great domestic happiness with a young bride: they seemed almost to be playing at being a married couple. The house was surprisingly modest; as governor of Spain Pompey had a mere fifty legionaries to protect him, and they were billeted on the neighbouring properties. Otherwise he was without executive authority, having given up his consulship amid universal praise for his wisdom. In fact I would say he was at the summit of his popularity. Crowds of locals stood around outside hoping to catch a glimpse of him; once or twice a day he would sally forth to shake hands and pat the heads of infants. He was quite corpulent now, breathless and rather an unhealthy purplish colour. Cornelia fussed over him like a little mother, trying to restrain his appetite at meals and encouraging him to take walks along the seashore, his guards following at a discreet distance. He was idle, somnolent, uxorious. Cicero presented him with a copy of *On the Republic*. He expressed great pleasure but immediately laid it aside and I never saw him open it.

Whenever I look back at this three-day interlude, it seems to stand out in my memory like some sunlit glade in the middle of a vast and darkening forest. Watching the two ageing statesmen throwing a ball for Marcus, or standing with their togas hitched up, skimming stones across the waves, it was impossible to believe that anything sinister was impending – or if it was, that it would amount to much. Pompey exuded absolute confidence.

I was not privy to all that passed between him and Cicero, although Cicero told me most of it afterwards. The political situation in essence was this: that Caesar had completed his conquest of Gaul; that the Gallic leader, Vercingetorix, had surrendered and was in custody; and that the enemy's army was wiped out (the final engagement had been the capture of the hilltop fortress of Uxellodunum along with its garrison of two thousand Gallic fighters, all of whom, on Caesar's orders, according to his *Commentaries*, had had both hands cut off before being sent home, *so that everyone might see what punishment was meted out to those who resisted Rome's rule*; there had been no trouble since).

Given all this, the question now arose of what to do with Caesar. His own preference was to be allowed to stand for a second consulship *in absentia* so that he could enter Rome with legal immunity for all the crimes and misdemeanours he had committed during his first; at the very least he wanted his command extended so that he could remain as ruler of Gaul. His opponents, led by Cato, believed that he should return to Rome and submit himself to the electorate just like any other citizen; and failing that, he should be forced to give up his army, it being intolerable to have a man in control of what was now eleven legions, sitting on the Italian border issuing diktats to the Senate.

'And what is Pompey's view?' I asked.

'Pompey's view varies according to the hour of the day you ask him. In the morning he thinks it entirely proper, as a reward for his achievements, that his good friend Caesar should be permitted to stand for the consulship without entering Rome. After lunch he sighs and wonders why Caesar can't simply come home and canvass face to face like anybody else: after all, that was what he did in Caesar's position, and what was so undignified about that? And then by evening, when – despite the best efforts of the good Lady Cornelia – he is flushed with wine, he starts shouting, "To hell with bloody Caesar! I'm sick of hearing about Caesar! Let him just try and set one toe in Italy with his bloody legions, and you'll see what I can do – I'll stamp my foot and a hundred thousand men will rise up at my command and come to the defence of the Senate!"'

'And what do you think will happen?'

'My guess is that if I were here I could probably just about persuade him to do the right thing and avoid civil war, which would be the ultimate calamity. My fear,' he added, 'is that when the vital decisions are being taken, I shall be a thousand miles from Rome.'

XLVI

I do not propose to describe in any detail Cicero's time as governor of Cilicia. I am sure history will judge it as of minor importance in the scale of things; Cicero judged it minor even at the time.

We reached Athens in the spring and stayed for ten days with Aristus, the principal professor of the Academy, who was at that time the greatest living exponent of the philosophy of Epicurus. Like Atticus, who was also a devoted Epicurean, Aristus took a practical, material view of what makes for a happy life: a healthy diet, moderate exercise, pleasant surroundings, congenial company and the avoidance of stressful situations. Cicero, whose god was Plato and whose life was full of stress, disputed this. He believed that Epicureanism amounted to a kind of anti-philosophy: 'You say happiness depends on bodily well-being. But continual physical well-being is beyond our control. If a man is suffering an agonising illness, say, or if he is being tortured, then in your philosophy he cannot be happy.'

'Perhaps he cannot be *supremely* happy,' conceded Aristus, 'but happiness will still be there in some form.'

'No, no, he cannot be happy *at all*,' insisted Cicero, 'because his happiness is entirely contingent on the physical. Whereas the most magnificent and fruitful promise in the entire history of philosophy is the simple maxim: *nothing is good except what is morally good*. From this we can prove that *moral goodness is sufficient by itself to create the happy life*. And from that derives a third maxim: *moral goodness is the only sort of good there is*.'

'Ah, but if I torture you,' objected Aristus, with a knowing laugh, 'you will be every bit as unhappy as I am.'

Cicero, however, was very serious. 'No, no, because if I remain morally good – which I am not claiming is easy, by the way, let alone that I have achieved it – then I must remain happy, however great my pain. Even as my torturer falls back in exhaustion there will be something beyond the physical that he cannot reach.'

Naturally I am simplifying a long and complicated discussion that lasted several days as we toured the buildings and antiquities of Athens. But this was what it boiled down to, and it was now that Cicero began to conceive of the idea of writing some work of philosophy that would not be a set of high-flown abstractions but rather a practical guide to achieving the good life.

From Athens we sailed down the coast and then hopped from island to island across the Aegean in a fleet of a dozen vessels. The Rhodian boats were large, cumbersome and slow; they pitched and rolled in even moderate seas and were open to the elements. I remember how I shivered in a rainstorm as we passed Delos, that melancholy rock where up to ten thousand slaves are said to be sold in a single day. Everywhere the crowds that turned out to see Cicero were immense; among Romans only Pompey and Caesar, and I suppose just possibly Cato, can have been more famous in the world. At Ephesus our teeming expedition of legates, quaestors, lictors and military tribunes, with all their slaves and baggage, was transferred to a convoy of ox carts and pack mules and we set off along the dusty mountain roads into the interior of Asia Minor.

It was a full fifty-two days after leaving Italy that we reached Laodicea, the first town in the province of Cilicia, where Cicero was immediately required to begin hearing cases. The poverty and exhaustion of the common people, the endless shuffling queues of petitioners in the gloomy basilica and the glaring white-stone forum, the constant moans and groans about customs officials and poll taxes, the petty corruption, the flies, the heat, the dysentery, the sharp stink of goat and sheep dung that seemed always in the air, the bitter-tasting wine and oily spicy food, the small scale of the town and the lack of anything beautiful to look at, or sophisticated to listen to, or savoury to eat – oh, how Cicero hated being stuck in such a place while the fate of the world was being decided back in Italy without him! I had barely unpacked my ink and stylus before he was dictating letters to everyone he could think of in Rome, pleading with them to make sure his term was restricted to a year.

We had not been there long when a dispatch arrived from Cassius reporting that the King of Parthia's son had invaded Syria at the head of such a massive force he had been obliged to withdraw his legions to the fortified city of Antioch. This meant Cicero had to set off immediately to join his own army at the foot of the Taurus mountains, the immense natural barrier separating Cilicia from Syria. Quintus was greatly excited, and for a month there seemed a real possibility that Cicero might have to command the defence of the entire eastern flank of the empire. But then a fresh report came from Cassius: the Parthians had retreated before the impregnable walls of Antioch; he had pursued and defeated them; the king's son was dead and the threat was over.

I am not sure whether Cicero was more relieved or disappointed. However, he still managed to have a war of sorts. Some of the local tribes had taken advantage of the Parthian crisis to rise in revolt against Roman rule. There was one fortress in particular, named Pindessium, where the rebel forces were concentrated, and Cicero laid siege to it.

We lived in an army camp in the mountains for two months, and Quintus was as happy as a schoolboy building ramps and towers, digging moats and bringing up artillery. I found the whole adventure distasteful, and so I think did Cicero, for the rebels stood no chance. Day after day we launched arrows and flaming projectiles into the town, until eventually it surrendered and our legionaries poured into the place to ransack it. Quintus had the leaders executed. The rest were put in chains and led off to the coast to be shipped to Delos and sold into slavery. Cicero watched them go with a gloomy expression. 'I suppose if I were a great military man like Caesar I would have all their hands amputated. Isn't that how one brings peace to these people? But I can't say I derive much satisfaction from using all the resources of civilisation to reduce a few barbarian huts to ashes.' Still, his men hailed him as imperator in the field, and afterwards he had me write six hundred letters – that is, one to every member of the Senate – requesting that he be awarded a triumph: a tremendous labour for me, working in the primitive conditions of an army camp, that left me prostrate with exhaustion.

Cicero placed Quintus in command of the army for the winter and returned to Laodicea. He was rather shocked by the relish with which his brother had crushed the rebellion, and also by his brusque manner with subordinates (*irritable, rude, careless*, as he described him to Atticus); he did not care much for his nephew, either – *a boy with a fine conceit for himself.* Quintus Junior liked to make sure everyone knew who he was – his name alone saw to that – and he treated the locals with great disdain. Still, Cicero tried to do his duty as an affectionate uncle, and at that spring's Festival of Liberalia, in the absence of the boy's father, he presided over the ceremony at which young Quintus became a man, personally helping him to shave his wispy beard and dress in his first toga.

As for his own son, young Marcus gave him cause for concern in a different way. The lad was affable, lazy, fond of sport and somewhat slow on the uptake when it came to his schoolwork. Rather than study Greek and Latin, he liked to hang around the army officers and practise swordplay and javelin throwing. 'I love him dearly,' Cicero said to me, 'and he is certainly a good-hearted fellow, but sometimes I wonder where on earth he comes from – I detect nothing in him of me at all.'

Nor was that the end of his family worries. He had left the choice of Tullia's new husband up to her and her mother, having made clear simply that his own preference was for a safe, worthy, respectable young aristocrat such as Tiberius Nero or the son of his old friend Servius Sulpicius. But the women had set their hearts instead on Publius Cornelius Dolabella, a most unsuitable match in Cicero's view. He was a notorious rake, only nineteen – about seven years younger than Tullia – yet remarkably he had already been married once, to a much older woman.

By the time the letter announcing their choice reached him, it was too late for Cicero to intervene: the wedding would have taken place before his answer arrived in Rome – a fact the women must have known. 'What is one to do?' he sighed to me. 'Well, such is life – let the gods bless what is done. I can understand why Tullia wants it – no doubt he's a handsome, charming type, and if anyone deserves a taste of life at last, it's she. But Terentia! What is *she* thinking of? It sounds as though she's half in love with the fellow herself. I'm not sure I understand her any more.'

And here I come to the greatest of all Cicero's personal worries: that something clearly was amiss with Terentia. Recently he had received a reproachful letter from the exiled Milo demanding to know what had happened to all that property of his that Cicero had bought so cheaply at auction: his wife, Fausta, had never received a penny. As it happened, the agent who had acted on Cicero's behalf – Philotimus, Terentia's steward – was still hoping to persuade Cicero to adopt some dubious money-making scheme and was due to visit him in Laodicea.

Cicero received him in my presence and told him bluntly that there was no question of him or any member of his staff or family engaging in any shady business. 'So you can save your breath as far as that's concerned and tell me instead what's become of Milo's bankrupt estate. You remember the sale was fixed so you got it all for next to nothing, and then you were supposed to sell it at a profit and give the proceeds to Fausta?'

Philotimus, plumper than ever and already sweating in the summer heat, flushed even redder and started to stammer that he couldn't recall the details precisely: it was more than a year ago; he would have to consult his accounts and they were in Rome.

Cicero threw up his hands. 'Come now, man, you must remember. It's not that long ago. We're talking about tens of thousands. What has become of it all?'

But Philotimus would only repeat the same tale over and over: he was very sorry; he couldn't remember; he would need to check.

'I'm beginning to think you've pocketed the money yourself.'

Philotimus denied it.

Suddenly Cicero said, 'Does my wife know about this?'

At the mention of Terentia, a remarkable change came over Philotimus. He stopped squirming and became completely silent, and no matter how many times Cicero pressed him, he refused to say another word. Eventually Cicero told him to clear off out of his sight. After he had gone he said to me, 'Did you note that last piece of impertinence? Talk about defending a lady's honour – it was as if he thought I wasn't fit to utter my own wife's name.'

I agreed it was remarkable.

'*Remarkable* – that's one word for it. They were always very close, but ever since I went into exile ...'

He shook his head and didn't finish the sentence. I made no reply. It did not seem proper to comment. To this day I have no idea whether his suspicions were correct. All I can say is that he was deeply perturbed by the whole affair and wrote at once to Atticus asking him to investigate discreetly: *I can't put all I fear into words.*

A month before the end of his official term as governor, Cicero, escorted by his lictors, set off back to Rome taking me and the two boys with him and leaving his quaestor in charge of the province.

He knew he could face censure for abandoning his post prematurely and for placing Cilicia in the hands of a first-year senator, but he calculated that with Caesar's governorship of Gaul about to come to an end, most men would have bigger issues on their minds. We travelled via Rhodes, which he wanted to show to Quintus and Marcus. He also desired to visit the tomb of Apollonius Molon, the great tutor of oratory whose lessons almost thirty years before had started him on his political ascent. We found it on a headland looking across the Carpathian Straits. A simple white marble stone bore the orator's name, and beneath it was carved in Greek one of his favourite precepts: *Nothing dries more quickly than a tear.* Cicero stood looking at it for a long time.

Unfortunately the diversion to Rhodes slowed our return considerably. The Etesian winds were unusually strong that summer, blowing in from the north day after day, and they trapped our open boats in harbour for three weeks. During that period the political situation in Rome worsened sharply, and by the time we reached Ephesus there was a sackful of alarming news waiting for Cicero. *The nearer the struggle approaches,* wrote Rufus, *the plainer the danger appears. Pompey is determined not to allow Caesar to be elected consul unless he surrenders his army and provinces; whereas Caesar is persuaded that he cannot survive if he leaves his army. So this is what their love affair, their scandalous union has come to – not covert backbiting, but outright war!*

In Athens, a week later, Cicero found more letters, including ones from both Pompey and Caesar, each complaining about the other and appealing to his loyalty. *As far as I am concerned, he may be consul or he may keep his legions,* wrote Pompey, *but I am certain that he cannot do both; I assume that you agree with my policy and will stand resolutely on my side and on the side of the Senate as you have always done.* And from Caesar: *I fear that Pompey's noble nature has blinded him to the true intentions of those individuals who have always wished me harm; I rely upon you, dear Cicero, to tell him that I cannot be, should not be, and will not be left defenceless.*

The two letters plunged Cicero into a state of acute anxiety. He sat in Aristus's library with both laid on the table before him and looked back and forth from one to the other. *I fancy I see the greatest struggle that history has ever known,* he wrote to Atticus. *There looms ahead a tremendous contest between them. Each counts me as his man. But what am I to do? They will try to draw a statement of my views. You will laugh when I say it, but I wish to heaven I was still back in my province.*

That night I lay shivering despite the Athens heat, my teeth chattering, hallucinating that Cicero was dictating a letter to me, a copy of which had to go to both Pompey and Caesar, assuring each of his support. But a phrase that would please one would infuriate the other, and I spent hour after hour in a panic trying to construct sentences that were utterly neutral. Whenever I thought I had managed it, the words would become disorganised in my head and I would have to start again. It was utter madness yet at the same time it seemed absolutely real, and when morning came I realised in a lucid interval that I had lapsed back into the fever that had afflicted me at Arpinum.

That day we were due to set off again by ship to Corinth. I tried hard to carry on as normal. But I guess I must have looked ghastly and hollow-eyed. Cicero tried to persuade me to eat but I was unable to keep food in my stomach. Although I managed to board the boat unaided, I spent the day's voyage almost comatose, and when we landed at Corinth that evening, apparently I had to be carried off the ship and put to bed.

The question now arose of what should be done with me. I was desperate not to be left behind, and Cicero did not want to abandon me. But he needed to get back to Rome, firstly to do what little was in his power to avert the impending civil war, and secondly to try to lobby for a triumph, of which, unrealistically, he still had slight hopes. He could not afford to waste days in Greece waiting for his secretary to recover. In retrospect I should have stayed in Corinth. Instead we gambled that I would be strong enough to withstand the two-day journey to Patrae, where a ship would be waiting to take us to Italy. It was a foolish decision. I was wrapped in blankets and placed in the back of a carriage and conveyed along the coastal road in great discomfort. When we reached Patrae, I begged them to go on without me. I was sure a long sea voyage would kill me. Cicero was still reluctant, but in the end he agreed. I was put to bed in a villa near the harbour belonging to Lyso, a Greek merchant. Cicero, Marcus and young Quintus gathered around my bed to say goodbye. They shook my hand. Cicero wept. I made some feeble joke about our parting scene resembling the deathbed of Socrates. And then they were gone.

*

Cicero wrote me a letter the following day and sent it back with Mario, one of his most trusted slaves.

> *I thought I could bear the want of you not too hard, but frankly I find it unendurable. I feel I did wrong to leave you. If after you are able to take nourishment you think you can overtake me, the decision is in your hands. Think it over in that clever head of yours. I miss you but I love you. Loving you I want to see you fit and well; missing you I want to see you as soon as possible. The former therefore must come first. So make it your chief concern to get well. Of your countless services to me this is the one I shall most appreciate.*

He wrote me many such letters during the time I was ill – once he sent three in a single day. Naturally I missed him as much as he missed me. But my health was broken. I could not travel. It was to be eight months before I saw him again, and by then his world, our world, was utterly transformed.

Lyso was an attentive host and brought in his own doctor, a fellow Greek named Asclapo, to treat me. I was purged and sweated and starved and hydrated: all the standard remedies for a tertian fever were attempted when what I really needed was rest. Cicero, however, fretted that Lyso was *a little casual: all Greeks are*, and arranged for me to be moved after a few days to a larger and more peaceful house up the hill, away from the noise of the harbour. It belonged to a childhood friend of his, Manius Curius: *All my hopes of your getting proper treatment and attention are pinned on Curius. He has the kindest of hearts and the truest affection for me. Put yourself entirely in his hands.*

Curius was indeed an amiable, cultured man, a widower, a banker by profession, and he looked after me well. I was given a room with a terrace looking westwards to the sea, and later, when I started to feel strong enough, I would sit outside for an hour in the afternoons watching the merchant ships going in and out of the harbour. Curius was in regular touch with all sorts of contacts in Rome – senators, equestrians, tax farmers, shipowners – and his letters, plus mine, together with the geographical situation of Patrae as the gateway to Greece, meant that we received the political news as quickly as anyone could in that part of the world.

One day around the end of January – this must have been about three months after Cicero's departure – Curius came into my room with a grim expression and asked me whether I was strong enough to take bad news. When I nodded, he said, 'Caesar has invaded Italy.'

Years afterwards, Cicero used to wonder whether the three weeks we had lost on Rhodes might have made the difference between war and peace. If only, he lamented, he could have reached Rome a month earlier! He was one of the few who was listened to by both sides, and in the short time he was on the outskirts of Rome before the conflict broke out – which was barely a week – he told me he had begun to broker the beginnings of a compromise: Caesar to give up Gaul and all his legions apart from one, and in return to be allowed to stand for the consulship *in absentia*. But by then it was far too late. Pompey was dubious about the deal; the Senate rejected it; and Caesar, he suspected, had already made up his mind to strike, having calculated that he would never be stronger than at that moment: 'In short, I was among madmen wild for war.'

The moment he heard that Caesar had invaded, he went straight to Pompey's house on the Pincian hill to pledge his support. It was packed with the leaders of the war party – Cato, Ahenobarbus, the consuls Marcellinus and Lentulus: fifteen or twenty men in all. Pompey was enraged, and he was panicking. He was under the misapprehension that Caesar was advancing at full strength, with perhaps fifty thousand troops. In fact, that inveterate gambler had crossed the Rubicon with only a tenth of that number and was relying on the shock effect of his aggression. But Pompey did not yet know that, and so he decreed that the city should be abandoned. He was ordering every senator to leave Rome. Any who remained behind would be regarded as traitors. When Cicero demurred, arguing that this was a mad policy, Pompey turned on him: 'And that includes you, Cicero!' This war would not be decided in Rome, he declared, or even in Italy – that was to play into Caesar's hands. Instead it would be a world war, fought in Spain, Africa, the eastern Mediterranean and especially at sea. He would blockade Italy. He would starve the enemy into submission. Caesar would rule over a charnel house.

I shuddered at the kind of war intended, wrote Cicero to Atticus, *savage and vast beyond what men yet envision.* Pompey's personal hostility towards him was also a shock. He left Rome as ordered and withdrew to Formiae and brooded on what course to take. Officially he was placed in charge of sea defences and recruitment in northern Campania; practically he did nothing. Pompey sent him a cold reminder of his duties: *I strongly urge you, in view of your outstanding and unswerving patriotism, to make your way over to us, so that in concert we may bring aid and comfort to our afflicted country.*

Around this time, Cicero wrote to me: I received the letter about three weeks after I learned of the outbreak of war.

From Cicero to his dear Tiro, greetings.

My existence and that of all honest men and the entire commonwealth hangs in the balance, as you may tell from the fact that we have left our homes and the mother city herself to plunder or burning. Swept along by some spirit of folly, forgetting the name he bears and the honours he has won, Caesar seized Ariminium, Pisaurum, Ancona and Arretium. So we abandoned Rome – how wisely or how courageously it is idle to argue. We have reached the point when we cannot survive unless some god or accident comes to our rescue. To add to my vexations, my son-in-law Dolabella is with Caesar.

I wanted you to be aware of these facts. Mind you don't let them upset you and hinder your recovery. Since you could not be with me when I most needed your services and loyalty, make sure you do not hurry or be so foolish as to undertake the voyage either as an invalid or in winter.

I obeyed his instruction and thus I found myself following the collapse of the Roman Republic from my sick room – and in my memory, my illness and the madness being played out in Italy are forever merged in a single fevered nightmare. Pompey and his hastily assembled army headed to Brundisium to embark for Macedonia to begin their world war. Caesar chased after him to stop him. He tried to blockade the harbour. He failed. He watched the sails of Pompey's troopships dwindle into the distance, then turned round and marched back the way he had come, towards Rome. His route along the Via Appia took him past Cicero's door in Formiae.

Formiae, 29 March
From Cicero to his dear Tiro, greetings.

So I have seen the madman at last – for the first time in nine years, can one believe it? He appeared quite unchanged. A little harder, leaner, greyer, and more lined perhaps; but I fancy this life of brigandage suits him. Terentia, Tullia and Marcus are with me (they send their love, by the way).

What happened was this. All yesterday his legionaries were streaming past our door – a wild-looking lot, but they left us unmolested. We were just settling down to dinner when a commotion at the gate signalled the arrival of a column of mounted men. What an entourage, what an underworld! A grimmer group of desperadoes you have never seen! The man himself – if man he is: one starts to wonder – was alert and audacious and in a hurry. Is he a Roman general or is he Hannibal? 'I could not pass so close without stopping for a moment to see you.' As if he was a country neighbour! To Terentia and Tullia he was most civil. He refused all hospitality ('I must press on') and we went into my study to talk. We were quite alone. He came straight to the point. He was summoning a meeting of the Senate in four days' time.

'On what authority?'

'This,' he said, and touched his sword. 'Come along and work for peace.'

'At my own discretion?'

'Naturally. Who am I to lay down rules for you?'

'Well then, I shall say that the Senate should not give its approval if you plan to send your troops to Spain or Greece to fight the armies of the republic. And I shall have much to say in defence of Pompey.'

At this he protested that these were not the sort of things he wanted said.

'So I supposed,' I replied, 'and that is just why I don't want to be present. Either I must stay away or speak in that strain – and bring up much else besides which I could not possibly suppress if I was there.'

He became very cold. He said I was in effect passing judgement against him, and that if I was reluctant to come across to him, others would be too. He told me I should think the matter over and let him know. With that he got up to leave. 'One last thing,' he said. 'I should like your counsels, but if I cannot have them I shall take advice wherever I can, and I shall stop at nothing.'

On that note we parted. I don't doubt our meeting has put him out of humour with me. It is becoming ever clearer that I cannot remain here much longer. I see no end to the mischief.

I did not know how to reply, and besides, I was frightened that any letter I sent would be intercepted, for Cicero had discovered that he was surrounded by Caesar's spies. The boys' tutor, Dionysius, for example, who had accompanied us to Cilicia, turned out to be an informant. So too, much more shockingly to Cicero, was his own nephew, young Quintus, who sought an interview with Caesar directly after his visit to Formiae and told him that his uncle was planning to defect to Pompey.

Caesar was at that time in Rome. He had pressed ahead with the plan he had outlined to Cicero and had summoned a meeting of the Senate. Hardly anyone attended: senators were abandoning Italy on almost every tide to join Pompey in Macedonia. But by an unbelievable stroke of incompetence, in his eagerness to flee, Pompey had forgotten to empty the treasury in the Temple of Saturn. Caesar went to seize it at the head of a cohort of troops. The tribune L. Caecilius Metellus barred the door and made a speech about the sanctity of the law, to which Caesar replied, 'There is a time for laws and a time for arms. If you don't like what is being done, save me your speeches and get out of the way.' And when Metellus still refused to move, Caesar said, 'Get out of the way or I shall have you killed, and you know, young man, that I dislike saying this more than I would dislike doing it.' Metellus moved out of the way very swiftly after that.

Such was the man to whom Quintus betrayed his uncle. The first clue Cicero had about his treachery was a letter he received a few days later from Caesar, on his way now to fight Pompey's forces in Spain.

En route to Massilia, 16 April
Caesar Imperator to Cicero Imperator.

I am troubled by certain reports and therefore I feel I ought to write and appeal to you in the name of our mutual goodwill not to take any hasty or imprudent step. You will be committing a grave offence against friendship. To hold aloof from civil quarrels is surely the most fitting course for a good, peace-loving man and a good citizen. Some who favoured that course were prevented from following it by fears for their safety. But you have the witness of my career and the judgement implied in our friendship. Weigh them well, and you will find no safer and no more honourable course than to keep aloof from all conflict.

Cicero told me afterwards that it was only when he read this letter that he knew for certain that he would have to take ship and join Pompey – 'by rowing boat if necessary' – because to submit to such a crude and sinister threat would be intolerable to him. He summoned young Quintus to Formiae and gave him a furious dressing-down. But secretly he felt quite grateful to him, and persuaded his brother not to treat the young man too harshly. 'What did he do, after all, except tell the truth about what was in my heart – something I had not had the courage to do when I met Caesar? Then when Caesar offered me a funk hole where I could sit out the rest of the war in safety while other men died for the cause of the republic, my duty suddenly became clear to me.'

In strictest confidence he sent me a cryptic message via Atticus and Curius that he was travelling *to that place where you and I were first visited by Milo and his gladiator, and if, when your health permits, you would care to join me there again, nothing would give me greater joy.*

I knew at once that he was referring to Thessalonica, where Pompey's army was now assembling. I had no desire to become involved in the civil war. It sounded highly dangerous to me. On the other hand, I was devoted to Cicero and I supported his decision. For all Pompey's faults, he had shown himself in the end to be willing to obey the law: he had been given supreme power after the murder of Clodius and had then surrendered it; legality was on his side; it was Caesar, not he, who had invaded Italy and destroyed the republic.

My fever had passed. My health was restored. I, too, knew what I had to do. Accordingly, at the end of June, I said farewell to Curius, who had become a good friend, and set off to chance my fortunes in war.

XLVII

I travelled by ship mostly – east across the Bay of Corinth and north along the Aegean coast. Curius had offered me one of his slaves as a manservant but I preferred to journey alone: having once been another man's property myself, I was uneasy in the role of master. Gazing at that ancient tranquil landscape with its olive groves and goatherds, its temples and fishermen, one would never have guessed at the stupendous events now in train across the world. Only when we rounded a headland and came within sight of the harbour of Thessalonica did everything appear different. The approaches to the port were crammed with hundreds of troopships and supply vessels. One could almost have walked dryfooted from one side of the bay to the other. Inside the port, wherever one looked there were signs of war – soldiers, cavalry horses, wagons full of weapons and armour and tents, siege engines – and all that vast concourse of hangers-on who attend a great army mustering to fight.

I had no idea amid this chaos of where to find Cicero, but I remembered a man who might. Epiphanes didn't recognise me at first, perhaps because I was wearing a toga and he had never thought of me as a Roman citizen. But when I reminded him of our past dealings, he cried out and seized my hand and pressed it to his heart. Judging by his jewelled rings and the hennaed slave girl pouting on his couch, he seemed to be prospering nicely from the war, although for my benefit he lamented it loudly. Cicero, he said, was back in the same villa he had occupied almost a decade before. 'May the gods bring you a swift victory,' he called after me, 'but not perhaps before we have done good business together.'

How odd it was to make that familiar walk again, to enter that unchanged house, and to find Cicero sitting in the courtyard on the same stone bench, staring into space with the same expression of utter dejection. He jumped up when he saw me, threw wide his arms and clasped me to him. 'But you're too thin!' he protested, feeling the boniness of my shoulders and ribs. 'You'll become ill again. We must fatten you up!'

He called to the others to come and see who was here, and from various directions came his son, Marcus, now a strapping, floppy-haired sixteen-year-old, wearing the toga of manhood; his nephew, Quintus, slightly sheepish as he must have known his uncle would have told me of his malicious blabbing; and finally Quintus senior, who smiled to see me but whose face quickly lapsed back into melancholy. Apart from young Marcus, who was training for the cavalry and loved spending his time around the soldiers, it was plainly an unhappy household.

'Everything about our strategy is wrong,' Cicero complained to me over dinner that evening. 'We sit here doing nothing while Caesar rampages across Spain. Far too much notice is being taken of auguries, in my opinion – no doubt birds and entrails have their place in civilian government, but they sit badly with commanding an army. Sometimes I wonder if Pompey is quite the military genius he's cracked up to be.'

Cicero being Cicero, he did not restrict such opinions to his own household but voiced them around Thessalonica to whoever would listen, and it was not long before I realised he was regarded as something of a defeatist. Not surprisingly Pompey hardly ever saw him, but then I suppose this may have been because he was away so much training his new legions. Close to two hundred senators with their staffs were crammed into the city by the time I arrived, many of them elderly. They hung around the Temple of Apollo with nothing to do, bickering among themselves. All wars are horrible, but civil wars especially so. Some of Cicero's closest friends, such as young Caelius Rufus, were fighting with Caesar, while his new son-in-law, Dolabella, actually had command of a squadron of Caesar's fleet in the Adriatic. Pompey's first words to Cicero when he arrived had been a curt 'Where's your new son-in-law?' To which Cicero had replied, 'With your old father-in-law.' Pompey had grunted and walked away.

I asked Cicero what Dolabella was like. He rolled his eyes. 'An adventurer like all of Caesar's crew; a rogue, a cynic, too full of animal spirits for his own good – I rather like him actually. But oh dear, poor Tullia! What kind of husband has she landed herself with this time? The darling girl gave birth at Cumae prematurely just before I left but the child didn't last out the day. I fear another attempt at motherhood will kill her. And of course the more Dolabella wearies of her and her illnesses – she's older than him – the more desperately she loves him. And still I haven't paid him the second part of her dowry. Six hundred thousand sesterces! But where am I to find such a vast sum when I'm trapped here?'

That summer was even hotter than the one when Cicero was exiled – and now half of Rome was exiled with him. We wilted in the humidity of the teeming city. Sometimes I found it hard not to take a certain grim satisfaction at the sight of so many men who had ignored Cicero's warnings about Caesar – who had been prepared indeed to see Cicero driven from Rome in the interests of a quiet life – and who now found themselves experiencing what it was like to be far from home and facing an uncertain future.

If only Caesar had been stopped earlier! That was the lament upon everyone's lips. But now it was too late and all the momentum of war was with him. At the height of the summer's heat, messengers reached Thessalonica with the news that the Senate's army in Spain had surrendered to Caesar after a campaign of just forty days. The news provoked intense dismay. Not long afterwards the commanders of that defeated army arrived in person: Lucius Afranius, the most loyal of all Pompey's lieutenants, and Marcus Petreius, who fourteen years earlier had defeated Catilina on the field of battle. The Senate-in-exile was flabbergasted at their appearance. Cato rose to ask the question on the minds of them all: 'Why are you not dead or prisoners?' Afranius had to explain somewhat shamefacedly that Caesar had pardoned them, and that all the soldiers who had fought for the Senate had been allowed to return to their homes.

'Pardoned you?' raged Cato. 'What do you mean, *pardoned* you? Is he now a king? You are the legitimate leaders of a lawful army. He is a renegade. You should have killed yourselves rather than accept a traitor's mercy! What's the use of living when you've lost your honour? Or is the point of your existence now just so that you can piss out of the front and shit out of the back?'

Afranius drew his sword and declared in a trembling voice that no man would ever call him a coward, not even Cato. There might have been serious bloodshed if the two had not been jostled away from one another.

Cicero said to me later that of all the clever strokes that Caesar pulled, perhaps the most brilliant was his policy of clemency. It was, in a curious way, akin to sending home the garrison of Uxellodunum with their hands cut off. These proud men were humbled, neutered; they crept back to their astonished comrades as living emblems of Caesar's power. And by their very presence they lowered morale across the entire army, for how could Pompey persuade his soldiers to fight to the death when they knew that if it came to it they could lay down their arms and return to their families?

Pompey called a council of war to discuss the crisis, consisting of the leaders of the army and of the Senate. Cicero, who was still officially the governor of Cilicia, naturally attended, and was accompanied to the temple by his lictors. He tried to take Quintus in with him but he was barred at the door by Pompey's aide-de-camp, and much to his fury and embarrassment Quintus had to stay outside with me. Among those I watched going in were Afranius, whose conduct in Spain Pompey staunchly defended; Domitius Ahenobarbus, who had managed to escape from Massilia when Caesar besieged it and now saw traitors wherever he looked; Titus Labienus, an old ally of Pompey's who had served as Caesar's second in command in Gaul but had refused to follow his chief across the Rubicon; Marcus Bibulus, Caesar's former consular colleague, now admiral of the Senate's huge fleet of five hundred warships; Cato, who had been promised command of the fleet until Pompey decided it would not be wise to give so fractious a colleague so much power; and Marcus Junius Brutus, who was only thirty-six and Cato's nephew, but whose arrival was said to have given more joy to Pompey than anyone else's, because Pompey had killed Brutus's father back in Sulla's time and there had been a blood feud ever since.

Pompey, according to Cicero, exuded confidence. He had lost weight, had put himself on an exercise regime, and looked a full decade younger than he had in Italy. He dismissed the loss of Spain as inconsequential, a sideshow. 'Listen to me, gentlemen; listen to what I have always said: *this war will be won at sea*.' According to Pompey's spies in Brundisium, Caesar had less than half the number of ships that the Senate possessed. It was purely a question of mathematics: Caesar did not have sufficient troop transports to break out of Italy in anything like the strength he would need to confront Pompey's legions; therefore he was trapped. 'We have him where we want him, and when we are ready we shall take him. From now on, this war will be fought on my terms and according to my timetable.'

*

It must have been about three months after this, in the middle of the night, that we were roused by a furious hammering on the door. We gathered bleary-eyed in the tablinum, where the lictors were waiting with an officer from Pompey's headquarters. Caesar's forces had landed four days earlier on the coast of Illyricum, near Dyrrachium; Pompey had ordered the entire army to begin moving out at dawn to confront them. It would be a march of three hundred miles.

Cicero said, 'Is Caesar with his army?'

'So we believe.'

Quintus said, 'But I thought he was in Spain.'

'Indeed he *was* in Spain,' replied Cicero drily, 'but apparently now he's here. How strange: I seem to remember being categorically assured that such a thing was impossible because he didn't have sufficient ships.'

At daybreak we went up to the Egnatian Gate to see if we could discover any more. The ground was vibrating with the weight of the military traffic on the road – a vast column was passing through the town, forty thousand men in all. I was told it stretched for thirty miles, although of course we could only see a fraction of it – the legionaries on foot carrying their heavy packs, the cavalrymen with their javelins glinting, the forest of standards and eagles all bearing the thrilling legend 'SPQR' ('The Senate and People of Rome'), trumpeters and cornet players, archers, slingers, artillerymen, slaves, cooks, scribes, doctors, carts full of baggage, pack mules laden with tents and tools and food and weapons, horses and oxen dragging crossbows and ballistae.

We joined the column around the middle of the morning, and even I, the least military of men, found it exhilarating; even Cicero for that matter was filled with confidence for once. As for young Marcus, he was in heaven, moving back and forth between our section and the cavalry. We rode on horseback. The lictors marched in front of us with their laurelled rods. As we tramped across the plain towards the mountains, the road began to climb and I could see far ahead the reddish-brown dust raised by the endless column and the occasional glitter of steel as a helmet or a javelin caught the sun.

At nightfall we reached the first camp, with its ditch and earthen rampart and its spiked palisade. The tents were already pitched, the fires lit; a wonderful scent of cooking rose into the darkening sky. I remember especially the clink of the blacksmiths' hammers in the dusk, the whinnying and movement of the horses in their enclosure, and also the pervading smell of leather from the scores of tents, the largest of which had been set aside for Cicero. It stood at the crossroads in the centre of the camp, close to the standards and to the altar, where Cicero that evening presided over the traditional sacrifice to Mars. He bathed and was anointed, dined well, slept peacefully in the fresh air, and the following morning we set off again.

This pattern was repeated for the next fifteen days as we made our way across the mountains of Macedonia towards the border with Illyricum. Cicero constantly expected to receive a summons to confer with Pompey, but none came. We did not know even where the commander-in-chief was, although occasionally Cicero received dispatches, and from these we pieced together a clearer picture of what was happening. Caesar had landed on the fourth day of January with a force of several legions, perhaps fifteen thousand men in all, and had achieved complete surprise, seizing the port of Apollonia, about thirty miles south of Dyrrachium. But that was just one half of his army. While he stayed with the bridgehead, his troopships had set off back to Italy to bring over the second half. (Pompey had never factored into his calculations the audacity of his enemy making two trips.) At this point, however, Caesar's famous luck ran out. Our admiral, Bibulus, had managed to intercept thirty of his transports. These he set on fire and all their crews he burnt alive, and then he deployed his immense fleet to prevent Caesar's navy returning.

As matters stood, therefore, Caesar's position was precarious. He had his back to the sea and was blockaded, with no chance of resupply, with winter coming on, and was about to be confronted by a much larger force.

As we were nearing the end of our march, Cicero received a further dispatch from Pompey:

Pompey Imperator to Cicero Imperator.

I have received a proposal from Caesar that we should hold an immediate peace conference, disband both our armies within three days, renew our old friendship under oath, and return to Italy together. I regard this as proof not of his friendly intentions but of the weakness of his position and of his realisation that he cannot win this war. Accordingly, knowing that you would concur, I have rejected his offer, which I suspect was in any case a trick.

'Is he right?' I asked him. 'Would you have concurred?'

'No,' responded Cicero, 'and he knows perfectly well I wouldn't. I would do anything to stop this war – which of course is why he never asked for my opinion. I cannot see anything ahead of us except slaughter and ruin.'

At the time I thought that Cicero was being unduly defeatist even for him. Pompey deployed his vast army in and around Dyrrachium, and contrary to expectations, he once again settled down to wait. No one in the supreme war council could fault his reasoning: that with every passing day Caesar's position became weaker; that he might eventually be starved into submission without the need for fighting; and that in any case, the best time to attack would be in the spring when the weather was less treacherous.

The Ciceros were billeted in a villa just outside Dyrrachium, built up high on a headland. It was a wild spot, with commanding views of the sea, and I found it odd to think of Caesar encamped only thirty miles away. Sometimes I would lean out over the terrace and crane my neck to the south in the hope that I might see some evidence of his presence, but naturally I never did.

And then at the beginning of April a very remarkable spectacle presented itself. The weather had been calm for several days, but suddenly a storm blew up from the south that howled around our house in its exposed position, the rain whipping down on the roof. Cicero was in the middle of composing a letter to Atticus, who had written from Rome to inform him that Tullia was desperately short of money. Sixty thousand sesterces was missing from the first payment of her dowry, and once again Cicero suspected Philotimus of shady dealing. He had just dictated the words *You tell me she is in want of everything; I beg you not to let this continue* when Marcus came running in and said that a great number of ships were visible out at sea and that he thought a battle might be in progress.

We put on our cloaks and hurried into the garden. And there indeed was a vast fleet of several hundred vessels a mile or more offshore, being tossed up and down in the heavy swell and driven at speed by the wind. It reminded me of our own near-shipwreck when we were crossing to Dyrrachium at the start of Cicero's exile. We watched for an hour until they had all passed out of sight, and then gradually a second flotilla began to appear – making, as it seemed to me, much heavier weather of it, but obviously trying to catch up with the ships that had gone before. We had no idea what it was that we were watching. To whom did these ghostly grey ships belong? Was it actually a battle? If so, was it going well or badly?

The next morning Cicero sent Marcus to Pompey's headquarters, to see what he could discover. The young man returned at dusk in a state of eager anticipation. The army would be breaking camp at dawn. The situation was confused. However, it appeared that the missing half of Caesar's army had sailed over from Italy. They had been unable to make land at Caesar's camp at Apollonia, partly because of our blockade but also because of the storm, which had blown them more than sixty miles north along the coast. Our navy had tried to pursue them, without success. Reportedly, men and materiel were now coming ashore around the port of Lissus. Pompey's intention was to crush them before they could link up with Caesar.

The next morning we rejoined the army and headed north. It was rumoured that the newly arrived general we would be facing was Mark Antony, Caesar's deputy – a report Cicero hoped was true, for he knew Antony: a young man of only thirty-four with a reputation for wildness and indiscipline; Cicero said he was not nearly as formidable a tactician as Caesar. However, when we drew closer to Lissus, where Antony was supposed to be, we found only his abandoned camp, dotted with dozens of smouldering fires where he had burned all the equipment his men could not carry with them. It turned out that he had led them east into the mountains.

We performed an abrupt about-turn and marched back south again. I thought we would return to Dyrrachium. Instead we passed by it in the distance, pressed on further south and after a four-day march took up a new position in a vast camp around the little town of Apsos. And now one began to get a sense of just how brilliant a general Caesar was, for we learned that somehow he *had* linked up with Antony, who had brought his army through the mountain passes, and that although Caesar's combined force was smaller than ours, nevertheless he had retrieved a hopeless position and was now on the offensive. He captured a settlement to our rear and cut us off from Dyrrachium. This was not a fatal disaster – Pompey's navy still commanded the coast, and we could be resupplied by sea across the beaches as long as the weather was not too rough. But one began to experience the uneasy sensation of being hemmed in. Sometimes we could see Caesar's men moving on the distant slopes of the mountains: he had control of the heights above us. And then he began a vast programme of construction – felling trees, building wooden forts, digging trenches and ditches and using the excavated earth to erect ramparts.

Naturally, our commanders tried to interrupt these works, and there were many skirmishes – sometimes four or five in a day. But the labour went on more or less continuously for several months until Caesar had completed a fifteen-mile fortified line that ran all the way round our position in a great loop, from the beaches to the north of our camp to the cliffs to the south. Within this loop we built our own system of trenches facing theirs, with perhaps fifty or a hundred paces of no man's land between the two sides. Siege engines were brought up and the artillerymen would lob rocks and flaming missiles at one another. Raiding parties would creep across the lines at night and slit the throats of the men in the opposing trench. When the wind dropped, we could hear them talking. Often they shouted insults at us; our men yelled back. I remember a constant atmosphere of tension. It began to prey on one's nerves.

Cicero fell ill with dysentery and spent most of his time reading and writing letters in his tent. 'Tent' was something of a misnomer. He and the leading senators seemed to vie with one another to see who could make their accommodation the most luxurious. There were carpets, couches, tables, statues and silverware shipped over from Italy on the inside, and walls of turf and leafy bowers outside. They dined with one another and bathed together as if they were still on the Palatine. Cicero became particularly close to Cato's nephew Brutus, who had the tent next door, and who was seldom seen without a book of philosophy in his hand. They would spend hours sitting up talking late into the night. Cicero liked him for his noble nature and his learning but worried that his head was actually crammed too full of philosophy for him to make practical use of it: 'I sometimes fear he may have been educated out of his wits.'

One of the peculiarities of this style of trench warfare was that one could also have quite friendly contact with the enemy. The ordinary soldiers would periodically meet in the unoccupied middle ground to talk or gamble, although our officers inflicted severe penalties for fraternisation. Letters were lobbed over from one side to the other. Cicero received several messages by sea from Rufus, who was in Rome, and even one from

Dolabella, who was with Caesar less than five miles away, and who sent a courier under a flag of truce:

> *If you are well I am glad. I myself am well and so is our Tullia. Terentia has been rather out of sorts, but I know for certain that she has now recovered. Otherwise all your domestic affairs are in excellent shape.*
>
> *You see Pompey's situation. Driven out of Italy, Spain lost, he is now, to crown it all, blockaded in his camp – a humiliation which I fancy has never previously befallen a Roman general. One thing I do beg of you: if he does manage to escape from his present dangerous position and takes refuge with his fleet, consult your own best interests and at long last be your own friend rather than anybody else's.*
>
> *My most delightful Cicero, if it turns out that Pompey is driven from this area too and forced to seek yet other regions of the earth, I hope you will retire to Athens or to any peaceful community you please. Any concessions that you need from the commander-in-chief to safeguard your dignity you will obtain with the greatest ease from so kindly a man as Caesar. I trust to your honour and kindness to see that the courier I am sending you is able to return to me and brings a letter from you.*

Cicero's breast could barely contain all the conflicting emotions aroused by reading this extraordinary missive – delight that Tullia was well, outrage at his son-in-law's impudence, guilty relief that Caesar's policy of clemency still extended to him, fear that the letter could fall into the hands of a fanatic like Ahenobarbus who might use it to bring a charge of treason against him …

He scribbled a cautious line to say that he was well and would continue to support the Senate's cause, and then he had the courier escorted back across our lines.

As the weather began to turn hotter, life became more unpleasant. Caesar had a genius for damming springs and diverting water – it was how he had often won sieges in France and Spain, and now he used the same tactic against us. He controlled the rivers and streams coming down from the mountains and his engineers cut them off. The grass turned brown. Water had to be brought in by sea in thousands of amphorae and was rationed. The senators' daily baths were forbidden on Pompey's orders. More importantly, the horses began to fall sick from dehydration and lack of forage. We knew that Caesar's men were in an even worse state – unlike us, they could not be resupplied with food by sea, and both Greece and Macedonia were closed to them. They were reduced to making their daily bread out of roots they grubbed up. But Caesar's battle-hardened veterans were tougher than our men; they showed no sign of weakening.

I am not sure how much longer this could have gone on. But about four months after our arrival in Dyrrachium, there was a breakthrough. Cicero was summoned to one of Pompey's irregular war councils in his vast tent in the centre of the camp, and returned a few hours later looking almost cheerful for once. He told us that two Gallic auxiliaries serving in Caesar's army had been caught stealing from their legionary comrades and sentenced to be flogged to death. Somehow they had managed to escape and come over to our side. They offered information in return for their lives. There was, they said, a weakness in Caesar's fortifications some two hundred paces wide, close to the sea: the outer perimeter appeared sound but there was no secondary line behind it. Pompey warned them they would die the most horrible death if what they had said proved to be false. They swore it was true, but begged him to hurry before the hole was plugged. He saw no reason to disbelieve them, and an attack was fixed for dawn the following day.

All that night our troops moved stealthily into position. Young Marcus, now a cavalry officer, was among them. Cicero fretted sleeplessly about his safety, and at first light he and I, accompanied by his lictors and Quintus, went over to watch the battle. Pompey had brought up a huge force. We could not get close enough to see what was happening. Cicero dismounted and we walked along the beach, the waves lapping at our ankles. Our ships were anchored in a line about a quarter of a mile offshore. Up ahead we could hear the noise of fighting mingling with the roar of the sea. The air was dark with clouds of arrows, occasionally lit up by flaming missiles. There must have been five thousand men on the beach. We were asked by one of the military tribunes not to proceed any further because of the danger, so we sat down under a myrtle tree and had something to eat.

Around midday the legion moved off and we followed it cautiously. The wooden fort Caesar's men had built in the dunes was in our hands, and in the flat lands beyond it thousands of men were deploying. It was very hot. Bodies lay everywhere, pierced by arrows and javelins or with horrible gaping wounds. To our right we saw several squadrons of cavalry galloping towards the fighting. Cicero was sure he spotted Marcus among them and we all cheered them loudly, but then Quintus recognised their colours and announced that they were Caesar's. At that point Cicero's lictors hustled him away from the battlefield and we returned to camp.

The battle of Dyrrachium, as it became known, was a great victory. Caesar's line was irretrievably broken and his entire position thrown into danger. Indeed he would have been utterly defeated that very day had it not been for the network of trenches that slowed up our advance and meant we had to dig in for the night. Pompey was hailed as imperator by his men on the field, and when he got back to the camp in his war chariot, attended by his bodyguards, he raced around inside the perimeter and up and down the torchlit tented streets, cheered by his legionaries.

The next day, towards the end of the morning, far in the distance in the direction of Caesar's camp, columns of smoke began to rise over the plain. At the same time reports started coming in from all around our front lines that the trenches opposite were empty. Our men ventured out cautiously at first but were soon wandering over the enemy's fortifications, astonished that so many months of labour could be so readily abandoned. But there was no doubt about it: Caesar's legionaries were marching off to the east along the Via Egnatia. We could see the dust. Whatever equipment they could not take was burning behind them. The siege was over.

Pompey summoned a meeting of the Senate-in-exile late in the afternoon to decide what should be done next. Cicero asked me to accompany him and Quintus so that he could have a record of what was decided. The sentries guarding Pompey's tent nodded me through without question and I took up a discreet position, standing at the side, along with the other secretaries and aides-de-camp. There must have been almost a hundred senators present, seated on benches. Pompey, who had been out all day inspecting Caesar's positions, arrived after everyone else, and was given a standing ovation, which he acknowledged with a touch of his marshal's baton to the side of his famous quiff. He reported on the situation of the two armies after the battle. The enemy had lost about a thousand men killed and three hundred taken prisoner. Immediately Labienus proposed that the prisoners should all be executed. 'I worry they will infect our own men who guard them with their treasonous thoughts. Besides, they have forfeited the right to life.'

Cicero, with a look of distaste, rose to object. 'We have achieved a mighty victory. The end of the war is in sight. Isn't now the time to be magnanimous?'

'No,' replied Labienus. 'An example must be made.'

'An example that can only cause Caesar's men to fight with even more determination once they learn the fate that awaits them if they surrender.'

'So be it. This tactic of Caesar's of offering clemency is a danger to our fighting spirit.' He glanced pointedly at Afranius, who lowered his head. 'If we take no prisoners, Caesar will be forced to do the same.'

Pompey spoke with a firmness that was designed to settle the matter. 'I agree with Labienus. Besides, Caesar's soldiers are traitors who have taken up arms illegally against their own countrymen. That puts them in a different category to our troops. Let's move on.'

But Cicero wouldn't let the matter drop. 'Wait a moment. Are we fighting for civilised values or are we wild beasts? These men are Romans just like us. I would like it to be recorded that in my view this is a mistake.'

'And I would like it to be recorded,' said Ahenobarbus, 'that it isn't only those who have fought openly on Caesar's side who should be treated as traitors, but all those who have tried to be neutral, or have argued for peace, or had contact with the enemy.'

Ahenobarbus was warmly applauded. Cicero's face flushed and he fell silent.

Pompey said, 'Well then, that's settled. Now it is my proposal that the entire army, bar let's say fifteen cohorts which I'll leave behind to defend Dyrrachium, should set off in pursuit of Caesar with a view to offering him battle at the first opportunity.'

This fateful pronouncement met with loud grunts of approval.

Cicero hesitated, glanced around and then stood up again. 'I seem to find myself playing the role of perennial contrarian. Forgive me – but is there not a case for seizing this opportunity and instead of chasing Caesar eastwards, sailing west instead to Italy and regaining control of Rome? That is after all supposed to be the point of this war.'

Pompey shook his head. 'No, that would be a strategic error. If we return to Italy, there will be nothing to stop Caesar conquering Macedonia and Greece.'

'Let him – I'd trade Macedonia and Greece for Italy and Rome any day. Besides, we have an army there under Scipio.'

'Scipio can't beat Caesar,' retorted Pompey. 'Only I can beat Caesar. And this war won't end merely because we're back in Rome. This war will end only when Caesar is dead.'

At the end of the conference, Cicero approached Pompey and asked for permission to remain behind in Dyrrachium rather than join the army on the campaign. Pompey, plainly irritated by his criticism, looked him up and down with something like contempt, then nodded. 'I think that's a good idea.' He turned from Cicero as if dismissing him, and began discussing with one of his officers the order in which the legions should depart the next day. Cicero waited for their conversation to end, presumably intending to wish Pompey good fortune. But Pompey was too engrossed in the logistics of the march, or at any rate he pretended to be, and eventually Cicero gave up and left the tent.

As we walked away, Quintus asked him why he didn't want to go with the army.

Cicero said, 'This global strategy of Pompey's means we could be stuck out here for years. I can't support it any longer. Nor to be frank can I face another journey through those damned mountains.'

'People will say it's because you're afraid.'

'Brother, I *am* afraid. So should you be. If we win, there'll be a massacre of good Roman blood – you heard Labienus. And if we lose …' He left it at that.

When we got back to his tent, he made a half-hearted attempt to persuade his son not to go either, even though he knew it was hopeless: Marcus had shown much bravery at Dyrrachium and despite his youth had been rewarded with the command of his own cavalry squadron. He was eager for battle. Quintus's son was also determined to fight.

Cicero said, 'Well then, go if you must. I admire your spirit. However, I shall stay here.'

'But Father,' protested Marcus, 'men will speak of this great clash of arms for a thousand years.'

'I'm too old to fight and too squeamish to watch others doing it. You three are the soldiers in the family.' He stroked Marcus's hair and pinched his cheek. 'Bring me back Caesar's head on a stick, won't you, my darling boy?' And then he announced that he needed to rest and turned away so that no one could see that he was crying.

Reveille was scheduled for an hour before dawn. Plagued by insomnia it seemed to me that I had barely fallen asleep when the infernal caterwauling of the war horns started. The legion's slaves came in and began dismantling the tent around me. Everything was timed exactly. Outside the sun had yet to show over the ridge. The mountains were still in shadow. But above them loomed a cloudless blood-red sky.

The scouts moved off at dawn, followed half an hour later by a detachment of Bythinian cavalry, and then, a further half-hour after that, Pompey, yawning loudly, surrounded by his staff officers and bodyguards. Our legion had been chosen for the honour of serving as the vanguard on the march and therefore was the next to leave. Cicero stood by the gate, and as his brother and son and nephew passed, he raised his hand and called farewell to each in turn. This time he did not try to conceal his tears. Two hours later, all the tents were down, the refuse fires were burning and the last of the baggage mules was swaying out of the deserted camp.

With the army gone, we set off to ride the thirty miles to Dyrrachium escorted by Cicero's lictors.

Our road took us past Caesar's old defensive line, and soon we came upon the spot where Labienus had massacred the prisoners. Their throats had been cut and a gang of slaves was burying the corpses in one of the old defensive ditches. The stench of ripening flesh in the summer heat and the sight of the vultures circling overhead are among the many memories of that campaign I would prefer to forget. We spurred our horses and pressed on to Dyrrachium, reaching it before dusk.

We were billeted away from the cliffs this time for safety, in a house within the walls of the city. Command of the garrison should, in principle, have been awarded to Cicero, who was the senior ex-consul and who still possessed imperium as governor of Cilicia. But it was a sign of the mistrust in which he had come to be held that Pompey gave the position instead to Cato, who had never risen higher than praetor. Cicero was not offended. On the contrary, he was glad to escape the responsibility: the troops Pompey had left behind were his least reliable, and Cicero had serious doubts about their loyalty if it came to fighting.

The days dragged by very slowly. Those senators who, like Cicero, had not gone with the army acted as if the war was already won. For example they drew up lists of those who had stayed behind in Rome, and who would be killed on our return, and whose property would be seized to pay for the war; one of the wealthy men they proscribed was Atticus. Then they squabbled over who would get which house. Other senators fought shamelessly over the jobs and titles that would fall vacant with the demise of Caesar and his lieutenants – Spinther I remember was adamant that he should be pontifex maximus. Cicero observed to me, 'The one outcome worse than losing this war will be winning it.'

As for him, his mind was full of cares and anxieties. Tullia continued to be short of money and the second instalment of her dowry remained unpaid, despite Cicero's instructions to Terentia to sell some of his property. All his old worries about her relationship with Philotimus and their fondness for questionable money-making schemes came crowding back into his mind. He chose to convey his anger and suspicion by writing her infrequent, short and chilly letters in which he did not even address her by name.

But his greatest fears were for Marcus and Quintus, still on the march somewhere with Pompey. Two months had passed since their departure. The Senate's army had pursued Caesar across the mountains to the plain of Thessalonica and had then struck south: that much was known. But where exactly they were now, no one knew, and the further Caesar drew them away from Dyrrachium and the longer the silence went on, the more uneasy the atmosphere in the garrison became.

The commander of the fleet, Caius Coponius, was a clever but highly strung senator who had a strong belief in signs and omens, especially portentous dreams, which he encouraged his men to share with their officers. One day, when there was still no news from Pompey, he came to dine with Cicero. Also at the table were Cato and M. Terentius Varro, the great scholar and poet, who had commanded a legion in Spain and who, like Afranius, had been pardoned by Caesar.

Coponius said, 'I had an unsettling encounter just before I set off to come here. You know that immense Rhodian quinquereme, the *Europa*, anchored offshore down there? One of the oarsmen was brought to see me to recount his dream. He claims to have had a vision of a terrible battle on some high Grecian plain, with the blood soaking into the dust and men limbless and groaning, and then this city besieged with all of us fleeing to the ships and looking back and seeing the place in flames.'

Normally this was just the sort of gloomy prophecy Cicero liked to laugh at, but not this time. Cato and Varro looked equally pensive. Cato said, 'And how did this dream end?'

'For him, very well – he and his comrades will enjoy a swift voyage back to Rhodes, apparently. So I suppose that's hopeful.'

Another silence fell over the table. Eventually Cicero said, 'Unfortunately, that merely suggests to me that our Rhodian allies will desert us.'

The first hints that some terrible disaster had occurred began to emanate from the docks. Several fishermen from the island of Corcyra,[1] about two days' voyage to the south, claimed to have passed a group of men encamped on a beach on the mainland, who had shouted out that they were survivors from Pompey's army. Another merchant vessel put in the same day with a similar tale – of desperate, starving men crowding the little fishing villages trying to find some means of escape from the soldiers they cried out were pursuing them.

Cicero attempted to console himself and others by saying that all wars consisted of rumours that frequently turned out to be false, and that perhaps these phantoms were merely deserters, or the survivors of some skirmish rather than a full-scale battle. But I think he knew in his heart that the gods of war were with Caesar: I believe he had foreseen it all along, which was why he did not go with Pompey.

Confirmation came the next evening, when he received an urgent summons to attend Cato's headquarters. I went with him. There was a terrible atmosphere of panic and despair. The secretaries were already burning correspondence and account books in the garden to prevent them falling into enemy hands. Inside, Cato, Varro, Coponius and some of the other leading senators were seated in a grim circle around a bearded, filthy man, badly cut about the face. This was the once-proud Titus Labienus, commander of Pompey's cavalry and the man who had slaughtered the prisoners. He was exhausted, having ridden non-stop for ten days with a few of his men across the mountains. Sometimes he would lose the thread of his story and forget himself, or nod off, or repeat things – occasionally he would break down entirely – so that my notes are incoherent and perhaps it is best if I simply say what we eventually discovered happened.

1 Corfu

The battle, which at that time had no name but afterwards came to be called Pharsalus, should never have been lost, according to Labienus, and he spoke bitterly of Pompey's generalship, calling it vastly inferior to Caesar's. (Mind you, others, whose tales we heard later, blamed the defeat partly on Labienus himself.) Pompey occupied the best ground, he had the most troops – his cavalry outnumbered Caesar's by seven to one – and he could choose the timing of the battle. Even so, he had hesitated to engage the enemy. Only after some of the other commanders, notably Ahenobarbus, had openly accused him of cowardice had he drawn up his forces to fight. Labienus said, 'That was when I saw his heart wasn't in it. Despite what he said to us, he never felt confident of beating Caesar.' And so the two armies had faced one another across a wide plain; and the enemy, at last offered his chance, had attacked.

Caesar had obviously recognised from the start that his cavalry was his greatest weakness and therefore had cunningly stationed some two thousand of his best infantry out of sight behind them. So when Labienus's horsemen had broken the charge of their opponents and gone after them in an attempt to turn Caesar's flank, they suddenly found themselves confronted by a line of advancing legionaries. The cavalrymen's attack broke upon the shields and javelins of these fierce unyielding veterans and they galloped from the field, despite Labienus's attempts to rally them. (All the time he was speaking I was thinking of Marcus: a reckless youth, he, I was sure, would not have been one of those who fled.) With their enemy's cavalry gone, Caesar's men had fallen upon Pompey's unprotected archers and wiped them out. After that, it was a slaughter as Pompey's panicking infantry had proved no match for Caesar's disciplined, hardened troops.

Cato said, 'How many men did we lose?'

'I cannot say – thousands.'

'And where was Pompey amid all this?'

'When he saw what was happening, he was like a man paralysed. He could barely speak, let alone issue coherent orders. He left the field with his bodyguard and returned to camp. I never saw him after that.' Labienus covered his face with his hands; we waited; when he had recovered, he went on: 'I'm told he lay down in his tent until Caesar's men broke through the defences and then he got away with a handful of others; he was last seen riding north towards Larissa.'

'And Caesar?'

'No one knows. Some say he's gone off with a small detachment in pursuit of Pompey, others that he's at the head of his army and coming this way.'

'Coming this way?'

Knowing Caesar's reputation for forced marches and the speed at which his troops could move, Cato proposed that they should evacuate Dyrrachium immediately. He was very cool. To Cicero's surprise, he revealed that he had already discussed precisely this contingency with Pompey, and that it had been decided that in the event of a defeat, all the surviving leadership of the senatorial cause should attempt to make for Corcyra – which, as an island, could be sealed off and defended by the fleet.

By now, rumours of Pompey's defeat were spreading throughout the garrison, and the meeting was interrupted by reports of soldiers refusing to obey orders; there had already been some looting. It was agreed that we should embark the next day. Before we returned to our house, Cicero put his hand on Labienus's shoulder and asked him if he knew what had happened to Marcus or Quintus. Labienus raised his head and looked at him as if he were crazy even to ask the question – the slaughter of thousands seemed to swirl like smoke in those staring, bloodshot eyes. He muttered, 'What do I know? I can only tell you that at least I did not see them dead.' Then he added, as Cicero turned to go, 'You were right – we should have returned to Rome.'

XLVIII

And so the prophecy of the Rhodian oarsman came true, and the following day we fled from Dyrrachium. The granaries had been ransacked and I remember how the precious corn was strewn across the streets and crunched beneath our shoes. The lictors had to clear a passage for Cicero, striking out with their rods to get him through the panicking crowds. But when we reached the dockside, we found it even more impassable than the streets. It seemed that every captain of a seaworthy craft was being besieged by offers of money to carry people to safety. I saw the most pitiful scenes – families with all the belongings they could carry, including their dogs and parrots, attempting to force their way on to ships; matrons wrenching the rings from their fingers and offering their most precious family heirlooms for a place in a humble rowing boat; the white doll-like corpse of a baby dropped from the gangplank by its mother in a fumble of terror and drowned.

The harbour was so clogged with vessels it took hours for the tender to pick us up and ferry us out to our warship. By then it was growing dark. The big Rhodian quinquereme had gone: Rhodes, as Cicero had predicted, had deserted the Senate's cause. Cato came aboard, followed by the other leaders, and immediately we slipped anchor – the captain preferring the dangers of a night-time voyage to the risks of remaining where we were. When we had gone a mile or two we looked back and saw an immense red glow in the sky; afterwards we learnt that the mutinying soldiers had set all the ships in the harbour on fire so that they could not be forced to sail to Corcyra and continue to fight.

We rowed on throughout the night. The smooth sea and the rocky coastline were silvered in the moonlight. The only sounds were the splash of the oars and the murmur of men's voices in the darkness. Cicero spent a long time talking alone with Cato. Later he told me that Cato was not merely calm, he was serene. 'This is what a lifetime's devotion to stoicism can do for you. As far as he's concerned, he has followed his conscience and is at peace; he is fully resigned to death. He is as dangerous in his way as Caesar and Pompey.'

I asked him what he meant. He took his time replying.

'Do you remember what I wrote in my little work on politics? How long ago that seems! "Just as the purpose of a pilot is to ensure a smooth passage for his ship, and of a doctor to make his patient healthy, so the statesman's objective must be the happiness of his country." Not once has either Caesar or Pompey conceived of their role in that way. For them, it is all a matter of their personal glory. And so it is with Cato. I tell you, the man is actually quite content simply to have been right, even though this is where his principles have led us – to this fragile vessel drifting alone in the moonlight along a foreign shore.'

He was utterly disillusioned with it all – recklessly so, in truth. When we reached Corcyra, we found that beautiful island crowded with refugees from the carnage of Pharsalus. The tales of chaos and incompetence were appalling. Of Pompey, there was no word. If he was alive, he sent no message; if he was dead, no one had seen his body: he had vanished from the earth. In the absence of the commander-in-chief, Cato called a meeting of the Senate in the Temple of Zeus, on its promontory overlooking the sea, to decide the future conduct of the war. That once-numerous assembly was now reduced to about fifty men. Cicero had hoped to be reunited with his son and brother, but they were nowhere to be found. Instead he saw other survivors – Metellus Scipio, Afranius and young Gnaeus, the son of Pompey, who had convinced himself that his father's ruin was entirely the result of treachery. I noticed how he kept glaring at Cicero; I feared he could be dangerous. Cassius was also present. But Ahenobarbus was not – it turned out that he was one of the many senators who had been killed in the battle. Outside, it was hot and dazzling; inside, cool and shadowy. A statue of Zeus, twice the size of a man, looked down with indifference upon the deliberations of these beaten mortals.

Cato began by stating that in Pompey's absence the Senate needed to appoint a new commander-in-chief. 'It should go, according to our ancient custom, to the most senior ex-consul among us, and therefore I propose it should be Cicero.'

Cicero burst out laughing. All heads turned to look at him.

'Seriously, gentlemen?' responded Cicero with incredulity. 'Seriously – after all that has occurred, you think that *I* should assume direction of this catastrophe? If it was my leadership you wanted, you should have listened to my counsel earlier, and then we would not be in our present desperate straits. I refuse this honour absolutely.'

It was unwise for him to have spoken so harshly. He was exhausted and overwrought, but then so were they all, and some were also wounded. The cries of protest and disgust were eventually stilled by Cato, who said, 'I take it from what Cicero says that he regards our position as hopeless, and that he would sue for peace.'

Cicero said, 'I would, most certainly. Haven't enough good men died to satisfy your philosophy?'

Scipio said, 'We have suffered a reverse but we are not defeated. There are still allies loyal to us all over the world, especially King Juba in Africa.'

'So that is what we have sunk to, is it? Fighting alongside Numidian barbarians against our fellow Romans?'

'Nevertheless, we still have seven eagles.'

'Seven eagles would be fine if we were fighting *jackdaws*.'

'What do you know of fighting,' demanded Gnaeus Pompey, 'you contemptible old coward?' And with that he drew his sword and lunged at Cicero. I was sure that Cicero was about to die, but with the skill of an expert swordsman Gnaeus checked his thrust at the last moment and left the tip of his blade touching Cicero's throat. 'I propose we kill this traitor, and I ask the Senate's permission to do the deed this instant.' And he pressed just a fraction harder so that Cicero had to tilt his head right back to avoid having his windpipe pierced.

'Stop, Gnaeus!' cried Cato. 'You will bring shame on your father! Cicero is a friend of his – he wouldn't want to see him insulted in this way. Remember where you are and put your sword down.'

I doubt whether anyone else could have stopped Gnaeus when his blood was up. For a moment or two the young brute hesitated, but then he withdrew his sword, and swore and stamped back to his place. Cicero straightened and stared directly ahead. A trickle of blood ran down his neck and stained the front of his toga.

Cato said, 'Listen to me, gentlemen. You know my views. When our republic was under threat, I believed it was our right and duty to compel every citizen, the lukewarm and the bad included, to support our cause and protect the state. But now the republic is lost …' He paused and looked around; no one challenged his assertion. 'Now that our republic is lost,' he repeated quietly, 'even I believe it would be senseless and cruel to compel any individual to share in its ruin. Let those who wish to continue the fight remain here, and we shall discuss our future strategy. Let those who wish to retire from the struggle depart from this assembly now – and let no man do them harm.'

At first no one moved. And then very slowly Cicero rose to his feet. He nodded to Cato, whom he knew had saved his life, and then turned and walked out – out of the temple, out of the senatorial cause, out of the war and out of public life.

Cicero feared that if he stayed on the island he would be murdered – if not by Gnaeus then by one of his associates. Accordingly we left that same day. We could not sail back north again in case the coast had fallen into enemy hands. Instead we found ourselves drifting further south, until after several days we arrived in Patrae, the port where I had spent my illness. As soon as the ship docked, Cicero sent word by one of his lictors to his friend Curius to say that we were in the city, and without waiting for a reply, we hired litters and porters to transport us and our baggage to his house.

I believe the lictor must have lost his way, or perhaps he was tempted by the bars of Patrae, for all six lictors in their boredom since our departure from Cilicia had fallen into the habit of drinking heavily. At any rate, we arrived at the villa before our messenger did, only to be told that Curius was away for two days on business, at which point we heard male conversation emanating from the interior. The voices sounded familiar. We glanced at one another, neither of us quite believing what we were hearing, then hurried past the steward and into the tablinum to discover Quintus, Marcus and Quintus Junior seated in a huddle. They turned to stare at us in amazement, and I sensed at once a certain embarrassment. I am fairly certain they must have been speaking ill of us – or rather of Cicero. This awkwardness, I should add, was over in an instant – Cicero never even noticed it – and we fell upon one another and kissed and embraced with the sincerest affection. I was shocked by how haggard they looked. There was something haunted about them, as there had been with the other survivors of Pharsalus, although they tried not to show it.

Quintus said, 'This is the most wonderful good fortune! We'd engaged a ship and were planning to set off for Corcyra tomorrow, having heard that the Senate was assembling there. And to think we might have missed you! What happened? Did the conference end earlier than expected?'

Cicero said, 'No, the conference is still going on, as far as I know.'

'But you're not with them?'

'Let us discuss that later. First let us hear what happened to you.'

They took it in turns to tell their story, like runners in a relay race handing on the baton – first the month-long march in pursuit of Caesar's army and the occasional skirmishes along the way, and then at last the great confrontation at Pharsalus. On the eve of the battle Pompey had dreamed that he was in Rome entering the Temple of Venus the Victorious, and that the people were applauding him as he offered the goddess the spoils of war. He awoke content, thinking this a good omen, but then someone pointed out that Caesar claimed direct descent from Venus, and immediately he decided the meaning of the dream was the opposite of what he'd hoped. 'From that moment on,' said Quintus, 'he seemed resigned to losing and acted accordingly.' The Quinti had been in the second line and so had avoided the worst of the fighting. Marcus, though, had been in the middle of the struggle. He reckoned he had killed at least four of the enemy – one with his javelin, three with his sword – and had been confident of victory until the cohorts of Caesar's Tenth Legion had seemed to rise up out of the ground before them. 'Our units lost formation: it was massacre, Father.' It had taken them the best part of a month, much of it spent living rough and dodging Caesar's patrols, to escape to the western coast.

'And Pompey?' asked Cicero. 'Is there news of him?'

'None,' replied Quintus, 'but I believe I can guess where he went: east, to Lesbos. That's where he sent Cornelia to await news of his victory. In defeat I'm certain he would have gone to her for consolation – you know what he's like with his wives. Caesar must have guessed the same. He's after him like a bounty hunter in pursuit of a runaway slave. My money is on Caesar in that particular race. And if he catches him, or kills him, what do you think that will mean for the war?'

Cicero said, 'Oh, the war will go on, it seems, whatever happens – but it will continue without me,' and then he told them what had happened at Corcyra. I am sure he did not mean to sound flippant. It was simply that he was happy to have found his family alive, and naturally that light-hearted mood coloured his remarks. But as he repeated, with some satisfaction, his quip about eagles and jackdaws, and mocked the very idea that he should take command of "this losing cause", and derided the bone-headedness of Gnaeus Pompey – 'He makes even his father look intelligent' – I could see Quintus's jaw beginning to work back and forth in irritation; even Marcus's expression was clenched with disapproval.

'So that's it, then?' said Quintus in a cold, flat voice. 'As far as this family is concerned, it's over?'

'Do you disagree?'

'I feel I should have been consulted.'

'How could I consult you? You weren't there.'

'No, I wasn't. How could I have been? I was fighting in the war you encouraged me to join, and then I was trying to save my life, along with those of your son and your nephew!'

Too late Cicero saw how casually he had spoken. 'My dear brother, I assure you, your welfare – the welfare of all of you – has ever been uppermost in my mind.'

'Spare me your casuistry, Marcus. Nothing is ever uppermost in your mind except yourself. *Your* honour, *your* career, *your* interests – so that while other men go off to die, you sit behind with the elderly and the womenfolk, polishing your speeches and your pointless witticisms!'

'Please, Quintus – you are in danger of saying things you will regret.'

'My only regret is that I didn't say them years ago. So let me say them now, and you will do me the courtesy of sitting there and listening to *me* for once! My whole life has been lived as nothing more than an appendix to yours – I am no more important to you than poor Tiro here, whose health has been broken in your service; less important, actually, as I don't have his skills as a note-taker. When I went out to Asia as governor, you tricked me into staying for two years rather than one, so that you could have access to my funds to pay off your debts. During your exile I almost died fighting Clodius in the streets of Rome, and my reward when you came home was to be packed off again, to Sardinia, to appease Pompey. And now here I am, thanks largely to you, on the losing side in a civil war, when it would have been perfectly honourable for me to have stood side by side with Caesar, who gave me command of a legion in Gaul …'

There was more in this vein. Cicero endured it without comment or movement, apart from the occasional clenching and unclenching of his hands on the armrests of his chair. Marcus looked on, white with shock. Young Quintus smirked and nodded. As for me, I yearned to leave but couldn't: some force seemed to have pinned my feet to the spot.

Quintus worked himself up into such a pitch of fury that by the end he was breathless, his chest heaving as if he had shifted some heavy physical load. 'Your action in abandoning the Senate's cause without consulting me or considering my interests is the final selfish blow. Remember, my position wasn't exquisitely ambiguous like yours: I *fought* at Pharsalus – I am a marked man. So I have no choice: I shall have to try to find Caesar, wherever he is, and plead for his pardon, and believe me, when I see him, I shall have something to tell him about *you*.'

With that he stalked out of the room, followed by his son; and then, after a short hesitation, Marcus left too. In the shocking silence that ensued, Cicero continued to sit immobile. Eventually I asked if there was anything I could fetch him, and when still he made no response, I wondered if he might have suffered a seizure. Then I heard footsteps. It was Marcus returning. He knelt beside the chair.

'I have said goodbye to them, Father. I will stay with you.'

Wordless for once, Cicero grasped his hand, and I withdrew to let them talk.

Cicero took to his bed and remained in his room for the next few days. He refused to see a doctor – 'My heart is broken and no Greek quack can fix that' – and kept his door locked. I hoped that Quintus would return and the quarrel might be repaired, but he had meant what he said and had left the city. When Curius got back from his business trip, I explained what had happened as discreetly as I could, and he agreed with me and Marcus that the best course was for us to charter a ship and sail back to Italy while the weather was still fair. Such, then, was the grotesque paradox we had reached: that Cicero was likely to be safer in a country under Caesar's control than he would be in Greece, where armed bands belonging to the republican cause were only too eager to strike down men perceived as traitors.

As soon as his depression had lifted sufficiently for him to contemplate the future, Cicero approved this plan – 'I'd rather die in Italy than here' – and when there was a decent south-easterly wind we embarked. The voyage was good, and after four days at sea we saw on the horizon the great lighthouse at Brundisium. It was a blessed sight. Cicero had been away from the mother country for a year and a half, I for more than three years.

Fearful of his reception, Cicero remained in his cabin below decks while I went ashore with Marcus to find somewhere for us to stay. The best we could manage for that first night was a noisy inn near the waterfront, and we decided that the safest course would be for Cicero to come ashore at dusk wearing an ordinary toga belonging to Marcus rather than one of his own with the purple stripe of a senator. An additional complication was the presence, like the chorus in a tragedy, of his six lictors – for absurdly, although he was entirely powerless, he still technically possessed imperium as governor of Cilicia, and was reluctant even now to break the law by sending them away; nor would they leave him until they had been paid. So they too had to be disguised and their fasces wrapped in sacking and rooms hired for them.

Cicero found this procedure so humiliating that after a sleepless night he resolved the next day to announce his presence to whoever was the most senior representative of Caesar in the town and accept whatever fate was decreed for him. He had me search through his correspondence for Dolabella's letter guaranteeing his safety – *Any concessions that you need from the commander-in-chief to safeguard your dignity you will obtain with the greatest ease from so kindly a man as Caesar* – and I made sure I had it with me when I went to the military headquarters.

The new commander of the region turned out to be Publius Vatinius, widely known as the ugliest man in Rome, and an old opponent of Cicero's – indeed it was Vatinius, as tribune, who had first proposed the law awarding Caesar both the provinces of Gaul and an army for five years. He had fought with his old chief at the battle of Dyrrachium and returned to take control of the whole of southern Italy. But by a great stroke of good fortune Cicero had made up his quarrel with Vatinius at Caesar's request several years before and had defended him in a prosecution for bribery.

As soon as he learned of my arrival, I was shown straight into his presence and he greeted me most affably.

Dear gods, he *was* ugly! His eyes were crossed, and his face and neck were covered in scrofulous growths the colour of birthmarks. But what did his looks matter? He barely even glanced at Dolabella's letter before assuring me that it was an honour to welcome Cicero back to Italy, that he would protect his dignity as he was sure Caesar would wish, and that he would arrange for suitable accommodation to be provided while he awaited instructions from Rome.

The latter phrase sounded ominous. 'May I ask who will issue these instructions?'

'Well indeed – that is a good question. We are still sorting out our administration. Caesar has been appointed dictator for a year by the Senate – *our* Senate, that is,' he added with a wink, 'but he is still away chasing your former commander-in-chief, and so in his absence, power is vested in the Master of Horse.'

'And who is that?'

'Mark Antony.'

My spirits sank further.

That same day Vatinius sent a platoon of legionaries to escort us with our baggage to a house in a quiet district of the town. Cicero was carried all the way in a closed litter so that his presence remained a secret.

It was a small villa, old, with thick walls and tiny windows. A sentry was posted outside. To begin with, Cicero was simply relieved to be back in Italy. Only gradually did he realise that he was in fact under house arrest. It was not so much that he was physically prevented from leaving the villa – he did not venture beyond the gate, so we never discovered what orders the guards had been given. Rather, Vatinius implied, when he came to check how Cicero was settling in, it would be dangerous for him to leave, and, worse, disrespectful towards Caesar's hospitality. For the first time we tasted life under a dictatorship: there were no freedoms any more; no magistrates, no courts; one existed at the whim of the ruler.

Cicero wrote to Mark Antony asking permission to return to Rome. But he did so without much hope. Although he and Antony had always been polite to one another, there was a long-standing enmity between them, born of the fact that Antony's stepfather, P. Lentulus Sura, had been one of the five co-conspirators of Catilina that Cicero had had executed.

Therefore it was no surprise when Antony refused Cicero's request. Cicero's fate, he said, was a matter for Caesar, and until Caesar made a ruling, he must stay in Brundisium.

I would say that the months that followed were the worst of Cicero's life – worse even than his first exile in Thessalonica. At least then there had still been a republic to fight for, there was honour in his struggle, and his family was united; now these supports had gone, and all was death, dishonour and discord. And so much death! So many old friends gone! One could almost smell it in the air. We had only been in Brundisium a few days when we were visited by C. Matius Calvena, a wealthy member of the equestrian order and a close associate of Caesar, who told us that both Milo and Caelius Rufus had died trying to stir up trouble together in Campania – Milo, at the head of a ragamuffin army of his old gladiators, had been killed in battle by one of Caesar's lieutenants; Rufus had been put to death on the spot by some Spanish and Gallic horsemen he had been trying to bribe. The death of Rufus at the age of only thirty-four was a particular blow to Cicero, and he wept when he heard of it – which was more than he did when he learned of the fate of Pompey.

Vatinius brought us the news of that himself, his hideous features especially composed for the occasion into a simulacrum of grief.

Cicero said, 'Is there any doubt?'

'None whatever – I have a dispatch here from Caesar: he has seen his severed head.'

Cicero blanched and sat down, and I pictured that massive head with its thick crest of hair and that bull neck: it must have taken some effort to hack it off, I thought, and been quite a sight for Caesar to behold.

'Caesar wept when he was shown it,' Vatinius added, as if he had seen into my mind.

Cicero said, 'When did this happen?'

'Two months ago.'

Vatinius read aloud from Caesar's account. It transpired that Pompey had done exactly as Quintus had predicted: he had fled from Pharsalus to Lesbos to seek solace with Cornelia; his youngest son, Sextus, was also with her. Together they had embarked in a trireme and sailed to Egypt, in the hope of persuading the Pharaoh to join his cause. He had anchored off the coast at Pelusium and sent word of his arrival. But the Egyptians had heard of the disaster at Pharsalus and preferred to side with the winner.

Rather than merely send Pompey away, they saw an opportunity to gain credit with Caesar by taking care of his enemy for him. Pompey was invited ashore for talks. A tender was sent to fetch him, containing Achillas, general of the Egyptian army, and several senior Roman officers who had served under Pompey and now commanded the Roman forces protecting the Pharaoh.

Despite the entreaties of his wife and son, Pompey had boarded the tender. The assassins had waited until he was stepping ashore and then one of them, the military tribune Lucius Septimius, had run him through from behind with his sword. Achillas then drew his dagger and stabbed him, as did a second Roman officer, Salvius.

'Caesar wishes it to be known that Pompey met his death bravely. According to witnesses, he drew his toga over his face with both hands and fell down upon the sand. He did not beg or plead but only groaned a little as they finished him off. The cries of Cornelia, who watched the murder, could be heard from the shore.

'Caesar was only three days behind Pompey. When he arrived in Alexandria he was shown the head and Pompey's signet ring on which is engraved a lion holding a sword in its paws; he encloses it with this letter as proof of the story. The body having already been burnt where it fell, Caesar has given orders for the ashes to be sent to Pompey's widow.'

Vatinius rolled up the letter and handed it to his aide.

'My condolences,' he said, and saluted. 'He was a fine soldier.'

'But not fine enough,' said Cicero, after Vatinius had gone.

Later he wrote to Atticus:

As to Pompey's end I never had any doubt, for all rulers and peoples had become so thoroughly persuaded of the hopelessness of his case that wherever he went I expected this to happen. I cannot but grieve for his fate. I knew him for a man of good character, clean life and serious principle.

That was all he had to say. He never wept over the loss, and thereafter I barely heard him mention Pompey again.

Terentia did not offer to visit Cicero and he did not ask to see her; on the contrary: *There is no reason for you to leave home at present*, he wrote to her. *It is a long, unsafe journey, and I do not see what good you can do if you come.*

He sat by the fire that winter and brooded on the state of his family. His brother and nephew were still in Greece and writing and speaking about him in the most poisonous terms: Vatinius and Atticus both showed him copies of their letters. His wife, whom he had no desire to meet, was refusing to send him any money to pay for his living expenses; when finally he arranged for Atticus to advance him some cash via a local banker, he discovered that she had deducted two thirds of it for her own use. His son was out all hours drinking with the local soldiers and refusing to attend to his studies: he yearned for war and often did not trouble to hide his contempt for his father's situation.

But mostly Cicero brooded on his daughter.

He learned from Atticus that Dolabella, who had returned to Rome as tribune of the plebs, now ignored Tullia entirely. He had left the marital home and was having affairs all over the city, most notoriously with Antonia, the wife of Mark Antony (an infidelity that enraged Antony, even though he lived quite openly with his own mistress, Volumnia Cytheris, a nude actress; later he divorced Antonia and married Fulvia, the widow of Clodius). Dolabella gave Tullia no money for her upkeep, and Terentia – despite Cicero's repeated pleas – was refusing to pay off her creditors, saying it was her husband's responsibility. Cicero blamed himself entirely for the wreckage of his public and private lives. *My ruin is my own work,* he wrote to Atticus. *Nothing in my adversity is due to chance. I am to blame for it all. Worse than the rest of my afflictions put together, however, is that I shall leave that poor girl despoiled of her father, of her inheritance, of all that was supposed to be hers …*

In the spring, with still no word from Caesar who was said to be in Egypt with his latest paramour, Queen Cleopatra, Cicero received a letter from Tullia announcing her intention of joining him in Brundisium. He was alarmed that she should undertake such an arduous expedition alone. But it was too late for him to stop her – she had made sure she was already on the road before he learned of her intentions – and I shall never forget his horror when at last she arrived, after a month of travelling, attended only by a maid and one elderly male slave.

'My darling girl, don't tell me this is the extent of your entourage … How could your mother have allowed it? You might have been robbed, or worse.'

'There's no point in worrying about it now, Father. I'm here safe and well, aren't I? And to see you again is worth any risk or discomfort.'

The journey showed the strength of the spirit that burned within that fragile frame, and soon her presence was brightening the entire household. Rooms shut up for the winter began to be cleaned and redecorated. Flowers appeared. The food improved. Even young Marcus tried to be civilised in her company. But more important than these domestic improvements was the revival in Cicero's spirits. Tullia was a clever young woman: if she had been born a man, she would have made a good advocate. She read poetry and philosophy and – what was harder – understood them well enough to hold her own in a discussion with her father. She did not complain, but made light of her troubles. *I believe her like on earth has never been seen*, Cicero wrote to Atticus.

The more he came to admire her, the less he could forgive Terentia for the way she had treated her. Occasionally he would mutter to me, 'What kind of mother allows her daughter to travel hundreds of miles without an escort, or stands by and allows her to be humiliated by tradesmen whose bills she cannot pay?' One night when we were having dinner he asked Tullia straight out what she thought could explain Terentia's behaviour.

Tullia answered simply, 'Money.'

'But that's ridiculous. Money – it's so demeaning.'

'She's got it into her head that Caesar will need to raise a huge sum to pay for the costs of the war, and the only way he'll get it is by confiscating the property of his opponents – you chief among them.'

'And for that reason she lets you live in penury? Where's the logic in that?'

Tullia hesitated before replying. 'Father, the last thing I want to do is to add to your anxieties. That's why until this moment I've said nothing. But now that you seem stronger, I think you ought to know why I wanted to come, and why Mother wanted to stop me. She and Philotimus have been plundering your estate for months – perhaps years. Not just the rent from your properties, but your houses themselves. You'd barely recognise some of them any more – they've been almost entirely stripped.'

Cicero's first reaction was disbelief. 'It can't be true. Why? How could she do such a thing?'

'I can only tell you what she said to me: "He may sink into ruin because of his own folly but I shan't let him take me with him."' Tullia paused and added quietly, 'If you want the truth, I believe she's been taking back her dowry.'

And now Cicero began to grasp the situation. 'You mean she's divorcing me?'

'I don't think she's fully decided yet. But I believe she's taking precautions in case it comes to that and you no longer have the means of repaying her yourself.' She leaned across the table and grasped his hand. 'Try not to be too angry with her, Father. Money is her only means of independence. She still has very strong feelings for you, I know it.'

Cicero, unable to control his emotions, left the table and went out into the garden.

Of all the disasters and betrayals that had struck him over recent years, this was the worst. It completed the collapse of his fortunes. He was numbed by it. What made it harder was that Tullia begged him to say nothing about it until such time as he could confront Terentia face to face, otherwise her mother would know it was she who was his informant. The notion of a meeting seemed a remote prospect. And then, out of the blue, just as the heat of the summer was starting to become uncomfortable, a letter arrived from Caesar.

Caesar Dictator to Cicero Imperator.

I have received various messages from your brother complaining of dishonesty on your part towards me and insisting that but for your influence he would never have taken up arms against me. I have sent these letters to Balbus to pass on to you. You may do with them as you wish. I have pardoned him, and his son. They may live where they please. But I have no desire to renew relations with him. His behaviour towards you confirms a certain low opinion I had begun to form of him in Gaul.

I am travelling ahead of my army and will return to Italy earlier than expected next month, landing at Tarentum, when I hope it will be possible for us to meet to settle matters regarding your own future once and for all.

Tullia was greatly excited when she read this: she called it 'a handsome letter'. But Cicero was secretly thrown into confusion. He had hoped he would be allowed to make his way back quietly to Rome, without fuss.

He viewed the prospect of actually meeting Caesar with dread. The Dictator would doubtless be friendly enough, even if the gang around him were rough and insolent. However, no amount of politeness could disguise the basic truth: that he would be begging for his life from a conqueror who had usurped the constitution. Meanwhile fresh reports were coming in almost every day from Africa, where Cato was raising a huge new army to continue to uphold the republican cause.

He put on a cheerful face for Tullia's sake, only to collapse into agonies of conscience once she had gone to bed. 'You know that I have always tried to steer the right course by asking myself how history would judge my actions. Well, in this instance I can be certain of the verdict. History will say that Cicero wasn't with Cato and the good cause because in the end Cicero was a coward. Oh, I have made such a mess of it all, Tiro! I actually believe Terentia is quite right to salvage what she can from the wreckage and divorce me.'

Soon afterwards Vatinius brought the news that Caesar had landed at Tarentum and wished to see Cicero the day after tomorrow.

Cicero said, 'Where exactly are we to go?'

'He is staying in Pompey's old villa by the sea. Do you know it?'

Cicero nodded. No doubt he was recalling his last visit, when he and Pompey had skimmed stones across the waves. 'I know it.'

Vatinius insisted on providing a military escort, even though Cicero said that he would prefer to travel without ostentation: 'No, I'm afraid that's out of the question: the countryside is too dangerous. I hope we will meet again soon in happier circumstances. Good luck with Caesar. You will find him gracious, I'm sure.'

Afterwards, as I was showing him out, Vatinius said, 'He doesn't seem very happy.'

'He feels his humiliation keenly. The fact that he will have to bow the knee in his old chief's former home will only add to his discomfort.'

'I might let Caesar know that.'

We set off the next morning – ten cavalrymen in the vanguard, followed by the six lictors; Cicero, Tullia and me in a carriage; Marcus on horseback; a baggage train of pack mules and servants; and finally another ten cavalry bringing up the rear. The Calabrian plain was flat and dusty. We saw almost no one apart from the occasional shepherd or olive farmer, and I realised that of course our escort wasn't for our protection at all, but to make sure

Cicero didn't escape. We stayed overnight at a house reserved for us in Uria and continued the following day until around the middle of the afternoon, when we were only two or three miles from Tarentum, and then we saw a long column of horsemen in the distance, coming towards us.

In the rising heat and dust they seemed mere watery apparitions. It wasn't until they were only a few hundred paces away that I recognised by the red crests on their helmets and the standards in their midst that they were soldiers. Our column halted, and the officer in charge dismounted and hurried back to tell Cicero that the oncoming cavalry was carrying Caesar's personal standard. They were his praetorian guard and the Dictator was with them.

Cicero said, 'Dear gods, is he planning to have me done in by the roadside, do you suppose?' Then, seeing Tullia's horrified expression, he added, 'That was a joke, child. If he'd wanted me dead it would have happened long ago. Well, let's get it over with. You'd better come, Tiro. It will make a scene in your book.'

He clambered out of the carriage and called to Marcus to join us.

Caesar's column had drawn up about a hundred paces away and deployed across the road as if for battle. It was huge: there must have been four or five hundred men. We walked towards them. Cicero was between Marcus and me. At first I couldn't make out which of them was Caesar. But then a tall man swung himself out of his saddle, took off his helmet and gave it to an aide, and began to advance towards us, stroking his thin hair flat across his head.

How unreal it felt to watch the approach of this titan who had so dominated everyone's thoughts for so many years – who had conquered countries and upended lives and sent thousands of soldiers marching hither and thither and had smashed the ancient republic to fragments as if it were nothing more substantial than a chipped antique vase that had gone out of fashion – to watch him, and to find him, in the end ... just an ordinary breathing mortal! He walked in short strides with great rapidity – there was something curiously birdlike about him, I always thought: that narrow avian skull, those glittering watchful dark eyes. He stopped just in front of us. We stopped too. I was close enough to see the red indentations that his helmet had made in his surprisingly soft pale skin.

He looked Cicero up and down and said in his rasping voice, 'Entirely unscathed, I am glad to see – exactly as I would have expected! I have a bone to pick with you,' he said, jabbing a finger at me, and for a moment I felt my insides turn to liquid. 'You assured me ten years ago that your master was at death's door. I told you then he would outlive me.'

Cicero said, 'I'm glad to hear of your prediction, Caesar, if only because you are the one man in a position to make sure it comes true.'

Caesar threw back his head and laughed. 'Ah yes, I've missed you! Now look here – do you see how I've come out of the town to meet you, to show you my respect? Let's walk in the direction you're headed and talk a little.' And so they strolled on together for perhaps half a mile towards Tarentum, Caesar's troops parting to allow them through. A few bodyguards walked behind them, one leading Caesar's horse. Marcus and I followed. I could not hear what was said, but observed that Caesar occasionally took Cicero's arm while gesturing with his other hand. Afterwards Cicero said that their conversation was friendly enough, and he roughly summarised it for me as follows:

Caesar: 'So what is it you would like to do?'

Cicero: 'To return to Rome, if you'll permit it.'

Caesar: 'And can you promise you will cause me no trouble?'

Cicero: 'I swear it.'

Caesar: 'What will you do there? I'm not sure I want you making speeches in the Senate, and the law courts are all closed.'

Cicero: 'Oh, I'm finished in politics, I know that. I shall retire from public life.'

Caesar: 'And do what?'

Cicero: 'I thought I might write philosophy.'

Caesar: 'Excellent. I approve of statesmen who write philosophy. It means they have given up all hope of power. You may go to Rome. Will you teach the subject as well as write it? If so, I might send you a couple of my more promising men for instruction.'

Cicero: 'Aren't you worried I might corrupt them?' Caesar:

'Nothing worries me when it comes to you. Do you have any other favours to ask?'

Cicero: 'Well, I would like to be relieved of these lictors.'

Caesar: 'It's done.'

Cicero: 'Doesn't it require a vote of the Senate?'

Caesar: 'I am the vote of the Senate.'

Cicero: 'Ah! So I take it you have no intention of restoring the republic ...?'

Caesar: 'One cannot rebuild using rotten timber.'

Cicero: 'Tell me – did you always aim at this outcome: a dictatorship?'

Caesar: 'Never! I sought only the respect due to my rank and achievements. For the rest, one merely adapts to circumstances as they arise.'

Cicero: 'I wonder sometimes, if I had come out to Gaul as your legate – as you were kind enough once to suggest – whether all of this might have been averted.'

Caesar: 'That, my dear Cicero, we shall never know.'

'He was perfectly amiable,' recalled Cicero. 'He allowed no glimpse of those monstrous depths. I saw only the calm and glittering surface.'

At the end of their talk, Caesar shook Cicero's hand. Then he mounted his horse and galloped away in the direction of Pompey's villa. His action took his praetorian guard by surprise. They set off quickly after him, and the rest of us, Cicero included, had to scramble into the ditch to avoid being trampled.

Their hooves threw up the most tremendous cloud of dust. We choked and coughed, and when they had thundered past, we climbed back up on to the road to clean ourselves off. For a while we stood watching until Caesar and his followers had dissolved into the haze of heat, and then we began our journey back to Rome.

PART SIX

REDUX

47–43 BC

'Defendi rem publicam adulescens; non deseram senex.'

'I defended the republic in my youth; I will not desert it in old age.'
Cicero, Second Philippic, 44 BC

XLIX

This time no crowds turned out to cheer Cicero on his way home. With so many men away at war, the fields we passed looked untended, the towns dilapidated and half empty. People stared at us sullenly; either that or they turned away.

Venusia was our first stop. From there Cicero dictated a chilly message to Terentia:

I think I shall go to Tusculum. Kindly see that everything is ready. I may have a number of people with me and shall probably make a fairly long stay there. If there is no tub in the bathroom, get one put in; likewise whatever else is necessary for health and subsistence. Goodbye.

There was no term of endearment, no expression of eager anticipation, not even an invitation to her to meet him. I knew then he had made up his mind to divorce her, whatever she might have decided.

We broke our journey for two nights at Cumae. The villa was shuttered; most of the slaves had been sold. Cicero moved through the stuffy, unventilated rooms and tried to remember what items were missing – a citrus-wood table from the dining room, a bust of Minerva that had been in the tablinum, an ivory stool from his library. He stood in Terentia's bedroom and contemplated the bare shelves and alcoves. It was to be the same story in Formiae; she had taken all her personal belongings – clothes, combs, perfumes, fans, parasols – and he said, 'I feel like a ghost revisiting the scenes of my life.'

At Tusculum she was waiting for us. We knew she was inside because one of her maids was looking out for us by the gate.

I recoiled at the prospect of another terrible scene, like the one between Cicero and his brother. In the event, she was gentler than I had ever known her. I suppose it was the effect of seeing her son again after such a long and anxious separation – he was certainly the person she ran to first and she clutched him to her tightly; it was the only time in thirty years I saw her cry. Next she embraced Tullia and finally she turned to her husband. Cicero told me later that he felt all his bitterness drain away the moment she came towards him, for he saw that she had aged. Her face was creased with worry; her hair flecked grey; her once proud back was slightly stooped. 'Only at that moment did I realise how much she must have suffered, living in Caesar's Rome and being married to me. I cannot say I felt love for her any more, but I did feel great pity and affection and sadness, and I resolved there and then to make no mention of money or property – it was all done with, as far as I was concerned.' They clung to one another like strangers who had survived a shipwreck, then parted, and as far as I know they never embraced again for the remainder of their lives.

Terentia returned to Rome the following morning, divorced. Some regard it as a threat to public morality that a marriage, however long its duration, may be broken so easily, without any form of ceremony or legal document. But such is the ancient freedom, and at least on this occasion the desire to end the partnership was mutual. Naturally I was not present for their private talk. Cicero said it was amicable: 'We had been apart too much; amid the vast upheaval of public events our old shared private interests were gone.' It was agreed that Terentia would live in the house in Rome until she moved into a property of her own. In the meantime, Cicero would remain in Tusculum. Marcus chose to go back to the city with his mother; Tullia – whose faithless husband Dolabella was about to sail to Africa with Caesar to fight Cato – stayed with her father.

If one of the miseries of being human is that happiness can be snatched away at any moment, one of the joys is that it may be restored equally unexpectedly. Cicero had long relished the tranquillity and clear air of his house in the Frascati hills; now he could enjoy it uninterrupted, and in the company of his beloved daughter. As it was to become his principal residence from now on, I shall describe the place in more detail. There was an upper gymnasium that led to his library and which he called the

Lyceum in honour of Aristotle: this was where he walked in the mornings, composed his letters and talked with his visitors, and where in the old days he had practised his speeches. From here one could see the pale undulation of the seven hills of Rome, fifteen miles in the distance. But because what went on there was now entirely beyond his control, he no longer had to fret about it and was free to concentrate on his books – in that sense paradoxically dictatorship had liberated him. Below this terrace was a garden with shady walks like Plato's, in whose memory he called it his Academy. Both these areas, Lyceum and Academy, were adorned with beautiful Greek statues in marble and bronze, of which Cicero's favourite was the Hermathena, a Janus-like bust of Hermes and Athena staring in opposite directions, given to him by Atticus. From the various fountains came the soft music of trickling water, and that combined with the birdsong and the scent of the flowers created an atmosphere of Elysian tranquillity. Otherwise the hillside was quiet because most of the senatorial owners of the neighbouring villas were either fled or dead.

It was here that Cicero lived with Tullia for the whole of the next year, apart from occasional excursions to Rome. Afterwards he regarded this interlude as the most contented period of his life, as well as his most creative, for he made good on his undertaking to Caesar to confine his activity to writing. And such was the force of his energy, no longer dispersed into the law and politics but channelled solely into literary creation, that he produced in one year as many books on philosophy and rhetoric as most scholars might in a lifetime, turning them out one after another without pause. His objective was to put into Latin a summary of all the main arguments of Greek philosophy. His method of composition was extremely rapid. He would rise with the dawn and go straight to his library, where he would consult whatever texts he needed and scrawl notes – he had poor handwriting: I was one of the few who could decipher it – and then when I joined him an hour or two later he would stroll around the Lyceum dictating. Often he would leave me to look up quotations, or even to write whole passages according to the scheme he had laid out; usually he did not bother to correct them, as I had learned very well how to imitate his style.

The first work he completed that year was a history of oratory, which he named *Brutus* after Marcus Junius Brutus and dedicated to him. He had not seen his young friend since their tents stood side by side in the army camp at Dyrrachium. Even to choose such a subject as oratory was provocative, given that the art was no longer much valued in a country where the elections, the Senate and the law courts were under the control of the Dictator:

> *I have reason to grieve that I entered on the road of life so late that the night which has fallen upon the republic has overtaken me before my journey was ended. But I grieve more deeply when I look on you, Brutus, whose youthful career, faring in triumph amidst the general applause, has been thwarted by the onset of a malign fortune.*

A malign fortune ... I was surprised at the risk Cicero was willing to run in publishing such passages, especially considering that Brutus was now an important member of Caesar's administration. Having pardoned him after Pharsalus, the Dictator had recently appointed him governor of Nearer Gaul, even though Brutus had never been praetor let alone consul. People said it was because he was the son of Caesar's old mistress Servilia, and that the promotion was meant as a favour to her, but Cicero dismissed such talk: 'Caesar never does anything out of sentiment. He has given him the job in part no doubt because he is talented, but mostly because he is Cato's nephew and this is a good way for Caesar to divide his enemies.'

Brutus, who along with a certain lofty idealism also had a good share of his uncle's perversity and stiffness, did not like the work named in his honour, nor a companion volume, *Orator*, which Cicero wrote not long afterwards and also dedicated to him. He sent a letter from Gaul to say that Cicero's speaking style had been fine in its day but was too high-flown both for good taste and for the modern age – too full of tricks and jokes and funny voices: what was needed was absolute flat, emotionless sincerity. I considered it typical of Brutus's conceit that he should presume to lecture the greatest orator of the age on how to speak in public, but Cicero always respected Brutus for his honesty and refused to take offence.

These were oddly happy, I would almost say carefree, days. The old Lucullus property next door, which had long stood empty, was sold, and the new occupant turned out to be Aulus Hirtius, the immaculate young aide to Caesar whom I had met in Gaul all those years ago. He was now praetor, though the law courts met so rarely he was mostly at home, where he lived with his elder sister. One morning he came round to invite Cicero to dinner. He was a noted gourmet and had grown quite plump on such delicacies as swan and peacock. He was still in his thirties, like nearly all Caesar's inner circle, with impeccable manners and exquisite literary taste. He was said to have written many of Caesar's *Commentaries*, which Cicero had gone out of his way to praise in *Brutus* (*they are like nude figures, upright and beautiful, stripped of all ornament of style as if they had removed a garment*, he dictated to me, before adding, not for publication, 'yes, and as characterless as stick figures drawn in the sand by an infant'). Cicero saw no reason not to accept Hirtius's hospitality. He went round that evening accompanied by Tullia, and so began an unlikely country friendship; often I was invited too.

One day Cicero asked if he could give Hirtius anything in return for all these splendid dinners he was enjoying, and Hirtius replied yes, as a matter of fact, he could: that Caesar had urged him, if he ever got the chance, to study philosophy and rhetoric 'at the feet of the Master' and that he would appreciate some instruction. Cicero agreed and started to give Hirtius lessons in declamation, similar to those he had received as a young man from Apollonius Molon. The lessons took place in the Academy beside the water clock, where Cicero taught him how to memorise a speech, to breathe, project his voice and use his hands and arms to make gestures that would better convey his meaning. Hirtius boasted about his new skills to his friend Gaius Vibius Pansa, another young officer from Caesar's Gallic staff, who was scheduled to replace Brutus as governor of Nearer Gaul at the end of the year. As a result, Pansa too became a regular visitor to Cicero's villa that year and he also learned how to speak better in public.

A third pupil in this informal school was Cassius Longinus, the battle-hardened survivor of Crassus's expedition to Parthia and the former ruler of Syria, whom Cicero had last seen at the war conference on the island of Corcyra. Like Brutus, to whose sister he was married, he had surrendered to Caesar and been pardoned; now he was impatiently awaiting a senior appointment. I always found him hard company, taciturn and ambitious, and Cicero didn't much care for his philosophy either, which was extreme Epicureanism: he picked at his food, never touched wine and exercised fanatically. He once confided to Cicero that the greatest regret of his life was accepting his pardon from Caesar: that it ate away at his soul from the start and that six months after his surrender he attempted to kill Caesar when the Dictator was returning from Egypt after the death of Pompey. He would have succeeded, too, if only Caesar had moored for the night on the same side of the Cydnus river as Cassius's triremes; instead he had unexpectedly chosen the opposite bank, and by then it was too late at night and he was too far away for Cassius to reach him. Even Cicero, who was not easily shocked, was alarmed by his indiscretion and advised him not to repeat it, and certainly not to do so under his roof in case Hirtius and Pansa got to hear of it.

Finally I must mention a fourth visitor, and he in many ways was the least likely of the lot, for this was Dolabella, Tullia's errant husband. She believed he was in Africa, campaigning with Caesar against Cato and Scipio, but at the beginning of spring Hirtius received a report that the campaign was finished and that Caesar had just won a great victory. Hirtius cut short his lesson and hastened back to Rome, and a few days later, first thing in the morning, a messenger brought Cicero a letter:

From Dolabella to his dear father-in-law, Cicero.

I have the honour to inform you that Caesar has beaten the enemy and that Cato is dead by his own hand. I arrived in Rome this morning to give a report to the Senate. I called at my house and was told that Tullia is with you. May I have your permission to come out to Tusculum and see the two people who are dearest to me in the world?

'Shock after shock after shock,' observed Cicero. 'The republic beaten, Cato dead and now my son-in-law asks to see his wife.' He stared bleakly over the countryside towards the distant hills of Rome, blue in the early spring light. 'The world will not be the same place without Cato in it.'

He sent a slave to fetch Tullia, and when she came, he showed her the letter. She had spoken so often of Dolabella's cruelty towards her that I assumed, as did Cicero, that she would insist she didn't want to see him. Instead she said it was up to her father and that she didn't much care either way.

Cicero said, 'Well, if that is really how you feel, then perhaps I shall let him come – if only so that I can tell him what I think of the way he's treated you.'

Tullia said quickly, 'No, Father, I beg you, please don't do that. He's too proud to submit to a scolding, and besides, I have only myself to blame – everyone warned me what he was like before I married him.'

Cicero was uncertain what to do, but in the end, his desire to hear at first hand what had happened to Cato overcame his distaste at having such a scoundrel under his roof – a scoundrel not just as a husband, incidentally, but as a rabble-rousing politician in the mould of Catilina and Clodius, who favoured the cancellation of all debts. He asked me if I would go to Rome at once with an invitation for Dolabella. Just before I left, Tullia took me aside and asked if she could have her husband's letter. Naturally I gave it to her; only afterwards did I discover she had none of her own and wanted it as a keepsake.

By midday I was in Rome – a full five years after I had last set foot in the city. In the fervid dreams of my exile I had pictured wide streets, and fine temples and porticoes clothed in marble and gold, all filled with elegant, cultured citizens. I found instead filth, smoke, rutted muddy roads much narrower than I remembered them, unrepaired buildings and limbless, disfigured veterans begging in the Forum. The Senate building was still a blackened shell. The places in front of the temples where the law courts used to meet were deserted. I was amazed at the general emptiness. When a census was taken later that year, the population was found to be less than half what it had been before the civil war.

I thought I might find Dolabella attending the Senate, but no one seemed to know where it was or even if it was in session these days. In the end I went to the address on the Palatine that Tullia had given me, which was where she said she had last lived with her husband, and there I found Dolabella in the company of an elegant, expensively dressed woman who I later discovered was Metella, daughter of Clodia. She behaved as if she was the mistress of the house, ordering refreshment for me and a chair to be brought, and I saw at a glance the hopelessness of Tullia's situation.

As for Dolabella, he was striking for three attributes: the fierce handsomeness of his features, the obvious strength of his physique, and the shortness of his stature. (Cicero once joked, 'Who has tied my son-in-law to that sword?') This pocket Adonis, for whom I had long tended an intense dislike because of the way he treated Tullia, even though I had never met him, read Cicero's invitation and declared that he would return with me immediately. He said, 'My father-in-law writes here that this message is brought to me by his trusted friend Tiro. Would that be the Tiro who created the famous shorthand system? Then I am delighted to meet you!

My wife has always talked of you most fondly, as a kind of second father to her. May I shake your hand?' And such was the charm of the rogue that I felt my hostility immediately begin to wilt.

He asked Metella to send his slaves after him with his luggage, and then joined me in the carriage for the journey to Tusculum. Most of the way he slept. By the time we reached the villa, the slaves were preparing to serve dinner, and Cicero ordered an extra place to be set. Dolabella made straight for Tullia's couch and reclined with his head in her lap. After a while I noticed she began to stroke his hair.

It was a fair spring evening with the nightingales calling to one another, and the incongruity between the charm of the setting and the horror of the story Dolabella unfolded made it all the more unsettling. First there was the battle itself, named Thapsus, at which Scipio had commanded the republican force of seventy thousand men in alliance with King Juba of the Numidians. They had used a shock force of elephant cavalry to try to break Caesar's line, but volleys of arrows and flaming missiles from the ballistae had caused the wretched beasts to panic, turn and trample their own infantry. Thereafter it was the same story as at Pharsalus: the republican formations had broken on the iron discipline of Caesar's legionaries, only this time Caesar had decreed there would be no prisoners taken: all ten thousand who surrendered were massacred.

'And Cato?' asked Cicero.

'Cato was not present at the battle but was three days' journey away, commanding the garrison at Utica. Caesar went there straight away. I rode with him at the head of the army. He wanted very much to capture Cato alive so that he could pardon him.'

'A wasted mission, I could have told you that: Cato would never have accepted a pardon from Caesar.'

'Caesar was sure he would. But you are right, as always: Cato killed himself the night before we arrived.'

'How did he do it?'

Dolabella pulled a face. 'I'll tell you if you really want to know, but it's not a fit subject for a woman's ears.'

Tullia said firmly, 'I'm quite strong enough, thank you.'

'Even so, I think it would be better if you withdrew.'

'I shall certainly do no such thing!'

'And what does your father say about that?'

'Tullia is stronger than she looks,' said Cicero, adding pointedly, 'She has had to be.'

'Well, you asked for it. According to Cato's slaves, when he learned that Caesar would arrive the next day, Cato bathed and dined, discussed Plato with his companions, and retired to his room. Then when he was alone he took his sword and slashed himself just here.' Dolabella reached up and drew a finger under Tullia's breastbone. 'All his guts spilled out.'

Cicero, squeamish as ever, winced, but Tullia said, 'That's not so bad.'

'Ah,' said Dolabella, 'but that's not the end of the story. He failed to make the wound fatal and the sword slipped out of his bloodied hand. His attendants heard his groans and rushed in. They summoned a doctor. The doctor arrived and pushed his intestines back in to the cavity and sewed up the wound. I might add that Cato was entirely conscious throughout. He promised he would not make another attempt, and his staff believed him, although as a precaution they took his sword away. As soon as they had gone, he tore the wound open with his fingers and dragged his intestines out again. That killed him.'

The death of Cato had a powerful effect on Cicero. As the lurid details became more widely known, there were those who said it was proof that Cato was insane; certainly this was Hirtius's view. Cicero disagreed. 'He could have had an easier death. He could have thrown himself from a building, or opened his veins in a warm bath, or taken poison. Instead he chose that particular method – exposing his entrails like a human sacrifice – to demonstrate the strength of his will and his contempt for Caesar. In philosophical terms it was a good death: the death of a man who feared nothing. Indeed I would go so far as to say he died happy. Neither Caesar, nor any man, nor anything in the world could touch him.'

The effect on Brutus and Cassius – both of whom were related to Cato, the one by blood and the other by marriage – was if anything even stronger. Brutus wrote from Gaul to ask if Cicero would compose a eulogy of his uncle. His letter arrived at the same time as Cicero learned that he had been named in Cato's will as one of the guardians of his son. Like the others who had accepted Caesar's pardon, Cicero found the suicide of Cato shaming. So he ignored the risk of offending the Dictator, complied with Brutus's request, and dictated a short work, *Cato*, in little more than a week.

Sinewy in thought and person; indifferent to what men said of him; scornful of glory, titles and decorations, and even more of those who sought them; defender of laws and freedoms; vigilant in the public interest; contemptuous of tyrants, their vulgarities and presumptions; stubborn, infuriating, harsh, dogmatic; a dreamer, a fanatic, a mystic, a soldier; willing at the last to tear the very organs from his stomach rather than submit to a conqueror – only the Roman Republic could have bred such a man as Cato, and only in the Roman Republic did such a man as Cato desire to live.

Around this time Caesar returned from Africa, and soon afterwards, at the height of summer, he staged finally four separate triumphs on successive days to commemorate his victories in Gaul, the Black Sea, Africa and on the Nile – such an epic of self-glorification as even Rome had never seen. Cicero moved back into his house on the Palatine in order to attend – not that he wanted to: *In civil war*, as he wrote to his old friend Sulpicius, *victory is always insolent*. There were five wild-beast hunts, a mock battle in the Circus Maximus that included elephants, a naval battle in a lake dug out near the Tiber, stage plays in every quarter of the city, athletics on the Field of Mars, chariot races, games in honour of the memory of the Dictator's daughter Julia, a banquet for the entire city at which meat from the sacrifices was served, a distribution of money, a distribution of bread, endless parades of soldiers and treasure and prisoners coiling through the streets – that noble leader of the Gauls, Vercingetorix, after six years of imprisonment, was garrotted in the Carcer – and day after day we could hear the vulgar chanting of the legionaries even from the terrace:

Home we bring our bald whoremonger,
Romans, lock your wives away!
All the bags of gold you lent him
Went his Gallic tarts to pay!

Yet despite their bombast, or perhaps because of it, Cato's reproachful ghost seemed to haunt even these proceedings. When a float went by during the Africa triumph depicting him tearing out his entrails, the crowd let out a loud groan. It was said that Cato's death had a particular religious meaning: that he had done it to bring down the wrath of the gods on Caesar's head. When that same day the axle on the Dictator's triumphal chariot broke and he was pitched to the ground, it was held to be a sign of divine displeasure, and Caesar took the crowd's disquiet seriously enough to lay on the most extraordinary spectacle of all: at night, with forty elephants on either side of him ridden by men holding flaming torches, he mounted the slope of the Capitol on his knees to atone to Jupiter for his impiety.

Just as some particularly faithful dogs are said to lie by the graves of their masters, unable to accept that they are dead, so there were those in Rome who clung to the hope that the old republic might yet twitch back into life. Even Cicero fell briefly victim to this delusion. After the triumphs were over, he decided to attend a meeting of the Senate. He had no intention of speaking. He went partly for old times' sake and partly because he knew that Caesar had appointed several hundred new senators and he was curious to see what they looked like.

'It was a chamber full of strangers,' he said to me afterwards, 'a few of them actually foreign, many not elected – and yet somehow it was still a Senate for all that.' It met on the Field of Mars, in the same room within Pompey's theatre complex where it had assembled in emergency session after the old Senate house was burned down. Caesar had even allowed the large marble statue of Pompey to remain in its original position, and the image of the Dictator presiding from the dais with Pompey's statue behind him gave Cicero hope for the future. The issue for debate was whether the ex-consul, M. Marcellus, one of the most intransigent of Caesar's opponents, who had gone into exile after Pharsalus and was living on Lesbos, might be allowed to return to Rome. His brother Caius – the magistrate who had sanctioned my manumission – led the appeals for clemency, and he was just finishing his speech when a bird seemed to appear from nowhere, fluttered over the senators' heads and swooped out of the door. Caesar's father-in-law, L. Calpurnius Piso, immediately got up and declared it to be an omen: the gods were saying that Marcellus too should be given the freedom to fly home. Then the whole Senate, Cicero included, rose as one and approached Caesar to appeal for clemency; Caius Marcellus and Piso actually fell to their knees at his feet.

Caesar gestured at them to return to their seats. He said, 'The man for whom you all plead has heaped more deadly insults upon me than any other person living. And yet I am touched by your entreaties and the omen seems to me especially propitious. There is no need for me to place my dignity above the unanimous desire of this house: I have lived long enough for nature or for glory. Therefore let Marcellus come home and dwell in peace in the city of his distinguished ancestors.'

This was received with loud applause, and several of the senators sitting around Cicero urged him to rise and make some expression of gratitude on behalf of them all. The scene so affected Cicero that he forgot his vow never to speak in Caesar's illegitimate Senate and did as they asked, lauding the Dictator to his face in the most extravagant terms: 'You seem to have vanquished Victory herself, now that you have surrendered to the vanquished all that Victory had gained. Truly you are invincible!'

Suddenly it seemed possible to him that Caesar might rule as 'first among equals' rather than as a tyrant. *I thought I saw some semblance of reviving constitutional freedom*, he wrote to Sulpicius. The next month he pleaded for the pardon of another exile, Quintus Ligarius – a senator almost as detestable to Caesar as Marcellus – and again Caesar listened and gave judgement in favour of clemency.

But the notion that this amounted to a restoration of the republic was an illusion. A few days afterwards, the Dictator had to leave Rome in a hurry in order to return to Spain and deal with an uprising led by Pompey's sons, Gnaeus and Sextus. Hirtius told Cicero that the Dictator was in a rage. Many of the rebels were men he had pardoned on condition they did not take up arms again; now they had betrayed his forgiving nature. There would be no further acts of clemency, Hirtius warned: no more gracious gestures. For his own sake Cicero would be well advised to stay away from the Senate, keep his head down and stick to philosophy: 'This time it will be a fight to the death.'

Tullia was pregnant again by Dolabella – the result, she told me, of her husband's visit to Tusculum. At first she was delighted by the discovery, believing it would save her marriage. Dolabella seemed happy too. But when she returned to Rome with Cicero to attend Caesar's four triumphs, and when she went to the house she shared with Dolabella intending to surprise him, she discovered Metella asleep in her bed. It was a terrible shock and to this day I feel the most profound guilt that I failed to warn her of what I had seen when I went there earlier.

She asked my advice and I urged her to divorce Dolabella without delay. The baby was due in four months. If she was still married when she gave birth, he would be entitled under the law to take the child; however if she were divorced, the situation would be much more complicated. Dolabella would have to take her to court to prove paternity, and at the very least, thanks to her father, she would have the best legal counsel available. She talked to Cicero and he agreed: the baby would be his sole grandchild and he had no intention of seeing it taken away from his daughter and entrusted to the care of Dolabella and the daughter of Clodia.

Accordingly, on the morning that Dolabella was due to leave with Caesar for the war in Spain, Tullia went to his house, accompanied by Cicero, and informed him that the marriage was over but that she wished to look after the baby. Cicero told me Dolabella's reaction: 'The scoundrel merely shrugged, wished her well with the child, and said that of course it must remain with its mother. Then he drew me aside to say that there was no way at the moment that he could repay her dowry and he hoped this would not affect our relations! What could I say? I can hardly afford to make an enemy of one of Caesar's closest lieutenants, and besides, I still can't bring myself entirely to dislike him.'

He was anguished and blamed himself for allowing the mess to develop. 'I should have insisted that she divorce him the moment I heard of the way he was carrying on. Now what is she to do? An abandoned mother of thirty-one with a weak constitution and no dowry is hardly the most marriageable of prospects.'

If there was any marrying to be done, he realised grimly, the person who would have to do it would be him. Nothing could have suited him less. He liked his new bachelor existence, preferred living with his books to the prospect of living with a wife. He was now sixty, and although he still cut a handsome figure, sexual desire – never a strong part of his character even in his youth – was waning. It is true that he flirted more as he got older. He liked dinner parties where pretty young women were present – he even once attended the same table as Mark Antony's mistress, the nude actress Volumnia Cytheris, a thing he would never have countenanced in the past. But murmured compliments on a dining couch and the occasional love poem sent round by a messenger the next morning were as far as things went.

Unfortunately, he now needed to marry to raise some money. Terentia's clandestine recovery of her dowry had crippled his finances; he knew Dolabella would never repay him; and although he had plenty of properties – including two new ones, at Astura on the coast near Antium and at Puteoli on the Bay of Naples – he could barely afford to run them. You might ask, 'Well why did he not sell some of them?' But that was never Cicero's way. His motto was always 'Income adjusts to meet expenditure, not the other way round.' Now that his income could no longer be expanded by legal practice the only realistic alternative was once again to take a rich wife.

It is a sordid story. But I swore at the outset to tell the truth, and I shall do so. Three potential brides were available. One was Hirtia, the elder sister of Hirtius. Her brother was immensely rich from his time in Gaul, and to get this tiresome woman off his hands he was prepared to offer her to Cicero with a dowry of two million sesterces. But as Cicero put it in a letter to Atticus, she was *quite remarkably ugly*, and it struck him as absurd that the cost of keeping his beautiful houses should be to install in them a hideous wife.

Then there was Pompeia, the daughter of Pompey. She had been the wife of Faustus Sulla, the owner of Aristotle's manuscripts, recently killed fighting for the Senate's cause in Africa. But if he married her, that would make Gnaeus – the man who had threatened to kill him at Corcyra – his brother-in-law. It was unthinkable. Besides, she bore a strong facial resemblance to her father. 'Can you imagine,' he said to me with a shudder, 'waking up beside Pompey every morning?'

That left the least suitable match of all. Publilia was only fifteen years old. Her father, M. Publilius, a wealthy equestrian friend of Atticus, had died leaving his estate in trust for his daughter until she married. The principal trustee was Cicero. It was Atticus's idea – 'an elegant solution', he called it – that Cicero should marry Publilia and so gain access to her fortune. There was nothing illegal about this. The girl's mother and uncle were all for it, flattered by the prospect of forming a connection with such a distinguished man. And Publilia herself, when Cicero hesitantly broached the subject, declared that she would be honoured to be his wife.

'Are you sure?' he asked her. 'I am forty-five years older than you – old enough to be your grandfather. Do you not find that … unnatural?'

She stared at him quite frankly. 'No.'

After she had gone, Cicero said, 'Well, she seems to be telling the truth. I wouldn't dream of it if she was repulsed by the very thought of me.' He sighed heavily and shook his head. 'I suppose I had better go through with it. But people will be very disapproving.'

I could not help remarking, 'It isn't *people* you have to worry about.'

'What are you referring to?'

'Well, Tullia, of course,' I replied, amazed that he hadn't considered her. 'How do you think she is going to feel?'

He squinted at me in genuine puzzlement. 'Why would Tullia be opposed? I'm doing this for her benefit as much as mine.'

'Well,' I said mildly, 'I think you'll find she *will* mind.'

And she did. Cicero said that when he told her of his intention she fainted, and for an hour or two he feared for her health and that of the baby. When she recovered, she wanted to know how he could possibly think of such a thing. Was she really expected to call this child her stepmother? Were they to live under the same roof? He was dismayed by the strength of her reaction. However, it was too late for him to back out. He had already borrowed from the moneylenders on the expectation of his new wife's fortune. Neither of his children attended the wedding breakfast: Tullia moved to live with her mother for the final stages of her pregnancy, while Marcus asked his father for permission to go out and fight in Spain as part of Caesar's army. Cicero managed to persuade him that such an action would be dishonourable to his former comrades, and instead he went to Athens on a very generous allowance to try to have some philosophy dinned into his thick skull.

I did attend the wedding, which took place in the bride's house. The only other guests from the groom's side were Atticus and his wife Pilia – who was herself, of course, thirty years her husband's junior but who seemed quite matronly beside the slender figure of Publilia. The bride, dressed all in white, with her hair pinned up and wearing the sacred belt, looked like an exquisite doll. Perhaps some men could have carried the whole thing off – Pompey I am sure would have been entirely at ease – but Cicero was so obviously uncomfortable that when he came to recite the simple vow ('Where you are Gaia, I am Gaius'), he got the names the wrong way round, an ill omen.

After a long celebratory banquet the wedding party walked to Cicero's house in the fading daylight. He had hoped to keep the marriage secret and almost scuttled through the streets, avoiding the gaze of passers-by, gripping his wife's hand firmly and seeming to drag her along. But a wedding procession always attracts attention, and his face was too famous for anonymity, so that by the time we reached the Palatine we must have been trailing a crowd of fifty or more. At least that number of applauding clients was waiting outside the house to throw flowers over the happy couple. I had worried that Cicero might injure his back if he tried to carry his bride over the threshold, but he hoisted her easily and swept her into the house, hissing at me over his shoulder to close the door behind us, quick. She went straight upstairs to Terentia's old suite of rooms, where her maids had already unpacked her belongings, to prepare for her wedding night. Cicero tried to persuade me to stay up a little longer and take some wine with him, but I pleaded exhaustion and left him to it.

The marriage was a disaster from the start. Cicero had no idea how to treat his young wife. It was as if a friend's child had come to stay. Sometimes he played the role of kindly uncle, delighting in her playing of the lyre or congratulating her on her embroidery. On other occasions he was her exasperated tutor, appalled at her ignorance of history and literature. But mostly he tried to keep out of her way. Once he confided to me that the only workable basis for such a relationship would have been lust, and that he simply did not feel. Poor Publilia – the more her famous husband ignored her, the more she clung to him, and the more irritated he became.

Finally Cicero went to see Tullia to plead with her to move back in with him. She could have the baby at his house, he said – the birth was imminent – and he would send Publilia away, or rather he would get Atticus to send her away for him, as he found the situation too upsetting to deal with. Tullia, who was distressed to see her father in such a state, agreed, and the long-suffering Atticus duly found himself having to visit Publilia's mother and uncle to explain why the young woman would have to return home after less than a month of married life. He held out the hope that once the baby was born the couple might be able to resume their relationship, but for now Tullia's wishes took priority. They had little option but to agree.

It was January when Tullia moved back into the house. She was brought to the door in a litter and had to be helped inside. I recall a cold winter's day, everything very clear and bright and sharp. She moved with difficulty. Cicero fussed around her, telling the porter to close the door, ordering more wood for the fire, worrying that she would catch a chill. She said that she would like to go to her room to lie down. Cicero sent for a doctor to examine her. He came out soon afterwards and reported that she was in labour. Terentia was fetched, along with a midwife and her attendants, and they all disappeared into Tullia's room.

The screams of pain that rang through the house did not sound like Tullia at all. They did not sound like any human being in fact. They were guttural, primordial – all trace of personality obliterated by pain. I wondered how they fitted in to Cicero's philosophical scheme. Could happiness remotely be associated with such agony? Presumably it could. But he was unable to bear the shrieks and howls and went out into the garden, walking around and around it, for hour after hour, oblivious to the cold. Eventually there was silence and he came back in again. He looked at me. We waited. A long time seemed to pass, and then there were footsteps and Terentia appeared. Her face was drawn and pale but her voice was triumphant.

'It's a boy,' she said, 'a healthy boy – and she is well.'

She was well. That was all that mattered to Cicero. The boy was robust and was named Publius Lentulus, after his father's adopted patronymic. But Tullia could not feed the infant and the task was assigned to a wet nurse, and as the days passed following the trauma of the birth, she did not seem to get any stronger. Because it was so cold in Rome that winter, there was a lot of smoke, and the racket from the Forum disturbed her sleep. It was decided that she and Cicero should go back to Tusculum, scene of their happy year together, where she could recuperate in the tranquillity of the Frascati hills while he and I pressed on with his philosophical writings. We took a doctor with us. The baby travelled with his nurse, plus a whole retinue of slaves to look after him.

Tullia found the journey difficult. She was breathless and flushed with fever, although her eyes were wide and calm and she said she felt contented: not ill, just tired. When we reached the villa, the doctor insisted she went straight to bed. Afterwards he took me to one side and said that he was fairly certain now that she was suffering from the final stages of consumption and she would not last the night: should he inform her father, or would it be better if I did it?

I said that I would do it. After I had composed myself, I found Cicero in his library. He had taken down some books but had made no attempt to unroll them. He was sitting, staring straight ahead at nothing. He didn't even turn to look at me. He said, 'She's dying, isn't she?'

'I'm afraid she is.'

'Does she know it?'

'The doctor hasn't told her, but I think she's too clever not to realise, don't you?'

He nodded. 'That was why she was so keen to come here, where her memories are happiest. This is where she wants to die.' He rubbed his eyes. 'I think I shall go and sit with her now.'

I waited in the Lyceum and watched the sun sink behind the hills of Rome. Some hours later, when it was entirely dark, one of her maids came to fetch me, and conducted me by candlelight to Tullia's room. She was unconscious, lying in bed with her hair unpinned and spread across her pillow. Cicero sat on one side, holding her hand. On her other side, her baby lay asleep. Her breathing was very shallow and rapid. There were people in the room – her maids, the baby's nurse, the doctor – but they were in the shadows and I have no memory of their faces.

Cicero saw me and beckoned me closer. I leaned over and kissed her damp forehead, then retreated to join the others in the semi-darkness. Soon afterwards her breathing began to slow. The intervals between each breath became longer, and I kept imagining she must have died, but then she would take another gasp of air. The end when it came was different and unmistakable – a long sigh, accompanied by a slight tremor along the length of her body, and then a profound stillness as she passed into eternity.

L

The funeral was in Rome. Only one good thing came out of it: Cicero's brother Quintus, from whom he had been estranged ever since that terrible scene in Patrae, came round to offer his condolences the moment we got back, and the two men sat beside the coffin, wordless, holding hands. As a mark of their reconciliation, Cicero asked Quintus to deliver the eulogy: he doubted he would be able to get through it himself.

That apart, it was one of the most melancholy occasions I have ever witnessed – the long procession out on to the Esquiline Field in the freezing winter dusk; the wail of the musicians' dirges mingled with the cawing of the crows in the sacred grove of Libitina; the small enshrouded figure lying on its bier; the racked face of Terentia, like Niobe's seemingly turned to stone by grief; Atticus supporting Cicero as he put the torch to the pyre; and finally the great sheet of flame that suddenly shot up, illuminating us all in its scorching red glow, our rigid expressions set like masks in a Greek tragedy.

The following day, Publilia turned up on the doorstep with her mother and uncle, sulky that she had not been invited to the funeral and determined to move back into the house. She made a little speech that had obviously been written out for her and that she had memorised: 'Husband, I know that your daughter found my presence difficult, but now that this impediment has been removed, I hope that we can resume our married life together and that I may help you to forget your grief.'

But Cicero didn't want to forget his grief. He wished to be enveloped by it, consumed by it. Without telling Publilia where he was going, he fled the house that same day, carrying the urn containing Tullia's ashes. He moved in to Atticus's place on the Quirinal, where he locked himself away in the library for days on end, seeing no one and compiling a great handbook of all that has ever been written by the philosophers and poets on how to cope with grief and dying. He called it his *Consolation*. He told me that while he worked, he could hear Atticus's five-year-old daughter playing in her nursery next door, exactly as Tullia had done when he was a young advocate: 'The sound was as sharp to my heart as a red-hot needle; that kept me at my task.'

When Publilia discovered where he was, she began to pester Atticus for admittance, so Cicero fled again, to the newest and most isolated of all his properties – a villa on the tiny island of Astura, at the mouth of a river, only a hundred yards or so from the shore of the Bay of Antium. The island was entirely deserted and covered with trees and groves, cut into shady walks. In this lonely place he shunned all human company. Early in the day he would hide himself away in the thick, thorny wood, with nothing to disturb his meditations but the cries of the birds, and would not emerge till evening. *What is the soul?* he asks in his *Consolation. It is not moist or airy or fiery or compounded of the earth. There is nothing in these elements that accounts for the power of memory, mind or thought, that recalls the past, foresees the future or comprehends the present. Rather the soul must be counted as a fifth element – divine and therefore eternal.*

I remained in Rome and handled all his affairs – financial, domestic, literary and even marital, as now it fell to me to fend off the hapless Publilia and her relatives by pretending I had no idea where he was. As the weeks passed, his absence became increasingly difficult to explain, not just to his wife but to his clients and friends, and I was aware that his reputation was suffering, it being considered unmanly to surrender to grief so completely. Many letters of condolence arrived, including a line from Caesar in Spain, and these I forwarded to Cicero.

Eventually Publilia discovered his hiding place and wrote to him announcing her intention of visiting him in the company of her mother. To escape such a fraught confrontation, he abandoned the island, ashes in hand, and finally nerved himself to write a letter to his wife setting out his desire for a divorce. No doubt it was cowardly of him not to do it face to face. But he felt that her lack of sympathy over Tullia's death had made their ill-conceived relationship entirely untenable. He left Atticus to sort out the financial details, which entailed selling one of his houses, and then he invited me to join him in Tusculum, saying he had a project he wished to discuss.

By the time I arrived, it was the middle of May. I had not seen him for more than three months. He was seated in his Academy reading when he heard my approach, and turned to look at me with a sad smile. His appearance shocked me. He was much gaunter, especially around the neck. His hair was greyer, longer and unkempt. But the real change was beneath the surface. There was a kind of resignation about him. It showed in the slowness of his movements and the gentleness of his manner – as if he had been broken and remade.

Over dinner I asked him if he had found it painful to return to a place where he had spent so much time with Tullia.

He replied: 'I dreaded the prospect of coming, naturally, but when I arrived it was not so bad. One deals with grief, I have come to believe, either by never thinking of it or by thinking of it all the time. I chose the latter path, and here at least I am surrounded by memories of her, and her ashes are interred in the garden. Friends have been very kind, especially those who have suffered similar losses. Did you see the letter Sulpicius wrote me?'

He passed it to me over the table:

I want to tell you of something which has brought me no slight comfort, in the hope that perhaps it may have some power to lighten your sorrow too. As I was on my way back from Asia, sailing from Aegina towards Megara, I began to gaze at the landscape around me. There behind me was Aegina, in front of me Megara, to the right Piraeus, to the left Corinth; once flourishing towns, now lying low in ruins before one's eyes. I began to think to myself: 'Ah! How can we manikins wax indignant if one of us dies or is killed, ephemeral creatures as we are, when the corpses of so many towns lie abandoned in a single spot? Check yourself, Servius, and remember that you were born a mortal man.' That thought, I do assure you, strengthened me not a little. Can you really be so greatly moved by the loss of one poor little woman's frail spirit? If her end had not come now, she must none the less have died in a few years' time, for she was mortal.

'I never thought Sulpicius could be so eloquent,' I remarked.

'Nor I. You see how all of us poor creatures strive to make sense of death, even dry old jurists such as him? It's given me an idea. Suppose we were to compose a work of philosophy that helped relieve men of their fear of death.'

'That would be an achievement.'

'The *Consolation* seeks to reconcile us to the deaths of those we love. Now let us try to reconcile ourselves to our own deaths. If we were to succeed – well, tell me, what could bring humanity greater relief from terror than that?' I had no answer. His proposition was irresistible. I was curious to see how he would manage it. And so was born what is now known as the *Tusculan Disputations*, upon which we started work the following day. From the outset, Cicero conceived it as five books:

1. *On the fear of death*
2. *On the endurance of pain*
3. *On the alleviation of distress*
4. *On the remaining disorders of the soul*
5. *On the sufficiency of virtue for a happy life*

Once again we assumed our old routine of composition. Like his hero Demosthenes, who hated to be beaten to the dawn by a diligent workman, Cicero would rise in the darkness and read in his library by lamplight until the day had broken; later in the morning he would describe to me what was in his mind and I would probe his logic with questions; in the afternoon while he napped I would write up my shorthand notes into a draft, which he would then correct; we would discuss and revise the day's work over dinner in the evening, and finally before retiring we would decide the topics for the following morning.

The summer days were long and our progress swift, mostly because Cicero decided to cast the work in the form of a dialogue between a philosopher and a student. Usually I played the student and he was the philosopher, but occasionally it was the other way round. These *Disputations* of ours are still widely available, so it is unnecessary, I hope, for me to describe them in detail. They are the summation of all that Cicero had come to believe after the battering of recent years: namely, that the soul possesses a divine animation different to the body's and therefore is eternal; that even if the soul is not eternal and ahead of us lies only oblivion, such a state is not to be feared as there will be no sensation and therefore no pain or misery (*the dead are not wretched, the living are wretched*); that we should think about death constantly and so acclimatise ourselves to its inevitable arrival (*the whole life of a philosopher, as Socrates said, is a preparation for death*); and that if we are determined enough, we can teach ourselves to scorn death and pain, just as professional fighters do:

> *What even average gladiator has ever uttered a groan or changed expression? Which has ever disgraced himself after a fall by drawing in his neck when ordered to suffer the fatal stroke? Such is the force of training, practice and habit. Shall a gladiator be capable of this while a man who is born to fame proves so weak in his soul that he cannot strengthen it by systematic preparation?*

In the fifth book, Cicero offered his practical prescriptions. A human being can only train for death by leading a life that is morally good; that is – to desire nothing too much; to be content with what one has; to be entirely self-sufficient within oneself, so that whatever one loses, one will still be able to carry on regardless; to do none harm; to realise that it is better to suffer an injury than to inflict one; to accept that life is a loan given by Nature without a due date and that repayment may be demanded at any time; that the most tragic character in the world is a tyrant who has broken all these precepts.

Such were the lessons Cicero had learned and desired to impart to the world in the sixty-second summer of his life.

About a month after we started work on the *Disputations*, in the middle of June, Dolabella came to visit. He was on his way back to Rome from Spain, where he had once again been fighting alongside Caesar. The Dictator had been victorious; the remnants of Pompey's forces were smashed. But Dolabella had been wounded in the battle of Munda. There was a slash from his ear to his collarbone and he walked with a limp: his horse had been killed beneath him by a javelin, throwing him to the ground and rolling on him. Still, he was as full of animal spirits as ever. He wanted particularly to see his son, who was living with Cicero at this time, and also to pay his respects at the place where Tullia's ashes were buried.

Baby Lentulus at four months old was a large and rosy specimen, as healthy-looking as his mother had been frail. It was almost as if he had sucked all the life out of her, and I am sure that was the reason why I never saw Cicero hold him or pay him much attention – he could not quite forgive him for being alive when she was dead. Dolabella took the baby from the nurse and turned him around and examined him as if he were a vase, before announcing that he would like to take him back to Rome. Cicero did not object. 'I have made provision for him in my will. If you wish to discuss his upbringing, come and see me any time.'

They strolled together to view the spot where Tullia's ashes were resting, beside her favourite fountain in a sunny spot in the Academy. Cicero told me later that Dolabella knelt and placed some flowers on the grave, and wept. 'When I saw his tears I ceased to feel angry with him. As she always said, she knew the type of man she was marrying. And if her first husband was more of a school friend to her than anything, and her second just a convenient way of escaping her mother, at least her third was someone she loved passionately, and I am glad she experienced that before she died.'

Over dinner Dolabella, who was unable to recline because of his wound but had to eat sitting up in a chair like a barbarian, described the campaign in Spain, and confided to us that it had been a near-disaster: that at one point the army's line had broken and Caesar himself had been obliged to dismount, seize a shield and rally his fleeing legionaries. 'He said to us when it was over, "Today for the first time I fought for my life." We killed thirty thousand of the enemy, no prisoners taken. Gnaeus Pompey's head was stuck on a pole and publicly displayed on Caesar's orders. It was grim work, I can tell you, and I fear you and your friends will not find him as amenable as before when he gets home.'

'As long as he leaves me alone to write my books, he'll get no trouble from me.'

'My dear Cicero, you of all men have no need to worry. Caesar loves you. He always says that you and he are the last two left.'

Late in the summer Caesar returned to Italy, and all the ambitious men in Rome flocked to welcome him. Cicero and I stayed in the country, working. We finished the *Disputations* and Cicero sent it to Atticus so that his team of slaves could copy it and distribute it – he particularly asked for one to be sent to Caesar – and then he began composing two new treatises, *On the Nature of the Gods* and *On Divination*. Occasionally the barbs of grief still pierced him and he would withdraw for hours into some remote part of the grounds. But increasingly he was contented: 'What a lot of trouble one avoids if one refuses to have anything to do with the common herd! To have no job, to devote one's time to literature, is the most wonderful thing in the world.'

Even in Tusculum, however, we were aware, as if it were a storm in the distance, of the Dictator's return. Dolabella had spoken correctly. The Caesar who came back from Spain was different to the Caesar who had gone out. It was not simply his intolerance of dissent; it was as if his grasp on reality, once so terrifyingly secure, had at last begun to loosen. First he circulated a riposte to Cicero's eulogy of Cato, which he called his *Anti-Cato*, full of vulgar gibes that Cato was a drunkard and a crank. As nearly every Roman had at least a grudging respect for Cato, and most revered him, the pettiness of the pamphlet did the Dictator's reputation far more harm than it did Cato's. ('What is this restless desire of his to dominate everyone?' Cicero wondered aloud when he read it. 'That requires him to trample even on the dust of the dead?') Then there was his decision to hold yet another triumph, this time to celebrate his victory in Spain: it seemed to most people that the annihilation of thousands of fellow Romans, including the son of Pompey, was not a thing to glory in. There was also his continuing infatuation with Cleopatra: it was bad enough that he installed her in a grand house with a park beside the Tiber, but when he had a golden statue of his foreign mistress erected in the Temple of Venus, he offended the pious and the patriotic alike. He even had himself declared a god – 'the Divine Julius' – with his own priesthood, temple and images, and like a god began to interfere in all aspects of daily life: restricting overseas travel for senators and banning elaborate meals and luxurious goods – to the extent of stationing spies in the marketplaces who would burst into citizens' homes in the middle of dinner to search, confiscate and arrest.

Finally, as if his ambition had not caused enough bloodshed in recent years, he announced that in the spring he would be off to war again at the head of an immense army of thirty-six legions, to eliminate Parthia first of all, in revenge for the death of Crassus, and then to wheel around the far side of the Black Sea in a vast swathe of conquest that would encompass Hyrcania, the Caspian Sea and the Caucasus, Scythia, all the countries bordering on Germany and finally Germany itself, before returning to Italy by way of Gaul. He would be away three years. Over none of this did the Senate have any say. Like the men who built the pyramids for the pharaohs, they were mere slaves to their master's grand design. In December, Cicero proposed that we should transfer our labours to a warmer climate. A wealthy client of his on the Bay of Naples, M. Cluvius, had died recently, leaving him a substantial property at Puteoli, and it was to this that we headed, taking a week over the journey and arriving on the eve of Saturnalia. The villa was large and luxurious, built on the seashore, and even more beautiful than Cicero's nearby house at Cumae. The estate came with a substantial portfolio of commercial properties located inside the town and a farm just outside it. Cicero was as delighted as a child with his new possession, and the moment we arrived he took off his shoes, hoisted his toga, and walked down the beach to the sea to bathe his feet.

The following morning, after he had handed out Saturnalian gifts to all the slaves, he called me into his study and gave me a handsome sandalwood box. I assumed that the box was my present, but when I thanked him, he told me to open it. Inside I found the deeds to the farm near Puteoli. It had been transferred to my name. I was as stunned by the gesture as I had been on the day he granted me my freedom.

He said, 'My dear old friend, I wish it were more and I wish I could have given it to you sooner. But here it is at last, that farm you always wanted – and may it bring you as much joy and comfort as you have brought to me over the years.'

Even though it was a holiday, Cicero worked. He had no family anymore with whom to celebrate – dead, divorced and scattered as they were – and I suppose that writing eased his loneliness. Not that he was melancholy. He had started a new work, a philosophical investigation of old age, and he was enjoying it (*O wretched indeed is that old man who has not learned in the course of his long life that death should be held of no account*). But he insisted that I, at any rate, should have the day off, and so I went for a walk along the beach, turning over in my mind the extraordinary fact that I was now a man of property – a farmer indeed. It felt like the end of one part of my life and the start of another, a portent that my work with Cicero was almost done and that we would soon part.

All along that stretch of coast one encounters large villas looking west across the bay towards the promontory of Misenum. The property next door to Cicero's was owned by L. Marcius Philippus, a former consul a few years younger than Cicero, who had been awkwardly placed during the civil war, given that he was Cato's father-in-law and yet was also married to Caesar's closest living relative, his niece Atia. He had been granted permission by both sides to keep out of the conflict, and had sat it out down here – a cautious neutrality that perfectly suited his nervous temperament.

Now, as I drew closer to the boundary of his estate, I saw that the beach was blocked off by soldiers who were preventing people passing in front of the house. For a moment I wondered what was happening, and when at last I worked it out, I turned and hurried back to tell Cicero – only to find that he had already received a message:

Caesar Dictator to M. Cicero.

Greetings.

I am in Campania inspecting my veterans and shall be spending part of Saturnalia with my niece Atia at the villa of L. Philippus. If it is convenient, my party and I could visit you on the third day of the festival. Please let my officer know.

I asked, 'How did you reply?'

'How else does one reply to a god? I said yes, of course.'

He pretended to be put-upon, but I could tell that secretly he was flattered, although when he enquired as to the size of Caesar's entourage, which he would also have to feed, and was told it consisted of two thousand men, he had second thoughts. His entire household were obliged to postpone their holiday, and for the remainder of that day and the whole of the next made frantic preparations, emptying the food markets of Puteoli and borrowing couches and tables from neighbouring villas. A camp was pitched in the field behind the house and sentries were posted. We were given a list of twenty men who were to dine in the house itself, headed by Caesar and including Philippus, L. Cornelius Galba and C. Oppius – these last two Caesar's closest associates – and a dozen officers whose names I have forgotten. It was organised like a military manoeuvre, according to a strict timetable. Cicero was informed that Caesar would be working with his secretaries in Philippus's house until shortly after noon, that he would then take an hour's vigorous exercise along the seashore, and would appreciate it if a bath could be provided for his use before dinner. As to the menu, the Dictator was following a course of emetics and so would have an appetite equal to whatever was provided, but he would particularly appreciate oysters and quail if they were available.

By this time Cicero was heartily wishing he had never agreed to the visit: 'Where am I to find quail in December? Does he think I am Lucullus?' Nevertheless, he was determined, as he put it, 'to show Caesar that we know how to live', and took pains to provide the finest of everything, from scented oils for the bathroom to Falernian wine for the table. Then, just before the Dictator was due to walk through the door, the ever-anxious Philippus hurried round with the news that M. Mamurra, Caesar's chief engineer – the man who had built the bridge across the Rhine, among many other amazing feats – had died of apoplexy. For a moment it looked as if the occasion might be ruined. But when Caesar swept in, red-faced from the exertion of his walk, and Cicero broke the news to him, his expression did not even flicker.

'That's too bad for him. Which way is my bath?'

No further mention was made of Mamurra – and yet, as Cicero observed, he must have been one of Caesar's closest comrades for more than a decade. Oddly, that brief insight into the coldness of Caesar's character is the thing I remember most clearly of his visit, for I was soon distracted by the house being full of noisy men, spread between three dining rooms, and naturally I was not at the same table as the Dictator. In my room they were all soldiers – a rough crowd, polite enough to begin with but soon drunk, and there was a lot of trooping in and out between courses to vomit on the beach. All the talk was of Parthia and the forthcoming campaign. Afterwards I asked Cicero what had passed between him and Caesar.

He said, 'It was really surprisingly pleasant. We avoided politics and talked mostly of literature. He said that he had just read our *Disputations* and was full of compliments – "Except," he said, "I have to tell you that I am the living refutation of your principal proposition." "And what is that?" "You claim that one can only conquer one's fear of death by living a good life. Well, according to your definition I have hardly done that, and yet I have no fear of dying. What is your answer?" To which I replied that for a man with no fear of dying, he certainly travelled with a large bodyguard.'

'Did he laugh?'

'No he did not! He turned very serious, as if I had insulted him, and said that as the head of state he had a responsibility to take proper precautions, that if anything happened to him there would be chaos, but this didn't mean that he was afraid to die – far from it. So I probed a little further into the subject and asked why it was that he was so unafraid: did he believe the soul was eternal, or did he think we all die with our bodies?'

'And what was his reply?'

'He said that he didn't know about anyone else, but that obviously *he* wouldn't die along with his body because *he* was a god. I looked to see if he was joking but I'm not sure that he was. At that moment, I tell you honestly, I ceased to envy him all his power and glory. It has driven him mad.'

The only time I saw Caesar again that night was when he left. He emerged from the principal dining room, leaning on Cicero and laughing at some remark he had just made. He appeared slightly flushed with wine, which was rare for him as he usually drank in moderation, if at all. His soldiers formed into lines as an honour guard and he lurched off into the night supported by Philippus and followed by his officers.

The next morning Cicero wrote an account of the visit to Atticus: *Strange that so onerous a guest should leave a memory not disagreeable. But once is enough. He is not the kind of person to whom one says, 'Do drop round the next time you are in the neighbourhood.'*

As far as I know, that was the last time Cicero and Caesar ever spoke to one another.

On the eve of our return to Rome, I rode over to look at my farm. It was difficult to find, almost invisible from the coastal road, at the end of a long track leading up into the hills: an ancient, ivy-covered building commanding a wonderful panorama of the island of Capri. There was an olive grove and a small vineyard surrounded by low dry-stone walls. Goats and sheep grazed in the fields and on the nearby slopes; the tinkle of their neck bells rang soft as wind chimes; otherwise the place was entirely silent.

The farmstead was modest but fully appointed: a courtyard with portico, barns containing an olive press and stalls and feed racks, a fish pond, a vegetable and herb garden, a dovecote, chickens, a sundial. Beside the wooden gate a shaded terrace with fig trees faced out to sea. Inside, up a stone staircase, beneath the terracotta roof, was a large, dry, raftered room where I could keep my books and write: I asked the overseer to have some shelves built. Six slaves maintained the place and I was glad to see that all appeared healthy, unfettered and well fed. The overseer and his wife lived on the premises and had a child; they could read and write. Forget Rome and its empire: this was more than world enough for me. I should have stayed and told Cicero that he would have to return to the city on his own – I knew it even at the time. But that would have been poor thanks for his generosity, and besides, there were still books he wanted to finish and my assistance was needed. So I bade farewell to my little household, undertook to return to them as soon as I could, and rode back down the hill.

The Spartan statesman Lycurgus, seven hundred years ago, is said to have observed:

When falls on man the anger of the gods,
First from his mind they banish understanding.

Such was to be the fate of Caesar. I am sure Cicero was correct: he *had* gone mad. His success had made him vain, and his vanity had devoured his reason.

It was around this time – 'since the days of the week are all taken', as Cicero joked – that he had the seventh month of the year retitled 'July' in his honour. He had already declared himself a god and decreed that his statue should be carried in a special chariot during religious processions. Now his name was added to those of Jove and the Penates of Rome in every official oath. He was granted the title Dictator for Life. He styled himself Emperor and Father of the Nation. He presided over the Senate from a golden throne. He wore a special purple and gold toga. To the statues of the seven ancient kings of Rome that stood on the Capitol, he added an eighth – himself – and his image was introduced on the coinage – another prerogative of royalty.

Nobody spoke now of the revival of constitutional freedom – it was surely only a matter of time before he was declared monarch. At the Lupercalian festival in February, watched by a crowd in the Forum, Mark Antony actually placed a crown upon his head, whether mockingly or as a serious gesture none could say; but it was placed there, and the people resented it. On the statue of Brutus – the distant forefather of our contemporary Brutus – who had driven out the kings of Rome and established the consulship, graffito appeared: *If only you were alive now!* And on Caesar's statue someone scrawled:

Brutus was elected consul
When he sent the kings away;
Caesar sent the consuls packing,
Caesar is our king today.

He was scheduled to leave Rome at the start of his campaign of world conquest on the eighteenth day of March. Before he left, it was necessary for him to decree the results of all the elections for the next three years. A list was published. Mark Antony was to be consul for the remainder of the year alongside Dolabella; they would be succeeded by Hirtius and Pansa; Decimus Brutus (whom I shall henceforth call Decimus, to distinguish him from his kinsman) and L. Munatius Plancus would take over the year after that. Brutus himself was to be urban praetor and thereafter governor of Macedonia; Cassius was to be praetor and then governor of Syria; and so on. There were hundreds of names; it was drawn up like an order of battle.

The moment he saw it, Cicero shook his head in amazement at the sheer hubris of it: 'Julius the god seems to have forgotten what Julius the politician never would: that every time you fill an appointment, you make one man grateful and ten resentful.' On the eve of Caesar's departure, Rome was full of angry, disappointed senators. For example, Cassius, already insulted not to be chosen for the Parthian campaign, was offended that the less-experienced Brutus should be given a praetorship superior to his. But the greatest resentment was Mark Antony's at the prospect of sharing the consulship with Dolabella, a man whom he had never forgiven for committing adultery with his wife, and to whom he felt greatly superior; in fact such was his jealousy, he was actually using his powers as an augur to block the nomination on the grounds that it was ill-omened. A meeting of the Senate was summoned in Pompey's portico for the fifteenth, three days before Caesar's departure, to settle the issue once and for all. The rumour was that the Dictator would also demand to be granted the title of king at the same session.

Cicero had avoided the Senate as much as possible. He could not bear to look upon it. 'Do you know that some of these upstarts from Gaul and Spain that Caesar has put into the place can't even speak Latin?' He felt old and out of touch. His eyesight was poor. Nevertheless, he decided to attend on the Ides – and not merely to attend, but to speak for once, on behalf of Dolabella and against Mark Antony, whom he regarded as another tyrant in the making. He suggested that I should accompany him, as in the old days, 'if only to see what the Divine Julius has done to our republic of mere mortals'.

We set off two hours after dawn, in a pair of litters. It was a public holiday. A gladiator fight was scheduled for later in the day and the streets around Pompey's theatre, where the contest was to be held, were already packed with spectators. Lepidus, whom Caesar shrewdly judged weak enough to be a suitable deputy and therefore was the new Master of Horse, had a legion stationed on Tiber Island, ready to embark for Spain, of which he was to be governor; many of his men were heading for a final visit to the games.

Inside the portico, a troop of about a hundred gladiators belonging to Decimus, the governor of Nearer Gaul, practised their lunges and feints in the shadow of the bare plane trees, watched by their owner and a crowd of aficionados. Decimus had been one of the Dictator's most brilliant lieutenants in Gaul, and Caesar was said to treat him almost as a son. But he was not widely known in the city and I had hardly ever seen him. He was stocky and broad-shouldered: he could have been a gladiator himself. I remember wondering why he needed so many pairs of fighters for what were only minor games. Around the covered walkways several of the praetors, including Cassius and Brutus, had set up their tribunals, conveniently closer to the Senate than the Forum, and were hearing cases. Cicero leaned out of his litter and asked the porters to set us down in a sunny spot so that we could have some spring warmth. They did as ordered, and while he reclined on his cushions and read through his speech, I enjoyed the sensation of the sun upon my face.

Presently, through half-closed eyes, I saw Caesar's golden throne being carried through the portico and into the Senate chamber. I pointed it out to Cicero. He rolled up his speech. A couple of slaves helped him to his feet and we joined the throng of senators queuing to go in. There must have been three hundred men at least. Once I could have named almost every member of that noble order, and identified his tribe and family, and told you his particular interests. But the Senate that I knew had bled to death on the battlefields of Pharsalus, Thapsus and Munda.

We filed into the chamber. In contrast to the old Senate house it was light and airy, in the modern style, with a central aisle of black-and-white mosaic tiles. On either side rose three wide, shallow steps, along which the benches were arranged in tiers, facing one another. At the far end, on its dais, stood Caesar's throne beside the statue of Pompey, upon the head of which some subversive hand had placed a laurel wreath. One of Caesar's slaves kept jumping up, trying to knock it off, but much to the amusement of the watching senators he couldn't quite reach it. Eventually he fetched a stool and climbed up to remove the offending symbol and was rewarded with mocking applause. Cicero shook his head and rolled his eyes at such levity and went off to find his place. I stayed by the door with the other spectators.

After that, a long time passed – I should say at least an hour. Eventually Caesar's four attendants came back in from the portico, walked up the aisle to the throne, hoisted it on to their shoulders with difficulty (for it was made of solid gold) and carried it out again. A groan of exasperation went round the chamber. Many senators stood to stretch their legs; some left. Nobody seemed to know what was happening. Cicero strolled down the aisle. He said to me, 'I don't much want to deliver this speech in any case. I think I'll go home. Will you find out if the session is definitely cancelled?'

I went out into the portico. The gladiators were still there, but Decimus had gone. Brutus and Cassius had given up listening to their petitioners and were talking together. I knew both men well enough to approach them – Brutus the noble philosopher, still youthful-looking at forty; Cassius the same age, but grizzled, harder. About a dozen other senators were hanging round them, listening – the Casca brothers, Tillius Cimber, Minucius Basilus and Gaius Trebonius, who had been designated by Caesar to be governor of Asia; I also remember Quintus Ligarius, the exile whom Cicero had persuaded the Dictator to allow home, and Marcus Rubrius Ruga, an old soldier who had also been pardoned and had never got over it. They fell silent and turned to look at me as I approached. I said, 'Forgive me for disturbing you, gentlemen, but Cicero would like to know what's happening.'

The senators looked sideways at one another. Cassius said suspiciously, 'What does he mean by "what's happening"?'

Puzzled, I replied, 'Why, he simply wants to know if there will be a meeting.'

Brutus said, 'The omens are unpropitious, therefore Caesar is refusing to leave his house. Decimus has gone to try to persuade him to come. Tell Cicero to be patient.'

'I'll tell him, but I think he wants to go home.'

Cassius said firmly, 'Then persuade him to stay.'

It struck me as odd, but I went and relayed the remark to Cicero. He shrugged. 'Very well, let's give it a little longer.'

He returned to his seat and looked at his speech again. Senators came up and spoke to him and drifted away. He showed Dolabella what he was planning to say. Another long wait ensued. But eventually, after a further hour, Caesar's throne was carried back in and placed upon the dais. Clearly Decimus had persuaded him to come after all. Those senators who had been standing around talking resumed their places, and an air of expectation settled over the chamber.

I heard cheering outside. Turning, I saw through the open door that a crowd was streaming into the portico. In the middle of the throng, like battle standards, I could see the fasces of Caesar's twenty-four lictors, and swaying above their heads the golden canopy of the Dictator's litter. I was surprised there was no military bodyguard. Only later did I learn that Caesar had recently dismissed all those hundreds of soldiers he used to travel around with, saying, 'It is better to die once by treachery than live always in fear of it.' I have often wondered if his conversation with Cicero three months earlier had anything to do with this piece of bravado. At any rate, the litter was carried across the open space and set down outside the Senate, and when his lictors helped him out of it, the crowd was able to get very close to him. They thrust petitions into his hands, which he passed immediately to an aide. He was dressed in the special purple toga embroidered with gold that he alone was permitted by the Senate to wear. He certainly looked like a king; all that was missing was the crown. And yet I could see at once that he was uneasy. He had a habit, like a bird of prey, of cocking his head this way and that, and looking about him, as if searching for some slight stirring in the undergrowth. At the sight of the open door to the chamber, he seemed to draw back. But Decimus took him by the hand, and I suppose the momentum of the occasion must also have propelled him forwards: certainly he would have lost face if he had turned round and returned home; there were already rumours that he was ill.

His lictors cleared a path for him and in he came. He passed within three feet of me, so close I could smell the sweet and spicy scent of the oils and unguents with which he had been anointed after his bath. Decimus slipped in after him. Mark Antony was just behind Decimus, also on his way in, but Trebonius suddenly intercepted him and drew him aside.

The Senate stood. In the silence Caesar walked down the central aisle, frowning and pensive, twirling a stylus in his right hand. A couple of scribes followed him, carrying document boxes. Cicero was in the front row, reserved for ex-consuls. Caesar did not acknowledge him, or anyone else. He was glancing back and forth, up and down, flicking that stylus between his fingers. He mounted the dais, turned to face the senators, gestured to them to be seated, and lowered himself into his throne.

Immediately various figures rose and approached him offering petitions. This was normal practice now that the debates themselves no longer mattered: they had become instead rare opportunities to give the Dictator something in person. The first to reach him – from the left, both his hands stretched out in supplication – was Tillius Cimber. He was known to be seeking a pardon for his brother, who was in exile. But instead of lifting the hem of Caesar's toga to kiss it, he suddenly grabbed the folds of fabric around Caesar's neck and yanked so hard on the thick material that Caesar was pulled sideways, effectively pinioned and unable to move. He shouted angrily, but his voice was half strangled so I couldn't quite make it out. It sounded something like, 'But this is violence!' A moment later, one of the Casca brothers, Publius, strode towards him from the other side and jammed a dagger into Caesar's exposed neck. I couldn't believe what I was seeing: it was unreal – a play, a dream.

'Casca, you villain, what are you doing?' Despite his fifty-five years, the Dictator was still a strong man. Somehow he grabbed the blade of Casca's dagger with his left hand – he must have torn his fingers to shreds – squirmed free of Cimber's grasp, then swung round and stabbed Casca in the arm with his stylus. Casca cried in Greek, 'Help me, brother!' and an instant later his brother Gaius knifed Caesar in the ribs. The Dictator's gasp of shock echoed round the chamber. He dropped to his knees. More than twenty toga-clad figures were now stepping up on to the dais and surrounding him. Decimus ran past me to join in. There was a frenzy of stabbing. Senators rose in their places to see what was happening. People have often asked me why none of these hundreds of men, whose fortunes Caesar had made and whose careers he had advanced, attempted to go to his aid. I cannot answer except to say that it was all so fast, so violent and so unexpected, one's senses were stupefied.

I could no longer see Caesar through the ring of his assailants. I was told afterwards by Cicero, who was closer than I, that by some superhuman effort he briefly regained his feet and tried to break away. But such was the force, the desperate haste and the closeness of the attack that escape was impossible. His assailants even wounded one another. Cassius knifed Brutus in the hand. Minucius Basilus stabbed Rubrius in the thigh. It is said that the Dictator's last words were a bitter reproach to Decimus, who had tricked him into coming: 'Even you?' Perhaps it is true. I wonder, though, how much speech he was capable of by then. Afterwards the doctors counted twenty-three stab wounds on his body.

Their business done, the assassins drew back from what a moment before had been the beating heart of the empire and was now a punctured skein of flesh. Their hands were gloved in blood. Their gory daggers were held aloft. They shouted a few slogans: 'Liberty!' 'Peace!' 'The republic!' Brutus even called out 'Long live Cicero!' Then they ran down the aisle and out into the portico, their eyes staring wildly in their excitement, their togas spattered like butchers' aprons.

The moment they had gone, it was as if a spell had been broken. Pandemonium erupted. Senators clambered over the benches and even over one another in their panic to get away. I was almost trampled in the rush. But I was determined not to leave without Cicero. I ducked and twisted my way through the oncoming press of bodies until I reached him. He was still seated, staring at Caesar's body, which lay entirely unattended – his slaves having fled – sprawled on its back, its feet pointed towards the base of Pompey's statue, its head lolling over the edge of the dais, facing the door.

I told Cicero we needed to leave, but he did not seem to hear me. He was staring at the corpse, transfixed. He murmured, 'No one dares go near him, look.'

One of the Dictator's shoes had come off; his bare depilated legs were exposed where his toga had ridden up his thighs; his imperial purple was ragged and bloodied; there was a slash across his cheek that exposed the pale bone; his dark eyes seemed to stare, outraged, upside down, at the emptying chamber; blood ran from his wound diagonally across his forehead and dripped on to the white marble.

All those details I see today as clearly as I saw them forty years ago, and for an instant there flashed into my mind the prophecy of the sibyl: that Rome would be ruled by three, then two, then one, and finally by none. It took an effort for me to drag my gaze away, to seize Cicero by the arm and pull him to his feet. Finally, like a sleepwalker, he allowed himself to be led from the scene, and together we made our way out into the daylight.

LI

The portico was in chaos. The assassins had gone, escorted by Decimus's gladiators. No one knew their destination. People were rushing to and fro trying to find out what had happened. The Dictator's lictors had thrown away their symbols of authority and made a run for it. The remaining senators were also leaving as fast as they could; a few had even stripped off their togas to disguise their rank and were trying to infiltrate themselves into the crowd. Meanwhile, at the far end of the portico, some of the audience from the gladiator fights in the adjacent theatre had heard the commotion and were pouring in to see what was going on.

I sensed that Cicero was in mortal danger. Even though he'd known nothing in advance of the conspiracy, Brutus had called out his name; everyone had heard it. He was an obvious target for vengeance. Caesar's loyalists might even assume he was the assassins' leader. Blood would demand blood.

I said, 'We have to get you away from here.'

To my relief, he nodded, still too stunned to argue. Our porters had fled, abandoning their litters. We had to hurry out of the portico on foot. Meanwhile the games continued oblivious. From Pompey's theatre welled the roar of applause as the gladiators fought. One would never have guessed what had just occurred, and the more distance we put between ourselves and the portico, the more normal things seemed, so that by the time we reached the Carmenta Gate and entered the city it appeared to be a perfectly ordinary holiday and the assassination felt as if it had been a lurid dream.

Nevertheless, invisible to us, along the back streets and through the markets, conveyed on running feet and in panicky whispers, the news was travelling faster than we could – so that somehow, by the time we reached the house on the Palatine, it had overtaken us, and Cicero's brother Quintus and Atticus were already arriving from separate directions with garbled versions of what had happened. They did not know much. There had been an attack in the Senate, was all they had heard: Caesar was hurt.

'Caesar is dead,' said Cicero, and described what we had just seen. It seemed even more fantastical in recollection than it had at the time. Both men were at first disbelieving and then overjoyed that the Dictator was slain. Atticus, normally so urbane, even performed a little skipping dance.

Quintus said, 'And you truly had no idea this was coming?'

'None,' replied Cicero. 'They must have kept it from me deliberately. I ought to be offended, but to be honest I'm relieved to have been spared the anxiety. It demanded far more nerve than I could ever have mustered. To have come to the Senate with a concealed blade, to have waited all that time, to have held one's nerve, to have risked massacre by Caesar's supporters, and finally to have looked the tyrant in the eye and plunged in the dagger – I don't mind confessing I could never have done it.'

Quintus said, 'I could!'

Cicero laughed. 'Well, you're more used to blood than I am.'

'And yet do none of you feel any sorrow for Caesar, simply as a man?' I asked. 'After all,' I said to Cicero, 'it's only three months since you were laughing with him over dinner.'

Cicero looked at me with incredulity. 'I'm amazed that you should ask me that. I imagine I feel as you must have felt on the day you received your freedom. Whether Caesar was a kind master or a cruel one is neither here nor there – master he was, and slaves was what he made us. And now we have been liberated. So let's have no talk of sorrow.'

He sent out a secretary to see if he could discover the whereabouts of Brutus and the other conspirators. The man came back soon afterwards and reported that they were said to be occupying the upper ground of the Capitol.

Cicero said, 'I must go at once and offer my support.'

'Is that wise?' I asked. 'As things stand, you bear no responsibility for the killing. But if you go and show your solidarity with them in public, Caesar's supporters may not see much difference between you and Cassius and Brutus.'

'Let them. I intend to thank the men who've given me back my liberty.'

The others agreed and we set off at once, all four of us, with a few slaves for protection – along the slope of the Palatine, down the steps into the valley and across the road of Jugarius to the foot of the Tarpeian Rock. The air was eerily still and torpid with an approaching storm; the thoroughfare, normally busy with ox carts, was deserted apart from a few people wandering in the direction of the Forum. Their expressions were stunned, bewildered, fearful. And certainly if one sought for portents one had only to glance up at the sky. Massy dense black clouds seemed to be pressing down upon the roofs of the temples, and as we began to climb the steep flight of steps there was a flash and a crack of thunder. The rain was cold and heavy. The stones became slippery. We had to pause halfway to recover our breath. Beside us a stream ran over the green mossy rock and turned into a waterfall; below us I could see the curve of the Tiber, the city walls, the Field of Mars. I realised then how shrewd a piece of military planning it had been to retire straight from the scene of the assassination to the Capitol: its sheer cliffs made it a naturally impregnable fortress.

We pressed on until we came to the gate at the summit, which was guarded by gladiators, fearsome-looking characters from Nearer Gaul. With them was one of Decimus's officers. He recognised Cicero and ordered the men to admit us, then he conducted us himself into the walled compound, past the chained dogs that guarded the place at night, and into the Temple of Jupiter, where at least a hundred men were gathered, sheltering in the gloom from the rain.

As Cicero entered he was greeted with applause and he went round shaking hands with all of the assassins apart from Brutus, whose hand was bandaged because of the wound Cassius had accidentally inflicted on him. They had changed out of their bloodied clothes into freshly laundered togas, and their demeanour was sober, even grim, with nothing left of the euphoria that had immediately followed the killing. I was amazed to see how many of Caesar's closest followers had rushed to join them: L. Cornelius Cinna, for example, the brother of Caesar's first wife and uncle of Julia – Caesar had recently made him praetor, yet here he was with his ex-brother-in-law's murderers. And here too was Dolabella – the ever-faith-less Dolabella – who had raised not a finger to defend Caesar in the Senate chamber, and who now had his arm round the shoulder of Decimus, the man who had lured their old chief to his doom. He came over to join in the conversation that Cicero was having with Brutus and Cassius.

Brutus said, 'So you approve of what we have done?'

'Approve? It's the greatest deed in the history of the republic! But tell me,' asked Cicero, with a glance around the sombre interior, 'why are you all cooped up here out of sight like criminals? Why aren't you down in the Forum rallying the people to your cause?'

'We are patriots, not demagogues. Our aim was to remove the tyrant, nothing more.'

Cicero stared at him in surprise. 'But then who is running the country?'

Brutus said, 'At the moment, no one. The next step is to establish a new government.'

'Shouldn't you simply declare yourselves to be the government?'

'That would be illegal. We didn't pull down a tyrant in order to set ourselves up as tyrants in his place.'

'Well then summon the Senate here now, to this temple – you have the power as praetors – and let the Senate declare a state of emergency until elections can be held. That would be entirely legal.'

'We think it would be more constitutional if Mark Antony, as consul, summoned the Senate.'

'Mark Antony?' Cicero's surprise was turning to alarm. 'You mustn't let him anywhere near this business. He has all of Caesar's worst qualities and none of his best.' He appealed to Cassius to back him up.

Cassius said, 'I agree with you. In my view we should have killed him at the same time as we killed Caesar. But Brutus wouldn't tolerate it. Therefore Trebonius delayed him on his way in to the chamber, so that he could get away.'

'And where is he now?'

'Presumably in his house.'

'That I would doubt, knowing him,' said Dolabella. 'He will be busy in the city.'

Throughout these exchanges I had noticed Decimus talking to a couple of his gladiators. Now he hurried across, his expression grim. He said, 'There's a report that Lepidus is moving his legion off Tiber Island.'

Cassius said, 'We'll be able to see for ourselves from here.'

We went outside and followed Cassius and Decimus around the side of the great temple to the raised paved area to the north that gives a view for miles over the Field of Mars and beyond. And there was no doubt of it: the legionaries were marching across the bridge and forming up on the riverbank nearest the city.

Brutus betrayed his anxiety by a constant tapping of his foot. He said, 'I sent a messenger to Lepidus hours ago but he hasn't returned an answer.'

Cassius pointed. 'That's his answer.'

Cicero said, 'Brutus, I implore you – I implore you all – go down to the Forum and tell the people what you've done and why you've done it. Fire them with the spirit of the old republic. Otherwise Lepidus will trap you up here and Antony will take control of the city.'

Even Brutus could now see the wisdom of this, and so a procession of the conspirators – or assassins, or freedom fighters, or liberators: no one ever could agree exactly what to call them – descended the twisting road that led from the summit of the Capitol around behind the Temple of Saturn and down into the Forum. At Cicero's suggestion they left their bodyguard of gladiators behind: 'It will make the best possible impression of our sincerity if we walk alone and unarmed; besides, if there is trouble, we can retreat quickly enough.'

It had stopped raining. Three or four hundred citizens had gathered in the Forum and were standing around listlessly among the puddles, apparently waiting for something to happen. They saw us coming when we were still quite a long way off, and moved towards us. I had no idea how they would react. Caesar had always been a great favourite of the mob, although latterly even they had come to weary of his kingly ways – to dread his looming wars and to pine for the old days of elections when they had to be courted by the dozens of candidates with flattery and bribes. Would they applaud us or try to tear us apart? In the event they did neither. The crowd watched in absolute silence as we entered the Forum and then parted to let us pass. The praetors – Brutus, Cassius and Cinna – went up on to the rostra to address them, while the rest of us, including Cicero, stood at the side to watch.

Brutus spoke first, and although I can remember his sombre opening line – 'As my noble ancestor Junius Brutus drove the tyrant-king Tarquin from the city, so today have I rid us of the tyrant-dictator Caesar' – the rest of it I have forgotten. That was the problem. He had obviously laboured hard over it for days, and no doubt as an essay on the wickedness of despotism it read well. But as Cicero had long tried to convince him, a speech is a performance, not a philosophical discourse: it must appeal to the emotions more than to the intellect. A fiery oration at that moment might have transformed the situation – might have inspired the crowd to defend the Forum and their liberty from the soldiers who even now were massing on the Field of Mars. But Brutus gave them a lecture that was three parts history to one part political theory. I could hear Cicero beside me muttering under his breath. It did not help that while he was speaking, Brutus's wound began to bleed beneath its bandage; one was distracted from what he was saying by that gory reminder of what he had done.

After what felt like a long time, Brutus ended to applause best described as thoughtful. Cassius spoke next, and not badly either, for he had taken lessons in oratory from Cicero in Tusculum. But he was a professional soldier who had spent little time in Rome: he was respected but he was not much known, let alone loved. He received less applause even than Brutus. The disaster, however, was Cinna. He was an orator of the old-fashioned, melodramatic school, and tried to inject some passion into proceedings by tearing off his praetorian robe and hurling it from the rostra, denouncing it as the gift of a despot that he was ashamed to be seen wearing. The hypocrisy was too much to bear. Someone yelled out, 'You didn't say that yesterday!' The remark was cheered, which emboldened another heckler to shout: 'You'd have been nothing without Caesar, you old has-been!' In the chorus of jeering, Cinna's voice was lost – and the meeting with it.

Cicero said, 'Now this is a fiasco.'

'You are the orator,' said Decimus. 'Will you say something to retrieve the situation?' and to my horror I saw that Cicero was tempted. But at that moment Decimus was handed a new report that Lepidus's legion appeared to be moving towards the city. He beckoned urgently to the praetors to come down off the rostra, and with as much confidence as we could muster, which was little, we all trooped back up to the Capitol.

It was typical of Brutus's other-worldliness that he should have believed right up until the last moment that Lepidus would never dare to break the law by bringing an army across the sacred boundary and into Rome. After all, he assured Cicero, he knew the Master of Horse extremely well: Lepidus was married to his sister Junia Secunda (just as Cassius was married to his half-sister Junia Tertia).

'Believe me, he's a patrician through and through. He won't do anything illegal. I have always found him an absolute stickler for dignity and protocol.'

And at first it seemed he might be right, as the legion, after crossing the bridge and moving towards the city walls, halted on the Field of Mars and pitched camp about half a mile away. Then soon after nightfall, we heard the plaintive notes of the war horns. They set the dogs barking in the walled compound of the temple and sent us hurrying out to see what was going on. Heavy cloud obscured the moon and stars but the distant lights of the legion's campfires shone clearly in the darkness. Even as we watched, the fires seemed to splinter and rearrange themselves into snakes of fire.

Cassius said, 'They are marching with torches.'

A line of light began wavering along the road towards the Carmenta Gate. Presently on the moist night air we heard the faint tramp of the legionaries' boots. The gate was almost directly beneath us, obscured from sight by outcrops of rock. Lepidus's vanguard found it locked and hammered for admittance and cried out to the porter. But I guess he must have run away. There was a long interval when nothing happened. Then a battering ram was brought up. A series of heavy thuds was followed by the noise of splintering wood. Men cheered. Leaning over the parapet, we watched the legionaries with their torches slip quickly through the ruptured gate, deploy around the base of the Capitol and fan out across the Forum to secure the main public buildings.

Cassius said, 'Will they attack us tonight, do you think?'

'Why should they,' replied Decimus bitterly, 'when they can take us at their leisure in the daylight?' The anger in his tone suggested he held the others responsible, that he regarded himself as having fallen in among fools. 'Your brother-in-law, Brutus, has proved more ambitious and more daring than you led me to believe.'

Brutus, his foot tapping ceaselessly, did not respond.

Dolabella said, 'I agree, a night attack would be too hazardous. Tomorrow is when they'll make their move.'

Now Cicero spoke up. 'The question is surely whether Lepidus is acting in alliance with Antony or not. If he is, then our position is frankly hopeless. If he isn't, then I doubt Antony will want him to have the sole glory of wiping out Caesar's assassins. That, gentlemen, I fear, is our best hope.'

Cicero was now obliged to take his chances with the rest: it would have been far too risky to attempt to leave – not in darkness, with the place surrounded by potentially hostile soldiers and with Antony at large in the city. So there was nothing for it except to settle down for the night. It was to our advantage that the summit of the Capitol can only be approached in four ways: by the Moneta Steps to the north-east, the Hundred Steps to the south-west (the route we had climbed that afternoon) and by the two routes that lead up from the Forum – one a flight of stairs, the other a steep road. Decimus strengthened the guard of gladiators at the top of each and then we all retreated to the Temple of Jupiter.

I cannot say we got much rest. The temple was damp and chilly, the benches hard, the memory of the day's events too vivid. The dim light from the lamps and candles played upon the stern faces of the gods; from the shadows of the roof the wooden eagles looked down with disdain. Cicero talked for a while with Quintus and Atticus – quietly, so as not to be overheard. He couldn't believe how ill-thought-out the assassination had been. 'Was ever a deed carried through with such manly resolution and yet such childish judgement? If only they *had* brought me into their confidence! I could at least have told them that if you are going to kill the devil, there's no point in leaving his apprentice alive. And how could they have neglected Lepidus and his legion? Or let an entire day go by with no attempt to seize control of the government?'

The edge of frustration in his voice, if not the words themselves, must have carried to Brutus and Cassius, who were sitting nearby, and I saw them look across at Cicero and frown. He noticed them too. He lapsed into silence and sat propped up against a pillar, huddled in his toga, doubtless brooding on what had been done, what hadn't, and what might be done yet.

With the dawn it became possible to see the main event that had occurred overnight. Lepidus had moved perhaps a thousand men into the city. The smoke from their cooking fires rose over the Forum. A further three thousand or so remained encamped on the Field of Mars.

Cassius, Brutus and Decimus convened a meeting to discuss what should be done. Cicero's proposal of the previous day, that they should summon the Senate to the Capitol, had plainly been overtaken by events. Instead it was decided that a delegation of ex-consuls, none of whom had been party to the assassination, should go to the house of Mark

Antony and ask him formally, as consul, to convene the Senate. Servius Sulpicius, C. Marcellus and L. Aemilius Paullus, the brother of Lepidus, all volunteered to go, but Cicero refused to join them, arguing that the group would do better to approach Lepidus directly: 'I don't trust Antony. Besides, any agreement reached with him will only have to be approved by Lepidus, who at the moment is the man with the power, so why not deal with him and cut out Antony altogether?' But Brutus's argument that Antony had legal if not military authority carried the day, and in the middle of the morning the former consuls set off, preceded by an attendant carrying a white flag of truce.

We could do nothing now except wait and watch developments in the Forum – literally so, for if one was willing to scramble down to the roof of the public records office, one had a clear view of proceedings. The entire space was packed with soldiers and civilians listening to speeches from the rostra. They crammed the steps of the temples and clung to the pillars; more still were pressing to enter from the Via Sacra and the Argiletum, which were backed up as far as the eye could see. Unfortunately we were too far away to be able to hear what was being said. Around noon, a figure in full military uniform and the red cloak of a general began to address the crowd and spoke for well over an hour, receiving prolonged applause: that, I was told, was Lepidus. Not long afterwards, another soldier – his Herculean swagger and his thick black hair and beard identifying him unmistakably as Mark Antony – also appeared on the platform. Again, I could not hear his words, but it was significant simply that he was there at all, and I hastened back to tell Cicero that Lepidus and Antony were now apparently in alliance.

The tension on the Capitol by this time was acute. We had had little to eat all day. Nobody had slept much. Brutus and Cassius expected an attack at any time. Our fate was out of our hands. Yet Cicero was oddly serene. He felt himself to be on the right side, he told me, and would take the consequences.

Just as the sun was starting to go down over the Tiber, the delegation of ex-consuls returned. Sulpicius spoke for them all: 'Antony has agreed to call a meeting of the Senate tomorrow at the first hour in the Temple of Tellus.'

Joy greeted the first part of his statement, groans the second, for the temple was right across town, on the Esquiline, very close to Antony's house. Cassius said at once, 'That's a trap, to lure us out of our strong position. They'll kill us for sure.'

Cicero said, 'You may be right. But you could all stay here and I could go. I doubt they'd kill me. And if they did – well, what does it matter? I'm old, and there could be no better death than in defence of freedom.'

His words lifted our hearts. They reminded us why we were here. It was agreed on the spot that while the actual assassins would remain on the Capitol, Cicero would lead a delegation to speak on their behalf in the Senate. It was also decided that rather than spend another night in the temple, he and all the others who were not actually part of the original conspiracy would return to their homes to rest before the debate. Accordingly, after an emotional farewell, and under the flag of truce, we set off down the Hundred Steps into the gathering twilight. At the foot of the stairs, Lepidus's soldiers had erected a checkpoint. They demanded Cicero go forward and show himself. Fortunately he was recognised, and after he had vouched for the rest of us, we were all allowed to go through.

Cicero worked on his speech late into the night. Before I went to bed he asked if I would accompany him to the Senate the next day and take it down in shorthand. He thought it might be his last oration and he wanted it recorded for posterity: a summation of all he had come to believe about liberty and the republic, the healing role of the statesman and the moral justification for murdering a tyrant. I cannot say I relished the assignment but of course I could not refuse.

Of all the hundreds of debates Cicero had attended over the past thirty years none promised to be tenser than this one. It was scheduled to begin at dawn, which meant that we had to leave the house in darkness and pass through the shuttered streets – a nerve-racking business in itself. It was held in a temple that had never before served as a meeting place for the Senate, surrounded by soldiers – and not just those of Lepidus but many of Caesar's roughest veterans, who on hearing the news of their old chief's murder had armed themselves and come to the city to protect their rights and take revenge on his killers. And finally when we had run the gauntlet of pleas and imprecations and entered the temple, it proved so cramped that men who hated and distrusted one another were nonetheless packed into close proximity so that one sensed that the slightest ill-judged remark might turn the thing into a bloodbath.

And yet from the moment Antony rose to speak it became clear that the debate would be different to Cicero's expectation. Antony was not yet forty – handsome, swarthy, his wrestler's physique fashioned by nature for armour rather than a toga. Yet his voice was rich and educated, his delivery compelling. 'Fathers of the nation,' he declared, 'what is done is done and I profoundly wish it were not so, because Caesar was my dearest friend. But I love my country more even than I loved Caesar, if such a thing is possible, and we must be guided by what is best for the commonwealth. Last night I was with Caesar's widow, and amid her tears and anguish that gracious lady Calpurnia spoke as follows: "Tell the Senate," she said, "that in the agony of my grief I wish for two things only: that my husband be given a funeral appropriate to the honours he won in life, and that there be no further bloodshed."'

This drew a loud, deep-throated growl of approval, and to my surprise I realised the mood was more for compromise than revenge.

'Brutus, Cassius and Decimus,' continued Antony, 'are patriots just as we are, men from the most distinguished families in the state. We can salute the nobility of their aim even as we may despise the brutality of their method. In my view enough blood has been shed over these past five years. Accordingly I propose that we show the same clemency towards his assassins that was the mark of Caesar's statecraft – that in the interests of civic peace we pardon them, guarantee their safety, and invite them to come down from the Capitol and join us in our deliberations.'

It was a commanding performance, but then of course Antony's grandfather was regarded by many, including Cicero, as one of Rome's greatest orators, so perhaps the gift was in his blood. At any rate he set a tone of high-minded moderation – so much so that Cicero, who spoke next, was entirely wrong-footed and could do little except praise him for his wisdom and magnanimity. The only point with which he took issue was Antony's use of the word 'clemency':

'Clemency in my view means a pardon, and a pardon implies a crime. The murder of the Dictator was many things but it was not a crime. I would prefer a different term. Do you remember the story of Thrasybulus, who more than three centuries ago overthrew the Thirty Despots of Athens? Afterwards he instituted what was called an amnesty for his opponents – a concept taken from their Greek word *amnesia*, meaning "forgetfulness". That is what is needed here – a great national act not of forgiveness but of forgetfulness, that we may begin our republic anew freed from the enmities of the past, in friendship and in peace.'

Cicero received the same applause as Antony and a motion was immediately proposed by Dolabella offering amnesty to all those who had taken part in the assassination and urging them to come to the Senate. Only Lepidus was opposed: not I am sure out of principle – Lepidus was never a man for principles – so much as because he saw his chance of glory slipping away. The motion passed and a messenger was dispatched to the Capitol. During the recess while this was being done, Cicero came to the door to talk to me. When I congratulated him on his speech, he said, 'I arrived expecting to be torn to pieces and instead I find myself drowning in honey. What is Antony's game, do you suppose?'

'Perhaps there isn't one. Perhaps he is sincere.'

Cicero shook his head. 'No, he has some plan, but he's keeping it well hidden. Certainly he's more cunning than I gave him credit for.'

When the session resumed, it soon became not so much a debate as a negotiation. First Antony warned that when the news of the assassination reached the provinces, particularly Gaul, it might lead to widespread rebellion against Roman rule: 'In the interests of maintaining strong government in a time of emergency, I propose that all the laws promulgated by Caesar, and all appointments of consuls, praetors and governors made before the Ides of March should be confirmed by the Senate.'

Then Cicero rose. 'Including your own appointment, of course?'

Antony replied, with a first hint of menace, 'Yes, obviously including my own – unless, that is, you object?'

'And including Dolabella's, as your fellow consul? That was Caesar's wish as well, as I recall, until you blocked it by your auguries.'

I glanced across the temple to Dolabella, suddenly leaning forward in his place.

This was obviously a bitter draught for Antony to swallow – but swallow it he did. 'Yes, in the interests of unity, if that is the will of the Senate – including Dolabella's.'

Cicero pressed on. 'And you confirm therefore that both Brutus and Cassius will continue as praetors, and afterwards will be the governors of

Nearer Gaul and Syria, and that Decimus will in the meantime take control of Nearer Gaul, with the two legions already allotted to him?'

'Yes, yes and yes.' There were whistles of surprise, some groans and some applause. 'And now,' continued Antony, 'will your side agree: all acts and appointments issued before Caesar's death are to be confirmed by the Senate?'

Later Cicero said to me that before he rose to make his answer, he tried to imagine what Cato would have done. 'And of course he would have said that if Caesar's rule was illegal, it followed that his laws were illegal too and we should have new elections. But then I looked out of the door and saw the soldiers and asked myself how we could possibly have elections in these circumstances – there would be a bloodbath.'

Slowly Cicero got to his feet. 'I cannot speak for Brutus, Cassius and Decimus, but speaking for myself, since it is to the advantage of the state, and on condition that what goes for one goes for all – yes, I agree that the Dictator's appointments should be allowed to stand.'

'I cannot regret it,' he told me afterwards, 'because I could have done nothing else.'

The Senate continued its deliberations for the whole of that day. Antony and Lepidus also laid a motion calling for Caesar's grants to his soldiers to be ratified by the Senate, and in view of the hundreds of veterans waiting outside, Cicero could hardly dare to oppose that either. In return Antony proposed abolishing forever the title and functions of dictator; it passed without protest. About an hour before sunset, after issuing various edicts to the provincial governors, the Senate adjourned and walked through the smoke and squalor of the Subura to the Forum, where Antony and Lepidus gave an account to the waiting crowd of what had just been agreed. The news was greeted with relief and acclamation, and this sight of Senate and people in civic harmony was almost enough to make one imagine the old republic had been restored. Antony even invited Cicero up on to the rostra, the first time the ageing statesman had appeared there since he had addressed the people after his return from exile. For a moment he was too emotional to speak.

'People of Rome,' he said at last, gesturing to quiet the ovation, 'after the agony and violence not just of the last few days but of the last few years, let past grievances and bitterness be set aside.' Just at that moment a shaft of sunlight pierced the clouds, gilding the bronze roof of Jupiter's temple on the Capitol, where the white togas of the conspirators were plainly visible. 'Behold the sun of Liberty,' cried Cicero, seizing the moment, 'shining once again over the Roman Forum! Let it warm us – let it warm the whole of humanity – with the beneficence of its healing rays.'

Shortly afterwards Brutus and Cassius sent a message down to Antony that in view of what had been decided at the Senate, they were willing to leave their stronghold, but only on condition that he and Lepidus sent hostages to remain on the Capitol overnight as a guarantee of their safety. When Antony went up on to the rostra and read this aloud, there were cheers. He said, 'As a token of my good faith, I am willing to pledge to them my own son – a lad of barely three, who the gods know I love more than any living thing. Lepidus,' he said, holding out his hand to the Master of Horse who was standing next to him, 'will you do the same with your son?'

Lepidus had little choice but to agree, and so the two boys – one a toddler, the other in his teens – were collected from their homes and taken with their attendants up on to the Capitol. As dusk fell, Brutus and Cassius appeared, descending the steps without an escort. Yet again the crowd roared its pleasure, especially when they shook hands with Antony and Lepidus, and accepted a public invitation to dine with them as a symbol of reconciliation. Cicero was also invited but he declined. Utterly exhausted by his efforts over the past two days, he went home to sleep.

At dawn the following day the Senate met again in the Temple of Tellus; and once again I went with Cicero.

It was astonishing to enter and see Brutus and Cassius sitting a few feet away from Antony and Lepidus and even from Caesar's father-in-law, L. Calpurnius Piso. There were far fewer soldiers hanging around the door and the atmosphere was tolerant, indeed notable for a certain dark humour. For example when Antony rose to open the session he welcomed back Cassius in particular and said that he hoped this time he wasn't carrying a concealed dagger, to which Cassius replied that he wasn't, but would certainly bring a large one if ever Antony tried to set himself up as a tyrant. Everyone laughed.

Various items of business were transacted. Cicero proposed a motion thanking Antony for his statesmanship as consul, which had averted a civil war; it passed unanimously. Antony then proposed a complementary motion thanking Brutus and Cassius for their part in preserving the peace; that too was accepted without objection. Finally Piso rose to express his thanks to Antony for providing guards to protect his daughter Calpurnia and all Caesar's property on the night of the assassination.

He went on: 'It remains for us now to decide what to do with Caesar's body and with Caesar's will. As regards the body, it has been brought back from the Field of Mars to the residence of the chief priest, has been anointed and awaits cremation. As regards the will, I must tell the house that Caesar made a new one six months ago, on the Ides of September, at his villa near Lavicum, and sealed and deposited it with the Chief Vestal. No one knows its contents. In the spirit of openness and trust that has now been established, I move that both these things – the funeral and the reading of the will – should be conducted in public.'

Antony spoke strongly in favour of the proposal. The only senator who rose to object was Cassius. 'This seems to me a dangerous course. Remember what happened the last time there was a public funeral for a murdered leader – when Clodius's followers burned down the Senate house? Just as we've established a fragile peace, it would be insanity to put it at risk.'

Antony said, 'From what I've heard, Clodius's funeral was allowed to get out of hand by some who might have known better.' He paused for laughter: everyone knew he was now married to Clodius's widow, Fulvia. 'As consul, I shall preside over Caesar's funeral, and I can assure you order will be maintained.'

Cassius indicated by an angry gesture that he was still opposed. For a moment the truce threatened to break. Then Brutus rose. He said, 'Caesar's veterans who are in the city will not understand it if their commander-in-chief is denied a public funeral. Besides, what sort of message will it send to the Gauls, already said to be contemplating rebellion, if we dump the body of their conqueror in the Tiber? I share Cassius's unease, but in truth we have no alternative. Therefore in the interests of concord and amity I support the proposal.'

Cicero said nothing and the motion carried.

*

The reading of Caesar's will took place the following day, a little way up the hill in Antony's house. Cicero knew the place well. It had been Pompey's main residence before he moved out to his palace overlooking the Field of Mars. Antony, in charge of auctioning the confiscated assets of Caesar's opponents, had sold it to himself at a knockdown price. It was not much changed. The famous battering rams of the pirate triremes, trophies of Pompey's great naval victories, were still set into the outside walls. Inside, the elaborate decoration had scarcely been touched since the old man's day.

Cicero found it unsettling to be back – the more so when he was confronted by the scowling face of the villa's new mistress, Fulvia. She had hated him when she was married to Clodius, and now that she was married to Antony she hated him all over again – and made no attempt to hide it. The moment she saw him, she ostentatiously turned her back and began talking to someone else.

'What a shameless pair of grave-robbers,' Cicero whispered to me, 'and how typical of that harpy to be here. Why *is* she, in fact? Even the widow isn't here. What business of Fulvia's is the reading of Caesar's will?'

But that was Fulvia. More than any other woman in Rome – more even than Servilia, Caesar's old mistress, who at least had the grace to operate behind the scenes – Fulvia loved meddling in politics. And watching her move from visitor to visitor, ushering them towards the room where the will was to be read, I felt a sudden sense of unease: what if hers was the brain behind Antony's skilful policy of reconciliation? That would put it in a very different light.

Piso stood on a low table so that everyone could see him, and with Antony on one side and the Chief Vestal on the other, and with all the most prominent men of the republic listening in the audience, he first displayed the wax seal to show that it had not been tampered with, then broke it open and started to read.

To begin with, its meaning buried in legal jargon, the will seemed entirely innocuous. Caesar left his whole estate to any son that might be born to him after the drawing up of the document. However, in the absence of such a son, his wealth passed to the three male descendants of his late sister: that is to Lucius Pinarius, Quintus Pedius and Gaius Octavius, to be divided in the proportions one eighth each to Pinarius and Pedius and three quarters to Octavius, whom he now adopted as his son, henceforth to be known as Gaius Julius Caesar Octavianus …

Piso stopped reading and frowned, as if he was not sure what he had just announced. *An adopted son?* Cicero glanced at me, screwed up his eyes in an effort at memory and mouthed, 'Octavius?' Antony meanwhile looked as if he had been struck in the face. Unlike Cicero, he knew at once who Octavius was – the eighteen-year-old son of Caesar's niece Atia – and for him it must have been a bitter disappointment as well as a total surprise: I am sure he must have hoped to be named as the Dictator's main heir. Instead, he was merely mentioned as an heir in the second degree – that is, one who would inherit only if the first heirs died or turned down their legacy – an honour he shared with Decimus, one of the assassins! In addition, Caesar bequeathed every citizen of Rome the sum of three hundred sesterces in cash, and decreed that his estate beside the Tiber should become a public park.

The meeting broke up into puzzled groups, and afterwards, walking home, Cicero was full of foreboding. 'That will is a Pandora's box – a posthumous poisoned gift to the world that lets loose all manner of evils amongst us.' He was thinking not so much of the unknown Octavius, or Octavian as he was now restyled, who promised to be a short-lived irrelevance (he was not even in the country but was in Illyricum); it was the mention of Decimus combined with the gifts to the people that troubled him.

All through the remainder of that day and throughout the next, preparations went on in the Forum for Caesar's funeral. Cicero watched them from his terrace. A golden tabernacle, built to resemble the Temple of Venus the Victorious, was erected on the rostra for the body to lie in. Barriers were put up to control the crowds. Actors and musicians rehearsed. Hundreds more of Caesar's veterans began to appear on the streets, carrying their weapons: some had travelled a hundred miles to attend. Atticus came round and remonstrated with Cicero for having allowed such a spectacle to go ahead: 'You and Brutus and the others have all gone mad.'

'It's easy for you to say that,' replied Cicero, 'but how was it to be prevented? We control neither the city nor the Senate. The crucial mistakes were made not *after* the assassination but *before* it – a child should have foreseen the consequences of simply removing Caesar and leaving it at that. And now we have the Dictator's will to contend with.'

Brutus and Cassius sent messages to say that they intended to remain indoors throughout the day of the funeral: they had hired guards and advised Cicero to do the same. Decimus with his gladiators had barricaded his house and turned it into a fortress. Cicero, however, refused to take such precautions, although he prudently decided not to show himself in public. He suggested instead that I might attend the funeral and report back to him.

I did not mind going. No one would recognise me. Besides, I wanted to see it. I could not help feeling a certain secret regard for Caesar, who over the years had always been civil to me. Accordingly I went down into the Forum before dawn (this was now five days after the assassination – it was hard, amid the rush of events, to keep track of time). The centre of the city was already packed with thousands, women as well as men – not so much the polite citizenry but mostly old soldiers, the urban poor, many slaves, and a large contingent of Jews, who revered Caesar for allowing them to rebuild the walls of Jerusalem. I managed to work my way around the vast crowd to the corner of the Via Sacra, where the cortège would pass, and a few hours after daybreak I saw in the distance the procession start to leave the official residence of the chief priest.

It paraded right in front of me, and I was amazed by the planning that had gone into it: Antony and I am sure Fulvia had left out nothing that might be relied upon to inflame the emotions. First came the musicians, playing their haunting plangent dirges; then dancers dressed as spirits from the Underworld, who ran up shrieking to the front of the crowd striking poses of grief and horror; then came household slaves and freedmen carrying busts of Caesar; then not one but five actors went marching past representing each of Caesar's triumphs, wearing masks of the Dictator fashioned from beeswax that were so incredibly lifelike one felt he had risen from the dead five-fold in all his glory; then, carried on an open litter, came a life-size model of the corpse, naked except for a loincloth, with each of the stab wounds, including that to his face, depicted as deep red gashes in the white wax flesh – this caused the spectators to gasp and cry and some of the women to swoon; then came the body itself, lying on an ivory couch, carried on the shoulders of senators and soldiers and shrouded from view by covers of purple and gold, followed by Caesar's widow Calpurnia and niece Atia, veiled in black and holding on to one another, accompanied by their relatives; and finally came Antony and Piso, Dolabella, Hirtius, Pansa, Balbus, Oppius, and all the leading supporters of Caesar.

After the cortège had passed, there was a strange hiatus while the body was taken to the steps behind the rostra. Neither before nor afterwards did I ever hear such a profound silence in the centre of Rome in the middle of the day. During this ominous lull the leading mourners were filing on to the platform, and when at last the corpse appeared, Caesar's veterans began banging their swords against their shields as they must have done on the battlefield – a terrific, warlike, intimidating din. The body was placed carefully into the golden tabernacle; Antony stepped forward to deliver the eulogy, and held up his hand for silence.

'We come to bid farewell to no tyrant!' he declared, his powerful voice ringing round the temples and statues. 'We come to bid farewell to a great man foully murdered in a consecrated place by those he had pardoned and promoted!'

He had assured the Senate he would speak with moderation. He broke that assurance with his opening words, and for the next hour he worked the vast assembly, already aroused by the spectacle of the procession, to a pitch of grief and fury. He flung out his arms. He sank almost to his knees. He beat his breast. He pointed to the heavens. He recited Caesar's achievements. He told them of Caesar's will – the gift to every citizen, the public park, the bitter irony of his honouring of Decimus. 'And yet this Decimus, who was like a son to him – and Brutus and Cassius and Cinna and the rest – these men swore an oath – they made a sacred promise – to serve Caesar faithfully and to protect him! The Senate has given them amnesty, but by Jupiter what revenge I should like to take if prudence did not restrain me!' In short he used every trick of oratory that the austere Brutus had rejected. And then came his – or was it Fulvia's? – masterstroke. He summoned up on to the platform one of the actors wearing Caesar's lifelike mask, who in a rasping voice declaimed to the crowd that famous speech from Pacuvius's tragedy *The Trial for Arms*:

That ever I, unhappy man, should save
Wretches, who thus have brought me to the grave!

The impersonation was uncannily good. It was like a message from the Underworld. And then, to groans of horror, the manikin of

Caesar's corpse was raised by some mechanical contraption and rotated full circle so that all the wounds were shown.

From that point onwards Caesar's funeral followed the pattern of Clodius's. The body was supposed to be burned on a pyre already prepared on the Field of Mars. But as it was being borne down from the rostra, angry voices cried out that it should instead be cremated in Pompey's Senate chamber, where the crime was committed, or on the Capitol, where the conspirators had taken refuge. Then the crowd, with some collective impulse, changed its mind and decided that it should be burned on the spot. Antony did nothing to stop any of this but looked on indulgently as once again the bookshops of the Argiletum were ransacked and the benches of the law courts were dragged into the centre of the Forum and stacked in a pile. Caesar's bier was set upon the bonfire and torched. The actors and dancers and musicians pulled off their robes and masks and threw them into the flames. The crowd followed suit. They tore at their own clothes in their hysteria and these along with everything else flammable went flying on to the fire. When the mob started running through the streets carrying torches, looking for the houses of the assassins, I finally lost my nerve and headed back to the Palatine. On my way I passed poor Helvius Cinna, the poet and tribune, who had been mistaken by the mob for his namesake the praetor Cornelius Cinna, whom Antony had mentioned in his speech. He was being dragged away screaming with a noose around his neck, and afterwards his head was paraded around the Forum on a pole.

When I staggered back into the house and told Cicero what had happened, he put his face in his hands. All that night the sounds of destruction went on and the sky was lit up by the houses that had been set on fire. The following day Antony sent a message to Decimus warning that the lives of the assassins could no longer be protected and urging them to withdraw from Rome. Cicero advised them to do as Antony suggested: they would be more useful to the cause alive than dead. Decimus went to Nearer Gaul to try to take control of his allotted province. Trebonius travelled by a circuitous route to Asia to do the same. Brutus and Cassius retreated to the coast at Antium. Cicero headed south.

LII

He was finished with politics, he said. He was finished with Italy. He would go to Greece. He would stay with his son in Athens. He would write philosophy.

We packed up most of the books he needed from his libraries in Rome and Tusculum and set off with a large entourage, including two secretaries, a chef, a doctor and six bodyguards. The weather had been unseasonably cold and wet ever since the assassination, which of course was taken as yet another sign of the gods' displeasure at Caesar's murder. My strongest memory of those days spent travelling is of Cicero in his carriage composing philosophy with a blanket over his knees while the rain drummed continuously on the thin wooden roof. We stayed one night with Matius Calvena, the equestrian, who was in despair over the future of the nation: 'If a man of Caesar's genius could find no way out, who will find one now?' But apart from him, in contrast to the scenes in Rome, we found no one who was not glad to see the back of the Dictator. 'Unfortunately,' as Cicero observed, 'none of them has control of a legion.'

He sought refuge in his work, and by the time we reached Puteoli on the Ides of April, he had completed one entire book – *On Auguries* – half of another – *On Fate* – and had begun a third – *On Glory* – three examples of his genius that will live for as long as men are still capable of reading. And no sooner had he got out of his carriage and stretched his legs along the seashore than he began sketching the outline of a fourth, *On Friendship* (*With the single exception of wisdom, I am inclined to regard it as the greatest of all the gifts the gods have bestowed upon mankind*), which he planned to dedicate to Atticus. The physical world might have become a hostile and dangerous place for him, but in his mind he lived in freedom and tranquillity.

Antony had dismissed the Senate until the first day of June, and gradually the great villas around the Bay of Naples began to fill with the leading men of Rome. Most of the new arrivals, like Hirtius and Pansa, were still in a state of shock at Caesar's death. The pair were supposed to take over as consuls at the end of the year, and as part of their preparation they asked Cicero if he would give them further lessons in oratory. He didn't much want to – it was a distraction from his writing, and he found their doleful talk about Caesar irritating – but in the end he was too easy-going to refuse. He took them on to the beach to learn elocution as Demosthenes had done, by speaking clearly through a mouth full of pebbles, and to learn voice projection by delivering their speeches into the crashing waves. Over the dinner table they were full of stories of Antony's high-handedness: of how he had tricked Calpurnia on the night of the assassination into giving him custody of her late husband's private papers as well as his fortune; of how he now pretended these documents contained various edicts that had the force of law, whereas in fact he had forged them in return for enormous bribes.

Cicero said, 'So he has his hands on all the money? But I thought three quarters of Caesar's fortune was supposed to go to this boy Octavian?'

Hirtius rolled his eyes. 'He'll be lucky!'

Pansa added, 'He'll have to come and get it first, and I wouldn't give much for his chances.'

Two days after this exchange, I was sheltering from the rain in the portico, reading the elder Cato's treatise on agriculture, when the steward came up to me to announce that L. Cornelius Balbus had arrived to see Cicero.

'Then tell the master he's here.'

'But I'm not sure that I should – he gave me strict instructions that he was not to be disturbed, no matter who came to call.'

I sighed and laid aside my book: Balbus was one man who would have to be seen. He was the Spaniard who had handled Caesar's business affairs in Rome. He was well known to Cicero, who had once defended him in the courts against an attempt to strip him of his citizenship. He was now in his middle fifties and owned a huge villa nearby. I found him waiting in the tablinum with a toga-clad youth I took at first to be his son or grandson, except when I looked more closely I saw that he couldn't be, for Balbus was swarthy whereas this boy had damp blond hair badly cut in a basin style; he was also rather short and slender, pretty-faced but with a pasty complexion pitted by acne.

'Ah, Tiro,' cried Balbus, 'will you kindly drag Cicero away from his books? Just tell him I have brought Caesar's adopted son to see him – Gaius Julius Caesar Octavianus – that ought to do it.'

And the young man smiled shyly at me, showing gapped uneven teeth.

Naturally Cicero came at once, overwhelmed by curiosity to meet this exotic creature, seemingly dropped into the tumult of Roman politics from the sky. Balbus introduced the young man, who bowed and said, 'It is one of the greatest honours of my life to meet you. I have read all your speeches and works of philosophy. I have dreamed of this moment for years.' His voice was pleasant: soft and well educated.

Cicero fairly preened at the compliment. 'You are very kind to say it. Now please tell me, before we go further: what am I to call you?'

'In public I insist on Caesar. To my friends and family I am Octavian.'

'Well, since at my age I would find another Caesar hard to get used to, perhaps it could be Octavian for me as well, if I may?'

The young man bowed again. 'I would be honoured.'

And so began two days of unexpectedly friendly exchanges. It turned out that Octavian was staying next door with his mother Atia and his stepfather Philippus, and he wandered back and forth quite freely between the two houses. Often he appeared on his own, even though he had brought an entourage of friends and soldiers over with him from Illyricum, and more had joined him at Naples. He and Cicero would talk in the villa or walk along the seashore together in the intervals between showers. Watching them, I was reminded of a line in Cicero's treatise on old age: *just as I approve of the young man in whom there is a touch of age, so I approve of the old man in whom there is some flavour of youth ...* Oddly enough, it was Octavian who sometimes seemed the older of the two: serious, polite, deferential, shrewd; it was Cicero who made the jokes and skimmed the stones across the sea. He told me that Octavian had no small talk. All he wanted was political advice. The fact that Cicero was publicly aligned with his adopted father's killers appeared to be neither here nor there as far as he was concerned. How soon should he go to Rome? How should he handle Antony? What should he say to Caesar's veterans, many of whom were hanging around the house? How was civil war to be avoided?

Cicero was impressed: 'I can understand entirely what Caesar saw in him – he has a certain coolness rare in one of his years. He might make a great statesman one day, if only he can survive long enough.' The men around him were a different matter. These included a couple of Caesar's old army commanders, with the hard, dead eyes of professional killers; and some arrogant young companions, two in particular: Marcus Vipsanius Agrippa, not yet twenty but already bloodied by war, taciturn and faintly menacing even in repose; and Gaius Cilnius Maecenas, a little older, effeminate, giggling, cynical. '*Those*,' said Cicero, 'I do not care for *at all*.'

On only one occasion did I have an opportunity to observe Octavian closely for any length of time. That was on the final day of his stay, when he came to dinner with his mother and stepfather, along with Agrippa and Maecenas; Cicero also invited Hirtius and Pansa; I made up the nine. I noticed how the young man never touched his wine, how quiet he was, how his pale grey eyes flicked from one speaker to another and how intently he listened, as if he was trying to commit everything they said to memory. Atia, who looked as if she might have been the model for a statue commemorating the ideal Roman matron, was far too proper to voice a political opinion in public. Philippus, however, who certainly did drink, became increasingly voluble, and towards the end of the evening announced, 'Well if anyone wants to know *my* opinion, I think Octavian should renounce this inheritance.'

Maecenas whispered to me, '*Does* anyone want to know his opinion?' and he bit on his napkin to stifle his laughter.

Octavian said mildly, 'And what leads you to that opinion, Father?'

'Well, if I may speak frankly, my boy, you can *call* yourself Caesar all you like but that doesn't *make* you Caesar, and the closer you get to Rome the greater the danger will be. Do you really think Antony is just going to hand over all these millions? And why would Caesar's veterans follow you rather than Antony, who commanded a wing at Pharsalus? Caesar's name is just a target on your back. You'll be killed before you've gone fifty miles.'

Hirtius and Pansa nodded in agreement.

Agrippa said quietly, 'No, we can get him to Rome safely enough.'

Octavian turned to Cicero. 'And what do you think?'

Cicero dabbed carefully at his mouth with his napkin before replying. 'Just four months ago your adopted father was dining precisely where you are now and assuring me he had no fear of death. The truth is, all our lives hang by a thread. There is no safety anywhere, and no one can predict what will happen. When I was your age, I dreamed only of glory. What I wouldn't have given to be in your place now!'

'So you would go to Rome?'

'I would.'

'And do what?'

'Stand for election.'

Philippus said, 'But he's only eighteen. He's not even old enough to vote.'

Cicero continued: 'As it happens, there's a vacancy for a tribune: Cinna was killed by the mob at Caesar's funeral – they got the wrong man, poor devil. You should propose yourself to fill his place.'

Octavian said, 'But surely Antony would never allow it?'

Cicero replied, 'That doesn't matter. Such a move would show your determination to continue Caesar's policy of championing the people: the plebs will love it. And when Antony opposes you – as he must – he'll be seen as opposing them.'

Octavian nodded slowly. 'That's not a bad idea. Perhaps you should come with me?'

Cicero laughed. 'No, I'm retiring to Greece to study philosophy.'

'That's a pity.'

After the dinner, when the guests were preparing to leave, I overheard Octavian say to Cicero, 'I meant what I said. I would value your wisdom.'

Cicero shook his head. 'I fear my loyalties lie in the other direction, with those who struck down your adopted father. But if ever there was a possibility of your reconciling with them – well then, in such circumstances, in the interests of the state, I would do all I could to help you.'

'I'm not opposed to reconciliation. It's my legacy I want, not vengeance.'

'Can I tell them that?'

'Of course. That's why I said it. Goodbye. I shall write to you.'

They shook hands. Octavian stepped out into the road. It was a spring evening, not yet entirely dark, no longer raining either but with moisture still in the air. To my surprise, standing silently in the blue gloom across the street were more than a hundred soldiers. When they saw Octavian they set up the same din I had heard at Caesar's funeral, banging their swords against their shields in acclamation: it turned out these were some of the Dictator's veterans from the Gallic wars, settled nearby on Campanian land. Octavian went over with Agrippa to talk to them. Cicero watched for a moment, then ducked back inside to avoid being seen.

When the door was shut I asked, 'Why did you urge him to go to Rome? Surely the last thing you want is to encourage another Caesar?'

'If he goes to Rome he'll cause problems for Antony. He'll split their faction.'

'And if his adventure succeeds?'

'It won't. Philippus is right. He's a nice boy, and I hope he survives, but he's no Caesar – you only have to look at him.'

Nevertheless, he was sufficiently intrigued by Octavian's prospects to postpone his departure for Athens. Instead he conceived a vague idea of attending the Senate meeting Antony had summoned for the first of June. But when we arrived in Tusculum towards the end of May, everyone advised him not to go. Varro sent a letter warning that there would be murder. Hirtius agreed. He said, 'Even I'm not going, and no one's ever accused *me* of disloyalty to Caesar. But there are too many old soldiers in the streets too quick to draw their swords – look what happened to Cinna.'

Octavian, meanwhile, had arrived in the city unscathed and sent Cicero a letter:

From G. Julius Caesar Octavianus to M. Tullius Cicero, greetings.

I wanted you to know that yesterday Antony finally agreed to see me at his house: the one that used to be Pompey's. He kept me waiting for more than an hour – a silly tactic that I believe shows his weakness rather than mine. I began by thanking him for looking after my adopted father's property on my behalf, invited him to take from it whatever trinkets he desired as keepsakes, but asked him to hand over the rest to me at once. I told him I needed the money to make an immediate cash disbursement to three hundred thousand citizens in accordance with my father's will. The rest of my expenses I asked to be met by a loan from the public treasury. I also told him of my intention to stand for the vacant tribunate and asked him for evidence of the various edicts he claims to have discovered in my father's papers.

He replied with great indignation that Caesar had not been king and had not bequeathed me control of the state; that accordingly he did not have to give an account of his public acts to me; that as far as the money went, my father's effects were not as great as all that, and that he had left the public treasury bankrupt so there was nothing to be got from there either;

as for the tribunate, my candidacy would be illegal and was out of the question.

He thinks because I am young he can intimidate me. He is wrong. We parted on bad terms. Among the people, however, and among my father's soldiers my reception has been as warm as Antony's was cold.

Cicero was delighted at the enmity between Antony and Octavian and showed the letter to several people: 'You see how the cub tweaks the old lion's tail?' He asked me to go to Rome on his behalf on the first of June and report back what happened in the Senate meeting.

I found Rome, as everyone had warned us, teeming with soldiers, mostly Caesar's veterans whom Antony had summoned to the city to serve as his private army. They stood around on the street corners in sullen, hungry groups, intimidating anyone who looked as though they might be wealthy. As a result, the Senate was very thinly attended, and there was no one brave enough to oppose Antony's most audacious proposal: that Decimus should be removed from the governorship of Nearer Gaul and that he, Antony, should be awarded both of the Gallic provinces, together with command of their legions, for the next five years – exactly the same concentration of power that had set Caesar on the road to the dictatorship. As if this were not enough, he also announced that he had summoned home the three legions based in Macedonia that Caesar had planned to use in the Parthian campaign and placed these under his own command as well. Dolabella did not object, as might have been expected, because he was to receive Syria, also for five years; Lepidus was bought off with Caesar's old position of pontifex maximus. Finally, as this arrangement left Brutus and Cassius without their anticipated provinces, he arranged for them to be offered instead a couple of Pompey's old corn commissionerships – one in Asia, the other in Sicily; they would have no power at all; it was a humiliation; so much for reconciliation.

The bills were approved by the half-empty Senate and Antony took them to the Forum the next day to be voted on by the people. The inclement weather continued. There was even a thunderstorm halfway through proceedings – such a terrible omen that the assembly should have been dismissed at once. But Antony was an augur: he claimed to have seen no lightning and ruled that the vote could go ahead, and by dusk he had what he wanted. There was no sign of Octavian. As I turned to leave the assembly I saw Fulvia watching from a litter. She was soaked from the rain but did not seem to notice, so engrossed was she in her husband's apotheosis. I made a mental note to myself to warn Cicero that a woman who hitherto had been nothing more than a nuisance to him had just become a far more dangerous enemy.

The following morning I went to see Dolabella. He took me to the nursery and showed me Cicero's grandson, the infant Lentulus, who had just learnt to take a few wobbling steps. It was now more than fifteen months since Tullia's death, yet still Dolabella had not repaid her dowry. At Cicero's request I began to broach the subject ('Do it politely, mind you: I can't afford to antagonise him'), but Dolabella cut me off at once.

'It's out of the question, I'm afraid. You can give him this instead in full and final settlement. It's worth far more than money.' And he threw across the table an imposing legal document with black ribbons and a red seal. 'I've made him my legate in Syria. Don't worry, tell him – he doesn't have to *do* anything. But it means he can leave the country honourably and gives him immunity for the next five years. My advice, tell him, is that he should get out as soon as he can. Things are worsening by the day and we can't be held responsible for his safety.'

I took the message back to Tusculum and relayed it verbatim to Cicero, who was sitting in the garden beside Tullia's grave. He studied the warrant for his legateship. 'So this little piece of paper has cost me a million sesterces? Does he really imagine that waving this in the face of some illiterate half-drunk legionary would deter him from sticking his sword in my throat?' He had already heard what had happened at the Senate and in the public assembly, but wanted me to recite my precis of the speeches. At the end he said, 'So there was no opposition?'

'None.'

'Did you see Octavian at all?'

'No.'

'No – of course not – why would you? Antony has the money, the legions and the consulship. Octavian has nothing but a borrowed name. As for us, we daren't even show our faces in Rome.' He slumped against the wall in despair. 'I tell you something, Tiro, between you and me – I'm starting to wish the Ides of March had never happened.'

There was to be a family conference with Brutus and Cassius on the seventh day of June in Antium to decide their next steps: he had been invited and he asked me to accompany him.

We set off early, descending the hills just as the sun came up, and crossed the marshy land in the direction of the coast. The mist was rising. I remember the croaking of the bullfrogs, the cries of the gulls; Cicero barely spoke. Just before midday we reached Brutus's villa. It was a fine old place built right on the shoreline with steps cut into the rocks leading down to the sea. The gate was blocked by a strong guard of gladiators; others patrolled the grounds; more were visible walking on the beach – I guess there must have been a hundred armed men in all. Brutus was waiting with the others in a loggia filled with Greek statuary. He looked strained – the familiar nervous tapping of his foot was more pronounced than ever. He told us he had not left the house for two months – amazing considering he was urban praetor and not supposed to be out of Rome for more than ten days a year. At the head of the table sat his mother, Servilia; also present were his wife Porcia and his sister Tertia, who was married to Cassius. Finally there was M. Favonius, the former praetor known as Cato's Ape on account of his closeness to Brutus's uncle. Tertia announced that Cassius was on his way.

Cicero suggested I might fill in the time while we waited by giving a detailed account of the recent debates in the Senate and the public assembly, whereupon Servilia, who had ignored me up to that point, turned her fierce eye upon me and said, 'Oh, so this is your famous *spy*?'

She was a female Caesar – that is the best way I can describe her: quick-brained, handsome, haughty, bone-hard. The Dictator had presented her with lavish gifts, including estates confiscated from his enemies and huge jewels picked up on his conquests, yet when her son arranged his murder and she was given the news, her eyes stayed as dry as the gemstones he had given her. In this too she was like Caesar. Cicero was slightly awed by her.

I stammered my way through the transcript of my notes, all the while conscious of Servilia's stare, and at the end she said with great contempt, 'A grain commissionership in Asia! It was for this that Caesar was assassinated – so that my son could become a corn merchant?'

'Even so,' said Cicero, 'I think he should take it. It's better than nothing – certainly better than staying here.'

Brutus said, 'I agree with you on your last point at least. I can't stay hidden from view any longer. I'm losing respect with every day that passes. But Asia? No, what I really need to do is go to Rome and do what the urban praetor always does at this time of year – stage the Games of Apollo and show myself to the Roman people.' His sensitive face was full of anguish.

'You can't go to Rome,' replied Cicero. 'It's far too dangerous. Listen, the rest of us are more or less expendable, but not you, Brutus – your name and your honour make you the great rallying point of freedom. My advice is to take this commission, do some honourable public work far away from Italy in safety, and await more favourable events. Things will change: in politics they always do.'

At that moment Cassius arrived and Servilia asked Cicero to repeat what he'd just said. But whereas adversity had reduced Brutus to a state of noble suffering, it had put Cassius in a rage, and he started pounding on the table: 'I did not survive the massacre at Carrhae and save Syria from the Parthians in order to be made a grain collector in Sicily! It's an insult.'

Cicero said, 'Well then, what will you do?'

'Leave Italy. Go abroad. Go to Greece.'

'Greece,' observed Cicero, 'will soon be rather crowded, whereas first of all Sicily is safe, second you'll be doing your duty like a good constitutionalist, and third and above all you'll be closer to Italy to exploit opportunities when they arise. You must be our great military commander.'

'What sort of opportunities?'

'Well, for example, Octavian could yet cause all sorts of trouble for Antony.'

'Octavian? That's one of your jokes! He's far more likely to come after us than he is to pursue a quarrel with Antony.'

'Not at all – I saw the boy when he was on the Bay of Naples, and he's not as ill-disposed towards us as you might think. "It's my legacy I want, not vengeance" – those were his very words. His real enemy is Antony.'

'Then Antony will crush him.'

'But Antony has to crush Decimus first, and that's when the war will start – when Antony tries to take Nearer Gaul away from him.'

'Decimus,' said Cassius bitterly, 'is the man who has let us down more than any other. Just think what we could have done with those two legions of his if he'd brought them south in March! But it's too late now: Antony's Macedonian legions will outnumber him two to one.'

The mention of Decimus was like the breaking of a dam. Denunciations flowed from everyone round the table, Favonius especially, who maintained he should have warned them he was mentioned in Caesar's will: 'That did more to turn the people against us than anything else.'

Cicero listened in growing dismay. He intervened to say that there was no point in weeping over past errors, but couldn't resist adding, 'Besides, if it's mistakes you're talking about, never mind Decimus – the seeds of our present plight were sown when you failed to call a meeting of the Senate, failed to rally the people to our cause, and failed to seize control of the republic.'

'Well upon my word!' exclaimed Servilia. 'I never heard anything like it – to be accused of a lack of resolution by you of all people!'

Cicero glowered at her and immediately fell silent, his cheeks burning either with fury or embarrassment, and not long after that the meeting ended. My notes record only two conclusions. Brutus and Cassius agreed grudgingly at least to consider accepting their grain commissionerships, but only after Servilia announced in her grandest manner that she would arrange for the wording of the Senate resolution to be couched in more flattering terms. And Brutus reluctantly conceded that it was impossible for him to go to Rome and that his praetorian games would have to be staged in his absence. Apart from that the conference was a failure, with nothing decided. As Cicero explained to Atticus in a letter dictated on the way home, it was now a case of 'every man for himself': *I found the ship going to pieces, or rather its scattered fragments. No plan, no thought, no method. Hence, though I had no doubts before, I am now all the more determined to escape from here, and as soon as I possibly can.*

The die was cast. He would go to Greece.

As for me, I was almost sixty and had privately resolved that the time had come for me to leave Cicero's service and live what remained of my life alone. I knew from the way he talked that he wasn't expecting us to part company. He assumed we would share a villa in Athens and write philosophy together until one or other of us died of old age. But I could not face leaving Italy again. My health was not good. And love him as I did, I was tired of being a mere appendage to his brain.

I dreaded having to tell him and kept postponing the fateful moment. He undertook a kind of farewell progress south through Italy, saying goodbye to all his properties and reliving old memories, until eventually we reached Puteoli at the beginning of July – or Quintilis, as he still defiantly insisted on calling it. He had one last villa he wished to visit, along the Bay of Naples in Pompeii, and he decided he would leave on the first leg of his journey abroad from there, hugging the coast down to Sicily and boarding a merchant ship in Syracuse (he judged it too dangerous to sail from Brundisium, as the Macedonian legions were due to start arriving any day). To convey all his books, his property and household staff, I hired three ten-oared boats. He took his mind off the voyage, which he dreaded, by trying to decide what literary composition we should undertake while at sea. He was working on three treatises simultaneously, moving between them as his reading and his inclination took him: *On Friendship*, *On Duties* and *On Virtues*. With these he would complete his great scheme of absorbing Greek philosophy into Latin and of turning it in the process from a set of abstractions into principles for living.

He said, 'I wonder if this would be a good opportunity for us to write our version of Aristotle's *Topics*? Let's face it: what could be more useful in this time of chaos than to teach men how to use dialectics to construct reasoned arguments? It could be in the form of a dialogue, like the *Disputations* – you playing one part and I the other. What do you think?'

'My friend,' I replied hesitantly, 'if I may call you that, I have wanted for some time to speak to you but have not been sure how to do it.'

'This sounds ominous! You'd better go on. Are you ill again?'

'No, but I need to tell you I have decided not to accompany you to Greece.'

'Ah.' He stared at me for what felt like a very long time, his jaw moving slightly as it often did when he was trying to find the right word. Finally he said, 'Where will you go instead?'

'To the farm you so kindly gave me.'

His voice was very quiet: 'I see, and when would you want to do that?'

'At any time convenient to you.'

'The sooner the better?'

'I don't mind when it is.'

'Tomorrow?'

'It can be tomorrow if you like. But that is not necessary. I don't want to inconvenience you.'

'Tomorrow then.' And with that he turned back to his Aristotle.

I hesitated. 'Would it be all right if I borrowed young Eros from the stables and the little carriage, to transport my belongings?'

Without looking up he replied, 'Of course. Take whatever you need.'

I left him alone and spent the remainder of the day and the evening packing my belongings and carrying them out into the courtyard. He did not appear for dinner. The next morning there was still no sign of him. Young Quintus, who was hoping for a place on Brutus's staff and staying with us while his uncle tried to fix an introduction, said that he had gone off very early to visit Lucullus's old house on the island of Nesis. He put a consoling hand on my shoulder. 'He asked me to tell you goodbye.'

'He didn't say more than that? Just goodbye?'

'You know how he is.'

'I know how he is. Would you please tell him I'll come back in a day or two to say a proper farewell?'

I felt quite sick, but determined. I had made up my mind. Eros drove me to the farm. It was not far, only two or three miles, but the distance seemed much greater as I moved from one world to another.

The overseer and his wife had not been expecting me so soon but nonetheless seemed pleased to see me. One of the slaves was called from the barn to carry my luggage into the farmhouse. The boxes containing my books and documents went straight upstairs into the raftered room I had selected earlier as the site for my little library. It was shuttered and cool. Shelves had been put up as I requested – rough and rustic, but I didn't care – and I set about unpacking at once. There is a wonderful line in one of Cicero's letters to Atticus in which he describes moving into a property and says: *I have put out my books and now my house has a soul.* That was how I felt as I emptied my boxes. And then to my surprise in one of them I discovered the original manuscript of *On Friendship*. Puzzled, I unrolled it, thinking I must have brought it with me by mistake. But when I saw that Cicero had copied out at the top of the roll in his shaking hand a quotation from the text, on the importance of having friends, I realised it was a parting gift:

> *If a man ascended into heaven and gazed upon the whole workings of the universe and the beauty of the stars, the marvellous sight would give him no joy if he had to keep it to himself. And yet, if only there had been someone to describe the spectacle to, it would have filled him with delight. Nature abhors solitude.*

*

I allowed two days to pass before I returned to the villa in Puteoli to say my proper goodbye: I needed to be sure I was strong enough in my resolve not to be persuaded out of it. But the steward told me Cicero had already left for Pompeii and I returned at once to the farm. From my terrace I had a sweeping view of the entire bay, and often I found myself standing there peering into the immense blueness, which ran from the misty outline of Capri right round to the promontory at Misenum, wondering if any of the myriad ships I could see was his. But then gradually I became caught up in the routine of the farm. It was almost time to harvest the vines and the olives, and despite my creaking knees and my soft scholar's hands, I donned a tunic and a wide-brimmed straw hat and worked outside with the rest, rising with the light and going to bed when it faded, too exhausted to think. Gradually the pattern of my former life began to fade from my mind, like a carpet left out in the sun. Or so I thought.

I had no cause to leave my property save one: the place had no bath. A good bath was the thing I missed most, apart from Cicero's conversation. I couldn't bear to wash myself only in the cold water from the mountain spring. Accordingly I commissioned the construction of a bathhouse in one of the barns. But that couldn't be done until after the harvest, and so I took to riding off every two or three days to use one of the public baths that are found everywhere along that stretch of coast. I tried many different establishments – in Puteoli itself, in Bauli and in Baiae – until I decided Baiae had the best, on account of the natural hot sulphurous water for which the area is famous. The clientele was sophisticated and included the freedmen of senators who had villas nearby; some of whom I knew. Without even meaning to, I began to pick up the latest gossip from Rome.

Brutus's games had passed off well, I discovered: no expense spared, even though the praetor himself was not present. Brutus had amassed hundreds of wild beasts for the occasion and, desperate for popular acclaim, he gave orders that every last one of them should be used up in fights and hunts. There were also musical performances and plays, including *Tereus*, a tragedy by Accius that contained copious references to the crimes of tyrants: apparently it received knowing applause. But unfortunately for Brutus, his games, although generous, were quickly overshadowed by an even more lavish set that Octavian gave immediately afterwards in honour of Caesar. It was the time of the famous comet, the hairy star that rose every day an hour before noon – we could see it even in the brilliantly sunny skies of Campania – and Octavian claimed it was nothing less than Caesar ascending into heaven. Caesar's veterans were greatly taken with this notion, I was told, and young Octavian's fame and reputation began to soar with the comet.

Not long after this I was lying one afternoon in a hot pool on a terrace overlooking the sea when some men joined me who I soon gathered by their talk were on the staff of Calpurnius Piso. He had a veritable palace about twenty miles away at Herculaneum and I suppose they must have decided to break their journey from Rome and complete their travelling the next day. I didn't consciously eavesdrop but I had my eyes closed and they may have thought I was sleeping. At any rate, I quickly pieced together the sensational intelligence that Piso, the father of Caesar's widow, had made an outspoken attack on Antony in the Senate, accusing him of theft, forgery and treason, of aiming at a new dictatorship and of setting the nation on the road to a second civil war. When one of them said, 'Aye, and there's not another man in Rome with the courage to say it, now that our so-called liberators are all either hiding or have fled abroad', I thought with a pang of Cicero, who would have hated to know that he had been supplanted as an upholder of liberty by Piso, of all people.

I waited until they'd moved on before I climbed out of the pool. I remember I thought I would have a massage while I pondered what I'd just heard. I was moving towards the shaded area where the tables were set out when a woman appeared carrying a pile of freshly laundered towels. I cannot say I recognised her at once – it must have been fifteen years since I had last set eyes on her – but a few paces after we had passed one another I stopped and looked round. She had done the same. I recognised her then all right. It was the slave girl Agathe whose freedom I had bought before I went into exile with Cicero.

This is Cicero's story, not mine; it is certainly not Agathe's. Nevertheless, our three lives were entwined, and before I resume the main part of my story I believe she deserves some mention.

I had met her when she was seventeen and a slave in the bath chambers of Lucullus's great villa in Misenum. She and her parents, by then dead, had been seized as slaves in Greece and brought to Italy as part of Lucullus's war booty. Her beauty, her gentleness and her plight all moved me. When I saw her next she was in Rome, one of six household slaves produced as witnesses at the trial of Clodius to support Lucullus's contention that Clodius, his former brother-in-law, had committed incest and adultery in Misenum with his ex-wife. After that I glimpsed her just once more, when Cicero visited Lucullus before going into exile. She seemed to me by then to be broken in spirit and half dead. Having some small savings put aside, on the night we fled Rome I gave the money to Atticus so that he could purchase her from Lucullus on my behalf and set her free. I had kept an eye out for her in Rome over the years but had never seen her. She was thirty-six, still beautiful to me, although I could tell from her lined face and raw-boned hands that she still had to work hard. She seemed embarrassed and kept brushing back loose strands of grey hair with the back of her wrist. After a few awkward pleasantries there was a difficult silence and I found myself saying, 'Forgive me, I am keeping you from your work – you will be in trouble with the owner.'

'There will be no trouble on that score,' she replied, laughing for the first time. 'I *am* the owner.'

After that we began to talk more freely. She told me she had tried to find me when she was freed, but of course by then I was in Thessalonica. Eventually she had come back to the Bay of Naples: it was the place she knew best and it reminded her of Greece. Because of her experience in the household of Lucullus, she had found plentiful work as an overseer in the local hot baths. After ten years some wealthy clients, merchants in Puteoli, had set her up in this place, and now it belonged to her. 'But all this is because of you. How can I ever begin to thank you for your kindness?'

Live the good life, Cicero had said: *learn that virtue is the sole prerequisite for happiness*. As we sat on a bench in the sunshine, I felt I had proof of that particular piece of his philosophy, at least.

My sojourn on the farm lasted forty days.

On the forty-first, the eve of the Festival of Vulcan, I was working in the vineyard in the late afternoon when one of the slaves called out to me and pointed down the track. A carriage, accompanied by twenty men on horseback, was bouncing over the ruts, throwing up so much dust in the shafts of summer sunshine, it looked as if it was travelling on golden clouds. It drew up outside the villa and from it descended Cicero. I suppose I had always known in my heart that he would come looking for me. I was fated never to escape. As I walked towards him, I snatched off my straw hat and swore to myself that on no account would I be persuaded to return with him to Rome. Beneath my breath I whispered, 'I will not listen … I will not listen … I will not listen …'

I could see at once from the swing of his shoulders as he wheeled round to greet me that he was in tremendous spirits. Gone was the drooping dejection of recent times. He put his hands on his hips and roared with laughter at my appearance. 'I leave you alone for a month and see what happens! You have turned into the elder Cato's ghost!'

I arranged for his entourage to be given refreshment while we went on to the shaded terrace and drank some of last year's wine, which he pronounced to be not bad at all. 'What a view!' he exclaimed. 'What a place to live out one's declining years! Your own wine, your own olives …'

'Yes,' I replied carefully, 'it suits me very well. I shan't be going far. And your plans? What happened to Greece?'

'Ah well, I got as far as Sicily, whereupon the southerly winds got up and kept blowing us back into harbour and I began to wonder if the gods weren't trying to tell me something. Then, while we were stuck in Regium waiting for better weather, I heard about this extraordinary attack on Antony made by Piso. You must have heard the commotion even here. After that, letters came from Brutus and Cassius saying that Antony was definitely starting to weaken – they were to be offered provinces after all, and he had written to them saying he hoped they would soon be able to come to Rome. He has summoned the Senate for a meeting on the first of September and Brutus has sent a letter to all former consuls and praetors asking them to attend.

'So I said to myself: am I really going to run away at this of all moments, while there's still a chance? Will I go down in history as a coward? I tell you, Tiro, suddenly it was as if a thick mist that had enshrouded me for months had cleared and I saw my duty absolutely. I turned right around and sailed back the way I had come. As it happened, Brutus was at Velia, preparing to set sail, and he practically went down on his knees to thank me. He's been given Crete as his province; Cassius has Cyrene.'

I could not help pointing out that these were hardly adequate compensation for Macedonia and Syria, which was what they had been allotted.

'Of course not,' replied Cicero, 'which is why they're resolved to ignore Antony and his wretched illegal edicts and go straight to their original provinces. After all, Brutus has followers in Macedonia, and Cassius was the hero of Syria. They will raise legions and fight for the republic against the usurper. A whole new spirit has infused us – a flame pure white and sublime.'

'And you will go to Rome?'

'Yes, for the meeting of the Senate in nine days' time.'

'Then it sounds to me as though you have the most dangerous assignment of the three.'

He waved his hand dismissively. 'So what is the worst that can happen? I'll die. Very well: I'm past sixty; I've run my race. And at least this will be a good death – which as you know is the supreme objective of the good life.' He leaned forwards. 'Tell me: do I seem happy to you?'

'You do,' I conceded.

'That's because I realised when I was stuck in Regium that finally I have conquered my fear of death. Philosophy – our work together – has accomplished that for me. Oh, I know that you and Atticus won't believe me. You'll think that underneath I'm still the same timid creature I always was. But it's true.'

'And presumably you expect me to come with you?'

'No, not at all – the opposite! You have your farm and your literary studies. I don't want you to expose yourself to any more risk. But our earlier parting was not what it should have been, and I couldn't pass your gate without remedying that.' He stood and opened his arms wide. 'Goodbye, my old friend. Words are inadequate to express my gratitude. I hope we meet again.'

He clasped me to him so firmly and for so long that I could feel the strong and steady beating of his heart. Then he pulled away, and with a final wave he walked towards his carriage and his bodyguards.

I watched him go, his familiar gestures: the straightening of his shoulders, the adjustment of the folds of his tunic, the unthinking way he offered his hand to be helped into his carriage. I glanced around at my vines and my olive trees, my goats and my chickens, my drystone walls, my sheep. Suddenly it seemed a small world – a very small world.

I called after him: 'Wait!'

LIII

If Cicero had pleaded with me to return with him to Rome, I probably would have refused. It was his willingness to set off without me on the last great adventure of his life that piqued my pride and sent me chasing after him. Of course my change of heart did not surprise him. He knew me far too well. He merely nodded and told me to gather what I required for the journey, and to be quick about it: 'We need to make good progress before nightfall.'

I called my little household together in the courtyard and wished them luck with the harvest. I told them I would come back as soon as possible. They knew nothing of politics or Cicero. Their expressions were bewildered. They lined up to watch me leave. Just before the place disappeared from view, I turned to wave, but they had already returned to the fields.

It took us eight days to reach Rome, and every mile of the journey was fraught with peril, despite the guards that had been provided for Cicero by Brutus, and always the threat was the same: Caesar's old soldiers, who had sworn oaths to hunt down those responsible for the assassination. The fact that Cicero had known nothing of it beforehand did not concern them: he had defended it afterwards, and that was enough to render him guilty in their eyes. Our route took us across the fertile plains that had been given to Caesar's veterans to farm, and at least twice – once when we passed through the town of Aquinum and then soon afterwards at Fregellae – we were warned of ambushes up ahead and had to halt and wait until the road was secured.

We saw burnt-out villas, scorched fields, slaughtered livestock; even once a body hanging from a tree with a placard reading 'Traitor' round its neck. Caesar's demobbed legionaries roamed Italy in small bands as if they were back in Gaul, and we heard many stories of looting, rape and atrocities. Whenever Cicero was recognised by the ordinary citizens, they flocked to him, kissed his hands and clothes and pleaded with him to deliver them from terror. Nowhere was the common population's devotion more evident than when we reached the gates of Rome on the day before the Senate was due to meet. His welcome was even warmer than when he returned from exile. There were so many deputations, petitions, greetings, handshakes and sacrifices of thanks to the gods that it took him nearly all day to cross the city to his house.

In terms of reputation and renown I guess he was now the pre-eminent figure in the state. All his great rivals and contemporaries – Pompey, Caesar, Cato, Crassus, Clodius – had died violent deaths. 'They are not cheering me as an individual so much as the memory of the republic,' he said to me when finally we got inside. 'I don't flatter myself – I'm merely the last left standing. And of course demonstrating in support of me is a safe way of protesting against Antony. I wonder what *he* makes of today's outpouring. He must want to *crush* me.'

One by one the leaders of the opposition to Antony in the Senate trooped up the slope to pay their respects. There were not many but I must mention two in particular. The first was P. Servilius Vatia Isauricus, the son of the old consul who had recently died aged ninety: he had been a strong supporter of Caesar and had only just returned from governing Asia – a difficult and arrogant man, he was deeply envious of Antony's dominant position in the state. The second opponent of Antony I have already mentioned: Lucius Calpurnius Piso, the father of Caesar's widow, who had been the first to raise his voice against the new regime. He was a sallow, stooping, hairyfaced old man with very bad teeth who had been consul at the time Cicero went into exile: for years he and Cicero had hated one another, but now they both hated Antony even more, and so in politics at least that made them friends. There were others present, but this was the pair who mattered most and they were of one voice in warning Cicero to stay away from the Senate the next day.

'Antony has laid a trap for you,' said Piso. 'He plans to propose a resolution tomorrow calling for fresh honours in memory of Caesar.'

'Fresh honours!' cried Cicero. 'The man is already a god. What other honours does he need?'

'The motion will state that every public festival of thanksgiving should henceforth include a sacrifice in honour of Caesar. Antony will demand to know your opinion. The meeting will be surrounded by Caesar's veterans. If you support the proposal, your return to public life will be destroyed before it even starts – all the crowds who cheered you today will jeer you as a turncoat. If you oppose it, you will never reach home alive.'

'But if I refuse to attend I'll look like a coward, and what sort of leadership is that?'

Isauricus said, 'Send word that you're too exhausted from your journey. You're getting on in years. People will understand.'

'None of us is going,' added Piso, 'despite his summons. We'll show him up as a tyrant whom no one will obey. He'll look like a fool.'

This was not the heroic return to public life that Cicero had planned, and he was reluctant to hide away at home. Still, he saw the wisdom of what they were saying and the following day he sent a message to Antony pleading tiredness as his excuse for not attending the session. Antony's response was to fly into a rage. According to Servius Sulpicius, who gave Cicero a full report, in front of the Senate he threatened to send a team of workmen and soldiers round to Cicero's house to tear down his door and drag him to the meeting. He was only deterred from such extreme action when Dolabella pointed out that Piso, Isauricus and a few others had also stayed away: he could hardly round up all of them. The debate went ahead and Antony's proposal to honour Caesar was passed, but only under duress.

Cicero was outraged when he heard what Antony had said. He insisted he would go to the Senate the next day and make a speech, regardless of the risk: 'I haven't returned to Rome in order to cower under my blankets!' Messages went back and forth between him and the others, and in the end they agreed to attend together, reasoning that Antony wouldn't dare to massacre them all. The following morning, shielded by bodyguards, they walked down in a phalanx from the Palatine – Cicero, Piso, Isauricus, Servius Sulpicius and Vibius Pansa (Hirtius could not join them because he really was ill) – right the way through the cheering crowds to the Temple of Concordia on the far side of the Forum, where the Senate was due to meet. Dolabella was waiting on the steps with his curule chair. He came over to Cicero and announced that Antony was sick and that he would be presiding in his place.

Cicero laughed. 'So much illness going around at the moment – the entire state seems to be ailing! One might almost imagine that Antony shares the common characteristic of all bullies: eager to dish out punishment, unable to take it.'

Dolabella replied coldly: 'I trust you won't say anything today that will put our friendship in jeopardy: I've reconciled with Antony and any attack on him I'd regard as an attack on myself. Also I'd remind you that I did give you that legateship on my staff in Syria.'

'Yes, although actually I'd prefer the return of my dear Tullia's dowry, if you don't mind. And as far as Syria is concerned – well, my young friend, I should make haste to get there, or Cassius might be in Antioch before you.'

Dolabella glared at him. 'I see you have abandoned your usual affability. Very well, but be careful, old man. The game is getting rougher.'

He stalked away. Cicero watched him go with satisfaction. 'I have wanted to say that for a long time.' He was like Caesar, I thought, sending his horse to the rear before a battle: he would either win where he stood or die.

The Temple of Concordia was the place where Cicero had convened the Senate as consul all those years before, in order to debate the punishment of the Catiline conspirators; from here he had led them to their deaths in the Carcer. I had not set foot in it since and I felt the oppressive presence of many ghosts. But Cicero seemed immune to such memories. He sat on the front bench between Piso and Isauricus and waited patiently for Dolabella to call him – which he did, as late in proceedings as he could and with insulting offhandedness.

Cicero started quietly, as was his way: 'Before I begin to speak on public affairs, I will make a brief complaint of the wrong done to me yesterday by Antony. Why was I so bitterly denounced? What subject is so urgent that sick men should be carried to this chamber? Was Hannibal at the gates? Who ever heard of a senator being threatened with having his house attacked because he failed to appear to discuss a public thanksgiving?

'And in any case, do you think I would have supported his proposal if I had been here? I say: if a thanksgiving is to be given to a dead man, let it be given to the elder Brutus, who delivered the state from the despotism of kings and who nearly five hundred years later has left descendants prepared to show similar virtue to achieve a similar end!'

There was a gasp. Men's voices are supposed to weaken as they age; but not Cicero's on that day.

'I am not afraid to speak out. I am not afraid of death. I am grieved that senators who have achieved the rank of consul did not support Lucius Piso in June, when he condemned all the abuses now widespread in the state. Not one single ex-consul seconded him by his voice – no, not even by a look. What is the meaning of this slavery? I say these men have fallen short of what their rank requires!'

He put his hands on his hips and glared around him. Most senators could not meet his eye.

'In March I accepted that the acts of Caesar should be recognised as legal, not because I agreed with them – who could do that? – but for the sake of reconciliation and public harmony. Yet any act that Antony disagrees with, such as that which limits provincial commands to two years, has been repealed, while other decrees of the Dictator have been miraculously discovered and posted after his death, so that criminals have been brought back from exile – by a dead man. Citizenship has been given to whole tribes and provinces – by a dead man. Taxes have been imposed – by a dead man.

'I wish Mark Antony were here to explain himself – but apparently he is unwell: a privilege he did not grant me yesterday. I hear he is angry with me. Well, I will make him an offer – a fair one. If I say anything against his life and character, let him declare himself my most bitter enemy. Let him keep an armed guard if he really feels he needs it for his own protection. But don't let that guard threaten those who express their own free opinions on behalf of the state. What can be fairer than that?'

For the first time his words drew murmurs of agreement.

'Gentlemen, I have already reaped the reward of my return simply by making these few remarks. Whatever happens to me, I have kept faith with my beliefs. If I can speak again here safely, I shall. If I can't, then I shall hold myself ready in case the state should call me. I have lived long enough for years and for fame. Whatever time remains to me will not be mine, but will be devoted to the service of our commonwealth.'

Cicero sat to a low rumble of approval and some stamping of feet. The men around him clapped him on the shoulder.

When the session ended, Dolabella swept out with his lictors, no doubt heading straight to Antony's house to tell him what had happened, while Cicero and I went home.

*

For the next two weeks the Senate did not meet and Cicero stayed barricaded in his house on the Palatine. He recruited more guards, bought a ferocious new watchdog, and fortified the villa with iron shutters and doors. Atticus lent him some scribes, and these I set to work making copies of his defiant speech to the Senate, which he sent to everyone he could think of – to Brutus in Macedonia, to Cassius en route to Syria, to Decimus in Nearer Gaul, to the two military commanders in Further Gaul, Lepidus and L. Munatius Plancus, and to many others. He called it, half seriously and half in self-mockery, his Philippic, after the famous series of orations Demosthenes had delivered in opposition to the Macedonian tyrant Philip II. A copy must have reached Antony: at any rate, he made known his intention to reply in the Senate, which he summoned to meet on the nineteenth day of September.

There was never any question of Cicero attending in person: being unafraid of death was one thing, committing suicide another. Instead he asked if I would go and make a record of what Antony said. I agreed, reasoning that my natural anonymity would protect me.

The moment I entered the Forum, I thanked the gods that Cicero had stayed away, for Antony had filled every corner with his private army. He had even stationed a squadron of Iturean archers on the steps of the Temple of Concordia – wild-looking tribesmen from the borders of Syria, notorious for their savagery. They watched as each senator entered the temple, occasionally fitting arrows into their bows and pretending to take aim.

I managed to squeeze in at the back and take out my stylus and tablet just as Antony arrived. In addition to Pompey's house in Rome, he had also commandeered Metellus Scipio's estate at Tibur, and it was there that he was said to have composed his speech. He looked badly hungover as he passed me, and when he reached the dais, he leaned forward and vomited a thick stream into the aisle. This drew laughter and applause from his supporters: he was notorious for being sick in public. Behind me his slaves locked and barred the door. It was against all custom to take the Senate hostage in this manner, and clearly intended to intimidate.

As to his harangue against Cicero, it was in essence a continuation of his vomit. He spewed forth years of swallowed bile. He gestured around the temple and reminded senators that it was in this very building that

Cicero had arranged for the illegal execution of five Roman citizens, among them P. Lentulus Sura, Antony's own stepfather, whose body Cicero had refused to return to his family for a decent burial. He accused Cicero ('this bloodstained butcher who lets others do his killing') of having masterminded the assassination of Caesar, just as he had the murder of Clodius. He maintained that it was Cicero who had artfully poisoned the relations between Pompey and Caesar that had led to civil war. I knew the charges were all lies, but also that they would be damaging, as would the more personal accusations he made – that Cicero was a physical and moral coward, vain and boastful and above all a hypocrite, forever twisting this way and that to keep in with all factions, so that even his own brother and nephew deserted him and denounced him to Caesar. He quoted from a private letter Cicero had sent him when he was trapped in Brundisium: *I shall always, without hesitation and with my whole heart, do anything that I can to accord with your wishes and interests.* The temple rang with laughter. He even dragged up Cicero's divorce from Terentia and his subsequent marriage to Publilia: 'With what trembling, debauched and covetous fingers did this lofty philosopher undress his fifteen-year-old bride on her wedding night, and how feebly did he perform his husbandly duties – so much so that the poor child fled from him in horror soon afterwards and his own daughter preferred to die rather than live with the shame.'

It was all horribly effective, and when the door was unlocked and we were released into the light, I dreaded having to return to Cicero and read it back to him. However, he insisted on hearing it word for word. Whenever I tried to miss out a passage or a phrase, he spotted it at once and made me go back and put it in. At the end he looked quite crumpled. 'Well, that's politics,' he said, and tried to shrug it off. But I could tell he was shaken. He knew he would have to retaliate in kind or retire humiliated. Trying to do so in person in the Senate, controlled as it was by Antony and Dolabella, would be too dangerous. Therefore his counter-charge would have to be made in writing, and once it was published there could be no going back. Against such a wild man as Antony, it was a duel to the death.

Early in October, Antony left Rome for Brundisium, in order to secure the loyalty of the legions he had brought over from Macedonia, and which were now bivouacked just outside the town. With Antony gone, Cicero also decided to retire from Rome for a few weeks and devote himself to composing his riposte, which he was already calling his Second Philippic. He headed off to the Bay of Naples and left me behind to look after his interests.

It was a melancholy season. As always in late autumn, the skies above Rome were darkened by countless thousands of starlings arriving from the north, and their chattering shrieks seemed to warn of some imminent calamity. They would nestle in the trees beside the Tiber only to rise in huge black flags that would unfurl overhead and sweep back and forth as if in panic. The days became chilly; the nights longer; winter approached and with it the certainty of war. Octavian was in Campania, very close to where Cicero was staying, recruiting troops in Casilinum and Calatia from among Caesar's veterans. Antony was trying to bribe the soldiers in Brundisium. Decimus had raised a new legion in Nearer Gaul. Lepidus and Plancus were waiting with their forces beyond the Alps. Brutus and Cassius had hoisted their standards in Macedonia and in Syria. That made a total of seven armies, formed or forming. It was merely a question of who would strike first.

In the event, that honour, if honour is the word, fell to Octavian. He had mustered the best part of a legion by promising the veterans a staggering bounty of two thousand sesterces a head – Balbus had guaranteed the money – and now he wrote to Cicero begging his advice. Cicero sent the sensational news to me to pass on to Atticus.

> *His object is plain: war with Antony and himself as commander-in-chief. So it looks to me as though in a few days' time we shall be in arms. But who are we to follow? Consider his name; consider his age. He wanted my advice as to whether he should proceed to Rome with three thousand veterans or hold Capua and block Antony's route or go to join the three Macedonian legions now marching along the Adriatic coast, which he hopes to have on his side. They refused to take a bounty from Antony, so he says, booed him savagely, and left him standing as he tried to harangue them. In short, he proffers himself as our leader and expects me to back him up. For my part I have recommended him to go to Rome. I imagine he will have the city rabble behind him, and the honest men too if he convinces them of his sincerity.*

Octavian followed Cicero's recommendation and entered Rome on the tenth day of November. His soldiers occupied the Forum. I watched as they deployed across the centre of the city, securing the temples and the public buildings. They remained in position throughout that night and the whole of the following day while Octavian set up his headquarters in Balbus's house and tried to arrange a meeting of the Senate. But the senior magistrates were all gone: Antony was trying to win over the Macedonian legions; Dolabella had left for Syria; half the praetors, including Brutus and Cassius, had fled Italy – the city was leaderless. I could see why Octavian was pleading with Cicero to join him on his adventure, writing to him once and sometimes twice a day: Cicero alone might have had the moral authority to rally the Senate. But he had no intention of putting himself under the command of a mere boy leading an armed insurrection with precarious chances of success; prudently he stayed away.

In my role as Cicero's eyes and ears in Rome, I went down to the Forum on the twelfth to hear Octavian speak. By this time he had abandoned his attempts to summon the Senate and instead had persuaded a sympathetic tribune, Ti. Cannutius, to convene a public assembly. He stood on the rostra under a grey sky waiting to be called – slender as a reed, blond, pale, nervous; it was, as I wrote to Cicero, 'a scene both ridiculous and yet oddly compelling, like an episode from a legend'. He was not a bad speaker, either, once he got started, and Cicero was delighted by his denunciation of Antony ('this forger of decrees, this subverter of laws, this thief of rightful inheritances, this traitor who is even now seeking to make war upon the entire state …'). But he was less pleased when I reported how Octavian had pointed to the statue of Caesar that had been set up on the rostra and praised him as 'the greatest Roman of all time, whose murder I shall avenge and whose hopes in me I swear to you by all the gods I shall fulfil'. With that he came down from the platform to loud applause and soon afterwards left the city, taking his soldiers with him, alarmed at reports that Antony was approaching with a much larger force.

Events now moved with great rapidity. Antony halted his army – which included Caesar's famous Fifth Legion, 'the Larks' – a mere twelve miles from Rome at Tibur and entered the city with a bodyguard of a thousand men. He summoned the Senate for the twenty-fourth and let it be known that he expected them to declare Octavian a public enemy. Failure to attend would be regarded as condoning Octavian's treason and punishable by death. Antony's army was ready to move into the city if his will was thwarted. Rome was gripped by the certainty of a massacre.

The twenty-fourth arrived, the Senate met – but Antony himself did not appear. One of the Macedonian legions that had booed him, the Martian, encamped sixty miles away at Alba Fucens, had suddenly declared itself for Octavian, in return for a bounty five times the size of that Antony had offered them. He raced off to try to win them back, but they mocked him openly for his stinginess. He returned to Rome, summoning the Senate for the twenty-eighth, this time to meet in an emergency session at night. Never before in living memory had the Senate gathered in darkness: it was contrary to all custom and the sacred laws. When I went down to the Forum intending to make my report for Cicero, I found it full of legionaries drawn up in the torchlight. The sight was so sinister I lost my nerve and did not dare to enter the temple, but instead stood around with the crowd outside. I saw Antony arrive, hotfoot from Alba Fucens, accompanied by his brother Lucius, an even wilder-looking character than him, who had fought as a gladiator in Asia and slit a friend's throat. And I was still there an hour later to see them both leave in a hurry. Never will I forget the rolling-eyed look of panic on Antony's face as he rushed down the temple steps. He had just been told that another legion, the Fourth, had followed the example of the Martian and had also declared for Octavian. Now he was the one who risked being outnumbered. Antony fled the city that same night and went to Tibur to rally his army and raise fresh recruits.

While all this was going on, Cicero finished his so-called Second Philippic and sent it to me with instructions to borrow twenty scribes from Atticus and ensure it was copied and circulated as soon as possible. It took the form of a long speech – had it been delivered, it would have lasted a good two hours – and therefore rather than set each man to work making a single copy, I divided the roll into twenty parts and shared the pieces between them. In this way, once their completed sections were glued together, we were able to turn out four or five copies a day. These we sent to friends and allies with a request that they either make copies themselves or at least hold meetings at which the speech could be read aloud.

News of it soon spread. On the day after Antony withdrew from the city, it was posted in the Forum. Everyone wanted to read it, not least because it was filled with the most venomous gossip, for example that Antony had been a homosexual prostitute in his youth and was always falling down drunk and had kept a nude actress as his mistress. But I ascribe its phenomenal popularity more to the fact that it was also full of detailed information no one had dared disclose before – that Antony had stolen seven hundred million sesterces from the Temple of Ops and had used part of it to pay off personal debts of forty million; that he and Fulvia had forged Caesar's decrees to extort ten million sesterces from the king of Galatia; that the pair had seized jewels, furniture, villas, farms and cash and had divided it all up among themselves and their entourage of actors, gladiators, soothsayers and quacks.

On the ninth day of December, Cicero finally returned to Rome. I had not been expecting him. I heard the watchdog barking and went out into the passage to discover the master of the house standing there with Atticus. He had been away for nearly two months and looked to be in exceptionally good health and spirits. Without even taking off his cloak and hat he handed me a letter he had received the previous day from Octavian:

I have read your new Philippic and think it quite magnificent – worthy of Demosthenes himself. I only wish I could see the face of our latter-day Philip when he reads it. I learn he has decided against attacking me here, no doubt nervous that his men would refuse to take the field against Caesar's son, and instead is marching his army rapidly to Nearer Gaul with the intention of wresting that province from your friend Decimus.

My dear Cicero, you must agree my position is stronger than we ever could have dreamed of when we met at your house in Puteoli. I am here now in Etruria seeking fresh recruits. They are flocking to me. And yet as ever I am in sore need of your wise advice. Can we not contrive a meeting? There is no man in all the world I would sooner speak with.

'Well,' said Cicero with a grin, 'what do you think?'

I replied, 'It's very gratifying.'

'Gratifying? Come now – use your imagination! It's more than that! I've been thinking about it ever since I got it.'

After a slave had helped him out of his outdoor clothes, he beckoned me and Atticus to follow him into his study and asked me to close the door.

'Here is the situation as I see it. Were it not for Octavian, Antony would have taken Rome and our cause would be finished by now. But fear of Octavian forced the wolf to drop his prey at the last moment and now he's slinking north to devour Nearer Gaul instead. If he defeats Decimus this winter and takes the province – which he probably will – he will have the financial base and the forces to return to Rome in the spring and finish us off. All that stands between us and him is Octavian.'

Atticus said sceptically, 'You really think Octavian has raised an army in order to defend what's left of the republic?'

'No, but equally is it in his interests to allow Antony to take control of Rome? Of course not. Antony at this juncture is his real enemy – the one who has stolen his inheritance and denies his claims. If I can persuade Octavian to see that, we may yet save ourselves from disaster.'

'Possibly – but only to deliver the republic from the clutches of one tyrant into those of another; and a tyrant who calls himself Caesar at that.'

'Oh, I don't know if the lad is a tyrant – I think I may be able to use my influence to keep him on the side of virtue, at least until Antony is disposed of.'

'His letter certainly seems to suggest he would listen to you,' I said.

'Exactly. Believe me, Atticus, I could show you thirty such letters if I could be bothered to find them, going all the way back to April. Why is he so eager for my counsel? The truth is the boy lacks a father figure – his natural father is dead; his stepfather is a goose; and his adopted father has left him the greatest legacy in history but no guidance on how to gain hold of it. Somehow I seem to have stepped into the paternal role, which is a blessing – not so much for me as for the republic.'

Atticus said, 'So what are you going to do?'

'I shall go and see him.'

'In Etruria, in the middle of winter, at your age? It's a hundred miles away. You must be mad.'

I said, 'But you can hardly expect Octavian to come to Rome.'

Cicero waved away these objections. 'Then we'll meet halfway. That villa you bought the other year, Atticus, on Lake Volsinii – that would suit the purpose admirably. Is it occupied?'

'No, but I can't vouch for its comfort.'

'That doesn't matter. Tiro, draft a letter from me to Octavian proposing a meeting in Volsinii as soon as he can manage it.'

Atticus said, 'But what about the Senate? What about the consuls-designate? You have no power to negotiate on behalf of the republic with anyone, let alone with a man at the head of a rebel army.'

'Nobody is wielding power in the republic any more. That's the point. It's lying in the dust waiting for whoever dares to pick it up. Why shouldn't I be the one to seize it?'

Atticus had no answer to that and Cicero's invitation went off to Octavian within the hour. After three days of anxious waiting Cicero received his reply: *Nothing would give me greater pleasure than to see you again. I shall meet you in Volsinii on the sixteenth as you propose unless I hear that that has become inconvenient. I suggest we keep our rendezvous secret.*

To ensure that no one would guess what he was up to, Cicero insisted we left in the darkness long before dawn on the morning of the fourteenth of December. I had to bribe the sentries to open the Fontinalian Gate especially for us.

We knew we would be venturing into lawless country, full of roaming bands of armed men, and so we travelled in a closed carriage escorted by a large retinue of guards and attendants. Once across the Mulvian Bridge we turned left along the bank of the Tiber and joined the Via Cassia, a road I had never travelled before. By noon we were climbing into hilly country. Atticus had promised me spectacular views. But the dismal weather Italy had endured ever since Caesar's assassination continued to curse us, and the distant peaks of the pine-covered mountains were draped in mist. For the entire two days we were on the road it barely seemed to get light.

Cicero's earlier ebullience had faded. He was uncharacteristically quiet, conscious no doubt that the future of the republic might depend on the coming meeting. On the afternoon of the second day, as we reached the edge of the great lake and our destination came into view, he began to complain of feeling cold. He shivered and blew on his hands, but when I tried to cover his knees with a blanket, he threw it off like an irritable child and said that although he might be ancient, he was not an invalid.

Atticus had bought his property as an investment and had only visited it once; still, he never forgot a thing when it came to money and he quickly remembered where to find it. Large and dilapidated – parts of it dated back to Etruscan times – the villa stood just outside the city walls of Volsinii, right on the edge of the water. The iron gates were open. Drifts of dead leaves had rotted in the damp courtyard; black lichen and moss covered the terracotta roofs. Only a thin curl of smoke rising from the chimney gave any sign it was inhabited. We assumed from the deserted grounds that Octavian had not yet arrived. But as we descended from the carriage, the steward hurried forward and said that a young man was waiting inside.

He was sitting in the tablinum with his friend Agrippa and he rose as we entered. I looked to see if the spectacular change in his fortunes was reflected at all in his manner or person, but he seemed exactly as before: quiet, modest, watchful, with the same unstylish haircut and youthful acne. He had come without any escort, he said, apart from two chariot drivers, who had taken their teams to be fed and watered in the town. ('No one knows what I look like, so I prefer not to draw attention to myself; it is better to hide in plain sight, don't you think?') He clasped hands very warmly with Cicero. After the introductions were over, Cicero said, 'I thought Tiro here could make a note of anything we agree on and then we could each have a copy.'

Octavian said, 'So you're empowered to negotiate?'

'No, but it would be useful to have something to show to the leaders of the Senate.'

'Personally, if you don't mind, I would prefer it if nothing were written down. That way we can talk more freely.'

There is therefore no verbatim record of their conference, although I wrote up an account immediately afterwards for Cicero's personal use. First Octavian gave a summary of the military situation as he understood it. He had, or would have shortly, four legions at his disposal: the veterans from Campania, the levies he was raising in Etruria, the Martian and the Fourth. Antony had three legions, including the Larks, but also another entirely inexperienced, and was closing in on Decimus, whom he understood from his agents had retreated to the city of Mutina, where he was slaughtering and salting cattle and preparing for a long siege. Cicero said that the Senate had eleven legions in Further Gaul: seven under Lepidus and four under Plancus.

Octavian said, 'Yes, but they are the wrong side of the Alps and are needed to hold down Gaul. Besides, we both know the commanders are not necessarily reliable, especially Lepidus.'

'I shan't argue with you,' said Cicero. 'The position boils down to this: you have the soldiers but no legitimacy; we have the legitimacy but no soldiers. What we do both have, however, is a common enemy – Antony. And it seems to me that somewhere in that mixture must be the basis for an agreement.'

Agrippa said, 'An agreement you've just told us you have no authority to make.'

'Young man, take it from me, if you want to make a deal with the Senate, I am your best hope. And let me tell you something else – it will be no easy task to convince them, even for me. There'll be plenty who'll say, "We didn't get rid of one Caesar to ally ourselves with another."'

'Yes,' retorted Agrippa, 'and plenty on our side who'll say, "Why should we fight to protect the men who murdered Caesar? This is just a trick to buy us off until they're strong enough to destroy us."'

Cicero slammed his hands on the armrests of his chair. 'If that is how you feel, then this has been a wasted journey.'

He made as if to rise, but Octavian leaned across and pressed down on his shoulder. 'Not so fast, my dear friend. No need to take offence. I agree with your analysis. My sole objective is to defeat Antony, and I would much prefer to do that with the legal authority of the Senate.'

Cicero said, 'Let us be clear: you would prefer it even if – and this is what it *would* mean – you have to go to the rescue of Decimus, the very man who lured your adopted father to his death?'

Octavian fixed him with his cold grey eyes. 'I have no problem with that.'

From then on, there was no doubt in my mind that Cicero and Octavian would make a deal. Even Agrippa seemed to relax a little. It was agreed that Cicero would propose in the Senate that Octavian, despite his age, be given imperium and the legal authority to wage war against Antony. In return, Octavian would place himself under the command of the consuls. What might happen in the longer term, after Antony was destroyed, was left vague. Nothing was written down.

Cicero said, 'You will be able to tell if I have fulfilled my side of my bargain by reading my speeches – which I shall send you – and in the resolutions passed by the Senate. And I shall know from the movements of your legions if you are fulfilling yours.'

Octavian said, 'You need have no doubts on that score.' Atticus went off to find the steward and came back with a jug of Tuscan wine and five silver cups which he filled and handed round. Cicero felt moved to make a speech. 'On this day youth and experience, arms and the toga, have come together in solemn compact to rescue the commonwealth. Let us go forth from this place, each man to his station, resolved to do his duty to the republic.'

'To the republic,' said Octavian, and raised his cup.

'To the republic!' we all echoed, and drank.

Octavian and Agrippa politely refused to stay the night: they explained that they needed to reach their nearby camp before darkness as the next day was Saturnalia and Octavian was expected to distribute gifts to his men. After much mutual backslapping and protestations of undying affection, Cicero and Octavian said goodbye to one another. The young man's parting phrase I still remember: 'Your speeches and my swords will make an unbeatable alliance.' When they had gone, Cicero went out on to the terrace and walked around in the rain to calm his nerves while I out of habit cleared away the wine cups. Octavian, I noticed, had not touched a drop.

LIV

Cicero had not expected to have to address the Senate until the first day of January, when Hirtius and Pansa were due to take over as consuls. But on our return we discovered the tribunes had summoned an emergency meeting to be held in two days' time to discuss the looming war between Antony and Decimus. Cicero decided that the sooner he made good on his promise to Octavian the better. Accordingly he went down to the Temple of Concordia early in the morning to show his intention of speaking. As usual I went with him and stood at the door to record his remarks.

Once word spread that Cicero was in his place, people began pouring into the Forum. Senators who might not otherwise have attended also decided they had better come to hear what he had to say. Within an hour the benches were packed. Among those who changed his plans was the consul-designate, Hirtius. He rose from his sickbed for the first time in weeks, and his appearance when he walked into the temple drew gasps. The plump young gourmet who had helped write Caesar's *Commentaries* and who used to entertain Cicero to dinners of swan and peacock had shrivelled to barely more than a skeleton. I believe he was suffering from what Hippocrates, the father of Greek medicine, calls a *carcino*; he had a scar on his neck where a growth had been recently removed.

The tribune who presided over the session was Appuleius, a friend of Cicero. He began by reading out an edict issued by Decimus denying Antony permission to enter Nearer Gaul, reiterating his determination to keep the province loyal to the Senate and confirming that he had moved his forces into Mutina. That was the town where I had delivered Cicero's letter to Caesar all those years before, and I recalled its stout walls and heavy gates: much would depend on whether it could hold out against a long siege by Antony's superior forces. When he had finished reading,

Appuleius said, 'Within days – perhaps even already – the republic will be gripped once more by civil war. The question is: what are we to do? I call on Cicero to give us his opinion.'

Hundreds of men leaned forwards in anticipation as Cicero rose.

'This meeting, honourable gentlemen, comes not a moment too soon in my opinion. An iniquitous war against our hearths and altars, our lives and fortunes, is no longer just being prepared but is actually being waged by a profligate and wanton man. It is no good our waiting for the first day of January before we act. Antony does not wait. He's already attacking the eminent and remarkable Decimus. And from Nearer Gaul he threatens to descend on us in Rome. Indeed, he would have done so before now had it not been for a young man – or almost rather a boy, but one of incredible and near-god-like intelligence and courage – who raised an army and saved the state.'

He paused to allow his words to register. Senators turned to their neighbours to check they had heard correctly. The temple became a hubbub of surprise mingled with some notes of indignation and gasps of excitement. Did he just say the boy had saved the state? It was a while before Cicero could continue.

'Yes, this is my belief, gentlemen, this is my judgement: had not a single youth stood up to that madman, this commonwealth would have utterly perished. On him today – and we are here today, free to express our views, only because of him – on him we must confer the authority to defend the republic, not as something merely undertaken by him, but as a charge *entrusted to him by us*.'

There were a few cries of 'No!' and 'He's bought you!' from Antony's supporters but these were drowned by applause from the rest of the Senate. Cicero pointed to the door. 'Do you not see the packed Forum and how the Roman people are encouraged to hope for the recovery of their liberty? That now, after a long interval, when they see us assembled here in such numbers, they hope we have met together as free men?'

Thus opened what became known as the Third Philippic. It turned Roman politics on its axis. It lavished praise on Octavian, or Caesar, as Cicero now called him for the first time. ('Who is more chaste than this young man? Who more modest? What brighter example have we among youth of old-world purity?') It pointed the way to a strategy that might yet lead to the salvation of the republic. ('The immortal gods have given us these safeguards – for the city, Caesar; Decimus for Gaul.') But perhaps even more important, for tired and careworn hearts, after months and years of supine acquiescence, it fired the Senate with fighting spirit.

'Today for the first time after a long interval we set our feet in possession of liberty. It is to glory and to liberty we were born. And if the final episode in the long history of our republic has arrived, then let us at the least behave like champion gladiators: they meet death honourably; let us see to it that we too – who stand foremost of all nations on the earth – fall with dignity rather than serve with ignominy.'

Such was the effect that when Cicero sat down a large part of the Senate immediately stood and rushed to crowd around him with their congratulations. It was clear that for the time being he had carried all before him. At Cicero's behest a motion was proposed thanking Decimus for his defence of Nearer Gaul, praising Octavian for his 'help, courage and judgement', and promising him future honours as soon as the consuls-elect convened the Senate in the new year. It passed overwhelmingly. Then, most unusually, the tribunes invited Cicero rather than a serving magistrate to go out into the Forum and report to the people on what the Senate had decided.

He had told us before he went to meet Octavian that power in Rome was lying in the dust merely waiting for someone to pick it up. That was what he did that day. He climbed on to the rostra, watched by the Senate, and turned to face all those thousands of citizens. 'Your incredible numbers, Romans,' he bellowed at them, 'and the size – the greatest I can ever remember – of this assembly, inspire me to defend the republic and give me the hope of re-establishing it!

'I can tell you that Gaius Caesar, who has protected and is protecting the state and your liberty, has just been thanked by the Senate!' A great swell of applause arose from the crowd. 'I commend,' shouted Cicero, struggling to make his voice heard, 'I commend you, Romans, for greeting with the warmest applause the name of a most noble young man. Divine and immortal honours are due for his divine and immortal services!

'You are fighting, Romans, against an enemy with whom no peace terms are possible. Antony is not just a guilty and villainous man. He is a monstrous and savage animal. The issue is not on what terms we shall live, but whether we shall live at all, or perish in torture and ignominy!

'As for me, I shall spare no efforts on your behalf. We have today, for the first time after a long interval, with my counsel and at my instance, been fired by the hope of liberty!'

With that he took a pace backward to signal that his speech was over, the crowd roared and stamped their feet in approval, and the last and most glorious phase of Cicero's public career began.

From my shorthand notes I made a transcript of both speeches, and once again a team of scribes worked in relays to make copies. These were variously posted up in the Forum and dispatched to Brutus, Cassius, Decimus and the other prominent men in the republican cause.

Naturally they were also sent to Octavian, who read them at once and replied within a week:

From G. Caesar to his friend and mentor M. Cicero.

Greetings!

I enjoyed your latest Philippics very much. 'Chaste... modest ... purity ... godlike intelligence' – my ears are burning! Seriously, don't lay it on too thick, mon vieux, as I can only be a disappointment! I would love one day to talk to you about the finer points of oratory – I know how much I could learn from you, on this as on other matters. And so – onwards! As soon as I hear word from you that my army has been made legal and I have the necessary authority to wage war, I shall move my legions north to attack Antony.

All men now waited anxiously for the next meeting of the Senate, due to be held on the first day of January. Cicero fretted that they were wasting precious time: 'It is the most important rule in politics always to keep things moving.' He went to see Hirtius and Pansa and urged them to bring the session forward; they refused, saying they did not have the legal authority. Still, he believed he had their confidence and that the three of them would present a united front. But when the new year dawned, and the sacrifices had been conducted on the Capitol in accordance with tradition, and the Senate retired to the Temple of Jupiter to debate the state of the nation, he received a nasty shock. Both Pansa, who presided and made the opening speech, and Hirtius, who spoke next, expressed the hope that, grave though the situation was, it might still be possible to find a peaceful solution with Antony. This was not at all what Cicero wanted to hear.

As the senior ex-consul, he had expected to be called next and rose accordingly. But instead Pansa ignored him in favour of his father-in-law, Quintus Calenus, an old supporter of Clodius and a crony of Antony, who had never been elected consul but had only been appointed to the office by the Dictator. He was a stocky, burly figure, built like a blacksmith, and no great speaker, but he was blunt and heard with respect.

'This crisis,' he said, 'has been made out by the learned and distinguished Cicero to be a war between the republic on the one side and Mark Antony on the other. That's not correct, gentlemen. It's a war between three different parties: Antony, who was made governor of Nearer Gaul by a vote of this house and by the people; Decimus, who refuses to surrender his command; and a boy who has raised a private army and is out for all he can get. Of the three, I know and personally favour Antony. Perhaps as a compromise we should offer him the governorship of Further Gaul instead? But if that's too much for the rest of you, I propose we should at the very least stay neutral.'

When he sat, Cicero stood again. But again Pansa ignored him and called Lucius Piso, Caesar's ex-father-in-law, whom Cicero had also naturally counted as an ally. Instead Piso made a long speech, the gist of it being that he had always regarded Antony as a danger to the state, and still did, but having lived through the last civil war, he had no desire to live through another and believed the Senate should make one last attempt at peace by sending a delegation to Antony to offer him terms. 'I propose that he should submit himself to the will of the Senate and people, abandon his siege of Mutina and withdraw his army to the Italian side of the Rubicon but no closer to Rome than two hundred miles. If he does that, then even at this late stage war may be averted. But if he does not, and war does come, at least the world will have no doubt who bears the blame.'

When Piso had finished, Cicero did not even bother to stand, but sat with his chin sunk on his chest, glowering at the floor. The next speaker was his other supposed ally, P. Servilius Vatia Isauricus, who delivered himself of a great many platitudes and spoke bitterly of Antony, but even more bitterly of Octavian. He was a relative by marriage of Brutus and Cassius and raised a question that was in many minds: 'Ever since he arrived in Italy Octavian has made the most violent speeches, swearing to avenge his so-called father by bringing his killers to justice. In so doing he threatens the safety of some of the most illustrious men in the state. Have they been consulted about the honours now being contemplated for Caesar's adopted son? What guarantees do we have that if we proceed to make this ambitious and immature would-be warlord the "sword and shield of the Senate" – as the noble Cicero suggests – he won't turn round and use his sword against *us*?'

These five speeches, coming after the ceremonial opening, took up all of the short January day, and Cicero returned home with his prepared oration undelivered. 'Peace!' He spat out the word. Always in the past he had been an advocate of peace; no longer. He jutted his chin in belligerence as he complained bitterly of the consuls: 'What a pair of spineless mediocrities. All those hours I spent teaching them how to speak properly! And to what end? I would have been better employed teaching them how to think straight.' As for Calenus, Piso and Isauricus, they were 'addle-headed appeasers', 'faint hearts', 'political monstrosities' – after a time I stopped making a note of his insults. He retired to his study to rewrite his speech and the next morning sallied forth for the second day of the debate like a warship in full battle array.

From the moment the session began he was on his feet, and stayed there, signalling that he expected to be called next and would not take no for an answer. Behind him his supporters chanted his name, and eventually Pansa had no option but to indicate by his gestures that Cicero had the floor.

'Nothing, gentlemen,' Cicero began, 'has ever seemed longer to me in coming than the beginning of this new year and with it this meeting of the Senate. *We* have waited – but those who wage war against the state have not. Does Mark Antony desire peace? Then let him lay down his arms. Let him ask for peace. Let him appeal to our mercy. But to send envoys to a man on whom thirteen days ago you passed the heaviest and severest judgement is beyond a joke and is – if I must give my real opinion – madness!'

One by one, like the impact of missiles thrown by some mighty ballista, Cicero demolished the arguments of his opponents. Antony did not have any legal title to be governor of Nearer Gaul: his law was pushed through an invalid assembly in a thunderstorm. He was a forger. He was a thief.

He was a traitor. To give him the province of Further Gaul would be to give him access to 'the sinews of war: unlimited money' – the idea was absurd. 'And it is to this man, great heavens, that we are pleased to send envoys? He will never obey anybody's envoys! I know the fellow's madness and arrogance. But time meanwhile will be wasted. The preparations for war will cool – they have already been dragged out by slowness and delay. If we had acted sooner we should not now be having a war at all. Every evil is easily crushed at birth; allow it to become established and it always gathers strength.

'So I propose, gentlemen, that we should send no envoys. I say instead that a state of emergency should be declared, that the courts should be shut, that military dress should be worn, that recruitment should be started, that exemptions from military service should be suspended throughout Rome and the whole of Italy, and that Antony be declared a public enemy …'

A spontaneous roar of applause and stamping feet drowned out the remainder of his sentence but he carried on speaking through it:

'… if we do all that, he will feel that he has begun a war against the state. He will experience the energy and strength of a Senate with one mind. He says this is a war of parties. What parties? This war has not been stirred up by any parties but by him alone!

'And now I come to Gaius Caesar, upon whom my friend Isauricus heaped such scorn and suspicion. Yet if he had not lived, who of us could have been alive now? What god presented to the Roman people this heaven-sent boy? By his protection the tyranny of Antony was thwarted. Let us therefore give Caesar the necessary command, without which no military affairs can be administered, no army held together, no war waged. Let him be pro-praetor with the maximum power of a regular appointment.

'On him our hope of liberty rests. I know this young man. Nothing is dearer to him than the republic, nothing more important than your authority, nothing more desirable than the opinion of good men, nothing sweeter than genuine glory. I shall even venture to give you my word, gentlemen – to you and to the Roman people: I promise, I undertake, I solemnly pledge that Gaius Caesar will always be such a citizen as he is today, the citizen that we all most earnestly wish and pray that he should be.'

That speech, and in particular that guarantee, changed everything. I believe it can truly be asserted – and it is a rare boast for any oration

– that if Cicero had not delivered his Fifth Philippic, then history would have been different, for opinion in the Senate was almost evenly divided, and until he spoke, the debate was running Antony's way. Now his words stemmed the tide and the votes started to flow back in favour of war. Indeed, Cicero might have won on every point if a tribune named Salvius had not interposed his veto, prolonging the debate into a fourth day, and giving Antony's wife Fulvia the chance to appear at the door of the temple to plead for moderation. She was accompanied by her infant son – the one who had been sent up to the Capitol as a hostage – and by Antony's elderly mother, Julia, who was a cousin of Julius Caesar and greatly admired for her noble bearing. They were all dressed in black and made a most affecting spectacle, three generations walking down the aisle of the Senate with their hands clasped in supplication. Every senator was aware that if Antony was to be named a public enemy, all his property would be seized and they would be thrown out on to the streets.

'Spare us this humiliation,' cried out Fulvia, 'we beseech you!'

The vote to declare Antony an enemy of the state was duly lost, while the motion to send a delegation of envoys to make him a final peace offer was carried. The rest, however, was all for Cicero: Octavian's army was recognised as legitimate and incorporated with Decimus's under the standard of the Senate; Octavian was made a senator, despite his youth, and also awarded a pro-praetorship with power of imperium; as a nod to the future, the age requirement for the consulship was lowered by ten years (although it would still be another thirteen before Octavian was eligible to stand); the loyalty of Plancus and Lepidus was bought, the one being confirmed as consul for the following year, the other being honoured by a gilded equestrian statue on the rostra; and the raising of new armies and the imposition of a state of military preparedness in Rome and all across Italy was ordered to begin immediately.

Once again the tribunes asked Cicero, rather than the consuls, to convey the Senate's decisions to the thousands gathered in the Forum. When he told them that peace envoys were to be sent to Antony, a collective groan went up. Cicero made a soothing gesture with his hands. 'I gather, Romans, that this course is also repudiated by you, as it was by me, and with good reason. But I urge you to be patient. What I did earlier in the Senate I will do before you now. I predict that Mark Antony will ignore the envoys, devastate the land, besiege Mutina and raise more troops. And I am not afraid that when he hears what I have said, he will change his plans and obey the Senate in order to refute me: he is too far gone for that. We shall lose some precious time, but never fear: we shall have victory in the end. Other nations can endure slavery, but the most prized possession of the Roman people is liberty.'

The peace delegation left the next day from the Forum. Cicero went with an ill grace to see them off. The chosen envoys were three ex-consuls: Lucius Piso, who had come up with the idea in the first place and so could hardly refuse to take part; Marcus Philippus, Octavian's stepfather, whose participation Cicero called 'disgusting and scandalous'; and Cicero's old friend Servius Sulpicius, who was in such poor health that Cicero begged him to reconsider: 'It's two hundred and fifty miles in midwinter, through snow and wolves and bandits, and with only the amenities of an army camp at the end of it. For pity's sake, my dear Servius, use your illness as an excuse and let them find someone else.'

'You forget I was at Pompey's side at Pharsalus. I stood and watched the slaughter of the best men in the state. My last service to the republic will be to try to stop that happening again.'

'Your instincts are as noble as ever, but your hold on reality is poor. Antony will laugh in your face. All that your suffering will accomplish is to help prolong the war.'

Servius looked at him sadly. 'What happened to my old friend who hated soldiering and loved his books? I rather miss him. I certainly preferred him to this rabble-rouser who stirs up the crowd for blood.'

With that he climbed stiffly into his litter and was borne away with the others to begin the long journey.

Preparations for war now slowed to a half-hearted pace, as Cicero had warned they would, while Romans awaited the outcome of the peace mission. Although levies took place across Italy to recruit four new legions, there was no great sense of urgency now that the immediate threat seemed to have been lifted. In the meantime, the only legions the Senate could draw on were the two encamped near Rome that had declared for Octavian – the Martian and the Fourth – and after receiving permission from Octavian, these agreed to march north to relieve Decimus under the command of one of the consuls. Lots for the office had to be drawn in accordance with the law, and by a cruel jest of the gods it went to the sick man, Hirtius. Watching this ghostly figure in his red cloak painfully ascend the steps of the Capitol, perform the traditional sacrifice of a white bull to Jupiter and then ride off to war filled Cicero with foreboding.

It was to be almost a month before the city's herald announced that the returning peace envoys were approaching the city. Pansa summoned the Senate to hear their report that same day. Only two of them came into the temple – Piso and Philippus. Piso stood and in a grave voice announced that the gallant Servius had no sooner reached Antony's headquarters than he had died of exhaustion. Because of the distance involved, and the slowness of winter travel, it had been necessary to cremate him on the spot rather than bring the body home. 'I have to tell you, gentlemen, that we found that Antony has surrounded Mutina with a very powerful system of siege works, and throughout our time in his camp he continued to pound the town with missiles. He refused to allow us safe passage through his lines to talk to Decimus. As to the terms you had empowered us to offer him, he rejected them in favour of terms of his own.' Piso produced a letter and began to read. 'He will give up his claim to the governorship of Nearer Gaul but only if he is compensated by the award instead of Further Gaul for five years together with the command of Decimus's army, raising his total strength to six legions. He demands that all the decrees he has issued in Caesar's name should be declared legal; that there should be no further investigation into the disappearance of the state's treasury from the Temple of Ops; that his followers should be given an amnesty; and finally that his soldiers should be paid what they are owed and also awarded land.'

Piso rolled up the document and tucked it into his sleeve. 'We have done our best, gentlemen. I am disappointed, I will not hide it. I fear this house must recognise that a state of war exists between the republic and Mark Antony.'

Cicero got to his feet, but yet again Pansa called his father-in-law, Calenus, to speak first. He said: 'I deplore the use of the word "war". On the contrary, I believe we have here, gentlemen, the basis for an honourable peace. It was my suggestion, first made in this Senate, that Antony should be offered Further Gaul, and I am glad that he has accepted it. Our main points are all met. Decimus remains as governor. The people of Mutina are spared any further misery. Roman does not take up arms against Roman. I can see by the way he shakes his head that Cicero does not like what I am saying. He is an angry man. But more than that, I venture to say that he is an angry *old* man. Let me remind him that it will not be men of our age who die in this new war. It will be his son, and my son, and yours, gentlemen – and yours, and yours, and yours. I say let us have a truce with Antony and reconcile our differences peacefully as our gallant colleagues Piso, Philippus and the lamented Servius have shown us how to do.'

Calenus's speech was warmly received. It was clear that Antony still had his supporters in the Senate, including his legate, the diminutive Cotyla, or 'Half-Pint', whom he had sent south to report on the mood in Rome. As Pansa called speaker after speaker – including Antony's uncle, Lucius Caesar, who said he felt duty-bound to defend his nephew – Cotyla ostentatiously made notes of their remarks, presumably so that he could report them back to his master. It had an oddly unnerving effect, and at the end of the day, a majority of the house, including Pansa, voted to remove the word 'war' from the motion and declare instead that the country was in a state of 'tumult'.

Pansa did not call Cicero until the following morning. But once again this worked to Cicero's advantage. Not only did he rise in an atmosphere of intense expectation; he was able to attack the arguments of the previous speakers. He started with Lucius Caesar: 'He excuses his vote because of his family connections. He is an uncle. Fair enough. But are the rest of you uncles too?'

And once he had his audience laughing – once he had softened the ground, so to speak – he proceeded to pulverise them with a cataract of invective and derision. 'Decimus is being attacked – there is no war. Mutina is being besieged – not even this is war. Gaul is being laid waste – what could be more peaceful? Gentlemen, this is a war such as has never been seen before! We are defending the temples of the immortal gods, our walls, our homes, and the birthrights of the Roman people, the altars, hearths and tombs of our ancestors; we are defending our laws, law courts, liberty, wives, children, fatherland. On the other side, Mark Antony fights to wreck all this and plunder the state.

'At this point my brave and energetic friend Calenus reminds me of the advantages of peace. But I ask you, Calenus: what do you mean? Do you call slavery peace? Heavy fighting is in progress. We have sent three leading members of the Senate to intervene. These Antony has repudiated with contempt. Yet you remain his most constant defender!

'With what dishonour did yesterday dawn upon us! "Oh, but what if he were to make a truce?" A truce? In the presence, before the very eyes of the envoys he pounded Mutina with his engines. He showed them his works and his siege train. Not for a moment, although the envoys were there, did the siege find a breathing space. Envoys to this man? Peace with this man?

'I will say it with grief rather than with insult: we are deserted – deserted, gentlemen – by our leaders. What concessions have we not made to Cotyla, the envoy of Mark Antony? Though by rights the gates of this city should have been closed to him, yet this temple was open. He came into the Senate. He entered in his notebooks your votes and everything you said. Even those who had filled the highest offices were currying favour with him to the disgrace of their dignity. Ye immortal gods! Where is the ancient spirit of our ancestors? Let Cotyla return to his general but on condition that he never returns to Rome.'

The Senate sat stunned. They had not been shamed in such a fashion since Cato's day. At the end, Cicero laid a fresh motion: that those fighting with Antony would be given until the Ides of March to lay down their arms; after that, any who continued in his army, or who went to join him, would be regarded as traitors. The proposal passed overwhelmingly. There was to be no truce, no peace, no deal; Cicero had his war.

A day or two after the first anniversary of Caesar's assassination – an occasion that passed without notice apart from the laying of flowers on his tomb – Pansa followed his colleague Hirtius into battle. The consul rode off from the Field of Mars at the head of an army of four legions: almost twenty thousand men scoured from every corner of Italy. Cicero watched with the rest of the Senate as they paraded past. As a military force it was less impressive than it sounded. Most were the rawest of recruits – farmers, ostlers, bakers and laundrymen who could barely even march in time. Their real power was symbolic. The republic was in arms against the usurper Antony.

With both consuls gone, the most senior magistrate left behind in the city was the urban praetor, Marcus Cornutus – a soldier picked by Caesar for his loyalty and discretion. He now found himself required to preside over the Senate even though he had minimal experience of politics. He soon placed himself entirely in the hands of Cicero, who thus, at the age of sixty-three, became the effective ruler of Rome for the first time since his consulship twenty years before. It was to Cicero that all the imperial governors addressed their reports. It was he who decided when the Senate should meet. It was he who made the main appointments. His was the house that was packed all day with petitioners.

He sent an amused account of his *redux* to Octavian:

> *I do not think I boast when I say that nothing can happen in this city these days without my approval. Indeed it is actually better than a consulship because no one knows where my power begins or ends; therefore rather than run the risk of offending me, everyone consults me on everything. Actually it is even better, come to think of it, than a dictatorship, because nobody holds me to blame when things go wrong! It is proof that one should never mistake the baubles of office for actual power – another piece of avuncular advice for your glittering future, my boy, from your devoted old friend and mentor.*

Octavian wrote back at the end of March to report that he was doing as he had promised: his army of nearly ten thousand men was striking camp just south of Bononia, beside the Via Aemilia, and moving off to join the armies of Hirtius and Pansa in relieving the siege of Mutina:

> *I am placing myself under the command of the consuls. We are expecting a great battle with Antony within the next two weeks. I promise that I shall endeavour to perform as valiantly in the field as you have in the Senate. What was it that the Spartan warriors said? 'I shall return either with my shield, or on it.'*

Around this time, word began to reach Cicero of events in the east. From Brutus in Macedonia he learned that Dolabella – heading for Syria at the head of a small force – had reached as far as Smyrna on the eastern shores of the Aegean, where he had encountered the governor of Asia, Trebonius. Trebonius had treated him civilly enough and even allowed him to proceed on his way. But that night Dolabella had secretly turned back, entered the city, seized Trebonius while he was asleep, and subjected him to two days and nights of intensive torture, using whips, the rack and hot irons, to force him to disclose the whereabouts of his treasury. After that, on Dolabella's orders, his neck was broken. His head was cut off and Dolabella's soldiers kicked it back and forth through the streets until it was completely crushed, while his body was mutilated and placed on public display. 'Thus dies the first of the assassins who murdered Caesar,' Dolabella was said to have declared. 'The first – but he will not be the last.'

Trebonius's remains were shipped to Rome and subjected to a post-mortem examination to confirm the manner of his death before being passed to his family for cremation. His grisly fate had a salutary effect on Cicero and the other leaders of the republic. They knew now what to expect if they fell into the hands of their enemies, especially when Antony issued an open letter to the consuls pledging his loyalty to Dolabella and expressing his delight at Trebonius's fate: *That a criminal has paid the penalty is a matter for rejoicing.* Cicero read the letter out loud in the Senate: it strengthened men's determination not to compromise. Dolabella was declared a public enemy. It was a particular shock to Cicero that his former son-in-law should have exhibited such cruelty. He lamented to me afterwards: 'To think that such a monster stayed under my roof and shared a bed with my poor dear daughter; to think that I actually *liked* the man … Who knows what animals lurk within the people who are close to us?'

The nervous strain under which he lived during those early days of April, while waiting for word from Mutina, was indescribable. First there would be good news. After months without contact, Cassius at last wrote to say that he was taking complete control of Syria: that all sides – Caesareans, republicans and the last remaining Pompeians – were flocking to him and that he had under his command a united army of no fewer than eleven legions. *I want you to know that you and your friends at the Senate are not without powerful support, so you can defend the state in the best interests of hope and courage.* Brutus also was meeting with success and had raised a further five legions, some twenty-five thousand men, in Macedonia.

Young Marcus was with him, recruiting and training cavalry: *Your son earns my approval by his energy, endurance, hard work and unselfish spirit, in fact by every kind of service.*

But then would come more ominous dispatches. Decimus was in desperate straits after more than four months trapped in Mutina. He could only communicate with the outside world by carrier pigeon, and the few birds that got through brought news of starvation, disease and low morale. Lepidus meanwhile was moving his legions closer to the scene of the impending battle with Antony, and he urged Cicero and the Senate to consider a fresh offer of peace talks. Cicero was so incensed by this weak and arrogant man's presumption that he dictated to me a letter that went off that same night:

> *Cicero to Lepidus.*
>
> *I rejoice at your desire to make peace among citizens but only if you can separate that peace from slavery. Otherwise you should understand that all men of sense have taken a resolution to prefer death to servitude. You will act more wisely in my judgement if you meddle no further in this affair, which is not acceptable either to the Senate or the people, or to any honest man.*

Cicero was under no illusions. The city and the Senate still harboured hundreds of Antony's supporters. If Decimus surrendered, or if the armies of Hirtius, Pansa and Octavian were defeated, he knew he would be the first to be seized and murdered. As a safety precaution he ordered home two of the three legions stationed in Africa to defend Rome. But they would not arrive until the middle of the summer.

It was on the twentieth day of April that the crisis finally broke. Early that morning, Cornutus, the urban praetor, hurried up the hill. With him was a messenger who had been dispatched by Pansa six days earlier. Cornutus's expression was grim. 'Tell Cicero,' he said to the messenger, 'what you've just told me.'

In a trembling voice the messenger said, 'Vibius Pansa regrets to report a catastrophic defeat. He and his army were surprised by the forces of Mark Antony at the settlement of Forum Gallorum. The lack of experience of our men was immediately evident. The line broke and there was a general slaughter. The consul managed to escape but is himself wounded.'

Cicero's face turned grey. 'And Hirtius and Caesar? Any news of them?'

Cornutus said, 'None. Pansa was on his way to their camp but was attacked before he could join them.'

Cicero groaned.

Cornutus said, 'Should I summon a meeting of the Senate?'

'Dear gods, no!' To the messenger Cicero said, 'Tell me the truth – does anyone else in Rome yet know about this?'

The messenger bowed his head. 'I went first to the consul's home. His father-in-law was there.'

'Calenus!'

Cornutus said grimly, 'He knows it all, unfortunately. He's in the Portico of Pompey at this very moment, on the exact spot where Caesar was struck down. He's telling anyone who'll listen that we're paying the price for an impious killing. He accuses you of planning to seize power as dictator. I believe he's gathering quite a crowd.'

I said to Cicero, 'We ought to get you out of Rome.'

Cicero shook his head emphatically. 'No, no. *They're* the traitors, not I. Damn them, I'll not run away. Find Appuleius,' he ordered the urban praetor briskly, as if he were his head steward. 'Tell him to call a public assembly and then to come and fetch me. I'll speak to the people. I need to steady their nerves. They must be reminded that there's always bad news in war. And you,' he said to the messenger, 'had better not breathe a word of this to another soul, do you understand, or I'll have you put in chains.'

I never admired Cicero more than I did that day, when he stared ruin in the face. He went into his study to compose an oration, while I, from the terrace, watched the Forum begin to fill with citizens. Panic has its own pattern. I had learned to recognise it over the years. Men run from one speaker to another. Groups form and dissolve. Sometimes the public space clears entirely. It is like a cloud of dust drifting and whirling before the onset of a storm.

Appuleius came toiling up the hill as requested and I took him in to see Cicero. He reported that the current rumour going round was that Cicero was to be presented with the fasces of a dictator. It was a trick, of course – a provocation that would be the pretext for his murder. The Antonians would then ape the tactics of Brutus and Cassius and seize the Capitol and try to hold it until Antony arrived in the city to relieve them.

Cicero asked Appuleius, 'Will you be able to guarantee my security if I come down to address the people?'

'I can't give an absolute guarantee, but we can try.'

'Send as big an escort as you can. Allow me one hour to get myself ready.'

The tribune went away, and to my astonishment Cicero then announced that he would have a bath and be shaved, and change into a fresh set of clothes. 'Make sure you write all this down,' he said to me. 'It will make a good end for your book.'

He went off with his body slaves, and by the time he came back an hour later, Appuleius had assembled a strong force out in the street, consisting mostly of gladiators along with his fellow tribunes and their attendants. Cicero braced his shoulders, the door was opened, and he was just about to cross the threshold when the lictors of the urban praetor came hurrying up the road, clearing a path for Cornutus. He was holding a dispatch. His face was wet with tears. Too out of breath and emotional to speak, he thrust the dispatch into Cicero's hands.

From Hirtius to Cornutus. Before Mutina.

I send you this in haste. Thanks be to the gods, we have this day retrieved an earlier disaster and won a great victory over the enemy. What was lost at noon has been recouped at sunset. I led out twenty cohorts of the Fourth Legion to relieve Pansa and fell upon Antony's men when they were celebrating prematurely. We have captured two eagles and sixty standards. Antony and the remnants of his army have retreated to his camp, where they are trapped. Now it is his turn to taste what it is like to be besieged. He has lost the greater part of his veteran troops; he has only cavalry. His position is hopeless. Mutina is saved. Pansa is wounded but should recover. Long live the Senate and people of Rome. Tell Cicero.

LV

What followed was the greatest day of Cicero's life – more hard-won than his victory over Verres, more exhilarating than his election to the consulship, more joyful than his defeat of Catilina, more historic than his return from exile. All those triumphs dwindled to nothing in comparison to the salvation of the republic.

That day I reaped the richest of rewards for my many days of labour and sleepless nights, wrote Cicero to Brutus. *The whole population of Rome thronged to my house and escorted me up to the Capitol, then set me on the Speakers' Platform amid tumultuous applause.*

The moment was all the sweeter for having been preceded by such bitter despair. 'This is your victory!' he shouted from the rostra to the thousands in the Forum. 'No,' they called back, 'it is *your* victory!' The following day in the Senate he proposed that Pansa, Hirtius and Octavian should be honoured by an unprecedented fifty days of public thanksgiving, and a monument erected to the fallen: 'Brief is the life given us by nature; but the memory of a life nobly sacrificed is everlasting.' None of his enemies dared oppose him: either they stayed away from the session or voted tamely as he asked. Every time he stepped out of doors he was cheered. He was at his zenith. All he needed now was the final official confirmation that Antony was dead.

A week later came a dispatch from Octavian:

From G. Caesar to his friend Cicero.

I am scribbling this by lamplight in my camp on the evening of the twenty-first. I wanted to be the first to tell you that we have won a second great victory over the enemy. For a week, my legions, in close alliance with those of the gallant Hirtius, probed the defences of Antony's camp for weaknesses. Last night we found a suitable place and this morning we attacked. The fighting was bloody and obstinate, the slaughter great. I was in the midst of it. My standard bearer was killed beside me. I shouldered the eagle and carried it. This rallied our men. Decimus, seeing that the decisive moment had arrived, at last led his forces out of Mutina and joined the battle. The greater part of Antony's army was destroyed. The villain himself, with his cavalry, has fled, and judging by the direction of his flight he means to cross the Alps.

So much is wonderful. But now I must tell you the hard part. Hirtius, despite his failing health, advanced with great spirit into the very heart of the enemy camp and had reached Antony's own tent when he was struck down by a fatal sword thrust to his neck. I have retrieved his body and will return it to Rome, where I am sure you will see that he receives the honours due to a brave consul. I shall write again when I can. Perhaps you will tell his sister.

When he had finished reading, Cicero passed me the letter, then clenched his fists together and raised his eyes to heaven. 'I thank the gods I have been allowed to see this moment.'

'Though it is a pity about Hirtius,' I added. I was thinking of all those dinners under the stars in Tusculum.

'True – I am very sorry for his sake. Still: how much better to die swiftly and gloriously in battle rather than lingeringly and squalidly on a sickbed. This war has been waiting for a hero. I shall make it my business to put Hirtius on the vacant plinth.'

He took Octavian's letter with him to the Senate that morning, intending to read it aloud, to deliver 'the eulogy to end all eulogies' and to propose a state funeral for Hirtius. It was a measure of his buoyant spirits that he could take the loss of a consul so lightly. On the steps of the Temple of Concordia he met the urban praetor, who was also just arriving. Senators were streaming in to take their places. The auspices were being taken. Cornutus was grinning. He said, 'I surmise by your expression that you too have heard the news of Antony's final defeat?'

'I am in raptures. Now we must make sure the villain doesn't escape.'

'Oh, take it from an old soldier – we have more than enough men to cut him off. A pity, though, that it cost us the life of a consul.'

'Indeed – a wretched business.' Side by side the two men began to climb the steps towards the entrance. Cicero said, 'I thought I would deliver a eulogy, if that is all right by you.'

'Of course, although Calenus has already asked me if *he* might say something.'

'Calenus! What business is it of his?'

Cornutus stopped and turned to Cicero. He looked surprised. 'Well, because Pansa was his son-in-law ...'

'What are you talking about? You've got it the wrong way round. Pansa isn't dead; it's Hirtius who has died.'

'No, no. It's Pansa, I assure you. I received a message from Decimus last night. Look.' And he gave the dispatch to Cicero. 'He says that once the siege was lifted, he set off directly for Bononia to consult with Pansa on how they should best pursue Antony, only to discover that he had succumbed to the wounds he received in the first battle.'

Cicero refused to believe it. Only when he read Decimus's letter did he have to concede there was no doubt. 'But Hirtius is dead as well – killed while storming Antony's camp. I have a letter here from young Caesar confirming that he has taken custody of the body.'

'*Both* consuls are dead?'

'It's unimaginable.' Cicero appeared so dazed by the news, I thought he might topple backwards down the steps. 'In the entire existence of the republic, only eight consuls have died during their year in office. Eight – in nearly five hundred years! And now we lose two in the same week!'

Some of the passing senators had stopped to look at them. Conscious that they were being overheard, Cicero drew Cornutus to one side and spoke to him in a quiet, urgent voice. 'This is a dark moment, but we must live through it. Nothing can be allowed to impede our pursuit and destruction of Antony. That is the alpha and omega of our policy. There are plenty of our colleagues who will try to exploit this tragedy to create mischief.'

'Yes, but who will command our forces in the absence of the consuls?'

Cicero made a sound that was something between a groan and a sigh and put his hand to his brow. What a mess this made of all his careful planning, of all his delicate balancing of power! 'Well, I suppose there's no alternative. It will have to be Decimus. He's the senior in age and experience, and he's the governor of Nearer Gaul.'

'What about Octavian?'

'Leave Octavian to me. But we will need to vote him the most extraordinary thanks and honours if we're to keep him in our camp.'

'Is it wise to make him up to be so mighty? One day he'll turn on us, I'm sure of it.'

'Perhaps he will. But we can deal with him later. He can be raised, praised and erased.'

It was the sort of cynical remark Cicero often made for effect: a play on words; a knowing joke, nothing more. Cornutus said, 'Very good, I must remember that – *raised, praised, erased*.' Then the two discussed how best to break the news to the Senate, what motions should be proposed and how the votes should be taken, and after that they proceeded into the temple.

'The nation has sustained a triumph and a tragedy in the same breath,' Cicero told the silent Senate. 'A mortal danger has been lifted but only at a mortal price. The news has just been received that we have won a second and decisive victory at Mutina. Antony is in flight with his few remaining followers, to where we do not know – to the north, to the mountains, to the gates of hell itself for all we care!' (My notes record cheers at this point.) 'But gentlemen, I have to tell you: Hirtius is dead. Pansa is dead.' (Gasps, cries, protests.) 'The gods demanded a sacrifice in expiation for our weakness and our folly over recent months and years, and our two gallant consuls have paid it in full measure. In due course their earthly remains will be returned to the city. We will lay them to rest with solemn honours. We will build a great monument to their valour that men will gaze upon for a thousand years. But we will honour them best by finishing the task they so nearly completed and extirpating Antony once and for all. (Applause.)

'I propose that in the light of the loss of our consuls at Mutina, and mindful of the need to prosecute the war to its end, Decimus Junius Albinus be appointed commander-in-chief of the Senate's armies in the field and that Gaius Julius Caesar Octavianus should be his deputy in all matters; and that in recognition of their brilliant generalship, heroism and success, the name of Decimus Junius Albinus should be added to the Roman calendar to mark his birthday for eternity, and that Gaius Julius Caesar Octavianus should be awarded the honour of an ovation as soon as it is convenient for him to come to Rome to receive it.'

The ensuing debate was full of mischief. As Cicero wrote to Brutus, *That day I realised that gratitude has considerably fewer votes in the Senate than spite.* Isauricus, as jealous of Octavian as he had been of Antony, objected to the idea of awarding him an ovation, which would allow him to parade with his legions through Rome. In the end Cicero was only able to carry his proposal by agreeing to give Decimus the even greater honour of a triumph. A commission of ten men was set up to settle the remuneration, in cash and land, of all the soldiers: the idea was to draw them away from Octavian, reduce their bounty and put them on the payroll of the Senate. To add insult to this injury, neither Octavian nor Decimus was invited to join the commission. Calenus, dressed in mourning, also demanded that his son-in-law's doctor, Glyco, be arrested and examined under torture if necessary to determine whether Pansa's death was murder: 'Remember we were assured to begin with that his injuries were not serious, but now we can see that certain persons stand to gain greatly by his removal' – an obvious reference to Octavian.

All in all it was a bad day's work, and Cicero had to sit down that night and explain to Octavian what had happened.

I am sending you by the same courier the resolutions that have today been agreed by the Senate. I hope you will accept the logic of our placing you and your soldiers under the command of Decimus, just as you were previously subordinate to the consuls. The Commission of Ten is a bit of nonsense I shall try to have rescinded: give me time. You should have been there, my dear friend, to hear the encomia! The rafters rang with praise of your daring and loyalty, and I am glad to say that you will be the youngest commander in the history of the republic to be granted the distinction of an ovation. Press on with your pursuit of Antony, and keep that place in your heart for me that I keep in mine for you.

After that there was silence.

For a long time Cicero heard nothing from the theatre of operations. That was not surprising. It was remote, inhospitable country. He comforted himself by imagining Antony with his lonely band of followers struggling along the inaccessible narrow mountain passes while Decimus raced to try to cut him off. It was not until the thirteenth day of May that news arrived from Decimus – and then, as is often the way with these things, not one but three dispatches arrived all at once. I took them straight to Cicero in his study; he opened the document case greedily and read them aloud in order. The first was dated the twenty-ninth of April and put Cicero on his guard at once: *I shall try to ensure that Antony is unable to maintain himself in Italy. I shall be after him immediately.* 'Immediately?' said Cicero, checking again the date at the head of the letter. 'What is he talking about? He's already writing eight days after Antony fled Mutina ...'

The next dispatch was written a week later, when Decimus was finally on the march:

> *The reasons, my dear Cicero, why I was unable to pursue Antony at once are these. I had no cavalry, no pack animals. I did not know of Hirtius's death. I did not trust Caesar until I had met and talked to him. So the first day passed. Early on the next I had a message from Pansa summoning me to Bononia. As I was on my way, I received the report of his death. I hastened back to my own apology for an army. It is most sadly reduced and in very bad shape through lack of all the necessities. Antony got two days' start of me and made far longer marches as the pursued than I as the pursuer, for he went helter-skelter, while I moved in regular order. Wherever he went he opened up the slave bar racks and carried off the men, stopping nowhere until he reached Vada. He seems to have made up a pretty sizeable body. He may go to Lepidus.*
>
> *If Caesar had listened to me and crossed the Apennines I should have put Antony in so tight a corner that he would have been finished by lack of supplies rather than cold steel. But there is no giving orders to Caesar, nor by Caesar to his army – both very bad things. What alarms me is how this situation can be straightened out. I cannot any longer feed my men.*

The third letter was written a day after the second and dispatched from the foothills of the Alps: *Antony is on the march. He is going to Lepidus. Please look to future action in Rome. You will counter the world's malice towards me if you can.*

'He has let him get away,' said Cicero, resting his head in his hand and reading the letters through again. '*He has let him get away!* And now he says that Octavian can't or won't obey him as commander-in-chief. Well, this is a pretty mess!'

He wrote a letter at once for the courier to take back to Decimus:

From what you write, the flames of war, so far from having been extinguished, seem to be blazing higher. We understood that Antony had fled in despair with a few unarmed and demoralised followers. If in fact his condition is such that a clash with him will be a dangerous matter, I do not regard him as having fled from Mutina at all but as having shifted the war to another theatre.

The next day, the funeral cortège of Hirtius and Pansa reached Rome, escorted by an honour guard of cavalry sent by Octavian. It passed through the streets to the Forum at dusk, watched by hushed and sombre crowds. At the base of the rostra the Senate, all in black togas, waited by torchlight to receive it. Cornutus gave a eulogy that Cicero had written for him, and then the vast assembly walked behind the biers to the Field of Mars, where the pyres had been prepared. As a mark of patriotic respect the undertakers, actors and musicians refused to take any payment; Cicero joked that when an undertaker won't take your money, you know you are a hero. But beneath his public show of bravado, in private he was profoundly troubled. As the torches were put to the base of the pyres, and the flames shot up, Cicero's face in the firelight looked old and hollowed with worry.

Almost as worrying as the fact that Antony had escaped was that Octavian either would not or could not obey Decimus's order. Cicero wrote to him, pleading with him to abide by the Senate's edict and place himself and his legions under the governor's command: *Let any differences be sorted out after victory has been attained; believe me, the surest way to achieve the highest honour in the state will be to play the fullest part now in destroying its greatest enemy.* Ominously, he received no reply.

Then Decimus wrote again:

Labeo Segulius tells me that he has been with Octavian and that a good deal of talk about you took place. Octavian to be sure made no complaints about you, he says, except for a remark which he attributed to you: 'The young man should be raised, praised and erased.' He added that he had no intention of letting himself be erased. As for the veterans, they are grumbling viciously about you and you are in danger from them. They mean to terrorise you and replace you with the young man.

I had long warned Cicero that his fondness for making puns and amusing asides would one day land him in trouble. But he couldn't help himself. He had always enjoyed a reputation as a caustic wit, and as he grew older he had only to open his mouth and people would flock around him, eager to laugh. The attention flattered him and served to inspire him to make ever more cutting remarks. His dry observations were quickly repeated; sometimes phrases were attributed to him he had never even uttered: indeed, I have compiled a whole book of these apocrypha. Caesar used to delight in his barbs, even when he was himself the target – for example, when as dictator he changed the calendar and someone enquired whether the Dog Star would still rise on the same date, Cicero replied, 'It will do as it is told.' Caesar was said to have roared with laughter. But his adopted son, whatever his other merits, was deficient when it came to a sense of humour, and for once Cicero took my advice and wrote a letter of apology.

I gather that confounded fool Segulius is going round telling all and sundry about some joke I am supposed to have made, and that now word of it has reached your ears. I cannot remember making the remark but I shall not disown it, for it sounds the sort of thing I might have said – lightly delivered, meant for the moment, not fit to be examined as a serious statement of policy. I know I do not need to tell you how fond I am of you, how zealously I guard your interests, how determined I am that you should play the leading part in our affairs in the years to come; but if I have caused offence, I am truly sorry.

His letter drew this response:

From G. Caesar to Cicero.

My feelings for you are unchanged. No apology is needed, although if it pleases you to make one, naturally I accept it. Unfortunately my supporters are not so easygoing. They warn me every day that I am a fool to put my faith in you and in the Senate. Your unguarded remark was catnip to them.

Really – that Senate edict! How could I have been expected to place myself under the command of the man who lured my father to his death? My relations with Decimus are civil but we never can be friends, and my men, who are my father's veterans, will never follow him. There is only one circumstance, they say, that would make them fight for the Senate without reservation: if I am made consul. Is that impossible? Both consulships are vacant after all, and if I can be pro-praetor at nineteen, why not consul?

This letter made Cicero blanch. He wrote back at once to say that, divinely inspired though Octavian was, the Senate would never agree to a man not yet even twenty becoming consul. Octavian replied equally swiftly:

My youth, it seems, is not an impediment to my leading an army on the field of battle but it is to my becoming consul. If age is the only issue, could I not have as a consular colleague someone who is as old as I am young, and whose political wisdom and experience would make up for my lack of it?

Cicero showed the letter to Atticus. 'What do you make of this? Is he suggesting what I think he is?'

'I'm sure that's what he's implying. Would you do it?'

'I can't pretend the honour would be meaningless to me – very few men have been consul twice; that would mean immortal glory, and I'm doing the job in all but name in any case. But the price! We've already had to confront one Caesar with an army at his back demanding an illegal consulship, and we ended up fighting a war to try to stop him. Do we now have to confront another, and this time tamely surrender to him? How would it look to the Senate, and to Brutus and Cassius? Who is planting these ideas in the young man's head?'

'Perhaps he doesn't need anyone to plant them there,' Atticus replied. 'Perhaps they arise quite spontaneously.'

Cicero made no reply. The possibility did not bear contemplating.

Two weeks later, Cicero received a letter from Lepidus, who was encamped with his seven legions at Pons Argenteus in southern Gaul.

After he had read it, he leaned forwards and rested his head on his desk. With one hand he pushed the letter towards me.

> *We have long been friends but I have no doubt that in the present violent and unexpected political crisis my enemies have brought you false and unworthy reports about me, designed to give your patriotic heart no small disquiet. I have one earnest request to make of you, dear Cicero. If previously my life and endeavour, my diligence and good faith in the conduct of public affairs have to your knowledge been worthy of the name I bear, I beg you to expect equal or greater things in time to come, as your kindness places me further and further in your debt.*

'I don't understand,' I said. 'Why are you so upset?'

Cicero sighed and sat up straight. To my alarm I saw that he had tears in his eyes. 'Because it means he intends to join forces with Antony and is providing himself with an alibi in advance. His duplicity is so clumsy it's almost endearing.'

He was right of course. On that very day, the thirtieth of May, when Cicero was receiving Lepidus's false assurances, Antony himself – long-haired and bearded after almost forty days on the run – was arriving on the riverbank opposite Lepidus's camp. He waded chest-deep through the water wearing a dark cloak, went up to the palisade and began talking to the legionaries. Many recognised him from the Gallic and the civil wars; they flocked to hear him. The next day he brought all his forces over the river and Lepidus's men welcomed them with outstretched arms. They tore down their fortifications and let Antony stroll unarmed into the camp. He treated Lepidus with the greatest respect, called him by the title 'Father' and insisted that if he joined his cause he would retain the rank and honours of a general. The soldiers cheered. Lepidus agreed.

Or that at least was the story they cooked up together. Cicero was sure they had been partners from the start and that their rendezvous had been arranged in advance. It simply made Lepidus seem less of the traitor he was if he could pretend he had bowed to *force majeure*.

It took nine days for Lepidus's dispatch announcing this shattering turn of events to reach the Senate, although panicky rumours ran ahead of his messenger. Cornutus read it out in the Temple of Concordia:

I call on gods and men to witness how my heart and mind have ever been disposed towards the commonwealth and freedom. Of this I should shortly have given you proof, had not Fortune wrested the decision out of my hands. My entire army, faithful to its inveterate tendency to conserve Roman lives and the general peace, has mutinied; and, truth to tell has compelled me to join them. I beg and implore you, do not treat the compassion shown by myself and my army in a conflict between fellow countrymen as a crime.

When the urban praetor finished reading, there was a great collective sigh, a groan almost, as if the whole chamber had been holding its breath in the hope that the rumours would turn out not to be true. Cornutus gestured to Cicero to open the debate. In the ensuing silence as Cicero rose to his feet one could feel an almost childlike yearning for reassurance. But Cicero had none to offer.

'This news from Gaul, which we have long suspected and dreaded, comes as no surprise, gentlemen. The only shock is the impudence of Lepidus in taking us all to be idiots. He begs us, he implores us, he entreats us – this creature! No, not even that: these bitter, squalid dregs of a noble line that merely assume the form of a human being! – he begs us not to regard his treachery as a crime. The cowardice of the fellow! I would have more respect for him if he came right out and told the truth: that he sees an opportunity to further his monstrous ambitions and has found a fellow thief to be his partner in crime. I propose that he be declared a public enemy forthwith and that all his property and estates be confiscated to help us pay for the fresh legions we shall require to replace those he has stolen from the state.'

This drew loud applause.

'But it will take us a while to raise new forces, and in the meantime we must face the salutary fact that our strategic situation is perilous in the extreme. If the fires of rebellion in Gaul spread to Plancus's four legions – and I fear we must brace ourselves for that possibility – we may have the best part of sixty thousand men ranged against us.'

Cicero had decided beforehand that he would not try to disguise the extent of the crisis. Silence gave way to murmurs of alarm.

'We should not despair,' he continued, 'not least because we have that number of soldiers ourselves, assembled by the noble and gallant Brutus and Cassius – but they are in Macedonia; they are in Syria; they are in

Greece; they are not in Italy. We also have one legion of new recruits in Latium, and the two African legions that are even now at sea and on their way home to defend the capital. And then there are the armies of Decimus and Caesar – although the one is enfeebled and the other truculent.

'We have every chance, in other words. But there is no time to be lost.

'I propose that this Senate orders Brutus and Cassius immediately to send back to Italy sufficient forces to enable us to defend Rome; that we intensify our levies to raise new legions; and that we impose an emergency tax on property of one per cent to enable us to purchase arms and equipment. If we do all of this, and if we draw strength from the spirit of our ancestors and the justice of our cause, it remains my confident belief that liberty will triumph in the end.'

He delivered his closing remarks with all his usual force and vigour. But when he sat down, there was scant applause. The dreadful stench of likely defeat hung in the air, as acrid as burning pitch.

Isauricus rose next. Hitherto this haughty and ambitious patrician had been the staunchest senatorial opponent of the presumptuous Octavian. He had denounced his elevation to a special praetorship; he had even tried to deny him the relatively modest honour of an ovation. But now he delivered a paean of praise to the young Caesar that amazed everyone. 'If Rome is to be defended against Antony's ambitions, backed up now by the forces of Lepidus, then I have come to believe that Caesar is the man upon whom we must chiefly rely. His is the name that can conjure armies from thin air and make them march and fight. His is the shrewdness that can bring us peace. As a symbol of my faith in him, I have to tell you, gentlemen, that I have lately offered him the hand of my daughter in marriage, and I am gratified to be able to tell you he has accepted.'

Cicero twitched suddenly in his seat as if he had been caught by some invisible hook. But Isauricus hadn't finished yet: 'To bind this excellent young man to our cause still further, and to encourage his men to fight against Mark Antony, I propose the following motion: that in view of the grave military situation created by the treachery of Lepidus, and mindful of the service he has already rendered to the republic, the constitution be so amended that Gaius Julius Caesar Octavianus may be permitted to stand for the office of consul *in absentia*.'

Afterwards Cicero cursed himself for not having seen this coming. It was obvious, once one stopped to think about it, that if Octavian could not persuade Cicero to stand for the consulship as his partner, then he would ask someone else. But occasionally even the shrewdest statesman misses the obvious, and now Cicero found himself in an awkward spot. He had to assume that Octavian had already done a deal with his putative father-in-law. Should he accept it with good grace or should he oppose it? He had no time to think. All around him the benches were abuzz with speculation. Isauricus was sitting with his arms folded, looking very pleased with the sensation he had created. Cornutus called upon Cicero to respond to the proposition.

He stood slowly, adjusting his toga, glancing around, clearing his throat – all his familiar delaying tactics to purchase some time to think. 'May I first of all congratulate the noble Isauricus on the excellent family connection he has just announced? I know the young man to be honourable, moderate, modest, sober, patriotic, valiant in war and of calm good judgement – everything in short that a son-in-law should be. He has had no stronger advocate in this Senate than I. His future career in the republic is both glittering and assured. He will be consul, I am sure. But whether he should be consul when he is not yet twenty and solely because he has an army is a different matter.

'Gentlemen, we embarked upon this war with Antony for a principle: the principle that no man – however gifted, however powerful, however ambitious for glory – should be above the law. Whenever in the course of my thirty years in the service of the state we have yielded to temptation and ignored the law, often for what seemed at the time to be good reasons, we have slipped a little further toward the precipice. I helped to pass the special legislation that gave Pompey unprecedented powers to fight the war against the pirates. The war was a great success. But the most lasting consequence was not the defeat of the pirates: it was to create the precedent that enabled Caesar to rule Gaul for almost a decade and to grow too mighty for the state to contain him.

'I do not say that the younger Caesar is like the elder. But I do say that if we make him consul, and in effect give him control of all our forces, then we will betray the very principle for which we fight: the principle that drew me back to Rome when I was on the point of sailing to Greece – that the Roman Republic, with its division of powers, its annual free elections for every magistracy, its law courts and its juries, its balance between Senate and people, its liberty of speech and thought, is mankind's noblest creation, and I would sooner lie choking in my own blood upon the ground than betray the principle on which all this stands – that is, first and last and always, the rule of law.'

His remarks elicited warm applause and entirely set the course of the debate – so much so that Isauricus, with icy formality and a glare at Cicero, later withdrew his proposal and it was never voted upon.

I asked Cicero if he intended to write to Octavian to explain his stand. He shook his head. 'My reasons are in my speech and he will have it in his hands soon enough – my enemies will see to that.'

In the days that followed he was as busy as he had ever been – writing to Brutus and Cassius to urge them to come to the aid of the tottering republic (*the commonwealth is in the gravest peril because of the criminal folly of M. Lepidus*), overseeing the tax inspectors as they set about raising revenue, touring the blacksmiths' yards to cajole them into making more weapons, inspecting the newly raised legion with Cornutus, who had been appointed military defender of Rome. But he knew the cause was hopeless, especially when he saw Fulvia being carried openly in a litter across the Forum, accompanied by a large entourage.

'I thought we were rid of that shrew, at least,' he complained over dinner, 'yet here she is, still in Rome and flaunting herself around, even though her husband has at last been declared a public enemy. Is it any wonder we're in such desperate straits? How is it possible, when all her property is supposed to have been seized?'

There was a pause and then Atticus said quietly, 'I lent her some money.'

'You?' Cicero leaned across the table and peered at him as if he were some mysterious stranger. 'Why on earth would you do that?'

'I felt sorry for her.'

'No you didn't. You wanted to put Antony under an obligation to you. It's insurance. You think we're going to lose.'

Atticus did not deny it, and Cicero left the table.

At the end of that wretched month, 'July', reports reached the Senate that Octavian's army had struck camp in Nearer Gaul, crossed the Rubicon, and was marching on Rome. Even though he had been half expecting it, the news still struck Cicero as a tremendous blow. He had given his word to the Roman people that if 'the heaven-sent boy' was given imperium, he would be a model citizen. *Every imaginable evil chance has dogged us in this war,* he lamented to Brutus. *As I write, I am in great distress, because it hardly looks as though I can make good my promises in respect to the young man, boy almost, for whom I went bail to the republic.* It was then he asked me if I thought he was honour-bound to kill himself, and for the first time I saw that he was not saying it for effect. I replied that I did not think it had come to that yet.

'Perhaps not, but I must be ready. I don't want these veterans of Caesar's torturing me to death as they did Trebonius. The question is how to do it. I'm not sure I could face a blade – do you think posterity will reckon the less of me if I choose Socrates's method and take hemlock instead?'

'I am sure not.'

He asked me to acquire some of the poison on his behalf and I went to see his doctor that same day, who gave me a small jar. He did not ask why I wanted it; I suppose he knew. Despite the wax seal, I could smell its rank odour, like mouse droppings. 'It's made from the seeds,' he explained, 'the most poisonous part of the plant, which I have crushed into a powder. The smallest dose, no more than a pinch, swallowed with water, should do the trick.'

'How long does it take to work?'

'Three hours or thereabouts.'

'Is it painful?'

'It induces slow suffocation – what do you think?'

I put the jar into a box in my room, and placed the box inside a locked chest, as if by hiding it away, death itself could be postponed.

The next day, gangs of Octavian's legionaries began to appear in the Forum. He had sent four hundred on ahead of his main army, with the aim of intimidating the Senate into granting him the consulship. Whenever they saw a senator, they surrounded him and jostled him and showed him their swords, although they never actually drew their weapons. Cornutus, as an old soldier, refused to be threatened. Determined to visit Cicero on the Palatine, the urban praetor pushed and shoved them back until they let him through. But he advised Cicero that on no account should he venture out himself unless he had a strong escort: 'They hold you as much responsible for Caesar's death as they do Decimus or Brutus.'

'If only I *had* been responsible! Then we would have taken care of Antony at the same time and we wouldn't be in the mess we are today.'

'Well here is some better news for you: the African legions arrived last night, and we didn't lose a single ship. Eight thousand men and a thousand cavalry are disembarking at Ostia even as I speak. That should be enough to hold off Octavian, at least until Brutus and Cassius send us help.'

'But are they loyal?'

'So their commanders assure me.'

'Then bring them here as quickly as possible.'

The legions were only a day's march from Rome. As they approached the city, Octavian's men slipped away into the surrounding countryside. When the vanguard reached the salt warehouses, Cornutus ordered the column to parade through the Trigemina Gate and across the Forum Boarium in full view of the crowds in order to steady civilian morale. Then they took up position on the Janiculum. From these strategic heights they controlled the western approaches to Rome and could deploy rapidly to block any invading force. Cornutus asked Cicero if he would come out and inspire the men with a rousing speech. Cicero agreed, and he was carried out of the city gates in a litter accompanied by fifty legionaries on foot. I rode on a mule. It was a hot, muggy day without a tremor of wind. We crossed the River Tiber over the Sublician Bridge and traipsed along a road of dried mud through the shanty towns that have for as long as I can remember filled the flat plain of the Vaticanum. It was notoriously malarial in the summer, and swarming with hostile insects. Cicero's litter had the protection of a mosquito net but I did not, and the insects whined in my ears. The whole place stank of human filth. Children, pot-bellied with hunger watched us listlessly from the doorways of tumbling shacks, while all around them, disregarded and pecking away at the rubbish, were hundreds of the crows that nest in the nearby sacred grove. We passed through the gates of the Janiculum and went up the hill. The place was teeming with soldiers. They had pitched their tents wherever they could find some space.

On the flatter ground at the top of the slope Cornutus had drawn up four cohorts – almost two thousand men. They stood in lines in the heat. The light on their helmets dazzled as brightly as the sun, and I had to shield my eyes. When Cicero stepped out of his litter there was absolute silence. Cornutus conducted him to a low platform beside an altar. A sheep was sacrificed. Its guts were pulled out and examined by the haruspices and declared propitious: 'There is no doubt of ultimate victory.' The crows circled overhead. A priest read a prayer. Then Cicero spoke.

I cannot remember exactly what he said. All the usual words were there – liberty, ancestors, hearths and altars, laws and temples – but for once I listened without hearing. I was looking at the faces of the legionaries. They were sunburnt, lean, impassive. Some were chewing mastic. I saw the scene through their eyes. They had been recruited by Caesar to fight against King Juba and the army of Cato. They had slaughtered thousands and had been stuck in Africa ever since. They had travelled hundreds of miles crammed together in boats. They had been force-marched for a day. Now they were lined up in the heat in Rome and an old man was talking at them about liberty, ancestors, hearths and altars – and it meant nothing.

Cicero finished speaking. There was silence. Cornutus ordered them to give three cheers. The silence continued. Cicero stepped off the platform and got back into his litter and we returned down the hill, past the saucer-eyed starving children.

Cornutus came to see Cicero the following morning and told him that the African legions had mutinied overnight. It seemed that Octavian's men had crept back from the countryside in the darkness, infiltrated the camps and promised the soldiers twice as much money as the Senate could afford to pay them. Meanwhile Octavian's main army was reported to be moving south along the Via Flaminia and was barely a day's march away.

'What will you do now?' Cicero asked him.

'Kill myself,' came the reply, and he did, that same evening, pressing the tip of his sword to his stomach and falling upon it heavily rather than surrender.

He was an honourable man and deserves to be remembered, not least because he was the only member of the Senate who took that course. When Octavian was close to the city, most of the leading patricians went out to meet him on the road to escort him into Rome. Cicero sat in his study with the shutters closed. The air was so close it was hard to breathe. I looked in from time to time but he did not seem to have moved. His noble head, staring straight ahead and silhouetted against the faint light from the window, was like a marble bust in a deserted temple. Finally he noticed me and asked where Octavian had set up his headquarters.

I replied that he had moved into the home of his mother and stepfather on the Quirinal.

'Perhaps you could send a message to Philippus and ask him what he suggests I should do.'

I did as he requested and the courier returned with a scrawled reply that Cicero ought to go and talk to Octavian: 'You will find him, I am sure, as I did, disposed to mercy.'

Wearily Cicero got to his feet. The big house, usually thronged with visitors, was empty. It felt as if no one had lived in it for a long time. In the late summer afternoon sun the silent public rooms glowed as if made of gold and amber.

We went together, in a pair of litters accompanied by a small escort, to the house of Philippus. Sentries guarded the street and the front door but they must have been given orders to let Cicero through, for they parted at once. As we crossed the threshold, Isauricus was just leaving. I had expected him, as Octavian's future father-in-law, to give Cicero a smile of condescension or of triumph; instead he scowled at him and hurried past us.

Through the heavy open door we could see Octavian standing in a corner of the tablinum dictating a letter to a secretary. He beckoned to us to enter. He seemed in no hurry to finish. He was wearing a simple military tunic. His body armour, helmet and sword lay scattered on a couch where he had flung them. He looked like a young recruit. Finally he ended his dictation and sent the secretary away.

He scrutinised Cicero in an amused way that reminded me of his adopted father. 'You are the last of my friends to greet me.'

'Well, I imagined you would be busy.'

'Ah, is that it?' Octavian laughed, revealing those terrible teeth of his. 'I was presuming that you disapproved of my actions.'

Cicero shrugged. 'The world is as it is. I have given up the habit of approving and disapproving. What's the point? Men do as they please, whatever I think.'

'So what is it you want to do? Do you want to be consul?'

For the merest fraction of a moment Cicero's face seemed to flood with pleasure and relief, but then he understood that Octavian was joking and immediately the light went out of it again. He grunted, 'Now you're toying with me.'

'I am. Forgive me. My colleague as consul will be Quintus Pedius, an obscure relative of mine of whom you will never have heard, which is the whole point of him.'

'So not Isauricus?'

'No. There seems to have been some misunderstanding there. I shan't be marrying his daughter either. I shall spend some time here settling matters and then I must go and confront Antony and Lepidus. You can leave Rome too if you like.'

'I can?'

'Yes, you can leave Rome. You can write philosophy. You can go anywhere you please in Italy. However, you cannot return to Rome in my absence, nor can you attend the Senate. You cannot write your memoirs or anything political. You cannot leave the country and go to Brutus or Cassius. Is that acceptable? Will you give me your word? I can assure you my men would not be so generous.'

Cicero bowed his head. 'It is generous. It is acceptable. I give you my word. Thank you.'

'In return I will guarantee your safety, in recognition of our past friendship.' He picked up a letter to signal that the audience was at an end. 'One last thing,' he said as Cicero turned to leave. 'It makes no difference, but I would like to know: was it a joke, or would you really have erased me?'

'I believe I would have done exactly the same as you are doing now,' replied Cicero.

LVI

After that, he seemed to become an old man very suddenly. He retired to Tusculum the next day and immediately started complaining about his eyesight. He refused to write or even read: he said it gave him a headache. He took no solace from his garden. He visited no one and no one visited him, apart from his brother. They would sit together for hours on a bench in the Lyceum, mostly in silence. The only subject Quintus could tempt him to discuss was the distant past – their shared memories of childhood and of growing up in Arpinum – and for the first time I heard Cicero talk at length about his father and mother. It was unnerving to see him, of all men, so disconnected from the world. Throughout his life he had demanded to know the latest news from Rome. Now, when I told him what I had heard was happening – that Octavius had set up a special court to try the assassins of Caesar, or even that he had left the city at the head of an army of eleven legions to fight Antony – he made no comment, save that he preferred not even to think about it. A few more weeks of this, I thought to myself, and he will die.

People often ask me why he did not try to run away. After all, Octavian did not yet have any firm control of the country. The weather was still clement. The ports were not watched. Cicero could have slipped out of Italy to join his son in Macedonia: I am sure Brutus would have been only too pleased to offer him sanctuary. But the truth was he lacked the will to do anything so decisive. 'I am finished with running,' he sighed to me. He couldn't even summon the energy to go down to the Bay of Naples. Besides, Octavian had guaranteed his safety.

I guess it must have been about a month after our retreat to Tusculum that he sought me out one morning and told me he would like to review his old letters: 'This constant talk with Quintus about my early years has stirred the sediment of my memory.' I had preserved them all, however fragmentary, incoming and outgoing, over more than three decades, and had sorted them by correspondent and arranged them on rolls chronologically. I carried the cylinders into his library and he lay on the couch while one of his secretaries read them out. It was all there, an entire life, from his early struggles to gain election to the Senate, through the hundreds of legal cases he took to make his name famous and which culminated in the epic prosecution of Verres, his election to aedile and then to praetor and finally to consul, his struggles with Catilina and Clodius, his exile and return, his relations with Caesar and Pompey and Cato, the civil war, the assassination, his return to power, Tullia and Terentia …

For more than a week he relived his life, and at the end he had recovered something of his old self. 'What an adventure it has been,' he mused, stretching out on the couch. 'It has all come back to me, the good and the bad, the noble and the base. I truly believe I can say, without being immodest, that these letters add up to the most complete record of an historical era ever assembled by a leading statesman. And what an era! No one else saw so much, and wrote about it while it was still fresh. This is history composed without any benefit of hindsight. Can you think of anything to compare with it?'

'It will be of immense interest a thousand years from now,' I said, trying to encourage his new good mood.

'Oh, it's more than merely of interest! It's the case for my defence. I may have lost the past and lost the present, but I wonder if with this I might not yet win the future.'

Some of the letters showed him in a bad light – vain, duplicitous, greedy, wrong-headed – and I expected him to weed out the most egregious examples and order me to destroy them. But when I asked him which letters he wished me to discard, he replied, 'We must keep them all. I can't present myself to posterity as some improbable paragon – no one will believe it. If this archive is to have the necessary authenticity, I must stand before the muse of history as naked as a Greek statue. Let future generations mock me for my follies and pretensions however much they like – the important thing is that they will have to read me, and in that will lie my victory.'

Of all the sayings associated with Cicero, the most famous and characteristic is: 'While there is life there is hope.' He still had life – or the semblance of it, at least; and now he had the faintest gleam of hope.

Beginning that day, he concentrated what remained of his strength on the task of ensuring his papers survived. Atticus eventually agreed to help, on condition he was allowed to retrieve every letter he had ever written to Cicero. Cicero rather despised him for his caution but in the end agreed: 'If he wants to be a mere shadow in history, that's his lookout.' With some reluctance I returned the correspondence I had carefully assembled over so many years and watched as Atticus lit a brazier and – not trusting the task to a servant – burnt with his own hand all the rolls on which his letters had been preserved. Then he put his scribes to work. Three complete sets of the collected letters were produced. Cicero kept one, Atticus another and I the third. I sent mine down to my farm along with locked boxes containing all my shorthand notes recording thousands of meetings, speeches, conversations, witticisms and barbed remarks, as well as the dictated drafts of his books. I told the overseer that it all should be hidden in one of the barns and that if anything happened to me he should give it to Agathe Licinia, the freedwoman who owned the baths of Venus Libertina at Baiae. Quite what she would do with it, I was not sure, but I sensed that I could trust her above all people in the world.

At the end of November, Cicero asked me if I would go back to Rome to make sure the last of his papers had been removed from his study, and to carry out a final general inspection. The house was being sold on his behalf by Atticus, and much of the furniture had already gone. It was the start of winter. The morning was chilly, the light gloomy. I wandered between the empty rooms as if I were an invisible spirit, and in my imagination I repeopled them. I saw the tablinum once again filled with statesmen discussing the future of the republic, heard Tullia's laughter in the dining room, saw Cicero bent over his books of philosophy in the library attempting to explain why fear of death was illogical … My eyes were blurred with tears; my heart ached.

Suddenly a dog began to howl – so loudly and frantically that my bittersweet fantasies vanished in an instant. I stopped to listen. Our old dog had gone. This had to be a neighbour's. It was a most piteous wailing and it set off others. I went out on to the terrace. The sky was dark with swirls of starlings, and all across Rome dogs were howling like wolves.

Indeed it was later said that at this very moment a wolf was seen darting across the Forum; that statues sweated blood and a newly born baby spoke. I heard the sound of running feet and looking down saw a group of men whooping with delight, racing towards the rostra and tossing to one another what I thought at first was a football but then realised was a human head. A woman started screaming in the street. Without thinking what I was doing I went out to see who it was and found the wife of our elderly neighbour, Caesetius Rufus, crawling on her knees in the gutter, while behind her the trunk of a corpse gushed blood from its neck across the threshold. Her steward, who I knew quite well, was running hopelessly to and fro. Panicking, I grabbed his arm and shook him until he told me what had happened – Octavian, Antony and Lepidus had joined forces and had published a list of hundreds of senators and equestrians who were to be killed and their fortunes seized. There was a bounty of a hundred thousand sesterces for each head that was brought to them. Both of the Cicero brothers were named on the list, and Atticus.

'That cannot be true,' I assured him. 'We have a solemn promise.'

'It's true,' he cried. 'I've seen it.'

I ran back to the house, where the few remaining slaves were gathered, frightened, in the atrium. 'Everyone must scatter,' I told them. 'If they catch us they will torture us to try to make us reveal the whereabouts of the master. If it comes to it, say he is in Puteoli.' I scribbled out a message to Cicero: *You and Quintus and Atticus are proscribed – Octavian has betrayed you – the death squads are looking for you – make at once for your house on the island – I will find you a boat.* I gave it to the ostler and told him to take it by his fastest horse to Cicero in Tusculum. Then I went to the stables and found my carriage and driver and ordered him to set off for Astura.

Even as we clattered down the hill, gangs of men armed with knives and staves were running up on to the Palatine, where the richest human pickings would be found, and I banged my head against the side of the carriage in my anguish that Cicero hadn't made good his escape from Italy while he had the chance.

I made that unfortunate driver whip his poor pair of horses until their flanks bled so that we could arrive in Astura before nightfall. We found the boatman in his hut, and even though the sea was beginning to get up and the light was dim, he rowed us the hundred yards over to the little island where Cicero's villa stood secluded in the trees. It had not been visited by him for months, and the slaves were amazed to see me, and not a little resentful at having to light fires and heat the rooms. I lay down on my damp mattress and listened to the wind buffeting around the roof and rustling the trees. As the waves crashed against the rocky shore and the house creaked, I was full of terror, imagining that every sound might be the arrival of Cicero's murderers. If I had brought that jar of hemlock, I almost think I might have taken it.

The next morning the weather was calmer, although when I walked through the trees and contemplated the huge expanse of grey sea with the lines of white waves running in to the shore, I felt utterly desolate. I wondered if this was a foolish plan and that we would do better to make directly for Brundisium, which at least was on the right side of Italy for a voyage east. But of course news of the proscriptions and the vast bounty for a severed head would race ahead of us, and nowhere would be safe. Cicero would never reach the harbour alive.

I sent my driver off in the direction of Tusculum with a second letter for Cicero, saying that I had arrived 'on the island' – I kept it vague in case the message fell into the wrong hands – and urging him to make all speed. Then I asked the boatman to go to Antium to see if he could charter a vessel to carry us down the coast. He looked at me as if I were mad to make such a request in winter, when the weather was so treacherous, but after some grumbling he went away, and came back the following day to say that he had procured a ten-oared boat with a sail that would be with us as soon as they could row the seven miles from Antium. After that there was really nothing I could do except wait.

The wooded islet of Astura was the place where Cicero had gone to ground after Tullia had died. He had found the absolute silence, except for the sounds of Nature, soothing; I found the opposite: they jangled my nerves, especially as day after day passed when nothing happened. I kept a regular lookout, but it wasn't until late in the afternoon on the fifth day that there was a sudden eruption of activity on the shoreline. Two litters arrived through the trees accompanied by a retinue of slaves. The boatman rowed me over to take a look, and as we drew closer, I saw that on the beach stood Cicero and Quintus. When I hurried over the sand to greet them, I was shocked by their appearance. Neither had changed his clothes or shaved; both were red-eyed from crying. A light rain was falling. Drenched, they looked like a pair of indigent old men. Quintus, if anything, was in a worse state than Cicero. After a sorrowful greeting, he took one look at the boat I had hired, pulled up on to the beach, and announced he would not set foot in it for a moment.

He turned to Cicero. 'My dear brother, this is hopeless. I don't know why I've let you drag me here, except that all my life I have done what you have told me. Look at us! Old men, we're in failing health. The weather is poor. We have no money. We would be better off following Atticus's example.'

I asked, 'Where is Atticus?'

Cicero said, 'He's gone into hiding in Rome.' He started to cry. He made no attempt to disguise it. And then, as quickly as he had started, he stopped and continued speaking as if nothing had happened. 'No, I'm sorry, Quintus, I can't live in someone's cellar, trembling every time there's a knock at the door. Tiro's plan is as good as any. Let's see how far we can get.'

Quintus said, 'Then I'm afraid that we must part, and I shall pray to meet you again – if not in this life then the next.'

They fell into one another's arms and clung to each other tightly, then Quintus broke away. He embraced me. None of those watching the scene could restrain their tears. Certainly I was overcome by the sadness of it all. After that, Quintus climbed back into his litter and was borne away up the track and into the trees.

It was too late for us to set off that day, and so we were rowed over to the villa. While Cicero dried himself at the fire, he explained that he had lingered for two days in Tusculum, unable to believe that Octavian had betrayed him, sure that there must have been some mistake. This much he had discovered: that Octavian had met Antony and Lepidus in Bononia, on an island in the middle of the river – just the three of them, with a couple of secretaries: they had left their bodyguards behind and had searched one another for concealed weapons – and that over the next three days, working from dawn till dusk, they had divided up the carcass of the republic between them, and to pay their armies had compiled a death list of two thousand wealthy men, including two hundred senators, whose property would be seized. 'I am told by Atticus, who heard it from the consul Pedius, that each of the criminals, as a token of good faith, was required to mark for death someone who was precious to them. Thus

Antony gave up his uncle, Lucius Caesar, even though he spoke in his defence in the Senate; Lepidus yielded his brother, Aemilius Paullus; and Octavian offered me – Antony insisted, although Pedius maintained the boy had been reluctant to agree.'

'Do you believe it?'

'Not particularly. I have looked into those pale grey soulless eyes of his once too often. He is no more affected by the death of a man than he is by the death of a fly.' He let out a sigh that seemed to shake his entire body. 'Oh Tiro, I am so tired! To think that I, of all people, have been outwitted at the last by a young man who has barely started to shave! Do you have that poison I asked you to get?'

'It's in Tusculum.'

'Well then, I can only pray to the immortal gods to allow me to die tonight in my sleep.'

But he did not die. He woke depressed, and the next morning, when we were standing on the little quay waiting for the sailors to pick us up, he suddenly announced that he would not leave after all. Then when the boat came within earshot, one of the sailors shouted up to us that he had just seen a unit of legionaries on the road from Antium, heading in our direction, led by a military tribune. That immediately shook Cicero out of his lethargy. He held out his hand and the sailors helped him down into the boat.

Our voyage quickly began to repeat the pattern of our first flight into exile. It was as if Mother Italy could not bear to allow her favourite son to leave her. We had gone about three miles, hugging close to the shore, when the grey sky began to fill with immense black clouds rolling in from the horizon. A wind got up, stirring the sea into steep waves, and our little boat seemed to rise almost to the perpendicular, only to crash down again, bow first, and saturate us with salt water. If anything, it was worse than before, because this time there was no shelter. Cicero and I sat huddled in hooded cloaks while the men tried to row us crosswise into the oncoming waves. The hull began to fill and the vessel became dangerously low. We all had to help bail, even Cicero, frantically scooping up the freezing water with our hands and tipping it over the side to stop ourselves sinking. Our limbs and faces were numb. We swallowed salt. The rain blinded us. Eventually, after rowing bravely for many hours, the sailors were exhausted, and told us they needed to rest. We rounded a rocky promontory and headed towards a cove, rowing as close to the beach as we could before we all had to jump out and wade ashore. Cicero sank in almost to his waist and four of the sailors had to carry him on to the land. They laid him down and went back to help their crewmates with the boat, hauling it right up on to the beach. They laid it on its side and propped it up using branches cut from the nearby myrtle trees, and with the sail and the mast they built a makeshift shelter. They even managed to light a fire, although the wood was wet, and the wind blew the smoke this way and that, choking us and making our eyes smart.

Darkness soon came, and Cicero, who had not uttered a word of complaint, appeared to sleep. Thus ended the fifth day of December.

I woke at dawn on the sixth after a fitful night to find calmer skies. My bones were chilled, my damp clothes stiff with salt and sand. I stood with difficulty and looked about me. Everyone was still asleep, except for Cicero. He had gone.

I looked up and down the beach and peered out to sea, then turned to scan the trees. There was a small gap, which turned out to lead to a path, and I set off, calling his name. At the top of the path was a road. Cicero was lurching along it. I called to him again but he ignored me. He was making slow and unsteady progress in the direction from which we had come. I caught him up and fell in beside him and spoke to him with a calmness I did not feel.

'We need to get back in the boat,' I said. 'The slaves in the house may have told the legionaries where we are headed. They may not be far behind us. Where are you going?'

'To Rome.' He did not look at me but kept on walking.

'To do what?'

'To kill myself on Octavian's doorstep. He will die of shame.'

'He won't,' I said, and caught his arm, 'because he has no shame, and the soldiers will torture you to death like they did Trebonius.'

He glanced at me and stopped walking. 'Do you think so?'

'I know it.' I took him by the arm and tugged him gently. He did not resist but lowered his head and allowed me to lead him like a child back through the trees to the beach.

How melancholy it is to relive all of this! But I have no choice if I am to fulfil my promise to him and tell the story of his life.

We put him back on to the boat and launched it once more into the waves. The day was grey and vast, as at the dawn of time. We rowed on for many hours, assisted by a breeze that filled the sail, and by the end of the afternoon had covered, by my reckoning, a further twenty-five miles or thereabouts. We passed the famous Temple of Apollo that stands a little above the sea on the headland at Caieta, and Cicero, who had been slumped, staring vacantly towards the shore, suddenly recognised it, sat up straight and said, 'We are nearly at Formiae. I have a house here.'

'I know you do.'

'Let us put in here for the night.'

'It's too risky. You're well known to have a villa at Formiae.'

'I don't care about that,' replied Cicero with something of his old firmness. 'I want to sleep in my own bed.'

And so we rowed towards the shore and tied up at the jetty that was built out into the sea a little way from the villa. As we moored, a great flock of crows rose cawing from the nearby trees as if in warning, and I asked Cicero at least to allow me to make sure his enemies weren't lying in wait for him before he disembarked. He agreed, and I set off up the familiar path through the trees, accompanied by a couple of the sailors. The path led us to the Via Appia. By now it was almost dusk. The road was empty. I walked about fifty paces to where Cicero's villa stood behind a pair of iron gates. I went up the drive and knocked firmly on the oak door, and after a short interval and a great noise of bolts drawn back, the porter appeared. He was startled to see me. I looked past his shoulder and asked if any strangers had come looking for the master. He assured me they had not. He was a good-hearted, simple fellow. I had known him for years, and I believed him.

I said, 'In that case, send four slaves with a litter down to the jetty to pick up the master and bring him to the villa, and meanwhile have a hot bath drawn for him and fresh clothes and food prepared, for he is in a poor state.'

I also sent two other slaves with fast horses to keep a lookout along the Via Appia for this mysterious and ominous detachment of legionaries that seemed to be on our trail.

Cicero was carried into the villa, and the gate and door were locked behind him.

I saw little of him after that. As soon as he had had his bath, he took a little food and wine in his room and then retired to sleep.

I slept myself – and very deeply, despite my anxieties, for such was my exhaustion – and the following morning had to be roughly woken by one of the slaves I had stationed along the Via Appia. He was out of breath and frightened. A force of thirty legionaries on foot, with a centurion and a tribune on horseback, was marching towards the house from the north-west. They were less than half an hour away.

I ran to wake Cicero. He had the covers up to his chin and refused to stir, but I tore them off him anyway.

'They are coming for you,' I said, bending over him. 'They're almost here. We have to move.'

He smiled at me, and laid his hand on my cheek. 'Let them come, old friend. I am not afraid.'

I pleaded with him: 'For my sake, if not for yours – for the sake of your friends and for Marcus – please *move*!'

I think it was the mention of Marcus that did it. He sighed. 'Very well, then. But it is quite pointless.'

I withdrew to let him dress and ran around issuing orders – a litter to be ready immediately, the boat prepared to sail with the sailors at their oars, the gate and the door to be locked the moment we were out of the villa, the household slaves to vacate the premises and hide wherever they could.

In my imagination I could hear the steady tramp of the legionaries' boots becoming louder and louder …

At length – far too great a length! – Cicero appeared looking as immaculate as if he were on his way to address the Senate. He walked through the villa saying goodbye to everyone. They were all in tears. He took a last look around as if saying farewell to the building and all his beloved possessions, and then climbed into the litter, closed the curtains so that no one could see his face, and we set off out of the gate. But instead of the slaves all making a run for it, they seized such weapons as they could find – rakes, brooms, pokers, kitchen knives – and insisted on coming with us, forming a homely rustic phalanx around the litter. We went the short distance along the road and turned down the path into the woods. Through the trees I could glimpse the sea shining in the morning sun. Escape seemed close. But then, at the bottom of the path, just before it opened out on to the beach, a dozen legionaries appeared.

The slaves at the front of our little procession cried out in alarm, and those carrying the litter scrambled to turn it round. It swayed dangerously and Cicero was almost pitched to the ground. We struggled back the way we had come, only to discover that more soldiers were above us, blocking access to the road.

We were trapped, outnumbered, doomed. Nevertheless, we determined to make a fight. The slaves set the litter down and surrounded it. Cicero drew back the curtain to see what was going on. He saw the soldiers advancing rapidly towards us and shouted to me: 'No one is to fight!' Then to the slaves he said: 'Everyone lay down your weapons! I am honoured by your devotion, but the only blood that needs to be shed here is mine.'

The legionaries had their swords drawn. The military tribune leading them was a hirsute, swarthy-looking brute. Beneath the ridge of his helmet his eyebrows merged together to form a continuous thick black line. He called out, 'Marcus Tullius Cicero, I have a warrant for your execution.'

Cicero, still lying in his litter, his chin in his hand, looked him up and down very calmly. 'I know you,' he said, 'I'm sure of it. What's your name?'

The military tribune, plainly taken aback, said, 'My name, if you must know it, is Caius Popillius Laenas, and yes, we do know one another: not that it will save you.'

'Popillius,' murmured Cicero, 'that's it,' and then he turned to me. 'Do you remember this man, Tiro? He was our client – that fifteen-year-old who murdered his father, right at the beginning of my career. He'd have been condemned to death for parricide if I hadn't got him off – on condition he went into the army.' He laughed. 'This is a kind of justice, I suppose.'

I looked at Popillius and indeed I did remember him. Popillius said, 'That's enough talk. The verdict of the Constitutional Commission is that the death sentence should be carried out immediately.' He gestured to his soldiers to drag Cicero from his litter.

'Wait,' said Cicero, 'leave me where I am. I have it in mind to die this way,' and he propped himself up on his elbows like a defeated gladiator, threw back his head and offered his throat to the sky.

'If that's what you want,' said Popillius. He turned to his centurion. 'Let's get it over with.'

The centurion took up his position. He braced his legs.

He swung his sword. The blade flashed, and in that instant for Cicero the mystery that had plagued him all his life was solved, and liberty was extinguished from the earth.

Afterwards they cut off his head and hands and put them in a sack. They made us sit down and watch them while they did it. Then they marched away. I was told that Antony was so delighted with these extra trophies that he gave Popillius a bonus of a million sesterces. It is also said that Fulvia pierced Cicero's tongue with a needle. I do not know. What is certainly true is that on Antony's orders the head that had delivered the Philippics and the hands that had written them were nailed up on the rostra, as a warning to others who might think of opposing the Triumvirate, and they stayed there for many years, until finally they rotted and fell away.

After the killers had gone, we carried Cicero's body down to the beach and built a pyre, and at dusk we burned it. Then I made my way south to my farm on the Bay of Naples.

Little by little I learned more of what had happened.

Quintus was soon afterwards captured with his son and put to death.

Atticus emerged from hiding and was pardoned by Antony because of the help he had given Fulvia.

And much, much later, Antony committed suicide together with his mistress Cleopatra after Octavian defeated them in battle. The boy is now the Emperor Augustus.

But I have written enough.

Many years have passed since the episodes I have recounted. At first I thought I would never recover from Cicero's death. But time wipes out everything, even grief. Indeed, I would go so far as to say that grief is almost entirely a question of perspective. For the first few years I used to sigh and think, 'Well, he would still be in his sixties now,' and then a decade later, with surprise, 'My goodness, he would be seventy-five,' but nowadays I think, 'Well, he would be long since dead in any case, so what does it matter how he died in comparison with how he lived?'

My work is done. My book is finished. Soon I will die too.

In the summer evenings I sit on the terrace with Agathe, my wife. She sews while I look at the stars. Always at such moments I think of Scipio's dream of where dead statesmen dwell in *On the Republic*:

> *I gazed in every direction and all appeared wonderfully beautiful. There were stars which we never see from earth, and they were all larger than we have ever imagined. The starry spheres were much greater than the earth; indeed the earth itself seemed to me so small that I was scornful of our empire, which covers only a single point, as it were, upon its surface.*

'If only you will look on high,' the old statesman tells Scipio, 'and contemplate this eternal home and resting place, you will no longer bother with the gossip of the common herd or put your trust in human reward for your exploits. Nor will any man's reputation endure very long, for what men say dies with them and is blotted out with the forgetfulness of posterity.'

All that will remain of us is what is written down.

CAST OF HISTORICAL CHARACTERS

AFRANIUS, LUCIUS an ally of Pompey's from his home region of Picenum; one of Pompey's army commanders in the war against Mithradates; consul in 60 BC

AGRIPPA, MARCUS VIPSANIUS Octavian's closest associate, aged twenty

AHENOBARBUS, LUCIUS DOMITIUS patrician senator; praetor in 58 BC; married to Cato's sister; a determined enemy of Caesar

ANTONY, MARK (MARCUS ANTONIUS) renowned as a brave and enterprising soldier under Caesar's command in Gaul; grandson of a famous orator and consul; stepson of one of the Catiline conspirators executed by Cicero

ARRIUS, QUINTUS a former praetor and military commander, closely allied to Crassus

ATTICUS, TITUS POMPONIUS Cicero's closest friend; an equestrian, an Epicurean, immensely wealthy; brother-in-law to Quintus Cicero, who is married to his sister, Pomponia

AURELIA mother of Julius Caesar

BALBUS, LUCIUS CORNELIUS wealthy Spaniard originally allied to Pompey and then to Caesar, whose *homme d'affaires* he became in Rome

BIBULUS, MARCUS CALPURNIUS Caesar's colleague as consul in 59 BC, and his staunch opponent

BRUTUS, MARCUS JUNIUS direct descendant of the Brutus who drove the kings from Rome and established the republic in the sixth century BC; son of Servilia, nephew of Cato; the great figurehead of the constitutionalists

CAESAR, GAIUS JULIUS former consul; a member of the 'triumvirate' with Pompey and Crassus; governor of three Roman provinces – Nearer and

Further Gaul and Bithynia; six years Cicero's junior; initially married to Pompeia, with whom he lives along with his mother, Aurelia, and daughter, Julia; later married to Calpurnia, daughter of L. Calpurnius Piso

CALENUS, QUINTUS FUFIUS an old crony of Clodius and Antony; a supporter of Caesar and an enemy of Cicero; father-in-law of Pansa

CASSIUS, GAIUS LONGINUS senator and able soldier; married to Servilia's daughter, Junia Tertia, and thus Brutus's brother-in-law

CATILINA, LUCIUS SERGIUS former governor of Africa, beaten by Cicero for the consulship

CATO, MARCUS PORCIUS half-brother of Servilia; great-grandson of Cato the Censor; uncle of Brutus; a Stoic and a stern upholder of the traditions of the republic

CATULUS, QUINTUS LUTATIUS former consul, member of the College of Priests, one of the most experienced men in the senate, leader of the patrician faction

CELER, QUINTUS CAECILIUS METELLUS brother-in-law of Pompey (who married his sister), husband of Clodia, brother of Nepos; member of the College of Augurs; praetor; head of the most extensive and powerful family in Rome; a war hero with a powerful military reputation

CETHEGUS, GAIUS CORNELIUS patrician senator, one of Catilina's co-conspiritors

CICERO, MARCUS TULLIUS JUNIOR Cicero's son

CICERO, QUINTUS TULLIUS Cicero's younger brother; senator and soldier; married to Pomponia, the sister of Atticus; governor of Asia, 61–58 BC

CICERO, QUINTUS TULLIUS JUNIOR Cicero's nephew

CLODIA daughter of one of the most distinguished families in Rome, the patrician Appii Claudii; the sister of Clodius; the widow of Metellus Celer

CLODIUS PULCHER, PUBLIUS scion of the leading patrician dynasty, the Appii Claudii; a former brother-in-law of L. Lucullus; the brother of Clodia, with whom he is alleged to have had an incestuous affair; lieutenant of Murena, the governor of Further Gaul; at his trial for sacrilege Cicero gave evidence against him; transferred to the plebs at the instigation of Caesar and elected tribune

CORNUTUS, MARCUS one of Caesar's officers, appointed urban praetor in 44 BC

CRASSIPES, FURIUS Tullia's second husband; a senator; a friend of Crassus

CRASSUS, MARCUS LICINIUS former consul; member of the 'triumvirate'; brutal suppressor of the slave revolt led by Spartacus; the richest man in Rome; a bitter rival of Pompey

CRASSUS, PUBLIUS son of Crassus the triumvir; cavalry commander under Caesar in Gaul; an admirer of Cicero

DECIMUS properly styled BRUTUS, DECIMUS JUNIUS ALBINUS, but not to be confused with BRUTUS (above); brilliant young military commander in Gaul; a protégé of Caesar

DOLABELLA, PUBLIUS CORNELIUS Tullia's third husband; one of Caesar's closest lieutenants – young, charming, precocious, ambitious, licentious, brutal

FULVIA wife of Clodius; subsequently married to Mark Antony

GABINUS, AULUS a former tribune from Pompey's home region of Picenum, he promulgated the laws that gave Pompey his extended command in the East; rewarded Pompey with a legateship in the war against Mithrades

HIRTIUS, AULUS one of Caesar's staff officers in Gaul, groomed for a political career; a noted gourmet, a scholar who helped Caesar with his *Commentaries*

HORTENSIUS HORTALUS, QUINTUS former consul, for many years the leading advocate at the Roman bar, until displaced by Cicero; brother-in-law of Catulus; a leader of the patrician faction; immensely wealthy; like Cicero, a civilian politician and not a soldier

HYBRIDA, CAIUS ANTONIUS Cicero's colleague as consul, descendant of one the most illustrious families in Rome, but nevertheless once expelled from the senate for corruption and bankruptcy

ISAURICUS, PUBLIUS SERVIUS VATIA (SENIOR) former consul, one of the grand old men of the Senate alongside Catulus

ISAURICUS, PUBLIUS SERVILIUS VATIA (JUNIOR) a patrician (son of the above), who nevertheless chose to support Caesar; a tough and highly decorated soldier, having triumphed twice; a former consul and member of the College of Priests; elected praetor in 54 BC

LABIENUS, TITUS a soldier and former tribune from Pompey's home region of Picenum; a tribune in Caesar's and Pompey's interests; one of Caesar's ablest commanders in Gaul

LEPIDUS, MARCUS AEMILIUS patrician senator, married to a daughter of Servilia; member of the College of Pontiffs

LUCULLUS, LUCIUS LICINIUS former consul and commander of the Roman army fighting in the East against Mithrades until supplanted by Pompey; haughty, aristocratic and vastly rich, his enemies in the senate contrived for several years to deny him a triumph and keep him waiting outside Rome; bitterly divorced from one of the sisters of Clodius and Clodia

METELLUS, LUCIUS governor of Sicily at the time of Cicero's investigation into Verres; brother of Quintus and Marcus (see below)

METELLUS, MARCUS elected praetor in 70 BC, to serve as president of the extortion court in 69 BC

METELLUS, QUINTUS consul in 69 BC; head of one of the leading families in Rome; brother of Lucius and Marcus (above)

MILO, TITUS ANNIUS a tough street-wise politician, an owner of gladiators

NEPOS, QUINTUS CAECILIUS METELLUS brother of Celer and brother-in-law of Pompey, who sends him back from his legateship in the East to stand for tribuneship and guard his interests in Rome; consul at the time of Cicero's return from exile

OCTAVIAN, GAIUS JULIUS CAESAR Caesar's great-nephew and heir

PANSA, GAIUS VIBIUS one of Caesar's commanders in Gaul

PHILIPPUS, LUCIUS MARCIUS consul soon after Cicero's return from exile; married to Caesar's niece, Atia, and thus the stepfather of Octavian; owner of a villa next door to Cicero's on the Bay of Naples

PHILOTIMUS Terentia's business manager, of questionable honesty

PISO, LUCIUS CALPURNIUS consul at the time of Cicero's exile, and thus an enemy of Cicero's; Caesar's father-in-law

PIUS, QUINTUS CAECILIUS METELLUS pontifex maximus; sixty-six years old and ailing; the adoptive father of Scipio

PLANCIUS, GNAEUS quaestor of Macedonia; his family were friends from the same region of Italy as the Ciceros

PLANCUS, LUCIUS MUNATIUS close lieutenant of Caesar, appointed governor of Further Gaul in 44 BC

POMPEY, GNAEUS MAGNUS born in the same year as Cicero; for many years the most powerful man in the Roman world; a former consul and victorious general who has already triumphed twice, he was away from Rome fighting in the East for four years; a member of the 'triumvirate' with Caesar and Crassus; initially married to Mucia, the sister of Celer and Nepos; later married to Caesar's daughter, Julia

RUFUS, MARCUS CAELIUS Cicero's former pupil, the son of one of his political supporters in the provinces; the youngest senator in Rome – brilliant, ambitious, unreliable

SERVILIA ambitious and politically shrewd wife of Junius Silanus, a candidate for the consulship; half-sister of Cato; the long-term mistress of Caesar; the mother of three daughters and a son Brutus, by her first husband

SERVIUS SULPICIUS RUFUS contemporary and old friend of Cicero, and a former praetor, famed as one of the greatest legal experts in Rome; candidate for the consulship; married to Postumia, a mistress of Caesar

SILANUS, DECIMUS JUNIUS married to Servilia, the long-term mistress of Caesar; a member of the College of Priests; defeated once for the consulship and plans to stand again

SPINTHER, PUBLIUS CORNELIUS LENTULUS consul at the time of Cicero's return from exile; an enemy of Clodius and friend of Cicero

SURA, PUBLIUS CORNELIUS LENTULUS former consul, once expelled from the senate for immorality; married to the widow of Hybrida's brother, and stepfather to the youthful Mark Antony; making a political comeback as urban praetor, and closely allied to Catilina

TERENTIA wife of Cicero; ten years younger than her husband, richer and of nobler birth; devoutly religious, poorly educated, with conservative political views; mother of Cicero's two children, Tullia and Marcus

TIRO Cicero's devoted private secretary, a family slave, three years younger than his master, the inventor of a system of shorthand

TULLIA Cicero's daughter

VATINIUS, PUBLIUS a senator and soldier famed for his ugliness; a close ally of Caesar

GLOSSARY

aedile an elected official, four of whom were chosen annually to serve a one-year term, responsible for the running of the city of Rome: law and order, public buildings, business regulations, etc.

auspices supernatural signs, especially flights of birds and lightning-flashes, interpreted by the **augurs**; if ruled unfavourable no public business could be transacted

Carcer Rome's prison, situated on the boundary of the Forum and the Capitol, between the Temple of Concord and the Senate house

century the unit in which the Roman people cast their votes on the Field of Mars at election time for consul and praetor; the system was weighted to favour the wealthier classes of society

chief priest see **pontifex maximus**

consul the senior magistrate of the Roman Republic, two of whom were elected annually, usually in July, to assume office in the following January, taking it in turns to preside over the senate each month

comitium the circular area in the Forum, approximately 300 feet across, bounded by the senate house and the rostra, traditionally the place where laws were voted on by the people, and where many of the courts had their tribunals

curia in its original form, the main assembly of the Roman tribes (of which, prior to 387 BC, there were thirty), consisting of a senior member of each

curule chair a backless chair with low arms, often made of ivory, possessed by a magistrate with imperium, particularly consuls and praetors

dictator a magistrate given absolute power by the senate over civil and military affairs, usually in a time of national emergency

equestrian order the second most senior order in Roman society after the Senate, the 'Order of Knights' had its own officials and privileges, and was entitled to one-third of the places on a jury; often its members were richer than members of the Senate, but declined to pursue a public career

Gaul divided into two provinces: **Nearer Gaul**, extending from the River Rubicon in northern Italy to the Alps, and **Further Gaul**, the lands beyond the Alps roughly corresponding to the modern French regions of Provence and Languedoc

haruspices the religious officials who inspected the entrails after a sacrifice in order to determine whether the omens were good or bad

imperator the title granted to a military commander on active service by his soldiers after a victory; it was necessary to be hailed imperator in order to qualify for a triumph

imperium the power to command, granted by the state to an individual, usually a consul, praetor or provincial governor

legate a deputy or delegate

legion the largest formation in the Roman army, at full strength consisting of approximately 5,000 men

lictor an attendant who carried the fasces – a bundle of birch rods tied together with a strip of red leather – that symbolised a magistrate's imperium; consuls were accompanied by twelve lictors, who served as their bodyguards, praetors by six; the senior lictor, who stood closest to the magistrate, was known as the proximate lictor

manumission the emancipation of a slave

Order of Knights see **equestrian order**

pontifex maximus the chief priest of the Roman state religion, the head of the fifteen-member College of Priests, entitled to an official residence on the Via Sacra

praetor the second most senior magistrate in the Roman republic, eight of whom were elected annually, usually in July, to take office the following January, and who drew lots to determine which of the various courts – treason, embezzlement, corruption, serious crime, etc. – they would preside over; see also **urban praetor**

prosecutions as there was no public prosecution system in the Roman Republic, all criminal charges, from embezzlement to treason and murder, had to be brought by private individuals

public assemblies the supreme authority and legislature of the Roman people was the people themselves, whether constituted by **tribe** (the *comitia tributa*, which voted on laws, declared war and peace, and elected the tribunes) or by **century** (the *comitia centuriata*, which elected the senior magistrates)

quaestor a junior magistrate, twenty of whom were elected each year, and who thereby gained the right of entry to the Senate; it was necessary for a candidate for the quaestorship to be over thirty and to show wealth of one million sesterces

rostra a long, curved platform in the Forum, about twelve feet high, surmounted by heroic statues, from which the Roman people were addressed by magistrates and advocates; its name derived from the beaks (*rostra*) of captured enemy warships set into its sides

senaculum an open space in front of the senate house where it was traditional for senators to assemble before the start of a session

Senate *not* the legislative assembly of the Roman Republic – laws could only be passed by the people in a tribal assembly – but something closer to its executive, with 600 members who could raise matters of state and order the consul to take action or to draft laws to be placed before the people; once elected via the quaestorship (see **quaestor**) a man would normally remain a senator for life, unless removed by the censors for immorality or bankruptcy, hence the average age was high (*senate* derived from *senex* = old)

tribes the Roman people were divided into thirty-five tribes for the purposes of voting on legislation and to elect the tribunes; unlike the system of voting by **century**, the votes of rich and poor when cast in a tribe had equal weight

tribune a representative of the ordinary citizens – the plebeians – ten of whom were elected annually each summer and took office in December, with the power to propose and veto legislation, and to summon assemblies of the people; it was forbidden for anyone other than a plebeian to hold the office

triumph an elaborate public celebration of homecoming, granted by the Senate to honour a victorious general, to qualify for which it was necessary for him to retain his military imperium – and as it was forbidden to enter Rome whilst still possessing military authority, generals wishing to triumph had to wait outside the city until the Senate granted them a triumph

urban praetor the head of the justice system, senior of all the praetors, third in rank in the republic after the two consuls

ACKNOWLEDGEMENTS

My greatest debt is to the Loeb edition of Cicero's collected speeches, letters and writings, published by Harvard University Press. I have been obliged to edit and compress Cicero's words, but wherever possible I have tried to let his voice come through. Loeb has been my Bible.

I have also made constant use of the great nineteenth-century works of reference edited by William Smith: his *Dictionary of Greek and Roman Antiquities, Dictionary of Greek and Roman Biography and Mythology* (three volumes) and *Dictionary of Greek and Roman Geography* (two volumes); these are now freely available online. *The Magistrates of the Roman Republic, Volume II, 99* BC – *31* BC by T. Robert S. Broughton was also invaluable, as was *The Barrington Atlas of the Greek and Roman World* edited by Richard J. A. Talbert. Again, wherever possible I have followed the facts and descriptions offered in the original sources – Plutarch, Appian, Sallust, Caesar – and I thank all those scholars and translators who have made them accessible and whose words I have used.

Biographies of, and books about, Cicero, which have given me numberless insights and ideas, include: *Cicero: A Turbulent Life* by Anthony Everitt, *Cicero: A Portrait* by Elizabeth Rawson, *Cicero* by D. R. Shackleton Bailey, *Cicero and his Friends* by Gaston Bossier, *Cicero: The Secrets of his Correspondence* by Jérôme Carcopino, *Cicero: A Political Biography* by David Stockton, *Cicero: Politics and Persuasion in Ancient Rome* by Kathryn Tempest, *Cicero as Evidence* by Andrew Lintott, *The Hand of Cicero* by Shane Butler, *Terentia, Tullia and Publia: the Women of Cicero's Family* by Susan Treggiari, *The Cambridge Companion to Cicero* edited by Catherine Steel, and – still thoroughly readable and useful – *The History of the Life of Marcus Tullius Cicero,* published in 1741 by Conyers Middleton (1683–1750).

Biographies of Cicero's contemporaries which I have found particularly useful include: *Caesar* by Christian Meier, *Caesar* by Adrian Goldsworthy, *The Death of Caesar* by Barry Strauss, *Pompey* by Robin Seager, *Marcus Crassus and the Late Roman Republic* by Allen Ward, *Marcus Crassus, Millionaire* by Frank Adcock, *The Patrician Tribune: Publius Clodius Pulcher* by W. Jeffrey Tatum and *Catullus: A Poet in the Rome of Julius Caesar* by Aubrey Burl.

For the general ambience of Rome – its culture, society and political structure – I have drawn on three works by the incomparable Peter Wiseman – *New Men in the Roman Senate, Catullus and His World* and *Cinna the Poet and other Roman essays.* To these I must also add *The Crowd in Rome in the Late Republic* by Fergus Millar, which analyses how politics might have operated in Cicero's Rome. Also valuable were *Intellectual Life in the Late Roman Republic* by Elizabeth Rawson, *The Constitution of the Roman Republic* by Andrew Lintott, *The Roman Forum* by Michael Grant, *Roman Aristocratic Parties and Families* by Friedrich Munzer (translated by Thérèse Ridley) and (of course) *The Roman Revolution* by Ronald Syme and Theodore Mommsen's *History of Rome.*

For the physical recreation of Republican Rome I relied on the scholarship of *A New Topographical Dictionary of Ancient Rome* by L. Richardson Jr, *A Topographical Dictionary of Rome* by Samuel Ball Platner, the *Pictorial Dictionary of Ancient Rome* (two volumes) by Ernest Nash and *Mapping Augustan Rome,* the *Journal of Roman Archaeology* project directed by Lothar Haselberger.

A special word of thanks should go to Tom Holland whose wonderful *Rubicon: The Triumph and Tragedy of the Roman Republic* (2003) first gave me the idea of writing a fictional account of the friendships, rivalries and enmities between Cicero, Caesar, Pompey, Cato, Crassus and the rest.

My research into the ancient world began in 2000, when I started work on *Pompeii* (2003). One of the great pleasures of these years has been meeting scholars of Roman history who have been without exception encouraging, even to the extent of electing me a proud if notably undistinguished President of the Classical Association in 2008. For various offers of encouragement and advice over the years I would like to thank in particular Mary Beard, Andrew Wallace-Hadrill, Jasper Griffin, Tom Holland, Bob Fowler, Peter Wiseman and Andrea Carandini. I apologise to those I have forgotten, and naturally absolve all those listed above of any responsibility for what I have written.

The two publishers who first commissioned me to write about Cicero were Sue Freestone in London and David Rosenthal in New York. Like the Roman Empire, they have both moved on, but I would like to thank them for their original enthusiasm and continued friendship. Their successors, Jocasta Hamilton and Sonny Mehta, have stepped into the breach and skilfully steered the project to its conclusion. Thanks also to Gail Rebuck and to Susan Sandon, for gallantly staying the course. My agent, Pat Kavanagh, to my great sadness and that of all her authors, did not live to see the work which she represented completed; I hope she would have enjoyed it. My thanks go to my other agents, Michael Carlisle of Inkwell Management in New York, and to Nicki Kennedy and Sam Edenborough of ILA in London. The estimable Wolfgang Muller, my German translator, once again acted as an unofficial copy-editor. Joy Terekiev and Cristiana Moroni of Mondadori in Italy literally shared the journey to Tusculum and Formiae.

Finally – *finally* – I would like to thank, as always, my wife, Gill Hornby, and our children, Holly, Charlie, Matilda and Sam, whose childhoods were lived in the shadow of Vesuvius and Cicero. *The Cicero Trilogy* is dedicated to them.